「變亂」

"TURMOIL"
~ BATTLE FOR THE HAN EMPIRE ~

BY T. P. M. THORNE

COVER ART BY T. P. M. THORNE

Published by PaMat Publishing

Cover art: *artistic depiction of China with a radiating 'cracks' from the Yan Province region in which the cities of Xuchang (Cao Cao's temporary imperial capital) and Guandu (the site of a famous battle in 200AD between two prominent warlords for control of the imperial court, and the main subject of the last act of this work) are situated. The 'domains' of the two mightiest warlords of that time are shaded differently, with the northern area being under the control of Commander-in-Chief Yuan Shao and the other being under the control of Excellency of Works Cao Cao.*

TABLE OF CONTENTS

FOREWORD

"Turmoil" is a direct sequel to my earlier work, '"Yellow Sky" – Crisis for the Han Dynasty', and my fourth foray into the era known as 'Three Kingdoms' (approx. 184AD – 280AD when including the Yellow Turban Rebellion and the decline of the Han that precedes it). I had not originally intended a sequel work, but as my first effort, 'Crouching Dragon – The Journey of Zhuge Liang', begins with the Battle of Guandu as an offstage crisis, I wanted to bridge "Yellow Sky" with it somehow. I initially hoped that my third work, 'East of the River – Home of the Sun Clan' would be that bridge, but that ended a full year before the Guandu crisis and left that important event without proper coverage.

The problem is that I did not intend any 'series' of any kind when I started out: this era is so fascinating and filled with great stories and anecdotes, however, that I am finding it difficult to know when and where to stop. This time, the book spans a much shorter time period of 5 years (the other works covered decades) but has a lot to cover. The years 195-200AD saw a lot of change and sees many of the most famous figures (Cao Cao, Yuan Shao, Liu Bei, Guan Yu, Sun Ce and Lü Bu, to name but a few) at their peak. Some of the most famous stories – Lü Bu's last stand, the Battle of Guandu, Guan Yu's service under Cao Cao, and Sun Ce's final years – occur during this time frame: only the latter is omitted. Why...? Well, unsurprisingly, including the many exploits of the Sun clan of Jiangdong in tandem with the rest is logistically impossible if I wanted to do them justice.

This work continues the long story of the Han Dynasty's demise: I have once again opted to give time to lesser-known figures such as Zang Ba, Yufuluo and Zhang Yang. The book begins where "Yellow Sky" ended, with the Chang'an Regency ruling China: the end of that regency is the focus of Acts I-III. Acts IV-VII follow the new government's attempts to rein in the various rebels, but the events of Act V lead to the warlord Yuan Shu finally declaring as an alternative emperor; the final acts (VII-IX) depict the last days of Yuan Shu, Gongsun Zan and the notorious Lü Bu along with the destined clash between Yuan Shao and Cao Cao.

Once again, I have tried to write as original a work as possible, partly by looking at figures and events that are usually ignored or downplayed, and mainly by drawing on history rather than folktales, although, as always, there are some instances of 'artistic license' for the sake of telling a story. And once again, all I can hope is that this book inspires or entertains someone out there as much as I have enjoyed writing it.

T. P. M. Thorne, the author

PROLOGUE: A FAMILIAR CHAOS

The vast lands of China were once again in turmoil. The people had lost count of the number of times that such nationwide chaos had disrupted their lives; this time the cause was the consequences of great peasant uprising – itself due to chaos of another kind – that had led to the death of the emperor. The cause – be it regicide or suicide – had the same effect: the army all but disintegrated, and the people nervously awaited the announcement of who would be their new masters. But for some, it was just another story, a story that bore an unnerving resemblance to events from centuries before.

"It's just like the days of the 'Three Kingdoms', hundreds of years ago, when the Han Dynasty collapsed," a middle-aged traveller said to his growing audience of peasant villagers that were looking for some form of escapism. "Everyone in the south says that."
"**Tell us about something from that time!**" one man said. "**Tell us about-!**"
"**Don't do Dong Zhuo! We heard that already!**" one woman insisted.
"**Tell us about Liu Bei!**" a child shouted.
"**No, tell us about Cao Cao!**" another child said; the crowd was divided on which of those great northern heroes would be the subject of the story.
"…In the south, all they want to hear about is the Sun clan," the traveller noted. "It's different in every place…"
"Will it be Cao Cao or Liu Bei…?" a woman asked.
"Their lives were mostly intertwined," the traveller chuckled. "To speak of one usually invites speaking of the other. But their lives were long, and their exploits many. What shall I speak about…? The later days, or-?"
"Nobody ever talks about how they got strong!" one boy complained. "My father says there was an idiot called Yuan-something, and… I forgot."
"Ah! Thank you, young man," the traveller said. "I shall talk about the Yuans, Shao and Shu, and the famous Lü Bu, about the Battle of Guandu."
The crowd chattered excitedly.
"Of course, there are a lot of different versions of that story, spoken and written," the traveller continued. "Chunyu Qiong the drunk, Guan Yu's exploits, and so on… but we'll start with… mm… where should I…?"
The traveller pondered the stories that he had heard and read, and wondered where he should truly begin. The story that he would tell would be different to the one in the records of history, it would be different to the centuries-old written works attributed to 'Luo Guanzhong', and it would be different from the one in his mind's eye: this would be a story told in many ways and for many different audiences in the ages to come.

****

ACT I: AN UNWELCOME STABILITY

1

"...My, how much has changed in recent times."

It was a reflective, sombre and somewhat haunted Cao Cao – Governor of Yan Province in eastern-central Han China – that had uttered those words as he stared out of his horse-drawn carriage and took in the sights of Yè, the walled capital city of Ji Province. Cao Cao then stroked his short, prematurely-grey beard and turned to look at his only company in the carriage: a gaunt, weary adviser in pale blue robes. After a pause, Cao Cao smiled strangely and said, "Your expression betrays the desire to ask me a question, Wenruo."

"You... are wondering if you should have come here, my lord," the adviser Xun Yu – whose courtesy name was Wenruo – replied cautiously.

"That was more of an inference statement than a question, but it is correct nonetheless," Cao Cao said with a sigh. "Ji Province... the seat of my old friend Benchu... or is that 'Lord Yuan Shao' now...? Are we friends now, or are we lord and vassal...? ...I prefer the former, but it is becoming increasingly obvious that he prefers the latter."

Xun Wenruo hummed thoughtfully and said, "Before we left, you summoned us all and made similar statements, and it was my belief that you had resolved your concerns about this invitation."

"But every one of those concerns has been replaced by a worse one still!" Cao Cao replied desperately. "Yes, I have decided that he does not intend a similar fate for me as the one he inflicted upon his predecessor; he cannot, for all of his arrogance, govern Ji, Bing, Qing and Yan Provinces simultaneously, and he knows that I would never betray him, and am hence best left in my seat of authority in Yan, despite my 'obvious difficulty in keeping it'."

The last words were said with evident bitterness; Xun Wenruo smiled sadly.

"...I say again, Wenruo, that a lot – too much – has changed," Cao Cao continued. "I had to determine who invited me here... who Yuan Shao now is. I had to wonder if he is Benchu, the friend that I have known since we were boys at school, the noble gentleman that I collaborated with to curb the vicious ambitions of the 'Ten Attendants', protect the so-called 'Partisans', and fight the tyrant Dong Zhuo... or whether he is... something else now, something closer to his wretched brother-cousin Shu. Some things still point to that friend I had, while others... like the state of things in the land as a whole, in particular the current state of things in Xu Province and Chang'an... say that 'Benchu', like 'Mengde', is... is *fading away*, Wenruo, leaving something much less... human."

Xun Wenruo hummed purposefully rather than respond with words. Cao Cao's final words were self-referential: his old friend Yuan Shao, the governor of Ji Province, had indeed been a lifelong friend that he had known only by his courtesy name 'Benchu' in past times, while Cao himself had enjoyed being referred to by his own courtesy name, 'Mengde'. 'Courtesy' - or 'style' – names not only implied closeness or respect between friends or acquaintances: they were names that men chose with care, names that they would use to give themselves a sense of identity and personification in a world where all men gave their family name before their given name and status was everything. Cao Cao was a troubled man, and he often wondered whether his sense of self was as established as it had been in more peaceful times: his hands were steeped in blood, and he had made decisions that he could not live with comfortably.

"…Is he Benchu…? …And… am I Mengde…?" Cao Cao whispered.

Xun Wenruo covered his face with his long sleeve and coughed nervously: he knew that the words were not for him to hear or answer.

"…**Why did so much have to change???**" Cao Cao cried suddenly. "**The needed changes were made, Wenruo! Why did**… *how* did… it all go… so *wrong*…?"

"If I knew, I would be better counsel than I am," Xun Wenruo replied.

"…But I am digressing; I know that," Cao Cao said. "Am I here because I am a friend, and he seeks my opinions on some matter, or am I here as a subordinate…? …Am I here to discuss the disgusting situation that our sovereign – whether he is to be truly accepted or not – endures in Chang'an…? …Am I here to be reprimanded for my 'failure' to keep Lü Bu out of my province and my difficulty in subsequently ejecting him from it…? …Or am I to be politely warned not to chase Bu into Xu Province and 'do any further harm to that place', now that Benchu considers it part of his growing sphere of influence…? …Or… or is it to ask me whether Zhang Miao suffered…?"

"…I truly wish that I knew, Lord Cao, so that I might be of better service," Xun Wenruo replied.

"…Let it be the overdue rescue of the emperor and the court that I am here to discuss," Cao Cao said with a bitter tone. "That matter has gone on too long, surviving even the death of Dong Zhuo and the exile of his evil stepson: I accept Li Jue and Guo Si's 'Regency' because I lack the military might to do something alone. Let it be *that*, Wenruo: let it be a discussion about ending the ridiculous feuds with his brother-cousin Shu and Gongsun Zan, reviving the Eastern Pass Coalition and finishing what we started five years ago! Let it be *that*, Wenruo, and not… not more personal nonsense, not more hankering, not more… *more*…"

Cao Cao's voice trailed; Xun Wenruo exhaled loudly in response.

Han Dynasty China did not know peace in any quarter; it was, like most of the rest of the world, a place beset with power struggles as new clans sought greater influence and older clans struggled to maintain the status quo. In the vast Roman Empire, a number of men had declared their own intent to rule and the wounds left by a crisis known as the 'Year of the Five Emperors' were still festering after almost two years. The victor of that war and self-appointed Emperor, Septimius Severus, had guaranteed the support of Britain's governor and rival Clodius Albinus for his battles with the other remaining claimants by allowing Albinus to take the title 'Caesar' and consider himself a future ruler; but Severus was, at the same time, desperately aligning himself more closely with former emperors Marcus Aurelius and Commodus while preparing his own sons – most notably his eldest son, the future tyrant nicknamed 'Caracalla' – to truly succeed him. The

Parthian king Vologases V – who feared Severus' intentions for his own kingdom – had backed Syrian governor Pescennius Niger as Roman Emperor, but the latter was defeated by Severus within a year; Vologases nonetheless continued to encourage uprisings against Severus in neighbouring provinces. The embattled Septimius Severus would, however, eventually conquer his enemies and expand the reach of Roman rule; by contrast, the young Han Emperor Xian would continue to suffer great indignities as he awaited help from his feuding warlords.

The Han Dynasty had existed for over two centuries, and it had only known one crisis that had unseated the ruling Liu clan, namely Wang Mang's usurpation. Wang Mang introduced the idea of the 'Mandate of Heaven', which stated that a clan could lose – or gain – the right to rule the empire, and that bloodlines were not as important as fitness to govern. Wang Mang fell afoul of his own changes, however, and the Han Empire was restored after a rebellion led by a surviving member of the Liu clan. The restoration was not without lasting consequences, and the most obvious was the chosen centre of power. The original imperial capital, Chang'an, was located in the northwest of China, and was geographically close to Hanzhong Province, which was the administrative seat and dynastic namesake of the Han founder Liu Bang, but it was also close to areas that were frequently targeted for raids by the Xiongnu peoples that lived beyond the Great Wall to the north, and the area also endured regular uprisings by the indigenous non-Han tribes that lived there. An administration – regardless of its title or reach – is always perceived as weak, or at the very least weaker or surmountable, once it has been toppled once, and the Han Emperor was no exception. The Xiongnu and their like became increasingly confident in their incursions, and Wang Mang's 'Mandate of Heaven' remained in the consciousness of the people, so the new Han Emperor moved the capital eastward, to the city of Luoyang.

For decade after decade, China and its neighbours traded and scuffled, but the Han Emperors retained superficial control of their empire: under the surface, the families of Empresses and Empress Dowagers were often the ones that held the power over sovereigns that were too young, too old, too frail, too naïve or too dependent on trustworthy counsel to keep their grip on authority. Cao Cao had been a child when the most recent crisis had begun: the Liang clan's hold over the young Emperor Huan had been broken by the emperor and his eunuch attendants, but those attendants then enjoyed absolute trust that some – who were later known collectively as the 'Ten Attendants', regardless of actual number – abused for personal gain, just as the Liangs and other consort's families had done for decades before. Within a few years, the 'Ten' had administrative power that far exceeded their perceived role as personal attendants to the emperor and his harem, and they had secretly-amassed wealth that exceeded that of noble families that had known centuries of favour.

The intelligentsia often rebuked the 'Ten' and their allies publicly, which annoyed Emperor Huan but solicited no serious reaction: that changed, however, when a famous medium with ties to the 'Ten' was executed for murdering a man ahead of an as-yet unannounced general amnesty that the 'Ten' had informed him of for the benefit of his prognostications. The Magistrate that ordered his death was arrested by Emperor Huan at the request of the 'Ten', and the subsequent show of mass support by unsuspecting courtiers and academics frightened the 'Ten' and drove them to seek the destruction of their many enemies. The 'Partisan Crisis', as it came to be known, saw thousands of men arrested, stripped of all rank and either exiled or executed: it left the Han court a gutted shell that was quickly refilled with men that the 'Ten' could control.

The power of the 'Ten' persisted when the childless Emperor Huan died and his child heir, a relative, became Emperor Ling: most reluctantly accepted the situation, and any who did not – including the new Empress Dowager's father, Dou Wu – were quickly defeated by the devious range of political and armed counterattacks that the 'Ten' employed. The persecution of 'Partisans' – which had been relaxed by Emperor Huan after his father-in-law Dou Wu's remonstrations – resumed under Emperor Ling, who had been tricked into thinking that his life was under threat from any who opposed the 'Ten': Cao Cao and his friend Yuan Shao were two of many young men who chose to shelter the 'Partisans' and discuss ways to remove the 'Ten'. To them, a court ruled from the shadows by a band of greedy, murderous eunuchs that did not tolerate any form of criticism was itself intolerable and could only lead to ruin.

And while the nation was not in ruins, it had certainly descended into chaos: Emperor Ling's aloof rule allowed the 'Ten' to tighten their grip, and even an uncle of the emperor was not spared demands for tribute or the punishment that met the defiant. Corruption and incompetence were rife, and still matters worsened: when crops failed, the 'Ten' failed to allocate relief funds to any but their friends; when the Khan of the Xianbei Confederacy led an army into China, the 'Ten' appointed unqualified allies as commanders and sent men into battle with such inadequate resources that some did not even have clothes or weapons; and when a Taoist cult known as the 'Way of Peace' started to sway the minds of the desperate people, the 'Ten' and their allies dismissed the threat and continued to behave in the same way. When a 'Way of Peace' coup within the capital failed, their leader, Zhang Jue, had his acolytes – who numbered in the hundreds of thousands – adopt the treasonous symbol of a yellow turban and attack every part of the Han infrastructure. The 'Yellow Turban Rebellion' was quelled by private militias led by men like Cao Cao, since the 'Ten Attendants' and their friends had embezzled the majority of the treasury monies: that, combined with other rebellions and a poorly-made decision to promote many of the Provincial Inspectors to semi-autonomous Governors created the right conditions for ambitious men to carve out their own territories.

When Emperor Ling died, his 13-year-old eldest son became Emperor Shao: Shao's mother, Empress Dowager Hè, and her brother Hè Jin then repeated the pattern of the past and seized control of the court. The 'Ten' were able to blackmail Empress Dowager Hè, since she had murdered the mother of her son's half-brother, Prince Liu Xie: they were in turn opposed by Hè

Jin, who was Commander-in-Chief of the Imperial Army. The political plotting culminated in the death of Hè Jin and the subsequent destruction of the 'Ten' by none other than Yuan Shao: the power vacuum was filled by the corrupt and sociopathic warlord Dong Zhuo, whose sizeable army and collection of formidable officers and cunning advisers made him powerful beyond expectation. Dong Zhuo tricked the prodigious and intimidating warrior Lü Bu into joining his service and murdering his own loyalist lord and stepfather, Bing Province Governor Ding Yuan: Dong Zhuo subsequently appointed himself as Chancellor of State, killed Empress Dowager Hè, deposed and then killed Emperor Shao, appointed Liu Xie as Emperor Xian and slaughtered the clans of dissenting officials.

The grieving Yuan Shao – whose clan was among those decimated by Dong Zhuo – then led what was known as the 'Eastern Pass Coalition' – a confederacy of provincial governors, prefectural administrators and militias – in a blockade attack on Dong Zhuo's defending forces in the capital Luoyang. After destroying priceless bronze statues – for the purpose of minting new coin to buy supplies – and causing crippling inflation, Dong Zhuo looted the capital – and any nearby imperial tombs – and murdered many of the capital's inhabitants before fleeing to the old capital Chang'an with Emperor Xian and his senior courtiers as hostages. A feud between Yuan Shao and his half-brother Yuan Shu caused the dissolution of the Eastern Pass Coalition, and that was, as Cao Cao recalled with regret, the on-going situation after 4 years: the Yuans were still feuding, and Emperor Xian was now a hostage of Dong Zhuo's former associates, the latter having been assassinated, ironically enough, by his own stepson, Lü Bu.

"It is difficult to know what to say about such times," Cao Cao suggested.
"The sooner that they are history – a memory of worse times – the better," Xun Wenruo replied.

****

2

"...Here we are, Wenruo: the home of Governor Yuan Shao of Ji Province," Cao Cao chuckled as his governor's carriage slowed in front of a large mansion. "We shall soon have to part company; I truly hope that he does not expect you to talk to any of his more wretched followers."
Xun Wenruo sighed miserably.
"I shall see if Xu Yòu is about," Cao Cao promised. "He is an old friend, as you know, and shall treat you well; better that than Chunyu Qiong or one of his other insufferable toadies."
"All of whom I know, Lord Cao, as a former adviser that 'defected'," Xun Wenruo noted pointedly. "One of the worst, if you recall, is my younger brother."
"...Oh, yes, of course," Cao Cao realised at last. "All those subtle hints, but I was so preoccupied with my own reservations... forgive me, my friend."
"...It was me or Mister Cheng!" Xun Wenruo joked.
Cao Cao smiled, laughed and said, "Indeed! I would be a bigger fool for bringing that bad-tempered and painfully honest man here! I might owe him much for his role in regaining my province, but he would probably ruin everything if he decided to speak to Benchu as he speaks to me. Benchu's 'touchiness' has already cost him good officers and more than one good official; I'd rather it didn't cost him any of mine. ...But will you be alright, Wenruo?"
"I will be fine as long as I don't have to converse with the likes of Chunyu Qiong," Xun Wenruo replied. "In fact, I hear that... ... ...never mind."
"...What...?" Cao Cao prompted.
"...I would prefer not to make promises," Xun Wenruo said. "There's nothing worse, I think, than promising a good thing and delivering nothing."
"...Agreed," Cao Cao chortled. "That's the cause of all of our woes, methinks. In fact, as I will doubtless mention at some point, it's Benchu's failure to-! ...But then, I *cannot* mention it, can I...? I can mention *nothing*... nothing that would either make me a hypocrite or him an enemy. ...In which case, I have to make discussing the weather last for the entire evening... ... ...should I turn us around...?"
"You know as well as I do that we're really here to determine his state of mind, Lord Cao," Xun Wenruo replied. "Do not let fear of what you will learn-"
"'Prevent you from moving forward': yes, I remember Mister Cheng's words as well as you do, Wenruo," Cao Cao interrupted. "I admit that I am afraid... of what I will learn about us both... he and I."
Xun Wenruo was about to reply, but he was halted – and startled – by a sudden cry:
"MENGDE...!"
Cao Cao leant out of the carriage and smiled cynically: he knew that the voice was that of Xu Yòu, a mutual friend of Cao Cao and Yuan Shao that knew the two from their shared days at school.
"...Why that face, Mengde...?" the short, nondescript Xu Yòu asked as he neared the carriage and fidgeted with the sleeve of his

brown robe. "Do *you* doubt my honesty as well...?"

"Not at all, Ziyuan," Cao Cao replied. "I just marvel at how old we all look these days."

"...You once composed a poem, if I remember, where you said that great power actually robs you of freedom," Xu Yòu said. "You forgot to mention that it puts twenty years on you as well."

"...I should really write them down," Cao Cao chuckled. "But yes, I do remember that one vaguely... it was when I was..."

Suddenly, Cao Cao's expression changed.

"It was... when I was appointed for... some role or other..."

Xu Yòu coughed nervously; Cao Cao was feigning his inability to recollect the day, and the reason was obvious. Cao Cao had been appointed as the District Captain of Luoyang, and he had invited his friends to celebrate the moment. Among that circle of friends were Yuan Shao, Xu Yòu, and three other men whose faces and names haunted Cao Cao: the reckless Wei Zi, who had died during a badly-planned attack on Dong Zhuo's forces that Cao had personally ordered; the honest Lü Boshe, whose family died at Cao Cao's own hands during an unfortunate misunderstanding; and Zhang Miao, who was loved and respected by all who knew him but died at Cao's command after he turned against Cao Cao and allowed the notorious wandering warlord Lü Bu to invade and seize Yan Province.

"...It is no surprise that the memory is blurred, Mengde, since much time has passed," Xu Yòu said carefully. "My point is made, so let's say no more of it."

"...Zhang Miao betrayed us all," Cao Cao retorted. "He did not merely betray me, Xu Ziyuan: as Benchu's appointed governor of Yan, he-!"

"I... I understand, Mengde," Xu Yòu insisted. "Only a madman or a fool would make a friend of Lü Bu, much less invite him to cause more damage to the Empire: it is a similar shame that Dong Gongren – whose decency I'd have sworn to the Heavens – has similarly lost his mind and fled to Bu's friend Zhang Yang rather than answer some questions about his conduct. You did what you had to do with Zhang Miao. Perhaps... perhaps it indicates that Lord Yuan was right to dissociate himself from the man years ago, rather than cling to the notion that his 'unparalleled decency' was something else altogether."

"...Perhaps," Cao Cao replied numbly. "...Will you be joining Benchu and I for dinner...?"

"What, and be myself in the company of my lord...?" Xu Yòu chortled. "Not a chance, Mengde: he'd never allow me to treat him as a friend now."

"And... and I can expect the same...?" Cao Cao prompted.

"To him, you are an equal, or near enough," Xu Yòu replied. "Anyhow... I am to escort Wenruo to-"

"*Wenruo*...?" Xun Wenruo said with surprise.

"You have shifted your allegiance to a friend of my lord, and I know you to be a good man, and you were 'Wenruo' to me before, Mister Xun," Xu Yòu replied. "If I am not being presumptuous, I would still like to refer to you as such."

"I'm glad that Wenruo is in good hands," Cao Cao said. "Now I must go to meet Benchu... since he does not come to meet me."

"He will meet you in the hall," Xu Yòu chuckled. "He's still a little paranoid about Lü Bu sending someone to repay him for the assassination attempt, even though the man and his followers are penniless vagrants hiding in Xu Province."

"…I shall go to the hall then," Cao Cao sighed. "Farewell for now, Wenruo."

Xun Wenruo clasped his hands together and bowed slightly before he said, "I hope that you enjoy the banquet, Lord Cao."

Cao Cao smirked, turned to Xu Yòu and said, "You'd better move so I can get out of the carriage."

Xu Yòu laughed apologetically and turned to move away: his gaze was immediately met by a towering hulk of a man with crazed eyes and a strange, toothy grin.

"**AYAH!** I-! I…? …Wh-wha…? …*What*…?" Xu Yòu bumbled as he stopped his instinctive retreat, regained his composure and turned to Cao Cao, who was laughing uncontrollably.

"…This is *Dian Wei*, Mister Xu," Xun Wenruo said as he gestured toward Cao Cao's giant, muscular bodyguard. Dian was wearing fresh leather armour over plain brown robes, and he carried a sword at his side; his toothy grin had been replaced by a humble smile and his eyes had calmed, but he was still somehow terrifying.

"I apologise for startling you, Mister Xu," Dian Wei said quietly.

Xu Yòu started to laugh strangely as he replied, "I should have looked where I was going, fool that I am! …*Aiee*… I thought I was dead then, for certain!"

"Oh, I needed cheering up!" Cao Cao cackled. "Now I am ready for my banquet!"

"I shall wait here until you return, Mister Xu," Xun Wenruo prompted.

"I… I'll take you inside, Mengde," Xu Yòu replied as he tried, in vain, to turn his gaze away from Dian Wei.

"He won't devour you if you turn your back on him, Ziyuan!" Cao Cao teased.

"…*Ayah*… really, I thought I was dead," Xu Yòu mumbled as he turned to enter the mansion; the guards parted and the doors opened.

"See you later, Wenruo!" Cao Cao chuckled as he started to follow Xu Yòu with the protective Dian Wei at his side; the guards stared at Dian Wei and silently prayed that they would not have to confront him at any point in their lives.

"…Yes, Lord Cao," Xun Wenruo murmured inaudibly.

"**Brother!**"

"…*Aiee*… not *him*," Xun Wenruo muttered as he turned to face his fresh-faced younger brother, Xun Chen.

"**I'd heard that you'd returned to us!**" Xun Chen cried as he finished his swift approach; he was accompanied by a slimmer, older man that Xun Wenruo was even less glad to see.

"…I think you know – *both of you* – that I am here with my lord Cao Cao," Xun Wenruo retorted. "Still, I am glad to be cordial as the vassal of your lord's most trusted and closest friend… greetings, brother Youruo, and Mister Guo Gongze."

Xun Wenruo clasped his hands together and bowed to both men.

"Brother," Xun Chen said with enforced disappointment as he returned the bow.

"Mister *Xun Yu*," the adviser Guo Tu replied icily; he did not return the bow.

"...So that's how it is, Guo Tu," Xun Wenruo retorted. "I call you 'Gongze' because I see no cause for bad blood between us."

"Do you not...?" Guo Tu said theatrically. "You *abandoned your lord*: what sort of man would-!"

"This is not like our joint departure from Han Fu's service, Mister Guo, which could just as easily be called 'abandonment'," Xun Wenruo retorted. "Did I join Yuan Shu, or Dong Zhuo...? No, I joined your lord's closest friend who this day joins your lord in this house for an informal banquet... a friend who, if I recall, had just lost Zhou Renming... to your lord. I was simply correcting a balance, if defending my decision is required."

"...Well met... *Wenruo*," Guo Tu grumbled.

"Now... am I to understand that you both ambushed me to prod my conscience and coerce me to return to Yuan Shao's service...?" Xun Wenruo asked calmly.

"How could you think such things of me, brother?" Xun Chen replied with exaggerated emotion in his tone. "We were merely passing by, saw you, and thought that we would greet you!"

Xun Wenruo bowed again and said, "And that you have done. I hope that we shall meet again in less uncomfortable circumstances."

"...Good day, brother," Xun Chen replied as he returned the bow and started to back away.

"...Good day, Mister Xun," Guo Tu said with obvious irritation.

"What a pair of fools," Xun Wenruo muttered once Xun Chen and Guo Tu were far enough away. "Chen... how can he and I share blood and a name...?"

Moments later, Xu Yòu returned.

"*Aiee*... that Dian Wei!" Xu Yòu chuckled. "He frightened every man that set eyes upon him, except, perhaps, Zhang Hè and Yan Liang... though they might be better actors than the rest of us... ... ...Is something wrong, Wenruo...?"

"Guo Tu and my fool brother leapt on me as soon as you were gone," Xun Wenruo replied bitterly. "They were not subtle in their intent."

"I'm sorry, Wenruo, and I swear that I know nothing of it," Xu Yòu insisted.

"You value your friendship with Lord Cao too much to be involved in such a blatant and nonsensical stunt," Xun Wenruo replied. "Forget about it. Shall we go to my hotel...?"

"You'll have quarters on the grounds," Xu Yòu explained. "I'll take you now..."

****

3

"...I was saying to Wenruo, on the way here... how much has changed in recent times."

Cao Cao uttered the words as he sat cross-legged on the floor, facing his old friend Yuan Shao: the two were strong, nourished noblemen that were close to 40 years of age, but their grey hairs and leathery skin betrayed years of military service and political stress. They both wore expensive patterned robes and had their uncut hair wound and covered by silk turbans: an empty banquet tray and a small tea kettle separated them.

"...Does something bother you, Benchu...?" Cao Cao asked.

Yuan Shao turned his gaze toward the doorway, where the titan Dian Wei was stood: he now wore plain robes rather than armour, but he carried a halberd, wore a sword at his side and had a hate-filled expression that filled Yuan Shao with dread.

"...You fear Dian Wei...?" Cao Cao chuckled. "You shouldn't."

"...Perhaps, but does his presence not imply that *you* fear *me*?" Yuan Shao countered.

"I... I don't fear *you*, but... I trust no-one fully anymore," Cao Cao admitted. "After Zhang Miao... how can I...? How can *we*...?"

Yuan Shao exhaled loudly.

"You were right," Cao Cao muttered. "I should have let you kill him back then, when he was rude to you. You said that he didn't 'understand', and you were right... I'm sorry I obstructed you."

"Don't be," Yuan Shao insisted. "In fact... I think that we maybe miss his naïve honesty more than we like to admit."

Cao Cao lowered his head, smiled, and said, "I sometimes wear a white garment under my clothes for him... not for long, just... for the moments where I want to weep for his idealism being so very, very out of place in this mad world we live in."

"...Yes," Yuan Shao replied.

"...Xu Yòu said that he would not attend," Cao Cao prompted.

"...He often elopes on 'private business'," Yuan Shao scoffed. "He's not here because it would be inappropriate, since he is a direct vassal of mine now. But... but since Zhang Miao... *before*, perhaps, if I am honest... I wonder about him as well, sometimes."

"He's not like us," Cao Cao suggested. "We're heroes... he isn't."

"What, I wonder, is a 'hero', Mengde...?" Yuan Shao sighed.

Cao Cao hummed thoughtfully.

Yuan Shao was the head of the Yuan clan of Ru County in Yu Province, whose collective closeness to the emperors of past times was well known. His distant ancestor, Yuan An, enjoyed commemorative odes and statues; his paternal grandfather, father and uncles enjoyed some of the highest administrative posts in the empire; Shao himself had been a close confidante of Hè Jin, the last Commander-in-Chief of the Han Imperial armed forces before the administration in the capital Luoyang had collapsed and power had coalesced into the hands of the warlord Dong Zhuo.

Cao Cao was the son of Cao Song, a man who had been adopted – and hence elevated – by an imperial court eunuch: this was at the time of Emperor Huan when, in contradiction to their intended status as sub-human, the eunuchs were some of the most influential individuals in Han China, since they enjoyed a social intimacy with the emperor and his courtesans that no normal man could. Cao Song became a rich and powerful man in his own right, and even received similar administrative responsibilities to the ones that members of more established clans like the Yuans were considered to be exclusively entitled to: Cao Song's sons went to the same schools as the children of those clans, and Cao Cao was unquestionably part of Han nobility as a result of that.

Under other circumstances, the lofty Yuan Shao might have considered Cao Cao to be his social inferior, but his own lineage was 'tainted': his biological father had sired him with a housemaid at a time when his wife and consorts had yet to give him a much-wanted son and heir, and by the time that he sired a 'legitimate' heir – Shao's half-brother Shu – the clan chief had no male heirs, and Shao was adopted by that important uncle to remedy the situation. That left Shao and Shu as cousins, but it had also robbed Shu of any possibility – in his own mind, at least – of somehow being elevated to clan chieftain himself someday.

"You sheltered 'partisans'... we both did," Cao Cao replied. "You fought the 'Ten'... hah! You actually went into the capital, in a mad rage, and cut them all up! I remember you castigating me once for petitioning against them; how feeble my little words seem when compared to your solution!"
"...What did we achieve, though?" Yuan Shao asked.
"I'm not sure," Cao Cao replied. "We have an emperor that we neither of us want, but all the best alternatives are dead... hah! And here's me saying that, when I was so against having Liu Yu!"
"Who was so cruelly murdered by Gongsun Zan, who still hankers after this province and Qing as well," Yuan Shao complained. "But my hands are tied: I am forbidden from marching against him, by imperial decree! But whose decree...? I am currently a vassal of men that slaughtered my clan!"
"I have the man that probably did it as a next-door neighbour," Cao Cao sighed. "I tell you, I *will not rest* until Lü Bu is a corpse."
"...But you do not intend to march into Xu again...?" Yuan Shao asked before taking a sip of his heated tea.
"...That would be encroachment into your domain," Cao Cao replied coldly. "I vowed to you that I would not."
"...Good," Yuan Shao replied before taking a second sip.
The mood was souring: Cao Cao sought a lighter discussion – if indeed it could be called that – by saying, "Liu Yan faltered."
"What a fool he was, allying with the Qiang!" Yuan Shao chortled. "Still, the other lot managed to obtain support from Yufuluo."
"He's still dipping in and out of Yan with his bandit friends," Cao Cao complained. "I wish he'd either make peace with his brother and join the confederacy, or surrender, or... or *something*. He used to lend aid to Han armies... now he's little more than a thief."
"Liu Yan used to be a ceremonial director, didn't he...?" Yuan Shao said. "Now he's a dead criminal. Oh, I know I could thank him, in a way, for the power-devolvement idea, but at the same time, it's the reason we'll probably not have peace for the next ten years."
"...Is that how long you see it going on for...?" Cao Cao prompted.
"Oh, yes," Yuan Shao chortled. "I'm not far off pacifying Bing,

now, I think... and when the proper moment arises, I'll ignore the regents' silly decree and march on Yòu Province. Once my son Tan and I have dealt with Gongsun Zan and taken Qing and Yòu, and once I've coerced my puppet governor in Xu, Liu Bei, to kill Lü Bu, that leaves Central Province, Jing, Yi, Yang and Hanzhong."

Cao Cao sipped his tea and listened quietly.

"My upstart brother will get bored eventually I think, and 'come home'," Yuan Shao continued. "Until then, he'll make silly deals with the likes of Gongsun and Sun Ce, but what of it...? Liu Biao is ostensibly an ally, but I'll still rein him in at some point, since I doubt he'll stay 'neutral' – or to use another word, cowardly – for long. We can deal with the White Wave Bandits and the Black Mountain Bandits together, and then that leaves Li Jue and Guo Si, and Yi and Hanzhong. With Liu Yan gone, I don't see Yi being independent for long; that wretched cultist Zhang Lu will try and seize the place, and Liu Zhang will need allies to keep it."

"Your advisers are very thorough," Cao Cao joked.

Yuan Shao frowned and said, "Of course I have to admit that these are ideas that have been bandied about at court... I'm sure that your court is the same."

"Of course!" Cao Cao chuckled. "I'm not so clever... Chen Gong was my brains in the early days, and now I have... other men."

"Yes... 'Wenruo'," Yuan Shao scoffed. "Wasn't he one of mine?"

"Be fair," Cao Cao retorted. "Xun Wenruo came to me; Zhou Renming went to you. Men make their own choices."

"...I suppose you're right," Yuan Shao sighed. "It's strange; as children, we happily lent one-another things, didn't we? Now I get annoyed when friends 'borrow' my vassals. I know that it isn't exactly the same, but-"

"I do understand," Cao Cao promised. "...I nearly passed up some really fine men because of where they came from. Yu Jin, from Wang Lang... and Dian Wei, from Zhang Miao."

"I inherited a lot of men from Han Fu," Yuan Shao noted. "A few, such as Dong Zhao and Qu Yi, have not worked out: others – such as Ju Shou, Zhang Hè, Guo Tu, and Xun Chen – are invaluable."

"What a lot of people we've met!" Cao Cao said. "When you start to think about it, it's quite incredible... that thirty years ago, I was the son of a wealthy minister, and you were heir to one of the most famous and influential clans in the land... we had a relatively small circle of friends, and certainly no 'vassals'! Now look at us, Benchu... look at what we've become."

Cao Cao had been smiling when he had started talking; both he and Yuan Shao were melancholy by the time he had finished.

"We need *wine*, not *tea*," Yuan Shao grumbled. "*Bloody locusts*... curse them all, every last little one of them!"

"What food will we eat?" Cao Cao wondered. "*Is* there any food?"

"Yes," Yuan Shao said. "We have stocks... forgive me if I don't say where, since like you, I have trouble with trusting people... not necessarily you, but if you were to mention anything to one of your more entrepreneurial advisers, then-"

"I understand," Cao Cao promised.

"Ah... what a world," Yuan Shao said. "I haven't been home at all."

"Me neither," Cao Cao realised. "Juancheng is my home now. I don't have much to go 'home' to, now. My family is in Yan now."

"...As most of mine – the part I acknowledge in these troubled times – is here, in Yè," Yuan Shao said. "Oh, Mengde, why must my cousin – who is, in truth, my brother – be so foolish…? Why did he have to be so spiteful? So many of our clan were cruelly slaughtered by Dong Zhuo, and yet he continues this feud! All that he has to do is apologise, Mengde, and accept me as the head of the clan, and we could be brothers again, and pay respects at the tombs of our ancestors and kin! Why must he do this to us…?"

"I wish I knew," Cao Cao sighed.

Four of Yuan Shao's servants brought trays of cooked meat and rice and a jug of wine.

"Go easy on the wine, though, since we can't waste rice on it at the moment," Yuan Shao whispered as his staff placed the trays on the floor between them.

"…Do you ever think that we'll save the emperor…?" Cao Cao asked once the servants were gone.

"The problem, Mengde, is what we call an emperor these days," Yuan Shao replied. "Is 'Xiandi' really mandated, or is he still the Prince of Chenliu? Have we an emperor…?"

"Until the locusts, I was a lot more certain!" Cao Cao joked.

"Yes, and you're not the only one," Yuan Shao chortled as he took a piece of seasoned chicken from a tray. "Some of my staff grumble about it, and I hear them; in some regions, they're calling the locusts' appearance another 'sign'."

"…Yes, I think that it's not going unnoticed by the majority of the poor," Cao Cao said sadly. "In fact… and I know you're not going to like me saying this… but…"

"…But what…?" Yuan Shao asked.

Cao Cao lowered his head and exhaled loudly.

"…You suspect that the Yellow Turbans will rise up again," Yuan Shao realised. "But they would need leaders, and it's my understanding that the likes of Liu Pi now serve my brother-cousin as paid mercenaries."

"Are they the only leaders the fools could find…?" Cao Cao said.

"…I cannot worry about possible threats when actual ones are so pressing," Yuan Shao said miserably. "Besides, wouldn't a Yellow Turban uprising force us all to cooperate, perhaps force my brother-cousin to abandon his selfish ambitions and return to the fold…? And wouldn't Gongsun Zan surrender his bloodstained seal of Yòu Province in the face of mass unrest…? And wouldn't all of that allow us to do everything else that we want to do…?"

Cao Cao looked up and hummed purposefully.

"When the famine has fully abated and the numerous rebels and bandits are quelled, then we can petition the court about Lü Bu, finally deal with my brother-cousin Shu, Zhang Yang in Henei and Gongsun Zan in Yòu Province, and then I will see about some form of reparation from the Tao clan for the loss of your father."

"*Blood* **is all that I want, Benchu!**" Cao Cao barked. "**I-!**"

"Mengde… *no*," Yuan Shao ordered. "I do not like to remind you that I am still, in many senses, your lord and commander, but it seems that I must."

Cao Cao did his best to hide his anger.

"…You talk of changes, and rightly so," Yuan Shao continued. "When I heard of your massacres in Xu… of bodies in the tens of thousands damming the Si River… of cannibalism, wiping villages and even cities out of existence, I… I…"

Cao Cao fought tears as he said, "Felt sick…? …Wondered if you could still be a friend to a monster that could massacre the 'innocents' so guiltlessly…? …Marvelled at how accurately the appraiser Xu Shao had prejudged me as a 'Crafty Villain' all those years ago…? …Perhaps wondered if I am another Dong Zhuo, a-"

"No," Yuan Shao insisted. "To avenge my friend Hè Jin, I… I ordered the massacre of every palace eunuch… some of them boys, recently 'converted'… I killed many of them myself. Many of them were 'innocents'… but I did not care. So long as the deaths of a thousand innocents led to the death of one or two dogs that had brought misery to the country, then… then I did not care."

The two men fell silent for a few moments.

"…But now, Benchu, how does it feel…?" Cao Cao asked at last. "How does it feel – as a man that once sheltered the 'Partisans', the 'innocents', from the 'Ten' – to know that you shed so much innocent blood and didn't care, so long as the ends were met…?"

Yuan Shao tipped the entire contents of his wine dish into his mouth before he replied, "I… I live with it. The 'Ten' were vanquished. We're not like Dong Zhuo or the 'Ten', Mengde. They did what they did to remove threats to their own greedy ambitions; we did what we did to avenge good men and punish the wicked. No man in our position can say that they have never said or will never say or do something that could cause someone harm: Zhang Miao aided a heartless murderer, a man that he knew to be evil, because he judged you – wrongly – to be worse."

"…I do not regret my actions in Xu as much as I probably should," Cao Cao admitted. "I would do it again if I had the time and the moment again. My father was the centre of my world, Benchu, the person that shaped me: that villain Tao Qian had him killed for his money. Liu Bei, like Zhang Miao, feigns piousness and innocence while he befriends murderers and hankerers, and-!"

"Liu Bei will remain in his post until I can spare someone suitable," Yuan Shao insisted. "I need Shen Pei, Ju Shou, Xun Chen… and you need your men to defend your own borders from Yufuluo and perhaps, you suggest, the Yellow Turbans as well. Liu Bei must wait, Lü Bu must wait… one and all, they must *wait*."

Cao Cao nodded slowly and silently.

"…It is good to have you here," Yuan Shao said with a smile. "One day, when the chaos has ended and we have our rightful places in the imperial court… in whatever form that takes… we will be able to have banquets for our friends, and celebrate a new era of enduring peace; it may seem like an impossible dream, Mengde, but all it takes is one good turn, and Heaven will surely deliver us that boon any day now!"

"…After the locusts, I don't share your optimism," Cao Cao replied dryly. "But just this once, Benchu, I will pander to it, because… because Heaven knows, we have all of us suffered enough."

"That I can drink to," Yuan Shao said as he poured more wine into his dish. "No more politics, Mengde! From here on in, imagine better times and let us sing and share poems and anecdotes!"

"I need to… *escape*, just for a while, so… just this once, I shall," Cao Cao replied.

The banquet continued for several hours: when it finally ended, Cao Cao left Yuan Shao and journeyed to his appointed quarters with Dian Wei and a worried Xu Yòu as an escort.

"What concerns you, old friend...?" Cao Cao asked drunkenly.

"...Nothing," Xu Yòu lied.

"Suit yourself, Ziyuan!" Cao Cao chuckled as Dian Wei passed him and entered their quarters.

"...Alright, alright, I admit that your 'bodyguard' unnerves me," Xu Yòu said at last.

"That's why I did not have him in the carriage," Cao Cao replied. "But do you see how he reviews my quarters for safety now...?"

"Yes," Xu Yòu said. "But Mengde, he has the glare of a madman! Don't you fear him turning on you in some moment of delusion...?"

"Not at all, Ziyuan, because I treat him well, and his 'madness' is common bloodlust," Cao Cao replied. "Is *she* on her way...?"

"...*Yes*," Xu Yòu sighed.

"Do not judge me," Cao Cao growled.

"Would I dare...?" Xu Yòu chortled. "I just find it quite... unusual... for a governor, or indeed anybody except a travelling brothel-keeper, to have a live-in prostitute that goes with them on business journeys... or indeed *any journey*."

"That is because other men have not got my foresight," Cao Cao said calmly. "In years to come, maybe all men will follow my example."

"...What, and insist on travelling with a psychopath and a prostitute...?" Xu Yòu chuckled. "An amusing thought, but unlikely. Anyhow, Mengde, I must see to Ben- ...I-I mean Lord Yuan. Will you be staying long...?"

"I'm going back in the morning," Cao Cao said regretfully. "I came all the way here, so I hoped to stay longer, but our enemies have changed our plans."

"Yufuluo," Xu Yòu supposed.

"And, perhaps, the Yellow Turbans of Runan," Cao Cao replied. "Anyway, I...I'm a little drunk, a little tired... I need to retire."

Xu Yòu clasped his hands, bowed and said, "Goodnight then, Mengde."

Cao Cao clasped his hands together clumsily, returned the bow as best he could and said, "Indeed, Ziyuan... indeed."

Xu Yòu turned and walked away: Cao Cao hesitated before he entered his quarters.

"Wei Zi... Lü Boshe... Zhang... *Mengzhuo*," Cao Cao whispered; it was the first time in a long time that he had used the courtesy name of his friend Zhang Miao.

"Lord Cao."

Cao Cao turned to the door of his quarters as it opened fully: Cao's bodyguard, Dian Wei, towered over him and left him momentarily startled.

"I have checked: there is nothing to fear," Dian Wei continued.

"...Thank you, Dian Wei," Cao Cao replied as his composure returned. "I shall sleep safely, then... *if* I can sleep."

Dian Wei stepped aside so that his lord and master could enter his room: Cao Cao retreated into his quarters and quietly hoped that he would not be haunted by the past any further.

****

4

"A lot has certainly changed in ten years," the northern warlord Gongsun Zan muttered as he threw down a letter from the governor of Xu Province, Liu Bei, and flicked the long, baggy sleeve of his elaborate robe as a popular sign of contempt.
Gongsun's blue-robed adviser, Guan Jing, looked on silently.
"Ten years ago, that man was my friend, a man I'd grown up with and studied with under Lu Zhi," the swarthy Gongsun Zan said as he gestured toward the crumpled cloth letter. "Ten years ago, he and I fought side-by-side against the Yellow Turbans as brothers! That man and I swore eternal loyalty to state and friendship! Now look at what he does to me, Mister Guan. I risked my life for him so many times, gave him work when he was mistreated by the state, gave him money, trusted him like *kin*... and..."
Liu Bei – who was of the same Liu clan as the Han emperors, but was part of a disinherited and disgraced line – had received lesser rewards for his service against the Yellow Turbans than Gongsun had; his life prior to the rebellion had been spent as a sandal and mat weaver and scholarship student.
"...He argues that he had no choice," the adviser Guan Jing said.
"**Didn't he???**" Gongsun Zan barked. "**Of all men, why Yuan Shao???** Of all men, why the man that murdered my nephew and reneged on countless promises???"
Guan Jing hesitated; he knew that his master had not finished.

The history between Yuan Shao and Gongsun Zan had been far from simple. The two had not, as many might have expected, fought together against the Yellow Turbans, as Yuan Shao was in ritual mourning for his father at the time and saw no service; their first collaboration was then supposed to be against Dong Zhuo as officers of the Eastern Pass Coalition, but Gongsun's lord, Yòu Province Governor Liu Yu, resisted calls to join the coalition and instead focussed on continued quelling of the never-ending regional rebellions and tribal incursions from the northern side of the Great Wall, for which he received praise and rewards.

As tensions between Chancellor Dong Zhuo and Yuan Shao's Coalition intensified and a chance of some form of resolution appeared to be nearing, Yuan Shao insisted that the coalition should not accept Dong Zhuo's appointed Emperor, Xian, and turned to imperial relative Liu Yu as an alternative: Liu Yu publicly rebuked Yuan Shao and remained loyal to Emperor Xian, and he expected Gongsun Zan – the true champion of his suppressions and repulsions in Yòu Province – to do the same, though Gongsun 'rented' cavalry divisions to individual coalition leaders as a private venture regardless.

When neighbouring Ji Province's governor, Han Fu, reneged on his obligations to the unstable Eastern Pass Coalition and put the supply chain at risk of collapse, Yuan Shao approached Gongsun Zan independently with a proposal: if Gongsun Zan would move south with his legendary 'White Horse Cavalry' and attack Han Fu whilst citing border defence to Liu Yu, then Han Fu would be forced to invite Yuan to take and relieve Ji Province, and Gongsun would receive part of the province as part of the feigned peace negotiations. Gongsun Zan agreed, since that would have enabled him to have his own independent territory, but once Han Fu ceded Ji, Yuan Shao reneged on the deal and Gongsun Zan received nothing. Gongsun Zan swore revenge for what he saw as an affront, despite the entire enterprise being a treasonous territory annexation.

"Mister Guan, Tian Kai sent Bei to Xu Province with my blessing to *keep the place from Yuan Shao and his friends* – not *cede it to them*!" Gongsun Zan cried.
"The only other choice was Yuan Shu," Guan Jing replied.
"Yuan Shu is our *ally*!" Gongsun Zan whined. "He shouldn't be, and I'd rather he wasn't, but…! …Oh, this makes my head hurt!"
"…Your despair at the political complexity is understandable," Guan Jing replied unhelpfully.

Gongsun Zan's opportunity for 'revenge' against Yuan Shao had come when Yuan Shu decided to publicly challenge Shao for control of the Eastern Pass Coalition and the chieftainship of the Yuan clan, citing Yuan Shao's lineage and military record as reasons for his unworthiness. Gongsun sent his nephew Yue and some cavalry as aid to Yuan Shu's general Sun Jian in repelling Yuan Shao's reprisal attacks in Yu Province, but the battles cost Gongsun Yue his life, and Gongsun Zan held Yuan Shao, rather than the local commander Zhou Renming, personally responsible and added it to the list of affronts. In the meantime, Gongsun Zan was finally confronted by Liu Yu and responded by assassinating Liu and declaring himself the rightful governor of Yòu Province. Not being content with that, Gongsun had his subordinate, Tian Kai, lead an army southeast into Qing Province to try and seize that as well: Yuan Shao met Tian Kai's advance with his valiant eldest son Yuan Tan. Liu Bei was invited to join Tian Kai and received his first proper army of infantry and cavalry as a result: the commission had also introduced Bei to Zhao Yun, a junior officer that would one day be famous for his exploits as a senior general under Bei.

"Of all the things to happen, this was the thing I expected least of all!" Gongsun Zan continued. "Ten years ago, we fought the Yellow Turbans together, he and I, and only recently I made a leader of men out of him… and… and now we are enemies!"
"…*Enemies*…?" Guan Jing exclaimed.
"…I hope our paths never cross, but yes, we are," Gongsun Zan replied. "In this world of chaos, we are allies by our choice of enemies, and enemies by our choice of allies. Yuan Shu opposes his brother, so he and I are allies. By that same rule, if Yuan Shao is Xuande's lord now, then… then he and I are enemies."

Gongsun Zan was initially content to aid the Black Mountain Bandits that plagued the western regions of Yòu and Ji Provinces, but he eventually met Yuan Shao in a famous encounter at Ji Bridge: few foresaw Gongsun as being beatable, but Yuan's army humiliated Gongsun, decimated his famous White Horse Cavalry using stratagem, and sent Gongsun Zan home to Yòu Province as the loser. An imperial decree prevented Gongsun from making another incursion and forced him to return to aiding the Black Mountain Bandits and Yuan Shu from the shadows.

But the rest of the country was just as unstable as the northern frontier: the governor of the western-central province of Xu, Tao Qian, had granted passage to Yan Governor Cao Cao's father, Cao Song, despite the two technically being on opposite sides of the Yuan feud. Cao Cao lauded Tao for his magnanimity and sent his father word that it was safe to leave the troubled north and go home to Pei County: Cao Song did not survive the journey. His entire entourage was slaughtered and their not-inconsiderable cargo of money and treasures was seized by what Tao Qian insisted were bandits: Cao Cao did not believe his neighbour and declared all-out war on him. Cao Cao's army marched eastward into Xu and razed every settlement that they encountered: Tao Qian pleaded for assistance from Yuan Shu – who declined assistance – and the horrified Tian Kai, who despatched Liu Bei – a former vassal of Tao Qian's – to Xu Province immediately. Liu Bei arrived just as Cao Cao launched a second, even more violent attack on western Xu that had forced the civil administration to flee the capital: Bei's efforts were futile, and Cao Cao only retreated after his own best friend Zhang Miao and senior adviser Chen Gong rebelled and invited Lü Bu to help them seize Yan Province from their master's loyalists. The aging and ailing Tao Qian died shortly thereafter, and Liu Bei somehow – reports were vague as to the exact circumstances – inherited the province, rather than Tao's two adult sons.

"You say that Yuan Shu is an ally, but… I beg to differ," Guan Jing said nervously.
"Oh, I know," Gongsun Zan chortled. "I… I know who he is, what he is… but like I said, our allies are determined by our enemies."
"You would judge your friend so harshly…?" Guan Jing prompted.
"Xuande betrayed me, just as Yuan Shao betrayed me!" Gongsun Zan barked half-heartedly. "He… *he*…!"
"…And Yuan Shu has not…?" Guan Jing said pointedly.
"Yuan Shu and I were never as brothers as Xuande and I were!" Gongsun Zan retorted. "His is the worse offence! He… he…!"
"…But yet you still call him 'Xuande'," Guan Jing noted.

With Liu Bei holding Xu – which had a border with southern Qing – and Gongsun Zan holding Yòu and northern Qing, the next step might have been the two working together to annex Qing entirely and then turning to the weakened Yuan Shao, whose reputation had been damaged for his blatant territory annexations, his failure to defeat Dong Zhuo, his apparent acceptance of the regency government and the actions of his friend Cao Cao; but Yuan Shu – whose agenda was entirely his own – had decided to wrest Xu Province from whoever governed it. He had, initially, vied with Tao Qian for territory in the southeast, and made no changes to his plans when Cao Cao – the closest ally of his rival Yuan Shao – attacked Xu as well; when Liu Bei accepted the seal of office from Tao Qian's officials and took control of the province, Yuan Shu immediately demanded that Bei cede the province to him or face invasion. Liu Bei had an unrepentant and murderous Cao Cao on his western border, Yuan Shao's forces at his northwest border,

Yuan Tan looming to the north and Yuan Shu posturing to the south: Xu Province could not survive another attack by the first of those men, and the last of them would not guarantee any stability. Liu Bei had decided – against much public remonstrance from many of Xu's officials and his own preferred allegiances – to surrender to Yuan Shao on the condition that he forced Cao Cao to stay his hand. Yuan Shao had ignored Cao Cao's feelings and accepted the surrender; Yuan Shu vowed that he would soon invade Xu Province, but further massacres had been averted.

"It's quite simple!" Gongsun Zan cried. **"He aids my enemy!"**
"Surely this is not as simple as you make it sound," Guan Jing said. "Surely you know that, and surely the best course of action now is–"
Gongsun Zan exhaled noisily, buried his head in his hands and said, "Leave me be."
Guan Jing groaned miserably, bowed slightly, and said, "As you wish, Lord Gongsun."
Once Guan Jing was gone, Gongsun Zan groaned miserably. His feud with Yuan Shao was not over, and he had the next phase of that conflict to plan for; now he had to factor his closest friend into his list of potential enemies, and that hurt him greatly.

"...I wonder if my friend Gongsun Bogui will reply...?"
The Governor of Xu Province, Liu Bei, asked the question of a gathering of his miserable, hesitant allies in his new provincial capital Xiapi. He was knelt in the host's place of his private meeting room and overlooking his small entourage, who were sat in rows to Bei's left and right.

The closest on Bei's right – all of whom were the men that Bei had adventured with for a decade – was Jian Yong, a childhood friend that was known for his irreverent mischief, frankness and unwavering loyalty; next to Jian Yong was Guan Yu, a tall and intimidating fugitive-turned-officer with a lofty air and famously well-kept beard that had joined Bei to fight the Yellow Turbans; next to Guan Yu was Zhang Fei, a swarthy, wild-eyed, thick-whiskered and ill-mannered former pig butcher that had not only fought at Bei's side but financed Bei's first militia with his own savings.

The advisers – who sat to Bei's left – were sat in order of influence. The closest was the wealthy Mi Zhu, a former vassal of Bei's predecessor Tao Qian; Zhu's brother, Mi Fang, was sat at his side; after Fang was Mister Sun Qian, an older man that had also served Tao Qian; next was Chen Yuanfang, a learned scholar and elder statesman that had fled the court in Luoyang some time before Dong Zhuo destroyed the city and entered Liu Bei's service by pure circumstance; the last was Chen Yuanfang's son, Chen Qun, whose great wisdom and foresight made him more valuable to Liu Bei than his father.
"Reply...? ...And say *what*, Xuande...?" Jian Yong asked in response to Liu Bei's question. "Gongsun Zan won't like what you've done."
"I... I know that, Xianhe, I know that," Liu Bei conceded. "But it is as we have discussed it so many times, and... and what's done is done. My concern now is where we might go from here."
"And more importantly, who might come here," Chen Qun said.

"…Yuan Shu," Guan Yu muttered.

"…Lü Bu," Jian Yong said with concern.

"Or even a triumphant Yuan Shao, a 'disobedient' Cao Cao, a vengeful Gongsun Zan… we must be ready for a lot of possibilities," Chen Qun said. "We must be ready for anything."

"Would Gongsun really attack Xuande…?" Zhang Fei asked.

"…I truly believe that we must be prepared for anything," Chen Qun reiterated.

"…It's *stupid*!" Zhang Fei exclaimed. "How did we get ourselves in such a mess, mm…? We were fine in Qing Province, helping Tian Kai fight Yuan Tan for Gongsun Zan: how'd we end up back here in Xu, having to put up with men like that bloody Cao Bao, and-"

"**Yide!**" Liu Bei chortled.

"…You've turned my style name into a rebuke, Xuande," Zhang Fei complained. "I swear you only use it to tell me off."

"I use it to remind you that I only reprimand you for your own good!" Liu Bei retorted. "Will you please leave Chancellor Cao alone…?"

"…**He was rude to you! He's *always* rude!**" Zhang Fei snapped.

"He is concerned – and rightly so – about the state of things here in Xu," Chen Yuanfang suggested. "Tao Qian's sons are still aggrieved that they were passed over for the governorship, and-"

"What can they do against Cao Cao… or *Lü Bu*, for that matter?" Zhang Fei asked. "A pair of educated dandies… they're fit for nothing but-!"

"*Yide*," Liu Bei said through laughter.

"…Alright, alright," Zhang Fei grumbled. "I can see that Yunchang isn't going to back me up, so I'll shut up."

Guan Yu coughed deliberately and said, "I have already said that I am worried about Lü Bu, Yide, and I agree about the Tao brothers as well. I do not like Cao Bao either, but he is a pedant toady, and such types are like so many pieces of chaff in any court, hard to sift from the finer stuffs that are always so lacking."

"*Aiee*… was that aimed at us?" Mister Sun complained.

"No, no!" Liu Bei insisted. "Yunchang would never say such things to you!"

"…Forgive me, Lord Liu, but shouldn't we be talking about Lü Bu, who is either poised to enter Xu Province or has done so already…?" Mi Zhu proposed.

Zhang Fei pointed at Mi Zhu and said, "There, look! A man that sees what I'm trying to say! We don't want Bu here!"

"…Don't we…?" Chen Qun asked.

"**What nonsense are you spouting???**" Zhang Fei barked. "**He's evil and stupid! He killed his stepfather, Ding Yuan, and joined Dong Zhuo! He helped to kill hundreds of people in Luoyang for Dong Zhuo! He helped Dong Zhuo to kill the Son of Heaven and loot the tombs of His Majesty's ancestors!**"

Liu Bei groaned as a sign of his grief at the fate of his ancestors and relations.

"I never saw you as caring much for the emperor, Yide!" Jian Yong teased.

"**This is no time for clowning about, Jian Yong!**" Zhang Fei continued. "**I'm serious! We have enough trouble with idiots like Cao Cao and Yuan Shu without inviting that walking**

disaster to stay here!"

"He might be a useful *buffer* against Cao Cao," Chen Qun suggested.

"Or a bloody good *excuse* for Cao Cao to use to come back here and start killing helpless people again!" Zhang Fei retorted.

"…I never thought I'd say it, but Yide is making very good sense," Liu Bei said. "Mister Chen Qun, I appreciate that intrigue can sometimes involve compromising one's values and making odd choices, but have I not done that enough…? Many – doubtless including Gongsun Bogui – are cross with me for coming here to repel Cao Cao and then capitulating to his master; what would people say if I now allowed Lü Bu – Dong Zhuo's infamous attack dog – to come and live here…?"

"What will happen if we attempt to turn him away…?" Chen Yuanfang asked.

Even Zhang Fei was silent in response; Guan Yu, Mi Zhu, Mi Fang, Jian Yong and Chen Qun nodded slowly and purposefully.

"This is *Lü Bu* we're talking about," Chen Yuanfang continued. "The man is a rabid dog in the midst of a battle, and near-unstoppable in single combat: I was forced to attend quite a few banquets where his jousting was part of the entertainment, and not *once* did anyone best him fairly… not *once*. His men and his peers may not necessarily like him, but they admire his martial prowess and fear his athleticism and his strength. His only weaknesses are his insatiable greed, recklessness and susceptibility to flattery and beautiful women. I do not count his dishonesty and untrustworthiness as weaknesses because they are oftentimes more harmful to his enemies than to himself. Add to that his latest advantage – the assistance of not one, but *three* of Cao Cao's adviser-officials, and the cunning Chen Gong *alone* would be enough of a worry – and we must surely consider cordiality over aggression."

Liu Bei turned his gaze from Chen Yuanfang to Zhang Fei.

"…We could fight him, surely, all of us…?" Zhang Fei protested. "Me, Yunchang, Chen Dao, and Mi Zhu, Mi Fang, Sun Qian, the Chens, Jian Yong-"

"What am *I* doing, Yide…? …Pulling silly faces to scare him away?" Jian Yong asked irritably. "Elder Chen is right, sad to say: if we intimidate Bu, he'll turn nasty. That's bad enough: in the old days when he didn't have advisers, he could be tricked. But Chen Gong outwitted *Cao Cao* – the 'Crafty Villain' – and turned a lot of his allies – including lifelong friends – against him. Yeah, I know, a lot of them defected because of what he did here, but look how many were prepared to work with Lü Bu – *Lü Bu*, who helped to kill an emperor and loot the tombs, like you said!"

"…But Chen Gong might abandon Bu and join us," Mister Sun suggested.

"Unlikely," Chen Qun said. "We're powerless against Cao Cao's full forces, while Bu was able to stay in Yan for what, a *year*…? …If not for the locusts, he'd probably still be there, and maybe he'd have won. Think what Bu could do to us, then, if Chen Gong agreed to help him. We must be careful in dealing with such men… we must use them to our advantage, as a buffer against Cao Cao."

"Lü Bu personally aided in the slaughter of the Yuan clan," Guan

Yu noted. "His sanctioned presence might trigger military action against us by one or even *both* of the brothers, separately or even *coordinated*. We must be prepared for such things as well. Yuan Shao might *ask* Cao Cao to resume his attacks on us, or even-"

"***Ayah*! Why does Heaven hate me???**" Liu Bei cried. "Has my allotted time as a man of means expired...? Is this a sign that I must return to my mats and sandals...?"

Chen Qun scoffed discreetly in response to Liu Bei's outburst.

"...I would not take it so personally, Governor Liu," Chen Yuanfang said carefully. "I would take it as being Xu Province's burden to bear, rather than yours alone. Tao Qian no doubt wondered if it was a curse, as you do."

"...Yes, I am being selfish," Liu Bei conceded as he turned to face Chen Yuanfang; he clasped his hands together and bowed slightly before he added, "I must do what is right for the province... whatever that might be."

"And the choices are, sadly, poor, one and all, and each fraught with its own dangers," Chen Qun said. "The first is to oppose Lü Bu without requesting any help: that will doubtlessly lead to more desertions than those we've suffered from abandoning Gongsun Zan, our army's true master, and almost surely lead to our losing the province by surrender or death."

Liu Bei shook his head and said, "A route with next to no chance of victory is not at all sound. What is the second choice?"

"The second is to oppose Lü Bu after requesting the help of Yuan Shao," Chen Qun continued. "The first and most obvious risk is whether that aid will arrive before we are outed and routed. The second is what we would have to concede to gain the aid, and that might mean losing the province anyway if Yuan Shao decides that we are unfit to remain here. The third is what form the aid – if any – will take: a good officer is unlikely to be spared, so will one of Yuan's pampered younger sons come here, or one of his toady officials, or will he send *Cao Cao*...?"

"*Aiee*... forget that choice," Liu Bei insisted. "What is the third...?"

"The third is to renege on our agreement with Yuan Shao and form a new alliance with Yuan Shu that would allow us to reduce desertions and perhaps call upon Gongsun to send more men to support us here," Chen Qun continued. "That, of course, would be the ideal outcome, which is highly unlikely: it also allows Yuan Shu to demand that we cede the province to him, and that's if he doesn't just tell Bu that he can stay here and-"

"*Ayah*! Why bother with this list of ever-worsening 'choices'?" Liu Bei cried. "'Choice four' is to make peace with Yuan Shu *and* Bu and have Yuan Shao and Cao Cao immediately descend upon us, and lose the province to them or our 'allies'. I think we can guess the fifth and last one, but go ahead and tell us anyway."

"...We arrange a meeting with Lü Bu and Chen Gong and try to negotiate a defence pact," Chen Qun continued. "In exchange for supplying his might to strengthen our western and southern borders, we provide any supplies that he might need and do our best to placate Yuan Shao."

"Why would Yuan Shao agree to us helping Lü Bu?" Zhang Fei asked cuttingly.

"I think I understand," Liu Bei said. "We would tell Yuan Shao that in exchange for Cao Cao restricting his actions to empty threats, we will place Bu on our southern border to fight his treasonous brother, which 'tames a wild tiger and puts it to use'."

"Yuan Shao will quickly realise that the alternatives to accepting that are having a reinvigorated and hungry Lü Bu sitting on a border with Qing, Ji or Yan, or our losing the province to his brother or Bu while he pontificates and procrastinates as usual," Chen Qun proposed. "He might follow up his agreement with a request that we kill Bu at a later date, or let Cao Cao attack us, but… that will be then. Right now, we have to do what we can achieve right now."

"…And plan for other, better choices while we play this unfortunate game," Liu Bei said thoughtfully. "…Alright, we'll talk to Lü Bu."

Zhang Fei groaned miserably.

"Of course, we'll have to consult the wider court," Mi Zhu said.

"**Sod what Cao Bao thinks!**" Zhang Fei barked. "**If he's got a problem with it, then he should get off of his fat, pampered bottom, get a sword and go and-!**"

"**Yide!**" Liu Bei cried. "Please! There are others besides Cao Bao that must have their say! What of Chen Gui and Chen Deng, for example…? Their financial and moral support is as essential as that of the Mi clan!"

Mi Fang sighed audibly, which angered his elder brother Zhu and led to his eyeing Fang disappointedly.

"…The Chens are not here," Mi Fang whispered as Liu Bei and his friends continued to discuss the matter in their own way. "We both know why."

Mi Zhu relaxed his gaze and grunted apologetically: Mi Fang was right to note that Chen Gui and Chen Deng – who had once approved of inviting Liu Bei to Xu Province – had excused themselves from the meeting and were otherwise putting distance between themselves and their new governor in many ways. Liu Bei was seen by many as a disappointment at best, and that left Mi Zhu with the worry that some might be seeking an alternative ruler for Xu Province yet again.

****

5

"…Why consult us, Governor Liu, when you have obviously decided what to do already…?" the gaunt City Chancellor Cao Bao asked as soon as Liu Bei had finished putting his proposal to the divided Xiapi court.

"Shut your mouth, Cao Bao, or I'll shut it for you!" Zhang Fei screamed.

"Sit down, Yide!" Liu Bei ordered as Zhang Fei started to rise from his place.

"…*Aiee*. What is more frightening: Lü Bu – who yields to Chen Gong whenever wisdom or tact is needed – or that uncultured northern pig butcher and his master's inability to control him…?" the aging head of the Xiapi County Chen clan, Chen Gui, whispered to his son and heir Chen Deng.

"His master scares me more," the slim, weary Chen Deng replied quietly. "First we yield to Cao's master, and now we court a man that will surely draw Cao back here to finish what he started."

Chen Gui smiled and said, "I have a different view… but I must pick my moment."

Mi Zhu noted the private conversation between Chen Gui and his son with concern.

"…Do we have a resource allocation plan, Governor, if we now intend to start feeding Lü Bu's hordes in addition to our own long-suffering populace…?" Cao Bao asked as calmly as he could. "Surely our locust-ravaged fields and depleted stores have been factored into your decision-making…?"

"BASTARD!" Zhang Fei bellowed as he rose from his seat yet again. **"Do you think that we-!"**

"Yide!"

"No, Xuande, I will not sit down again, not while he-!"

"YIDE!"

Liu Bei was now on his feet, glaring wildly: the court silently awaited the outcome.

"…He acts as though we *want* to be friends with Lü Bu!" Zhang Fei protested. "He acts as though we *want* to give him all our food!"

Liu Bei gestured silently, and Zhang Fei returned to his seat amongst the rows of officers; Liu Bei then sat down, turned to Chancellor Cao Bao and said, "Forgive Yide, as you have had to do more times than I would like… but his passion is rooted in valid concern for the people."

Cao Bao clasped his hands together, bowed slightly and said, "The fault is also mine, Governor. I am aware that the exigencies of the day are more rooted in military matters, and that we are surrounded by enemies through no fault of yours. If Lü Bu must be placated, then so be it."

"…If I might be so bold, I have a viewpoint that we must all consider," Chen Gui said as he got to his feet.

Mi Zhu, Mi Fang and Mister Sun awaited the influential nobleman's words apprehensively.

"Lü Bu was a villain when he slew Ding Yuan and dealt repeated affronts against the Son of Heaven and his esteemed ancestors for Dong Zhuo, we all agree on that," Chen Gui continued. "But a man is born flawed, and it is by the acts by which he seeks to redeem himself that he must sometimes be judged."

Many of Tao Qian's loyalists hummed agreeably.

"Lü Bu aided Wang Yun's plot to destroy Dong Zhuo's regime," Chen Gui continued, "and although that plot ultimately failed to remove all of Dong's followers – some say because of Bu's arrogance – it was Bu that killed the tyrant Dong Zhuo, and for that we must thank him."

"Your words are valid," Liu Bei declared. "Please, Mister Chen, do go on."

"Thank you, Governor," Chen Gui said with little evident reverence in his tone. "I might say the same of Dong's adviser Jia Xu, who now keeps a tight leash on the regents' bloodlust and makes shrewd political decisions, but that is another conversation entirely. Bu fled Chang'an after that debacle, and after wandering aimlessly for a time, he aided Yuan Shao in an assault on the Black Mountain Bandits that severely weakened them and relieved many suffering people. Thirdly – and most importantly – he aided the benevolent Chen Gong's coup in Yan Province, an act that was carried out to spare us further harm."

Mi Zhu sensed additional intent in Chen Gui's charismatic oration and exhaled heavily.

"Like it or not, the actions of Lü Bu, Chen Gong and Zhang Miao are the sole reason that we were not ground into dust," Chen Gui said as he turned to face Mi Zhu. "They saved us… so the least we can do is repay that great debt we owe."

Most of the officials murmured agreement with Chen Gui's words.

"You do not need to convince *me*, Mister Chen," Mi Zhu retorted.

Chen Gui smiled and asked, "Then why did you sigh…?"

Liu Bei sensed the tension between the two influential clan chieftains and said, "I do not think that we need to discuss this further, gentlemen."

"I quite agree," Chancellor Cao Bao declared. "I shall personally inspect the stores and ensure that the rations are revised to account for the extra mouths. And now that we can view our visitors as friends, we should actually hope that there are many, many mouths."

Zhang Fei sneered at Cao Bao and flicked his sleeve; Liu Bei noted his actions and glared at him silently.

The warlord Lü Bu and his entourage neared the Yan-Xu border after several bouts of fighting with Cao Cao's forces: Lü Bu remained at the rear of his battered army so that he could preserve as many men as possible, but the toll of his failed invasion of Yan Province had been high.

"**They're pursuing again!**" Lü Bu's cousin Wei Xu said as he fled from an attack on a scouting party. "**It's-!**"

"**I don't care who it is, Wei Xu!**" the tall, athletic Lü Bu declared as he readied his heavy halberd. "**They're all chaff to me! Let them come!**"

"**We should have Chen Gong, Wang Kai or Xu Si here to give us advice,**" a tall, powerful officer suggested. "**It may be Li Dian again, or-**"

"**Shut up, Gao Shun!**" Lü Bu retorted. "**I need no advisers to scatter some rats!**"

Another intimidating cavalry officer pointed his spear and said,

"**They approach.**"
"**The let us smash them, Zhang Liao!**" Lü Bu replied.
The small Yan pursuit force comprised fifty infantrymen and twenty riders; two of the riders charged at Lü Bu simultaneously.
"**Worthless!**" Lü Bu heckled as he struck down one man, twirled his halberd as though it weighed nothing at all and swung it at the second, horrified horseman.
"**These men must have been too enthusiastic for their own good!**" Gao Shun said as he charged at the infantry and ploughed through them, killing four men in his single pass and wounding two others.
"**You throw your lives away!**" Zhang Liao taunted as he fought a short duel with an outmatched cavalry captain and cut him down with ease.
"**WHO DARES TO SEND SUCH WEAKLINGS TO CHALLENGE THE 'MAN AMONG MEN'?**" Lü Bu proclaimed as he cut down two more riders and charged at the remaining infantry. "**THAT MAN WILL DIE A THOUSAND TIMES FOR INSULTING ME!**"
Lü Bu's control of his large, reddish-brown Arabian horse was close to flawless; man and steed were as one as he moved this way and that, cutting down the men with such ease that one could be mistaken for thinking that they were not trying to attack or evade him at all. Zhang Liao, Gao Shun, Wei Xu and the rest of Lü Bu's rear guard were also impressive as they provided their reckless commander with support.
"**Back! Back to the camp!**" one Yan cavalry captain ordered; the decimated pursuit force retreated gladly.
"**Your men can go, but you'll stay here!**" Lü Bu cackled as he charged at the fleeing captain and felled him in a single swipe.
"*Aiee…* **I saw other forces in the distance!**" Wei Xu cried.
Gao Shun followed Lü Bu and shouted, "**You mustn't stray too far, my lord! Li Dian is not far behind these men and–**"
"**I need none of your prattling! We're going now!**" Lü Bu snapped as he ended his attack and turned to follow his army.
"…Yes, my lord," Gao Shun said as he followed Lü Bu once again.

"*…Aiee… aiee…!* …Bu knows no decency!" the Yan officer Li Dian complained as he surveyed the scene of Lü Bu's improvised massacre an hour later. "There are men cut down as they tried to retreat; these were good men!"
"What now, sir…?" a cavalry captain asked. "He's almost at the border!"
"…We report back to my brother and ensure that these men are given dignified burials," Li Dian replied. "After that… we chase him down until he is dead or, less ideally, in Xu Province. We can't be careless – these poor men prove that – but we can't give up either. Bu *has to be dealt with*."

Li Dian's pursuit would not lead to Lü Bu's capture or death: Bu's forces reached and crossed the border before any more battles could take place. Lü Bu's forces coalesced and started to set up a camp at some distance from the Yan-Xu border.
"So here we are… Xu Province," the former Yan Province official and exiled rebel Wang Kai said needlessly.
"We can only hope that we'll be well received," Wang Kai's

colleague and co-conspirator Xu Si said.

"I have lost so many men," Lü Bu complained. "Do you know that I lost Xue Lan *and* Li Feng in Chengshi?"

The adviser Chen Gong frowned irritably and said, "Yes."

"And Qiao Long…?" Lü Bu continued.

"Are you going to list them all one by one…?" Chen Gong scoffed. "I am your chief adviser, Lord Lü! I know who is alive and who is dead, and what we gained and what we lost! Do you not think that I am as annoyed as you are…? In fact, I am more annoyed than you could ever be: I instigated the entire sorry affair, so now I have a reputation as a betrayer of masters, regardless of the nobility of my motives! Cao Cao will hate me for my treachery, and he will not rest until I am dead, just like that poor naïve fool Zhang Miao!"

"I'm as dead as both of you for my part in this," Wang Kai suggested.

"As am I," Xu Si lamented. "Why did Heaven favour such a wicked man???"

"Why ask?" Chen Gong replied. "What's done is done, gentlemen."

"…So what can we achieve here in Xu Province?" Lü Bu prompted.

"Liu Bei is a hero of the age," Chen Gong retorted. "If you think that I am going to scheme against him after what just happened, then the answer is 'No'."

"So we're just going to hide here, then," Lü Bu grumbled.

"Let's meet Liu Bei, and see what happens," Chen Gong pleaded. "Perhaps he will give you his other 'holding', Yu Province, since he cannot govern both at the same time. Or perhaps he will send you north to Qing to bolster Kong Rong, or south to aid Liu Yao against Sun Ce. Let's see what happens."

"As long as I am not left idle, I shall be grateful," Lü Bu replied. "All that I fear is that I will be rebuked by the world and exist without purpose."

"That's highly unlikely," Chen Gong promised.

The imposing yet humble officer Gao Shun gestured that he would like to speak, but Lü Bu glared at him and said, "I can well do without any of your condescending criticism right now, Gao Shun! In fact, I'd rather you stayed silent!"

Gao Shun bowed silently.

"…I will meet Liu Bei," Lü Bu continued. "…And Bei should hope that he impresses me… he will not like what happens if I am not suitably impressed."

****

6

Liu Bei, Guan Yu and Mister Sun gathered a small force and travelled west to the settlement of Xiaopei, where Lü Bu had settled temporarily: they were met at the gates of the field camp by two of Lü Bu's subordinates.

"Welcome, Governor Liu," Chen Gong said with a humble bow. "I am Chen Gong, and this is General Zhang Liao."

"Your presence is appreciated, Governor Liu," Zhang Liao said as he bowed to each of the three main visitors in turn: Guan Yu bowed slightly in response and studied the tall, imposing Zhang Liao as though he were a strategic text.

"I have with me Mister Sun Qian and my 'right arm', Guan Yu," Liu Bei explained as he gestured toward his followers.

"*Guan Yu…* ah, yes, I have heard of Guan Yunchang," Chen Gong admitted. "Your face is not as red as I had heard, but your long beard is as magnificent."

Guan Yu bowed slightly and silently.

"Mister Chen," Mister Sun hailed. "You are one of the masterminds behind the rebellion against the villain Cao Cao, are you not…?"

"Sadly, yes," Chen Gong replied. "…I say 'sadly' because it failed, and many good men, like the benevolent Zhang Miao of Chenliu, are missing, most likely dead, and we achieved nothing."

"But it saved Xu Province," Liu Bei suggested. "For that, you have my eternal gratitude, Mister Chen Gong. Your noble actions were brave, and they will surely earn you praise for all time."

Chen Gong smiled sheepishly and said, "I am not entirely sure whether I should be praised so highly, because I do not know entirely what I was trying to achieve, Governor. Was I trying to save Xu Province…? …I suppose I was. Cao Cao had turned from man to monster, and he had to be stopped… whether we stopped him for Xu Province or for what we feared he would do in the future, I cannot say. But enough of this! Surely we should hurry to Lord Lü, so that he can thank you for your aid in this dark hour."

Liu Bei nodded silently, and Chen Gong led the visitors to Lü Bu's command tent; Guan Yu focussed his attentions on Zhang Liao, since any plot would doubtless involve a man of his obvious strength and stature. As Liu Bei and Mister Sun entered the command tent, Guan Yu turned to Zhang Liao and said, "Your master is renowned for his treachery… yet in your countenance I sense honour and pride. How is it that you serve such a man…?"

Zhang Liao smiled and replied, "He is my lord, Mister Guan."

"You should seek a better lord in the future," Guan Yu retorted.

"Xuande!" Lü Bu cried as he saw Liu Bei for the first time.

"…Lü Fengxian," Liu Bei replied uneasily: Lü Bu was physically intimidating, and travellers' stories suddenly came back to him.

"I sense a weakness in your voice, born of fear, but you need not fear!" Lü Bu chuckled. "I am your brother, Xuande, because of what you have done for me! You have allowed me to come here and live, even after all that I have done."

"What you heard was not weakness, but emotion," Liu Bei insisted. "I have long heard about Lü Bu, the noble vassal of Ding Yuan, who was so cruelly swayed from the light by Dong Zhuo's honeyed words… your redemption was achieved by slaying the tyrant, and you will be a legend for certain."

Lü Bu's smile was replaced by a solemn frown.

"I had heard of your great strength, your unmatched skill in all individual athletic exploits, and your heroism against the Black Mountain Bandits, both before and after the fall of Luoyang," Liu Bei continued. "We in Xu owe you much for your actions in Yan."

"I was a fool," Lü Bu sighed theatrically. "When I was washing the blood of Ding Yuan from my hands, I knew that I had made a mistake. But at the time, I did not know how to atone… instead, I made matters worse. When he destroyed villages, I aided him, because he convinced me that they were his enemies, and that they were being righteously punished."

"…Cao Cao said the same of Xu," Chen Gong volunteered.

"When the Eastern Pass Coalition formed against Dong Zhuo, I wanted to join it," Lü Bu continued. "Oh, how I wanted to turn against him, but I was surrounded on all sides by men that would have cut me down before I could act! Instead, I allowed him to manipulate me once again, and helped him to sack the capital, to loot the tombs of former emperors…"

Liu Bei's eyes filled with tears, and he said, "As they are my ancestors, I must weep openly and feel sadness… please, go on."

"…I have been a terrible villain," Lü Bu sighed. "But I have tried to atone since then, Xuande. When the opportunity arose to kill the tyrant, I did so without hesitation, for the good of the land."

Zhang Liao recalled the true reason for the assassination – Lü Bu's fear of punishment for craving one of Dong Zhuo's maids – and started to think about what sort of man his master was.

"I then left Chang'an when the wretches like Li Jue, Guo Si, Li Ru, Jia Xu and the fickle Hu Zhen besieged me," Lü Bu continued: he paused, wiped a false tear from his eye, and added, "I tried to save Director Wang Yun, my associate in the plan to stabilise the capital, but I could not."

"You did what you could," Liu Bei suggested.

"Yes, but it was not enough!" Lü Bu chuckled miserably. "I was forced to flee, abandoning my family; it is only recently that I have been reunited with them. I had with me the head of the tyrant, and I went to Yuan Shu, but he turned me away. I then went to my old friend and colleague Zhang Yang, but he was a prisoner of his own corrupt vassals, and he could not receive me. I then went to Yuan Shao, but he proved his reputation as a man that uses and discards as being quite true: he feigned having buried his hatred for me, had me help him to defeat the Black Mountain Bandits, and then he tried to kill me!"

"…I admit that I worry about having him as my lord," Liu Bei said.

"You should," Lü Bu warned. "I only barely escaped… but then I travelled south, where I met poor Zhang Miao, who, like me, was trapped serving a vicious master that he had mistaken for a hero. We became friends, Mengzhuo and I: when I think that his clan was probably slain for his so-called treachery, I feel responsible."

Chen Gong stifled laughter at such a blatant lie.

"We are all responsible, my lord," Wang Kai sighed.

"Ah, Mister Wang and Mister Xu," Liu Bei said as he looked at the defectors from Yan Province. "It is good that you also survived."

"Were it only that the Zhangs were as lucky!" Xu Si replied.

"…So terrible," Liu Bei sighed. He then turned to Lü Bu – who was visibly irritated at being interrupted in the middle of telling his tale of woe – and said, "Go on, please, Fengxian, and tell us what happened after first meeting Zhang Miao."

"I again went to Zhang Yang, but was forced to hide, because Li Jue and Guo Si, the wicked captors of the sovereign, still seek my head for my failed efforts to depose them and stabilise the nation," Lü Bu continued. "I was then offered the opportunity to aid Chen Gong, Wang Kai, Xu Si, Zhang Chao and poor, dear Mengzhuo in their fight against Cao… the rest, you know."

"…And I thought that *I* had been bounced from place to place, enduring ridiculous misfortune!" Liu Bei cried. "You, Fengxian, have been made to suffer! Perhaps your service under Dong Zhuo was inexcusable, but you have made up for it as well as any man could: for your efforts to save Xu from Cao, you have atoned as far as I am concerned, and your soul should be at peace."

Lü Bu bowed humbly and said, "You are too kind, Brother. Now please, come and meet my family!"

Liu Bei agreed; his bodyguard Chen Dao tried to follow, but Liu Bei dismissed him with a silent gesture before he followed Lü Bu.

"*Aiee*: should he always be so trusting?" Mister Sun whispered.

"Every man here will die by my hand if Lord Liu is harmed," Guan Yu replied audibly. "Why should we worry about treachery?"

Chen Gong looked at the fearless Guan Yu and said, "Lord Lü is sincere in his invitation, I promise you that."

Mister Sun suspected that Lü Bu intended to provoke an invitation to the capital, which would be more beneficial than a murder attempt on the border: he bowed humbly and replied, "I do not doubt that. I spoke generally, for Lord Liu is like this with everyone: he would allow *Cao Cao* a private audience without a bodyguard, I think, if Cao Cao were polite enough."

"Is that so…?" Chen Gong chuckled. "Xuande has a kind and honest heart, then, as I had heard. A deceitful man would never be so trusting of others."

"Quite," Mister Sun replied.

Lü Bu led Liu Bei to his personal tent, had him sit on the bed reserved for his wife, and said, "My lady, please show courtesy toward my brother Xuande."

Lü Bu's wife, Lady Yan, knelt before Liu Bei and said, "You are now my husband's brother, and hence my brother-in-law. You are welcome here as family. I shall now prepare tea for you."

"This is too much!" Liu Bei insisted as Lady Yan got to her feet and moved to a nearby kitchen area. "It is I that should be grateful!"

"You saved us from Cao Cao's wrath," Lü Bu retorted. "I cannot be grateful enough. Daughter! Come and greet your new uncle!"

Lü Bu's teenaged daughter, Lady Lü – who had been sat on the opposite side of the room – got up, neared Liu Bei, bowed penitently, and said, "Greetings, worthy uncle."

Liu Bei was close to tears once again: he bowed, got to his feet, and said, "You are being far too kind, far too kind! I am indebted to you, and it should therefore be me that extends such humility to you, Fengxian! We should go to Xiapi, where-"

"I could not ask for such an honour," Lü Bu insisted as he Lady Lü with a terse gesture. "Let us stay here in Xiaopei and use our worthless lives to buffer you against Cao Cao."

"Ayah! Ayah! You cannot expect me to abandon my region's

saviour to a violent death!" Liu Bei replied. "I will not hear of it! You say that you are my brother, Fengxian: should my brother not be in the capital…?"
Lü Bu hid a smile as he bowed and said, "If you must insist."

Liu Bei and Lü Bu returned to the command tent; Mister Sun guessed the new situation and groaned reflexively.
"Something affects you, Mister Sun?" Chen Gong prompted.
"Oh, uh… I have pains in my feet," Mister Sun lied. "It looks like we will all be travelling to Xiapi, Governor!"
"Indeed yes," Liu Bei revealed. "Fengxian and I are to protect this province together. Neither of the Yuan brothers is trustworthy, and Cao Cao is a constant threat: we'll need to be as solid as a stone wall to keep this poor province safe from the villains on all sides. We shall leave as soon as it is possible!"
"Not before I throw a banquet, Xuande!" Lü Bu insisted. "I must let the world see that you are my respected younger brother!"
Guan Yu grunted irritably at Lü Bu's reference to his lord as a 'younger brother', since that also implied that Liu Bei would be the subordinate in their relationship.
"I'll assist with the preparations, my lord," Chen Gong promised.
"We'll retire to the guest tents that you have kindly provided, Fengxian, rather than go into Xiaopei City," Liu Bei said. "Today… today, we have begun a great partnership of heroes! Now, the nation might one day know the peace that we both strive to see!"
Lü Bu, Chen Gong, Wang Kai and Xu Si bowed humbly, and the visitors retreated with their guide Zhang Liao. Minutes later, Gao Shun entered the tent and said, "My lord, I have carried out reconnaissance: be sure that Liu Bei has come to us sincerely."
"Don't you think I can see that???" Lü Bu retorted. "Get out!"
Gao Shun bowed, turned and left the tent.
"Gao Shun is a thinker, and should have stayed," Chen Gong said.
"He's arrogant and *rude*, and questions me *continuously* and *needlessly*," Lü Bu insisted. "We don't 'need' him; if I 'needed' him, and he was such a great 'thinker', then I wouldn't have needed all of *you*."
Chen Gong bowed slightly as a sign of deference; all of the advisers were aware that Lü Bu valued Gao Shun's loyalty, skill, efficiency and shrewdness yet envied and detested him for those same attributes at the same time. They were also aware that Lü Bu could have avoided many of the predicaments that he had found himself in if he had listened to Gao Shun, and so was Bu himself: they sensed that Bu was completely intolerant of Gao Shun this day and did not question the matter further.
"…Liu Bei's naïve beyond belief… that, or a different kind of thinker," Lü Bu continued. "Still, that doesn't matter: either way, we're now going to the capital."
"I already told you that I will not plot against Liu Bei," Chen Gong insisted. "All I wanted to do was get you – *us* – away from the Yan border. Before Liu Bei arrived, I received a messenger from Chenliu: Zhang Miao is definitely dead, and Cao Cao is only concerned with the famine now. Xiapi is in the east of the province, on the other side of the Si River, so Cao Cao cannot surprise us if we're there. If the capital had still been in the west, I'd have found us a way to go to Donghai."

"So what next…?" Xu Si wondered.

"We learn what we can," Chen Gong replied. "Yuan Shao, Yuan Shu and Cao Cao will learn of this and act accordingly; Liu Bei's own vassals will also have opinions, so we must be cautious. If Liu Bei is proven to be an incompetent governor, then we'll seize the place, as you obviously want to. If not… we wait and see."

"Lord Liu Xuande, you cannot genuinely trust Lü Bu," Guan Yu said once the group from Xiapi were settled in their guest tents.

"Of course not," Liu Bei sighed. "I am worldly enough to know a hankerer when I meet them. However, a man in a weak position must always wonder if a deception is in order when–"

"*Weak position*…?" Mister Sun scoffed. "His army is decimated and has no grain! You're a provincial governor twice over! You have strong men in your retinue that can match that rustic thug!"

"Ah, yes, but do I have a man like *Chen Gong* on my side?" Liu Bei retorted. "I have no proper advisers, gentlemen. I have no professional schemer that can anticipate the actions of men like Chen Gong. I have politicians like you and Chen Yuanfang; I have warriors, like Yunchang, and Yide; but where are my proper advisers? I must ingratiate myself with Bu and hope that Chen Gong has no plan like the one he used against Cao Cao… because if those two men intend to steal my province… there is very little that I can do about it."

"There is," Guan Yu said plainly. "You can order me to fight them. I'm not afraid of Lü Bu. Get Yide here, and put the Danyang Brigades and Chen Dao's unit on your front lines. Only Zhang Liao and Gao Shun concern me: the rest are scruffy bandits."

"A reckless plan!" Liu Bei cried. "Lü Bu is unmatched in single combat, and his men are every bit the equal of my Danyang men, who are more likely to defect to him than his to me! No… if I antagonise him, he will definitely defeat me and seize Xu… and I cannot inflict that on the people."

Guan Yu sighed sadly and replied, "I think that you are wrong, but… I concede. But I shall watch the man and his allies nonetheless, and act of my own free will if I see no choice."

Liu Bei endured the banquet despite Lü Bu repeatedly calling him 'Younger Brother' and treating him in a patronising manner once the alcohol removed his ability to feign good nature. Chen Gong, Wang Kai and Xu Si observed Liu Bei with disdain, since the timid countenance of the man did not reflect the power that Bei held as a provincial governor; Chen Gong's greatest disdain was reserved for Lü Bu, however, who undid all of his previous attempts at civility with his drunken behaviour.

The next day, everyone began preparations for the long journey east to the Xu Provincial capital, Xiapi: however, Lü Bu agreed to remain in Xiaopei with his followers when he saw the reactions of Liu Bei's vassals to his behaviour at the banquet. Chen Gong was quietly disappointed, but their being in Xu Province at all would suffice for what he had planned.

∗∗∗∗∗∗∗∗∗∗∗∗

7

Cao Cao returned to his court in Yan Province, which had temporarily relocated from the capital Juancheng – based to the east in Dong Prefecture – to Xuchang City in the west.

"I hope that we do not leave Lü Bu with an easy route to return by consolidating here," Cao Cao said as he looked at the mass of seated officials and officers. "I am sure that my cousin Hong will do a fine job of routing the troublemakers and building better relationships with the people, but that won't be enough if Bu-"

"Bu hasn't the men or the grain to attack us again, and I have left talented men to guard the key positions while your cousin plays 'mediator', as you should have expected of me," a towering, thin, sour-faced middle-aged adviser retorted as he got to his feet and glared at his lord with irritated eyes.

"Ah! How are you, Mister Cheng…?" Cao Cao teased.

"Well enough for a man of over fifty that has to keep gallivanting back and forth from one place to another, 'un-muddling the minds' of important men – that are important for no good reason – by explaining the obvious," Cheng Yu grumbled. "My main regret of living fifty years is the sheer number of idiots that I have been forced to meet and endure: had I died as a child, then I would only know my own village, and they were more than enough."

"So you are old today, then," Xun Wenruo chuckled.

"You were like a chicken with no head, Xun Yu, running around and panicking when Lü Bu came here at Chen Gong's treacherous invitation!" Cheng Yu heckled. "Who pacified – and, where possible, replaced – the fools that were appointed to manage important places like Fan County and Cangting Ford?"

Xun Wenruo was not offended; he smiled and said, "You were a calming voice in a great storm, Mister Cheng. How does the supply acquisition plan go…?"

Many officials balked reflexively, as Cheng Yu had a reputation – deserved or otherwise – for introducing human meat to the supply chain when food was scarce or, sometimes, when such meat was simply easier to obtain.

"We do not need to know that, Wenruo," Cao Cao pleaded. "If our eastern borders are guarded, then we can focus on Yufuluo."

"That mantra is rumoured as being heard in village to the east of Runan," another man said.

"…'Mantra', Gongda…?" Cao Cao prompted. "I hope that you do not mean the sixteen-word mantra of the Yellow Turbans."

Xun Wenruo's slightly older nephew, Xun Yòu – whose courtesy name was 'Gongda' – bowed slightly and said, "Sadly, my lord, I mean the very same. The locusts have evidently inflicted another infestation upon us."

"If the vast majority of people weren't as stupid as the livestock, this wouldn't keep happening," Cheng Yu complained. "They'll rise up, waste countless barrels of dye making those ridiculous yellow scarves, and then they'll smash and burn everything left that's of value around them, all as a protest, they'll say, against having nothing! They'll make their farming tools into weapons and leave the fields untilled, while complaining that they starve! They'll march against us, and-!"

"I… have done this before, Mister Cheng, many times, and if I must fight the Yellow Turbans again, then so be it," Cao Cao interrupted. "Perhaps I will end up with another legion, like the Qing Corps."

"Who routinely desert, assault and rob other soldiers, and switch sides in the middle of battles," Cheng Yu heckled. "You cannot make fine cuisine out of millet!"

"Then what do you suggest that I do with a hundred thousand men with nothing else to do…?" Cao Cao retorted. "…Never mind, I know that you're just being crotchety, and you were one of the advocates for organising them in the first place. We must focus on Yufuluo for now, and only worry about the Yellow Turbans if they bleed out of Runan. Wenruo, Gongda, and *wise old Mister Cheng*, I would appreciate your views… among others."

"Yufuluo is doing what he always does: sending men this way and that to harass this village and that village, with no real concentrated force to repel," Cheng Yu explained. "His Xiongnu followers are bolstered by bandits, most likely enterprising Black Mountain Bandits. The only way to defeat such things is the same old way; the 'normal, innocent people' are going to have to do their part in defending their own worthless hides instead of waiting for someone else to do it."

"And I can think of nobody better to rally them than you, Mister Cheng," Xun Gongda said dryly. "What a shame it is that you will be too busy and the responsibility will have to fall to others."

"My advice to those 'lucky' enough to have that burden would do well to learn from me," Cheng Yu retorted. "If needs be, feign an attack or two to 'inspire' them. Like all animals, they sometimes need a good kick to get going."

"*Aiee*… what a man you are, Mister Cheng Yu," Xun Wenruo said. "But you are right, at least in part: we'll need local help to repel Yufuluo, just as we did against the Yellow Turbans."

Cao Cao turned to face a young officer whose normally-fierce face was currently wearing a broad smile: he laughed and said, "You are enjoying the proceedings, Cousin Yuanrang."

"Old Cheng is always amusing, Cousin Mengde," the irrepressible Xiahou Dun replied. "Am I going on this campaign…?"

"*Ayah*! Why take such a careless man?" Cheng Yu protested. "He'll probably get himself caught by Yufuluo, just as he let himself be caught by Lü Bu!"

"I've learned my lesson, Old Cheng," Xiahou Dun retorted. "Anyhow, it'll be nice to get out of this area and go see Miaocai. Let me go along, Mengde!"

"I intended to take you, Yuanrang, though our chances of spending much time with Cousin Miaocai are slim," Cao Cao said. "My main concern is about who should go, and who should stay in case Yuan Shu attacks our southern border or Lü Bu does an about-turn…"

"Bu is good as gone to be Liu Bei's problem now," Cheng Yu insisted. "His army is broken; if he came back, he'd be food for the dogs and-"

"Or our troops!" Xiahou Dun joked.

Cheng Yu harrumphed irritably.

"*Please*, Yuanrang," Cao Cao sighed.

"… It would only be funny if it weren't likely *true*," Xun Gongda muttered.

"As I was saying before I was interrupted… he'd be finished, and his remaining forces would probably defect to us to survive, handing the likes of Chen Gong and Xu Si over to us in the process, and the traitors know that," Cheng Yu continued. "They'll want to stay in Xu Province or go to Yuan Shu in northern Yang. Yuan Shu would kill him, as Yuan Shao would or we would. Liu Bei, unless his wits were woven into one of his peasant mother's straw mats at some point, will know that the only solution to the 'Lü Bu problem' is to do what anyone else would do."

Cao Cao laughed and said, "Fine! Well, I suppose that Li Qian's sons are part of the force at the Xu border, in addition to my cousin Hong…"

"They are," Cheng Yu replied. "I believe that they might have personally eliminated the men that killed their father. Li Dian, the younger one, is a natural officer and one to watch, so I understand."

"Oh…?" Cao Cao exclaimed. "Well then, I shall look forward to him reaching his full potential! What of Yue Jin, Yu Jin, Han Hao, and-"

"Do you not see them among your officers here…?" Cheng Yu asked gruffly.

"…I do," Cao Cao replied wearily. "Mister Cheng, you are especially cantankerous today. Xue Ti, Man Chong, Liu Yan, Mao Jie and Zao Zhi are administrating Dong Prefecture, I sense…"

"I will remain here, and either Wenruo or his nephew Gongda can accompany you, since there's no need for both," Cheng Yu suggested. "You have no need to take two geniuses to deal with one fool. As for officers – as per your earlier, unfinished question that I interrupted with my 'cantankerousness' – I would say that you can take your pick… the more that you take, the faster you'll be back."

"Very good!" Cao Cao chuckled. "When can we be ready to leave…?"

"Gongda and I were already preparing the supplies and ordering the regiments before you got back from talking to your muddled friend in Ji Province," Cheng Yu replied. "Taking your own preparations and those of your chosen company into account, I'd say two days at the most, Lord Cao."

"Very good indeed!" Cao Cao declared. "I'll relish the opportunity to finally – and personally – put that troublesome barbarian to rest… permanently!"

"Liu Pi is behaving strangely, my lord."

The Ru County nobleman, Yuan Shu, glared at the whole of his Jiujiang court with lofty, disparaging eyes before he answered his adviser Han Yin by saying, "What exactly do you mean by 'strange'? He is a former Yellow Turban, is he not? Doesn't 'strange' best describe his rabble?"

"He's… he's recruiting around Runan, but he doesn't inform us of his whereabouts or intentions as he usually does," Han Yin explained. "There is a concern that the famine has driven his faction back to their old ways, and-"

"That's nonsense!" Yuan Shu scoffed. "We pay them well enough; why would he forfeit my patronage to don his headscarf and divide the peasants again?"

46

"Anger, frustration… desperation," Han Yin said. "We should monitor their movements carefully."

"…Alright," Yuan Shu grumbled. "But there is one thing that those fanatics said that I cannot disagree with: change is coming. I will be at the forefront of that change, gentlemen! I will soon be ready to make my announcement to the world!"

The officials were as nervous as they always were, but they were as silent as always.

"And I hear that Cao Cao has moved west," Yuan Shu prompted.

A second adviser said, "He has, Lord Yuan. Word is that the Yan rebellion is all but quelled now, so he is probably doing so to challenge Yufuluo's advance through his northwest counties."

"…That would make sense, Mister Yan Xiang," Yuan Shu replied thoughtfully. "But Cao's 'cousin' Xiahou Yuan – 'Miaocai' – is a stalwart guardian in those parts."

"The chaos left by the rebellion of his northwest administrators – such as Zhang Miao – has probably done little to help Xiahou maintain order," Han Yin suggested.

"…Lü Bu will flee to Xu Province or seek peace with me," Yuan Shu said. "Liu Bei continues to defy me, and Cao Cao has weakened his eastern defences…"

Han Yin shook his head and said, "I don't doubt that Cao Cao has left forces in the east of his province to deal with Lü Bu or anything else that may arise. He has a few good advisers to replace Chen Gong, like Cheng Yu and Xun Yu."

"…**Cao Cao will regret taking sides with my 'cousin', Yuan Shao!**" Yuan Shu cried as sudden anger overtook him. "**That bastard peasant-spawn should never have been made head of our clan! *I* am the rightful heir! I AM!**"

Yuan Shu's officials were used to his repetitive outbursts and remained silent.

"But why should we expect Cao Cao to see things clearly?" Yuan Shu scoffed. "Is he not the son of a man of no merit that was adopted by one of those corrupt eunuchs that ruined this country and made it as it is now…? People still blame me for the collapse of the Eastern Pass Coalition, but was my Sun Jian not the only man that confronted Dong Zhuo…? Was he not the only one of them all that cleared the armies from the surrounding lands, entered Luoyang, repelled Lü Bu, chased Dong Zhuo westward, put out the fires and resealed the tombs…?"

The officials murmured agreeably.

"What did Yuan Shao do, mm…?" Yuan Shu asked.

"*Aiee…! Every… single… day*, we have to listen to this," one junior official muttered involuntarily; those that heard him agreed silently and did not betray him.

"He procrastinated while a Son of Heaven met his end like a fatted pig! He lied, made shady deals, and sought to grow his territories!" Yuan Shu continued. "My only 'crime' was to challenge his record as chieftain and commander, and his response – to turn his hitherto-idle forces away from Dong Zhuo and against his own half-brother, for that is what he is in truth – only shows that my criticisms had touched a nerve, and is the true reason that the coalition achieved nothing!"

Some officials struggled to hide their pained expressions; Yuan Shu's 'challenge' was an infamous open letter that had spoken of

Yuan Shao in a highly derogatory and offensive manner and left Shao with no alternative but to respond aggressively in order to restore his shattered pride.

"And for all of my so-called 'failures', do I not have most of Yu Province, Jiujiang Prefecture, and soon Lujiang Prefecture as well, which then gives me all of northern Yang...?" Yuan Shu continued. "While he kills his best generals and chases his best officials away with false accusations of corruption, do I not make good use of good men and grow my forces...? Do I have mass-murderers as my best friends...?"

The officials gave their lord the agreeable murmurings that he wanted.

"...Forgive my interruption, Lord Yuan, but you refer to Lujiang, and there are new and encouraging reports from there," Han Yin said. "Sun Ce has repelled a number of the bandits that were supporting Lu Kang's spirited defence, and we might have success there sooner than expected."

"I'll believe it when I see it, Lord Yuan," a lofty, well-dressed official scoffed. "Our best forces have been chipping away at that old goat for what seems like an age: Sun Ce would have to be a prodigy equalling or bettering his father to deliver victory outside of a year."

"...Perhaps he *is* such a tiger, Mister Liu Xun," Yuan Shu murmured.

"...And in that case, would you give him Lujiang if he takes it for you, as you promised, Lord Yuan...?" Liu Xun asked pointedly.

"...I will decide that, Mister Liu, when or if the time comes that I must," Yuan Shu replied. "In fact... I think I now know who *should* receive Lujiang when it rightly falls into my hands..."

"And your reaction to Cao Cao's movements will be...?" Han Yin asked timidly.

"...Nothing, *yet*, as is obviously preferred," Yuan Shu replied. "We'll see how he fares against the bandits; no, my main focus should be the northeast... *Liu Bei*..."

****

8

Cao Cao's thousands-strong force marched to the region southeast of Chenliu Prefecture's capital and prepared to make their first strikes against the invaders.

"They currently attack the small village to the west of Kuang Town," Cao Cao noted. "They number in the hundreds… against such a tiny village… such cowardice deserves great humiliation, and besides, that place lost much when Li Jue's men attacked it, so it should not lose any more."

"This will be easier than Li Jue and Guo Si's attacks during the 'Dong Zhuo crisis', or Yuan Shu's invasion of Fengqiu," Xun Gongda suggested.

"The former was truly a challenge; the latter was, thankfully, a farce," Cao Cao retorted. "…It makes me think of that fine young man that I had in my employ as an adviser during that first incursion that you mention… what a shame that Mister Xi succumbed to illness, just as Heaven had found use for him."

"Heaven's design is often hard to fathom," Xun Gongda sighed.

"…Let's act quickly, before word gets back to their leaders," Cao Cao decided. "I need no stratagem to deal with the attacks on the villages! **Xiahou Dun, Yu Jin, Dian Wei, Yue Jin!**"

"*Dian Wei*…?" Xun Gongda exclaimed as the four officers rode forth and turned to face their lord and hear his orders.

"We need to scare them, Gongda," Cao Cao said. "Have you a better way to do so…?"

"…I am not Cheng Yu, so any true answer to that is beyond me," Xun Gongda replied dryly.

Cao Cao laughed and said, "Well met! Xiahou Dun, Yu Jin: you will attack from the east and west. Yue Jin: you will attack from the north. Dian Wei… you will charge from the south and *destroy* any bandit that you encounter. I expect you all to act as ferociously as you did in Xu Province, but the people of the village are to be saved, not slain… understood? I want the people to chant our names when this is done."

The four officers placed their right fists to their chests, shouted, **"AS YOU COMMAND!"** as one, and rode to their units to ready them for the attack.

"Cousin Mengde!"

Cao Cao smiled and turned to his young cousin Cao Xiu.

"Let me fight, Cousin Mengde!" Cao Xiu pleaded.

"…Once again, young Xiu, you are the excitable 'enduring horse'!" Cao Cao chuckled. "Never a dull moment for you since you were a flag-bearer for my battles with Dong Zhuo, mm…?"

"You never let me carry the flag into battle, Cousin," Cao Xiu complained. "I always ended up staying in the camp."

"You weren't ready for battle then," Cao Cao retorted. "Since then, you've become a fine major, so I gladly have you along for this campaign. As for letting you fight the bandits head on…"

"How else will I grow as a general?" Cao Xiu asked.

"…A fair point," Cao Cao sighed. "Very well: join Xiahou Dun."

"I shall not disappoint you!" Cao Xiu promised.

"Will you be taking part, Lord Cao?" Xun Gongda asked quietly.

"Not today," Cao Cao replied. "I am enjoying a rare day without a headache, and the smells of war are likely to change that if I am in close proximity to them."

Xun Gongda nodded silently.

The attack was, as Cao Cao ordered, ferocious: the screams of the villagers as they begged for mercy were quickly drowned out by the chanting soldiers as they set upon the bandits. Dian Wei was the first to enter the village, and his methods immediately had the bandits terrified: he slashed and swiped at the enemy with his halberd as he rode back and forth, laughing and screaming like a tribal warlord, and his soldiers seemed almost superfluous.

"Somebody get him!" one senior bandit cried. **"*QUICKLY!*"**

One bandit archer managed to knock Dian Wei from his horse, and for a moment, there was relief as the wounded horse bolted: but when the angry Dian Wei got to his feet, it was as though a wild tiger had appeared in his place. Men howled in agony as the unseated officer slashed, kicked, punched and even bit any man that neared him as he moved in random directions; Dian's soldiers were afraid to stray too close to their frenzied commander in case they became one of his victims.

"He's mad! He's truly mad!" one bandit wailed as he fled from Dian Wei with one hand over his face: blood was seeping from the gaps between his fingers, and a mangled piece of what was left of his nose hung down above his lip.

"Everyone rush at them!" the bandits' leader ordered.

"Bugger off! *You* attack him!" a subordinate retorted as he led his battered men away from Dian Wei's small force.

"Oh no! *More!*" a man screamed.

The bandits were afraid to turn their attention away from Dian Wei and his men, but Yu Jin's force had now arrived: they were chasing another group of bandits toward Dian Wei with the help of a small group of armed villagers.

"Don't come this way!" the bandit leader cried. **"There's-!"**

The leader suddenly fell silent; Dian Wei had lunged at him as he threw orders at his men and plunged his halberd blade into the top of the man's head.

"Run, lads, run! Run, or we're dead!" another bandit cried.

Dian Wei tore the halberd from the head of his latest victim and started toward the self-appointed replacement leader, screaming, **"YOU ALL DIE TODAY!"**

Yue Jin and Xiahou Dun arrived, but their participation was not required; the morale of the bandits was utterly broken, and most of them were dropping their weapons and fleeing.

"I'll pursue!" Xiahou Dun's subordinate, Han Hao, declared.

"I'll join you!" Cao Xiu said.

"You left none for me!" Xiahou Dun complained as he looked at the gore-laden Dian Wei, who started to laugh.

"Then I'll go with Cao Xiu and Han Hao!" Xiahou Dun decided. **"I want my share of enemy heads too!"**

"...I wonder if Lord Cao will count that mess as one head or two," the short, stocky Yue Jin said as he stared at the mangled corpse of the bandit leader.

Cao Cao and Xun Gongda rode into the town an hour later, after every last bandit had been repelled; the armed villagers cheered and waved their improvised weapons above their heads while the old and young alike tried to offer gifts of food.

"**We are here so that you might keep your food, people!**" Cao Cao bellowed. "**We will take no gifts!**"

"**Heaven bless you, Governor!**" one elderly woman cried.

"…I wonder if am now as popular as Zhang Miao was in these parts," Cao Cao murmured. "That… is all I ask."

"Pardon, Lord Cao…?" Xun Gongda prompted.

"…I… was asking a selfish question of the Heavens," Cao Cao replied. "What matters, Gongda, is that we have made our intentions clear. Now we shall see what our enemies will decide to do; if they have any sense, they'll go back to Bing Province with their rat's tails between their legs. If they stay, then I'll show no mercy… because these incursions have to end, once and for all."

"It won't take long for this to get back to Yufuluo," Xun Gongda chortled. "Such danger… will surely make him think again."

Word of Cao Cao's advance reached the ears of the rebel coalition leadership in northwest Yan, who immediately gathered on a wooded hill to the northwest of Fengqiu to discuss their strategy for meeting the threat: the two overall commanders were the Xiongnu warrior Yufuluo and 'Fixed Gaze', a senior member of the 'Black Mountain Bandits'.

The tall, fierce-faced Yufuluo was the chieftain of an exiled Southern Xiongnu tribe: he had been the Han's chosen 'Chanyu', or king, of all of the Southern Xiongnu peoples, but the other chieftains rejected him as a 'Han puppet', cast him and his followers out and appointed an alternative. Yufuluo requested military assistance from the Han government, but it had all occurred at a time of great upheaval: the 'Ten'-led court disintegrated and its replacement – the regime led by Dong Zhuo – was not about to assist Yufuluo when it had problems of its own. Yufuluo briefly joined Yuan Shao's Eastern Pass Coalition, but he quickly tired of the inaction, imprisoned his assigned collaborator Zhang Yang and tried to seize Bing Province for himself. Yufuluo established a base in Ping County in the south of the province, but he had his own Southern Xiongnu peoples to contend with and could not extend further north. Collaborations with the Black Mountain Bandits and attacks on the Han loyalists followed, but Yufuluo dreamed of being accepted by his people as a whole, especially when the man chosen to replace him died and his successor was named as none other than Yufuluo's brother, Huchuquan, with whom he was on good terms. Yufuluo's eldest son, Liu Bao, was a minor chieftain in his own right and was active in Liang Province and the region north of Chang'an: his Chinese name indicated his blood connection to the ruling Han Dynasty by marriage, but he showed no interest in anything but pillaging and expanding his harem.

The uncouth, scruffy 'Fixed Gaze' was a founder member of the criminal coalition of smaller bandit gangs that operated in the northern Bing, Ji and Yòu Provinces. A fateful alliance between 'Oxhorn' Zhang and 'Flying Swallow' Chu Yan and the subsequent disastrous raid on a well-defended village left the latter with control of both men's followers and a decision to make, and Chu Yan chose to adopt not only the followers of his popular rival, but his family name: 'Flying Swallow' Zhang Yan, as he was known thereafter, invited the rival gangs to consider an alliance against the weakened Han government for maximum benefit, and the 'Black Mountain Bandits' – named for their main base – were born. The coalition numbered in the hundreds of thousands at its strongest times, and none but the most powerful warlords – such as Yuan Shao of Ji, Cao Cao of Yan and Gongsun Zan of Yòu – could effectively counter their activities: but Gongsun Zan had decided to work with rather than against the bandits, and he often gave them support in their attacks on his enemy Yuan Shao.

The combined might of Yufuluo's thousand-strong tribal following and the multitudes of bandits allowed for attacks beyond either group's normal scope: Yan Province had been a repeated target since Yuan Shu – who did not care how Yuan Shao's ally, Cao Cao, was ejected from that place – was supplying assistance and had briefly fought Cao simultaneously in the Fengqiu region of Yan before being ignominiously expelled. This time, however, there would be no Yuan Shu to help the rebels, and Gongsun Zan was too far away to lend aid, so Cao Cao's aggressive reaction to the latest incursions was worrying.

"To run is to be like the cowardly deer, fleeing from a harmless dog that barked," Yufuluo suggested.

"...We've run away before," Fixed Gaze countered. "And what I'm hearing about doesn't scream 'harmless', my friend."

"Yes, we ran before, and then the dog Cao Cao turned back to his home, because he has no teeth behind his bark!" Yufuluo insisted. "So his men killed some of your men; that is what happens in war! If we run, we waste time! If we stay, we will win!"

"This isn't Zhang Miao we're dealing with now!" a lesser bandit leader suggested angrily. "He was a soft touch that much less hit us as tapped us on the wrist; Xiahou Yuan is tough, yeah, but he's understaffed and don't do much; this is Cao Cao, the provincial governor, and word is that he has some nutter called 'Dian Wei' working for him that-!"

"*Dian Wei*...?" another bandit exclaimed. "Did you say 'Dian Wei', Brother Big Eyes...?"

"I did," 'Big Eyes' replied. "You heard of him too, Thin Wang?"

"...Someone local told me about a 'Dian Wei'... that he was paid to kill someone once, and instead of just killing that one man he went in the house and killed *everything*; men, women, children, animals, everything!" 'Thin Wang' explained. "They said the people that found 'em couldn't tell who was who and what was what, 'cause he didn't leave enough of 'em to be sure!"

The other bandits chattered nervously.

"They call him 'The Coming Evil' in that village!" Thin Wang continued. "The people that pursued him to kill him, he tore them apart with his bare hands and just walked away! He-!"

"I heard a very different version o' that story, a version told by someone other than friends o' the man that he killed," Fixed Gaze said irritably. "And even if that was true, he's one man! *One man*! We're going to get ourselves in a knot over one man...?"

"But you want to run!" Big Eyes shouted. **"It's 'Nobody's Chanyu' there that wants to stay and pick a fight, isn't it?"**

Yufuluo growled and raised his sword; Fixed Gaze gestured that the Xiongnu chieftain should calm down and turned to his bandit ally, replying, "I'm saying that we may have to consider running, yeah. But only if we really have to; if we're seen to run from a bogeyman like 'Dian Wei', we'll look stupid, especially if Cao's not so dangerous besides that. His men surprised ours, and I have to factor that into it: in a fair fight – or better yet, one where *we* get the drop on *them* – we'll-"

"CAO CAO'S COMING!"

Every man turned and either gasped or groaned as a scout staggered into the meeting area, fell to the ground and struggled to find the strength to follow his warning with some information.

"...**Enough talk!**" Yufuluo bellowed. "**I go to meet him! Any real men here can join me; the rest can scurry back to Bing!**"

The Xiongnu contingent left the meeting and started down the hill; a few bandits followed, but most waited for Fixed Gaze to tell them what to do.

"...We can't stay here on a wooded hill, can we, in case he uses fire," Fixed Gaze murmured.

The bandits looked at each other disconcertedly.

"...**C'mon lads; let's be real men and see if we can't chase Cao back to Dong Prefecture!**" Fixed Gaze said with feigned determination. "**Damned if want to run again away: we'd only be running away to come back, anyhow!**"

The Black Mountain Bandits hollered and chanted as they took up their weapons and started down the hill after their Xiongnu allies.

"Ah, so they decided to meet us," Cao Cao chuckled as Yufuluo and Fixed Gaze led their forces toward the patch of ground that Cao Cao had carefully chosen to be intercepted on.

"Orders...?" Xun Gongda prompted.

"Your topography notes were most helpful," Cao Cao replied. "I know exactly what to do, and I think you do as well... so why don't you give the orders...?"

Xun Gongda smiled, nodded, and turned to the eager officers Dian Wei, Xiahou Dun and Yu Jin.

"Dian Wei... you'll remain here, by Lord Cao Cao, because Yufuluo will certainly try and charge at us," Xun Gongda began. "If his charge falters or he fails to charge, then you, Yu Jin, will lead a force forward, feign weakness and allow the repelling force to drive you toward the hills to the southwest."

"And I should retreat through the valley...?" Yu Jin guessed.

"Quite right, for I have someone ready there... Yue Jin, who has a contingent of archers, cavalry and infantry waiting on the high ground," Xun Gongda continued. "Xiahou Dun, you will have your men make repeated strikes toward their left flank, while Yu Jin will attack the right until the proper moment is upon us. If Yufuluo charges through the centre, then we counter and chase them into the trap; if he holds on his front line, then Yu Jin's actions will divide his forces and we'll charge whoever doesn't follow Yu Jin. It isn't a classic stratagem, but it works well for these sorts."

"We accord completely," Cao Cao said. "Follow Gongda's orders, gentlemen, and we will certainly win today."

The Xiongnu-Bandit coalition leaders finished arraying their forces in their usual disorderly fashion and urged chanting and heckling that drowned out the counter-chants of the Yan forces; Xun Gongda smiled and raised a small wooden fan that would now serve as a signalling device. Xiahou Dun and Yu Jin led their forces forward and struck at the lines of Xiongnu warriors; the response was savage, and both officers were genuinely forced to retreat before they lost too many of their infantry.

"**A poor start,**" Cao Cao shouted over the din.

"**Yufuluo will now attack, for certain,**" Xun Gongda replied.

"**You should stay put until we know if they have a plan, Chanyu!**" Fixed Gaze pleaded, but Yufuluo was too determined to bring an end to the battle to listen to him.

"**Wild Fox! Young Wolf! We will charge!**" Yufuluo ordered, and the two lesser Xiongnu leaders responded eagerly. "**A shame that my son is not here: he would take many enemy heads as trophies today – maybe he may have taken Cao's head!**"

"*Aiee…* **charge if you must, but be careful!**" Fixed Gaze said.

Yufuluo scoffed and started his charge; Dian Wei rode forward with his horsemen and blocked the path to his lord as soon as the charge was confirmed. Yufuluo gasped as Dian Wei met every strike that Young Wolf made and unseated the talented Xiongnu warrior with a violent shove; Wild Fox advanced and tried to push Dian Wei back so that he might rescue his ally, but Dian's horse trampled Young Wolf as Dian himself lunged at the Xiongnu warriors and felled two more with ease. Wild Fox sensed that he would die pointlessly and started to retreat; Yufuluo also abandoned the effort and returned to his line with less than half of his horsemen and two thirds of his infantry.

"**I will go back to Lord Cao!**" Dian Wei said. "**Others may follow them!**"

Cao Xiu led a small cavalry unit after Yufuluo's retreat.

"**Well done, Dian Wei!**" Cao Cao said as his grinning bodyguard returned with bloodied halberd in hand. "**I wish that I could let you pursue!**"

"**Your safety comes first, Lord Cao Cao,**" Dian Wei replied.

"**Where is Fixed Gaze???**" Yufuluo barked upon his return to the coalition front lines.

"**Fixed Gaze and Thin Wang went after an officer that tried to pincer you: they went west!**" Big Eyes replied.

"…**We must fight on!**" Yufuluo decided. "**I cannot lose here!**"

Wild Fox nodded angrily and said, "**I want blood for blood!**"

"**We shall have it!**" Yufuluo replied. "**Next time we all charge!**"

"**Wait 'til Fixed Gaze comes back!**" a bandit insisted.

The bandit Fixed Gaze was pursuing Yu Jin into the hills, as Cao Cao and Xun Gongda had planned: his forces were caught off-guard by the ambush team that waited there, and he was forced to retreat. Yu Jin and Yue Jin met in the valley and laughed at the small victory; Fized Gaze had lost a dozen horsemen, his ally Thin Wang, and almost forty of his trusted and valued men.

"We'll chase him and finish him off!" Yue Jin suggested.

"You may lead!" Yu Jin replied. "Zhu Ling and I will support you!"

Yu Jin's aide Zhu Ling smiled and said, "Victory is assured!"

"…**We're done!**" Fixed Gaze cried as he stopped his wounded horse next to the irritated Yufuluo. "**I lost a lot o' friends just now! We have to-**"

"**Coward!**" Yufuluo screamed. "**If I had not waited for you, Cao would be ground bones! I will charge without you!**"

Fixed Gaze tried to protest, but it was in vain; Yufuluo charged, but the combined force of Cao Cao, Dian Wei and Xiahou Dun at the front, Yu Jin to the left and Yue Jin to the rear left the rebel coalition with no choice but to retreat and find a place to regroup.

"*AIEE*! **Is this Dian Wei???**" Fized Gaze cried as Xiahou Dun rode alongside him and swung his sword back and forth.

"**No, but you're still dead!**" Xiahou Dun cackled maniacally; it was only due to the intervention of a Xiongnu warrior that Fixed Gaze was able to get away unscathed.

"**Their leader is getting away, Yuanrang!**" Cao Xiu said.

Xiahou Dun ascertained Cao Xiu's intent from his gestures and signalled to his men that they should pursue Fixed Gaze at once; he finally got the better of the Xiongnu horseman and charged after the leader of the Black Mountain Bandits.

"**I'm going to die here because of an old nag!**" Fixed Gaze lamented. "**Come on, you stupid horse!**"

Cao Xiu reached Fixed Gaze and tried to strike at him with his sword, but some fearless Xiongnu riders blocked his path.

"**I'm outmatched!**" Cao Xiu realised; he turned his horse and retreated to join Xiahou Dun, and the veteran riders pursued him.

"**Together!**" Xiahou Dun suggested. "**Everyone fight together!**"

One rider in Cao Xiu's unit sensed that there would soon be needless deaths, so he detached from the group and hurried toward Xun Gongda.

"**Barbarian scum!**" Xiahou Dun screamed. "**Today you all die!**"

"**I'm with you, Yuanrang!**" Cao Xiu promised.

Many minutes later, Xun Gongda ran to Cao Cao's side and shouted, "**Some are straying from the plan.**"

"**No one must pursue!**" Cao Cao ordered. "**Dian Wei, you will make it known! No one follows: let them flee!**"

"**DO NOT PURSUE!**" Dian Wei bellowed as he rode around the battlefield and slashed at any stragglers that had failed to retreat with the main force. "**LORD CAO CAO ORDERS IT!**"

Every man that heard Dian Wei felt a chill run down their spine.

"**I will not run next time, Cao, you cheating coward!**" Yufuluo heckled as he fled the battlefield. "**Next time, you die!**"

Cao Cao could not have heard the words, but he knew what Yufuluo was most likely thinking and smiled as he watched his enemies retreat.

"…Why must we let them go again…?" Xiahou Dun grumbled as he ended his pursuit and started toward his lord and cousin.

"**We've minimised our own casualties,**" Xun Gongda reported to his lord. "**Theirs are- …I can barely hear myself think over our men's chanting and hollering, let alone report, Lord Cao!**"

"**I am not blind, Gongda,**" Cao Cao replied. "**They were smashed: next time, they will be crushed!**"

Cao Cao's men – and local men more than any other – chanted his name and revelled in their triumph. Once again, Cao Cao noted that many of those local men had once served his former friend Zhang Miao, and some might have opposed his rule only a short time ago; their reverence made the victory all the sweeter.

****

9

In the northwest of the country, the level of chaos was at a surprising low. A decade earlier, the administrative corruption had driven the local people – Han Chinese and other ethnic groups, such as the Qiang and the Di – to rise up in rebellion that became increasingly organised. Many Han officials joined that rebellion by choice or by force, and two – the former major Ma Teng and the former Attendant Official Han Sui – had even forsaken their Chinese roots, married Qiang women and later rose to the rank of chieftains of rival tribes. The northwest province of Liang was considered by some to be a lost cause as the rebels captured settlement after settlement and gained recruits from across the social spectrum: the Han court could not allow the loss of the region, primarily because it would place the former Han capital, Chang'an – then a thriving trade city and symbol of authority and stability – at risk of being seized.

Many were sent from the current Han capital Luoyang to deal with that rebellion – most notably Sun Jian, a hero of past and later campaigns, and Tao Qian, Liu Bei's predecessor as Governor of Xu Province – but none were truly successful. Two men came close to victory after four years of intermittent campaigning: one was a decorated commander of the loyalist coalition that defeated the first Yellow Turban uprising, Huangfu Song, and the other was the local warlord Dong Zhuo. They were recalled when Emperor Ling died suddenly and left the nation with yet another source of chaos, this time a dynastic crisis as the supporters of the heir, Liu Bian, and his younger half-brother, Liu Xie, fought with pen and dagger. The rebels took advantage of the opportunity to create independent states for themselves, and Dong Zhuo – who was supposed to remain in the Liang region to quell them – courted them instead and grew his own base in southern Mei County. Dong Zhuo was invited to the capital by Commander-in-Chief Hè Jin and his aide Yuan Shao, their intent being to use Dong Zhuo's fearsome reputation as a subjugator of rebels and barbarians to intimidate the Empress Dowager – Hè Jin's own sister – into signing an arrest – and, technically, death – warrant for the 'Ten Attendants'; but by the time that Dong Zhuo had arrived, the 'Ten' had killed Hè Jin and abducted the young emperor and his brother, and Yuan Shao had led a force into the palace to chase down and kill the 'Ten'. Dong Zhuo's found Emperor Shao and Prince Liu Xie before better men could, and that gave him the first platform that he needed to become Chancellor of State and a near-unstoppable tyrant.

Dong Zhuo had now been dead for three years after ruling for two: now the capital Luoyang was in ruins and its Emperor Shao dead, the result of Dong Zhuo's plans to rule from Chang'an – due to its closeness to his Liang Province allies – with Liu Xie as Emperor Xian. In the aftermath of Lü Bu's assassination of his former stepfather, Dong's subordinates had formed two camps: one – those that Director of the Imperial Secretariat Wang Yun deemed 'unforgivable' – coalesced to plot yet another coup, while the others joined Lü Bu in restoring order in Chang'an. But Wang

Yun's successful coercion of Lü Bu to murder Dong Zhuo had only given him the briefest of victories: Dong's senior advisers, Jia Xu and Li Ru, outwitted Lü Bu, regained the support of Dong's ally Hu Zhen, and retook Chang'an. Wang Yun committed suicide for the sake of his clan; Lü Bu fled the capital with his followers; and Li Jue and Guo Si – now the most powerful of Dong Zhuo's former vassals – seized power as joint regents with Jia Xu and Li Ru as their guides.

The teenaged Emperor Xian tried to impose his will on his new regents, but they were as irreverent as Dong Zhuo: it was only the intervention of other former vassals, like Jia Xu, Li Ru, Hu Zhen and Zhang Ji, that prevented another regicide. But there would be one more drama before the current – relative – calm: Liu Yan – the Governor of Yi Province in the far west of Han China, and a relative of the Han Emperor – made a pact with the Qiang warlords Ma Teng and Han Sui and launched an attack on Chang'an, though whether his intent was to rescue or supplant the emperor was not clear. The attack cost Liu Yan his three eldest sons and shortened his life, while Ma Teng and Han Sui escaped relatively unscathed; Regent Li Jue used the campaign to promote his nephew Li Li, and some of his more powerful allies – including General Hu Zhen – met sudden and suspicious ends. The regents were, at the end of the campaign, more powerful than ever, having humiliated Liu Yan and earned the begrudging respect of their Qiang neighbours. Incursions and rebellions all but ceased in the south of Liang, and with Jia Xu as a guiding force – Li Ru having 'retired' after a public rebuke from Emperor Xian over his part in the deaths of Empress Dowager Hè and Emperor Shao – the regents seemed to be a somewhat acceptable medium between the weak, corrupt Han government of recent times and Dong Zhuo's violent dictatorship. For some, however, a return to the norms of Han Dynasty rule was the only acceptable future.

"Everyone be seated and be silent! The Emperor approaches!" Regent Guo Si's words solicited a lot of involuntary grumblings as the large collection of Han officials – each one dressed identically in brown robes and black headdresses – knelt in their places and faced the empty imperial throne. Li Jue and Guo Si were dressed in patterned robes and had more elaborate headdresses than the other officials, while their shared adviser, the prematurely-aged Jia Xu, opted to dress in the uniform brown. No man wore shoes on their socked feet, as was the protocol; none but the grey-robed eunuch guards that lined the walls carried weapons, and that included the small collection of Liang warlords that held all of the most powerful positions in the land. Li Ju and Guo Si sat to the left of the imperial seat, although Li Jue seemed reluctant to move too far from it, as though it called to him somehow.
"Here he comes," Li Jue murmured as the first of Emperor Xian's blue-robed eunuch attendants shuffled into the hall through a side door; five years before, a similar band of eunuchs – the famous 'Ten' – would have been met by discreetly-flicked sleeves and mumbles of defiance at their near-absolute power, but their replacements were the timid, humble 'creatures' that they were supposed to be.

The Emperor's entry to the hall caused every loyal man

to press his head to the floor in reverence: the near-universal kowtow was silent, so the shuffling sounds made by Emperor Xian and his attendants could still be heard as they took their places. The 16-year-old sovereign was dressed in red robes adorned with dragons and streaks of gold: he wore a black, T-shaped mortarboard hat atop his head that had beads secured at the longest ends to partially obscure his face. The Regents' adviser, Jia Xu, had remained standing until the last possible moment: he fell to his knees, kowtowed, and whispered, "Your Majesty."

Emperor Xian stifled a sigh; he was now used to shows of empty reverence from Li Jue, Guo Si and the other Liang warlords, and he did not consider Jia Xu – one of their and Dong Zhuo's most trusted schemers – to be any more sincere. Once the Emperor was seated and his fawning eunuchs were huddled together near the side door, Li Jue nodded to Jia Xu purposefully.

"...We shall begin if it pleases Your Majesty," Jia Xu said.

"It pleases us that we should begin," Emperor Xian replied dryly.

"...There isn't much to talk about today, is there," Guo Si said. "In fact, we should be done before-"

"We actually have quite a few things to discuss," Li Jue said.

"Like what?" Guo Si asked. "You've been planning without me...?"

"*Aiee*... even now, they are like children," the latest Director of the Imperial Secretariat, Shisun Rui, muttered as the officials endured another bout of verbal combat between the two regents.

"Hush," another man – Minister Yang Biao – pleaded quietly.

Shisun Rui closed his eyes and tried to control his anger.

"...And that was all that we discussed without you," Li Jue said to an irritated Guo Si. "You were busy organising the northern defences, so why bother you...?"

"...Alright," Guo Si muttered. "I guess I should have realised that."

"And speaking of those defences, Regent Li and Regent Guo, I take it that we can enjoy some respite from the Qiang *and* the Xiongnu now...?" Minister Yang Biao asked.

"We can indeed, Minister Yang," Li Jue replied. "Ma Teng and Han Sui are not going to attack us again any time soon; Song Jian seems content to sit in his little 'kingdom' and do nothing, which we'll let him do until we're ready to deal with him; the other Qiang tribes aren't going to do anything unless any of those three do anything; and as for the Xiongnu, they seem to have withdrawn to Bing Province now that the chaos around Chang'an has subsided. They were just exploiting an opportunity, as all barbarians do."

Shisun Rui scowled at the hypocritical statement.

"All in all, everything's going pretty well!" Guo Si chuckled.

Many officials stifled groans.

"And what of the nationwide famine, the Black Mountain Bandits, the White Wave Bandits, the general rebel activity, the feud between the Yuans of Ru County, and the whereabouts of the traitor, Lü Bu...?" Emperor Xian asked calmly.

Li Jue bowed reluctantly and said, "Your Majesty, Lü Bu was last reported as attacking Yan Province. There are conflicting reports as to whether he is still in Yan or he has gone elsewhere, but we will keep the court informed."

"And we're doing everything that we can about the famine, Your Majesty," Jia Xu promised. "The bandits and feuding warlords in the east do, admittedly, make it difficult to reach some areas, but

we're doing everything possible."
Emperor Xian sensed sincerity in Jia's tone and nodded gladly.
"We've sent supplemental petitions to remind Yuan Shao, Yuan Shu, Gongsun Zan, Cao Cao and the rest of the rabble that they are to put the state before their personal ambitions and squabbles," Li Jue said. "The-"
Guo Si started giggling.
"...What are you doing...?" Li Jue asked irritably.
Guo Si grinned and replied, "No, sorry, I just think that's funny coming from us when-! ...I shouldn't laugh."
"...No Regent Guo, you shouldn't," Li Jue said coldly. "We've put our past behaviour behind us now that we are servants of His Majesty, and we are now doing what we can to set a good example... an example that men like Yuan Shao – men that can claim better lineages than some of the officials here – should be setting as well, not scrapping for land that isn't theirs. But we've sent more petitions, and they seem to be heeding them and confronting the rebels that His Majesty mentioned. There is, in addition, the faction of rebel Xiongnu that will also be dealt with."
"And this rumour that our distant relative Liu Bei has 'seized' Xu Province...?" Emperor Xian prompted.
"That... is unconfirmed," Li Jue said awkwardly. "If he has, then-"
"If he has, then he had no right, since he's disinherited," Guo Si said. "If old Tao Qian had sons, then-"
"I was answering perfectly well without your help!" Li Jue chortled.
"...Sorry, Regent Li," Guo Si sighed.
"Liu Bei is, indeed, *rumoured* to be the *acting* governor after Tao Qian's death, and we also have word that correspondence is on the way here, Your Majesty," Jia Xu said. "Any news will be immediately presented to the court."
"Very good, Mister Jia Xu," Emperor Xian said politely.
"...Marquis Zhang, you had a matter to raise...?" Li Jue said as he alternated his gaze between Jia Xu and the smiling emperor.
Zhang Ji – who was one of the few that remained of Dong Zhuo's other senior vassals – bowed slightly and said, "I was going to suggest that we strengthen our border with Hanzhong, Regent Li."
"Against *Liu Zhang*...?" Li Jue chuckled.
"No, Regent Li; against Zhang Lu, ruler of Hanzhong," Zhang Ji replied. "I am well aware that Liu Zhang has done nothing but send tribute since taking power, and that he is not the threat that his ambitious father was; but Zhang Lu's kind are benefitting greatly from the chaos caused by the famine and the warlords bickering, and while he rules Hanzhong and calls it 'Han'ning', it should be of concern."
"We quite agree, Marquis Zhang," Emperor Xian said, "but have we the forces to spare for a greater defence against this avaricious heretic that defiles our dynasty's birthplace...?"
"I suppose that you want to post Huche'er to the border so that he can gain merit," Guo Si heckled.
"...And have him nowhere near me at such a dangerous time...?" Zhang Ji retorted. "I have no desire to be as vulnerable as Fan Chou, Hu Zhen or Wang Fang at any point in time."
"What's that supposed to mean...?" Guo Si asked.
"He means that we should all be careful," Li Jue replied as he glared at Zhang Ji. "...And he's right. I'll despatch additional men

to build more signal towers and checkpoints... and dismantle some of the roads into the province. That should be enough."
"I agree," Zhang Ji said with a smile.
"We feel much safer with that decision made," Emperor Xian said.
"Then we should move on, discuss any remaining matters quickly and get back to our duties," Li Jue suggested. "Mister Jia Xu...?"
Jia Xu coughed deliberately and prepared to announce the next item on the agenda.
"...Should I not be playing a greater role in this...?" Shisun Rui complained quietly. "Surely I am Director in name only!"
"You are surprisingly agitated today, and should calm down," Yang Biao replied. "When this farce is over, come to my office."
Shisun Rui nodded silently.

Minister Yang Biao had been waiting for a moment to act since Regent Li Jue's public execution of former ally Fan Chou at a banquet: although the given reason for the execution had been for allowing the Qiang warlord Han Sui to escape after the failed attack on the capital, the remaining warlords and officers – particularly Marquis Zhang Ji and Li Jue's fellow regent Guo Si – were becoming suspicious of Li Jue and each other, since each new death added more power to those that were left, and Li Jue was obviously ambitious. Minister Yang had watched two attempts to remove Dong Zhuo and his minions come to nothing, and he was determined to make his own effort a successful one. To that end, he had explored every possibility, and when direct attempts to divide the warlords failed, he resorted to a secondary target for division – the warlords' wives and consorts.

"Marquis Zhang's wife is legendary for her beauty," Director of the Imperial Secretariat Shisun Rui said as he sat in a private conference with Yang Biao.
"Yes, but Zhang Ji is not the greatest threat," Yang Biao replied. "Our target is the regents. I have done some very careful research, and my target is Lady Qiong, the wife of Regent Guo Si."
"A fair-looking woman, but with a sneering face," Shisun Rui recalled.
"Bitter and vengeful, jealous and spiteful... her only competition in Guo Si's household are terrified lesser consorts, many if not all of them women that were kidnapped from their ransacked villages and forced to live with him," Yang Biao explained. "She can terrorize and control them easily, but she frets that someone – a relative of an official, perhaps – might catch her husband's roaming eye and take her place. She is everything that we want in our unwitting accomplice, just as Lü Bu's negative traits were essential for the late Director Wang Yun's scheme. The difference is that we will do nothing: there will be no coup, no military gatherings, no enlisting of barbarian chieftains... we'll simply sow the seed of jealousy in Lady Qiong's mind via a bit of gossip, and she'll do the rest."
Shisun Rui smiled, bowed, and said no more.

****

10

A week later, Regent Guo Si returned to his lavish residence after a long day in the court: his principal wife, Lady Qiong, greeted him upon his return and followed him to the living quarters.

"You're a bit more excitable today," Guo Si noted as he sat and watched as Lady Qiong prepared tea. "All smiles… what is it?"

"Nothing," Lady Qiong replied. She was lying: she had heard that Guo Si was secretly meeting with one of Li Jue's consorts, and she was determined that she would prevent her husband from spending any more time at Li Jue's house.

"I don't believe you," Guo Si chuckled. "You're usually sneering at me, asking me who this woman was, who that woman was… come on, what is it?"

"Nothing… well, not exactly nothing, rather I am… concerned," Lady Qiong sighed theatrically. "I… I was looking for the proper moment to tell you that I think you may be in danger."

Guo Si frowned.

"Your friend, Li Jue, means to kill you," Lady Qiong declared.

Guo Si grinned and said, "What do you know? Alright, his behaviour can be a little bit much sometimes, but *kill me…*? He needs me to help him run the country."

"He has that 'Jia Xu' person," Lady Qiong retorted. "All you are to him is a rival."

"Look, you don't know anything," Guo Si said irritably. "What do you know about Li Jue? We've been to one-another's homes a few times, you've met his women, he's-"

"Yes, I have," Lady Qiong interrupted. "His consorts are very pretty… don't you think…?"

"What's that got to do with anything?" Guo Si asked obliviously.

"…He wants everything, you can see it in his eyes," Lady Qiong suggested. "He plans your death… so that he can rule alone."

"*Nonsense*!" Guo Si chortled. "He's had loads of opportunities to be rid of me, and I'm still here! Him and me, we're friends!"

"…I hope that you're right," Lady Qiong giggled. "So we are to 'enjoy' the gifts that he sent you, of food and wine…?"

Guo Si frowned again and said, "I was waiting… but if it'll shut you up, we can eat some of it now, to show you he means well."

Guo Si got up and walked into his kitchen: his staff scattered, as they assumed that they were about to be punished for something.

"…You'll not get me to eat anything given to us by Li Jue," Lady Qiong scoffed as she followed her husband into the kitchen.

"Why?" Guo Si chuckled. "You're afraid that it's poisoned now…?"

"…Let's just say that I would rather test it on a dog first," Lady Qiong replied.

Guo Si scowled, took up some of the seasoned meat in his hands, and walked into the garden; a mangy guard dog ambled over, and Guo Si chucked the meat onto the ground in front of it.

"Such a waste of good roasted pork," Guo Si complained as the dog gorged on the food. "Why do I do it…? You're the most untrusting person I know, so-"

Suddenly, the dog started to behave strangely: Guo Si backed away in horror as the animal convulsed, vomited, and collapsed.

"…Th-that… that…!" Guo Si whimpered.

"I told you, he wants you dead!" Lady Qiong declared. "Perhaps he suspects you of carrying on with his women, or-"

"Look, he knows that I wouldn't!" Guo Si cried. "We had a deal: he stays away from mine, I stay away from his! That way, we wouldn't...! ...**How can this be???**"

A group of household staff congregated around the dying dog: Lady Qiong smirked and said, "Perhaps you don't know each other as well as you thought you did."

"...You did it," Guo Si decided as he looked at his wife. "You put poison in the food to make me mistrust him, didn't you???"

"If you want to believe that, fine," Lady Qiong replied. "But you'll see the truth about Li Jue soon enough... he'll kill you eventually."

Lady Qiong turned and retreated into the house; Guo Si stood and stared at the dog, muttering, "It has to have been her... it *can't have been Li Jue...!*"

Days passed.

"...Where is Guo Si?" Jia Xu asked as he waited in the chancellery meeting hall with Regent Li Jue. "Did he not receive the request to meet us here, Lord Li...?"

"Look, Mister Jia, I'm not his keeper," Li Jue grumbled. "He turned up at my door drunk the other night, going on about a dog. If he isn't here, he isn't here."

"A dog...?" Jia Xu mused. "Ah, yes; I heard that there was some disturbance at the Guo residence a few days ago... a guard dog was poisoned."

"Perhaps a burglar killed his favourite dog, and he'd come to complain about it," Li Jue sighed. "I'll be honest, Mister Jia, I didn't care: I told him to go back home, and then he said something about his wife, and staggered off somewhere."

"...Odd," Jia Xu murmured. "Still: until he arrives, perhaps we should discuss what I was-"

"Mister Li... Mister Jia," Guo Si said as he walked into the spacious chancellery audience hall and advanced towards the other two men: he was visibly armed.

"I thought we agreed that we wouldn't needlessly carry swords anymore!" Li Jue barked. **"After all the fights that we used to have, we-!"**

"I feel *safer* with it," Guo Si retorted as he sat opposite Li Jue.

"...Suit yourself," Li Jue replied uneasily. "I suppose that I shall have to start wearing one again, then."

"*Ayah*; only if you want me to retire again!" Jia Xu said angrily.

"...Alright then, I won't," Li Jue conceded. "But why are you wearing one, Guo Si? Why are you acting so strangely? Is this because of this dog that died? Was it a burglar?"

Guo Si glared at Li Jue, looking for a trace of guilt: he found no sign of insincerity, and so he smiled awkwardly and said, "I... I fear that I've been made a fool of by my wife."

"*Again*...?" Li Jue cackled. "Surely, Guo Si, you have the most evil woman as your principal spouse! She poisoned your dog? Why...?"

"...Forget about it," Guo Si pleaded.

"Alright then, I shall!" Li Jue replied. "Well, we're not waiting for anyone else: Mister Jia, you can talk now."

Jia Xu was wondering if there was more to the poisoned dog story, but he decided not to press the matter further: he coughed deliberately and said, "We are really making progress. The Yuans are no longer fighting openly, and I think that means that we can consider inviting them both to meet and declare a truce."

"…And Cao Cao…?" Guo Si prompted.

"That awful mess appears to have resolved itself," Jia Xu replied. "We've had a petition from Liu Bei, asking that his own position as Governor of Xu be ratified by His Majesty – to silence critics loyal to Tao Qian's sons, no doubt – and recommending Kong Rong as Governor of Qing Province."

"Why not?" Li Jue chuckled. "Liu Bei and Kong Rong are no threat. Oh, yes… speaking of meetings, I'm holding a banquet in a few days; you're both invited as honoured guests."

"Hey, why would I say no?" Guo Si replied. "You have some of the finest wine outside the imperial store: I haven't got drunk *properly* since… well, I can't remember!"

"You wouldn't do, you were drunk," Li Jue joked. "Alright then! I think we're owed a bit of a frolic, what with all the serious work we've been doing… something that isn't just a reward for a battle victory or whatever… just a banquet, so we can all relax for once."

"Normally, I'd say 'No', but I accept," Jia Xu said politely. "Shall we return to business now…?"

"Oh, right, yes!" Li Jue chuckled. "We discussed Liu Bei and Kong Rong last… so who's next…?"

The two regents were reconciled, despite neither knowing nor bothering to find out why they were on the verge of feuding again. Li Jue's banquet was uneventful, which convinced Guo Si that his wife had been wrong, or even manipulative; many banquets followed, and all thought of betrayal was quashed. Minister Yang Biao was unfazed, because he was certain that the peace could not endure: others were not so optimistic.

"We… *I*… fear for the future."

Emperor Xian was sat in his private quarters with his beloved consort Lady Fu, who had recently been created his empress: the two were as close as ever, and they were also as insecure and afraid of their own court as ever. Emperor Xian had dismissed his courtiers so that he could abandon protocols and tell Empress Fu how he felt, although there was no need: she knew him well and felt the same.

"I want to believe that my elevation is some form of sign that the court is once again loyal to Your Majesty and peace is restored," Empress Fu replied "But like Your Majesty, I am tired of groundless optimism. The court does nothing about the regents!"

Emperor Xian smiled sadly, straightened the left sleeve of his dragon-patterned robes and said, "The loyal men that followed me here from Luoyang have been repeatedly purged; very few of them remain now. I can only hope that nearby relatives, like Liu Biao and Liu Zhang, are mindful of the consequences of the house of Han collapsing. But what can they do? What can *anyone* do…?"

Empress Fu sighed loudly and lowered her head; Emperor Xian touched her hand and held his false smile.

****

11

Cao Cao's forces started to fragment as Cao's desire to end the campaign against Yufuluo overtook his instinctive caution; the vanguard reached the outskirts of an abandoned village that was the perfect place for any number of misfortunes.

"We should really tighten the formation," Xun Gongda suggested.

"My head...!" Cao Cao complained. "These blasted bandits and savages are vexing me to the point where I fear that my brains will explode!"

"Rushing and tripping isn't advised," Xun Gongda retorted. "We're now open to an ambush, and I strongly suggest that we-"

A sudden cry ended Xun Gongda's advice; arrows felled men and horse alike, and Cao Cao was suddenly in danger.

"*Ayah*! **We have to get out of here!**" Cao Cao cried.

"**I will protect you!**" Dian Wei said. "**Go to the east, Lord Cao, and I will follow!**"

"**I'll send a man to alert the army!**" Xun Wenruo promised. "**Cao Xiu, accompany the lord!**"

Cao Cao galloped away from the village ruin while Xun Gongda and Dian Wei did their best to distract the ambush party; but within minutes of his escape, Cao Cao was being pursued again and Cao Xiu was forced to stop and keep the enemy busy.

"...**Damn these headaches! They are my ruin!**" Cao Cao lamented as he rode further and further away from the ruined town and his army. One rider after another volunteered to keep the enemy busy until Cao was completely alone.

"...To die at the hands of bandits and Yufuluo's renegades... my ancestors will laugh at me!" Cao Cao sobbed as he rode through unfriendly foliage. He had no choice but to avoid using the roads, but the way was more treacherous and tiring for his already-exhausted horse. "...Ah Man's alone and tired, a horse his only friend; what better way for such a fool to meet his early end?" Cao Cao chuckled as his sanity started to fail him.

Xun Gongda and Dian Wei repelled the force around the deserted town, but it was obvious that Cao Cao was still in danger.

"...I should not have underestimated them!" Xun Gongda cried.

"I will follow his intended route," Dian Wei said.

"That's... that's best, General Dian," Xun Gongda replied. "I shall send search parties in other directions in case he had to deviate from that route."

Dian Wei kicked his horse and had it gallop to the east.

"...Heaven forgive me, but this wasn't my fault," Xun Gongda whispered. "His headaches are more pain to us than to him..."

Cao Cao happened upon a cottage as he fled: he dismounted, ran toward the small house and started to pound on the door.

"**Alright, alright!**" a voice complained. "**I'm coming, alright?**"

"**Hurry, please!**" Cao Cao urged. "**Your governor is here!**"

"*Governor*...? **Governor Cao Cao...?**" the voice exclaimed.

"Wait... I know that voice," Cao Cao realised. "...*Qin Bonan*...?"

The door opened, and a man of a similar age to Cao Cao immediately grabbed the governor's arms and said, "Mengde!"

"Please, I must get indoors, Bonan," Cao Cao replied.

"You're in trouble…?" Qin Bonan asked.

Cao Cao pushed his way past Qin Bonan and replied, "Yes. I only ask that you tell any passer-by that I rode on; have you a servant that can unsaddle my horse and pretend it to be your own…?"

"Yes," Qin Bonan said. "**LAD! Come here!**"

A servant boy ran into the living quarters and bowed humbly.

"Go and take the horse that's outside around the back and remove everything from it, and quickly," Qin Bonan ordered. "Hide the saddle and harness as best you can."

The boy retreated to complete his tasks.

"…*Mengde*…!" Qin Bonan whispered. "To think that we last met what, a decade ago…? What a hero you've become…!"

"I disagree," Cao Cao replied as he removed his dented battle helmet and dropped it to the floor. "I've made a mess of things, Bonan. The Black Mountain Bandits *and* Yufuluo of the Xiongnu are after me. My vanguard, my campaign adviser, my cousin Xiu, my bodyguards… might all be dead."

Qin Bonan frowned and said, "What will you do…?"

"I don't know," Cao Cao replied; he was now haunted by what was a very familiar situation. His eyes filled with tears, and he added, "You know that I would never hurt you or your family, Bonan."

"Of course!" Qin Bonan said cheerfully. "Now you should be rid of all that armour, else your pursuers will know who you are."

"…Maybe six years or so ago, I was close to alone, just like this," Cao Cao said as he removed his cloak and arm guards. "I happened upon the house of a friend, just like this…"

"…Lü Boshe," Qin Bonan sighed. "I have heard that story from Zhang Miao. That villain told me that you killed Boshe's family for no good reason, but I know you to be better than that."

"I… panicked," Cao Cao admitted. "He was not home, and-"

"Mengde, you need not explain the details," Qin Bonan insisted. "Just be rid of your armour, but keep your sword, obviously."

"…You truly trust me…?" Cao Cao asked.

"Zhang Miao allied himself with the villain Lü Bu and tried to seize the province," Qin Bonan replied. "I've watched the rest: Xu Yòu and Yuan Shao are up north, becoming property magnates; Yuan Shu is to the south, funding the rebels that you're now running from; you're the only one that's tried to make a difference, Mengde. I never had what it took to be anything much, so I came here to be a farmer; you, you're a famous hero now. My life is that much more meaningful for having met you here today."

"…You flatter me," Cao Cao murmured. "I-"

The servant boy suddenly returned and said, "Master Qin! Master Qin! There are riders coming! Twenty men at least!"

"…Hide in the kitchen, Mengde," Qin Bonan suggested. "Lad, go and tend the horse. Try and act normally; oh, and have my son accompany you in suitable attire."

Cao Cao suspected that Qin Bonan was planning something and said, "Don't waste your life, Bonan. If they-"

"If they come here, they'll meet me, not you," Qin Bonan interrupted. "Go and hide in the kitchen. There are clothes in there that are due to be laundered: find a robe."

Cao Cao wanted to do more, but the headache was impeding his vision and making it hard to focus; he staggered into the kitchen.

Minutes later, the door was being rapped upon yet again.
"**Alright, alright!**" Qin Bonan chuckled theatrically. "**I'm-!**"
The door gave way as a large bandit shoulder-barged it at speed; a dozen men entered the house and surrounded Qin Bonan.
"Where is Cao Cao...?" the bandits' leader asked.
"What...?" Qin Bonan retorted. "Why would the governor be here?"
"Isn't that his helmet on the floor...?" another bandit heckled.
"...No more delays," the bandits' leader growled. "Where is he?"
Cao Cao was crouched by the kitchen door, watching fearfully; he could only turn away and bite his hand when Qin Bonan said, "Do you not have the breeding to know a noble when you see one...?"
The bandits exchanged confused glances.
"I entered this cottage and killed the master in order to assume his identity, but I was not fast enough," Qin Bonan continued. "I have lived many years, but I have sinned once too many times, and Heaven has confounded me. Take my head to your masters, for unlike you they will recognise me straight away."
"...This is too easy," a third bandit said.
"Heaven is playful," Qin Bonan chortled. "All too often, great men are thwarted by the lowest kind; my father died at the hands of bandits, so why shouldn't I...? Kill me and be done with it."
"He's convinced me!" the bandits' leader chuckled; Cao Cao stifled a yelp as he heard the sounds of Qin Bonan being stabbed and then beheaded by the bandits. Cao rocked back and forth as he waited for the inevitable suggestion that they should search the house, but instead the leader added, "Let's hurry! We'll get a good reward for this!" and ushered his men from the property.
"...Heaven, you are cruel," Cao Cao sobbed. "This... is not *right*...!"

Dian Wei found Cao Cao after hours of searching; Cao was riding his saddled horse along the road, and he was obviously mortified.
"Are you hurt...?" Dian Wei asked.
"They will all die, Dian Wei, every last one of them," Cao Cao replied. "I want some men to visit the home of Qin Bonan; his family will need support, and his body requires proper burial."
Dian Wei was confused.
"...A man gave his life for me, Dian Wei, and I will not let his sacrifice be without purpose or reward," Cao Cao explained. "Qin Bonan's immediate household will know my generosity, and his murderers will know suffering. Where is the army...?"
"At the ruin," Dian Wei replied. "And Cao Xiu is safely with them."
"...Very good," Cao Cao said tonelessly. "We press on as one, so that there will be no more mistakes. We must kill them all."
"I will grind them to paste, Lord Cao," Dian Wei replied.

Jing Province's governor, Liu Biao, received word of Cao Cao's activities via a polite letter from Xun Wenruo; he retired to his private meeting room to read it.
"...Well, at least he's letting me know," Liu Biao grumbled. "Mister Kuai, are we likely to see any of these 'bandits and Xiongnu renegades' adding themselves to our own troubles...?"
Liu Biao's only company – his senior adviser, Kuai Liang – smiled and replied, "No, Lord Liu. The Runan mercenaries sit between them and Jing if they go southwest, and they're unlikely to try and seize Nan County, since that means deviating from the path that

would take them back into Bing Province and safety."

"...So it is the Sun clan and Yuan Shu that I must concern myself with, as usual, but nothing more," Liu Biao sighed. "I am so... *tired* of all this now, Mister Kuai. They all want Jing, and... and there are days when I would gladly cede it to know peace."

Liu Biao's strong physique had long since withered from time spent in various courts around Jing, and his handsome features were eroded by age and stress; he covered his face with his hands and exhaled noisily.

"I shall leave you," Kuai Liang said.

"Keep me informed!" Liu Biao ordered. "I must know everything..."

Cao Cao led his army toward the closest enemy camp and arrayed the infantry and cavalrymen at some distance away from it; Fixed Gaze got word of the activity and gathered his senior allies.

"It sounds like a proper military array," Fixed Gaze said. "We'd do well to avoid it and stick to shock attacks when he isn't prepared."

Yufuluo entered the meeting with his own followers and shouted, **"We won't run again, bandit! I will break his stupid army this time, with or without your help!"**

"...Well then we have to help, don't we?" Fixed Gaze sighed.

"Where's your son, 'Nobody's Chanyu'...?" Big Eyes heckled. "I thought he was helping us, or has he gotten scared...?"

"Quiet, runt!" Yufuluo barked. **"My son is no coward!"**

"Don't upset the help, Big Eyes," Fixed Gaze complained. "We're dead enough as it is. Any word from Poison Yu...?"

"No, and don't expect it either," Big Eyes replied. "His lot are set on attacking Yè again."

"...If they were hitting *Henei*, I'd understand," Fixed Gaze said.

"Are you helping me smash Cao or not???" Yufuluo asked.

"Yes, yes!" Fixed Gaze grumbled. **"Get ready, lads."**

"Remember that I want them *smashed*," Cao Cao said as the Xiongnu rebels and Bandits gathered for the battle.

"They will be," Xun Gongda promised.

The Yan Province army was divided into 8 blocks of infantry with cavalry at front and rear and a large, elevated drum – with dual drummers – placed behind each unit. The Bandit-Xiongnu alliance was typically disordered; Yufuluo rode back and forth with his subordinate chieftains and bodyguards while the entire rebel force hurled insults and hollered at the government force.

"EVERYONE IS IN POSITION!" Dian Wei bellowed.

"...**DO IT!**" Cao Cao ordered.

Xun Gongda raised a small flag; the drummers started to beat out a rhythmic pattern, and the units shifted about to form groups of perpendicular human walls.

"The Han men dance for us!" Yufuluo heckled. **"Charge them!"**

The horde of Xiongnu rebels charged at the Yan array without fear or restraint; they picked a unit that looked vulnerable, but that was exactly what Xun Gongda had intended.

"I don't like it!" Big Eyes said to Fixed Gaze. **"Arrays are bad!"**

"Yufuluo should know that, what with Xiongnu men being used in Han arrays so much!" Fixed Gaze replied. **"He's either arrogant or ignorant!"**

"Both!" Big Eyes retorted. **"What do we do?"**

"...**Pray...?**" Fixed Gaze said as he watched his Xiongnu allies disappear into the maze of enemy soldiers; Xun Gongda signalled for a second time, and the drummers changed the beat that they were playing shortly afterward.

"**Tricks! Stupid, weak tricks!**" Yufuluo complained as he and his men realised that the shifting walls of men were now closing around them; the Yan cavalry moved freely, as they knew the carefully-rehearsed opening well, but the Xiongnu were confused as open spaces quickly became phalanxes and solid walls became enticing paths to they-knew-not-what. One by one, the Xiongnu men fell, but they were doing little damage in return.

"**We'll have to charge!**" Fixed Gaze decided.

The Black Mountain Bandit force charged at the outside of the array; Xun Gongda raised another flag, whereupon signalmen carried further messages to the ends of the battle lines. Within seconds, Cao Xiu and Xiahou Dun led two forces forward from the flanks and Dian Wei charged from the centre, dealing demoralising savagery on the men that he encountered.

"**Smash through! Get Yufuluo out!**" Fixed Gaze ordered.

But the bandits were faltering in the face of the new attack, and some of the smaller groups within the confederacy were fleeing the battle to save themselves. Archers at the rear of the array fired at the charging bandits, and many were felled and killed.

"...**Damn it, damn it!**" Fixed Gaze cried as he broke off his attack and turned to flee. "**Sorry, Chanyu! You're on your own!**"

Yufuluo and his dwindling cavalry darted through the gaps in the array while doing their best to avoid the spears, swords and pikes that jutted out of the human walls and the cavalrymen that awaited them at seemingly random points; Yufuluo was hurt several times before he decided that a suicidal charge at one part of the infantry wall would be his only chance, however slim. The gamble worked; Yufuluo was stabbed in the thigh, but he and his decimated force cut through and escaped the trap.

"**Move, move!**" Yufuluo ordered. "**We have to go!**"

The battlefield became a sea of death that was accompanied by a cacophony of orders, cheers, yelps and screams of pain and the sounds of feet, hooves and blades; Cao Cao's head was pounding, and all that he could think of was the need to destroy his enemies.

"**DO NOT LET THEM ESCAPE!**" Cao Cao screeched as he raised his sword of authority aloft. "**NONE OF THEM MUST LIVE! NONE OF THEM! I WILL SLAY THEM MYSELF!**"

Cao Cao was about to charge at the fleeing rebels, but Xun Gongda restrained him by grabbing his arm; Cao Cao spun around to face his adviser and glared at him with hateful eyes.

"**CORNERED TIGERS FIGHT HARDEST!**" Xun Gongda protested. "**WHY SEND YOURSELF TO THE NETHERWORLD...?**"

Cao Cao stopped struggling and clutched his forehead.

"**LET OTHERS FIGHT NOW!**" Xun Gongda continued.

"The smells, the sounds... are *intolerable*," Cao Cao complained.

The Bandit-Xiongnu alliance lost dozens of its cavalrymen and hundreds if not thousands of its infantrymen; there would be other battles, but the momentum was now with the Yan Province army and its leader, Governor Cao Cao.

Cao Cao's army reached the western border of Chenliu Prefecture, having fought a series of small battles with Fixed Gaze's faction of Black Mountain Bandits and Yufuluo's rebels as he moved: Cao gazed westward at the lands of Central Province and sighed.

"It pains us all, Lord Cao, to know that Luoyang still lies in ruins and the Son of Heaven is still a hostage," Xun Gongda suggested.

"You and your uncle should, in a sane world, have the same privileged places in that court that your fathers and grandfathers did," Cao Cao replied. "Instead, you toil for an unstable 'villain' and fight rebels and bandits."

"Xu Shao's appraisal looms over you, but it shouldn't," Xun Gongda said. "If it must, then remember all of his words…"

"…I do," Cao Cao chortled. "He called me 'An able statesman in times of peace, and a crafty villain in times of chaos'. He didn't want to share his opinion of me, no doubt for fear of what it might trigger within me… and he was right. Since then, Gongda, all there has been is chaos… and I yearn for peace so that I can be the good man that I want to be."

"But he has done more than appraise you, Lord Cao: he has explained what must be done to restore order," Xun Gongda suggested. "No man that tries to resort purely to honest tactics will put an end to this chaos… it is the never-ending struggle to rationalise 'what is right versus what is necessary'. There will always be those that will try and make the unjustifiable seem necessary for personal ends… but one cannot beat an immoral enemy without, at certain times, meeting them on common ground. Would Yuan Shao have defeated the corrupt eunuchs by continuing to petition the court *they controlled*, as so many cold bones tried to…? Dou Wu, Chen Fan, Hè Jin… none were successful because they were too fair to their enemy. The 'Ten' *had* to be put to the sword, one and all, because they were never going to change their evil ways by polite request, and they would not have stopped until there was not a good man left."

"…It is men like Benchu and I, so-called 'heroes', that do what must be done to finally bring peace," Cao Cao said tonelessly.

"I… I believe so," Xun Gongda replied. "So does my uncle. So does Cheng Yu. So do we all, Lord Cao. History will look kindly upon you, Lord Cao, for any minor wrongdoings that you might be forced to commit in the pursuit of everlasting peace, if that is what you truly strive for. The Heavens know that there is no other way, and so will all men, one day."

"…But I feel so *powerless*, Gongda," Cao Cao admitted. "My army is not great enough to face the Liang warlords and their fair-weather Qiang allies and take Chang'an. …We struggled against *Yufuluo*! …If the Yuans do not make peace and the warlords of the east do not act soon, then… then will we one day be told that Li Jue and Guo Si have once again slain the Son of Heaven…?"

"There will still be good men close to His Majesty," Xun Gongda replied. "They will give us time… time to put things right."

Cao Cao nodded and said, "Then let us relieve the last of the settlements and return to Xuchang; I feel a cold wind, and worry that it's Zhang Miao's fallen kin prodding at my conscience."

****

12

Yufuluo's battered Xiongnu warriors and Fixed Gaze's bandits retreated separately across Central Province and toward the sandy, surging currents of the Yellow River; their marches would take them past the ruins of the capital Luoyang and privately-managed lands – including a fief awarded to former Yellow Turban pacifier Zhu Jun – that had once been attacked and pillaged by Li Jue and Guo Si in their days as Dong Zhuo's generals.

"We're probably going back to a purge by Yuan Shao," Fixed Gaze muttered as he rode across the scarred landscape. "Poison Yu's lack o' sense in knowing what to attack has really left us in it."

"Where's 'Nobody's Chanyu'…?" Big Eyes sniggered. "He ran from that last battle before we did!"

"I think he was hit during his charge this time, Big Eyes," Fixed Gaze replied. "I don't reckon he'd be running like this if he wasn't hurt, not after seeing how angry he was, and 'specially after he said his son was joining us soon…"

"P'raps his son lost his nerve and isn't coming, and that's why he's running," Big Eyes suggested.

"Yufuluo is brave, if nothin' else," Fixed Gaze replied. "His son is pretty brave too, so that ain't it. No, I reckon Yufuluo was hurt and hurt *bad*, in which case… in which case our next trip into Yan might be on our own."

Another bandit coughed before he asked, "Are we going to raid anywhere, boss…? A lot o' the lads are hungry."

"I don't know what to do," Fixed Gaze replied.

"What about Henei…?" Big Eyes suggested. "Zhang Yang's not got a big army to counter us, and he usually just let us run wild when he was in Bing, didn't he…? He doesn't seem to have so much of a problem with us now that he doesn't have Ding Yuan, Lü Bu and Zhang Liao to work with."

"Yufuluo broke his spirit when he locked him up, that much is obvious," Fixed Gaze chuckled. "…I know the feeling."

"So are we stopping in Henei when we get there, then…?" Big Eyes prompted.

"…Yeah," Fixed Gaze replied. "I might, yeah… for a while."

"…It's been five years since he killed Ding Yuan."

Henei Prefecture's Administrator Zhang Yang turned to his gaunt adviser Dong Zhao – whose courtesy name was 'Gongren' – as he added, "And he still doesn't know the right thing to do. Now Zhang Miao is dead, and there's even more chaos! His entire journey there was for nothing, and more good men are gone! Oh, and if he's lost Yan Province, then don't I have to worry about the man coming back here again if his plans don't work out?"

"Lü Bu is your friend, not mine, so you are the best judge," Dong Gongren replied.

"…He writes that he goes east… to Xu," Zhang Yang mused. "I wonder what he plans to do there."

Dong Gongren coughed deliberately and said, "Forgive my frankness, my lord, but… as long as his actions do not drag us into a pit, I do not care."

"…You're quite right, of course," Zhang Yang said. "Our worries

are many: the regents to the west, Yuan Shao to the east, The Black Mountain Bandits and Yufuluo's men just about everywhere, Cao Cao to the south; there is no end to the chaos…"
Dong Gongren nodded silently.
"The Xiongnu in Bing Province are growing bolder," Zhang Yang continued. "I think that they intend to exploit the chaos and take Bing over altogether… and I do not like the idea of an independent Xiongnu state on my northwest border, not after being imprisoned by Yufuluo for all that time."
"Yuan Shao will not tolerate it," Dong Gongren said with increasing impatience.
"…You still feel resentful that you were slandered and forced to flee Ji Province, and you care little for my problems," Zhang Yang supposed.
"I care for all of the world's legitimate problems," Dong Gongren retorted. "I just find it difficult to worry about men like Lü Bu; I still find the fact that you risked an imperial arrest warrant to shelter that man – *twice* – quite preposterous."
"…I think that I am damaged by what I have seen, heard and felt," Zhang Yang said. "Our lord, Ding Yuan, was a true hero. I-"
"And Bu killed him," Dong Gongren noted. "He then went on to serve Dong Zhuo."
"He is misunderstood!" Zhang Yang protested. "He-!"
"I know, I know," Dong Gongren said. "Bu was 'fooled' by Dong Zhuo's seemingly rational arguments, and failed to notice, somehow, that he was an evil, violent madman that tortured and killed innocent men, women and children, razed entire villages for personal amusement and murdered the Son of Heaven."
"Fengxian killed Dong Zhuo personally!" Zhang Yang retorted.
"*Ayah*… yes, *eventually*," Dong Gongren said wearily. "But do we truly know that he did it for the right reasons…?"
"Any reason will do when the outcome is the death of an evil man," Zhang Yang replied. "Fengxian is swayed by his emotions, but I genuinely believe that he will one day become the hero that a man with his talent demands to be."
"…Enough about Lü Bu, Lord Zhang," Dong Gongren pleaded. "Yuan Shao plots our destruction, and Yufuluo is retreating from Yan and coming this way; he is poised to do *something*, though I know not what. He may, I hope, just be content with fleeing to Bing Province… but he may also attack Henei."
"And gain what…? …A fine view of the ruins of Luoyang that lay across the Yellow River…?" Zhang Yang chortled. "He'll cause trouble in Bing, Yu and Yan, most probably just Bing for now, if Cao Cao's beaten him again. As for Yuan Shao… the regents have forbidden him to take action against recognised Han officials or Gongsun Zan. He has been ordered to focus on defeating the Black Mountain Bandits… and Cao Cao will have far, far too much to do to attack us on his behalf…"

＊＊＊＊＊＊＊＊＊＊＊

13

Word of Lü Bu and Liu Bei's alliance of convenience in Xu Province finally started to reach their closest neighbours at around the time that Cao Cao completed his return march to Xuchang: the reactions were understandably emotional.

"Liu *Bei*...!" Cao Cao growled as he read the written report.
"My lord, we must discuss this with everyone," Xun Gongda pleaded as he dismissed the messenger from Cao Cao's near-empty audience hall with a benign wave of his hand.
"...I... I know," Cao Cao replied as he clutched the side of his head. "Oh, Gongda, these men aim to kill me with headaches born of anger and worry! But I swear that I'll tear out their hearts with my teeth first!"
"My uncle is hurrying here, and Mister Cheng as well," Xun Gongda continued.
"Liu Bei...! Liu *Bei*...!" Cao Cao said with growing anger. "First you save the father-killers of Xu from my righteous wrath, and now you harbour that treacherous animal, that killer of fathers *and* sovereigns! It is *your* name that will be forever synonymous with 'crafty villainy', Liu Bei, and not *mine*! I am as I am by *circumstance*, Liu Bei, but *you* are wicked by *choice*!"
"Hating Liu Bei solves nothing, Lord Cao," Xun Gongda suggested.
"...No, you... you're right," Cao Cao replied as he found the strength to fight his anger. "He... he is not... he is not right, not in anything he does, but... but maybe I must be objective. I must give all men the same benefit of the doubt until I am sure of all of the facts... but my head hurts so, Gongda. It hurts, and I really cannot believe that I have to come back from a successful campaign to... to *this*."
"It is unfair," Xun Gongda agreed. "I expect that the Yuans will be similarly aggrieved. Let us hope that it unites them, and then – maybe – some good might come of this."
"Unlikely," Cao Cao said as he passed the report to Xun Gongda. "I truly wonder if there is anything that could reconcile those two... Benchu is too stubborn, and the other one is a delusional fanatic. I think this only ends with Yuan Shu's death."
Xun Gongda silently agreed.

Ji Governor Yuan Shao summoned his advisers to his court in Yè City and asked, "Why should I tolerate Liu Bei sheltering Lü Bu? These words that he sends me are surely foolish nonsense!"
The gaunt, world-weary, middle-aged adviser Tian Feng was currently in possession of Liu Bei's letter, which he was reading for a second time while his master ranted.
"My lord, let me march against Xu Province," the adviser-general Chunyu Qiong pleaded. "I have been unable to prove my true worth to you yet: I have been an adviser – just another voice among men like Tian Feng, Pang Ji, Xun Chen, Shen Pei, and Ju Shou – but when have I been the warrior that I am at heart? Was I not, like you and Cao Cao, a colonel of the Army of the Western Garden...? I know that I showed that I was every bit the equal of General Qu Yi in the second campaign against Gongsun Zan, but I

yearn for more opportunities! Let me take to the field against the villain Lü Bu and avenge your clan on your behalf!"

"Are you mad?" the adviser Pang Ji chortled. "This is *Lü Bu* that we talk about! You're no match for that man in battle. And what about his best generals, Zhang Liao and Gao Shun?"

"Pang Ji is right," the adviser Shen Pei suggested. "Send General Chunyu with Zhang Hè, Gao Lan, Yan Liang and Wen Chou."

"Do I need all that help for one friendless Lü Bu and his overrated, conscripted subordinates?" Chunyu Qiong scoffed. "I think that you are just trying to humiliate me, gentlemen."

"Zhang Liao and Gao Shun are not 'conscripted'," Tian Feng said wearily. "They have followed Bu since the days of Ding Yuan; as for 'friendless', it is my understanding that Administrator Zhang Yang did not expel him willingly."

"Yes, well, I'll deal with *him* soon enough," Yuan Shao muttered.

"Zhang Yang is appointed Administrator of Henei by the imperial court," Tian Feng noted. "To attack him is to attack the empire."

"I know that!" Yuan Shao retorted. "I... I know that. I will petition if nobody else does, citing his refusal to obey the edict and apprehend Lü Bu! ...But enough about him! What do I do about Liu Bei??? And *no*, Mister Chunyu, I do not intend a march against my own province! Not if there is some other way to deal with him!"

"And after the recent attack on this very capital by the Black Mountain Bandits, our resources cannot be reallocated to Xu anyway," Ju Shou suggested.

"Are the bandits that great a threat?" the adviser Xun Chen asked.

"Of course they are!" Ju Shou chortled. "They got to the city walls! Their commander, 'Poison Yu', was paces away from-!"

"I don't need reminding!" Yuan Shao barked. "Yes, I know, I cannot spare my men for an attack on Xu anyway... not while the bandits and their ally Yufuluo are still so powerful. We shall have to march west and annihilate them, but that does solve the long-term Liu Bei problem! What can I do right now?"

"Write to Liu Bei, demanding that he expel or eliminate Lü Bu," Tian Feng suggested. "If he disobeys, then we should have the court direct the original arrest edict at him."

"A sound idea," Yuan Shao decided. "I'll write to Liu Bei at once."

Cao Cao waited until his senior officials had gathered and called a meeting to discuss Lü Bu and Xu Province.

"Everything that I hate is in one place," Cao Cao said irritably. "But here I am, shackled by famine, rampant disease, and my lifelong friend Yuan Shao's muddle-headedness! I should be able to leave Xuchang and march east: I should be able to ride into Xu Province, tear Lü Bu's tiny heart from his chest, dissect Chen, Wang and Xu for their treachery, and impale that mat weaver Liu Bei's head on a spike!"

Xun Gongda expected Cheng Yu to say something, but the adviser sat silently and gave no indication of his thoughts; Gongda then turned to his uncle, Wenruo, who gestured that he should continue.

"...But that isn't going to happen," the adviser Xun Gongda suggested. "Instead, you're going to mediate, if you're going to do anything at all; we agreed that."

"Yes, yes, I know... we all knew that Bu was going to hide with Liu

Bei," Cao Cao admitted. "You, Mister Cheng and your uncle Wenruo have already convinced me of the need for calm and patience. I have a headache again today, and it is vexing me."

"Some music would soothe you more than tearing Xu Province apart again," Xun Gongda joked. "Shall I summon the musicians?"

"No," Cao Cao replied. "I'll go and rest. I just hope, Gongda, that you're right about those two ending up as enemies; oh! That reminds me: Lu Kang. I wonder if we know more about that valiant man's efforts to hold onto Lujiang."

"Sadly, we do," Xun Gongda said. "Lu Kang... is dead."

"*Ayah*... really...?" Cao Cao lamented. "That man was a good, honest fellow... a better man than I could ever hope to be. What happened? I know that he tried to remain neutral in the pointless bickering between the Yuans, and that Yuan Shu didn't much appreciate it; so Shu's army actually managed to break through Old Lu's famously-solid defences?"

"In the end, Yuan Shu used Sun Ce," Xun Gongda explained. "It seems that Mister Lu made a mistake: he refused to see Sun Ce at some point after the man's father was killed in Jing, and Ce carried a grudge. His failing to see Sun Ce and his father as anything more than Yuan Shu's dogs is the heart of the matter: Sun Ce sieged Lu Kang's stronghold with such aggression that no man alive could have held that place, or so Yuan Shu would have us believe. Frankly, I believe it."

"What a waste," Cao Cao sighed. "But I cannot castigate young Sun Ce, can I...? Not after what I have done to Xu Province in the name of *my* father..."

"Go and rest," Xun Gongda pleaded.

Cao Cao nodded sadly and withdrew from the hall.

"...Our weakness condemns us," Xun Gongda muttered.

"...I suppose that ends proceedings: thank you all for attending," Xun Wenruo declared, and the majority of the officials dispersed.

"I'm surprised that you have nothing to contribute, Mister Cheng," Xun Wenruo said to the unreadable Cheng Yu; something was different about his appearance, but neither Xun Wenruo nor Xun Gongda could immediately identify what it was.

"Today is... not a good day for me," Cheng Yu replied.

"Has there been some personal tragedy...?" Xun Wenruo asked.

"No, no, Wenruo, I am just... unable to show my usual resolve today," Cheng Yu replied. "Every man has days where they are of little use to anyone, including themselves, and today is such a day. But I have taken in what has been said, and I will certainly put my ideas in writing if I cannot put them into words. Good day to you both."

Cheng Yu walked away slowly and forlornly; Xun Gongda finally ascertained what was different about Cheng and said, "He's put colour in his hair... to darken it..."

"...He is the last person that I expected to suffer from aesthetic vanity," Xun Wenruo admitted. "Professional vanity, maybe, but... not his appearance... I suppose that his age worries him."

"But then he has a toadying side that surfaces rarely as well," Xun Gongda said as he and his uncle started to walk toward the main entrance to the audience hall.

"Oh, yes," Xun Wenruo replied. "He refused a very respectable post from Liu Dai when offered and was rude to him in addition,

but took a vastly inferior post from Lord Cao and was very humble about it. His 'confidence' comes and goes like the weather... as does his strange hatred of his fellow men. He's very complicated."
"Aren't we all...?" Xun Gongda chuckled.

"**Curses!**" the warlord Yuan Shu screamed as he loomed over a terrified messenger. "***Curse them*, the defiant wretches!**"
"My lord, the messenger has done no wrong," the adviser Han Yin suggested.
"...You're right," Yuan Shu sighed; he turned his gaze back to the messenger, waved his hand dismissively and said, "Get out."
The messenger bowed penitently, turned, and fled.
"...So Cao Cao defeated the bandits and Yufuluo, and chased them out of Yan Province, and he's definitively defeated Lü Bu's forces as well," the adviser Yan Xiang mused.
"**I can read!**" Yuan Shu heckled as he waved the report angrily. "**I do not need you to tell me what I already know!**"
"At least the situation in Lujiang was resolved quickly," Han Yin suggested. "When added to Jiujiang, it means that the whole of Northern Yang Province is now yours; Liu Xun and Chen Ji are both dependable administrators, and therefore cannot lose them. That means that you can finally consider moving south *or* north, Lord Yuan."
"...Why not south *and* north...?" Yuan Shu retorted. "Hui Qu and Sun Ce will surely defeat Liu Yao and his allies, and Ji Ling, Lei Bo, Chen Lan and Liang Gang are all ready to march, are they not...?"
"They should rest after the exertions in Lujiang," Yan Xiang suggested.
"Does Sun Ce rest...?" Yuan Shu heckled. "All of my officers are tigers! They should all bear their claws at the same time!"
"...But Lü Bu will be looking for a new sanctuary, most likely in Xu, with or without Liu Bei's blessing; Liu Biao has strengthened Jing's defences, and Cao Cao's morale is peaked," Han Yin replied. "We must be careful not to overextend, especially with the rumours coming out of Runan that Liu Pi and Huang Shao are-"
"**Nonsense!**" Yuan Shu shrieked. "**There is no popular Yellow Turban uprising in Runan! Liu Pi has not returned to his old ways!** That... that is **ridiculous! He**... he would not ***dare!***"
But Yuan Shu was worried: he relied on the support of the Black Mountain Bandits, Yufuluo and Gongsun Zan in the northern provinces, Liu Pi and Huang Shao's mercenaries in Yu Province and various pirates in the southeast, and many of those self-serving associates were either reconsidering their position or finally crumbling under the pressure that was being inflicted upon them. Yuan Shu's dreams of greatness were, in truth, gradually slipping away, but the more distant they became, the more tightly he clung to the idea that he was destined to rule not just Yu Province or the Yuan clan, but all of China.
"...It is only a matter of time now," Yuan Shu muttered as he retreated from the meeting hall in a daze. "All I need is a sign, and then I will finally ascend...!"

****

14

The Southern Xiongnu exile Yufuluo had retreated to his base in Ping County in Bing Province after his last crushing defeat by Cao Cao: he would normally lick his minor wounds and begin plans for another campaign, but this time, he would never campaign again. Yufuluo was wounded seriously during his more recent skirmishes, and now he was slowly dying of fatigue and despair. His brother – the Southern Xiongnu *Chanyu*, Huchuquan – and his eldest son Liu Bao heard of his condition and hurried to be at his side.

"Your son will be my heir," Huchuquan declared as he clasped Yufuluo's hand. "You could not be Chanyu... your son will have that which you were denied."

Yufuluo nodded and smiled.

"...**Father, you are strong, with many years left to live: why don't you fight it???**" the brawny Liu Bao cried.

"Where... are my family...?" Yufuluo asked. "I hear... my son..."

"Here I am, Father," Liu Bao said as he crouched next to his father. "I have brought with me my women and my children. See here, Father, my newest, a *son*...!"

Liu Bao turned to a young woman that was wearing traditional Xiongnu clothing, but she was certainly not of Xiongnu origin: she was Cai Yan, eldest daughter and only surviving child of the once-revered and now disgraced Han official Cai Yong, whose actions were many and impressive throughout his middle career. Cai Yan was, like her father, possessed of a quick and intelligent mind, but that meant nothing to the man that had abducted her, ordered the slaughter of her mother and siblings and taken her for a concubine; to Liu Bao, she was a beautiful girl that would do chores and bear him strong children, and nothing more. Cai Yan approached her husband mechanically and handed her fur-wrapped, gurgling baby to him.

"A son...! A son...!" Yufuluo croaked. "Strong... strong...!"

"We will all be strong," Huchuquan vowed. "Today, no more division: all of us shall come together, and live here in this region together. Today, I lead, but one day, your son, and then his son. Heaven demands it."

Yufuluo started to cough feebly, and a Xiongnu physician ordered everyone to give him space; Liu Bao handed his son back to Cai Yan, who stared at her child with lifeless, weary eyes.

"How long...?" Liu Bao asked of the physician.

"...Soon," Huchuquan said as he stared at his brother. "Why ask, Nephew...? It is obvious that... it will be soon. Days, weeks... a few months, perhaps, if he tries to fight... but it is all 'soon'."

Liu Bao looked to the physician, who said, "His Highness is correct, Prince Bao."

"...**I will have many sons!**" Liu Bao proclaimed. "**Father, I will be a great king! I will give you many grandsons, and they will be great kings too! I will not disappoint you! Father, your spirit will know happiness! *Father*...!**"

Yufuluo was still coughing, but he extended his hand to reach out to his son; Liu Bao extended his own hand, briefly held his father's hand, and then drew back as Yufuluo's strength failed and the outstretched arm fell to his side.

"**I will not leave! I will give him strength to fight!**" Liu Bao insisted. "**Women, go! I will stay!**"

Cai Yan and the other two women – one Chinese, one Xiongnu – did as they were told and retreated mechanically.

"I will be great… and you will be known to all men in the world!" Liu Bao promised as his father's eyes slowly closed. "Your descendants will rule the world…! Father, you are strong, you have always been strong… why will you not fight???"

Yufuluo tried to smile at his son's comforting words, but he lacked the strength to do anything: he had lost the will to fight his ailments, and he would soon lose the will to live altogether.

"Soon… and then we will be one again," Huchuquan murmured.

Yufuluo's eventual demise would, as Huchuquan said, mark an end to division of the Southern Xiongnu. Yufuluo's son Liu Bao would be Huchuquan's heir as Chanyu of all of the tribes, and until that day, Bao would be a king with control over five tribes and answer to none but his uncle. The possibility of a Southern Xiongnu consolidation worried some, but to others it meant a possible return to the days when the settlers would provide horses and cavalrymen to the Han army in exchange for permission to live as they chose. There would be one long-term consequence of Liu Bao and his descendants – who had, from marriage alliances, Han Imperial blood flowing in their veins – becoming the future Chanyus, but history would have China and its succession of rulers wait for over a century before it learned of – and suffered – that consequence. In the meantime, a new peace could be dreamed of between the empire and its settlers: but at the same time that one enemy to the empire melted away, another was ready to announce its return.

"**Our time is here once again!**" the battle-hardened mercenary Liu Pi said to a vast army of followers that had gathered on the outskirts of a village in Runan Prefecture, Yu Province. For some time – close to decade, in fact – Liu Pi had been a wandering bandit and later a hired sword that worked with Yuan Shu and his subordinate general Sun Jian: now he was about to return to the role that had brought him to the attention of those famous men.

Liu Pi had abandoned his plain turban and now wore the military symbol of his old master, Zhang Jue, the founder of the 'Way of Peace': a piece of plain yellow cloth that was the epitome of treason, an open defiance of the rule that only the emperor could wear yellow 'above the head'. His long-term ally Huang Shao – who was stood at side - was attired in the same farmer's clothes and yellow turban, and every single man and woman in the crowd wore yellow turbans to show their contempt for an emperor that was seen to have abandoned them.

"**The time is right to let the enemies of Heaven see that we have grown strong again!**" Liu Pi continued. "**Let them see that we will seize their hidden grain, defy their curfews, and build fortresses to house our families! We will strike down those that harm the people, and give the land back to all men and women!**"

"**Let Heaven hear that you know its will!**" Huang Shao screamed. "**Let the enemies of Heaven know their fate! Let**

us be like the locusts they brought upon us, and devour them!"

The angry, desperate crowd then began to chant the mantra that had inspired and propagated the original Yellow Turban Rebellion a decade earlier:

**"Han's mandate has passed!
Yellow Sky, soon here!
In this renewing year,
Prosperous all, at last!"**

"...Are we *sure* that we are ready...?" Huang Shao asked of Liu Pi as the crowd continued their monotonous chanting.

"I am tired of hiding," Liu Pi replied. "We may not win, but what good has being silent done...? My only regret is surrendering to Sun Jian the first time."

Huang Shao nodded, turned his gaze back to the crowd and shouted, **"More! Make the ground shake! Shout until the liars and the thieves in Chang'an hear you and feel the despair that they have inflicted upon us! Let them know your will!"**

The crowd chanted endlessly:

**"Han's mandate has passed!
Yellow Sky, soon here!
In this renewing year,
Prosperous all, at last!"**

"...We might be ready, and we might not; either way, it starts now," Liu Pi said. "Once Hè Man and Hè Yi get here, we'll start by going north... to the border with Yan."

"*Yan*...?" Huang Shao exclaimed.

"Yuan Shu won't stop us if he thinks we're hurting his enemies," Liu Pi explained. "Let's use him for a change... he might even fund us!"

Huang Shao laughed, raised his hands and cried, **"Our enemies are fools, so how can we lose? Prosperous all at last, people; prosperous all, at last!"**

The Yellow Turbans would soon attract the attention of Yuan Shu and Cao Cao, but their diminished threat was the least of the Han's problems. Those looking for further unrest could now turn eastward to Xu Province – where ambitions would finally manifest as actions – or westward to Chang'an, where the Li-Guo co-regency was about to be shaken to its core and the young Emperor Xian was to finally have an opportunity to restore his clan's authority.

****

ACT II: THE BATTLE FOR CHANG'AN

15

Han Dynasty China was now a greatly divided place. In Liang Province to the far northwest, the northern frontier regions – known as Xiliang – were now under the control of three Qiang tribal leaders – Ma Teng, Han Sui, and Song Jian – and the south was controlled by the self-appointed regents, Li Jue and Guo Si, who still had the Han Emperor, Xiandi, as a hostage-ruler within the current capital Chang'an. The Qiang and the 'regents' were surrounded on all sides: the Di and Xiongnu tribes were in the north, east and west; the cult leader Zhang Lu governed Hanzhong Province to the south; Liu Zhang ruled Yi Province to the south of Hanzhong; and a multitude of powerful warlords existed in the east, beyond the border with Central Province, where the true capital, Luoyang, still lay in ruins after five years.

The eastern warlords were still, after five years, fighting personal battles: the Governor of Jing Province and imperial relation, Liu Biao, ignored the situation in Chang'an and maintained his defences against the vassal-warlord Sun Ce, whose family bore a grudge for the death of their patriarch, the famous hero Sun Jian; the ruler of the 'Southern Xiongnu' tribal confederacy, Huchuquan, was restoring order amongst his people after the defeat of his rebellious brother Yufuluo by Han loyalists; Bing, Ji, Yan and Yòu Provinces were still being targeted by the million-strong criminal coalition of 'Black Mountain Bandits', which led to them being targeted in turn by Cao Cao and Yuan Shao, who were now two of the most powerful warlords in China. Yuan Shao ruled Ji Province – which was to the north of Luoyang – while Cao Cao still governed Yan Province with Yuan Shao's blessing. The northernmost Yòu Province was still ruled by the warlord Gongsun Zan, who had murdered and usurped the governor, Liu Yu, three years before; he was now contending with Yuan Shao for Qing Province, which was south of Yòu and east of Ji, and he had the Black Mountain Bandits as less-than-secret allies in addition to his own formidable cavalry.

Cao Cao's father's death at the hands of robbers was still, in his mind, the responsibility of the entire population of Xu Province, and he did not consider his two previous 'visits' to be the end of the matter. Xu's new governor, Liu Bei – a disinherited scion of the royal house – had already upset many by taking the role at the expense of his predecessor's sons, and he now courted further controversy by giving shelter to the fugitive warlord Lü Bu, whose crimes included being an accessory to regicide, civilian massacres, personally murdering Bing Province Inspector Ding Yuan and Chancellor Dong Zhuo – who were each serving as his stepfather at the time of their deaths – and attempting to seize Cao Cao's domains. Liu Bei had now given Cao Cao a second reason to plot further incursions, and it was only an unpopular treaty with Yuan Shao that saved the province from harm.

Lastly, there was the vast and sparsely-populated Yang Province in the southeast of Han China: the northern part of the province that lay above the Yangtze River was governed by Yuan Shao's ambitious brother Yuan Shu, while the south was contested by Yuan Shu's vassal Sun Ce and the regency-appointed governor,

Liu Yao. Yuan Shu's agenda was still the same. At least for now: he continued his feud with Yuan Shao, whose role as clan chieftain was a desirable prize. But as the Yuans and their allies fought each other for personal gain, the Black Mountain Bandits and the 'White Wave Bandits' around Luoyang benefitted from the lack of policing and the 'Yellow Turbans' – the cultist army that had destabilised the Han administrations across China a decade earlier – were about to resurface in Yu Province, where the Yuan clan's ancestral home, Ru County, was situated. Many worried that the future of the Han depended on the Yuans ending their feud and turning their attentions back to challenging the regency government in the northwest, but reconciliation was becoming increasingly unlikely as new grudges were heaped on top of the old and agendas quietly changed.

In the capital Chang'an, the officials that were loyal to the Han Dynasty had given up on waiting for the divided Yuan brothers to reunite for the sake of the nation, but they were hopeful that two other men – Regents Li Jue and Guo Si – could be divided and hence offer a chance to liberate the young emperor.

"I admit that I grow impatient," Minister Yang Biao said to his dwindling group of allies. "So many good men have died..."

"Perhaps we should leave this administration be," the Director of the Imperial Secretariat, Shisun Rui, suggested. "Jia Xu has now appointed Huangfu Song as Commander-in-Chief; surely that shows a change in policy! Great men like Huangfu and Zhu Jun are finally being recognised again, and-"

"All too late to be a real change," Yang Biao insisted. "Huangfu Song is ill, and it is still Li Jue that holds the military power. Zhu Jun is also ill, and will never take a position in a court run by the men that hounded his region and committed such atrocities there. Don't forget, Director Shisun, that this is the same Li Jue and Guo Si that sacked villages and raped and murdered the good people in them with their master, Dong Zhuo; and they were still active until Dong Zhuo's death in such activities, long after Dong himself had moved onto growing fat in the chancellery and torturing *us* on a daily basis. We've lost a lot of colleagues to these two men and their wicked master: we can't afford to forget that, because if something were to happen to Jia Xu, they would revert to their true nature, and we would soon see the emperor die. Remember, gentlemen, that one of our 'contacts' within the fold has already told us that it was Fan Chou and Zhang Ji that stopped the regents from murdering His Majesty and assuming power: one of those men was executed in front of us at a banquet, and the other fears for his life; when Zhang Ji is inevitably killed, then who will stop them from committing regicide, as their master once did...?"

"...That is true," Shisun Rui conceded. "...And I knew that."

"We must hope that 'our lady' does her part," Yang Biao continued. "If she does not, then we must do something... Li Jue and Guo Si *must* be removed... they simply *must*."

But there were more banquets, and the regents seemed to be inseparable until a day when Li Jue made an off-guard remark that shook Guo Si to the core. Another banquet loomed, and Guo Si was haunted.

"...Why are you going...?" Guo Si's wife, Lady Qiong, asked plainly.
"I am in no danger!" Guo Si insisted. "It's *you*, you spiteful woman, filling my head with nonsense about him wanting to kill me... he's my *friend*."
"Men with power don't have friends," Lady Qiong scoffed. "Men with power have rivals. You're a fool, a dreamer! He's waiting patiently, like he did with Fan Chou!"
"Fan Chou let Han Sui-! ...Wait, why am I arguing with you about this anyway...?" Guo Si said. "What do you know about Fan Chou?"
"I hear things," Lady Qiong retorted. "Heed my words, husband: he'll kill you eventually. First Fan Chou, then Zhang Ji, then you... then he can rule alone."
"Leave me alone!" Guo Si said. "I'm sick of your troublemaking!"
"But I'm still here," Lady Qiong chortled. "You know I'm right."
"...I'm going to the banquet," Guo Si grumbled. "I intend to get drunk – very, very drunk – and enjoy myself."
"Enjoy yourself with who...? Li's women...?" Lady Qiong taunted.
"What is the matter with you...?" Guo Si complained. "...I'm going."
Guo Si left his house and began the journey to the home of his co-regent, but the seed of doubt had long since been planted, and he was very nervous.

The banquet was a grand affair, and the court officials attended as requested. Li Jue welcomed Guo Si as his honoured guest, and the two joked as friends.
"They are friendlier than ever!" Shisun Rui hissed as he sat alongside a calm and stoic Yang Biao. "We are stuck with them!"
"Patience," Yang Biao replied. "Even if it takes a decade, we will be rid of them."
The last of the officials arrived and took their seats: Li Jue then invited Guo Si, his lofty nephew Li Li, Marquis Zhang Ji and Jia Xu to sit close to him as honoured guests, while other former followers of Dong Zhuo and his clan, such as Dong Cheng, Duan Wei and Zhang Ji's nephew Zhang Xiu, also sat in places that showed their favoured positions. With the death of Fan Chou, other officers had seen a rise in fortunes; one, Wu Xi, was now a close ally of Guo Si, while another, a former White Wave Bandit called Yang Feng, was part of Li Jue's following.
"Welcome all!" Li Jue began. "Why are we here, some of you might ask...? We're here because the country is stabilising, and things are getting better! Now is a time to celebrate the fact that, each and every day, the traitors dwindle in number, and the land is nearing a day of peace!"
"...Traitors...?" Zhang Ji murmured; he looked at the curtains around the room, recalled the fate of Fan Chou, and wondered if Li Jue intended another 'execution'.
"I am glad to see Commander Huangfu Song!" Li Jue said as he looked at the withered hero of the Yellow Turban Rebellion. "You once fought alongside us in Liang Province: we could have used your expertise against those same traitors, Han Sui and Ma Teng, when we fought them recently, esteemed Mister Huangfu!"
Huangfu Song smiled falsely and bowed.
"You shouldn't be bowing to me, venerable Mister Huangfu!" Li Jue said condescendingly. "All of us here should be bowing to you... men like you are the reason that peace is a certainty."

"*Peace*...? Are we in the same country?" the pale, gaunt Chang'an Magistrate Zhong Yao muttered. "And this banquet is supplied too well, far too well, while the country starves! This is-!"
"Hush," Yang Biao pleaded.
"That's enough introductions!" Li Jue decided. "Let's enjoy ourselves, gentlemen! We've earned it, I think!"
"Yeah, we have!" Guo Si cackled: he had started drinking immediately, and the strong rice wine was already going to his head. "Let's drink!"
"Yes, let's," Li Jue said tonelessly.
Zhang Ji eyed Li Jue and wondered whether he would survive the evening; Jia Xu guessed the situation and asked, "Does something bother you, Marquis Zhang?"
"No, Mister Jia," Zhang Ji lied. "Please ignore my expression."
Jia Xu turned his gaze to the regents and hummed thoughtfully.

For an hour, the festivities were boisterous but uneventful: Li Jue and Guo Si joined in with the songs sung by their musicians, and they even tried to join in with the dancing. Minister Yang Biao and his allies despaired; but then, entirely unexpectedly, the atmosphere changed.
"...You... really know how... to throw a banquet, Li Zhiran," Guo Si said to Li Jue as he drunkenly struggled with a piece of chicken.
"Yes, well... I'm the descendant of great men, Mister Guo," Li Jue replied with a tone that was strange and ambiguous in intent. "I, Jue, am a descendant of *Li Guang*, the 'Flying General', who was in turn a descendant of the sage of Heaven, Lao Tzu. So how could I not know how to throw a banquet?"
"...I'm just saying," Guo Si said defensively. "...I don't remember you ever telling me you were a descendant of the Flying General. Oh, no, wait... I knew that, I just forgot. Wasn't he really, really *useless*, though...? Didn't he make a lot of really stupid mistakes, because he never planned nothing properly...?"
"...*I* don't," Li Jue replied icily. "I'm *very careful*, Mister Guo."
Guo Si froze: he looked at the half-eaten piece of chicken in his hands, and a terrible thought crossed his mind. He recalled the poisoned dog, and his wife's continual protestations, and suddenly, he was looking at his offended co-regent with fear. Guo Si looked around the room with drunken eyes, and struggled to gain focus: suddenly, he was worried about the cause of his haziness, and the fear overwhelmed him.
"So, Marquis, how is your family?" Jia Xu asked of Zhang Ji.
"Fine, fine," Zhang Ji replied. "So tell me, Mister Jia, how you plan to deal with the unrest in the east: are the Yuans ever going to-?"
The sound of Guo Si's sudden, violent retching forced every man that was present to stop eating and turn their attention to the host seats: Guo Si flailed comically as he tried to regurgitate his food, and the sight amused as much as it offended.
"...What are you doing?" Li Jue asked irritably.
"**Poison! Poison! *Bastard*!**" Guo Si screamed. "**Someone bring me something to be sick! I *have to be sick*!**"
"*Here*?" Zhang Ji chortled.
"**What's the matter with you???**" Li Jue shrieked.
"**Bastard!**" Guo Si replied between his bouts of futile retching.
Two terrified servants had already retreated to the grounds at the rear of the residence; they returned with a bowl of slurry, which

was immediately offensive to the guests before Guo Si had even done anything with it.

"Oh, this is disgusting," Yang Biao complained. "He's not-!"

"He is," Shisun Rui sighed as he pushed his tray of food away.

"**Ayah! What the hell are you doing, you fool???**" Li Jue screamed as Guo Si put the bowl of foulness to his mouth; seconds later, Guo Si was vomiting violently and the other attendees were getting up and moving to the far end of the hall. When Guo Si was satisfied that he was safe, he wiped the mess from his mouth with his sleeve and pointed at Li Jue silently.

"...What... *what*... **D'AAAAAGH! This is the most disgusting thing that you have ever done, that I have ever...! You *creature*, Guo Si!**" Li Jue cried. "**My banquet is ruined! *Explain yourself*, you-!**"

"P-poison! You... tried... t'*kill me*!" Guo Si croaked.

Zhang Ji frowned angrily.

"...The smell is foul, and I can't stay here," Huangfu Song said.

A few of the officials took the former hero Huangfu Song's words as a cue to leave; at the same time, Li Jue and Guo Si glared at each other with hatred.

"**Gentlemen... regents, please calm down!**" Jia Xu cried.

"You... want it *all*, Li Jue!" Guo Si said as he got to his feet.

"You're drunk, and demented!" Li Jue retorted. "It's bad enough that you threw up everywhere, but you've poured pig shit all over my floor as well! You'll pay for this to be cleaned up, or-!"

"You tried t'*kill me*!" Guo Si growled. "You... you poisoned my food again, jus' like when you... you put poison in the other food you sent to me! My wife was right! You want me *dead*!"

"...Regent Guo... Regent Li... please don't do this," Jia Xu said powerlessly. "I'll go back to my village for good this time if you do this... I won't come back if-"

"**How dare you, Guo Si!**" Li Jue barked. "**You come here, ruin my banquet, deface my home, and then resort to accusing me of treachery??? Where is the 'Hongmen'? Where are the killers? You just want to get out answering for your disgraceful, drunken antics! But you won't! In front of everyone here, I swear that I-!**"

"**You want your... family to... to rule!**" Guo Si said as he staggered backwards and produced a concealed knife from his belt. "**You let Wang Fang be killed by Ma Chao... then you had Li Li frame Fan Chou... next, you want t'kill Zhang Ji... next it was me, after him, but you... you got impatient!**"

Zhang Ji silently wished that he was armed.

"**That's the last insult!**" Li Jue cried as he produced a concealed weapon of his own, and the extent of the existing mistrust became evident. "**You dare point a blade at me in my own home, and accuse me of...! War, Guo Si... WAR!**"

Minister Yang Biao smiled silently as Guo Si fled the house to prepare his men and Li Jue issued orders of his own; his scheme had worked, and the battle of the regents had begun.

****

16

"Why are we moving to the palace complex…?" Jia Xu asked as he did his best to keep up with the furious – and shaken – Li Jue.

"He'll attack my house for certain, Mister Jia, and it is not designed to repel sieges," Li Jue replied.

Jia Xu laughed desperately and asked, "Can we not nego-?"

"**Did he seem ready to negotiate to you???**" Li Jue screamed.

"Why are we hurrying?" Yang Feng teased. "He lives what, a few doors down, so it will take him at least twenty minutes to-"

"I do not appreciate your sense of humour!" Li Jue retorted. "Jia Xu, we must know who is with us and who is against us."

"…And who is 'us'…?" Jia Xu asked calmly.

Li Jue stopped, turned to Jia Xu and replied, "Perhaps I was wrong to assume that-"

"Can we afford to stop?" Yang Feng prompted.

Li Jue grunted angrily and ordered the retreat to resume.

"…I must be seen to try and bring you both to your senses, and right now I am unsure of what I can achieve where Guo Si is concerned," Jia Xu conceded. "For now, I am 'on your side', Regent Li, but rest assured that I will do all I can to-"

"And I will certainly not try to stop you," Li Jue interrupted. "Guo Si and I are allies by circumstance and by Heavenly design, not by choice, and we must find unity again before Han Sui and Ma Teng smell blood and make another attempt to seize the capital."

"…Good," Jia Xu murmured. "I'm glad that you understand."

"…I *don't* understand!" Li Jue cried desperately. "What is going on? One minute we are as brothers, and then he's eating slurry, throwing up on my floor and accusing me of trying to murder him! We were talking casually about my ancestors and the nature of organising banquets… there was no cause for this!"

"I sense intrigue, most certainly by his spiteful wife but inspired, perhaps, by others," Jia Xu said. "Let's hope he can be placated."

"If he cannot, then I must kill him and assume sole responsibility as regent, for the good of the nation," Li Jue declared. "In fact, I wonder if I should not do that anyway, regardless of how this is resolved. We cannot afford to have this happen again!"

Jia Xu hummed thoughtfully.

"Is your head clearer now?" Marquis Zhang Ji asked as he rode alongside the agitated Guo Si; the two were also on their way to the palace complex. Guo Si been able to wash, change clothes and obtain a weapon since fleeing from Li Jue's mansion, but he was still far from composed; he did not respond to Zhang Ji's question save for a grunt.

"…I just hope that this isn't a mistake," Zhang Ji continued.

Guo and Zhang were riding ahead of a small army of their followers – of which only a few wore armour, and that mostly consisted of confiscated leather breastplates over their robes – and many of the civilian banquet guests, who were not accompanying the procession by choice.

"This was not part of my plan, Director," Minister Yang Biao said to an irritated Shisun Rui.

"But it is the outcome," Shisun Rui replied. "Now we are prisoners

of a man that is clearly quite deranged… drunk *or* sober."
"Guo Si is a monster!" Magistrate Zhong Yao whimpered. "How can he abduct us like this!? We are-!"
"Hush," Yang Biao pleaded. "We will live longer by cooperating… and, if possible, getting Guo Si to calm down."
"And make peace with Li Jue…?" Shisun Rui chortled.
Yang Biao harrumphed, but his tone suggested embarrassment.
"…We're damned either way," Shisun Rui continued. "Why did we loiter like lost goats, and not leave the banquet with Huangfu Song? At least we'd have had time to learn of this and flee!"
"And abandon His Majesty, for whom we instigated this…?" Yang Biao retorted.
"I'm sure that His Majesty will thank us profusely," Shisun Rui scoffed. "I'm sure that the Son of Heaven will be eternally grateful that we have caused Guo Si to descend upon the palace complex with an army to seize him! I'm sure that this second armed breach of sacred walls to take him into custody in what – six years is it…? – will make legends of us, just as it did for Yuan Shao and the 'Ten'! Statues of us will be erected everywhere, forged from melting down all those worthless bronze coins that Dong Zhuo made out of the old ones!"
Yang Biao harrumphed again.
"We even have some unscrupulous, irreverent warlords nearby to seize power afterwards, just as before!" Shisun Rui heckled. "Three sets, in fact: the ones that did it last time, the Yuan brothers and their friends, and the Qiang barbarians!"
"The Yuans will surely hear of this, abandon their feud and rush to Chang'an," Yang Biao insisted. "And Liu Zhang of Yi will-"
"Liu Zhang is a toady, and even if he wasn't, he has to march through Hanzhong, and that would add Zhang Lu to our list of problems," Shisun Rui interrupted. "And the Yuans will do *nothing*: that's why we resorted to the plan that got us into this. Face facts, Minister Yang, as I have… we failed, collectively. Though I mock you, I do so because… because I am pathetic. We all are. My plans were as worthless as everyone else's; we were always going to fail. For whatever reason, this is Heaven's design."
"**No!**" Zhong Yao cried. "**That cannot be-!**"
"**Will you all be QUIET???**" Guo Si shrieked as he turned his horse and rode toward the group of captives with his glaive raised.
"*Aiee*… **Guo Si, will you calm down?**" Zhang Ji pleaded. "**We have to hurry, in case Jia Xu told Li Jue to take the palace!**"
"I think that he did, and that we might be too late," Zhang Ji's nephew, Zhang Xiu, said uncomfortably; he had spotted Li Jue's ally, Duan Wei, blocking the road to the palace, and he and his men were wearing far more armour.
"*Ayah*! **Jia Xu is too clever!**" Guo Si exclaimed. "**Why did that clever man have to side with that treacherous bastard Li Jue??? Does he not think that he will be eliminated too, when his usefulness has ended???**"
"Perhaps Mister Jia's hoping to double-cross everyone: he's certainly cunning enough," Zhang Ji chuckled. "Perhaps it's Li Jue that should be scared."
"This is bad, but… but we will not give up so easily!" Guo Si decided. "**Zhang Ji, Wu Xi: create a path to the palace!**"
Wu Xi looked at Zhang Ji and awaited his response.

"…That is risky," Zhang Ji replied. "We're too poorly equipped to-"
"Your foreign man, Huche'er, is a demon, another Lü Bu or Ma Chao, and could rid us of Duan Wei single-handed, with or without armour!" Guo Si suggested. "Send *him* forth!"
Many turned their eyes toward the imposing Huche'er: he was visibly unlike the Han Chinese, Xiongnu or other ethic tribes that inhabited China, but few knew which part of the lands beyond the Great Wall had produced him. He was not wearing any armour over his robes at all – having ceded what little there was to superiors and subordinates alike – but he towered over many men, and he wielded his heavy halberd with ease that betrayed an immense strength and skill.
"…**He's good, but not good enough to get out of an ambush, which is what that will be if Jia Xu planned this!**" Zhang Ji heckled. "**Did drinking that slurry not sober you up enough? *Think*, Guo Si! We have to-!**"
"**He's charging!**" Zhang Xiu announced. "**Duan Wei, he's-!**"
"Then this isn't Jia Xu's doing," Zhang Ji decided. "But we've no time to think! **Alright! Wu Xi, Huche'er: you lead our-!**"
"**I give the orders, Zhang Ji!**" Guo Si shrieked. "**I'm the-!**"
"**I'm doing what you told me to do, you…! …*Aiee*! I am punished for I know not what!**" Zhang Ji complained as he readied his weapon and his horse.
"*Punished*…? With what, your *wife*…?" Guo Si muttered as Zhang Ji left him and charged at Duan Wei.
"**Ayah! Zhang Ji is with Guo Si!**" Duan Wei cried as Huche'er reached his force and dealt a series of powerful strikes that unseated three riders. "**Someone tell Lord Li, and QUICKLY!**"
A rider turned and fled from the battle.

Li Jue's small army was nearing the main gates of the imperial palace complex when Duan Wei's messenger reached them.
"…Somebody is approaching from the direction of our homes," Li Jue's nephew, Li Li, announced. "It is one of Duan Wei's men."
The small convoy slowed.
"…*Trouble*," Jia Xu said as the rider halted in front of Li Jue.
"Duan Wei has been attacked by forces belonging to Guo Si!" the rider reported. "They are trying to break through and come this way! They are great in number!"
"*Aiee*… so Guo Si has had the same idea," Li Jue sighed.
"Who attacks Duan Wei…?" Yang Feng asked.
"Zhang Ji and Guo Si… and Wu Xi as well," the rider replied.
"They are all with Guo Si…?" Li Jue exclaimed.
"I guess they don't trust you like I do," Yang Feng said dryly.
"Yang Feng, Xu Huang: go and help Duan Wei," Jia Xu ordered.
Yang Feng – who was tall and thin, but strong – turned and nodded to his subordinate Xu Huang, who was tall, brawny and intimidating, although his face betrayed an intelligence that went beyond his rank. The two men gestured to their force – which consisted of lightly-armed infantry and a small team of riders – and started down the city streets toward the battle between Duan Wei and Guo Si.
"Will they be enough…?" Li Jue wondered. "Or must I leave procuring the emperor to you, Mister Jia, and face Guo myself…?"
Jia Xu blanched involuntarily at the thought of being left with the

responsibility of abducting the emperor for a second time; after a notable moment to compose his thoughts, Jia Xu shook his head and said, "Lord Li, we must, since you have started this, finish it: we will need to approach His Majesty together. Yes, we should we be prepared for a direct confrontation with Guo Si before or even after we breach the palace, but I cannot 'procure' him alone."

"...'Breach'...?" Li Jue scoffed. "I am Regent! How can I 'breach' the palace, Mister Jia...?"

"That is right, *Regent*, but *I* would certainly be breaching the palace if I went alone, for I lack your authority," Jia Xu countered.

"...Sly as always, but you're quite right," Li Jue conceded. "What a pity that I lack the followers to overwhelm Guo Si quickly. We should gather as many of the officials as we can, to further legitimise our work."

"That will be difficult," Jia Xu admitted. "When you retreated from the banquet hall, Guo's men started to herd them together and..."

"...And he has the entire court as hostages," Li Jue sighed. "...But he won't have Huangfu Song. He left early."

"Huangfu Song is gravely ill!" Jia Xu retorted. "He's got months at the most, even without all of this stress! Leave that poor man be!"

"Will Guo Si leave him be...?" Li Jue heckled. "He's Commander-in-Chief of the army at your behest!"

"...Let that be on Guo Si's conscience!" Jia Xu countered. "Huangfu Song is of no use to you! His role is ceremonial at best; your nephew, Li Li, holds all of the military power, at *your* behest!"

"Mister Jia is right, Uncle," Li Li suggested. "Leave Guo Si with that worthless old relic: it'll only make him look like a worse villain if he causes Huangfu's death."

Jia Xu groaned and said, "I-! ...*Aiee*... that isn't what I meant by-!"

"That's what it *sounded like*, Mister Jia," Li Jue retorted. "Let's continue: we might not have much time."

"...First I aid Dong Zhuo, and now Li Jue and Guo Si; is it my destiny to continually offend the Han...?" Jia Xu lamented.

Huche'er and his riders were tearing into Duan Wei's infantry when Yang Feng and Xu Huang arrived to support Duan; Wu Xi signalled to Huche'er, and the two retreated to consolidate and avoid needless losses.

"You are sent by Heaven, Yang Feng!" Duan Wei chuckled.

"I'm just glad that we stopped them breaking through," Yang Feng replied. "Y'know, I'm starting to think that I might need to call on some old friends in the east to help us out here, and-"

"**They have regrouped!**" a soldier screamed.

Huche'er and Wu Xi had begun a counterattack, and they were now joined by Zhang Ji and a frenzied Guo Si.

"**They're poorly armoured!**" Yang Feng noted. "**We-!**"

"**Two divisions have gone around us, and are headed for the palace!**" a second soldier reported.

"**Damn it! We have to aid Li Jue!**" Yang Feng cried desperately.

"**He is *Regent* Li!**" Duan Wei barked. "**And we have to-!**"

"**We need to aid 'Regent Li' quickly, Duan Wei!**" Yang Feng said urgently. "**There ain't no time for protocol! You go ahead, and me and Xu Huang'll guard the rear!**"

Duan Wei did as he was asked, or rather told; Yang Feng and Xu Huang had their men form a rear guard as Huche'er finally reached them. Huche'er lunged at Xu Huang, who barely defended against the strike with his own glaive; Yang Feng engaged Guo Si, who showed why he was a powerful Liang warlord by displaying the prowess that had once allowed him to survive – though only barely – a long duel with Lü Bu.

"Get out of my way, you idiot!" Guo Si screamed.

"Not a chance!" Yang Feng retorted, but Zhang Ji added his own considerable strength to Guo Si's, and Yang Feng's team was forced to fall back.

"Ignore them and break through!" Guo Si ordered as he forced Yang Feng's riders aside with violent swipes of his halberd and rode toward the palace. **"Zhang Ji, do as we planned!"**

Huche'er and his master Zhang Ji now served as a rear guard to a force that was pursuing Duan Wei: Xu Huang ended his attempts to defeat Huche'er and regrouped with Yang Feng.

"We… need to get back to Li Jue," Yang Feng groaned.

"Are you alright…?"Xu Huang asked.

"Yeah, I am, though I feel a little weak right now," Yang Feng replied. "*Aiee*… Guo Si may be a fool, but the man's still strong, even with all that laying around and drinking and feeding his face that he does…"

"…So what do we do…?" Xu Huang asked.

"Attacking Zhang Ji and Huche'er will be pointless and wasteful," Yang Feng replied. "The best thing that we can do now is go around them, like they went around us. I just hope that Duan Wei survives the pincer and Li Jue survives the ambush."

Director of the Imperial Secretariat Shisun Rui stared at the soldiers that were escorting his group of senior officials to the chancellery building and sighed woefully.

"…We did not aid this latest plot, Yang Zan, yet we are condemned anyway," the official Huang Wan – who was a veteran of Wang Yun's plot to oust Dong Zhuo – said bitterly.

"Are we both being punished by Heaven for the last time, I wonder…?" the official Yang Zan replied with a wistful smile.

"Perhaps we could try and escape while Guo Si and the other senior officers are busy fighting," Yang Biao said thoughtfully. "Two captains, a dozen men… and they're no better protected from attacks than we are, most of them…"

"The 'dozen men' wear whatever armour their commanders didn't confiscate while we have our robes between the air and our flesh; and their weapons are real, whereas ours exist only in your vivid imagination, Minister Yang," Shisun Rui replied.

"…I know, I know… but our situation is unbearable!" Yang Biao groaned. "I worked in the chancellery briefly: to think that I will now be held prisoner there, along with every other worthy man in the world, while our regents wage open war on the streets of Chang'an! I am not sure if our poor country has ever suffered such indignity as this!"

"If the Qiang, the Xiongnu, the Xianbei, or our various foreign neighbours learn of this and decide to act, then the Han is done for… if it is not already beyond rescue!" Shisun Rui lamented.

"We have lived in a truly awful time!" Zhong Yao declared. "First we watched as great men like Chen Ji and Lu Zhi were persecuted by the 'Ten'; we quivered while the Yellow Turbans ravaged the

land; we cowered helplessly while men like Cai Yong and Ma Midi were forced to condemn their reputations by fawning on Dong Zhuo, while others, like Chen Ji and Wang Can, fled and others, like Zhou Bi, were put to death in the vilest ways that the sadist Dong could contrive! And then Wang Yun-"
"I know, Zhong Yao, but please, enough," Shisun Rui said quietly.
"...I agree," Huang Wan said. "Such words solve nothing."
Zhong Yao shook his head obliviously and added, "The progeny of noble, pious Yuan An have become greedy hegemons that even wage war against their own kin, Empresses became regicidal schemers, humble peasants have become armies of bandits and cultists that tear their own provinces apart, once-passive Xiongnu settlers have become ransacking mobs, and even the meek and modest eunuchs became notorious criminals that-!"
"*Enough*, Magistrate Zhong... *enough*," Shisun Rui pleaded. "Let us not go from endeavouring to save the Han to composing the odes that mark its demise. Perhaps we will see fortune smile upon our young majesty soon... perhaps there is someone as yet unheard or not thought of that will deliver us from this hell."
"Perhaps His Majesty will think of something," the official Fu Wan – whose daughter was Empress – suggested optimistically.
"...Perhaps, Mister Fu," Shisun Rui replied.
The dozens of captive officials – who were added to during the journey by pre-planned hunting missions – continued on their way to the chancellery building without offering any real resistance.

"**Major Duan Wei is caught in a pincer!**" a rider reported to a frustrated Li Jue.
"**Ayah! I cannot afford to lose Duan Wei! I have too few followers as it is!**" Li Jue cried. "**Jia Xu, we must temporarily abandon our mission and repel Guo Si!**"
Jia Xu buried an urge to smile and said, "We should use this opportunity to talk him down, Regent Li, and make him see-"
"*Reason...?*" Li Jue scoffed. "**He'll see my blade! He'll know death! Li Li, you will be my second! Jia Xu, you will stop trying to remain neutral and advise me!**"
Jia Xu sighed miserably.
"**You tried to escape your responsibilities once before, but there is no Niu Fu for you to find refuge with now!**" Li Jue heckled. "**You will *advise me*, Jia Xu, or the capital will never be stabilised! Think about it, and quickly!**"
"...Alright," Jia Xu replied.
Li Jue raised his sword and shouted, "**FORWARD!**"
"...This is ten steps *backwards*," Jia Xu muttered.

"**Li Jue is here!**" the courtier-turned-officer Dong Cheng yelped as the regent tried to unseat him with a sudden lunge; like Guo Si and Zhang Ji, Li had rediscovered the brute strength and martial skill that had been necessary when he was building his reputation and growing his power in Liang Province in years gone by. The two dispersed and interspersed armies briefly clashed, separated, and reformed on clear opposing sides; the people that lived in the surrounding houses cowered and prayed that they would be spared harm in the event of a major encounter.
"Li Jue is stronger than I expected," Dong Cheng admitted.

"**I will challenge him!**" Guo Si declared.

"...**Is that wise?**" Wu Xi asked. "**Our lack of armour is-**"

"**I need no armour!**" Guo Si boasted. "**All I need is one opportunity to separate his head from his neck with my-!**"

"**GUO SI! ARE YOU SOBER ENOUGH TO TALK?**" Li Jue heckled. "**OR MUST I PROVIDE MORE SLURRY FOR YOU...? BUT THEN, WOULD YOU NOT REGURGITATE IT AGAIN, IN FITTING PLACE OF YOUR USUAL WORDS OF WISDOM...?**"

Guo Si pointed his glaive at Li Jue and shrieked, "**You...! You're trying to outwit me by putting it in a funny way, but aren't you just saying that I've always talked a load of-!**"

"**Calm down, Guo Si! He's trying to provoke you!**" Zhang Ji pleaded. "**You mustn't try and charge him without armour!**"

"**ZHANG JI!**" Li Jue bellowed. "**MARQUIS ZHANG JI! WHY ARE YOU WITH THAT DEMENTED THUG? AREN'T ALL THE WITS IN THE LAND OVER HERE...?**"

"**Demented thug???**" Guo Si screamed. "**I-!**"

"**I AM HERE BECAUSE YOU CANNOT BE TRUSTED, LI JUE!**" Zhang Ji replied. "**WHERE ARE FAN CHOU, HU ZHEN, AND WANG FANG, AND WHY WOULD I WANT TO JOIN THEM IN THE NETHERWORLD BY HELPING YOU...?**"

"**GUO SI DECEIVES YOU!**" Li Jue retorted. "**I DID NOT-!**"

"**AND IF WE HAVE ALL OF THE CLEVER OFFICIALS, AREN'T 'ALL THE WITS IN THE LAND' – EXCEPT THAT TWO-FACED JIA XU – ALL OVER *HERE*?**" Guo Si taunted.

"...**DOG!**" Li Jue screamed.

"...This is *pointless*," Jia Xu protested. "We should be trying to-!"

"We should be trying to resume our march to the palaces," Li Jue interrupted. "**Li Li: I can see that they're not properly armed, any of them; secure arrows and select your best archers.**"

Li Li nodded, bowed and retreated.

"**Duan Wei, Yang Feng: prepare to charge with everything you have,**" Li Jue ordered. "**I think that they will want to preserve their unprotected innards, and that means that they'll fall back.**"

Duan Wei and Yang Feng did as they were asked, and Guo Si was forced to issue orders to retreat. Zhang Ji and Huche'er served as a defending force once again, but Zhang Ji was visibly starting to tire of the situation.

"**YOU'RE A COWARD, LI JUE!**" Guo Si screamed as his forces started to withdraw. "**WHY DO YOU NOT CHARGE...? IS IT NOW BENEATH YOU, 'DESCENDANT OF LAO TZU'...?**"

"Heckle me all you want... soon I'll have the emperor!" Li Jue said.

"**What did he say?**" Jia Xu asked. "**I couldn't hear!**"

"I don't know, Mister Jia, and what's more, I don't care," Li Jue replied. "**Let's get back to our mission before someone tells Guo to get some armour and turns him into a threat.**"

Jia Xu was unhappy at the thought of returning to Li Jue's plan to abduct Emperor Xian, but he had nowhere to run, just as Li Jue had said.

✶✶✶✶✶✶✶✶✶✶✶✶

17

Guo Si assembled his forces in preparation for another attack on Li Jue's entourage.

"What can we achieve...?" Zhang Ji asked. "We need more armour! We need more weapons! We need to secure food supplies, water supplies, arrows, siege materials, barricade materials-"

"**Alright-alright-shut-up-shut-up!**" Guo Si snapped. "Fine, we'll get armour and all that other stuff that you said! But what are we supposed to do with all that if he's gotten into the palace and he has the emperor...?"

"...Cite that we're trying to save the emperor from a man that wanted to kill him and take the throne for himself," Zhang Ji retorted. "We have enough officials to draft a thousand edicts and petitions, while he will have, at the most, some second-rate relief staff and a half-accepted boy sovereign that has never had power to know what to do with it."

Guo Si pondered the point, smiled slightly and said, "I want to agree, but a part of me wants to try and get Li Jue before he establishes himself in the palace complex properly. So here's what we'll do... you do everything that you think that we need to do, and I'll do what I want to do."

"Deal," Zhang Ji chuckled; Guo Si and Wu Xi then assembled an assault team and started toward the palace complex once again while Zhang Ji, Zhang Xiu and Dong Cheng began a coordinated series of resource acquisitions.

"Oh no... not again," Duan Wei complained as Guo Si and Wu Xi advanced on his defensive position; the people fled once again as another bout of fighting began. The two small armies smashed into one-another, and men screamed in reaction to wounds inflicted and received.

"**Why do you stay with the friendless liar Li Jue...?**" Guo Si asked as he locked weapons with the determined Duan Wei.

"**I don't... serve fools!**" Duan Wei replied as he pushed Guo Si and his horse back.

"**You're no match for me!**" Guo Si barked. "**Move or die!**"

"**I will do neither!**" Duan Wei insisted, but Guo Si was a better fighter despite lacking adequate armour; Wu Xi and one half of the cavalry-and-infantry force remained to keep Duan Wei busy while Guo Si took the other half and continued toward the Imperial palace.

"**Ayah! Back, back!**"

Guo Si turned his horse and fled after issuing the desperate order: Li Li had ordered archers to repel any force that was fortunate enough to pass Duan Wei.

"That's all of them turned back," a captain said to a triumphant General Li Li.

"And my uncle is in the palace at last," Li Li replied. "Now Guo Si has a serious problem! Can he raise a sword against the guardians of the Son of Heaven...?"

Emperor Xian and Empress Fu – who were in the emperor's

private quarters in the Northern Palace – were warned of the current situation by a loyal eunuch attendant.

"They were in the Southern Palace, and about to breach the gates that lead to the interconnecting tunnel to this palace, when I came to inform you, Your Majesty!" the attendant reported between repeated kowtows.

"…Someone must tell the Gate Guards that they should offer no resistance," Emperor Xian ordered.

"Your Majesty, the Gate Guards are duty-bound to defend you to the death!" the attendant replied as he continued to kowtow before his emperor. "But a man serving Li Jue has asked that they surrender their weapons to avoid harm inadvertently coming to them or your heavenly manifestation!"

"…Jia Xu, no doubt," Emperor Xian mused. "We hope that the Gate Guards comply. We have lived through one such incursion already in our past life as the Prince of Chenliu, and many lives were needlessly lost. Go, and negotiate with these men that bring arms into our sacred palace."

The attendant kowtowed for one last time and retreated.

"…I wonder if any of our ancestors had to endure this twice, and in a different capital each time," Emperor Xian murmured. "…And if they loot and burn Chang'an, where will they take the court to next…? …Chengdu…?"

"…What is going on, Your Majesty…?" Empress Fu wondered.

"One could wonder if the regents *planned this*," Emperor Xian chuckled. "I–"

Emperor Xian halted his informal reply when he realised that many of his attendants and a number of Gate Guards were still loitering.

"…*We* had heard that there was to be a grand banquet at the home of Regent Li Jue, held in honour of the regents' successful efforts to restore order in our empire," Emperor Xian continued in a more formal tone. "Every senior official would be in attendance, which means that the palace – and the surrounding city – will currently be administrated by the subordinates of those officials, and little true order will exist. Perhaps our vassals have been imprisoned – or slain – and the regents have finally gotten their wish that we be removed – and they ascended – fulfilled."

"We would sooner die than allow it, Your Majesty!" one scrawny eunuch wailed.

"…You are not the 'Ten'," Emperor Xian replied. "You can do nothing against such men."

The meek eunuch attendants began a collective sobbing and wailing; Emperor Xian and Empress Fu exchanged weary glances and waited for the men that would inform them of their fate.

Zhang Ji smiled when he saw the frustrated expression on Guo Si's face; Wu Xi was following the demoralised regent after an undignified retreat from Duan Wei, and he was equally forlorn.

"Don't say it, Zhang Ji," Guo Si growled.

Zhang Ji bowed slightly and said, "I was going to report that we have lots of armour, more weapons, supplies, and we've even managed to recruit more men."

"…I thank you," Guo Si replied half-heartedly. "You'll be my co-regent when Li Jue's dead and this is over."

"I am content with being a marquis," Zhang Ji promised. "You can be a lone regent for all I care, so long as Li Jue is dead at the end of this. The more I think about it all, Guo Si – especially Fan Chou's 'execution', and the way Hu Zhen 'just died' – the more it makes my blood boil. We've achieved what we've achieved as allies, but he wants it all for himself and always did. As bad as Dong Zhuo was sometimes, he at least made sure we were all rewarded... he didn't start trying to kill us all."
Guo Si snorted angrily; Wu Xi nodded slowly and sighed.
"...But enough of that," Zhang Ji continued. "Now we have everything we need, it doesn't matter whether he has the emperor or not; let's set up barricades, reinforce the chancellery, and have Wu Xi harass the palace."
"I am ready to confront them again whenever you see fit, Regent Guo and Marquis Zhang," Wu Xi said obediently.

The regents' long-time adviser, Jia Xu, sat in the audience hall of the Northern Palace and stared at the decorated walls around him: every now and then, a scream or a loud crashing sound made him wince. He had been forced to choose which regent he would follow in a moment of crisis and, rightly or wrongly, he had chosen Li Jue. Jia Xu knew that Guo Si was now in command of the chancellery building with Zhang Ji and Wu Xi as senior officers and most of the civil administration as hostages; Li Jue was in the process of securing the emperor, despite Jia Xu's pleas for the sovereign to be left out of the conflict.
"...Now I am an accomplice to a traitor... *again*," Jia Xu lamented.
Minutes later, Li Jue emerged from the corridor that led to Emperor Xian's private chambers: he gestured toward Jia Xu and said, "Are you with me or not?"
"...I am," Jia Xu replied as he got to his feet. "The reports are that-"
"I've got the emperor," Li Jue continued. "We can leave the palace now and-"
"*Leave*...?" Jia Xu chortled. "Leave the palace with His Majesty...?"
"You said there are reports," Li Jue prompted.
"...Major Duan reports that Guo Si has now ordered Wu Xi to seize the emperor; he's advancing – yet again – as we speak," Jia Xu said numbly.
"Then we must fight!" Li Jue declared.
"*Again*...?" Jia Xu complained. "We fought Guo Si what, maybe *three times* on the way here...? We should retreat via the-"
"Retreat...? From *Wu Xi*...?" Li Jue scoffed. "I'll have my nephew go and- ...No... no, maybe *Yang Feng* or that fine officer of his, Xu Huang, can challenge that mediocrity! If he'd sent *Zhang Ji*, or *Huche'er*, then I might worry!"
"Can you two not stop this?" Jia Xu pleaded.
"Must I reiterate the situation for you, even with all your sense...? Guo Si has accused me of attempting to poison him in front of the courtiers!" Li Jue said as Emperor Xian emerged from the rear corridor with a retinue of nervous eunuch attendants and maids. "Not to mention that he-! ...I won't say what else he did, not in front of the emperor... but *you* know what he did, Jia Xu! You know what he did! How can we be friends now...?"
Emperor Xian sighed wearily.

"So what do you intend to do with His Majesty…?" Jia Xu asked worriedly.

"He can't stay here," Li Jue said irreverently. "He can go in a battle tent near the marketplace… we need to be near food and water supplies, just as Guo Si has made sure to do."

"You're going to put the Son of Heaven in a *tent*?" Jia Xu exclaimed.

"He goes in a tent for hunting expeditions, doesn't he?" Li Jue scoffed. "This is an emergency, you pedant! How can we stay here in one place, where we can be surrounded???"

"If Guo Si or anyone else – especially anyone else – attacks the palace, then he is guilty of treason and heresy!" Jia Xu protested. "He knows that taking arms into the palace is the worst of crimes, so he wouldn't dare do that!"

"…Perhaps you're right, since that's true," Li Jue said.

Emperor Xian looked at the armed men that were dotted about and sighed at the hypocrisy that was being shown by his captors.

"…But who will present him with the charges?" Li Jue continued. "He has the entire Imperial Secretariat as hostages! He has most of the imperial court! There are no bureaucrats to do anything! But he won't get the emperor! The emperor is *mine*!"

Emperor Xian sighed miserably once again.

"I… I cannot apologise enough, Your Majesty," Jia Xu pleaded as he kowtowed to the young sovereign.

"We can see that you are currently without influence," Emperor Xian replied tonelessly and somewhat empathetically.

"Stop grovelling, Jia Xu!" Li Jue barked. **"Help me move him out of here!"**

The attendants wailed and moaned as Li Jue and his soldiers ushered the imperial entourage out of the hall.

"…How did it come to *this*…?" Jia Xu groaned.

There would be several battles, small and large, as the two sides moved their hostages about and gained and ceded ground: the entire city of Chang'an slowly turned into a walled battlefield as the conflict between Li Jue and Guo Si escalated. The Qiang warlords Han Sui, Ma Teng and Song Jian learned of the chaos, but they were too busy with their own internal matters to take advantage of it; Hanzhong's ruler Zhang Lu was being controlled by the outwardly timid but cunning Yi Province Governor Liu Zhang, who kept Zhang Lu's family as hostages in order to ensure his obedience; and in the east of the country, the various rulers were either oblivious to or indifferent to any news that trickled out of the northwest region. The majority were watching the eastern province of Xu where another, almost simultaneous period of chaos was about to begin.

****

18

Xu Province Governor Liu Bei summoned his weary officials to hear the latest news from the Xu-Yang provincial border. The gathering sat silently and awaited a report from Liu Bei's trusted aide, Mister Sun Qian.

"...It's... official," Mister Sun reported. The politician paused before he added, "General Ji Ling is marching northward to try and take Xu Province for Yuan Shu."

The ensemble remained silent and looked to their wartime governor, Liu Bei.

"We must repel him immediately," Liu Bei fretted. "How can I lose this place when I was so trusted by Tao Qian to protect it...?"

The late Governor Tao Qian's middle-aged sons – who were amongst the group of mid-ranking officials – glared at Liu Bei.

"So what do you intend to do...?" Chancellor Cao Bao asked dryly.

"**You-! Damn you, Cao Bao, you bastard!**" Zhang Fei heckled. "**How dare you-!**"

"Yide, for all of the people under Heaven will you **please stop making trouble!**" Liu Bei snapped. "Chancellor Cao, I apologise yet *again* for Zhang Fei's language and behaviour. To answer your question, I intend to march personally."

"Is that wise?" Cao Bao suggested. "You're the appointed governor."

"It's best that I go," Liu Bei retorted.

"Don't you have *anyone* that you can trust to lead the army for you...?" Cao Bao chortled. "Have you *nobody* that-"

Zhang Fei leapt to his feet, pointed at the Chancellor of Xiapi and screamed, "**Cao Bao! Damn you, Cao Bao, you-!**"

"**YIDE!**" Liu Bei cried. "**Stop making me look incompetent!**"

"...It's a bit late for that," the influential Chen Gui muttered.

"Chancellor, I would send Mister Sun and Guan Yunchang, but I worry that some of my vassals from Pingyuan and Zhuo follow *me specifically*," Liu Bei explained uneasily. "Besides, I think that showing that I am a man of action is very important."

"...So who would stay here in Xiapi and guard the capital...?" Chancellor Cao asked. "Are you going to invite Lü Bu to-"

"*No*," Mi Zhu scoffed. "*General of the Household Xu Dan* will keep a large contingent of the Danyang forces here."

The tall, imposing Xu Dan bowed humbly from where he sat and said, "I shall guard Xiapi with my life."

"I shall also leave Zhang Yide here," Liu Bei suggested.

Cao Bao groaned involuntarily: Zhang Fei leapt up again before the chancellor could apologise and said, "**You should *watch yourself*, Cao Bao! You might think that I'm a stupid pig butcher, but I don't need to be smarter than you to-!**"

"*Zhang Yide*," Guan Yu said before Liu Bei could speak.

"He groaned!" Zhang Fei protested. "What have I done to him???"

"I apologise for my rude gesture, General Zhang," Cao Bao said meekly. "Governor Liu, I am your capital's chancellor, and I shall abide by your decisions."

"Very good," Liu Bei replied with strange cheer. "Let's prepare to march against this threat that approaches us!"

Cao Bao looked at Chen Gui and Chen Deng: all of them had lost faith in Liu Bei and were secretly pondering the idea of writing to Lü Bu's adviser, Chen Gong.

Tao Qian's sons, Shang and Ying, went to Cao Bao's chancellery office once the emergency meeting was over.
"This is intolerable, Mister Cao!" Tao Shang began. "Liu Bei was invited here and given the authority that is rightly ours in order to protect this province from harm: where is the security that he is supposed to embody? His ruffian friend Zhang Fei is probably a greater threat than this 'Ji Ling' that comes here!"
"Bei inspires no confidence; even the men that invited him here are starting to drift toward alternatives," Tao Ying suggested. "I implore you, Chancellor, to consider opening a dialogue with the heroes of Yan Province, Lü Bu and Chen Gong."
Cao Bao hummed thoughtfully and said, "I have considered doing that very thing, my lords. Like you, I do not see a hero in Liu Bei; Zhang Fei is a volcano waiting to erupt; Guan Yu is arrogant and irreverent; and I use that last word cautiously, since I must then describe Jian Yong, for whom 'irreverent' could never be too great a euphemism, with respect to any aspect of basic social interaction. Liu Bei simpers and whines when he deals with them, and he is no more impressive in combat: Cao Cao defeated him with painful ease when he first arrived, and that was before a lot of Gongsun Zan's borrowed men deserted him in the wake of his embarrassing surrender to Yuan Shao. But can we – or I – challenge him, I wonder...?"
"General Xu Dan estimates Liu Bei poorly also," Tao Shang replied. "If a hero like Lü Bu were to offer his aid to us, as he did to the people of Yan..."
"I... I worry about Lü Bu's true nature," Cao Bao admitted. "Yes, his recent acts are commendable, but his motives are suspect. We must not invite a wolf into the house to help us be rid of a troublesome dog."
"...Might I volunteer an opinion...?"
Tao Shang, Tao Ying and Cao Bao turned to Chen Gui and Chen Deng, who had entered the office unannounced.
"I am here a friend, I assure you," Chen Gui continued. "The lords Tao Shang and Tao Ying invited me, but I was waylaid by our acting governor wanting my opinion on something as well."
"*Ayah*... you scared me for a moment, Mister Chen!" Cao Bao chuckled. "What is your esteemed opinion...?"
"As you know, I was in full agreement with my peer, Mi Zhu, when defending this province was the matter at hand," Chen Gui continued. "But when it came to the succession and the subsequent surrender to Yuan Shao, our opinions diverged. Mi Zhu was obviously out for himself all along, and saw Liu Bei as a way to elevate his already-privileged clan to greater heights. He obviously suspects that the crimes that Liu Bei's disinherited ancestors committed will be pardoned by His Majesty, and that his connection by marriage to Bei will give him a place in future imperial courts... while my only interest is making Xu Province a safe place to be for everyone that lives here."
"It is good to have an ally, Mister Chen," Tao Shang said.
"Alas, we haven't enough allies at present," Chen Gui replied. "Liu Bei is unpopular, yes, for his surrender to the murderer Cao Cao's

friend... but others see it as a necessary evil, a way to prevent further incursions by having Yuan Shao restrain his close friend as no enemy could hope to do. But in doing what he did, he has unleashed Yuan Shu upon us, but Yuan Shao will certainly lend no aid because he hates us; the whole thing is a nonsense! We invited Liu Bei here rather than surrender to Cao Cao; why would we invite him here so that he could then surrender to Cao's friend...? The people of Xu would have preferred that we stood firm, endure another short-term hardship – with the aid of that criminal Zang Ba, if needs must – and then meet the threat of Cao Cao with better friends than Liu Bei has been."

"You put a strong case for talking to Chen Gong, Mister Chen Gui," Cao Bao admitted. "I fear Zhang Fei's reaction, since there will be no Liu Bei or Guan Yu to restrain him... but he'll still be unfettered if we do nothing."

"We should be cautious, see what Chen Gong's motives are; and Lü Bu's as well, naturally, for like you, I worry that the animal that killed the noble Ding Yuan is still in there somewhere, waiting for another Dong Zhuo to awaken it," Chen Gui replied. "Chen Gong and I may share a family name, but any connection is distant, like the distance between us and the Chens that aid Liu Bei, so I do not trust Chen Gong automatically. His motives may be as suspect as his master's."

"But are they worse than Liu Bei...?" Tao Shang proposed.

"We must be sure that we really want to know the answer to that question, for it involves inviting Lü Bu and Chen Gong to replace Liu Bei as our military guardians," Chen Gui retorted. "We must be sure that they will allow the Taos to take their rightful place and not hanker for their place as Liu Bei has done."

Tao Ying hummed thoughtfully and said, "That is quite right."

"...The Chens that are with Bei surprise me," Cao Bao admitted.

"Chen Yuanfang is a wise old man that has seen the inside of the Han court and enjoyed high rank in his later years, but suffered the pain of exile in his younger years, thanks to the wretched 'Ten'," Chen Gui explained. "His father was a 'Partisan', and he was too by design... so his great literary talent went unused. His own son, Chen Qun, grew up an exile too, but did not share Yuanfang's bitterness toward the Han court that saw him reject initial offerings when the madness of the Partisan Crisis subsided.

"Yuanfang fled the court when Dong Zhuo took control of the government, all but abolished the 'Three Excellences' and restored the overly-powerful role of 'Chancellor of State' so that he might have it for himself; Dong Zhuo, deranged oddity that he was, revered Yuanfang, much as he admired poor Cai Yong, who was forced to be his resident pet scholar after spending years in exile for slandering the 'Ten'... but unlike Cai Yong, who died a dog's death at the hands of Director Wang Yun for being an accomplice to Dong Zhuo – an accusation that was unfairly made, and I think Wang Yun knew that at the end – Yuanfang and his son were lucky enough to fool the tyrant into letting them escape to Qing Province, where they fell into Liu Bei's newly-arrived camp by pure circumstance and nothing more.

"They do not strike me as loyalists to Liu Bei, as Guan Yu, Zhang Fei, Jian Yong and – wretched traitors that they are – Mi Zhu, Mi Fang and Sun Qian can be best described; Chen

Yuanfang and Chen Qun are his travelling companions while they look for a safe haven."

"...Then we must make those great scholars see that we admire them and desire their presence here in a peaceful Xu," Tao Shang suggested. "And... and we must refrain from inviting further disaster upon ourselves. Let us see whether Liu Bei can repel Ji Ling, and whether Zhang Fei can show more restraint when given proper responsibility. If not, then – and only then – we consider inviting Chen Gong and Lü Bu to aid us in restoring order."

Chen Gui bowed slightly and replied, "I think that is the best course of action."

"It was a fortunate thing indeed that we had your advice, Mister Chen Hanyu," Cao Bao said. "We shall be patient and observe."

"Now, if you'll excuse me," Chen Gui said politely; the five men exchanged bows, and Chen Gui and Chen Deng departed.

"You were strangely silent," Chen Gui said to his son as they returned to their residence.

"Your words were all that were needed, Father," Chen Deng replied. "I agreed with all of them, so why speak...?"

"I only hope that Liu Bei – and, more than him, Zhang Fei – do not prove themselves to be as unreliable as my worst scenario," Chen Gui admitted. "Lü Bu scares me, and Ji Ling's attack must certainly be repelled."

"Whatever happens, we'll react as best we can," Chen Deng said.

To the northeast of Xu Province was a city called Kaiyang, named for the county. Kaiyang was usually considered to be part of Langya Prefecture in southeast Qing Province, but boundaries were a contentious thing in the age of the warlord-governor and Kaiyang was close to – and therefore argued to be a part of – Xu Province. But in recent times, it no longer mattered whether Kaiyang was part of Qing or Xu; it was completely autonomous, and was governed by the bandit king Zang Ba. Zang had once been the naïve and idealistic son of an honest prison warder that worked in a city in Mount Tai Prefecture, which was itself a chaotic and troubled part of Qing Province. During the time that the 'Ten Attendants' controlled the government and decided who held the power in the provinces, corruption reached every part of the region, and power was split between dishonest officials and criminal gangs; when Zang's father questioned the imprisonment of innocent – but 'troublesome' – officials while criminals operated openly and unpunished, he was wrongfully arrested and thrown in a prison wagon for transportation to the capital. Since there were no honest local officials to appeal to, Zang Ba was forced to approach the local criminal underworld – the very people that he had been raised to despise – instead, and they were happy to oblige. Zang's father was freed from the prison cart by a criminal gang, and father and son were forced to hide in the hills and live as bandits: the situation warped Zang Ba's view of the world and left him bitter.

When the Yellow Turbans rose up, Zang Ba and his bandit allies volunteered to aid the loyalist cause, expecting that it would lead to amnesty and a new, less corrupt society. Neither amnesty nor reforms were apparent after the Yellow Turbans were defeated, so Zang Ba and his allies travelled south to Kaiyang and exploited the fractured leadership in Xu Province to secure a foothold in the county capital. Neither Xu's governor, Tao Qian, nor the Buddhist cultist Chancellor of Xiapi, Ze Rong – of whom the latter was the more powerful at the time due to his religiously-founded manipulation of the other administrators – tried to do something about Zang Ba, so Kaiyang became a fortified crime city that people simply accepted. But Zang Ba knew that one day, if the nation ever stabilised, he would be confronted and perhaps lose everything. He feared Cao Cao's rampages across the province in recent times, especially since criminal gangs were blamed for the death of Cao's father; now Ji Ling and Liu Bei were of concern, since Bei was known to be inflexibly strict in his attitude towards banditry and Ji Ling might destroy the province as Cao Cao had tried to.

"We shall have to watch ourselves," Zang Ba said to his assembled subordinates. "Cao's still waiting for an opportunity to come back here, and Bei's probably going to try and 'clean the province up' if he ever feels we're an internal threat... you've something to say, Wu Dun...?"

Wu Dun nodded and said, "Me and Chang Xi, we've been talking, and we reckon that we could work with Yuan Shu, like how Liu Pi and the Black Mountain Bandits are said to work with him."

The bandit Cheng Xi nodded to confirm his solidarity with Wu Dun.

"*If* that's true, and nobody's sure that it is," Zang Ba retorted.

"Oh, course it is, boss!" Cheng Xi said. "They never attack Yuan Shu, but they attack everyone that's fighting him, don't they! Yuan Shu and Gongsun Zan, they both work with the Black Mountain Bandits: hasn't Gongsun contacted *us*...?"

"...Yeah, he has done, a couple o' times," Zang Ba replied. "But I've heard nothing from Yuan Shu or Ji Ling, yet I'm getting word that Ji Ling's already over the border; and if *they* don't talk to *us*, that's that. They don't intend on allying with us, friends. We have to be worried about all of 'em, not just Liu Bei and Cao Cao."

"...What about helping Liu Bei...?" Wu Dun suggested. "I mean, we helped the government fight the Yellow Turbans, and..."

Many of the bandits laughed at the idea.

"...**Shut up, you bastards!**" Wu Dun whined. "**I was just-!**"

"**Quiet down, lads!**" Cheng Xi chuckled. "**The boss isn't done!**"

The other bandit leaders gradually fell silent.

"Look, Wu Dun, that's just silly," Zang Ba said. "*Help Liu Bei*...? ...*Liu Bei*, a *Legalist*...? If it was left up to him, we'd all be bald and dick-less with no hands or feet, and a big tattoo on our foreheads saying 'Thief'... and that's whether we help him or not."

The bandits laughed quietly and nervously for a few moments and then fell silent.

"...Yeah, you're right to not find it *too* funny," Zang Ba continued. "His idea of thanks would be the 'Five Pains', and that doesn't appeal. If Bei wins, we think about moving north; if he loses, we sit tight and see what Cao Cao and Ji Ling do... *alright*...?"

The bandits murmured in accord, and no more was said.

****

19

Liu Bei was still preparing to leave Xiapi when he received a letter from his master Yuan Shao. Bei summoned Guan Yu, Zhang Fei, Jian Yong, Mi Zhu, Mi Fang, Mister Sun, Elder Chen Yuanfang and his son Chen Qun to his private audience chamber so that he could discuss the content with them.

"…He demands that I betray Lü Bu," Liu Bei revealed. "Can I risk such action, especially when I am about to face Ji Ling…?"

"That Lü Bu's a nuisance!" Zhang Fei said angrily. "He calls you 'Younger Brother' all the time! How dare he!"

"That isn't a good reason to make war against him," Chen Qun suggested. "His main adviser, Chen Gong, is a truly marvellous man. Even the Danyang Brigades respect Chen Gong for his good nature and his heroic stand against Cao Cao."

"That worries me," Mi Zhu admitted. "What if they start to switch their allegiances to Lü Bu as a result…? Won't Lord Liu lose the province?"

"Hasn't he lost it already…?" Chen Qun said wearily. "Didn't he lose it when he surrendered it to Yuan Shao?"

"…So I shouldn't do as Yuan Shao asks, then," Liu Bei prompted.

"Of course not!" Chen Qun replied. "How can we attack Lü Bu, the hero that tried to rescue Yan Province from the tyrant Cao Cao – and in doing so rescued this place???"

"…So should I tell Lü Bu that Yuan Shao has asked me to do this thing…?" Liu Bei asked further.

"There's no need for that," Mister Sun insisted. "He'll know that you'll be pressured by Yuan Shao and others; he isn't a fool, and Chen Gong isn't either."

"Oh, for an end to the needless wars and the petty intrigue!" Liu Bei cried. **"Can't I just run the province???"**

Chen Yuanfang and his son Qun looked at one-another with tired eyes; they were becoming unbearably frustrated with Liu Bei.

The preparations were swiftly completed. Liu Bei began his march toward the Xu-Yang border with a sense of brave determination, although he was not free from concerns about the safety of his capital and his place as governor.

"…I'm not sure," Liu Bei said as he rode alongside Jian Yong.

"It'll be fine," Jian Yong insisted. "I mean, Yide is reckless, yes, but he's not a fool, and he has Old Chen and Chen Qun to help him. What can he do…?"

"He's hot-headed; he makes mistakes," Liu Bei complained.

"The same can be said of *you*, Xuande," Jian Yong sighed. "Why are you not now the Magistrate of Anxi, if that isn't the case…?"

Liu Bei harrumphed, but after a few moments, he smiled and said, "I suppose so."

"Yide is reckless beyond belief at times," Guan Yu suggested. "But like Lord Liu Xuande, I am sure that he will be sensible at the critical moment."

"He'd better be," Mi Zhu hoped. "We cannot afford to compromise our already precarious situation right now."

Yuan Shu finally learned of Lü Bu's location and role in Xu

Province from General Ji Ling's scouts and summoned his advisers to a meeting in his court at Shouchun.

"Well?" Yuan Shu barked. "What now? It's all confirmed: first Liu Bei steals the province from Tao Qian's sons and hands himself over to my brother-cousin, and now he invites the murderer of my clan, Lü Bu, to guard the place with him!"

"You simplify it too much," the adviser Han Yin chuckled. "Lü Bu is now the guest of a man that is controlled by Yuan Shao; didn't Yuan Shao try and kill Lü Bu? Don't you think that he'll be angry that his puppet governor, Liu Bei, now shelters the man that not only murdered the clan as you say, but tried to take Ji Province from him, humiliated him in front of his court by sacking his domains, and aided a rebellion in Yan to unseat his ally Cao Cao?"

Yuan Shu hummed thoughtfully.

"Lü Bu killed the man that ordered the death of your clan," the adviser Yan Xiang suggested. "Do you punish the blade for what the executioner did? Lü Bu was to Dong Zhuo a mindless tool, at best, or at worst, an obedient dog: whatever his current master ordered, he did it. 'Fight the Black Mountain Bandits!' Ding Yuan ordered, and Lü Bu did as he was asked. 'We shall fight Dong Zhuo in the capital!' Ding Yuan suggested, and Lü Bu did not question. 'Murder Ding Yuan!' Dong Zhuo ordered: he did it. 'Murder the Yuans!' Dong Zhuo said: he did it. 'Sack the imperial tombs!' he commanded: Lü Bu obeyed, just as he always has. But then Lü Bu killed Dong Zhuo without a shred of conscience, on the order of Wang Yun! By employing Lü Bu, we don't employ the murderer of your clan, because Lü Bu did not do it maliciously: he did it, if he did it at all, because he was asked or told to. 'Fight the Black Mountain Bandits!' Yuan Shao ordered, and Lü Bu obeyed, bringing things full circle: why should you not have your chance at wielding such a dangerous weapon...?"

Yuan Shu smiled and said, "Put like that, I can work with him."

"Write to him," Han Yin suggested. "If his response is favourable, we can have him aid Ji Ling's march on Xu Province and pincer Liu Bei; if he is less accommodating, then we can find some other way of playing him against Yuan Shao, Liu Bei or Cao Cao and benefit from the outcome."

Yuan Shu laughed and said, "I like it! I shall write immediately!"

Yuan Shu's general Ji Ling had opted to march to the northeast from the border and set up a camp in Huaiyin, a region in the north of Guangling Prefecture that was considered part of Xu Province or Yang Province by various contenders. Liu Bei camped nearby and prepared for battle while he sent scouts to ascertain the size of Ji Ling's army. The news was bad: Ji Ling's army was larger than expected.

"We'll have to confront him all the same," Guan Yu said as Liu Bei groaned at the prospect of another rout. "Let me fight this man Ji Ling. If we kill their commander, they'll surely retreat."

"I... ... ...alright, go," Liu Bei sighed. "But be careful, please."

Mi Zhu waited until Guan Yu had bowed and left the command tent before he said, "I won't lie to you, Lord Liu: I'm concerned. Ji Ling only suffered in the past when he has been subject to Yuan Shu on the battlefield, such as the defeats he suffered against Liu Biao in Nan County and Cao Cao at Fengqiu. Unfettered, Ji Ling is a force to be reckoned with."

"So why let me send Yunchang to fight him?" Liu Bei retorted.

"Guan Yunchang is among the most intelligent of the fighting men today, in addition to being one of the strongest," Mi Zhu replied. "I do not fear for his safety, rather I fear for ours. Guan will retreat when he sees that the situation is beyond him; it is Ji Ling's subsequent actions that concern me."

"I'll formulate a plan," Mister Sun promised.

Guan Yu took an elite contingent of cavalry and advanced on Ji Ling's camp, but the enemy general was ready for him. What met Guan Yu was a vast horde of men, predominantly infantry but augmented by a small cavalry presence: Guan knew that his enemy was not going to be an easy target, so he withdrew. Ji Ling's spotters detected Guan's movements and informed their delighted commander.

"I will pursue this man personally," Ji Ling decided. "If I can take the head of Liu Bei's prize general, he'll be finished!"

Ji Ling's appointed advisers, Yang Hong and Yuan Huan, looked at each other silently; Ji Ling noticed this and said, "You have other ideas, gentlemen...?"

"No," Yang Hong replied.

"Not as such," Yuan Huan said. "I think that Guan Yu should be treated with caution... but you know that, General Ji."

"I do," Ji Ling chuckled. "Let's go!"

Ji Ling led a force of infantry and cavalry after Guan Yu, finally catching up to the retreating Xu Provincial force when their camp was within sight.

"General, let me challenge him!" the officer Chen Lan pleaded. "I was denied a chance to gain real merit in Lujiang, and-"

"There will be other opportunities for gaining merit," Ji Ling promised as he prepared to charge. "This man is my prize, and mine alone!"

"But is Guan Yu a real champion?" the officer Lei Bo asked.

"He is said to be a hero of the age," Yuan Huan replied as Ji Ling charged.

Guan Yu turned his horse about and met Ji Ling personally: the two exchanged blows while their subordinates engaged in their own battles. Guan Yu smiled as he used his custom-made Green Dragon pole sword to block one powerful downward strike by Ji Ling; he knew that the other man was a match for him, but he also knew the importance of returning to Liu Bei. Guan used his superior strength to push Ji Ling away and followed the repelling action with a powerful swipe: Ji Ling narrowly avoided the counter and urged his horse backwards, allowing Guan Yu space to continue his retreat.

"...**THERE'LL BE A NEXT TIME!**" Ji Ling screamed.

Guan Yu laughed and shouted, "**I LOOK FORWARD TO IT!**"

"Will you pursue...?" Yuan Huan asked as he reached Ji Ling.

"...No," Ji Ling replied. "As you no doubt intend to suggest, this might've been an attempt at a trap... but I'll have the final say, I promise you that."

Ji Ling threw his arm upward as a gesture that his men should withdraw; they complied immediately.

Guan Yu entered Liu Bei's command tent and said, "Lord Liu, his forces are well-organised, brave and obedient. Ji Ling himself is not without talent, although I know I could best him. But this fight will be difficult."

"…We must request reinforcements from Xiapi!" Liu Bei said.

"And leave Xu Province exposed…?" Mister Sun exclaimed.

"…No… no, you're right," Liu Bei sighed. "We'll just have to do our very best."

"Or ask Lü Bu for help," Mi Fang suggested dryly.

Guan Yu glared at Mi Fang; Liu Bei also stared at the younger Mi brother, but with an expression that betrayed a genuine consideration of the notion.

"Your tone suggests that you jest; hopefully, brother, you *do*," Mi Zhu chortled. "I would not invite that inconstant man here… I'm worried enough about him being stationed in Xiaopei. If he were distanced from his enemy Cao Cao, he could become a threat to us… so *no*."

"On the other hand, he'd be where we could see him!" Mi Fang joked. "I'm as worried as you: hopefully, our fears are without grounds…"

Yuan Shu's promised letter reached Lü Bu several days after Liu Bei reached Huaiyin; the tenant-warlord elected to read the letter privately before he conferred with his advisers.

"General Lü Fengxian,

I hope that you are in good health. What troubled times we live in! In such times, a man can miss opportunities with ease, and I write to you now to state that I am aware that I missed an opportunity when you visited me in Nan County. Now that place is not mine, though it will be again very soon. Now you are in Xu Province, and I wonder whose it is and whose it should be.

3 years ago, Dong Zhuo seized control of the court, committed regicide, and slaughtered my clan. I then took up arms against the villain, but I could not defeat him: you, Fengxian, slayed him and brought me his head. That was the first great favour that you did for me, and I am grateful.

Not so long ago, I travelled into Yan Province to lay rightful claim to it, and despatched a man to assume the office of Inspector. Cao Cao harried my friend, chased me from the province and inflicted indignity upon me: you, Fengxian, invaded Yan Province, humbled the villain Cao, and showed the world that I have good friends, thus restoring my standing. That was the second great favour that you did for me, and I am grateful.

Right now, despite my never having heard of Liu Bei as such and having no quarrel with him, he wages war against me from the province that he has stolen from the honest, unfortunate Tao Qian. If you were to rise up against this craven, vicious thief for me, Fengxian, then that would be the third great favour that you had done for me, and I would be grateful.

If you had done those three favours for me, then I would place all of my faith in you, and entrust you with all matters of state, if that were within my power to do. I imagine that your army must be tired and hungry from years of fighting and the famine that curses the north! I will send you enough grain to feed your men, and I will throw my doors open to you. If what I send is not enough, ask and I shall send more; no request is too great for you, Fengxian. If you need weapons, ask and they shall be sent: no request is too great for you, Fengxian.

Your grateful friend Yuan Gonglu bids you farewell for now."

"This is ideal," Lü Bu chuckled quietly.

Chen Gong had suspected that Lü Bu had received important correspondence: he entered the command tent and said, "I saw a messenger come and go; is there something that I should know about, my lord?"

Lü Bu laughed and replied, "You're an insightful man, Mister Chen. I have here a letter from Yuan Shu!"

Chen Gong took the letter, read it, smiled, and said, "Perfect. We should agree to this and begin a march to Xiapi, but… I want us to have the maximum number of defectors to our cause. We'll not get that by attacking Liu Bei without provocation; we need a catalyst."

"A catalyst such as…?" Lü Bu wondered.

"This plan I have is reliant on Liu Bei making bad decisions… and fortunately for us, he is obviously inept and devoid of good counsel," Chen Gong chuckled. "Chen Gui and Chen Deng, the heads of the influential Chen clan of this province, are already fed up with him, and the Danyang Brigades look up to you for your martial prowess; if he's marched against Ji Ling, then we should find out who went and who stayed. If he left that clown Jian Yong or that violent moron Zhang Fei in charge of Xiapi, then we'd be asked to take the province from Bei, I think. If he's taken all of his friends with him, then Chancellor Cao Bao is the man to approach. I'll find out and plan accordingly."

"I marvel at you advisers," Lü Bu sighed. "I'll entrust everything to you."

"…Thank you, my lord," Chen Gong replied.

Chen Gong had Lü Bu's forces march toward Xiapi while the oblivious Liu Bei was fighting in Huaiyin. Success for Liu Bei now depended on Guan Yu's prowess as a general and Zhang Fei's effectiveness as a diplomat; in the latter case, Liu Bei was doomed before he had ever left his capital.

****

20

Zhang Fei stood on the battlements of Xiapi City and stared at the distant, snake-like form of the Si River as a messenger concluded a report on two on-going situations. He did not respond when the messenger finished: after a few tense and silent moments, the younger of the Xiapi Chen clan leaders, Chen Deng, dismissed the messenger with a pursed smile and a hand wave.

"...Don't get angry, Mister Zhang," Chen Gui pleaded.

"Why shouldn't I get angry?" Zhang Fei barked as he turned to face Chen Gui, Chen Deng and Chen Qun. "Xuande and Yunchang are in trouble against this 'Ji Ling' fellow down south, and now Lü Bu is moving east towards Xiapi without being asked to! Yunchang'll get that Ji Ling, so I won't worry too much about that, but the other thing... Lü Bu... I didn't ask him to move, so there's only one person around here that could and did."

"Yes... his adviser, Chen Gong," Chen Gui protested.

"**No, it's that bloody *Cao Bao*!**" Zhang Fei snapped. "**He's conniving! He's up to something, and I'm going to-!**"

"Don't do anything," Chen Deng pleaded. "Cao Bao would not dare ask Bu to march east; this is Chen Gong's doing, no one else's."

Zhang Fei smirked and said, "S'funny, you Chens condemning another Chen: so many good Chens around us... Old Chen Yuanfang, Chen Dao, you three... and then we have this Chen Gong messing everything up for us, when we were told he was a really great man! I tell you this: if this Chen Gong is making trouble, I'll kill him; but if he isn't the problem, and I'm right about Cao Bao... I'll kill *him*."

With that said, Zhang Fei left the wall of Xiapi City. After a few moments of contemplation, Chen Qun sighed deliberately, bowed to Chen Gui and Chen Deng, and said, "Farewell for now, gentlemen... we shall no doubt encounter each other later."

The three Chens bowed to each other, and then Chen Qun retreated; Chen Gui and Chen Deng were left alone to stare at the landscape that surrounded the city.

"...I cannot believe that we ever really thought Liu Bei was a future hero," Chen Gui said with a sigh. "And you can see the same thought in the eyes of Chen Qun... Liu Bei is a fool surrounded by bigger fools, and men like Mi Zhu and Chen Qun can only hope that awful situation will change."

"Sadly, Father, I agree completely," Chen Deng said. "I need no persuasion: Liu Bei will definitely lose this place because he values oafs and ignores good counsel."

"I admit – to you, for you were there, but never to the Tao brothers – that I agreed with the plan to put him in charge here, and that I really resented Chen Qun for being so defiant about it," Chen Gui continued. "But Chen Qun could see what we could not... even if he really is as benevolent and honest as he projects himself to be, Liu Bei is doomed to failure because he has Guan Yu, Zhang Fei and Jian Yong as his closest allies and confidantes. A lofty egomaniac, an irrational brute and an irreverent clown; those three men can only bring misfortune on others and themselves. Bei is also spineless: he could not stand up to Lü Bu if he had to, and I'm sure that the same applies when considering

Cao Cao, Yuan Shu and every other 'hero' of the age... I say 'hero', of course, because I wonder if we were as wrong about those other men as we were about Bei."

"Even if Lü Bu is a thug, he has good counsel now," Chen Deng mused. "If we are dealing with Chen Gong – a man that almost bested Cao Cao, if not for Heaven cursing his plans with a famine – then we are dealing with a rational, clever man..."

"...The sort of man that could protect Xu Province," Chen Gui said. "Cao Bao agrees, though he is still being understandably reticent in public. Zhang Fei senses the doubt and hates him, and I doubt that will end well."

Chen Deng nodded silently.

Within days of Lü Bu's forces reaching the region to the west of Xiapi and setting up an encampment, the inevitable came to pass.

"**AAAAAAAAGH! That damn Cao Bao!**" Zhang Fei screamed as his subordinates looked on with increasing dread. "**I'll break him! I'll kill him! I'll feed him to-!**"

"General Zhang, regain your head! You really must calm down!" General of the Household Xu Dan pleaded.

"**I hate Cao Bao!**" Zhang Fei retorted. "**Arrogant bastard! What good is he??? How dare he make noise! Dare he?!**"

"...What exactly is the problem...?" Chen Deng whispered.

"Rumours are that Cao Bao made disparaging comments about the passing of power from Tao Qian to Lord Liu," Xu Dan replied quietly. "There are also rumours that he is considering going to Lü Bu and requesting his aid in 'regime change' within Xu."

"*Ayah*... This could mean blood spilling!" Chen Deng exclaimed.

"**What are you two whispering about?!**" Zhang Fei bellowed; every man present winced at Zhang's voice, which was akin to a giant at the bottom of a well.

"General Zhang, you must be *measured*," Xu Dan pleaded. "Chancellor Cao Bao is a man of high status, and-"

"**He'll taste the metal of my pike!**" Zhang Fei roared.

"The words that circulate are *rumours*!" Chen Deng pleaded. "You cannot act so absolutely when your act is based on *rumours*!"

"**The man has always looked down on us!**" Zhang Fei growled. "**Funny looks, always sneering at me and Guan Yunchang, like we're worthless! Well, enough is enough! He wants things to change, does he...? Well then, I'll help him!**"

"No!" Chen Qun said as Zhang Fei departed. "You *mustn't*...!"

Lü Bu was sat in his command tent with his three advisers – Chen Gong, Wang Kai and Xu Si – when a major under General of the Household Xu Dan brought eventful news on that same night.

"**General Lü, I bring urgent news!**" Major Zhang Kuang began. "**General Zhang Fei has attacked Chancellor Cao Bao!**"

"He's done *what*...?" Wang Kai chortled.

Lü Bu leant forward and smiled a hankering smile.

"Chancellor Cao is no longer in control!" Major Zhang reported.

"...He's *dead*...?" Xu Si asked.

"That... is likely," Major Zhang replied carefully. "But the city is now disrupted... order has broken down... I was sent here to inform you of this by General of the Household Xu Dan!"

"And there's an obvious reason *why* he'd want me to know this,"

Lü Bu chuckled.

"Forgive me Major, but we must discuss this further," Chen Gong said. "Zhang Liao will certainly ensure that you are given food and accommodation if you need it."

Major Zhang bowed humbly and withdrew from the command tent with his cautious escort, Zhang Liao.

"Surely this is a moment to exploit...?" Lü Bu prompted.

"I think so," Chen Gong said.

"You have thoughts...?" Lü Bu asked of Wang Kai and Xu Si.

"I am in agreement with Chen Gong," Xu Si said.

"We're asked to do this: where is the problem?" Wang Kai said.

"Precisely," Chen Gong said. "Liu Bei's subordinates are obviously incompetent, petty fools that allow quarrels to lead to disaster. I am aware that Zhang Fei is a hot-headed butcher from a small place called Yan in the north, a man who put all of his money into following Liu Bei and fought at his side against the Yellow Turbans. He is known to be intolerant of men that he regards as 'toadies and pedants', and often reacts aggressively or even violently toward men that 'look down upon him'. Cao Bao is not a man that is easy to read, and being the Chancellor of Xiapi, he would be above Zhang Fei and hence prone to having every move read as condescending or threatening. Obviously he had concerns about being left with Zhang Fei – so would I – and some correspondence has gone back and forth between our camps. But I never thought it would come to this."

"Yes, yes, but do you agree that we can feel justified in 'rescuing' Xiapi?" Lü Bu said impatiently.

"I think so," Chen Gong said once again. "But if we do this, we do this to a man that has offered us shelter, a man that has the respect of talents and merchants... this may only further damn you in the eyes of your contemporaries as a man of-"

"It's a bit late for all that, Mister Chen," Lü Bu chuckled. "I am an 'untrustworthy wretch' that murders adoptive fathers and hankers for other men's land. That's my legacy now, damned to from the minute that I killed Ding Yuan and served Dong Zhuo. Liu Bei trusted me... but he'll lose the province to Yuan Shu if I don't act now, since he entrusts his life to idiots. We'll move immediately."

"...A-and... and after Zhang Fei killed Chancellor Cao Bao... Lü Bu... Lü Bu, h-he...! He...! He-he seized... seized Xiapi, and...! And...!"

The messenger from Xiapi could say no more: he broke down in tears and awaited the wrathful response of the inhabitants of Liu Bei's command tent in Huaiyin.

"*Ayah*! **Our cause is ruined!**" Liu Bei cried.

"Bloody fool," Jian Yong sighed. "We're homeless *again*."

"You may go," Mi Zhu said to the messenger, who fled gladly.

"What nonsense was it over...?" Jian Yong asked.

Mister Sun read the letter left by the messenger.

"*Well*...?" Jian Yong prompted impatiently.

"...It doesn't say," Mister Sun said.

"Yide never did like Cao Bao," Jian Yong noted. "There was always some manner in which the man really rubbed Yide up the wrong-"

"**He's condemned us to vagrancy!**" Liu Bei shrieked. "**I don't care what fool 'reasons' he had for this! He killed a prominent man, and caused the city to descend into chaos,**

and then he didn't even have the decency to be ready to defend it from that faithless scoundrel Lü Bu! I'm not sure that beheading him would be punishment enough for this!"

"You speak that way of *Yide*, a brother-in-arms from our first days, when we shared rooms, and lived as family," Guan Yu protested. "*I* am angry at him for this, Lord Liu, but-"

"My family… *our* families… are now hostages, Yunchang," Liu Bei said pointedly. "My wives, daughters, *all* our families, are now at the mercy of *Lü Bu*. Hah! **How much worse can things get???**"

"I can answer that for you now, if you want," Jian Yong chortled. "We're still fighting Ji Ling, and word is that Yuan Shu intends to send him more support. We can't stay here now: Lü Bu is the most treacherous dog of our age, and he'll probably write to Yuan Shu and suggest an alliance, if he hasn't already. What was our covered back is now our exposed weakness, and-"

"Enough, **enough!**" Liu Bei whined. "Mister Sun… Mister Mi Zhu, Mister Mi Fang… what can we do…?"

"We'll need to return to Xiapi at once, and try and regain control from Lü Bu," Mi Zhu suggested.

Liu Bei ordered a retreat from the battlegrounds at Xuyi and Huaiyin and tried to leave Guangling Prefecture; but as he fled, Yuan Shu's general Ji Ling pursued and applied unrelenting pressure on the already-demoralised army, causing it to disintegrate. Liu Bei, Guan Yu, Mister Sun, Mi Zhu and Mi Fang could only hope that there was some way to regain Xiapi from Lü Bu and chase Ji Ling from Xu Province; as the army shrank and supplies dwindled, many wondered – even Guan Yu – if Zhang Fei could or should be forgiven for his thoughtless and costly act.

When Liu Bei finally reached Xiapi City, he had very few of his 10,000 troops left. Zhang Fei was encamped to the east of Xiapi, and he was forced to welcome an exasperated Liu Bei back to what was now a base for Lü Bu.

"…Xuande," Zhang Fei said as Liu Bei fixed his steely gaze on the butcher from Yan and was seemingly trying to destroy him with it.

"So what was it, uh…?" Liu Bei said with a tone that married disbelief, amusement and rage. "Did he not show you enough respect…? Did he 'look at you funny' at a banquet…? What ridiculous, wretched, self-destructive excuse to bring disaster down on us all met the standards that you always set so high???"

"Calm down, Xuande," Jian Yong pleaded. "Yide looks ready to commit suicide."

The furious Liu Bei instinctively screamed, "**Perhaps he *should*!**"

"…*Aiee*… *no*, Lord Liu," Guan Yu whispered.

"…If that's what it takes, then I will," Zhang Fei said with emotion.

Liu Bei's senses returned; his gaze softened, and he turned his head sideways as he tried to find a reason to spare Zhang Fei.

"…Yide can atone with good service in the future," Guan Yu suggested. "We all have the potential for failure, Lord Liu… I do not expect to render perfect service myself, despite the will to do so. Yide is better as a living example than a guilt-ridden ghost."

"I agree," Jian Yong said. "Yide's might and courage're invaluable; if we have to execute anything, then his *attitude* will do."

"Okay… okay!" Liu Bei chuckled as he stifled tears and looked at the mortified Zhang Fei with forgiving eyes. "Be glad that I have sound counsel on this matter if no other, Zhang Yide… and that I value good men above their mistakes, however bad. Perhaps Lü Bu can be reasoned with, and we can recover our families, at least, if not the city."

Zhang Fei smiled feebly and kowtowed to show penitence and sorrow at his catastrophic error of judgement.

"Bei's back," Lü Bu said as he walked away from the battlements of the walled city of Xiapi. "How should we proceed…?"

"He's finished," Chen Gong scoffed. "Get rid of him: tell him that our roles are reversed, and that *he* can go to Xiaopei, across the river, as a subordinate ally, and that *you* are the governor now."

"And if he refuses those terms…?" Lü Bu prompted.

"Then he must be driven away," Chen Gong replied. "While I hold Liu Bei in high regard for his morals, his subordinates are a rowdy, undisciplined bunch that will certainly lose him anything that he gains, if his own floundering doesn't do it first. In such times, a man must know his followers, and govern with conviction. As you have already said, allowing him to regain 'control' of the city will only leave it open to further mishap. I am not the only man to have doubts about Liu Bei… else we would not now have the support of most of his former vassals and the wealthy and influential Chen family, would we…?"

"No," Lü Bu snickered. "Well then, I suppose that we had better send a man to dictate the terms to 'Former Governor Liu', then!"

"*That…!*" Liu Bei exclaimed as Mister Sun finished reading the letter from Lü Bu.

"Xuande, I… I'm sorry," Zhang Fei bleated. "This is my fault… I know that you forgave me, but–"

"And that is that," Liu Bei insisted.

Mister Sun passed the letter to Mi Zhu, who read it and said, "The Chens have betrayed us…? Not only Chen Gui and Chen Deng of Xu Province… but Elder Chen Ji and Chen Qun as well!"

"**What???**" Liu Bei cried.

"Faithless wretches!" Guan Yu said with anger. "The Chens of Xu are of no concern to me, but Old Chen and his son were–!"

"Wait," Liu Bei said. "Mister Sun, you did not–"

"I read the part that was relevant to our predicament at this moment," Mister Sun protested. "The loyalty of the 'two lines of Chens' is irrelevant to us now. And they have not 'betrayed us', Lord Liu… rather they have opted to remain within the capital as vassals of 'Acting Governor' Lü Bu to ensure order is maintained."

"…And Bu will keep our families as hostages," Mi Zhu noted.

"That much, I guessed," Liu Bei said with resignation.

"**I'll tear Lü Bu's throat out with my teeth if ever get the chance!**" Zhang Fei bellowed. "**Just give the order and I'll–!**"

"If you were a match for him in a duel, then I would suggest one, but you're not," Liu Bei replied. "Lü Bu is a prodigy of the age in terms of personal prowess, even if he is entirely dependent on the counsel of that villain Chen Gong."

"Eventually, even Chen Gong will tire of supporting Bu," Jian Yong said reassuringly. "Lü Bu is undisciplined, reckless… eventually, he'll do something stupid, like he did under Dong Zhuo."

"But in the meantime, we must flee… *again*," Liu Bei said.

"We're stuck in a pincer between Lü Bu and Ji Ling," Mi Zhu mused. "We cannot accept these ridiculous terms, not straight away at least; we must return to Guangling, and be seen to resist Ji Ling so that he – the greater threat – does not realise how endangered and isolated we are. But Lü Bu is playing his usual self-serving game... he'll harry us as we turn about to fight Ji Ling, or he may even try and tender his services to Yuan Shu, and help Ji Ling to pincer us properly."

"We lost most of the army on the way back, to desertion!" Mister Sun protested. "I cannot advocate a direct attack on Ji Ling; we were doing badly enough when we had a proper army."

"If we do not," Mi Zhu warned, "he will realise how weak we are. He must be made to think that any appearance of weakness is a ruse, to confuse him."

"He is unlikely to fall for that," Guan Yu suggested. "However, I am forced to agree, since we have no other logical choice right now. While Ji Ling pursues us, we are helpless; if we stay here without capitulating, Lü Bu will attack us, alone or in concert with Ji Ling; if we try and flee, one or both will pursue us and finish us off. We have to go back to Guangling, and hope that Lü Bu doesn't work with Ji Ling."

"...Fine," Liu Bei conceded. "A bold front it is, then."

"Liu Bei is leaving," Wang Kai reported to an ecstatic Lü Bu.

"It isn't as good as ceding the province, but it'll do!" Lü Bu cackled. "He can't attack us, not when we have his family. So where does he flee to...?"

"He doesn't," Wang Kai said. "He's turned about to bluff Ji Ling."

"Oh...?" Lü Bu chortled. "...Well, that's a surprise... that's what *I'd* do. Perhaps he isn't as worthless or cowardly as I thought..."

After a short silence, Chen Gong coughed and said, "You are acting governor now. Perhaps you should make some appointments, in order to stabilise the city."

"I thought *you* were doing that," Lü Bu grumbled.

"If you are happy to leave it to me, then very well," Chen Gong said with a smile.

Liu Bei returned to Guangling with what was left of his army and arrayed them as best he could against the larger force led by Yuan Shu's general, Ji Ling. The outcome, however, was foregone; Zhang Fei and Guan Yu rode out and challenged Ji Ling and his subordinate generals to duels, but the outcomes were inconclusive, and Ji Ling's army stormed Liu Bei's positions, crushing his weak defensive lines. Within days, Liu Bei was preparing to retreat from Guangling for a second time.

"Where will we go...?" Liu Bei asked.

"...North, since any other way is too risky," Mister Sun supposed.

"North takes us past Bu again," Guan Yu said. "Is that not risky?"

"Northwest is Xiaopei," Jian Yong said. "We could go there, and-"

"North is safer," Mi Zhu insisted. "I suggest Haixi, a well-fortified city in Donghai. We can 'weather the storm' there, and write to potential allies for help."

"*Haixi*...?" Guan Yu exclaimed. "Is there not a large criminal confederacy operating in and around Haixi, led by a 'Chen Yu'...?"

"Haixi is no more or less bothered by bandits than most places

these days, and 'Haixi Chen' is hardly likely to help Ji Ling or Lü Bu," Mi Zhu said. "As I already said, we can 'weather the storm' and write to potential allies for-"
"Like who...?" Guan Yu scoffed. "Zang Ba...? *Cao Cao...?*"
"...If needs be," Mi Fang said. "But I'd start with Yuan Shao."
"This is ignominious," Liu Bei complained. "Why did I not just stay in Zhuo, and weave mats...? Am I not going to end up with nothing in the end, laughed at for being a man that could lose just about anything that I'm given???"
"...We move north," Jian Yong conceded after an uncomfortable silence. "Haixi... how will we live?"
"Even if I exhaust every bit of wealth I have and every favour I'm owed, I will do all I can to support Lord Liu," Mi Zhu promised.
"Like my brother, I am committed to restoring order, and I believe that – even if all looks bleak now – Lord Liu is the man that will restore that order," Mi Fang declared. "Even if I must eat rice husks, every bit of my wealth is now Lord Liu's."
Liu Bei looked at his willing subordinates with reddened eyes and sobbed, saying, "I am a fortunate man indeed, to have met such good, wise, and honest men... it is more than I deserve. No, all I deserve is *Zhang Fei.*"
Zhang Fei lowered his eyes and exhaled noisily.
"Don't be too critical of Yide," Jian Yong suggested. "There may be a good reason – conceived by fate – why he did what he did... I doubt we'll ever truly know what it is, but he would never betray you willingly, and that's what counts."
"None of us would," Mi Fang promised.
"...Perhaps you're right," Liu Bei sighed. "Alright, then... let's salvage a dignified retreat, if we can, and go to Haixi."

"...*Haixi...?*" Lü Bu exclaimed as Chen Gong finished relaying the contents of a report to his small group of trusted aides that now included Chen Gui, Chen Deng, Chen Yuanfang and Chen Qun.
"Apparently, yes," Chen Gong replied. "It's a sound choice for a siege – which is what he will inevitably face – but that isn't saying much. He's got few supplies, and the nationwide famine does limit his options for procuring more; so unless he gets a lot of help... that siege will be a most unpleasant experience, and that's if he isn't routed by Haixi Chen's bandits or the citizens don't kill him and open the gates after the first month."
"Oh dear!" Lü Bu chuckled. "Poor, poor Liu Bei! He has lost his reputation, his governorship, his army... and now he must endure a siege that will strip him of any dignity! He should have heeded Heaven's word and been content as a daydreaming peasant!"
Most of Lü Bu's officers and the advisers Wang Kai and Xu Si laughed without shame; Zhang Liao, the officer Gao Shun, Chen Gong and those that had defected from Liu Bei were not quite so amused. For some, it was guilt; for others, it was simply a case of not finding humour in the total humiliation and suffering of others. But their reactions did not matter: Liu Bei was about to suffer an unbearably long siege, while in the Han capital Chang'an, another costly standoff was soon to come to an end.

★★★★★★★★★★★★

21

The warring Han 'co-regents', Li Jue and Guo Si, assembled battle camps at opposite ends of Chang'an, and the vast central marketplace – where thriving commerce normally drove the local economy – was designated as the main battleground. Each morning, the citizens would try and ascertain where and when the skirmishes between the regents would take place: those that were lucky enough to guess correctly would be able to go about their business for a while before that area became a battleground; those that guessed incorrectly would be collateral damage as arrows flew this way and that and improvised cavalry and infantry charges toppled established stalls and left corpses and rubbish everywhere. On the most active days, it was not unusual for a dozen fights to take place around the capital, and Emperor Xian and his vassals were always potential victims when those battles neared the headquarters of Li Jue, the regent that held them captive. The other regent, Guo Si, would sometimes take terrified courtiers from his collection of hostages in the chancellery and parade them to taunt Li Jue: they, too, could be hit in the ensuing battles, and many had been left horrifically injured or dead.

Jia Xu alternated his time between the imperial tent and Li Jue's command tent, as he was eager to ensure the health and safety of his sovereign: he was always humble and penitent, which made Emperor Xian increasingly certain that he could somehow work with or manipulate Jia to achieve peace or, better still, escape from Chang'an.

"Your Majesty," Jia Xu hailed as he entered the imperial tent after one day of fighting; he spied a hole in the enclosure and asked, "Was anyone hurt...?"
"We are fine," Emperor Xian replied. "But we are anxious that this cease as soon as possible. We have been here for many weeks now, and it is intolerable."
Jia Xu kowtowed and said, "I have tried many times to mediate without success, Your Majesty. I will never stop trying, I promise."
"There are reports that people are leaving the city," Emperor Xian prompted. "We are hearing that many valuable men have been killed, and that death and suffering are a way of life."
"I... I am afraid that it is true, that it is all true, Your Majesty," Jia Xu replied. "I am trying to find a solution."
"We have formulated a solution," Emperor Xian declared.
"I await your instruction, Your Majesty!" Jia Xu said meekly.
"It is obvious that Li Jue and Guo Si cannot rule together, but that they will not relinquish power to others," Emperor Xian continued. "Therefore, we propose the following: Li Jue can be the Western Regent and rule the west of the nation on our behalf from Chang'an; Guo Si can be the Eastern Regent and rule on our behalf in the east from Luoyang. As our recent ancestors are buried in the east, we would travel to the east and return to our original capital, Luoyang."
Jia Xu was silent as he pondered the declaration.
"Is there a problem?" Emperor Xian asked pointedly.
Jia Xu kowtowed and said, "Not at all, Your Majesty... I... I can find

no better solution, and cannot disagree. If you would commit your seal to an edict that I shall prepare as Acting Preparer of Documents, I shall do what I can to have this proposal of yours enacted in full and as quickly as possible."

"Very good," Emperor Xian said calmly. "Prepare the edict."

Li Jue and Guo Si marched to the centre of the main marketplace in Chang'an and levelled their spears at each other.

"**Bastard and usurper!**" Guo Si heckled.

"**Liar and hankerer!**" Li Jue retorted.

Li Jue ordered Duan Wei to charge; Guo Si ordered Wu Xi to oppose the charge. Both of the regents then ordered full cavalry charges: rotten animal carcasses, mouldy vegetables and unburied human corpses were trampled as the horsemen clashed amid the remains of the trading hub.

"**Yang Feng! Xu Huang!**" Li Jue cried. "**Attack now!**"

The two men rode to the front line of Li Jue's army.

"This is ridiculous," Yang Feng muttered. "Still... orders are orders. Captain Xu!"

"As you command," Xu Huang replied; the two men led a second cavalry advance.

"**Zhang Ji! Zhang Xiu! Huche'er!**" Guo Si shrieked. "**Counter! Counter!**"

"Am I aiming just for the men, or shall I try and spear us a couple of chickens...?" Zhang Ji quipped as he passed Guo Si on his tired, scruffy horse.

"**Don't backtalk me, you smug bastard!**" Guo Si barked. "**Your life's in danger as well! You, your nephew... and who'll get your pretty wife if you die...?**"

"You think I don't know that...?" Zhang Ji grumbled. "Alright, Nephew, let's get this over with."

"Yes, Uncle," Zhang Xiu replied.

"**Huche'er!**" Zhang Ji cried. "**Forward at once!**"

The foreign-featured Huche'er nodded silently and charged with his elite force; the two Zhangs then followed with their cavalry. Huche'er met Xu Huang, and the two clashed violently; each man was strong and skilled, so there would be no quick or bloodless end to the encounter.

"**WITHDRAW! WITHDRAW!**" Jia Xu cried as he rode toward the battle with the reins of his horse in one hand and the edict from the emperor in the other. "**HIS MAJESTY ORDERS THE IMMEDIATE CESSATION OF VIOLENCE!**"

"**I DON'T CARE!**" Guo Si retorted. "**GO AWAY, YOU TRAITOR!**"

Zhang Ji rode back to Guo Si's side and said, "**Wait! Let's hear them out.**"

"**Why???**" Guo Si barked. "**That bastard Li Jue fed me poisoned meat! He was going to kill you as well, or did you forget again already?**"

"**Jia Xu's up to something... and whatever it is he's come up with might benefit us,**" Zhang Ji suggested. "**I'm going to listen: HUCHE'ER! WITHDRAW!**"

"**...WITHDRAW!**" Guo Si ordered.

When Li Jue saw that Guo Si's forces were retreating, he shouted "**WITHDRAW!**"

Both sides retreated to their command tents, and Jia Xu rode toward Guo Si's camp.

"Why should I be listening to you?" Guo Si heckled as Jia Xu dismounted at the improvised wall of debris that marked the perimeter of the camp.
"Did I want this?" Jia Xu replied. "I begged the two of you to stop, didn't I?"
"...True," Guo Si conceded. "But why did you side with Li Jue? Did I ever harm you, Mister Jia...?"
"Li Jue intended to take His Majesty hostage, and I had to be sure that the Son of Heaven was going to be safe," Jia Xu replied. "I already went along with one regicide... my tortured soul couldn't bear being responsible for another. If you had reached His Majesty first, then I would have switched to your side immediately for the same purpose."
"...I see and understand, Mister Jia, but only because I must," Guo Si said sadly.
"...So what is your proposal, Mister Jia Xu...?" Zhang Ji prompted.
"I'll not patronise the two of you by reading it out," Jia Xu sighed. "Let's go to your command tent... I am unarmed and alone, so what can I do...?"
"True enough," Guo Si chuckled. "Let's go."
       Guo Si and Zhang Ji finished reading – and re-reading – the imperial edict less than an hour later; the two men looked at each other, and then at Jia Xu.
"Well...?" Jia Xu prompted.
"So we would govern independently...?" Guo Si mused. "...It seems like a good idea, Mister Jia... and if I had the emperor, I'd be the stronger man, especially since I automatically get to keep all of the officials as well... well, those that are left, alive, anyway. Why would Li Jue agree to that?"
"He hasn't... yet," Jia Xu admitted. "He will, though... because he hates His Majesty, and doesn't want him anyway. Rest assured that he'll love governing the west without the Son of Heaven to worry about."
"He'll spend most of his time fighting Ma Teng and Han Sui," Zhang Ji chuckled. "I hope that Li Jue adopts the plan, Mister Jia... I will be glad to leave this place behind and travel to Luoyang with Regent Guo. You can appoint me Director of Retainers, and I'll oversee the rebuilding."
"Oh, wait! That's right! Luoyang's still all burned down!" Guo Si realised. "What sort of plan is this...? Why would you suggest making the emperor live in a pile of rubble if you like him so much, Mister Jia...?"
"It was His Majesty's idea, not mine," Jia Xu admitted.
"...His Majesty suggested this?" Zhang Ji exclaimed. "That boy's cunning; couldn't there be some sort of trap?"
"I thought of that, but he has no active allies anymore," Jia Xu replied. "I have been receiving news from the east regularly: Yuan Shao and the Black Mountain Bandits are still fighting in Ji Province, Cao Cao is settling Yan Province after the famine, and Liu Biao has chased Yuan Shu back into Yang Province, so the path to Luoyang has just one obstacle to worry about: the White Wave Bandits."
"...A faithless rabble," Zhang Ji scoffed: he then smiled and added,

"Alright, I won't argue anymore: we've none of us anything to gain by letting the emperor escape, have we...?"

"No," Jia Xu replied. "I'd have a death sentence given to me for my supposed part in Shaodi's death, I know that."

"If Li Jue agrees, then I agree," Guo Si said. "Go and tell him."

Jia Xu bowed to Guo Si and Zhang Ji before he retreated to Li Jue's camp.

"...Rebuilding Luoyang will be a lot of work," Guo Si grumbled.

"Does it matter...?" Zhang Ji chortled. "We'll never have to worry about that treacherous Li Jue trying to murder us again, and we can have things exactly as we want them, Regent Guo. This is perfect."

Guo Si smiled gratefully at the prospect.

An hour later, Li Jue finished reading the edict and lowered the document slowly.

"...You're dissatisfied, I can tell," Jia Xu said nervously. "But before you lose your temper, consider the benefits."

"What *benefits*???" Li Jue shrieked. "Guo Si and Zhang Ji get to go east to Luoyang, where they can then bully an edict out of the emperor demanding another coalition, this time against *me*! If I agree to this, I can count the days before I'll have Yuan Shao, Yuan Shu, Cao Cao, Liu Biao and goodness-knows-who-else marching here with two million troops to demand my head! I'll have Han Sui, Ma Teng and Song Jian biting at my ankles the whole time as well! **Why would I agree to this???**"

"Yuan Shao and Yuan Shu are not going to stop fighting," Jia Xu replied calmly. "Cao Cao is too busy looking for an opportunity to destroy Xu Province, and Yuan Shu is too busy looking for an opportunity to seize it from Liu Bei. Gongsun Zan will probably launch a campaign against Yuan Shao at the very moment that it's known that His Majesty's left Chang'an, Song Jian is keeping himself to himself, and Ma Teng and Han Sui are too busy fighting each other nowadays. Guo Si and Zhang Ji are going to be governing a burned-out husk of a city, while you get to keep Chang'an; when the market is cleaned up, it'll be back to normal, while rebuilding Luoyang will take years."

"...I thought that you were worried about the emperor," Li Jue snickered.

"It was His Majesty's idea, not mine," Jia Xu replied. "But the Son of Heaven wouldn't be staying here with us if it was my idea anyway. He needs to be far away from Ma Teng, Zhang Lu and–"

"With 'us'...? ...You're not going to Luoyang...?" Li Jue realised.

"I cannot go there," Jia Xu said tonelessly. "I do not believe that His Majesty would allow one of Dong Zhuo's advisers to live: look at what he wanted to do to Li Ru."

"Oh, yes," Li Jue gasped as recalled his one-time second adviser. "Well, I'll certainly need you here anyway. If there's no danger of an edict against me, then go ahead and tell Guo Si that he can go to Luoyang and take the boy with him."

"I shall tell His Majesty as well," Jia Xu said gladly.

More than an hour later, Emperor Xian was startled by the arrival of Jia Xu and one of Guo Si's vassals, Captain Dong Cheng.

"Don't be scared, Your Majesty," Jia Xu pleaded as he fell to his knees in penitence; Dong Cheng quickly followed his example.

"Who is this man that accompanies you, Mister Jia...?" Emperor Xian asked. "He seems familiar to us."

"...This is Captain Dong Cheng, recently arrived from Guo Si's camp to assist in Your Majesty's preparations for the journey to Luoyang," Jia Xu explained.

"We are glad to hear that our proposal was not contested, but... *Dong* Cheng...?" Emperor Xian prompted. "Which Dong clan does this man belong to...?"

Dong Cheng was silent.

"...To the Dong clan that the Grand Dowager belonged to," Jia Xu said after a notable pause. "The clan of Dong Zhuo was *exterminated*, Your Majesty, by the late Director Wang Yun."

"...We would hope so," Emperor Xian grumbled as he turned to one of his eunuch attendants and gestured that he should like to be fanned. "We would not wish to be in the company of any relative of that wicked man, that murderer of our brother."

"...Naturally," Jia Xu replied nervously. "No, Mister Dong Cheng is a distant relative of the late Grand Dowager that played such a valuable part in Your Majesty's early tutelage."

"If that is so, then we are glad to have you in our service," Emperor Xian said to a relieved Dong Cheng. "We hope that your allegiances are clear."

Jia Xu shuddered; Dong Cheng kowtowed repeatedly and said, "I am loyal to Your Majesty first and foremost."

Emperor Xian smiled and said, "Very good. We are appeased."

"I... I h-have things to arrange, Your Majesty," Jia Xu bumbled.

"You may go," Emperor Xian replied.

Jia Xu kowtowed repeatedly and retreated from the imperial tent; he knew that Emperor Xian might have a plan of some sort that could doom Li Jue, Guo Si and himself at the very least – if not all of Dong Zhuo's former vassals – but had decided to say nothing.

"...If that is how it is to be," Jia Xu decided, "then... so be it."

Two of the three Qiang 'super-warlords' in Liang Province – Han Sui and Ma Teng – met on the outskirts of the late Dong Zhuo's power base in Mei County to discuss the situation in Chang'an.

"The fighting in the capital is subsiding now," Han Sui said to his sometimes-ally and sometimes-rival, Ma Teng. "We've missed an opportunity."

"After our last attempt to take the capital went so wrong, I don't see where there's an opportunity," Ma Teng retorted. "Liu Yan's army was crushed, you barely escaped with your life, and-"

"You *dare*...!" Han Sui growled as he stood up and placed his hand on his sword hilt.

"...Do you try to intimidate my father, Han Sui...?" the brawny Ma Chao said as he readied his own sword.

"You'll use your head properly or lose it, Han Sui!" the younger Ma Tie cried.

Han Sui's bodyguards raised their weapons; Han Sui smirked and said, "You have fine sons, Ma Teng, but they are too brave for their own good."

"Is that so?" Ma Chao replied. "You have achieved what, you-!"

"Enough, son," Ma Teng ordered. "You're too touchy, Han Wenyue. I was not trying to say that you were weak, I-"

"Save your cowardly explanations for a man that cares, Ma Teng,"
Han Sui retorted. "I came here to hear you out and end our own
feud, and then the regents started to fight: now they've stopped
fighting and it seems that we must start again."
"You're lucky that I want to talk," Ma Teng countered. "Your last
attack on me killed my favourite consort and one of my
daughters!"
"Your last attack on me killed a favourite nephew and *two* of *my*
daughters, Ma Teng," Han Sui growled. "I still have one last head
to claim, then."
Every man present took an offensive stance and raised their
weapon.
"You're either brave or stupid to make a challenge when you're in
enemy territory, Han Sui," Ma Chao suggested. "I'll kill you, your
guards, and then I'll kill every one of your family, and-!"
"*Enough*, son," Ma Teng ordered once again; he then turned to his
rival and added, "Don't make me try and restrain my eldest again,
Han Sui, because I doubt that he'll listen: you've seen him in
battle, and so you know that you won't survive."
"My death will only bring pain on your entire clan," Han Sui
retorted. "I have sons too, Ma Teng, and any one of them is as
good as your eldest."
"...Get out," Ma Teng said. "Get out, go back to Longxi and think
about everything... carefully."
Han Sui grinned at Ma Chao, laughed and slowly retreated from
the central tent with his entourage.
"...*Aiee*... but he's right, though, that we missed an opportunity,"
Ma Teng admitted. "If we'd only put aside our differences while
there were no serious grudges! We could have killed Li Jue and
Guo Si and taken the capital!"
"We don't need Han Sui," Ma Chao suggested. "Last time we killed
their vanguard generals, and since then they've been killing each
other. We could still-"
"No, son... no," Ma Teng insisted. "If we attacked Li Jue and Guo
Si now, Han Sui would wait until we were close to victory and
exhausted, and then he would kill us *and* the regents."
"...Some of the lesser chieftains think we're being weak," Ma Tie
suggested.
"*Aiee*... why must everything be about strength and weakness all
the time...?" Ma Teng complained. "What is the point of dying to
prove that we're strong...?"
Ma Chao harrumphed and said, "I will kill anyone that challenges
you, Father."
"...I don't doubt that!" Ma Teng chuckled. "But let's be sensible.
Han Sui intends war, my sons, and we will have plenty of chances
to show how strong we are by fighting and beating Han Sui."
"Han Sui will see his entire clan die," Ma Chao said. "His heart will
know great pain, Father: I will personally see to it!"
"...I don't doubt that either," Ma Teng sighed.

✱✱✱✱✱✱✱✱✱✱✱✱

22

Inside Haixi City on the opposite side of the country, morale –
along with everything else – was dwindling quickly.
"…Two weeks."
"Two weeks??? Have you finally lost your mind altogether…?" a
scruffy and dirty Zhang Fei heckled as he glared at the haggard
form of Jian Yong. "We've been here for two bloody months and-!"
"Save… your strength, Yide," Liu Bei pleaded. "Jian Xianhe… was
referring to… the last time… that any of us had a full meal."
Zhang Fei turned to Jian Yong, saying, "Sorry, alright…? …Sorry."
"So… you should be," Liu Bei said. "This… is *your fault*, you-!"
"Now who's wasting strength, Xuande…?" Jian Yong wheezed. "…I
really need water. At least there's water from the well… until they
find a way to pollute it or cut it off, anyway."
"I'm… so tired, Xianhe," Liu Bei sighed. "I'm not built for this."
"Who *is*…?" Jian Yong retorted. "Who, exactly, is built for… for
being trapped in a walled city for months while someone tries to
smash their way in daily and… and there's barely any food…?"
"…Maybe I *should* surrender to Lü Bu," Liu Bei muttered.
"Never!" Zhang Fei protested. "Xuande, we can't do that! He's let
us know that our families are safe, but us, he'll kill us if we let
him, and then our families when he doesn't need them anymore!"
"…But he just wants my seal of office and the governorship," Liu
Bei retorted. "Why would he kill us once he has them…?"
"He's working with Yuan Shu!" Zhang Fei barked. "He'll hand us
over to Cao Cao! …Or he'll give us to Yuan Shao, who'll punish us
for losing the place!"
"…Where is… Mister Sun Qian…?" Liu Bei asked.
"Mister Sun… is with the Mi brothers and Yunchang, defending the
walls," Jian Yong replied. "Ji Ling's attacking them again."
"I could hear… but… … …then why are you here, Yide?" Liu Bei
said as he turned to Zhang Fei. "If you have… the strength to
shout at Xianhe… then why are you not at the walls…?"
Zhang Fei snorted miserably before he replied, "Mi Zhu, that
defeatist, he… he ordered me to…!"
"…He fears losing the walls today…?" Liu Bei exclaimed. "Well
why… did you not say so before, you fool…? I will go and defend
them in person! Jian Yong, Chen Dao, ready your-"
"*Ayah*; why am I here, if not to protect you???" Zhang Fei
despaired. "How can I do that if you are on the bloody wall???"
Liu Bei got to his feet, coughed uncomfortably and said, "I… have
lost a little sleep and feel a little strange after… all that smoke I
breathed in from the fires… but I am alright! How can I inspire
everyone to keep fighting by hiding in here w-with you and Chen
Dao…? If things got that bad, what were you going to do…? …Lack
of food has made my brother-in-law Mi Zhu simple-minded."
Liu Bei was still coughing as he retrieved his sword and dressed in
armour; Jian Yong shook his head and got to his feet, saying, "I
might as well die with you, Xuande. Nobody else will want me."
Liu Bei started to laugh painfully as he followed Zhang Fei out of
the private residence.

The horrors of the siege of a walled city were always two-fold. On the outside, the besiegers – regardless of their morals and motives – faced a daily war of attrition if they chose to bring the matter to a speedy conclusion rather than starve the occupants; that was the strategy more often than not, since most sieges took place in hostile territory where relief forces could arrive, supplies were a factor and securing other military targets required swift movement. The most common tactic was attempting to scale the walls: men would be sent to those walls – sometimes having to pass a wet or dry moat or artificial mounds first – and place wooden siege ladders that they would then try to climb. If they somehow passed the gauntlet of rocks, boiling oil or water, and the simple tactic of pushing the ladder away from the wall, then they would engage the defenders on the wall and try to reach the devices that allowed the gates to be opened or the drawbridge to be lowered: that would allow the rest of the invading army to storm the city. Other options included sappers that would try and tunnel under the walls, siege ramps and towers that were vulnerable to fire, catapults for attacking the occupants, diverting rivers to either flood the city or deprive it of water, or building mounds to give archers better shots at the defenders on the battlements. If time was not an issue – and for Ji Ling, it was not, as Lü Bu neither aided Liu Bei nor harmed Ji Ling's supply route – then the besieger could simply sit and wait for the city to succumb to starvation and disease.

For the besieged, resources were the key to survival and everything became a commodity. People were a resource that had to be maintained or reduced depending on needs; fewer food resources made a smaller population preferable, but if supplies were adequate then a large population gave opportunities for sudden attacks on the besiegers and solid defence of the walls. Food and water were a given; weapons – arrows, swords, and projectiles like rocks, flammable straw balls and oil – were equally important if the attackers were attacking continually. Sometimes a wall might be breached, or a gate might be punctured; it was therefore essential that there were materials available to repair the damage and artisans that could do the job properly. Every pair of hands had to do their part, and if they did – and supplies did not run out – then a siege was survivable, since the enemy could withdraw due to sustaining too many casualties while climbing the walls, running out of supplies of their own or a relief force arriving to provide external support. But if time was not an issue – and, for Ji Ling, it was not – a siege would definitely leave the defenders without supplies, desperately low on morale, and beset by hygiene and health problems that would inevitably lead to the spread of diseases in addition to malnutrition; if injuries were sustained from projectile attacks, fights with besiegers that made it to the wall or day-to-day accidents, then matters got worse still. Liu Bei knew that if the siege went on too long, then some very difficult choices would need to be made; some would be painful, but others would have the defenders come face-to-face with their own humanity and risk losing it. Liu Bei needed help, but whether he would get any or not was another matter entirely.

"...Liu Bei is under attack...?"
The lord of Yòu Province, Gongsun Zan, read the urgent report

from Xu Province and eyed Liu Bei's filth-encrusted messenger with conflicting emotions.

"…My lord, what will you do…?" the adviser Guan Jing prompted.

"Why does Yuan Shao, his *master*, not help him…?" Gongsun Zan asked of the messenger, who fell to the floor and sobbed.

"Is Liu Bei not your friend…?" Guan Jing said.

"He *betrayed me*!" Gongsun Zan replied angrily. "He dares beg me for help after all of his duplicitous behaviour???"

"Forgive me, my lord, but… we've all been duplicitous at some point," Guan Jing said. "What matters in the end is friendship."

"We studied together as children, and fought together a few times as men, and that is all," Gongsun Zan retorted. "I have problems of my own, Guan Jing! Xu Province is too far away, and while I have not fought Yuan Shao personally of late, his son Yuan Tan still harasses my forces in northern Qing, and my… 'allies'… still draw blood on my behalf elsewhere! Who can I send…? The last man I sent to save someone came back in a coffin."

"Our lord *needs you*, Lord Gongsun!" the messenger pleaded.

"**Get out!**" Gongsun Zan screamed. "**Do not come back! 'You'll get no help from me, Liu Bei, not after you helped my nephew's killer!' Tell him *that*, messenger: tell him *that*!**"

"*Aiee*… are you sure…?" Guan Jing asked as the messenger fled the empty audience hall in tears.

"…I do not do what I do easily," Gongsun Zan replied. "I have no cooperation pact with Haixi Chen or Zang Ba, who are the only men in the area that are equipped to fight Ji Ling; my Black Mountain Bandit friends were routed by Lü Bu when they last fought, and that was when Bu only had a few men under his command… so even Chen and Zang combined – even if they *were* my allies – would be powerless against a Bu with a governor's power behind him and doubtlessly the famous Danyang Brigades as well. I daren't go to Xuande's aid in person, or I'd lose Yòu Province; no, Mister Guan, the sad fact is that Xuande is on his own. And before you question that decision, remember that-"

"He took your borrowed men and surrendered to your enemy, so why would you risk everything for a man that clearly isn't prepared to do the same…?" Guan Jing supposed. "I was ensuring that you were doing what you truly wanted to do, my lord."

"I truly want to help him, Mister Guan, but we're ambitious warlords with pressing problems now, not carefree friends," Gongsun Zan replied dolefully. "When this is over, if he still lives… and if *I* still live… then we'll share a jar of wine, apologise to each other, and enjoy the new era of peace as neighbours and friends again. Until then, we must be pragmatic."

Guan Jing smiled, bowed and said, "I quite agree."

"**Fool! Wretched, incompetent buffoon!**" Yuan Shao shrieked as his secretary Chen Lin finished reading the letter that Liu Bei had sent from Haixi. The two were in a command tent in a base within eastern Bing Province, as Yuan Shao had secretly advanced to the region – without alerting the ambitious Gongsun Zan – in order to personally deal with 'Poison Yu', a very active senior commander of the Black Mountain Bandits that had almost compromised Yuan's capital in Ji Province.

"Will you help?" Chen Lin asked.

"...How can I, my friend...?" Yuan Shao replied. "If we were in Yè, then perhaps I might react differently... unlikely, but possible. But I am on campaign!"

Chen Lin nodded sadly and said, "I expected better of a man that was spoken of so highly, even if that was by our enemies... a close friend of Gongsun Zan, a hero of the Ji Province front of the Yellow Turban campaign, a man considered capable of opposing Cao Cao by Gongsun *and* Tao Qian... perhaps he didn't try."

"Oh, he tried, else he wouldn't send me *this*," Yuan Shao scoffed. "I've half a mind to ask Mengde to 'help him'!"

Chen Lin laughed and said, "The other so-called heroes that were named alongside you are all proving to be a disappointment."

"When I think back to before those dangerous days in Luoyang, before the day when you saved me from assassination by the 'Ten', I wonder where the heroes have gone," Yuan Shu replied. "My brother-cousin has become a hankering lunatic that fraternises with bandits; Cao Mengde, too, has lost some of his sanity somewhere along the line, and contents himself with strange trysts with hired women and vendettas against entire provinces for the crimes of one man; and as for Liu Bei, whose reputation I valued too... that reputation has not just been proven to be unfounded... it has proven to be a cruel and tasteless *joke*!"

Chen Lin smiled silently.

"This fool, this sandal weaver that I trusted to run Xu – Heaven forgive my idiocy for doing so – has done everything wrong that *can* be done wrong and *more besides*!" Yuan Shao complained. "This nonsense he writes about some ruffian friend of his killing the chancellor over a petty dispute, and allowing Lü Bu to be invited into Xiapi, and my spiteful brother-cousin's general besting him repeatedly in Guangling and then being able to just casually march into the province... if Liu Bei were here, now, I'd have him taken into the yard and strangled with a cord like the simpering, gutless, womanly creature that he is!"

"I don't need to guess your response," Chen Lin joked.

"There will be no response... yet," Yuan Shao replied. "When I can be sure that the bandits don't threaten my capital anymore, and Mengde is done with the 'Yellow Turbans' – if that is truly what they are, and not some false vision created by my deceitful brother-cousin – then I will station Zhang Hè on my northern border to guard against Gongsun Zan, place Yan Liang and Wen Chou in the vanguard and march against Lü Bu and Ji Ling in person. I will place a trusted man in Xu to govern it, and Liu Bei – who is obviously no more worthy than Liu Zhang of Yi – can be placed under house arrest in my capital until I decide what to do with him. His notorious followers – the ones of value, anyway – can join me, retire or die."

"Very good," Chen Lin said. "Now, for news from Yingchuan..."

"...Liu Bei has lost Xu Province...?"

Cao Cao was taken aback by the news; he was on campaign in Yingchuan in the northwest of his province, this time against splinter groups of Black Mountain Bandits and the Runan Yellow Turbans led by Liu Pi and Huang Shao.

"In all but that he's ceded the seal – which he obviously hasn't – it seems so," the adviser Xun Wenruo reported. "Lü Bu failed here

because there were more men with you than against you, while Liu Bei enjoyed no such popularity, it seems."
Cao Cao smiled and started to laugh.
"...What will you do...?" Xun Wenruo asked.
"Nothing, naturally," Cao Cao chuckled. "Benchu would order me to halt if I went anywhere near Xu... though that may change. Now don't get me wrong, I hate Lü Bu – more than I hate Liu Bei, for obvious reasons – but that idiot losing Xu to *anyone* is still music to my ears. There's nothing I hate more than cowards that hide in the shadows, and Bei did that when he went to Benchu to save his own hide. Tao Qian was an old dog, but he was a *brave* old dog."
"Will anyone help him...?" a brawny, thick-whiskered man asked.
"Unlikely, Miaocai," Cao Cao replied as he turned to his 'cousin' Xiahou Yuan. "Benchu wouldn't, even if he wasn't busy. Liu Bei betrayed Gongsun Zan, and Gongsun does not forgive 'betrayals' easily, even though he's guilty of quite a few himself. ...There's Kong Rong in Qing, but he's on the verge of losing any power he pretends to have and needed Taishi Ci to rescue him from a few Yellow Turbans two years ago; he has no army to send! And Bei's nearest powerful neighbours besides that are both bandit kings... Haixi Chen would rob him afterwards; Zang Ba... I'm not sure. His father was one of the most honest men in the land, so I hear, and Zang's motives for seizing Kaiyang are not entirely selfish."
"...So Liu Bei's only hope is Lü Bu having a change of heart, then!" Xun Wenruo chuckled. "He's a very unlucky man..."

Kong Rong, the Chancellor of Beihai – and, supposedly, the Inspector or Governor of Qing Province at Liu Bei's suggestion – stared at the desperate letter from his friend Liu Bei and sighed.
"...I probably won't last another year here in Qing, Liu Xuande," Kong Rong said as he read the words for a second time. "Oh, if I had but a fraction of my famous ancestor's wisdom, I would gladly help you, but... I cannot...!"
The frail Kong Rong allowed the cloth letter to fall from his hands and land on his desk; he was 42 years of age, but he looked and felt like a man in his 60s after having endured sieges and the upheavals caused by Dong Zhuo's rule. The post in Qing Province had been relentlessly stressful, and Kong Rong – whose famous ancestor was none other than the philosopher Confucius – almost relished the day when he would be told to cede his role to someone else and go somewhere that had fewer problems.
"I can do nothing," Kong Rong sighed. "But... I wish you luck..."

Liu Bei's would need the luck that Kong Rong spoke of; Ji Ling besieged him mercilessly, depriving his forces of every essential resource without conscience. Many would resort to the most drastic of measures in order to stay alive while Ji Ling's men made attempt after attempt to climb or breach the city walls. Xu Province's newest Acting Governor, Lü Bu, laughed at each report he received and awaited the day when his Acting Chancellor, Chen Gong, would tell him what to do next; the unreadable Chen Gong watched and waited quietly.

****

23

In the western capital Chang'an, open warfare had given way to a strange calm: people were able to repair damage, bury bodies, clear away rubbish and begin a return to normality while the feuding regents, Li Jue and Guo Si, put their mutual enmity aside and worked – albeit separately and independently – towards the planned departure of Emperor Xian and his entourage.

Li Jue and Guo Si even elected to avoid any face-to-face meetings on the actual day of the young emperor's departure from Chang'an; Li Jue's absence would be conspicuous and controversial. The royal procession itself was far from acceptable when going by the standards that custom demanded – the emperor's carriage had been destroyed, so a modified minister's carriage would be used instead – but Emperor Xian was only interested in getting away from at least one of his regents, so no complaints were made.

"It is almost impossible to believe...!" the haggard Shisun Rui said as he met with his recently-liberated allies.
"Free from the madness at last... and it was the wisdom of His Majesty that finally resolved it, after all of our futile scheming!" Magistrate Zhong Yao said cheerfully.
Shisun Rui groaned and said, "But so many did not get this far..."
There was a moment's silence.
"...So many of my colleagues are gone," Shisun Rui continued miserably. "It's a pity that some of them – particularly those that lived through the scheme that rid us of Dong Zhuo, and were mercifully left out of the later plans only to die in the street anyway and lie unburied next to rotting fruit, animal carcasses and barbarian soldiers – did not live to see His Majesty return to Luoyang at last."
"...But what *remains* of Luoyang...?" Zhong Yao whimpered.
"I... cannot say," Shisun Rui replied. "Some say it is just a few houses that were destroyed, and the Southern Palace; others say... that... that *nothing* remains."
Some officials started to sob.
"It is better than remaining here and enduring the regents' feuding!" Shisun Rui protested. "We can rebuild Luoyang together! Once we have a competent Director of Retainers, we'll round up some of those White Wave Bandits that used to attack us and rob us as we travelled on the roads years ago, and make them rebuild Luoyang! It is Heaven's will!"
"Now I'm hearing more things about the east, I worry," Minister Yang Biao said as he clutched a bandaged wound beneath his ribcage. "Lu Kang... dead... Zhu Jun... sick, maybe dead... Liu Yu's son Hè... dead... Xu Province... governed by... by *Lü Bu*...!"
"*Liu Bei*," Shisun Rui insisted. "You misheard, Mister Yang... *Liu Bei* rules Xu Province... Lü Bu is said to be there by some, but... *governing Xu*...? ...Nonsense."
"...If Li Jue and Guo Si... can be regents, then... why can't... can't Lü Bu be a provincial governor...?" Yang Biao retorted. "The world... is broken enough for that to be true, Mister Shisun. Any world where... where a hero like Huangfu Song dies a forgotten,

powerless man, sick and miserable, surrounded by... by the people that he used to fight, like Ma Teng and Han Sui, who are all... quite well and... quite powerful..."

"Save your strength, Mister Yang," Shisun Rui pleaded. "The cruelty of that is not lost on me either; he should have died in a better place and in happier times, as a hero, not as a... ... ...enough. We're losing the point of this conversation, gentlemen! We survived the great darkness, and now we're going to begin rebuilding! Soon, everything will be as it should be... and the Han will be great once again, with a shrewd and erudite young emperor that wants what is best for his people! The dark period is almost over, gentlemen... almost..."

Emperor Xian had returned to his evacuated Northern Palace at the soonest opportunity; he could not convince his paranoid attendants to give him any privacy, but he still spoke as candidly as he could with Empress Fu.

"We will soon be away from Chang'an," Emperor Xian said. "We are under no illusion that this journey will be easy, but we have endured cowering in tents while our regents turned this city into a rubbish tip, and that is incentive enough to risk the journey to our true home in Luoyang."

The eunuch attendants – who had heard every rumour about the state of Luoyang from the court officials – looked at each other and wondered if their emperor truly knew what awaited him at the end of the journey.

"When we are there, we can begin planning for the future, rather than dwelling in and fearing the nature of the present," Emperor Xian continued. "We can force our bickering vassals to turn their eyes, minds and hearts back to the needs of the state, and we can finally punish the chaos-makers and resume trading with the larger world. We yearn for a larger world after knowing only the inside of palaces for so long... and we crave true authority after being a puppet for our entire reign."

"...But Regent Guo Si accompanies us," Empress Fu noted.

Emperor Xian smiled and said, "That is his intention, yes."

The attendants exchanged confused glances.

"What... has Your Majesty set in motion...?" Empress Fu asked.

"There is nothing to fear," Emperor Xian replied. "We have not directly set anything in motion, but we are confident that the good and honest peoples will deliver us from the problems that insist on accompanying us."

"...I hope that is true, Your Majesty," Empress Fu said. "The nation has gone without the peace your divine presence brings to them for too long, and the people hunger for normality."

Emperor Xian laughed and said, "Were it only so, dear Empress; most would simply desire a meal, we think, and miss little else."

Guo Si entered his palatial home and looked at the walls.

"Isn't Luoyang still in ruins...?" Guo Si's wife, Lady Qiong, heckled as she followed him. "We're quite comfortable here; Li Jue must want to stay here for a very good reason for him to be content with letting you go to Luoyang. Have you thought of that...?"

"...Shut up," Guo Si muttered.

"My words saved you from Li Jue," Lady Qiong continued. "If I had not exposed him, where would you be...?"

"...Now I've more time to think, I wonder if you really exposed anything," Guo Si retorted. "Yeah, we were always going to fight, but there was probably no need for-"

"Coward!" Lady Qiong hissed. "You know he killed the others, but you still want to believe in him because you're scared of him! That's why you surrendered!"

"I didn't surrender!" Guo Si chortled. "You're mad! Really, truly, you are! I should leave you here, and just take the consorts!"

"You'd leave the mother of your heir to the mercy of your murderous 'friend' and run away to Luoyang...? Is there no end to your wickedness...?" Lady Qiong retorted theatrically. "You'd leave a woman that married you willingly, the woman that bore you your heir, and take women that you enslaved when you and your 'friend' were raiding the lands around the old capital...?

Guo Si clenched his fists and closed his eyes.

"...I wonder if they'll be so quiet and obedient when they're that much closer to the graves of their families, the ones you killed while you were taking them," Lady Qiong taunted. "Perhaps Li Jue won't need to poison you... perhaps, without me to watch them as I have done since you 'acquired them', they will-"

"**ENOUGH!**" Guo Si shrieked. "**You mock me relentlessly, but remember that I am no joke!**"

"Such anger...! But I am alive and unharmed, which means that you know me to be right once again," Lady Qiong heckled.

Guo Si unclenched his hands and sighed miserably.

"You need me, like it or not," Lady Qiong continued. "What you are, I allow and protect, for *I* need *you*... like it or not."

"...Are you fully prepared for the journey...?" Guo Si asked bitterly.

"More than you, I imagine," Lady Qiong replied. "I hope that you are aware of who you can and cannot trust."

Guo Si nodded seriously and walked to the garden, where he hoped to have time to think before he continued his preparations.

"...You make it all worthwhile."

Marquis Zhang Ji grinned like a naïve, love-struck youth as he stared at his wife, Lady Zou; her staggering beauty had been infamous for years, and she was still among the most attractive women in the land.

"I worry about Guo Si," Lady Zou said in response. "He is a famous hankerer."

"He knows that I would gut him for any sign of disrespect toward you," Zhang Ji insisted. "Has even tried to smile at you...?"

"Not recently," Lady Zou admitted. "But I am more concerned about you. He would take me for himself at worst, but you are a popular man here in Liang Province, and you have strong officers... he has always been jealous of that."

"Li Jue is the one that I worry about, and we'll soon be far, far away from him and his followers," Zhang Ji said calmly. "Oh yes, we might need to worry about Li Jue sending people to try and harm us, but Guo Si will be protecting us by protecting himself, so I am not that worried."

Lady Zou smiled and said, "If you are truly calm, then I am calm. Where is our nephew...?"

"He is assisting the emperor's entourage with their preparations,"

Zhang Ji replied. "...He will be my heir... and I could not hope for a better one. He risked everything to save us when Dong Zhuo was assassinated and Wang Yun put that ridiculous and indiscriminate warrant out for our arrest; and since then, he has been my most trusted aide, competent with the pen and the sword."
"It is true that he is almost like a son to us," Lady Zou said.
"When we reach Luoyang, I... I wonder what our place will be," Zhang Ji murmured.

Once every single person was ready for the journey, Jia Xu met with Guo Si at the gates of the western capital so that he could speak with him one last time.
"...This feels strange," Guo Si admitted. "You're sure that you won't join me, Mister Jia...? I'd make you an Excellency, or Grand Tutor... whatever role you want, it's yours."
"My job now is stopping the two of you from fighting anymore," Jia Xu replied. "When I know that you're safely installed in Luoyang, I intend to retire again."
Guo Si then turned to Zhang Ji and said, "Are you ready...?"
"We are," Zhang Ji replied. "No jokes about my wife though, please, Guo Si, I'm not in the mood."
"...I am not in the mood for jokes either, Zhang Ji," Guo Si replied.
Zhang Ji and Zhang Xiu led their small army out of the gates.
"I hope that this is truly a good idea, Mister Jia," Guo Si said.
Yang Feng and Dong Cheng rode up to Guo Si and bowed slightly; Dong Cheng smiled and said, "We're ready to leave, Lord Guo."
"...Fine, fine, very good," Guo Si whimpered. "You two... go and... go and get back to the front."
Dong Cheng and Yang Feng rode away.
"I'll leave you now," Jia Xu said quietly.
"...Yeah," Guo Si sighed. "You take care, Mister Jia."
"I shall," Jia Xu said as he bowed humbly; the former adviser to Dong Zhuo then retreated so that he could inform Li Jue of the successful departure.
Yang Feng and Dong Cheng reached the front of the train of horses and wagons and inspected them for one last time; the two men had been on opposite sides of the violent feud between the Regents only weeks before, but they were now united by a new and grander purpose.
"We'll soon be out of here," Dong Cheng said tonelessly.
"Yes," Yang Feng replied. "Everything's going well."
Dong Cheng smiled.
"**We're ready?**" Guo Si asked as he and his ally Wu Xi rode to the front of the procession.
"**We are, Regent Guo!**" Dong Cheng replied.
"**Let's go then!**" Guo Si ordered.

And so Emperor Xian left Chang'an after 3 years of being retained there as a puppet ruler, and he began the journey eastward to his capital. Emperor Xian's loyalists' paralysing fear of upsetting the Son of Heaven had left him unaware of the full extent of the damage that had been done to his former capital, Luoyang, which had been left untouched – and therefore in a state of total disrepair – by the feuding warlords in the east. He was also unaware of the actual extent of the rampant banditry, the return –

if they ever really disappeared – of the Yellow Turbans, the number of general rebellions, the irreverence of privileged and peasant alike, and, most importantly, the damage done by the recent famine.

Emperor Xian smiled obliviously: his plan had succeeded, and he was free of Li Jue. All that was left to do, he supposed, was rid himself of Guo Si, and there were some among his travelling companions that would gladly help him.

One man that watched the newest situation in Chang'an was Zhang Lu, the ruler of what had once been called Hanzhong Prefecture but was now known, at his demand, as the state of Han'ning; he learned of the emperor's movements and reluctantly sent a messenger to Chengdu, the capital of Yi Province and the seat of Governor Liu Zhang.

"What am I to do, gentlemen…?" the thin, unimpressive Liu Zhang asked of his courtiers. "Zhang Lu's man speaks of one of the regents taking the emperor to the east, most likely to Luoyang: should I be providing men to accompany the escort…?"

"Remain out of this, my lord," the weary middle-aged adviser Dong Fu insisted. "As an adviser to your father, I watched as disaster befell us. We-"

"We wouldn't be attacking, Mister Dong Fu," Liu Zhang's brother-in-law Wu Yi said. "Isn't that right, Lord Liu?"

"It is absolutely right," Liu Zhang replied. "I have no quarrel with the regents. I merely wanted to provide assistance to the Son of Heaven, who is my distant relative as well as my sovereign."

"There are many that remember that your father attacked the capital with the aid of Han Sui and Ma Teng less than two years ago," Dong Fu warned. "The men I refer to will wonder whether your intentions are good, my lord."

"*Aiee…* have I not paid tribute enough times since becoming governor…?" Liu Zhang complained. "Did I not come here at the court's request to rebuke my father for his part in that plot?"

Some of the older vassals that Liu Zhang had inherited from his father grumbled in reaction to being reminded of the events.

"I reiterate that we should stay out of it," Dong Fu said. "Ma Teng and Han Sui are feuding at present; Li Jue and Guo Si may start fighting again; word is bleeding out of Yu and Yang Provinces that we have possible threats from Yellow Turbans and men like Sun Ce and Yuan Shu. We shouldn't add to our woes unnecessarily."

"But how is aiding the sovereign and being seen to be loyal 'adding to our woes'…?" Liu Zhang protested.

"I can guarantee you that the offer of aid will be rejected," Dong Fu replied. "By all means try, Governor, but we must do more to prove that things are different before we can expect the loyal men around His Majesty – or the regents – to trust us."

Liu Zhang sighed miserably and said, "Very well then… I shall be seen to maintain distance. I only hope that it is the right course."

"It is the only course," Dong Fu insisted.

****

24

"...I really am losing count of the days now."
Liu Bei stared vacantly as Jian Yong rambled; both were filthy from the need to conserve Haixi's water for drinking, and neither had consumed anything resembling a proper meal in weeks.
"...I don't know if I can... I can stomach... *that*, over an' over," Jian Yong continued. "I really don't know, Xuande, whether I can..."
Liu Bei lowered his head and whimpered childishly.
"But... but you can't *surrender*, I see that you can't do *that*," Jian Yong said seriously. "We'll all do whatever it takes, Xuande..."
A painfully gaunt Mi Zhu staggered into Liu Bei's audience room and said, "Nothing... to report, Lord Liu."
"...They don't even attack us that much now," Jian Yong chortled.
"Why *bother*...?" Liu Bei sobbed.
"Lord Liu, I don't want to ask this," Mi Zhu said sternly, "but-"
"Then *don't*," Liu Bei said; his tone was icy, but his eyes pleaded.
"...I must," Mi Zhu insisted. "People are starving... people are dying... *we're* dying, Lord Liu, if only slowly."
Liu Bei snorted ambiguously; Jian Yong watched with concern.
"...No one wants to make the sort of decision that you and you alone must make," Mi Zhu continued. "If I could do it, I would, Lord Liu, and gladly, but... as Governor, it must be you."
Liu Bei started to shudder.
"...Lord Liu, I have refrained from pressing you about this," Mi Zhu continued as Guan Yu and Zhang Fei – who were also visibly thinner and unkempt – entered the hall and awaited the response.
"...Xuande," Jian Yong prompted. "Xuande, you have to-"
"NO! NO! I WILL NOT! NO! I CANNOT!" Liu Bei shrieked as the enormity of it all finally caused him to lose his composure – and, perhaps, his sanity – altogether. Guan Yu and Zhang Fei ambled forward and restrained Liu Bei, who was now screaming incoherently and flailing as if he were suffering a seizure.
"...Perhaps I should go," Mi Zhu sighed.
"He has to decide!" Guan Yu insisted. "Lord Liu, you *must*-!"
"NO! NO! I CAN'T! YOU CANNOT MAKE ME DO THIS THING!" Liu Bei screamed. **"I WILL NOT! NEVER! NO!"**
"Others have already been forced to for days now!" Zhang Fei cried emotionally. **"It's too late, Xuande! All you're doing is giving them permission to-!"**
"NEVER, ZHANG FEI! NO!" Liu Bei shrieked. **"HEAVEN WOULD NEVER FORGIVE ME! WHO**...? ...Who would forgive me...?"
Every man – even Guan Yu – was moved to tears.
"What... what you ask... to willingly consume the flesh of men and women... robs us of our right to call ourselves Heaven's children!" Liu Bei sobbed. "What you ask – that I *condone it*, that I... that I *order it* – robs me of the right to call myself *anything*!"
Zhang Fei frowned as he whimpered, "B-but Xuande, I... but others have already... *I* have already...!"
The horrified Liu Bei stared into Zhang Fei's miserable eyes.
"As... as have *I*, Lord Liu... we did it so that you would continue to eat the food of men for as long as possible," Guan Yu admitted.
Liu Bei's eyes darted back and forth between his two old comrades as he tried to decide whether he should be disgusted or grateful.

"And… regrettably… I have done so too," Mi Zhu sighed.

"B-but…! No…!" Liu Bei cried as he turned to face Jian Yong. "But y-you-! …Your eyes, they… no. …You too…? No, Xianhe, not…!"

Liu Bei collapsed to his knees and lowered his eyes.

"Where exactly d'you think that I got 'wolf meat' from, Xuande…? One that Ji Ling fired over the wall to attack us…?" Jian Yong retorted. "You rebuked me for not sharing… now you see why."

"…I… I…!" Liu Bei sobbed.

"You *what*, Xuande…?" Jian Yong asked.

"I… … …until this day, I never knew the lows to which a man can stoop when he is desperate," Liu Bei began.

"*What*???" Jian Yong barked. "You-!"

"*But*," Liu Bei continued, "I also never knew how lucky I truly am… to have such friends, such brothers as you."

One by one, every other man fell to his knees and started to sob.

"…To think that you did everything you could to protect me from the horror that we are forced to face by the villain, Lü Bu, rather than simply forcing me to endure it with you, or even easier, to convince me to yield the province so that you could recover your families and go home… no man ever had friends and brothers like mine," Liu Bei said with a strange smile. "It is when a man faces hardship that he truly knows who his friends and brothers are; who else could count them in as high a number as I…?"

After a painful silence, Mi Zhu wiped the tears from his eyes and asked, "Will you… give the order…?"

"Would it not be easier for me to cede the province…?" Liu Bei retorted. "I ask that not to avoid the act – I will do it even once to show my solidarity and share your pain. I ask because I truly wonder if my keeping this province is worth such suffering."

"…You must fight on," Jian Yong declared. "I… I can't live comfortably with what I've done, but I must try, because yielding this place to a man that once served Dong Zhuo – a man that did what we are forced to do by choice, so I hear, and made others do it for his amusement – would be the greater sin."

"Lü Bu being governor would bring Cao Cao here, who had his men eating the bodies of their victims when he came here before," Zhang Fei noted. "…Xuande, I… I was expected to help 'prepare', what with me being a butcher, and knowing what… what to do, and… and for all that I have done to deserve it, I am truly sorry! For killing Cao Bao, and for losing Xiapi to that bastard Lü Bu and forcing us to come here, I-!"

"Yide, you need not say more," Liu Bei said gently.

"You must continue to resist, Lord Liu," Guan Yu insisted. "We must not surrender… we cannot. We must fight on…"

Liu Bei looked up at Mi Zhu, smiled again and said, "I need not ask your view, dear brother-in-law. The heartless Ji Ling will push us until we break, and Lü Bu and his faithless villain of an adviser, Chen Gong, will never accept anything less than our total submission… and even then, they'll come for the seal of office and then turn back and leave us at Ji Ling's 'mercy' anyway."

Mi Zhu nodded silently.

"…And to do so might doom this province to further horrors, most likely from Cao, Bu and Yuan Shu tearing it apart as they quarrel for it," Liu Bei continued. "You all know that as I know that, and that is why we hold onto the seal, and what it represents… even

when that means losing everything else that we value."
Mi Zhu coughed deliberately and asked, "What are your orders…?"
"Y-you will give… *my* permission… as Governor, for… for the procurement of rations from the bodies of the naturally deceased," Liu Bei said with great difficulty. "None must be slaughtered for the purpose of supplying rations, unless… unless circumstances deteriorate further and leave us with… with no choice, and the deed must be done humanely in that case."
Zhang Fei – who would be the most likely candidate for such slaughtering – covered his face with his hands and sobbed quietly.
"…How many are 'aware'…?" Liu Bei asked apprehensively.
"Only those that participated in its preparation or were shrewd enough to deduce it are aware, Lord Liu," Mi Zhu lied.
"Is that so…?" Liu Bei chuckled.
Mi Zhu sighed, closed his eyes and said, "No, it… it is not. Lord Liu, I have seen things that I hoped that I would never see! Men I've spoken to and knew as being *good* men – and even women, and children! – tearing at the flesh of the dead, and of their neighbours, dead *and* living, as the urge to live overtook the urge to live as something *decent*! I will never sleep soundly again! I-!"
"Hush, dear brother-in-law," Liu Bei said with a strange, musical tone. "It… it is Heaven's design. I know not why, but… this is all Heaven's design. We must be strong and… and survive this, so that we might do better."
After a tense silence, Mi Zhu snorted violently, got to his feet, swept his robes mechanically and said, "I shall… issue your order."
Liu Bei nodded, and Mi Zhu left the hall.
"…Will you be alright, Lord Liu…?" Guan Yu asked.
"I have no right to expect that question, not when you have suffered so readily to spare me the same," Liu Bei replied. "You and I are brothers; you, me, Yide, and Xianhe, we're brothers… and from now on, I *insist* that you call me 'Xuande'."
"…I am honoured, Liu Xuande," Guan Yu said emotionally. "We – Yide and I – should go and accompany Mi Zhu. It is unlikely that there will be unrest, since the people of Haixi made a lot of choices before we did, but… we should be there, just in case."
Liu Bei nodded silently; Guan Yu helped the mortified Zhang Fei to his feet, and the two generals departed. For a short time, Liu Bei and Jian Yong sat in total silence.
"…What are you thinking about, Xianhe…?" Liu Bei asked at last.
Jian Yong sighed and said, "I was wondering what *I* taste like."
Liu Bei went into uncontrollable, frenzied hysterics, despite Jian Yong's toneless words being meant as a genuine thought rather than a joke in poor taste: he cackled maniacally, slapped the unnerved Jian Yong's arm and said, "***Terrible*, Xianhe: *terrible*!**"
Liu Bei's laughter continued as his grasp on his sanity failed; Jian Yong forced nervous laughter until Liu Bei's giggling turned to tears, at which point the Governor of Xu Province buried his head in his hands and rocked back and forth like a child.
"**Xianhe! *Xianhe*!**" Liu Bei wailed. "I…! I-I gave *permission* to…!"
"It'll be fine," Jian Yong said as he patted Liu Bei's arm. "This can't go on forever, it just can't… soon it'll end, and… we'll be fine."

****

25

The imperial entourage's journey took it through some rugged and hazardous terrain: as the procession neared Tong Pass – which served as a border of sorts between Chang'an and the path toward Luoyang – Guo Si suddenly started to become agitated. He stopped the procession, gathered his officers and said, "I wonder if we should go back."
"What?" Yang Feng chortled. "Why? Do you actually like fighting with Li Jue?"
"Don't be rude to me!" Guo Si barked. "Remember who I am! ...Wait a moment, why are you with me anyway??? **Aren't you one of Li Jue's men???**"
"I'm here because I want to get out of Chang'an!" Yang Feng retorted. "And yes, I served Li Jue, because Dong Zhuo made me; but ever since I've been serving Dong Zhuo and you two regents, I've wondered if I picked the right side. I still wonder that now... whether I should have helped *any of you*."
Guo Si's expression hardened: he raised his spear and said, "You want to fight?"
Zhang Ji, Zhang Xiu, Huche'er and Wu Xi were now positioned to aid Guo Si; Dong Cheng remained where he was, despite his being a subordinate of Guo Si as well.
"Of course not," Yang Feng scoffed. "I don't have enough men, even if I wanted to. I'm just glad to be protecting the emperor."
Guo Si sneered and lowered his weapon; Zhang Ji, Zhang Xiu, Huche'er and Wu Xi backed away and returned to their original positions.
"So are we going back, then, Regent Guo...?" Dong Cheng asked.
"...No," Guo Si replied. "Yang Feng's right: all I ever did was fight against Li Jue. Why would I want to go back to that when I can rule alone in Luoyang? Let's keep moving."

Empress Fu and her small retinue of ladies-in-waiting and eunuch attendants had been entrusted with the remnants of the imperial treasury's silk for the journey to Luoyang: they were forced to carry it in their arms as they sat in or on the carriages and carts, which made the valuable goods painfully visible to the Liang Province soldiers that accompanied them.
"...S'at real, d'ya think?" one of Guo Si's men said to a colleague as they walked alongside Empress Fu's carriage.
"I reckon so," the second soldier replied. "Imperial silk... one little piece o' that on the market is worth... I dunno... a lot more than the crap silk we're paid with sometimes, I know that."
"...Don't see why they should get to keep it," the first soldier grumbled. "The Han's nothing now... and where we're going is burned down."
The second soldier stared at the carriage and said, "Her guards are just eunuch servants... and they're nowhere near as well trained as the Gate Guards. What d'ya reckon...? Shall we see if we're alone in our thoughts...?"
The first soldier smiled and nodded, and then the second dropped back to speak to other colleagues. The men were tired, poorly-paid, poorly-equipped and completely irreverent, so the number of

those that agreed with the idea of confiscating the silk was considerable: within minutes the small group of soldiers had stopped the empress's procession and surrounded it.

"What is the meaning of this???" Empress Fu exclaimed.

"The silk," a captain demanded. "Hand it over."

"Wretched thieves!" Empress Fu's senior lady-in-waiting heckled.

"Shut up," the captain ordered. "Just hand it over, or else."

The eunuch attendants had gathered to ready their weapons as the soldiers made their demands, but they were anticipated: they launched their attack, but a second group of men caught them in a pincer and slaughtered them. Blood showered the carriages and their occupants, and the women cried out in terror.

"**WHAT'S GOING ON???**" a voice shrieked.

"Go, *go!*" the thieves' captain hissed, and after snatching the bloodied silk from the terrified women, the men fled.

"Oh...! Oh, I'm sorry, Your Highness," Dong Cheng said as he approached the scene with some of his own infantrymen. "I should have placed my own men to-"

"**After them... after them, I say!**" Empress Fu cried.

"**Do as the Empress commands!**" Dong Cheng barked: half of his men then pursued the thieves.

"...My guards...!" Empress Fu gasped as she leant out of her carriage and viewed the mutilated bodies of her eunuch attendants. "They... they're all...!"

"I will take you to the Son of Heaven," Dong Cheng said. "You should ride with him from now on, Your Highness. I assure you that the perpetrators will-"

"Please! Please... no promises," Empress Fu interrupted. "Just... just do what you can, and say no more."

Dong Cheng nodded sombrely and ordered the remainder of his force to assist the survivors of the attack.

Once the empress was installed within Emperor Xian's carriage, Dong Cheng took Yang Feng to one side and said, "No more waiting: one way or another, I'm definitely getting rid of Guo Si and his men *now*."

Yang Feng looked at the Emperor's carriage. Empress Fu was sat opposite her mortified husband and sovereign: she was shivering nervously, and she was still spattered with the blood of her murdered guards. The empress' ladies-in-waiting were now on different transport carts, and they were sobbing pitifully as the events of the last hour haunted their thoughts.

"*Harming the empress*...?" Dong Cheng whined angrily. "That is-!"

"They stole silk, and if the guards hadn't resisted, that would have been it," Yang Feng said sternly. "If our plan works, there may be more 'incidents' like that with the next men that are assigned to 'protect' them... it may be wise to inform His Majesty that possessions are replaceable and lives are not."

Dong Cheng huffed angrily.

"Hey: it's them or Guo Si's lot," Yang Feng said.

"I know, I know!" Dong Cheng grumbled. "How will we do it...?"

A third man joined Yang Feng and Dong Cheng: it was Yang Feng's subordinate, Xu Huang, who bowed humbly.

"You and Xu Huang will come in on my signal," Yang Feng explained. "First, I'll get everything and everyone where they need to be, and then..."

Tensions raised between the different factions as Emperor Xian's entourage passed into Hongnong, a prefecture and former principality that was situated to the west of Luoyang. Guo Si ordered the procession to halt once again, and he called the officers together.

"I'm hearing about fights," Guo Si said angrily. "No fighting, please! We're supposed to be going to-"

"Do we all look stupid to you?" Yang Feng barked. "We know where we're going, Guo Si! We're going to Luoyang, the former capital that was burned down by Lü Bu on the orders of Dong Zhuo!"

Guo Si tensed.

"Didn't you and Li Jue sack *this* region a lot?" Yang Feng heckled.

"Watch your tongue," Guo Si's general Wu Xi growled.

"Don't threaten me, Wu Xi," Yang Feng retorted. "I just want to be sure that we're not going to be asked to loot the emperor now, because I won't do it!"

"You're starting to get on my nerves, Yang Feng!" Guo Si screamed.

"...**NOW!**" Yang Feng ordered.

Guo Si did not have time to react as Dong Cheng and Yang Feng's subordinate Xu Huang descended on his position with a large group of cavalry.

"I'm a *fool*!" Zhang Ji said as he dodged a strike by Xu Huang, spurred his horse and tried to find a way to lead his men into a counterattack. Huche'er rushed to defend Zhang Ji, but he had not recovered from injuries sustained during the last marketplace encounter, and he was hurt yet again by one of Xu Huang's horsemen. Huche'er knew that he could do little else but accompany Zhang Ji, so he turned and followed him.

"Uncle!" Zhang Xiu cried as he tried to control his horse. **"Uncle, wait!"**

"TRAITORS!" Guo Si cried. **"TRAITORS AND-!"**

"Save it for the netherworld, you scum!" Yang Feng shouted bravely; he then engaged Wu Xi and put Guo Si's lieutenant to flight.

"Why??? HOW???" Guo Si said as he fought his way out of the pincer and galloped westward with a small group of loyal followers.

"After Zhang Ji!" Yang Feng ordered. **"Him and his man Huche'er have to die!"**

Yang Feng personally led the force that would intercept Zhang Ji.

"We are pursued," Huche'er said to his lord, Zhang Ji.

"We must fight, then!" Zhang Xiu supposed.

"No!" Zhang Ji ordered. **"What about our families?"**

Zhang Xiu silently agreed.

"I'll try and negotiate!" Zhang Ji insisted. **"We had to go back anyway!"**

Zhang Ji and his forces halted and turned to face their pursuers.

"...**Prepare to attack!**" Yang Feng urged.

"Wait!" Zhang Ji said as Yang Feng advanced toward him.

"Do you surrender or join us?" Yang Feng asked.

"Neither, but I won't fight you," Zhang Ji replied. **"I... I've had enough. I'm not with Guo Si, so I won't try and fight you. Let me take my men, my family and my men's families, and go south into Jing."**

"...Should we trust him...?" one of Yang Feng's riders wondered aloud.

"...No choice, Yang Ding," Yang Feng replied; he then pointed his spear at Zhang Ji and said, **"You don't come back."**

Zhang Ji nodded, turned to his followers and said, **"You'll all hold at a distance, weapons down!"**

Once Huche'er, Zhang Xiu and his other men had retreated, Zhang Ji nodded respectfully toward Yang Feng, turned his horse and galloped westward toward the baggage train so that he could retrieve his civilian entourage.

"Yang Ding: take your men and follow him," Yang Feng ordered.

Yang Ding and his loyal followers did as they were asked.

Emperor Xian was startled once again as Dong Cheng rode to the side of his carriage and asked, "Your Majesty, are you well?"

"We are fine, but we are confused," Emperor Xian replied. "What is going on?"

"General Yang Feng and I have repelled Guo Si!" Dong Cheng said with cheer. "We can now go on to Luoyang without Your Majesty being humiliated by him and his wretched barbarian soldiers anymore!"

Empress Fu smiled appreciatively.

"...We are grateful to be rid of him before the time and place that was naturally expected," Emperor Xian sighed. "But how far will we get before Guo returns with Li Jue and an army...?"

"We intend to request help from the White Wave Bandits," Dong Cheng replied. "General Yang is an old friend of Han Xian, the leader of the bandits."

Emperor Xian was rattled by the idea: he frowned and said, "We had... we had understood Yang Feng's 'reinforcements' to be of a slightly different nature. How can we feel safe in the company of bandits? ...And were the White Wave Bandits not *Yellow Turbans* before they were bandits...? Weren't the Yellow Turbans dedicated to our *destruction*...?"

Empress Fu also frowned as she awaited the answer.

"Those days of heretics are over," Dong Cheng promised. "I am reliably informed by Yang Feng that Han Xian is a good man that was forced into taking up banditry by the 'Ten Attendants', as many a man was. His loyalty to the Han is undimmed, and he will willingly and joyously assist Your Majesty at this desperate hour."

"...We shall have to place our trust in Yang Feng and hope that he is right," Emperor Xian conceded. "Once it is possible to do so, we should like to have calls for assistance sent out to all of the nearest governors and inspectors, telling them to rise up in our defence against the traitors!"

Dong Cheng was far more aware of the situation in the east than his sovereign: he was morbidly silent for a few moments before he said, "We shall send messages to all of the governors and inspectors, Your Majesty... as desired."

Emperor Xian guessed the reason for Dong Cheng's hesitation and sighed, saying, "Are the rulers of the provinces really so absorbed in their own interests that they would not answer the call of their sovereign...?"

"...They surely will," Dong Cheng replied half-heartedly.

Yang Feng returned to the front of the procession and found Dong Cheng just as the latter had left his audience with Emperor Xian.

"**Well...?**" Yang Feng asked.

"**All is well,**" Dong Cheng declared. "**His Majesty is fine!**"

"**Can Guo Si easily regroup?**" Yang Feng asked.

"**I don't know, but his forces are still scattered!**" Dong Cheng reported.

"**Come with me, and let's be certain!**" Yang Feng suggested.

Guo Si had halted in order to coordinate with General Wu Xi; he had then ordered Wu to retrieve their families from the procession. Wu Xi's men had achieved their task, but Wu was now acting as a rear guard and fighting Yang Feng's ally Xu Huang to the north of Guo's position.

"...*Fool*," Lady Qiong hissed as she passed her husband in her carriage. "Fool! This-!"

"**Someone hasten the procession!**" Guo Si barked.

"**Fine! Hurry me along! But you're still a fool!**" Lady Qiong heckled as her carriage moved away at greater speed.

"...*Shut up*," Guo Si muttered.

Many minutes passed, and the last of the rescued families passed Guo Si's position and moved westward. Another group of horsemen arrived, and Guo Si assumed it to be Wu Xi and his men: he was wrong.

"**THERE'S GUO!**" Yang Feng cried. "**MAKE SURE HE DIES!**"

Yang Feng and Dong Cheng's attack caught Guo's weary followers off-guard, and they scattered once again.

"**BASTARDS! ROTTEN BASTARDS!**" Guo Si cried as he tried to turn the situation around.

"**Why are you still here, idiot?**" Yang Feng cackled as he lunged at Guo Si; the veteran general avoided the attack with ease but retreated rather than risk being surrounded. Yang Feng laughed as he watched Guo Si flee and shouted, "**Where will you go, Guo Si...? Back to Chang'an...?**"

"*Bastards*...!" Guo Si sobbed quietly. "Where else... can I go...?"

"...Good riddance to them," Yang Feng said as Guo Si and his followers disappeared from view.

"What now?" Dong Cheng asked of Yang Feng.

"We'll go and get the emperor moving again," Yang Feng replied. "I expect that Xu Huang will be back soon, since Wu Xi is no threat to him... and Guo Si won't challenge us again, not without Zhang Ji or Li Jue."

"Where *is* Zhang Ji...?" Dong Cheng asked.

"He's promised that he's done with fighting, and I believe him," Yang Feng replied. "He's fetched his men's families and gone south."

"So it is just the regents now, then," Dong Cheng mused. "Them... and *Jia Xu*."

Yang Feng shuddered; the thought of fighting the regents was daunting enough, but the thought of their being assisted by a desperate Jia Xu – whose advice had toppled far smarter men than Yang Feng – truly caused concern.

"What do we do, Uncle...?" Zhang Xiu asked as he rode alongside the demoralised Liang Province general Zhang Ji; Yang Feng's ally Yang Ding had seen the surrendered marquis to the region to the north of the Jing border, but he had now gone back to the emperor, and Zhang was free to move without being monitored.
"I... I do not know," Zhang Ji admitted as he turned his horse so that he could observe the carriage that carried his wife, Lady Zou. "We have to find shelter... oh, why didn't I join Yang Feng??? Did I even *like* Li Jue and Guo Si? Was I even looking to harm the emperor for them??? Why did I flee???"
"...But we *did* flee, and that is that," Zhang Xiu suggested. "Now, we must plan for our future: we are now about to leave Central Province and enter Jing. Now that Yang Ding is gone, do we turn and go back to Chang'an, or do we go on...?"
"You're thinking; you're a good man, Xiu, better and wiser than I," Zhang Ji said sadly. "We *cannot... must not... will not* go back to Chang'an. Li Jue will surely execute us for desertion or perhaps treason, depending on what Guo Si will decide to tell him: no, we must create a new fortune for ourselves now. Yuan Shu once held Wan City for some time: if we continue to Wan, perhaps we will find the place accommodating. We'll surrender to Yuan Shu or Liu Biao if needs be."
"I'll follow you, Uncle, no matter what happens," Zhang Xiu promised. "You can rely on me always."

"Why are we not allowed to see our sovereign???" Chang'an Magistrate Zhong Yao cried as he walked with a mixture of fellow officials and civilian emigrants from the western capital.
"...Fu Wan has been allowed to see the Son of Heaven and his daughter the empress," Director of the Imperial Secretariat Shisun Rui said as calmly as he could.
"Who knows what horrors the sovereign endures with such men as his so-called guardians!" another official whined.
"...Fu Wan said they were *fine*," Shisun Rui groaned.
"This whole affair is ridiculous!" Zhong Yao complained. "Our place is with the Son of Heaven, not here!"
Shisun Rui exhaled fiercely as his patience started to fail him.
"We're being kept away by Yang Feng and Dong Cheng!" Minister Yang Biao said weakly. "We... we're His Majesty's vassals, his ministers, his-!"
"Look, save your strength, you bloody fools!" Shisun Rui said with as much strength as he could muster. **"We're walking the entire way to Luoyang now, it seems, and we'll probably be harassed by the regents and the bandits for the entire journey! If you want to get there standing on your feet instead of lying down in a box, calm down and shut up!"**
"Sorry, Mister Shisun, I... I don't understand... where is my composure...?" Zhong Yao wondered. "Where is my usual strength...? I am over 40! I'm better than this!"
"I, too, am too old to be acting like this," Yang Biao said. "I am not my usual self... surely it isn't fear, after all we've endured...?"
"This isn't a usual situation," Shisun Rui admitted. "And believe me, gentlemen... I'm as scared as you, and we have good cause to

be. Never has the Han been so fragile, so vulnerable as it is right now. But whimpering and moaning will just waste our remaining strength, so… so try and control your feelings, gentlemen, or we won't make it."

The travellers whimpered and moaned regardless, but it would not serve them: there would be no improvement to their lot, and the advance would continue from fear of the pursuers that would surely come.

"…This is not how I envisaged it," Emperor Xian muttered as he stared out of his carriage. "This… this is intolerable."

Empress Fu stared at the bloodstains on the fronts of her robes and sighed miserably.

"Have I unwittingly condemned us to worse suffering…?" Emperor Xian continued. "I know that the situation in Luoyang is bad, but no one will tell me *how* bad… I wonder, is it… is the place even habitable…?"

"Your Majesty, I am scared!" Empress Fu admitted. "I do not want to be 'guarded' by bandits! They killed the attendants, and they… they…!"

"They were… not bandits, but rather they were enemies of the state, enemies that I swear – *we* swear – will be destroyed as soon as an edict can be safely written," Emperor Xian said sternly. "Luoyang cannot be that far away, and no matter what state it is in, our authority will be restored… well, not restored… for we never had any, did we…? …O Heaven, all we ask is a chance to restore our dynasty to its former glory! We have had our Wang Mang: now let us have our rebirth!"

"Do not say such things, Your Majesty!" Empress Fu pleaded.

"No, that's right, I – *we* – should never beg favours of Heaven, for we are Heaven's manifestation on earth, and *others* ask things of *us*," Emperor Xian said as he tried to regain his composure. "This is a test, and we shall pass it, as we have passed every other. Our dynasty *will* shine again!"

Emperor Xian's flight from Chang'an had only just begun. Guo Si reluctantly continued his journey back to Chang'an to alert his fellow regent, Li Jue, and their long-term adviser Jia Xu of the situation while Zhang Ji and his followers continued their journey south to Wan City in Jing Province. News of the situation would take time to reach the warlords in the east, where personal feuds and the desire for power continued to dominate the political landscape. Han Dynasty China had changed, and the young Emperor Xian was about to find out exactly how much it had changed, and what his place within his own empire now was.

✳✳✳✳✳✳✳✳✳✳✳✳

ACT III: THE DISPLACED SOVEREIGN

26

An eventful year in Han Dynasty China had reached a mid-point, but nothing was resolved. The young ruler of the Han Empire, Emperor Xian, had exploited a contrived rift between the self-appointed co-regents, Li Jue and Guo Si, and managed to escape the old capital Chang'an, but his intended journey eastward to the current capital Luoyang – which was still in ruins after Chancellor Dong Zhuo's tyrannical reign – was far from over. Guo Si – the 'regent' that had chosen to accompany Emperor Xian to Luoyang – had been routed and chased away by former allies Dong Cheng and Yang Feng, who apparently intended to liberate the court from the regents' control; Guo's closest ally, Zhang Ji, decided to move south after the rout and occupy a part of Jing Province as an independent warlord, which left Guo Si with no choice but to return to Chang'an and seek help from the Qiang tribal warlords of Xiliang or his estranged co-regent, Li Jue.

While the Emperor travelled, his eastern warlord-vassals were mostly fixed in place: the most powerful of them all, the Yuan brothers of Ru County, were still fighting over chieftainship of their clan, and their influence still forced all of the provincial governors and administrators to support one or the other militarily. The elder brother and chosen chieftain of the clan, Yuan Shao, had control of Ji Province in the north and partial control of neighbouring Bing and Qing Provinces; Yuan Shu controlled most of Yu Province in central China and the northern half of the vast Yang Province in the southeast; Yuan Shao's ally Cao Cao governed Yan Province to the east of Yu, while Gongsun Zan still controlled Yòu Province in the far north without sanction; southern Yang was on the verge of being taken from the court-appointed governor by Yuan Shu's vassal Sun Ce; and in the middle of the eastern and western situations, Governor Liu Biao of the central-western Jing Province did his best to maintain neutrality and protect his domains from Yuan Shu and Sun Ce. All eyes, however, were focussed on the eastern province of Xu, where the politics were as complicated as ever.

Yan Governor Cao Cao's notorious revenge on all of the people of Xu Province for the untimely death of his father had all but removed many of the settlements in the west of Xu and driven the governor Tao Qian to an early grave; Tao's successor, Liu Bei, had surrendered to Cao Cao's friend and master Yuan Shao almost immediately in order to save the province from a third ravaging, but the unpopular move drove detractors within Xu's government to invite the roaming warlord Lü Bu and his adviser Chen Gong – who had recently fled from a failed takeover of Yan Province and settled in western Xu with Liu Bei's blessing – to seize power in Xu, which Bu gladly and immediately did. Liu Bei's army – which had been fighting Yuan Shu – collapsed, and Bei led the remnants to the northern city of Haixi, where his fate was made very clear: suffer countless months of relentless, dehumanising sieging by invading forces belonging to Yuan Shu – with whom Lü Bu had a secret pact – or surrender all of his power to Lü Bu and suffer an unknown fate thereafter. Some in the Xu government started to suspect that they had made a mistake by allying with Lü Bu when they bore witness to his vicious nature, but it was now too late: even if Liu Bei never surrendered the seal of office, Lü Bu controlled Xu Province.

And in the midst of the in-fighting between the various governors and administrators of the eastern provinces, other opportunists thrived: parts of northern Xu and southern Qing Provinces were controlled by gangs led by vigilante-turned-crime lord Zang Ba; Bing Province was under partial control of the 'Black Mountain Bandit' confederacy led by 'Flying Swallow' Zhang; Han Xian's 'White Wave Bandits' roamed Central Province – where the capital Luoyang was located – in the tens of thousands; and the 'Yellow Turbans' – the militant faction of the 'Way of Peace' cult that had once numbered in the hundreds of thousands and threatened to bring down the Han Empire completely – had been revived by two of the movement's veteran generals in Yu Province.

Emperor Xian would be forced to acquaint himself with many of the factions that now roamed or ruled the eastern side of his empire. The young ruler was used to politically complex situations from his forced immersion in the situation in the west: the seat of his dynasty's founder – Hanzhong Province in the central-west – had been seized by the leader of the 'Way of Five Pecks' cult, Zhang Lu, and renamed Han'ning; Yi Province Governor Liu Zhang – the son of Liu Yan, who was the man that enabled the cultists to seize Hanzhong – controlled his northern neighbour Zhang Lu by keeping the cultist's family as hostages, but Liu was otherwise timid and unthreatening; and Liang Province in the northwest was ruled by Regent Li Jue, other former allies of Li Jue's dead master Dong Zhuo, numerous small rebel groups and tribes, and the Qiang tribal leaders Han Sui, Ma Teng, and Song Jian. But even a cynical familiarity with the complex western political landscape could not prepare Emperor Xian for what would unfold over the next year.

Several days after being repelled and forced to retreat, the remnants of Regent Guo Si's army returned to Chang'an and prepared for the possibility that Regent Li Jue might not be welcoming or receptive.
"What in the...!" a guard captain exclaimed as Guo Si's tiny vanguard rode up to the western gates of Chang'an. "I-it's Guo Si! Guo Si has come back!"
"Let me in, fool, or we're all dead!" Guo Si shouted angrily.
"...Somebody fetch General Duan," the captain ordered.
"...What are you doing back here...?" Li Jue asked as Duan Wei led the battered and distressed Guo Si down the aisle of the Southern Palace audience hall.
"It is nice to see that you have made the imperial palace your residence, Li Jue, no doubt in preparation for your coronation as 'First Emperor of the Western Liang Dynasty'!" Guo Si retorted. "While I have been *betrayed*, you have-!"
"Zhang Ji betrayed you...?" Li Jue supposed.
"No, although the least the *coward* could have done is *stay*!" Guo Si replied. "No, it was Yang Feng and Dong Cheng... they ambushed us, scattered the men, and-"
"Wait, so... so the emperor is free!" Li Jue realised at last. "Guo Si,

he'll have us condemned!"

"**I *know*!**" Guo Si cried. "We have to forget all our past stupidity! We have to trust each other, put differences aside, and get him back! Where's Jia Xu?"

"In the chancellery," Li Jue said. "Are you okay to hurry there with me now, Mister Guo?"

"I have no choice!" Guo Si replied.

The regents – now united once again by fear of what the emperor could do to harm them – hurried to their adviser.

"…So that's it, Mister Jia," Guo Si wheezed as he finished a truncated account of recent events.

"…This is a disaster," Jia Xu said as he looked at the terrified regents. "There is no telling what a liberated emperor with a grudge could do."

"Save us!" Guo Si cried.

"How?" Jia Xu scoffed. "Only *you* can save you now, Guo Si: you have to take everything you have and go after Yang Feng and Dong Cheng. You – both of you – have to pursue with intent, and do whatever must be done to retrieve His Majesty and bring him back here to Chang'an."

"What will *you* do, Mister Jia…?" Li Jue asked pointedly.

"What will *I* do…?" Jia Xu chortled. "Han Sui and Ma Teng are like wild animals! If they smell blood, they will descend on Mei County and Chang'an and occupy them! I have to stay here and ensure that Chang'an retains some semblance of order!"

"…We'd better get going," Li Jue said worriedly.

"Wu Xi was going to try and reassemble my forces and lead them back here," Guo Si reported. "I'll send someone to find them and tell them to wait at the border."

"Good," Li Jue sighed. "I'll get Duan Wei to ready my men… we'll have to hope that Zhang Ji finds his way back here as well."

Li Jue and Guo Si hurried out of the chancellery: as soon as they were gone, Jia Xu snorted irritably and muttered, "This is the end of those two, perhaps… how sad it is that I must fall with them… *if*, indeed, I *must*…"

Instead of pondering the defence of Chang'an, Jia Xu planned an escape: he was desperate to dissociate himself from the regents yet again, but he knew that retirement was not an option.

Yi Province's governor, Liu Zhang, received more correspondence from his reluctant ally Zhang Lu, the ruler of Han'ning. Liu Zhang summoned his Chengdu court and said, "If this is all true, the regents have been chased away from His Majesty by the White Wave Bandits! Surely, gentlemen, we-?"

"*Aiee… no*, my lord! Stay away!" Dong Fu interrupted.

"Let me *finish*, Mister Dong!" Liu Zhang said. "The regents-!"

"My lord, I must agree with Mister Dong," Wu Yi admitted. "This situation is anything but simple!"

Liu Zhang smiled coldly and said, "Very well, Wu Yi: because you are my brother-in-law and your father was a close friend of my father, and because you are one of my most trusted supporters, I shall allow your interruption."

All eyes turned to Wu Yi, who said, "If we march an army northwards, we do so through Zhang Lu's territory. Yes, he is a vassal, but not by choice, and we cannot fully trust him. If we make it through 'Han'ning' without incident – a feat in itself, since there will be a need to build a strong supply line and trust Zhang and his 'Way of Five Pecks' acolytes to leave it unmolested – then we will be traversing the treacherous winding plank roads that lead to Liang Province. If we somehow get past them without losing half of our oxen and horses, most of our grain and maybe some of our men, then we face two, possibly three, or maybe even four or five enemies, depending on who is currently allied with whom."

"**Listen to Wu Yi!**" a middle-aged politician cried.

"I *am* listening, Mister Yang," Liu Zhang insisted. "Please, Mister Wu, go on."

"First there are the Qiang warlords, Ma Teng and Han Sui, who are still fighting to the west of the province," Wu Yi continued. "Song Jian is remaining out of the fighting at the moment, but will he do so forever...? If we were to suddenly appear in Liang, might they all forget their personal feuds and attack us...?"

"...That is a valid argument," Liu Zhang conceded. "Go on."

"If I might take over, Mister Wu," Dong Fu said.

Wu Yi nodded silently.

"The second matter is the regents," Dong Fu continued. "They were fighting before, but now they are united against the White Wave Bandits; if we appear now, will they presume us to be exploiting the chaos and making another play for the capital..? Might the Qiang warlords wonder the same...? What of the Han loyalists, who are a separate faction to any of the aforementioned? Do we know who fights for whom, and to what end...? Are the White Wave Bandits *abducting* the Son of Heaven or *rescuing him*...?"

Liu Zhang's eyes wandered.

"And that's all without the other madness," Dong Fu grumbled. "Yellow Turbans in Runan, at least two bandit confederacies operating in the central provinces, the Di, Qiang, and even the Xiongnu causing havoc in Liang; we're walking into an utter mess, Lord Liu, and we won't know if we're making matters better or worse. If we are to act, then let's do so when we know more. By all means send a man to pay tribute to the Son of Heaven when we know where he is, but for now, *wait*."

"*Aiee...* I accept your counsel, gentlemen, but only because I must," Liu Zhang said. "Gather more information, and the second that we have the Son of Heaven's whereabouts and who guards him I want to send aid!"

"The information will be gathered," Dong Fu promised.

"...So my 'master', Liu Zhang, will do nothing... *again*," the ruler of Han'ning, Zhang Lu, muttered as he read a response from Yi Province. He then turned to his adviser Yan Pu and said, "Should I act alone?"

"No, Great Master," Yan Pu replied. "Heaven does not indicate that our moment is here, as you are aware. We should let the Han die a natural death if that is what must now occur and then act in response to that; if the Han survives then we must accept it until Heaven deigns us ready to change the land as we have changed Han'ning."

"…I tire of serving as a buffer for Liu Zhang," Zhang Lu admitted. "I think that it is time that I demanded the return of my family and the independence that his father promised."

Another official, Yang Bo, shook his head and said, "Liu Zhang may be timid, but he is also suspicious and harsh when dealing punishment to perceived wrongdoers. If you oppose him publicly, he'll certainly-"

"If he dares to harm a hair on the head of my mother or any other member of my family, that wretched heretic will die a dog's death," Zhang Lu growled. "I will have no more of this condescending nonsense from that cowardly pedant that bends at the knee to Dong Zhuo's puppet emperor! At least his father was a real man; to take orders from Liu Zhang is like a master taking orders from his servant, and I will not have it!"

Zhang Lu's defiance would cost him dearly.

And in western Liang Province, the latest news forced the Qiang chieftains Ma Teng and Han Sui to call for a ceasefire once again, although the orders would take time to reach every combatant. Ma Chao had led a force to the northwest of Mei County to destroy Han Sui's southern supply lines, and he was one of the last to learn of the decision to lay down arms.

"**You're all chaff to Ma Chao!**" the eldest son of Ma Teng declared as he rode his black horse through a line of Han Sui's Qiang and Han Chinese infantry; men fell in all directions as the young prodigy struck them with his spear. Several of Han Sui's elite cavalrymen challenged Ma Chao and his riders, but Ma was almost as impressive as Lü Bu when it came to horseback combat.

"**General Ma!**" a messenger cried as he rode up to Ma Chao's battle lines on a scruffy brown horse. "**General Ma! Where is General Ma?!**"

"**He's charged,**" an infantry major replied. "**What is it?**"

"**Commander Ma Teng orders all combat to end!**" the messenger reported.

"**Tell that to Han Sui!**" the major retorted.

"**He'll soon order the same!**" the messenger said. "**But Commander Ma worries that-!**"

Ma Chao had broken off his attack while the messenger and the major were talking; he approached them with his elite cavalry and asked of his major, "**Who is this...?**"

"**I've been sent by Commander Ma,**" the messenger replied. "**The enemy-**"

"**They suddenly retreated: Han Sui's man sounded a horn, and they didn't fire after me either,**" Ma Chao noted. "**Has there been another ceasefire...?**"

Before the messenger could answer, a signalman cried, "**A MAN APPROACHES!**"

"**…I already know the answer,**" Ma Chao said as he turned to face the approaching envoy from Han Sui's forces.

"**We're retreating to camp!**" Han Sui's man said.

"**…We'll do the same,**" Ma Chao replied.

Ma Chao's younger brother Ma Tie had been coordinating the far end of the battle line; he approached as Han Sui's messenger retreated and asked, "**Has there-?**"

"**Yes, *again*!**" Ma Chao complained. "**We should just have it

**out and be done with it! We'll only be back here fighting
again before long!"**
Ma Teng's messenger smiled nervously and said, **"General Ma,
the commander-"**
"I know," Ma Chao grumbled. **"Tell him I'm on my way."**

Ma Teng and Han Sui were already in conference in a specially-
constructed neutral encampment when Ma Chao and Ma Tie
arrived and joined them.
"...Behave, my sons," Ma Teng ordered as Ma Chao entered the
command tent.
"They have no need to 'misbehave', Ma Shoucheng," Han Sui
chuckled. "We're both a little less 'touchy' this time, eh...?"
Ma Teng laughed and said, "Indeed."
Many of the officials and officers that were gathered in the tent
could scarcely believe that Ma Teng and Han Sui could be so
cordial after the many personal losses that they had inflicted upon
each other, but they did not comment upon it.
"As we were saying, the moment may again be right to act,
'General Who Pacifies the East'," Han Sui continued. "You and me,
we're both recognised Han generals; yes, the regents that got us
those appointments are now enemies of the state by the looks of
things, but if we were to be *careful*..."
Ma Teng hummed thoughtfully and said, "You believe the news
that the White Wave Bandits actually 'saved' the emperor...?"
"I don't see why not," Han Sui replied. "The emperor is said to be
sending out requests for aid to protect him from the *regents*, not
the bandits."
"...So you suggest attacking the regents," Ma Teng supposed.
"I suggest not attacking each other, at least," Han Sui replied.
"We both started this, so let's both finish it, Ma Shoucheng. We've
both spilled the kin blood of the other, but we're not beyond
stopping before we destroy ourselves."
"...Or weakening ourselves so much that Song Jian, the regents or
one of the Han warlords could take advantage," Ma Teng mused.
"Or, of course, if the emperor were saved and issued a decree
calling for all the 'western villains' to be killed..."
One full-blooded Qiang leader yawned loudly.
"Are we boring you...?" Ma Teng heckled. "Get out if you don't
want to listen."
"This is weak talk!" the Qiang leader complained as he pushed
his way past several officials and left the meeting.
"...We can attack the regents, or we could wait and see what the
Han does, and then we could help them or kill them," Han Sui
suggested. "If the emperor wasn't so far away I'd say that we
could go and get him, but that would be dangerous."
"Either way, our own feud has to stop," Ma Teng said. "I agree
with you on that, Han Wenyue."
Han Sui smiled, and the two Qiang warlords clasped hands as a
sign that they were reconciled, if only for the time being.

＊＊＊＊＊＊＊＊＊＊＊＊

27

Jing Governor Liu Biao was quietly pondering his next move against his main enemies – Yuan Shu, who controlled Yu Province to Jing's east, and Yuan's vassal Sun Ce, who was actively seizing Yang Province to the southeast – when his senior adviser Kuai Liang entered his private audience hall and coughed deliberately.

"...Wouldn't 'My lord, might I say something?' be a more appropriate way of getting my attention...?" Liu Biao said irritably.

"I... I didn't know how to put what I had to say," Kuai Liang admitted.

"You, lost for words...?" Liu Biao said nervously. "What is it...? Who attacks me, and from where...?"

"...The... the regents' ally, the Liang warlord *Zhang Ji*, attacks Wan City," Kuai Liang replied apprehensively.

Liu Biao gasped and said, "The *regents* attack me??? B-but... *why*...? I have resisted my better judgement and avoided any confrontation with them, so why do they attack me???"

"I... I honestly don't know, but Wan can only hold for so long against a professional soldier like Zhang Ji," Kuai Liang replied.

"...But who can I spare...?" Liu Biao groaned. "I need your brother Yue and Huang Zu to remain in the south and defend against Sun Ce, and I need Cai Mao to monitor the situation in Yu, especially now that Yuan Shu is apparently staging a new 'Yellow Turban Rebellion' there in order to attack me!"

"The 'Yellow Turbans' – or whatever they truly are – are more concerned with attacking Cao Cao and securing a foothold in the east of Yu, it seems," Kuai Liang replied. "Zhang Ji is terrifying when unfettered, and we could well do without his kind as hostile tenants; uprooting him, should he secure a foothold, will be a thousand times harder than uprooting Yuan Shu."

"...Then Cai Mao will have to go to Wan," Liu Biao decided.

"I will have regular reports sent back here from the front, and if needs be I'll go in person," Kuai Liang suggested.

"...Zhang's a mindless thug, isn't he...?" Liu Biao asked bemusedly.

"No," Kuai Liang replied. "He's one of Dong Zhuo's more intelligent supporters in Liang Province. But that isn't why I'd go; there's been no word about Li Ru in recent years, but that doesn't mean that the co-architect of the regicide doesn't still live and serve as an adviser... and then there's Jia Xu, who is well known to still live and exercise a lot of influence from the shadows. That cunning fox's presence would require a more agile mind than Cai Mao's to counter. But as you say, something is going on in Central Province, and it seems to involve the Son of Heaven somehow: this might be connected, but I need more information."

"...I want to know every little detail," Liu Biao ordered.

Kuai Liang bowed low, turned and left the room.

"...Yuan Shu craves my land as a personal estate; Sun Ce desires my very life as compensation for his father's; what do the regents want...?" Liu Biao wondered miserably. "I have stayed out of the nonsense that surrounds me, so... *why*...?"

Zhang Ji and Zhang Xiu observed the besieged walls of Wan City and wondered how long it would take to seize the place.

"Will such a small army be enough...?" Zhang Ji murmured.

"Your men are some of the fiercest in all of the land, Uncle," Zhang Xiu said. "Why shouldn't we take Wan within the month...?"

"My main concern is not what Liu Biao will do," Zhang Ji admitted. "I have not sent word of my activities to either of the two idiots, Li and Guo... so they'll suspect – rightly – that I've gone my own way. Knowing them, they'll probably attack me first."

"I disagree," Zhang Xiu replied. "You're not capable of drafting an edict for their heads, Uncle, but the emperor is. You have nothing to fear from the regents – either of them – or Yang Feng and the emperor: the latter two will be proving problematic to each other, and the regents know, despite being as irrational as they can often be, that they have no choice but to focus all of their efforts on recovering the men that can condemn them. The only thing that we'll get from the regents is a begging letter, perhaps reminding you that you might have to worry about any edicts that are written as well: and that's an empty threat, because Dong Cheng knows that you opposed the emperor being overthrown or killed on many occasions... and even if the loyalists choose to forget that fact, you deserted the field rather than aid the regents in recapturing the emperor, and they at least owe you that."

Zhang Ji smiled and said, "I have in you a wise heir, Nephew. Liu Biao will be my only worry then... but what can he do...? We know that he is surrounded by the useless Liu Zhang, hankering Yuan Shu and vengeful Sun Ce on three sides, and that the latter two consume all of his time and resources."

"He'll send someone," Zhang Xiu suggested. "You're well known to the warlords that govern provinces close to Liang, Uncle, and he'll fear you. He won't send Huang Zu of Jiangxia, but he may send someone else that he relies upon."

"Mm... we could do with having a strategist," Zhang Ji said thoughtfully. "It's a genuine pity that we don't have a man like Jia Xu... but at least we have Huche'er, who compensates us with his strength and skill."

Zhang Ji and Zhang Xiu turned their attentions back to the siege of Wan: their champion Huche'er was bellowing orders to the veteran men at the west wall, and the defenders – whose numbers were sparse after several emigrations in the wake of occupation by Yellow Turbans and Yuan Shu – looked on fearfully as another group of Zhang's men prepared to attack.

"...In a way, the Yellow Turbans, Yuan Shu and the famine have done us great favours," Zhang Ji said. "Their supplies are stretched, while ours are more-or-less ample for a month; the people are few, and already demoralised; and Yuan Shu and his cultist allies will reduce the scale of the response from the governor. You're right, Nephew: in a month or less, we will have Wan City, and once we have that, we only need to show a small measure of sense and the rest of Nan County will be ours as well!"

"And from there, Uncle, who knows what we can achieve," Zhang Xiu replied.

Zhang Ji smiled optimistically and said, "Indeed."

The emperor's procession had moved across western Central Province as quickly as its burdens would permit, but resources were running dangerously low and fatigue had overwhelmed men, horses and oxen alike. When the travellers were finally forced to stop and rest, a spacious tent was prepared for the emperor and the baggage train was contracted to give the inevitable pursuers less to attack.

Emperor Xian tired of watching his tent being assembled and had Dong Cheng summon Yang Feng so that he could ask what was planned: he was quietly resigned to more powerless misery after so many years, but a part of him hoped that this would be a turning point.

"All we can do is wait, Your Majesty, and hope that the White Wave Bandits get here before Li Jue and Guo Si can regroup and come after us," Yang Feng said in response to the emperor's query. "I've got two of my best – Yang Ding and Xu Huang – taking the rear, so we won't be caught off-guard: Administrator Zhang Yang will be here soon as well, hopefully."

"...*Bandits*," Emperor Xian scoffed. "We are to be saved by an army of *bandits*... while our appointed governors do *nothing*."

"Sadly, Your Majesty, that is the world," Yang Feng said plainly. "Would I dare even *look at you* in any other circumstances?"

"*No*, you *wouldn't*!" a weary eunuch attendant heckled.

Yang Feng laughed tactlessly and said, "When we get to Luoyang, I'll apologise for my lack of etiquette. For now, all I care about is *saving* the Son of Heaven."

Xu Huang rode up to the gathering and said, "Li and Guo have been sighted. They're bringing an advance force of a thousand cavalrymen. Yang Ding is delaying them, but he won't last long."

"Don't panic," Yang Feng insisted. "Without Zhang Ji's lot to worry about, we can hold against those idiots for a fair while!"

"If we lose, they will kill us all, for certain," Dong Cheng said.

"Oh, I don't doubt it... but we won't lose!" Yang Feng cackled as he levelled his spear. "Look at who comes here!"

Every man's eyes turned to the east, where a small army of horsemen and infantry could be seen: they carried simple banners that identified them as being members of the notorious White Wave Bandits.

"I knew that Han Xian wouldn't let me down," Yang Feng chuckled. "Right, then! **Let's go and show those two 'regents' that their day is over!**"

Yang Feng's battle cry gave his small army morale, and they turned and prepared to engage the regents' larger force.

Li Jue and Guo Si swept Yang Ding's delaying force aside with ease and advanced on the vulnerable encampment: the destruction of the supply train followed.

"**Find the emperor!**" Li Jue ordered. "**Ignore the rest! Let them come to us!**"

Li Jue's forces did as they were asked, but as they moved east, they met a resistance force led by Dong Cheng.

"**This is as far as you go!**" Dong Cheng screamed.

"**A coffin for *you*, you traitor!**" Li Jue retorted. "**KILL HIM!**"

Dong Cheng's men moved forward to provide a much-needed barrier between the attackers and the main camp.

"**You're a brave little maggot, Dong Cheng!**" Li Jue heckled.

"**You'll regret betraying me, Dong Cheng!**" Guo Si suggested.

"**You're not a maggot: no, you're food for the maggots!**"

"**I'm not alone!**" Dong Cheng retorted.

Xu Huang arrived with a second force from the northwest, and the regency's isolated vanguard was forced onto the defensive.

"**You should have counted your men before you attacked!**" Xu Huang taunted.

"**You think this is it?**" Guo Si barked. "**We have a whole army coming! But we don't need it, not for you two and your scruffy followers! Wu Xi: attack Xu Huang! Make up for your past losses!**"

"**I shall, Your Excellency!**" Wu Xi replied.

Xu Huang engaged Wu Xi and forced him to retreat: he then charged at Guo Si, who was a more effective fighter.

"**I've held my own against Lü Bu!**" Guo Si cackled. "**What chance do you have, just a little lackey of Yang Feng...?**"

"**NOW!**" Yang Feng cried as he charged with his Bandit cavalry.

"**Forward, you men!**" the White Wave leader, Han Xian, shouted as he advanced on his brown steed; Li Jue's forces were now outnumbered, and the regents ordered a retreat to regroup.

"**We mustn't lose here!**" Guo Si screeched. "**Li Jue, we can't–!**"

"**The first infantry are here, so we can counter now!**" Li Jue interrupted. "**We hit them with everything!**"

Guo Si turned and looked at the approaching infantry with delight.

"**Push them back! Kill them all!**" Li Jue ordered. "**No one walks away! Not Yang Feng, not Dong Cheng, not even the emperor! The Han ends now!**"

The thousands-strong Chang'an infantry reacted to Li Jue's gestures, but could not hear his words – many might have hesitated if they had. They charged at the imperial encampment, but before they could reach it, they were attacked on all sides by horsemen led by Yang Feng, Han Xian, Dong Cheng and Xu Huang. Li Jue and Guo Si urged their own cavalry onward, but the White Wave Bandit infantry vanguard had arrived: the raucous, violent mob numbered over 20,000, and the sight was enough to terrify the regency forces and cause many men to scatter.

"**Don't we *pay you*, you ingrates???**" Li Jue cried as he watched his infantry disintegrate. "**It's just a horde of bandits! Regroup! REGROUP!**"

"**Kill the regents!**" Han Xian ordered. "**Then on to Chang'an!**"

Li Jue and Guo Si were suddenly as scared as their men: the day was obviously lost, and the emperor was definitely free of their control. Guo Si was the first to turn about and flee; it was only when half of his men had been cut down or forced to surrender that Li Jue finally gave up on his quest and retreated to the relative safety of the western capital.

"**VICTORY!**" Yang Feng bellowed.

The thousands of Bandits cheered along with the Han forces.

"**It's been a long time since we fought together, mate,**" Han Xian said as he rode alongside Yang Feng. "**I hope this isn't the last time.**"

"**We must ensure that His Majesty is safe,**" Yang Feng replied.

"**O' course,**" Han Xian chuckled. "**I keep forgetting you're an imperial general.**"

The two friends rode to the tent where the emperor was actually housed, since the imperial tent had been left empty as a decoy: they dismounted in front of the enclosure and prepared to pay homage to the sovereign.

"…Your Majesty," Yang Feng said as he entered the tent and immediately kowtowed.

"…Your Majesty," Han Xian said with as much grace as he could muster: his kowtow was clumsy but apparently sincere.

"You have both done well," Emperor Xian replied. "The false regents are now in full retreat, we presume…?"

"They are," Yang Feng confirmed. "Shall we pursue?"

"Our priority is to reach Luoyang safely," Emperor Xian decided.

"We'll ensure there's a strong rear guard, and begin preparations to start moving again," Han Xian said as Dong Cheng entered the tent and kowtowed silently.

"You have both done well," Emperor Xian reiterated. "You, Dong Cheng, are also to be commended. Rewards will be forthcoming as soon as it is appropriate, but now we must seek more help. We cannot simply rely on an army of disaffected commoners for protection, because their loyalties may be fickle. If you have not already done so, you must send word to the governors, inspectors and administrators of Eastern Central Province, Jing, Yan, Xu, Ji, Bing and Yu, and have them provide support. They *must* and *will* provide support."

"It has been done," Dong Cheng said. "We must be… patient."

The officers knew that the situation was even more urgent than their emperor supposed. Li Jue and Guo Si had managed to destroy a lot of the supplies despite the measures taken to disperse them throughout the camp, which meant that there was very little food; there were a lot of mouths to feed, and that would start to become a problem very quickly.

"Everywhere I look, there are *criminals*!" Director of the Imperial Secretariat Shisun Rui cried as the White Wave Bandits continued their staggered arrival. "Bandits, bandits, this way and that! How can I tell others to… to be calm when… when…!"

"**They multiply before my very eyes!**" another official screamed hysterically. "**Hundreds become thousands, thousands become tens of thousands… they are the locusts taking human form, come to devour us all!**"

Shisun Rui coughed painfully and said, "I could… I could almost believe it… that they *are* the locusts, returned as men to… to consume us…!"

Minister Yang Biao noted his colleague Shisun Rui's mental deterioration and sighed miserably; two other men – Empress Fu's father, the official Fu Wan, and Chang'an Magistrate Zhong Yao – stood at his side and shared his observations and his distress.

"Shisun Junrong tried to keep us sane, and now he falters so quickly," Zhong Yao lamented. "I understand, though; he has lost friends and family both, he is ill now, and these White Wave Bandits are the worst threat yet. He has reached his limit."

"Whose idea was this…?" Minister Yang Biao wondered as he turned to observe the disorderly hordes of White Wave Bandits.

"…I think it is a plot of His Majesty's design gone wrong," Fu Wan replied miserably. "My daughter spoke in a way that implied His Majesty's involvement, but… I think that Yang Feng deliberately misled His Majesty about the force of rescuers that he was going to summon."

"They're former Yellow Turbans, or at least some of them are," Yang Biao recalled. "Perhaps, if they are shackled to some sort of faith, they will restrict their criminality to looting and petty theft; perhaps we will be spared worse."

"Let us hope that they steal some food from someone else and bring it here," Zhong Yao said as he stared at the smouldering supply train. "We have barely enough left to feed the Son of Heaven, Her Highness the Empress, the attendants, the imperial guards and the other important people, like senior officials, senior officers and elite soldiers; how can we hope to feed the hundreds of people that accompanied us and the thousands of bandits that now 'guard' us as well...?"

Yang Biao and Fu Wan silently agreed.

"I almost wish that I was still hysterical, so that I did not have to think about it," Zhong Yao continued. "Minister Yang, Mister Fu, I was a student of Cai Yong, and I am proud to say so! I am – was – the Magistrate of Chang'an! I would hope to be appointed Magistrate of Luoyang when we get there, if no other worthier man is found! But a solution to this problem – a problem that I would be expected to ponder at the very least – escapes me!"

"Do not... feel... responsible, Zhong Yuanchang," Yang Biao groaned. "I..."

"Your injuries are worse than I had realised," Zhong Yao noted.

"I have no intention of dying here!" Yang Biao insisted. "I did not live for fifty-three years and survive Dong Zhuo and those accursed regents in order to die in the wilderness at the hands of bandits, or to starve to death, or to succumb to a little injury! I will see Luoyang again, and I will see the warlords humbled and the Han restored!"

"We must all do our best to survive," Zhong Yao replied. "His Majesty needs us."

But as the White Wave Bandits increased in numbers, their brazenness grew as well: they started to show greater and greater disrespect for the very people that Yang Feng had invited them to the region to protect. As the days passed, many started to wonder whether they would actually prove to be a worse 'protector' than the regents had been; some recalled the arrival of Dong Zhuo in Luoyang, and how the jubilation at finally being rid of the 'Ten Attendants' was quickly replaced by the realisation that in many ways, Dong Zhuo would be far worse, and they wondered whether fate – or Heaven, if they truly believed in it – would continue to torment them with ever-worsening transitions of power.

"...So now we are guarded by thieves."

Empress Fu's toneless words were nonetheless laced with hatred for the White Wave Bandits.

"I cannot believe what Heaven subjects us to," Emperor Xian moaned. "A tent... a *tent*...! Now the 'Son of Heaven' reviews the nation from a *tent*...! First the seditious eunuchs, then my brother's mother and *her* brother, then Dong Zhuo, and then those two bumpkin regents... and now I am in a tent in the middle of nowhere, 'guarded', I am told, by the White Wave Bandits! *Bandits*! Those men are-!"

"Hush," Empress Fu said suddenly.

Emperor Xian fell silent: moments later, two White Wave Bandits entered the tent, grinned fearlessly, and departed again.

"...They steal from others and their own, like animals," Empress Fu whispered. "They do not respect anything. My ladies are terrified, although they have not harmed them so far. They are content with valuables... so far, at least."

"Even the days of Wang Mang were not said to have been as bad as this," Emperor Xian lamented. "Truly, one wonders if the prognostications were true... one can truly wonder if-"

"Say no more," Empress Fu pleaded. "May Your Majesty and Heaven forgive me for my frankness, but... say no more!"

Emperor Xian nodded silently: no more needed to be said. In the minds of many, whatever had been the lowest point for the Han Dynasty before that moment had been exceeded in terms of severity; they wondered whether there was any lower point that could be reached, and whether there truly was a way back from such a point. Most wondered if there was any hope of recovery from where they already were; Emperor Xian and his traumatised empress certainly did.

The son of the man whose advice to Emperor Xian's predecessor had empowered the warlords that now ignored their emperor – Liu Zhang, the Governor of Yi Province – received the defiant words of his neighbour and vassal Zhang Lu and reacted instinctively.

"Gather his family," Liu Zhang said to his brother-in-law Wu Yi. "Gather them all together and-"

"You need to summon everyone to discuss this," Wu Yi pleaded.

"Discuss what???" Liu Zhang chortled. "This man, this cultist beast, now writes to me to tell me that he will no longer 'bow and scrape' to 'a craven supporter of the men that defy the will of Heaven'! He must be punished!"

"The entire reason that my father and your father had Zhang Lu send his family here was to keep them as hostages," Wu Yi protested. "Kill them, Lord Liu, and what do you have over him then...?"

"He defies me now, while they are here," Liu Zhang retorted. "Their continued presence here incites insurrection; if I send them back alive, I look weak. If I kill them, I send a message that I am not to be crossed."

"I can't dissuade you...?" Wu Yi asked.

"Not you, not anyone," Liu Zhang said. "They must all die."

"...Alright," Wu Yi replied. "I'll do as you ask."

Within a day, every member of Zhang Lu's family that was a 'guest' in Chengdu had been gathered in one place and beheaded or strangled. Some lauded the move as a long-overdue message to a cultist dictator, while others worried that it could compromise the security of the already-isolated Yi Province, since the only friendly – or, more accurately, neutral – neighbour was now Liu Biao of Jing Province to the east. Time would certainly tell.

****

28

Li Jue passed through the territorial boundary known as Tong Gate and gathered his battered officers together for a meeting to discuss what to do next.
"Where's Guo Si?" Duan Wei asked.
"That coward fled ahead of us... I saw his banner on the ground as we marched," Li Jue replied bitterly. "If he'd stayed, we might have been able to regroup and-!"
"That's unlikely," Duan Wei suggested.
"My nephew is bringing a second infantry force," Li Jue explained. "Once we're together, we can go back and try again."
"Without Guo Si's force, we'll not achieve much," Duan Wei insisted. "There are close to a hundred-thousand White Waves, and they're guarding the emperor! They were the only thing we were afraid of when we were pillaging in Central Province, so how can we win when we're weaker now than we were then...?"
"...You're right," Li Jue sighed. "We brought this on ourselves without realising it; how many of those people we harmed caused more to join the White Waves?"
"Let's just go back to Chang'an," Duan Wei suggested. "Jia Xu can help us plan the reconstruction, and we can try and get support from the Qiang. It isn't over."
"You've gotten smarter," Li Jue chortled. "Alright... we retreat. Yang Feng and Dong Cheng have won, and the emperor has won... for now. But once Jia Xu gives us a plan, we can pull ourselves back out of the pit. **Onward, to Chang'an!**"

But while Li Jue and his allies retreated to Chang'an, the emperor's requests for aid were being taken to the surrounding provinces by desperate messengers.
"A letter from His Majesty...?" Jing Governor Liu Biao exclaimed as an imperial messenger was led into his Xiangyang audience hall in the north of the province; the court showed the appropriate level of penitence to the imperial representative.
"This proclamation shall be brief and devoid of some of the usual protocol, due to the urgency of the hour," the messenger began. "His Majesty has been given an opportunity to flee the wicked clutches of the villains Li Jue and Guo Si, but danger remains: they have been repelled, but they intend to pursue and recapture His Majesty as he makes his way to Luoyang. This is a formal request for any aid that can be provided: troops, food, or shelter."
Liu Biao kowtowed and said, "We shall discuss how we can help. You will be well cared for until a decision is reached, and I promise a swift answer."
"I must hurry on to other places, so you will have to forward your response to His Majesty directly, preferably when you act," the messenger retorted.
"...We shall discuss how we can help," Liu Biao reiterated.
The messenger turned and retreated without saying another word.
"We *cannot* help," the adviser Kuai Liang sighed once the messenger was gone.
"Can I refuse a request from His Majesty...?" Liu Biao asked.
One of Liu Biao's newest advisers – Wang Can, who was a young

prodigy and former pupil of the famous scholar Cai Yong – nodded and said, "We are too far away to be of use to His Majesty."

Liu Biao laughed and said, "So you are not distracted by the brays of your beloved creatures today, Wang Can…? Very good, but your geography is poor; how can I reply to His Majesty that 'we are too far away' when we are closest to His Majesty's procession…?"

All eyes turned to Wang Can, who was also notorious for being unable to concentrate when he heard the sound of donkeys; there were none nearby to muddle his mind at that moment, however, so his true ability could properly manifest.

"Wan City in Nan County might have served as a temporary base, but not now that it's under siege again by Li Jue's ally Zhang Ji," Wang Can explained. "We could bring His Majesty past that place and here to Xiangyang, or southward to Jiangling… but that would, in effect, make that place the temporary imperial capital – with all of the financial burdens that one would expect – and the responsibility for rebuilding Luoyang would then fall to the host governor, namely-"

"I've heard enough, 'Friend of the donkeys'," Liu Biao chuckled. "I haven't got the strength to fight that sort of battle anymore… Sun Jian and Yuan Shu have made me old before my time. If I took the emperor in, I'd probably be called 'another Liu Yan' and accused of taking him hostage by the other warlords… and I'd have to follow his every command and pay for everything too! Even though I am a member of the royal clan, I cannot help."

"We'll ignore this request, then," Kuai Liang said. "But I suggest sending more men to Wan City: we don't want to lose it again."

"Do it," Liu Biao ordered. "If needs be, I'll go personally."

The Henei Administrator Zhang Yang received the same imperial request for aid from a different messenger within a few days of Liu Biao declining assistance.

"…I cannot refuse," Zhang Yang decided. "Messenger, tell His Majesty that I am at his disposal."

"You shall be rewarded!" the messenger said joyously.

"I am happy to be doing the right thing," Zhang Yang replied.

"I must move on!" the messenger said. "Heaven will reward you!"

Zhang Yang turned to his adviser Dong Gongren and said, "Please see this vassal of our sovereign has everything that he needs."

"I shall," Dong Gongren replied.

As Dong Gongren and the messenger withdrew from the audience hall, Zhang Yang looked at his vassals and said, "Many of you have been in the employ of the villains Li Jue and Guo Si… but who do you serve now…?"

The courtiers were silent.

Zhang Yang turned to two of his loyal officers and said, "Sui Gu, Yang Chou: ready the elite forces to greet His Majesty. He must feel safe from the very first moment."

The officers did as they were asked; Zhang Yang, meanwhile, smiled at the thought that he, like the emperor, was freed from the far-reaching clutches of the two regents. He relished the idea of helping the emperor, who would need his assistance as quickly as he could provide it.

Yuan Shu's appointed Administrator of Lujiang, Liu Xun, received an imperial messenger and listened to his plea. Once the messenger had been escorted from the hall unanswered, Liu Xun turned to his senior adviser Liu Yè and asked, "Do I help...?"

"I would not do anything without forwarding the request to Lord Yuan Shu and awaiting his orders," Liu Yè replied. "Like you, I am a distant relative of His Majesty, so I feel pain at the thought of a relative suffering, but... like it or not... our lord is Yuan Shu, and he insisted that we have his approval for everything and anything."

"...You're right," Liu Xun said reluctantly; he was about to issue the order to forward the message, but he hesitated as another thought entered his mind.

"You're unsure," Liu Yè guessed.

"...What do the rest of you think...?" Liu Xun said as he looked at the collection of politicians and advisers.

"We agree with Liu Yè," one man replied; the others then murmured agreeably.

"...Not one of you sees the benefits of responding to this independently...?" Liu Xun asked desperately. "Haven't we got strong generals to fight for the sovereign?"

Many eyes turned to the battle-hardened officers Qi Ji and Qin Yi, who had been promoted for their efforts against the former administrator Lu Kang and assigned to lead the security forces within the prefecture.

"We have General Qi and General Qin, yes, and also General Liang Gang, *perhaps*, but we lack a militia of sufficient size to repel whoever Lord Yuan Shu sends here to relieve you of the seal of office and serve the Son of Heaven in any significant way," Liu Yè replied. "And that, of course, is if Qi Ji and Qin Yi wish to potentially oppose their lord's wishes...?"

Qin Yi lowered his gaze; Qi Ji grunted quietly and turned his eyes to the ceiling.

"...Well put!" Liu Xun chuckled; he was privately angry, but he knew Liu Yè's words to be correct. After a pause, Liu Xun added, "We'll forward the message to Lord Yuan immediately."

Yan Province Governor Cao Cao's temporary court in the city of Xuchang received two messengers from the west: one told of the emperor's plight, the other of General Zhang Ji's assault on Wan City in Nan County.

"My lord, we should help the sovereign," Xun Wenruo said. "That goes without saying, I think. As for Zhang Ji... he cannot be allowed to settle in Nan County. Even if he now independent as the report suggests, he is a former general under Dong Zhuo and too close to His Majesty's convoy for comfort."

Cao Cao hummed thoughtfully, turned to the recently-arrived Cao Hong, and said, "You're reckless but brave, and your efforts in pacifying eastern Yan have impressed everyone, I would think, so my sending you is as good as going myself."

"Don't send him," Cheng Yu scoffed. "This is the *Son of Heaven* asking this of you, not some petty official! You must go yourself!"

"I cannot agree this time, Mister Cheng," Cao Cao retorted. "To the south, I have Yuan Shu. To the west, I have Yellow Turbans and Yuan Shu's mercenaries, be they one and the same or not. To the east, I have Liu Bei and Lü Bu. To the north, I have Yuan Shao, and I am now unsure whether that's a good thing or not.

Liu Biao may already feel I've let our alliance down, so I must watch him too! But if Zilian can go and do this great double mission for us – save the sovereign and aid the liberation of Nan County – we'll have Liu Biao for a friend and His Majesty's blessing. I'd love to go, but with so many enemies around me, I cannot risk it."

"…You know best," Cheng Yu sighed.

"Cao Hong: ready a force of three-thousand and go to Central Province at once," Cao Cao ordered.

Cao Hong bowed and said, "It shall be done."

When the messenger that had been sent to Henei returned to the imperial encampment in the wastelands of western Central Province, he was greeted with relief.

"So *someone* had the decency to help His Majesty," Dong Cheng scoffed. "Zhang Yang will surely know Heaven's gratitude; Liu Biao, by contrast, is a wretch that deserves to lose everything!"

"…We are genuinely saddened that another relative shirks his responsibilities," Emperor Xian sighed. "Let us hope that he is more of a Liu Yu than a Liu Yan at heart, and that we will not suffer some treachery at a later date."

"Liu Biao has good reason, Your Majesty," Yang Feng insisted. "We now know that Zhang Ji is making trouble in Nan County; how can we evade Li and Guo by walking straight into their closest ally?"

"…You are quite right," Dong Cheng conceded. "Curse Zhang Ji, and curse our foolishness for letting him go!"

Yang Feng grunted irritably, since the decision to release Zhang Ji had been his and his alone.

"But what of Yan, Yu, Xu, Bing and Ji…?" Dong Cheng continued. "Are the men in those places heartless?"

"The messengers must travel further to reach them and return," Yang Feng suggested. "Let's… let's be patient."

The officers looked about them at the dire situation; it would take weeks for the procession to reach the ruins of Luoyang, and food supplies were almost exhausted. The need to supply the emperor with fitting sustenance at all costs meant that some of the emperor's vassals were already eating crudely extracted plant matter so that he could have any proper food that was left; others – including some of the famished bandits – were cannibalising the bodies of people that had been left unburied after fighting Li Jue and Guo Si.

"…It's tragic," Yang Feng sighed: those that knew what he meant by those words could not disagree.

General Zhang Ji and his nephew Zhang Xiu had found Wan City to be sparsely defended, since Liu Biao had not had the time or the resources to adequately repopulate it after expelling its previous squatter, Yuan Shu: their siege of the city had gone well, but Zhang Ji learned of Liu Biao's latest movements and called an urgent meeting of his senior followers.

"We must end this siege within the week, gentlemen!" Zhang Ji urged. "Liu Biao has written to Cao Cao and sent one of his senior naval commanders up the Yu River to harry us; in addition, the emperor has been sending requests for aid, and we'll probably have militias answering the call from all over! We could have one or both of the Yuan brothers, Cao Cao, Zhang Yang and Liu Biao attacking separately or even teaming up against us, citing our former alliance to the regents and Dong Zhuo: that would certainly suit Liu Biao!"

"Taking the place quickly changes what, if you do not mind me asking, my lord...?" the foreign-featured Huche'er asked as politely as he could.

"If we have Wan and are safely within its walls, they'll not waste precious resources trying to get it back until the regents are defeated," Zhang Ji replied. "If we are still fighting, they'll surround and beat us while we're exposed."

"Haste is never advised during a siege," Huche'er noted. "Haste leads to mistakes."

"You're right, my friend, but I have no choice!" Zhang Ji retorted. "We cannot negotiate until we have Wan. I'll join the siege efforts personally, since this is my battle and, perhaps, my folly."

Zhang Xiu shook his head and said, "Huche'er is right, Uncle. We must be patient and whittle them down slowly, and if we cannot do that then-"

"We have nowhere to run," Zhang Ji interrupted. "We cannot go back to Chang'an; we cannot go to Yi or Hanzhong in the west; we cannot go to Bing, Ji or Yòu to the north; we cannot go to Yu, Yan, Qing or Xu in the east; we cannot trespass any further southward into Jing, or flee to Yang; we must make a life here or die."

Zhang Xiu and the other officers nodded slowly and silently.

"Move out: we must win, and *quickly*," Zhang Ji ordered.

The defenders of Wan City were startled by the ferocity of the new attack, but they immediately noticed the presence of Zhang Ji and his close proximity to the walls as his bloodlust overwhelmed his senses; the Wan City Magistrate ordered his archers to the wall and had them concentrate on hitting the exposed commander.

"**Someone tell Lord Zhang to withdraw!**" Huche'er cried; he had guessed what the defenders intended and feared the worst.

"**Uncle, you must move back!**" Zhang Xiu shouted as he rode toward Zhang Ji, but he was too late; Zhang Ji was struck by arrow and thrown from his horse.

"...What... happened...?" Zhang Ji croaked as Zhang Xiu and two other men started to drag him away from Wan's walls; Huche'er ordered that the siege be intensified and did his best to hide Zhang Ji's condition from his men.

"Did we not get the commander...?" Wan's Magistrate wondered as he peered over the wall and watched the activity below.

"We certainly did," the Wan City archery captain replied. "Perhaps he was a decoy, or his men fight on like a snake without a head; either way, we've almost exhausted our arrows trying to hit him."

"...These Liang men are like demons," the magistrate complained. "Our chances are hopeless at this rate. If we do not repel them by the end of tomorrow, I will order a general surrender or an evacuation."

The magistrate's advisers did not protest.

"Uncle, they're evacuating the city!"

Zhang Ji turned his head and forced his eyes to open slightly; he was bedridden in his command tent, so the siege of Wan City was now a series of second-hand reports that came to him through his nephew, Acting Commander Zhang Xiu.

"...It's... night...?" Zhang Ji asked.

Zhang Xiu nodded and replied, "They waited until dark and opened the east gate; now they've sent a letter begging us to accept their surrender. It's over!"

"...Good," Zhang Ji said. "And... and the naval fleet...?"

Zhang Xiu exhaled fiercely and replied, "It still approaches."

Zhang Ji smiled painfully and said, "We must hurry into the city, then. But... keep my lady from my bedside, Nephew. She cannot... see me like this... until... I am ready."

Zhang Xiu nodded obediently and said, "I'll prioritise your movement, Uncle."

Liu Biao's naval officer, Cai Mao, reached the lands west of Wan half a day later, but had arrived too late to save the city. The attempt at retaking the city lasted for several days, but Acting Commander Zhang Xiu and the officer Huche'er proved to be too effective as a defender, and the governor's forces withdrew.

"Worthy uncle... they're gone," Zhang Xiu whispered as he knelt at Zhang Ji's bedside once again.

"Very good, nephew... very good," Zhang Ji wheezed.

Zhang Ji's wife, the beautiful Lady Zou, watched the two men talk and sobbed silently.

"You're going to be fine, Uncle!" Zhang Xiu insisted.

"We need... a p-plan," Zhang Ji panted.

"...Alright," Zhang Xiu said quietly.

"My lady... p-please withdraw to... another room, so that... can talk, p-privately, with... with Xiu," Zhang Ji asked of Lady Zou: she reluctantly obeyed.

"You are being morbid," Zhang Xiu suggested.

"You must... take care of her, nephew," Zhang Ji pleaded.

"But-!"

"Promise me," Zhang Ji insisted.

"I promise," Zhang Xiu whispered.

"I'm tired," Zhang Ji said quietly. "Let me sleep."

Zhang Xiu left his gravely injured uncle to rest.

The cost of the victory had been high, but Zhang Ji had achieved two very significant things when he seized Wan City: he had broken all ties with the regents Li Jue and Guo Si, and he had secured a strong base for his small army and their families. Even the most powerful of warlords would have difficulty liberating Wan City, and one of the most powerful would famously try to do so in times to come; the result of that encounter would have ramifications that would shape the nation in ways that few could have foreseen.

****

29

Yuan Shu's appointed Administrator of Lujiang, Liu Xun, reluctantly passed the imperial messenger's request for aid to his master in the Yang Provincial capital Shouchun in Jiujiang Prefecture; Yuan Shu was keen to know of the fate of the sovereign, as he had designs of his own.
"The emperor is now without a base… all the signs that have been seen were true," Yuan Shu said to an audience of officials. "The Han is all but extinguished."
"All the same, I think you should send aid," the adviser Han Yin pleaded. "Send someone, my lord, or you will be scorned."
"…I'll send aid, but I need my best men for attacking Liu Bei," Yuan Shu replied.
"The Son of Heaven should take priority, surely!" Han Yin chortled.
"Which one, Han Yin…?" Yuan Shu retorted. "Dong Zhuo's puppet that languishes in the wilderness, waiting for his regents to recapture him…? Liu Yu's charming son Hè, who doubtless inherits my fool brother's appointment to the role from his unfortunate father, and who still resides as a 'guest' in my lands and enjoys my hospitality…? …Or are you being fanciful and referring to someone else…? I'll send aid because Xiandi is the only emperor we have right now… but that, gentlemen, is right now… later, there will surely be another!"
Many of the Shouchun courtiers mumbled uneasily: Yuan Shu was obviously planning the announcement that they all dreaded.
"…And Lü Bu makes another request for you to send him everything that you promised," the official Yan Xiang prompted.
"All in good time, gentlemen!" Yuan Shu cackled.
"…My lord, it is his third, perhaps fourth request, and his cooperation is essential to Ji Ling's continued success against Liu Bei," Han Yin said nervously.
"Am I inundated with grain, horse and weapons…?" Yuan Shu retorted. "Bu is a pragmatist and knows that the land has resource shortage problems; furthermore, he needs my cooperation as much as I need his. He will wait and accept it."
"…I hope so," Yan Xiang murmured.

When the Yuan clan's chosen head, Ji Governor Yuan Shao, received the messenger from the emperor, he was forced to assemble his advisers to discuss the request.
"You *must* invite the emperor to Ji Province," Ju Shou declared.
"I agree," Tian Feng said. "He must be brought here to Yè City and given a proper home while Luoyang is rebuilt."
"It is the only correct thing to do, and is a decision weighed down with advantages," Ju Shou added.
"It seals your position as the hero that you are!" Xu Yòu said.
"And *Zhang Yang* is nearby," Pang Ji noted. "He will certainly lend aid… but how can that be right…?"
"…Quite right: can I leave Zhang Yang – a man that now gives refuge to men like Lü Bu and that churl Dong Zhao – with the responsibility of the Son of Heaven…?" Yuan Shao said. "Doesn't the sovereign belong here, with me, in Ji Province? Is it not the case that I have sweat blood for the Majesty, and my duty now is

to continue to serve him in any way that I can? I committed a treasonous act to save Shaodi from the 'Ten'; I lost my clan contesting Dong Zhuo's schemes to commit regicide; I put my reputation at risk when I formed the Eastern Pass Coalition to rescue the capital from that same Dong Zhuo. After all that, can I now leave His Majesty in the care of a scruffy knave, a man that betrayed Ding Yuan's memory by taking an appointment from the man that plotted Ding's murder? Didn't Zhang Yang then harbour the murderer Lü Bu not once, in fact, but *twice*?"

"Precisely," Pang Ji agreed. "It also eliminates your greatest worry at present: the claims made by Yuan Shu. By securing the sovereign, you can have it confirmed that you are Governor of Bing, Governor of Ji, Governor of Qing, Governor of Yan, Governor of Xu, and head of your clan. It will all be imperially sanctioned."

"...Yes!" Yuan Shao chuckled. "That is right as well!"

"Is it...?" Chunyu Qiong scoffed.

"*Aiee*... how is it *wrong*?" Tian Feng groaned.

"Invite the emperor here, my lord, and you'll be his vassal," Guo Tu suggested. "You will have to bend at the knee: you'll never be given all those provinces, Lord Yuan. The emperor will want those provinces given to relatives, just as he always has! It'll then be *your* responsibility – financial and otherwise – to rebuild Luoyang! Who, then, will fund the fight against Gongsun Zan and the Black Mountain Bandits? Has either of them disappeared suddenly...? Yes, you are back in Yè after a short campaign, but is Poison Yu – or any of the other senior bandits – no longer a threat...?"

Yuan Shao was silent.

"No! Do not listen to Chunyu Qiong and Guo Tu!" Ju Shou protested. "Invite the sovereign here! There are only advantages!"

"...Being made to kowtow in the corridors of my own capital...?" Yuan Shao retorted snidely. "Being made to spend my own money rebuilding Luoyang, after all that I did to stop Dong Zhuo destroying it in the first place...? Why should *I* pay to repair the place? Why should *I* act as though I am somehow to blame? That might not be how it is intended, but that is how it will feel."

"What about Yuan Shu?" Tian Feng pleaded. "Sheltering the sovereign ends the-"

"There is no guarantee that the emperor will be impartial or biased in your favour, my lord," Chunyu Qiong suggested. "His Majesty's father was muddle-headed, sad to say... I recall our time as colonels of the Western Garden Army with despair."

"Oh, goodness, yes," Yuan Shao chortled. "That was ridiculous. What if the emperor wants me to put on parades, and waste my money providing him with a harem, or building him a palace here...? No, now that I think about it, I don't want him here."

"*Ayah*! You'd let the Son of Heaven live in the ruins of Luoyang???" Ju Shou exclaimed.

"I have already expended vast amounts of wealth and grain on his predecessor, the *chosen* Son of Heaven," Yuan Shao scoffed. "To expend more on a puppet, and lose my autonomy as well... no."

"This is folly," Ju Shou protested.

"I'll hear no more!" Yuan Shao said. "I have my own problems! If a man is to be charitable, it is as it was when I harboured the 'partisans' in the days of the 'Ten': I must have something to give! If I am torn between war and maintaining the emperor's luxurious lifestyle, I will be ruined and of use to no one! If matters change, so be it... but with the bandits all around us, Gongsun lurking in the north and my wicked cousin still hankering for all that he sees in the south – oh, and that animal Lü Bu, lest we forget – I cannot risk damage to my capacity to fight!"

No more was said. Yuan Shao was a changed man: this time, he would not risk all for his sovereign, and none would argue otherwise, no matter how they felt.

Lü Bu's court in Xu Province received the emperor's request for help and reacted with genuine surprise.

"It's actually addressed to me, and not to Liu Bei...?" Lü Bu exclaimed.

"It seems so, though notably not as a governor," Chen Gong replied. "Zhang Yang is nearby; perhaps he told the sovereign about your bragging letters. If so, my lord, he also spoke *very kindly about you.*"

"I'm forgiven," Lü Bu realised. "I aided the man that killed his brother... I failed the man that tried to save him from Li Jue and Guo Si... I've even overthrown the boy's relative to seize this place... and yet... I'm forgiven...? ...What a kind sovereign."

"We should send help," Wang Kai suggested.

"I... I truly want to... but I can't," Lü Bu replied. "I'm understaffed; Yuan Shao, Yuan Shu and Cao Cao surround me; and Liu Bei still has friends. But I'll write back nonetheless... and apologise in the strongest possible terms."

"Do that," Chen Gong said.

"We could do more if we received the supplies that Yuan Shu promised," Xu Si suggested. "Has there still been no response...?"

"No, there hasn't," Chen Gong sighed. "But-"

"He has another... month," Lü Bu decided. "After that, I chase his man Ji Ling out of my province."

"And *free Liu Bei*...?" Wang Kai exclaimed. "But-!"

"Bei's a completely broken man," Chen Gong said indifferently. "He writes with tales of what he and his fellow 'besieged' endure: they have been pushed to do things that make him ashamed to be alive on some days, he says. He still talks of truces, of Lord Lü being his General of the Household and my being his chancellor, or giving us full control of one half of the province... and once – though just once – he hints that he might – if categorically promised that he and his followers will be spared – cede the province altogether."

"And you place faith that the single hint is enough to risk rescuing him...?" Xu Si challenged.

"If he does not concede, then he will face a siege by General Zhang Liao!" Lü Bu chuckled. "And that, Mister Xu, will have him begging for Ji Ling to return!"

"That's all, of course, only if Yuan Shu fails to keep his word," Chen Gong noted. "For his sake – and everyone else's – let us hope that he does."

Yuan Shu and Cao Cao's forces allied with the White Wave Bandits and did battle with the scout forces sent by Li Jue while Zhang Yang led the demoralised emperor into Henei City.

"We are glad to be in a safe place," Emperor Xian said as he

walked toward the host seat of Zhang Yang's residential audience hall. "After living in a tent, we find the latest accommodation to be temporarily fitting… although there will need to be vast improvements made if we are to rule from here."
Zhang Yang shuddered involuntarily.
"Have you a large militia…?" Emperor Xian asked.
"N-no, Your Majesty," Zhang Yang replied.
"…So we will need the protection of external armies to continue," Emperor Xian said with disappointment. "Are the forces supplied by the governors adequate?"
"Impossible to say, Your Majesty: the militias sent by Li Jue and Guo Si are still formidable," Dong Cheng replied uneasily.
"…So we need the continued 'protection' of the White Wave Bandits," Emperor Xian realised.
"Hey, we're pretty cheap to hire, all in all!" a White Wave Bandit leader joked.
"**Silence!**" Dong Cheng cried. "**How dare you address your sovereign thus!**"
"**Ooh! A thousand pardons!**" the bandit and his friends heckled in unison.
"…Shouldn't you be fighting outside?" Zhang Yang said as he glared at the bandits.
"For you, Mister Zhang, we'll go away," one of the bandits said. "You've quite the reputation, and we don't want a fight."
Some of Zhang Yang's officials were former Black Mountain Bandits that Zhang Yang had forced to surrender: they laughed as the White Wave Bandits withdrew.
"Shall I make sure they leave?" the Henei general Sui Gu asked.
"Please," Zhang Yang replied.
As Sui Gu and a small group of soldiers followed the retreating bandits, Zhang Yang kowtowed to the emperor and said, "I do indeed have a reputation amongst their type: I only hope it is enough to keep them from disrespecting Your Majesty any further."
"…So do we," Emperor Xian replied.

It would be some time before Zhang Yang realised the financial burden of hosting the whole of his sovereign's entourage: at first, he was as gracious and grateful a host as any could be, and Emperor Xian was glad to be safe.

＊＊＊＊＊＊＊＊＊＊＊＊

<h1 style="text-align:center">30</h1>

Within a month of Emperor Xian's arrival in Henei, the situation in Xu Province was about to evolve yet again.

"**REPORT!**"
General Ji Ling turned his gaze from his desk to the messenger that had entered his Haixi command tent and asked, "What news…?"
"A force led by Generals Zhang Liao and Hao Meng approaches from the south!" the messenger reported. "They have attacked our rear guard! They-!"
"They're *Lü Bu's men*!" Ji Ling exclaimed. "The treacherous rat! I… I will have to withdraw! After everything I've achieved here, I… I…! …**D'AAAAAGH!**"
Ji Ling threw his desk to one side and leapt to his feet; the messenger cowered fearfully and started mumbling prayers.
"…I have no quarrel with you, soldier," Ji Ling said as his composure returned. "Go and… get something to eat… you look starved."
The messenger rambled hysterically, bowed and fled the tent.
"I heard you scream!" the adviser Yuan Huan said as he entered the tent with the officer Chen Lan. "What-?"
"Bu's attacking our rear guard!" Ji Ling replied. "We must get out of Xu Province!"
Yuan Huan tried to speak, but he was momentarily dumbstruck.
"Why should we run from Bu's men?" Chen Lan asked. "Can't we-"
"I… I appreciate your courage, Mister Chen, but no," Ji Ling insisted. "We have to retreat, or we risk being trapped."
"*Aiee*… the fool!" Yuan Huan cried. "You're quite right, General, but… we will need to ascertain why he thinks that he can-"
"Lord Yuan probably delayed providing him with the supplies that they discussed," Ji Ling muttered as he set his desk upright and picked up his scattered bamboo military texts. "Does Bu not see that there are more battle-fronts than there are stars in the sky, and that there has just been a famine…?"
Yuan Huan hummed thoughtfully and said, "Perhaps we should hold our ground as Chen Lan says and send word back to our lord that-"
"I… I want to, but we have Zang Ba, Haixi Chen, Liu Bei and two of Lü Bu's best generals to worry about now," Ji Ling interrupted. "We're better off going back; we'll be sent back here with others soon enough. Chen Lan…"
"I shall go at once, inform Lei Bo and the other officers, and then I'll begin my own preparations," Chen Lan said as he turned and left the tent.
"…A smart one in his own way, that Chen Lan," Ji Ling sighed.

"*Aiee*… retreat…?" the officer Lei Bo groaned.
"Look, it's Ji Ling's order," Chen Lan protested. "You and me, we're old friends, and so you know this annoys me."
"…Yeah," Lei Bo sighed.
"It's like General Ji always says: 'There will be other chances to gain merit'," Chen Lan continued. "I never wanted to stay here

and starve Liu Bei out anyway, to be honest... Lu Kang was bad enough. It doesn't seem right, does it, for men like Guan Yu to die like that, holed up in a city with no supporters, surrounded by enemies and slowly starving to death... not if he's a 'hero'..."
"...No," Lei Bo agreed. "We'll be sent back another time, and fight properly!"
"Now let's get our men ready to leave, before Bu's men get here," Chen Lan urged.

Haixi's residents reacted excitedly to the news that Yuan Shu's general Ji Ling had suddenly retreated: none of the defenders knew why, and nobody cared, because it meant the end of a siege that had taken every last shred of humanity from most of them and left them broken. But the reason for the withdrawal soon became clear: months after forcing Liu Bei to retreat to Haixi in the first place, the warlord Lü Bu had sent a force to Haixi, led by the adviser Xu Si and Generals Zhang Liao and Hao Meng. The trio camped outside the city and sent a messenger to the gates to deliver a personal message from Lü Bu himself.
"...What now, I wonder...?" Jian Yong asked of his lord and long-time friend Liu Bei as they sat together in the audience hall of the city administrator's house.
"I... I don't know," Liu Bei whimpered.
Every man was a physical and emotional mess; none had enjoyed a diet free from horror, and every man was unkempt and suffering from malnutrition.
"...Well you're the one that can answer, Xuande, which is why I asked," Jian Yong said.
Liu Bei had Lü Bu's letter in his hand: he read it again with tired eyes and replied, "After all those letters I've sent, begging for some form of truce – trying to make him understand what the people of Haixi have suffered, and reaching out to his sense of humanity, to no avail – he's asking me to yield... but *kindly* this time, more or less."
Jian Yong smiled sadly and asked, "Will you yield...?"
"...I must!" Liu Bei replied. "Oh, I know the consequences: I felt sick to the stomach enough when I yielded to Yuan Shao, but by doing this I make an enemy of both Yuans at the same time!"
"But we have no choice," Jian Yong said as he took the letter from Liu Bei and started to read. "If we don't yield, Bu's army will either attack us or turn back and let Ji Ling or Haixi Chen finish us off."
"Mister Sun and Mi Zhu said the same," Liu Bei admitted.
"...I expected as much," Jian Yong said. "As for the future, if I may; Cao Cao is our only other possible 'ally', I think, but-"
"Never," Liu Bei insisted. "Cao Cao's evil brought us here to Xu Province, Xianhe! He brought us here with his brutality, and that means that we two cannot live under the same sky willingly!"
"...So we're going to Lü Bu then," Jian Yong chuckled. "His letter is vague... I wonder what his full terms will be this time."
"Something *humiliating*... that much is certain," Liu Bei muttered.
"Yide is the sorriest men alive," Jian Yong said sombrely. "I-"
"He's not to blame," Liu Bei interrupted. "Bu was invited here by me, wasn't he? Yide was one of the clever ones that said we should expel him... so how can I blame him? He warned me about Chancellor Cao Bao, too; it can only be Cao Bao that was colluding

with Bu's adviser Chen Gong. And he never liked Chen Gui and-"

"Even Yide would disagree with what you're saying, Xuande," Jian Yong chuckled. "He's a pig-headed, violent idiot, and that's that. He hated me too, once... and Mi Zhu, and Mister Sun... he only liked Yunchang, Chen Dao and Zhao Yun straight away, and-"

"Oh, for Zilong to be here with us!" Liu Bei cried. "He might have been the help that Yunchang and Yide needed to repel Ji Ling!"

"Maybe," Jian Yong said. "Where's Chen Dao, by the way? What's the point of a bodyguard if he isn't here guarding your body?"

"Who's here to harm me?" Liu Bei scoffed. "I let him rest awhile... he's been eating millet and drinking foul water... he looks very ill."

"Haven't we all suffered...?" Jian Yong chortled. "...Still, you're right... he needs a rest. When will we go to Lü Bu?"

"...Tomorrow," Liu Bei replied. "I think that Haixi is full of too many bad memories for everyone... after what, a year of this place, of... of being less than human...? ...I for one cannot bear to linger for a single day more than I have to."

Jian Yong nodded soberly and said, "It can't be worse than this."

Within hours, the remnants of Liu Bei's army opened the gates to confront Xu Si, Zhang Liao and Hao Meng.

"...This will be terrible," Liu Bei muttered; his army was reduced to less than 200 men, and they were a pitiful sight. Zhang Liao and Hao Meng led a small contingent of men to the city gates to intimidate any defiant inhabitants, but they quickly realised that it would not be necessary.

"...They have endured the worst of hardships," Zhang Liao said as he looked at Guan Yu, who was noticeably thinner and weaker.

"Don't pity them too much," Hao Meng suggested.

"I'm not a fool, General," Zhang Liao said. "Address them, Xu Si."

"**LIU BEI!**" Xu Si cried. "**WHY ARE YOU HERE!**"

Guan Yu observed Xu Si with disdain and muttered, "Wretch."

"He's lucky; I'm saving my strength for Bu," Zhang Fei grumbled.

"**I'm here to**... to...!" Liu Bei said: his voice failed as the enormity of his intended announcement brought him close to tears.

"**TO WHAT?**" Xu Si heckled.

"...**To**... to yield... **to yield the province!**" Liu Bei cried.

Many of Liu Bei's men started to sob; Hao Meng sighed and said to Zhang Liao, "I'm not made of stone: fool though he is, I pity him."

"All the same, let's escort him to Lord Lü," Zhang Liao replied.

The bandit ruler of Kaiyang City, Zang Ba, received the news that Ji Ling had retreated and summoned his senior followers to his meeting hall; he smiled and told his allies, "Liu Bei is free, and the Haixi siege is over... Lü Bu saved him. That can only mean one thing: Liu Bei's handed control of the province over to Bu."

Many of the bandits chattered excitedly.

"He's famous for fighting the Black Mountain Bandits, lads, so I wouldn't get too cheerful about this," the bandit Chang Xi said.

"That's quite right," Zang Ba said. "Bu might deploy Bei here to attack us, or come here himself; there's no guarantee that he'll accept us like Tao Qian was forced to."

"We'll soon know!" Wu Dun chuckled. "Why not make a bit of trouble around here, and-"

"No," Zang Ba interrupted. "We wait until we know what's what, old friend: Ji Ling ran, but Yuan Shu's got a lot more generals where he came from, and he's powerful. If he sent a load of his best men back here, even Lü Bu and the Danyang Brigades couldn't keep him out of Xu Province."

"That's true," Wu Dun conceded. "Any word from Sun Guan…?"

"Yeah," Zang Ba replied. "Zhongtai's managed to get some more o' the lads around Mount Tai to join us, and we might need the extra hands more than I ever anticipated. They're great for expanding north, plus they'll be a help if Yuan Shu or Bu try and attack us."

"And Yin Li…?" Chang Xi asked pointedly.

Yin Li was a former Han official that had later turned to banditry: he operated in the Mount Tai region, but his allegiances were considered suspect by some.

"Don't judge, Chang Xi," Wu Dun protested. "Remember that Zang's father was a Han official, a warder in a prison, and he raised Zang to hate what he's doing now."

Zang Ba sighed and said, "Too right. Yin Li's the same… he's turned on the government because of what he saw and heard, same as me."

Chang Xi nodded soberly; Zang Ba and Yin Li were but two of many bandits around the country that had resorted to criminality because the actions of the 'Ten' and others had corrupted their local governments and left them with no income, no support in times of crisis, no faith in the legal system and no protection from raids carried out by the same criminal gangs that they now belonged to.

"We focus on building our influence in the north, around Mount Tai," Zang Ba ordered. "We need to get everyone together, and be a confederacy: we need to be like the Black Mountain Bandits in Ji and Bing. We need to be so many, so strong, and so spread out that Bu, the Yuans and every other fool that tries to fight us ties themselves up in knots and runs home with nothing. We'll live longer, and we'll certainly be remembered."

Many of the bandits hollered enthusiastically at the prospect of becoming as powerful a force as the Black Mountain Bandits: a new series of diplomatic talks – a bizarre concept in itself – began between the various factions of bandits that operated in the embattled region around Mount Tai in Qing Province. The leaders – of whom Zang Ba, Chang Xi, Wu Dun, Yin Li and Sun Guan were the most notable – negotiated successfully and began the first steps towards becoming the confederacy that would be known as the *Mount Tai Bandits*. They would make that region – and most of the rest of Qing – a place that no isolated government administrator could hope to govern properly. The places that were considered as part of Xu as well as Qing – such as Langya, the ancestral home of the famous Zhuge family and the place where Cao Cao's consort Lady Bian was raised – would also be the responsibility of the Governor of Xu Province, whoever that might be in the wake of the Haixi siege.

****

31

"*...Idiot.*"

Yuan Shao threw the latest report on Xu Province to the ground at his feet; his audience hall was mostly silent as the officials awaited their lord's opinions.

"Worthless, cowardly idiot," Yuan Shao continued. "Mengde was right; I was a fool to leave that man as my governor in Xu. Now the place is Lü Bu's, which is almost as bad as my brother-cousin taking it!"

"He could do little else," the adviser Ju Shou suggested.

"The poor man that rushed that report here did so in vain, for there's nothing *I* can do," Yuan Shao complained. "Zhang Hè reports activity from Gongsun's border armies, so I must yet again take to the saddle to intimidate the barbarians."

"My lord, let me go," the adviser-general Chunyu Qiong pleaded.

"Normally I'd agree, my friend, but Gongsun's men are getting confident," Yuan Shao replied. "I must show strength."

"But what if it another ploy to get you out of Yè and weaken its defences...?" Ju Shou asked. "We've been lucky: my lord, we should consider closing and fortifying the city to-"

"I can't do that!" Yuan Shao chortled. "I know that the bandit attacks are a pain, Mister Ju, but if my capital were a fort it would suggest that I fear my enemies! They always number in small amounts and do minor damage before they flee: when I return from the north I intend to march against 'Poison Yu' again, and next time it will be to arrest the little ruffian and put him in chains for the world to see! Perhaps I will give him over to my Director of Retainers and force him to repair the damage that he's done to my capital. Administrator Li...?"

The Administrator of Wei Prefecture, Li Cheng, bowed humbly.

"You'll ensure that there are vigilant men placed as guards on every gate of every city in the prefecture at *all times*, Administrator Li: I want the word sent out," Yuan Shao ordered. "If 'Poison Yu' dares to come back here then I want him caught and shamed; other than that, I want trade to carry on as normal. There can be no sign of weakness. I allowed Lü Bu to scare me just that once, I confess, but I will not allow scruffy bandits to do the same."

"As you command, Governor Yuan," Li Cheng replied.

"Guo Tu, Pang Ji, Tian Feng: you'll accompany me as my counsel," Yuan Shao continued. "Chen Lin, have word sent to General Zhang that I am on my way."

Yuan Shao's secretary, Chen Lin, bowed slightly and said, "It shall be done, my lord governor."

Very good," Yuan Shao sighed. "Onward, then, to remind Gongsun Zan of who he deals with..."

Lü Bu's court in Xiapi was silent as the adviser Chen Gong entered the audience hall and walked towards his lord with a letter in his right hand.

"Well...?" Lü Bu grunted.

Chen Gong smiled dryly, raised his right arm and said, "Liu Bei has returned with Xu Si, my lord."

Chen Gong's words made his lord Lü Bu sit up and lean forward; the audience hall was packed with courtiers that had once served Liu Bei, but only a few hung their heads in shame.

"So he yielded after all," Lü Bu chortled. "Or so I hope: all I care about is making Liu Bei see that he is no longer governor, Mister Chen Gong."

"He will understand," Chen Gong said. "Let's bring him here…"

"To be paraded in front of this court…?" the influential Chen Gui challenged. "I have no love for Liu Bei, but he should surely be seen privately after all that has gone on in Haixi…?"

"I agree with Mister Chen, Lord Lü," General Gao Shun said. "We do not know Liu Bei's state of mind, and-"

"**Silence!**" Lü Bu shouted. "**Am I now stupid…? Did I say that I wanted him 'paraded' at any point…? Of course I will see him privately, Gao Shun!**"

Gao Shun bowed slightly and said no more; Chen Gui was quietly glad that Bu saved his anger for his own general.

"This meeting is adjourned!" Lü Bu continued. "I must prepare for my meeting with Liu Bei!

"You are beginning to wonder if we made a mistake," Chen Deng prompted as he left the audience hall with his father Chen Gui.

"Hah! I am past 'beginning to wonder'," Chen Gui replied bitterly. "Bu is unstable, and I wonder if he is any more likely to listen to sound counsel than Bei was, now that he is set to become the governor."

Chen Gui and Chen Deng watched as the distressed Tao brothers, Shang and Ying, fled the hall at speed and sought a place where they could lament their situation privately.

"This was not my vision," Chen Gui continued. "Those two, they'll never have power in this province; in fact, I wonder whether Bu will have them quietly assassinated, which is something that Liu Bei would never have done."

"I hear the stories of how Hè Jin and Yuan Shao invited Dong Zhuo to the capital to help them get rid of the 'Ten', and I hurt inside when I consider that we might have made the same mistake," Chen Deng admitted.

"There is no 'might' here, my son; we have brought a terrible scourge here," Chen Gui replied. "We were right when we summoned Liu Bei, and wrong when we helped him become acting governor when a military rank sufficed; we were right to want Chen Gong, but not to want Lü Bu as well. Now Liu Bei – the only man that could rid us of Bu – has been reduced to a shadow of a man, stripped of every shred of strength that he had and forced to come back here to tender the seal to that smirking demon. And worse awaits us, I fear."

"We should meet with Chen Yuanfang, Chen Qun, Xu Dan and the Taos to discuss how we might counter the problems," Chen Deng suggested.

"Forgive me for speaking of our late lord's sons so, but… they are nothing now," Chen Gui replied. "They are an irrelevance: their timidity and lack of experience as military leaders made them unfit to govern Xu through the Cao Cao crisis, which is why we invited Liu Bei here in the first place. Once Bei became governor, they became history, and to the world it is Bei – not the Taos –

that Bu steals the province from. Neither Bu nor Bei should rule this place, but the Taos are not the answer: the question, my son, is who should take Bu's place when the opportunity arises."

"...And to that, I have no answer," Chen Deng sighed miserably.

"Ah... Liu Xuande!" Lü Bu said as a dejected and infuriated Liu Bei entered the governor's private meeting room that he had once called his own; Bei and his followers had been able to wash, change clothes and start to take larger meals as their stomachs recovered, but their experiences had left physical marks that would take time to disappear.

"...Acting Governor Lü," Liu Bei replied as he bowed low in reluctant respect.

"Rise, please, Xuande!" Lü Bu cackled. "Now please, sit, as my honoured guest!"

Guan Yu was forced to restrain Zhang Fei and drag him from the audience room as Liu Bei sat in a guest seat to the left of Lü Bu; Mister Sun, Mi Zhu, Mi Fang and Jian Yong sat in a row to the left of Liu Bei.

"Remain vigilant," Liu Bei's bodyguard Chen Dao said to his carefully chosen band of men, who then discreetly scanned the room for signs of hidden assassins.

"...I'm sorry that it had to come to this, Xuande," Lü Bu said insincerely. "You left that oaf butcher here to guard the city; I understand that you needed Yunchang on the battlefield, but if you were that desperate, why did you not ask me to provide you with Zhang Liao or Gao Shun... or even fight in person... so that a man with greater wit and intelligence could be left with such an important task...?"

"It is entirely my own fault that I am in this position, as usual," Liu Bei said as he bowed low once again from his seated position. "I think that you were wise to act so quickly, and save the city from disaster."

Chen Gong – who was sat to Lü Bu's right with Wang Kai and Xu Si – frowned and said, "Then why did you not tender the seal of office to Lord Lü and insist on clinging to power that you are currently so ill-placed to keep...?"

Mister Sun harrumphed quietly; Mi Zhu and Mi Fang shuddered involuntarily; Jian Yong exhaled noisily in a public show of irritation at Chen Gong's words that was not usual within the boundaries of etiquette.

"You have something to say...?" Lü Bu said as he looked at Jian Yong with menace.

"My friend Jian Xianhe must be forgiven, for though he is completely sincere he is reckless beyond belief, and somewhat uncultured at times," Liu Bei protested.

"So are many of your followers, it seems," Chen Gong scoffed. "It becomes ever more apparent that whoever you left here, the result would have been the same. As I have often said to Lord Lü... while I respect you for your good character, I cannot justify your place as governor of this province if you insist on staffing the capital with uncultured, undignified idiots just because they're your friends. How do you expect to retain power without sound counsel and wise officials...?"

"There may be some truth in what you say," Liu Bei replied with restraint. "I now accept the situation as it stands, and I am placing myself and my followers – who choose, despite everything, to stay in my service – in your hands. Wherever you put me, I will stay, and whatever you have me do, I will do it."

"Very good!" Lü Bu said with cheer. "So you will accept your role as defender of Xiaopei, and assist me in my own personal battle with Yuan Shu, who now demands that I cede the province to him…?"

"We were fighting Yuan Shu before," Mister Sun said cuttingly. "All that would be changing, 'gentlemen', are the morals and reasons behind that fight."

"I shall ignore that," Lü Bu said as he glared at Mister Sun. "Liu Xuande, I wish you well on your journey to Xiaopei: may your followers find escape from the memory of the horrors of deliberate cannibalism, uncleanliness and rampant disease that have wracked them these past months, and when you are all recovered, then perhaps we can face Yuan Shu together!"

"You… are most kind," Liu Bei said with difficulty.

"Oh, I am not even started!" Lü Bu said. "Despite the harsh words of my adviser, I do not think you to be completely incompetent. As a gesture of goodwill, I appoint you 'Inspector of Yu Province'."

"***Inspector*???**" Mister Sun shrieked.

"Yes, 'Inspector'," Lü Bu said as he glared at Mister Sun yet again.

"You… are most generous," Liu Bei said with even greater difficulty.

"And you, Liu Xuande, are most gracious," Lü Bu chuckled. "You may retire now: good day to you!"

Liu Bei and his followers got up and left the audience room.

"He has been suitably shamed, and yet he did not rise to it," Wang Kai noted once Lü Bu and his three advisers were the only men present.

"…The fools following him did," Lü Bu scoffed.

"Mister Sun is probably regretting his choice of allegiances, and Jian Yong is an old friend from Bei's hometown; pay them no mind," Chen Gong said dismissively. "Jian's well known for having no idea how to conduct himself; he thinks that everything is a big joke. Well, I think that for Liu Bei and Jian Yong, there is little to laugh at right now. Liu Bei has lost this province and is now our subordinate, providing a necessary pair of eyes to the west."

"Do we have to fear betrayal…?" Xu Si wondered.

"If he has not already gone to Cao Cao, he never will," Chen Gong decided. "Liu Bei cannot bring himself to work alongside a man that killed a hundred-thousand of this province's civilian population… he knows that would be very unpopular. He cannot go to Yuan Shu either, not after he refused to cede the province."

"He could go to Yuan Shao," Lü Bu supposed. "…Or Gongsun Zan."

"Neither man offers a safe haven; the two are fighting each other!" Chen Gong replied. "Remember, his old friend Gongsun allied himself with our mutual enemy Yuan Shu, while Yuan Shao is a close relative and reluctant adversary of that same Yuan Shu. Liu Bei has very few choices, and he knows it."

"Liu Biao of Jing…?" Lü Bu fretted.

"Now you are being fanciful," Chen Gong scoffed. "Liu Biao might be in contention with Yuan Shu and his lackey Sun Ce, but that is the very reason that he cannot send help. We are far to the east of the land, and all of his allies are in the west. Liu Bei is isolated, as we are, and has nothing to gain by facing us when he has next to no men left, and no money either."

"...Then I am content that his surrender is genuine, born of a real understanding that he has no choice," Lü Bu decided. "I shall return the families of his vassals to him, to show goodwill and ensure that he regains some trust in my sincerity on the matter of allying against Yuan Shu, who shall regret breaking his promises."

Chen Gong nodded and said, "A wise move, I think."

Liu Bei's first action upon reaching his camp outside Xiapi City was to sob.

"Couldn't put it better myself," Jian Yong sighed.

"I say we fight him!" Zhang Fei barked.

"That's unwise, Yide," Guan Yu said. "We're weak, tired... and we have no friends here. At least we might find friends in Xiaopei, as we did once before."

"Was I so terrible a governor...?" Liu Bei bleated. "I have earned the contempt of five Chens! They are united not by blood by their lack of any respect for me! Chen Gong, bad enough; Chen Gui and Chen Deng, worse still; but to have lost the faith of *Elder Chen Yuanfang* and *Chen Qun*...? What did I do wrong?"

"Blame me if you must blame anyone," Mi Zhu suggested. "I was tempted to come before you bound in rope for execution, Lord Liu... this was my folly."

"Then it is mine also, for the crime committed by one of us is a crime committed by both of us," Mi Fang said. "We compelled you to seize Xu Province from the Tao clan, Lord Liu. Chen Qun said we would not hold the province, and he also said that Lü Bu might be the man to take it from us... he is a wise man indeed."

"Yes, and now he serves Lü Bu!" Liu Bei sobbed. "I should have stayed in Zhao... weaving mats and shoes is all I'm good for!"

"Don't say that, Xuande," Zhang Fei pleaded.

"It's true," Liu Bei continued. "I lost Anxi County, bad enough; I lost Xu Province, and now the brigand Bu has reduced me to 'Inspector of Yu'! Tao appointed me *Governor* of Yu... and for that I seized his province from his dead hands, right in front of his heirs. To the world – and perhaps myself – I am not just a fool, I'm a hypocrite and a liar and a hankerer."

Many of Liu Bei's junior officers started to weep for him; Zhang Fei sneered and said, "You're being weak. We're suffering another setback, that's all. Lü Bu can't keep Xu Province: Yuan Shao and Cao Cao will fight him for it from the west, and Yuan Shu will fight him for it from the south!"

"Yes, and in both cases, where will their campaign of violence start...?" Liu Bei snapped. "It will start in Xiaopei: *we* will die first!"

Zhang Fei lowered his head and exhaled noisily.

"Let's get out of Xiapi," Jian Yong suggested. "Let's go now, before Bu starts to get paranoid. We'll take our families – I assume that's allowed – go to Xiaopei, and build a new army, and then we'll see what we can do. We're not done yet, Xuande."

"A fine statement, Jian Yong, thankfully devoid of your usual irritating and inappropriate clownery," Guan Yu declared. "I shall begin preparations to leave."

"I'll help you," Zhang Fei said.

Once Guan Yu and Zhang Fei were gone, Liu Bei turned to his remaining advisers – Mi Zhu, Jian Yong, Mister Sun and Mi Fang – and said, "If any of you want to join Chen Yuanfang and Chen Qun, I will not hold it against you."

"We're your vassals to the last," Mi Zhu insisted.

Liu Bei was silently grateful. The journey to Xiaopei was long and arduous, but free from combat: and for a while, Liu Bei and his allies would be safe to rebuild and put the memories of the Haixi siege behind them.

To the northwest of Xu – in the forested hills in the east of Bing Province – the Black Mountain Bandit leader 'Poison Yu' received word that Yuan Shao had departed for the northern border with Yòu Province and taken most of his army with him.

"This time, we don't mess about," Poison Yu said to a larger audience than he was used to. "A lot o' you blokes have come down from the north, and we even have some Xiongnu with us this time."

A minor Southern Xiongnu chieftain grinned and gestured regally.

"Yuan Shao's still leaving his doors open, and this time we hurt him bad," Poison Yu continued. "Anything valuable that can be taken, we take it; anything valuable that can't be taken, we smash it; any*one* valuable that can be killed, we k-"

"Uh... wait a minute," the bandit leader 'Floating Cloud' chuckled. "Let's stick to 'smashing things and stealing stuff', shall we, 'boss'...? If we start massacring important people in Yuan's capital, that'll-"

"Our 'friend in the north' pays us well, and we have to earn that pay," Poison Yu retorted. "This time, we do Yuan some serious damage. If influential people don't feel safe, they'll leave and take their money with them. That's the plan."

"...Alright," Floating Cloud sighed. "Don't say I didn't warn you, though."

"Right then, lads, let's get ready," Poison Yu said. "This time, Yè won't know what hit it!"

****

32

The warlord Li Jue's return to Chang'an was a solemn affair; Jia Xu met him at the gates of the city and awaited an explanation.

"Emperor Xian escaped us," Li Jue reported. "Of all the insane things that could have happened, I did not expect that the *White Wave Bandits* would come to his rescue, Mister Jia."

"The White Wave Bandits...?" Jia Xu exclaimed.

"Apparently, their leader Han Xian is an old friend of Yang Feng; it's a pity that I didn't know it before," Li Jue sighed. "It's also a pity that I didn't know about Yang Feng's real feelings: I hear that he's been contemplating betrayal since before Dong Zhuo died, but never acted due to cowardice. He's probably been helping the other traitors from the shadows, though."

"...Possibly," Jia Xu replied numbly. "I am more annoyed that I did not sense it, since I am supposed to be the one that anticipates or deduces such things. So Yang Feng betrayed us after careful planning; not impulsively, as it seemed. Dong Cheng, Yang Feng... what about Zhang Ji? Do we know anything new about him...?"

"Zhang Ji's gone south, and attacked Nan County; I don't know why. It certainly wasn't an attempt to help us, because his nephew turned our messenger back," Li Jue explained. "Guo Si's gone too; where, I don't know."

"Mei City," Jia Xu revealed. "He wrote to me, wanting advice."

"Why is he in Mei?" Li Jue asked. "Does he still have that ridiculous idea in his head about me wanting to kill him?"

"He doesn't want anything to do with you," Jia Xu said. "He did not say why, but that's the likely reason, yes. My lord, you must-"

"Yes, I'm back to being 'My lord' now, aren't I, now I'm not the regent," Li Jue realised. "Mister Jia, you're my last hope. What do I do? I sent men back and forth to harass the bandits, to try and bribe the bandits, and whatever else seemed plausible, and nothing worked; and last I heard, militias were arriving from the south, probably from Cao Cao or Yuan Shu. What if the warlords have decided to aid him after all...? Should I go after the boy again, or should I go and try and talk to Guo Si, or should I-?"

"Just... just give me time to think," Jia Xu pleaded. "I am certain that we can win Zhang Ji over, and if he has taken Wan City, he'll be the key to our regaining our lost strength. Let the eastern warlords aid His Majesty: aid him to do what, exactly...? Luoyang is in ruins, so whoever helps him must spend their own monies to do so, and that can't sustain, not even for the wealthier ones like the Yuans. Even if one of them did take him in, they'll want rid of him again before they end up a beggar, and that just leaves the White Wave Bandits... who can surely be bought. You just failed to find their price."

"Alright," Li Jue said passively.

"...I shall travel to Wan City and visit Zhang Ji," Jia Xu continued. "If he's taken the city, fine: I'll negotiate with him, and see if we can use it as a base from which we can launch attacks on Luoyang and get His Majesty back to Chang'an. If he hasn't, I'll either help him take the city by stratagem, or I'll see if I can get him to come back to Chang'an to aid our mutually beneficial task. If he won't return in that instance, fine: we know where we stand, and can deal with him later."

"You seem to know what to do to save us all, Mister Jia," Li Jue said lifelessly. "You do whatever you need to do, and use whatever resources you need to use. I'll... I'll be at home."

Jia Xu watched Li Jue, Li Li, Duan Wei and the other officials as they led their soldiers into the city. The adviser exhaled quietly, made a decision, and travelled to the chancellery to begin execution of a plan. He wrote a letter to Zhang Ji and had it rushed to Jing Province ahead of his arrival; he would continue to correspond as he travelled, as he was anxious to build a strong relationship with the man that would be his new master. He quickly learned that Zhang Ji was seriously hurt from the man's nephew, Marquis Zhang Xiu; Jia Xiu cultivated a friendship with Zhang Xiu in his replies and continued the journey nonetheless.

To the west, Zhang Lu – the ruler of Han'ning – received delayed word from Yi Province that left him a broken, vengeful man.

"*All of them...!*" Zhang Lu sobbed. "*He...!*"

"Heaven demands that you show restraint, Great Leader," the adviser Yan Pu said.

Zhang Lu waved the letter from Yi Province back and forth and cried, "**Liu Zhang has put each and every one of them – every single one of my family members that I entrusted to his father – to the sword, Mister Yan!**"

"I know," Yan Pu replied.

"Even my mother, who was old and helpless," Zhang Lu continued. "There will be no peace between us now, Mister Yan: I had only sought independence from Liu Zhang, but now I demand *reparation...* blood for blood!"

"Such things take time to plan, especially since he'll be ready for you," Yan Pu suggested. "Do not react for now. Have him think that his 'show of discipline and strength' – which is an act of gross idiocy in addition to being an atrocity – has taught you a lesson."

Zhang Lu scowled and said, "Heaven will *punish him...!*"

Yuan Shu's adviser Han Yin rushed into his master's private audience room and said, "Forgive me, my lord, but we have an urgent communication from Ji Ling."

Yuan Shu and another of his advisers, Yan Xiang, had been conferring when Han Yin entered the room: they ended their discussion, and Yuan Shu asked, "Has Liu Bei been defeated...?"

"...No," Han Yin said with obvious irritation. "Forgive my rudeness, my lord, but I warned you what would happen if you reneged on your supply deal with Lü Bu, even if you gave good reasons for it! I warned you about making and breaking promises with regard to Sun Ce as well, so I can only hope this serves as-"

"Bu has saved Liu Bei, hasn't he?" Yuan Shu said with disbelief and anger. "...**Damn that impatient, inconstant fool! I-!**"

"My lord, he's written to say that he is tired of waiting for you to keep your promises!" Han Yin said with despair. "What did you think he would do?"

"**I gave him good reasons!**" Yuan Shu cried.

"And he didn't consider them to be good enough," Han Yin retorted. "He's chased Ji Ling away from Haixi and brought Liu Bei back to Xiapi: why he truly did so – and how that situation will resolve itself – we don't know. But if you think about making any more promises, my lord, then do one of two things: keep them, or don't make them in the first place."

"...**That fool!**" Yuan Shu barked. "**He'll regret this! I vow it!**"

Han Yin and Yan Xiang stared at one-another with what was now a usual sense of dread.

A week passed: Jia Xu and his retinue – which, unbeknownst to Li Jue, included his entire family and household staff from Chang'an – arrived at the gates of Wan City.

"Mister Jia Xu...!" Zhang Xiu said as he welcomed the adviser into the city personally. "Mister Jia Xu, it is good to see you!"

"Let's talk somewhere privately," Jia Xu suggested.

Zhang Xiu and Jia Xu continued their conversation in the private audience chamber of the administrator's residence.

"I am glad that you took and held this place," Jia Xu began. "How is your uncle now...?"

"...Gone," Zhang Xiu sighed. "We had to have a simple funeral..."

Jia Xu exhaled loudly as a lament.

"My aunt is devastated, but we have had to worry about supplies, attacks by Liu Biao... perhaps another siege," Zhang Xiu continued. "Some surrendered to Liu Biao already, Mister Jia; can we get help from Chang'an, or is that cause lost?"

"...I shall have to secure a white garment," Jia Xu said sadly. "I will not let Marquis Zhang be forgotten, for he and I have been good acquaintances since our days serving Niu Fu together. To answer your question, the situation is Chang'an is critical: the regents are finished, and... and if I might be so bold, I shall say that it is probably for the best, since neither truly earned their exalted roles."

Zhang Xiu smiled and said, "It has long been my secretly-held belief that Li Jue is a hankering braggart that would one day harm my uncle as he did Fan Chou and Hu Zhen, or abandon him at the critical moment as he did Wang Fang. Guo Si is a violent idiot, and no friend or master worth having... but wait... your words suggest that... Mister Jia, are you...?"

"Consider me to be *your* adviser now, Mister Zhang, and I shall start by suggesting that you negotiate peace with Liu Biao," Jia Xu declared. "We do not want His Majesty ordering our destruction, and peace with Liu Biao is the best way to avoid that, since it affirms our desire to be independent from Li and Guo and frees Liu Biao to concentrate his efforts elsewhere. Yes, if Li Jue and Guo Si somehow regained their strength, we could ally with them again and allow them to use this place as a foothold into the east to recapture the Son of Heaven, but... I never wanted to hold His Majesty hostage, not for them or Dong Zhuo. I'd rather let that chapter of history go; Zhang Ji would agree with me, I'm sure."

"So am I," Zhang Xiu murmured. "I know that it is *my* wish."

"Of course, Li Jue and Guo Si will probably try and threaten us and call us deserters, but we have nothing to fear from them," Jia Xu continued. "Offer your services as a guardian of Nan County, and Liu Biao – who is understaffed after the losses he incurred against Yuan Shu and Sun Jian – will surely accept. We can then try and broker a peace with His Majesty, work towards amnesty... and distance ourselves from what we've been part of in the past."

Zhang Xiu nodded silently.

"I cannot allow Cao Cao's agents near the emperor!"
Zhang Yang's protest was met with a slight smile by his adviser Dong Gongren.
"Allowing his lackey to fight for us outside is one thing, but to allow him to be inside the city, within striking distance of the sovereign...?" Zhang Yang continued. "And what are you smiling about...? Cao's the butcher of Xu Province! He tries to harm my friend Fengxian! He's *allied to your enemy Yuan Shao*!"
"We're in a new age now," Dong Gongren replied. "Let Cao Hong come and guard His Majesty: is it any less dangerous than allowing Liang Gang, an officer serving the hankering Yuan Shu...? That man finances the Black Mountain Bandits, and yet I don't hear any objections from you!"
Zhang Yang exhaled noisily and said, "The bandits are altogether different to Cao Cao! The bandits are the disaffected having lost restraint! Cao Cao is a nobleman's son that should know better! He'll want to get an amnesty for his atrocities... atrocities that make him another Dong Zhuo!"
"You're wrong," Dong Gongren insisted. "Allow Cao Hong to help us to protect the emperor; Cao Cao is not another Dong Zhuo, he is another Fengxian. Let him atone, my lord, or we might unleash a worse beast in the future."
Zhang Yang nodded and said, "Mm... That's a fair argument. The entire regency farce was born out of a failure to give amnesty..."
"So Cao Hong can enter Henei...?" Dong Gongren prompted.
After a conspicuously long pause, Zhang Yang sighed and replied, "Yes... Heaven forgive me if I am wrong, but... yes."

Another week passed: in Yuan Shao's capital, Yè City, a hitherto-peaceful day was suddenly turned to a day of terror.
"**Administrator! Administrator!**" a city guard captain screamed as he ran into the office of the Administrator of Wei Prefecture, Li Cheng; every one of the busy officials stopped working and turned to face the battered, bloodied soldier.
"What is it, captain? Bandits...?" Li Cheng exclaimed.
"They're everywhere!" the captain sobbed. "The people, the-!"
"Alright, alright, calm down," Li Cheng said. "We'll have to organise the guard; where is Ju Shou? Is Mister Xun Ch-"
Administrator Li Cheng was suddenly interrupted by an attack on his office; the guard captain was cut down and killed by the first bandit that entered the room.
"**Wretches!**" Li Cheng cried. "**You'll all die dog's deaths!**"
"**Yeah?**" the bandits' leader said. "**As bad a death as yours...?**"
"**Heaven smite you!**" Li Cheng retorted.
The bandits' leader gave a signal, and his men descended on the administrator and his staff and hacked them to death.
"**The Administrator's head goes to Poison Yu,**" the bandits' leader said. "**I'll take it myself!**"
The Black Mountain Bandits were finally confronted by Ju Shou's defence militia and forced to leave Yè, but not before they had left many buildings in flames and killed several civilians, soldiers and officials. It would not take long for word to reach Yuan Shao; many of the Bandits expected that his reaction would

be violent, and they would not be proved wrong.

More time passed: after 7 years of the Han imperial court being at the mercy of Dong Zhuo and his associates, the imperial court was safely installed in Henei. But there was still no visible sign of strength, and that concerned Emperor Xian; the court gathered in the audience hall of Henei's administrator's residence so that the young sovereign could have his will made known.
"What we do not understand is why so many of our forces still follow the traitor Li Jue," Emperor Xian said to his courtiers. "Do they not know that he imperils us…?"
Henei Administrator Zhang Yang kowtowed and said, "We are trying to make the soldiers that we encounter understand, but it is complicated, Your Majesty. Some are loyal to Your Majesty, and they are easily swayed; others are loyal to Dong Zhuo's former retainers, and their allegiances are harder to fathom or sway; others are borrowed from the tribal forces led by the likes of Ma Teng and Han Sui, so they are-"
"We know of their intentions," Emperor Xian sighed. "They would be rid of us, and hurl the nation into anarchy… would Li Jue not want us dead if he were to retrieve us, Mister Zhang…?"
"…Possibly, Your Majesty," Zhang Yang replied. "We are sending new requests for aid… for it is surely time for Your Majesty to return to your capital and-"
"How can we return to our capital?" Emperor Xian interrupted. "Which capital would we return to, Mister Zhang? One is governed by our would-be-assassin, the other is utterly destroyed!"
Zhang Yang kowtowed yet again and said, "I am gathering men all the time, Your Majesty; I will serve as Acting Director of Retainers and personally oversee the reconstruction of Luoyang. Your Majesty can return to the palace as soon as it is habitable, and-"
"How would we live…?" Emperor Xian scoffed. "How would we live in such a place, Mister Zhang…? Time and again you insist upon this, and time and again we must refuse: when will our divine word be heeded without question…?"
Zhang Yang kowtowed and replied, "I shall say no more today, Your Majesty… but your divine presence is not meant to be in a place like this. Your Majesty belongs in the palace of Luoyang, and if I must rebuild it with my own hands… then so be it."
Emperor Xian was visibly unimpressed; the nominal court continued for another 10 minutes before the emperor dissolved it.

"…We are at breaking point," Zhang Yang complained as he walked the corridors of his new residence – a former nobleman's mansion – with his adviser Dong Gongren and his officer Sui Gu. "It is nearing a *year*: Henei cannot endure this for much longer! We have forces stationed in and around here that were sent by the rival warlords Cao Cao and Yuan Shu; they constantly engage in private skirmishes! Some of my forces had to be repelled because they were Li Jue's cronies, which was costly…"
Sui Gu hummed sadly.
"Worse still, there is not ample food… famine is spreading, and food is scarce," Zhang Yang continued. "His Majesty must always be kept fully nourished and surrounded by comfort, regardless of what others must then suffer… and suffer they do. I almost feel

sorry for the eunuch attendants when I watch them staggering around, trying to tend to His Majesty's every need with little more than a plant root for a day's sustenance... we will soon be eating millet, I expect, and I know that some of the White Wave Bandits that we rely on as our muscle are already killing and eating people. What to do, my friend... what to do...?"
"How will being in Luoyang be any better...?" Sui Gu wondered.
"Even in its dilapidated state, Luoyang is a better shield against the forces sent by Li Jue," Zhang Yang replied. "The capital is bigger, and once the palace is rebuilt, I suspect that many of the more... how shall I put it... 'frugal' warlords will suddenly have an interest in assisting the Son of Heaven, and then maybe we can finally rid ourselves of the need to tolerate having the White Wave Bandits as bodyguards and soldiers. I *must* convince His Majesty to relocate... else things can only get worse."
"Speak to Dong Cheng," Dong Gongren suggested. "He's gained great favour... he might be the 'voice of reason' that you need."

Zhang Yang took Dong Gongren's advice and spoke to Dong Cheng in the latter's temporary home in Henei.
"Like you, I desire a return to the capital," Dong Cheng said after Zhang Yang had stated his case. "I am in an ever-more advantageous position, save for the ambitious Yang Feng and Han Xian and their White Wave allies pushing for more at everyone else's expense as reward for their part in saving His Majesty."
"His Majesty must be made to understand that he cannot stay in Henei, Mister Dong!" Zhang Yang protested. "You've heard my promises, and I intend to keep them... like my former master, Ding Yuan, who was so cruelly slain while trying to protect-"
"The late Prince of Hongnong," Dong Cheng said pointedly.
"...Ah, yes," Zhang Yang sighed.
"Your late master was fighting Dong Zhuo to prevent His Majesty from becoming the Son of Heaven, remember...?" Dong Cheng continued. "While it was being done to prevent a regicide, it was also a rebuke, so be careful how you frame your arguments."
"They should make no mention of Ding Yuan," Zhang Yang said.
"Ding Yuan was a fine man," Dong Cheng replied. "But all the same, he would have become part of a coalition to depose and possibly punish His Majesty for 'his role in Dong Zhuo's plot'. The Eastern Pass Coalition does not fill His Majesty with joy."
"...And suddenly, I regret being a part of it, no matter how insignificant," Zhang Yang said. "To think that we were contemplating all manner of things... including the appointment of Governor Liu Yu as the Son of Heaven! What would we have done with the incumbent, whom the leaders depicted as a traitor...?"
"His Majesty will have thought about that," Dong Cheng promised. "He worries that Yuan Shao, Cao Cao and Yuan Shu were all prominent members of that coalition as well, and that his distant relatives, Liu Bei and Liu Biao, are currently being attacked by the last of those men while he sends Liang Gang here to 'help'."
"Not to mention Lü Fengxian's behaviour," Zhang Yang sighed. "I am not afraid to admit that His Majesty's calm acceptance of Fengxian's overthrow of Liu Bei was a complete shock. His Majesty even wrote to Fengxian for help!"
"His Majesty is clever and cynical," Dong Cheng said. "But I am

sure that we can win an argument to relocate: after all, Administrator, where better to starve to death than the capital, if one had the choice…?"

Zhang Yang smiled and said, "Perhaps *you* should suggest that."

Another busy week passed: Emperor Xian had his court meet in order to make a reluctant announcement.

"We will travel… to Luoyang," Emperor Xian declared. "It will be rebuilt by Acting Director of Retainers, Zhang Yang… beginning with the restoration of our palaces, north and then south."

"We'll keep you prop'ly safe, Your Majesty," Han Xian said.

The remark was met with quiet contempt by the withered courtiers, as the White Wave Bandits that Han Xian commanded had long been the main source of trouble around Luoyang.

"We are grateful," Emperor Xian replied carefully. "We should like to begin preparations immediately… court dismissed."

One of the emaciated eunuch attendants shuffled forward to help the young emperor to his feet: the rest of the court groaned painfully as their hunger-ravaged bodies fought against them while they got up to leave.

"Director Shisun, you were the lucky one," Minister Yang Biao groaned. "You died at just the right time."

"Too true," Chang'an's former Magistrate, Zhong Yao, replied.

"…What a sorry mess," Cao Hong muttered as he turned to Yuan Shu's general Liang Gang.

"I'm here to protect the emperor, not talk to you, shameless minion of Cao Cao," Liang Gang retorted as he walked away.

"So you're Cao Cao's boy, are you?" Han Xian noted as he stared at the isolated Cao Hong.

"I'm his cousin and a trusted officer," Cao Hong replied.

Han Xian laughed icily and said, "Well, so long as you ain't here to massacre the locals like you did in Xu Province, we'll be fine working together, won't we…?"

The White Wave commander whistled a tune as he walked away; Cao Hong clenched his fists and fought an overwhelming urge to attack the man.

"My friend's making a fair point," Yang Feng said as he placed a hand on Cao Hong's shoulder that was immediately swatted away.

"Xu Province was a personal matter!" Cao Hong protested.

"Naughty-naughty! State always comes first," Yang Feng teased. "I hear you intend to start harassing northern Jing."

"We can't allow Zhang Xiu – a former ally of Dong Zhuo and the so-called 'regents' – to sit in Wan City and act as a communications post for Chang'an!" Cao Hong retorted. "His Majesty needs to be safe from harm, and-"

"I'd leave that place alone," Yang Feng warned. "I hear that while Zhang Ji is dead, his nephew now administrates that place with *Jia Xu* as his adviser and *Huche'er* as the muscle."

"Should I care?" Cao Hong heckled.

"If you want to live, yes," Yang Feng replied. "Yeah, you probably don't care that Huche'er is a titan of a man, since your lord has that Dian Wei fellow; but Jia Xu is probably one of the main reasons that everything is in such a mess, Mister Cao. He advised Dong Zhuo, and then he made powerful regents out of Guo and Li. His abandoning the fools is the reason that their threat to us has lessened... but he's a coiled snake. Leave him be, and that's that; poke him, and you'll die."

"...I am under orders to guard His Majesty," Cao Hong said after a long pause. "I'll accompany him to Luoyang, in the vanguard."

"It's better to do that," Yang Feng suggested. "Take your men over the Yellow River as soon as you can and set up a defensive camp... Luoyang isn't far away, but Heyang Ford and several other defensive positions near to the capital couldn't be hurt by some bolstering... I'll ask Liang Gang to secure the ford, I think."

Cao Hong bowed reluctantly and said, "You have escorted His Majesty this far... I shall trust your judgement, General."

Yang Feng reciprocated the courtesy, and Cao Hong withdrew from the audience hall; the latter's intention was to write to Cao Cao's adviser Xun Wenruo to inform him of the latest decision. The messenger would not reach Yan Province before the Emperor set out on his latest journey; that journey was fraught with danger as Emperor Xian's military escort fought with mercenary groups and contingents of Qiang and imperial infantry that had been sent by the desperate Li Jue. But Dong Cheng, Yang Feng and Han Xian put their own forces to good use, and the Emperor reached Luoyang unscathed.

What awaited Emperor Xian could almost be called a foreshadowing of what was to come: Luoyang was a hollowed shell of a city, emptied of life and meaning and full of terrible reminders of how much had changed in the last 8 years. None of the burnt-out houses made suitable accommodation, so the inhabitants would have to live in tents around their husks, including the young emperor. Acting Director of Retainers Zhang Yang and his army of convict labourers immediately set about the reconstruction of the northern palace while the various defence forces bickered amongst themselves; food was still scarce as the regional famine continued in an unrelenting fashion, and only the emperor would fully escape the horror of what that would entail.

Days passed: Yuan Shao's army had barely had time to reach the Ji border when a messenger from Yè brought word of the damage that the Black Mountain Bandits led by 'Poison Yu' had done in his absence. The command tent was silent as each man absorbed the news and grasped the enormity of it.

"...*Gongsun* planned this... and he'll die a dog's death too after I...!" Yuan Shao could not finish the sentence; he slumped forward and moaned like a wounded animal.

"My lord, the enemy have mostly retreated, but some still lurk," the imposing General Zhang Hè said. "I regret that I have brought you here and am therefore-"

"No, General, you are blameless," Yuan Shao insisted. "Continue your fine work here. I will return to Yè to prepare my personal retaliation. I will throw everything at this 'Poison Yu' this time, gentlemen; not enough of him will be *left* to display in public!"

"Poor Mister Li," Guo Tu sighed. "They are animals, Lord Yuan."

"And they'll *die* like animals," Yuan Shao promised.

✳✳✳✳✳✳✳✳✳✳✳✳

33

Another month passed. While the appointed Governor of Xu Province, Liu Bei, endured being a gate guardian in Xiaopei in western Xu, the man that usurped his governorship – the warlord Lü Bu – waited to see whether the Governor of neighbouring Yan Province, Cao Cao, would act: Cao Cao was aware of the situation, but he was more interested in the movements of the super-warlord Yuan Shu and the fate of the marginalised Emperor Xian.

"I am probably safe for now," Lü Bu said as he looked at his courtiers. "Here in Xiapi, I have order: Cao Cao can't come after me here without a fight that he won't quickly forget, and Yuan Shu is trying to smash a rock with an egg. If he annoys me too much with his sending Ji Ling after Liu Bei, I'll deal with him personally."

"Perhaps you should write to *Zhang Yang*, my lord," General Gao Shun suggested. "We're all old friends, aren't we? He is close to The Son of Heaven at the moment, and His Majesty acknowledges your place here; that can only be-"

"*Disaster* is all it can be!" Lü Bu interrupted. "The emperor surely hates me and wants me dead: that much will be true! He *cannot* have genuinely forgiven me! That's *impossible*!"

"Why, my lord?" Gao Shun retorted. "We helped His Majesty get rid of Dong Zhuo."

"He'll never forgive me for the tombs!" Lü Bu replied. "Wang Yun could never have saved my life once things were back to normal! I am living on borrowed time! You should know that, Gao Shun: you're not as smart as you think you are!"

Gao Shun exhaled noisily and refrained from saying any more.

"There can be no good from the emperor being in Henei," Lü Bu muttered.

"But we're all men of that region," General Hao Meng said. "We all go back a long way, fighting the Black Mountain Bandits with Ding Yuan. You have a province now, my lord: Zhang Yang has Henei. We're all doing well! An alliance that's given assent by the emperor could be-"

"**That won't happen, fool!**" Lü Bu barked. "**I'll be lucky if the boy doesn't demand my head! I'm only glad it's Zhang Yang he has to ask, or I'd be dead already! Now *shut up*, Hao Meng: you're talking too much these days!**"

Hao Meng lowered his head and grumbled irritably.

"…All we're doing is arguing," Chen Gong said. "Dismiss the court, *Governor*."

Lü Bu made a terse gesture and grunted, "Dismissed."

The former Han scholar Chen Yuanfang, his son Chen Qun, the Xiapi nobleman Chen Gui and his son Chen Deng left the court together and began the walk to their homes: as they travelled, Chen Deng said, "Lü Bu was *drunk*: I'm *sure of it*! Is he really better than Liu Bei?"

"Lü Bu becomes *Dong Zhuo*," Chen Yuanfang sighed.

The other three nodded silently.

"Liu Bei was, at worst, incompetent; he was not a wicked man," Chen Yuanfang continued. "This idiot Bu will start killing us if anything happens to Chen Gong, so we must hope that sagacious man does not die any time soon."

"But can we waver again...?" Chen Qun asked. "I fear that Zhang Fei will tear us apart if Liu Bei ever regained power... and it is Zhang Fei that we must consider."

"Quite," Chen Gui said. "Chen Gong can control Lü Bu, I think... but Zhang Fei could not be controlled. Let's trust Chen Gong and not scheme ourselves into any more trouble; that's how we ended up with Liu Bei and Lü Bu, after all."

The two Chen factions agreed to let fate determine events in future; meanwhile, one of Lü Bu's officers had finally had enough of his rude and disrespectful master.

A week later, Lü Bu was woken by an anxious subordinate.

"Why are you barging into my sleeping quarters in the middle of the night, cousin???" Lü Bu complained as the officer Wei Xu tried to pull the warlord out of his bed; Bu's wife was wailing incoherently, which prompted Bu to add, "**Shut up, whiney woman! How can I hear what the problem is if-!**"

"Treachery!" Wei Xu said. "You must escape!"

Lü Bu could hear the sounds and voices of the men that were attacking his residence, and he knew that he had no time. He was only dressed in undergarments, but he had no time to dress or arm himself: he took his wife and fled through the rear of the building while Wei Xu rescued Bu's daughter.

Lü Bu fled Xiapi with his wife and daughter: he then left them with Wei Xu and went to the camp of General Gao Shun, who was stationed outside the city's west gates to guard against possible attacks by their many enemies.

"...Why are you half-dressed and ambling around in the middle of the night?" Gao Shun asked as Lü Bu entered his command tent. "Please don't tell me you're drunk again, Lord Lü... this is a bad time."

"Someone is attacking my home!" Lü Bu said with a tone that betrayed a rare emotion in the man: fear. "I don't know who it was, but- ...Wait a minute... was it *your* men, Gao Shun???"

Lü Bu backed away as paranoia overwhelmed him: Gao Shun smirked and replied by saying, "Your occasional rebukes have not diminished my sense of honour. If I had intended to leave your service, I'd have done it when we were in Chang'an. What do you know about the men? What were they armed with?"

Lü Bu calmed slightly and said, "I didn't actually see them... I only heard them. They- ...Wait. They... they spoke with central-northern accents... Henei accents!"

"*Henei*...?" Gao Shun said. "...Then there is a very strong likelihood that-! ...Never mind. I'll go into the city and repel the attackers if they're still there... you stay here and arm yourself with my supplies. Are your wife and daughter safe...?"

"Yes," Lü Bu replied. "They're with Wei Xu. He's the one that warned me."

"That's good," Gao Shun said. "I shall get going then."

Gao Shun left the tent with sword in hand; Lü Bu frowned thoughtfully, but his thoughts did not include gratitude.

Gao Shun returned an hour later and said, "My lord, the attackers have been repelled." He then noted that Wei Xu had arrived, and added, "Your quick thinking saved us a lot of trouble."

"He only does what he can to serve," Lü Bu said pointedly.

"…Quite," Gao Shun replied; he could sense that Lü Bu was suspicious, so he added, "It's as I suspected. I placed people to watch the gates, and sure enough, there were men spotted fleeing to Hao Meng's camp at the south gate. He and his men are all Henei locals, so-"

"Hao Meng will die a slow, painful death," Lü Bu growled. "I only hope it's him and him alone that I have to worry about."

"My suggestion is that I take a retinue and attack his camp before he has time to reinforce it," Gao Shun continued. "If I have your permission, my lord, I'll do that now."

"Maybe we should consult Chen Gong," Wei Xu suggested.

Lü Bu glared at Gao Shun and said, "Go ahead… attack Hao Meng. We'll see what happens afterwards."

Once Gao Shun had retreated yet again, Wei Xu asked, "Why were you staring at him like that…?"

"Gao Shun always offers advice that I don't want," Lü Bu replied.

"What's that got to do with anything?" Wei Xu wondered.

"He's clever," Lü Bu continued. "Hao Meng isn't smart enough to betray me: no… someone else is behind this…"

"Hao Meng isn't a fool," Wei Xu said. "And Gao Shun is a good man, a loyal man."

"…I hope so," Lü Bu grunted.

Hao Meng's assassin force had returned to their camp without achieving anything: they were greeted by Hao Meng's highest-ranking subordinate, Major Cao Xing.

"Prepare for any possible attack!" Hao Meng ordered.

"What's going on…?" Cao Xing asked.

"Don't question me!" Hao Meng barked. "Just do it!"

"Who are we fighting…?" Cao Xing asked as Hao Meng pushed his way past him.

"…Gao Shun, most likely," Hao Meng replied. "But Bu himself, maybe, if-"

"**What have you done???**" Cao Xing cried as he drew his sword and pointed it at Hao Meng. "**You… you actually did it! You betrayed our lord! How dare you!**"

"**How dare *I*???**" Hao Meng retorted as he raised his spear; his other subordinates backed away, as they were unsure as to whether they wanted to be associated with him anymore.

"**You tried to assassinate Lord Lü while he slept!**" Cao Xing realised. "**Dog! Wretch!**"

"***He's* the animal! *He's* the wretch!**" Hao Meng retorted. "**He's bringing down the wrath of every man in the land on us! He'll be the death of us all, and yet he punishes us for our loyalty! Well I, for one, will take no more!**"

"**Sneaking out in the middle of the night to cut his throat is no way to do justice to such a man, you coward!**" Cao Xing said as he lunged with his sword.

Hao Meng was able to repel Cao Xing's sword strikes with his spear, and he quickly made a successful strike against his major's left arm. But Cao Xing was not done: he learned how to dodge Hao Meng's slow lunges and swipes, found an opening, and dealt a blow with the edge of his sword that almost severed Hao's arm from his body. Hao Meng screamed and retreated with his spear clutched tightly in his working hand; Cao Xing wanted to advance and finish him, but Gao Shun arrived with a small cavalry force and rode straight toward Hao Meng, running Hao through with his spear and ending his life.

"Gao Shun!" Cao Xing exclaimed.

"**Don't attack, General Gao!**" a captain serving Cao Xing pleaded. "**Major Cao was-!**"

"I can see and understand well enough without an explanation," Gao Shun said as he dismounted and approached Cao Xing. "Well done, and thank you… betraying Hao Meng was not an easy decision to make, I'm sure."

"Betraying Lord Lü was the only other option, and I could never do that," Cao Xing said as he turned to the men that had accompanied Hao Meng on his assassination mission: they had been apprehended by their own colleagues, and they were resigned to a painful death.

"Come to my command tent, Major Cao," Gao Shun said kindly. "Lord Lü is there, and he will be pleased to know he has a man like you in his service."

"What of Hao Meng…?" Cao Xing asked as he looked at the twitching body of his former superior.

"…I'll bring his head with us," Gao Shun replied. "But don't worry: our lord will know your pivotal role in his destruction."

Cao Xing smiled gratefully.

Lü Bu's eyes were untrusting slits when Gao Shun entered his command tent with Cao Xing. Chen Gong and General Zhang Liao had joined him, but neither man had a judgemental expression.

"…Is that the head of Hao Meng?" Lü Bu asked tersely.

Gao Shun raised the severed head of the traitor to chest height and said, "It is."

"What happened?" Chen Gong asked.

"As I have already explained to Lord Lü, I chased the men as they fled from his residence and traced their movements to Hao Meng's camp," Gao Shun replied. "Lord Lü had already identified the would-be-assassins as men from Henei, and Hao Meng was an obvious suspect."

"*Very obvious indeed*," Lü Bu said through gritted teeth.

"…I went to Hao's camp as ordered, whereupon I found Major Cao Xing engaged in bloody battle with him," Gao Shun continued. "Major Cao had already incapacitated him, so all that was left was a final strike to end his life… I was eager to do my part, so I apologise to Major Cao for 'stealing the kill', as it were!"

"Good that he's dead," Wei Xu growled. "Good riddance, the-!"

"But if he is dead, Wei Xu, then how can we know who his associates were?" Lü Bu asked snidely.

"Associates…?" Gao Shun chuckled.

"You didn't look that surprised at Hao Meng's plan," Lü Bu said.

"Of course not," Gao Shun scoffed. "You were rude to him, my lord, as you are so very often rude to many of your own men when your passion overtakes you. Hao Meng was impulsive: he did not take kindly to being stationed outside the capital, and-"

"And what about *you*…?" Lü Bu asked. "Are *you* happy…?"

Gao Shun frowned and replied, "Of course not, but I understand the need for-"

"Well, you needn't be unhappy anymore, *Mister* Gao Shun!" Lü Bu barked.

"Ayah! No!" Chen Gong cried. "My lord, don't-!"

"Consider yourself relieved of duty, Gao Shun," Lü Bu continued.

"...I knew you'd do this," Gao Shun sighed.

"Your men will serve Wei Xu from now on," Lü Bu said.

"Don't do this to General Gao, Lord Lü!" Zhang Liao pleaded.

"So you think I should leave him with a command, Zhang Liao, when his role in what just happened is very, very suspicious...?" Lü Bu chortled. "Why was he so keen to slay Hao Meng before we could question him, I wonder...?"

Gao Shun threw Hao Meng's head to the floor and said, "I accept your decision, Lord Lü, but not your summary of my character. If I wanted to challenge you, I'd meet you on the battlefield... and die knowing I'd fought a hero first."

"GET OUT!" Lü Bu shrieked.

Gao Shun stifled his rage, bowed humbly, and left what was now Wei Xu's command tent.

"Cao Xing: you seem to have known that Hao Meng was plotting *something*," Lü Bu said as he fixed his gaze on Hao Meng's major. "What do you know? What other conspirators were you made aware of?"

"...He did try to involve me in plans to challenge you openly, but I refused," Cao Xing replied. "He only mentioned one name when discussing 'friends': Chen Gong."

Chen Gong scowled angrily but said nothing.

"...He was lying," Lü Bu said with self-targeted insistence. "Hao Meng was a lying dog. So... so he tried to involve you in open revolt?"

"He did, but I warned him that you are the greatest warrior that ever lived, a hero by Heaven's decree, and that only a fool would do such a thing," Cao Xing replied.

Lu Bu's caution gave way to his vanity: he laughed and said, "That, gentlemen, is a true general! You'll receive Hao Meng's army as your own as reward for your insight and loyalty. Return to your camp."

"Thank you, Lord Lü," Cao Xing replied quietly.

Lü Bu turned to Zhang Liao and said, "Go with him."

Zhang Liao sighed miserably and accompanied Cao Xing to the southern camp.

"You should not have punished Gao Shun," Chen Gong said. "You hate him because he is honest, my lord, but he is a man that will gladly die for you!"

"...I know," Lü Bu admitted. "But... I will hear no more."

Wei Xu and Chen Gong did not challenge Lü Bu any further. Hao Meng was dead, and Cao Xing was given Hao Meng's command and promoted to a general. Observers such as Chen Gui and Chen Qun saw the friction in Lü Bu's camp and wondered whether that would be the last betrayal: Lü Bu would wonder the same.

****

34

Yan Province Governor Cao Cao's court in Xuchang City convened at Xun Wenruo's request.

"All is ready," Cheng Yu said once all men were present.

"Xun Wenruo!" Cao Cao hailed. "I always know that I am to be blessed whenever you proffer your wisdom! Speak, my friend, to my ready ear and mind."

"My lord," Xun Wenruo began, "I have talked at length with Mister Cheng, and we agree that the time is right for you to make an auspicious invitation."

The officials looked at each other with bewilderment.

"Oh...?" Cao Cao said. "And what or who would I be inviting...?"

"His Majesty," Cheng Yu revealed, "to your new stronghold here at Xuchang."

The court was silent.

"...I have long deliberated the matter of His Majesty's safety," Cao Cao admitted. "I sometimes think of the divine majesty's plight, living in the ruins of his capital, surrounded on all sides by hordes of hankering bandits, eking out an existence on whatever can be found... and I weep inside."

Governor Cao Cao gave a show of emotion, and his officials followed his lead.

"...But I force you away from your point," Cao Cao continued after a minute of group lamentation. "Please, Wenruo, Zhongde, I would hear your reasoning."

"You shall put it best, I think," Xun Wenruo said to Cheng Yu.

"My lord," Cheng Yu said, "no man has attempted to relocate His Majesty, and with good reason; His Majesty belongs in the capital Luoyang, and none but the villain Dong Zhuo can take responsibility for the state of that former jewel. The times are uncertain; no man, not even the wealthiest and most influential, such as Yuan Shao, can hope to rebuild Luoyang, and even a joint effort would leave us unable to face the other perils, such as the Qiang, the Xianbei, the Nan, the remnants of the Yellow Turbans, and so on and so forth. We must, therefore, take the difficult step of temporarily removing His Majesty and his attendants from that beleaguered place and bring him here, where his divine manifestation will be safe."

"Well put," Cao Cao sighed. "But there must be some caveats; else why has no other man – such as my good friend, Yuan Shao – pondered and acted thus far...?"

"Forgive me, my lord, but... he was my master before you were, and I left him to join you with good reason," Xun Wenruo answered reluctantly.

Cao Cao laughed and said, "Again, well put! Sadly, Benchu is now a bit muddle-headed, which is mainly due to the confusing counsel of fools like Guo Tu, Shen Pei and the former Garden Army colonel, Chunyu Qiong. I imagine that he was told that such a venture would be 'burdensome'...?"

"You guess the situation correctly, my lord," Xun Wenruo confirmed. "My brother confirmed it to me in a private letter that I only reveal for its importance."

"We are not without burdens," Cao Cao challenged. "What has

supposedly changed here in Yan Province?"

"We have less to bear than we did," Xun Wenruo insisted. "The famine's effects have lessened, and most importantly, the renegade Southern Xiongnu chieftain Yufuluo is dead, his followers returned to their benign and chosen king Huchuquan, and the Black Mountain Bandits – now robbed of Yufuluo's men and maybe Yuan Shu's support as well – are unable to move beyond Bing and Ji Provinces, such is the ferocity of Yuan Shao's assault upon them. The White Wave Bandits are also a diminished threat, so apart from incursions by the Yellow Turbans in Runan…"

"…Which I intend to deal with once and for all, and very, very soon," Cao Cao promised.

"…The main problems are the usual ones," Xun Wenruo concluded.

"I might not be as wealthy as Benchu, but even with my lesser means, I will still shoulder that divine burden that he has refused!" Cao Cao declared. "It is the least I can do for the state… I have dedicated myself to preserving it, have I not, what with sheltering partisans, and openly defying those wretched eunuchs, regardless the threat it posed to my life…? Did I not expend my own wealth to form a militia to fight the Yellow Turbans, and then again, to destroy Dong Zhuo…? Life is about burdens, and a real man accepts them! …But what burden is there in guarding our sovereign, who is the image of divine will…?"

"I am glad that you see things that way, my lord," Xun Wenruo said politely. "With the emperor safely installed here in Xuchang, you can then 'control the rebellious in the name of the emperor', and be proven just at all times. No other man has your devotion to His Majesty… no other man will guard his sagely life without harbouring wicked thoughts… no other man but *you*, my lord, can do this."

Cao Cao hummed thoughtfully and said, "You have convinced me, both of you. I shall send word to Cao Hong in Luoyang, and have him bring the emperor here, where he will be truly safe. We can then begin a great expedition against all of the traitors, starting with those foolish Yellow Turbans in Runan!"

"An expedition that requires *fed men*," Cheng Yu suggested.

"*Ayah*! Why must you always imply such horrors, Mister Cheng???" Xun Gongda cried.

"Are they not existing horrors…?" Cheng Yu chortled. "Do the Son of Heaven's courtiers not eat roots and the flesh of-"

"Yes, they do, and so do some poor souls here in Yan Province," Xun Wenruo interrupted. "My nephew simply makes a protestation about your need to elaborate needlessly… which you met with another elaboration. What we need, however, is a solution…"

Cheng Yu, Xun Wenruo and Xun Gongda turned their gazes to the official Zao Zhi, who was physically weak and noticeably timid despite his keen mind.

"Yes… our supplies must be more guaranteed in future," Cao Cao mused. "We must be careful not to overstretch ourselves, but there is also the problem of the cost this is having. With so much unrest, a standing army is an effort to feed, and we don't want to have to resort to pillaging our neighbours like bandits."

Zao Zhi gestured that he would like to speak.

"Ah! Mister Zao Zhi," Cao Cao said with strange cheer. "You have something important that you would like to say…?"

"My lord, you know that I am an advocate of balance," Zao Zhi declared. "In times of peace, men are farmers, while in times of war, they are soldiers. But when the situation is as it is now, a balance must be found. Men must be both providers and consumers if there is to be victory."

"...Oh...?" Cao Cao exclaimed. "...Do go on."

"I would hope that you have heard of the concept that I call *tuntian*," Zao Zhi continued. "The principle is simple: when there is the ability to do so, the soldiers must work on the fields – alongside the local villagers, or alone – to produce the food that, at least in part, they will then consume when they are on a campaign. That way, men are not idle, and they are seen by all as men; part of a community, not some aloof element that brings misery. Order is maintained, and growth is only to be expected: the men will settle, have families, and create an even stronger army in addition to a stronger community."

Cao Cao was silent, and Zao Zhi was suddenly afraid.

"...You are not in favour of Mister Zao's plan...?" Xun Wenruo prompted.

"...Oh! No, no, you misunderstand me!" Cao Cao said with genuine cheer. "I am, in fact, glad of this advice! Mister Zao, you have provided a long-term solution to the oldest of military problems! It shall be adopted immediately!"

Zao Zhi smiled with relief, bowed, and said, "I am glad to be of assistance."

Cao Cao retired to his private audience hall after the meeting; Xun Wenruo asked to join him and said, "The news from the south haunts you."

"...Yes and no," Cao Cao replied. "Mister Xu Shao... that brilliant mind, the appraiser of men's characters that seemed to be infallible – and the man that gave me my destiny as the 'Crafty Villain' – is dead; naturally, that gives me a cause for thought."

"For his being dead, or how he died...?" Xun Wenruo asked.

Cao Cao smiled and replied, "He's not the only man who recognised me, Wenruo; you are quite right to infer that I ponder his failure at the end to see the situation in front of him. He supported Liu Yao, which is fine; he invited the famed Taishi Ci to Yang, which is understandable; but from there, it unravels. How did he fail to see the threat that Sun Ce posed... or if he did, how did he fail to convince a shrewd man like Liu Yao to show caution...? How did such a keen mind allow Liu Yao to be crushed in battle and flee to the far-flung corner of his own province...? How did such a genius, such a practiced prognosticator meet such an ignominious end in that same wretched corner of the province...? ...How did they fall foul of *Ze Rong*...?"

"Tao Qian was no fool, and he was deceived by Ze Rong's false religion, enough to let the man make a fortified money pot out of Xiapi," Xun Wenruo replied. "And aside from that, Xu Shao was an appraiser of men, not situations: you can know every man around you as well as you know yourself, and yet a situation can change anything and anyone, even your own sense of self. Xu Shao did not misread anyone, in my opinion; he misjudged the situation. In war, luck and the weather can sometimes be more important than the enemy general. He might have defeated every man in Sun

Ce's army in his own mind, only to be felled by heavy rain or an arrow that did as it pleased."

"…Well put again," Cao Cao sighed. "But then that only makes me fear that…"

"…That Xu Shao's appraisal can still be true…?" Xun Wenruo supposed.

"If he was not gifted, then I am freed," Cao Cao replied. "If he was, then I am still doomed to be a 'Crafty Villain' in this age of unrelenting chaos!"

"And an able statesman when peace is restored," Xun Wenruo retorted. "And that duality suggests that Xu Shao saw in you a flexible, clever man that adjusts his behaviour to suit the times in which he lives… which is no crime. Xu Shao, at the critical moment, could not be flexible, and died as an appraiser in a place and at a time when knowing men was unimportant."

"Yet again, I am resolved," Cao Cao said with a smile. "Thank you, Wenruo. Now I can return to the more important task at hand; readying our men for unfamiliar *tuntian* and too-familiar war."

While Cao Cao began preparations to revolutionise military resource production, a messenger sped a letter to the impatient and weary Cao Hong in Luoyang. He acted initially by announcing his intention to the imperial court: their response was not universally favourable.

"Deputy Director Zhang! Deputy Director Zhang!" Dong Cheng cried as he ran into the partially-reconstructed audience hall of the northern imperial palace; conscripted workmen were toiling to restore the room to its former glory while Zhang Yang and his subordinate Dong Gongren looked on with a genuine sense of pride.

"Deputy Director Zhang!"

Zhang Yang's concentration was only broken by the third utterance of his name: he turned to Dong Cheng and said, "You look concerned about something."

"They're fighting!" Dong Cheng said. "Cao Hong, Liang Gang, they're-!"

"Aren't they always?" Zhang Yang scoffed.

"No, no, I mean that they are actually fighting!" Dong Cheng said. "You must aid us, Director Zhang! Cao Hong must be chased away!"

"…So you and Liang Gang are allied against Cao Hong?" Zhang Yang asked with obvious lack of interest.

"We should all be!" Dong Cheng retorted. "Did you not hear the man's words?"

"I did," Zhang Yang sighed.

"And it does not bother you???" Dong Cheng chortled. "It is bad enough that the White Wave Bandits and that Yang Feng do nothing, but how can *you* react like that??? You came to me with an insistence that His Majesty must be in Luoyang! How can you now allow him to be taken to Xuchang after being so anxious to remove him from Henei?"

"I know where that argument's leading," Zhang Yang growled. "I am here, am I not? I am spending my own money rebuilding parts of this palace! I did not want rid of His Majesty from Henei! But what can I do to help you get rid of Cao Hong? He has what, a thousand men, maybe two…? So does Liang Gang! And Han Xian has thousands, maybe *tens of thousands*! Why am I needed anywhere but here, restoring the palace…?"

"…You are quite right," Dong Cheng sighed. "I shall leave you…"

Dong Cheng turned and hurried out of the audience hall.

"He frets for his place, my lord," Dong Gongren suggested.

"As do we all," Zhang Yang suggested. "Han Xian and Yang Feng are far, far too powerful; I am now 'Deputy Director' because 'Commander-in-Chief Han Xian' also wanted the role of Director of Retainers, even though he does nothing to fulfil it. And Yang Feng…? I forget if he's an Excellency or General of the Left: perhaps he is both! Those men are another Li Jue and Guo Si!"

Dong Gongren hummed sadly.

"The Imperial army is fractured, with the barbarian contingents favouring the Chang'an mob led by Li Jue and the rest being fickle or reticent," Zhang Yang continued. "Cao Cao wants His Majesty in Xuchang… that's not at all ideal, no. But as you have rightly stated, is His Majesty any safer here, under the 'protection' of fifty-thousand ex-Yellow Turbans that once wanted his family exterminated…? I… I have no answer."

Dong Gongren said nothing: there was nothing more that he could say. Both men continued to observe the work on the imperial palace while a battle raged in and around the burnt-out capital: it would, as Zhang Yang had predicted, be Cao Hong that would be chased away by the forces of Liang Gang and Dong Cheng while the White Wave Bandits looked on and did nothing. In addition, Yuan Shu's general seemed to be maintaining constant and purposeful communication with his master in Shouchun: that worried some, and with good reason.

Cao Hong sent a messenger to Xuchang to report his failure to acquire the emperor; the irritated Cao Cao summoned his court to ask his advisers' opinions yet again.

"Don't do anything," Xun Wenruo said.

"**It was your idea in the first place!**" Xiahou Dun barked.

"Dun is quite right," Cao Cao said as he stared at Xun Wenruo.

"I did not expect such resistance," Xun Wenruo admitted. "But I don't expect that to last. Right now, the Son of Heaven is 'protected' by a collection of bandits: there will be men around His Majesty that will see the folly of that and invite the warlords to rescue the Son of Heaven once again."

"Yes, and no doubt *Benchu* will respond to that invitation next time," Cao Cao grumbled.

"Yuan Shao will do nothing, Lord Cao," Xun Wenruo promised. "Just be patient."

"…Fine," Cao Cao sighed. "I will wait."

Over the next few weeks, life in the ruins of the imperial capital Luoyang was consistently dire. The officials continued their pampering of their emperor whilst suffering themselves, and Zhang Yang continued to oversee the reconstruction of the imperial palace. As time went on, however, the coalition of rescuers was becoming as fractured as the Eastern Pass Coalition that had preceded it. Han Xian and Yang Feng were becoming increasingly familiar at court meetings, and some factions of the

White Wave Bandit confederacy were beginning to bully civilians and each other as the awareness of their strength grew. Dong Cheng observed the situation with dread and asked his supposed ally Liang Gang to come to his encampment to discuss it privately.

"You wanted to speak with me, General Dong…?" Liang Gang said as he entered Dong Cheng's tent.

"Surely it has not escaped you that our victory against Cao Hong was ours, and ours alone, General Liang," Dong Cheng replied. "The most that the White Wave Bandits did was to pursue the defeated force and raid them for supplies."

"…I take it that you refer to our friend Han Xian's announcement that he got rid of Cao Hong with Yang Feng's help," Liang Gang chuckled. "Don't worry about it."

"But I *do* worry about it!" Dong Cheng said. "His Majesty cannot be allowed to think that these criminals mean him any good! I have seen this before: they are acting like the regents, taking titles for themselves and mistreating the weak! They must be got rid of. Can your lord send more help?"

"…I'm afraid not," Liang Gang replied cagily. "Lord Yuan is currently tied up near the Xu Provincial border, fighting Lü Bu."

"*Lü Bu*?" Dong Cheng exclaimed.

"Time has not stopped outside the capital, General," Liang Gang continued. "The upstart usurper Liu Bei that stole that province from the son of my lord's ally Tao Qian was himself overthrown by Lü Bu some time ago. You knew that. But Lü Bu reneged on an agreement to work with my lord, and now he intends to make Xu Province an independent state from which he can sow more anarchy."

"That's not ideal at all!" Dong Cheng gasped. "And yet here we have his old friend and colleague Zhang Yang rebuilding the palace… for *whom*, I wonder…?"

"Zhang Yang and Lü Bu are friends, yes, but they are two entirely different men," Liang Gang suggested. "Zhang Yang would not have killed Ding Yuan and joined Dong Zhuo. He *did not*, to be more precise."

"Quite true," Dong Cheng sighed.

"Why did you want more help…?" Liang Gang asked. "Did you plan on confronting the White Wave Bandits…?"

"Yes," Dong Cheng admitted. "Foolish, maybe, but they're only slightly better than the rebels in the west! It won't be long before they kill His Majesty, I just know it!"

"Yes… the Han is truly weakened," Liang Gang sighed theatrically.

"And we must do all that we can to restore its glory!" Dong Cheng declared.

"Naturally," Liang Gang said. "I shall write again, but all of my lord's forces are busy. To the west, guarding against Liu Biao and Zhang Xiu; to the south, fighting Liu Yao; to the east, against Lü Bu; and, sad to say, to the north, against that wicked ally of my lord's brother."

"*Cao Cao*, you mean," Dong Cheng murmured. "Yes…"

"…As I say, I shall write again," Liang Gang prompted.

"Oh! Oh, yes, thank you," Dong Cheng said. "That was all; many thanks to you, General Liang, for all that you have already done." Liang Gang bowed and retreated.

"…Cao Cao… *yes*… but will he forgive me…?" Dong Cheng

wondered as he took up a quill and planned a letter in his mind.

"As you promised, Wenruo!" Cao Cao chuckled as he waved a cloth letter back and forth and smiled at his assembled courtiers. "It is just as you promised!"
"Guessed, at best," Xun Wenruo said humbly.
"Guessed, promised, all the same!" Cao Cao continued. "We are invited this time! And this time, I shall go in person! Cao Ren, Cao Anmin, Cao Xiu, Xiahou Dun, Yue Jin: ready your men! Xun Wenruo, you shall accompany me as my adviser, since this was your marvellous idea: your nephew Gongda shall look after Xuchang in our absence! Xiahou Yuan shall guard the west, Li Zheng the east, and-"
"What of me, Father?"
All eyes turned to the 19-year-old Cao Ang: the tall youth certainly looked the part of a warrior, as he was athletic and stern-faced.
"You take Anmin and Xiu: why not me?" Cao Ang continued.
Cao Cao's nephew Anmin was also an athletic man, though shorter than Ang and not so imposing; he nodded agreeably and said, "Cousin Ang differs only a little in age from me, Uncle. Why can he not join us...?"
"My Ang wants to accompany me on this campaign!" Cao Cao said with pride. "I do not think that is wise, though, my son. Anmin and Xiu have combat training that exceeds yours; there are a million White Wave Bandits at least, and-"
"Father, we both know that number is an exaggeration of their true fighting force," Cao Ang interrupted. "The White Wave Bandits include their women and children in their counts, so their numbers are closer to the tens of thousands."
"That is quite true," Xun Gongda admitted.
"But my own forces are smaller these days," Cao Cao lamented. "My Qing Province Corps halved during and after the Xu Province campaign, partly due to famine but partly due to so many wanting to return to their old ways. Nowadays, I have around fifty-thousand men myself, and I need to leave many of them in Yan to guard against Yuan Shu and Lü Bu. Besides, I always intended for you to be a politician or a peacetime governor, my son, not a warlord like me! With that being the case, why would I want you with me...?"
Cao Ang sighed and said, "As you wish, Father."
"**Now that is settled, let us march!**" Cao Cao bellowed.
Preparations were swift, as Xun Wenruo had predicted the outcome and readied Cao Cao's forces in advance: a force of 10,000 marched northwest toward Luoyang with the intention of defeating the White Wave Bandits and securing the emperor.

∗∗∗∗∗∗∗∗∗∗∗∗

35

In Bing Province – which was to the northwest of the drama that was unfolding in Luoyang – Yuan Shao received word of the emperor's situation and pondered what he should do.

"My lord, leave Yan Liang and Wen Chou to destroy the bandits and return to Yè for now," Tian Feng pleaded. "Whether you decide to change your mind and help His Majesty or not, your presence in Yè will soothe hearts – especially the family of Li Cheng, who have twice requested an audience to thank you for attending his funeral – and enable you to react to any attack from any direction. If you remain here too long, Gongsun might march south or your son might need aid to-"

"All that you say is true," Yuan Shao decided. "I shall return to Yè for now. Oh, I'll be back, gentlemen, as soon as I know what's going on to the south… but for now, my people need me to be in my capital, being their governor."

"I shall not disagree," the adviser Guo Tu sighed.

"Neither shall I, Governor," the adviser Pang Ji muttered as he stared at Tian Feng.

Within a week, General Liang Gang was forced to send his master Yuan Shu a report of the latest developments in Luoyang.

"**What's this???**" Yuan Shu cried as he read Liang Gang's despatch. "Cao Cao has turned up in Luoyang with an army, and he's been *invited*, this time by *Dong Cheng*!"

The Shouchun court was silent.

"…Faithless ingrate!" Yuan Shu continued. "My Liang Gang aided Dong Cheng when he was in peril, and this is the thanks I get??? I should order Liang Gang to kill him!"

"But you won't of course," the adviser Yan Xiang suggested. "After all, this is Cao Cao's moment; we did not send more help, so Dong Cheng has gone to the next warlord. He could have gone north, since Ji Province is as close as Yan… and Yuan Shao and Cao Cao are not as close these days."

"…No… no, that's right," Yuan Shu conceded. "I won't be ordering Liang Gang to resist Cao Cao. I'll order him to act as rear guard until the emperor is in Yan Province, and then withdraw to Yang Province: if Cao Cao wants a fight, then let it be with the White Wave Bandits."

"And if the bandits win…?" Yan Xiang wondered.

"You'd suggest that I have Liang Gang repel Cao Cao with them, to stay close to the emperor, no doubt," Yuan Shu scoffed. "Liang Gang will remain neutral this time. Dong Cheng is close to the emperor; his daughter is now an imperial consort. That's an enemy I can do without."

"A sensible decision, my lord!" the adviser Han Yin said with relief.

"…But the signs for the Han are not good," Yuan Shu added.

Many of Yuan Shu's officials sighed inwardly: their lord could only mean one thing when he said that, and they dreaded the day when he made his feelings public.

Han Xian and Yang Feng learned of Cao Cao's approach and gathered their forces on a stretch of land to the south of Luoyang;

Dong Cheng volunteered to act as rear guard and Han Xian agreed, assuming that they still regarded Cao as a mutual foe.
"Oy! Cao Cao! Where's the one we already beat up?" Han Xian taunted as he rode back and forth on one of the few horses that had not been slaughtered for food: Cao Cao smirked, as he could see that the White Wave Bandits were poorly nourished and tired from fighting Li Jue's mercenaries and each other. Cao Cao's men were better fed, though not as well as any would have hoped for: they were still outnumbered by around 5 to 1, but Cao Cao's men were also better trained.
"Cao Hong's men are waiting to the west," Xun Wenruo reported. "It looks like Yuan Shu's men are staying out of it: Liang Gang has retreated to Heyang Ford."
"Excellent," Cao Cao said. "Us to the south of them, Cao Hong to the west, and Dong Cheng in the capital to ensure that they cannot abduct His Majesty; all is ready. Let's attack at once!"
"No," Xun Wenruo said. "Dong Cheng has a plan, I think."

Dong Cheng hurried to Emperor Xian's furnished tent as soon as Han Xian and Yang Feng were out of the capital.
"What now...?" Emperor Xian sighed.
"I have had no opportunity to report while the seditious Han and Yang were insisting on staying close," Dong Cheng began.
"What have they done?" Emperor Xian asked wearily.
"They harass the courtiers, they pillage nearby places, they hanker for titles, and they take credit for victories won by others!" Dong Cheng explained. "I don't doubt that when Li Jue finds their price, they will hand you back to him."
"We worry about the same eventuality," Emperor Xian admitted.
"There is no way to guarantee Your Majesty safety here now," Dong Cheng continued. "Governor Cao has returned with an army to escort Your Majesty to Yan Province, where the court can reside until Zhang Yang has completed the restoration of the palace and the inner city. Remain here, and either Li Jue or Han Xian could harm Your Majesty."
"...So we must move again," Emperor Xian sighed. "...So be it."
The eunuch attendants sobbed miserably; their bodies were no more than skin and bone, and their numbers had dwindled.
"Han Xian and Yang Feng shall be stripped of their titles," the emperor continued. "Zhang Yang shall be restored as Director of Retainers. Cao Cao and your good self shall be rewarded appropriately when we reach Yan Province."
"I only ask to serve!" Dong Cheng said as he kowtowed.

Dong Cheng hurried out of the city and approached Han Xian and Yang Feng with a force of loyal men.
"You're supposed to be guarding the city, Dong Cheng!" Yang Feng shouted.
"You will surrender, and let Cao Cao pass!" Dong Cheng said.
"On whose authority, little man...? Yours, and your couple o' hundred walking corpses...?" Han Xian growled.
Dong Cheng smirked and held the temporary imperial seal aloft.
Yang Feng's subordinate Xu Huang gasped and said, **"He's sanctioned by His Majesty! We have to surrender!"**
"Not a chance!" Han Xian barked.

"…**Wait,**" Yang Feng said as he looked at Cao Cao's army. "**If the emperor's decided we're not in charge no more, then–**"

"**I'll fight!**" Han Xian bellowed: he threw his right arm upward and charged toward Cao Cao's forces with his bandit infantry.

"**No, no, wait!**" Yang Feng cried. "**Damn! Now *I* have to fight!**"

"**No you don't!**" Xu Huang pleaded. "**We could *join* Cao Cao!**"

"**Not a chance!**" Yang Feng retorted. "**The Butcher of Xu Province will never know my service!**"

Yang Feng followed Han Xian's charge, but they were met with a hail of arrows and an infantry charge. The White Wave Bandits lacked a cavalry, so they were easily scattered by the small cavalry force that Cao Cao possessed. Dong Cheng harried the rear of the bandit force so they could not retreat into Luoyang: both of the bandit commanders were left with the sudden and inescapable understanding that their time as high-ranking officials was over, just like Li Jue and Guo Si before them. The leaders of the individual groups of men within the White Wave confederacy realised that they were no longer going to have their own way, and many retreated from Luoyang immediately.

"**We'll have to flee!**" Han Xian said as he turned his horse.

Yang Feng began his own retreat, but he quickly realised that his friend and subordinate Xu Huang was not following him.

"**What are you doing???**" Yang Feng cried.

Xu Huang and many of his soldiers did not move.

"…**Fool!**" Yang Feng said as he abandoned Xu Huang and fled with the men that had chosen to remain with him.

"No," Xu Huang sighed. "I see the changes."

Xiahou Dun neared Xu Huang and said, "**You surrendering?**"

Xu Huang fell to one knee and said, "**I am.**"

Every one of Xu Huang's small group of men followed his example.

"…Who is this interesting man, Yuanrang…?" Cao Cao said as he stopped his horse alongside Xiahou Dun.

"I dunno," Xiahou Dun replied; he then turned to the surrendered men and shouted, "**Hey you, the leader! Who are you?**"

"**For what it is worth, I am Xu Huang, and I tender my meagre service to Lord Cao Cao so that I can continue to protect His Majesty with all my being,**" Xu Huang replied.

"…**I have gained another champion!**" Cao Cao chuckled as he looked at the brawny Xu Huang. "**Rise, Xu Huang, and get to know your new friends! You are most welcome!**"

Xu Huang stood up, bowed humbly, and smiled. He was glad of the opportunity to do good after his former master's recent misdemeanours, but he could not know how important he would be to Cao Cao's future endeavours.

The White Wave Bandit leaders Han Xian and Yang Feng fled southward, where they were confronted by Liang Gang and his thousand-strong force.

"**We just want to pass!**" Yang Feng protested as most of his vastly reduced following fell to their knees and begged for mercy. "**We were allies! Don't that count for nothing???**"

"It does," Liang Gang replied. "**Bring your followers here, and you can rebuild your 'army'; it's that or die.**"

Han Xian and Yang Feng kowtowed as silent thanks: they did not want to owe Yuan Shu, but they both knew that they had no choice. The two brought their followers into Yu Province and sent word to former colleagues that Yuan Shu would give them shelter.

Emperor Xian had asked to be taken to the gutted palace audience hall in order to see the progress that had been made. As the young emperor walked about – flanked as always by terrified eunuchs that felt his actions were against protocol – Director Zhang Yang and Dong Gongren watched nervously.

"Cao Cao has been invited here to state his intentions," Dong Gongren said quietly.

"A request, if I may, Gongren," Zhang Yang asked.

"You want me to accompany the Son of Heaven to Xuchang and watch Cao Cao," Dong Gongren supposed.

"I know there's probably very little that I can do if the man ends up being untrustworthy, but I would still want the chance to do something," Zhang Yang said.

"I was going to ask your permission to go, so this suits us both," Dong Gongren admitted. "I shall be vigilant, my lord… I promise."

"We are pleased," Emperor Xian said suddenly; he sighed, turned to Director Zhang and said, "We are pleased to be home. Your progress also pleases us."

The former Magistrate of Chang'an, Zhong Yao, entered the hall at that moment and said, "Your Majesty, Cao Cao is here."

Emperor Xian walked to a silk cushion that had been placed where his stolen throne should have been, knelt upon it and said, "We will see Governor Cao Cao at once."

"The officials will be assembled as well, Your Majesty," Zhong Yao said penitently.

Once the remnants of the imperial court were gathered and sat on simple blankets on the scarred floor of the hall, Dong Cheng said, "Your Majesty, Yan Governor Cao Cao approaches."

Cao Cao entered, stopped in front of Emperor Xian, and kowtowed penitently, saying, "I, Cao, live for Your Majesty's divine will."

"You are here to bring us to Xuchang," Emperor Xian prompted.

"I have come here to propose such a move," Cao Cao replied.

"Years ago, you were very familiar with this place," Emperor Xian said as he stared at Cao Cao with conflicting emotions. "You once attended court as a vassal of our ancestor: you were a colonel in his 'Army of the Western Garden'."

"That is so, Your Majesty," Cao Cao replied.

"…You fought alongside Yuan Shao, leader of the Eastern Pass Coalition," the emperor continued. "Was that coalition not committed to our removal…?"

"Your Majesty, I was also part of that coalition!" Zhang Yang said as he kowtowed repeatedly. "But its intention was the removal of Dong Zhuo! Your Majesty will know only my devout loyalty!"

"Director Zhang speaks truthfully!" Cao Cao protested. "We were fighting to restore the glory of the Han Dynasty!"

"…But you do not deny that our removal was part of that 'restoration'…?" Emperor Xian asked pointedly.

"Dong Zhuo committed regicide," Cao Cao replied. "We did not know what part Your Majesty might have had in that, uninformed as we were! Had we been aware of all of the facts, we would have recognised your divine self as mandated! It was only when your unfortunate relative, Governor Liu Yu, refused to take your place

196

that we understood! I am here before you now as your subject, your vassal and your unyielding shield against the evils of the day! Trust me, Your Majesty, and I will bring the court safely to Xuchang and exhaust my energies in exterminating Your Majesty's enemies, wherever they might be!"
The courtiers voiced approval for Cao Cao's rhetoric, and murmurs suggested that the court was mostly happy to follow Governor Cao to Yan Province. Emperor Xian's court continued to suffer a lack of food and basic amenities, and he lost at least one courtier a day to sickness or death: Emperor Xian knew that he had no choice.
"Very well," Emperor Xian declared. "We… will go to Xuchang."

Emperor Xian returned to his makeshift private chambers and dismissed his attendants and consorts with a terse wave of his hand; once he and his empress were alone, he sighed and said, "Nothing is as simple as it should be."
"…We are in more trouble…?" Empress Fu prompted.
"Perhaps, perhaps not," Emperor Xian replied. "It depends on what our latest 'guardian' intends when we get to Yan."
"…Yan…?" Empress Fu exclaimed. "Cao Cao, the-"
"Yes, the one that attacked Xu Province," Emperor Xian chortled. "The White Wave Bandits called him a 'butcher'; he was part of that 'Eastern Pass Coalition' as well, so I don't know what to say."
"…So he is the Chancellor of State now…?" Empress Fu supposed.
Emperor Xian smirked; there had been no appointment to that role as yet, as the last power-holders had promoted themselves to regents and Jia Xu – who operated out of the chancellery, and had chancellor's powers when it suited the regents – was never formally named as such. The 'Chancellor of State' was an old role that Dong Zhuo had revived when he seized power seven years before; it was one of an older set of the 'Three Excellence' – or 'Three Ducal Minister' – titles, along with 'Imperial Counsellor' and 'Grand Commandant'. The 'Chancellor of State' had been replaced by the less-powerful 'Excellency over the Masses', who could be investigated by the 'Excellency of Works' – formerly the 'Imperial Counsellor' role – as part of a proper accountability structure; 'Grand Commandant' likewise evolved into 'Commander-in-Chief' but gradually shifted from a military role to a civilian post. Whoever held those three titles would be the most powerful Han subjects in the land, and it was likely that Cao Cao would either retain the older forms and become 'Chancellor of State' or return to the modern forms and become 'Commander-in-Chief', since that was the most powerful of the three.
"…So we are truly unaware of anything," Empress Fu guessed.
"As always, yes," Emperor Xian replied. "As always, we are left blindly hoping and waiting to see; it must be Heaven's will."

Within days, the entire imperial court would move for the second time in a year and the third time in seven years: it would go to Xuchang, where Cao Cao was master, and none knew what that might lead to.

∗∗∗∗∗∗∗∗∗∗∗∗

36

Word of the emperor's latest movements travelled quickly: Yuan Shao's court in the Ji Provincial capital Yè learned of the relocation to Xuchang while the emperor was still travelling.

"**AAAAAGH! How dare that two-faced knave!**" Yuan Shao cried as he absorbed the news of Cao Cao's actions. "He would 'rescue' the Son of Heaven, uh...?"

Chunyu Qiong coughed nervously and said, "My lord, Cao Cao does wrong today, and he will answer for it."

"...But perhaps it should have been me," Yuan Shao pondered.

Tian Feng shook his head sorrowfully and said, "What's done is done. Now Cao Cao is installing His Majesty in Xuchang: we can only wait and see why he has suddenly decided to do this. Perhaps he only seeks His Majesty's safety, as you do."

"That is true," Yuan Shao agreed. "Mengde... Mengde is an upstanding man, a man that has tirelessly served His Majesty. He has done this because I failed to act; if anything, he has made me look selfish at the very least, if not stupid, and I suppose that I must admit that is the reason why I am angry."

"You're wrong to be angry, or feel stupid or selfish," Chunyu Qiong protested. "You cannot afford to take on the emperor and become a target of accusations of evil hankering! Cao Cao has not given the emperor refuge... he has taken the emperor hostage! And that will become clear, my lord, you mark my words!"

Yuan Shao eyed Chunyu Qiong irritably and said, "You speak ill of my friend, Mister Chunyu. Mengde would not do such a thing... he *could not*."

"It would not be his first offence!" Guo Tu cried.

"Cao Cao massacred the innocents... you insisted that he would not and could not do that until you heard it from the lips of a multitude!" Chunyu Qiong said. "Cao Cao is afflicted by madness... it erodes his thinking! Does he not suffer 'strange headaches', and then do irrational things...?"

"...He has suffered from headaches for much of his life, yes, and he is capable of some strange and irrational behaviour," Yuan Shao admitted. "But he has a swathe of advisers around him now, as I do! This is another man's scheme, not his, I'm sure of it. What do *you* think, Xu Ziyuan...?"

All eyes turned to Xu Yòu, who smiled and said, "It sounds like the work of Xun Wenruo, who was always talking about the fate of the Han. He'd suggest this. We've both known Mengde for years, and this wouldn't be him, no... it's Wenruo."

"Many others suggested it," Xun Chen said angrily. "Your slander against my brother is designed to harm my career, Xu Yòu! Do you do it to save your own...?"

"You have no time for your brother!" Xu Yòu barked. "I meant no slander anyway! You have started this utterly self-serving line of questioning so that you can-!"

"Stop bickering!" Yuan Shao ordered. "Do Cao Cao's advisers bicker as you all do? *No*, and that's why he is always seen to be more decisive... I need to rest."

Chunyu Qiong smiled; he knew that Yuan Shao meant 'get drunk' when he said 'rest', and that he would soon speak no more of the matter at hand.

"We will keep you informed of any important matters," Tian Feng promised. "You go and *rest*, my lord."

"...I shall," Yuan Shao said as he left the audience hall by way of a side door and retreated into his private chambers.

"*Aiee...* muddle-headed *fool*!" Tian Feng muttered as he left the hall by way of the main entrance.

Emperor Xian viewed the relatively simple audience hall in Xuchang with disappointment as Cao Cao led him toward the host seat; the young sovereign sat on the cushion and sighed.

"Your Majesty will be safe here," Cao Cao chuckled nervously.

"We might be safe, but will we be *comfortable...*?" Emperor Xian retorted. "Is this place a seat of resplendent majesty, like Chang'an, and Luoyang, that hungry foreign kings will see and then decide that we are not easy prey for their armies...?"

Cao Cao was unavoidably irritated; he coughed and replied, "Chang'an, Your Majesty, is under the control of enemies of the state at present, else I'd take Your Majesty back there until Luoyang was rebuilt."

"Our ancient western capital is besieged by rebels and barbarians; our eastern capital is in ruins; and now, after a year of tents, we are displaced to a hamlet," Emperor Xian complained. "What ill fortune... what ignominy!"

Cao Cao gritted his teeth, kowtowed, and said, "All will be done to restore order by your loyal subjects, Majesty. But at present, there is no man given the right to wield the sword of truth and bring that order in your stead. Forgive my impertinence, but Your Majesty should appoint a man to lead your forces, and quickly."

The attendants around the emperor eyed Cao Cao with contempt.

"...And which great statesman would you suggest for such a great task...?" Emperor Xian asked cuttingly.

"There are many great men in the land," Cao Cao said as he continued to kowtow. "I could have a list prepared for Your Majesty's inspection."

"...But then, that would be a poor show of gratitude," Emperor Xian decided. "We sometimes forget that there are still kind men... oh, how long we have lived in ruins, wondering what would become of our dynasty, while the warlords bickered and fought amongst themselves for some scrap of land or other, some small measure of improvement to their material fortune... while we, the manifestation of their spiritual fortune, were left to rot. Only you, Governor Cao, have tried to do something to restore order: so it is perhaps fair to say that only you can actually achieve it."

Many of Cao Cao's loyal retainers were forced to stifle anticipatory smiles or cover their mouths with their sleeves.

"I am unworthy!" Cao Cao said as he continued to kowtow.

"You shall be proved worthy," Emperor Xian declared. "We elevate you to Excellency of Works, Acting Commander-in-Chief, Acting Excellency over the Masses, and also the Marquis of Wuping."

"I thank you, Your Majesty!" Cao Cao sobbed as he kowtowed further. "I will strive to find men to fill the posts I occupy so undeservedly!"

"You shall continue to serve tirelessly in the restoration of the land, fighting seditious enemies wherever they appear," Emperor

Xian ordered.

"I shall, Your Majesty!" Cao Cao promised.

"This shall be our provisional capital until order is restored," Emperor Xian said with less enthusiasm.

"And it shall be made into a place befitting your divine presence, Your Majesty!" Cao Cao insisted. "A palace shall be built, a place suitable for the Son of Heaven until Luoyang is restored!"

"…We should certainly hope so, if we do not wish to add foreign powers to our already-considerable list of problems," Emperor Xian sighed quietly. "Now… we have had it said to us that Lü Bu, the villain that once aided our nemesis Dong Zhuo yet assassinated him to free us, still acts as governor but without merit. Some have suggested tolerating him: what is your opinion, Mister Cao…?"

"…Forgive me, but… we should placate him further," Cao Cao replied. "His friend Zhang Yang now rebuilds your capital: Zhang speaks fondly of a man that has 'strayed from the light but found it again'. Liu Bei, the man he took the province from, was ill-equipped to keep it. I have my own history with Lü Bu and his adviser Chen Gong, but I have to admit that Bu is a great warrior. Grant him the title 'General of the Left' and reward him with a noble title, and he will be Your Majesty's sharpest sword: we will need him to defeat Gongsun Zan, Yuan Shu and the other rebels. After that, we will let him be his own judge and act accordingly."

"…It shall be so," Emperor Xian decided. "Is there anything else…?"

When the court session ended, Cao Cao and his most trusted vassals met in the newly-appointed imperial chancellery, Cao's old home having been occupied by the emperor and his entourage.

"*Marquis of Wuping*…?" Xiahou Dun said with confusion.

"It technically removes me from here," Cao Cao replied. "It is designed to tell me that I no longer hold sway in Xuchang; but no matter, since my new role entitles me to a home in the capital. The great work is about to begin!"

"This is a great day!" Xun Wenruo sobbed. "To think that we have saved His Majesty from destitution, and given him much-needed refuge…! Oh, my soul is warmed, my ancestors content that-!"

Cao Cao coughed deliberately, and Xun Wenruo fell silent.

"It's going to cost me a fortune to redecorate Xuchang and remodel it into an imperial capital," Cao Cao suggested. "I sense little real gratitude… which leads me to worry whether His Majesty trusts me."

"Oh, I'm sure that he does!" Xun Wenruo insisted. "As you say, the great work is about to begin… but we must first alert the warlords to your appointments."

"…Yes," Cao Cao murmured. "I can almost hear the congratulatory chants now."

"While we're here, I thought I should say that Yuan Shu has withdrawn his forces from the defence coalition," Xun Wenruo said. "In fact, it looks like Liang Gang aided the White Wave Bandits' retreat. Sad to say, it looks like there will be no voluntary peace."

"I expected that," Cao Cao sighed. "There's only one way to get the peace that you speak of: I must ask His Majesty for edicts to punish the enemies of the state."

"What'll that involve?" Xiahou Dun asked.

"Cousin Dun, it will involve what it always involves: violence, or the threat of violence," Cao Cao replied. "But I keep asking myself: where will I start…?"

"You should start where the worst of the trouble is," Xun Wenruo suggested. "In this case, the real trouble is in the west of the country."

"Isn't Lü Bu a worse problem…?" Xiahou Dun asked.

"No," Cheng Yu insisted. "Bu is a meandering thug: yes, I know, he has our friend-turned-foe Chen Gong advising him, but where can he go? What can he do…? Lord Cao was right to suggest placating his faction with rank; we can have him help us get rid of the rest and then destroy him afterwards."

Xiahou Dun laughed appreciatively.

"I agree, Mister Cheng," Xun Wenruo said. "No, the main problem is the last of Dong Zhuo's loyal vassals. Li Jue and Guo Si are still quite influential in the northwest, as they've absorbed many of their former colleagues' armies into their own and have some support from the anarchistic Qiang tribes and rebels in Liang Province. They should be eliminated as quickly as possible. But to get to them, we must remove Dong Zhuo's adviser Jia Xu and General Zhang Ji's nephew Zhang Xiu from Nan County. That means attacking northern Jing Province, and since Liu Biao has accepted their surrender… it means attacking Liu Biao."

"That's not good at all," Cao Cao murmured. "He's been on our side up to now."

"In the self-serving 'war' between the Yuans of Ru County," Cheng Yu scoffed. "Their time is over, Lord Cao: you're the chancellor now in all but name, and the Yuans are just another pair of pampered nobles, while Liu Biao is a lazy traitor that didn't help his own kin. You're also the Commander-in-Chief, so the imperial army is yours to command… what there is of it, anyway."

"That's quite right," Xun Wenruo said. "We must reassemble the army, organise it, implement *tuntian* at a nationwide level, and begin systematic elimination of the enemies of the state. First Zhang Xiu in Nan County, and if necessary, Liu Biao as well; after him, Li Jue and Guo Si, and their allies Ma Teng, Han Sui and Song Jian; since we'll be in that region, we should demand loyalty from Yi Province governor Liu Zhang and Hanzhong 'governor' Zhang Lu, though we should work toward removing the latter, disgusting cultist parasite that he is. When the west is pacified, we'll turn to the east: first we'll liaise with Liu Bei, and then-"

"We'll do no such thing!" Cao Cao chortled. "He's my enemy!"

"Hear me out," Xun Wenruo insisted. "First we placate him, in order to deal with Lü Bu later: after that, we'll deal with Liu Bei if needs be."

Cao Cao grunted ambiguously.

"Then we have to manage Sun Ce, Yuan Shu, Yuan Shao and Gongsun Zan so far as warlords go, because Yang Governor Liu Yao is a court vassal, and therefore His Majesty's to command," Xun Wenruo continued. "That leaves the various bandit, cultist and rebel factions: but when the warlords are brought under control, they'll be easier to deal with. Once they're gone, Lü Bu and Liu Bei can be dealt with."

"Bringing Yuan Shao 'under control'… the thought disturbs me," Cao Cao admitted. "He's been quietly building power while he's been in Ji Province: he has a lot of Bing Province, all of Ji Province, and most of Qing Province. He commands an army of close to a hundred-thousand trained men… all that stands between him and total control of the north of the country is Gongsun Zan."

"And his own stupidity," Cheng Yu suggested. "That'll be his ruin."

"But he's still my friend… I think," Cao Cao said. "But after this…"

"…Might I suggest that you talk to someone…?" Xun Wenruo asked nervously.

"Am I not talking to many people now…?" Cao Cao chortled. "Who would you have me talk to now…?"

"…I have been waiting for the right time to tell you of a marvellous young man," Xun Wenruo continued. "He is an age ahead of his years, and honest with it. If you spoke to this man, you would feel better."

"…Who is this man…?" Cao Cao asked.

"His family name is Guo, his given name Jia, his style 'Fengxiao'," Xun Wenruo replied. "He-"

"*Guo Jia*?" Xun Gongda exclaimed. "Uncle, you…! …You have got us *Guo Jia*???"

"Who's this 'Guo Jia' for us to be getting so excited?" Xiahou Dun grumbled.

"He is not famous – not yet – but at only twenty-six, he's a match for any man," Xun Wenruo insisted. "If anyone can sway you toward optimism and give you schemes to save the realm, my lord, then it is Guo Fengxiao."

"You want Mengde to take advice from a twenty-six year old nobody?" Xiahou Dun scoffed. "Mengde, he-!"

"I'll speak with this man," Cao Cao said. "Where is he now…?"

"He's in Xuchang: I'll invite him here immediately, if you wish," Xun Wenruo replied.

"Do it," Cao Cao said.

Emperor Xian retired to his personal quarters after the meeting: Empress Fu greeted him with a smile that still lacked any kind of optimism. Emperor Xian dismissed all of the servants with a terse gesture and had Empress Fu sit opposite him so that they could talk privately.

"…I feel like a creature reincarnated," Emperor Xian muttered. "It's the same again: he is another Dong Zhuo, I just know it."

Empress Fu's forced smile disappeared.

"He's Excellency of Works, Commander-in-Chief, a Marquis twice over, and… and yet I don't know what else that man will demand before he is satisfied," Emperor Xian continued. "The greed radiates from him… and the things I hear, about his actions in Xu Province… they do little to distinguish him from the men I have suffered before."

"What will we do…?" Empress Fu asked.

Emperor Xian looked to the sky and laughed desperately.

✷✷✷✷✷✷✷✷✷✷✷✷

37

The slim, frail Guo Jia walked into Cao Cao's private audience chamber later that evening. Cao Cao was immediately disturbed by the youth's wasted appearance and asked, "What sickness ravages you?"
"Vice," Guo Jia replied. "I am my own worst enemy."
Cao Cao smiled: the only other men present were Cao Cao's imposing and sociopathic bodyguard Dian Wei and the adviser Xun Wenruo, and both smiled reflexively when they noted Cao Cao's expression.
"Sit, sit!" Cao Cao urged, and Guo Jia took a seat to the right of Cao Cao.
"Fengxiao, you are even more pallid than before!" Xun Wenruo realised. "If you want to serve Lord Cao, you should learn to resist life's urges a little more!"
"Men die," Guo Jia replied. "Lord Cao, I should like to say a few words, and you can decide on whether you want my help when I have finished."
Cao Cao smirked and said, "Go ahead."
"The Han is at a precipice," Guo Jia began. "Whether it lives or dies as an institution is now entirely down to you. The army is destroyed: it was mostly conscripts and foreign battalions anyway, and poor governance at the highest level is the reason for its erosion, along with the erosion of the state as a whole. The 'Ten Attendants' stole what they could not borrow, and killed who they could not control: your friend Yuan Shao killed the eunuchs, but then Dong Zhuo finished what the eunuchs started, committing regicide and destroying the economy. Liu Yan, late governor of Yi Province, also dealt wounds when he advised provincial semi-autonomy: that has evolved into total autonomy and given rise to the era of the warlord-governor. While it has given you the foothold that you needed to make more of a difference than you could when you fought and lost at Xingyang, it-"
"*Ayah*! What are you saying???" Xun Wenruo cried.
"Let him talk, Wenruo," Cao Cao chuckled. "He's being honest, as you promised."
"...It has also given rise to lesser men, such as Yuan Shu and Gongsun Zan, being able to expand territories that were never theirs to begin with," Guo Jia continued. "If the former minions of Dong Zhuo and their barbarian friends are not dealt with, the west will never know peace; if the warlords are not subjugated, then it is only a matter of time before one of them decides to form their own independent state, or worse yet, declare as an alternative emperor. I hear that one of the fools might be poised to do that as we speak."
"...Yes, I have heard the same," Cao Cao admitted. "Do go on."
"To save the Han, a long and difficult fight must be fought," Guo Jia continued. "Destroy Li Jue, Guo Si, Zhang Xiu and Jia Xu – in the last case, it is regrettable but maybe necessary – to pacify the west, for the rebel armies will respect your strength and accept nominal appointments while we turn to the east. Sun-"
Guo Jia was forced to stop talking in order to cough uncomfortably; Cao Cao winced at every wheeze and awaited the

moment when the younger man would speak again. Xun Wenruo sighed miserably; after a few moments, Guo Jia brought his cough under control and continued.

"…Sun Ce is more of a threat than Yuan Shu, and his faction may perhaps be the most insurmountable threat in the long term if he is not bought with the promise of respect and recognition, for he has in his employ many great warriors and the educated sons of former courtiers.

"Next are the Yuans and Gongsun Zan… Gongsun is a horse trainer in the end, and will not be difficult to beat – after all, Yuan Shao beat him – while the Yuans are stubborn, ignorant and lofty, and therefore impossible to tame with words. Shu will hopefully destroy himself – signs are that he will – while Shao has two choices: obey the will of the sovereign, or fight for power and lose. The various factions that I have not spoken of are tribes, rebels, pirates, bandits and cultists: the cure to those ills is fairness. After them, Liu Bei is a future threat and must be eliminated as quickly as possible once peace is achieved elsewhere; Lü Bu is a dog of war that must be tamed or slain, else he'll cause trouble when there are no more wars to fight. If the people are fed and occupied with rewarding work, the majority will go back to their old lives, and then the job is done! …Or at least, that is my opinion.

"I have said what I wanted to say, Governor Cao… what happens next is up to you. Oh, and, uh… does this city have a reasonable brothel…?"
Xun Wenruo stared at Guo Jia with disbelief; Dian Wei studied the weak and visibly insignificant man with curiosity; Cao Cao smiled and started to laugh.
"…Lord Cao…?" Xun Wenruo prompted.
"You are employed, Guo Fengxiao!" Cao Cao said through laughter. "Today, I have gained another genius!"
Guo Jia coughed painfully and said, "It'll be nice to have something interesting to do. Is there anything that I can help with straight away…?"

Cao Cao and Guo Jia remained in the private room and talked for several hours, after which they parted company as like-minded friends as well as colleagues; of all of the advisers that Cao Cao would acquire, it could be argued that Guo Jia was the most important. But while Cao Cao celebrated an increase in influence and the acquisition of another great mind, the man that lost Guo Jia's service – Yuan Shao – would take no joy from the news coming out of Xuchang.

✳✳✳✳✳✳✳✳✳✳✳✳

38

Yuan Shao's Ji Province court met to receive the first imperial proclamation to come out of the temporary capital of Xuchang. Yuan Shao tensed as it was read aloud; he then took the written version with trembling hands and examined it in anger as his officials waited patiently. Once the imperial messenger was gone, the adviser Pang Ji coughed deliberately and said, "Lord Yuan, you-"

"**WRETCH!**" Yuan Shao shrieked as he threw the proclamation to the floor. "**Cao Cao is a treacherous, self-serving DOG!**"

"I did warn you," Chunyu Qiong said smugly.

"This might not be as it seems," Xu Yòu protested. "Mengde would-"

"Cao Cao is a liar, always has been: did he not slander his own uncle to escape punishment for bad behaviour...?" Yuan Shao said irritably. "This is perfectly in character for a man once described as 'A crafty villain in a time of chaos'! Oh, how gifted you were, Xu Shao, that you saw in a glance what I missed for *thirty years*!"

"My lord and friend, *write to him*, and be honest, if that is what you feel you must do," Xu Yòu suggested. "He might have you appointed to a grand title."

"Like *what*...?" Yuan Shao scoffed. "He has pinched all of the best ones for himself! Commander-in-Chief *and* Excellency of Works...? It is the work of a greedy knave, a wretch, a hankering charlatan of a man!"

"Write to him," Tian Feng agreed. "He will see your anger, and act accordingly, if he has a shred of decency."

"...He'll *regret this*," Yuan Shao muttered as he snatched a quill from its container and dipped it in ink.

"*Aiee*... and now, once again, I am losing a friend," Cao Cao said as he lowered the letter from Yuan Shao to his lap. For a few moments, his chancellery audience hall was silent.

"Tell him to drop dead," Xiahou Dun scoffed. "Where was he when the country needed him...? He failed to take the initiative against Dong Zhuo, he did nothing at all against the Yellow Turbans... and he did nothing for the emperor either. Seriously, Mengde, a less capable or competent man exists where...?"

"He is my *friend*," Cao Cao sighed miserably. "I cannot simply ignore or rebuke him. He did *try* to fight Dong Zhuo, and he had reasons why he did not fight the Yellow Turbans; in fact, now that I know what it is to lose a beloved father, I wonder if I could have fought them if I had been him. As for the emperor, well... if I am honest, I understand his reluctance in that venture quite well myself now. All it has brought me is trouble."

"You do not mean that," Xun Wenruo protested.

"...No, maybe I don't," Cao Cao said sadly. "But I definitely did not mean to offend Benchu, so I must make amends."

"I say nay," Xiahou Dun declared.

"Oh, will you be *sensible* for a moment...?" Cao Cao said desperately. "He has an army of a hundred-thousand, and control of Ji, eastern Bing, southern Qing and more besides! If he were a less noble man, he'd have already declared himself the rightful

holder of the Mandate of Heaven by now!"
Xiahou Dun mumbled angrily and lowered his head.
"Benchu is a good man," Cao Cao insisted. "He is muddled by the message that my latest act sends, and thinks that I have abducted His Majesty. I shall write back to him, offering him the chance to have a title befitting his own service to restoring stability... yes, and I shall do it now."
Guo Jia smirked silently.

Lü Bu's court was the next to receive a proclamation from Xuchang: it was read aloud before a mesmerised audience.
"...**Cao Cao is promoted to Acting Excellency over the Masses and Commander-in-Chief! Lü Bu is officially acknowledged as Governor of Xu Province!**" the messenger said. "**In addition, he is hereby created 'Marquis of Pingtao', and promoted in military rank to 'General of the Left' for his great service to the Han! Yuan Shao is promoted to 'Excellency of Works'! More announcements will follow in due course! That is all!**"
The imperial messenger handed the written declaration to a shuddering Chen Gong and left the audience hall.
"...Congratulations, General," Chen Gui said as he stared at Lü Bu.
"Can it be that I am truly forgiven...?" Lü Bu bleated.
"It... would seem so," Chen Gong replied numbly. "But... am *I*...?"
"*Indeed*, Mister Chen," Wang Kai moaned. "Are *we*...? Are *we*...?"
Xu Si – the third of the trio that had once betrayed Cao Cao – nodded sullenly.
"Your war with Cao Cao was personal," Chen Gui suggested. "This is a state matter, gentlemen, and Cao Cao does the right thing. I admit, I'm impressed: I half expected Cao to order a punitive expedition against Xu Province! He *is* a great statesman after all, when his mind is clear."
"I must reply," Lü Bu said. "I must reply... yes, *now*, expressing my desire to serve the Han! This is my rebirth complete!"
"His, maybe... but what of us???" Wang Kai whispered to Xu Si, who nodded sadly.
"Wait until the general's seal arrives, my lord," Chen Gong urged. "Until I see a seal... I cannot be certain."
Lü Bu saw Chen Gong's concern and stopped smiling: he too would wait until Cao Cao's true intentions were known.

Another messenger from Xuchang entered the court of Yuan Shao and advanced toward the lord with another imperial decree. The officials – including Yuan Shao – kowtowed, and the messenger began his oration.
"**This is an official declaration of the will of the Son of Heaven! The following promotion is granted with immediate effect: Yuan Shao, Governor of Ji Province, is hereby elevated to the position of 'Excellency of Works' and created the Marquis of Yè! Further promotions are indicated in the written document! That is all!**"
The imperial messenger passed the written decree to Tian Feng and confidently withdrew with his mission accomplished; Tian Feng passed the proclamation to Yuan Shao, who was already shaking once again.

"…Well…?" Xu Yòu prompted as Yuan Shao read and re-read the announcement from his old friend's court in Xuchang with increasing rage.

"… … …**Churl!**" Yuan Shao barked. "**Knave! Crafty, shifty creature!**"

"My lord, be specific in your concerns," Tian Feng pleaded. "We can gain nothing, or advise you well, from a tirade of potentially misdirected insults. What is wrong? Your ancestors have been Excellences, and it is only right that-"

"**He *dares* to write to me as 'Acting Excellency over the Masses' – a *Chancellor* in truth, like Dong Zhuo! – promising me the 'grand title' of 'Excellency of Works'!**" Yuan Shao said furiously.

"But… but 'Excellency of Works' is a high title indeed," Xu Yòu protested.

"Higher than his own titles of 'Commander-in-Chief' and 'Acting Excellency over the Masses'…?" Yuan Shao retorted. "Are you to try and tell me that 'Excellency of Works' truly excels *either position*…?"

Chunyu Qiong shook his head theatrically and said, "Such a devious man."

"Quite," Yuan Shao chortled. "The man insults me, and humiliates me! I have always been his better, my family far more exalted than *his*, coming from a line of adoptions by court eunuchs as it does; his father that I so readily mourned despite all my reservations was a court lackey, readily taking bribes and offering them to advance his own status; when he met his end on that road in Xu Province, it was as a man richer than I, perhaps, and how so, I wonder…? Cao Song even served the heinous Dong Zhuo loyally, and even when his son rebelled, he kept his head when my entire family lost theirs for the same crime! Yet for all I've done to support Cao Cao – ignoring the Xu Province massacre, offering him references, mediating with his self-inflicted enemies on his behalf – he shamelessly commits this affront, and ends all bonds of friendship that I ever foolishly assumed there were between us."

"Don't say that, my lord and friend," Xu Yòu pleaded. "Cao Mengde offers you something in all sincerity here, I am sure of it; he has a flawed understanding of the exact level of titles, for many men would be blindly overwhelmed at the prospect of becoming an Excellency. Write back and explain your position, and I believe that he will rectify this apparent mistake."

Yuan Shao's fury reduced him to statue-like immobility; his advisers awaited a response and wondered what it would be.

"…He will have one last chance, because I still harbour childhood memories of friendship," Yuan Shao decided at last. "But I warn you all now: if he does not show me the respect that I deserve, I will hear no dissent from any of you, and I will immediately march upon his puppet capital and rescue the emperor from the wolf's fold with my own two hands."

"We would none of us stop you," Xu Yòu promised. "I'd be as angry as you."

Cao Cao received the latest correspondence from Yuan Shao with a growing feeling of anger and disappointment; he summoned

Xun Wenruo and Guo Jia to a private meeting to discuss what he should do.

"He feels that 'Excellency of Works' is beneath him," Cao Cao scoffed as he threw his old friend's letter to one side.

"That's why we're both here instead of there, my lord," Guo Jia chuckled as he gestured toward Xun Wenruo. "He's not just a little muddle-headed, I fear; he's greedy, jealous, selfish, and, I'm afraid to say, just a mite stupid as well."

Xun Wenruo awaited the response to this frank disassembly of the character of Cao Cao's best friend with trepidation.

"I'm sadly inclined to agree now, Fengxiao," Cao Cao declared. "He implies in his correspondence that our friendship is on the line; how wrong he is, for that friendship ended the moment that he demanded a title the first time. I was offered my titles by His Majesty for saving him! And I deserve them, I think, because I have not just saved His Majesty once; I saved him once by being a voice against the 'Ten', and then again when I fought the Yellow Turbans, and then again when I fought Dong Zhuo! Yuan Shao is all the things you say, Guo Fengxiao, and more."

Xun Wenruo smiled as he turned to Guo Jia and said, "You are already my better, Guo Fengxiao, and serve our lord peerlessly with your concise and frank counsel."

"I say the truth, and that is that," Guo Jia insisted. "But before you lavish me with too much praise, Wenruo, be mindful that my advice on how to remedy this might be enough to undo me."

"...Ah, so we think alike!" Cao Cao chuckled. "You propose that I concede to him the title 'Commander-in-Chief' that he so blatantly hankers for, and request the 'Excellency' title for myself as a 'consolation'."

"Quite so," Guo Jia confirmed. "It will placate the man for long enough for you to build your own forces to a level where you can meet him on the battlefield and stand a chance of defeating him."

"What...!" Xun Wenruo exclaimed.

Cao Cao frowned and said," You really believe that it will come to that, Guo Fengxiao?"

Xun Wenruo stared at Guo Jia nervously as the latter replied by saying, "I do."

"...I'll admit, this is no revelation to me," Cao Cao sighed. "Only you have seen it, or maybe chose to voice it... for that, Fengxiao, I am glad, because I have long desired an opportunity to discuss that terrible thing, should it happen, and how to survive it."

"We two – Wenruo and I – are but two of many men that have left or will leave him as his feeble nature continues to erode his grip," Guo Jia said surely. "Trust me, my lord, in this if nothing else; if you act correctly, Yuan Shao will bait himself into a trap, lose all of his followers to you, and be easily subjugated. From there, he can be, how shall we say, 'rehabilitated', him and his rebellious sibling-cousin Yuan Shu, and turned back toward their destined intention... maintaining the glory of the Han."

Cao Cao nodded and said, "Then I will try and act correctly. I could not bear to lose Benchu, fool that he has become... for like me, he is guilty of making mistakes, as all men do, and at heart, he is worth saving."

Guo Jia smiled, bowed, and replied, "And you shall. But to return to the present, I should say that this appointment should be in the form of a warning."

"...I understand," Cao Cao said. "He must see that I am law on His Majesty's behalf."

"I would go further than that," Guo Jia insisted. "You now have the power to go directly to the emperor, and have edicts drawn up. I suggest that you do that, and-"

"Wait, wait: that would make me look like a villain!" Cao Cao chortled.

"Not so," Guo Jia replied. "Yuan Shao is conquering the north, is he not? He is doing this with imperial sanction, is he...?"

Xun Wenruo smiled and nodded agreeably.

"He conquers the entire north, and then what will he do...?" Guo Jia asked. "I'll tell you; he'll claim that his conquests make him a more worthy commander of the army and chancellor – as a 'deliberate mistake' in his letter accuses *you* of being – and he'll demand the emperor. He'll then use the emperor to issue edicts condemning his enemies, and use those edicts as a basis for systematic invasion and conquest of the whole country. And once he's done, he'll gradually set events in motion that will eventually culminate in his declaration of a new dynasty... the dynasty of the *Yuans*... and the Han will die."

"Yes, that's quite right!" Xun Wenruo realised. "My lord, Fengxiao is right!"

"...*Benchu*...?" Cao Cao said with disbelief. "Yuan Shu, yes, but *Benchu*...?"

"Your friend is not that different to his brother," Guo Jia suggested. "Most of the perceived differences derive from circumstance. If it were Shu that were the elder son and bastard born of a maid, and Shao the younger, legitimate son born of a wife... would Shao simply accept it...?"

"...No," Cao Cao realised. "Taking other matters and words, and applying them contextually... no, he would certainly not. You're right... they are the same."

"Which means that his declaration will not be born of desperation, but hubris," Guo Jia said. "That hubris will come from domination that must not, *cannot* happen."

"But can we be *sure*...?" Cao Cao asked desperately.

"I shall propose one last thing... or rather, I shall ask a question that leads to a point," Guo Jia retorted. "Where is Kong Rong?"

Cao Cao frowned and said, "Kong Rong? Is he imperilled?"

"Yes, and by none other than Yuan Tan, your friend's son," Guo Jia reported. "I know that Kong Rong was recommended as 'Governor of Qing' by Liu Bei, and that you resented his support of Liu Bei, but we can agree that Mister Kong only saw the matter from the outside."

"I do concede that," Cao Cao murmured. "So Kong Rong is good as dead...?"

"His capital is attacked by Tan, and friends seek aid for him," Xun Wenruo said. "But Guo Fengxiao is terribly, painfully right... Yuan Shao allows and orders such awful things, and he must be stopped before he can do worse."

Cao Cao nodded and asked, "What must I do...?"

"To stop him, you must issue an edict condemning his actions before you give him what he wants, so he won't dare ask for any more," Guo Jia suggested.

"...That is sound," Cao Cao conceded. "We'll do that. Now: what about Lü Bu, and the matter of his as-yet-to-be-received General's Seal?"

"Follow the plan we already discussed," Guo Jia suggested. "Apologise for the 'loss'. Make your 'true intentions' known to him. Tell him that we'll see whether we can procure some materials in the meantime, and all will be well."

"...Yuan Shao will soon receive my barbed proclamation," Cao Cao muttered. "I doubt, therefore, that all will be well."

"...How *dare he*."

Yuan Shao lowered the latest imperial edict to his lap and started to sob silently.

"But my lord, you are Commander-in-Chief now!" Xu Yòu protested.

"Only after being soundly *rebuked*!" Yuan Shao said through angry tears. "He has labelled me a hankering *seditionist* with this thing! He has labelled me as the very thing *he is at heart*! And I am *powerless*; I cannot refute this, because he has rewarded me at the same time, and any action I took would then be seen not only as ingratitude, but *treason*! Oh, Cao Cao, you have not just lost me as a friend... you have made an *enemy* of me now."

Yuan Shao and Cao Cao's mutual friend Xu Yòu was dumbstruck.

"...But as you say, you can do nothing," Tian Feng said calmly. "So you must order the generals to halt their preparations for marching on Yan Province before word leaks out."

"... ... ...Do it, Mister Tian, and quickly," Yuan Shao said as he got to his feet. "I... I need a rest."

"B-but what of the titles...?" Xu Yòu asked.

"Cao Cao has no right to give the 'Excellency of Works' title to himself," Yuan Shao replied. "It is mine and therefore mine to give, and I want it known that I cede the title to the elder statesman Chen Yuanfang, citing his 'greater worthiness of the role'. That should rake up some muck between him and Lü Bu, if nothing else."

Xu Yòu nodded slowly.

"As for the 'Commander-in-Chief' and marquisate that my dear friend has seen fit to bestow upon me... he can choke on those as well," Yuan Shao continued. "When I have wreaked divinely-requested retribution upon him, I will receive titles from the Son of Heaven directly: *nothing* that second-rate Wang Mang 'gives me' can ever truly mean a thing."

As Yuan Shao fled his audience hall, the officials looked at one-another and wondered what would happen next. But Yuan Shao knew when he was beaten, and he halted all plans to march on Yan Province. His 'revenge' would take time to prepare for, and it would lead to one of the greatest battles of the age.

✱✱✱✱✱✱✱✱✱✱✱✱

39

A contemplative Cao Cao dismissed all of his officials and sat alone in his chancellery office. He looked at his surroundings with a sense of pride: he had achieved much since those heady days in Luoyang, but there was still a lot to do.

"...So many problems... can this 'Hero of Chaos' solve them all...?" Cao Cao murmured.

And there were many problems to solve. In the far west, the meek Liu Zhang governed Yi Province quietly and endured a border with the theocratic state of Han'ning that was governed by his father's old ally Zhang Lu.

"...Liu Zhang must wait until last," Cao Cao decided. "Zhang Lu... the same."

To the north of Han'ning, the various rebel groups of the northwest still controlled Liang Province: of them all, the three large confederacies led by Han Sui, Ma Teng and Song Jian were the most formidable.

"...To get to them, I must first rid the west of Dong Zhuo's men," Cao Cao said as he inspected a map of that region.

Only three of Dong Zhuo's former generals remained in the west: Li Jue held Chang'an, Guo Si held Mei County, and Zhang Xiu – with the help of Dong Zhuo's mastermind Jia Xu – held Nan County in northern Jing Province. The rest of Jing Province was still governed by Liu Biao and his ally Huang Zu.

"I must fight Nan County, so I must fight Liu Biao," Cao Cao said with regret.

Bing Province lay to the north of Jing and western Central Province: that region was still overrun by Black Mountain Bandits, and now that Zhang Yang was relocated to Henei, only Yuan Shao remained to fight them.

"Yuan Shao will take Bing when he defeats the bandits," Cao Cao muttered.

Yuan Shao had already seized Ji Province, which lay to the east of Bing; he was also on the verge of taking Qing Province, which lay to the east of Ji, from his rival Gongsun Zan.

"...Gongsun Zan... mm," Cao Cao said.

Gongsun Zan was governing the northern Yòu Province without imperial sanction, and he had murdered an imperial relative – the fiercely loyalist Liu Yu – to acquire it: Cao Cao suspected that he might be asked to destroy Gongsun by the young emperor, but he could not be sure. In addition, Yuan Shao's renegade half-brother Shu still had Liu Yu's son as a hostage, and that was troublesome.

"Yuan Shu means no good," Cao Cao supposed.

Many had heard rumours that Yuan Shu harboured ideas about being some sort of independent ruler, while others suggested that he wanted to be emperor: either was unacceptable, and he would have to be reined in eventually. But that was easier said than done: Yuan Shu and his vassals controlled most of Yu Province, most of Yang Province and the Yang-Xu border.

"Xu Province... Lü Bu and Liu Bei..."

Dong Zhuo's former foster son was now appointed governor of Xu Province, but no one intended that to be anything but temporary. Lü Bu was a wild stallion that might never be tamed, and that meant that he was an obstacle to order that would need to be removed: but his vassals were cunning, especially Cao Cao's former adviser Chen Gong. In addition, Liu Bei and his followers were unwilling subordinates to Lü Bu, but their hatred of Cao Cao for his previous actions in Xu Province might mean that they would rather help Bu than the chancellor.

"...The south will have to wait," Cao Cao decided. "Sun Ce and Yuan Shu must be divided somehow, else they will cause me no end of problems. Xu Province must also wait... unfortunately."

Cao Cao knew that the White Wave Bandits that hounded Central Province would return, despite their defeat at his hands. In addition, another large Yellow Turban uprising in Runan Prefecture was threatening the Yu-Yan border: and whether it was being supported by Yuan Shu or not – and it probably was – it had to be dealt with before anything else.

"They... *they* are where I must begin," Cao Cao said with certainty.

"The Yellow Turbans of Runan...?" a voice asked.

Cao Cao looked up and smiled dryly as Guo Jia entered his private chambers, sat opposite his master, coughed uncomfortably, picked up a spare wine dish and gestured toward a wine jug that Cao Cao had by his side.

"*Yes*, Fengxiao," Cao Cao replied as he passed the wine jug to his bold adviser.

"But what of Zhang Yang, who may become troublesome when the palace is rebuilt...?" Guo Jia asked. "And what of Dong Cheng, who fawns on the emperor and expresses open distaste at your 'monopoly on power'...? You have a plan for your enemies *without*, 'Hero of Chaos'... but do you have a plan to deal with your enemies *within*...?"

Cao Cao smiled, raised his wine dish, and said, "One at a time."

****

ACT IV: THE HERO OF CHAOS

40

After 7 years of being a puppet ruler, Emperor Xian of the Han Dynasty enjoyed the feeling – however superficial it might eventually turn out to be – that his authority was recognised and the dynasty was on the road to full restoration.

Emperor Xian had begun a new reign era to mark his arrival in the third imperial capital of his reign. His first capital, Luoyang, had been the second capital of the Han Dynasty as a whole: his second, Chang'an, had been the place where the dynastic founder, Liu Bang, had first presided over the land. Now the 17-year-old Emperor Xian was in Xuchang, the relatively modest capital city of Yan Province: he was unhappy with the arrangement, but he had little choice. His first capital, Luoyang, had been looted and burned to the ground by his infamous former Chancellor of State, Dong Zhuo: his second, Chang'an, was now in the hands of the warlord Li Jue, a man that had, until recently, been holding Emperor Xian as a hostage and ruling as a 'co-regent' with his long-time ally Guo Si. With neither capital being fit to house the sovereign, a temporary solution was found, and despite concerns from many around the country, the governor of Yan Province – the warlord Cao Cao – had escorted the young emperor to the city of Xuchang in his own province, where he was lord and master. Emperor Xian pondered this as he entered the imperial audience hall though a side door at the rear of the room: his courtiers – who were knelt on the floor in rows, awaiting his arrival – immediately kowtowed. At first glance, Emperor Xian could not tell one man from another, as they were identically dressed in familiar brown robes and black caps: but after greater scrutiny he located some familiar figures among the audience, though they were few and far between.

The emperor's journey from Chang'an to Xuchang had been fraught: the procession had been looted by its own escort and then pillaged by the bandit army that rescued them from that escort. Although two rest stops had been made – the first in Henei, a city north of Luoyang that was on the opposite side of the ferocious Yellow River, and the second in Luoyang itself – neither brought peace nor comfort. Henei was under constant attack by Li Jue's mercenaries, and Luoyang was a ruin: during the stay in the latter, the travellers were forced to live in tents and eat whatever they could find: many of Emperor Xian's most trustworthy vassals – eunuch attendants, ladies and maids, courtiers, soldiers and officers alike – had perished before or during that journey, so many of the men in his new court were Cao Cao's followers, and their true loyalties could not be easily ascertained.

The emperor's saviour Cao Cao was unsurprisingly present at the gathering: he was now 'Excellency of Works', and 'Acting Excellency over the Masses', and in addition to that he was 'Acting Commander-in-Chief', since the holder of that position – the nobleman Yuan Shao – had refused to play a part in what he described as another attempt to take the emperor hostage. Cao Cao, in his acting capacity as all three of the 'Three Excellencies', would therefore open proceedings once the sovereign was seated. Cao Cao's face betrayed bitterness derived not only from the years of war and loss, but also the vast financial burden that the imperial retinue had become to him: Emperor Xian could almost taste the anger in Cao Cao's expression, but he hid his fear as he had always done. The elaborate red robes that the emperor wore were a slight impediment to his movement: he shuffled forward on his socked feet and took his seat facing the rows of penitent courtiers. Xian stifled an urge to swat away the row of beads that dangled from his hat and partially obscured his face, but ritual was ritual, no matter how pointless it all seemed to him now. One by one, the courtiers sat up, but few dared to look upon their emperor: one man that did without fear – Excellency Cao Cao – got to his feet, moved to the emperor's side and prepared to address the sea of men before him.

"Your Majesty, and gentlemen of the court: I have requested this meeting to discuss the immediate future," Cao Cao began. "The land has suffered enough at the hands of rebels. In my short life, I have seen far too much harm done to my land and its divine sovereigns... I think that we all ache for a time of peace, and it may be at hand at last."

Many of the officials murmured cynically.

"I can sense the question on the tip of every wise tongue: where is this peace?" Cao Cao continued. "Thousands of Yellow Turbans wreak havoc in Runan Prefecture to the west of us, the million-strong Black Mountain Bandits sow terror in Bing and Ji Provinces to the far north, rebel gangs and barbarians now control Liang Province, a heretic rules Hanzhong, and the warlords that operate without remit or restraint are unacceptable! 'Where is this impending peace?' you ask, for you have not seen the signs of it."

The small number of Han officials that had followed the emperor murmured uneasily: the rest – who were Yan Province officials and therefore sympathetic to Cao Cao – silently wondered where Cao Cao's speech was leading.

"The White Wave Bandits are in hiding, but when they resurface, they will be dealt with," Cao Cao continued. "The Black Mountain Bandits are fewer in number these days, primarily because of the heroic efforts of Commander-in-Chief Yuan Shao, whose absence today is... unfortunate. I agree with the many petitions that I have received about the Yellow Turbans in Runan: they are a menace, and I intend to make an announcement about them. The rebels in Liang are an inherited disaster, but one that can be managed once Li Jue and Guo Si are eliminated; in fact, I have formulated a plan to deal with them, although some patience will be required. Those of you that recall the Liang Province Rebellion will know that the situation flummoxed some of our greatest forebears, such as Fu Xie and Huangfu Song, and they did not have Li Jue, Guo Si and the other remnants of Dong Zhuo's evil to deal with. But rest assured that I have a plan for them, once others are dealt with."

Cao Cao's loyalists murmured agreeably.

"Might I have my say...?" a wizened scholar asked.

"...Indeed you may, Zheng Xuan!" Cao Cao chuckled. "A man that has lived for seventy years has much to contribute. I am in awe of your teacher, Ma Rong, and have followed your own teachings: you are a welcome re-addition to the court after being forced to hide for so long, and you may be as frank as you like."

"You have failed to address the warlords," Zheng Xuan said. "Yuan

Shao and Yuan Shu continue to bicker like princes over a mere clan chieftainship; the first of those men, Yuan Shao, is also guilty of consolidating the north under his own banner without imperial sanction, yet all that has been offered is a friendly rebuke and some promotions; the other Yuan is trying to seize the south with his pirate friends, yet little is now being done to stop him anymore, and one could wonder why; Gongsun Zan is, sadly, transformed from the best of youths that served under my friend Lu Zhi into a disgrace of a man that murders imperial relatives and leads armies to attack the people like a Wuhuan chieftain; Jing Governor Liu Biao failed to answer the Son of Heaven's calls for aid despite being one of the closest men to him, and now he harbours Zhang Xiu and Jia Xu, two villains that deserve death for their roles in Dong Zhuo's regime; Li Jue and Guo Si are just sitting there, leaving the serving men of the land confused and wondering who truly leads the army; and perhaps worst of all, Lü Bu has overthrown an imperial relative, Liu Bei, and seized Xu Province, yet for some bizarre reason this court sees fit to treat Bu – who is, if I recall, Dong Zhuo's foster son, bodyguard and senior general, and the man that looted the imperial tombs – as the legitimate successor to the governorship! I have, I think, been frank; what is your response…?"

The tirade provoked a number of responses: Emperor Xian stared at Cao Cao and awaited a response to the valid points that had been made; the Han loyalists started to heckle Cao Cao; some of Cao Cao's allies started to heckle Zheng Xuan; Cao Cao himself smiled and relished the challenge.

"**Silence, please!**" Cao Cao barked. When the noise finally subsided, he laughed and said, "I shall try my best to explain, Elder Zheng. The Yuans are old family friends, but the lack of action is not betrayal of Confucian values. As I have already said, there is a need for patience. Has anyone before me just done a dance or chanted a mantra, and then found that all of the problems in the land have just vanished…? I think not. It may be fair to say that this court faces the largest number of problems ever faced at once, and it will take many heroes to solve them all. What I propose is a one-at-a-time solution, starting with problems that can ease pressure on resources and make it easier to deal with others. I think you know what I mean."

Zheng Xuan – amongst others – nodded silently.

"The Yuans will be last, if they have not ended their feud before I have ended my campaign," Cao Cao continued. "Gongsun Zan will destroy himself; Li Jue and Guo Si must wait until the bandits and eastern rebels are quelled; must I go on…?"

"…No," Zheng Xuan said quietly. "You've proved that you have considered everything, Excellency Cao, and that is all that anyone should be asking for in such troubled times."

"I should hope so," Cao Cao replied. "First, we must crush the last faction of Yellow Turbans. That will dishearten the derived elements – such as the remnants of the White Wave Bandits – and make it easier to deal with them. I will lead the army into Runan and destroy the heretics personally, if His Majesty so permits."

Emperor Xian smiled slightly and said, "We do."

Cao Cao kowtowed to his sovereign and said, "I'll march soon. The pacification of Runan is urgent, since they are on Yan's southern border and now harass Yingchuan. When they are destroyed, I shall call the court to discuss which of our long-term problems will be dealt with next, if Your Majesty permits."

Emperor Xian was suddenly disturbed by Cao Cao's choice of words: his smile disappeared, and he said, "We do... *Excellency*."

Cao Cao noted the emperor's tone and shuddered.

Cao Cao returned to his chancellery office after the court session and said to his assembled advisers, "It is clear that His Majesty still doesn't trust me."

The sickly Guo Jia – who was as frail as a man three times his 26 years of age – smiled and asked, "Can you blame him? He's known nothing but intrigue."

"You are both worrying too much!" Xun Wenruo protested. "His Majesty meant nothing by his tone! You have permission to march, so let's march!"

"But what about Zheng Xuan and those of a like mind...?" Cao Cao said. "His input was unexpected and, if I am honest, unwanted, Wenruo. I almost regret that he chose to return to the court."

"He's crotchety, but certainly no worse than our own Cheng Yu," Xun Wenruo replied. "Had he wanted to, he could have said things that were far more damaging. He remembers your efforts to save the 'partisans', as many others do, and he respects you. To men like him that once signed a young Cai Yong's petition to create the Xiping Stones, seeing you where you are now is seeing history play out."

"...I suppose so!" Cao Cao said.

"He went on too long about Lü Bu," Cheng Yu grumbled. "Are we supposed to drop everything, ignore the 'disturbing threat' of the Yellow Turbans in Runan that he himself raised as an issue with me in private correspondence, and go and rescue Liu Bei?"

"Even if I agreed with him, I could not," Cao Cao replied. "The very notion of confronting Bu reminds me of a genuine problem that we must face sooner or later: the people of Xu Province hate me! How long will it take them to understand that any third expedition I make into the place will not be to avenge my father's death, mm...? They'll see my banners, and every last peasant will take up arms at Lü Bu's side to defend themselves from 'The Butcher of Xu Province'! I'm the man that dammed the Si River with the corpses of the innocent, Wenruo! I...! I...!"

Cao Cao's eyes were filled with tears: he then fell silent and lowered his head.

"*Aiee...* if only you were wrong about the people of Xu," Xun Wenruo lamented.

Cheng Yu laughed and said, "Does this matter? We did what we did. Excellency Cao, Mister Xun, and everyone else... stop talking about Xu Province for now. We will deal with that miserable place as and when we must."

Cao Cao sighed and said, "Mister Cheng Yu's honesty is as well-timed as ever. But I expected Guo Fengxiao to speak first."

"I was busy thinking," Guo Jia said. "Mister Cheng is quite right: Xu must wait, and Lü Bu must wait... although Bu may not wait if he doesn't get his seal for the office of 'General of the Left' soon. If it is true that he only helped Liu Bei because Yuan Shu was late in delivering promised supplies, then it might be said that if we

delay too long, the fickle 'Man among men' may let his distrust –
or Chen Gong – dictate his actions and turn back to Yuan Shu."
"I've written to him," Cao Cao replied. "He'll understand. No, the
focus now isn't my old friend Yuan Shao's posturing, Yuan Shu's
ambitions, Gongsun Zan's feral rampaging, Lü Bu's land-grabbing
or anything else: Runan is on our border, and if the Yellow
Turbans break Yingchuan, we'll be in trouble. My only concern,
though, is… is what Yuan Shao will do when I march to Yu."
Guo Jia noted Cao Cao's pained expression and said, "It still
harms your soul to contemplate war with a man that you once
saw as a brother of sorts, my lord."
"I still want to call him 'Benchu' as I always have, but those days
are gone," Cao Cao lamented. "How… sad."
Xun Wenruo hummed thoughtfully.
"Yes… how sad," Cao Cao continued. "Now he's just another
hankering warlord… and his letters become ever-more aggressive.
He refuses all titles and roles because they aren't grand enough
for him, or just to spite me. Hah: roles that were good enough for
his wealthy, influential ancestors are not good enough! How far
we've come, gentlemen, from the man that once sat at tables and
cried rivers for the disadvantaged! How far we've come, friends,
from the saviour of the 'partisans' and the slayer of the corrupt
'Ten'! Now he hankers for power, just like the men he once
reviled… it's sad and pathetic."
"But if we might return this conversation to the relevant issues,
and say what needs to be said…?" Guo Jia said. "You fear that he
will attack Yan Province while you're in Yu Province fighting the
Yellow Turbans. So do I. But he is still fighting the Black Mountain
Bandits, and their recent attack on his capital killed his City
Administrator and left him needing to assert authority. He'll be in
Bing Province for the next couple of months at least."
Cao Cao nodded slowly and asked, "So I am free to advance…?"
"If you leave a trustworthy vassal like Cao Ren to guard the
capital and your northern border, then you may advance freely,"
Guo Jia replied.
"Very true," Cheng Yu said.
"You should only use the generals that prefer attacking to
defending," Xun Wenruo suggested. "The rest can stay here."
"…Yu Jin will be my vanguard," Cao Cao decided. "Yue Jin and
Xiahou Dun should go too… yes… Cao Ren can guard the capital…
and once Yingchuan is relieved, Xiahou Yuan can remain there."
"And I shall return to Dong Prefecture until you are victorious,"
Cheng Yu said. "That way, your northern and eastern borders are
more secure."
"But what of my southeast border…?" Cao Cao fretted. "What
about Yuan Shu?"
"He'll go after Lü Bu first, and besides, most of his army is tied up
in the south," Guo Jia replied. "You're safe to march, my lord."
Cao Cao smiled, laughed and said, "Then I shall!"

****

41

The court-appointed governor of Xu Province, Lü Bu, sent messengers to all of the men that he thought to be his subordinates: one of those men was Liu Bei, his reluctant guardian of Xiaopei; another was Zang Ba, the self-appointed ruler of the city of Kaiyang; yet another was Xiao Jian, a man appointed as Administrator of Langya Prefecture in southeast Qing Province by Gongsun Zan and Tao Qian, but whose base was in Ju City to the immediate east of Xiapi.
"This man's letter is a thinly-disguised demand for tribute," Xiao Jian complained to his small retinue of officials. "This uncultured ruffian should not possess such authority in Xu, but regardless, I answer to another, not to him."
One adviser said, "Lord Xiao, what do you intend to do…?"
"My prefecture is under attack from bandits and heretics; what do I have to spare for this greedy oaf in Xiapi…?" Xiao Jian scoffed. "He'll get no proper response from me."
The officials murmured nervously; Lü Bu's temper was as infamous as the man himself, and many feared the reaction to the response.

"Calm down!" the adviser Chen Gong pleaded as Lü Bu threw his desk to one side and roared like a wounded animal; the other courtiers were understandably fearful.
"The man wonders why you approached him!" the officer-turned-courtier Gao Shun said. "I mean that in the sense that-"
"**AAAAGH! I should have known that you would volunteer another of your unwanted opinions, you smug fool!**" Lü Bu shrieked as he turned his anger against the powerless Gao Shun. "**Even when you are stripped of your rank, you cannot stop your mouth moving and your tongue wagging! Ju is practically walking distance away from here, moron! What do you mean 'The man wonders why I approached him'…?**"
Gao Shun did not respond.
"…Why could you have not been silent in the first place, mm, and saved us your idiotic heckling?" Lü Bu taunted.
"All this fuss over a fantasising pedant," the nobleman Chen Gui scoffed. "What for?"
Lü Bu turned to face Chen Gui and silently awaited an elaboration.
"I know Xiao Jian: he's a native of Donghai Prefecture, and has attended this court in the days before Liu Bei as a vassal of Tao Qian," Chen Gui continued. "He looks at maps and sees drawn boundary lines and names of places, not spheres of influence, despite knowing the world to be run on them and being a victim of it. Of course he reacted this way, Lord Lü: yes, he is in Ju, but his pedant heart is in his seat in *Langya*, the prefectural seat awarded to him by Tao Qian and Gongsun Zan that he has never been able to truly occupy!"
Lü Bu frowned.
"And in his meaningless capacity as Gongsun Zan's chosen Administrator of Langya – therefore meaning that in his own mind he answers to Gongsun's chosen Inspector of *Qing* Province, Tian Kai, and not you – he wondered why you approached him, my

lord," Gao Shun said calmly.

"But he's in *Ju*, which is *here*, in *Donghai*, in *Xu* Province!" Lü Bu countered.

"Yes, because he cannot be in Yangdu, or some other place to the north, because the region is overrun with Mount Tai Bandits and militarily controlled by Yuan Tan," Chen Gui noted. "He 'administrates' places like Kaiyang that have dubious status, but even they are off-limits to him as they are the playground of the Mount Tai Bandits, who treat it as they do the rest of Langya. Think of it as the same as 'Liu Bei, Inspector of Yu', who is master of nothing and lives in a tent in Xiaopei."

Lü Bu smirked and grunted ambiguously.

"Southern Langya has long been fought for, contested... is it part of Qing or part of Xu...? ...I don't know, it depends," Chen Gui continued. "Tao Qian said it was part of Xu, the various Inspectors of Qing, Gongsun Zan and Yuan Shao all say it is part of Qing, though they differ as to why. To the people of Langya, it is Langya, and they'd probably say that they don't care what province they belong to, so long as they have peace."

"...What is your point...?" Lü Bu asked bemusedly.

"The point," Chen Gui replied, "is that Xiao Jian will get no peace for 'his people' as part of Qing Province; he's not even safe to be there himself, really, which reinforces that point. Yes, Gongsun Zan appointed Tian Kai as Inspector of Qing, but he's never been able to advance as far as Langya, and the Chang'an court appointed Kong Rong, *supposedly*, and Kong Rong is inept: he is so inept, my lord, that no one is entirely sure if he is truly the provincial governor or if he is still the Chancellor of Beihai, including Kong Rong himself. It should be noted that Kong Rong couldn't even defend Beihai, and needed help from Taishi Ci; he is descended from Confucius, *supposedly*, but... I wonder what was passed down."

Lü Bu laughed tersely and said, "Go on."

"Xiao Jian should be made to understand that Langya's best interests lie with an allegiance to *you*, not the provincial government of Qing, which has always been corrupt and weak, or to Tian Kai, who will never get past Yuan Tan," Chen Gui continued. "Even Cao Cao could not tame Ji'nan when the 'Ten' put him there. Mount Tai is little more than a namesake for a bandit army that grows by the day in reaction to government incompetence. If Xiao Jian does not find better friends, his appointed prefecture – which, amusingly enough, is somewhere that he may never have even been to or seen – will be devoured by the criminal gangs, and the whole of Langya will be like Kaiyang."

"...So I should write back to this strange, demented daydreamer and remind him that I am strong and he is weak, that Tian Kai is a long way away while I am within marching distance, and that ignoring me isn't a good idea," Lü Bu prompted.

"...I'd say that you should promote better communication, but refrain from threats," Chen Gui replied. "He'll deduce any threats by himself, once he has a moment to think about it."

"He's an avid student of the classics, and loves references to them: he considers gratuitous references and homages to classic texts as some sort of sign of intelligence, for some reason," Chen

Deng volunteered. "Include some classical references in your next communication with him, and he'll change his opinion of you and understand his predicament in one stroke."
"Knowing them vaguely myself, I know the very situation to refer to," Lü Bu replied.

Lü Bu's letter left Xiapi and reached Ju City within days; Administrator Xiao Jian – who suspected potentially humbling content – dismissed his small court, retreated to his private audience room and asked Registrar Ji Jian to read it aloud.
"…Well…?" Xiao Jian prompted after a few silent minutes.
"My lord, I, uh… I think this letter is better read," Ji Jian said nervously.
"Give it here," Xiao Jian sighed; he took the cloth letter from the nervous registrar and started to read.

> "Mister Xiao Jian,
>
> You know me.
>
> Many years ago now, the warlords of the east rose up as one against Dong Zhuo, with whom I had an unfortunate – and thankfully short – alliance that was far from convenient. Dong Zhuo defeated the Eastern Pass Coalition and went west, to Chang'an. I followed, hoping to remain close to His Majesty. When the time was right I allied with Director Wang Yun and killed Dong Zhuo, but I was forced to retreat because I lacked the support to finish what I had started, and Wang Yun died thereafter, having achieved little.
>
> I went east, back to where it had begun, where I hoped to find the able men and willing leaders to aid my quest to rescue and restore His Majesty; instead I found warlords feuding with each other over petty matters, and not one that I approached put the state beyond their own ambitions.
>
> I am from Wuyuan, which is, as you know, beyond the Great Wall some five-thousand li away from Xu Province, where we both of us now are. I have therefore travelled far, but I did not come here to this place to fight for it. Ju City and Xiapi City are not too far from each other, so it is very easy to upkeep good communications between them. Why, then, has this not been the case?
>
> You, Mister Xiao, Administrator of Langya in Qing Province, who resides in Ju City in Donghai Prefecture in Xu Province – this province, and also my province – act as though you are an emperor – but of little more than a prefecture – or a king – but of little more than a county! How is it that a man in your position can show such disrespect?

I hear that you are well read. Very well: consider this. When Yue Yi of old times attacked the Qi State, he conquered in excess of seventy cities in Qi, but he could not take Ju or Jimo because of Tian Dan.

I know that I am not Yue Yi. But then, you are not Tian Dan.

You can and should seek the advice of wiser men with regard to this letter if you do not quite understand it.

I look forward to your swift response.

General of the Left Lü Bu
Marquis of Pingtao
Governor of Xu Province"

"...Aiee... *aiee*...! I must reply to this at once!" Xiao Jian cried. "Don't just sit there, fool: get a pen, and paper, and be ready to write what I say!"
"Yes, my lord," Ji Jian replied wearily.

Langya Administrator Xiao Jian sent Lü Bu 5 horses and an ingratiating letter as a response. In exchange, Lü Bu promised that he would provide any support that Xiao Jian needed in his battles with the Mount Tai Bandits in the future.

****

42

To the southwest of Xu Province, a disaffected official had made an important decision; the thin and frail Liu Fu, a survivor of the chaos in Lujiang Prefecture in Yang Province, prepared to make the journey north to Yan Province and the new seat of imperial power in Xuchang.
"...Mister Liu."
Liu Fu halted his preparations and turned to his front door; a nervous servant had allowed Qin Yi, a high-ranking officer in Yuan Shu's army, to enter the house.
"Ah! General Qin," Liu Fu said fearlessly. "Do come in."
Qin Yi bowed slightly and asked, "Are you still set on going north...?"
"I am," Liu Fu replied. "And have you had time to consider what I have discussed with you...?"
"I have," Qin Yi confirmed. "I have also spoken with General Qi Ji, and he also desires an opportunity to serve the Son of Heaven."
"...And you are both sure...?" Liu Fu prompted. "After all, your lord Yuan Shu is-"
"Yuan Shu is, as you have made us see, a vile hankerer, a would-be pretender," Qin Yi interrupted. "Mister Liu, he intends only harm, and we desire stability. We helped Yuan Shu to take Lujiang from Administrator Lu Kang because we were told that he was a rebel; little did we know that our lord was the true rebel, and now we want to make amends."
The servant looked at Liu Fu and frowned purposefully.
"...Very good," Liu Fu said. "General, I shall be ready to leave Lujiang within the next two days. Have your men ready, for we might have to fight our way out of Lujiang; my very distant relatives, Administrator Liu Xun and his adviser Liu Yè, are unlikely to take news of your departure well."
"None shall prevent our returning to the light," Qin Yi replied.

Liu Fu, Qin Yi, Qi Ji and a small army of Yuan Shu's disaffected former followers departed Lujiang within the next two days and began the journey northward to Xuchang City in Yan Province, and their emperor. When Liu Fu next returned to Lujiang, it would be to reform the entire administration and begin construction of one of the most famous fortresses of the age.

The ruler of the bandit city of Kaiyang, Zang Ba, finally received his demand for tribute from Lü Bu and reacted to it with unsurprising irreverence.
"We must all kneel, 'criminal' friends, to Lü Bu, the Marquis of Pingtao!" Zang Ba cackled as he waved Lü Bu's letter aloft.
"We must kneel, 'lawless' friends, to General of the Left Lü Bu, the lord of Xu Province!"
The assembled senior bandits laughed along with their leader.
"I say 'How dare he?' This man is worse than any of us!" Zang Ba said as his amusement turned to anger. **"He killed the Son of Heaven! He helped Dong Zhuo! Never in all that time did he or the regents that followed him get us a pardon or look our way! Now here he is, demanding tribute!"**

Many of the bandits began a chorus of condemnations that were aimed at Lü Bu.

"**What do you want to do…?**" the bandit chieftain Yin Li asked.

"**Oh, don't worry, I'm not stupid enough to fight Bu,**" Zang Ba chortled. "**But I want to teach him a lesson. To the east of Xiapi is Ju City, where that little puffed-up coward Xiao Jian, 'Administrator of Langya', is hiding.**"

The bandit Sun Guan smiled and asked, "**You planning on robbing him, old mate?**"

"**I am, Zhongtai,**" Zang Ba replied. "**That little mouse has been gathering funds to build a militia to take Kaiyang from us, so I hear; well, that money'll do us nicely for any future fights that we need to have with him and Bu, won't it?**"

"**Use his own money to fight him! I like it!**" the bandit Wu Dun cackled. "**When do we leave?**"

"**In a week, I hope, but we'll need to be sneaky,**" Zang Ba replied. "**Bu'll try and take Ju City, so we have to have it and be in there before he reacts; that place is strong enough to keep him out, and he'll look like the fool that he is. If the plan works, it won't matter if he wins, though, 'cause we'll have cleared the treasury and moved it all to Kaiyang!**"

The bandits chattered and gesticulated excitedly.

"**…Ju is pretty close to Xiapi, boss,**" the bandit Chang Xi noted. "**We won't have much time.**"

"**Against a useless coward like Xiao Jian, we won't need the time,**" Zang Ba promised. "**Get yourselves ready, friends: this'll be fun!**"

****

43

Excellency Cao Cao was elated when he heard that Wang Lang – a former senior subordinate of Xu Governor Tao Qian – was on his way to his home village and early retirement.

"Do you hope to assassinate him...?" Xun Gongda asked.

"Mm...? Assassinate who...?" Cao Cao said as he pored over a letter from another man. "...Wang Lang...? No, no. I got my prize general Yu Jin from that man, and he abandoned the villain Tao Qian, so he is not my enemy."

"So you hope to recruit him, then...?" Guo Jia said with a smile.

"...Mm...? ...Oh, uh... yes, yes I do, Fengxiao," Cao Cao replied.

"You are lost in that letter, Mengde," Xiahou Dun chuckled. "Is it a naughty love poem from your Lady Bian...?"

Cao Cao laughed, lowered the letter and said, "No! It is from a Mister Liu Fu in Lujiang, in Yang Province."

"...Not a name that carries much weight," Cheng Yu suggested.

"Liu Fu, style 'Yuanying', is a distant imperial relative that was born in Xiang County, in Pei Prefecture," Cao Cao explained. "I knew him as a youth: he is very smart, a truly nice fellow with some good ideas for social development. He fled Pei when Dong Zhuo was causing chaos and the resurgent Yellow Turbans were causing trouble in the region. He ended up in Lujiang, and... well..."

"He wants to come to Xuchang," Guo Jia guessed.

"Better than that, Fengxiao!" Cao Cao replied. "He not only comes here as we speak, but he brings with him two – *two*! – of Yuan Shu's generals: a 'Qi Ji' and a 'Qin Yi', and all of their men!"

"...Mediocrities," Cheng Yu grumbled. "Ji Ling, or Liang Gang, perhaps, would interest me, but not two 'generals' promoted by that fool Liu Xun that-"

"I knew Liu Xun as well, Mister Cheng," Cao Cao chuckled. "He's lofty, for sure, and perhaps not very talented... certainly not as talented as Liu Fu, anyway. But to get back to your point, I care little whether these generals are future heroes; they are defectors from Yuan Shu's cause, and that will harm him. Furthermore, they surrender to the Han, not to me or to Yuan Shao, which is ideal."

"It stops Yuan Shao whinging about it," Guo Jia said.

"I wouldn't care if he did," Cao Cao replied. "No... Liu Fu is an excellent addition to the imperial court... an excellent addition!"

"And Wang Lang...?" Guo Jia prompted.

"I want that clever and resourceful man in my service, but getting him will be difficult," Cao Cao admitted. "I-"

"*Resourceful*...?" Cheng Yu scoffed. "Isn't it true that he allied with bandits and failed to defeat Sun Ce's lesser officers, and that his incompetence cost the Zhou brothers of Kuaiji their lives...? Isn't it true that his adviser Xu Jing, brother of the famed appraiser Xu Shao, fled to the barbarian territories rather than serve him any longer...?"

"*One* of those Zhou brothers, maybe, and they were fools," Xun Wenruo suggested. "Didn't Zhou Renming leave our lord's service, he was so short-sighted...? And didn't they lose every place that they were given to guard...?"

"Mister Cheng is right to say that Wang Lang is a poor strategist when the options are few," Cao Cao said. "But he is a man of the pen primarily, and in that he is very highly skilled. I am trying to rebuild the court, gentlemen, and I'll need to look far and wide: Wang Yun, Zheng Tai, Cai Yong, Ma Midi, Shisun Rui… all gone. But young prodigies like Wang Can, old luminaries like Chen Yuanfang, and men like the eight Simas of Li County, Liu Fu and Wang Lang are just what we need to replace the fallen ones."

"And Jia Xu…?" Guo Jia chuckled.

"*Aiee*… Dong Zhuo's brain trust…? He should be put to death a thousand times, not given a good job!" Xun Gongda heckled.

"…We must be prepared to consider anything and everything," Cao Cao said.

A messenger entered the private audience room; Xun Wenruo took the messenger's wooden letter tube and dismissed him with a polite wave of his hand and a smile.

"More…?" Cao Cao chuckled. "My, this is a busy day!"

"A moment," Xun Wenruo pleaded as he removed two cloth letters from the tube and unfurled it. "This is sent urgently from Xue Ti, in Dong Prefec-"

Cao Cao frowned and said, "Is the place in danger?"

"No, Lord Cao," Xun Wenruo replied as he studied the first letter. "The first, it is… old, relatively speaking, and is originally from Qing Province… from Governor Kong Rong."

"The chaos around the Qing-Yan border has temporarily subsided due to a minor outbreak of something, so messages can get through more easily," Cheng Yu suggested. "That must be the cause of the delay. What does the descendant of the great philosopher have to say, then…?"

"He is under attack," Xun Wenruo explained.

"Not again!" Xiahou Dun cackled. "Yellow Turbans again, I suppose. Why doesn't he beg help from-?"

"Last time, he got help from his friend Liu Bei, and the lone wolf Taishi Ci… or so I hear from some, since others say that it was Bei's general Guan Yu that delivered Beihai from the Yellow Turbans," Xun Gongda said. "Isn't that so, Uncle…?"

"…Yes, there are a few conflicting accounts of the event," Xun Wenruo replied. "When Kong Rong gets here, we'll have to have him tell us which is true."

"…'When he gets here'…?" Cao Cao prompted. "What nonsense! How can he abandon his post and come here amid such-"

"He's got little choice, Excellency," Xun Wenruo said. "The 'Mount Tai Bandits' – as Zang Ba of Kaiyang and his merry friends have now appeared to rename themselves – are tearing Mount Tai, Langya and Beihai Prefectures apart, and Yuan Tan, Tian Kai, the Yellow Turbans, unaffiliated bandits, rebels, criminals and waterway pirates are wrecking whatever they have not touched. Eastern Qing is completely lost, and-"

"He has men to aid him," Cao Cao scoffed. "And wouldn't Yuan Tan be likely to aid him in the event of-?"

"Yuan Tan… is the one that has attacked Kong Rong," Xun Wenruo said nervously.

"…Again…?" Guo Jia murmured. "And after being warned…?"

Cao Cao scowled.

"…Don't get one of your headaches and start screaming and throwing things, Mengde," Xiahou Dun pleaded.

"Give me the letters," Cao Cao growled.

Xun Wenruo laughed nervously as he passed Cao Cao the correspondence and said, "The second letter is from Xue Ti, and it says that the situation has escalated since Governor Kong sent that-"

Cao Cao exhaled fiercely and repeatedly as he read and re-read Kong Rong's letter.

"So Governor Kong is now Yuan Tan's prisoner, then," Guo Jia supposed.

Xun Wenruo smiled sadly and replied, "He is."

"So do we have to abandon our plan to go west and fight the Runan Turbans, then...?" Xiahou Dun asked. "Are we going east to fight Yuan Tan and Zang Ba?"

"...No," Cao Cao replied angrily. "No, Yuanrang, we're still going to focus our efforts on those worthless heretics. Runan is next to us, and Eastern Qing is not; I do not desire a return to Ji'nan right now, where I am probably less popular than I am in Xu Province; nor do I desire a fight with my old friend's son, whether Yuan Shao is my friend anymore or not. Wenruo, send word to Li Dian and have him provide the 'escort' that Mister Kong requests."

Xun Wenruo understood the true meaning of Cao Cao's words and said, "I shall do as you ask, but... does this not strain the relationship with Yuan Shao still further...?"

Cao Cao nodded silently.

"...You are angry that your lifelong friend – and, at your decree, Commander-in-Chief of the Han forces – has ordered this attack," Guo Jia said calmly. "An attack on a court-appointed governor – even if it was Jia Xu that appointed him and Liu Bei that recommended him – is treason."

"He has done this to *test me*," Cao Cao replied through gritted teeth. "He has done this precisely because he was told not to."

"So Yuan Tan and Zang Ba will have to wait," Cheng Yu sighed.

"*We*...! ...We cannot spare the resoucres that are required," Cao Cao retorted. "We shall just have to hope that Zang Ba's arrogance leads him to make a mistake."

"And Yuan Tan...?" Cheng Yu asked.

"...I have no words," Cao Cao replied.

"This has one benefit, my lord," Guo Jia suggested.

"*Ayah*... what benefit could be had from losing Qing Province to a treasonous Yuan Tan and an army of bandits???" Xun Gongda exclaimed. "Mister Guo, this is the worst news since Lingdi's time, when the army lost Liang Province to Ma Teng and Han Sui!"

"We have a man that knows Wang Lang, and can approach him for us if our pleas continue to fall on stubborn ears," Guo Jia replied casually. "Heaven may take Eastern Qing, but it gives us Liu Fu, Qin Yi, Qi Ji, Kong Rong and Wang Lang, and weakens Yuan Shu: that is not so unfair a trade."

"...I shall try and see it as such," Cao Cao said miserably.

Qing Province Governor Kong Rong was brought to his own audience hall by a triumphant Yuan Tan – the eldest son of Yuan Shao – and forced to cower below his own host's seat that the brawny Tan now occupied.

"Greetings, Mister Kong Rong!" Yuan Tan chuckled as he leant forward and ruffled his wiry beard. "You look well! I am sure that my father will be glad to be reunited with you after so many years!"

"I am appointed by the Han court, by the Son of Heaven!" Kong Rong protested.

"Are you now...?" Yuan Tan heckled. "What 'Son of Heaven' would this be...? The second son of Lingdi, born of Consort Wang, that the seditious Dong Zhuo placed on the throne after committing regicide...?"

"Xiandi has been universally accepted!" Kong Rong retorted.

"Only, as my father always says, 'for lack of choice'," Yuan Tan said coldly. "Cao Cao, the cruel and faithless wretch that he is, makes Xiandi his emperor and issues proclamations from his self-serving court in Xuchang, but your appointment does not even come from that godless place, oh no; your appointment comes from the regents in Chang'an, at the request of the mat weaver Liu Bei!"

Yuan Tan's courtiers laughed derisively.

"I... am court-app-appointed... G-Governor... of Qing...!" Kong Rong sobbed.

"No, Mister Kong; *I* am Acting Governor of Qing now, until Father decides upon a permanent appointment," Yuan Tan declared. "I am a man of the sword: if I am considered unsuited to civil nonsense, it doesn't bother me, as I prefer the rush of battle. You, you're a traitor that fraternises with the likes of Liu Bei and accepts appointments from Liang warlords that kidnapped the imperial court and murdered the sovereign. You'll be incarcerated until my father decides what to do with you."

Kong Rong noticed a familiar face among Yuan Tan's vassals and cried, "Mister Xin Ping... Mister Xin Zhongzhi...! Xin Zhongzhi, reason with your lord! This cannot-!"

"You are condemned by your own hand, Kong Rong," Xin Ping said coldly. "Your esteemed ancestor would be ashamed. Guards: take this man to the prison."

"**No!**" Kong Rong pleaded. "**My family! What will you do with my family???**"

"Your family will be kept comfortable until we know your fate," Yuan Tan replied. "Now please, Mister Kong, show some dignity at this crucial moment, so that I have good things to tell my father!"

"**Heaven forgive you, Yuan Tan!**" Kong Rong screamed as he was led away by two guards. "**You commit treason! Repent before you feel Heaven's wrath, Yuan Tan! Show righteous mercy, Yuan Tan! YUAN TAN!**"

"...Idiot," Yuan Tan scoffed; he then turned to Xin Ping and asked, "What are the chances of Cao Cao reacting?"

"He'll stage a prison break at worst, I think, and Kong Rong is no loss," Xin Ping replied. "He daren't engage you on the battlefield; he has too many other things to worry about."

"And so does Gongsun Zan... so Qing is ours, then," Yuan Tan chuckled. "Someone bring me the governor's seal! I should like to hold it."

****

44

Lü Bu sat in his living quarters and stared at the latest letter that he had received from Cao Cao. He read every word over and over again, searching for every possible meaning; after an hour had passed, his radiant wife, Lady Yan, shuffled into the room and sat opposite him with a smile on her face.
"…I said that I wanted to read this on my own!" Lü Bu scolded.
"But what good is there to be had in reading it and not deciding anything?" Lady Yan replied. "Why don't you talk to Gongtai?"
"…'Gongtai' is hardly likely to be impartial!" Lü Bu suggested. "But… but I have to admit that you are right, my lady: I am too stupid to come to my own conclusion."
"You're not stupid, Husband, but you are not aware of all of the methods of intrigue," Lady Yan replied. "Speak to them all. Summon all of your advisers and speak to them."
Lü Bu nodded tersely and said, "I know it's late, but I'll do it now."

Lü Bu summoned Chen Gong and six other men to his governor's office, but four of those six men met beforehand at the house of the eldest – the famed scholar and author Chen Yuanfang.
"Father, they have arrived," Chen Yuanfang's son, Chen Qun, said as he entered the living quarters.
The host was in his sixties and very weary of the intrigue now: he smiled and said, "My father and I were victims of the 'Partisan Crisis' thirty years ago, and by birth, you were too, Qun. When does the madness end, I wonder…?"
Chen Qun was silent.
"…Show them in," Chen Yuanfang sighed.
Chen Qun went to the front door, greeted the two guests – the nobleman Chen Gui and his son Chen Deng – and brought them to the living quarters, where Chen Yuanfang was sat waiting for them in the host seat. The four men exchanged ritual bows and cynical glances when they met, but for a few moments, nothing was said.
"Welcome, Mister Chen Gui and Mister Chen Deng," Chen Yuanfang hailed at last.
"My thanks, Elder Chen," Chen Gui replied.
Chen Yuanfang harrumphed and said, "Bu's disturbed our evening. Do we know what this is about, Chen Hanyu…?"
"We do," Chen Gui replied. "My son and I have already discussed it at length."
"So what is it about…?" Chen Qun asked impatiently.
Chen Deng smiled and said, "A letter… a letter from *Cao Cao*."
"…From *Cao Cao*?" Chen Yuanfang exclaimed. "He almost got me killed once already with that unwanted promotion to 'Excellency of Works'! What does that reckless man want to do now?"
"Nothing that harms us this time," Chen Gui promised. "It's about Bu's promotions. It's a 'placating ruse': Chen Gong, Wang Kai and Xu Si will see right through it, though, unfortunately."
"My father and I are not in favour with Bu because of that promotion nonsense," Chen Qun complained. "It's up to the two of you now."
"But you're both invited to this meeting as well," Chen Gui said.
"To be *heckled*, no doubt," Chen Yuanfang scoffed. "First I am

forced to flee from Dong Zhuo, and now this: if I had known that my misery would not end with the partisan amnesty, I would have retired to the hills and become a hermit, and I certainly wouldn't have cursed Qun with life either."

"I am sure that everything will be fine, Father," Chen Qun said.

"I feel the same," Chen Gui declared. "Though we're different Chen clans, our paths have crossed by Heaven's mischievous design. You Chens of Yingchuan have suffered ups and downs, while we Chens of Xiapi have enjoyed power and influence here in Xu Province: now we're tied together because the governor of your ancestral province, Cao Cao, pledged to destroy our governor Tao Qian. Thanks to that destructive misunderstanding, my son and I have had Liu Bei and now Lü Bu for masters, and Xu Province is no happier; you two had Liu Bei assigned as your master by pure luck when hiding in Qing Province, and ended up here when he was invited by Tao Qian. And now, despite our different paths, we're all trapped and miserable! I only hope that Deng forgives me for my part in this mess."

"Of course, Father," Chen Deng insisted. "But if it were only *three* Chen clans united against Lü Bu! I already know the answer but I will still ask: why can't Chen Gong see sense...? He saw Cao Cao's evil, so why not Lü Bu's...?"

"He sees it," Chen Yuanfang grumbled. "But he's still convinced that Cao Cao will kill him if he doesn't ensure that Lü Bu prevents their meeting."

"So for the sake of three men that miscalculated a risk – Chen Gong, Wang Kai, and Xu Si – an entire province must suffer," Chen Qun said. "It is only because their insurrection saved this province from Cao Cao that I am not livid at their craven selfishness. But we ramble on pointlessly: what can we do?"

"Our mission is to convince Bu that he must listen to Cao Cao, but we are unlikely to succeed, since Chen Gong and the other two will feed his neurosis," Chen Gui replied. "As you said, it may be up to me and my son, if Bu still mistrusts you."

"He'll mistrust us more if we keep him waiting, I suppose," Chen Yuanfang groaned as he got to his feet. "You two should go first: oh, and thank you for coming and warning us. We'll try and act as if we're surprised, of course..."

Chen Gui and Chen Deng bowed respectfully and departed.

"We can trust the Chens of Xiapi," Chen Qun decided.

"Oh, I know that," Chen Yuanfang replied. "It's Chen Gong that we need to fear."

"And Cao Cao," Chen Qun suggested.

"Of course!" Chen Yuanfang chortled. "The 'Hero of Chaos' is not beyond harming this poor province again. O Fate, why do you keep forcing men to choose from two evils...? Why can there be no *kind* heroes...?"

"Is there such a thing?" Chen Qun sighed.

The Chens of Xiapi would be the second group of men to arrive at Lü Bu's office: the advisers Chen Gong, Wang Kai and Xu Si were already there, and their greeting was noticeably frosty.

"You assume the worst of us," Chen Gui said with a smile.

"Rumours abound of a letter from Xuchang," Chen Gong replied. "Cao Cao writes here... did you know of it...?"

Chen Gui frowned and said, "No: is this more appointments...?"
"I don't know," Chen Gong admitted. "We-"
Lü Bu appeared and barked, "**Where are the other Chens?**"
"...They got the summons," Chen Gong promised. "I-"
"Are we late...?" Chen Yuanfang asked as he entered the office.
"If we are, I apologise for us both," Chen Qun said.
"**It doesn't matter!**" Lü Bu cried. "**Shut up and sit down!**"
The 7 advisers sat in two lines to the left and right of Lu Bu's host seat: to Bu's left, Chen Gong sat closest to their lord, followed by Wang Kai and then Xu Si; to Bu's right, Chen Gui, Chen Deng, Chen Qun and Chen Yuanfang sat in a row with Yuanfang placed furthest from his master.
"I'll get to the point," Lü Bu grunted as he thrust a cloth letter into Chen Gong's hands. "Knowing you, you already know, but-"
"A personal letter from *Cao*...?" Chen Gong exclaimed theatrically.
"Read it for yourselves, gentlemen," Lü Bu said. "He is very humble, very apologetic... he speaks of regret at having 'lost the general's seal' in an incident in Shan County, and then he speaks of eliminating just about everybody in the land, with the exception of *Yuan Shao*. It's that particular omission that bothers me."
"Gongsun Zan... Yuan Shu, which would encompass the Suns of Fuchun... Han Xian and Yang Feng of the White Wave Bandits... but no Yuan Shao," Chen Gong mused as he read the letter. "I am not surprised though, since Yuan Shao was promoted to Excellency of Works in the first proclamation, and then to Commander-in-Chief in that bizarre follow-up. They're old friends, he and Cao."
"And Yuan Shao's my old enemy," Lü Bu suggested. "Yuan Shao wants me dead! If I am 'General of the Left', and he is 'Commander-in-Chief', doesn't that mean I'm subordinate to Yuan Shao? **How can that work???**"
Nobody answered.
"And as a point, how are you, dear 'Excellency of Works'...?" Lü Bu asked as he stared at Chen Yuanfang. "I still wonder... *why*...? What *for*...?"
"Elder Chen is a famous statesman!" Chen Gui protested. "He knew the famed Cai Yong, the noble Zheng Tai, Wang Yun, and more besides!"
"Yes... I did," Chen Yuanfang sighed. "I knew them all."
"And you yourself told me that he once gave Dong Zhuo valuable advice that should have been heeded, or don't you remember...?" Chen Gui continued. "Elder Chen's been an asset and a friend to us, my lord: don't turn on him now."
Lü Bu nodded tersely and said, "I am being too paranoid. Master Chen Yuanfang, I apologise. You're too good for this place, and I sometimes forget that."
Chen Yuanfang bowed humbly and replied, "I am just glad to serve a good lord."
"Enough undeserved praise," Lü Bu grunted. "Chen Gong, what are your views?"
"Cao Cao means us no harm at present," Chen Gong decided.
"How can you know that?" Wang Kai asked.
"Cao Cao is vindictive: he tore this province apart for one man's supposed crime against his father!" Xu Si heckled. "How can you now speak of him as-!"
"Gentlemen, please listen," Chen Gong said calmly. "Cao Cao has

other worries: he is afraid of attacks on his capital by the Yellow Turbans of Runan and from the north, by his friend Yuan Shao."

"So you agree that it's a ruse?" Wang Kai asked.

"Oh yes, of course!" Chen Gong chuckled. "But sometimes being the victim of a ruse has benefits: in this case, he is forced to placate our lord with the second-highest military rank in the land! What is given insincerely will be true nonetheless, once we have the seal of office."

"But he clearly states that there *isn't one*!" Lü Bu protested.

"Ah, but he's promised it in writing," Chen Gong retorted. "That means that he must do as he promises, or he will be seen either as dishonest or incompetent."

"But how long must I wait?" Lü Bu asked.

Chen Gong smiled and replied, "He promises you a seal when the materials can be procured to fashion a new one: knowing the state of things, I can believe that finding the gold and coloured silk required will be a struggle."

"...Yes... As the man that helped the man that made things this way, I not only believe it... I see the irony and justice in it," Lü Bu said. "I'll write to the emperor all the same, stating my own intentions and making my own apologies."

"A fine idea," Chen Gong replied. "But... word it very carefully."

"How so...?" Chen Qun asked. "To what end must our lord 'word it carefully'?"

"If this is an attempt to destroy our lord after placating him with false promises, the world must know," Chen Gong replied. "Our lord has bad history with the Han Dynasty that must be addressed before others can address it and apologised for before others can claim there has been no repentance."

"That is quite right," Wang Kai said. "Cao Cao is wily... a public statement to the court will force Cao to abide by his promises."

"If you must do that, then write a simultaneous letter to Cao Cao that explains matters in an equally careful way," Chen Gui suggested. "Your theatrical exercises are sound if Cao Cao is playing games, Chen Gong, but if he is not, then it is unsolicited provocation that will backfire."

"...Also true," Wang Kai conceded. "Write to throne and minister, my lord, and ensure that both are informed and placated."

"Fine: very good!" Lü Bu said. "I'll need a pen and ink then!"

"Remember: this isn't Xiao Jian," Chen Gong warned. "Be *polite*."

Within hours, a messenger was on his way from Xiapi in eastern Xu Province to Xuchang in western Yan Province; and at around the same time, the would-be courtier Liu Fu was finishing his own journey to Xuchang. Cao Cao heard of Liu Fu's arrival and had a welcoming party ready for him at the gates of the temporary imperial capital.

"Greetings, Mister Liu," Zhang Yang's former adviser, Dong Gongren, began. "His Excellency Cao Cao will be most pleased that you have arrived."

Liu Fu bowed low and replied, "You are too kind."

"I am Dong Zhao," Dong Gongren said. "To my left, Xun Yòu..."

Xun Gongda bowed politely.

"...And to my right is General Yu Jin," Dong Gongren concluded as he gestured toward the stern, silent officer.

"I am truly surprised that I am being greeted by one of His Excellency's champions and one of his senior advisers in addition to your good self, Mister Dong Zhao," Liu Fu replied warily. "Generals Qi Ji and Qin Yi accompany me, as I'm sure you know."

Yu Jin bowed to the two apprehensive officers from Lujiang and said, "Your names are familiar to me, gentlemen; I see that you have brought quite a few of your men with you."

"They are not our men, they are the Empire's men, born to serve the Son of Heaven, and to be used as His Excellency Cao Cao sees fit," Qi Ji replied. "We, too, are at His Excellency's disposal, as His Majesty would desire."

The two officers bowed low as a sign of deference.

"...Very good," Xun Gongda said. "General Yu, they will serve the Han well. See that they are introduced to their new colleagues, and have everyone quartered appropriately."

General Yu Jin gestured politely, and the former vassals of Yuan Shu followed him out of the main city and towards a visitor's barracks.

"You may return to your duties, Mister Dong Zhao," Xun Gongda said politely. "I shall escort Mister Liu Fu to see His Excellency."

Dong Gongren bowed silently and departed.

"...It's been some time, Liu Yuanying," Xun Gongda chuckled. "I remember you well, as does His Excellency. Won't you please follow me...?"

Liu Fu bowed slightly, smiled, and said, "It will be a pleasure, Gongda. My, what work goes on here! Are you building a palace for His Majesty...?"

All eyes turned to a great mound of earth: a series of exquisitely crafted stone steps already dressed one side, and the beginnings of a grand southern palace already stood atop it.

"Yes, and an expensive business it is too, though worth every coin," Xun Gongda replied as the two men made their way through the busy streets of Xuchang. "It will not be as grand as the palace in Luoyang, of course, but it will serve its purpose until that great capital is restored to its former glory, which... which will take some time, I fear."

"So I hear," Liu Fu said diplomatically.

"Mister Dong Zhao is – was – the main adviser to the current Director of Retainers, Zhang Yang, who is in Luoyang as we speak," Xun Gongda continued. "Zhang is a former general under Ding Yuan, and a fine man, unlike his former comrade Lü Bu, who currently acts as Governor of Xu Province."

"That place has been unfortunate," Liu Fu said sadly. "First the heretic Ze Rong, then Tao Qian's poor choice of allies led to the tragedy involving His Excellency's father, and then the whole mess with Liu Bei and Lü Bu... I hope that some stability comes to the province and its people soon."

"And I could say the same for Lujiang, and Yang Province in general," Xun Gongda prompted. "Tell me, what sort of government does Yuan Shu preside over...?"

"A nonsensical mess, Gongda," Liu Fu chortled. "The man is incompetent! He makes enemies of everyone! He demands excessive taxes, distributes wealth poorly, rankles the influential, allows problems to go unsolved... it's things like that that led to the Yellow Turbans, and nobody can tell him. I almost feel sorry for some of his vassals, like Sun Ce and Wu Jing; others, like Han Yin and Chen Ji, are harder to pity."

"Liu Xun...?" Xun Gongda wondered.

"...Difficult to fathom," Liu Fu admitted. "He's well educated, and should know better than to side with the likes of Yuan Shu, but... but as you know, the allegiances are complicated. They all of them actually think that Shu is the rightful leader of the Yuan clan, citing Shao's... 'background'."

"As you may or may not know, His Excellency and Commander-in-Chief Yuan are not on good terms at present," Xun Gongda said. "You're trusted, so I can tell you: Qing Governor Kong Rong is currently a hostage of Yuan Tan."

"*Ayah*... madness," Liu Fu lamented. "Oh, well; what can I do...? I am no strategist, so I cannot save Mister Kong, but if there's anything that I can do to improve development here in Xuchang, I will work until I drop."

Xun Gongda smiled gratefully; Liu Fu would later meet Cao Cao and be assigned a mid-level role in the Xuchang government, and that would be just the beginning.

****

45

Lü Bu was informed of the sudden arrival of a messenger from Ju City; he dressed appropriately, left his private meeting room, entered his packed audience hall and awaited the unexpected communication from his ally Xiao Jian.

"This man Xiao Jian is extreme: first he ignores me, and now this!" Lü Bu joked.

"My lord, this is serious," the adviser Chen Gong replied. "Go on, messenger."

"A siege!" the messenger wailed. "The *Mount Tai Bandits*! They-!"

"**How DARE THEY!**" Lü Bu cried. "**They dare encroach on Xu Province like this??? They will know death! I will exterminate them personally for this!**"

"My lord, be measured," the former general Gao Shun suggested. "Your reputation as a peerless duellist and the slayer of Dong Zhuo is firm as a rock right now, but if you march on Ju City in person and fail to expel them, the-"

"**Shut up, you dog!**" Lü Bu heckled. "**You have no rank! You are NOTHING! How DARE you tell me what to do! How DARE you insinuate that I can't defeat a few scruffy bandits! I made my name destroying creatures like them!**"

Gao Shun bowed politely and said, "It is true that I have no rank, my lord, but-!"

"**SHUT UP!**"

"…If you would just hear me out, I-"

"**SHUT UP!**"

"…Ju City has repelled all manner of attackers, even Yue Yi of the age of Warring States, as you so recently had to point out to Xiao Jian!" Gao Shun protested. "Its walls are as troublesome as Wan City in Jing! If Zang Ba's men have the city when you get there, you will need to withdraw, and I could not bear to see you humbled by the likes of-"

"**AAAAAAGH! AAAAAAGH! Someone drag this man out into the street so that I might flog his back until his spine is exposed!**" Lü Bu screamed as he leapt to his feet. "**How DARE YOU, Gao Shun, you… you dog! I…! I…! No, I will drag you into the street myself, you-!**"

"Punish him later, when he is proven wrong, my lord," Chen Gong urged. "Save your strength for Zang Ba."

Lü Bu was breathing erratically as he glared hatefully at Gao Shun; it took almost a minute before he found the composure to step back and sit down again.

"…Governor, how will you proceed against Zang Ba…?" Chen Gui asked calmly.

"As… I said… I will march upon Ju City in person, and tear the man's head from his neck," Lü Bu replied at last. "I am a man among men… I am *the* man among men! None have ever beaten me in battle; I have only been foiled by petty intrigue in the past, and what do bandits know of intrigue, uh…? I will be back before my letters reach Xuchang!"

Gao Shun looked at Chen Gong, who secretly agreed with Gao's assessment; Chen smiled sadly, turned his gaze to Lü Bu and said, "Who will you take as your adviser, Governor…?"

"I had no advisers in the days when I served under Ding Yuan!" Lü Bu retorted. "I had no advisers when I fought the Black Mountain Bandits for him, and then for Yuan Shao! They are fools, weak fools, and I will crush them!"
"You should take an adviser," Chen Gong pleaded.
"…Alright, alright!" Lü Bu snapped. "I will take Wang Kai! You stay here and wait for Cao Cao's reply, in case I am delayed!"
Chen Gong bowed slightly and said, "As you wish."
"**Qin Yilu! Wei Xu!**" Lü Bu barked.
Lü Bu's cousin Wei Xu and the officer Qin Yilu bowed humbly.
"You two should gather your men," Lü Bu ordered.
Gao Shun looked at Wei Xu – who now commanded Gao's elite unit – and sighed miserably.
"**We will move immediately!**" Lü Bu continued. "**Every last bandit dies!**"
Lü Bu stormed out of the packed audience hall, which immediately fell silent.

"…This is a disaster," Chen Gong muttered as he entered the city chancellery half an hour later; Xu Si and a silent, thoughtful Chen Gui followed him.
"Poor Wang Kai," Xu Si lamented. "He will be to blame for this catastrophe!"
"No he won't: Xiao Jian is to blame," Chen Gong replied. "He lost the city to-"
"There was no mention of the city being lost," Xu Si said bemusedly.
"Xiao Jian is a coward," Chen Gong retorted. "You think he'll stay and defend it, after what happened to Liu Bei in Haixi…?"
"…Xiao Jian's no Liu Bei," Xu Si conceded.
"No… he isn't," Chen Gong sighed. "And speaking of Liu Bei, he is the man that should be going to Ju City to be humiliated, not Lord Lü. Gao Shun is right: we'll never regain Ju from Zang Ba."
"…I wouldn't be concerned, gentlemen," Chen Gui suggested. "Lü Bu's reputation as a hero will be undamaged; did losing to the regents affect him at all…?"
"Losing to Li Jue, Guo Si and an army of hardened barbarians is quite unlike losing to a disjointed collection of bandits, Mister Chen Gui," Chen Gong retorted. "Our lord did indeed make his name as the scourge of the Black Mountain Bandits…"
"…Who were defeated…?" Chen Gui said pointedly.
"No, they were not," Chen Gong conceded. "So… so perhaps you are right… oh, I hope you are right, Chen Hanyu. We are negotiating with Cao Cao, and cannot afford to look weak, especially not after the wording of those letters…"
"Fret not," Chen Gui insisted. "At worst, we'll be forced to wait for Zang Ba to ask for a truce while he retreats to Kaiyang with his spoils: after all, who wants an infuriated, oft-drunken, humiliated and vengeful Lü Bu for a close neighbour…?"
Chen Gong stifled a telling smile and replied, "It is as you say."

Lü Bu left a trail of destruction as he moved out of Xiapi and went east: every person that was identified as a bandit was violently massacred. The warlord governor reached Ju City within days, but – just as Chen Gong had predicted – Xiao Jian had given up the city and fled.

"That cowardly mouse!" Lü Bu complained. "If he had just held on for a few more days, then…!"

"But surely we'll take the city easily," General Qin Yilu said.

"Why is it always men like you that have the most beautiful wives…?" Lü Bu heckled. "Zhang Ji has – or had – Lady Zou, and you have Lady Du, and yet you haven't the slightest bit of sense! Are the most beautiful women attracted to the greatest fools…?"

Qin Yilu lowered his head and sighed.

"…So Gao Shun was right, then," Wei Xu said.

"I…! …Yes, he was right, alright?" Lü Bu replied angrily. "I wanted to be here before they took the city because it is close to impregnable if the defenders have enough supplies, and Xiao Jian has been stockpiling for a march for ages now!"

"…The worthless fool!" Wang Kai whined. "He's given Zang Ba a foothold in Donghai!"

"There will be no 'Donghai Bandits' as long as I live!" Lü Bu insisted. "I will make Zang Ba understand that he will not win! Damn him, damn them all: I'll do what I can to get him out of there! It's just as I said to Xiao Jian: I'm not Yue Yi, but Zang isn't Tian Dan either!"

"…*Aiee*… such a predicament," Wang Kai muttered.

And within Ju City's walls, Zang Ba sat in the Administrator's residence's private quarters and rocked back and forth silently.

"…Want to share your thoughts…?" the bandit Sun Guan asked as he entered the room.

"He's a demon," Zang Ba chuckled hauntingly. "He… there's stories that-!"

"Yeah, I know," Sun Guan interrupted. "He's gutted blokes, left their heads on spikes, dragged 'em to death with horses, all sorts; nobody wants to stay outside and fight him. He earned his reputation in Bing Province, and no mistake."

"…We'll have to hold out, and hope he has to retreat when his supplies run out," Zang Ba suggested. "Any other time that'd be a dream, what with Xiapi being so close, but after a famine, and with him having other enemies, like Yuan Shu, there's a hope."

"I'll hope with you," Sun Guan said. "I'll… go back to the wall."

Zang Ba nodded gratefully, and Sun Guan left him to his thoughts.

In Xiaopei – which was to the west of Ju City – life was starting to get back to a state of relative normality after the destruction wreaked by Cao Cao two years before.

"…We're getting word of messengers going back and forth between Xiapi and Xuchang," Mister Sun Qian said to Liu Bei's small court.

"I just can't believe that His Majesty accepted Bu as the governor," Zhang Fei complained. "The man killed His Majesty's brother and looted his ancestors' tombs! How can he-?"

"I… I know, Yide," Liu Bei said kindly. "It vexes me too, because I know that Cao Cao is behind the appointment, but… what's done is done. At least Cao hasn't asked Bu to attack us."

"*Yet*," Jian Yong suggested. "He hasn't asked him *yet*."

"I preferred you when you were an awful comedian, Jian Yong," Zhang Fei heckled. "Stop being so pessimistic! Even if Bu comes for us, so what...? Me and Yunchang are back to full strength now, and that siege made us both tougher: let him come here, and-!"

"I'd rather he didn't, Yide," Liu Bei pleaded. "Don't wish that on us. Anyhow... Mister Sun, you think that the correspondence is ominous...?"

"It might be, or it might be good for us," Mister Sun explained. "It seems that Cao Cao has not provided Bu with a general's seal, which means that his appointment as 'General of the Left' is just empty air at present. I think that the delay is contrived, and that Cao will renege on his deal with Bu as soon as he's dealt with the other problems that he faces."

"But there is little chance of us being restored to Xiapi," Liu Bei suggested. "In fact, I wonder what 'His Excellency Cao' does have in mind for us; oh, I hope that he reserves his anger for me and me alone."

Mi Zhu, Mi Fang, Sun Qian, Jian Yong, Zhang Fei and Guan Yu bowed as one, and Guan Yu said, "We disagree. We are your brothers and vassals, and we will share your fate, whatever that may be."

The Haixi siege had changed every man within the group in some way, and given them a shared memory of horror that united them forever: Liu Bei fought tears at hearing Guan Yu's words, and he said, "I am truly blessed."

Elsewhere, at Ju City, Lü Bu's frustration peaked as he failed to breach the defences yet again.

"YOU'RE ALL FOOD FOR THE PIGS!" Lü Bu cried defiantly.

"D'you think he'll ever give up, boss?" the bandit Wu Dun asked as he peered over the high wall and watched Lü Bu's forces withdraw.

"Difficult to say, mate," Zang Ba replied uneasily.

"Your voice is cracking, Xuangao," Sun Guan noted. "I'm not the only one that's getting worried that we've overstretched, then."

"Bu's mad at us," Zang Ba replied. "We've lost him quite a few men, and we've held the place, and he won't like that. He obviously underestimated us and didn't bring enough men, but if he goes and comes back too quickly, we're dead... even if it takes ten years, he'll hole us up in here until we're dead."

"So do we contact Yin Li and get some help...?" Sun Guan asked.

"No, we get out of here as soon as the chance comes," Zang Ba replied. "We take what we can, and then we see if we can have a truce with Bu. We can't afford him coming after us."

Lü Bu returned to his command tent and threw his battle helmet to the ground.

"What do we do...?" Wang Kai asked. "We're out of supplies, and-"

"What else are we going to do???" Lü Bu snapped. "We have to... to... we have to retreat! We have no choice!"

"It's for the best," Wang Kai said. "We shouldn't waste supplies on bandits, not at a time like this."

"Xiao Jian is a dead man if he ever shows his face in my court," Lü Bu growled. "If he'd just held out... for a few more days...!"

"We know now that he didn't stand a chance against them, Governor," Wang Kai retorted. "The fact is, the-"

"The fact is that... that *Gao Shun*... that *Gao Shun*, that smug bastard, he was *right*, wasn't he…?" Lü Bu complained. "Why he has to be right… I *hate him*!"

"He wasn't entirely right," Wang Kai replied. "Your reputation will not be tarnished."

"It… it should be," Lü Bu grunted.

"*Aiee…* nonsense!" Wang Kai cried.

"Have Generals Wei and Qin issue the orders at once," Lü Bu continued. "I… I may need to fill my ears to drown out the heckling that we'll get, else I might do something else that I'll regret afterwards."

Lü Bu's demoralised army retreated to Xiapi, and Zang Ba's haunted bandits left Ju City immediately thereafter. Neither leader had anything to gain from dwelling too long on the encounter itself, but both had learned a lesson: Lü Bu was forced to admit that he was not infallible in his confrontations with bandits, and Zang Ba had learned that the rumours about Bu's savage ferocity were far from exaggerated, and that his own strength was limited. Lü Bu went home to Xiapi with the intention of turning his attentions back to negotiations with the court in Xuchang, while Zang Ba returned to Kaiyang with the intention of discussing a future truce with Bu.

****

46

Yuan Shu was deeply disturbed by many of the reports that he was receiving; the fear of appearing to be weak in front of a full court consumed him, so he summoned two of his weary senior advisers to his private meeting room.

"The false emperor in Xuchang; Cao Cao preparing to march, but with no clear intention; Lü Bu, of all men, made General of the Left, and my brother-cousin made Commander-in-Chief; and worst of all, my name on a list of traitors that are to be brought under heel!" Yuan Shu fretted. "Liu Xun has informed me that Qi Ji and Qin Yi have deserted and gone to Xuchang as well!"

"What do you want to do...?" Han Yin asked.

"I do not want to yield to a false emperor!" Yuan Shu replied. "The nation needs – nay, *demands* – a strong, unifying sovereign, and Dong Zhuo's last legacy, the wrongly-elevated Prince of Chenliu, is not that sovereign! Cao Cao is another Dong Zhuo that even recruits the same Lü Bu and prince-puppet, and my wretched half-brother forgets our clan's fate and willingly acts as his Hua Xiong!"

"Word is that Yuan Shao and Cao Cao are, in fact, at odds," Yan Xiang said calmly. "I would be patient; Lü Bu betrayed everyone that placed faith in him, and he will do so again. But... but Lord Yuan, Xiandi is now accepted by all, and-"

"Not by me!" Yuan Shu barked. "Not by me, not by the people! They rise up once again in defiance of Dong Zhuo's puppet, that traitor that benefitted from the regicide of his own brother!"

"...All the same, there are greater advantages to 'procuring' the Son of Heaven – rescuing him, to put it a better way – than pursuing the 'other course'," Yan Xiang protested. "If Cao Cao marches north, as we expect him to do, then-"

"My first priority is that traitor Lü Bu!" Yuan Shu insisted. "When that slayer of fathers, looter of tombs and guardian of tyrants is dead, the path to Xuchang will be clear! Perhaps I should have my Sun Ce challenge him, since so many obstacles in the south have been eliminated now!"

"A rebellion around Danyang and the constant uprisings by the Shanyue and bandits make it unlikely that Sun Ce can be reallocated to the Xu campaign," Han Yin said. "We must instead send Ji Ling back there: that has two advantages."

"...I can guess the first," Yuan Shu chortled. "Liu Bei guards Xiaopei, and he will balk at the first sighting of the man that robbed him of his humanity for a year."

"Indeed," Han Yin replied. "The second is Ji Ling's dual desires for revenge against Bu for ruining the Haixi campaign and finishing what he started against Bei. No other man will give you blood as Ji Ling will."

"...Then when the time is right, Ji Ling will launch a full-scale assault on southeast Xu," Yuan Shu decided. "When Bei and Bu are eliminated, and Xu is ours, Cao Cao will try and march east to take Xu for himself; we will then attack Xuchang while he is distracted, take their false emperor, and deprive Cao and my half-brother of their convenient justification for conquest! All eyes will then turn to me, and my moment will have arrived!"

"*Aiee*... be careful, Lord Yuan," Yan Xiang pleaded. "Your plan-"

"I cannot fail!" Yuan Shu declared. "Heaven is with me! Victory and ascension are inevitable! My moment will soon be here!"
Han Yin shuddered; Yan Xiang sighed disapprovingly.

Within a week of Lü Bu's retreat from Ju City, his messenger reached Xuchang.

"We understand that our vassal, General of the Left and Marquis of Pingtao Lü Bu, has sent us a memorial," Emperor Xian said to his assembled courtiers: his tone was noticeably dry, as he had never really liked the idea of Lü Bu being given rank. The unreadable Cao Cao did not answer, so after a few moments of uncomfortable silence Emperor Xian added, "We should like an answer to our question."
"There is, indeed, a memorial," Xun Wenruo said.
"We should like to hear it," Emperor Xian ordered.
"Mister Zhong Ji...?" Xun Wenruo prompted.
Lü Bu's memorial was presented to the imperial court in Xuchang by an official named Zhong Ji, who was noticeably nervous despite his maturity and rank.
"What can Lü Bu intend, Uncle...?" the fretful Xun Gongda whispered to Xun Wenruo.
"Evil or good," Xun Wenruo replied.
"...Read the memorial," Cao Cao said uncomfortably.
"It reads: 'I, Bu, pay humblest respects to Your Majesty, and also convey humblest and sincerest apologies'," Zhong Ji narrated. "'I was filled with joy when I learned that I had been forgiven for past misdeeds, but I was, as I have stated previously, unable to find the resources to be of immediate use. I am now in a stronger position, and I would have come to Luoyang to protect Your Majesty personally, but then I heard that Cao Cao had come to your aid, and-'"
Xun Wenruo gasped involuntarily.
"...Please continue reading, Mister Zhong," Cao Cao ordered.
"...'I heard that Cao Cao had come to your aid, and that Cao Cao has shown fealty and escorted Your Majesty to the new capital Xuchang while the repairs to Luoyang are conducted'," Zhong Ji continued. "'In recent times, I have fought bitter battles with Cao Cao, and now he is Your Majesty's principal defender and Excellency of Works. I, in contrast to Cao Cao's long-standing position in the land, am a general on the outside of normal politics, and I worried that if I came to escort Your Majesty at Cao Cao's side, there might be some misunderstanding with regard to my motives. Therefore, I chose to remain here in Xu Province and wait for Your Majesty to reprimand me for my disobedience. I did not dare to show inappropriate autonomy; rather I felt it best to act on instruction. I hope that this explanation is acceptable, and I offer my unworthy self to Your Majesty, and may I not fail to serve you well again. Your humble servant, General Lü Bu, Governor of Xu Province'."
"He speaks well enough," Emperor Xian said. "Mister Cao, we sensed tension, but there is no cause for concern, I hope."
Cao Cao smiled and replied, "None at all."
The court session continued and ended without further incident.

"That... was more than just 'tense'," Cao Cao chortled as he returned to his chancellery office later that afternoon. "I really thought that... ... ...but he didn't."

The advisers Guo Jia, Xun Wenruo and Xun Gongda had followed Cao Cao to the office: Guo Jia smiled and said, "Bu seems to be afraid of you."

"I sensed it too," Cao Cao replied. "A surprise, I admit! So, Bu's nerves are frayed, and he feared that I'd try and destroy him..."

A weary junior official appeared before Cao Cao could continue, and said, "I have a letter for His Excellency, brought here from Governor Lü Bu of Xu Province."

"Oh...?" Cao Cao exclaimed. "No need to read it to me, lad: hand it over, and then you may go."

The messenger handed the cloth scroll to Cao Cao and retreated.

"...Mm... interesting," Cao Cao said as he read Lü Bu's words.

"I'm sure that it is," Guo Jia chuckled.

"He once again apologises for 'disobeying the emperor', and states that he 'deserves punishment according to the law'," Cao Cao explained. "Then he starts to fawn... he thanks me for my 'comforting and encouraging words', and-"

"*Lü Bu*???" Xun Gongda giggled. "*Lü Bu* wrote such things???"

Cao Cao laughed and said, "I know, they're not really the words of a 'Man among men', are they...? Anyhow, he goes on to say that he looks forward to the imperial decree that orders him to destroy Yuan Shu 'and others', and that he'll do whatever it takes to fulfil the wishes of His Majesty."

"There is no decree, and we haven't a seal of office for him as yet," Xun Wenruo said thoughtfully. "How shall we reply...?"

"For now, I won't," Cao Cao said. "This does not demand an immediate reply, and as you have implied, I can hardly have His Majesty issue a decree to a general that doesn't have a seal. Let's wait and see, because the situation in Xu Province is changeable, like its current governor. I wonder if Lü Bu's eagerness to destroy Yuan Shu will endure if he's bribed again."

"That's quite right," Guo Jia declared. "Lü Bu might be opposing Yuan Shu *now*, but what about two months' time? We have other matters to plan before the decree that he – or rather, his barbed and biased counsel – rightly predicts can be finalised. But this proves the point once and for all: Lü Bu is no threat until peace is achieved elsewhere, provided he is managed properly."

"And he shall be," Cao Cao chuckled. "He *shall be*, Guo Jia."

The communications between Excellency Cao Cao and Governor Lü Bu would be safely suspended: Cao Cao could concentrate his energies on smashing the defiant Yellow Turban factions in Yingchuan – a prefecture that straddled the border between Yu and Yan Provinces – and Runan Prefecture in eastern Yu Province. This would probably have multiple benefits to the pacification mission, since the Yellow Turbans were most likely allied to the warlord Yuan Shu and causing trouble on his behalf, just as the Black Mountain Bandits were.

* * * * * * * * * * * *

47

The Yellow Turbans of Runan were a paradox: the uprising had once been popular, but the doctrine of the newest incarnations owed more to banditry and anarchy than the original theological and reformist mantras. Poor villages and underfunded towns that had once been sources of new recruits were now targets for raids: people that had once defied their parents and joined the Yellow Turbans were now determined to be rid of the constant threat.

The symbol that defined the rebel army – the yellow scarf that bound their uncut hair – was now more than flagrant disobedience of the rule that no one other than the emperor could wear yellow above their head and a declaration that power was destined to shift from the few to the many; it was now more than a manifestation of the belief that the Han Dynasty had exhausted its mandate. It still meant those things to some, but to many others it merely represented a complete breakdown of society. To many, the Yellow Turbans was now nothing more than a thousands-strong criminal gang that had no benevolent intentions. Some within the Yellow Turbans still felt that they were fighting for the people, and that the villages that rebuked them were 'collaborators': there was no clarity anymore, just a cycle of violence that men like Cao Cao hoped to end.

One man in Runan was already taking the fight to the Yellow Turbans: he was almost two metres tall, and his physique was muscular yet flabby from his vast food consumption. His strength was immense, and he commanded the respect of his entire village, despite his low intellect and lack of wit: that man's name was Xu Chu, and his style name was Zhongkang.

The chief of Xu Chu's village suggested that the Yellow Turbans could only be defended against if the people relocated to a fortress: Xu Chu agreed, and he set about the construction immediately. The finished fort was made of wood and stone, and the Yellow Turbans marvelled at how quickly it had appeared: what amazed them more, however, was that Xu Chu had been working with little rest and could take credit for at least a third of the work.

The leaders of the Runan Yellow Turbans, Liu Pi and Huang Shao, were veteran officers that fought during the original uprising 12 years previously, so they knew the importance of strategy and symbolism. They knew that Xu Chu's fortress was strategically important, and they knew that it was going an inspiration to others that might be contemplating defying the Yellow Turbans; they also knew that destroying it was going to be a challenge, so they brought an army of 10,000 with them.

"This man's too dangerous to be left," Liu Pi said as he stared at the fort. "This 'Xu Chu' either joins us or he dies, Huang Shao."

Huang Shao nodded and said, "**Agreed! Begin the assault!**"

"**They're attacking! Zhongkang, they're attacking!**" a lookout screamed as the Yellow Turbans approached the fort: Xu Chu ambled up the steps and joined him on the battlements.

"This won't be hard," Xu Chu insisted. "We'll shoot at them."

"We haven't enough arrows to repel ten-thousand men!" the

lookout retorted.

"Let's fire anyway," Xu Chu said calmly, "and I'll think of something if we run out before they go home."

"*Aiee...* this is my last day!" the lookout cried as he ran toward a colleague at the other end of the wall. Archers hurried to the battlements, and the Yellow Turbans were briefly repelled by the thin volley of arrows that followed.

"They can't repel us like that!" Liu Pi insisted. "They can't have enough arrows! We should just keep charging!"

"**KEEP GOING, MEN!**" Huang Shao ordered, and the Yellow Turbans pressed their attack. Men reached the walls with their siege ladders, but when they reached the top, men pushed their ladders back or Xu Chu was waiting with a strange smile on his face. The latter was a worse fate: Xu Chu would grab the climber's head and press his thick thumbs into the man's eye sockets. When that ceased to entertain him, Xu Chu hurled the blinded, howling victim away from the wall or twisted his head to snap his neck before letting the body fall onto the next climber. That continued until the arrows started to run low: the village chief hurried to Xu Chu and said, "We'll soon have no defence against them, Zhongkang! What do we do?"

"I know," Xu Chu said cheerfully. "Fetch many, many stones, little ones, and bring them to the walls. Make big piles at each wall."

The chief was perplexed, but he could see no other choice but to do as Xu Chu had asked. As the last of the arrows left the south wall, Xu Chu picked up a stone and said, "I'll do the rest!"

Xu Chu leant over the wall and hurled his stone at the nearest climber with all of his might: the tiny projectile cracked the man's skull and killed him almost instantly.

"*Ayah!* **Back, back!**" another climber shrieked as he watched the spectacle from a nearby ladder. The men below him descended as quickly as they could, but it was not fast enough to save them from being struck by the tiny projectiles that Xu Chu now wielded with such incredible force.

"**What in Heaven is going on up there???**" Liu Pi cried.

""He's... throwing little *stones* at the men!" Huang Shao exclaimed. "The men're falling like leaves! This man is a monster!"

Once word of Xu Chu's actions had reached the climbers on the other ladders across the southern wall, the siege climbers abandoned their mission altogether; Xu Chu laughed merrily and moved to the west wall to repeat the violence, and that soon led to another retreat. When the northern wall was relieved, Liu Pi and Huang Shao knew that the morale of their force was gone and retreat was inevitable.

"One man... *one man*!" Liu Pi complained as he fled with his army.

"We'll try again!" Huang Shao replied.

Xu Chu was hugged and praised by the people of the fortress, and the day was won. The evening was spent collecting the fired arrows from the ground around the fortress while Xu Chu was entertained with a modest banquet derived from the meagre supplies that remained.

But the Yellow Turbans were not defeated, and they returned within days; and after many days of being besieged, the food in the fortress stores ran out.

"Let me get food," Xu Chu said to the exhausted chief.

"Where from...?" the chief asked cynically.

Xu Chu turned to look at a large ox that was chewing at dried foliage nearby.

"You can't kill it!" the chief exclaimed. "Besides, how can one ox feed us all??? There are hundreds of us!"

"I can trade it for food," Xu Chu suggested.

"With who...?" the chief asked disdainfully.

"With the Yellow Turbans," Xu Chu replied.

"With the-! ...*No*," the chief chortled. "How can we deal with them, you big silly man??? They'll rush the fort and kill us when they know that we have no food!"

"They're rebelling because of the way that people are hungry and miserable," Xu Chu said. "They wouldn't rebel for that and then let us starve!"

"*Aiee*... alright, go on," the chief sighed. "We were dead already if not for you... let's see if you can give us another miracle."

Xu Chu climbed onto the ox and rode the animal toward the gates of the fortress.

"You... you'll never guess what's happening now," Huang Shao snickered as he approached Liu Pi. "That big fat idiot Xu Chu has actually come to us with an ox, looking to trade it for food!"

Liu Pi grinned and giggled, "Stop winding me up."

"No, really!" Huang Shao continued. "He's here with it, asking us if we have any food for them! He wants to swap!"

"I need to see this for myself," Liu Pi said through laughter.

Liu Pi and Huang Shao hurried to the gates of their camp: the Yellow Turban guards were awestruck at the sight of the giant Xu Chu and his large ox, and they did not want to approach him after word of his stone-throwing feats of recent days.

"So, here you are: the champion of Runan," Liu Pi heckled as he approached Xu Chu with sword in hand. "I hear you want to trade that mangy ox for food."

"*Mangy*...? There's nothing wrong with this ox!" Xu Chu retorted. "It's big, and strong – I rode it here, and I'm very, very heavy, you know."

"...Yes, you do appear to be," Liu Pi replied condescendingly. "So, uh... how much food were you planning on swapping it for?"

"We really don't have much," Xu Chu replied honestly. "Enough for everyone – there are about a thousand of us – to have two small meals would be good; I'll find something else to trade when we need more."

"...Uh huh... 'When you need more'," Liu Pi chuckled. "Alright."

"Don't think that I don't trust you – I don't – but I'm going to ride back now, and when you bring the food, then you can have the ox," Xu Chu continued. "I just realised that I can't carry it all back on my own, so that would make more sense."

"It probably would," Liu Pi chortled. "I'm sure they're missing your protection anyway."

"My family and the other people in my village are very brave, and they're protecting the fortress while I'm here," Xu Chu replied. "They care about me, yes, but the fortress has protection, plenty of protection, so they don't need me."

Liu Pi's face fell as a new thought entered his mind.

"...I should go," Xu Chu added. "Although I said I'm not needed, I'm sure they're worried, and-"
"Yes, yes, fine," Liu Pi grumbled.
Huang Shao – who was oblivious to the concerns that now weighed on Liu Pi's mind – laughed and said, "Go on then, friend: see you soon."
Xu Chu smiled, remounted his ox, and returned to the fortress.
"...A *thousand*...?" Liu Pi mused. "And how many... are as big and strong as him?"
"He may be big, but Heaven blessed him with a very small brain," Huang Shao joked. "He's also far too trusting. And come to think of it, I don't see why we didn't kill him while he was-"
"Hey, we're supposed to be fighting for the *people*, and they *are* the people," Liu Pi scolded. "We're only fighting them until they renounce the Han, Huang Shao. Let him go back, and we'll do this deal properly. If we're kind, maybe they'll see sense and *join us*, and then he'd be *our* big idiot."
Huang Shao nodded agreeably, and preparations began to collect the food.

"You said WHAT???"
The elders of the village were dumbstruck: only the chief was angry enough to overcome his fear and confront Xu Chu upon his return from the Yellow Turban camp.
"Don't be scared," Xu Chu chuckled. "They'll do as I asked."
"...*Aiee*... we're dead. **We're *dead*!**" the chief cried.
The nearby villagers groaned miserably.
"No we're not!" Xu Chu said. "Soon we'll be fed and happy again!"
The reaction to that statement was more groaning, but nobody had a plan, so they waited for what they thought to be the only possible outcome of Xu Chu's actions.

Liu Pi and Huang Shao led the Yellow Turban trading delegation, which stopped at a distance from the fort: they had brought a quantity of grain that met the needs that Xu Chu had described. Xu Chu had the gates opened, and he rode out of the fortress on the ox: when he reached Liu Pi and Huang Shao, he said, "Here I am. As you can see, the ox is very strong. Can your men bring the food to the gates? It isn't that I don't trust you – I don't – but-"
"Yeah, yeah, alright," Liu Pi sighed. "Lads: carry the stuff to the gates."
The Yellow Turbans brought the food to the gates and left it on the ground; they then backed away and Liu Pi said, "Now give us the ox, big fellow."
Xu Chu rode to Liu Pi once again, dismounted, and said, "You've been very honest. Thank you."
"Look, just... just go away, yeah...?" Liu Pi sighed. "Consider this a last gesture of goodwill. We're still enemies, Xu Chu, and I will still destroy your fort if you don't surrender soon."
"We'll see, since we won't give up easily," Xu Chu replied. "Goodbye, then."
Xu Chu returned to the gates without looking back.
"...He really trusts us, despite what he says," Huang Shao whispered.
Liu Pi sighed and said, "I suppose so; either that or- ...**HEY!**"

246

The ox had wrested itself free of its Yellow Turban minders, turned, and fled toward the gates of the fortress: the Yellow Turbans drew their swords, and Huang Shao shouted, "**YOU TRICKED US!**"

Xu Chu turned, realised that the ox had followed him and laughed, saying, "Silly thing. You don't live here anymore! Come on, I'll take you back!"

Xu Chu mounted the ox again and rode the animal back to Liu Pi and Huang Shao.

"You think your performing ox is very amusing, but I'm not laughing," Liu Pi growled. "Don't play games with us!"

"It's a bit silly, that's all," Xu Chu replied. "I'm sure it understands now that I've brought it back."

Xu Chu dismounted and returned to the gates, but within minutes, the ox was free and trotting back to the fortress once again. When Xu Chu returned for the second time, Liu Pi said, "I'm going to kill the thing in a minute, and maybe you as well, you big-!"

"Don't be angry," Xu Chu said. "If it runs again, I'll bring it back."

"**Yeah, and how often do we do that???**" Huang Shao cried.

"One more time at the most, I promise," Xu Chu replied as he dismounted again.

"...That fat oaf is up to something... he must be," Liu Pi grumbled as he watched Xu Chu walk away. "There's a plan, a scheme, a- ...Here we go again."

The latest group of ox-minders were lying on the floor and groaning, and the ox was running after Xu Chu yet again: Huang Shao lost his temper and bellowed, "**XU CHU! YOU'LL DIE TOMORROW, IF NOT TODAY, XU CHU!**"

Xu Chu turned, looked at the ox, smiled, and said, "Naughty thing! This time, I'm going to make you understand that you don't live here with us anymore! I didn't want to scare you, but now I have no choice!"

What Xu Chu did next left the defenders and the Yellow Turbans without words: he pushed the ox onto its side, grabbed the flailing animal's tail and dragged it toward Liu Pi and Huang Shao, shouting, "**I think it will stay with you this time!**"

"...Run... **RUN!**" Liu Pi cried as his courage left him completely: the sight of a man dragging such a large and heavy beast of burden made every single one of the Yellow Turbans lose their nerve and flee without collecting their ox.

"He's Heaven-sent!" the village chief gasped as he watched the spectacle from the fortress wall: people surged out of the gates to marvel at Xu Chu, who released the terrified ox and laughed childishly.

Xu Chu's fortress would not be bothered by the Yellow Turbans again. That would not be the end of the problems that the Yellow Turbans of Runan faced, however: Cao Cao's army would arrive within weeks, and that would be the greatest threat that they had faced since the coalition that had defeated their original rebellion.

＊＊＊＊＊＊＊＊＊＊＊＊

48

Cao Cao's army attracted a lot of attention as it moved westward toward the capital of Yingchuan Prefecture: villagers were fearful of the reputation of such forces, but Cao Cao had told his officers that the penalty for looting was death. This was an army that would not begrudge that instruction, however: they were better fed, better equipped and better trained than what had become an unfortunate norm in China for the last 40 years.

Each soldier had at the very least a filled water pouch, a filled food pouch, a shirt, trousers, a leather chest plate, a leather helmet, a sword, pike, spear or bow and arrows, and shoes on his feet: there would be no barefoot or even naked infantrymen on this campaign, as there had been at the lowest points for the Han army. The cavalry were few in number, but the horses were nourished and had fine saddles, and the men that rode them were better equipped than the foot soldiers. Each of Cao Cao's officers had their own horse and a grand battle standard bearing their name and the name of their lord: even the advisers enjoyed the relative comfort of riding horses, although the majority were dressed in their usual robes rather than armoured.

"This will be a grand first victory," Cao Cao said with pride: he wore a gilded helmet topped with a red plume and gilded armour, and looked every bit the grand hero. Cao Cao's ever-present bodyguard-general, Dian Wei, remained tirelessly vigilant in the face of possible assassination attempts.

"We should be mindful that the Qing Province Corps might have divided loyalties," Xun Wenruo warned.

"It's not lost on me, Wenruo," Cao Cao sighed. "I lost a lot after Xu Province: I expect the odd brigade to mutiny here and there."

Xiahou Dun shook his head and said, "Why bring them then, Mengde? Why do we pit Yellow Turban against Yellow Turban?"

Cao Cao did not answer.

"Major Xiahou Dun... it's 'Major', isn't it...?" Guo Jia said.

"Like I know," Xiahou Dun grumbled. "What are you, Mister Guo?"

"A senior adviser to the Excellency of Works," Guo Jia replied.

"Who's the-? ...Oh, right, yeah, Mengde's the Excellency of Works, isn't he," Xiahou Dun said. "Me, I dunno: am I a major...? A general...? I dunno. I just smash things when I'm asked to."

Cao Cao laughed at the words.

"But nobody answered my question!" Xiahou Dun complained.

"I intended to," Guo Jia replied. "We need to use the Qing Province Corps at present. We have a 'personnel shortage'."

"We're the imperial army now!" Xiahou Dun retorted. "Get that smug bastard *Yuan Shao* to provide some men! He's Commander-in-Chief, isn't he??? That, or what about the army that-!"

"Yuan Shao's men... are Yuan Shao's men," Cao Cao interrupted. "The army is fractured; many still serve Li Jue, and you *know that*, Xiahou Yuanrang."

"AAAAH! I *know*, but I don't see *how*!" Xiahou Dun cried.

"The imperial army was a mess at best, a joke at worst," Guo Jia replied. "Dong Zhuo reorganised it after he sacked Luoyang, and a lot of good Han officers have died since. The actual army was always made up of paid mercenaries, donated Southern Xiongnu

tribesmen, convicts, conscripts and whatnot. Many Liang Province locals joined the army when Dong Zhuo moved the capital."
Xiahou Dun was silent.
"…Did I answer your question…?" Guo Jia prompted.
"**Yes, you did!**" Xiahou Dun barked. "**But it's still *ridiculous*!**"
"Yuanrang has a point," Cao Cao conceded. "The Qing Province Corps are conscripted Yellow Turbans from that region: how will they react to being pitted against their own kind…?"
"You already answered your own question," Guo Jia replied. "But we'll be fine, my lord. Liu Pi and Huang Shao are 'old friends of yours', are they not?"
Cao Cao snorted and said, "Yes. I already had the joys of fighting those two idiots in Yingchuan over a decade ago. This time they don't have better men like Bo Cai to rally them: I hear that they were recently bested by a lone warrior – a 'demon giant' – that held off ten-thousand of their best recruits from a wooden fortress that was otherwise manned by a few hundred inexperienced peasants from his village. Some say he did it with pebbles."
"Tavern gossip is fun, isn't it?" Guo Jia chuckled. "I've been wondering if it's true since I heard it."
"Whether it's true or not, the end of the Yellow Turbans is nigh," Cao Cao declared. "I won't permit their kind to cause havoc anymore. Liu Pi and Huang Shao will either surrender or die."

The Yellow Turban army heard about Cao Cao's advance and consolidated around the capital of Yingchuan, which was being defended by Cao Cao's close ally Xiahou Yuan. A sea of campsites greeted the imperial army's vanguard: Xun Wenruo and Guo Jia oversaw the assembly of fenced camps and then ordered the officers to meet in the command tent.
"Why are we talking?" Xiahou Dun complained. "They're there, we're here: let's just smash them, rescue Miaocai, and-!"
"You sound like that fool brute Zhang Fei that cost Liu Bei the governorship of Xu Province," Cao Cao said admonishingly. "Use your head! There are at least fifty-thousand of them! We number only ten-thousand at present!"
"There's reinforcements on the way, Mengde, but we won't need them," Xiahou Dun replied.
"Don't you remember Xingyang?" Cao Cao asked. "Don't you remember the pain of losing? Don't you remember the loss of poor Wei Zi? Do you want to put Miaocai's life at risk needlessly???"
"Liu Pi and Huang Shao are not in the same league as Xu Rong," Xiahou Dun scoffed. "They're mediocrities. They're stupid scum: the Yellow Turbans are all-!"
A scruffy infantry major coughed deliberately.
"…What's your problem?" Xiahou Dun barked.
"He is a former Yellow Turban," Cao Cao explained. "You're the one that brought up the composition of my army before, Yuanrang: the Qing Corps are an invaluable part of it. Now, if you don't mind I'd like to get something done today. Xun Wenruo, Guo Fengxiao, Xun Gongda: please share your thoughts."
The three advisers gathered around an easel and studied the map that was set upon it.
"The situation is classic," Xun Wenruo began. "There are a lot of them, but they have been exhibiting signs of fragmentation. If we

use their huddling tactic against them by surrounding them and cutting them off from the river, we can then destroy their camps, scatter them, and liberate the city. If they do not surrender, we can coordinate with Xiahou Yuan."

The short, stern-faced Yue Jin gestured that he would like to speak and asked, "What if they attack before we can surround them, gentlemen...?"

"A fair point, Yue Jin," Xun Gongda replied. "Our camp is adequate for resisting a limited number of attacks of a limited magnitude: if they were to launch an all-out assault, we could be surrounded ourselves. But we've planned for that. Scouts have been placed by your colleague, the vanguard commander Yu Jin."

Yue Jin turned to the innocuous Yu Jin and nodded respectfully.

"We have barricades that can be erected if an attack is imminent, and we can use variations on the 'empty camp ruse' if needs be," Xun Gongda continued. "The key thing to remember is – and I hope that the Qing Corps representatives can forgive me for saying so – that the Yellow Turbans are a coalition of disaffected peoples that fight for a range of reasons. The chance of their remaining together when enough pressure is applied is unlikely, and we hope to win some of them over with our reform plans."

"Reform plans...?" Xiahou Dun chuckled.

"We're not here to murder people," Guo Jia replied. "We're here to pacify the region. We're going to try and make them understand that the Han government is freed from the corruption that engulfed it and aggravated them in the past, and that the future should be discussed around tables, not fought for on battlefields. We're here to curb wrongfully obtained military power and grant a different form of empowerment to the deserving: a voice, a chance to speak and be listened to."

"And the 'undeserving'...?" a Qing Corps captain asked.

"You were in Qing Province: you know the answer," Cao Cao said. "Anarchists and criminals will be crushed: the disaffected and misguided will be heard. You must trust that the correct distinctions will be made."

Some of the junior Qing Corps officers murmured uneasily, as they were ostracised by some of the populace for their deciding to stay with Cao Cao's army after the Xu Province campaigns that made no distinctions whatsoever.

"Liu Pi and Huang Shao are frustratingly unrepentant," Cao Cao continued. "This is the second time that those two have chosen to wear that treasonous article at their brow and harm the people: I am in a forgiving mood, but this is their last chance."

Guo Jia noticed the discontent among the Qing Corps officers and said, "That is all, gentlemen: detailed instructions will be passed to the senior officers, who will then brief subordinates appropriately. All but those senior officers are dismissed."

The lower-ranking officers gradually dispersed, leaving Cao Cao, Guo Jia, Xun Wenruo, Xun Gongda, Xiahou Dun, Yue Jin and Yu Jin to continue their discussions.

"We'll lose a fair few again this time," Guo Jia supposed.

"To desertion or defection...?" Yu Jin wondered. "The latter could be problematic."

"Why bring them in the first place then???" Xiahou Dun cried.

"We've had a few hundred men join us as we've travelled," Xun

Wenruo said optimistically.

"Yes, but not the famed 'giant' that humbled the Yellow Turbans already," Cao Cao sighed. "Have our scout forces been able to locate him?"

"We might have the location of his 'fortress', but the inhabitants of the place we've found are so aggressive that they might be bandits," Guo Jia reported.

"Leave them," Xun Wenruo suggested. "Whether they're bandits or defensive locals, they're not who we're after."

"My uncle is quite right," Xun Gongda said. "The people are not our enemy, as you have said yourself, Excellency Cao."

"...'Excellency Cao'," Cao Cao chortled. "How strange that sounds, even after so long. I can't help but wonder if Yuanrang was right about our 'Commander-in-Chief', though: even if he now hates me, Yuan Shao's ancestral home of Ru County is under threat, and besides that he should want to help His Majesty regain the-"

"Yuan Shao's presence would be a threat," Guo Jia interrupted. "Letting even one of his cronies near the Son of Heaven would be a mistake; allowing him to deploy forces near or even close to Yan Province would be a disaster."

Cao Cao nodded sadly and replied, "I know that. I know that, Fengxiao. I just... I just want things to be different."

"Then we should break the Yellow Turbans here and push them back into Runan," Guo Jia said. "That will make a significant first difference."

Cao Cao smiled, turned to Yu Jin, and said, "When you came to me from Wang Lang, you were not shown trust: much time has passed, and I now trust you to be my vanguard. We'll waste no more time: deploy your men immediately and hit them hard."

Xiahou Dun grunted as a sign that he was mystified.

"If we do nothing, they'll know that we have a better long-term plan," Cao Cao explained. "We must 'feign ignorance'."

"Oh, right," Xiahou Dun said. "What do I do?"

"Xiahou Dun, Yue Jin: you'll ready your men to pincer their encampment from the north and west and march as soon as you're ready," Cao Cao ordered. "I will personally lead the southern force."

The three officers bowed and departed.

"...A calm before a storm," Cao Cao murmured.

Xun Wenruo frowned and said, "Pardon, Excellency?"

"A great storm is coming," Cao Cao replied. "The 'Yellow Sky' that the Turbans predicted has not come to pass: instead, dark clouds gather that will rain defeat upon them. After that, a chill wind will harm the bandits of the north... and after that, violent winds and rains will batter the warlords into submission, and the fire of a Han renewed will purify the land. They will all wish that they had stayed indoors."

Guo Jia laughed at the words; Xun Wenruo and Xun Gongda smiled slightly, but they were concerned that Cao Cao might be suffering one of his 'headaches' and do something costly.

Yu Jin led his forces toward the eastern side of the Yellow Turban encampment, turned to his battle-hardened deputy Zhu Ling and said, "Do you wish you'd stayed with your old master yet?"

Zhu Ling sighed miserably and replied, "No, commander. I do not miss Yuan Shao's 'leadership'."

"I'm teasing," Yu Jin promised. "The men are nervous... and so am I, but not because of the fighting."

"The Qing Corps brigades concern you," Zhu Ling guessed. "Isn't that why we're setting them against the enemy first?"

Yu Jin smiled silently and signalled to his army drummer: the rhythmic beating of the war drum roused the men and indicated the start of the attack.

"By the heavens!" Huang Shao exclaimed as he tried to secure his sword-belt. "I thought they were going to-!"

"Better for us that they're stupid," Liu Pi interrupted. "We outnumber them, so they probably hoped a shock attack would cause a panic. They're about to learn otherwise, aren't they?"

Liu Pi and Huang Shao left their command tent and went to the eastern edge of their camp. The Yellow Turbans had not been scattered by Yu Jin's attack, and the attackers had been additionally blunted by a small number of defections by Qing Province Corps soldiers and officers.

"...I'd heard that Cao Cao was some foretold as some sort of 'Hero of Chaos' by a famous appraiser," Huang Shao said with contempt. "He's certainly a hero *to* chaos: who'd pit former Yellow Turbans against Yellow Turbans if they had any sense?"

"He's arrogant," Liu Pi replied. "They all are. We-"

A sudden, noisy panic among the Yellow Turbans camped close to the city walls silenced Liu Pi: Yu Jin had led a spirited charge that had cut through the defensive lines and left a trail of dead and wounded men in its wake.

"**Arrows!**" Huang Shao cried. "**Shoot him, idiots! SHOOT HIM!**"

A thin volley of arrows rained down on Yu Jin and his horsemen, who promptly retreated: they had done a lot of damage to morale, however, and Liu Pi knew it.

"...He's gone," Huang Shao said with relief.

"I hope we got a lot of new friends from Qing Province," Liu Pi said fearfully. "If that man that just charged us is typical of Cao Cao's forces, we'll need them."

The city was reacting in the wake of the realisation that a relief force had come: the defenders were firing arrows at the camps at the base of the eastern wall.

"If that man was typical, would we have people leaving them and joining us?" Huang Shao retorted. "I'll lead a force against them tomorrow. They'll soon get the message that Yingchuan is ours: after that, we'll get Cao Cao, advance north and take Xuchang, throw that boy emperor off of his gilded throne, and take the country for the people!"

"...I won't argue, but be careful," Liu Pi replied.

Yu Jin and Zhu Ling advanced toward Cao Cao's command tent with expressions on their faces that betrayed their fear of what their lord would say.

"...I'll go in alone," Yu Jin decided.

"Agreed: he'll only want to speak to you, anyway," Zhu Ling supposed. "He hates me."

"He doesn't much like me either," Yu Jin sighed. "I've probably got a demotion coming to me at the very least."

"...We did our best," Zhu Ling replied.

When the two men reached the command tent, Yu Jin smiled and said, "You go back to the men and reassure them that everything is going to be fine… you're a far better liar than I am."
Zhu Ling laughed desperately and retreated.
"Ah! General Yu," Guo Jia hailed.
Yu Jin shuddered nervously, bowed low and said, "M-Mister Guo. I am here to-"
"This way!" Guo Jia chuckled. "You're expected!"
Yu Jin bowed for a second time and followed Guo Jia into the tent.
"General Yu," Cao Cao said with a smile. "I understand that you drew blood at the foot of the walls and alerted the defenders, thus giving them hope! You've exceeded my expectations."
Yu Jin kowtowed and said, "But I failed you, Excellency! Men defected and deserted! We were forced to retreat!"
"So…?" Cao Cao chuckled. "Nothing was beyond my expectation… except for your bravery, General Yu. In fact, I've had a Qing Corps captain in here speaking very highly of you, saying that a lot of men that were contemplating defection changed their minds when they saw what a demon you were in battle!"
"If anything, General Yu, you've helped us to retain men and maintain the morale in the city," Xun Wenruo suggested.
"From now on, I'll have no more doubts about you," Cao Cao promised. "You're a hero: let no man say otherwise! Dian Wei!"
Cao Cao's titan bodyguard advanced toward Yu Jin with a jar of wine in his tree-like arms: Yu Jin stared upward at the fearsome man with involuntary terror.
"Enjoy, General," Dian Wei said as he thrust the wine jar into Yu Jin's hands.
"Th-th-thank you, M-Mister Dian Wei, and thank you, Your Excellency," Yu Jin stammered. "I… I am-"
"Don't you dare say that you're unworthy!" Cao Cao said as Dian Wei returned to his side. "Tomorrow, they'll probably attack: you may go and rest now. Enjoy that wine, but not too much. You'll need you wits to repel the force they send against us. Oh, and I vow that your men will be rewarded at a safer moment."
"Y-yes, Excellency!" Yu Jin replied. "I will do better tomorrow!"
Yu Jin bowed gratefully and retreated.
"…A future hero, indeed," Cao Cao said. "But I'll need more."
"You'll find none of the heroes that you seek amongst these Yellow Turbans in Runan," Guo Jia sighed.
"Oh, I know that," Cao Cao said. "But I got Xu Huang from the White Wave Bandits: he's almost here with the rest of the army, isn't he Wenruo…?"
"He's shown incredible skill at getting men moving at speed," Xun Wenruo replied. "It must be because of his time fighting the Qiang in the northwest, or maybe some bandit history, conducting flash raids. …Or maybe he's just got a natural gift. Whatever the reason for it, he's an asset."
"We'll deploy him here," Cao Cao decided. "Ah… I almost look forward to tomorrow. I think it will prove to be quite decisive."
Cao Cao's counsel agreed silently.

∗∗∗∗∗∗∗∗∗∗∗∗

49

The Yellow Turban co-commander Huang Shao led a force toward Cao Cao's fenced camps at dawn. His standard was simple – his name and the title 'General of the People' on a piece of plain white cloth – and his soldiers were dressed in little more than their ordinary clothes and a simple leather chest plate: their bright yellow scarves were the only defining and consistent feature from one man – or woman – to another. Cao Cao's forces – who were uniform in appearance – arrayed so professionally that the Yellow Turban general was left wondering if the Han really had experienced an improvement in their fortunes. Huang Shao's followers were less daunted: some of the officers had even encouraged their units to chant the old mantra that had been taught to them by the founder of the 'Way of Peace', Zhang Jue:

**"Han's mandate has passed!
Yellow Sky, soon here!
In this renewing year,
Prosperous all, at last!"**

The words haunted the souls of the Qing Province Corps that Cao Cao commanded: those words had once roused the impoverished and indignant to take up arms against the state, and the Han officers were aware of their power.
"We're bound to have more defections from this," Yu Jin complained.
"I don't hear any chanting on our side," Zhu Ling replied.
Some men were trying to leave the Han battle lines, but their officers did their best to keep them where they were.
"We have to stick to the plan," Yu Jin insisted. **"They'll charge if we hold."**
        Huang Shao's heckling officers became increasingly nervous when they realised that the Han lines were holding firm.
"What do we do?" a Yellow Turban major asked.
"...Charge," Huang Shao ordered. **"What's wrong with me? They're outnumbered! This'll be easy! CHARGE!"**
Thousands of Yellow Turbans descended on the smaller Han army: Yu Jin and Zhu Ling met the charge with a line of shields and pikes, and the Yellow Turbans incurred serious casualties that caused immediate panic.
"Second wave! Second wave!" Huang Shao cried. **"I'll charge them too! Come on everyone! 'Yellow Sky soon here'! 'Prosperous all'! 'Prosperous all'!"**
Huang Shao led his men toward the Han lines, but it was a trap: Xu Huang led a second force of Han soldiers from the west, trapping Huang Shao's men in a pincer. Huang Shao tried to fight his way out, and initially seemed to be capable of doing so, until a new force arrived: it was led by Cao Cao's bodyguard, Dian Wei.
"*Ayah*! It's the demon man!" a Turban from Yingchuan cried.
"Dian Wei of Jiwu!" another local exclaimed. **"The evil comes! The evil comes!"**
Dian Wei lived up to his reputation: he rode straight into the Yellow Turban forces and howled like a wild animal, scattering

men in all directions with violent, effortless swings of his heavy halberd. Men's heads were cleaved open, limbs were parted from bodies and brains were dashed on the ground. The impact of the carnage was immediate: hundreds of men fled, and Huang Shao sensed that the end was near. Dian Wei leapt from his horse and continued his rampage: he destroyed any man that strayed too close to him in the confusion of the normal exchanges between Han and Turban infantry that were happening all around him.

"**Keep fighting! Keep fighting!**" Huang Shao pleaded, but many of his followers did not have the heart to fight against former Turbans from Qing Province and the likes of Dian Wei. Xu Huang's force was more measured, but the former White Wave Bandit was still making easy work of harrying Huang Shao's rear lines: his horsemen were formidable enough, but the athletic Xu Huang was intimidating enough on his own. Xu Huang was not as strong as Dian Wei, but he still wielded his halberd with ease and knocked down man after man as he rode along the lines of Turbans.

"**Where is Cao Cao???**" Huang Shao screamed desperately. "**He's a coward! Here is Huang Shao: where is Cao Cao???**"

"**I'll take your head to him!**" Yu Jin bellowed through laughter as he and his horsemen charged at Huang Shao and his elite bodyguards: the bodyguards were quickly overwhelmed, and Huang Shao fell shortly afterward. The Yellow Turbans scattered completely once they knew that their leader was dead, and the battlefield was filled with Han victory cries.

"**Prosperous Han! Prosperous Han!**" Dian Wei chanted mischievously as he paraded the severed head of a Yellow Turban major. "**What colour is the sky?**"

"**Azure! Azure!**" the Han soldiers replied. "**Glory to the Han!**"

"...Yingchuan is saved," Yu Jin said as he surveyed the battlefield.

"I wonder if we're to hurry there," Zhu Ling replied.

The news of the victory was taken to Cao Cao along with Huang Shao's severed head for ritual inspection.

"...I never really knew the man for this to have much of a point," Cao Cao said dryly. "But we're sure this is Huang Shao...?"

"The retreat suggests that it was," Yu Jin replied.

Cao Cao looked at the grinning, gore-laden Dian Wei and said, "You had fun, I see."

"Many fled at the sight of General Dian," Xu Huang said.

"I expect that they did!" Cao Cao chuckled.

"Some locals have even surrendered to us and either burned or submitted their yellow scarves as a sign of their 'enlightenment'," Yu Jin reported. "When news reaches Liu Pi, he'll surely retreat."

"Hopefully," Cao Cao scoffed. "Poor Miaocai has been trapped in there for too long as it is. Are Yuanrang and Yue Jin ready to advance, Wenruo?"

"They are, my lord," Xun Wenruo replied. "Do you still intend to lead the fourth army?"

"...No," Cao Cao decided. "Xu Huang: you shall lead it."

Xu Huang bowed humbly and said, "I am truly blessed to have your trust, Your Excellency. I shall not disappoint you."

"If we can move immediately, we should," Guo Jia suggested.

"Very good," Cao Cao replied.

Liu Pi's mood was sombre when he heard the news of his colleague's demise from recently-returned survivors of the failed attack on Cao Cao's camp.

"I never liked him," Liu Pi chortled.

His officers were silent.

"That was... a bad joke," Liu Pi sighed. "How bad is it now?"

A major coughed uncomfortably and said, "There's little hope of holding Yingchuan now, General Liu. The city knows about our defeats, and our scouts report that Cao Cao is on his way here."

"Other scouts report strange goings-on in nearby villages," a captain said. "It may be that they have more men."

"More...?" Liu Pi exclaimed. "So... so we've been outwitted? They've positioned armies on all sides to-!"

"**ENEMY ATTACK!**" a bloodied scout cried as he scrambled into the command tent on his hands and knees. "**ENEMY-!**"

"**I know!**" Liu Pi barked. "**Everyone get moving!**"

The officers hurried out of the command tent. Liu Pi stared at the scout, who was now kneeling on the floor and sobbing.

"...What village are you from, lad?" Liu Pi asked.

"Nandun," the scout whimpered. "Nandun, in Runan."

"...Lucky you, then," Liu Pi continued. "You're going home soon. When you can, go and pass on that we're retreating. Can you go now? Are you hurt...?"

The scout got to his feet, wiped tears from his eyes and left the tent without answering his commander.

"...Cao Cao, the Butcher of Xu Province, and 'Crafty Villain': why does Heaven love you so...?" Liu Pi chuckled miserably. "Why, when all we ever wanted was a *life*, instead of an *existence*... are we so *hated*...?"

Liu Pi sighed woefully and started to gather the few campaign-planning materials that he used in order to imitate a professional military commander.

While Liu Pi continued his mechanical, emotionally-disconnected preparations for departure, the rest of the Yellow Turban army did what it could to repel the attack by Yu Jin. The situation was already bleak when Xiahou Dun suddenly began an attack on the southern camps: he was quickly joined by Yue Jin, who laid siege to the northern camps. When Liu Pi finally finished entrusting the contents of his abandoned command tent to a female subordinate, he journeyed to the eastern front to see the situation for himself.

Liu Pi searched the rear lines for an officer, and when he found one he tugged him away from the barricades and said, "Report."

The captain fought tears as he replied, "The south, the north... and now someone called 'Xu Huang' is-"

"Xu Huang... a former White Wave Bandit, or so I'd hope he was 'former'," Liu Pi grumbled. "So rumours that they're still helping the Han are probably true; bastards. Two-faced, selfish-!"

"**ARROWS!**"

Liu Pi and the captain ducked to avoid a volley of Han arrows: when the short burst ended, Liu Pi said, "So we're surrounded on all sides: I know what'll come next, because it's obvious. We need to get away from Yingchuan. As we discussed, alright...? Men stay and cover, others-"

"Yes, *sir*," the captain replied cynically.

Liu Pi sensed the indignation in the captain's voice and smiled humbly before he withdrew to issue orders to the camps that were close to the city. But he was too late: the northern, western, southern and eastern gates of Yingchuan City all opened and small armies of angry conscripts poured out of them with their weapons raised and hollering curses at the Yellow Turbans that had been besieging them. At the head of the eastern force was a man with a surprisingly kind face hidden by thick whiskers and a black battle helmet: his standard – which was being carried by a youth in leather armour – read, 'Xiahou Yuan, Administrator of Chenliu'. The morale of the Yellow Turbans – who were now being attacked by 8 armies on all sides – disintegrated, along with any military order that they still had.

"By the heavens," Liu Pi whimpered. "Didn't I get this so very wrong, Huang Shao: and I thought *I* was the smart one. You were the smart one after all... by *dying*."

Liu Pi spotted a horse nearby: its rider was slumped lifelessly along the animal's neck.

"...This is no time for ritual," Liu Pi decided.

Liu Pi ran to the horse, pulled the corpse from the saddle and let it fall unceremoniously to the ground. Liu Pi contemplated some form of apology, but there was no time: he leapt into the saddle and galloped southward. Scouts were already relaying a series of retreat orders whether Liu Pi had told them to or not: the Han commanders ordered their men not to pursue anyone that fled, but the fate of any that stayed and fought was final.

"**Cousin Miaocai!**" Xiahou Dun cried when he spotted Xiahou Yuan. "**Miaocai, you're alive!**"

"Of course!" Xiahou Yuan chuckled. "It wasn't so bad."

"Mengde says we can't pursue," Xiahou Dun complained. "I want to tear them all apart for what they did to you!"

"Don't fret," Xiahou Yuan insisted.

"...You're thinner," Xiahou Dun noted.

"I was thinner before they attacked," Xiahou Yuan replied. "Honestly, Yuanrang; you have to stop worrying!"

Xiahou Dun bowed slightly and exhaled as signs of emotion.

"...So many dead," Xiahou Yuan said as he looked at the chaos around him. "Men and women both... fought and died for this terrible cult. Mengde already lived through this once; I hope his soul can cope with it."

"He'll want to see you," Xiahou Dun suggested.

"And I want to see Mengde too!" Xiahou Yuan chuckled. "Let's go and find him, Cousin Yuanrang. The fighting's over, I think."

The two men rode through the sea of bodies to find their lord.

Cao Cao embraced Xiahou Yuan like a brother when the two met outside the former's command tent.

"I'd suggest that you come into the city, Mengde, but it's a little disorderly," Xiahou Yuan said. "You've done wonders here!"

"If killing angry commoners is a wonder," Cao Cao sighed. "You and Yuanrang should follow me to my personal tent: Xun Wenruo, Xun Gongda and Guo Fengxiao can manage things for me here."

Xiahou Dun and Xiahou Yuan followed Cao Cao and his bodyguard Dian Wei on a short walk to the second tent.

"You're haunted by events, I assume," Xiahou Yuan said as he entered the rest tent and sat to the left of the entrance.

"Haunted...?" Xiahou Dun scoffed as he took a seat next to Xiahou Yuan. "The Yellow Turbans had that coming."

Cao Cao sat in his host seat, and Dian Wei stood behind him.

"Any violence is jarring," Xiahou Yuan suggested.

"Quite right, Miaocai," Cao Cao said. "I've lost a few hundred Qing Corps soldiers on this campaign... and the carnage here will only cause more to desert. Huang Shao's death is beneficial, but Liu Pi lives, and as a 'hero' of the original rebellion, he will continue to inspire until he is crushed. Yes, I had a victory here, but just as many joined the Turbans as surrendered to us. I say what I say now to you, and you only, because we are as family: the Turbans are something that I cannot prevent, because the root cause – imperial ignorance – has not faded."

Xiahou Yuan frowned and said, "I thought that the young Majesty was quite shrewd."

"Compared to previous ones, yes," Cao Cao said with a sigh. "Dong Zhao – Henei Administrator Zhang Yang's former adviser, and now mine – tells me that His Majesty's first demands upon his arrival in Henei were the decorating of the administrator's residence – so that it better resembled a palace 'worthy of our presence' – and a fine meal 'as befits the Son of Heaven'. He cannot be blind or deaf: there was a famine, he'd been living in a tent, his Empress was robbed at blade-point by Guo Si's thugs, and his courtiers were dying of starvation! He was in the care of the White Wave Bandits, yet he never once thought about their motivations...? He had just escaped Li Jue and Guo Si, and in the process he's lost Huangfu Song, Shisun Rui, and more besides... and before that, he'd already lost Wang Yun, Cai Yong-"

"Yeah, yeah, we get it," Xiahou Dun grumbled. "He just whinged about being 'mistreated' and wanted to live in luxury while everyone else went without: that's the sort of oblivious nonsense that caused the first rebellion."

"Exactly," Cao Cao sighed.

"And... His Majesty's attitude is unchanged...?" Xiahou Yuan asked.

"It's *worse*," Cao Cao scoffed. "His first order when he got to what's left of Luoyang was the reconstruction of the Northern *and* Southern Palaces, but not a word about the homes that his loyal subjects need: Zhang Yang's still there now, overseeing it and paying for it all with his own money *and* mine!"

Xiahou Yuan shook his head disapprovingly.

"Yeah, and the emperor wants Xuchang remodelled as an imperial capital as well, even though he's not staying long!" Xiahou Dun chortled. "Mengde's paying for that as well!"

"His Majesty is draining the already-exhausted coffers – the imperial treasury and those of his loyalists – on *pomp*," Cao Cao complained. "Yes, there's little vice, which is a blessing, but he's building a harem now. Once the princes and princesses start appearing, all of my poor father's hard-earned legacy will be frittered away with as little effort as taking something from a sack. His Majesty can give me a million titles, but they'll be no compensation for being penniless."

"And then the people will hear of it all," Xiahou Dun grumbled.

"They're already angry," Cao Cao continued. "It's... it's that phrase again, Miaocai. 'Making the Old Mistake'. I've seen it all before, perhaps less than two decades ago... and it's having the same impact as it did then. As long as the empire fails to learn the lessons and rein in its self-indulgence, the Yellow Turbans will keep reappearing, and eventually there won't be anyone that can stop them... or worse yet for the Han... there won't be anyone that will *want* to stop them."

"*Aiee*... I feel like a man that's been in another land, yet I'm only a short distance away," Xiahou Yuan said. "You said nothing of this in your letters, Meng- ...Ah, yes, well I suppose that complaining in writing would be dangerous."

"Treason accusations aside, I have enemies," Cao Cao replied. "I suspect that Zhang Yang doesn't like or trust me; Dong Cheng certainly doesn't; and, worst of all, *Yuan Shao* is now my enemy."

"That's... not entirely a surprise to me," Xiahou Yuan admitted. "He's an idiot that I never liked. I suppose that I'm surprised that he's an 'enemy'; 'no longer a close friend', perhaps, but not an enemy. So you fear that he'll plot against you?"

"I do," Cao Cao replied. "Then there're the usual suspects: Lü Bu, Chen Gong, Wang Kai and Xu Si; the hankering Yuan Shu..."

After a long pause, Xiahou Yuan said, "We'll not be seeing each other again for a while, I suppose."

"I must now go south into Runan and defeat Liu Pi once and for all," Cao Cao replied. "After that, I must immediately return to the capital. There are many enemies – state and personal – that I must deal with, while you must, regrettably enough, remain here as a gate guard a little longer."

"Great men with plans are always parted from kith and kin by their ambitions," Xiahou Yuan suggested. "You're not the first, and you won't be the last."

Cao Cao's eyes filled with tears as he said, "Zhang Miao said something like that to me once... long ago... oh, poor Zhang Miao... and Wei Zi...!"

"Don't start mourning now, Mengde!" Xiahou Dun scolded. "This isn't the time! And especially not for *Zhang Miao*! That bastard betrayed you! He betrayed us all!"

"...Sorry," Cao Cao whimpered. "Zhang Miao once guarded Chenliu for me, as Miaocai does now... and he protected my family too. Despite his treachery... which some say I deserved... I miss him. He was the most honest man I ever knew."

"...Let's not waste our few hours together mourning and moping!" Xiahou Yuan suggested. "Come on, Mengde, and share with us some of the wine that you must have brought with you!"

Cao Cao smiled warmly and said, "A fine idea."

The three men enjoyed a drink and spoke of better times before they had to part company and prepare for the roles that fate had demanded of them: Xiahou Yuan would remain in Yingchuan and guard it from further threats, and Cao Cao and Xiahou Dun would advance to Runan together and eliminate the Yellow Turbans once and for all.

✳✳✳✳✳✳✳✳✳✳✳✳

50

Liu Pi was forced onto an immediate defensive upon reaching Runan Prefecture in Yu Province. Cao Cao's pursuit had been immediate and organised, but orders had been given that the Yellow Turbans should not be ruthlessly cut down as they fled. Liu Pi had his depleted forces camp around the first friendly village that he encountered, and preparations began for retaliation while word went out to the significant numbers of Yellow Turban sympathisers in the prefecture: Cao Cao camped north of Liu Pi and immediately summoned his officials.

"Any news that I should know about?" Cao Cao asked.

"Yuan Shu has sent Ji Ling to Xiaopei," Xun Wenruo replied.

"Oh...?" Cao Cao exclaimed. "That's where Lü Bu put Liu Bei, isn't it? ...Has Lü Bu requested assistance?"

"We learned of it from 'other sources'," Xun Wenruo replied. "Bu doesn't seem to be interested in telling us what's going on in 'his province'."

"...I hope that doesn't mean that he's contemplating turning back to Yuan Shu," Cao Cao fretted. "That would be a serious problem. What would I give the greedy man to win him back then...? He's already 'General of the Left'! All there is to award is one of the 'Three Excellences', and there's no way that I'm making that man an Excellency!"

"Worry about Lü Bu after Liu Pi surrenders," Xun Wenruo replied.

"Liu Pi has no intention of giving up," Cao Cao complained.

"Why should he?" Guo Jia suggested dryly. "He's got a lot of support here in Runan, and it has to be said that an errant member of the most prominent family in Ru County might have a lot to do with Liu Pi's ability to acquire resources and rally so effectively."

"How can Yuan Shu still have money for such things?" Xun Wenruo wondered. "He's been fighting his cousin for what is it now...? Six years...?"

"Closer to seven, I think," Cao Cao grumbled. "But Guo Jia makes a valid point: if Yuan Shu is funding the Yellow Turbans, then they can put up a solid defence now that they're back in Runan. But I can't afford a long campaign! If I'm away from Xuchang for too long, the White Wave Bandits may attack, or Yuan Shao may invade, or-!"

"Forget 'ors' and 'maybes'," Guo Jia interrupted. "War is often about shows of strength, not strength itself, and the most important strength is often *speed*, not power. Liu Pi will certainly stand a chance of trapping us here if he can entrench himself and call on a near-inexhaustible supply of reinforcements, but he has to have time to do that. He's expecting us to sit here and recover our strength and our wits before attacking: that's where he needs to be wrong."

"*Ayah*. You cannot expect the men to fight so soon!" Xun Wenruo protested.

"If we wait, they'll wish they'd fought the fatigue earlier," Guo Jia retorted. "We're still dependent on Qing Corps men that are far more likely to defect in a place like this than they ever were in Yingchuan. Right now, we face maybe two or three thousand

Turbans: if we wait until the camp is established and the men are rested, we'll be facing five to ten thousand. By the time we're getting somewhere against the five to ten thousand, twenty to a hundred thousand more will turn up from all over the province, the Qing Corps will defect, and we'll be resting here forever, in an unmarked pit."

"**He's right!**" Xiahou Dun cried. "**We need to destroy them now!** ...But wait... why didn't we hack them down as they fled, if we're now to do as you say...?"

"Cutting down fleeing peasant men and women is – and would definitely be seen as – cowardice and an atrocity, whether they were armed or not," Guo Jia replied. "Now they're here, they're an army again, and our actions are against an army. If we hit hard now after a show of mercy, it will have the opposite effect to massacring the defeated in flight."

"I understand," Xiahou Dun replied.

"...Yu Jin, Xu Huang: you'll attack the camps around the village – but not the village itself – at once," Cao Cao ordered. "Xiahou Dun, Yue Jin: you'll take your forces around and pincer them as before. We'll give them the south as an escape route... where I shall be waiting personally."

The officers retreated to prepare their men.

"...I pray this is it," Cao Cao murmured.

"Once this is done, you'll be free to go back," Guo Jia promised.

Cao Cao clutched his head and said, "Damned headaches...! ...Are we to spare Liu Pi, or is he to be made an example of...?"

"If we can keep him alive, keep him alive," Guo Jia insisted. "Yes, he may rebel again, but if we kill him, his successors may be unforeseen trouble, as they will be new, untested, potentially more fanatical than Liu Pi is and therefore more dangerous."

"That was not seen with Zhang Jue," Xun Wenruo said.

"I beg to differ," Guo Jia retorted. "Everyone said that with the death of Zhang Jue, the 'Way of Peace' would die... Now it is more like the 'Way of War'. His Yellow Turban foot soldiers – who still number in the tens of thousands in some provinces – are all that remains, unchained from any organisational doctrine or any plan for if they ever gained ground anywhere. They've either pursued parts of what Zhang Jue set out, or they've evolved into new and even greater threats, like the militant bandit confederacies in the north that even attack their own kind – the common people that they once belonged to – and seek nothing but chaos and destruction."

Xun Wenruo tried to interject, but Guo Jia indicated that he was not finished.

"Liu Pi is relatively organised, but his followers are not," Guo Jia continued. "If the Turbans of Ji Province – Zhang Jue's main base – evolved into the Black Mountain Bandits, and those around Central Province became the White Wave Bandits, then what will Liu Pi's following become...? The Blue River Bandits...? The Green Valley Bandits...? Make him surrender, and they'll do as he says: more importantly, we'll know what we're dealing with in future, because men with minds do not forget defeats as easily as headless mobs do."

"...I cannot argue," Xun Wenruo conceded.

Guo Jia smiled apologetically and said, "I do not mean to belittle you, Wenruo, as your tone implies to be your assumption. All men can be wrong; as a man that is knowingly destroying himself with vice, I cannot claim to be correct in all things. But I am right in this. My lord, gather your men for the ambush at once: time is against us."

Cao Cao got to his feet and said, "Very good! We march at once!"

Liu Pi was stunned by the ferocity of the attack by the Han forces. "…**Cao Cao is too clever!**" Liu Pi cried. "**He let us flee to feign benevolence, and now he stamps on us!**"

"What will we do?" a major asked.

"…Hè Yi and Hè Man's reinforcements aren't even halfway here yet," Liu Pi replied. "We're dead if we sit here… we'll need to leave and rendezvous with them on the road."

The officers agreed, and the preparations for a second major retreat began: Xiahou Dun and Yue Jin's pincer forces arrived just as the main Yellow Turban army was about to move, which left the Turbans with a southern road as the only available direction of escape. The Han forces quickly occupied the area as the Yellow Turbans fled: the villagers were surprised and relieved to find that they would not be punished for their obvious collaboration.

Liu Pi's retreat passed a small wood. Liu was fearful of an ambush, but his fears were realised before he could alert his officers; the majority of the soldiers scattered, and Liu Pi was left with a handful of devoted followers that awaited the judgement of Excellency Cao Cao.

"You've been a villain, Liu Pi," Cao Cao said as he loomed over the defeated Yellow Turban general from atop his warhorse. "You've harmed the people."

"What 'people'?" Liu Pi retorted. "You speak of Han collaborators that ignore the injustices toward the many so long as they are comfortable, and they deserve to be chastised!"

"That's very eloquent, relatively speaking: you've been studying," Cao Cao teased.

"…**Han's Mandate has passed!**" Liu Pi cried defiantly. "**Yellow Sky, soon-!**"

"**That's enough,**" Cao Cao ordered. "You want me to kill you, but that solves nothing. You'll be a memory, not a martyr. Your followers will find a new leader, but what will they do…?"

Guo Jia smiled as he realised that Cao Cao had heeded his words.

"Your mantra meant nothing when our swords crossed twelve years ago, and it means nothing now," Cao Cao continued. "The sky isn't yellow, and the Han is still here."

"**Only because men like you prop it up with your ceaseless toadying!**" Liu Pi replied. "**It isn't what the people want, or why would the emperor have spent years as a prisoner of Dong Zhuo? Why did he spend a year in the middle of nowhere, starving while-**"

"He was in the care of the White Wave Bandits for that year you speak of," Cao Cao interrupted. "I have White Wave Bandit commanders in my service."

"**They're traitors to the people!**" Liu Pi cried. "**The people still starved, and yet the White Waves fed themselves and fawned on a dead dynasty! The Han is its own worst**

enemy, and it will destroy itself if we don't do it!"

Cao Cao smiled coldly and replied, "If that's Heaven's will, Liu Pi… but you're not Heaven. You have no right and no mandate to dethrone the Han. You're a commoner with no ideas, no-"

"Master Zhang Jue had an idea until you killed him, you and your Han collaborators that grow fatter while others grow thinner!" Liu Pi said angrily. **"He was going to make all men and women equal! What good have you and your kind done for the world, Butcher of Xu? Your father was a famous wealthy toady, and you are a famous murderer of the innocents!"**

Cao Cao's smile disappeared as he said, "On another day, Liu Pi, I might have cut your head off for such words. But today I am recovering from a migraine, so I feel sorrow for other men in pain. You want to die. I understand that. You've been humbled, and your idealistic dreams have been shattered for a second time. But you'll serve the world better as a living example of the Han's mercy than you will as a martyr to a ridiculous cause."

"I'd rather die!" Liu Pi shrieked. **"I want this to be the year of my death!"**

"And to some, it will be," Cao Cao snickered. "Your cause is dead, Liu Pi. Your armies aren't coming. My men are everywhere, and the good people are sick of your looting and resist you."

"I'll never yield!" Liu Pi promised. **"You'll regret freeing me, Cao Cao! Let me live and I'll kill you and your emperor! Kill me, so I can haunt your soul!"**

"…Let's do a deal," Cao Cao chuckled. "You hate the Han… and after a decade, you probably don't even know why anymore. But if you give me a chance, as the Acting Excellency over the Masses, to put things right – end the corruption, restore order, put food on tables and money in hands – then you'll be justified in coming after me if I don't do it, but your dream of a better land will be part-fulfilled if I do. You'll never get the land where all men are equal – even Zhang Jue would have reneged on that eventually – but you'll get order and a better way of life if I succeed. Why die now and never know what might come next, when you can live, wait, and see…?"

Liu Pi was silent.

"I don't intend to kill any more of you if I can help it; I regret the deaths I've caused already," Cao Cao continued. "Live and lead them for me, Liu Pi. Don't let them stray from what you've encouraged them to believe in – a quest for national peace – by dying here now."

Liu Pi sobbed miserably and said, "You… you win. I surrender, Cao Cao… I surrender."

The other Yellow Turban captives cried and wailed at their leader's familiar words.

"Word will be sent… to the others… that our battle is over," Liu Pi continued. "They will stop fighting… as well…"

"Very good," Cao Cao replied.

"But know that I'll still be here watching!" Liu Pi cried. **"I warned you, Cao Cao! If you regret this later, don't complain! You brought it on yourself! When we come for you in your capital, don't sigh and weep! You'll have brought it on yourself for your crimes against the people!"**

"...I vow that I'll do all that I can to ensure that day never comes, Liu Pi," Cao Cao replied.

"...*Ayah*... I wanted to kill him!" Cao Cao admitted as he entered his command tent and threw his gilded helmet to the floor.
"But you didn't," Guo Jia said as he followed Cao Cao into the tent and retrieved the helmet. "You did the right thing: he was goading you, and as you said, it served no purpose."
Cao Cao sat in his host seat and clutched his aching head; Guo Jia sat to his left and watched as Xun Wenruo, Xun Gongda and Xiahou Yuan entered the tent and took seats to Cao Cao's right.
"...No," Cao Cao conceded. "No, it didn't; do we have any more news from anywhere?"
"Yuan Shao's still in Bing Province," Xun Gongda replied.
"And Yuan Shu is not moving," Xun Wenruo said. "His general Ji Ling is still in Xiaopei, as far as we know. Lü Bu is not sending any urgent communications, so we can only assume that he is either unconcerned or contemplating defection again."
"...Well, we're done here in Runan," Cao Cao replied. "We'll march back to Xuchang as quickly as we can: keep me informed of any new situations."
The advisers bowed humbly and quietly thanked the heavens that their lord had completed the campaign without causing any serious calamities.

Liu Pi's surrender marked the end of the Yellow Turban uprising in Runan. Huang Shao had finally met his end after 12 years of intermittent troublemaking, while Liu Pi kept his word and told his subordinates to cease their activities. But it would not be the last time that Liu Pi would fight Cao Cao.

∗∗∗∗∗∗∗∗∗∗∗∗

51

Cao Cao's victory over the Yellow Turbans was also a significant victory for the Han Empire, as there was no more visible sign of the erosion of its authority – at least so far as the emperor was concerned – as their unchecked activity. The bandits and rogue warlords were seen as a far smaller threat because they did not chant about the end the Han, but their impact was no less damaging for their lack of rhetoric. Some of those autonomous warlord-chieftains were now autonomous provincial governors: this was a far cry from the days when most of the provinces were run by loyalist relatives of the imperial Liu clan.

That thought haunted Liu Bei, the former governor of Xu Province: while his governorship – granted at the expense of his predecessor Tao Qian's sons at a time of crisis – had been mired in controversy, he had always expected it to be recognised by the Han court at some point. But fate had decided otherwise, and his current situation was miserable: he was now a vassal of the infamous Lü Bu, and he had been reduced to little more than an expendable buffer at the strategic settlement of Xiaopei to the west of Xu Province. Xiaopei would be an important target for any western or southern attacker: Cao Cao would need it to advance to the capital Xiapi in the east, and Yuan Shu would encounter it during a northern march from Yang Province. It was the latter – Yuan Shu – that now threatened Liu Bei, once again in the form of his fearsome general Ji Ling.

"…This is not good at all," the politician Mister Sun said as he read through a report from the Xu-Yang border.

"What are we worrying about now, Mister Sun…?" Mi Zhu asked.

"Ji Ling's showing no signs of slowing his advance," Mister Sun fretted. "More and more supplies and men are being sent from Jiujiang! He definitely means to take the south of the province for his master!"

Mi Zhu's brother, Mi Fang, turned to his lord, sighed sadly and asked, "What are your thoughts, Lord Liu…?"

All eyes turned to Liu Bei, who did little more than whimper.

"You must make a decision," Guan Yu said.

"I know that nobody probably wants to know what I think, but I'm going to say something anyway," Zhang Fei declared: his words were met with groans.

"I'd rather you didn't, Yide," Liu Bei said lifelessly.

"I'm going to speak, Xuande," Zhang Fei insisted. "We shouldn't just sit here! We should go and fight Ji Ling, and avenge our past suffering!"

"I agree!" Jian Yong said in a mischievous tone. "Come, Xuande! Let's you and I lead the charge! It's what we should have done in Haixi! We'll charge Ji Ling, and when we get to his front lines, we can imagine that they're big, long rows of delicious seasoned chicken pieces, and-!"

"I'll bloody eat *you*, Jian Yong!" Zhang Fei screamed. **"I preferred it when you became serious for a while! Take the piss out of me, will you??? I'll-!"**

"You'll what, 'Yide'?" Jian Yong heckled. "You're always the first one to go on about how terrible the situation we're in is, and how nobody's doing anything about it: *you caused it*."

Zhang Fei's bulging eyes receded: he was now the focus of everyone's attention and everyone's frustration, and he hung his head low with shame.

"…Sorry, okay, but I can't do another rant from you," Jian Yong grumbled. "We all came here together, and we've been together like this for twelve years when you count the time in Ji, Qing and Xu together… so I feel like I'm being cruel to a brother, especially after the ordeal we shared in Haixi. But Yide, you're a pain."

"Sad to say, Xianhe, you are right," Liu Bei said. "Yide, we have to show caution and remember what we cannot do. The question is, however, what we *can* do. Mi Zizhong…?"

All eyes turned to Mi Zhu, who said, "I know what worries you, Lord Liu. Our last encounter with Ji Ling has all but depleted the vast wealth and influence that my family once possessed, and more souls were harmed than ours."

"Last time we lost Elder Chen, Chen Changwen, Chen Hanyu, Chen Yuanlong and a ten-thousand-man army," Liu Bei lamented. "We haven't the monies or the morale to endure more pain at Ji Ling's hands! We're all weak, tired and angry, and our army is small! Those things have never won wars!"

"…How can you call those dirty Chens by familiar names, Xuande?" Zhang Fei asked miserably. "Do you also forgive those lying, two-faced men for betraying you to Lü Bu? Is that why you can still call me 'Yide'…?"

"I… I call them those names as a habit," Liu Bei insisted. "My anger at their actions is altogether different, Yide: you're a fool that did something with consequences that weren't obvious to you… while the Chens… all four of them… knew exactly what they were doing. I was invited here by two of them to save this province from a monster: and just because of a few men that they didn't warm to… they made another monster – a wicked, sinful man that looted the tombs of dead emperors and hacked the innocent to death without cause or remorse – into their governor. I understand you, Yide, I always have; but not the Chens. Their actions… defy understanding."

"This doesn't solve anything!" Mister Sun complained. "Forgive whoever you want to forgive, Lord Liu, and let us move back to deciding what to do about Ji Ling!"

Liu Bei nodded silently, but there was no discussion: the room fell silent as each man tried to think of something, but nothing came to mind.

"…Maybe we should ask Lü Bu to send aid," Jian Yong said at last.

"**Damn Lü Bu! Damn him! I'll eat his flesh before I ask him for help!**" Zhang Fei barked.

"Fortunately, Yide, this isn't your decision to make," Liu Bei sighed. "*Unfortunately*, it's *mine*."

"Don't ask him for help," Zhang Fei pleaded. "We must be able to turn this around! Yunchang can challenge Ji Ling, and-!"

"I'm still injured," Guan Yu interrupted.

"…**Then *I'll* go and fight the bastard!**" Zhang Fei said.

"Didn't we just do this?" Jian Yong complained.

"He won't fight you, Yide," Liu Bei replied. "He refuses all duels since Yunchang clipped his helmet and killed that major in our previous encounters. His camp is heavily guarded, so we can't storm it or launch a night attack. We need to win by way of traditional field combat, and we can't because his force is too big." Zhang Fei glared at Mi Zhu, Mi Fang and Mister Sun and said, "What's the point of you three…? All you do is sit there and-!"

"**Yide!**" Liu Bei cried. "The Mis are my brothers-in-law, uncles to my young daughters! They financed us through the horrors of Haixi, and-!"

"Alright, alright!" Zhang Fei said. "I… I'm sorry, Xuande. It's just that I don't want to lose here, not if I don't have to, and they're the brains, and-"

"Enough," Liu Bei ordered.

Another long silence ensued that was eventually broken by Mi Zhu, who said, "Sad to say, Mister Jian is right. We have no choice: this is Bu's problem as much as it's ours… more so, actually, since this is his province now."

"No, no, no!" Zhang Fei whined. "Not Lü Bu! Not *Lü Bu*! There *must* be another way! There *has* to be! We can't ask help from-!"

"Shut up, Yide," Liu Bei ordered. "Mister Mi, Xianhe, you both seem to agree that I have no choice but to beg help from that wretch; Yide disagrees, and I know Yunchang well enough that I know he'll accept the necessary, no matter how awful it is; Mister Sun, Mi Fang, what do you think…?"

"…I agree with my brother, as much as I don't want to," Mi Fang admitted.

"If there were another way, we'd all suggest it, Lord Liu," Mister Sun said.

"…Fine," Liu Bei sighed. "I'll send a messenger immediately."

"**Curse me!**" Zhang Fei cried. "**This is my own fault! He's our master because I got angry and killed that Cao Bao! You were wrong to forgive me, Xuande!**"

"…*Shut up*, Yide," Liu Bei grumbled.

Liu Bei's request for help reached Xiapi within days, whereupon it was read to the entire provincial court. Chen Gong dismissed the messenger as soon as he finished speaking, and all eyes turned to Governor Lü Bu. Silence followed: eventually, Bu's long-suffering subordinate Gao Shun – who was still demoted to a petty official, despite his accurate prediction of the outcome of the recent Ju City campaign – lost patience and said, "Lord Lü, you have to decide what to do. Like it or not, Liu Bei is your shield in Xiaopei: if he falls, Ji Ling will have a clear path to the Si River, and it will be your only viable defence against such an army. What we must do is-"

"Didn't I remove your rank?" Lü Bu interrupted. "Be quiet, Gao Shun, or I'll remove your head as well."

Gao Shun bowed low and said no more.

"Does anyone else have an opinion?" Lü Bu asked. "Chen Gong…?"

"…I agree with Gao Shun," Chen Gong replied. "Liu Bei must be saved, or the province might be lost."

"There is no other answer: Gao Shun is right," Wang Kai said as Lü Bu's eyes turned to him.

Lü Bu grunted irritably and looked at his court: his eyes singled out the elder statesman Chen Yuanfang, and he said with malice, "Do you have good advice, 'Excellency'…?"

"As I have *already said*, I turned the role down," Chen Yuanfang replied. "Yuan Shao only offered the title of 'Excellency of Works' to me as a slight against Cao Cao; I have no desire to leave here and live in Xuchang."

"Are you sure? You escaped Dong Zhuo with a similar trick once," Lü Bu heckled.

"You still think ill of me, Governor," Chen Yuanfang sighed. "That is regrettable."

Chen Yuanfang's son Qun got to his feet and said, "We're loyal to Xu Province, my lord, and you are Xu Province. We serve you and you alone. My father may or may not have an opinion about Liu Bei, but here's mine: he's too slow-witted and incompetent to defeat Ji Ling. If you don't go and save Bei, he'll cry himself to death and Ji Ling will certainly be at the Si River by the end of the year, and who knows what that may lead to."

Lü Bu laughed and said, "That's a very convincing and amusing argument."

The nobleman Chen Gui rose and said, "Go to Xiaopei at once, Governor, but show caution."

"*Caution...?*" Lü Bu scoffed.

"Chen Gui is right," the adviser Xu Si suggested. "You're too quick to prove your might against men like Ji Ling, but why bother? We all know he's no match for you, since he's supposedly a poor match for Zhang Fei and Guan Yu, who are both proven to be your inferiors. What you must do is find a way to settle the matter *peacefully*."

"And what sort of wimp would I appear to be then?" Lü Bu asked. "Xu Si, I am known as a man among men! I hated my forced choice of countenance with Cao Cao and the emperor enough: how can I resort to simpering requests for bloodless solutions to *Ji Ling*? I'll meet him in battle and behead him, and that's that!"

"He won't let you," Xu Si replied. "But he'd allow you to prove your worth in another way that satisfies your honour: negotiate."

"I'll do no such thing," Lü Bu scoffed. "I'll leave straight away... I know how to deal with this fool Ji Ling. Wang Kai: you'll accompany me. Chen Gong, Xu Si: you'll be in charge in my absence... just in case someone decides to double-cross me in the way that they double-crossed my poor, 'slow-witted' and 'incompetent' predecessor."

Chen Gui, Chen Deng, General of the Household Xu Dan, Chen Yuanfang and Chen Qun shuddered as one.

Lü Bu and his long-serving officers Zhang Liao and Qin Yilu prepared to depart for Xiaopei with a force of 2,000 and Gao Shun as a low-ranking auxiliary; Bu's relative, General Wei Xu – who had inherited Gao Shun's command – and General Cao Xing – who had been promoted after ending Hao Meng's mutiny against Lü Bu – would remain outside Xiapi and guard against any other possible attacks. Chen Yuanfang waited until the self-appointed governor was gone, and then he asked his son Qun for his views.

"...You intend to betray Lü Bu," Chen Qun realised.

"Not directly," Chen Yuanfang said. "Son, I am old. I cannot do this nonsense again. Lü Bu is only marginally better a man than Dong Zhuo."

"And Cao Cao...?" Chen Qun challenged.

"Cao Cao is a complicated man," Chen Yuanfang replied. "I abhor what he did to this province; the scars of his campaigns may never fully heal. But he now has many clever men serving him: Xun Yu and his nephew Xun Yòu, and Cheng Yu, to name but three; I knew Xun Yu's father and uncle well, and I know him as a genius that can tame Cao's spirit and make the hero of him that was predicted."

Chen Qun nodded thoughtfully and said, "That's true, Father."

"Furthermore, His Majesty is there with Cao Cao, safe and sound, after being held hostage by White Wave Bandits in Luoyang; word is that Cao Cao defeated the bandits and freed the Son of Heaven almost single-handedly!" Chen Yuanfang continued. "We have much to thank him for, and he might be the only way to rid ourselves of strife, ironic though that might seem to be."

"I've heard different accounts, but I have to admit, Cao Cao appears to be a man reformed, unlike Bu, who is perhaps worse now that he is independent," Chen Qun said. "What do you want to do?"

"Nothing, for now," Chen Yuanfang replied. "I will be patient, and wait for others to see things as we do and make it known... just as Chen Gong once did in Yan."

When Lü Bu arrived in Xiaopei he fought his way past Ji Ling's outer camps, stopped his brown war-steed at the gates of Liu Bei's camp and waited there with his custom-forged halberd in hand. Ji Ling's harassment force commanders, Chen Lan and Lei Bo, spotted the imposing and infamous warrior and hurried to their master's command tent with the news of his arrival.

"*Lü Bu*???" Ji Ling exclaimed. "What's he doing here???"

Ji Ling's advisers did not answer the pointless question.

"...Let's see what we're up against," Ji Ling sighed.

Ji Ling and his officials travelled to the area in front of Liu Bei's main camp, and Ji made sure that Lü Bu could see him.

"**JI LING!**" Lü Bu shouted. "**JI LING, WILL YOU AGREE TO A MEETING?**"

"...What should I do...?" Ji Ling asked as he turned to his robed advisers.

"Speak to him," the adviser Yuan Huan replied.

Ji Ling nodded slowly, turned to face Lü Bu again and replied by saying, "**WE'LL WITHDRAW, AND WE'LL ARRANGE A MEDIATION CAMP!**"

"**I'LL BE RIGHT HERE!**" Lü Bu replied.

Liu Bei had learned of Lü Bu's arrival and hurried to the gates to welcome him; Guan Yu, Mi Zhu and Mister Sun followed while Jian Yong and Mi Fang kept the furious Zhang Fei occupied.

"**Fengxian!**" Liu Bei cried from his place behind the locked gates. "You came here to aid me after all, Fengxian!"

"Of course, 'Xuande'," Lü Bu replied. "Open the gates."

"But what about Ji Ling?" Mister Sun fretted.

"We can't leave Fengxian without our support! **Open the gates!**" Liu Bei ordered.

"What on earth would I do without Liu Bei's support...?" Lü Bu snickered quietly.

"Where is Ji Ling's force?" Liu Bei wondered.

"I have arranged a parley," Lü Bu explained. "You and I will travel to a neutral location for a meeting shortly, wherein I will resolve this mess once and for all."

"How?" Mister Sun heckled.

"You dare address me in that manner, old bones, when you betrayed your previous lord and embarrassingly underserved your current one...?" Lü Bu countered. "I hear you were a politician, a diplomat: what plan do *you* have, uh...? Come on, tell me!"

"...*Aiee*! I should not have spoken!" Mister Sun sobbed.

"Retire, Mister Sun," Liu Bei said kindly. "Mi Zhu and I will go to this meeting."

Lü Bu watched Mister Sun withdraw and snorted contemptuously.

"Did you come alone?" Liu Bei asked.

"Do I look like a fool?" Lü Bu replied incredulously. "Zhang Liao and Qin Yilu are to the east with a force of two-thousand; Ji Ling will know it."

"Yes, I'm sorry, that was a silly question," Liu Bei sighed. "Excuse my apparent stupidity; it's from fatigue."

"Find the spirit that saved Pingyuan, else you're of no use to me in the future," Lü Bu replied bluntly. "Ah...! Ji Ling's men are setting up the parley now. Let's find a couple of trustworthy men and go to him."

Liu Bei turned to the silent Chen Dao and said, "You shall accompany me."

"I'll have Zhang Liao join us," Lü Bu decided.

Within an hour, Lü Bu, Liu Bei, Mi Zhu, Wang Kai, the intimidating Zhang Liao and Chen Dao were facing Ji Ling and three of his subordinate officers – who included Chen Lan and Lei Bo – in a specially-constructed tent.

"So what deal did you want to make, Lü Bu?" Ji Ling said once the ritual obeisance had ended. "What land will you yield in exchange for my withdrawal?"

"Oh, I haven't come here to make a deal like that," Lü Bu chuckled. "No, I've come here to make a far more respectable proposition."

"There's nothing else that I'll accept," Ji Ling growled. "Land or lives, Bu: choose."

"You're not in a position to threaten me," Lü Bu countered. "One of my men is worth ten of yours. Xiapi is guarded by the Si River, and beyond that, three-thousand full-time soldiers that include Danyang Brigades. Further to that, I have tens of thousands that I can call on with three words: 'Avoid another massacre'. Everyone remembers Cao Cao, and they'll rise up against you like cornered tigers. You'll get Liu Bei easily, but you'll get little else without losing a lot yourself."

Liu Bei tried to gasp, but he could make no sound.

"So what is it that you propose?" Ji Ling said irritably.

"A simple test of my prowess," Lü Bu replied.

"I'm not duelling with you," Ji Ling scoffed.

"I wouldn't put you through that," Lü Bu snickered. "No, I was thinking of a little archery contest. I've had Zhang Liao's men root a halberd outside the tent: I will walk until I am so far from that halberd as it looks like a twig, and then I will fire a single shot with my bow: if I hit the tip of the bayonet on the halberd on my first and only shot, then you must withdraw. If I miss, then I will withdraw, and whatever happens here is fate. The solution to our problem will be decided by an arrow."

Liu Bei tried to protest against the idea, but all that he could manage was a hoarse croak.

"...You're insane, Bu," Ji Ling chortled. "You'd wager your province on this?"

"I would," Lü Bu replied. "Would you wager your standing with Yuan Shu by accepting, or do you want to refuse? Refusing, I fear, means a fight here and now, and I don't think that your lackeys will be able to stop me taking your head."

Ji Ling's officers placed their hands on their swords, but Ji Ling said, "**Wait**; you win, Lü Bu. I'll accept... because your arrogance will finally be your undoing."

"Is that so...?" Lü Bu cackled. "After you, Ji Ling."

Ji Ling and his wary officers left the tent; Lü Bu, Wang Kai and Zhang Liao followed, but Liu Bei was frozen with fear and lost in a daze as he tried to absorb the magnitude of the deal that had just been struck.

"...Lord Liu?" Mi Zhu prompted.

Mi Zhu's words pulled Liu Bei's mind from the haze: he ran after the swaggering Lü Bu and grabbed his arm, saying, "**What have you done to me, Fengxian??? How can this be??? Fengxian, why have you tied my soul to your arrow???** *Fengxian*!"

Wang Kai sighed disdainfully and said to Zhang Liao, "It would be funny, if Liu Bei were not such a famous hero. How can this be the man from Pingyuan?"

"I am starting to suspect that he was broken by the siege of Haixi," Zhang Liao replied.

"Ah, yes... the famine in Yan Province left us all a little rattled, and Haixi was far, far worse," Wang Kai supposed. "I wonder if he will ever recover."

"For our lord's sake, I should probably say that I hope not," Zhang Liao replied.

Lü Bu enjoyed Liu Bei's hysterical outbursts as he walked to his chosen firing point; Ji Ling and one of his followers had gone in the other direction and stopped close to the rooted spear that Lü Bu intended to hit, while two remained close to Bu in order to react to any possible treachery. Once Lü Bu was ready, he nodded toward Zhang Liao, who turned to Chen Dao and said, "I do not wish to manhandle your lord and master, General Chen, but his remonstrations are somewhat obstructive. Might you restrain him so that my lord can save his life...?"

Chen Dao nodded respectfully and pulled the frantic Liu Bei away from Lü Bu.

"*Why*???" Liu Bei whined. "*Fengxian...!*"

"Such a lack of faith," Lü Bu snickered as Zhang Liao handed him a longbow and an arrow: Bu nocked the arrow with grace and speed that showed his skill, and with little apparent thought or preparation, he fired.

"*AYAH*! **My life!**" Liu Bei cried. "**My-!**"

"**IMPOSSIBLE!**"

Ji Ling's outburst silenced Liu Bei: Lü Bu's precision shot had struck the stabbing blade of the halberd and knocked the weapon backwards, just as Bu had boasted.

"...Heaven made you, Fengxian!" Liu Bei whispered as the grinning Lü Bu lowered his bow and walked toward the exasperated Ji Ling.

"**Amazing!**" Ji Ling said with laughter. "**You are truly a man among men!**"

"*Aiee*... he's a demon, and we tried to fight him in the tent: thank Heaven that General Ji stopped us!" Chen Lan whispered to Lei Bo, who nodded agreeably.

"**A bargain's a bargain, Ji Ling!**" Lü Bu cackled. "**Will you honour our deal...?**"

"**How can I refuse after seeing such a thing?**" Ji Ling shouted. "**This day is yours! Allow me to entertain you with a banquet before I withdraw!**"

"**I am glad to accept,**" Lü Bu replied.

Ji Ling and his subordinates retreated, and the siege of Xiaopei was over.

"Fengxian... Fengxian, you are a marvel, and every bit the hero that men speak of!" Liu Bei said as Lü Bu, Wang Kai and Zhang Liao approached him.

"Sad to say, *you're* not what *I'd* heard about," Lü Bu replied. "Why are you so weak nowadays, Liu Bei? What happened to the hero of the Yellow Turban Rebellion, the major-magistrate that fought Yuan Tan at Pingyuan...?"

Liu Bei was silent and humbled.

"Yuan Shu will find someone else to send here," Lü Bu continued. "Build your forces here in Xiaopei, so you won't be beaten so easily next time. Don't fail or cry to me for help again, Inspector Liu, or I'll have to replace you. Xiaopei *must be held*."

Lü Bu, Wang Kai and Zhang Liao withdrew to their camp and prepared for the banquet that would precede their return to Xiapi.

"...And that's that," Mi Zhu said.

Liu Bei stared at Ji Ling's retreating army and sighed miserably.

"...'Decided by an arrow', indeed," Mi Zhu scoffed. "What a reckless, demented idiot. If an unfavourable wind had blown up as he fired, we'd be finished now, all of us, including him."

Liu Bei's eyes steeled.

"We can't continue to be under the boot of that man, Lord Liu," Mi Zhu protested.

"I... I see that," Liu Bei replied calmly. "Fear and horror made a pathetic, cowardly fool of me... I see that now. He's right: I need to find my hero's spirit again. I must put the memory of Haixi and my other defeats behind me, and do exactly as he said. No, I'll never be what I was, and it will always be so, but I can use the assumptions of others to my advantage... for in perceived weakness, there is sometimes strength. No, today is a new beginning, not an end. I'll build my forces, gentlemen, and then... we'll see."

Mi Zhu and Chen Dao smiled: after a long period where it seemed that the hero Liu Bei had been consigned to legend, a glimmer of hope had returned to their hearts.

****

52

Excellency Cao Cao returned to Xuchang and delivered the obligatory report of his victory against the Runan Yellow Turbans to the Imperial court.

"...And so Liu Pi surrendered, Your Majesty, thereby bringing his rowdy mob under control," Cao Cao concluded. "While Liu Pi lives and fears us, there will be no more trouble from them."

"We are pleased," Emperor Xian said. "Your leadership is exemplary, and your success has already made your reputation great. We are optimistic at last for a return to peaceful times."

Cao Cao kowtowed and replied, "I am far from done. To the north, in Fengqiu, the Black Mountain Bandits have long been a nuisance, and the villains Zhang Xiu and Jia Xu still reside in northern Jing: I should like to march as soon as possible and expel them."

"You have our permission, Mister Cao," Emperor Xian said. "We only seek an end to being surrounded by bandits, heathens and anarchists, and it seems to be the case that you are the only man capable of doing it. Whatever must be done, do it."

"...I shall, Your Majesty," Cao Cao promised. "Peace and order are soon to be a reality."

Dong Cheng – one of the men that had invited Cao Cao to save the emperor from the White Wave Bandits – scowled angrily at Cao Cao's words.

"*Ayah*... he is lauded as the only capable man of the age!" Dong Cheng complained as he entered the living quarters of his home. "This is my fault... all of it. I invited the wolf into the house... and now the door is closing, Wang Fu."

Wang Fu – who was a trusted friend and fellow official – coughed nervously and asked, "Could it be that he is loyal after all...?"

"*Cao Cao*...?" Dong Cheng scoffed. "His hungry visage is plain for all to see."

"But if he stabilises the nation and does no harm, your words will mean nothing to people," Wang Fu said. "And you were the man that-"

"I know... I know," Dong Cheng sighed. "I am the Hè Jin to his Dong Zhuo, the fool that brought him to us while in pursuit of a saviour! The eunuchs were obvious in their wickedness because it affected everyone, and Dong Zhuo made a mockery of the word 'blatant': the wily Cao Cao will ensure that he is loved and respected by the very people that I must convince of his true intentions!"

"Be patient," Wang Fu said. "...I should go. But I say again, Dong Cheng: if he's honest after all, forget talk of plots. If he's what you suspect, then he'll let us know in time. Until then, enjoy his feats, because they bring us closer to peace."

Wang Fu left the cynical Dong Cheng to plan alone.

Cao Cao gathered his allies in his chancellery audience hall and said, "You were all in court, so you know my intentions."

"The destruction of the Black Mountain Bandits and any Xiongnu allies they might still have," Yu Jin replied. "I will gladly be the vanguard once again, my lord."

"Send me too," Xu Huang said. "I must prove to Your Excellency that I am reformed and as determined to destroy the bandits as any other man here."

"Such enthusiasm!" Cao Cao chuckled. "You'll both go, then."

"Does Zilian need help?" Xiahou Dun asked. "I hear that he's struggling."

"He is," Xun Wenruo said. "Zhang Xiu is too popular with the locals of Nan County, who aid the villain's defence!"

"I want to deal with Zhang Xiu, but not now," Cao Cao replied. "Cao Hong will have to wait until I can spare the resources and have a clearer marching path... which I cannot do until Fengqiu is pacified again, and properly this time."

"I understand that the new legitimate Southern Xiongnu chieftain is Yufuluo's brother, Huchuquan," Xiahou Dun said. "Isn't that a problem?"

"Ah: the wild warrior wants to know a bit now!" Cao Cao teased.

"You moaned about me being ignorant," Xiahou Dun grumbled.

"I'm afraid that you've still a lot to learn," Cao Cao continued. "Huchuquan's been their 'Chanyu' since... mm... the year that Dong Zhuo seized Luoyang, I think... it was certainly before the Eastern Pass Coalition was founded. And not at any point did he aid his brother, so I expect no reinforcements from Bing now."

"...Right," Xiahou Dun murmured.

"And that's if there are any more Xiongnu rebels here in Yan," Cao Cao continued. "Yufuluo's almost certainly dead, despite recent attempts to convince us otherwise, most likely by his son, with whom I have personal business that must sadly wait."

Xun Wenruo frowned; Guo Jia smiled knowingly.

"The battle between the Black Mountain Bandits' overall leader, 'Flying Swallow', and Yuan Shao is intensifying," Cao Cao continued. "If we strike now, we can free Yan Province from all disruptive elements and start thinking about dealing with external threats at last."

"Like Zhang Xiu," Xiahou Dun prompted.

"...I appreciate that you are worried about Cao Hong," Cao Cao replied. "So am I, but more because of my cousin's lack of restraint. I trust that we've had no more 'Dancing prostitute' incidents...?"

Guo Jia smiled and said, "My lord, he is now as pious as you or I."

Some of Cao Cao's older allies stifled laughter.

"...I deserved that," Cao Cao chuckled. "Alright, well, we're settled then: Cao Ren!"

The stout, serious Cao Ren bowed humbly.

"You're guarding Xuchang again," Cao Cao ordered. "Guo Jia, Xun Wenruo, Xun Gongda: you will join me, as always. Yu Jin, Xu Huang: you will be the vanguard. Yue Jin, Xiahou Dun: you will be responsible for supplies and general order in the-"

"Wait, wait!" Xun Wenruo pleaded. "We cannot march now! The army has only just returned from fighting Liu Pi!"

"Preparations are different to marching," Guo Jia suggested. "We'll have to wait a few weeks, of course, but we should wait no longer. Speed is *everything*, Wenruo."

"And it's a national emergency," Cao Cao said. "The men will understand. They have to. The faster we act, the sooner they'll have peace."

Cao Cao's followers agreed with the declarations that had been made and began immediate preparations for another campaign.

The warlord Yuan Shu summoned his weary officials to his court in Shouchun City to discuss Ji Ling's retreat from Xiaopei.
"Before anything else is said, my lord, might I ask what Ji Ling's fate will be?" the adviser Han Yin asked.
"He was neither right nor wrong to accept that ludicrous 'challenge'," Yuan Shu replied. "I'd have accepted, truth all told, because like Ji Ling, I would never have expected the man to do it. Lü Bu really is as amazing an athlete as people say."
"Your verdict is gratefully received," Han Yin said. "But does this mean the end of hostilities in Xu Province?"
"Ji Ling gave his word, but *I didn't*," Yuan Shu replied. "However, I am not a fool: Bu has shown his might yet again, and I think that he should be given a chance."
The adviser Yang Hong coughed deliberately and asked, "What do you mean?"
"One of you – I forget which – told me that I should see whether Bu can be made to serve me," Yuan Shu replied. "It was an oversight on my part that led to Bu welcoming Liu Bei into his fold and stationing him in Xiaopei: had I been quicker in providing the supplies that I promised, that would not have happened. While I have other plans that require all of my resources, Bu's allegiance is so advantageous as to take priority: I shall send him half of what I originally promised, plus something else… a mutually advantageous proposal."

Lü Bu was surprised and delighted when his general Zhang Liao entered his audience hall and said, "It's as initially reported, my lord: Yuan Shu has sent supplies. Bushels of grain, arrows, swords, meat, silks, even a small amount of gold."
"What's he up to now, I wonder," Chen Gong said cynically.
"Oh, look, he's just 'paid late', that's all!" Lü Bu chuckled.
"There is a letter, encased in a tube," Zhang Liao reported.
"…Alright, so he may be up to something after all," Lü Bu conceded. "But we should all keep an open mind. I'll read his letter in private."
The influential Chen Gui turned to his son Deng and frowned purposefully.
"*Alone*…?" Chen Gong asked.
Lü Bu shook his head and replied, "No, I'll have you, Wang Kai, Xu Si, the two Chens of Xu and the other Chens join me."
Chen Yuanfang and Chen Qun exchanged weary glances.
Lü Bu's eyes steeled as he added, "Why must I read private letters in public…?"
"B-because we're your advisers!" Chen Gong continued.
"I have five wise Chens in my service, but which ones can I *trust*, I wonder…?" Lü Bu growled.
"All of them, if treated well," Gao Shun said.
"You–! …Shut up! You're lucky you still have a job, Gao Shun! You're lucky to be *alive*!" Lü Bu retorted.
Gao Shun bowed silently.
"Bring me the letter," Lü Bu grunted as he got to his feet and left the audience hall.

Chen Gong turned to Zhang Liao and said, "Where is this letter...?"
"With the supplies that I brought here," Zhang Liao replied. "I shall fetch it."
"I'll come with you," Chen Gong said. "Wang Kai, Xu Si, Chen Gui, Chen Deng, Elder Chen, Chen Qun: you should go and join Lord Lü. I'll be along shortly."
The six advisers bowed respectfully and got to their feet to leave the hall.

The four Chens endured several minutes of Lü Bu's silent, intimidating stare before Chen Gong entered the private audience room with Yuan Shu's letter.
"Give," Lü Bu barked.
"Here," Chen Gong said as he proffered the wooden container; Lü Bu snatched the tube, extracted the letter with little finesse, and started to read. As Bu's eyes moved back and forth, his fierce scowl became an amused grin.
"He wants a marriage alliance," Lü Bu chuckled.
"Now I am *sure* that he's up to something," Chen Gong said. "Why would the man want a marriage alliance now, after everything that-"
"He cites my display of talent at Xiaopei as an awakening," Lü Bu said with thinly veiled arrogance. "He wants to see his son married to my daughter so that his descendants will have his noble name and my 'divine gift of might'."
"He flatters you now because he is preparing for something," Chen Gui suggested.
"So am I not deserving of this praise he offers...?" Lü Bu retorted.
"N-no... I mean, yes, you are, but this isn't praise; it's flattery," Chen Gui replied.
"Yuan Shu does not praise, he flatters," Chen Yuanfang agreed.
"I am an exception to any rule," Lü Bu suggested. "He does not praise other men, but in me he sees a man that he can work with! He has said as much!"
"I have heard dangerous rumours about him, my lord," Chen Deng said. "He wrote to your predecessors with talk of-"
"What have Tao Qian and Liu Bei got to do with this?" Lü Bu interrupted. "I care nothing for his correspondence with those fools. He wants to join my clan with his, gentlemen, and that can only be advantageous! My daughter will bring Yuans into the world! It will improve our fortunes! I cannot refuse this offer!"
"Dong Zhuo made all sorts of offers," Chen Gong said pointedly.
"This is nothing like that!" Lü Bu insisted. "Dong Zhuo made me his foster son, which turned out to be meaningless! This would be a marriage alliance! A joining of our clans by blood! My grandsons would be wealthy Yuans! This is perfect!"
"I disagree," Chen Gui said. "Yuan Shu is going to announce something ridiculous sooner or later, and you will regret having had anything to do with him. Delay your response, and wait for matters to become clearer."
"But... but he's the second in line to the Yuan chieftainship!" Lü Bu protested.
"Second?" Chen Gong chortled. "No, my lord, he is *fifth*. Yuan Shao has four sons, three of them healthy young men. Yuan Shao and all of his sons and all of their families would have to be killed

in some ridiculous accident to make Yuan Shu the chief of the clan: and even if every one of Yuan Shao's sons bore nothing but daughters, any sons that Shu's son had with your daughter would be what... eighth? Tenth...? Some other ridiculous distance from any meaning...?"

Lü Bu snorted irritably.

"This is all part of Yuan Shu's life-long fantasy about defeating his 'brother-cousin' and becoming the clan head," Chen Gong continued. "His last declaration made that clear: but I read that nonsense when Cao Cao got it, and his claim is based on one thing only. Yuan Shao was a 'bastard son of a chambermaid' that was undeservedly adopted by his uncle, at which point he became the heir to the clan, but Yuan Shu says that shouldn't have happened. But it did. If men with no blood ties can become the eldest sons and heirs to clan titles, why not a 'bastard accident' if the clan chief did not care...?"

"...But if he did beat Yuan Shao, then he'd be the clan chief... am I right, Wang Kai...?" Lü Bu asked.

"...If he was successful in defeating Yuan Shao and either forcing him to cede the title or exterminating his branch of the clan, then yes," Wang Kai replied.

"Well there it is!" Lü Bu chuckled. "If I do this, I can help him kill Yuan Shao and all of his children and his children's families, as he obviously plans to!"

"*Ayah*... Are you serious...?" Chen Gong exclaimed.

"Yuan Shao tried to kill me at least twice," Lü Bu replied. "If Yuan Shao wins, I die, but if Yuan Shu wins, my grandchildren will be wealthy nobility!"

"...I can't argue with that proposed outcome," Chen Gong said, "but I can argue with the morality of it and your suggestion that somehow, *somehow* you and Yuan Shu are going to defeat an army of a hundred-thousand men!"

"Yuan Shu has the Black Mountain Bandits, Gongsun Zan and his ten-thousand White Horse Cavalry, and that 'Sun Ce' boy as allies already," Lü Bu retorted. "Now that I think about it, he's got quite a few decent allies. If he had me, he could beat Yuan Shao, who only has *Cao Cao*."

"Yes, Cao Cao, *Excellency* Cao Cao, who has the *Son of Heaven* as his guest at Xuchang!" Chen Gong cried.

Lü Bu grunted again.

"Not long ago, we were genuinely glad that His Majesty had forgiven you, and we were relishing your appointment as 'General of the Left'," Chen Qun said. "We were waiting for a decree to destroy Yuan Shu... not imperial tidings on your daughter marrying his son. Such an act would be seen as unscrupulous."

"Yes, but where is my official seal...?" Lü Bu asked snidely. "Yuan Shu promised supplies, and they are here, real as you or I! But where is my seal...? Has it really been lost, or does Cao Cao lie to me...? Am I really 'General of the Left', or am I 'A walking corpse'...? *That* wouldn't need a seal, only a coffin, and it's far, far more likely, wouldn't you say...?"

"...I know when I'm wasting my time," Chen Gong sighed. "But be careful, my lord. Yuan Shu has reneged on a lot of promises during his life..."

Chen Gong got to his feet, bowed respectfully to each man, and left the room.

"Wang Kai…? Xu Si…?" Lü Bu prompted.

"This has advantages and disadvantages, but they depend on whether our other option is the imperial court or Cao Cao in truth," Wang Kai replied.

"Yuan Shu is not as safe an ally as others, but Cao Cao… is not someone that I can endorse at all," Xu Si suggested. "I am unsure, and can venture nothing certain."

"What do you two think?" Lü Bu asked as he turned to Chen Gui and his son Chen Deng.

"Yuan Shu is fickle and insincere," Chen Gui replied.

"I would not agree to this," Chen Deng said.

"And *you*???" Lü Bu said as he turned to Elder Chen Yuanfang and his son Chen Qun.

"What else is there to say…?" Chen Qun sighed.

"*Try*," Lü Bu growled.

"A man does not turn down gold and silk for empty promises," Chen Yuanfang said. "Yuan Shu is not just a man of empty promises: he is himself an empty promise. Cao Cao has seen fit to ensure that you are imperially appointed as governor, marquis and general: you are a statesman, a nobleman and a commissioned officer now. Why would you throw away all that has been given to you by the Son of Heaven for an alliance with an inconsequential liar, just because he has sent you a few overdue gifts from a deal long since expired…?"

But Lü Bu was not convinced: the only gold and silk that he had seen had come from none other than Yuan Shu, and the seal of authority from Xuchang seemed to be the empty promise. Furthermore, the thought of marrying his daughter into Yuan Shu's noble bloodline was too desirable a prospect, and Wang Kai and Xu Si's selfishly motivated reticence was compounding his doubts. Despite all of the protests, Lü Bu opened a dialogue with Yuan Shu, who saw it as yet another sign.

****

53

"...Is this true?"

Excellency Cao Cao was as bemused as any man at the latest report from Xu Province.

"Apparently, Lord Cao," Guo Jia replied. "Lü Bu turned Ji Ling back with an arrow."

"...Sometimes I wonder if I'm surrounded by lunatics," Cao Cao admitted. "What a fool! What sort of fool gambles everything that he had worked for like that, on the hope that the wind or some other factor might not ruin everything?"

"Anyone can be a fool," Guo Jia said. "Lü Bu just excels at it."

Cao Cao laughed, waved the cloth report back and forth and replied, "What can I say, mm...? This is what it is."

"It's another problem temporarily resolved," Guo Jia suggested. "That's never a bad thing when you have as many enemies as we do. Cao Hong is not getting anywhere in Jing Province – Zhang Xiu is too popular, amazingly enough – and the Black Mountain Bandits seem to be trying to gain ground here in Yan again, perhaps because they fear losing their base in Bing to Yuan Shao."

"...They've had their way for long enough," Cao Cao decided. "With the Yellow Turbans vanquished, why can't we deal with them?"

"Agreed," Guo Jia said. "The bandits must be routed this time."

Cao Cao hummed ambiguously.

"...Yuan Shao concerns you," Guo Jia supposed.

"We'll be fighting the same enemy this time," Cao Cao replied. "There was a time when I relished opportunities to work with old friends, but this time, I'm worried that he'll attack me or send more of the bandits toward Yan and make them my problem instead of his."

"We'll be doing the same," Guo Jia chuckled.

Cao Cao smiled guiltily and said, "We are, I suppose... but am I supposed to be writing to him and asking him to cooperate with me? He's the Commander-in-Chief of the Imperial armed forces! How can we not be speaking?"

"You tried," Guo Jia said. "Just focus on your own problems."

"...I'll do that," Cao Cao replied. "We're ready to march, so we will: the Black Mountain Bandits have annoyed us for long enough!"

Cao Cao's army advanced to Fengqiu and launched an immediate attack on the Black Mountain Bandits' disorderly camps. Yu Jin and Xu Huang were blunted by the unexpected and concentrated response and returned to Cao Cao's command tent for advice.

"...Perhaps I should coordinate with Yuan Shao after all," Cao Cao murmured.

"Do that at your peril," Xun Wenruo suggested. "Yuan Shao will sense your weakness and 'support you' with an army that will occupy Yan, seize His Majesty and ultimately destroy you."

"Maybe I won't do that, then," Cao Cao chortled. After a short silence, he added, "Oh, I know all of these things, gentlemen, but sometimes a man says the same things over and over in the hope that it will suddenly become a more feasible idea."

"Sometimes we must learn from the strangest of sources," Guo Jia said. "On this occasion, let's learn from Lü Bu... or, to be more specific, his mentor, Ding Yuan."

"…So I am to adopt Lü Bu and let him kill me," Cao Cao joked.

"*No!*" Guo Jia chuckled. "I meant-!"

"I know what you meant, Fengxiao," Cao Cao interrupted. "Ding Yuan was the first man to have any success against the Black Mountain Bandits; his subordinates included Lü Bu, yes, but they also included the more reliable *Zhang Yang*, who – fortunately enough for us – genuinely detests bandits. He's still rebuilding Luoyang, so-"

"We needn't write to him, my lord," Guo Jia insisted. "His tactics are favoured by me also: speed and confusion. Some enemies do require a waiting game, but stupid opponents like the bandits are best broken by sudden shock attacks on their camps. Lü Bu employed the tactic while working for Yuan Shao – on their leader Flying Swallow, no less – and it still worked, even after years of opportunity to learn."

"…Yu Jin, Xu Huang: wait until they are all settled, and do what you did before, but with random timing and greater emphasis on sudden retreats," Cao Cao ordered.

The Administrator of Henei, Zhang Yang, had requested regular reports from his former adviser Dong Gongren on the state of things in Xuchang: he had received word of the recent conflict between Cao Cao and the bandits, and it worried him greatly. Zhang Yang frowned thoughtfully as he watched enslaved labourers toiling on the palace in Luoyang: he was no more concerned about the dubious origins of the workers than he usually was, so his subordinates knew that something else was bothering him.

"Is there a problem, my lord?" a burly officer asked.

"…No, Major Yang," Zhang Yang replied. "Well, I say that but- …I'm being muddle-headed. My main focus should be – is – the reconstruction of the palaces."

"And that is going well," Yang Chou suggested. "But you're haunted by something, my lord, and ignoring it is as pointless as denying it."

"…The Black Mountain Bandits are now on either side of us," Zhang Yang said. "They're in Ji and Bing to the north and Yan to the south; if Cao Cao and Yuan Shao can't control them – and their lack of willingness to cooperate makes that likely, sad to say – they could decide to come here."

"The White Wave Bandits could reappear at any moment, since their leaders are in Yu and the rest are scattered all over Central Province," Yang Chou retorted. "It's all factored for, my lord."

"…The Son of Heaven is in Yan," Zhang Yang murmured. "If Cao Cao loses, then-"

"Cao won't lose," Yang Chou insisted. "Focus on the work here."

Zhang Yang forced a smile and said, "You're quite right. Gongren says the same… so I shall be optimistic."

Yang Chou left Zhang Yang to oversee the arrival of a new consignment of materials; Zhang Yang left the battered southern palace and returned to his temporary office in the northern palace site to compose his thoughts. His desk was littered with correspondence from the increasingly distant Dong Gongren and Zhang's former ally Lü Bu: it was Bu that concerned him most.

"What are you doing, Fengxian...?" Zhang Yang wondered as he stared at the most recent of Lü Bu's letters. "Why do you keep doing things like this...?"

The Black Mountain Bandits in Fengqiu lost their leader in one of their many encounters with Cao Cao's officers, and that caused them to fragment; the threat gradually subsided, and a jubilant Cao Cao had Guo Jia join him in his command tent to discuss the immediate future.
"So it is finally confirmed that Yufuluo is no more," Guo Jia said.
"They did a good job of keeping so many confused, but yes, he is definitely dead, and his brother wants no trouble," Cao Cao replied. "His son, that's a different story; I'll deal with him later."
Guo Jia smiled and said, "The Southern Xiongnu are no longer a threat, and we can safely say that Chenliu is saved and the Black Mountain Bandits are back to being your old friend Yuan Shao's problem. You can attack the target of your choice now."
Cao Cao hummed thoughtfully and said, "Any thoughts...?"
Guo Jia scanned the tent ambiguously.
"...Is there a fly in here?" Cao Cao asked.
"No, I was looking for thoughts," Guo Jia replied dryly. "You never know when one might go past you. Or maybe we should ask Xun Wenruo and Xun Gongda, my lord. My only thoughts are about the threat that those two men in Xu Province, Lü Bu and Liu Bei, pose to us: I have no idea who to attack next."
"...Why does Liu Bei scare you so?" Cao Cao asked. "Why is old Cheng Yu so scared of him? Liu Bei is a nonentity! He crumbles at the first signs of-"
"Recently, yes," Guo Jia interrupted. "But in the past, he fought well. While serving Yuan Shao, I met many men that fought in Ji Province during the Yellow Turban Rebellion: Liu Bei was in Yòu Province, and then he moved south, fighting in Qing and Xu. Every place that he visited was pacified eventually, and his nature is so quaint and so pleasant that men warm to him easily. Many Yellow Turban armies fell apart with far less bloodshed and far more dialogue."
"That's a man that could aid our work!" Cao Cao suggested.
"Ah, but Liu Bei is an imperial relative," Guo Jia noted. "He'll be brought into His Majesty's inner circle if elevated. What then?"
"My predecessor Liu Dai was a fool, but he meant no harm," Cao Cao said. "Liu Yu was so loyal to the Han that he refused to supplant His Majesty, even when we all thought that His Majesty had collaborated with Dong Zhuo to depose and kill his brother."
"Ah, but Jing's governor Liu Biao now harbours Jia Xu and Zhang Xiu, two men that once served Dong Zhuo: Jia Xu made Dong Zhuo's rise to Chancellor possible, quite possibly solely," Guo Jia retorted. "I know that I have advocated employing him when he is tamed, but who brings an unrepentant Jia Xu into their fold when that man's advice made a lesser god out of a monster...?"
Cao Cao laughed awkwardly and said, "Yes, but-!"
"And what of Liu Yan...?" Guo Jia continued. "Most clever men are united in the belief that Liu Yan tricked Lingdi into creating governors out of inspectors, tricked the eunuchs into sending him to Yi so that he could rule that remote place as though he were a prince, and then coerced Zhang Lu into seizing Hanzhong."

"He attacked the regents in the capital," Cao Cao argued.

"Yes, but *why*?" Guo Jia countered. "Did he do it to rescue His Majesty…? That's perhaps answered best by asking who he allied with to attack the capital – Ma Teng and Han Sui, two anti-Han rebel warlords – and why he wanted Hanzhong."

Cao Cao snorted a laugh.

"Hanzhong… seat of Liu Bang before he became First Emperor of the Han… the place the dynasty is named for," Guo Jia continued. "He wanted that place because he felt that it gave him the right to rule. The Liu that rules Hanzhong might one day rule the entire empire… so when Liu Yan attacked Chang'an, I believe that he did it to seize the throne for himself. One day, my lord, his worthless, craven son must be relieved of Yi and Hanzhong, because he has no right to them."

Cao Cao chuckled and said, "Now I'm destroying Liu Zhang! …But your arguments amuse me and enlighten me, so please continue."

"I shall," Guo Jia replied. "Liu Dai's brother, Liu Yao, accepted rank from the regents, and then he allied with the heretic Ze Rong that pillaged Xiapi and Guangling, murdering Han's appointed officials along the way. Liu Bei is, at the end of the analysis, a man, like any of us: my question, my lord, is 'What sort of man is he?' Past evidence points to a Liu Biao, a Liu Yan or a Liu Yao."

"…You do make a strong argument," Cao Cao admitted.

"Cheng Yu and I agree, so it is our joint argument," Guo Jia replied. "Liu Bei harboured Lü Bu – Dong Zhuo's muscle – just as Liu Biao now harbours Dong Zhuo's mastermind. Liu Bei used the influence of local magnates to steal Xu Province from Tao Qian, just as Liu Yan used Lingdi's misplaced trust to steal Yi and then used Zhang Lu's muscle to steal Hanzhong from its governor. He's allied to Gongsun Zan – who murdered Liu Yu to seize Yòu Province – and aided Tian Kai in his efforts to seize Qing Province without imperial sanction… which is uncomfortably reminiscent of Liu Yao's behaviour in southern Yang. He is the worst of all three of the rogue Lius combined, my lord, and he must not be allowed to gain any kind of foothold: he must be kept low, prevented from making influential friends, and destroyed at the first opportunity, or he will be a greater threat than any other man in the land."

Cao Cao was initially dumbstruck by the declaration: after a long silence, he sipped wine from a neglected dish and said, "Cold wine… is as strangely sobering as your words, Guo Jia. Now I hope that I shall never meet him again."

"Sadly, there are other men demand your immediate attention, but he must still be watched carefully," Guo Jia suggested. "At present, he's powerless; make sure he stays that way."

Cao Cao nodded slowly.

Cao Cao was not the only man that began to have new fears about Liu Bei. As the weeks passed after the relief of Xiaopei, the humiliated and demoted Liu Bei was growing in strength, and that concerned Lü Bu, who had only recently saved Liu Bei from death: now his thoughts were slowly turning to destroying him.

****

54

Excellency Cao Cao was not universally popular by any means: Dong Cheng exploited Cao's absence from the capital and asked some of the other courtiers to visit his home, ostensibly to have a banquet. But as soon as Dong Cheng was sure that there would be no espionage by Cao Cao's many agents in Xuchang, he sighed miserably and said, "We have another Wang Mang in our midst, gentlemen."
One of his guests – Minister Yang Biao – frowned and asked, "Who would you be referring to, Mister Dong…?"
"I need to speak his name, Mister Yang?" Dong Cheng retorted. "Who else do I mean…? Who else could I possibly mean but the-"
"That, gentlemen, is the point at which I must depart, I think," Fu Wan said.
"Mister Fu Wan…!" Dong Cheng chuckled nervously.
"My daughter is Empress," Fu Wan replied. "All is well at last… we have a place where food is available, where houses have roofs, where we are not bullied and heckled by bandits, and where we stand a chance of restoring order! Why are you determined to ruin it now?"
"I agree," Yang Biao said coldly.
"As do I," Zhong Yao said. "There is the promise of genuine order now, Dong Cheng: why risk further chaos?"
The other guests looked at one-another nervously.
"Remember, gentlemen, that I heard no name," Fu Wan continued. "No man here heard slander… and perhaps it would be best if that is how things were left."
Dong Cheng nodded silently.
"Now, I shall take my leave," Fu Wan added with false politeness.
Fu Wan bowed to each man and left the house: within minutes, all but two of the other guests got to their feet, bowed respectfully and left. The three men that remained – Dong Cheng, Zhong Ji and Wang Fu – stared at one-another nervously until a servant entered the hall and signalled that it was safe to speak.
"…*Aiee*… so they are all toadies and cowards," Dong Cheng sighed.
Wang Fu smiled and said, "Yang Biao is no coward. And they fear more than the 'Chancellor in an Excellency's garb'. They fear a loss of newly-restored order, as Mister Fu Wan does."
"*Order*…!" Dong Cheng chortled. "There is no peace or order anywhere! This is *Dong Zhuo* all over again! Cao Cao is going to be the poison cup that finally extinguishes the Han if-!"
"Forgive me, but must I again remind you that *you* invited him to Luoyang to rescue the Son of Heaven from the White Wave Bandits?" Zhong Ji said.
"…That, of course, is the reason why I lack credibility," Dong Cheng replied. "The two of you are forced to keep reminding me of that sad fact…"
"I don't mean to confound you," Zhong Ji said. "Like you, I fear Cao Cao's intentions; like you, I want to see him destroyed before he harms the sovereign; but like the others, I remember the horrors of the journey from Chang'an. I remember the White Wave Bandits, and I remember Guo Si's charming 'armed escort' that even assaulted the Empress's guards and stole articles from

the imperial treasury. Compared to the last eight years, this is a very good situation."

Dong Cheng snorted angrily and said, "All that you say is true. But Fu Wan is descended from the great Fu Sheng! He's also descended from a line of Han loyalists, yet he's a craven-"

"He's also the Empress's father," Wang Fu interrupted. "Don't you know the tale of Dou Wu and Chen Fan...? He does, I'll assure you. Even if Cao Cao's a threat-"

"And he is," Zhong Ji admitted. "A few times now, I've seen men's words get to him – even those of the Son of Heaven – and for a moment, there's a look in his eye that I've seen before... in the eyes of Dong Zhuo."

"And the event that he is most famous for – the ravaging of Xu Province, not once but twice – is an atrocity that Dong Zhuo would be proud of," Dong Cheng said. "Every man, woman, child, cat, dog, chicken, city, town, village, wall, stone and tree was destroyed by that man as he advanced on Xiapi! Such a murderous streak cannot be a good quality for an excellency to possess!"

"...If I may," Wang Fu said, "I would like to continue: as I was saying, such a man cannot be defeated without a plan. You're a military man as well as an official, but without a plan, how do you hope to defeat the minds around Cao Cao?

"When he first began his career, he had Chen Gong: that brilliant man betrayed him and joined Lü Bu after the atrocities in Xu Province, but Cao still has Xun Yu and his nephew Xun Yòu, Cheng Yu, and Guo Jia. Those four aren't the only advisers that he has, but they're enough... the rest just make him even more dangerous. And that's without the men that flock here to join his court; I hear that he has rescued Kong Rong from Yuan Tan, and Liu Fu brought men from Lujiang – Yuan Shu's seat – to join the court as well."

"But Xun Yu is a fierce Han loyalist," Dong Cheng protested.

"Wenruo's blind to Cao Cao's true nature," Wang Fu replied. "That poor man may be clever, but at the same time, he's too trusting: he won't realise what sort of man he serves until it's too late. And even if you were to somehow make Wenruo see sense, there's Cheng Yu and Guo Jia."

"*Aiee...* Guo Jia," Dong Cheng sighed.

"A clever young man with a self-destructive love of vice," Zhong Ji noted. "He'll not see our age – he'll kill himself way before then – but while he lives, he's a threat. And Cheng Yu is a man with no scruples. He'd probably have us minced up and fed to the troops if we were defeated."

"That's why I needed Mister Fu Wan!" Dong Cheng whined. "I wanted to-!"

"We know what you wanted to do," Zhong Ji interrupted. "But you have a beautiful daughter of your own that is in the imperial harem. If she gains favour, Heaven is with us. If she does not, then perhaps Heaven has decided... *something else*, shall we say."

"His Majesty is known for his devotion to Empress Fu," Dong Cheng replied.

"But he has an obligation to provide as many princes for the realm as possible, so he must engage with his consorts," Zhong Ji said. "Show patience. Let's not make the same mistakes as men like

Dou Wu, Zhou Bi, Wang Yun and Shisun Rui have made before us. While he obviously doesn't wish to intrigue further, Minister Yang Biao's plan to divide the regents worked because he was patient and careful, while Dou Wu failed because he rushed and involved too many people. Zhou Bi was too obvious at the critical moment, Wang Yun failed to make the right allies or pardon the right enemies, and Shisun Rui was not in full control of the men that might have aided him, and so they endangered him instead. Patience and care, Mister Dong Cheng: patience and care."

Dong Cheng agreed: his plan to defeat Cao Cao would have to wait. But as others had said, he was the man that had invited Cao Cao to the capital and allowed him to get close to the emperor: he therefore felt personally responsible for the current calamity, and he felt that he was duty-bound to put things right. But like many men before him, he was dependent on others to make his plan succeed: in this case, he needed his daughter, Consort Dong, to be alluring enough to win the emperor's attention and give him an opportunity, and that was a matter for fate to decide.

Yuan Shu smirked as he read the latest response from Lü Bu.

"We have him, gentlemen," Yuan Shu cackled. "He is ours to command…!"

Yan Xiang, Han Yin, Yuan Huan and Yang Hong were united in their distress; Han Yin coughed nervously and said, "My lord, you must not assume too much. This is Lü Bu, the most untrustworthy man in-"

"In this, we can be sure of his trustworthiness, gentlemen," Yuan Shu insisted. "The mere promise of becoming part of my illustrious clan, of partly wiping the stain of his own commoner's lineage from his grandchildren's faces, has rightly excited him! It is mutually beneficial: I have strong, athletic grandsons and beautiful granddaughters, and he has some genuine right to feel part of something special! In addition, I gain the strength of this era's mightiest champion!"

"…He sends a man here to parley further, I understand," Han Yin prompted.

"Some fellow called Qin Yilu," Yuan Shu replied dismissively. "He will have a price, and I can find and match it, I think. We will then have him to spy for us and learn of Bu's true intentions if they somehow differ from proper logic."

"…So we will not be campaigning against Xu Province again," Yan Xiang prompted.

"Of course not!" Yuan Shu snapped. "No, we can now focus on Yu and Yang… and perhaps Jing. Sun Ce has eliminated almost all of my adversaries in southern Yang, though I still wonder if I can trust him; I only hope that the threat of losing his family and the families of his trusted vassals is enough."

"And what about Qing Province…?" Han Yin asked.

"What can I do about Qing?" Yuan Shu retorted. "Gongsun's man is incompetent if he's been beaten by my villainous nephew. If Gongsun asks for help, and Bu is with us, then we'll take Qing for ourselves. Soon, all will be mine…"

The dejected former governor of Qing Province, Kong Rong, arrived in Xuchang while Cao Cao was concluding his return from

Fengqiu; Cheng Yu, Dong Cheng, Wang Fu, Yang Biao, Zhong Yao and Dong Gongren greeted him at the city gates.

"Oh, to see so many familiar faces...!" Kong Rong bleated. "Oh, but I am so ashamed of what has happened... and my family...!"

"Your family is being negotiated for, Mister Kong," Cheng Yu replied gruffly.

"...Your countenance suggests great disappointment, Mister Cheng," Kong Rong sighed.

"Mister Cheng is always like that, and with everyone, even His Excellency," Yang Biao chuckled. "It's good to have you here, anyway, Kong Wenju. A post awaits you, of course, and-"

"Can I assume a role after Qing Province...?" Kong Rong suggested. "Argue my helplessness against Yuan Tan all you want, gentlemen, but I could not handle a few Yellow Turbans either! If it weren't for Taishi Ci and Liu Bei-"

"Liu Bei is a fool, and Taishi Ci is a rebel," Cheng Yu grumbled. "You will need to acquaint yourself with current events, I think, Mister Kong. Now, if you'll excuse me, I have His Excellency's return and my own return to Dong Prefecture to plan for..."

Cheng Yu bowed slightly, turned, and retreated to the chancellery.

"...Such an unpleasant man," Dong Cheng scoffed.

"I knew Mister Cheng Yu, and I know Yang Biao, Dong Zhao, Wang Fu and Zhong Yao, but I am not sure that we have met, sir," Kong Rong said politely.

"My family name is Dong, my given name Cheng, Mister Kong," Dong Cheng replied. "I am a 'politician', apparently: I hold surprisingly low rank, given that I was the one that-"

"Mister Dong Cheng, now is not the time for venting frustration," Yang Biao said purposefully. "Mister Kong has just travelled from Qing Province, where he was held captive by a seditious-"

"I... should like to converse with you all about a great many things in the future," Kong Rong interrupted as he stared at the irritated Dong Cheng. "As for my time in captivity, I understand that Yuan Tan and his wicked aide, Xin Ping, have-"

"*Xin Ping*...?" Yang Biao exclaimed. "*Ayah*... that man had such promise."

"...Yes, well, he aids Yuan Tan now," Kong Rong chortled. "He did nothing to secure my release: in fact, I think that he suggested my imprisonment."

"We must meet and share a kettle of wine, Wenju, and discuss old times," Yang Biao said. "But for now, I must go; gentlemen..."

Yang Biao bowed humbly and retreated into the city.

"I, too, have matters to attend to," Dong Gongren said. "Gentlemen..."

Dong Gongren bowed respectfully and left Kong Rong, Dong Cheng and Wang Fu alone.

"Now, Mister Kong, let us escort you to the city, since the others have obviously been distracted," Dong Cheng said.

"...Please do not raise controversial matters now, Mister Dong Cheng!" Wang Fu hissed.

"I know not what you speak of, Wang Fu, but I must know something," Kong Rong said. "Cheng Yu spoke ill of my friend Liu Bei... and I have heard disturbing rumours on the way here."

"Mister Kong Rong, I think that you will be an asset to the court," Dong Cheng replied. "We should go to a tavern, and I shall update you on all matters: additionally, I shall tell you of Luoyang, and the White Wave Bandits, and Cao Cao."

"...The 'Crafty Villain', Xu Shao called him; to think that the man once threw away the role of District Captain to make a petty point... to think that a man once known for his mischief and vice is now the Excellency of Works!" Kong Rong chuckled. "Mengde – His Excellency, I mean – has saved me, though, so I should not judge him."

"Ah, but it is 'His Excellency' that slanders your friend Liu Bei, Mister Kong," Dong Cheng retorted.

"What...?" Kong Rong exclaimed. "B-but... why...?"

"Come, Mister Kong Rong, and we shall talk further," Wang Fu sighed; he knew that he could not prevent Dong Cheng from trying to involve Kong Rong in his plotting, so he had decided to accompany the two men and be aware of what was said.

"Cao Cao is not what he seems," Dong Cheng said as he led Kong Rong into the city. "We three shall go and speak of the events in Chang'an, Henei and Luoyang, and my part in them: then, perhaps, you will see things more clearly."

Kong Rong would come away from his first meetings in Xuchang as a man confused; he had wanted to kowtow to the Excellency of Works and thank him for saving his life, but he became increasingly opposed with every word that Cao's detractors said. Kong Rong awaited the return of men like Xun Wenruo so that he might hear a better appraisal, but he was doubtful that anything could sway him from the belief that Cao Cao had to be challenged with words at the very least.

＊＊＊＊＊＊＊＊＊＊＊＊

55

Cao Cao's return to the court was mostly greeted with muted congratulations for his victory over the Black Mountain Bandits; he expected the newly-arrived Kong Rong to be a humble and grateful supporter, but Kong Rong's attitude was noticeably cold, if not hostile.

"...I truly do not understand," Xun Wenruo murmured as he followed Cao Cao and Guo Jia into the chancellery. "The things that he said... are not at all like Kong Rong!"

"My enemies have obviously got to him before my allies could," Cao Cao retorted as he swept a pile of bamboo books from his desk and sat down in front of it.

"He's more likely annoyed at Yuan Shao's letter," Guo Jia chuckled. "I must admit, whoever came up with the justification for imprisoning Kong Rong was thinking clearly: the idea that Yuan Tan was 'removing a seditious fraud that was recommended by thieves and appointed by traitors, in the name of His Majesty' was simple and to the point. Do you not agree, Excellency...?"

Cao Cao stared at the empty desk and did not reply.

"...You wanted a paper and pen, Excellency...?" Xun Wenruo asked.

"I am surrounded by ingrates, Wenruo," Cao Cao muttered as he clutched his head. "I rescued the entire court from the White Wave Bandits, but I am treated like a villain! Even Kong Rong, whose life I saved from Yuan Tan, acts as though I am the one responsible for it! This is Xingyang all over again: I am the only one that makes an effort to do something, but all that I get in return is abuse and rebukes. Even His Majesty treats me like a villain, with all of his slights and sarcastic remarks! Did Dong Zhuo or the regents receive such treatment? No, because everyone was too scared of them to be so trivial! It is certainly true, Wenruo, that 'The man that serves himself knows only praises great, while the man that serves the land knows only jealous hate'. Others drive me to contemplate villainy, Wenruo, with their spiteful treatment of the just!"

"You have a headache," Xun Wenruo replied.

"Kong Rong vexes me more than most," Cao Cao admitted. "I risked all-out war with Yuan Shao to get that fool out of Qing Province, and now he openly chastises me! Why do men like him and Benchu have to be so arrogant???"

"...'Benchu'...?" Guo Jia noted.

"He... he should still be a friend, Fengxiao," Cao Cao retorted. "It is being dragged into this madness that separated us and made enemies of us! It is the quest for power that made us enemies, not any real reason! The Yuan brothers would be so different if they had not had that fortune to quarrel over! Will my own sons do the same...?"

"Probably," Guo Jia replied. "But you shouldn't concern yourself with other people. Rest, try not to think about the stresses of the day... spend some time with your family, instead of imagining them all fighting after you're dead."

Cao Cao laughed desperately and said, "You're quite right."

"I'll talk to Wenju, find out what – or rather, who – drove that strange behaviour at court... so that we can act," Xun Wenruo suggested.

"Who must I kill now...?" Cao Cao asked dryly. "I have led Wei Zi to his death, ordered the murder of Zhang Miao, and must one day fight Benchu to the death; who, I wonder, must die so that Kong Rong gets his sense back...?"

"I made no mention of killing anyone," Xun Wenruo replied. "There are other ways to 'act' besides killing people."

"Yes, but killing's usually the only thing that works," Cao Cao retorted as he leant forward and covered his head with his hands.

Guo Jia exchanged glances with Xun Wenruo and said, "Leave the court to us, Excellency, and get some rest at home."

"Thank you, gentlemen," Cao Cao replied miserably.

Cao Cao's domestic arrangements were mostly normal for the time: he had several wives and consorts, and they would increase in number as his status grew. Cao's principal wife was Lady Ding, but only because his first wife, Lady Liu – who was mother to his 3 eldest children, among them his heir Cao Ang – had passed away. Lady Ding knew that she was not as desirable as Cao's favourite, the former courtesan Lady Bian – whom Cao had met in a brothel and taken a liking to – and she had failed to produce further heirs, so she maintained her status by raising Cao Ang, Cao Shuo and the eldest Lady Cao – Lady Liu's children – as if they were her own. Lady Bian, by contrast, had already given Cao 4 sons – Cao Pi, Cao Zhang, Cao Zhi and Cao Xiong – and still caught Cao's eye. Another wife, Lady Huan, had recently given birth to another son, Cao Chong; Cao Cao had much to celebrate, as many sons meant many more descendants that would bear his family name.

"I am glad to see you all," Cao Cao said as his wives and consorts – over a dozen in all – lined up to greet their lord and husband. "Where are my children...?"

The children – who ranged from cradled babies to fully-grown teenagers and adults – were presented to their proud father.

"Father, it is good that you are home," the eldest, Cao Ang, declared.

"I am glad to be home, my son," Cao Cao replied; he then turned to Lady Bian's eldest and said, "I see that you have grown a little taller, Pi."

"Taller, yes, but never the tallest," Cao Pi replied. "Others will always tower over me."

Cao Cao snorted a laugh and said, "An interesting answer."

"A banquet has been prepared to celebrate your return, my lord," Lady Ding said.

"We are entitled to some sort of celebration, I think!" Cao Cao replied; he gestured purposefully, and the family turned as one to enter the mansion.

Cao Cao sat in the host's seat and observed his large family with pride: when the main banquet ended, he had his eldest sons – Ang, Shuo and Pi – sit before him and practice poetry and witticisms while Lady Ding and Lady Bian looked on.

"Pi, I think, has impressed me most, since he is young yet sharp," Cao Cao chuckled. "A fine lad... a fine lad. But that is not to say that I am not blessed by Ang and Shuo!"

The gaunt Cao Shuo smiled and said, "We all of us live to make you proud, Father."

"We hope that we will be as great as you someday, Father," Cao
Ang declared.
"You shall, you shall," Cao Cao replied.
"...There are three runners," the 8-year-old Cao Pi said suddenly,
"all equal in skill, who are challenged to race each other. The first
gets a head start, and has a shorter lap to run; the second has a
longer lap, starts second, has weights tied to his feet, and must
run backwards; the third must wait until he can barely see the
others before he can start running, must run sideways, is
weighted down at both ankles, and must run twice the distance
that the first has to run. Who wins the race...?"
Cao Cao smiled and replied, "The one who reaches his finishing
point first. Why do they race...?"
"To win," Cao Pi said.
"Win what...?" Cao Cao challenged.
"...Something good," Cao Pi replied. "They don't find out what it is
until they win."
Cao Cao laughed and said, "It would have to be very good indeed,
my son, for the 'second and third' of the three to participate in
such an unfair competition that they have so little hope of
winning!"
"They are just there so the first has someone to win against," Cao
Pi replied. "They are not meant to win."
Cao Cao frowned and said, "I think I understand your metaphor,
but little expected it from one as young as you. Are these your
own thoughts...?"
"Sometimes, after school, we play games that aren't fair," Cao Pi
replied. "That is one of them: I just wondered what you thought
about it, Father."
"...Ah, I see," Cao Cao murmured. "I thought- ...Never mind."
"For the second to win, the first must somehow fall," Cao Shuo
noted. "For the third to win, the first and second must fall; the
first only wins because he has an unfair advantage, the others
because of their friends' misfortune. What a horrible game."
"Isn't it, Elder Brother...?" Cao Pi said. "But everyone still tries,
though, even the third, because the other two *might* fall, mightn't
they...?"
"After being treated so unfairly, the third deserves to win
something," Cao Ang suggested. "Whoever thought of that game
is very cruel."
Cao Cao smiled, looked to Lady Ding and Lady Bian and said,
"What fine sons I have: they are a credit to you both. May all my
children be as these three."
Lady Ding smiled at Cao Ang as if he were her own and sighed
gratefully.

Xun Wenruo left the chancellery and journeyed to the Kong Rong's
new home in Xuchang. After a long session of exchanging
anecdotes over tea, Xun Wenruo said, "It is so good to have you
here, Kong Wenju! You have been away from the Son of Heaven
for too long!"
"It is good to be here," Kong Rong replied. "I cannot truly know
what role you or anyone else truly played in my escape from Yuan
Tan's clutches, but I am eternally grateful for your sincere and
wonderful friendship."

"If I could have broken you out of that prison with my own two hands, I would have," Xun Wenruo promised. "Ah… what times these are that we live in, Wenju. It's a shame that we have not had the chance to speak freely as we once did, about the matters of the day, and the concerns of the age. Such things have happened… Cai Yong, Wang Yun, Shisun Rui, Zheng Tai and so many others that we once looked up to are gone, and we must now continue their great work."

"…One of the reasons that I am glad that you came here was the need to speak freely and urgently," Kong Rong admitted at last. "Wenruo, I cannot understand what Cao Cao is doing. I used to respect the man, but-"

"You still should," Xun Wenruo interrupted. "Don't think of speaking rudely at court again, Wenju, because I may not be able to quell his anger on the wrong day."

"*Ayah*! But that is just it!" Kong Rong said. "You're supporting another Dong Zhuo, aren't you…? Since I've been here, Dong Cheng-"

"Dong Cheng is behind this…?" Xun Wenruo exclaimed. "…But it makes sense."

"Others – many others – have expressed concern at Cao Cao's rise to power!" Kong Rong insisted.

"Dong Cheng enjoys high status for a man with such little talent and such an unclear lineage, and his daughter is a consort to His Majesty, so I don't see what else he can want," Xun Wenruo scoffed. "The man allowed the White Wave Bandits to treat the Son of Heaven with egregious contempt for quite some time before he invited His Excellency to help him, so I have to say that his protestations are insulting to me."

"But-!"

"And Lord Cao is not another Dong Zhuo," Xun Wenruo continued. "I honestly can't believe that you say such things, Wenju! How can you say that of a man that once risked his life to face Dong Zhuo at Xingyang?"

"Times have changed," Kong Rong insisted. "Many whisper that he has His Majesty here as a hostage, much like Dong Zhuo did in Chang'an, and-"

"I would never allow that," Xun Wenruo interrupted. "When you attack Lord Cao, you attack *me*, Wenju."

Kong Rong sighed and said, "I apologise, Wenruo."

After a short silence, Xun Wenruo smiled a conciliatory smile and asked, "I know that you are erratic because you fear for your family. Any word…?"

Kong Rong smiled sadly and said, "Since being chased out of Qing Province by Yuan Shao's brute of a son, I have been lucky to live here in Xuchang, though negotiations for my captured family do not go well."

"I shall ask Lord Cao to write to Yuan Shao, demanding that his son returns your family," Xun Wenruo promised. "That man has been most obnoxious of late, demanding things and- …I digress. As I said, your request will be heard."

Kong Rong bowed and said, "Thank you."

Xun Wenruo smiled again and said, "Now, perhaps, you might do something for me and for the state…"

Kong Rong bowed slightly and said, "For the state, anything."

Xun Wenruo bowed gratefully and said, "Your friend Wang Lang has been in retirement since being defeated by the brigand Sun Ce, has he not...?"

"He has," Kong Rong sighed. "Does Excellency Cao desire his head on a spike?"

"...Not at all," Xun Wenruo replied disappointedly.

"But didn't Wang Jingxing serve as an adviser to Tao Qian, the only named suspect for the murder of Excellency Cao's poor father...?" Kong Rong asked snidely. "Didn't Wang Jingxing then go and become Administrator of Kuaiji and continue to aid the 'nefarious Tao Qian' from a distance, providing him with-"

"*Enough*," Xun Wenruo said. "Please hear me out, Wenju."

Kong Rong lowered his head and said, "I shall... but I cannot forget Xu Province."

"His Excellency deeply admires Wang Lang's talent and is grateful for his sending Yu Jin to serve in Yan Province," Xun Wenruo continued. "His Excellency wants to have Wang Lang come here, to Xuchang, and work for the court, as fate always intended. He has written to Mister Wang on several occasions, but the poor man's replies suggest that he is traumatised by his numerous defeats and considers himself unworthy of status."

"...So Excellency Cao would like me, as Wang Jingxing's old friend, to write on his behalf and convince him to come here," Kong Rong supposed.

"You are as wise as your ancestor," Xun Wenruo replied.

"Hardly... but I will gladly do it, because a man like Jingxing should not be wasting away," Kong Rong said. "I will have a letter ready and sent by the end of tomorrow."

"My thanks," Xun Wenruo replied.

Kong Rong could not resist making one further point: he smiled and said, "Wang Jingxing is a smart man... so he will be sure to make his own mind up about-"

"Do not spoil a moment of accord, Wenju," Xun Wenruo pleaded. "His Excellency is benevolent at heart, despite any faults that he has. Trust me in that."

Kong Rong sighed and said, "I shall have to."

Once Xun Wenruo had left his home, Kong Rong immediately began writing a letter to Wang Lang, a man that had been adviser to Governor Tao Qian of Xu Province and the semi-autonomous administrator of the southern prefecture of Kuaiji. Wang Lang had repeatedly insisted that he would not serve in another administration, but he did not refuse this request from a friend and began preparations to travel to Xuchang; this decision would be one of the most important in all of the era's history, because it would pave the way for the final victor in the famous 'Three Kingdoms' period that would begin within the next 25 years.

****

56

Lü Bu summoned his court and glared at the assembly with untrusting eyes. After a short silence, he said, "I hear that Liu Bei has suddenly found his strength again, and built a fine army."
"*Ayah… don't do it!*" Chen Gong pleaded.
"Has he or hasn't he got ten thousand men?" Lü Bu shrieked.
"He does, my lord," Wang Kai confirmed.
"And has he or hasn't he been heard bemoaning his status?" Lü Bu asked.
"That a rumour that cannot be clarified," Xu Si replied. "The-."
"It's enough for me," Lü Bu said. "I'll march against that little ingrate *personally*."
"My lord… this is not the right course of action!" Chen Gong pleaded. "You must not-"
"Liu Bei will know his place!" Lü Bu shouted angrily. **"I'll teach him a lesson!"**
Many of the courtiers exchanged weary, cynical glances.

On the day of the attack, Liu Bei heard of Lü Bu's approach and assumed that his lord and master had simply returned to gloat, or threaten him with replacement: he was completely thrown when Bu tore into his outlying camps and cut down many of the new recruits that Liu Bei had worked so hard to find.
"What is he doing???" Liu Bei sobbed.
"I'll fight him!" Zhang Fei cried: he charged at Lü Bu on his short brown steed, but Lü Bu matched his impressive strength with greater dexterity and unseated the burly Zhang from his horse with surprising ease. Guan Yu charged, but Bu was ready: he matched every one of Guan Yu's skilful attacks with his halberd, and his subordinate Wei Xu was forced to continue the assault on the camp.
"You're good," Lü Bu chuckled, **"but I'm the best!"**
Guan Yu was still recovering from an injury that he had sustained when he was fighting Ji Ling's forces: the fatigue overwhelmed him, and he was forced to retreat.
"No one can beat Lü Bu! NO ONE!" Lü Bu cried maniacally. **"Burn this place! Leave NOTHING!"**
"We'll… have to flee," Guan Yu groaned as he reached the despondent Liu Bei. "He is mad… and his arrogance and malice are peaked. We cannot stay, or he'll kill the civilians."
"Will this province never know peace…?" Liu Bei cried as Guan Yu and Chen Dao forced him to abandon what was left of his camps. Zhang Fei found his horse and aided the Mi brothers, Mister Sun and Jian Yong while the distracted Lü Bu destroyed Xiaopei's defences in an act of self-destructive violence.
"He's a monster!" Mister Sun cried as Mi Zhu led him away.

Lü Bu's mocking laughter filled the heads of the survivors long after the real sounds were far behind them.
"Where are we going?" Jian Yong asked of Mi Zhu.
"We have only one option open to us… Xuchang," Mi Zhu replied.
"No," Zhang Fei said. "No, you… you can't be… … …**I'll go back! I'll go back and fight him again! I'll kill him! I'll tear him**

apart! Just get the civilians out of the way, and-!"

"Yide, *please*... we have no choice," Liu Bei whimpered. "It goes against every fibre of my being, I promise you that it does... but we must go to Cao Cao. There is nobody else to turn to."

"What about Yuan Shao?" Jian Yong proposed.

"That's too far!" Liu Bei chortled. "How would we survive...?"

"But to go to *Cao Cao*...?" Jian Yong said with disbelief.

"Cao Cao supports His Majesty now," Liu Bei replied. "His past misdeeds are atoned for."

"**You said that about Lü Bu!**" Zhang Fei barked.

"And can you 'atone' for damming a river with tens of thousands of corpses of the innocent over a single man's supposed crime...?" Jian Yong added. "The-!"

"**It's Cao Cao or turning around and giving ourselves over to that madman for swift disposal!**" Liu Bei retorted. "**Where else is there???**"

"But... won't Cao Cao want us dead for blocking his path to Tao Qian...?" Jian Yong asked worriedly. "Won't he want us dead for Xuande inheriting Xu...?"

"He's put all that in the past, I think," Mi Zhu replied. "He promoted Lü Bu, and he did more harm to Cao than we ever did."

"Quite right," Liu Bei said. "Now let's say no more... and go to Xuchang. I may get the opportunity to meet my divine relative; that would be a wonderful thing."

"Get him to reverse your disinheritance," Zhang Fei grumbled.

Liu Bei sighed loudly and stared at the sky; he was as distressed as he had ever been in his life to that point. His vassals said no more as they made the long and difficult journey west, toward the Yan-Xu border.

Cao Cao was forced to allow Xun Wenruo, Guo Jia and Xun Gongda to have a meeting in the private chambers of his chancellery office when news of Liu Bei's arrival in Yan Province was announced.

"Don't let him in," Guo Jia pleaded. "Remember what I said!"

"The man is harmless," Cao Cao replied. "Yes, I remember your words, but there are alternate interpretations of Liu Bei's behaviour and actions."

"Like what?" Guo Jia challenged.

"One of the men that you compared him to was a schemer, and all of their actions were meticulously planned," Cao Cao suggested. "The other two can be argued as victims of circumstance."

Guo Jia whined desperately and cried, "Don't be fooled! He-!"

"I know your arguments, Guo Fengxiao, and it must be said that Liu Yao was forced to ally with Ze Rong, and that the accusations against Ze Rong are not fully proven," Xun Gongda said. "Liu Biao was given little choice but to allow Zhang Xiu – not Jia Xu – to stay in Wan. He'll eject him eventually, as he did with Yuan Shu."

"No he won't!" Guo Jia chortled. "Jia Xu's charm offensive is winning people over! He's becoming more and more entrenched!"

"But it remains the case that Liu Bei is his own man, and that his actions are all explainable as circumstantial," Xun Gongda insisted. "Other men argue the same."

"Yes, and I'm sure that they always will!" Guo Jia retorted. "Good schemers always make their work look like luck, fate or the work of others! Yuan Shao's acquisition of Ji is a fine example!"

"...*Aiee*... that's a good point," Xun Wenruo admitted.

"Did Han Fu know that it was a scheme until it was too late?" Guo Jia asked. "Your brother Chen aided that plot, did he not...?"

"He's my brother by blood," Xun Wenruo sighed.

"Han Fu took that invasion by Gongsun as a genuine incursion, not a deal struck between Gongsun and his own Administrator of Bohai!" Guo Jia continued. "He tendered that province to Yuan Shao based on barbed advice given by your brother and Shao's cousin Gao Gan! And then what...? Where is Han Fu now...?"

"...And I cannot argue, because Yuan Shao admitted the plot to me in not so many words," Cao Cao said numbly. "He called it 'benevolent subterfuge', or some nonsense like that. But only a few men know of it... most think it was Han Fu's own idea to cede the province, and that there was no plot."

"Yet another reason why Yuan Shao wants Gongsun Zan dead," Guo Jia suggested. "While Gongsun's anger at his nephew's death at the Battle of Yang City is the declared cause of their feud, it suits your former friend, my lord, because Gongsun could reveal Yuan Shao's plan to the world and ruin his reputation as an honest man. Gongsun will never be believed now, of course, since his reputation as a nominated *xiaolian* – a man of the highest integrity – is irrevocably destroyed after murdering Liu Yu and seizing Yòu Province... but a loose end is a loose end."

"...But what has Liu Bei done?" Cao Cao chortled. "He fought the Yellow Turbans nobly enough! He gave his men to Taishi Ci to liberate Beihai from yet more Yellow Turbans, and did not try and take credit for himself! Yes, he fought Yuan Tan at Pingyuan, but neither Tian Kai nor Yuan Tan had a proper claim to Qing! Yes, I know, I hated him for aiding Tao Qian... but it was the choice of the Xu officials to appoint him governor, Guo Fengxiao! He did not appoint himself as Liu Yan or Gongsun Zan did! He did not murder Tao Qian as Gongsun murdered Liu Yu! Yes, he allowed Lü Bu to shelter with him, but... can I blame him?"

"Don't allow guilt to determine matters," Guo Jia warned.

"I do nothing of the sort!" Cao Cao insisted. "It was a case of 'An enemy of my enemy is my friend', was it not...? I attacked Xu; Bu attacked Yan, thus saving Xu by forcing me to retreat; therefore, Lü Bu was Xu's saviour. It was a simplification of complex matters, but now Liu Bei sees things more clearly, doesn't he? Bu stole the province from him, and now he comes to me."

"*Ayah*... desperation drives him, nothing more!" Guo Jia protested. "He will soon forget gratitude and plot to get close to His Majesty! If you are perceived as an obstacle, then he will plot to remove you! He's an imperial relative: letting him near the throne is as bad as letting Liu Yan near Lingdi was, maybe worse!"

"We say all this about a man that we don't know, gentlemen," Cao Cao said. "I will not refuse him shelter, else men will call me a villain, and don't they already call me that without reason...? We'll let him state his case, and we'll let him move as he pleases; if he is a threat, then he'll let us know it soon enough."

"Heed the examples of history!" Guo Jia cried.

"The men you refer to were all influential; Liu Bei has no friends here," Cao Cao replied. "Elder Chen and his son deserted him; Chen Gui and Chen Deng betrayed him; Mi Zhu is no longer

wealthy; Gongsun Zan would be a very poor choice of hosts."
"Everything you say strengthens my case against him!" Guo Jia retorted. "Why did the Chens turn on him? Where did the Mi clan's wealth go? How can Liu Bei be a friend to Gongsun Zan without-"
"I was once a friend of Yuan Shao," Cao Cao said. "Friends can sometimes be as family are: a complex thing to argue. Let us give this complex man a chance: that's all I ask others to do for me."
Guo Jia sighed miserably and said, "Then we are to greet Liu Bei: so be it. Just try and keep him away from Dong Cheng and Kong Rong, mm...?"
Xun Wenruo and Xun Gongda exchanged worried glances, as Guo Jia's arguments had gravitas that they could not ignore.

Emperor Xian dismissed his attendants so that he might discuss recent events with his confidante Empress Fu in private; the empress was noticeably subdued, and Xian knew the reason.
"I deny nothing, but I admit something," Emperor Xian said. "My duty to the imperial line is, I cannot lie, enjoyable, but it is duty nonetheless, I assure you; I do not take them into my confidence as I do you, my lady."
"I am aware that you are simply doing what you must," Empress Fu replied. "After all, even the freest Son of Heaven, as with any normal man of means in the land, is duty-bound to ensure that he has produced as many children as he has consorts, time and enthusiasm. I knew this from before we were wed, Your Majesty, and I accept it, not just because I must but because I choose to."
"...I am not sure whether that comforts or disturbs me," Emperor Xian admitted. "But that is not what we are to discuss, it was just something that I had to say. No, I wanted to discuss a possible change in the situation: *Liu Bei* is here in Xuchang."
Empress Fu nodded and said, "Liu Bei has been very busy of late, if I recall."
"Liu Bei is not a seditious relative like Liu Yan or Liu Biao," Emperor Xian continued. "Yes, he is disinherited, but I was all but disinherited for a time, and offences committed by his ancestors should not condemn him. He fought the Yellow Turbans to aid the empire, serves wherever he is put, and has been a thorn in the side of every man that I detest, including the Excellency of Works. This is the man that will help me restore the Han."
"...If Your Majesty is sure that he will not disappoint, then I am happy that we have a new friend," Empress Fu replied. "What can he do...?"
Emperor Xian sighed miserably and said, "Very little at present, but if he is given rank and opportunities to build a base and an army, then he might achieve a lot. All that is needed is an opportunity, so we must hope that Heaven grants us one."

Kong Rong sat at the desk in his living quarters and smiled.
"Xuande, here in Xuchang...!" Kong Rong whispered. "With you here, Xuande... what could happen...?"

✳✳✳✳✳✳✳✳✳✳✳✳

57

Cao Cao welcomed Liu Bei and his retinue at the gates of Xuchang: Xiahou Dun, Cao Xiu, Xu Huang, Xun Wenruo and Guo Jia accompanied him.

"You've been done a wrong, Liu Xuande," Cao Cao said as he led Liu Bei into the city. "How glad I am of the opportunity to meet you properly, put my personal follies behind us, and greet you as the hero that you are."

"I am no hero, Your Excellency," Liu Bei whimpered. "Lü Bu stole Xu Province from me because I am incompetent."

"Call me Mengde," Cao Cao insisted. "Today, two heroes – perhaps the only true heroes in the land – meet at last, and that calls for a banquet!"

"You flatter me undeservedly," Liu Bei replied. "And I worry about Xiaopei: I had ten thousand recruits, and Bu was cutting them down like ripened wheat."

"...*Ten thousand*, you say...?" Cao Cao exclaimed.

Guo Jia smiled knowingly.

"...That's an impressive force for a man to gather when he is at a disadvantage," Cao Cao said with reluctant respect. "Xuande, you are a hero of future times."

Liu Bei sensed Cao Cao's caution and replied, "I would be content to save Xiaopei, since that was my responsibility. But now, I have no army again: what can I do?"

"I'll give you an army, and I'll make sure that you're promoted to 'Governor of Yu Province': and *properly* this time, not by a rogue warlord!" Cao Cao promised. "I'll help you to return to Xiaopei; you can watch Bu for me, until the appropriate moment arrives for us to deal with him."

Chen Dao, Mister Sun and Mi Zhu followed their master silently.

"Your allies are quieter than I'd heard," Cao Cao joked.

"It's better that they are," Liu Bei replied. "At least, that much is true with regard to Zhang Yide... who is not here. I left him with our families, who we were lucky to retrieve while Bu was on his mad rampage. I have only brought my advisers and bodyguard, who are all quiet and level-headed."

"I look forward to meeting them all," Cao Cao insisted.

Xiahou Dun sneered silently, which amused Guo Jia.

"His Majesty has insisted on meeting you," Cao Cao continued. "That is not a surprise, of course: the Son of Heaven has wanted to meet you for years."

"And I, His Majesty!" Liu Bei said excitedly. "Oh, to bask in his divine image...!"

"And you shall, Xuande," Cao Cao chuckled. "We'll go to him once you've bathed, rested and been given appropriate attire."

Emperor Xian was waiting for Liu Bei in the grand audience hall of the temporary palace: the penitent officials watched as Liu Bei – who had changed into court robes – entered the hall, neared his relative and sovereign, and kowtowed before him.

"...A distant uncle, now not so distant," Emperor Xian declared. "We are glad to know our loyal relative, Liu Bei. We are truly glad to finally know you."

Cao Cao shuddered at the warmth of Emperor Xian's address.

"I, Bei, am unworthy to sit in your presence, Your Majesty!" Liu Bei replied with tear-filled eyes. "My ancestors wronged, and I rightly pay a price!"

"You are our relative, and we know no wrong of yours," Emperor Xian said. "We know that you have urgent business in Xiaopei that no other man should rightly undertake, but we hope that in the future, you might be closer to the court, where we can enjoy your presence."

"I am honoured, Your Majesty," Liu Bei replied. "I shall soon be gone again, but when that matter in Xiaopei is resolved, I would be glad to serve Your Majesty here in Xuchang with every fibre of my being! I would serve Your Majesty as a horse would!"

"We look forward to your return, and feel sad for every day between that day and now," Emperor Xian said. "We agree to Mister Cao's request that you be promoted to Governor of Yu Province, and we give our assent to any undertaking that is necessary to restore order."

Liu Bei kowtowed and said, "Thank you, Your Majesty!"

Dong Cheng left the imperial court with a strange smile on his face: it was noticed by his allies Wang Fu and Zhong Ji, who followed him to his home.

"Aren't you two worried that our meeting will be reported?" Dong Cheng said as he entered his living quarters.

"Aren't you worried that you're wearing a schemer's smirk in public?" Wang Fu scolded. "If I could see it, others could see it: you see Liu Bei as a possible ally."

"Of course I do!" Dong Cheng replied. "He's what we've needed! I won't thank Lü Bu for many things, but I'll thank him for this: he's sent us the hero that our cause needed. My daughter has found favour, which is also good... fate is with us, gentlemen! When Lü Bu is dealt with, Liu Bei will return to the capital: when he does, all I then need to do is speak to him, learn of his thoughts, and find accord... which I shall do when the time is right."

Wang Fu and Zhong Ji left the house as worried men.

"...The sooner that Liu Bei is back in Xiaopei, the sooner I'll sleep easier," Cao Cao grumbled as he returned to his office later that day. "I have to have a banquet with him tonight... I hope to see something other than a future hero fighting fate."

"I did warn you that he's a future threat," Guo Jia said as he followed his master.

"He is just excitable, I'm sure," Xun Wenruo said. "He's a royal kinsman, and we'd do well to remember that."

"Yes... that is true," Cao Cao sighed. After a pause, he added, "Bu won't like this at all. But he brought it on himself."

"Send Liu Bei back quickly, and ensure that he has no time or privacy that allows him to converse with our court rivals for too long in the meantime," Guo Jia urged. "As you say, it is better for us all."

"I'll do as you suggest," Cao Cao replied thoughtfully. "Where is Bei now...?"

Cao Cao had turned to Xiahou Dun, who stared blankly and said nothing in response.

"...Who was appointed to escort him around the city...?" Guo Jia prompted.

"Not me," Xiahou Dun replied indifferently.

Cao Cao turned to Cao Xiu, who said, "Why look at me, Cousin...?"

"Oh dear," Guo Jia whispered.

"*Aiee*... who watches Bei???" Cao Cao exclaimed. "Where is he???"

At the same time, Liu Bei had accepted an invitation to a modest banquet at the home of Kong Rong.

"Oh, Xuande, I know I keep saying it, but how good it is that we are both in the same room at last, after so many years of knowing each other as words on pieces of paper!" Kong Rong said excitedly. "A man like you is sorely needed here in Xuchang: all is not as well as it appears."

"Forgive my selfishness, but my heart is in Xiaopei, which is the only place where I can currently do any good," Liu Bei replied. "I cannot stay here, and you heard that well enough in court, Wenju."

"Oh, yes, I know that you have to go back there and deal with Lü Bu for Cao Cao, but after that you can return to the capital, as His Majesty desires!" Kong Rong said. "At that point, 'Excellency Cao Cao' – if he has not become the 'Chancellor of State' by then – must be challenged at every turn, and with your voice added to my own, we-"

"Would I not be showing ingratitude by heckling him at court...?" Liu Bei asked.

Kong Rong sighed wearily and replied, "I am meant to be grateful for his saving me from Yuan Tan, but he did it to seem benevolent, not because he truly cares! He does not save you because he likes you, Xuande! He needs you to act as a buffer against Lü Bu!"

"Again, I am a buffer," Liu Bei chuckled miserably. "I am like the sandals that I used to weave, protecting the weak flesh from the hard earth! But is Cao Cao weak flesh...? Am I hardened straw...?"

A servant gestured to Kong Rong, who frowned, got to his feet, spoke with the servant and returned to Liu Bei, saying, "It seems that someone, a 'Zhu Ling', is out looking for you. I see that His Excellency wants an eye kept on you while you are in Xuchang."

"Then I should go, and be entertained by His Excellency," Liu Bei replied as he got to his feet and exchanged bows with his host. "It has been good to see you, Kong Wenju, and I hope that our next meeting will be longer and free of interruptions."

"So do I," Kong Rong said pessimistically; he watched Liu Bei leave the house and wondered if Liu Bei would be allowed to return to the capital at all.

Liu Bei and Chen Dao were escorted to the chancellery by Zhu Ling; Cao Cao greeted his guest at the door and said, "Apologies for dragging you away from...?"

"Kong Rong," Zhu Ling confirmed.

"*Kong Rong*," Cao Cao sighed.

Liu Bei nodded silently.

"...You need say nothing, Xuande," Cao Cao continued. "Why that man distrusts me, I do not know."

"Wenju fears for his family," Liu Bei replied.

"And I assure you that I do everything I can to get them here," Cao Cao said. "But I am being ungracious; please, after you."
"No, after you!" Liu Bei replied, as was the protocol; the two men entered the chancellery and took seats as host and guest. Guo Jia and Xun Gongda sat opposite Liu Bei and studied him intently; Mister Sun, Mi Zhu and Mi Fang arrived within minutes, escorted by Xun Wenruo, and each man took a seat; Chen Dao and Dian Wei stood behind their respective lords and viewed the other for signs of treachery.
"Such rain, and such noise...!" Liu Bei chuckled; the weather had changed, and there was now a violent thunderstorm brewing.
"It is Heaven's cry," Cao Cao replied. "Change comes at last."
The two men were silent for a few moments; the thunder and lightning caused the occasional jitter, and the rain clattered against the chancellery walls without pause.
"...His Majesty was very pleased to see you, as I promised," Cao Cao said.
"It was like seeing the sun for the first time," Liu Bei replied. "Even if I lose my life in Xiaopei, I can do so knowing that I have seen Heaven's manifestation and received forgiving words that free me from the guilt I carry for my ancestors' wrongdoings. That is enough for me, Excellency."
"I insist that you call me Mengde," Cao Cao said. "And to return to our previous conversation for a moment... Kong Rong, Dong Cheng and others are aggrieved that their ranks are not higher, but I have much to organise and few men to organise it, and I have the way of things to consider, where they perhaps do not. Where can I put a gentle scholar like Kong Rong to govern, when the world is so full of chaos...?"
Liu Bei nodded silently.
"And Dong Cheng is a former junior officer under Dong Zhuo's son-in-law Niu Fu that somehow, through the mysteries of fate, ended up in a position to assist the Han loyalists – men like poor Shisun Rui, who died on the way to Luoyang, and Yang Biao, who thankfully survived – militarily when the regents started feuding," Cao Cao explained. "It is fortunate that he invited me to Luoyang when he did, for the White Wave Bandits were probably days away from regicide; but I cannot give a man rank that he is not worthy of, no matter how much I regard him for his character. Dong Cheng is not senior officer material, else Dong Zhuo would have made more of him; he is not ministerial material, else Jia Xu would have used him better. If I am honest, I think that he probably aided Yang Feng's betrayal of Guo Si because he was bitter, not because he was loyal to the Han, else he would not have allowed the atrocities that His Majesty endured for so long; he likewise invited me to attack Yang Feng because Yang had gained favour – admittedly undeserved – and he had not."
"...It is probably as you say," Liu Bei replied carefully. "I have had no words with Dong Cheng, though Wenju briefly mentioned him."
"Hopefully, Dong Cheng's pretty daughter becoming part of His Majesty's harem will earn him favour by that other route, and he will get what he wants," Cao Cao chuckled. "As for me, I will make do with being a man that earns my posts, as you do."
"Alas, I have earned none of the posts that I have held, else I wouldn't have lost them," Liu Bei replied. "I haven't the

marvellous military record that you have."
Cao Cao thought of his own actions in Xu, fought the urge to scowl at what might have been a slight and said, "I have not been flawless, Xuande, as you know. Did you want to return to Xiaopei immediately...?"
Liu Bei sensed Cao Cao's meaning and replied, "As immediately as immediately can be, Excellency- ...Sorry, 'Mengde'. I would be back there now, looking for what is left of my army, if it was possible. I shall leave tomorrow or tonight if the option is there for me to do so."
Cao Cao laughed and said, "Such courage and tenacity! I shall have your army and escort ready to return to Xiaopei in one day from now, and you shall be quartered on my estate in the meantime; actually, I... I should confess before you learn of it elsewhere that I started preparing for your departure before we had finished our first encounter at the gates. I knew that you would want to leave *quickly*, you see."
Liu Bei smiled knowingly and replied, "I am grateful."
The two men raised their wine dishes silently; their followers exchanged glances and did their best to hide their thoughts about the meeting and the events that would arise from it.

Liu Bei received the resources that he needed to go back to Xiaopei and begin rebuilding his forces as soon as he was back there. Lü Bu was unhappy, but he knew that Liu Bei was now a favourite of the emperor and an appointed governor. The two would endure an uneasy truce while Liu Bei plotted a way to seize Xu Province from Bu and Bu pondered a way to be rid of all of his problems, including Liu Bei. And once again, Yuan Shu was watching the developments with increasing glee.

✳✳✳✳✳✳✳✳✳✳✳✳

ACT V: A COSTLY ERROR

58

The situation in the centre of Han China had reached a turning point: the resurgent Yellow Turbans of Runan had been pacified, and the Black Mountain Bandits were losing ground to Yuan Shao after being chased from Yan Province by Cao Cao. The imperial court – which had enjoyed a relatively stable but busy year in the temporary capital Xuchang, in Yan Province – now saw one large but identifiable obstacle as being left before lasting peace could be obtained, namely forcing the warlords – Chinese and Qiang alike – to end their enterprising activities and pledge unconditional allegiance to Emperor Xian; that would not be easy.

Of the many warlords that had initially existed, quite a few remained: the Qiang warlords Ma Teng, Han Sui and Song Jian and their sometimes-allies, the former regents Li Jue and Guo Si, controlled the northwest; Yi Province Governor Liu Zhang and the cultist ruler of Hanzhong, Zhang Lu, controlled the far west; Gongsun Zan controlled Yòu Province on the northeast frontier and the northern tip of Qing Province to the southeast of that; Yuan Shao – whose many titles included Commander-in-Chief of the Imperial Army and Governor of Ji Province – controlled not only Ji but most of Qing and Bing Provinces as well; Cao Cao, in addition to his capacities as Excellency of Works and Acting Excellency over the Masses, was forced to lead the imperial Army since Yuan Shao now refused to work with him; Liu Biao was governor of Jing Province, though his northernmost counties were controlled by Zhang Xiu, a fugitive warlord from the northwest, and his adviser Jia Xu; Director of Retainers Zhang Yang was still the Administrator of Henei Prefecture to the north of the ruined capital Luoyang; the notorious Lü Bu now had the title 'General of the Left' and served as Governor of Xu Province in the east; and last but not least, the ambitious Yuan Shu – Yuan Shao's brother, and self-styled contender for the chieftainship of the wealthy Yuan clan – controlled most of Yu Province and most of Yang Province to the southeast, although the latter was actually annexed by his reluctant vassal Sun Ce. Excellency Cao Cao would therefore have a staggering 11 warlords – 14 if Liu Zhang, Zhang Yang and the lofty Yuan Shao were not as obedient as they seemed to be – to defeat or placate if he was to end the chaos that had been the norm for as long as anyone could remember.

Cao Cao's cousin Cao Hong had been tasked with defeating Zhang Xiu, whose influence now extended beyond Wan City and into much of the rest of Nan County. The materialistic Cao Hong was not renowned for his reliability or seriousness, but he could charm people with relative ease when required; his reputation was proved correct when he arrived in the northeast of Nan County. Cao Hong's advisers – who were none of them veterans of Cao Cao's campaigns – were horrified when Cao Hong's first act upon setting up his camp was to invite a troupe of dancer-prostitutes to his command tent to entertain the officers and local men of influence. That had become a routine, and despite a string of losses against Zhang Xiu's small but formidable army – and resistance from an additional militia comprising local people who liked Zhang Xiu and disliked Cao Cao – Cao Hong continued to entertain in his command tent in the same way night after night.

"*Ayah!* We will be blamed for this!" one adviser sobbed; Cao Hong was clapping and laughing as the dancers writhed and turned to a tune by local musicians. The women wore no shoes, as was Cao Hong's preference, and they took it in turns to leap onto the drums that had been placed in the centre of the room in order perform their own beats with their carefully-timed, skilful dancing.

"We're ignored," a second adviser complained. "His Excellency knows his cousin well, and this worked in Yan *sometimes*, so-"

"We will still be blamed for not controlling him when we *inevitably lose!*" the first adviser hissed.

"...Perhaps we will be ambushed and killed tonight, and then it will be over," a third adviser said with what sounded like hopefulness in his tone.

"**More! More!**" Cao Hong cackled. "**More wine, more women, more dance!**"

But outside the tent, many of the soldiers – some of them originating from Cao Cao's ex-Yellow Turban 'Qing Corps' – grumbled about their living conditions and wondered if they should continue to serve their commander.

"These reports are ludicrous," Jing Governor Liu Biao complained to his court. "It is bad enough, gentlemen, that I am branded a villain by Cao Cao's puppet court now, and accused of collaborating with the likes of Zhang Xiu when he is an unwanted tenant; this strange fool of a relative that Cao Cao has sent here to 'pacify' me is forcing me to ally myself with Zhang Xiu in order to survive! Cao Cao makes the accusation, and then contrives the evidence to support his claim with cruel subterfuge!"

"But our 'alliance' with Zhang Xiu consists of local militias with a free hand that are doing nothing more than defending themselves from an incursion," the adviser Kuai Liang suggested.

"*Ayah!* They are *my* people, *my* provincial subjects, working side-by-side with Zhang Xiu and Jia Xu!" Liu Biao retorted. "Cao Hong is a Han officer, so any act of defence is also treason!"

"Like it or not, it's the only solution," the adviser and politician Huan Jie sighed.

"Agreed," Kuai Liang said. "My lord, we cannot let Cao Cao abuse his current position as Li Jue, Guo Si and Dong Zhuo did before him. We must be seen to resist attempts to destroy the government here and petition His Majesty directly about it."

"I have done as you say, but where is the proper answer...?" Liu Biao retorted. "Did Cao's cronies ever allow proper discussion?"

"...They certainly 'discussed it', and they inferred that you allow Zhang Xiu to remain here, since you 'have made no move to evict him as you did Yuan Shu'," the adviser Wang Can said. "Your initial attempts at expelling him are disregarded, and now we are where we are."

"Gentlemen, it is as Wang Can says," Liu Biao declared. "Zhang Xiu will continue to resist Cao Hong, and the local people will continue to resist as well because Zhang Xiu does not harm them but Cao Hong does with his supply demands and lavish night parties. It is only the shallow nobles, whores and street musicians of Nan County that love Cao Hong; the rest do not, and if I am seen to accept him, they will turn on me. So I am damned: I can resist the Han and be labelled a traitor, or I can aid Cao Hong and be ousted by my own disaffected subjects."

"…Or you can carry on as you are: let Cao and Zhang fight, keep fresh supplies moving into Nan for the people, continue to petition the court, and let the truth be the winner of this battle," Kuai Liang suggested. "Cao Cao will, eventually, be exposed for the schemer that he is, and he will turn his attentions elsewhere. His hungry quest for Jing will end as badly as Yuan Shu's did."

Liu Biao nodded and said, "Though it is a weak stance, I am not in a position to do anything else. Cai Mao can monitor the situation, but besides that I shall sit and wait; the truth is that I do not want either of them here – neither Zhang nor Cao – and I must hope that they destroy each other."

Zhang Xiu, meanwhile, was concerned about the situation that he and his followers were now enduring.

"Mister Jia, Cao Hong does not leave, even after countless setbacks," Zhang Xiu complained. "He pushes us and wastes our resources!"

"He's softening us up for Cao Cao, whether he knows it or not," Jia Xu replied. "Cao Hong might have been the right man for winning over counties in Yan that were sympathetic to Lü Bu, but he was the wrong man to send to Luoyang – that Cao knows too well – and in this very different matter he is inexperienced and incompetent. With that said, it can be deduced that Cao Cao did not send him here to win alone… or at least, one would hope so if one were His Majesty."

"Yes, but 'one' is not His Majesty, one is *me*, or rather *us*, and Cao Hong is proving to be a frightening nuisance now!" Zhang Xiu said. "If we are, as you say, being 'softened up', do we have to look for allies…?"

"We'll find none," Jia Xu retorted. "Li Jue and Guo Si are not men that we should be seen with, and note that Li Jue's unsolicited correspondence has been as hostile as the government's. The Qiang would not come here to help, and if they did, it would be to ravage Nan County, not defend it; Liu Zhang is a spineless mediocrity whose army is not fit for purpose, even if he had a great man to lead it, and he would never go up against the Han's Excellency of Works; Zhang Lu of 'Han'ning' is a worse ally to consider than the regents or the Qiang, because he offends the Son of Heaven with everything that he does; that leaves the likes of Zhang Yang and the Yuan brothers, and I need not elaborate there, I think."

Zhang Xiu had been pacing back and forth as Jia Xu spoke; he stopped, hummed thoughtfully and said, "So your judgement is that we sit here, resist Cao Hong as we have been doing, and accept the inevitable."

"We knew that the defence of Wan City would be difficult," Jia Xu replied. "We knew that Liu Biao would at the very least protest, and that the Han would seek 'revenge' on us for our affiliation with the Liang warlords. All this we knew, but the alternative was to surrender to the Han government, and that has worse risks. We are 'out in the open' and able to protest if we are here; let Cao Hong stay until he outstays his welcome altogether, and then let

Cao Cao come here, so that we can show our potential for doing good, make our case and force the Han to show discretion."
"Fine, Mister Jia," Zhang Xia said. "We shall do as you say."

Day after day, Cao Hong awoke, recovered from the excitement of the night before and led his forces into a battle in one part of Nan County or another: and day after day, Qing Corps soldiers deserted or quarrelled with their peers, locals rioted or engaged Hong's forces directly, and small detachments led by Zhang Xiu's general Huche'er blockaded roads and fought for the opportunity to remain in Jing. Eventually, Cao Hong was trapped inside his own camp and harassed by a variety of enemies; he was then forced to assemble his officers and officials for an altogether different type of meeting in his command tent.
"*Ayah*... what am I to do...?" Cao Hong said to his weary advisers. "I do what I can to be popular, but I am being rebuked by the fools that live here! Do they enjoy being pillaged and raped by Dong Zhuo's henchmen?"
"Li Jue and Guo Si were responsible for much of that, not Zhang Ji," one adviser replied. "Jia Xu is sly: he has had Zhang Xiu treat the people well, so the people like them. Liu Biao does not want to rile his people, so he allows local village chiefs and even magistrates to act as they please; those chiefs and magistrates benefit from Zhang Xiu, so they aid him in repelling us. They see *you* as the problem, my lord, for bringing war to a place that was relatively peaceful and prosperous."
Cao Hong whined angrily and said, "But I must clear the way for Cousin Mengde to go to Chang'an! How can these stupid peasants be so obstructive to such a cause...?"
"They won't care about that," the adviser replied. "The only way to pass Zhang Xiu without the 'stupid peasants' being 'obstructive' is to do so bloodlessly."
"But I am tasked with eliminating the villains!" Cao Hong said. "After all I did in eastern Yan, after we got rid of Lü Bu; there, I was a hero, but these idiots, they brand *me* the villain and-!"
"We will have to retreat," a second adviser warned. "We're incapable of making any progress here. We must retreat and ask His Excellency for help."
"I'll look incompetent!" Cao Hong cried. "How can I do that?"
"You have no choice," the first adviser said.
"...Curse the idiots of Nan County!" Cao Hong exclaimed. "Curse them all, the fools! Alright, alright, we'll retreat! Give the orders to break camp and retreat! And someone get me a pen and paper!"
The officers left the tent to issue their commander's orders while the advisers did all that they could to hasten Cao Hong's preparation of a letter to Xuchang; Cao Cao would be disappointed by his cousin yet again, but he had already guessed that he would one day have to go to Jing and deal with Zhang Xiu personally.

****

59

While Cao Cao contemplated his next move against Zhang Xiu, another of his future targets – Gongsun Zan, the self-styled Governor of Yòu Province – sat at the host's seat of his residence's private meeting room, looked at the latest reports from northern Qing Province and sighed miserably. His adviser Guan Jing – who was his only company – smiled and said, "We must maintain a belief that we can turn this around, Lord Gongsun. Tian Kai is very capable, and-"

"Yuan Tan is every bit the future hero, and Qing is all but lost," Gongsun Zan retorted angrily. "The famine is worsening, so I must change my plans."

"What do you intend to do?" Guan Jing enquired.

"As we discussed," Gongsun Zan replied, "I will develop Yijing so that it will serve as the greatest defensive structure ever-"

"*Defensive*...?" Guan Jing chortled. "You cannot think that Yuan Shao will have the strength to invade Yòu Province...?"

"Are you senile?" Gongsun Zan scoffed. "Bandits are still a problem, and the Wuhuan are still making noise, and now, to make it worse, 'Commander-in-Chief' Yuan Shao – promoted to that post by his friend Cao Cao! – has an imperial edict sanctioning an attack on me! If he has the might of the puppet emperor's word behind him, what do my depleted army and a few scruffy bandits led by Zhang Yan mean?"

"How can Zhang Yan lose when he has so many followers...?" Guan Jing asked.

"The Black Mountain Bandits are like any other confederacy," Gongsun Zan retorted. "They're allied until it doesn't suit someone, and then it all goes wrong. Yuan Shao is winning in Bing Province: I do not know exactly how, but he is winning, and once he has got Bing, he will want Yòu and the rest of Qing so that he has all of the northeast. Qing is almost lost... so soon, I will be fighting for my lands and my life."

"...We who serve you will fight – and if needs be, die – at your side, Lord Gongsun," Guan Jing promised. "But I maintain that we have the better army, and that Yuan Shao cannot prevail!"

Gongsun Zan laughed and said, "I hope you're right."

But the next few weeks saw Yuan Shao deliver blow after fatal blow against the Black Mountain Bandits in Bing Province. The Southern Xiongnu sat in Ping County and offered no resistance or support for the bandits; the bandit confederacy's overall leader, 'Flying Swallow' Zhang Yan, journeyed southward and met with his demoralised allies in the hills of southern Bing.

"What happened to your spirit, lads...?" Flying Swallow heckled; the large open-air gathering was silent in response, so he added, "We've been up against worse than Yuan Shao! Why-?"

"Yuan's like a mad dog," the bandit 'Poison Yu' interrupted. "Since me and my lads hit his capital and killed the prefectural administrator, he's looking to get his reputation fixed, and the only way he can do that is getting my head on a spike."

"He won't get it, Yu," Flying Swallow insisted. "I've come down here now, and-"

"He's got thousands of men here in Bing," Poison Yu interrupted. "They're well-trained… very well trained. And the Xiongnu aren't with us now that Yufuluo's dead, 'cept maybe some little bands of 'em, so-"

"What about going to Yufuluo's son, Liu Bao, then…?" Flying Swallow asked.

"He's been named heir to the whole mess," the bandit 'Big Eyes' grumbled. "As soon as that happened, he became 'Everyone's Chanyu' and forgot about us."

"…Without the Xiongnu, we might have problems," Flying Swallow admitted.

"Yeah, and what if Yuan – who's been named 'Commander-in-Chief' of the Han army now – gets cozy with the main Xiongnu lot, like the Han were in the past…?" Poison Yu suggested. "Some o' the lads reckon they've seen *Wuhuan* riders in his cavalry an' all… not rebels, *Tadun's lot*."

"…Blimey," Flying Swallow exclaimed. "I didn't think they'd help Yuan Shao; if that's true, Gongsun's in trouble too, and we need his help to-"

"**Maybe we should just give up!**" one lesser leader cried; his words were received favourably by some, while others jeered and threatened him.

"**There'll be no giving up!**" Flying Swallow barked. "**I promised Oxhorn that I'd lead you lot properly and get things done, and I will! I took that man's family name as my own, and I won't be seen to break a promise!**"

"You sound like one of them Han generals, with all their fancy rhetoric," Big Eyes heckled. "I'm fighting on 'cause all I have waiting for me now is slow-slicing; we'll get no mercy from Yuan or his mate 'Excellency' Cao Cao, the Butcher of Xu, will we…?"

The bandits murmured agreeably.

"Exactly," Flying Swallow said. "We'll storm his camp in the morning."

Ji Governor Yuan Shao spent most days in his command tent while his officers did the bulk of the fighting; on the morning after Flying Swallow Zhang Yan's arrival, he was woken early at his own request so that he could inspect his battle map and be prepared to receive a range of eagerly-anticipated reports.

"Commander Yuan, Mister Tian and Mister Guo are here," Yuan Shao's secretary, Chen Lin, announced.

"Ah, Mister Tian!" Yuan Shao said as the advisers Tian Feng and Guo Tu entered the vast tent. "And Mister Guo too! What news…?"

"General Yuan Tan reports that Tian Kai has ceded ground south of Pingyuan, and the complete seizure of Qing is a matter of weeks – or even days – away," Tian Feng replied. "And the bandits' loss of supplies from Yan Province has certainly done damage to their cause."

"Yes, well, it's about time that 'Excellency Cao' did something about his northern defences, isn't it…?" Yuan Shao said. "But the former news is splendid indeed! My son is a tiger! Oh, what a delightful-! …Oh, yes, sorry: Mister Guo…?"

"Gongsun is withdrawing into his shell," Guo Tu reported. "General Zhang Hè notes in-fighting and desertions in armies close to the border, and our agents have told us of defensive earthworks being created around a fortified city called Yijing."

"I know the place... it is near the western mountains. That is so that he can be close to his bandit friends, no doubt," Yuan Shao scoffed. "Well, his time is nearly at an end: let him 'withdraw into his shell', gentlemen, for shells can be cracked if the sword is sharp enough. What of the news that the bandits have sent reinforcements to aid 'Poison Yu'...?"

"The confederacy leader, Zhang Yan, is said to be among the reinforcements, who mostly arrived yesterday with no decorum or subtlety," Guo Tu replied. "They'll likely attack as soon as they can muster enough morale."

"Then we shall have to counter them quickly!" Yuan Shao said as his nephew Gao Gan and General Chunyu Qiong entered the tent. "Aha! General Chunyu, your timing could not be better! Are Yan Liang and Wen Chou ready...?"

"They are ready, Commander-in-Chief!" Chunyu Qiong replied enthusiastically.

"And are your forces ready, Nephew...?" Yuan Shao asked as he looked at the unimpressive Gao Gan.

"They are, Uncle and Commander-in-Chief," Gao Gan replied.

"Very good, very good... all very good!" Yuan Shao giggled. "Let's rid ourselves of these idiot criminals, so we can tell His Majesty of our fine work and show the court what a true hero looks like!"

Yuan Shao placed his gilded helmet on his head, adjusted it pedantically, and left the tent with his commander's sword in hand; Chen Lin, Tian Feng, Guo Tu, Gao Gan and Chunyu Qiong followed at a distance.

"...Uh... You are going to lead the assault...?" Tian Feng said at last.

"Why not...?" Yuan Shao retorted as he stopped next to his horse. "I want to see the looks on their faces for myself!"

"Aw, damn... he beat us to it!" Flying Swallow complained as a blood-drenched messenger staggered into his half-built camp at the foot of the hills.

"H-he... the...!" the messenger croaked.

"I get it, mate," Flying Swallow sighed. "Someone get him to somewhere that he can rest or die in peace...?"

The messenger collapsed into the arms of two comrades that dragged him up the nearest hill.

"Do we retreat up the hill?" Poison Yu asked.

"And get smoked out...?" Flying Swallow chortled. "Nah, we'll have to fight him head on. Gongsun suggested a few things, and here's what I reckon we'll do..."

Flying Swallow led a 'regiment' of around 3,000 bandits to intercept Yuan Shao's army, who were busy dispatching the last of the bandits' signal camps.

"The scoundrels come to meet us!" Yuan Shao sniggered. **"We shall smite them all here and now!"**

"That can't be all of them," Guo Tu fretted. **"Lord Yuan, they plan some sort of-!"**

"I'm not a fool, Guo Tu!" Yuan Shao retorted. **"Of course they plan to encircle us, but I fear them not! Their ruse is seen through, and we will trounce them soundly! Yan Liang!"**

General Yan Liang rode forward to await his orders: he was an impressive and imposing sight on his Wuhuan battle steed, and his elite men – both cavalry and infantry – were well-trained.

"**Do as they expect, Yan Liang, and charge their centre,**" Yuan Shao cackled.

"**It shall be done, Commander!**" Yan Liang replied.

Yan Liang led 200 men forward in a spear formation, with the faster cavalry at the head; Flying Swallow smirked and said, "**Let 'em come!**"

Yan Liang's cavalry suddenly put on speed as they neared the bandits' front line: they tore into the men that they encountered and felled close to 30 before they wheeled around and fled.

"**Bloody cowards!**" Flying Swallow cried as he ran back and forth trying to restore order in his scattered lines. "**Big Eyes! Big Eyes, where are you???**"

"**…Here,**" Big Eyes replied as he stumbled towards his leader. "**Got me in the arm, and… I dunno… me ribs hurt.**"

"**Where the hell is Poison Yu???**" Flying Swallow shrieked as Yan Liang turned about and charged again. "**Where are Circles and Yu???**"

At the same time, Poison Yu and 'White Circles' left the wooded areas that they had been hiding within and began their attacks on Yuan Shao's flanks, but they had been outmanoeuvred: Wen Chou and Chunyu Qiong led cavalry and infantry forces to pincer the bandits between themselves and Yuan Shao's main unit.

"**If I die here, I get Yuan Shao first!**" Poison Yu cried as he spied Yuan Shao's golden helmet amongst the fighters and hoped for a great opportunity.

"**My lord, be careful!**" a Han cavalry officer bellowed as he came between Poison Yu's riders and Yuan Shao; he then raised his halberd and said, "**To get to the commander, you must pass Jiang Yiqu!**"

"**Never heard of you!**" Poison Yu heckled as he tried to pass the thin wall of cavalrymen.

"**My lord, Wen Chou is here!**"

"Oh, hell," Poison Yu whimpered as Yuan Shao's elite general appeared and charged at his unit.

"**THUNDER LORD IS HERE!**"

Even Wen Chou was rattled by the voice of the approaching bandit chieftain; Poison Yu broke out of the encirclement and fled with half of his riders.

"**I'll never complain about your voice again!**" Poison Yu cackled as he met with 'Thunder Lord' Zhang.

"**WE'VE GOT TO RETREAT!**" Thunder Lord replied.

"I won't argue," Poison Yu sighed as he watched many comrades being hacked down at speed by Yuan Shao's forces.

"**Don't let that one get away! That was the wretch that killed Li Cheng!**" Yuan Shao shrieked. "**After that one! That was 'Poison Yu'!**"

Wen Chou and Yan Liang led a charge against the largest group of scattered bandits, and one in every five men fell.

"**We're being massacred!**" Flying Swallow cried. "**We have to retreat!**"

"**Yellow Dragon's lot have come!**" Big Eyes reported. "**About time they-!**"

"**So what?**" Flying Swallow retorted. "**He's only got three-hundred men!**"

But 'Yellow Dragon' had only brought around 200 men, and he was being pursued by a force led by Gao Gan.

"...S'over," Flying Swallow muttered.

Yuan Shao's forces were in every direction, and the slaughter continued; when Flying Swallow and his surviving followers finally broke out of the encirclement and fled northward, they left hundreds of their comrades behind as captives and corpses.

"Every live man that we caught is to be punished with the Five Pains," Yuan Shao ordered. "The dead are to be-"

"Isn't that a little harsh...?" Tian Feng asked. "By all means brand them, or take a hand from the identifiable leaders, but-"

"They are irredeemable, and softness only invites further incursions!" Yuan Shao retorted. "I want them to know that their crimes will-!"

"My lord, we're getting word that some splinter groups of Xiongnu are on their way, and they are with the bandits," a scout announced.

"...**Huchuquan will be lucky if I don't personally flay his back raw for this!**" Yuan Shao cried.

"They're splinter groups!" Tian Feng protested. "They might not even be Southern-"

"Nonsense!" Yuan Shao scoffed. "That sneaky barbarian is lending aid under a haze of subterfuge! He is no better than his churl of a brother Yufuluo!"

A nearby Wuhuan cavalry commander grunted angrily.

"They're treacherous, those people!" Yuan Shao continued obliviously. "I have not forgot Yufuluo's actions during our front against Dong Zhuo, when he-!"

"But my lord, we're getting word that some minor Wuhuan chieftains have lent Flying Swallow a cavalry," Tian Feng said pointedly.

Yuan Shao looked at the offended commander of his own Wuhuan cavalry unit, harrumphed irritably and said, "Perhaps Huchuquan can give us assistance in dealing with his rogue elements... and I concede that I was wrong to speak as I did."

The Wuhuan commander nodded sternly.

"Next time, we get Poison Yu," Yuan Shao continued. "I will not return to Ji Province without his head in a sack."

Wen Chou bowed slightly and said, "One of us will secure him next time, my lord."

"...Yes," Yuan Shao scoffed. "And no more jumping at the sound of some man's big voice, either, mm...? The man himself was nothing special."

"One can never be sure if a loud bark precedes a fierce bite, my lord," Guo Tu suggested. "That is especially true for enemies that lack subtle stratagem."

"...I know it," Yuan Shao said apologetically. "Now... I suggest that we rest briefly and then pursue."

"In this case, there is no fault in that idea," Tian Feng replied. "Our enemy is frightened, tired and disorganised: if we dally, their new reinforcements will make them too strong, and we would be here another month."

"That is enough for me, Mister Tian," Yuan Shao said. "**REST, AND THEN ONWARD!**"

The Black Mountain Bandits regrouped to the north of the site of their disastrous defeat.

"The help's still coming, but we've taken a pretty big knock," Flying Swallow said to a quiet and reflective Poison Yu.

"We lost a lot o' mates in that fight," Big Eyes sighed.

"Yeah, and you don't look too well yourself," Flying Swallow replied. "Sit the next one out; you won't be much use anyhow."

A bandit leader with a shoulder-length moustache sighed and said, "We're all dead, I reckon. Yuan's lot are acting like madmen."

"We obviously riled 'em bad this time, Zuo," Big Eyes replied.

"We should go north – far, far north – and try and gather everyone up," 'Eighty-foot Moustache' Zuo suggested further. "We'll be torn apart if we–"

"I knew I should have let the capital alone!" Poison Yu whined. "This is 'cause I hit the capital! The prefectural administrator must've been his father-in-law, or something! If I'd not got carried away, and–!"

"*Carried away…?*" Flying Swallow cackled. "We're *bandits*! The fancy blokes with the money, they're the people we rob! When – if – they fight back, we kill them! Yuan Shao's here 'cause you hit the bastard where it hurts, and that's nothing to be crying over: he can kill us all, and it won't bring his man back, will it? People'll go 'Why did he kill all them bandits?' and others, they'll say, 'He did it 'cause the bandits got right into Yè, and killed his administrator', and people'll say 'His capital must have had pretty poor defences, what an idiot'."

Some of the bandits laughed half-heartedly; Poison Yu smiled and said, "I don't feel any better, but thank you. We–"

"THEY'RE PURSUING!"

The scout's warning made many men's blood run cold.

"Oh, gods, no," Flying Swallow groaned. **"Where are the reinforcements?"**

"Wuhuan are close; the Xiongnu, dunno!" 'Eighty-foot Moustache' Zuo reported. **"Both are north-ways!"**

"We have to fight and retreat!" Flying Swallow ordered.

The Black Mountain Bandits did what they could against Yuan Shao's forces; Poison Yu led his riders past Yan Liang and Wen Chou's vanguard and toward Yuan Shao yet again, and this time he was determined to take the head of the lord of Ji Province.

"You again!" Jiang Yiqu bellowed as he blocked the path to the commander.

"That's him! That's 'Poison Yu'!" Yuan Shao cried. **"Bring me his head!"**

"I'm not called 'Poison Yu' for nothing, you pampered wimp!" Poison Yu shouted as he tried to pass Jiang Yiqu; but Chunyu Qiong added his own small force to Jiang's, and Poison Yu turned and fled once again.

"DO NOT LET HIM GO!" Yuan Shao ordered. **"Do not make me try and catch him myself!"**

"THUNDER GOD IS HERE!"

Chunyu Qiong faltered, but Jiang Yiqu was ready this time: he charged at the loud but unimpressive Thunder God and unseated him with a swipe of his halberd. At the same time, Yan Liang had turned about after slaying a number of mid-ranking bandits, and he spied Poison Yu retreating towards him. Poison Yu screamed defiantly and tried to bluff his way past the general, but his luck had run out: Yan Liang charged at the bandit leader and practically cleaved him in two with his halberd. Poison Yu's riders scattered: one raced toward Flying Swallow – who was retreating from an attack led by Wen Chou – and told him the news.

"*Dead...?*" Flying Swallow gasped. "Damn it, he was-!"

"**XIONGNU!**"

The cry was from one of Yuan Shao's men; the Xiongnu reinforcements numbered less than 60, but they were mostly on stout local horses or taller foreign horses and served as an experienced cavalry force.

"...**Keep moving back!**" Flying Swallow ordered as his composure returned. "**Back to the northern mountains, lads!**"

The message filtered through the bandit ranks, and the retreat continued with the help of the Xiongnu. Yuan Shao was keen to continue the pursuit, but he halted when Yan Liang presented the severed, gore-laden head of Poison Yu for inspection; the bandit's expression was resigned, which amused Yuan Shao.

"Hmm... not so confident without an army or a body, are you...?" Yuan Shao sniggered as he knocked Yu's nose with the knuckles of his right hand; the head was being held by its long, unfurled hair, and it briefly swung back and forth like a pendulum.

"Will we keep advancing?" Guo Tu asked. "Now that the Xiongnu are arrived, I-"

"It is my decision that we press them further," Yuan Shao replied. "I want a few more of the leader's heads to be presented to me before we go home. I want them to understand that for every important scalp they take, we will take ten of their miserable, relatively worthless hides in exchange. Yan Liang, give your prize to General Chunyu and resume your hunt."

Yan Liang threw the lifeless head of Poison Yu to Chunyu Qiong and replied, "As you command."

The bloodshed would continue for another two days: when Yuan Shao finally withdrew, thousands of the Black Mountain Bandits were injured or dead and the confederacy leader, Flying Swallow Zhang Yan, was moving at speed toward the northernmost mountain ranges with the intention of assuming a strictly defensive posture for the moment.

****

60

At around the same time that Yuan Shao had his revenge against the Black Mountain Bandits, his eldest son Tan was dealing a major blow to the Black Mountain Bandits' main supporter, Gongsun Zan, in Qing Province: Gongsun's appointed Inspector of Qing, Tian Kai, had finally been pushed out of the northwest and back to the border with Yòu Province. While Tian Kai remained within his defensive camp and wrote to Gongsun Zan for assistance, Yuan Tan established a new camp to the south of the Tian's camp and addressed his followers.

"Now, friends, we give Tian Kai one final nudge," Yuan Tan began. "We've been here fighting this talentless imbecile for far longer than should have been necessary, but I suppose we had the bandits, Yellow Turbans, crime syndicates and rebels delaying us for much of the time... oh, and Liu Bei, who now rots in Xu Province."

"What are your plans after Tian Kai is expelled...?" the adviser Xin Ping asked.

"Fret not, Mister Xin," Yuan Tan chuckled. "I do not intend to invade Yòu Province without permission! First and foremost, I serve my father and act only on his instruction. Now, to this final mission before our attentions turn to pacifying the region properly: Lü Kuang, Lü Xiang, Han Juzi!"

Three officers stepped forward and awaited their instructions.

"Nothing clever, just a straightforward night raid," Yuan Tan continued. "Han Juzi will accompany me on an attack on the south gate of his camp, Lü Kuang from the west, and Lü Xiang from the east. He will then be left with no choice but to retreat through his north gate."

The three officers bowed and responded as one, saying, "**As you command!**"

Xin Ping hummed thoughtfully; Yuan Tan noted the gesture and said, "You wish to say something, Mister Xin...?"

"...I wonder if I might make a minor addition to your plans," Xin Ping asked.

"I am ready for your instruction," Yuan Tan replied.

That evening, Tian Kai gathered his officers and officials in his command tent.

"...I worry that he'll strike," Tian Kai said.

"Oh, he certainly will," the officer-adviser Tian Yu replied. "We've set up some defences in preparation for night attack. But we have to decide whether we're trying to stay or trying to leave."

"...I wish Liu Bei were here," Tian Kai sighed.

"Do not," Tian Yu scoffed. "You seconded me to that idiot, if you remember, and I am back here because he was not the man that we thought him to be. By all means wish that his general Guan Yu was here, or that fine young man Zhao Yun that led his cavalry, but do not wish for Liu Bei."

"...I cannot believe that we are being chased out of the province by Yuan Shao's puppy!" Tian Kai complained. "This is humiliating."

"Everything has conspired against us, even the weather," Tian Yu said. "But that's all irrelevant. What are we to do?"

"…I will not simply cede this place!" Tian Kai decided. "We hold, and we hope that Lord Gongsun can spare some more cavalry, perhaps call upon our Wuhuan allies."

"We must hope that our Wuhuan *enemies* do not learn of this," one adviser said.

"…Quite right," Tian Kai replied. "But we must be especially vigilant tonight, gentlemen: Yuan Tan is unlikely to let us sleep."

That night, several small infantry raiding parties struck at the south, west and east gates of Tian Kai's camp: the wooden gates collapsed, and the raiders ran through the camp.

"**Where is Tian Kai?**" the eastern raiding party leader shouted as he reached the centre of the poorly-defended and poorly-lit enclosure.

"**We'll take your head to him!**" a cavalry captain replied: ambush parties appeared from the darkness, and the raiders retreated at speed. But the reaction to the ambush was, itself, bait for an ambush: once Tian Kai's forces had divided to pursue the three raiding parties back to the gates, three new forces appeared led by Han Juzi, Lü Kuang and Lü Xiang and caught the defenders in pincers. Tian Kai's main force gathered in the centre of the camp and tried to decide which of the beleaguered defensive regiments should be rescued, but they were then attacked by a fourth army from the north that was led by Yuan Tan and his subordinate Han Meng.

"**You shouldn't have tried to trap me!**" Yuan Tan heckled. "**Now I'll not let you live!**"

Tian Kai's militia briefly engaged Yuan Tan's, but the poor light and general panic meant that many attacks were being accidentally directed against allies; Yuan Tan intentionally gave way to the demoralised Tian Kai, who fled northward with what was left of his army.

"…**Qing Province is ours!**" Yuan Tan roared, and his men cheered wildly.

As they travelled into Yòu Province, Tian Kai's forces were met by the small and insufficient reinforcements that had been sent by Gongsun Zan; the demoralised Tian Kai placed them at the rear of his reduced force and moved west, toward Gongsun's last bastion at Yijing. There would be no reclamation of the lands lost in Qing Province: all that remained was the defence of Yòu Province, which would be more difficult than anyone dared to think about.

"Ah, yes… everything is going extremely well!" Commander-in-Chief Yuan Shao chuckled as he travelled at the head of his victorious army; he was back in Ji Province, and within sight of his capital city of Yè.

"More news," the adviser Guo Tu said. "What's left of the Black Mountain Bandits is coalescing in the northeast, on the Yòu Provincial border; the northern Wuhuan chiefs are showing considerable eagerness ahead of our meeting; Yuan Tan is close to taking the last part of Qing from Tian Kai – which, if it is accurate, probably means that he's done it by now – and we have defections from Gongsun Zan."

"Oh...? Who...?" Yuan Shao prompted.

"A 'Wang Men' has brought quite a few men over to us," Guo Tu continued. "It sounds like there may be thousands, in fact. In addition to that, Gongsun's got a very strange strategy for holding on to power that isn't working at all."

"Gongsun's consolidating all of the supplies in Yijing, but leaving the majority of his forces to fend for themselves," Tian Feng explained. "That's why Wang Men defected: many others are facing mutiny and losing their heads. Basically, Gongsun's lost control. The Wuhuan are running wild, the bandits are running wild, starving people are rebelling... which leaves his army in Yijing, the few hardened loyalists that may still exist, and Zhang Yan's bandits."

"This is all delightful to me!" Yuan Shao admitted. "The Heavens favour me at last! After years of being forced to tolerate Gongsun needlessly by those accursed regents, and having to suffer raids by the bandits, I am unfettered and given proper rank – or, at least, suitably fitting rank – and I have an army that no one can oppose! Once Gongsun is obliterated – and I must be unforgiving, for he killed a member of the Liu clan and usurped a provincial governorship – the only problems in the north will be the barbarians and the rebels, and all of the four northeast provinces will be mine to govern!

"My muddle-headed brother-cousin, meanwhile, is branded a rebel, holds some worthless, disease-ridden southern marshlands and part of our ancestral home, which is pitiful by comparison; and further to that, he is reliant on pirates, bandits and heretics for military support, which is hardly sustainable. Once I have all four of the northeast provinces, he will surely have to consider mediating."

"...*Mediating*...?" Tian Feng exclaimed. "You've been at war for seven years! Thousands – tens of thousands, or maybe *hundreds of thousands*! – have been injured and killed as a result of the feud! How is *mediation* possible???"

"At the end, we are kin," Yuan Shao replied dismissively. "He spoke some harsh words, and I reacted appropriately. Men took sides, but they are mostly fighting for their own causes rather than mine or Shu's: Cao Cao most certainly did not ravage Xu Province at my instruction! At the end, this is about rightful heirs to material things and whatnot, and I have proven that I am the rightful heir now, I think; I should hope that he will finally come to his senses, beg forgiveness for his rudeness and his treacherous ways, and then I can have him pardoned by the court and the past matters can be forgotten."

"*Aiee*... can it be that easy...?" Tian Feng protested. "Your brother split the Eastern Pass Coalition! His Majesty was forced to spend six years as a hostage and a vagrant because of it! Won't His Majesty want Yuan Shu punished severely? Isn't it *right* that he is punished severely...?"

"If *Lü Bu* can be forgiven, Shu can be forgiven," Shao retorted. "Anyhow: no more of this kind of talk! We will soon back in the capital, and I shall be able to write my *dear friend Mengde* a letter, informing him of my achievements..."

Tian Feng sighed miserably.

"...This is intolerable."

Cao Cao threw down a letter from his former friend Yuan Shao and grunted angrily; his only company in the chancellery meeting room – Xiahou Dun, Guo Jia, Xun Wenruo and Xun Gongda – remained silent.

"It is... no, gentlemen, there is no other word that I can use that is not unacceptably offensive to the ear!" Cao Cao continued. "It is intolerable! He *taunts me*!"

"...Intolerable, yes, but not unexpected," Guo Jia suggested.

"...'Dear Excellency Mengde; I hope you are well, despite everything!'" Cao Cao narrated angrily. "'We see so little of each other, for we are so busy! I understand that you have beaten a few heretics in Runan for me and chased the Black Mountain Bandits back into Bing so that I could dispose of them once and for all, and for that minor assistance, you have my thanks! I hope that the court will approve of my choice of Gao Gan for Governor of Bing, for I could not think of a talent close to you that could be spared at such a critical moment for your offices, acting and permanent both'...!"

"...So petty," Guo Jia snickered quietly.

"...'Your support for Kong Rong is disappointing but understandable in these morally ambiguous times, but his family will be released as agreed, and I would trust that a better man than he will be sent to replace my son at some point as Governor of Qing'...! ...This is *unnecessary*!" Cao Cao complained. "I gave him the title of 'Commander-in-Chief' as he wanted, and he is still snide and overbearing!"

"My lord," Xun Gongda said, "you shouldn't be so-"

"'I have also reunited the fragments of Qing Province,' he writes, 'and my son Tan has chased Gongsun Zan's lackey Tian Kai back to Yòu, which my next target: I wonder, what is yours?'" Cao Cao continued; he was not looking at the letter as he spoke, as the words were painfully burned into his short-term memory. "...'Will you deal with Lü Bu, now that you no longer need my permission to do so, or will you do something about the regents and their adviser in Jing that makes a fool of your cousin as we speak?'"

Xun Wenruo exhaled loudly.

"...'If you can be patient, I will deal with whatever you cannot manage when I have dealt with Gongsun Zan'," Cao Cao continued. "And then of course, his final heckle: 'Your long-standing supporter through all of your many troubles, *Marquis* Yuan Shao, *appointed* Commander-in-Chief of the armed forces and Governor of Ji Province.'"

The advisers said nothing.

"...**Intolerable!**" Cao Cao cried. "**He expected sympathy when Yuan Shu used words not unlike these to admonish him! He started a costly seven-year feud for goading words such as these!**"

"Why commit such rubbish to memory?" Guo Jia asked. "He is being pompous, but his words are private, not public as Shu's were, and they are not as harsh as you depict them: he writes that drivel because you are better than him and he knows it."

"And I intend to prove it," Cao Cao growled. "No more dallying: the road to Chang'an must be cleared. The regents must not fall to Yuan's blade, they must fall to *mine*. To reach Chang'an, I must pacify Nan County. So Zhang Xiu must die."

"…Or surrender," Xun Wenruo suggested.

"If he surrenders, fine," Cao Cao said. "But one way or another, I must have victory over the regents before Yuan defeats Gongsun Zan. Once he has Ji, Bing, Qing and Yòu fully under his boot, he'll have an army that's three-or-four-times the size of mine, and he'll certainly challenge me then. I estimate that I have… a year."

"You know that I always advocate speed, but I do not advocate *haste*… my lord, I insist that you should not be hasty," Guo Jia protested. "Make the proper preparations before you march west, or you will be handing yourself over to Yuan Shao, Yuan Shu or the regents."

"I agree," Xun Wenruo said. "Choose your moment and your method *carefully*!"

Cao Cao was too busy reflecting on Yuan Shao's correspondence to listen to his advisers; he was hurt, he was angry, and he was determined that his friend-turned-rival would have no more victories to boast of.

****

61

Henei Administrator and Director of Retainers Zhang Yang finally completed his work on the restoration of the Northern and Southern Imperial Palaces in Luoyang; he finished a final tour and left the complex to take one last look at a year of effort.

"…I feel content," Zhang Yang said with a smile.

"What will you do now…?" Zhang's officer Sui Gu asked.

"I have done all that I can," Zhang Yang replied. "The walls and gates of the city are repaired and given new strength; the guard posts and barracks are back to as they were; the palaces are filled with the basic requirements for the Son of Heaven; others have started coming here to oversee the restoration of the houses, shops, markets, temples and other places, and where their work begins, mine ends. This has been expensive yet rewarding, and now I must go back to my role in Henei."

"I wonder what rewards you will receive," Sui Gu said.

"I… have atoned for my failings," Zhang Yang replied. "Besides, I am already a marquis and 'General who pacifies the Nation'; what else could I want…? This was mainly about atonement for me, General. Governor Ding Yuan was foster father to my friend Lü Fengxian, who was misled and tricked into murdering a good man and committing many other atrocities besides; I was not able to prevent Fengxian from killing Ding Yuan and harming the emperor, and for that I am ashamed. Dong Zhuo had this placed burned to the ground; I was a captive of Yufuluo, so I could do nothing, but that does not excuse me, for my capture was due to my own carelessness. I then allowed what happened in Chang'an; I did not challenge the regents, rather I accepted rank from them, and for that I am ashamed. I do not regret my twice sheltering Fengxian when he needed a friend because I had hoped to show him how to be a friend to me and to others in the future, but… but I cannot understand his present course."

Sui Gu grunted tonelessly.

"I was clumsy, oblivious and fell short of what a man of my position is meant to achieve," Zhang Yang continued. "But now I have atoned: the Son of Heaven was in the wilderness, and I gave his divine manifestation sanctuary in Henei; the Son of Heaven ached to be within the walls of the true capital, and I brought the court here; the Son of Heaven asked that the palace be given new lustre, and I have realised the dream. I have made it possible for normality to return at last… the rest is up to greater men than I."

"…The Yuans, Cao Cao, and Lü Bu…?" Sui Gu supposed.

"Perhaps," Zhang Yang replied. "What will *you* do…?"

"I will go back to Henei with you, Lord Zhang, and so will General Yang and the others," Sui Gu said. "I do wonder what Dong Zhao will do, though."

"I wonder if Gongren has joined the government and is no longer my friend or vassal, since he did despair at my loyalty to Fengxian," Zhang Yang replied. "I… I think so. But he was always supposed to do much better, and if Excellency Cao gives him a chance to be a great man, then I am pleased that Yuan Shao's mistake has not harmed him."

"…I wonder if the land will return to normal," Sui Gu sighed.

"There has been enough suffering," Zhang Yang said. "Perhaps, with the restoration of the palace, we can have peace at last… I very much hope so."

Zhang Yang sent word of his intentions to Xuchang before he returned to Henei; the delighted Emperor Xian was only too happy to have Zhang Yang made Grand Marshal for his efforts and further rewarded with extra taxable households and other material gifts. Zhang Yang would play one last, minor role before he would be consigned to history, but his contribution to the restoration of the Han Dynasty was at an end: now, as he had said, it was up to others to finish the task.

****

62

Cao Cao left his home and travelled to the chancellery office to meet with Xun Wenruo and Guo Jia.

"Tian Chou, Cheng Yu, Dong Zhao and my nephew Gongda will attend the meeting as you requested," Xun Wenruo explained to an agitated Cao Cao. "Then… Excellency, are you suffering one of your headaches…?"

"My second son, Shuo, is ill again," Cao Cao replied. "I do not know if it is serious; he's been frail since the famine struck my home as it every home… but the lad was never that strong anyway."

"I am sorry to hear that," Xun Wenruo said.

"…And, of course, it strains the already-delicate relationship that I have with Lady Ding," Cao Cao continued. "She castigates me for continually extending the family; as you know, I have now taken Lady Yin, widow of Hè Xian, to be my wife."

"…A fine-featured young lady," Guo Jia said with a smile. "Excuse my not caring what Lady Ding thinks, for that is a private matter; how does Yuan Shao react to your marrying the daughter-in-law of his idol and former patron, Commander-in-Chief Hè Jin…?"

"I do not know, but I can guess," Cao Cao replied. "Hè Jin was not just the Commander-in-Chief and Yuan's 'patron', as you put it: he was the uncle of the previous emperor that was so cruelly slain by Dong Zhuo. If I then marry the widow of the late sovereign's maternal cousin, a woman who has a child by that first husband…"

"…Ah," Guo Jia chuckled. "I was not aware that she had a child!"

"The boy is two years old, nearly," Cao Cao explained. "I did not want to see the grandson of a hero like Hè Jin without a father; I could have married her to one of you, or one of my generals, but I worried that others might say I was not treating her with due respect. But that is not how Yuan will see it…"

"I wouldn't worry," Guo Jia replied. "If you became a monk, he'd find something to castigate you for. Enjoy life."

Xun Wenruo covered his face with his sleeve.

"*Aiee*… don't put it like that!" Cao Cao complained. "Anyhow… I am glad to hear that Tian Zitai and Dong Gongren are eager to join my growing army of advisers. When Mister Tian went home briefly, I assumed that it was to escape me!"

"That must have been quite the journey," Guo Jia suggested. "All the way to Yòubeiping… with a war between Yuan Tan and Tian Kai going on at the time!"

"He wanted to pay respects to the graves of his ancestors and also his former lord," Xun Wenruo said. "Liu Yu was good to him."

"I wanted to avenge the poor man myself, but it looks like Yuan Shao will get that privilege," Cao Cao grumbled. "But he will not get the regents! They are mine!"

"Which is what the meeting will be about," Xun Wenruo said. "Cheng Yu is speeding here as we speak and will be perhaps a day or two away now; his forwarded response was especially cantankerous, though, Excellency."

"I care little for his mood," Cao Cao retorted. "There are important matters to discuss. I must attack Zhang Xiu, and quickly."

Guo Jia shook his head and said, "I cannot emphasise this enough times, Excellency: *do not rush*."

"Remember Xingyang!" Xun Wenruo pleaded.

"...I am hardly likely to forget," Cao Cao retorted.

Emperor Xian sensed that another major announcement was due and invited Empress Fu to discuss it privately.

"I can only hope that it will be a return to Luoyang," Emperor Xian said excitedly. "Xuchang is not a capital that would impress foreign dignitaries, and I would hope that the inevitable return to stability would mean the people from the far north might start visiting us with their exotic treasures. I saw a few before Dong Zhuo looted them, and they were truly fascinating."

"...Does Your Majesty really expect a return to normality...?" Empress Fu asked cautiously.

"Oh, certainly," Emperor Xian replied dangerously. "The Excellency of Works has destroyed the Yellow Turbans; the Commander-in-Chief has humbled the bandits and pacified Bing Province, which has been troubled since my father's time; the villain Gongsun Zan is surrounded by enemies and is close to destruction; Yuan Shu is weakened by recent developments, and cannot expand his influence; the villains in the northwest bicker as they await final disposal by one or both of my Excellences; and my relative Liu Bei is poised to strike a fatal blow to the villains in Xu Province. The palaces and walls of Luoyang are restored, leaving only the homes of our subjects, and the last court session spoke of enthusiastic reconstruction work. Not since the times before my inattentive and flawed father has there been such promise! With no seditious eunuchs, barbarians and rebels to harm us, peace is assured!"

"...So Your Majesty is no longer wary of Excellency Cao...?" Empress Fu asked.

"He has achieved marvellous things and shown no signs of having designs on the throne," Emperor Xian replied. "He has unfortunate history, but then so does the man that has rebuilt the capital: they seek redemption, it seems, and if they keep their words they shall have it."

Empress Fu smiled and said, "I shall enjoy life in Luoyang."

Emperor Xian took Empress Fu's hand and smiled.

Cao Cao had decided to act: he summoned the advisers Xun Wenruo, Xun Gongda, Guo Jia, Cheng Yu, Dong Gongren and Tian Chou to the private audience room of his chancellery.

"I hope that my contributions will be heeded, my lord, for you drag me away from Dong Prefecture," Cheng Yu said frankly. "I was dealing with a very aggressive, skilled set of Yellow Turbans, some of whom are obviously ex-Qing Corps, and–"

"There will be time enough for that in the future," Cao Cao interrupted. "Right now, there are more important problems to deal with, Mister Cheng, and you know what – or rather, *who* – they are, *surely*."

"Li Jue, Guo Si, Zhang Xiu, Jia Xu, Lü Bu, Liu Bei, Ma Teng, Han Sui, Song Jian, Zhang Lu, Gongsun Zan, Sun Ce and Yuan Shu," Cheng Yu replied. "I am not ignorant of things just because I am in the east of Yan Province fighting brigands."

Cao Cao smirked and said, "Rude as ever! But I forgive you, as always. Mister Cheng, you have listed everyone significant, I think, except for Liu Biao."

"Liu Biao is of no threat," Cheng Yu retorted. "His harbouring Zhang Xiu and Jia Xu is incriminating but due to his situation... a situation that you know, *surely*."

"...Well put, but I must see him as a threat now," Cao Cao said. "I am planning the long-overdue expedition against the western rebels, and Zhang Xiu will be my first target. His destruction will send a message to the rest that I am serious and capable."

"Who will you take as adviser and mediator?" Cheng Yu asked.

"I will act in both capacities," Cao Cao replied.

"Are you serious?" Cheng Yu exclaimed.

"He is," Guo Jia sighed.

"None of us can change his mind," Xun Gongda complained.

"Do not speak of me as though I am not here!" Cao Cao chortled.

"But would it make a difference...?" Guo Jia retorted. "We talk as though you are not here because our words of wisdom are treated as though they are not spoken!"

"You have so many advisers that there is no need to leave them all here, Excellency," Tian Chou suggested.

"What is there to this fool Zhang Xiu?" Cao Cao asked.

"Jia Xu," Guo Jia replied. "...And Huche'er, if you consider officers."

"*Again*, you mention Jia Xu," Cao Cao scoffed.

"Guo Fengxiao does so because Jia Xu is truly dangerous!" Xun Wenruo protested.

"Jia Xu cannot make a man with such a small army into a king," Cao Cao said.

"He's made enough of a fool of Cao Hong for the last few months," Xun Gongda retorted. "Where is Cao Hong now? Is he not holed up in a city, besieged by forces loyal to Zhang Xiu that have aid from the local people...?"

"My cousin was unlucky," Cao Cao insisted. "Liu Biao gave aid to-"

"Zhang Xiu is liked by the Nan County populace," Guo Jia interrupted. "He governs well, and that's partly because he's being guided by Jia Xu. Liu Biao 'offered help' – or rather, declined to forbid local leaders from offering help – because he has seen in Zhang Xiu a man that he can work with in better times. We shouldn't be too quick to attack either of them... and Liu Biao especially."

"If I do not save Cao Hong and defeat Zhang Xiu and Liu Biao, how can I go beyond Jing to Chang'an, and defeat Li Jue, Guo Si and the Liang rebels...?" Cao Cao asked. "How else can I act? Won't Zhang Xiu aid his old allies...?"

"You haven't asked or tested the point," Guo Jia suggested. "You've assumed Zhang Xiu to be an ally of Li Jue and Guo Si, like his uncle, but that isn't necessarily so. They didn't provide aid to the mercenaries around Luoyang."

"No more of this!" Cao Cao snapped. "All of you should know that I am a man of conviction, and that this is something that I will do and do right!"

Cao Cao got up, flicked his sleeve and left the room.

"...Headache?" Cheng Yu whispered.

Xun Wenruo, Xun Gongda and Guo Jia nodded silently.

"We should probably go," Cheng Yu added, and the six advisers left the meeting room. As they walked through the public audience hall, Cheng Yu said, "Isn't there a doctor that could help him...?"

"I hear that there are a few marvellous physicians, but none that are based around here permanently," Xun Wenruo replied. "Lord Cao would need regular treatment."

"That's too bad," Cheng Yu said. "His irrational moods are more frequent, and they worsen in severity."

But each man's reservations were as pointless as any other's: Cao Cao was occupying two roles that made him an equivalent to a Chancellor of State, and he would have his way unless Emperor Xian publicly challenged his decision.

"...You cannot take our son!" Lady Ding protested as she followed her husband Cao Cao, who walked through his mansion and entered the serene garden. "What does Ang know of warfare...?"

"He cannot know less than Yuan Tan," Cao Cao retorted. "He has read every text that I have, I think, and-"

"And how can you leave when Shuo is gravely ill???" Lady Ding heckled.

"He is not 'gravely ill'!" Cao Cao snapped. "All he needs is rest and nourishment! And this is for the state! How can I be a good Confucian and disregard the needs of the state???"

"...Please do not take Ang," Lady Ding whimpered. "It is Xiu that normally-!"

"I must be ready for future times, and so must my heir," Cao Cao replied. "I should like to say that the world will be peaceful, but it won't; Yuan Shao will certainly challenge me, and the vendetta will be generational, with his sons committed to fighting mine. Ang, Shuo, Pi and the rest will have to be as adept with a sword as with a pen, whether either of us likes it or not."

Cao Cao's second wife, Lady Bian, had followed the arguing pair; she stopped short of joining the debate and watched from the doorway.

"...Heaven knows, woman, I do not want to take Ang, not after all the times that I have deliberately excluded him from my campaigns," Cao Cao continued. "But this time, I have little choice; Zhang Xiu is a tadpole, and therefore good practice, while every subsequent enemy will be a snake or a tiger. Xiu, Anmin and I will teach him everything that he does not already know, and he will be quite safe."

"You cannot know that," Lady Ding chortled. "I hear all your conversations, Husband; 'In war there are no certainties'."

Cao Cao clutched his forehead and said, "If I had a choice I would not take him but I do **not have a choice so that is the *end* of the matter, THANK YOU!**"

Lady Ding sobbed bitterly and lowered her head.

"...Tomorrow, I address the court," Cao Cao continued. "I leave in a week."

"**A *week*???**" Lady Ding exclaimed.

"Did I not say that there is no discussion...?" Cao Cao retorted.

Lady Ding snorted angrily and returned to the house; Lady Bian then approached Cao Cao and touched his arm.

"...I have no *choice*!" Cao Cao whined.

"I will support her and watch over Shuo with her," Lady Bian promised. "You will return to an ordered house as you always do, Husband."

"You are a tough woman, and a woman of your word," Cao Cao

replied. "I know not to doubt you. I only hope that... that *I* can keep *my* word."
"You will do your utmost, and that is all that you can do," Lady Bian replied.
Cao Cao smiled, touched Lady Bian's face and said, "You were quite a find."

Within a week, Cao Cao had petitioned the imperial court, received a muted response, and readied his forces for a battle with all of the Han's designated enemies in the northwest: the first would be – because of his 'tenants' in Nan County – Liu Biao, Governor of Jing Province and a man that he had been allied to only a few months before.
"Ah, the way of the world," Cao Cao sighed as he inspected his army. "...To think that I now have to fight another former ally."
"You really should have us with you, my lord," Guo Jia insisted.
"And I should be going!" Xiahou Dun protested. "I always get to-!"
"I only retained Yan Province when Lü Bu invaded because so many of my most trusted allies were here," Cao Cao countered. "Guo Jia, Xun Yu, Xun Yòu, Cheng Yu, Tian Chou, Dong Zhao: you must all remain here in Yan and make sure that this place endures. Remember, Yuan Shao is now a potential enemy, and he could strike at any time. I now march on Liu Biao, and if I succeed, it will be the first step toward ending the chaos, and at that point, I will need others to aid my march to Chang'an; if I do not, then I need a place to return to, mm...?"
The officials nodded uneasily.
"I need no counsel for this," Cao Cao chuckled. "No, I am smart enough not to leave myself exposed; see you all soon. Ang, Anmin, Xiu, Ren, Yu Jin, Yue Jin: ready yourselves."

And so Cao Cao began the march west to Jing Province: Cao's son Ang, cousin Xiu and nephew Anmin would be the vanguard generals on what Cao Cao deemed to be 'the straightforward and easy first step' of the northwest campaign, while Cao Cao – who travelled in a grand carriage – would be his own counsel, Cao Ren would have a rare offensive role and attack the surrounding region with Yue Jin while Yu Jin would serve as rear guard. The first point of attack would be Wan City in Nan County: that place had seen occupation by the Yellow Turbans during the initial uprising 13 years before, and it had only been saved by Sun Jian, who later ensured that it could be taken by his master Yuan Shu before dying during his siege of Xiangyang. Liu Biao had successfully expelled Yuan Shu, but now the place was occupied by Zhang Xiu and Jia Xu, who were both former allies of Dong Zhuo. Perhaps Cao Cao was mindful of the past and hoped that Liu Biao would chase his latest squatters out of the province; perhaps he intended to seize the province as punishment for Liu Biao's past inaction. Regardless of his innermost thoughts, Cao Cao was seemingly certain of victory and advanced without fear.

****

Cao Cao's vanguard travelled through northern Runan, and word quickly reached the courageous Xu Chu's fortress home: the giant feared that Cao Cao might mistake his settlement for a rebel stronghold, so he left his people and travelled toward the procession of soldiers with a small force of his own. When Xu Chu finally located the imperial army, he had his men wait at a distance and walked to the middle of the road. The single presence – even before they realised his size and strength – was enough to trigger a change in formation: Cao Ang and Cao Anmin moved to either side of Cao Cao's carriage, and the cavalry formed a solid block in front of it.

"What... in the name of...!" Cao Ang cried as he spotted Xu Chu on the road ahead. **"Father, what manner of demon is it???"**

"It's just a man," Cao Cao replied. "Dian Wei: be ready."

Dian Wei smiled as he relished the thought of a battle with a challenging opponent.

"YOU THERE, Y-YOU GIANT!" Cao Anmin shouted. **"WHO AND WHAT ARE YOU?"**

"'Who and what are you'...?" Cao Cao chortled. "It's just a man, Nephew!"

"Perhaps, but he's a very large man, Uncle," Cao Anmin replied nervously.

"...He *is*," Cao Cao realised as the procession neared Xu Chu.

"I'll shred him," Dian Wei growled.

"No, wait... he may want to talk," Cao Cao pleaded; he then leant out of the carriage and shouted, **"Speak, stranger!"**

Xu Chu neared the wary cavalrymen and said, **"I'm just surrendering, so you don't hurt my people. They live in a fortress over there, you see, and-"**

"Stay back!" Cao Ang ordered. "Father, what do we do with this large man?"

"...Honestly; you'd think they'd never seen a man of his girth before!" Cao Cao chuckled; he then got out of his carriage, approached Xu Chu with Dian Wei at his side, and said, "A man like you must be famous. What's your name?"

"Uh... my *name*?" Xu Chu bumbled as he stared at Dian Wei.

"You do have one, I hope," Cao Cao prompted. "What is it...?"

"Your friend is very tall, like me," Xu Chu said as he continued to stare at Dian Wei without fear. "I'm just surrendering, because-"

"What... is... your... name...?" Cao Cao said impatiently.

"Oh! Yes, it's Xu Chu, though everyone used to call me Zhongkang, because that's my style name," Xu Chu chuckled. "By everyone, I mean-"

"Your people," Cao Cao interrupted. "I know that name... Xu Chu... *Xu Chu*... ... ...Xu Chu! The same Xu Chu that repelled the Yellow Turbans of this region with mere pebbles, and dragged an ox as though it were a mouse...?"

"I have to be honest and say that I only dragged the ox a *very* short way, just to scare it and make it behave," Xu Chu replied. "But yes, that's me. I'm glad you know me, because that means my people are safe! ...Are you Excellency Cao Cao? I brought some men with me, and I was hoping that we could help you a bit, you know, to get rid of all the rebels."

Cao Cao looked Xu Chu up and down, laughed, and said, "This is my Fan Kuai!"

"You're going to *recruit him*?" Cao Ang exclaimed.

"Yes, of course!" Cao Cao chuckled. "*Look*, Ang! This man is a gift from Heaven! Now I have Dian Wei and Xu Chu, who or what should I fear?"

The imperial march continued with its latest recruits: Xu Chu was added to Cao Cao's bodyguard force as a captain, and he accepted his new situation gladly.

"...*Aiee*... **damn Zhang Xiu and Jia Xu, for they have brought about my ruin!**"

Liu Biao's Xiangyang court did not react to his lament.

"**Have none of you a thing to say???**" Liu Biao screamed. "**Or do you all intend to desert me now that Cao Cao marches on my province???**"

"This is anticipated; all that has changed – slightly – is the timing of it," the adviser Kuai Liang said calmly. "Nothing changes for us: continue to protest your innocence in this affair. If Zhang Xiu and Jia Xu are forward-thinking, then they will surrender, accept full responsibility, and offer their support to Cao Cao, who will then pass us by on his way to Chang'an."

"...Have I a choice...?" Lui Biao muttered.

Messengers brought news of Cao Cao's advance to the lord of Wan City, Zhang Xiu, who immediately summoned his adviser Jia Xu.

"*Ayah*... I admit, this might be bad," Jia Xu said. "He marches sooner than I had anticipated; Cao Cao is not the strongest of the warlords, but he acts with authority equivalent to a Chancellor of State, and-"

"I know, and besides, such things don't help me!" Zhang Xiu whined. "What must I do? He marches here with an army of thousands, and I have only hundreds, if that! Will Huche'er be enough to repel them? Do I ask for help from Governor Liu?"

"You may have to, but... but there is another way," Jia Xu proposed. "If we put up a fight, we might hold out, but would help arrive soon...? I advocate only one strategy here: surrender, and-"

"*Surrender*???" Zhang Xiu exclaimed.

"...Yes," Jia Xu continued. "Some say that 'Excellency' Cao Cao is shrewd and objective; if that is so, then he will quickly see that we are 'reformed', as it were, and the worst that can happen in that case is that we'll be forced to help him fight the former regents. But if he proves to be the villain foretold by Xu Shao, we can feign deference and await an opportunity to rid ourselves of him."

"But if there isn't an opportunity to be rid of him quickly, we could be irreversibly harmed," Zhang Xiu suggested.

"The worst case, then, is if no early opportunity arises; our humble stance will have earned Cao's respect and we will be allowed to live," Jia Xu insisted. "Then, if a later moment comes when we can smite him, we will be doubly successful. Cao Cao daren't, as Excellency of Works, be seen to act unprofessionally."

"...I hope you're right," Zhang Xiu muttered. "I'll ensure that he knows our intention to surrender before he gets here."

Cao Cao's force had stopped close to Cao Hong's besieged camp and built a camp of its own: Zhang Xiu's messenger arrived just as Cao Cao was preparing to relieve his humiliated cousin.

"Magnificent!" Cao Cao cackled as he read Zhang Xiu's declaration of surrender. "This man might disgust me with the ease with which he cedes his uncle's hard-fought legacy, but he saves me much-needed time with his craven capitulation!"

"...So what happens now, Father...?" Cao Ang asked.

"Well, I suppose that we will not have to face Liu Biao now, since his treacherous tenant has taken full responsibility for the unrest here – a wise move that was the self-serving Jia Xu's idea for certain, as he prepares to abandon yet another lord," Cao Cao replied. "We will establish ourselves in Wan City, pacify the locals, and suitably humble the two traitors for their part in Dong Zhuo's tyranny and the regents' ability to retain power. Li Jue and Guo Si will be made aware of our presence here, and then – after we have ensured reinforcements *from* and the security *of* Xuchang – we will begin the end of this long, awful farce."

"I want to take the head of one of the regents for the Son of Heaven, Uncle!" Cao Anmin said. "And surely we will take the head of the two traitors in Wan at some point too...?"

Cao Cao suddenly had another, more selfish thought; he smiled and said, "I wonder if Lady Zou still lives."

"Zhang Ji's wife is said to be one of the most beautiful women in the land, the envy of all of Zhang's peers," Yu Jin noted.

"...Yes, so I hear!" Cao Cao chuckled. "It would be a lucky man indeed that has Lady Zou. If she does still live, then I should like to ensure that she is cared for, and I can think of no better man to do so than I."

Dian Wei grinned at the words.

"...Yes, Excellency," Yu Jin said with well-hidden disappointment.

"REPORT!"

Cao Cao turned to the exhausted messenger and said, "Take your time lad: we appear to have more time than I had anticipated!"

"...General Cao Hong... has... has accepted the s-surrender... of the local militia," the messenger wheezed.

"So Jia Xu ensured that his allies knew his intentions... very organised," Cao Cao said. "As much as I despise the 'king-maker' Jia Xu, I must also respect his efficiency and attention to detail. When you get your breath back, messenger, return to Cao Hong and tell him to reorganise his men and join us at Wan. Or work is far from done!"

The messenger retreated immediately.

"...I shall leave 'Benchu' with no cause for pomposity," Cao Cao muttered. "Let him and his 'wonderful son' Tan beat timid pedants like Kong Rong and isolated barbarians like Gongsun Zan: I shall deliver the heads of the Liang warlords to His Majesty, and my son shall be a famous hero!"

"Pardon, Father...?" Cao Ang prompted.

"...Nothing, my son," Cao Cao replied. "I was just... thinking."

Cao Cao's confidence – and, unfortunately for him, his arrogance – peaked as Wan City came within sight: Liu Biao's surrender was highly likely to follow, and then Liang Province would be the last significant target before he could finally deal with Yuan Shu and –

if needs be – Yuan Shao as well.

The unruffled Yuan Shu, meanwhile, watched events play out from his base in northern Yang Province. The self-proclaimed 'rightful heir to the Yuan clan of Ru County' received regular reports from his spies: he monitored the situations in Xuchang, Xiaopei, Xiapi, Yè, Yijing and Nan County with great interest.

"…Cao Cao definitely marches on Liang Province," Han Sui said to his sometimes-ally, sometimes-rival Ma Teng. "He reminds us of our ranks as Han generals; that's good."
The two men were sat in the busy command tent of a military camp on the northwest border of Mei County; they had chosen to move to that position – which was also to the southwest of the western capital Chang'an – when rumours of Cao Cao's departure from Xuchang reached them.
"So we're fighting the regents for the Han, then," Ma Teng chuckled. "What do we do to them?"
"We should siege the areas around Chang'an and Mei County," Han Sui replied. "We should just take the heads of the regents and nothing else, I think; Cao Cao's said to have a strong army, and we'll need to know more before we think about opposing it."
"Agreed," Ma Teng said. "Which one do you want?"
"…Let's split our forces and each of us fight both," Han Sui replied. "That way, we're not risking any arguments between us."
"Once again, I agree," Ma Teng said. "I'll get my men ready."

The self-appointed co-regents would now be attacked by their former Qiang allies, who now perceived them as weak and too risky to be aligned with; Li Jue and Guo Si's followers would have their loyalty tested to its limits and beyond as attack after savage attack was launched against them by the tribal warlords.

****

Cao Cao entered the city of Wan with his bodyguard Dian Wei at his side. The sight of the large and terrifying General Dian – and the stories that accompanied his name – stole every last bit of desire to resist from Zhang Xiu's soldiers, who were suddenly grateful for their leader's apparently-cowardly actions.

"You're a smart man," Cao Cao chuckled as he received the seal of office from the humiliated Zhang Xiu; he then looked at Jia Xu – who immediately lowered his gaze – and added, "Or *someone* is, at least; Mister Jia Xu! 'Administrator' Zhang is the nephew of Dong Zhuo's well-known ally Zhang Ji: you must be drawn to former vassals of Dong Zhuo!"

"I am not a man that finds employment easily, Your Excellency," Jia Xu replied humbly. "That said, Lord Zhang is not-"

"Narrow-mindedness is to blame for your predicament," Cao Cao interrupted. "A man of talent should be cherished! ...And on that note, 'Administrator' Zhang... I return to you your seal of office."

"What...?" Zhang Xiu exclaimed as Cao Cao proffered the seal.

"I don't see the sense in replacing you here," Cao Cao said dismissively. "Now, would you kindly familiarise me with the facilities? I know little of Wan, to be honest; oh, and I have to say that the repairs are impressive! You'd never know this place was the scene of such horrors. Some places still bear the scars of the Yellow Turbans, you know, even after all this time, and yet Wan is as it was! I'm impressed."

"Well, I inherited the place, so my predecessors take most of the credit!" Zhang Xiu said with relief as he started to guide Cao Cao toward his residence.

"...So you're Huche'er," Dian Wei said as he suddenly halted and turned to confront the equally-tall general.

"I am," Huche'er replied.

"...A *foreigner*, uh?" Dian Wei heckled. "...I was looking forward to gutting you."

Huche'er smiled fearlessly and stared into Dian Wei's eyes.

"DIAN WEI!"

Cao Cao's call reminded Dian Wei of his duties as a bodyguard: he smirked at Huche'er and returned to his master's side.

At first, everything appeared to be fine: Cao Cao was entertained by a banquet at Zhang Xiu's home that same night, but it escaped neither the host nor his adviser's attentions that Cao Cao was showing a lot of interest in Lady Zou, whose legendary beauty had lost little of its allure, even with the absence of makeup and a choice of plain white and colourless clothes to signify her continued mourning for her husband Zhang Ji. Once the banquet was over, Zhang Xiu summoned Jia Xu to his private audience chamber to discuss it.

"I cannot believe the way he stared and leered at my aunt!" Zhang Xiu whined. "She's in mourning! Has he no shame???"

"I'm saddened," Jia Xu admitted. "It's Lü Bu and the maid all over again, only this time it is *my* problem, not Li Ru's! I'd hoped that the rumours about Cao Cao's lecherous nature were invented by his enemies; but he has a prostitute with him, just as they said, and he enquires about the brothels and taverns, just as I'd been warned that he would. When he was reciting poetry at the banquet, I was almost inspired to pledge my services to him, he was so profound and apparently sincere; so sad, then, that he is also depraved."

"Stop delivering speeches and *help me*, would you???" Zhang Xiu cried. "Did you prattle like this when Dong Zhuo and Li Jue asked your advice?"

"…Cao Cao suffers crippling headaches, and is weak to vice; no, it is his bodyguards, and especially Dian Wei, that we have to fear most," Jia Xu said soberly. "Cao lacks any counsel, opting instead to bring his eldest son and other family members as his vanguard generals, which is all the heights of vanity and arrogance… or maybe a desire to outdo someone. Either way, he'll be easily defeated if he carries on like this, luckily for us."

"He is obviously hankering for my aunt!" Zhang Xiu complained. "I'm scared, Mister Jia, for her dignity! What if he-"

"He… no, no, he wouldn't do that, it would be the heights of contempt," Jia Xu insisted.

But Jia Xu was wrong. Within a week of his arrival, Cao Cao had taken up residence in Zhang Xiu's residence and taken Lady Zou as a concubine. It was unclear whether Lady Zou was happy with the arrangement, but none contested it, and Cao Cao spent every free moment in her company.

"**This is *intolerable*!**" Zhang Xiu shrieked as he paced back and forth in the private audience chamber within his administrative office. "Mister Jia, you must contrive a plan to rid me of this unparalleled villain!"

"I will, I will, I promise," Jia Xu murmured.

"He was making love to her in *my bedroom* when I went to see him this afternoon," Zhang Xiu muttered bitterly. "You cannot know, Mister Jia, what it is to know that a man has taken your home, and made a whore of your widowed aunt, and in *your bed*. My uncle will start haunting me if I do not do something soon, and that is if I do not go mad first. *Think*, man!"

"I *am* thinking, my lord!" Jia Xu protested. "We cannot afford to make a mistake."

Zhang Xiu groaned with anguish, collapsed to his knees, and screamed, "**I want him humbled, Jia Xu! He ravages my aunt, and makes me look like a fool! For this affront on my family, I want Cao Cao begging for forgiveness at my feet!**"

"*Please*, my lord, *lower your voice*!" Jia Xu hissed.

But Cao Cao had installed two of his soldiers near Zhang Xiu's office, and the outburst was overheard. One soldier immediately hurried toward Zhang Xiu's home to warn Cao Cao.

Cao Cao smiled as the soldier entered the house; he was enjoying a drink in the company of Lady Zou, who was, in her capacity as his concubine, expected to wait on his every indulgence. The only other presence was Dian Wei, who eyed Lady Zou with lust equalling his master's.

"I know why you're here," Cao Cao said before the soldier could speak. "Answer me 'yes' or 'no'…"

The soldier nodded silently.

Cao Cao chuckled as he ran his finger down the arm of the unreadable Lady Zou, and then he said, "Retire, please, my lady."

"As you wish," Lady Zou said as she got to her feet and retreated into the sleeping quarters. Dian Wei watched her retreat, and once she was gone, he nodded sternly.

"…So he is *unhappy*, is he…?" Cao Cao snickered as he turned his attentions to his spy once again. "Details, please."

"All we heard was that he wants you humbled for offending his family," the soldier reported nervously.

"You want me to destroy him, my lord?" Dian Wei supposed.

"No, no, that… that's messy," Cao Cao chuckled softly. "He is, after all, the nephew of Lady Zou, and I would rather not upset her too much… there are other ways to rid myself of him. Perhaps suicide due to his distress at betraying his uncle; that way, I can keep Lady Zou, and she will be safe to keep."

Dian Wei grunted jealously.

"Do I not share enough with you…?" Cao Cao chortled.

Dian Wei growled submissively.

Cao Cao turned to the soldier and said, "Go back immediately, and continue to listen."

The soldier retreated immediately.

"…We'll return to camp," Cao Cao decided. "Have Lady Zou's maids prepare her luggage, for I would like her to accompany me on this campaign… she is a calming force for me."

Dian Wei nodded obediently and went to Lady Zou; but just as Zhang Xiu had been unaware of Cao Cao's spies, so it was the case that Cao Cao was totally unaware of forces loyal to Zhang Xiu. While Excellency Cao prepared to leave the administrator's home – all the while plotting Zhang's demise – a member of Zhang Xiu's household fled the house to warn his true master.

As soon as the report was delivered, Zhang Xiu and his adviser retreated into a rear corridor of his office that was out of earshot of Cao Cao's spies.

"We must act immediately," Jia Xu said.

"Yes, yes, but *how*???" Zhang Xiu pleaded.

"It will soon be night: he is returning to his camp, and Lady Zou will be busy packing, and hence in no danger," Jia Xu explained. "We attack tonight; he does not know of our awareness of his plans, so he believes that he has the upper hand. He will shortly know otherwise; I have secretly been gathering our forces and recruiting from nearby villages, and so we have close to five-thousand men."

Zhang Xiu was surprised and delighted at the news.

"Our weapons will be surprise and fire; but there is the matter of Dian Wei. The man is as incorruptible as he is evil; he won't take bribes, he refuses untested food and drink, and he sleeps with one eye open, so we will have no surprise attack on him. We must instead engage him correctly, and hope that his fearsome nature does not dissuade the poor men that will have to fight him. I will need your permission to–"

"You know what you are doing," Zhang Xiu said excitedly. "Just rid me of Cao Cao, and you can name your price!"

"Your gratitude will be enough," Jia Xu replied humbly.

Night fell, and the oblivious Cao Cao settled into his bed after an evening of reading some passages from *The Art of War*. For an hour, he slowly drifted in and out of sleep, and the only sounds were chirping insects and crackling fires. But just as it seemed as though the night would be a peaceful one, a sudden din erupted; Cao Cao was roused by his bodyguard Dian Wei, who said, "We are attacked."

"Attacked...?" Cao Cao mumbled. "Who...?"

"We must leave!" Dian Wei barked.

Cao Cao was still sleepy, but the fearsome voice of his bodyguard awakened and sobered him immediately; he hurriedly grabbed some armour and a sword and began a dash for a horse as the sounds of battle neared his tent. As he left the tent, Cao Cao was greeted by the faint smells of burning wood and flesh and the faint sounds of agony as men fought to the death to the west of the camp. But in the dark night, visibility was poor, and that lack of his primary sense panicked him.

"Ang, where are you???" Cao Cao shouted.

"Father, go quickly!" Cao Ang ordered as he neared his father on a well-behaved warhorse. **"I'll be right behind you!"**

A soldier brought a horse to Cao Cao, who mounted it and prepared to flee eastward. Cao Ang and Cao Anmin had a force of men ready to serve as a rear guard while Dian Wei rallied the rest to keep the enemy in the camp.

"Dian! DIAN WEI!" Cao Cao cried as he realised that his beloved bodyguard was not present.

"He must stay to fool them!" Cao Ang suggested. **"Get moving, Father!"**

Cao Cao finally started his retreat.

"Shall I stay or go?" Xu Chu asked; he was covered in gore from a multitude of kills, but he seemed to be completely unfazed.

"...Go with Father!" Cao Ang ordered. **"There's no sense in him losing all of his bodyguards – go Xu Chu! GO!"**

Xu Chu gathered what remained of Cao Cao's 'Tiger Guard' and pursued his lord; once Cao Ang was sure that he could do no more to buy time for his father, he followed the retreat.

Dian Wei had returned to the region around the command tent, knowing that was likely to draw his enemies away from Cao's true location. His group of ten elite men assisted him in a show of total defiance: this led to the false impression that Cao Cao was still within the tent, which in turn led to Zhang Xiu's forces pressing all of their efforts on the camp and largely ignoring the small group of riders that were fleeing eastward. One by one, Dian Wei's men fell, and he started a reluctant retreat toward the command tent. He was armed with two halberds, which he swung with characteristic vigour, and the enemy were understandably unwilling to challenge him. Those that did were immediately knocked aside by the halberds – and usually fatally – but despite his efforts, Dian Wei was receiving injuries. He howled and bellowed like an animal as he took several blows from blunt weapons and received cuts from swords, but he fought on, seemingly without an end.

"This man is a demon!" one major said as Dian Wei swept another of his men aside.

But Dian Wei was human all the same, and apparent insanity

could only serve as a shield to the limits of human endurance for so long. As Dian Wei neared the end, he further intensified his efforts to protect the lord that was not there and fought with even more vigour. As he knocked down the soldiers, Dian Wei made a point of trying to tear open their heads and maximise the gore for added menace.

"**COME AND FIGHT! I'LL DASH YOUR BRAINS!**" Dian Wei barked. "**I'LL MINCE YOU ALL UP, AND DEVOUR YOU!**"

Dian Wei was now a bloodied mess, but he had killed or wounded dozens, and the enemy were fearful beyond reason. Dian Wei grinned, exposing white teeth through a soot-and-blood-covered face, and the sight caused many men to step back in fear. Dian Wei bellowed once again, and the enemy generals ordered a final push against his position. The giant man repelled every man that approached him at first, but the wounds mounted, and his life started to ebb away, while his enemies started to increase as the gates of the camp were breached. Dian was then surrounded by hundreds of men, but he showed no fear: he screamed repeatedly instead, and fixed one of his halberds into the soil to keep him upright. He swung wildly with the other halberd, and the knowledge of the weight of the weapon struck fear into everyone, even the more important officers. Dian then fixed the second halberd at his other side and shouted, "**BASTARDS! COME AND FIGHT! I'LL KILL YOU ALL!**"

The enemy were struck dumb.

"**COME AND FACE... THE EVIL!**" Dian Wei bellowed. "**COME... and... FIGHT...!**"

The giant then glared at his enemies with wild eyes and slowly succumbed to his injuries. The terrified soldiers were more worried by the silent and immobile Dian Wei than they had been by the animated monster that had resisted them; they edged toward him like timid mice, and recoiled every time they heard a noise.

Xu Chu was forced to confront Huche'er as he pursued his lord: the two began a fearsome clash that caused the onlookers to forget their own private exchanges and watch with awe. Huche'er was odd enough with his foreign features, while his opponent was as fat as he was tall: their dexterity and skill was what truly marvelled the onlookers, as Xu Chu was a lot faster than he should have been, and Huche'er was genuinely in danger of losing his life, despite his own incredible strength and agility. Xu Chu fought like an animal, and his stamina remained undimmed after several minutes of continual strikes and counter-strikes with his heavy halberd; Huche'er, by contrast, was tiring, and he knew that he would soon be left exposed. Zhang Xiu's general did the only thing that he could, and retreated. Xu Chu did not follow: he knew that Cao Cao's welfare was paramount, so he continued on his way, and the soldiers returned to their own battles.

"...**He's dead,**" one captain said after 10 minutes of waiting for any further movement from the silent, gore-covered Dian Wei.

"**He's standing up! His eyes are open!**" a soldier screamed. "**How is he dead???**"

"**He's dead!**" the captain insisted; he edged forward slowly, however, since he was still terrified by the previous exploits of Cao

Cao's bodyguard. After three failed attempts to find the courage to touch Dian Wei, the captain shoved Dian's arm and the bodyguard toppled over lifelessly.

"**Quickly, before he comes back to life!**" one soldier cried, and another severed Dian Wei's head from his shoulders with a sword.

"**By the gods, what a monster!**" a major said with relief. "**Now we shall claim the head of his master! CAO CAO! WE ARE COMING FOR YOU!**"

But when the men entered the tent, all they found was a lumpy bed that was soon found to be padded out with clothing; Cao Cao had successfully evaded them.

"...This is bad," one infantryman muttered.

The exhausted Huche'er arrived moments later and asked, "**What's happened here?**"

"**We were deceived!**" a major said. "**Cao Cao isn't here!**"

Huche'er hummed thoughtfully and said, "So was that other man a decoy, or...?"

"...**The horsemen that went east!**" a scout said suddenly.

"**Then that big man was** *not* **a decoy! Quickly, we must go east, toward Wuyin! That must be where he went!**" Huche'er ordered. "**Move at once!**"

Cao Cao and his followers stopped on a road that led to the town of Wuyin and counted the cost of the expedition.

"*Dian Wei...!*" Cao Cao sobbed. "Oh, what will I do without you, Dian Wei...!"

"We can't afford to stop for long, Father," Cao Ang panted. "No matter how bravely he fights... our men were scattered, and there were maybe a few thousand of them. They'll realise you went this way... Father, we have to keep going."

"I would rather *die*!" Cao Cao cried. "I have lost Dian Wei... who will protect me from my enemies now??? I am naked without Dian Wei... I am dead anyway, without Dian Wei...!"

"Father, you must show more strength!" Cao Ang scolded. "You have Xu Chu now! You have many other men that will fight and die for you! I-!"

"**Enemy!**" Cao Anmin shouted. "**They're coming!**"

The twenty cavalrymen that were approaching were a small group of men that had been sent after the riders initially; they fired arrows from horseback, striking two horses and killing one of Cao Cao's soldiers. Cao Cao's nephew Anmin leapt onto one of the horses and sped toward the enemy; a small group of infantry followed.

"My lord, you must flee immediately!" an injured captain pleaded.

Cao Cao looked about for a horse, but most of them were injured or fleeing.

"A horse... **I need a horse!**" Cao Cao shrieked. "**I must find a horse, or I will die here!**"

Cao Ang – who was mounted on the only remaining horse – heard his father's cries, and sighed with resignation. Ang rode toward his desperate father and said with strange gentleness, "Father... Father, take my horse."

Cao Cao fixed his panicked gaze on his eldest son's face.

"Father," Cao Ang said with a smile. "Father... take my horse."

Cao Ang leapt from the horse and urged his confused father to mount it; once his father was safely in the saddle, Ang said, "I'll be right behind you," and urged the horse to a gallop.

"**Ang! ANG!**" Cao Cao screamed as the horse carried him away from his son once again. "**ANG! RUN, ANG! RUN!**"

"Shall I stay or go…?" Xu Chu asked for the second time on that eventful night.

"…Go," Cao Ang said hoarsely. "Protect him… *go*."

"Good luck, Lord Cao, and see you soon," Xu Chu replied: he and his fellow Tiger Guards then pursued their lord and left Cao Ang to his fate.

"…'See you soon'…! What a fool!" Cao Ang snickered.

"**Cao Cao is getting away!**" the enemy commander cried.

Cao Ang sighed, readied his sword, and prepared to resist the enemy while his father continued on a journey to safety.

Jia Xu and Zhang Xiu were grateful to see a calm messenger arriving to announce the outcome of the battle.

"**REPORT!**" the messenger began. "**Cao Cao's forces were completely routed!**"

Zhang Xiu was obviously elated.

"**His bodyguard, Dian Wei, had been confirmed dead, and his head will shortly arrive for inspection!**" the messenger continued.

Jia Xu smiled, as this was a confirmation that he had hoped for.

"**A 'Cao Ang' has also been killed! A 'Cao Anmin' has also been killed! Cao Cao is as yet unaccounted for!**"

The messenger stopped, and Zhang Xiu's face fell.

"…So Cao Cao escaped," Jia Xu guessed as his own expression hardened. "Kindly tell us everything you know."

"Cao Cao's bodyguard feigned his presence within the camp, and allowed Cao Cao to escape: further forces aided his flight to Wuyin," the messenger explained with a more muted tone. "Cao Cao had escaped eastward by the time that Huche'er reached his son's position."

"Thank you: you are dismissed," Jia Xu said to the messenger, who retreated immediately.

"So… so we are now the murderers of his son, *and* his nephew, *and* his bodyguard," Zhang Xiu said desperately. "**Bloody *fool*, Jia Xu! He tore Xu Province to pieces for the death of his father, and he wasn't even sure that Tao Qian was to blame! WHAT WILL HE DO TO *US*???**"

"Remain calm," Jia Xu replied. "We'll pursue and finish him off."

"…We have to try, or we're dead," Zhang Xiu said.

"I don't believe it to be necessary, if I'm honest," Jia Xu replied calmly. "But we'll pursue anyway, since he could do with getting a further reminder that he is not as strong as he thinks…"

****

65

A battered, half-starved and demoralised Cao Cao was carried into safer territory by his son's warhorse as dawn broke. As luck would have it, Cao Xiu's reserve unit was stationed on the route the horse had taken, and Xiu's men settled him into a tent for nourishment and recuperation.

"Someone has notified General Yu Jin, Cousin Mengde," Cao Xiu reported.

"…Ang… Dian Wei… Anmin…!" Cao Cao groaned as Xu Chu and another Tiger Guard helped him into a bed. "I… I…!"

"…If only I had not been left in reserve…!" Cao Xiu lamented. "I could have been there, Cousin Mengde! I-!"

General Yu Jin entered the tent at that moment and said, "Lord Cao! I had heard that you had been routed, but-!"

"**Stay away from me!**" Cao Cao screeched. "**You're from Wang Lang! Wang Lang was Tao Qian's! Everywhere I look, I see men that will take from me!**"

"…I offend you with my presence, but I shall prove my worth," Yu Jin replied.

"**Get out!**" Cao Cao cried. "**My son is dead! Dian Wei is dead! GET OUT!**"

"We're still being pursued," Cao Xiu said.

"I'll deal with that," Yu Jin promised.

Yu Jin led a force of men in a series of attack-and-run charges that successfully delayed Zhang Xiu's pursuit force; his efforts would not be enough to repel them altogether, however, and reinforcement was badly needed. Zhang Xiu and Jia Xu maintained their efforts, and Yu Jin's force dwindled in the face of Qing Corps desertions and general exhaustion.

"**REPORT!**"

Zhang Xiu and Jia Xu ordered their guards to allow the messenger into their open-air command area.

"Speak, messenger," Jia Xu ordered.

"Yu Jin has retreated slightly," the messenger explained. "Zhu Ling has moved northward. There has been another mutiny in their front line force."

"We have him," Zhang Xiu said. "The 'Crafty Villain' will die here!"

"…Perhaps," Jia Xu replied. "Are there any other reports, messenger…?"

"Han force military activity has ceased in the surrounding regions," the messenger replied.

"…That's exactly what I expected," Jia Xu said. "Lord Zhang, that means that Cao Ren and Yue Jin have gotten word of the situation and-"

"If Cao Ren and Yue Jin are on their way here, then we have to smash Cao *Cao* before they arrive, Jia Xu!" Zhang Xiu barked. "We must destroy that man or we'll be hunted down like-!"

Jia Xu coughed deliberately.

"…Dismissed," Zhang Xiu said as he stared at the messenger, who immediately retreated. Zhang then turned to Jia Xu and added, "I insist that we advance."

"Panic is unnecessary," Jia Xu retorted. "Cao Cao is a different type of warlord; he may seem like another Dong Zhuo, but there is more to him. He won't come back here straight away; in fact, he *can't*, not even if he were-"

"We advance," Zhang Xiu growled. "He defiled my aunt! He disrespected me in my own home! My bed reeks of his flesh! My aunt's dignity is irreparable! This is *personal*, Jia Xu!"

Jia Xu nodded and said, "We'll advance."

But Zhang Xiu's hopes were quickly shattered: his forces concentrated on trying to pass Yu Jin's defences, but Zhu Ling launched a sudden attack from the north, Yue Jin attacked from the southwest and Cao Ren arrived to the southeast to complete the pincer.

"We have to keep fighting!" Zhang Xiu protested as his small army faltered.

"No!" Jia Xu replied. **"He'll retreat, and then others will-!"**

"HERE IS CAO REN!"

Cao Cao's cousin charged Zhang Xiu's lines with his forces; Zhang Xiu was suddenly in great danger, and Huche'er was forced to end his attacks on Yu Jin and rescue his lord.

"Now! While they're confused!" Yu Jin ordered.

Yu Jin's force aided Cao Ren's, and the rout was reversed; Zhang Xiu was led to safety by Huche'er while Jia Xu issued retreat instructions to Zhang's fragmented militia.

"...You're Heaven-sent," Yu Jin said to Cao Ren.

"As are you, General Yu," Cao Ren replied. "Now let us rescue our lord from this wretch Zhang Xiu."

Yu Jin spied a white kerchief that was wrapped around Cao Ren's left bicep; he sighed woefully and said, "You know all the details, then, General Cao."

Cao Ren nodded tersely.

"...As you say, let's save Lord Cao," Yu Jin continued.

"Go: Yue Jin and I shall serve as rear guard," Cao Ren said. "They *will not pass us*."

Yu Jin left Cao Ren and escorted the remnants of Cao Cao's force to Wuyin.

Zhang Xiu retreated to the walls of Wan City and glared at Jia Xu with angry, frightened eyes.

"He *cannot* come back here, he knows that," Jia Xu insisted. "He *will not*, not *yet*."

"What rational man do you describe, Jia Xu???" Zhang Xiu shrieked. **"He molested the aunt of a surrendered enemy in the man's bed! He massacred a hundred-thousand innocents for the death of his father! I've killed his heir! His *HEIR*, Jia Xu! Why did I do this??? Why did...! ...This was *your* idea... now I will lose more than my pride, thanks to your nonchalant scheming!"**

Huche'er stared at Jia Xu and awaited Zhang Xiu's orders.

"...I think you'll find that he'll do nothing, Lord Zhang," Jia Xu insisted. "Cao Song's murder was unprovoked, an act of villainy; our actions were revenge for undeserved mistreatment, and Cao Cao knows it. We can petition the emperor, and that would be an enormous embarrassment that he won't want. He's surrounded by enemies that will demand his resignation from his prestigious

posts, or suspension at the very least while our claims are investigated."
Zhang Xiu calmed slightly.
"Seriously... 'Excellency' Cao Cao's going to admit that he lost an entire vanguard army because he got drunk and wanted to sleep with the recently-widowed aunt of a surrendered administrator?" Jia Xu chuckled. "He humiliated you without conscience and then threatened your life without reason, and you rightly humbled him in return. If his heir was that unready for battle, he should not have been here."
Zhang Xiu smiled and said, "We actually defeated him."
"And rightly so, my lord," Jia Xu insisted. "He'll not be back any time soon..."

"...How can I go back, Wenze?"
Yu Jin was startled by Cao Cao's use of his style name: he bowed low and replied, "Where do you refer to going back to, Lord Cao?"
"Wan City... or Xuchang, for that matter!" Cao Cao chortled as he toyed with a small knife. The tent was filled with guards and anxious medics, but the Excellency of Works was more or less fine; he sighed and added, "Where can a failure like me go now, I wonder...?"
"You didn't fail, you had a setback," Yu Jin insisted. "Cao Hong will be ready to fight soon, and we can request reinforcements! This needn't be the end."
Cao Cao looked at Yu Jin, smiled, and said, "You're a good man, Wenze. I've mistreated you, yet here you are, doing all you can for me. I won't forget your heroism and loyalty."
Yu Jin bowed low and replied, "I am unworthy of praise!"
"What nonsense etiquette we have... yet following it might have saved my son," Cao Cao said miserably. "Poor Dian Wei... he may have been completely insane, but when Dian cared for a man's well-being, that man could know he was safe."
"With your permission, I shall ensure that there are no more pursuers, Lord Cao," Yu Jin said.
"...You do that, Wenze," Cao Cao replied with a smile. "I have enough men here to listen to me bleat, I think."
Yu Jin bowed humbly and left the tent.
"Well...?" Major Zhu Ling asked as Yu Jin approached him.
"He is distraught," Yu Jin replied. "We should keep checking on him and doing sweeps of the area to make sure that Zhang Xiu doesn't catch us off-guard again."
Zhu Ling agreed, and the two found five men to conduct a patrol. They left the Wuyin camp and began a slow walk down an artery road: the patrol was uneventful at first, but as they were about to circle clockwise around the area, they were shocked at the sight of a group of naked men shuffling toward them, groaning with agony and clutching wounds on their upper bodies.
"A trap...?" Zhu Ling wondered.
"If it is, it could only spring from an odd mind like Jia Xu's," Yu Jin replied; he then raised his sword and shouted, "**YOU THERE! HALT IMMEDIATELY!**"
"**GENERAL YU!**" one of the men cried. "**PLEASE HELP US, GENERAL YU!**"
"I know that man!" Yu Jin realised. "**WHAT HAPPENED???**"

Yu Jin's soldiers used their tunics to partially cover some of the disrobed men, who were all part of a unit assigned to the protection of the camp: Yu Jin frowned and said, "Who did this, Captain?"

The man that had spoken before shook his head and whimpered, "It was those bloody *Qing Corps*! They turned on us when they heard that Lord Cao was beaten at Wan, and-!"

"I've heard enough," Yu Jin interrupted. "Wretched Yellow Turbans…! Once a rebel, always a rebel! I'll go and speak to Lord Cao at once, so that he is aware of the new danger. Zhu Ling: ensure that these poor men get clothes and food, and set up further defences on this road as we agreed."

"You can count on me," Zhu Ling promised.

Yu Jin was going to hurry to Cao Cao, but he realised that the Qing Corps might aid Zhang Xiu, so he had men from his own forces construct more defensive positions around Wuyin before he returned to his master. Zhu Ling realised that Yu Jin had not gone to their lord yet, so he sought Yu out and said, "What are you doing? If you don't go now, won't the Qing Corps speak to him first and try to slander you?"

"Let them," Yu Jin replied. "Even if he executes me, the camp will be safe. If I don't do this and Zhang Xiu gets to him, then I really will be a traitor."

"*Aiee*… then *I* will go to Cao Cao," Zhu Ling sighed.

When Zhu Ling reached Cao Cao's tent some time later, he was greeted by the dark, brooding stare that he had become accustomed to.

"Who are you…?" Cao Cao asked; but before Zhu Ling could reply, his expression softened slightly and he added, "Never mind… you're the man I got from Yuan Shao a few years back, aren't you… the one that chose to stay."

"I am," Zhu Ling replied.

"Where is your superior, Yu Jin…?" Cao Cao asked plainly.

Zhu Ling looked around the room discreetly, and he quickly found what – or rather who – he was looking for: a Qing Province Corps major was standing behind and to the left of Cao Cao, smirking confidently.

"…You may go, Major Deng," Cao Cao growled, and the Qing Corps major retreated, shoving Zhu Ling as he went. Once the major was gone, Cao Cao looked at Zhu Ling and asked, "What did you want, Major Zhu…?"

"…To tell you that my superior, General Yu, is currently reinforcing the camp against further risk," Zhu Ling explained. "It was not his order, but rather it was my belief that you should know."

"I'm sure I know *why*," Cao Cao snickered. "It's alright, Major; you may go."

Zhu Ling bowed, left the tent, and asked around the camp for word on what had been said: once he was aware of the situation, he hurried to Yu Jin.

"**General Yu!**" Zhu Ling cried when he found Yu Jin. "General Yu, the Qing Corps have already spoken to Lord Cao! The camp is rife with slander! You're branded a traitor!"

"Am I now," Yu Jin chuckled. "As I already said, we'll see what happens."

"**Are our wounds inflicted by General Yu?**" one soldier cried:

he was the captain of the looted men, now fully clothed and working again despite his injuries. The captain shook his fist and added, "We'll speak for the commander! And we'll give those Qing Corps scum a beating when we see them! They'd better flee if they know what's good for them!"

"I am not concerned," Yu Jin said to a desperate Zhu Ling. "Help me here."

Zhu Ling sighed woefully and assisted Yu Jin with the completion of a further two defensive camps before Yu Jin finally went to speak with Cao Cao.

"Ah! Yu Wenze," Cao Cao said as Yu Jin entered his tent with Zhu Ling; Cao Cao had a protective Cao Xiu at his side, but the atmosphere was relaxed.

"Excellency and lord, I have completed a new ring of defensive camps around Wuyin," Yu Jin reported. "Zhang Xiu will never get here now."

"I don't doubt that you're right," Cao Cao said with a smile. "Tell me, Wenze... about the rumours that I hear. Some tell me that my Qing Corps robbed and pummelled some of my other men, while others – my Qing Corps – accuse you of treachery. Do you have anything to say...?"

"Only that I have done what needed to be done," Yu Jin replied. "Your judgement shall be correct, Excellency, and I shall not dispute it."

Zhu Ling was about to intervene on Yu Jin's behalf when Cao Cao laughed and said, "I was right to keep you, Wenze! Sad to say, a number of my Qing Province Corps have deserted over the years since I first recruited them: many went after what happened in Xu Province, as you know. What I have left, I do not assume to be permanent... for nothing is permanent in such an age, not sons, not nephews or trusted vassals. Some of them fled while you were building your last camp, so you were right not to protest: they betrayed themselves in the end, as all criminals inevitably do. Are the men that were attacked in need of anything...?"

"I am pleased to say that their injuries are minor, and I have reimbursed their lost belongings from my own supplies," Yu Jin replied. "I shall forward your concerns."

Cao Cao clapped his hands together and said, "All is not lost! I have fine warriors, strong bodyguards, noble and honest counsel, and the best of generals. All is not lost: we shall recover, and the land will know peace after all!"

Yu Jin and Zhu Ling felt compelled to bow humbly at the words and declare their allegiance and admiration for their lord.

Cao Cao was forced to abandon his campaign, as he had lost his eldest son and heir, his nephew, his strongest bodyguard and most of his vanguard. But word of his defeat travelled slowly, and there would be one man who would pay an immediate and high price for sluggish communications.

"**Bastards! Bastards and traitors!**" the former regent, Guo Si, cried as he tried to think of a way to escape from the men that surrounded and sieged his home in the capital of Mei County.

"**Do something!**" Guo's wife, Lady Qiong, pleaded; she had a bloody knife in her hand that she had just used to slaughter Guo's enslaved consorts – and any others that she feared as rivals.

"**Do what???**" Guo Si screamed. "**That isn't Cao Cao's men out there! That's my own men! That's men like *Wu Xi*!**"

"What sort of worthless general were you that they can mutiny like this???" Lady Qiong heckled. "You're useless! Useless and-!"

The barricade of furniture that reinforced the front door finally gave way, and Guo Si's servants – his only remaining supporters – scattered as Wu Xi led a force of men into the house.

"Stay back," Guo Si said as he brandished his sword.

"...Kill everyone," Wu Xi ordered.

Wu Xi's men started to kill the terrified house-servants; Lady Qiong tried to flee, but two men ran her through.

"...There are dead women in the bedroom!" one man exclaimed.

"So you were in the process of killing your family, uh...?" Wu Xi chuckled as he stared at the isolated Guo Si.

"**I've been good to you, you bastard!**" Guo Si cried. "**How can you come here, after-!**"

The sound of one of his children emitting a dying scream made Guo Si halt his speech and wince.

"...You're rude, stupid, and dangerous," Wu Xi replied. "Cao Cao's in Wan City, getting ready to come here and kill us all, all of us, for what you and Li Jue did!"

"S-so you think killing me and Li Jue will save you...?" Guo Si chortled.

"No, I think killing you and taking your head to Li Jue will save us," Wu Xi retorted. "He was always the smart one, so if anyone'll survive, it'll be him. You, you always listened to that dead witch on the floor, and ruined everything."

Guo Si's gaze turned to the corpse of his wife Lady Qiong.

"So how do we do this, 'Regent Guo'...?" Wu Xi taunted.

"...I'm alone, and everything I had is gone," Guo Si chuckled miserably. "Does it matter how we do this...? Just... just end it."

Wu Xi raised his sword and ran Guo Si through with it; Guo fell to his knees, whereupon Wu Xi walked behind the former regent, grasped his turban, and severed his head with the sword. Guo Si's body twitched erratically and fell forward, while the head – which wore a sullen expression – remained in Wu Xi's hand.

"You should've had him *strangled*," one captain suggested. "Is his head actually worth anything?"

"...He was a great general once, a long time ago, and still deserved a man's death," Wu Xi replied. "And his head is worth *everything*; now let's go to Li Jue."

Wu Xi and his men left the house, the city and the county with their former master's preserved head in a sack; they would be greeted cautiously by Li Jue, who accepted them into his own depleted ranks and prepared for the future. The Qiang warlords, Ma Teng and Han Sui, learned of the betrayal and wondered what they should do in the face of an imminent attack by Cao Cao that would never come.

∗∗∗∗∗∗∗∗∗∗∗∗

66

Excellency Cao Cao would learn of yet another family tragedy as he travelled; a messenger from Xuchang met his returning procession and informed him that Cao Shuo, his second son, has succumbed to illness.

"…I cannot face her," Cao Cao muttered. "I can't… not now I…!"

The Excellency of Works cupped his lowered head in his hands; Yu Jin dismissed the messenger politely and awaited further instructions.

"…Yuan Shao will laugh," Cao Cao said at last. "That spiteful man will take delight in this, I know he will. His sons grow, and mine wither. Heaven favours him."

"Excellency, I… I am sorry," Yu Jin replied.

"Oh, at least we already wear white for our other losses, and haven't got to make another stop somewhere," Cao Cao said. "But… I am *humiliated*. Wenze! I am a *boulder* that has been smashed by the egg of some tiny, frail bird! I achieved nothing except the destruction of my family and the public embarrassment of the Han army!"

"You see an error that must be corrected," Yu Jin prompted.

"…I will make no move against Wan again, not for now at least," Cao Cao replied. "Those two must wait, because others will react to my failure, and it is they that must be prepared for."

"They will pay dearly one day, Cousin!" Cao Hong vowed.

"…I thank them," Cao Cao replied. "I thank them, Zilian, because they taught me a lesson. Jia Xu is a man that I must one day prove worthy of… a man that saw another strong warlord persecuting a weaker opponent and chose to smite the mightier, not join him as he did twice before. He, too, has learned lessons, and one day, if I am worthy and he survives, he and I will collaborate."

"I do not understand your thinking!" Cao Hong sobbed. "What of Ang… and Anmin…!"

"I have killed men's sons too, Zilian," Cao Cao replied. "It's… it's business."

But Cao Cao's principal wife, Lady Ding, was not in a forgiving mood when Cao Cao returned to his home.

"**You miserable excuse for a husband and father!**" Lady Ding screeched. "**You killed our sons! You left one to die unvisited in his bed, and then let the other one be killed by rebels! Shame on you! Shame on you, you talentless mediocrity! Shame on you, you worst of husbands and worst of fathers! Heaven will never forgive you!**"

To the surprise of all, Cao Cao kept his head bowed took the abuse quietly.

"Our husband has lost a son too, sister," Lady Bian protested.

"**You are not my sister, Lady Bian!**" Lady Ding retorted. "**They were not my blood sons, but they were my sons anyway, and they meant everything to me, and now they're dead! As far as I am concerned, I am no longer married! The man I married is not that man there! The man that I married is as dead as my sons!**"

Lady Ding pushed her way past Cao Cao and ran into the vast garden.

"Do not be angry at her, Mengde," Xiahou Dun said as calmly as he could.

"Forgive her, Husband!" Lady Huan pleaded.

"…Forgive her for what…?" Cao Cao said to the white-robed assembly, which included his wives, two of his lesser consorts, his close cousins Cao Hong and Cao Xiu, Xiahou Dun, Xun Wenruo, Xun Gongda and his eldest son Cao Pi.

"…'In war, there are no certainties'," Cao Cao continued. "I… I made mistakes, and I must atone for them. Lady Ding wants nothing more to do with me, and that is perfectly understandable. If she will accept a place at the outskirts of my estate, fine; if she would rather return to her ancestral home, I understand. Either way, she will receive an allowance and have complete freedom of movement; she is not at fault, after all, so why should she suffer further…?"

The assembly was silent apart from a few muted sobs.

"…Not long ago, son, you spoke of an unfair, childish game," Cao Cao said as he turned to Cao Pi, the boy that was now his heir. "You, your brothers and I discussed its unfairness, and how the third runner would only benefit from his rivals' misfortune; I'm sure that this real-world example has not gone unnoticed."

Lady Bian embraced her son and said, "Lord and Husband, you-!"

"I… mean nothing more than to note the matter, and draw strange academic solace from it," Cao Cao promised. "After all, this was fate; that eight-year-old boy did not kill my eldest sons… of everyone here, only this fool here, me, is in any way responsible for this… this *disaster*."

"What now, Mengde…?" Xiahou Dun asked. "You must want revenge for-!"

"There will be no revenge, only readiness for the consequences of my failure and a future campaign against Zhang Xiu to eliminate him *for the state*," Cao Cao interrupted. "And that reminds me that I have broken protocol by coming here first: the state should *always* come before personal matters, so I am once again at fault. I must now go to His Majesty and apologise for my mistakes."

"Don't apologise to that greedy boy, Mengde!" Xiahou Dun pleaded. "You-!"

"Do not refer to His Majesty as a 'boy', Yuanrang," Cao Cao scolded. "The Son of Heaven is our motivation, our purpose… now I must go, and you, Yuanrang, should stay here. Wenruo, Gongda, Zilian, Wenlie: let us depart."

Cao Cao turned and left the house with his advisers, Cao Hong and Cao Xiu.

"…*Aiee*… Lady Bian, I leave everything to you," Xiahou Dun said after a long silence. "I am no good at family disputes."

Lady Bian nodded silently, and Xiahou Dun left the house.

"Are we safe…?" Lady Huan whispered.

"Lord Cao is not a monster," Lady Bian insisted. "He would not intentionally harm his family."

"…So you have returned," Emperor Xian said with disappointment; each of the assembled officials looked at their humbled Excellency of Works with their own personal mixture of sympathy, empathy, disgust, disdain or quiet ambition. Emperor Xian shook his head and asked, "Have you anything to say…?"

"I have nothing to say to defend myself," Cao Cao replied. "I was my own ruin: I ignored petitions from Jing Governor Liu Biao that protested his innocence, and made an unnecessary enemy of him; I received a declaration of surrender from Zhang Xiu that handed me Wan bloodlessly, but then I offended him needlessly and brought great misfortune upon Your Majesty's army and, less importantly, my own family. As you know, I lost my son and a beloved nephew, which I will not likely be forgiven for, for others loved them too, and their grief and anger are rightly great."

"Personal loss is not an experience that is alien to us," Emperor Xian said. "We are sorry that you paid such a heavy personal price for a military blunder."

"Your words are truly valuable, Your Majesty," Cao Cao replied.

"…Your Majesty, Excellency Cao has made one mistake after many successes," Xun Wenruo suggested. "He might deserve a demotion, but his is a life worth preserving."

"Mister Cao made no oath that demanded his life in the event of failure," Emperor Xian noted. "And we do not see the purpose of demoting him when we are still surrounded by threats, either: Mister Cao, you shall correct your self-stated mistakes with your service from this moment."

Cao Cao smiled gratefully and kowtowed.

"So, uh… what can be expected now that this has happened, 'Excellency'…?" Dong Cheng asked.

"…Who can say…?" Cao Cao replied coldly. "My defeat is seen by all: what they do is down to their own conscience and their own ambition. We might see more rebels or heretics; we might see the regents march east; we might see Yuan Shu resume his territorial expansion; rest assured, Mister Dong Cheng, that I am a man that has learned a lesson and learned it well, and I will not fail the empire again."

But Cao Cao knew that promises of future caution were irrelevant and that the damage had already been done; so did his allies and, more importantly, so did his rivals and enemies.

✳✳✳✳✳✳✳✳✳✳✳✳

67

Yuan Shao received word of Cao Cao's defeat at Wan City as he prepared for his own campaign against Gongsun Zan.

"...As a father, I know that he will be suffering right now," Yuan Shao said to his assembled courtiers. "But his loss was entirely self-inflicted, and it only goes to prove that he is unfit to be the guardian of His Majesty. Ruining a vital western campaign over a woman; honestly, gentlemen, I laugh at the ridiculousness of it!"

"He was ill-prepared anyway, if our intelligence is correct," the adviser Guo Tu said with malice. "He only took with him as generals the relatives that he lost and a 'Yu Jin' that apparently failed to act. The-"

"Mister Guo, I cannot let you continue," the adviser Xu Yòu declared. "I know that the relationship between our lord and Cao Cao is strained right now, but that does not make it acceptable to laugh at his losing his beloved son and heir and a beloved nephew! Criticise his military failings by all means, but-!"

"Did I laugh...?" Guo Tu retorted. "Did I do anything but criticise his failings...? You allow your continued affection for childhood friends to cloud your mind and make you hear words and laughters that were never uttered, Xu Yòu."

"Indeed, Mister Guo," Yuan Shao said coldly. "We must be level-headed, Mister Xu Yòu: those childhood days are long gone, and complex men is all that remains of us. Cao erred, and I must wonder, as Commander-in-Chief, whether I should-"

"**REPORT!**"

The court fell silent as a messenger received permission to approach Yuan Shao and fell to one knee, adding, "**Liu Hè, The son of the late governor of Yòu Province Liu Yu, has reached the Ji border and requests an escort to this capital!**"

"...Liu Hè lives...?" Yuan Shao exclaimed. "My knave of a brother-cousin must have been-!"

"Lord Yuan – *Commander-in-Chief Yuan* – do not pursue a divergent path that might lead to ruin," Tian Feng urged.

"Accepting that fine relative of the imperial clan into my domains is hardly treason!" Yuan Shao chortled. "Chunyu Qiong: arrange the escort, and deliver him to me personally!"

Chunyu Qiong smiled, bowed and departed with the messenger.

"...His father, Governor Liu Yu, was your choice for an alternate sovereign," the adviser Ju Shou noted cautiously. "Does your lordship plan on-?"

"I plan nothing!" Yuan Shao snapped. "I failed the father, so now I want to honour the son! What's wrong with that?"

"...But how, after all this time, could he escape, I wonder...?" Xu Yòu mused. "Has something happened in Yuan Shu's domains to weaken his grip, and give Liu Hè the opportunity to escape...?"

"If such a thing has happened, it is only our good fortune, and only further good can come of it!" Yuan Shao retorted. "Ji is mine, Bing is mine, Qing is mine, and soon Yòu will also be mine: that last task will be made even easier with Liu Hè to rally his father's demoralised subordinates in that place and compel them to fight under my banner! And if my brother-cousin is weakened, all the

better, for it means that he will soon want to mediate and end the selfish feud that he started!"
"...But still," Xu Yòu said, "I wonder... what has happened...?"

"This is another sign that I am destined to succeed the eroded, exhausted Han, and I will wait no longer!"
Yuan Shu's assembled officials stared at their master and absorbed his words fearfully.
"What else can I be told that I must wait for?" Yuan Shu continued. "My name is auspicious, my place in the world is divinely approved, and the Han continues its slide into ruin! The voices of the noble Partisans rose up against this wreck of a dynasty at around the time that I was born, and were willing to give their lives for change that I embody! The Xianbei humbled the broken imperial army while the eunuchs grew fat on the unallocated war budget! The Yellow Turbans predicted the end and hastened it with violence! Men of the Liu clan did their part too, like Liu Yu, Liu Biao and most of all, Liu Yan! Dong Zhuo took the court over as easily as one pulls something from a sack! He held my fool brother-cousin's so-called 'coalition' at bay with no difficulty, save for the actions of my Sun Jian!"
Some of the officials murmured agreeably, but the majority were not swayed.
"When Dong Zhuo died, those two fools Li Jue and Guo Si were able to take Dong's puppet emperor for themselves!" Yuan Shu continued. "...And when the idiots lost him, who found him...? Near to no man would step forward to help the Han emperor save for me, and he languished in the wilderness for months, eating men's flesh and dried leaves! Now that nonentity *Cao Cao* has been able to snatch the Han emperor and hold him in Xuchang: yet he cannot defeat an enemy that is but a tenth of his supposed strength!"
Some of the officials recalled Cao Cao humbling Yuan Shu at Fengqiu with relative ease, but none spoke.
"Whereas *I*, gentlemen, have Sun Ce, who has taken the entire south for me!" Yuan Shu continued. "Oh yes, Lü Bu hesitates *now*, but when he sees my divine majesty manifest, he will surely pledge allegiance so that he can be at the side of the next Son of Heaven!"
"Caution! *Caution*, my lord!" the adviser Yan Xiang pleaded. "Sun Ce has written to say that he cannot agree, and that he will break ties with you if you-"
"Mere words!" Yuan Shu chortled. "He'll soon show his true nature when I have spoken! No, my friend, this is fate... destiny... the will of Heaven! I want it known throughout the land that from today, the Mandate of Heaven has rightly passed, and that the *Zhong Dynasty* rules the land, and that I am *First Emperor*! I want preparations made for an ascension ceremony at once! **All men will be invited to pay homage to ME!**"

Many had wondered if the defeat of the Han Dynasty's Excellency of Works by such a small force in Wan City was another sign that the Mandate of Heaven has truly passed to another, but few had truly guessed what was to come next.

For the second time in 7 years, a public declaration by Yuan Shu would divide the country and turn the attentions of the warlords to the Yuan family. The first announcement – that he was the rightful heir to the Yuan clan chieftainship and deserving leader of the Eastern Pass Coalition against Dong Zhuo – had led to the division of his clan, the final breakdown of the already-strained coalition and a series of self-serving inter-regional conflicts between the warlords in the east of China. This time, Yuan Shu was declaring the Han Dynasty's mandate as exhausted and announcing that he was the first ruler of his own self-created Zhong Dynasty: this time, the repercussions would be far-reaching, devastating and beyond everything that the warlords might have thought possible.

And once again, Han Emperor Xian would be facing the prospect of being the last of his dynasty.

✳✳✳✳✳✳✳✳✳✳✳✳

ACT VI: THE FALSE SOVEREIGN

68

The situation in Han Dynasty China had simplified slightly, but it had not improved. The number of rebellions, bandit attacks and religiously-motivated uprisings in the north had been reduced by the efforts of Excellency of Works Cao Cao and his former childhood friend, Commander-in-Chief Yuan Shao, but the number of troublesome warlord-governors was close to unchanged.

In the northwest, the number of warlords had reduced by just one: Guo Si, one of the two 'regents' that had inherited possession of the young Emperor Xian from the tyrant chancellor Dong Zhuo, had been killed by his own men, all of whom now served the other regent, Li Jue. Li's only company in the region – a number of powerful Qiang tribal warlords – watched the situation in the centre of the land and waited before they decided who would have their support. In the northeast, a long feud between the powerful nobleman Yuan Shao and the warlord-chieftain Gongsun Zan was reaching a possible end as Gongsun's grip on all but the northernmost province of Yòu was failing; the three neighbouring provinces – Bing, Ji and Qing – were now under the control of Yuan Shao and a variety of tribal chieftains and bandit confederacies. In the centre-east, the infamous warlord Lü Bu was enjoying apparent acceptance by the state as 'General of the Left', the fourth most powerful military role in the land, in addition to being Governor of Xu Province; but he kept a close eye on his tenant, the Han clansman Liu Bei, who was building an army in the western region of Xiaopei at the request of the government. In the centre of the land, Yu Province was being contested by Yuan Shao's ambitious brother Shu and Cao Cao, while Cao's own Yan Province was the temporary home of Emperor Xian. In the south, Yuan Shu's general Sun Ce had taken control of practically all of the vast Yang Province; the timid Liu Zhang and the cultist Zhang Lu ruled the westernmost provinces of Yi and Hanzhong. That left Jing Province in the centre-west – the seat of Governor Liu Biao – which was a place that would see a lot of conflicts in the years ahead.

The city of Wan in northern Jing was the capital of Nan County and a key strategic target for any ambitious man: Zhang Ji, a former vassal of Dong Zhuo, had died taking the city, and his nephew Zhang Xiu inherited the prize, along with Dong Zhuo's former mastermind, Jia Xu. Cao Cao had recently led an army to Nan County to seize it and use it as a base from which to attack the warlords in the northwest: Zhang and Jia had surrendered without a fight, but Cao Cao had been not only careless but contemptuous in his dealings with the pair, and he was dealt an unbelievable – and personally damaging – defeat as a result. Jia Xu was correct in his assumption that Cao Cao would not petition Emperor Xian for another attack on Wan, as he would not be able to justify it on moral grounds. Once he was back in the imperial capital Xuchang, Cao Cao bore the pain of losing his beloved son, nephew and bodyguard at Wan – and then his second son to illness – with false stoicism; he never fully recovered from any of the tragedies, and he was inwardly bitter. His defeat was seen by all, and none saw and exploited it more than Yuan Shu.

Yuan Shu had already been at war with his brother Yuan Shao for 7 years, but that was over the chieftainship of their wealthy and influential clan: now Yuan Shu had done the unthinkable and declared to his horrified followers that he was 'The First Emperor of the Zhong Dynasty'. Yuan Shu's domains were beset by chaos as every one of his subordinates and citizens tried to decide whether they would live under a non-Han emperor or challenge him as subjects of the Han: for some, that was an opportunity to pursue their own destiny – such as Sun Ce – or escape captivity – such as the Han clansman Liu Hè – but for others, it would be the most damaging thing that Yuan Shu had ever done, or could ever do. It would take time for the news to filter out of Yuan Shu's disorganised domains and reach his enemies, and until then, most were painfully oblivious to the madness that was to come.

A messenger was escorted into the private audience chamber of Cao Cao's residence by his advisers Guo Jia and Xun Wenruo. The two advisers were concerned about the reaction of their master the Excellency of Works: he was famous for his moods, but the range of behaviour had diversified since losing his beloved eldest son, his nephew and his bodyguard Dian Wei during the failed occupation of Nan County.

"What's this?" Cao Cao said as he entered the room with the servant that had alerted him to the visitors.

"Some very strange and unwanted news, my lord," Guo Jia said dryly. "Yuan-"

"Yuan Shao's sent me another condescending letter," Cao Cao supposed. "I didn't much like him before, but to send something like that after I'd just lost my heir?"

"It's worse than that... far worse," Guo Jia said.

"You need to hear this before His Majesty does," Xun Wenruo said with fear.

"*Worse*...?" Cao Cao exclaimed as he dismissed his servant. "Well go on then... what is it that I must hear...?"

Guo Jia turned and nodded at the messenger, who then said, "Report: Yuan Shu has issued a proclamation that he is to be named as *First Emperor of the Zhong Dynasty*, and-"

Cao Cao started laughing riotously, and the messenger stopped speaking.

"...You may go, messenger," Xun Wenruo said as Cao Cao's laughter gave way to a painful cough; the messenger handed a written report to Wenruo and retreated.

"...That's the best laugh that I've had in a long time, gentlemen!" Cao Cao admitted.

"You shall have to be slightly more serious when this is read to His Majesty, my lord," Xun Wenruo suggested as he read the letter.

"That – if you do not mind me saying, Wenruo – is obvious," Guo Jia chuckled. "Lord Cao, I think that it is only a man whose wits have completely left him that declares such a thing at his critical hour. Gongsun Zan is faltering; Tao Qian is dead, Liu Bei is usurped, and Xu Province is now in the hands of the inconstant Lü Bu; and Shu's best officer, Sun Ce, has long been rumoured to desire independence, and I imagine that this will provide him with a very noble excuse."

"Yuan Shu is doomed, now," Cao Cao said surely.

"Oh, most certainly, yes," Guo Jia agreed. "So tell us, Wenruo, now that we examine the matter more thoroughly, what he has cited as the reasoning behind this momentous declaration of suicide...?"

"*Auspicious signs*, and characters in his names," Xun Wenruo said with amusement.

"'Auspicious signs'???" Cao Cao cackled. "My, I wonder what the fool takes as *inauspicious*!"

"This will, I think, lead to yet another coalition of warlords, the third in thirteen years," Guo Jia said. "Yuan Shu is now guilty of heresy and treason both. He is therefore guilty of the crimes of Yellow Turban and Dong Zhuo alike: if each deserved a coalition, then both crimes deserves a punitive expedition to exterminate the man. An alliance like that could mend differences..."

"...I assume that you mean that it could be a good time for amnesties and forgetting old grudges," Cao Cao said. "But I will not forgive the crimes against my family, Guo Jia. Xu Province shall come under my jurisdiction as compensation, at the very least; and I shall not forget the way that Yuan Shao so callously expected me to forget the injustice because it suited his own purpose, and then had the cheek to-"

"I referred more to men such as Lü Bu," Guo Jia insisted. "Yes, he's untrustworthy, but his might is formidable, and some of his subordinates would make good acquisitions, like Gao Shun and Zhang Liao... and, dare I say it, Chen Gong would make a good *re*acquisition, if you can forget his past mistakes."

Xun Wenruo alternated his nervous gaze between the daring Guo Jia and Cao Cao.

"...We agree on that," Cao Cao admitted. "I'd like some of Liu Bei's men as well... Guan Yu is particularly impressive."

"And he gets on very well with some of the officers," Xun Wenruo noted. "Others... not so much; Xiahou Dun seems to dislike him intensely."

"That is because Guan is far, far too honest when he speaks," Guo Jia sighed. "I believe that he made some references to Lord Cao's excursions into Xu that were... extremely negative."

"I can see that the matter of Xu Province is difficult to grasp for any man that has little experience of true grief and loss," Cao Cao declared. "Hopefully, I will one day have an opportunity to win him around."

"...And *Jia Xu*...?" Guo Jia asked plainly. "Would you win *him* around...?"

"*Ayah*! What-! ...Are you insane, suicidal, or just mischievous...?" Xun Wenruo asked desperately. "Guo Fengxiao, how can-"

"Fengxiao is right," Cao Cao interrupted. "Jia Xu is a genius. If I can forgive and re-employ Chen Gong, I can understand and recruit Jia Xu."

"...I cannot understand," Xun Wenruo admitted. "I will not try to."

"Perhaps that is for the best," Cao Cao said. "Now, we prepare for the emperor..."

Emperor Xian was invited to a packed courtroom to hear news that many already knew: Cao Cao stepped forward in his capacity as Acting Excellency over the Masses and said, "Your Majesty, something new and troublesome has occurred. It is not fitting that the originator of the following 'announcement' be brought here, so I have instead taken it upon myself to prepare a version of the declaration that *is* suitable."

The 19-year-old emperor looked at the assembled officials and sighed before he said, "Whatever this news is, it is better heard quickly than endlessly prepared for. Soften the blow no longer, and tell us what calamity befalls us now."

"Your Majesty's treasonous and wretched so-called 'vassal', Yuan Shu of Ru County, has already been responsible for endangering you seriously six years ago, when he caused the collapse of the Eastern Pass Coalition with his slander," Cao Cao began. "Since then, he has forced men to fight needlessly over lands that are not theirs to own or seize. Now, he has committed the ultimate crimes, *heresy* and *treason*, and announced that he is First Emperor of-"

"**Enough!**" Emperor Xian cried over the gasps of astonishment that rippled around the room. "History repeats! Wang Mang was a trusted vassal also, and yet he overthrew our distant ancestor and caused years of unrest! Dong Zhuo first threatened us with this, and after him Li Jue and Guo Si: how ***dare*** **this dog Yuan Shu declare our mandate exhausted! He must be purged!**"

"...Naturally, Your Majesty, our first objective should be to assemble a coalition of governors and face Yuan Shu as one, in your name, just as good men rose up to fight the Yellow Turbans for your divine father," Cao Cao said. "My staff have been preparing a draft decree since this terrible news reached us; it shall be sent to you for approval and if it meets Your Majesty's standards, it will be sent out to Jing, Yi, Xu, Yang, Ji-"

"Forgive my interrupting, Excellency, but why send it to Yu or Yang?" the official Kong Rong said. "Aren't they under the control of this traitor? And isn't Ji the seat of the Marquis of Yè, Commander-in-Chief Yuan Shao, who is the traitor's brother?"

"...Mister Kong is right to note these things," Emperor Xian said. "Should Yuan Shao be allowed to retain his titles if he is close kin to the traitor?"

"The Yuan brothers have been feuding for years now, so they are the greatest of enemies," Xun Wenruo's nephew Gongda suggested. "Yuan Shao will fight for the empire, not to save his covetous wretch of a brother."

"And Yu and Yang are actually under the control of subordinates of Yuan Shu that have long sought autonomy," Guo Jia said. "We will not have to wait for long, I think, before Sun Ce, Wu Jing, Liu Xun and Sun Ben write to Xuchang and ensure that we know that they are not going to support this hankering fool... but I would send the decree to them anyway."

"Do whatever it takes," Emperor Xian said with a tone that implied as much fear as it did anger. "We want this heretic and traitor destroyed as soon as possible."

Dong Cheng looked at Cao Cao with bitter eyes and asked, "Who will lead this grand campaign, Excellency Cao, since Yuan Shao cannot be trusted to do so...?"

"I will lead it myself," Cao Cao replied with a smile. "I have learned valuable lessons since my failure to take Wan City, Mister Dong. I will have the invaluable aid of the majority of the warlords to the east of Chang'an..."

"And what about Chang'an and beyond...?" Kong Rong asked. "What can we expect of Li Jue, Guo Si, Ma Teng, Han Sui, Song Jian, Liu Zhang, Zhang Lu, and, closer to home, Zhang Xiu in-"

"I know them all, Kong Rong, and there is no need to relay them all to the court," Cao Cao interrupted. "They won't aid Yuan Shu, nor will they rise up. I have placated Han Sui, Ma Teng and Song Jian with nominal titles, so they will do nothing."

"And we can be sure of that...?" Kong Rong retorted. "You and I are old hands at this political game, Excellency. How many times have we both attended courts in the past where some official or other has blithely dismissed some threat or other, only to see it consume us within no time at all?"

"...I don't like to talk about defeats, but I shall, Mister Kong Rong, to allay your fears," Cao Cao replied icily. "If Li Jue, Guo Si or any of our other problems in the west were going to attack us, it would have been when I was repelled from Jing Province by Zhang Xiu. They did not move: in fact, I hear that 'Regent Guo Si' might already be dead. Zhang Lu of Hanzhong won't do anything unless provoked, Liu Zhang of Yi is harmless, the Qiang rebels in Liang Province are, as I have already said, managed; they will none of them aid Yuan Shu. Many of those mentioned don't want a *real* majesty, never mind a comical pretender."

Emperor Xian groaned with displeasure, and the eyes of the court turned to him.

"...Forgive my bluntness, Your Majesty," Cao Cao said as he kowtowed.

"It is true, though, so why not say it?" Emperor Xian replied. "We are as besieged as we ever were with enemies... we only hope that you can end them all, Mister Cao."

"If I can, I will," Cao Cao promised.

"Then let it be known that we assent to whatever must be done," Emperor Xian declared. "This 'Yuan Shu' must be eliminated, and the land restored!"

Cao Cao smiled as he kowtowed one last time: after years of unrest, the 'Hero of Chaos' was finally in a position to bring that chaos to an end.

****

69

Yuan Shao received his brother's proclamation and reacted with understandable alarm: after taking some time to digest what it may mean for his clan as a whole, he summoned his officials to his Yè City court.

"He means to destroy me with *this* now," Yuan Shao whined. "*Emperor*??? That bloody fool isn't content with claiming to be the head of our clan now, uh? Now he wants to be the Son of Heaven! But he is *neither*! Yet this is my burden to bear as much as his, gentlemen! He has cursed us both with this nonsense!"

"Your brother has always been like this, friend and lord," the adviser Xu Yòu said. "Despite what you say, this isn't your responsibility: none in the land held you responsible for his other acts of idiocy, so why should they castigate you for this?"

"The land did not have *Cao Cao* for a *chancellor* before," Yuan Shao retorted. "And he is Chancellor in all but name! He reprimanded me for all manner of nonsense in our last communications; he will surely see this as a chance to finish me off! He'll tell the emperor that-"

"He'll do no such thing," Xu Yòu insisted. "Mengde is-"

"**Don't use that man's courtesy name in my presence, Xu Yòu!**" Yuan Shao barked. "**If you still wish to see that brigand as a friend, then fine, I'll tolerate it; but I won't allow him to be seen as mine!**"

Xu Yòu bowed low and said, "Forgive me, my lord."

"What must I do?" Yuan Shao asked of his other officials. "I am a Confucian: I strive to put state before personal matters. But Confucius also taught the importance of family, and in this instance, I am torn! How can I wage bloody war on my own brother and chase him down and kill him, as though he were a crazed dog?"

"Isn't that what you've been trying to do for the last seven years?" the adviser Tian Feng asked.

Yuan Shao waved his hand dismissively and said, "Of all men, I did not expect that from you. As I have already told you at least four times, this battle between us over the chieftainship of our clan would always have been decided by a few words in the end. Yes, lives were and will be lost, but at the end of the day, we would have made our peace when he learned the error of his ways and apologised! But this is something else entirely! He hankers for the throne, and that can only have one outcome: he must die for it! But how can I be a party to that...?"

Some of Yuan Shao's junior officials were grumbling, since his admission that his feud with his brother might, were they to consider things properly, have bloodless solutions that no man sought was causing them difficulty. The adviser Ju Shou coughed deliberately and said, "Remain neutral unless ordered to help. You won't be, so that will be that."

"But my brother will be hunted down and killed by the others!" Yuan Shao cried.

Tian Feng frowned and said, "Could that not have happened in the last seven years...?"

"I... I expect so," Yuan Shao conceded. "My goodness, this has been a true folly. My feud with Gongsun Zan stems from this; my feud with Cao Cao stems from this; the condition of the land stems from this!"

"Indeed so," Tian Feng sighed.

"...I need a rest," Yuan Shao mumbled as he got to his feet and left the room.

"And again, he resorts to running away," Xu Yòu complained. "Will that rid us of the Black Mountain Bandits or defeat Gongsun Zan?"

"Our lord Yuan Shao is grieving about an irreconcilable situation, Xu Yòu!" the adviser-general Chunyu Qiong heckled. "What sort of friend are you?"

"The worst kind, if at all!" the adviser Xun Chen said with a sneer. "Always 'conducting business'... how much private wealth will be enough, I wonder...?"

Xu Yòu flicked his sleeve and left the hall without responding.

"...Gentlemen, let us not forget that Lord Yuan needs us to remain focussed on ending his problems," the adviser Xin Pi suggested. "That includes continuing our preparations for marching against Gongsun Zan."

"I say again that I will help in any way that I can," the newly-arrived Liu Hè announced. "I would do it to repay Governor Yuan for his kindness, but I cannot deny that killing Gongsun to avenge my poor father appeals greatly."

"Let us hope that Lord Yuan is still capable of completing that important task, Governor Liu," Ju Shou replied.

"...I have known Lord Yuan for many years, since we served side-by-side as Western Garden Army colonels," Chunyu Qiong said. "We've been through much, and yet... and yet I have never seen him so upset."

Tian Feng and Ju Shou nodded agreeably.

The news of Yuan Shu's self-appointment reached Jia Xu and Zhang Xiu in Wan City, and the two met privately to discuss it.

"Now Yuan Shu has gone mad," Zhang Xiu chortled. "Alright, he was never that stable, but this is complete insanity! Even Dong Zhuo at his worst was hesitant to do what he has done!"

"I beg to differ, my lord," Jia Xu retorted. "He might not have declared that he was the sovereign, but he did commit regicide."

"Oh, yes, of course," Zhang Xiu said. "So is this good or bad...? Will we have Cao Cao back here accusing us of being conspirators, or something...?"

"This can only be a good thing for us at present," Jia Xu replied. "Cao Cao cannot implicate us in this mess, and since Yuan Shu's holdings are all to his south and east, he cannot come to this region without looking very strange indeed; he might send a general or two to harass us again, but that will be all. It will take at least a year to destroy Yuan Shu, even if all of his more powerful vassals deserted him, which they surely will..."

"But what do we do when that time inevitably comes?" Zhang Xiu fretted. "When Cao Cao has united the eastern warlords under the banner of 'justice', won't he order them all to march west and eliminate us?"

Jia Xu smiled and said, "You give them all too much credit. They'll do what they do every time, my lord: they'll bicker amongst themselves about glory, land and suchlike, and then they'll turn on each other, just like the last two times."

"Do you really think so?" Zhang Xiu exclaimed.

"Of course!" Jia Xu replied. "Cao Cao is still hated by many for his actions in Xu Province... with some suggesting that his crimes there actually outweigh those of our former lord Dong Zhuo. The other warlords and their problems are of a different sort now: to the north, Gongsun Zan of Yòu Province and the northern frontier region holds steadfast, and his hatred of Yuan Shao is undimmed; Yuan Shao himself sits in Ji, desperately trying to add to his ill-gotten provincial holdings while trying to look like the obedient Han vassal; Yuan Tan serves his father as a governor in Qing Province, but he's too aggressive to keep the place and needs replacing; Liu Zhang of Yi and his neighbour Zhang Lu of Hanzhong are, at present, as irrelevant as they are distant, so I'll say no more of them; the Qiang chiefs Ma Teng, Han Sui and Song Jian are not going to get involved in eastern affairs, and Li Jue and Guo Si daren't; Liu Biao is content to be a turtle, and he knows that he'll soon have a vengeful Sun Ce biting at his southern heel; the prodigy Sun Ce will soon declare independence, and as I said, revenge against Liu Biao will be his priority once Yuan Shu is defeated; the fickle and belligerent Lü Bu now governs Xu Province, with the appointed governor Liu Bei as an unwilling vassal, and that can only end badly; the White Wave Bandits now owe a debt to Yuan Shu, but anything could happen there; Zhang Yang of Henei is too weak militarily to do anything other than watch; and then there are the minor warlords, like Wu Jing, Liu Yao, Liu Xun and so on, that will do whatever their minds tell them.

"Lü Bu will do what he always does, and go back and forth until he is humbled again, though this time may be his last, since Cao Cao hates him for his takeover of Yan Province and Liu Bei will surely want him dead; Sun Ce will, as I have said, stay in the south and do what it takes to unify it, which locks Liu Biao down for certain; and then, of course, everything will depend on the Yuans of Ru County, as it always seems to in the end. Yuan Shu will be isolated and destroyed, but will his brother Shao just sit there and allow his brother's blood to be spilt...? And then there is the fact that Yuan Shao and Gongsun Zan have unfinished business, and whoever wins – I believe it can only be Yuan Shao – will command Ji, Bing, Qing and Yòu Provinces: can that mean anything other than a consecutive play for Yan Province to take that too and snatch the Son of Heaven from Cao Cao...? There are many men with many reasons and excuses to wage war with Cao Cao, and I believe that such a war will follow Yuan Shu's destruction."

"You truly know all the men of the land, Mister Jia," Zhang Xiu said with admiration. "You are wasted serving me as an adviser."

"I am content to serve a man that has no ill intent," Jia Xu replied. "I do not like to speak ill of Dong Zhuo, but he was evil, and I cannot deny that. Li Jue and Guo Si were idiots, both of them, and working for them was a painful experience."

Zhang Xiu laughed and said, "My uncle despised them! What do you think their fate will be? Do you really think that it's true that Guo Si is dead?"

"If Li Jue doesn't kill Guo Si to seize Mei County, one of Guo's own disaffected vassals surely will," Jia Xu replied. "As for Li Jue, his time is short as well: when Yuan Shu is destroyed and Cao Cao has swept all of his other enemies aside he'll target Li Jue, and that will be the end of him one way or another."

"...But *we're* in his path when that happens!" Zhang Xiu cried.

"Trust me," Jia Xu said. "I will have a plan for that day, my lord."

Zhang Xiu nodded silently, content that Jia Xu would not disappoint him.

Gongsun Zan laughed maniacally as he read Yuan Shu's proclamation for a third time; his reduced gathering of loyal courtiers shook their heads and groaned.

"He actually sent that poor young man through Yuan Shao's territories to get this to Yijing!" Gongsun Zan cackled. **"Heaven knows what number of obstacles that messenger had to cross to get this to me! But it is an offer of help, a coordinating strategy to rid us both of his brother or provide me with any sort of support *at all*...?"**

The court mumbled quietly.

"He sent a healthy, useful man halfway across the country, braving guard towers and battle camps, to tell me that he is 'First Emperor of the Zhong Dynasty' and that he demands my 'unbending loyalty'...!" Gongsun Zan said with enduring disbelief. **"The man is mad... mad! I had hoped that he would be my saviour, but instead he is a curse that I must be rid of at once! How dare he send me this! I would rather bend at the knee to Liu Hè, though I'd surely lose my head in doing so! Being seen to side with this... this... what word can describe this man??? No word is enough!"**

"Rebuke him soundly and publicly," the adviser Guan Jing urged.

"What else would you imagine me doing, Mister Guan...?" Gongsun Zan heckled.

"Father, we should also pledge firm allegiance to Emperor Xian!" Gongsun Xu suggested. "We might be-"

"I have already wronged the Han by killing an imperial relative, son," Gongsun Zan replied. "The correspondence from the regents was polite enough, but that was because they were villains and the emperor was their hostage; the situation has changed, and the correspondence from Xuchang makes it perfectly clear that I am an enemy of the state, guilty of serious crimes and targeted for-"

"Lies, wicked slander and lies invented by Yuan Shao's friend Cao Cao!" Guan Jing cried. **"Liu Yu was plotting usurpation with Yuan Shao, and his destruction was beneficial to the Han! Liu Hè is in Yè, not Xuchang, and we all know why! The Yuans plot treason separately! Write to Xuchang, plead your case-"**

"A mad, unworkable plan," Gongsun Zan interrupted. "The emperor – whether we accept him or not – is a lifelong puppet of ambitious warlords. Cao Cao will intercept and destroy any petition I send to what is *his* capital first and foremost, a place filled with *his* vassals. All we can do, gentlemen, is wait out the famine, liaise with Zhang Yan, challenge Yuan Shao's advances when they happen, and hope that Cao Cao – like Dong Zhuo and the regents before him – is undone by a hero and the emperor is passed to a more receptive host."

"...Like who...?" Guan Jing wondered.

"I hope for a lot now, but... my old friend Liu Xuande, perhaps, or even Lü Bu, villain that he was," Gongsun Zan replied. "Zhang Yang is fair, and Liu Biao is approachable... who knows...? A shame that I must remove Yuan Shu from that list, though, since he was... since he was the most powerful, and most likely to...!"

Gongsun Zan threw Yuan Shu's proclamation to the floor.

"*Damn* that selfish fool," Gongsun Zan growled. "*Damn him...!*"

"...So what do I do?"

Xu Province Governor and General of the Left Lü Bu asked the question of his advisers Chen Gong, Wang Kai, Xu Si, Chen Yuanfang, Chen Qun, Chen Gui and Chen Deng; they were sat together in private discussion, since every man knew that their next moves were consequential ones and enemy spies were a possibility.

"Placate Liu Bei, correspond with Cao Cao, rebuke Yuan Shu," Chen Qun replied.

"Are you three are happy with that idea...?" Lü Bu asked as he stared at Chen Gong, Wang Kai and Xu Si. "Should I favour Cao over Yuan...?"

Wang Kai and Xu Si were once again hesitant, and both resorted to incoherent mumbling; Chen Gong sighed and said, "It isn't really simple enough a situation to answer simply, my lord."

"And are you two are happy with that idea, after what Cao Cao did to this province...?" Lü Bu asked as he stared at Chen Gui and Chen Deng. "My 'predecessor' that you two love to refer to at awkward moments, *Liu Bei*... was invited here to repel Cao Cao, wasn't he...? Wasn't I labelled a hero for keeping Cao away from here? How is it now alright to 'correspond with Cao Cao'? What has Yuan Shu done to Xu Province or any of us that I should 'rebuke' him and befriend another mass murderer? Have I not already served Dong Zhuo and paid a price for it...?"

"Did we not have this conversation a thousand times???" Chen Yuanfang despaired.

"...Things change," Chen Gui replied awkwardly. "Now Cao Cao is a redeemed Han Excellency: doesn't he deserve to be judged again on recent merits?"

Lü Bu was about to reply, but he realised that he would condemn himself with his arguments and remained silent.

"Cao was a redeemed Han Excellency until his catalogue of mistakes at Wan; now he is ridiculed and despised once again, just as he was when he invaded this province," Chen Gong retorted. "A wise man should always review a situation at a given moment, not rely on outdated conclusions."

"...Perhaps," Chen Gui conceded.

"We should not have invited Liu Bei here and made him governor," Chen Deng said. "We should have given Tao Qian over to Cao Cao. Tao allowed the wicked 'Buddhist cleric' Ze Rong to turn this city into a haven for cultists, and he took good men prisoner that now serve Sun Ce instead of the state. He used the Danyang Brigades as bullies, and he entered into self-serving alliances with villains. We did not see it: we forgave it all as incompetence, when that in itself was a crime for a man in such a position of responsibility. Even if he was in no way responsible for what happened to Cao Cao's father, we should have betrayed him to Cao, not to Liu Bei, for we have suffered worse calamities for our scheming."

"Like *me*," Lü Bu said cuttingly.

"Like Yuan Shao as our master and Yuan Shu as our enemy," Chen Gui retorted.

"That second problem can be fixed by answering this letter!" Lü Bu suggested as he waved a piece of correspondence aloft.

"Yes, with a resounding 'Die, traitor'," Chen Qun said sternly.

"...But a lot of what it says here has merit!" Lü Bu said as he held Yuan Shu's proclamation to chest height. "The Han are plagued with misfortune, and nothing can save that young emperor now. He's been Dong Zhuo's puppet, Li Jue's puppet, Zhang Yang's unpaying tenant, and now he's Cao Cao's puppet! His older brother was Hè Jin's puppet, and all the ones before that were letting eunuchs run the country! And wasn't I in the middle of marriage negotiations?"

"You'd marry your daughter to a treasonous heretic that's hated by all of the lords of the land, even his own vassals...?" Chen Gui asked plainly.

Lü Bu was silent.

"...My lord, do you remember what happened when you last allowed a man to sway you from what made sense...?" Chen Yuanfang asked coldly.

"Yes, I do," Lü Bu replied. "But Yuan Shu and Dong Zhuo are very different men."

"Yuan Shu is a hankering moron," Chen Qun retorted. "Have you already forgotten that he wooed you with promises of rewards in order to get you to overthrow Liu Bei and then reneged immediately by withholding what he had promised...?"

Lü Bu grunted angrily and said, "That's quite true."

"Dong Zhuo wooed you with promises of proper rewards in order to get you to kill Ding Yuan, but he at least had the sense to keep 'rewarding' you for a few years!" Chen Qun continued. "Yuan Shu is so stupid that he couldn't even manage what an oaf like Dong Zhuo could do! His noble blood is the only difference you're choosing to see, but Yuan Shu's claims and promises are all false, and any man that follows him will die!"

"...I'll march to the Huai River and confront Yuan Shu there," Lü Bu decided.

"Write to Cao Cao, promising to aid him, and publicly decry Yuan, so that Liu Bei or some other manipulative creature can't report your advance as a march to *join* Yuan Shu," Chen Qun suggested.

Lü Bu was silent.

"*Ayah*... you really are trying to keep your options open, aren't you?" Chen Qun realised. "Forget the marriage! Forget the presents! He's the world's enemy now!"

"Yuan Shu's advisers might be good," Lü Bu said. "Ji Ling's impressive enough to fight Cao Cao's followers, and-"

"If his advisers were any good, they would not have let him write that silly thing you have in your hand!" Chen Qun chortled. "And Ji Ling is but one general: his best, Sun Ce, will defect to Cao Cao, and he'll lose the entire south in one stroke!"

"Is Sun Ce so tough?" Lü Bu scoffed.

"…You see it as a *challenge*, too," Chen Qun realised. "You *must not*! Joining Yuan Shu would be *suicide*, it would be-!"

"**I already said I'd march to the Huai River, didn't I???**" Lü Bu barked. "**I'll destroy Yuan Shu! I'll humble him! If I can, I'll be the one to *behead him*!**"

"…Don't lose focus, Lord Lü," Chen Yuanfang warned. "You'll die if you do."

Lü Bu harrumphed, but he did not argue: however, that did not mean that he had conceded. Bu still desired the marriage alliance despite the altered circumstances, and the advisers that he had gained in Yan Province – Chen Gong, Wang Kai and Xu Si – were increasingly nervous of Cao Cao and fearing for their own necks before they worried for their master, so they would no longer do anything that swayed him toward Cao Cao and Xuchang. Chen Yuanfang, Chen Qun, Chen Gui and Chen Deng knew it well, and it concerned them greatly.

"**We shouldn't stay with him!**" the officer Chen Lan said to a gathering of confused and disaffected soldiers in northern Shouchun. "**Yuan Shu's a traitor now, and a heretic as well, no better than them Yellow Turbans!**"

"**Chen's right!**" the officer Lei Bo declared. "**We've nearly died being made to fight men like Lü Bu but he wasn't grateful, was he…? No, he was rude to Ji Ling, and nearly demoted him! And *then*, yeah, and *then* there was when he had us starving Liu Bei to death in Haixi, and that was cowardly! And *now* he says he's *emperor*!**"

The soldiers murmured nervously.

"**It won't be long before Zhang Xun goes, 'cause he's friends with Sun Ce, who's definitely gonna go: Qiao Rui thinks Sun Ce's a future hero an' all, so he'll probably go with Zhang Xun!**" Chen Lan suggested. "**All o' Sun's lot'll go their own way, and then what, ay…? Even if we really believed Yuan was emperor, what chance do we stand?**"

The soldiers mumbled agreeably; one eventually asked, "**Where would we go?**"

"**Yu Province,**" Chen Lan replied. "**We'll see if we're wanted by the Han, and if we're not, then we'll make our own way.**"

"**As *bandits*…?**" another soldier exclaimed.

"**If we have to!**" Lei Bo said. "**It's that or stay with Yuan Shu, which will only lead to our deaths!**"

More men stayed and listened than scoffed and returned to their lord Yuan Shu; Chen Lan and Lei Bo took their band of deserters and travelled from Jiujiang to Yu Province. Chen and Lei were just two of many of Yuan Shu's officers that would reconsider their allegiances, and most would choose to leave.

Within days of his announcement, Yuan Shu lost the support of Sun Ce, Ce's maternal uncle Wu Jing and Ce's cousin Sun Ben: that lost him all of the prefectures of Yang Province that lay below the Yangtze River and the part of the easternmost prefecture of Guangling that he controlled as well. That left Yuan Shu with some of Yu Province and the northern Yang prefectures of Jiujiang and Lujiang, but he was doggedly determined to fight on without his 'prize tiger'.

That fight would be difficult: Cao Cao rallied his forces for an attack on the Yan-Yu and Yan-Yang borders; the aforementioned Sun Ce immediately began to attack his hated former lord along their new borders. But that would, in essence, be almost all of the action taken against the pretender.

Yuan Shao remained neutral and focussed his attentions on his usual enemies, namely Gongsun Zan and the Black Mountain Bandits; Liu Biao was still angry that he had been targeted by Cao Cao, so he also remained neutral while guarding his borders against attacks by Yuan Shu or Sun Ce; Gongsun Zan tried to volunteer support for the campaign against Yuan Shu after more pressure from his vassals, but the offers were ignored; and then, as always, there was the fickle Lü Bu, who sent troops to the regions around the Xu-Yang border but made no definitive move to support either side.

Despite the nature of his predicament, more of Yuan Shu's vassals stayed loyal to him than might have been expected: advisers like Yan Xiang and Han Yin would continue their service; administrators like Chen Ji and Liu Xun would ensure that their domains worked for his cause; generals like Ji Ling and Zhang Xun remained as his vanguard. In addition, Yuan Shu could call upon the confederacy of White Wave Bandits led by Yang Feng and Han Xian, the Black Mountain Bandits led by Flying Swallow Zhang Yan, a lower-Yangtze bandit army led by a man called Zu Lang and a number of Shanyue tribes that lived in and around Yang Province. A self-proclaimed future emperor that relied almost entirely on rebels, non-Chinese tribes and bandits drew scorn from most, but this was an era of chaos: many Han loyalists wondered if Yuan Shu might actually win, and even the thought was terrifying to them.

****

70

The elderly scholar Zhao Qi invited his old friend Zheng Xuan, Kong Rong, Zhong Yao and the newly-arrived Wang Lang to his Xuchang residence for a banquet.

"…To see your completed work is so exciting, Master Zhao!" Kong Rong said as he perused Zhao Qi's contributions to 'Commentaries on Mencius'.

"To have it read by a descendant of the great man that mentored Mencius is exciting in its own way, Mister Kong," the 90-year-old Zhao Qi replied. "I have served the Han for my whole life, and willingly so; now I – with others – have left a legacy for the future minds to ponder. To think that men in a thousand years or more may know me for my efforts is warming, indeed."

"They surely shall," Kong Rong said as he handed the bamboo book to Wang Lang with care.

"I shall relish the opportunity to study it at length," Wang Lang said as he unfurled the book and started to skim through its neat lines of characters. "…But if I might be so bold, Master Zhao, I should forego the content without having had the time to enjoy it, and instead praise the calligraphy."

"I, too, am an admirer of the clarity and, if you'll excuse the choice of words, 'simplicity', Master Zhao," Zhong Yao chuckled.

Zhao Qi smiled and said, "I am no Hu Guang or Cai Yong."

"I meant no offence! Your work is exemplary!" Zhong Yao protested.

"I am teasing, Mister Zhong," Zhao Qi chuckled; his face suddenly fell, and he added, "Ah, Cai Yong… how I wish that marvellous man was still among us; he was cruelly taken from us, gentlemen, and worse still, by a man that thought he was doing the world a favour."

Zhong Yao lowered his head and said, "The late Wang Yun still has my respect, but measurably less for his ordering the death of my mentor and friend, sad to say."

"Is your fellow student of Mister Cai, Wang Can, still committed to serving Liu Biao?" Zheng Xuan asked.

"Yes, I'm afraid so," Zhong Yao chortled. "I can only think that Governor Liu has a lot of donkeys."

Kong Rong, Zhao Qi, Zheng Xuan and Wang Lang laughed as one.

"Oh, dear… what quirks Heaven curses us with to rob us of dignity!" Zheng Xuan said. "But will he insist on staying there if Excellency Cao marches on Jing again at a later date…?"

Kong Rong's smile vanished, and he said, "That man should not be able to march against a place and people that have done nothing to warrant it! Again, like Xu Province, he-!"

"*Aiee*… Wenju, please do not mention that unfortunate situation," Wang Lang pleaded theatrically. "I still have nightmares… I should have helped Governor Tao to evacuate the villages at the least, but I did not, and that grieves me to this day!"

"…Was Tao Qian responsible for the death of Cao Song…?" Zheng Xuan asked.

Wang Lang's face was unreadable as he replied, "I do not know, but my opinion is that he was not; Zhang Kai was independent, and Ze Rong has since been proved a fraud that probably killed

Guangling Administrator Zhao Yu and my friend Xue Li for little more than to have their possessions, so why wouldn't Ze Rong have killed Cao Song for his wealth as well…?"

The septuagenarian Zheng Xuan grunted ambiguously and said, "That is true. I knew Cao Song and Tao Qian, and respected them both; I want to believe that both men died needlessly and that they are now friends in a better place."

"I wonder, Mister Wang, if I might ask about Xu Jing…?" Zhao Qi prompted.

"Alas, I cannot talk about Mister Xu without mentioning my disastrous handling of the barbarous Sun Ce," Wang Lang replied. "Xu Jing was my adviser to the end of that regrettable mess in Kuaiji; I was forced to flee my capital when Sun Ce's hordes descended upon it, and a spirited defence was attempted further south. We lost place after place as Sun Ce made use of every wicked tool that he spied, so I was forced to match his villainy in ways that break my heart."

"…How so…?" Zhong Yao enquired.

"…I allied with bandits and tribes that harmed the local populace, for they were the only ones that were strong enough to repel the heretic Yuan Shu's attack dog," Wang Lang continued. "But such types are treacherous; despite my best efforts to negotiate a cessation of their wrongs against the people and instead focus on fighting our mutual enemy – with, of course, the promise of some small place to have autonomy – they persisted in that harming, and we lost support of key figures, including my capital's magistrate, who all joined Sun Ce. This is, I should note, *before* Sun Ce 'turned back to the light', as he has supposedly done."

"*Ayah*… that makes no sense at all!" Zhong Yao complained. "Please elaborate further, Wang Jingxing!"

"It makes sense when one considers the bizarre alliances that we see all around us," Zhao Qi suggested. "The recently-scattered Yellow Turbans of Runan were allied, most say, to the villain Yuan Shu, who is also said to aid the Black Mountain Bandits and give refuge to the White Wave Bandits that harmed the sovereign: a year ago, gentlemen, that left us puzzled, but now we know why! And then there is Gongsun Zan – a pupil of Lu Zhi – who-"

Zheng Xuan groaned miserably.

"…I speak no ill of your friend Lu Zhi," Zhao Qi insisted.

"I know, old friend, but I weep inside to think that Gongsun – a man that we both saw as a future hero – is a wicked hankerer, allied to the barbarians beyond the wall, and has the blood of Liu Yu on his hands!" Zheng Xuan replied. "And his other notable pupil, Liu Bei, was, until recently, repeatedly trapped in Xiaopei, little more than a buffer and a signal tower to warn us of any further acts of treason by that wretch Lü Bu, whose crimes are too many to number. And where are *my* students…?"

"I have tried to find many of them," Zhong Yao admitted. "Cui Yan is worse than a wandering hermit; every time I get word of him, it is to say 'He just left here'."

"…Leave them," Zheng Xuan grumbled. "Perhaps it is best that they do not come here… anyhow, we have digressed from asking Mister Wang to tell us of Kuaiji."

"There was little else to say," Wang Lang insisted. "The bandits and the tribes were humbled by Sun Ce's growing army of trained men – mostly pirates and other such types, but with such discipline! – and I was chased down like the hunted deer until I surrendered. He humiliated me in front of his allies, and then I was offered two choices: serve him, or go into exile. I chose the latter, and from there, here I am. Xu Jing was as committed as I, gentlemen, because Sun Ce was responsible – indirectly in some cases, *perhaps*, but responsible nonetheless – for the deaths of Lu Kang, whom we all knew and respected; Liu Yao, who was appointed governor and an imperial relative; and most notably Mister Xu's brother, Xu Shao, whose favour I never gained but whose brilliance was undeniable by all."

Zheng Xuan and Zhao Qi both moaned at the mention of the three familiar names.

"All of them pillars of the state," Zhong Yao declared. "Sun Ce has deprived the world of great talents, as Gongsun Zan and Lü Bu have, and Heaven will never forgive them."

After a short silence, Wang Lang coughed deliberately and said, "To conclude – and finally answer Mister Zhao's question – Xu Jing went into the hostile southern territories beyond Yang, where nothing is serving Heaven and a few civilised men struggle to maintain order; he hoped to secure us refuge, but I was captured before he could return, and I can only assume that he either stayed there or moved on to a better land, like Jing or Yi."

"Since this nonsense began all those years ago, it has been the fools harming the talented, and it is the learned yet gentle man that has suffered and shed the most blood," Zheng Xuan complained. "The belligerents all still have their heads, or most of them do: Guo Si *may* be dead at last, some say, but Lü Bu, Li Jue, Gongsun Zan, Yuan Shu, Sun Ce, the Qiang warlords of Liang and the myriad bandits thrive, while Zhu Jun, Lu Zhi, Cai Yong, Wang Yun, Xu Shao, Zhou Bi, Shisun Rui, and so, so many more… are cold bones."

"Excellency Cao aims to put an end to that," Zhong Yao said.

"You are too quick to trust him," Kong Rong retorted.

"And you are too quick to slander him," Wang Lang suggested. "Wenju, please remember that the times we live in are complex! While I agree with the laments about our lost friends, and I agree with you on most things, I cannot agree with your denunciations of Excellency Cao."

"Even after what he did to Xu Province, a situation that 'gives you nightmares'…?" Kong Rong countered. "Wang Jingxing, I am surprised at you."

"…I am surprised at myself, Wenju, but perhaps I see the world and how one survives in it, and you do not," Wang Lang said unapologetically. "When Dong Zhuo took charge of the capital, Governor Tao asked me whether we should fight him then and there: I said that he should not, for it would be fatal, and it was, for Ding Yuan. Had I answered otherwise, as my critics suggest, then Dong Zhuo might have had the Danyang Brigades."

"…Your point is sound," Zhong Yao conceded.

"When Sun Ce attacked Kuaiji, I did not have the army to face him properly, and defeat was inevitable," Wang Lang continued. "I allied with the tribes and the bandits in order to 'buy time', as it were, for I had hoped that someone else could be relied upon for aid, such as Liu Yao, who was hiding to my northwest and recovering from his recent defeats in Danyang; he had lost Xu Shao and lacked other decent counsel, so I was forced to rely entirely on my 'unwanted help'. Had I defeated Sun Ce, I would have reorganised Kuaiji, made decent men of the bandits, pacified the tribes, and built a stronger army to push Sun northward, but without the demoralised and inactive Liu Yao I was still doomed. If I had simply fought Sun with the militia that I had, I would have been defeated immediately, and the same critics would have said, 'Were there no temporary alliances that you could make?'"

"...I see *your* motivations," Kong Rong insisted, "but Cao Cao-!"

"Cao Cao went on the information that he had, which may have been wrong, or not, when he attacked Xu Province," Wang Lang continued. "'Cornered tigers fight hardest', as they say, and when Cao Cao was seen advancing eastward, the people put up a united, spirited defence against what they saw to be a hostile invader, and paid for their defiant obstruction with their lives, because 'Men must honour their fathers', and blood demanded blood. That is regrettable, but Tao and Cao were both at fault. Now Cao Cao is trying to be honourable; he made decent soldiers out of some of the Yellow Turbans of Qing Province, but – other than that single instance – he seeks no alliances with disreputable types, for he does not need or want their help."

Kong Rong laughed irritably and said, "Yes, but-!"

"While Yuan Shao, Yuan Shu and the rest of them did nothing to aid His Majesty, Cao Cao marched north, fought a bandit army that vastly outnumbered his own and won decisively," Wang Lang continued. "Dong Cheng – the man that invited him to do so – now complains that Cao Cao is a hankerer, when he happily served Niu Fu – son-in-law of the man that killed our previous sovereign – and then the regents that held our current sovereign hostage for many years. Cao Cao, since settling the emperor here, has defeated the Yellow Turbans, the Xiongnu rebels and the Black Mountain Bandits; his march against Zhang Xiu might have failed due to a moment of weakness, but it led to the Qiang warlords turning against the 'regents' and Liu Biao pledging allegiance to His Majesty and promising to be more helpful in future, so some good was achieved by indirect means; now Cao Cao plans expeditions against all of the enemies of the state, while his most recent predecessors – Dong Cheng's former masters – were content with being idle parasites that issued self-serving petitions and self-promotions... after they had razed Luoyang and slaughtered thousands without provocation."

Kong Rong exhaled loudly.

"His Excellency could have left you in Qing to rot, Wenju, because you were a friend of Liu Bei – a man he hated for aiding Tao Qian – and he seeks reconciliation with Yuan Shao, father of the man that captured you, *and*, further to that, you were appointed by the regents," Wang Lang continued. "Excellency Cao is flawed, as are we all, but he has my former officer Yu Jin as his vanguard and invited me here, despite my close allegiance to Tao Qian, *and* he saved not only you but Liu Bei – a man that he hated – as well, despite that also rankling the then-governor Lü Bu *and* his childhood friend Yuan Shao at a stroke. Consider those points."

Zhao Qi and Zheng Xuan – who kept their own opinions to themselves – exchanged glances before they turned to the mortified and bewildered Kong Rong.

"...I know that my small doubts about Excellency Cao are put to one side," Zhong Yao said.

"And isn't it true that your family is now safe...?" Wang Lang added as he stared at Kong Rong. "Who is to thank for that...? Dong Cheng...?"

"*Aiee*... alright, Jingxing, I shall give Excellency Cao a chance," Kong Rong conceded. "I see that I have seemed ungrateful, and while I will continue to challenge his poor ideas, I will not heckle him otherwise."

Wang Lang bowed slightly and said, "That is the proper course: and if any of his ideas are so poor that he needs to be challenged, you shall do so with my support."

"...But implementing *tuntian* alone deserves great praise," Zhong Yao noted.

Kong Rong laughed miserably, looked at Wang Lang and said, "One thing is for certain, Wang Jingxing: one way or another, my inviting you here on Cao Cao's behalf will be interesting."

****

71

Yuan Shu sat on a temporary throne and read various battle reports with eyes that were willingly blind to reality. After an hour of watching Yuan Shu lost in silent and pointless reading, his adviser Han Yin coughed loudly and deliberately.

"...Speak your mind," Yuan Shu said tonelessly.

"My- ...I mean, Your Majesty," Han Yin said with difficulty. "Your Majesty, I must insist that you listen to what is going on, since the reports are obviously failing to engage you."

"We are listening," Yuan Shu said with deranged grandeur.

"The attack on Chen County has been met by Cao Cao, but he is being repelled at present, and the White Wave Bandits are causing the required chaos," Han Yin reported. "The Shanyue are harassing Sun Ce, but we don't know how that will turn out. Lü Bu is not acting as yet: my- ...I mean, Your Majesty... he must be asked to aid us."

"I shall dispense with royal protocol, since this is a busy hour," Yuan Shu replied. "If Lü Bu is still interested in marrying his daughter to the Prince of Lujiang – it was Lujiang that we agreed upon as the heir's principality, wasn't it, or was it Lu County?"

"...I *forget*, Your Majesty," Han Yin sighed.

"...Well, he's a prince, and that's all that matters!" Yuan Shu chuckled. "Yes, uh... well, as we said, if Bu's still agreeable, you should manage the affair on our behalf."

"I'll write to Lü Bu immediately," Han Yin said.

A week passed.

Chen Qun hurried to Lü Bu's court when he heard that Yuan Shu had sent some correspondence: Bu and the 'Yan advisers' – Chen Gong, Wang Kai and Xu Si – were not present, but the Xiapi nobleman Chen Gui, Gui's son Chen Deng, Bu's officer Gao Shun and a number of other distressed officials were gathered for a possible discussion.

"...No... no, he *hasn't*...!" Chen Qun whined.

"I fear that he *has*," Chen Gui sighed. "He sent his man Qin Yilu in secret to advance the negotiations. I'll do what I can, Changwen."

"Why does he now ignore us...?" Chen Qun complained.

"That, I fear, is Lord Lü's way," Gao Shun said before he left the hall, sighing sadly.

"...But this is a *heretic's son* that he's marrying his daughter to!" Chen Qun cried.

"He doesn't see it that way," Chen Deng said. "He really believes that Yuan Shu can 'defeat Cao Cao, humble Sun Ce', and so on. Han Yin is on his way here."

"No, no, that won't do," Chen Qun mumbled. "Is there a way to delay Han Yin?"

"He's being escorted from the border by General Hou Cheng," Chen Deng replied. "Lord Lü fears interference by Liu Bei or interception by Cao Cao."

"Then... then there is nothing that we can do to stop Lord Lü's daughter travelling to Shouchun to marry Yuan Shu's son," Chen Qun said numbly. "After that... there will be nothing that we can

do to-"
"Leave it to me," Chen Gui insisted. "Even if she leaves here, it isn't over."
"If you can save us, Chen Hanyu, then I'll petition for you to be made Grand Tutor," Chen Qun said humbly.
"I'll have earned it!" Chen Gui joked. "Trust me, Changwen."

A few days later, Lü Bu's wife Lady Yan stood and watched with pride as Lü Bu inspected his daughter's face for one last time before she would depart for Shouchun.
"You shall make a fine princess," Lü Bu whispered.
"I hope that I am worthy, Father," the young Lady Lü replied.
"You're my daughter," Lü Bu retorted. "If not for the silliness that governs status, you'd already be a princess!"
Lady Lü smiled gratefully.
Lü Bu's relative and vassal Wei Xu appeared at the doorway, coughed quietly and said, "Han Yin is waiting."
Lü Bu ran his finger down the side of his daughter's face, smiled unintelligently, and said to his wife, "We are soon to be made great in all eyes, my lady, as is right."
"You will be the hero of the land, Husband, and of the *world*!" Lady Yan sobbed happily.
Lü Bu touched his wife's hand, turned to Wei Xu and said, "Let us go, then."

Han Yin bowed low when Lü Bu entered the private audience room to meet him.
"I shall leave you, and do as you asked," Wei Xu whispered.
Lü Bu nodded, and Wei Xu departed via the exit that led to the public audience hall.
"So you are Yuan Shu's emissary," Lü Bu said. "So, Mister Han Yin... I trust your journey was a comfortable one...?"
"All the more comfortable for knowing that I was to meet a hero such as you," Han Yin replied obsequiously. "Might we discuss what happens next?"
Lü Bu sat in his host seat and said, "Please, sit down. I wonder, Mister Han Yin, why you did not castigate me for referring to your master by his name, now that he is First Emperor...?"
"You are His Majesty's future relative, grandfather to His Majesty's divine progeny," Han Yin replied as he sat at the closest guest seat. "Besides, such times call for laxity in protocol."
Chen Gong, Wang Kai, Xu Si, Chen Gui, and Chen Deng entered the room via the same door that Wei Xu had used to leave it: Han Yin turned to the five men and bowed respectfully, and they reciprocated immediately.
"Chen Gong, Wang Kai, Xu Si!" Han Yin cawed. "What an honour it is to meet the men that humbled the 'Crafty Villain' and turned Lord Lü toward the light!"
"I can take no credit for the latter," Chen Gong replied.
Wang Kai and Xu Si bowed silently.
"...And Mister Chen Gui, and Mister Chen Deng!" Han Yin continued. "Your wealth and influence could have been used for personal gain, yet you used it to save this province from that same 'Crafty Villain', and then remove the deceitful Liu Bei before he could harm your people! You are truly noble!"

"...Quite," Chen Gui replied. "Mister Han Yin, you have served Yuan Shu for a long time. Does his audacious declaration not disturb you?"

Lü Bu glared at Chen Gui with anger.

"Of course," Han Yin replied calmly. "But the signs are there, Mister Chen, when one looks hard enough. Men will say that Sun Ce's defection is inauspicious, but the man was never like his father. Sun Ce is an undisciplined, hankering dog that has long been a concern. As for the rest, well... Liu Bang did not win over every man that he met! ...And yet he was First Emperor of the Han. The mandate of the Han is exhausted, gentlemen, else how could *Cao Cao*, of all men, have the former Prince of Chenliu in his clutches now...?"

Chen Gui looked at Chen Gong as he replied, "Perhaps that is so. We were invited here, and I am now anxious to know why."

"My daughter will leave here *tonight*," Lü Bu declared. "Mister Han will escort her to Shouchun, and when the time is right, I shall follow her with-"

"Why the rush?" Chen Gong asked.

"You of all men should know why!" Lü Bu replied. "You're the one that's been making the most noise, and now you feign ignorance of the matter??? No one must know about this until it is too late! Not Liu Bei, not Cao Cao, and not any of their agents that may be in our midst!"

"Is that why Elder Chen and Chen Qun were not invited?" Chen Gui asked.

"I am... concerned," Lü Bu replied. "Yes, I am concerned! Cao Cao offered the old man rank, high rank, and with no explanation as to why! How can I not be suspicious...? ...And after Hao Meng, how can I-!"

Chen Gong coughed deliberately, and Lü Bu fell silent.

"...Should I retire to my hotel?" Han Yin asked.

"Oh, uh... no, no," Lü Bu said as he suddenly realised that he was starting to discuss personal conflicts in front of a stranger. "Mister Han, we shall celebrate your presence here in private, and then we shall begin final preparations for your journey back to Shouchun. Wang Kai and Xu Si will go with you; Wei Xu will escort you to the border, and no further."

Han Yin bowed and smiled warily.

The returning general Hou Cheng was approached by several of his colleagues as he waited for further instructions from Lü Bu.

"...So is it true that Qin Yilu has abandoned his wife?" General Cao Xing asked.

"...Unbelievably, yes," Hou Cheng replied.

"*Aiee...* that is not acceptable!" General Zhang Liao said. "He has a son! How can he abandon his son and heir? Why would he do such a thing?"

"When he arrived in Shouchun – which, he says, was in chaos – Yuan Shu offered him the opportunity to marry 'a woman with some class'," Hou Cheng explained. "I wish I'd had the courage to ask him if I can take Lady Du as my consort."

"...Even when one ignores the children, the beautiful Lady Du is a woman that no man should willingly discard," Zhang Liao said with disbelief. "What blinding enchantment can he be affected by...?"

"The promise of social advancement," Gao Shun suggested. "It has made fools of smarter men than Qin Yilu."

"...Do you refer to our lord...?" Zhang Liao asked.

Gao Shun laughed and said, "I have nothing to say about our lord, General Zhang. I am loyal to him, and that is that."

Zhang Liao hummed thoughtfully and murmured, "But it applies..."

That night, Lü Bu and Lady Yan escorted their daughter to a carriage at the southern gates of Xiapi City: Wang Kai, Xu Si, Zhang Liao and Wei Xu were their only company. The young Lady Lü was wearing a thick cloak and had her hair covered by several scarves, and she was noticeably afraid.

"Soon, you shall be princess... and not long after that, you shall be an *empress*," Lü Bu whispered.

Han Yin approached the Lü family and said, "Your daughter has great beauty and a strength that can only have come from you and your fair lady wife, Lord Lü."

"You are every bit the imperial emissary, Mister Han!" Lady Yan said without thinking.

"We should hurry," Lü Bu decided; he helped his daughter into the carriage, bowed to Han Yin, and then he stepped aside so that Han Yin could take a seat in the carriage that faced Bu's lonely, terrified daughter. Lü Bu nodded to Wang Kai and Xu Si, and they followed Han Yin into the carriage; Lady Lü's expression did not change, even with her father's vassals for added company, since they were strangers too.

"Are your other advisers not here?" Han Yin asked suddenly.

"Why would I need advice right now?" Lü Bu chuckled softly. "May your journey be as swift as it is safe."

Han Yin bowed toward Lü Bu and Lady Yan, smiled at Lady Lü, and sat back to await the beginning of the journey.

"...Go," Lü Bu ordered.

Lü Bu did not stay to watch Wei Xu and the carriage depart: he took his wife's hand and ushered her back into the city.

"Our daughter...!" Lady Yan gasped.

"She'll soon be a princess, and soon after – *very soon after* – an empress," Lü Bu said without stopping. "That solves everything."

Zhang Liao was now the acting commander of the permanent camp outside the southern gates: Gao Shun – who held that role before Hao Meng's failed mutiny – approached Zhang Liao and said, "It is done, then?"

"...Because it is you, I shall answer," Zhang Liao replied. "You and I, we've followed Lord Lü for many years... so, so many years. He's made reckless decisions before... so, so reckless... but this might be the worst of them all."

"And yet, all the same, we'll serve him until our dying breaths," Gao Shun said. "I cannot turn against him, not even when I see him betray the whole country again by siding with his second Wang Mang in eight years. Am I a fool?"

"If you are, then... then so am I," Zhang Liao replied as he began a slow walk back to the command tent of the camp; Gao Shun followed silently.

Lü Bu returned his distressed wife to their home and went to the governor's office, where Chen Gui was waiting.

"I am here, Mister Chen, as you asked; oh, no Chen Gong...?" Lü Bu heckled childishly. "Has he gone to visit Cao in Xuchang...?"
"What a foolish thing to say, my lord," Chen Gui scoffed. "How can he go there?"
"...Ah, yes, that *would* be rather stupid, wouldn't it?" Lü Bu chuckled. "He's got to stay here, hasn't he... even if he really didn't want to. So what did you want?"
"The deed is done," Chen Gui sighed. "I just wanted to say that... that sometimes, a matter can seem to be done, and yet it is far from done. When you betrayed Ding Yuan and killed him, and pledged your soul to Dong Zhuo, and then became his foster son, it seemed to be the case that you were bound to the man forever; that was not the case, however. The same applies now."
"**Don't talk in riddles, Chen Gui!**" Lü Bu barked. "**What are you trying to say?**"
"I am not speaking in riddles, my lord governor," Chen Gui replied. "Nothing I have just said is complicated or shrouded in mystery. I stated fact. You might not see it now, but you will do in time..."
"...See *what*???" Lü Bu asked.
"You'll see that what you did tonight was the biggest mistake that you have ever made," Chen Gui replied. "And then, you'll weep, because it will seem to be beyond change... all I ask is that at that point, you remember Dong Zhuo, Ding Yuan, and Wang Yun. Things are only at an end when things reach their destination."
Lü Bu flicked his sleeve and left the office.
"...You'll soon change your mind, 'Fengxian'," Chen Gui chuckled. "You always do."

✻✻✻✻✻✻✻✻✻✻✻✻

72

Lü Bu retreated to his home and stayed there for the next four days; he drank heavily, rebuked any attempts at communication by his wife Lady Yan, and brooded quietly. At first, Lady Yan suspected that there may be another muse among the court dancers, but she quickly realised that he was having second thoughts about sending his daughter to Shouchun after all.
"Talk to Chen Gui," Lady Yan suggested on the fourth evening.
"*Aiee...* and admit that I am now wondering if I have made an irreversible mistake?" Lü Bu retorted. "I can't do that."
"You have to do *something*," Lady Yan said. "Our daughter nears a place that now fills your heart with doubts... perhaps she might already be there."
After several minutes of silent contemplation, Lü Bu got to his feet and staggered out of his living quarters to find his boots.
"Where are you going?" Lady Yan asked.
"To visit Chen Gui," Lü Bu replied. "He knew I'd... see."

Chen Gui had remained in the audience hall of the governor's office at the end of every evening, despite protestations by his son Deng: this night, his faith was rewarded when Lü Bu appeared and said, "I'm ready to listen."
"What made you change your mind?" Chen Gui asked.
Lü Bu collapsed into his public host seat and replied, "Funny, that... I must be even more selfish than I thought. I remembered everything that you said that I should remember, and then I remembered when I was wandering around Central Province with Dong Zhuo's head in a sack... I visited Yuan Shu, and he rebuked me, and put people to watch me, and eventually, I wondered if he'd kill me... so I fled. He was so spiteful, so angry, and... now I think about it, he'll never really forgive me for my part in his clan's destruction. His brother doesn't, and he's the sensible one."
Chen Gui smiled and said, "Was that all...?"
"He's saying he's the emperor... and I actually went along with it!" Lü Bu cried. "I am actually more intelligent when I am drunk, I think! How can that pampered, childish, lying, thieving idiot be the emperor? How could I have agreed to this nonsense idea of marrying my poor daughter off to him? ...Oh, we both know the answer to that, of course... she'd be a princess..."
"...And soon enough, she'd be an *empress...* and *all would be right*," Chen Gui said. "I could see it in your eyes. Why not help the man achieve his dreams and then smite him as you did Dong Zhuo, so that you could undo wrong with right? But that would not work, my lord... any more than it did when you killed Dong Zhuo."
"That was for selfish reasons too," Lü Bu admitted. "I didn't kill him because he was evil; I killed him because he'd found out that I was courting one of his favourite maids."
Chen Gui hummed thoughtfully.
"What a man I am, mm...?" Lü Bu chortled. "Oh, yes: a man among men... a dog among dogs. But tonight, I will put something right. I need to find Zhang Liao."
"He's... in the southern camp," Chen Gui replied.
Lü Bu got to his feet and left the hall. Chen Gui was rattled by the

Lü Bu that he had just spoken to, and he was now wondering if Xu Province might be better off without him. The problem was that the only man left that had the strength to rid the province of him was the greatest scourge that the province had ever known.

Lü Bu barged into the southern camp's command tent and said, "Zhang Liao, I need to gather a cavalry force to- ...What are you doing here?"
Gao Shun was alone in the command tent: he looked up from a military text and replied, "Zhang Liao trusts me, and he is only human; he needs sleep, like any man, Lord Lü. You said that you needed cavalry, so I shall go and wake him."
"...Do that," Lü Bu said. "You... you will accompany us, Gao Shun. Serve me well in this, and you will have regained *my* trust... and then I will restore your rank."
Gao Shun got to his feet and said, "That's all that I want, Lord Lü: your trust."
Lü Bu was left alone in the tent once Gao Shun was gone: his eyes filled with tears, and he whispered, "How can I not know who I can trust...? Is it because I... cannot trust *myself*...?"

Lü Bu personally led his cavalry in pursuit of Han Yin's carriage: he caught up to the small procession as it neared the border with Yang Province, and after a short battle with the men that Yuan Shu had sent to receive the carriage, he brought the dumbfounded Han Yin, the perplexed Wang Kai and Xu Si and the relieved Lady Lü back to Xiapi.
"...Now I'm confused," Chen Gong grumbled as he hurried to the gates of Xiapi to receive his master. "What's he up to now...?"
Han Yin was being roughly escorted by Zhang Liao, though he was not bound in any way: Lü Bu was smiling proudly, while his daughter held onto Wei Xu's arm and sobbed pitifully.
"...Might I ask what's going on?" Chen Gong said. "Wang Kai...?"
"...I am in the dark, same as you," Wang Kai replied irritably.
"...And Xu Si as well, I see," Chen Gong murmured.
"You've gone mad, Lü Bu!" Han Yin cried. **"You're mad! Completely mad!"**
"Shut up," Lü Bu retorted. "Mister Chen, I've changed my mind."
"...I guessed that, but I don't see what you intend to do," Chen Gong said. "You've sent her off, and now she's back; you welcomed this man, and now you're apparently going to imprison him. I don't see where this leads."
"I... am not sure myself," Lü Bu admitted. "But Chen Gui is right: I cannot just send my daughter off to Shouchun! What if she were held hostage?"
"*Chen Gui*...?" Chen Gong exclaimed quietly.
"*Ayah*! You're an idiot!" Han Yin shrieked. **"His Majesty was going to make a future empress of her! What you can hope for now, I do not know!"**
Lü Bu's expression changed, and he wavered again.
"Oh, this is ridiculous," Chen Gong grumbled. "General Zhang Liao: please escort Han Yin back to the hotel and keep him under guard. Wei Xu: please escort Lady Lü to the Lü residence and inform Lady Yan of what has happened... though I would prefer that you keep it simple if you can, for now."

Zhang Liao and Wei Xu followed their instructions.

"...Perhaps I have been hasty," Lü Bu murmured.

Wang Kai and Xu Si groaned desperately and covered their faces with their sleeves.

"Stop wavering, Lord Lü!" Chen Gong cried. **"Be decisive! Lives depend on this, including your own! What if *Cao Cao* learns of this nonsense???"**

"How could he know...?" Lü Bu scoffed.

But Lü Bu was wrong, as he often was: before he had even waved his daughter away from the gates of Xiapi, an agent of the court had sped westward to inform Cao Cao of the marriage alliance.

"...He insults us," Cao Cao growled as he finished listening to the private report.

"Worse... he betrays us," Guo Jia suggested. "But we must be careful, Excellency: Bu is dangerous, and we must be soft instead of stern now."

"Oh, I know," Cao Cao chortled. "I am used to this awful man now. His seal of office is ready to send: I shall send it, with a warning, just as I did with Yuan Shao."

"What will you say?" Xun Wenruo asked.

"Oh, I'll be polite, Wenruo!" Cao Cao promised. "As Fengxiao has advised, I shall say this..."

"He says: 'The officials in Shan County were distressed when the events there led to the loss of your seal, so they offered to produce another'," Chen Gong relayed to Lü Bu and his group of advisers: Lü Bu himself was sat at the host seat of his private audience room, clutching the immaculate seal that he had waited so long for.

"I'm a man of Yan Province: such a thing could not have been produced or paid for by Shan County clerks!" Wang Kai scoffed.

"It wasn't," Chen Gong said. "He goes on to say, 'Unfortunately, their own local stock of such supplies were inadequate, and in addition, the imperial coffers are empty. It was therefore necessary, in order to show my sincerity, to take the gold and purple silk required from my own personal wealth'."

"Oh my," Xu Si gasped. "The seal is paid for by Cao Cao alone?"

Lü Bu hummed thoughtfully as he continued to study the seal.

Chen Gong's expression changed: he looked up at Lü Bu and said, "He goes on to say, 'You are not being wise'."

Lü Bu froze, and his eyes met Chen Gong's.

"What... does he mean by that...?" Wang Kai asked.

Chen Gong's eyes returned to the letter, and he replied, "He says, 'Yuan Shu has declared himself as emperor, which is treason punishable by death: so, surely, you should break all of your connections with him'."

"He knows?" Chen Yuanfang gasped.

"One of you told him, and it is most likely *you*, old man!" Lü Bu shrieked. **"Don't act innocently when guilt is in your heart! Is that what your appointment as 'Excellency of Works' was for? A *reward*...? A *reward*, Chen Ji, for *spying for Cao Cao*???"**

"*Yuan Shao* deferred that dratted title to me!" Chen Yuanfang retorted. "I have nothing to gain by spying for Cao Cao!"

"My father has done nothing wrong," Chen Qun pleaded. "You-"
"Will you all be QUIET???" Chen Gong bellowed.
Chen Qun and Lü Bu fell silent and stared at Chen Gong, who continued by saying, "I-If I may, gentlemen... h-he says, in the end, 'The imperial court trusts you, else I would not send you this seal and reaffirm your commission. You once asked about a decree, addressed to you, to destroy Yuan Shu: that now exists, I assure you, and will soon be despatched. You should prove your loyalty to the Han when the opportunity arises'."
Lü Bu looked at the seal and grunted.
"What now...?" Wang Kai whispered.
Chen Gong and Xu Si started to drift into private thought and forgot about their master, who now turned to the exonerated Chen Gui for counsel.
"There is only one course of action left open to you, my lord," Chen Gui insisted.
Lü Bu looked at Chen Gui and said, "I know."

Within a week, Cao Cao was welcoming Chen Deng at the gates of Xuchang City.
"I received your 'advance gift'," Cao Cao chuckled. "Han Yin's head and body no longer know each other, and I hope that his master Yuan Shu will soon suffer for the indignities that he heaps upon the Son of Heaven. Won't you accompany me to my office, Mister Chen...?"
"It would be a pleasure, Excellency," Chen Deng replied.
        A short time later, Cao Cao and Chen Deng were sat in the private audience hall of the chancellery, enjoying tea.
"Mister Chen... I am glad you came here," Cao Cao said politely.
"I hope that my lord's gift of silk was ample thanks for your generosity," Chen Deng replied. "Though, if I might be very frank with you..."
"...Please, go ahead," Cao Cao urged.
"...Lü Bu is a fool and a monster that has learned not one lesson that life has thrown at him," Chen Deng said. "I have had the experience of three lords in recent times: Tao Qian, Liu Bei, and Lü Bu. The first, you know too well, and I can only convey my own personal sadness at the cruel and undeserved fate of your father."
Cao Cao bowed low and whispered, "My thanks to you."
"I cannot say what happened, because Tao Qian was a man that had dealings that were outside our knowledge," Chen Deng continued. "However, I do know that he died a broken man, surrounded by men that fought over who should succeed him. Liu Bei was the man chosen, and he quickly surrendered to Yuan Shao to save the province from your return; forgive my honesty, but I see no way to avoid this subject. Xu Province is my home, the place where I am known and respected..."
After a short silence, Cao Cao smiled and said, "I do not consider my actions in Xu Province to be my finest, Mister Chen. Perhaps we should move on to Liu Bei."
"Yes," Chen Deng agreed. "Liu Bei was, for want of a better word, useless. His vassal Zhang Fei is like an untamed dog, and Jian Yong acts like a man that knows nothing of basic etiquette. He wears dirty boots to meetings, passes foul gasses loudly and without apology..."

376

Cao Cao laughed at the notion.

"And Liu Bei did *nothing*!" Chen Deng chortled. "All we'd ever hear is the odd hollow rebuke, but nothing ever changed... until Liu Bei went to confront Ji Ling, and left Zhang Fei and Xiapi's chancellor Cao Bao in charge. Zhang hated Cao, and the outcome was simple enough: Zhang killed Cao, and Lü Bu was asked to come and diffuse the situation, because we had nobody else to turn to. Now, we're stuck with Lü Bu; but Your Excellency, that cannot be the way it is forever. You must one day destroy him before he destroys the land with his fickle, destructive idiocy."

Cao Cao smirked and said, "His destruction is in mind, Mister Chen, but it is not a priority. Yuan Shu must die first, unless Bu somehow proved an obstruction to that."

"I can't promise you that Lü Bu won't waver and join up with the man again in the future, but for now, my father and I can sway him," Chen Deng replied. "We'll keep you informed of everything that he does in future, so that you can act if need be."

"I thank you," Cao Cao said. "You're a good man: I only wish that you could stay here, but I know that we're both agreed that you're better placed in Xu Province."

Chen Deng bowed slightly and said, "That is so."

"...And the esteemed Chen Yuanfang and his son, Mister Chen Qun... they are also 'unhappy'...?" Cao Cao asked.

"Elder Chen, Chen Qun, General Xu Dan... and I'm sure that Bu's long-suffering general Gao Shun will one day see sense," Chen Deng replied. "One man, Hao Meng, already did, but sadly died alone; but others will turn from him, I am certain."

"...Then Lü Bu is closely watched, indeed," Cao Cao murmured. "That's good."

Chen Deng bowed, and the purposeful meeting ended.

But when Chen Deng returned to Xiapi, he was met at the gates by an angry, drunk and paranoid Lü Bu that asked, **"Is it true that you've received rank???"**

"...It is," Chen Deng replied. "I am appointed 'Administrator of Guangling'."

"And your *father*...?" Lü Bu asked further.

"He, too, has received rank," Chen Deng replied as he looked behind Bu, scanned the collection of advisers and met the gaze of his calm father, Chen Gui.

"...**Treachery!**" Lü Bu cried. **"I've been tricked! You tricked me into sending Han Yin to his doom, and now I've made an enemy of Yuan Shu for no good reason! A few days ago, I was his relative; now, I am his hated foe, while at the same time, you two get rank from Cao Cao! Is that a *reward*...? A *reward*, for tricking me into cutting my own throat???"**

Chen Yuanfang sighed woefully.

"Uh... maybe we should discuss this privately...?" Chen Gong prompted.

"What difference does it make *where* I talk???" Lü Bu retorted. **"Whatever I say and wherever I say it, Cao Cao will know! I'm encircled by liars and traitors!"**

"But we have secured for you a promise of liaisons with the imperial court," Chen Gui said. "You're a governor, a marquis, and a general... you now have the seal to prove your rank, so what is

wrong...? Yuan Shu is hated by all, and you will soon receive orders from the true sovereign to kill him. We have not condemned you... we have *saved you*."
Lü Bu's wild eyes calmed.
"And I am still your vassal," Chen Deng said. "If I am Administrator of Guangling, then Guangling is deemed part of Xu, not Yang, and is yours. Where is the harm in that...? Is that not an improvement in your fortunes, lord and governor...?"
Lü Bu nodded silently.
"Now come," Chen Gui said kindly. "Let's go and prepare for a public announcement of your appointment as His Majesty's fourth-most important officer! Let's discuss which nobles will want to marry your daughter, who is now their equal in *legitimate imperial eyes*! Let us be glad that we avoided a terrible mistake."
Lü Bu calmed completely, and he smiled, saying, "Yes... let's."
Chen Gui and Chen Deng escorted Lü Bu into Xiapi, and Chen Yuanfang and his son Qun followed quietly: that left Chen Gong, Wang Kai and Xu Si standing alone and feeling increasingly powerless.
"This is bad," Xu Si said.
Chen Gong frowned and murmured, "Now, gentlemen, he only listens to *them*..."
"That cannot be," Wang Kai warned. "If our lord is forgiven, it will be because Cao Cao can use him, as every other lord likes to... but what about us? We stole Cao's province from him, we humiliated him... and as far as he's concerned, we turned a childhood friend against him."
Chen Gong exhaled fiercely and said, "I know, gentlemen... I know it all too well."
"For Mengzhuo alone, we'll die, and no doubt by the Five Pains," Xu Si suggested.
"Our lord must be turned again, back toward Yuan Shu if that's what is needed," Wang Kai urged.
"Alright, yes, we'll push him back toward the 'Wang Mang' again, but only because it is our only other option!" Chen Gong snapped; but after a moment, he sighed and said, "I... I will do what I can. We all of us must, gentlemen, if we want to survive. Our... our path is rocky, and littered with awful perils, but... the only other path leads to certain death."
Wang Kai and Xu Si agreed: the three men would endeavour to sway Lü Bu away from Cao Cao and back toward an enemy of the state, if only to save themselves.

****

73

Yuan Shu's reaction to learning that Lü Bu had betrayed him and sent his loyal adviser Han Yin to Cao Cao for disposal was irrepressible anger. He did not have the resources to attack Bu with his own forces alone, however, since he was also fighting Cao Cao and Sun Ce on two other fronts: he therefore contacted Yang Feng and Han Xian, the leaders of the White Wave Bandits, and asked them to attack Xu Province in exchange for rewards unspecified. Yang Feng and Han Xian were now enemies of the Han, having been chased away from Luoyang by Cao Cao: they therefore decided that they had no choice, so they marched to the Yang-Xu border with Yuan Shu's generals Zhang Xun, Liang Gang and Qiao Rui, and Jiujiang's Administrator Chen Ji, who was disgruntled at being used as a field officer after years of service in senior court roles. But times were difficult: he had no choice but to do as he was asked.

"Are we fools…?" Zhang Xun asked of Qiao Rui as they marched side-by-side at the head of Yuan Shu's army.

"For not deserting our lord and going south to work with Bofu, or for leading this attack against the 'Man among men' with an army of criminals as our main force…?" Qiao Rui retorted.

Zhang Xun smiled and said, "Forget that I even spoke."

"I am now going to be attacked by up to a million White Wave Bandits, and it is because of your suggestion to betray Yuan Shu's generous offer!" Lü Bu said as he glared at Chen Gui; the two were sat in the private audience room of the governor's residence, which was now a second home for Chen Gui.

"…Yuan Shu attacks us with help, yes," Chen Gui replied.

"Liu Bei has proved his uselessness yet again and retreated in the face of the army, serving as little more than advance warning as my enemies advance toward Xiapi!" Lü Bu continued. **"And your son has taken good men that I needed here and gone to Guangling to fight pirates! What good is that to me???"**

"My son had little choice," Chen Gui replied. "Neither did Liu Bei."

"It was following your advice that triggered this!" Lü Bu shrieked. **"Make another suggestion: what do I do???"**

"I'm surprised at your lack of clarity or calmness," Chen Gui said. "You're *Lü Bu*, not some common officer. You once fought *two million* Black Mountain Bandits and bested them, did you not…?"

"…There were never two million," Lü Bu sighed. "There were always a lot less… … …and that's *always the case*, isn't it…?"

Chen Gui smiled and said, "It is."

"I am being cowardly," Lü Bu decided. "But nonetheless, I am still facing over a hundred-thousand, I would have thought."

"At the most," Chen Gui said. "Yang Feng and Han Xian lead the bandits, and Zhang Xun commands the armies belonging to Yuan Shu. Yang and Han are not planners, and Zhang Xun is a mediocrity elevated by circumstance. An alliance of those three fools is akin to three chickens tied together at the neck: an ambling, shambling mess. My son Deng has already formulated a plan, and if we follow it, this army might reach Xiapi, but it will

not last long after that."
"Tell me everything," Lü Bu said excitedly.

When Yuan Shu's 'Zhong Dynasty Army' reached the Si River, they divided: Liang Gang and Chen Ji remained on the west bank of the Si River, while Commander Zhang Xun and General Qiao Rui crossed to the east bank with the White Wave Bandits and set up a more permanent camp in preparation for the final, fateful march against Xiapi. But on the night before the march, Han Xian entered Yang Feng's command tent and said, "You'll never guess what I just had given t'me, mate. A letter from *Lü Bu*!"
"What's it say...?" Yang Feng asked.
"It's a guilt trip, pretty much," Han Xian said. "He reminds us that we rescued the emperor from Li Jue and Guo Si, and that he killed Dong Zhuo. He says that we're all men that've tried to help the emperor before, but that we're helping a man that's committed high treason and heresy, and we should think again, like he has."
Yang Feng hummed thoughtfully.
"Yeah, I gotta admit, I don't know what to do either," Han Xian continued. "He's made a good point, mate: Yuan Shu's no more the emperor than either of us are, and siding with him only digs us deeper graves. Bu reckons he's 'General of the Left', and that if *he* can get back in the emperor's favour after personally raiding the imperial tombs for Dong Zhuo, then so can we, if we help him get rid of Yuan Shu."
"I never really thought about that," Yang Feng murmured. "He actually opened the imperial coffins and rooted around the bodies for treasure; what a-"
"I don't care," Han Xian interrupted. "He's got a point, and I reckon we should do as he says in this here letter and double-cross Zhang Xun when we reach Xiapi. But I won't do it without you, 'cause we're mates and co-leaders, and all that."
"They're *your* bandits," Yang Feng chuckled. "My lot's a few hundred at the most, isn't it...? But yeah, I agree, we shouldn't stay with Yuan Shu. What's the plan...?"

Han Xian, Yang Feng and Zhang Xun marched on Xiapi once dawn broke the next morning. Zhang Xun had his campaign subordinate Qiao Rui ready a ram for destroying the southern gates while forces led by Han Xian and Yang Feng surrounded the city and went through the motions of attacking the other gates. Lü Bu and Chen Gui watched the scene from the White Gate Tower, an elaborate reinforced observation post above the southern gates of Xiapi City.
"Chen Gong, Wei Xu, Zhang Liao, Cao Xing, Hou Cheng and Gao Shun are ready," Chen Gui reported. "Once Han Xian and Yang Feng show their true intent, we'll rush out and finish Zhang Xun."
"And if their true intent is to destroy me, Mister Chen...?" Lü Bu asked snidely.
"They have already signalled that they are going to help us, my lord, by congregating around the other three gates and doing next to nothing but shout and throw small rocks," Chen Gui replied. "We have our allies... so now, we wait."
        Zhang Xun was about to deploy his siege ladders against the southern walls of Xiapi when Qiao Rui ran toward him, crying,

"**Betrayal, Zhang Xun!**"
"Betrayal…?" Zhang Xun exclaimed. "Who's- …**What???**"
The White Wave Bandits surged on Zhang Xun's position and overwhelmed his smaller army: Zhang Xun retreated, and Qiao Rui surrendered after holding back the White Wave Bandits for his friend and commander.
"There wasn't even much of a fight," Lü Bu complained as he watched from the White Gate Tower.
"Be thankful for that," Chen Gui retorted. "Yuan Shu's main army is divided between defending Shouchun and attacking Chen County, but it is still formidable enough. Liang Gang and Chen Ji are on the west bank of the Si with a substantial combined force of thousands, so we should chase them and rout them before they get any ideas about regrouping."
Lü Bu agreed, and he descended from the walls with his advisers.
Lü Bu confronted the surrendered Qiao Rui outside the city and said, "Are you proud of your achievements here today?"
"Just get it over with," Qiao Rui retorted. "I'm just sad that I lost to treacherous bandits, rather than in a battle against a hero like yourself or Sun Ce of Fuchun. But such is life, General. Kill me and be done with it."
"…We'll take him with us to the border, and release him when Yuan Shu's army is repelled," Lü Bu decided.
"Are you keeping your options open again?" Chen Gui sighed.
"A man like Qiao Rui deserves to die in a proper battle!" Lü Bu retorted. "We march west at once!"
"What about us?" Han Xian asked as he gestured toward his friend Yang Feng.
Lü Bu looked at the mass of White Wave Bandits and said, "You'll both be promoted, as I promised, and you'll keep whatever you take off the enemy."
"Yeah, fine, but do you want our help chasing Yuan Shu back to Yang Province?" Han Xian asked impatiently.
"Of course," Lü Bu replied. "We'll tear them apart!"
The coalition of Lü Bu's forces and the White Wave Bandits descended on Zhang Xun's retreating men with unyielding, merciless force; locals might have been forgiven for thinking that Cao Cao had returned, since the river was soon littered with the drifting bodies of the soldiers that ended up in the river in one way or another. Lü Bu cried out in triumph and ordered a pursuit, but Chen Gong was able to persuade him to wait until the enemy had left the western bank and began a full retreat to the border.

Zhang Xun, Liang Gang and Chen Ji regrouped on the west bank of the Si River and made the decision to go back to Yang Province. When they were half a day away from relative safety, Lü Bu and the bandits attacked again: men were strewn across the landscape as the 'Man among men' vented his frustrations and demonstrated his ability as a warrior and commander. A far smaller army returned to Yang Province than had left it; the three generals were relieved at having escaped, but that sense of relief did not last for very long. Lü Bu was not done: he charged into Yang Province with his allies and looted the inhabited regions on the path that led to Shouchun.
"What do we do?" Zhang Xun said to his campaign adviser, Yuan

Yin. "Your family has the most to lose if we fail, so suggest something!"

The thin, frail Yuan Yin frowned and said, "Lü Bu is slowing now. I suspect that he might withdraw once his bandit friends start to lose interest, since he will suddenly find himself at a disadvantage against us without them. We should go back to His Majesty and help him to reinforce Shouchun County."

"So… so if the bandits get their share of spoils, they might go home?" Liang Gang said. "What then? Do we turn about and attack Bu?"

"I wouldn't suggest it, General," Yuan Yin replied. "Let's just remain on the move."

The three generals agreed, and they continued their retreat.

Lü Bu, Han Xian and Yang Feng continued their march west toward Shouchun by land, although many of the White Wave Bandits seized boats from local fishermen and sailed down the Huai River, stopping only to loot riverside settlements. Zhang Xun's force retreated slowly and gradually until they were at the eastern border of Shouchun County. Bit by bit, northeast Jiujiang fell to the White Wave Bandits and Lü Bu's uncontained bloodlust: and then, just as victory against Yuan Shu seemed to be guaranteed, the White Wave Bandits started to slow.

"Why are your people turning and going back to Xu Province?" Lü Bu asked of the irreverent Han Xian.

"We're bandits, not soldiers," Han Xian chuckled. "Well, I prefer 'Rebels', but because we tend to steal from Han collaborators a lot, and they're seen as 'the innocent', we're seen as bandits and that's that, really, so-"

"I don't care what you want to call yourselves!" Lü Bu barked. **"Why are your people leaving the front???"**

"Hey, listen, Bu, we don't care about the Han empire," Han Xian said angrily. "They won't forgive us, and to be honest, we don't care if they do or not. Before the White Waves, we were Yellow Turbans… remember them?"

Lü Bu grunted.

"That's right… people that were fed up with the Han, and we still are," Han Xian continued. "We were left to starve, taxed to death, insulted and spat on by the fortunate few… and we had enough. Why should we fight to go back to that…?"

Lü Bu loomed over the smaller Han Xian and said, "You're going back to Yuan Shu's side, then, are you? You're sending men back to my province to-!"

"No, we're not siding with anyone," Han Xian said with a sigh. "That's all it is with you lot, isn't it…? Sides, factions, wars… who's at the top, who's at the bottom… we don't care. You promised we could settle in Xu, so we have. You promised us that we'd keep whatever we got from the campaign, and the situation is this: my men follow me, yeah, but only so far. We're a cooperative, see… a confederacy. Each little 'battalion' is a load o' people, usually form the same village or something, and they all follow me. The Black Mountain lot are set up in the same way. I ask my boys and girls to do something, and they either do it or they don't, see. The ones that're going back to Xu are either bored, tired or carrying so much stolen stuff that they can't carry any more. Do you see…?"

Lü Bu eyed Chen Gong and said, "Yes, Mister Han... I 'see'."
"Good, 'cause I'm getting fed up as well, to be honest," Han Xian continued. "Yuan Shu's holed up in Shouchun with his best men now, and that's a fight that'll cost lives... we started this to live, not die. Yuan Shu isn't an enemy of ours, nor is he a friend... do you see...?"
Lü Bu glared at Han Xian and said, "I get it. I'll go on alone, then."
"You can if you want," Han Xian chuckled as he turned to walk away. "I'm not your keeper, 'Fengxian': if your masters in Xuchang want you to go on, that's that."
Lü Bu shuddered angrily until Chen Gong stepped between him and the retreating Han Xian and said, "I'd advise a clever withdrawal from Yang Province now."
"I... always entertained the idea," Lü Bu replied. "We'll... release Qiao Rui, and then we'll go back to Xiapi. But I want one last laugh at Yuan Shu's expense first."
"If that helps," Chen Gong sighed, as it did nothing to help his own cause.

Yuan Shu was alarmed when a humbled Qiao Rui entered his Shouchun court and fell to one knee before him.
"...We heard that you were captured," Yuan Shu said as he stared at Qiao Rui.
"Lü Bu, in a show of mercy, spared my worthless life!" Qiao Rui replied as he held a letter aloft. "He gave me this to present to you, Your Majesty!"
Yuan Shu did not wait for any of his vassals to collect the letter from Qiao Rui: he got up from his throne and took it from the man's hand personally.
"Well...?" the adviser Yan Xiang asked as Yuan Shu started reading and became increasingly angry at a rapid pace.
"...**I'll tear his throat out!**" Yuan Shu cried. "**I'll rip his entrails out and dance on them, the wretched...!**"
Yuan Shu threw the letter to the ground and retreated to his private chambers; after a few tense moments, Yan Xiang picked up the letter and started to read.
"...What does it say?" the official Yuan Huan asked.
"Not here," Yan Xiang replied as he followed Yuan Shu.
"*Aiee*... Lü Bu deserves death," Yuan Huan grumbled as he followed Yan Xiang.
"He called me a rat!" Yuan Shu whined as Yan Xiang approached his host seat and took a subordinate seat at his side.
"Yes, *Your Majesty*," Yan Xiang sighed.
"I, we, all the same right now, I am too angry to care!" Yuan Shu continued. "He taunts me, when I offered him power! How dare he call me *inconstant*! What, then, is that wretch??? Is there a word for *his* nature if *I* am inconstant???"
"He's provoking you, but his words are petty and empty," Yan Xiang suggested. "He calls you a coward and a rat; he claims that he has 'dominated the Huai River region'; and yes, he calls you a liar... but they are all empty words, and flagrant hypocrisy too. He's bragging about turning the White Wave Bandits against you; that was never difficult. He's fallen for division ruses often enough himself: what happened with Ding Yuan...?"
Yuan Shu nodded silently.

"You want to challenge him, don't you?" Yuan Huan supposed.

"He urges me to meet him at the river," Yuan Shu replied. "He says, 'I am still close and await your reply to this letter'; how can I ignore it after he called me a coward and accused me of being 'trapped in Shouchun and unable to come out'? It will make a mockery of me!"

"Then march, and defeat him," Yan Xiang said. "I suspect that he is putting on a show of strength, however, so do not expect too much, Your Majesty."

Yuan Shu smiled icily and replied, "He had better not leave his neck exposed, Yan Xiang, or he'll know my blade across it; I promise you that. We march at once!"

Yuan Shu gathered 5,000 men and placed Qiao Rui and Ji Ling at the front for the march to the Huai River. Yuan marched in person: he was astride a white horse, robed in silk garments and wearing gilded battle armour in an attempt to affirm his self-appointed status as an emperor. Flag-bearers carried Yuan Shu's new 'Zhong Dynasty' insignia to add to the illusion of majesty; Yan Xiang rode at his side, but the weary adviser was certain that there would be no battle. Yan Xiang was proved correct: when Yuan Shu's men reached the south bank of the Huai River, they were greeted by the sight of Lü Bu's men on the northern bank, heckling and laughing.

"**Bastard!**" Yuan Shu exclaimed as he caught sight of the grinning Lü Bu. "**We must go the nearest ford at once and cross!**"

"What has he achieved?" Yan Xiang asked. "Calm yourself!"

"**I want to cross!**" Yuan Shu cried. "**I want to cross and-!**"

"Leave him," Yan Xiang said. "His bandit allies have obviously gone, and he will soon withdraw. Let him laugh: he'll not be alive this time next year."

Lü Bu turned his horse and began a slow retreat from the riverbank while his archers waited with arrows nocked and ready to fire: Yuan Shu smirked, turned to face his men, and said, "**He's no hero... let him laugh!**"

Yuan Shu's men heckled Lü Bu's dwindling presence on the northern bank, but there would be no more bloodshed. Lü Bu returned to Xiapi, and his bandit allies settled in his province, much to the irritation of the local people. Despite their cordial relations in recent times, Yuan Shu and Lü Bu were now bitter enemies, and that seemed to be an irreversible situation: but this was a time of chaos, and nothing was certain while clever, manipulative men had their own agendas.

****

74

As the weeks passed, Cao Cao's armies in Chen County started to gain ground and Cao Cao prepared to march against the pretender's army in person. Yuan Shu left the humiliated Chen Ji and Zhang Xun in Shouchun and took Ji Ling, Liang Gang and Qiao Rui northwest to Chen County – which was in the east of Yu Province and close to the Yuan ancestral home of Ru County – to bolster the force led by Generals Li Feng and Yue Jiu. The reinforcements gave Yuan Shu an initial change in fortunes, but when word reached his soldiers that Cao Cao, Yu Jin, Yue Jin, Xiahou Dun, Cao Ren, Cao Xiu, Cao Hong, Xu Huang and the fearsome Xu Chu were on their way with a force of 50,000, the mood changed.

"…How many deserters…?" Yuan Shu asked weakly.

Ji Ling bowed before his master and said, "Hundreds at the *most*, Your Majesty."

"I cannot afford to lose any more men!" Yuan Shu cried. **"Sun Ce has turned on me; Lei Bo and Chen Lan have gone; Zhang Xun has lost his nerve; Han Yin is dead; and Lü Bu… that wretch cost me the White Wave Bandits! The Runan Turbans don't want to fight Cao Cao, the Black Mountain Bandits are stuck fighting my accursed brother…! Who else can I lose, Ji Ling??? Who else???"**

"What are you going to do, Your Majesty?" Yuan Huan asked.

"I… must reinforce Shouchun," Yuan Shu decided. "To survive, I must accept that life is about victories and defeats… there is no sense in wasting my energy trying to gain Chen County, only to lose Shouchun! I must go now… I must go immediately!"

"So we should order a full retreat?" Yuan Huan supposed.

"Cao Cao will guess my plan," Yuan Shu replied. "Ji Ling, you will support my withdrawal to Shouchun: there is no need for the others to be aware of things, else there might be panic. We can go back there and formulate another plan to deal with Cao Cao and secure Chen County."

"…We're leaving the others to die," Ji Ling protested. "We mustn't do that, Your Majesty. We need every good man that we can-"

"Right now, only one thing matters: the emperor must survive!" Yuan Shu shrieked. **"Do as I say, General Ji, and prepare for my return to Shouchun!"**

Ji Ling bowed and replied, "As you command, Your Majesty."

Yuan Shu slipped away from Chen County, leaving Liang Gang, Qiao Rui, Li Feng and Yue Jiu to face Cao Cao and his army. The four generals did not realise that their commander and emperor was gone until Liang Gang tried to deliver a report to the command tent: he took the news to his horrified comrades and tried to start a discussion about what they should do.

"Flee!" Li Feng said. "That's the only option we have! Cao Cao will outnumber us by at least two-to-one! If we stay here now, we'll be destroyed!"

"His Majesty must have left instructions for us," Qiao Rui said. "It must be that some fool adviser forgot to issue them, or maybe Ji Ling will return."

"Or perhaps we were meant to know that we should follow once

His Majesty was safe in Shouchun, for that's the only place that he would go," Liang Gang suggested. "We should begin our own withdrawal, and join him there. What do you think, Yue Jiu?"
"I don't know," Yue Jiu replied honestly. "I've been here with Li Feng, fighting these men that still serve the Han Emperor, and... I don't know. Perhaps we were abandoned here, gentlemen."
"I refuse to believe that!" Liang Gang barked. "We must see that His Majesty had to withdraw to the capital, and that it is our duty to survive and protect him! What sense would there be in abandoning us?"
"...To buy time?" Yue Jiu retorted.
"Enough," Liang Gang ordered. "We'll stand up to the enemy if they arrive before we can leave, but if we can go quickly, then go we should!"
"...Alright," Yue Jiu sighed.
The four generals began a retreat, but it was too late: Cao Cao's forces had arrived. The Excellency of Works allowed his giant bodyguard Xu Chu to take the field, and the result was terrifying: like Dian Wei before him, the mild-mannered man became a wild animal when faced with his master's enemies, and men lay broken in all directions as he killed them with savagery that was strangely devoid of malice. Qiao Rui tried to challenge Xu Chu, but he was smashed and left quite dead, and his men deserted at the sight of it. Yu Jin and Xiahou Dun took their own forces forward, and Yue Jiu was isolated and killed in the melee. Liang Gang's force was the farthest from the Chen County camp, so he urged his men to hurry on while the last of the living generals – Li Feng – did his best to escape and fight another day. But Li Feng did nothing more than give Liang Gang more time: he was caught in a pincer by Cao Cao's forces and slain.
        "A fine victory," Cao Cao said as he inspected the remains of Yuan Shu's camp. "I have eliminated three more of the pretender's wicked henchmen, and broken his northern advance! All that remains now is to press forward and take Shouchun!"
"That is true," Guo Jia replied.
"...Am I forgetting anything...?" Cao Cao asked.
"If you were, I would tell you," Guo Jia replied. "Yuan Shu is not a difficult foe."
"Surprisingly not," Cao Cao chuckled. "For a man that dared to consider himself as a mandated Son of Heaven, he is quite ineffective and weak!"
"His might came from Sun Ce of Fuchun and little else," Guo Jia suggested. "Now that his southern tiger works against him, he's a dead man. We should press forward and eliminate him quickly, before the other warlords start to fidget."
"...That's a very kind way of putting it," Cao Cao said. "My 'coalition' consists of Sun Ce and Lü Bu, really... I had hoped that Zhang Yang might join us, but he went back to Henei as soon as the palace was rebuilt."
"Yes, I noticed that," Guo Jia sighed. "I hope he doesn't decide to help his old colleague Lü Bu when the time comes to rid ourselves of the man... it would be a waste of a fine statesman. But let us stay in the present! We must advance at once, Excellency, and give the man no breathing space. We must not allow either Sun Ce or Lü Bu to be the man that destroys the pretender, either, or

whoever does the deed will expect northern Yang as a reward."
"Oh, yes, of course!" Cao Cao gasped. "We should continue our march immediately!"

Liang Gang sent word to Shouchun that Cao Cao was on his way: he was dead by the time that the messenger arrived.
"...Four fine men... gone," Yuan Shu said as he allowed the letter to fall from his hand. "So now, I have... Ji Ling, Zhang Xun, Chen Ji, Hui Qu and Liu Xun."
"Lujiang Administrator Liu Xun is under attack by the Suns, and it isn't going well," the adviser Yuan Huan reported. "The Shanyue can only keep Sun Ce and Wu Jing distracted: Sun Ben is in Lujiang, and there are fears that we may-"
"**NO!**" Yuan Shu barked. "**I won't-!** ...I won't hear it. I won't hear that word. We will not lose Lujiang. We cannot afford to. Liu Xun will not fail me."
A youth of average stature stepped forward, coughed nervously, and said, "Father, perhaps we should negotiate with Sun Ce."
Yuan Shu turned to his son Yao and said, "That is not an option. And as my crown prince I expected more. This is your future that I'm protecting, your *empire*!"
"Forgive me, but we should discuss how we will defend Shouchun," the adviser Yan Xiang said. "Now that we are on this path, we must follow it to its conclusion. Administrator Chen, General Ji and General Zhang should begin a plan of increased fortification immediately."
"I will go to the border at once," Administrator Chen Ji declared.
"...I'd be alright if not for Lü Bu," Yuan Shu mumbled. "Damn that... *that*...!"

While Yuan Shu and his followers did what they could to defend against the onslaught by Cao Cao's imperial army, Liu Bei was beginning to tire of the White Wave Bandits' presence in Xu Province and summoned Mi Zhu, Mi Fang, Mister Sun, Jian Yong, Guan Yu and Zhang Fei to discuss it.
"Day after day, I get complaints from the residents of Xiaopei that these cruel and heartless bandits are pillaging their supplies and taking women for wives against their will," Liu Bei said to his assembled vassals. "Lü Bu does nothing, of course, because they are his friends..."
"Yang Feng once served Dong Zhuo as well," Mister Sun recalled. "The other one, Han Xian, is a Yellow Turban leader from the first uprising, isn't he?"
"Whether he is or he isn't, the problem is the same," Mi Zhu suggested. "Now, we must come up with a solution to that problem. What do we do about them?"
"I say that we round up their leaders and kill them," Zhang Fei said. "That lot don't understand anything but violence, and without leaders, they'll break up and go away, hopefully back to wherever it is that they came from."
The declaration was met with silence.
"...I'll shut up," Zhang Fei grumbled. "But before I do, I'll say this: stop inviting me to meetings if you don't want to hear what I have to s-!"
"No, no, you're right, Yide," Liu Bei said. "You're right, if only this

once; we must treat them as we treated the Yellow Turbans! Every defiant Yellow Turban that was treated kindly has since risen up again and needed to be put down by force, just as they should have been in the first place. And the White Wave Bandits are merely a breakaway group of former Yellow Turbans, so they should be treated in exactly the same way!"

"Sadly, I agree," Guan Yu said. "The good people have long since returned to their lives: whoever is left as part of these anarchist armies is no disgruntled civilian, they're just a thief or some other type of criminal."

Jian Yong yawned theatrically and said, "That didn't take long. Who gets the job of fighting them and arresting their leaders...? How many of them are there again...?"

"...*Aiee*... there is that, though," Liu Bei groaned. "They number in the tens of thousands..."

"But are they all in one place...?" Mi Zhu asked.

"They're spread all over the province, like a plague of rats," Mister Sun grumbled.

"But here in Xiaopei, we have both main leaders – no doubt here on Bu's instruction, looking for an opening to kill us for him – and only... I don't know... ten thousand proper bandits...?" Mi Zhu suggested. "The rest are the bandits' families. If we struck quickly, we could get both of them."

"I'll go after Yang Feng," Guan Yu declared. "Zhang Yide can go after Han Xian."

"Mi Fang will go with you," Liu Bei replied. "Mi Zhu and Mister Sun will accompany Yide, and I will remain here with Jian Yong."

"Why do I get two pedants and Yunchang only gets one?" Zhang Fei complained.

"Because you're twice as likely to do something stupid," Liu Bei retorted. "In Yunchang's case, I send Mi Fang to liaise with the other bandits if needs be and use his local influence for our benefit. In your case, Mi Zhu will do the same, and both will keep you from-"

"**Alright, alright!**" Zhang Fei cried. "Can I not go and smash this Han Xian now?"

"Apprehend him, Yide," Guan Yu said. "We want him alive so that he can be tried properly."

Zhang Fei smiled and said, "So long as that's fine by him, it's fine by me."

"Maybe Chen Dao should go, instead of Yide," Liu Bei fretted.

"I'm *joking*, Xuande!" Zhang Fei sighed. "Let's go."

Two days later, Han Xian and Yang Feng were brought before Liu Bei's court in Xiaopei.

"**Cowards!**" Han Xian heckled. "**Lousy government toadies! You should be ashamed of yourself!**"

"**Bei's related to the bloody emperor!**" Yang Feng snapped. "**Did you expect him to be anything else but a-!**"

"Be quiet, the pair of you," Liu Bei ordered. "You know why you're here, but I'll tell you anyway."

"**Yeah, love the sound of your own stupid voice!**" Han Xian heckled. "**I hope you and your emperor both-!**"

"**SHUT UP!**" Zhang Fei shrieked as he pressed his sword-blade to Han Xian's throat.

"...I pity you both," Liu Bei sighed. "Yang Feng, you once escorted the Son of Heaven from Chang'an to Luoyang...what happened...? Why did you stray...?"

"Get on with it," Yang Feng replied.

"And you, Han Xian... I need ask nothing," Liu Bei said with theatrical disdain. "You've been a thorn in the Han's side for over ten years now... hounding the noblest in society as they tried to go about their business..."

"I robbed rich bastards as they waddled in and out of the capital with their ill-gotten gains," Han Xian retorted. "What made one or two rich folks smile a bit for a few days kept thousands from starving and dying for months. I never killed none of 'em, and they had plenty more wealth than what we took: I was defending the poor, and you're defending corruption, murder and them bloody eunuchs that-!"

"Silence," Liu Bei ordered.

"**No, I won't be silent!**" Han Xian barked. "I'm dead now, whatever I say, so I'll say what I want to say! You're gonna drag me out of here an' execute me now, even if I cried and said I was sorry! This isn't a court: it's a play, with all the words already planned out! I'll tell you this: the Han are done. I may not be that religious if I'm honest with myself, but one thing that Zhang Jue said was right; the day's coming when all you lot get what's coming to you, and everyone gets a little yellow above their head, not just one little pampered, greedy, useless bastard in a palace! 'Yellow Sky', Liu Bei: one day, you'll all be dead, and the people will be free! It's only a matter of time!"

"...Your last words were poorly chosen," Liu Bei replied. "**Guards-**"

"Wait," Yang Feng said. "I have something to say as well. Yes, I helped the emperor. I saved him from Li Jue and Guo Si, after having felt guilty for ages that I didn't save him from Dong Zhuo. And I was proud – really, genuinely proud – of what I'd done. And then I *met him*."

Han Xian cackled maniacally.

"**DEATH TO YOU BOTH!**" Liu Bei shrieked. "**GUARDS! GUARDS! DEATH! DEATH! DEATH!**"

Four soldiers dragged the two White Wave Bandit leaders out the courtroom: both were laughing and screaming 'Yellow Sky!' at Liu Bei and his allies, but neither appeared to be afraid of what awaited them.

"...Death... to the *pair of you*...!" Liu Bei sobbed.

"Good riddance," Mister Sun grumbled. "They do not speak for the majority, Lord Liu!"

"They spoke for a *million people*," Jian Yong suggested. "Zhang Jue had *two million followers*. The Black Mountain Bandits-"

"Confused, angry *idiots*!" Liu Bei insisted. "Their way did no good! It only led to peasants looting peasants! Who here in Xu Province deserved to be pillaged, mm...? Who in Xu Province deserved those wretched bandits coming here and stealing from them? Little old men having their turbans stolen, and women being snatched... but where were the 'waddling wealthy' among them...? All that nonsense about 'helping the poor'... they helped *themselves*, as criminals always do! They were fighting for *Yuan Shu*! What does *he* want?"

"Firstly, I was just messing about, which I apologise for," Jian

Yong said. "Secondly, they're *dead now*, Xuande, and we have a few more leaders in custody that'll ensure that they all leave this province in a matter of days. It's over."
"…But the Han's still endangered, Xianhe," Liu Bei said. "Yes, I can kill a few criminals… but can I save the Han…?"

Liu Bei's friend Kong Rong was surprised by the arrival in Xuchang of a 25-year-old man named Mi Heng; Kong invited the younger scholar from Qing Province to his home and treated him as an honoured guest.
"You live well here in 'the capital'," Mi Heng said as Kong Rong's servants brought more tea and food to the two-person banquet in Kong's living quarters.
"I was a little doubtful of Cao Cao at first, but Wang Lang's made me see that I have to wait and watch," Kong Rong replied. "…Ah, to see you here, Zhengping!"
"It is good to see you again," Mi Heng said. "For us to be here like this is like Confucius reuniting with Yan Yuan."
"You're my friend, not my student!" Kong Rong chuckled.
"But you're older than me by a whole twenty years, which is enough for the comparison, Wenju," Mi Heng retorted.
"*Aiee*… don't remind me of my age!" Kong Rong sighed. "You're as tactless as ever, Zhengping. But wait; why are you here…?"
"Yuan Tan's a talentless brute, but Heaven's being mischievous again and given him an advantage over Tian Kai," Mi Heng scoffed. "I left Pingyuan before I ended up in some terrible and inappropriate situation."
"…His Majesty would benefit from your presence in court," Kong Rong decided. "Excellency Cao's on campaign against the heretic Yuan Shu at the moment, but when he returns I shall write to him and recommend you for service."
"Thank you, Wenju; I shall relish working for a deranged murderer like 'Excellency Cao'!" Mi Heng chortled.
"…If you're here, you might as well be doing something," Kong Rong replied. "But please, do not be so frank; Cheng Yu might get away with it, but others do not."
"I'll speak my mind, as all intellectuals should be able to do," Mi Heng retorted. "I thought Cao Cao and Yuan Shao once protected men like us."
"…Times and situations change," Kong Rong said. "Watch your words, Zhengping."
Mi Heng smirked; he had no intention of being careful at all, and that would be his undoing.

****

75

The deaths of Han Xian and Yang Feng – and the subsequent, inevitable collapse of the White Wave Bandit presence in Xu Province – were reported to the provincial governor Lü Bu within a few days.

"Liu Bei sent their heads to Xuchang," Chen Gong reported to Lü Bu's court.

"Liu Bei had no right to do that," Lü Bu growled. "I made a deal with them!"

"Actually… he did us a favour," Gao Shun suggested. "My lord, they were treating the local people very badly, and it was causing anger. If they'd been allowed to stay, you would have become very, very unpopular. Now, he's done what you could not for fear of looking like you'd broken your promises. You have an excuse to rid yourself of Liu Bei at a later date, and you're rid of an unwanted problem."

Chen Gong, Wang Kai and Xu Si glared at Gao Shun, but they did not put their self-serving feelings into words.

"Don't make me regret giving you your commission back, Gao Shun," Lü Bu said. "This is not a case of 'All is well, he did me a favour'! They were my allies against attacks by Yuan Shu, and maybe-!"

"Yuan Shu has been pushed into a corner," Chen Qun reported. "My 'observers' tell me that Cao Cao's army has killed Qiao Rui, Yue Jiu, Liang Gang, Li Feng and Chen Ji: Lei Bo and Chen Lan have left his service, and Sun Ce is on the verge of breaking Liu Xun in Liujiang. He won't attack you, my lord… he can't."

"And thank goodness that you didn't go through with that marriage, my lord!" Chen Gui chuckled. "If you had, where would you be then…?"

Lü Bu eyed his courtiers with seething mistrust as he replied, "Indeed, yes, Mister Chen… where would I be then…?"

"Like Yuan Shu, you'd be isolated!" Chen Gui continued. "You'd-"

"**On the other hand, perhaps I'd be father to a future empress!**" Lü Bu shouted angrily. "**Yuan Shu is only isolated because he lost the White Wave Bandits and me: *I* wonder, Mister Chen, what would have happened if I had not listened to YOU – for I think, Mister Chen, that *I* am isolated now!**"

The courtiers were silent as Lü Bu got up and left them: he was wavering yet again. Chen Gong, Wang Kai and Xu Si seized the opportunity and followed their lord immediately, and Gao Shun followed after a long pause for thought; Chen Qun turned to Chen Gui and said, "I shall write at once."

Chen Gui nodded silently; Chen Qun fled the court at the first available opportunity and had news of Lü Bu's state of mind sent to Cao Cao's court in Xuchang.

"Liu Bei… *Liu Bei*…!" Lü Bu growled as he paced back and forth in his private office.

"Shall I summon the Chens?" Gao Shun asked.

"Leave them, I'm not sure if I trust them," Lü Bu replied. "…But Liu Bei… oh, I'm sure about him… I want him watched more closely. He didn't kill Han Xian and Yang Feng for looting: he killed them to weaken me, and he did not just do that for himself! He is either working with Yuan Shu or Cao Cao, and I need to know which! Oh, I know what you're thinking... 'Yuan Shu? But Liu Bei is related to the emperor!' The Yuans don't do badly for killing each other, and princes have warred before. If he's working for Cao Cao, then I must rethink the situation."

"You... you don't mean that you intend to re-establish communications with Yuan Shu, do you...?" Gao Shun asked disbelievingly. "You... you wouldn't, my lord... you wouldn't, not when he is no close to destruction...!"

"And the Han Emperor isn't close to destruction...?" Lü Bu retorted. "I'll hear no more arguments... I'll be my own counsel."

Gao Shun bowed and said, "I'll have more men placed to watch Liu Bei at once."

Once Gao Shun was gone, Chen Gong asked, "My lord, what will you do...?"

"Get out, all of you," Lü Bu replied. "I want to think, and I can't do that with you all hovering around me like moths and telling me what to think."

Chen Gong sighed, bowed, and withdrew; Wang Kai and Xu Si were standing and staring at their lord, but they retreated as well when he growled at them.

"...To where do I turn...?" Lü Bu wondered. "...To *where*...?"

That night, Lü Bu wrote to his old friend the Grand Marshal Zhang Yang, Administrator of Henei for a possible answer.

Elsewhere, in the bandit-controlled Kaiyang County, the leader of the Mount Tai Bandits, Zang Ba, pondered recent events carefully with his friend and rival chieftain Sun Guan.

"...I really want to get back to my own territory, Xuangao," Sun Guan admitted.

"Look, I know that we're all bigger men than we were, with our own little 'fiefs' and all that, but if we don't think as one, it'll all end badly for us," Zang Ba replied. "Word is that Liu Bei's killed Han Xian and Yang Feng: fine, we didn't want the White Waves encroaching on our territory anyway, which they might've done, and a lot of 'em that don't want to go home to Central Province might join us. But if Bei starts on us next, what then...? We don't know what 'General of the Left' will do either; we've not got anything clear in writing, really, that says we're all friends, do we...? He probably hates us for not helping him against Yuan Shu."

"...I see your point," Sun Guan admitted. "What are you thinking of doing...?"

"At some point, Bu might be asked to attack Yuan Shu, and I say that we help him," Zang Ba replied. "On the other hand, he might be attacked, either by Yuan Shu or the government, and in that case we help him as well."

"...What, even if he's attacked by the government...?" Sun Guan chortled. "That's-!"

"We're *bandits*," Zang Ba retorted. "We're not county magistrates, we're bandits, and bandits are not getting a very good time amid all this, Zhongtai."

"...Okay, fine, we'll put our lots in with Bu," Sun Guan conceded.

"We have the option to abandon him any time we like," Zang Ba added. "If Cao Cao offers us a better deal, we'll hear him out. The only one I won't listen to is Yuan Shu, 'cause he's a dead man now, and only a fool would help him."

"...The same *could* be said of Bu," Sun Guan chuckled.

Cao Cao might have been forced to break Yuan Shu, but that did not stop him trying to deal with more personal issues; Jing Governor Liu Biao received correspondence from the Excellency of Works that contained a plan and a warning.

"Gentlemen, here we have another unexpected and unwanted pain," Liu Biao said to his court in Xiangyang. "Just when we thought that we were safe! Sun Ce and Cao Cao are distracted by Yuan Shu; the Yellow Turbans are destroyed; the White Wave Bandits have migrated to Xu Province and no longer harass the border region; and last but not least, I have cordial relations with my unwanted guests, Zhang Xiu and Jia Xu. But oh, my friends, was there ever a chance of peace enduring...?"

"...What has happened?" General Cai Mao asked.

Liu Biao smiled dryly and replied, "What has happened, brother-in-law, is that I am being asked to either aid or ignore – in other words, do not impede in any way – another attack on Zhang Xiu."

"*Ayah*... Cao Cao must enjoy pain," the adviser Kuai Liang said. "Has he already marched...?"

"No; he's sent some low-level officers to harass Nan County, and does not intend to come back to Jing 'yet'," Liu Biao explained.

"Ah, I see," Kuai Liang chuckled. "Cao Cao is just trying to remind Zhang Xiu that the matter is not resolved; Cao will either march or make peace with Zhang later. In that case, we need not fret: even if the local defence forces put up a fight, Cao won't punish us for it. He has other plans."

"...I yearn for the simpler times," Liu Biao muttered.

"I wonder, Mister Kuai, if you might explain to us why there is word of an in-law of yours seeking work with *Sun Ce*...?" the politician Huan Jie asked suddenly.

"*Aiee*... I was hoping that this matter would not arise, but that was a fool's hope," Kuai Liang sighed.

"...Your *in-law*, Mister Kuai...?" Liu Biao prompted.

"Yes, Lord Liu: Zhuge Jin, son of the former administrator that fled here from Qing Province," Kuai Liang explained. "The-"

"Zhuge Jin... wasn't he that miserable, withdrawn man that looked a bit like a donkey...?" Liu Biao chuckled.

"He *did*, didn't he...?" the adviser, politician and scholar Wang Can said excitedly.

"Mister Zhuge Jin was refused work on account of his apparent mediocrity and lack of trustworthiness," Kuai Liang continued. "In desperation, he journeyed to Yang."

"So he is not a spy of yours, then...?" Huan Jie asked.

"No, Mister Huan, he is not," Kuai Liang replied. "And I doubt that Sun Ce will give him work either. He's so miserable and uninspiring that he'd probably be rejected even if he wasn't from Jing Province and connected to me."

"...So this is not worth discussing any further," Liu Biao supposed.

"No, Lord Liu, it is not," Kuai Liang replied. "He's probably already on his way back here to work on his family farm."

Liu Biao nodded and said, "Then we will instead focus on how we shall respond to anything that Zhang Xiu might do."

The minor warlord Zhang Xiu summoned his adviser Jia Xu to Wan City's administrator's residence and asked, "Was this part of your plan, Mister Jia? He's already-!"
"Cao Cao has sent a pitiful harassment force, *just as I said that he might*," Jia Xu interrupted. "It's of no concern; I've already ordered Huche'er to send out his best men to bolster the towns and villages. There is not one senior general among them at present: a 'Cai Yang' and a 'Wang Zhong', who are led in turn by a 'Che Zhou', who is a civilian administrator with little military experience to speak of."
"...But they are here to make a point, aren't they, Mister Jia...?" Zhang Xiu supposed.
"Oh yes, of course they are, but not the point that you might think," Jia Xu replied. "Word will reach the Qiang warlords that Cao Cao has not been humbled after all, so they will maintain their attacks on the regents and drive them to destruction. After that, we'll be asked to surrender again."
"And am I supposed to do such a thing?" Zhang Xiu growled.
"This time will be different," Jia Xu promised. "This time, he will bestow rank upon you and apologise for the past mistakes."
"What need would he have for such an approach, Mister Jia...?" Zhang Xiu asked.
"Look around, for the answers are everywhere," Jia Xu replied. "The enemies of the Han – and Cao's personal foes – are still there, and of them all, two must come before he can do anything to us: Yuan Shu and Lü Bu. He cannot do anything until both of those men are dead, and that means making some sort of peace with us."
"...I'd do it for the sake of my men, but his crime against my poor aunt still angers me," Zhang Xiu admitted.
"We cannot revolve our every action around revenging a single wronged person, Lord Zhang, no matter who they are," Jia Xu retorted. "So many thousands have been harmed that we must look to a long-term peace that benefits the many. The chaos in Xu Province that Cao Cao must now deal with is entirely derived from his inability to restrain his need to avenge his father."
"...Then whatever it takes to bring peace, I'll do it, for what you say is true," Zhang Xiu decided.
"Trust me, my lord," Jia Xu said. "His next target after Yuan Shu will be Lü Bu."

Ding Yuan's former general and confidante, Grand Marshal and Henei Administrator Zhang Yang, had been enjoying a day of relatively simple work in his administrator's office when Lü Bu's letter arrived. Since finishing the reconstruction of the north and south palaces in Luoyang and returning to Henei, he had been partially reimbursed for his financial outlays while Emperor Xian had been in his care: as a result, things were going well.
"I heard that you got a letter from Bu," Zhang's general Sui Gu said as he entered his lord's office. "What does he want now? Not refuge again, I hope."
"He's still Governor of Xu," Zhang Yang replied thoughtfully. "He isn't asking me if I want to join him there now, though; he's

asking me who he should side with in the 'War of the emperors'. He's risking my ignoring him just for calling it that."

"That's exactly what you should do, my lord," a third voice urged: it was Yang Chou, another of Zhang's generals. "Forgive my interruption, but I can't let you throw yourself into the fire for that lying, treacherous man anymore."

"I do agree with Yang Chou, I'm afraid," Sui Gu sighed. "He's trouble, and is best ignored and rebuked."

"Perhaps I'm too nice, but I can't do that," Zhang Yang replied. "I saw the potential in him as much as poor old Ding Yuan. I know that he's done awful things, but no man is perfect. I'll write back and tell him to stay with Cao Cao."

Yang Chou bowed silently and left the office.

"Learn to ignore Lü Bu, 'Grand Marshal Zhang'," Sui Gu suggested. "Don't let him be the death of you as well."

Zhang Yang pondered the point long after Sui Gu had gone, but he replied anyway.

＊＊＊＊＊＊＊＊＊＊＊＊

76

Months passed, and Yuan Shu held onto Shouchun County with everything and everyone that he had left. Yuan Shao remained aloof, but he made sure that spies would bring him immediate word of his brother's arrest or escape. The Governor of Xu Province, Lü Bu, watched Shouchun and Xiaopei very closely as he decided what to do: his advisers became increasingly anxious, especially when he started to consult his politically-inexperienced wife, Lady Yan, on matters instead of them.

It was only because of their individual spies in their master's household that Chen Gong and Chen Gui learned of the arrival of a letter from Yuan Shu. Neither man knew of the other's intentions, so when Chen Gong arranged to speak with Chen Gui, Wang Kai, Xu Si, Chen Yuanfang and Chen Qun about a matter of great urgency, Chen Gui could only feign surprise while the other Chens gasped at a genuine shock.

"What I cannot believe at all, gentlemen, is that it's the exact same nonsense again!" Chen Gong despaired. "Marriage alliances; cooperation; promises of great rewards; it was ridiculous enough before, but Yuan Shu is close to the end of his days! Shouchun County is pressed on all sides, and only Ji Ling and Zhang Xun remain to delay the inevitable now!"

"So do we confront him and dissuade him?" Chen Qun asked.

"We cannot, else he'll know I'm spying on him," Chen Gong replied. "We can only wait for the announcement and have our best arguments ready."

"But do we *want* to dissuade him?" Wang Kai asked. "Isn't the only other option Cao Cao, who intends goodness-knows-what?"

"*Think*, Wang Kai! If Yuan is close to death, then he is now a worse choice than Cao Cao!" Chen Gong replied. "We'd be backing a failed seditionist!"

"If Yuan Shu is truly finished, then that's quite right, Mister Wang," Xu Si conceded.

"...But we can do nothing for now," Chen Gong said. "Let's go our separate ways."

The other advisers agreed, and the meeting ended. But while Chen Gong, Wang Kai and Xu Si returned to their duties, the other three went to the home of Chen Gui to discuss the matter further.

"Sorry I 'kept you in the dark', so to speak," Chen Gui said to Chen Yuanfang and Chen Qun. "Chen Gong called the meeting before I could find a proper moment to tell you. Unfortunately for Chen Gong, his spy is not as well informed as mine; Bu's going to order Gao Shun to attack Liu Bei without telling us first."

"*Ayah*... that will be met with anger by the court," Chen Yuanfang sighed. "But what am I saying...? His attack will be carried out at *Yuan Shu's request*! That will be our doom!"

"*His* doom, gentlemen," Chen Gui said. "We're serving the imperial court. It is only his loyal vassals that will pay a price. Despite everything... I actually feel sorry for Liu Bei. Last time, Bu was lost in the moment, and Bei escaped relatively easily: Gao Shun is one of Bu's best generals, so Bei may well die."

"There's nothing we can do," Chen Qun suggested. "All that we can hope is that his vassals are uncharacteristically professional and competent when Gao Shun arrives."

"While I am here, I should say that you might be in danger now, Hanyu," Chen Yuanfang said. "You should leave Xiapi."

"Your son and I arranged that already," Chen Gui admitted. "I am Chancellor of Pei: I shall go and take up that post now that the court demands it."

Chen Yuanfang smiled and said, "Very good! Your son builds an army in Guangling, and you will be in Pei, far from harm: perfect."

"It is only 'perfect' because Bu will not listen to me anymore, which is regrettable," Chen Gui replied. "A final word: do not be too stubborn when I'm gone from here, gentlemen. Let the other fools advise him now; it's as good as over."

"Indeed," Chen Yuanfang sighed. "Indeed."

Gao Shun reached Xiaopei within ten days and launched yet another sudden, merciless attack on Liu Bei: once again, the first target was Bei's outlying camps and the civilian settlement, although Gao Shun was holding back against the latter. Guan Yu and Zhang Fei – who were, once again, Liu Bei's only generals – were too busy trying to protect the civilians of Xiaopei from Gao Shun's apparently indiscriminate strikes: the latter knew Liu Bei's priorities, so the ruse was intentional. Liu Bei was pushed into the settlement, and Gao Shun blocked him from being able to attack or retreat; another humiliating siege was inevitable.

"**WHY???**" Liu Bei screamed. "**O Heaven, hear me! O Heaven, just tell me what I have done, and I will apologise! Just please, stop doing this to me!**"

"Where are we going to do?" Jian Yong asked of Mi Zhu.

"We have only one option open to us... we must write to Xuchang," Mi Zhu replied.

"No," Zhang Fei whined. "No! Not Cao Cao again!"

"Yide, *please*... we have no choice," Liu Bei whimpered. "We must go to Cao Cao again. There is nobody else to turn to."

"What about Yuan Shao?" Jian Yong proposed yet again.

"He's the brother of the traitor!" Liu Bei chortled. "How can I turn to the brother of a man that declares the mandate of my clan exhausted, and my kinsman as an unworthy sovereign...?"

"**We can't go back to Cao Cao!**" Zhang Fei cried.

"It's Cao Cao, Yuan Shao, Yuan *Shu*, or giving ourselves over to Gao Shun for disposal!" Liu Bei retorted. "**What else is there???**"

Zhang Fei was silent.

"But... won't Cao Cao take Xu Province this time...?" Jian Yong asked worriedly. "Won't he want Xu as a reward for ridding the province of Lü Bu...?"

"The worst is his seizing it in the name of His Majesty," Mi Zhu replied. "He can't take it for himself now."

"Quite right," Liu Bei said. "Now let's say no more... and write to Xuchang at once."

"I wonder who he will send!" Zhang Fei asked dryly. "Maybe he'll send that man that chops people up and feeds them to the soldiers! That'd be right!"

Liu Bei sighed loudly and covered his head with his hands: he was distressed to the point of collapse, and his mind raced at the thought of a repeat of the siege of Haixi.

Liu Bei's messenger was given an immediate audience at the chancellery in Xuchang, but the report had to be given to Xun Gongda, since Cao Cao was attacking the outskirts of Shouchun County in Yang Province. It was immediately forwarded to the intended recipient by one of Cao Cao's own men: when the vocal report had been delivered, Cao Cao dismissed the young soldier, perused Liu Bei's letter and groaned irritably.

"Why do you lament?" Guo Jia asked.

"I don't need this, Fengxiao," Cao Cao replied. "Bu has acted altogether too quickly! I expected an attack on Bei, but...!"

"Yes, this is earlier than expected... and at Yuan Shu's request, without a doubt," Guo Jia supposed.

"Xuande presumes as much," Cao Cao said as he passed the letter to Guo Jia.

"...'Xuande'...?" Guo Jia noted nervously. "You actually see him as a friend?"

"Let's not waste time discussing that, Fengxiao," Cao Cao insisted. "Who do I send to relieve Xiaopei? I cannot let the place fall, but I need to keep everything I have here to destroy Yuan Shu once and for all!"

"...Send Xiahou Dun," Xun Wenruo suggested.

"Dun...?" Cao Cao chortled. "Dun is altogether the wrong man, surely...? He's easily provoked, he's-!"

"He fights with great vigour, and may be a contrast to Gao Shun," Xun Wenruo said.

"I don't agree, but we need everyone else to be guarding Yan or attacking Yang," Guo Jia admitted. "Give him enough men to repel Gao Shun's thousand, and he won't fail."

"...He'll have fifteen-hundred: that should be enough," Cao Cao decided. "I'll send Dun... but I am afraid, gentlemen. I hold him dear as any brother, son or nephew that I have. He must come back unharmed!"

"We can't guarantee that for anyone, anywhere," Guo Jia replied.

"...No," Cao Cao sighed as he thought of Ang, Anmin, Dian Wei, Wei Zi, Yuan Shao's cousin Yi and most of all, his father Cao Song. He laughed strangely and said, "Fate, gentlemen: fate. Send Xiahou Dun."

Yuan Shao was delighted when Tian Feng announced the arrival of the gifted scholar Cui Yan.

"Long have I heard of your great wisdom!" Yuan Shao chuckled as Cui Yan bowed before his Yè City court. "You're a local man, Mister Cui, but has this region enjoyed your presence much...?"

"As you'll probably know, Governor Yuan, I have been the victim of circumstance," Cui Yan replied. "I longed to visit my tutor, Zheng Xuan, and resume the studies that were so cruelly cut short by the Yellow Turban Rebellion, but instead I have wandered the eastern provinces. I have seen Qing, where bandits were rampant and crime lords held sway; I have seen Xu, where the deviant Ze Rong misused religion to build a utopia for himself and his followers while others went hungry; I have seen Yan, where bandits and tribes made lives a misery; I have seen Yu, now seen by some as the heartland of the Yellow Turbans despite your esteemed clan hailing from there. I have seen and still see much chaos, but no solutions."

"Your words will be heard, Mister Cui," Yuan Shao promised. "Please, enlighten me."

Guo Tu sneered as Cui Yan replied, "Once, Master Xun said, 'If soldiers are poorly disciplined, the army will be weak: it could not win, even if it was led by King Tang of Shang or King Wu of Zhou'. As I moved through Ji, I saw that the famine has hit some parts of your territory with such ferocity that even the soldiers are turning from their duties and becoming criminals that are no better than the Black Mountain Bandits. People cry out, 'Where is Governor Yuan? Why does he allow theft, robbery, looting and murder, and allow the dead to be left to rot at the roadside?'"

"I know of it, Mister Cui, but I cannot be everywhere," Yuan Shao sighed. "What must I do?"

Cui Yan smiled and said, "Order the prefectural and county officials to bury the dead with all haste; extend aid to areas that are worst hit by famine; ensure that poor officers are replaced; show your knowledge of the benevolent acts of King Wen of Zhou and the people will love you for the hero that you are."

Yuan Shao got to his feet and said, "It shall be done! Ju Shou, Tian Feng, Guo Tu, Pang Ji, Xun Chen, Chunyu Qiong: all of you, do as Master Cui says, and retire to write letters to the prefectures and counties! Master Cui, you shall henceforth be a 'Cavalry Commandant' and lend your genius to bringing order to my army! We will soon require such order to bring peace to Yòu Province!"

"I shall serve you in any way that I can, Lord Yuan," Cui Yan replied humbly.

"Though I dislike the insinuation that we've done nothing to solve anything, I'm relieved that a wise man is here to sway Lord Yuan on these matters," Ju Shou said to Tian Feng as the two left the meeting hall.

"...How long, I wonder, before he ignores Cui Yan as he so often ignores us," Tian Feng replied. "How long, I wonder, before he contemplates the journey to Xuchang..."

Liu Bei laughed inanely when Mi Zhu reported the arrival of Cao Cao's reinforcements: Gao Shun cautiously withdrew to his camp to the east of Xiaopei, and Liu Bei personally led the welcoming party that would thank the new arrivals.

"Don't thank me, Bei," Xiahou Dun growled as Liu Bei tried to grasp his hands.

Zhang Fei's eyes bulged angrily, and he shouted, "**What-!**"

"I'm here to save Xiaopei," Xiahou Dun continued. "I didn't come here for you: if it were Yellow Turbans, Yuan Shu or Lü Bu guarding it, I'd still be here, because that's what I've been ordered to do."

Xiahou Dun had walked straight into a rebuke without realising it: Guan Yu smiled coldly and said, "That explains the horrors that you inflicted on this province the last time that you were here, Xiahou Dun: I'm so glad to know that it was 'nothing personal', and I'm sure the victims' families would be too."

Zhang Fei grinned at the well-timed slight, but Liu Bei's other vassals were not so amused.

"**I'LL KILL YOU!**" Xiahou Dun shrieked as he tried to lunge at Guan Yu: he had to be restrained by his subordinate Han Hao and another officer. Xiahou Dun struggled to free himself and shouted,

"RELEASE ME, HAN HAO! I WILL KILL YOU GUAN YU!"

"You've not harmed enough people here already...?" Guan Yu taunted. "And Han Hao is the name of a subordinate of Wang Kuang, is it not...? Didn't a 'Han Hao' once try and *save* the emperor...? Why do you now aid a man that-?"

"Enough, Yunchang," Liu Bei pleaded.

"My understanding was that you and your master played no part in the Eastern Pass Coalition, Guan Yu," Han Hao said as calmly as he could.

"'Me and my master' also played no part in wreaking vicious, spiteful destruction here in Xu Province," Guan Yu retorted. "If your master was here when that happened, Han Hao... weren't you here as well...?"

"I'LL TEAR OUT YOUR THROAT!" Xiahou Dun screeched.

Han Hao exhaled fiercely and said, "Say no more, Guan Yu, or you'll do more harm to this province... because we'll leave."

"And disobey orders...?" Guan Yu snickered. "I doubt that."

Xiahou Dun's struggling intensified, but he had lost the ability to speak and had reverted to angry, feral cries.

"Please, Yunchang, stop it," Liu Bei said half-heartedly. "General Xiahou, Major Han, please array your men in front of Xiaopei, and we'll do all we can to repair our own camps and add our strength to your own. I, for one, am grateful for your presence here, but I am sure that the people of Xu are collectively relieved."

Some of Liu Bei's local recruits bore expressions that betrayed feelings that were closer to Guan Yu's harsh analysis: Han Hao nodded and replied, "Thank you."

As Han Hao dragged the crazed Xiahou Dun away, Liu Bei turned to Guan Yu and hissed, "It's usually Yide that does things like that! What's the matter with you???"

"It needed to be said," Guan Yu replied calmly. "They are not going to find warm smiles and grateful welcomes here, and Xiahou Dun's initial attitude was so utterly crass and inappropriate that he needed to be reminded of his own mistakes. How dare he come here and chastise a state-appointed governor! How dare he think that he can brazenly admit that he's his master's, and not the state's! How dare he, above all else, admit that he has no conscience about who he harms and, perhaps more importantly, who he helps!"

"Sad to say, Yunchang is right," Mister Sun said. "Xiahou Dun needed putting in his place, Xuande, even if it jeopardised our alliance with his master."

"...And it sheds new light on Cao Cao, too, in a way, I think," Mi Zhu suggested.

"I cannot pursue that thought process, gentlemen!" Liu Bei pleaded. "Let's say no more of our unfortunate introduction and concentrate on repelling Gao Shun, who will certainly be back within the week."

Liu Bei's vassals agreed, and they re-entered the fortified settlement to begin preparations for the military turnaround.

"...That was wonderful, Yunchang," Zhang Fei chuckled as he walked alongside the remorseless Guan Yu. "I wish I could do that to people."

"He had it coming,," Guan Yu replied tersely.

Liu Bei and Xiahou Dun worked as separately as they did collaboratively, and the tension between the two militias never really receded. But regardless, they were able to restore the functionality of some of Liu Bei's exterior defence works before Gao Shun – who had been sending scouts to ascertain the size of the reinforcement army – was ready to return with his small army and resume his assault.

In Jing Province's northern capital Xiangyang, Governor Liu Biao summoned his adviser Kuai Liang and said, "Sun Ce and his allies are on the verge of breaking Liu Xun, if these reports are to be believed. What should I do…?"

"We must stop toing and froing and have a clear path," Kuai Liang replied. "The Pangs and Kuais are united on the issue, and newer members of your court, such as Huan Jie and Wang Can, also agree: you must ignore our unwanted tenant in Nan County, forget about Cao Cao's forces in that region, and even forget about the threats that are posed by various factions in Yu Province. My lord, you must strongly consider gradually relocating to Jiangling for now and collaborating more closely with Huang Zu in order to support Liu Xun against Sun Ce. That boy's the immediate threat once Yuan Shu is defeated, and Liu Xun's the only thing standing between Sun Ce and Jing."

"…But Liu Xun is a vassal of Yuan Shu," Liu Biao noted. "By helping Liu Xun, I also help a man that's dedicated to unseating my clan and usurping the throne!"

"That's the case now, yes… but I imagine that Liu Xun will quickly realign to His Majesty – who is, like you, kin to Liu Xun – once Yuan Shu is destroyed," Kuai Liang replied. "An independent Lujiang could ally with Jing against Sun Ce."

"…If that's how things transpire, that could be beneficial," Liu Biao said. "But wouldn't an independent Lujiang Prefecture be opposing the Han…?"

"That depends on how Cao Cao is viewed at that point," Kuai Liang replied. "He has enemies in the court and a flawed side to his character that could make him a liability to himself; already, there are some that call Cao 'the next Dong Zhuo' and even 'the new Wang Mang'… would an independent Lujiang be opposing the Han or another kidnapper intent on usurping the Han…?"

"*Ayah*… I say it again, Mister Kuai: I yearn for simpler times!" Liu Biao cried. "Nothing makes sense for more than a day anymore!"

"Accept it," Kuai Liang replied. "For quite some time to come, this is how it will be."

✱✱✱✱✱✱✱✱✱✱✱✱

77

The situation in Xiaopei went from bad to better to worse in quick succession; Gao Shun's efficiency was terrifying, and all of the efforts that Liu Bei and Xiahou Dun had made to fortify the area were quickly rendered meaningless and served as little more than a slight impediment.

"Gao Shun, it's said, is called 'The Camp Smasher' by the Black Mountain Bandits, and I can now believe it," Liu Bei whimpered as he pored over a map of the area in his command tent.

"All that is different is that we have that unhinged dog Xiahou Dun outside as a very thin buffer between us and Gao Shun's cavalry," Guan Yu complained.

"I sense a belief that retreat is inevitable," Mi Zhu said. "If I am right in sensing that, then you are right in thinking that, Yunchang. Gao Shun's too good a field general."

"So we must prepare for a strategic withdrawal," Mi Fang sighed.

"What will Xiahou Dun do, though?" Mister Sun wondered. "Would he-"

"**REPORT!**" a messenger cried as he ran into the command tent. "**Gao Shun attacks again! The last of the defence posts is lost! Xiahou Dun is engaging the enemy! Han Hao requests support!**"

"...But not Xiahou Dun himself," Mi Zhu murmured as Liu Bei silently dismissed the messenger. "Han Hao is being sensible, but what would Xiahou do if-"

"We can't just sit here," Liu Bei decided. "Jian Yong, Guan Yu, Sun Qian, Mi Fang: reinforce our position here and begin preparations for a retreat to Xuchang. Mi Zhu, Zhang Fei: we will go and provide the requested assistance to Xiahou Dun."

All men accepted their orders, and Liu Bei mentally prepared for the confrontation with Gao Shun.

Xiahou Dun's militia was engaging Gao Shun's on a stretch of flat land that allowed small formations: Gao Shun had arranged his infantrymen at a considerable distance from the Xiaopei defences and was relying entirely on his cavalry for the shock tactics that he enjoyed employing.

"**Something isn't right here,**" Han Hao protested as a seething Xiahou Dun prepared to charge Gao Shun's distant lines. "**Wait for Liu Bei.**"

"**You should never have requested Bei's help!**" Xiahou Dun retorted. "**I'll mince this Gao Shun and serve him to Lü Bu before I kill that bastard as well! You can stay here and wait for Bei, since you like him so much!**"

"*Ayah...* **Don't be a fool!**" Han Hao pleaded.

But Xiahou Dun was too angry to listen to good counsel: he readied his men and launched a direct attack on Gao Shun's lines.

"...He's every bit as aggressive, gullible and reckless as I'd heard," Gao Shun snickered as he watched Xiahou Dun's unguarded approach. "**Archers...!**"

Han Hao cried out with sympathetic anguish as man after man fell to Gao Shun's arrows: he could sense that Xiahou Dun must have been one of them, because his men were in disarray. Liu Bei, Mi

Zhu and Zhang Fei arrived as Gao Shun's second volley felled more men.

"**We must aid General Xiahou!**" Liu Bei ordered. "**FORWARD!**" Bei led his small force of elite cavalry forward without fear and showed his prowess as a mounted archer and general both; Zhang Fei charged Gao Shun's lines with greater ferocity than Gao Shun had expected, and Han Hao followed the lead. Mi Zhu arranged a quick formation of archers that provided additional pressure, and Gao Shun finally retreated.

"...**General Xiahou! GENERAL XIAHOU!**" Han Hao cried as he surveyed the battlefield. "**Be alive, General Xiahou! GENERAL XIAHOU!**"

Xiahou Dun's soldiers were sobbing, groaning, and crawling along the ground like dying animals: arrows protruded from open wounds, and struck horses flailed and jerked their necks in an effort to cling to life. Xiahou Dun would not be easy to find among the carnage, but somehow, Han Hao did manage to find his master quite quickly. Xiahou Dun was lying on his back, shaking as if he were cold; his face had no clear expression, but he did not need one, as the arrow that had perforated his left eye and remained lodged in the bone socket was expressive enough.

"...General Xiahou," Han Hao whispered as he knelt beside his commander; Han suddenly realised that his actions would not save Xiahou's life, so he shouted, "**SOMEONE GET HELP! THE COMMANDER NEEDS HELP!**"

"N-not... Liu Bei," Xiahou Dun pleaded through extreme pain. "N-not... not Bei...!"

"No...! No, not Liu Bei," Han Hao chuckled with disbelief; he decided that if Xiahou Dun was even managing to be his usual stubborn self in that condition, then he would certainly live. A rescue team arrived within minutes, and Xiahou Dun was taken to Xiaopei's infirmary for treatment.

"We'd better retreat now," Han Hao suggested to Liu Bei's officials as they gathered in the main command tent. "General Xiahou needs to go back to the capital, and you can't stay here or you'll be slaughtered when Gao Shun returns."

"We already ascertained as much," Liu Bei replied. "Preparations began just before this happened, but we'll need a few days. I'll be on the front lines if needs be."

"And what an asset you'd be," Han Hao admitted. "Your actions brought us back from an inevitable rout. When you're composed, Governor Liu, you're every bit the hero that His Excellency Cao says that you are."

"Enough undeserved praise!" Liu Bei chuckled softly. "Let's get out of Xiaopei. Lü Bu can have this victory... it is righteousness that will win in the end."

Gao Shun would only get one more chance to attack Liu Bei and what remained of Xiahou Dun's reinforcements: Liu Bei and Mi Zhu managed to use their resources wisely and within days, the Xiaopei defenders had fled westward to Xuchang. The retreat would not be without demoralising sacrifices, however; a few brave decoys withstood Gao Shun long enough to allow the army to escape, but Gao's pursuit led to the loss of the baggage train and the families of Liu Bei's forces.

"…Why don't we just give our wives to Bu and be done with it," Zhang Fei grumbled. "Him and his lot spend more time with our families than we do!"

"I do not expect them to be harmed," Liu Bei said as calmly as he could. "He did not harm them when we were trapped in Haixi; harming them now that I am a Han-appointed governor would only invite greater disaster upon him."

"I hope you're right about that, Xuande," Jian Yong replied. "A lot's changed…"

"Gao Shun let him ESCAPE???" Lü Bu shrieked at a terrified messenger from Xiaopei; the court was silent after Bu's arrogant announcement of his attack on Liu Bei. "I *knew* that I should have sent Zhang Liao, but I feared he'd be too kind to Guan Yu!" Lü Bu continued. "Liu Bei will go to Cao Cao. He will sob and weep as he always does… and Cao Cao will take pity… and he will send him back here with an army… an *imperial army*… I am *doomed*!"

Near to none of Lü Bu's inherited officials took pity on him for his predicament; his own vassals were visibly divided.

"…If Cao Cao comes here, we'll be killed," Wang Kai mumbled.

"He'll make examples of us!" Xu Si cried. "What will he do???"

"Calm, please, gentlemen… calm," Chen Gong pleaded, although he was secretly as fearful as Wang Kai and Xu Si. "We'll work something out. News of Xiahou Dun's defeat and possible death will rile Cao, yes, but he has to consider his own tenuous position: the land is still mired in chaos; Cao's been cut yet again; and General Gao reports that we have Bei's family again, which will provide us with a bargaining tool. This will partially relieve Yuan Shu as well: let's see if he is grateful."

Chen Yuanfang and Chen Qun were not warmed by what Chen Gong had to say; Wang Kai, Xu Si and Lü Bu visibly were. More ties to the ailing pretender were looking increasingly likely, while any chance of a bloodless solution was slowly and steadily slipping away. Lü Bu would probably fight to the death to keep Xu Province, and that was exactly what every sane person in Xu did not want.

"…And what about Gao Shun…?" Wang Kai asked. "Should he stay in Xiaopei?"

Lü Bu betrayed his true understanding of Gao Shun's ability and trustworthiness when he said, "No, I want him back here, defending the capital. Have him secure the region and then return to me at once."

"It shall be as you ask," Chen Gong promised.

"…And how do we react to Zang Ba's offer of cooperation…?" Chen Qun asked.

"We accept," Lü Bu replied immediately; his desperation was evident, since he had made it perfectly clear on a number of previous occasions that he was still upset by his forced retreat from Ju City and hated the Mount Tai Bandits for it.

"Administrator Xiao won't like that," Xu Si said. "Ju City will-"

"I don't care!" Lü Bu snapped. **"Tian Kai was defeated, Kong Rong was expelled, and Yuan Tan governs Qing now! Xiao Jian is no more the Administrator of Langya than I am now the General of the Left and Governor of Xu!"**

"My lord, it is not over," Chen Gong protested.

"I am ruined yet again, the victim of bad advice and worse luck," Lü Bu continued as he sank deeper and deeper into melancholy. "I could have been the father of an *empress*...! I could have been the founder of a *dynasty*...!"

Chen Yuanfang and his son Qun exchanged nervous glances.

"But yet again... I am undone," Lü Bu whimpered.

The triumphant general Gao Shun received Lü Bu's order and did as he was asked. Lü Bu's advisers expected immediate reprisals, but those reprisals never came; Bu remained on permanent alert regardless and grew increasingly suspicious of his officials, particularly those that he had inherited from Liu Bei and Tao Qian.

Over the next few weeks, the situation changed yet again: Cao Cao retreated from Yang Province when he heard that Xiahou Dun – a man that he saw as close family, and loved as dearly as a brother – had been severely wounded in Xiaopei, and the desperate Yuan Shu was unexpectedly relieved.

"Explain again, Fengxiao," Cao Cao said as he and his advisers rode back to Xuchang in a carriage.

"Will asking me to tell you over and over again somehow make the situation different or better...?" Guo Jia retorted.

Cao Cao clutched his aching head and said, "I... I must understand what has happened. To do so, I must hear it again."

Xun Wenruo looked at Guo Jia and frowned purposefully; Guo Jia sighed and began to read the report from Xiaopei yet again.

Xiahou Dun had many injuries, but the worst by far was the shot that had struck his left eye: the arrow was embedded in the eyeball, and both the arrow and the eye had to be removed. Cao Cao was relieved that Xiahou Dun had not died – as his friend Wei Zi had done during the battle at Xingyang years before – but Cao's hatred of Lü Bu and his determination that Bu would have to be killed had grown as a result of the encounter.

To add to Cao Cao's concerns, Liu Bei was now on his way back to Xuchang: he and some of his advisers feared that Cao's detractors would quickly gravitate toward the disinherited prince's descendant, as he was apparently a favourite of Emperor Xian and, to some, a possible alternative to Cao Cao. Guo Jia and some of Cao's other vassals pondered ways to politely expel Liu Bei as soon as he arrived, but Bei only had one place to go if he were to leave, and that was back to Xu Province yet again: he could not go back there until Cao Cao could aid him with an army, and Cao could not do that until he could be sure that neither Yuan Shao nor Yuan Shu would interfere or invade Yan Province in his absence. As with all military and political matters, the timing of any action was everything.

****

78

Cao Cao sat in his private meeting room in the chancellery and re-read a letter that he had received from his former critic Kong Rong; Guo Jia, Xun Gongda and Xun Wenruo arrived within minutes of each other and sat in guest places.

"...Greetings, gentlemen," Cao Cao mumbled.

"Still worried about Liu Bei?" Guo Jia supposed.

"...You're more worried about him than I am," Cao Cao retorted. "No, I'm preoccupied with Dun's injuries, my other recent personal losses, and this 'Mi Heng' fellow that Kong Rong's recommended to me."

"I've heard good things about Mi Heng of Pingyuan," Xun Wenruo said. "Why are you concerned...?"

"Because I do not know if Kong Rong is playing games," Cao Cao replied. "He has been far more affable since Wang Lang arrived in Xuchang, but I still worry that he is-"

"Don't concern yourself with Kong Rong," Guo Jia insisted. "He's a mediocrity in comparison with most of your inner circle, never mind his famous ancestor. I, too, have heard about Mi Heng, and he's potentially an asset... provided he's learned to be more tactful in recent times."

"But an honest man is a man that I need as part of my counsel, like you three and Cheng Yu," Cao Cao suggested.

"There's honest and there's Mi Heng," Guo Jia chuckled. "He's a man that knows he's talented, but he sometimes forgets that he is not entirely unique. He's a fine poet, musician and-"

"Oh...?" Cao Cao exclaimed. "Well then, I shall look forward to meeting him! It is men such as this 'Mi Heng' that will be the new Cai Yongs that the imperial court badly needs!"

"...Indeed," Guo Jia chuckled.

Cao Cao invited many of the Han's officials to a banquet in the chancellery's main audience hall; they included Kong Rong, Mi Heng, and three men from Cao's respected eastern Yan administration – General Li Dian and the officials Man Chong and Mao Jie.

"Firstly, I should like to welcome Mi Heng, a respected scholar from Pingyuan," Cao Cao said once every man was seated; the audience turned and bowed to Mi Heng, but his responses were noticeably muted and lofty.

"...We hope that you shall be an asset to the state, Mister Mi Heng," Cao Cao said as he glared at the mortified Kong Rong.

"Why are you acting so facetiously, Zhengping???" Kong Rong whispered.

"I shall act as I please in the company of such toadies and mediocrities," Mi Heng replied.

Cao Cao had turned his attentions to Man Chong and Mao Jie; he smiled and said, "So good to see you again, gentlemen! We have been apart too long. Man Chong: for your exemplary work as Magistrate of Gaoping, I promote you to Assistant Officer within my own administration."

"I am unworthy of the promotion," Man Chong insisted.

"If there were a prefectural administrator's position free, you'd be

getting that," Cao Cao retorted. "I shall assign a man – perhaps Zhao Rong – to serve as the general for the militia in Gaoping. Now for Mao Jie: you have served me well in getting Chenliu reorganised, and for that I must insist that you take the role of-"
Mi Heng yawned loudly.
"...That you take the role of 'Assistant Officer in the Provincial Headquarters'," Cao Cao continued as he fought the urge to glare at Mi Heng.
"I, too, am unworthy of such praise!" Mao Jie replied humbly.
"Nonsense!" Cao Cao chuckled. "Now, General Li Dian: I understand that you must feel frustrated that I do not recognise your obvious intelligence by giving you military ranks."
Li Dian bowed low and said, "You are misinformed, Excellency: I am glad to serve the Han in any capacity."
"But to make you a mere sword when you have a mind too is to waste a talent that could serve the nation better!" Cao Cao insisted. "I intend to promote you to 'Administrator of Lihu Prefecture', so you can wield the pen more often."
Li Dian smiled and bowed gratefully.
"Now," Cao Cao continued, "we-"
"Is there more to this gathering than egregious fawning, giving rank to allies as one passes the tea kettle, and patting one-another on the back for doing little more than your jobs...?"
There were few men that did not turn and glare at Mi Heng in the wake of his statement; Kong Rong laughed nervously as Cao Cao's other guests flicked their sleeves and harrumphed at the young scholar, who was noticeably enjoying the reaction.
"**Silence!**" Cao Cao barked; the room quietened immediately.
"...Excellency," Kong Rong chuckled, "I-!"
"Mi Heng, you seem to have learned little," Guo Jia sighed.
"And you still drink and fornicate like that third-in-line nobleman's son that knows he's never going to achieve anything," Mi Heng retorted. "You're an adviser to the Excellency of Works: have you no shame?"
"**Quiet, you pup!**" Cheng Yu snapped.
"...Disciplinary words from a man without restraint," Mi Heng chuckled. "Cheng Yu, you feed human flesh to the imperial army, and are therefore in no position to-"
"*Ayah*! Show some *respect*, Mi Zhengping!" Xun Wenruo pleaded.
"*Respect*...?" Mi Heng snickered. "Mister Xun Yu, it is nice to meet you! Didn't you work for Ji Governor Han Fu, or was that your brother...? I forget, since you're both so interchangeable. I know you both ended up working for Yuan Shao, and then you came here to help speed things up in Xu Province."
Many men started to flick their sleeves and heckle Mi Heng again; Cao Cao's eyes were locked onto Kong Rong, who was grinning bizarrely and staring at the tray of food in front of him.
Dong Cheng – who was sat with his political allies Zhong Ji and Wang Fu – smiled and said, "I honestly don't know whether to laugh or cry!"
"Don't show support for this man, or he'll destroy us," Zhong Ji replied quietly.
"How dare you treat respected men of talent with such shameful contempt, Mi Heng!" Xun Wenruo cried. **"You were**

invited as a guest, offered rank, and you-!"

"**What rank, I wonder...?**" Mi Heng interrupted. "**I was told that Xuchang was a place for great men to gather, a place where the talented would be rewarded with fitting titles: how so? A muscled county clerk called 'Li Dian', who already possesses a general's seal for what exactly, gets the title 'Administrator of Lihu', only minutes after a 'Magistrate Man Chong' gets a desk role in Xuchang and is told 'there are no Administrator's roles'; and who is Zhao Rong? Is Zhao Rong some hitherto-untold-of hero that 'His Excellency' thinks will defend Gaoping against-?**"

"**Watch your tongue!**" Cheng Yu growled.

"**Or else what...? ...Will I be the next course if I don't shut up?**" Mi Heng retorted. "**What sort of court is this? Kong Rong rots in a pedant's role, Dong Cheng has no military rank despite inviting Cao Cao to rescue the emperor, the Commander-in-Chief doesn't-!**"

"**SHUT UP!**" Xun Wenruo screamed.

"**You're an insult to your ancestors, Xun Yu, and the worst of the shameful!**" Mi Heng continued. "**Once, the Xuns were loyal and intelligent men that held high office! Now you're little more than a 'king-maker', a schemer-for-hire that makes lions out of tomcats!**"

The heckling intensified; all the while, Cao Cao glared at the terrified Kong Rong and wondered what should happen next.

"That... was Kong Rong's last mistake," Cao Cao said as he returned to his private audience room an hour later; he was followed by Guo Jia, Xun Wenruo, Xun Gongda, Dong Gongren, Cheng Yu and Tian Chou.

"I think that Kong Rong was as upset by it all as everyone else," Guo Jia chuckled.

"**How can you be so calm about it???**" Xun Wenruo cried.

"The man obviously hoped that his display of irreverent banter would earn him respect," Guo Jia said.

"That... was not 'banter', Fengxiao," Cao Cao replied angrily. "For that, he shall be humiliated. I was going to offer him a role in my counsel, but not now."

"So what role will you give him...?" Dong Gongren asked.

"...One befitting his musical talent," Cao Cao replied icily.

"*Ayah*... a *court drummer*...?" Kong Rong whined as Mi Heng strolled back and forth across Kong's living quarters.

"A *drum master*," Mi Heng replied with apparent pride.

"...*Still*... after the atrocious way that you conducted yourself, I'm actually surprised that he didn't kill you," Kong Rong said. "There are men that might have, Zhengping."

"But he is still trying to humiliate me, Wenju," Mi Heng chortled. "He should know better than to do such a thing, though, to someone that is his intellectual match at the very least. My predecessor in the role has already warned me of the dos and don'ts, and I am only too happy to take them to heart."

"Please... *please*, Mi Zhengping, do not do anything rash...!" Kong Rong whined.

"If Cao is the great mischief-maker of old, the 'Crafty Villain' – oh,

and the man that appreciates the higher mind – that people claim him to be, then I am merely proving that I am being neglected," Mi Heng retorted. "If not, then I will have exposed him for the mediocrity that he truly is. Where is the rashness in that?"
Kong Rong groaned and covered his face with his hands.

Cao Cao had another banquet within a week of the first, and many of the invitees were the same: one omission was Mi Heng, who would now be the drum master for the musical entertainment.
"What a waste of a fine mind," the elder statesman Zheng Xuan sighed as he took his seat.
"After last time, he's lucky he isn't in a prison cell," the minister Zhong Yao replied.
Kong Rong was the recipient of many nervous or judging stares as he entered the hall; he took a seat between Wang Lang and Zheng Xuan and exhaled loudly.
"You sound like a man about to be sentenced," Wang Lang teased.
"I might be," Kong Rong replied as Cao Cao entered the hall with his small group of trusted advisers.
        The banquet started and progressed uneventfully, but when it came to the musical entertainment, many wondered if it would be the last day for Mi Heng and, perhaps, Kong Rong as well. The musicians entered through the side door; many immediately noticed that Mi Heng was wearing scruffy, musty robes and stifled their reactions to it.
"Oh… *no…*!" Kong Rong whimpered.
Mi Heng looked at the infuriated Cao Cao and said, "I shall begin with a piece that everyone should find familiar, Excellency."
Guo Jia smiled and awaited Mi Heng's next act of defiance enthusiastically; the other attendees were not so amused. Mi Heng started to play his mid-sized drum, and the other musicians followed his lead.
"…*This…*?" Zheng Xuan croaked.
Mi Heng had chosen a tragic work that recalled terrible happenings in times gone by, and it was well known for its haunting melody; Cao Cao was both moved and enraged, as the music reminded him – and every one of the guests – of past tragedies and mistakes and reduced many to tears.
"…Such talent," Guo Jia whispered; even he was moved, despite his nonchalant attitude to everything, including his own mortality.
"…Have you dressed as one of the victims of Yuyang, drummer…?" one junior attendant heckled. "Why have you come here in such well-worn clothes?"
Mi Heng stopped, turned to the attendant, and said, "If my clothes offend, then I shall atone immediately."
Every man was forced to turn their gaze, cover their faces and stifle gasps or snickers as Mi Heng began to undress; Cao Cao covered his face with his hand and glared at Kong Rong through the gaps between his tensed fingers as Mi Heng – who was now naked from head to foot – resumed his drumming and the terrified musicians started to follow his lead once again.

"Alright, alright… my idea miscarried," Cao Cao grumbled as he retired to his private meeting room once again; his advisers followed as they always did, and even Xun Wenruo could not hide his amusement at the antics of a man that had slandered him so badly before.

"So what will you do...?" Guo Jia asked dryly.

"...I don't know," Cao Cao admitted. "He is trying to amuse and impress with his wit, I think, but I find him intolerable, and he appears to be that type of person that cannot be made to understand that *nobody finds them funny*."

"Quite," Cheng Yu chortled. "He does things that I would never stoop to in an attempt to gain recognition; all he's gaining right now is a-"

"When I next march, he'll accompany us," Cao Cao decided. "Perhaps his attitude will change when he sees the horrors of real life; perhaps he'll see that there is a need for him to behave and show his true worth..."

"And if he does not 'see'...?" Xun Wenruo asked.

"...Then I shall respectfully make him someone else's problem," Cao Cao replied. "I will not be the man that gives that man his final fate; perhaps I am getting old, and a different, less world-weary spirit is a better master for him. I know *just the fellow to send him to*, in that case..."

Cao Cao's advisers suspected that his words were not as kind and well-meaning as they appeared to be, but they did not comment.

Mi Heng was relieved of his role as the court's drum master and allowed to serve as a junior courtier, although he was never invited to any more banquets; he behaved well when he was in the presence of Emperor Xian, so many considered him to be a man that simply lacked an understanding of his limits. But Mi Heng was quickly forgotten when Liu Bei finally arrived in Xuchang and thoughts turned to what would have to be done about Lü Bu.

****

79

"**Xuande!**"
Dong Cheng had been eager to speak with Liu Bei, and at last, after weeks of Cao Cao's vassals being one step behind the visitor from Xu Province, security had lessened and a chance had come. Liu Bei stopped his leisurely walk through the streets of Xuchang upon hearing his style name, and said, "Who calls me?"
Liu Bei's bodyguard Chen Dao readied his halberd in case the call was a prelude to an attack of some kind.
"Xuande, we have been unable to speak, but now is a good time," Dong Cheng replied. "I must know your views on the Excellency of Works. Can we go to my home and talk, perhaps…?"
"…Mister Dong Cheng, you do not need to speak to me about Excellency Cao," Liu Bei said. "Is it not the case that you are father to an imperial consort?"
"Yes, and like Dou Wu of earlier times, it does me little good," Dong Cheng replied quietly. "Cao Cao is the law, as the eunuchs were in Dou Wu's day: please, we have to talk."
Liu Bei looked around him at the people going about their business: there was a noticeable military presence, and all of the soldiers were taken from Cao Cao's personal forces.
"Cao Cao is another Wang Mang, or at best another Dong Zhuo!" Dong Cheng pleaded. "Men like you are the only ones that can stop him, Xuande!"
"I owe the Excellency of Works for my life, Mister Dong Cheng," Liu Bei replied carefully. "I was chased out of Xiaopei once, and he gave me rank, allowed me to see the Son of Heaven and sent me back to my province with arms and grain. I was besieged and then chased out of Xiaopei again – only weeks ago, and the memory still haunts me – and it is His Excellency that I again owe for a safe place to rest and an opportunity to save Xu Province and its people. Which man is it that you refer to that I should hate and conspire to destroy…?"
"The real man under the façade," Dong Cheng retorted. "Cao Cao has not changed. He is the same man that wrought mischief in the capital as a youth, murdered the innocents in Xu, and brought His Majesty here from Luoyang so that he could control the court."
Liu Bei smiled dryly and said, "Ah, but wasn't Cao Cao invited to Luoyang to do that… by *you*…?"
Dong Cheng lowered his eyes and replied, "Yes. But that was because the only other choice was to allow the White Wave Bandits to 'protect' His Majesty! Have you never been made to pick the least bad of an awful set of choices…?"
Liu Bei stopped smiling and said, "That, Mister Dong Cheng, has been all I have ever been able to do. But what you ask makes no sense to me at present. Now, if you don't mind…?"
Dong Cheng smiled awkwardly, bowed and said, "Of course. Perhaps we shall have this conversation again when I have a better way of framing my arguments… or when you have understood what we face."
Liu Bei bowed silently, and Dong Cheng retreated.
"…Again, I am dragged into intrigue, and yet I know that only I will suffer for it," Liu Bei sighed. "Come, General Chen, let us be

on our way."

Chen Dao nodded, and the two men continued on their way.

"AAAH! Are you a man or a demon???"

Guan Yu laughed as the weary Yue Jin backed away from him, dropped his practice spear, and rubbed his arm; some of the high-ranking officers in Cao Cao and Liu Bei's armies had been testing each other's strength in the main barracks for almost two hours while Zhang Fei and others looked on, and Guan Yu was proving to be a difficult match for most of the challengers.

"You're every bit the champion that I'd heard about, Guan Yunchang," Xu Huang said.

Yue Jin and Han Hao voiced their reluctant agreement.

"Were I only a match for Lü Bu," Guan Yu sighed.

"You are," Zhang Fei insisted. "When have you fought him without an injury?"

"That is quite true, Yide, but even then I wonder," Guan Yu replied with unusual modesty. "A man must know his limits."

"Come on, 'Yide'," Yue Jin prompted. "You're up against your friend next."

"Nah," Zhang Fei chuckled. "That wouldn't be fair."

"Zhang Yide and I never cross our weapons," Guan Yu explained. "We used to, but we are as brothers now, and it would be wrong: we might as well raise arms against Lord Liu."

"I've never seen Zhang Fei in action yet," Yue Jin complained.

"Be careful what you wish for!" Zhang Fei joked. "I save my strength for enemies. I'm going now, Yunchang… you staying or going…?"

"I shall stay," Guan Yu replied. "We'll meet later."

Zhang Fei bowed slightly and retreated: he had a noticeable limp.

"Ah, I see… he's injured," Yue Jin said.

"He was hurt when we fought Lü Bu, and then again when we were protecting the civilians from Gao Shun," Guan Yu explained. "I, too, was hurt, though not so badly. Yide is like a tiger when he fights: while I cautiously retreat, Yide will tear men apart: he will not stop unless he is restrained by allies or killed by his foes."

"…So he's another Dian Wei," Yue Jin murmured. "That's good to know for the future."

"You were a near match for Bu, I heard," Han Hao said. "Although we have not had a perfect working relationship, Guan Yu, I have to admit that you are a future hero."

Guan Yu bowed slightly and replied, "You overpraise me. As I said, I know my limits: Bu is a rare athletic prodigy, and finding a true match will be hard."

"It's a shame that Xu Chu isn't able to join us," Yue Jin said. "I'd like to see Guan fight him; or maybe Zhang, when he is better."

"We do not know what the future might bring," Guan Yu suggested. "Would anyone care to have another bout…?"

"Don't you get tired…?" Yue Jin said. "Xu Huang! It's your turn to fight again."

"It's a pleasure," Xu Huang said as he readied himself.

Time passed.

A messenger from the office of the Excellency over the Masses brought a letter to the current lord of Wan City, Zhang Xiu, and his adviser Jia Xu; the two accepted the correspondence and moved to the private meeting room of the administrator's residence so that they could decipher its true intent.

"...A truce...?" Zhang Xiu exclaimed.

"A temporary cessation of hostilities for the purpose of freeing up all of his forces for a march into Xu Province to rid it – and the world – of Lü Bu," Jia Xu replied.

"Exactly as you promised," Zhang Xiu said with wonderment.

"I promised nothing," Jia Xu insisted. "There was always a chance that Cao Cao might do something extraordinary and ridiculous, but he did what any sensible man would do at a time like this. Now his forces will leave, and we must fortify every sympathetic settlement and do what we can to make others sympathetic to us while they are elsewhere; when they return, it will be as the victors of a great battle in Xiapi, and it might be the case that Yuan Shu is dead by then as well."

"...In which case, we'll be facing Cao's full wrath," Zhang Xiu said.

"Quite right," Jia Xu replied. "We both know that day will come..."

"...And that I will have to consider surrendering," Zhang Xiu said. "I... I cannot promise that I will have the strength to do that, but I will try to find it."

"The only other choice is to die for your cause, whatever you might think that is," Jia Xu replied. "Ponder carefully, my lord... ponder carefully."

More weeks passed.

Cao Cao had been waiting: Yuan Shu had been broken, and he was now maintaining a solid defence against his numerous enemies in his last remaining stronghold in Shouchun County; Lü Bu was maintaining a similar defence in Xiapi; the former co-regent Li Jue was yet another man that was refusing to move since he had lost the emperor almost 2 years before; Yuan Shao and Gongsun Zan were obviously poised for another confrontation, but Shao had been waiting until the majority of the Black Mountain Bandits were pacified. Every man was waiting for someone else to do something, and now, at last, one man made his move, setting a chain of events in motion.

"Yuan Shao's attacked Gongsun Zan," Xun Wenruo said as he hurried into Cao Cao's chancellery office.

"Oh...? Already...?" Guo Jia exclaimed.

"'Already'??? I thought that he never would!" Cao Cao chuckled.

"I thought the Black Mountain Bandits would last longer; Yuan Shu's financial incentives have been pared back, which means that he's going to run out of money within a year," Guo Jia explained. "Now that Yuan Shao has moved, so should we."

"Indeed," Cao Cao said enthusiastically. "The edicts for the western men are written; the army has been secretly planning for weeks; it is now or never."

"Then let it be now," Guo Jia replied. "I'll alert the generals."

"Yue Jin will go north to guard against a possible feint by Yuan Shao, and he should only join us once we are certain that Yuan is unable to return to Ji at a stroke," Cao Cao ordered. "Cao Ren will guard the capital. Yuan Shu's being attacked by Sun Ce from the

south, Wu Jing from the west and bandits in every direction at the moment, and is, therefore, of little concern: Cai Yang, Wang Zhong and Liu Dai can earn some merit there, perhaps, by harrying his northern positions. Cao Hong, Yu Jin, Xu Huang, Han Hao, Zhu Ling, Cao Xiu and Liu Bei will go with me immediately; Xun Gongda and Guo Jia will be my counsel."
Guo Jia bowed silently.
"I cannot disagree," Xun Wenruo said.
"Lü Bu! Your end is nigh!" Cao Cao said with glee.

The former regent, Li Jue, sat in his latest sanctuary – the chancellery office in the former western capital, Chang'an – and looked at the walls with nostalgia. He had once taken orders from Dong Zhuo in that same room; and then, after Dong Zhuo was assassinated, Li Jue had ruled Chang'an with his colleague Guo Si and met with his allies and advisers in that same room.
"Mister Li Ru… I wonder what happened to you."
Li Jue asked that question regularly now: Li Ru – the man that had been Dong Zhuo's adviser at the darkest moments – had walked out after being publicly rebuked by Emperor Xian, and he did not return. His fellow adviser, Jia Xu, had commented that he would likely commit suicide or be hunted down and killed for his role in the deaths of Emperor Shao and Lady Hè: either way, he was gone. Jia Xu, on the other hand, was safely installed in Wan City and serving the nephew of Li Jue's former subordinate Zhang Ji: Li Jue laughed at the way that Jia Xu had survived yet again.
"Wily Mister Jia… *wily Mister Jia…!*"
Jia Xu had supposedly escaped death a few times before Dong Zhuo recruited him: it was easy to believe. When Dong Zhuo's popularity plummeted, the adviser coerced Dong's son-in-law, Niu Fu, into recruiting him, allowing him to be far away from Luoyang when Dong Zhuo looted and burned the city, and was forced to fight Sun Jian; it also meant that he was in Anyi when Dong was assassinated, leaving Li Ru to manage the counter-coup that would save many lives, including Li Jue's. Jia Xu then, somehow, managed to be away from Anyi when Niu Fu, Niu's family and Niu's closest retainers were betrayed by a rogue adviser; and when the counter-coup succeeded, it was Jia Xu that reaped the rewards after he escaped rebuke and became the sole adviser to the regents. And just when Jia Xu's timing could not seem to be any more uncanny or careful, he fled the capital when the regents lost the emperor, severed ties with the regents in all senses bar saying it, and entered Zhang Xiu's service in Jing Province. Jia Xu had survived the disaster of losing Emperor Xian: Guo Si, Li Jue's fellow regent, had not.
"…Mister Guo…"
Li Jue toyed with a badly-soiled turban: it had been Guo Si's. The two regents did not speak or see each other again after losing Emperor Xian to the White Wave Bandits: the next time that he saw his old ally was when Guo's vassal Wu Xi brought his severed head as an offering and surrendered. Li Jue now clutched the turban that wrapped Guo Si's hair on the day that he died; at the time, Li Jue had smiled, as it meant that his own forces were bolstered, but now he craved a reliable ally, and Guo Si was gone.
"Lord Li."

Li Jue looked up and saw his vassal Duan Wei standing over him.
"Are they still outside…?" Li Jue asked.
"They are," Duan Wei replied. "Ma Chao has issued a challenge."
"Damn them," Li Jue chortled; his desperation then peaked, and he shouted, "**Damn Han Sui and Ma Teng! Damn Song Jian! They rose up against the Han before: why do they now help Cao Cao???**"
Although Li Jue asked the question, he already knew the answer. Weeks before, Yuan Shao had launched his campaign to destroy Gongsun Zan: within days, Cao Cao had sent edicts westward – issued in the name of Emperor Xian – demanding that the Qiang warlord recipients rise up and destroy 'The great traitor', Li Jue, and promising the government-sanctioned autonomy that they desired in exchange.
"They must know he'll renege," Li Jue said. "Han Sui, Ma Teng, Song Jian… they must surely know. The Han never cedes territory that easily… why don't they see??? …Or is this because we've fought before…? Is this… is this because of last time, when they joined Liu Yan…? Did I kill sons of theirs too…?"
"I don't know, Lord Li," Duan Wei replied.
"They think they're buying time," Li Jue scoffed. "But they're wrong; it's Cao Cao that's buying time, Duan Wei… he'll come here eventually, and they'll lose it all. Not now, not in a year's time, maybe… but he will. And they'll die… still… they'll last longer than I have, eh, Duan Wei…?"
Duan Wei raised his bloodied sword.
"My nephew fought well, I hope," Li Jue sighed. "Get it over with."
Duan Wei struck with all of his might, and the warlord Li Jue – who had enjoyed a decade of power in the west as a subordinate and then successor to Dong Zhuo – died at last. None of his family would be spared.

Li Jue's demise marked an end of an era, as he was the last of Dong Zhuo's vassal-generals to fall, and Chang'an was returned to government control. It also meant that Cao Cao had secured a fragile peace in Liang Province, because its rulers – Ma Teng, Han Sui, Song Jian, and a host of lesser tribal warlords – would gratefully accept the complete devolvement from Han rule that Li Jue's destruction delivered. Until the Han court decided otherwise, the west of China – Liang, Yi and Han'ning – would no longer be a major concern. Jing Province Governor Liu Biao and his forced ally Zhang Xiu were glad to be left alone and would cause no trouble; the Yellow Turbans of neighbouring Yu were scattered, if only temporarily; and the Black Mountain Bandits of Bing were piecing their shattered forces back together, so the centre of the land was also of no immediate concern. The east was the sole focus now: Yuan Shao and Gongsun Zan were locked in a bitter struggle for Yòu Province in the north; Yuan Shu was doing what he could to guard his borders in northern Yang; Sun Ce was pacifying the south; and in the middle, there was Lü Bu, whose moment for judgement had finally come.

∗∗∗∗∗∗∗∗∗∗∗∗

ACT VII: THE BATTLE OF XIAPI

80

Han Dynasty China knew many famous men in the period immediately following the Yellow Turban Rebellion: none, perhaps, was more famous – or infamous – than the warrior Lü Bu, who seemed to be at the core of every major event that occurred.

Bu had been born in a semi-autonomous region beyond the Great Wall that separated Han China from the hostile lands and tribes to the north; he chose to migrate southwards to the Southern Xiongnu-dominated central-northern province of Bing and joined militia of the provincial Inspector, Ding Yuan. At the time of the Yellow Turban Rebellion, the Southern Xiongnu were mostly passive migrants that exchanged service in the Imperial army for the right to live as they chose; the threat that Ding Yuan faced was the Black Mountain Bandits, a million-strong criminal confederacy that spawned from the defeated Yellow Turban army.

The majority of the Yellow Turbans had not been followers of the religious doctrine of the founder of the 'Way of Peace' sect, Zhang Jue, who had created the Yellow Turbans as a militant force to overthrow the Han Emperor when a carefully-planned coup was exposed and prevented by Han loyalists; they had risen up against their emperor due to economic and social injustice that could, in part, be traced back to the 'Ten Attendants', an ever-changing eunuch faction that had once saved the Han Emperor Huandi from his own Empress's ambitious relatives but then misused their accidental rise to power to build fortunes and populate the government – regional and central – with their own supporters. Ding Yuan did not care that some of the Turbans – and, later, the Bandits – were fighting for any particular cause, however: his aim was to restore stability, and he quickly earned a reputation for fairness and firmness in equal measure as he pacified Bing Province. Lü Bu was quickly recognised as a rare athletic and military talent, and Ding Yuan gradually promoted him and even took Bu as a foster son; Ding Yuan's close ally, General Zhang Yang, also respected Bu greatly and regarded him as a friend as well as a colleague.

Everything changed, however, when Emperor Ling died, five years after the Yellow Turban Rebellion: a succession dispute erupted between the family of Empress Dowager Hè – who was mother to the eldest of Lingdi's sons, Prince Bian – and Grand Empress Dowager Dong, Lingdi's mother and the appointed guardian of his second son, Prince Xie. The Hè family – which included the Commander-in-Chief of the army, Hè Jin – was the victor, and Prince Bian became Emperor Shao; that should have been the end of the matter, but Hè Jin decided to be rid of the 'Ten Attendants' once and for all, and the féud between them ended with the destruction of both sides. Hè Jin had asked Ding Yuan to move his forces to Henei, a city to the north of the capital Luoyang, as part of a plan to intimidate the eunuchs and his sister Empress Dowager Hè, so Ding was one of the first men to reach the capital after He Jin's closest aide, Yuan Shao, massacred the palace eunuchs to avenge Jin's murder by the 'Ten'; the chaos allowed another invited general, Dong Zhuo of Liang Province, to seize control after he was mistakenly rewarded for rescuing Emperor Shao and Prince Xie from the last of the fleeing eunuchs. Dong Zhuo quickly declared that Emperor Shao was unfit for purpose and suggested that Prince Xie should be elevated in his place: Ding Yuan was one of many detractors, and it was Lü Bu's decision to betray Ding, murder him and join Dong Zhuo that allowed the latter to become Chancellor of State, murder Emperor Shao and ascend Prince Xie as Emperor Xian. Lü Bu was one of Dong Zhuo's most powerful generals, and he personally oversaw many of the chancellor's atrocities, including the torture and murder of the immediate families of any who opposed Dong and joined Yuan Shao's Eastern Pass Coalition, the looting of the imperial tombs for their treasures and the subsequent razing of Luoyang as Dong Zhuo fled west to the old Han capital, Chang'an, with Emperor Xian and the court as hostages. The eastern warlords decried Lü Bu – whom Dong Zhuo took as his foster son to ensure his loyalty – as an irredeemable villain.

The Eastern Pass Coalition collapsed after its founders, the Yuan brothers, started a feud over the chieftainship of their clan, and it seemed that no one could or would stop Dong Zhuo; Lü Bu ensured his place in history once again when he joined forces with Director of the Imperial Secretariat Wang Yun and assassinated Dong Zhuo, ostensibly to atone for his past wrongs but more because his relationship with Dong has become strained over their mutual attraction to one of Dong's serving maids. Bu's arrogance left him unable to hold Chang'an, and he fled to the east while Wang Yun met his end at the hands of Dong Zhuo's loyalists, who then seized the young emperor and ruled as a regency government; Bu served Yuan Shao – whose once-dominant family was decimated by Dong Zhuo – and briefly resumed his career against the Black Mountain Bandits before being forced to flee for showing arrogance. Bu was once again decried as an irredeemable villain by Yuan Shao, though many others were left confused after his part in the death of Dong Zhuo; most expected his legacy to end in Henei, where he sought shelter from his many enemies with his former colleague Zhang Yang.

But Lü Bu was determined to continue making a name for himself; when Yuan Shao's childhood friend Cao Cao – who was now Governor of the eastern-central Yan Province – launched a savage and unfocussed attack on the eastern province of Xu to avenge the suspicious death of his wealthy father, Cao's senior adviser Chen Gong and childhood friend Zhang Miao rebelled and invited Bu to the region to provide them with military support. Lü Bu eagerly accepted Chen Gong's invitation and led his small but professional army into Yan Province, which forced Cao Cao to withdraw from Xu and paved the way for the militarily-weak Liu Bei to inherit the province from its ailing governor Tao Qian and gain his first serious appointment. Cao Cao chased Lü Bu from his province after a famine damaged the effectiveness of both factions; Bu sought shelter with the grateful inhabitants of Xu province, who labelled Bu a hero.

But Lü Bu was still determined that his role in history was not yet complete: when Yuan Shu attacked Liu Bei, Bu reneged on the mutual defence pact that he had agreed with Bei and allowed him to be besieged in the city of Haixi for a year. When Yuan Shu then reneged on his own deal with Bu, the latter finally decided to aid Liu Bei in exchange for Bei yielding the province; there were many in Xu that felt disdain for or even hated Liu Bei for surrendering to Yuan Shao a year earlier and his perceived weakness in general, so the action was barely contested. The Han Emperor – who had, in the meantime, finally been liberated from Chang'an, moved east to Yan Province and taken up temporary residence in Xuchang City – allowed his new Excellency of Works, Cao Cao, to appoint Lü Bu as Governor of Xu and 'General of the Left' while a more permanent solution to the man dubbed 'Man among men' and 'The Father Killer' could be formulated. The people scratched their heads and wondered who or what Lü Bu really was, and the Han court waited.

There were many matters that prevented Cao Cao from dealing with Lü Bu immediately. Firstly, he was now a rival of Yuan Shao, rather than a friend; Cao could not risk moving into Xu Province while the ambitious Yuan was poised to march in any direction, as he would most likely move south and seize Emperor Xian. Secondly, Yuan Shao's rebellious brother Shu had now declared that he was 'First Emperor of the Zhong Dynasty': the destruction of a man that had committed treason and heresy had to take precedence, but Yuan Shu had enjoyed so many temporary alliances with Bu – who had, in the past, shown that he could make kings out of generals – that many argued the necessity of Bu being eliminated first. Thirdly, Cao Cao has suffered a recent, catastrophic, self-inflicted and entirely avoidable defeat at the hands of two of Dong Zhuo's former vassals while marching west to eliminate the former regents; the man appointed as the Han's Excellency of Works had been publicly humbled and forced to retreat by a much weaker adversary, and that was simultaneously boosting Yuan Shu's claim that the Han Dynasty's 'Mandate of Heaven' had passed and Yuan Shao's claim that Cao was unfit to host Emperor Xian. There could be no more mistakes.

Now, after years of waiting for an excuse, Yuan Shao – head of the Yuan clan of Ru County, Governor of Ji Province and Commander-in-Chief of the Han Imperial army – had finally decided to attack Gongsun Zan, who was a friend of Liu Bei, a former Han county magistrate, a hero of wars against bandits and Wuhuan tribes in the northern frontier province of Yòu and the primary financier of the Black Mountain Bandits; Gongsun had once entered into a land-acquisition deal with Yuan Shao, but he then murdered Yòu's loyalist governor Liu Yu, took control of the province and waged war against Shao for his reneging on the terms of the land deal and being indirectly responsible for the death of a beloved nephew. Yuan Shao was now distracted, so Cao Cao could act: he would do so with frightening speed.

Lü Bu's chief adviser Chen Gong heard of Cao Cao's sudden advance and summoned the entire court to discuss it.
"He brings Liu Bei, a host of generals and soldiers by the

thousands," Chen Gong reported. "I should have seen this coming as soon as we got word that Yuan Shao had marched northwards! I'm a fool!"

"What good is it now, Chen Gong?" the adviser Wang Kai said. "He's on his way: that's all that matters!"

"We're doomed," Xu Si murmured. "We betrayed him in Yan… we'll not be forgiven… he'll slaughter us like fatted pigs…!"

Chen Gong and Wang Kai silently agreed with Xu Si's words.

"Cao Cao's letter clearly states that surrender is an option, does it not…?" the adviser Chen Qun prompted.

"It does," Lü Bu replied. "I am seriously considering it."

"You mustn't!" Xu Si protested.

"What letter?" Gao Shun asked.

"Cao Cao… sent Lord Lü a letter advising us to consider the benefits – rather than the disadvantages – of surrender," Chen Gong replied nervously.

"Then, as I said, perhaps surrender *is* a credible option," Chen Qun suggested.

"For *who*…?" Chen Gong retorted instinctively.

"…For our lord," Chen Qun replied with a smile.

"**How can surrender be an option???**" Wang Kai screeched. "**Lord Lü has twice attacked an imperial relative while in this province, and he wronged the entire Han Dynasty while he served Dong Zhuo!**"

Lü Bu shuddered angrily.

"Why has the wider court not been made aware of the letter before?" the officer Gao Shun asked with obvious irritation.

"I was… about to discuss it," Chen Gong replied.

"But you oppose the idea, and hope to dissuade Lord Lü from surrendering to the Han court," Gao Shun supposed. "How is that wise, Mister Chen…?"

"He'd be surrendering to Cao Cao!" Chen Gong retorted. "Cao Cao *is* the court!"

"Your argument is that Lord Lü will not be forgiven," Chen Qun said. "Why, then, does Lord Lü possess an authentic seal that proclaims him 'General of the Left'? Can there be any good reason for a man with rank to resist…?"

"…That's quite true," Lü Bu mused. "What are you up to now, I wonder, Chen Gong? Were you planning to hand me over to Cao Cao to save yourself…? Would you have me resist, and then show your own loyalty to the Han by-"

"Don't dare accuse me of conspiring or scheming with Cao," Chen Gong retorted. "I placed my life on the line to be rid of Cao Cao in Yan Province. I've done everything I can to keep him out of Xu. I *hate* Cao Cao."

"And that is precisely why you are not the best man to negotiate this," Chen Qun said. "My lord, the Han court is extending another chance for peace here. You've wronged the court by siding with the traitor Yuan Shu yet again – something that I strongly advised against, but you listened to Chen Gong and the others, and what's done is done. Twice now, you've harmed Liu Bei, and he's prepared to forgive you. Twice now, you've harmed Cao Cao, and he's prepared to forgive you. How many times have you harmed the Han, and yet His Majesty has forgiven you, and given you rank and title! Why do you cry 'Atonement!' and then throw the

mercy back in people's faces???"
Lü Bu snorted loudly.

"*There* is your conspirator, my lord," Chen Gong said as he pointed at Chen Qun. "*There* is your schemer! I've stayed here and sweated blood for you! When the famine ruined our great cause in Yan, I had the opportunity to blame others, apologise to Cao Cao, and abandon you, but I didn't! Look *there*, though, to Old Chen and his son Qun, who are old friends of Liu Bei, looking to ingratiate themselves with the man again now that he's an imperial favourite!"

"What *nonsense*," Chen Yuanfang scoffed.

"You would say that, Old Chen!" Chen Gong heckled. "*Excellency of Works*, *Palace Attendant*, and more besides: you've hidden here, awaiting a moment to toady your way back to greatness! You're famous for your books, but not for your heart and valour! I faced not one but *two* tyrants, Dong and Cao, and while I failed to beat either, I faced them! Where were you? You accepted rank and gave advice to Dong Zhuo willingly, and unlike Lord Lü, you knew he was evil!"

"That's right!" Wang Kai said.

"We three fought Dong and Cao, but where were the Chens of Yingchuan or the wealthy Chens of Xiapi?" Xu Si heckled. "And where are they now…? Chen Gui's run off to Pei; Chen Deng's in Guangling, fighting pirates! How does that help us?"

"You're scared for your own necks, so you propose a futile resistance," Chen Qun scoffed. "You just want Lord Lü to put up a defence while you plan your escape route. 'Where were we', you ask…? My father and grandfather threw away imperial recognition when they challenged the 'Ten', and faced exile for it. My father received rank from *Zhou Bi*, not Dong Zhuo, and that was so he had the prestige to encourage others to join the Eastern Pass Coalition! The Chens of Xiapi faced Cao Cao too, and invited Liu Bei here to save Xu from him!"

"And then *betrayed him*, after already betraying Tao Qian!" Wang Kai cackled. "Now your insincere, materialistic friends try to betray a third master!"

"Do not use that argument, Wang Kai," Lü Bu said sombrely. "I am accused of the same."

"But your 'betrayals' had reasons behind them, and the court has seen that," Chen Qun suggested. "Don't listen to the three men that will drive you to definite destruction, my lord. I was about to say an important thing when I was interrupted by Wang Kai: I was about to ask a question of your advisers from Yan. Wang Kai, Xu Si, Chen Gong: you ask where we *were*. That's now irrelevant. Where we are now, and where we will be is all that matters. We're here, and we'll remain here, in a peaceful Xu Province, if only you'll allow it. But where will you three be while your master fights a losing battle with the armies of the Han, and the poor people of this province endure more war and hardship, if you have your way…? …In Yang Province, perhaps, giving more flawed counsel to Yuan Shu or his former general Sun Ce…?"

Lü Bu turned to Chen Gong and said, "Have you a good answer to that question?"

"We can't trust Cao Cao!" Chen Gong protested. "He'll destroy us!"

"Your fear is that he'll destroy *you*, especially when he finds out that all the bad advice – attacking Xiaopei, wedding the lord's daughter to Yuan Yao, attacking Xiaopei again and injuring his much-loved cousin, Xiahou Dun – has come from *you*, in addition to the things that you have already done," Chen Qun suggested. "This isn't about saving Lord Lü or sparing the province more grief at all; it's about saving yourselves, gentlemen."

Lü Bu glared at Chen Gong, Wang Kai and Xu Si and awaited their arguments.

"M-my lord, this is *Cao Cao*!" Wang Kai chortled. "How can we surrender to the man that slaughtered thousands of innocents here in Xu Province?"

"Men and women speak of him as though he were a demon!" Xu Si said. "His name is a byword for evil! His evils are far from forgotten: villagers in the west are fleeing upon seeing his banners! There are peasants burning incense in temples and apologising to Heaven for uttering his name, fearing that he was summoned here again by that simple action!"

Lü Bu's eyes wandered.

"By inviting Cao Cao here, Liu Bei will have earned mistrust; by repelling him, you will be loved, and the people will repel him as well, ensuring our safety," Chen Gong said. "Welcome him, and the people will hate you, and they will attack you. Then they'll attack *him*, and then he'll 'pacify' them again. And if you survive all that, Cao Cao won't let you stay here: the letter mentions making a 'Che Zhou' governor, which means you'll either stay here as a guest or go back to Chang'an… and I wonder what might happen then. Will you be 'Marquis Lü, General of the Left', or will you be arrested, tried, and executed for your very long list of crimes against the Han, including serving Dong Zhuo, looting the imperial tombs and collaboration with the heretic Yuan Shu…?"

"Yes! Listen to Chen Gongtai!" Wang Kai said excitedly.

"*Ayah*… **no!**" Chen Qun whined. "**See *sense*, Lord Lü!**"

But sown fear and mistrust had won the day, and Lü Bu would listen to his advisers from Yan Province.

"…So what do you propose that I do, Gongtai…?" Lü Bu asked.

"No, Lord Lü!" Chen Qun protested. "**Do not listen to him!**"

"SILENCE!" Lü Bu screamed. "**Your advice will only condemn me further!**"

Chen Gong smiled and said, "We're not done yet, my lord. Wang Kai, Xu Si and I can save you."

"State your suggestions and I will abide by them," Lü Bu replied.

The many officials that had hoped for a quick surrender were desolate, and they glared angrily at Chen Gong, Wang Kai and Xu Si, the men that had ensured that the conflict would continue.

＊＊＊＊＊＊＊＊＊＊＊＊

81

Yuan Shao smashed his way through the demoralised Yòu Province forces that were scattered throughout the region but mostly positioned close to various settlements for supply reasons. One battle took place close to the town of Anxi, which Liu Bei had once lived in and managed as a county magistrate.

"So many of these armies have no competent leaders," Yuan Shao scoffed as he watched his Wuhuan cavalrymen cut down one confused soldier after another.

"They are like beasts with no heads," the adviser Guo Tu snickered. "Gongsun Zan's completely abandoned them to hide in Yijing, just as the reports stated!"

"I truly feared his tens of thousands, but if they will all be as easy a challenge as this, then destroying Gongsun will be as easy as taking something from a sack," Yuan Shao said. "Tan writes to say that Tian Kai has completely abandoned Qing Province, and that eastern Yòu will soon be under our complete control: we cannot be here for more than a year, I think!"

"We must still be cautious," the adviser Tian Feng suggested. "The Black Mountain Bandits-"

"You make gods out of dogs, Tian Feng!" the adviser Pang Ji heckled. "Weren't you on the campaign where Lord Yuan humbled the bandits, slayed their mightiest leaders and chased them into the hills? Are there more than ten of them now?"

"There are still close to a *hundred thousand*, Pang Ji, and Zhang Yan – their mightiest leader by far – still lives and no doubt bears a grudge," Tian Feng replied calmly. "We cannot rule out the possibility that they will aid their former sponsor."

"...Unlikely!" Pang Ji insisted. "Why should they risk further humiliation by Lord Yuan when-"

"ATTACK!"

The defenders of Anxi had decided to fight to the last in a moment of desperation; they charged Yuan Shao's position as one, and Yuan's army was forced to surround and destroy them. Generals Yan Liang and Wen Chou led their men away from the town and ordered their cavalry to show no mercy; the Wuhuan riders needed no explanations and hacked down the Yòu infantrymen with their axes, spears, halberds and swords.

"**Pathetic!**" Wen Chou said as he slashed at a poorly-equipped infantry captain and killed him in a single stroke. "**These men are already broken: it is broken eggs against rocks!**"

Yuan Shao turned to a young major and said, "**Ju Hu, go forth and make your father proud.**"

"**I shall, Lord Yuan!**" Ju Hu replied as he led a cavalry charge at the nearest group of enemy soldiers.

"**If he is capable, I shall promote him to a general,**" Yuan Shao suggested.

"**I wouldn't advise that,**" Guo Tu chuckled dismissively.

"**I agree: Ju Shou knows too much favour already,**" Pang Ji said. "**Promote his son, and-**"

"*Aiee*... **must you always divide us all...?**" Tian Feng cried. "**Ju Shou is one of the most loyal men in Ji! The-!**"

"**If he can betray one lord, Mister Tian Feng, then he can**

betray another," Guo Tu replied.

"...**Fool! You condemn yourself with your arguments, as you almost always do!"** Tian Feng heckled. "**You 'betrayed' Han Fu as well! In fact, he was opposed to it while you-!"**

"**Enough about Han Fu!"** Yuan Shao said guiltily. "**That man died a long time ago now, so why am I still hearing his name??? And Mister Tian is right: Ju Shou is an exemplary official and his son is a good man. Perhaps I will reconsider promoting him, yes, but he is still a fine officer! Look how he scatters the wretches as easily as Yan Liang and Wen Chou do!"**

Pang Ji sneered.

"...**Any word from General Chunyu Qiong or General Zhang Hè?"** Yuan Shao asked.

"**General Chunyu has met little opposition,"** Guo Tu reported. "**No word from General Zhang yet, but he's in western Changshan, so messengers will take a while longer."**

The Anxi defenders were either running away, dying or lying dead on the ground; Yuan Shao laughed and said, "**Zhang Hè is, like my Yan Liang and Wen Chou, a hero for the future times. He'll soon report the end of western resistance, and then it is on to Yijing Fortress and Gongsun Zan's last breath!"**

General Yan Liang, General Wen Chou and Major Ju Hu approached their leader; each man held the severed head of an enemy officer in his left hand and their polearm in their right.

"**Although the men you present are all mediocrities, they will still earn you merit,"** Yuan Shao declared while Guo Tu completed the gory task of collecting the battle trophies from each man. "**Arrange your men and prepare to press on! Glory to the Han!"**

"**As you command! Glory to the Han!"** Ju Hu said.

"**None shall withstand us! Glory to the Han!"** Yan Liang said.

"**Glory to the Han! Glory to the Commander-in-Chief!"** Wen Chou cried.

"When this is over, what will you do...?" Tian Feng asked as the officers retreated to ready their forces for the advance.

"That depends on my dear old friend Cao Cao, as it has done for some time," Yuan Shao replied coldly. "If he wins, we improvise; if he blunders again, I march on Yan. Let us go now."

Tian Feng nodded slowly as he tried to rationalise the path to inevitable conflict with Cao Cao that was being followed. Many of Yuan Shao's advisers had suggested that he destroy the weaker Cao Cao of earlier times, just as Cao's advisers were now suggesting that he destroy Liu Bei; now Cao Cao was very powerful, even if he was still far weaker militarily, and that would make any battle costly.

"...The right course, but we are too late in taking it," Tian Feng muttered as he followed his lord.

There would be many battles in Yòu Province as Yuan Shao led his forces northward to Yijing; some would be battles of the sword, while others would be battles of the mind. One battle that would not be fought with swords took place in Zhending, the capital of Changshan Prefecture in western Yòu.

"**He left us to fend for ourselves!"**

"All the food's in Yijing!"
"Haven't loads of others already surrendered?"
"I won't fight for Gongsun Zan!"
Cavalry Captain Zhao Yun – whose style name was 'Zilong' – listened to the many protestations that his subordinates were making and pondered his response.
"We joined Gongsun with you years ago, Zilong, but there's no way that we can help him now, not with all that we're finding out!" one cavalryman said. **"Sorry, but if you go back to him, you go without me."**
"And me!"
"Me too!"
"...But who do we serve, then...?" Zhao Yun asked.
"You *want* to go back to him???" another man heckled.
Zhao Yun smiled and replied, "I did not say that. I simply asked who it is that we serve. Yuan Shao is Commander-in-Chief of the Han. Gongsun Zan is – was – Magistrate of Zhou and a general in Governor Liu Yu's military, but now we know that Governor Liu was murdered and the province seized. We served Gongsun Zan after Governor Liu's death, but only because we were told that the death was not suspicious and that Yuan Shao intended harm and that Yuan Shu was virtuous; now Yuan Shu claims to be emperor and is hated by the world, Yuan Shao is the Han's sword and shield and Gongsun hides away in Yijing with all the food and lets everyone else fend for themselves."
The cavalrymen chattered agreeably.
""We're most of us men from right here, in Zhending," Zhao Yun continued. "We are most of us people that knew each other before all of this chaos. Any man that isn't was a man that we met on the way to Pingyuan or a man that we met while we were there."
"...That's an idea!" the first man said. "We could go to Liu Bei!"
"Forgive me, but that's not a good idea right now," Zhao Yun replied. "Gongsun Zan is Liu Bei's friend: we do not know if they are similarly fated to betray the Han as Gongsun already has. Liu Bei is in Xu Province, and the politics there is complicated; tavern gossip portrays many Liu Beis, and none of them are a man that we should be crossing the land to follow. I, like all of you, remember his kind leadership fondly, but times change and men change with them. Gongsun Zan was hailed as a hero not more than ten years ago... and now he is a villain."
"So we go to Yuan Shao," the cavalryman retorted.
"Let's surrender to Yuan Shao's generals and let them decide," Zhao Yun replied.

Zhao Yun led his men out of Zhending and took them to the camp of Yuan Shao's campaign generals Zhang Hè and Gao Lan; Zhang Hè greeted the cavalrymen at the gates of the fenced camp and watched as every man dismounted, fell to one knee and joined a collective pledge that they would not fight for Gongsun Zan.
"Please, all of you, rise," Zhang Hè said as Gao Lan joined him.
"Are we going to use them...?" Gao Lan whispered. "They look seasoned."
Zhang Hè turned to Zhao Yun and asked, "How much battle experience have you had?"
"We were stationed in Pingyuan, where we served under General

Tian Kai and then Major Liu Bei," Zhao Yun replied fearlessly.
"*Aiee*… Liu Bei's force in Pingyuan was very well respected, and their achievements are still notable, even if he's become a bit of a joke now," Gao Lan said. "These men are probably very good."
"Why are you here in Zhending, Captain Zhao?" Zhang Hè asked.
"My brother died some years ago, and I left Liu Bei's service to return home to Zhending and mourn his passing," Zhao Yun explained. "There were more tragedies after that, sad to say, and so I had to remain here; my friends and colleagues drifted back here as Tian Kai lost more and more of Qing Province, and now here we are."
Zhang Hè hummed thoughtfully and said, "Men like you are wasted as prisoners or battle fodder; would you be prepared to serve Commander Yuan Shao in even the slightest capacity? I cannot promise high rank or front-line service, but the alternatives are few and worse."
"We are here to serve the Han," Zhao Yun replied. "We will aid the Han cause in whatever way that we can, General Zhang."
"…Then your surrender and your service are both accepted," Zhang Hè declared. "I will have your ability and achievements made known to Commander Yuan."
Zhao Yun bowed humbly.

Yuan Shao's advance through Changshan was not always bloodless, but many were as keen to rebuke Gongsun Zan and serve the Han as Zhao Yun had been. Zhao would not know important service for some time, but by choosing to join Yuan Shao he had made it possible for his next lord to meet him again and make him one of the most famous figures of the era.

****

82

The next advice that Chen Gong, Wang Kai and Xu Si offered to Lü Bu was as obvious as it was self-destructive: Bu would be encouraged to repair his relationship with the pretender Yuan Shu, ask assistance of Zang Ba's Mount Tai Bandits and oppose Cao Cao and Liu Bei with everything that Xu Province could muster. In addition, Lü Bu wrote to Zhang Yang, his old colleague and friend from his days serving Inspector Ding Yuan in Bing Province: this time, he was writing for military support rather than advice, and Grand Marshal Zhang's allies were far from happy.

"Write to Dong Gongren, and have him put you straight," General Sui Gu pleaded.

"Fengxian is my friend!" Zhang Yang chortled. "Dong Zhao showed why Yuan Shao was better rid of him when he tricked me into letting that wretch Cao Cao near His Majesty, and then convinced me His Majesty was safer in Xuchang; you think I'm going to let him talk me into abandoning a man that is trying to-"

"Bu's allied to Yuan Shu!" General Yang Chou cried. "Yuan Shu seeks the demise of the Han, so how can Bu be trying to save it?"

Zhang Yang groaned and said, "You... you're right in a sense... but as Fengxian has said, the matter is complex! He's not allied to Yuan Shu by choice! Cao Cao has isolated him! What have Cao the Crafty Villain and the treacherous Liu Bei got planned after they've killed Fengxian and robbed the land of its only hero, mm...? What if Cao Cao plans a regicide, like Dong Zhuo did, and puts Bei on the throne? There will be no Fengxian to smite the new-"

"Bu is no hero," Yang Chou replied. "You're muddled, Lord Zhang."

"...I'll hear no more," Zhang Yang insisted. "Cao Cao is the enemy of the people: he kills the innocent, abducts the sovereign and oppresses the just. I'll not just sit here and watch while he eliminates the only man that can stop him!"

General Sui Gu sighed with anguish; General Yang Chou shook his head sadly, turned to a subordinate and whispered instructions.

"I want everybody to mobilise," Zhang Yang continued. "We're marching on Yan!"

Later that same afternoon, General Yang Chou visited Zhang Yang in his private office. Zhang Yang was reading a military manual; he looked up, smiled, and said, "How go the preparations...?"

Yang Chou lunged and ran the unarmed Zhang Yang through with his sword. The Grand Marshal gurgled, spluttered and grasped at empty air as Yang Chou stepped back prepared to strike again, but it was not necessary. Blood poured from Zhang Yang's mouth, and after one last grasp at the air above him – as though he were reaching for the heavens – Zhang fell to the floor and expired. Yang Chou walked to Zhang's official seal of office and grasped it tightly before he left the room and began a swift, regimented walk toward the training grounds.

"LISTEN TO ME!" Yang Chou cried as he stood on a raised area and viewed the hundreds of soldiers before him. **"Zhang Yang is dead! There will be no march against Yan or to Xu!"**

The soldiers looked at one-another bemusedly.

"We will tender our service to His Excellency Cao Cao!" Yang Chou continued. **"We will remain here, or we will join Cao Cao on his march against the traitors in the south!"**
Sui Gu approached Yang Chou and said, "What are you doing?"
"Don't challenge me, Sui," Yang Chou said as he held the administrator's seal aloft. "We're surrendering to the Han!"
Sui Gu spied Yang Chou's bloodied shirt, scanned the area to assess the number of supporters that Yang Chou had, and then he smiled, saying, "Why are we doing that? No one knows that Zhang pledged support to Bu, do they?"
Yang Chou lowered his confiscated seal and said, "He sent advance word to Bu before we even heard about it all, Sui. He never intended to give us a chance to talk him out of it. If that letter's intercepted, or found after Bu's dead, we're dead too."
The soldiers on the ground watched the exchange nervously.
"...Then you did the right thing," Sui Gu said purposefully. "We have to do the right thing. Have you sent word to His Excellency Cao yet...?"
"No, I killed Zhang and came straight here," Yang Chou replied thoughtlessly.
Most of the junior officers that surrounded Sui Gu and Yang Chou were unaware of Zhang Yang's death, including some of Yang Chou's own men: Sui Gu sensed the tension and said, "*Killed*...? Oh, I thought you'd locked him in his office. He's very popular, Yang Chou. That might have been unwise."
"I had no choice!" Yang Chou retorted as men neared him with angry expression on their faces. "He was going to-!"
"Y'know, it's funny; you were the one that went on most about Lü Bu, and yet you've just done to Zhang Yang *exactly* what Bu did to Ding Yuan," Sui Gu suggested. "You also said there was only one way to deal with men like Bu... and I agree."
Yang Chou tried to draw his sword, but he had the seal in his hand and was forced to drop it before he could do so: Sui Gu had no such impediment, and he immediately ran Yang Chou through with his own sword. As Yang Chou fell backwards and into a group of his loyalists, a fight seemed inevitable: it was short, and it only took one more fatality before Yang Chou's captains surrendered to the rest.
"...Now we need a new plan," Sui Gu sighed as he knelt and picked up Zhang Yang's gore-laden seal. He took the object in hand, stood up to address the soldiers, and said, **"We're not going to help Lü Bu. We're not going to Cao Cao either."**
"Then where are we going...?" a captain asked.
"There's only one man left with a halfway-good reputation," Sui Gu replied. **"Heaven knows, I don't want to work for him, not with the past I have, but we have no choice."**
"Who...?" the captain asked. **"Can't we just-?"**
"Stay neutral...?" Sui Gu chuckled. **"Nope: Liu Biao tried that, and so did Lord Zhang, Heaven rest his confused soul. We have to go to Cao Cao, Lü Bu, Liu Biao, or one of the Yuans, 'cause they're all that's left... so Yuan Shao it is."**
The junior officers did not argue, because they had no alternative suggestion; Sui Gu turned to the men and said, **"Back to barracks! There'll be no war for us today."**
The soldiers were gratefully dismissed; Zhang Yang was buried

honourably, while Yang Chou was buried as a traitor. Acting Administrator Sui Gu sent a letter to Yè City in Ji Province, pledging his allegiance to its governor Yuan Shao, and Shao's administration gratefully accepted.

The self-proclaimed 'Man among men', Lü Bu, had lost his only friend: he would not get help from Henei or anywhere else, so he would face Cao Cao alone.

Cao Cao, meanwhile, was tiring of one man that he had reluctantly allowed to join his third march into Xu Province in two years; that man was Mi Heng, Kong Rong's young friend, who elected to protest outside Cao Cao's command tent every time the army stopped to rest or fight Lü Bu's regional forces.

"...**Insufferable! He is *insufferable*!**"

Cao Cao's cry finally forced Guo Jia to say, "Then you must decide what to do with him, Excellency."

"Every time he sits out there he says things about *me*, about my *father*, about Grandfather Teng that kindly adopted my father!" Cao Cao continued. "He goes too far, gentlemen! He speaks of my last visits to this place, and-!"

"Then *do something*, Excellency, before he demoralises us any further," Xun Gongda suggested. "You said something about 'a fellow that you could send him to'; who was this 'fellow'...?"

Cao Cao finally calmed down and turned to Guo Jia, who said, "You're thinking of Liu Biao."

"*Liu Biao*...?" Xun Wenruo exclaimed.

"He tolerates Wang Can," Cao Cao replied. "As I said before, I am touchy and more affected by my high office and responsibilities than I had ever expected to be. Perhaps Liu Biao will find him to be more agreeable."

"I shall inform Mi Heng of your wishes at once, Excellency!" Xun Gongda said excitedly.

Xun Gongda left the command tent and spoke to Mi Heng, who was sat outside the tent, smacking the ground with a thin branch and hollering abuse at the occupants; Guo Jia turned to Cao Cao and asked, "Do you think that Liu Biao will thank you...?"

"As long as Mi Heng isn't my problem, I don't care," Cao Cao said.

Mi Heng sensed that he had outstayed his welcome; he gathered his things, left Cao Cao's army and began a lonely westward journey to Jing Province with a letter of recommendation from Excellency Cao Cao. The young scholar did not intend to stop in Xuchang, as he intended to write to Kong Rong once he was safely installed in the temperate Liu Biao's court in Xiangyang; Cao Cao quickly forgot about Mi Heng and turned his attentions back to the battle for Xu Province.

The 'White Horse General', Gongsun Zan, summoned his followers to his command room in Yijing and made a strategic proposal.

"Changshan is going, Liaoxi is gone, and we're about to lose control of every road to Yijing," Gongsun Zan said. "We can't suffer another direct attack by Yuan Shao's forces. Before we lost our access roads to the western mountains, I sent my son Xu to request aid from the Black Mountain Bandits."

"To what end...?" the adviser Guan Jing asked.

"There are two ways to end this, and the current choice – to sit here and withstand Yuan Shao's persistent attacks – is too damaging," Gongsun Zan replied. "The other is to somehow get the elite cavalry out of Yijing, meet with Zhang Yan and attack Ji Province while Yuan Shao's entire army is here in Yijing fighting a decoy force; he'll get word, turn around to defend Ji and-"
"*Ayah*… no, my lord, that's far too dangerous," Guan Jing insisted.
"More dangerous than sitting here and rotting, Mister Guan…?" Gongsun Zan retorted.
"If only you had waited to speak to me before you sent your son!" Guan Jing lamented. "Your plan would be sound if every man in the city fought with all his heart for you and you alone, but what happens when you're not here…?"
Gongsun looked at the rest of his tired, malnourished officials.
"Like it or not, Lord Gongsun, you lost a lot of men with your idea of coalescing the supplies and elite men in here and waiting Yuan out," Guan Jing continued. "If you now abandon this fortress as you abandoned the likes of Wang Men, they'll throw the gates open as soon as a heartfelt plea is made and you'll lose Yòu Province. What good will attacking Ji be then…?"
Gongsun Zan exhaled noisily.
"Yuan Shao has a supply line, and that can be cut when we know where it is," Guan Jing suggested. "Moreover, your son has gone to request help from Zhang Yan; that will add tens of thousands to our cause, and Yuan cannot possibly hope to stay here when he surrounded by bandits and far from home with dwindling supplies. We can then attack him as he retreats to Ji, which will have the same effect as your plan but with none of the risk of losing this province in the process."
"…Alright," Gongsun Zan conceded. "We… we hold."
Gongsun Zan's situation was not unlike that which Lü Bu – a man that had similarly taken his province from its imperial relative governor by force – would soon be enduring; two famous men were facing the prospects of ending their careers in the same ignominious fashion at more or less the same time, and each by one of the former defenders of the 'Partisans' in days gone by.

****

83

Lü Bu sat in the living quarters of his governor's residence and listened to the distant sounds of preparations for war. His wife Lady Yan sat opposite him, starting into his eyes and smiling strangely, while his daughter Lady Lü loitered near the entrance to her sleeping quarters and watched her parents cautiously.

"...Soon, Cao Cao will be here," Lü Bu said suddenly.

"Perhaps you should not have listened to Gongtai," Lady Yan said.

"And who should I have listened to...? *Chen Gui*...?" Lü Bu retorted. "That man tricked me into risking everything. Our daughter could be a princess now! I-!"

Chen Gong rushed into Lü Bu's living quarters with General Wei Xu and said, "My lord, scouts have reported that Cao Cao has reached Peng. His men will be exhausted after the long march and battles against the various militias we stationed along the-"

"So...?" Lü Bu sighed.

"Now is the moment to act," Chen Gong protested. "If we leave it any longer, Cao Cao will recover from his long march and cross the Si River. This is the stratagem of 'pitting the rested and healthy against the tired and weak': if we do that now, he'll be blunted, and we'll win for certain."

"...Didn't Tao Qian try and fight Cao Cao at Peng?" Lü Bu retorted. "His men were even more exhausted then, from destroying everything they'd met on the way, and yet they still won. And his men were already in Peng. Mine have to exhaust themselves crossing the river and marching there, and by the time they get there, who will be tired and who will be rested?"

Lady Yan smiled and nodded agreeably.

"...It doesn't work like that!" Chen Gong chortled desperately.

"But if we stay here, won't it be the case that my men will still be rested...?" Lü Bu continued. "And after crossing the Si River, won't his be even more tired...?"

Chen Gong shook his head slowly.

"And then, when they attack, we'll charge and push them back to the Si, and drown them in it, like we did to Zhang Xun!" Lü Bu continued. "That will be a victory that rids us of all our enemies!"

"...*Aiee*... **Lord Lü, we must attack at Peng, and at once!**" Chen Gong barked.

Lü Bu picked up a wine dish, gestured that Lady Yan should fill it for him, and said, "We'll let him cross the Si, Mister Chen."

Chen Gong growled with frustration and left Lü Bu's residence.

"...I'm right," Lü Bu decided. "Cao Cao will die here."

Cao Cao's forces were allowed to rest for a day at Peng, which meant that their march to the Si River was fast and unimpeded: they crossed, set up camps, and advanced on Xiapi with unbridled ferocity. Lü Bu's surprised and demoralised men were forced to go on an immediate defensive, and Chen Gong was left despairing.

"**Didn't I say this would happen???**" Chen Gong cried as Lü Bu paced back and forth in his living quarters: Bu's wife and daughter watched the exchange from the entrance to the sleeping quarters.

"...What do you want? **A reward for your worthless insight???**" Lü Bu retorted.

"It would not be 'worthless insight', my lord, if you'd only *listened*!" Chen Gong said. "Now all is lost!"

"I have to address my officers," Lü Bu grumbled. "There is only one course of action now. Have them gather in the keep of the White Gate Tower."

"...Alright," Chen Gong replied.

"Father, what will happen to us...?" Lady Lü asked once Chen Gong had departed.

"We'll be alright," Lü Bu replied. "I am a man among men, but I see now that I have erred in my actions. I intend to surrender, after all."

"But Cao Cao and Liu Bei will kill you!" Lady Yan exclaimed.

"No they won't," Lü Bu chuckled. "Bei is too noble, and Cao will be content with the heads of others that have wronged him worse than I have. Chen Gui was right before..."

Lü Bu left his family and went to the high keep of White Gate Tower: Chen Gong, Wang Kai, Xu Si, Chen Qun, Zhang Liao, Gao Shun, Wei Xu, Cao Xing, Hou Cheng and several subordinate officers were waiting for him. The sounds of war were not far away, and every now and then a projectile struck the reinforced observation tower and made the inhabitants flinch.

"Why have you called us all here now, Lord Lü?" Gao Shun asked. "We have defences to oversee!"

"**Be quiet!**" Lü Bu barked. "I have... I have an announcement."

"What have you decided...?" Chen Qun asked hopefully.

"I will surrender," Lü Bu declared. "Cao Cao is a wise man, and-"

"*Ayah*! Not again!" Chen Gong exclaimed. "**Stop wavering! Stop it, stop it! We cannot surrender to Cao Cao! He is the greatest villain under Heaven!**"

"Let the lord speak," Gao Shun said angrily. "This is about us all."

"Indeed," Lü Bu said. "Cao Cao is a clever man and a sensible one: he is not interested in any of you; I doubt he truly means me harm either, for he is forgiving too. He sieges us because we resisted needlessly, so if we-"

"**Fool!**" Chen Gong cried. "**This is *Cao Cao*! What was clever or sensible about what he did to this province??? If he's so forgiving, where is *Zhang Miao*? If he will stop a needless siege, where is *Zhang Chao*? If he is so wise, then will you explain his recent campaign against *Wan City* to me...?**"

Lü Bu faltered.

"He *never* keeps his word; understand that if nothing else," Chen Gong continued. "He'll promise you amnesty, but he won't abide by it. You're Lü Bu... the foster son of Dong Zhuo... the murderer of kind Ding Yuan... looter of tombs... kidnapper of sovereigns... murderer of princes-"

"**SHUT UP!**" Lü Bu cried emotionally.

"Betrayer of covenants... you're inconstant, untrustworthy, and above all, strong and a threat to everything that he tries to do," Chen Gong continued. "Really, my lord, be sensible: how can you expect to be spared...?"

Lü Bu lowered his head and exhaled noisily.

"...My lord, what are our orders...?" Gao Shun asked.

Lü Bu was silent for a few moments before he looked up and said, "We... we hold."

The junior officers grumbled inanely, and Chen Qun groaned as a sign of his anger at what was happening.

"Don't just stand there!" Lü Bu screamed. **"Return to your duties! Yes, I'm a fool! There will be no surrender! Of Cao, Bei and I, only one of us can live by the end of this, and it must be me! Now GO!"**

The officers and advisers filed out of the keep; Gao Shun, Chen Qun and others made a point of glaring at the relieved Chen Gong as they passed him.

"...So: now I have decided to fight, what do I do now...?" Lü Bu said as he looked at Chen Gong with tired, angry eyes.

"Write to Yuan Shu, my lord," Chen Gong replied. "Have him-"

Lü Bu grinned maniacally, laughed, and said, "The pretender again! Very good!"

"...Have him send aid," Chen Gong continued. "Cao's brought everything worth bringing to Xu, so Yuan Shu will have the men to support you: if he wants to survive, he'll need you now. Write at once... no, wait... trusted men must go."

"This is your idea, so why don't *you* go to him...?" Lü Bu chuckled. "You'll be safe then! Safe... safe and sound... while I am **TRAPPED, HUNTED DOWN AND KILLED LIKE A DOG! Oh, Chen Gong, you are my Jia Xu!"**

Chen Gong winced and said, "I seek no 'escape'! If someone must go, let it be Wang Kai or Xu Si!"

Lü Bu was silent: his eyes closed, and he appeared to calm down.

"Shall I send one of them at once...?" Chen Gong prompted. "Or did you have someone else in mind, my lord...?"

"Fine," Lü Bu replied. "Send *both*; do it now."

"And scouts bring word of Chen Deng," Chen Gong continued. "He's bringing an army quietly, no doubt to surprise Cao Cao. With his help, Zang Ba's harassment tactics and Yuan Shu's aid, we can still win!"

"...Just go and get on with it," Lü Bu muttered.

Chen Gong left his master and did as he was asked; Bu returned to his home and awaited news of further developments.

"...Why are you back here...?" Lü Bu heckled as Chen Gong entered his living quarters no more than an hour after dissolving the meeting at the White Gate Tower.

"I... I am afraid that Wang Kai and Xu Si cannot get through without a distraction," Chen Gong chuckled nervously.

"A *distraction*...?" Lü Bu replied warily.

"...A *big* distraction," Chen Gong said.

Lü Bu exhaled fiercely, got to his feet and shouted, **"Armour!"**

Han army scouts reported sudden activity on all sides of Xiapi City to Cao Cao.

"So the 'Man among men' has decided to make an appearance!" Cao Cao chuckled.

Xiapi's four sets of gates opened almost simultaneously; Zhang Liao and Cao Xing appeared at the southern gate, Gao Shun and Hou Cheng appeared at the eastern gate, and Wei Xu appeared at the northern gate where attacks were not as intensive. For a moment, there was silence at the western gates as the besiegers wondered who or what would confront them; amongst them were Liu Bei's forces that he led in person.

"Why're the men hesitating?" Zhang Fei complained. "We should–"
Many of the Han soldiers turned and fled from the walls as Lü Bu raced out of the western gates atop a huge, reddish-brown Arabian steed and tore into them with his heavy halberd; he then glared at his enemies fearlessly and screamed, "**HERE IS LÜ BU! WHERE ARE THE MEN THAT DARE TO CLAIM TO BE MY EQUALS? WHO WILL TRY AND END THIS WITH A DUEL...?**"
Zhang Fei snarled and prepared to engage Lü Bu.
"Don't be a fool!" Liu Bei hissed. "You're still not recovered fully from the rout at Xiaopei: he'll tear you apart!"
"**Then *I* will go!**" Guan Yu said as he rode forward with his Green Dragon pole sword raised.
"*Ayah!* **Neither are you, Yunchang! Come back, or you'll die!**" Liu Bei cried.
"**I'll help you, Yunchang!**" Zhang Fei said as he urged his own horse forward.
"...They were both really great men," Jian Yong sighed. "I'll miss them, Xuande."
"This is not a joking matter!" Liu Bei whined.
Lü Bu grinned and met Guan Yu's charge; the two failed to land any of their strikes and counter-strikes, but many expected that to change when Zhang Fei joined the fight.
"**AT LAST, A REAL CHALLENGE!**" Lü Bu cackled as he kicked at Zhang Fei and turned his horse sideways to best meet both men.
"**You can't fight us both!**" Zhang Fei barked.
"**Get back, Yide!**" Guan Yu protested. "**I want a fair fight!**"
"**Then fight elsewhere!**" Lü Bu said as he moved at speed and put both men off-balance with powerful shoves from his halberd; he was obviously enjoying the battle and knew the demoralising effect that it would have on his enemies.
"He's... *incredible*," Jian Yong admitted as Bu continued to guide his well-trained horse and deflect the blows of both of Liu Bei's generals at the same time.
"**He's like a demon, or a god!**" one Han soldier exclaimed.
"...*Aiee*...! **They deprive me of my best generals when they sacrifice themselves like this!**" Liu Bei complained. "**I might as well die too!**"
Liu Bei urged his horse and charged at Lü Bu with one of his swords raised; his lead bodyguard, Chen Dao, screamed "**Lord Liu!**" and sped after him.
"...**Well don't just sit there!**" Jian Yong shouted at the rest of Bei's bodyguards. "**Go and help!**"
"...**I WILL KILL YOU ALL!**" Lü Bu screamed as he spotted Liu Bei's approach. "**I WILL KILL YOU AS I SHOULD HAVE KILLED YOU BEFORE!**"
Several of Lü Bu's cavalrymen rode out of the gates to even the numbers, and the battle intensified.
"...He's mad," Chen Gong muttered as he watched the melee from the walls; the only man to hear his words – an archery captain – gave no response.
"**Master Chen Gong! Wang Kai and Xu Si have slipped past the besiegers at the east gate!**" a messenger reported.
"...Then it is time to rescue our lord before he gives Liu Bei a good reputation," Chen Gong chuckled desperately; he then turned to and shouted, "**ARCHERS!**"

Arrows rained down on Liu Bei's men; Liu Bei immediately broke off his attack and fled, and Guan Yu, Chen Dao and the other bodyguards followed.

"**YIDE!**" Liu Bei cried, as he sensed that his old ally was still trying to get the better of Lü Bu. "**YIDE, MOVE!**"

Zhang Fei could not hear his lord, but something told him that he was being scolded; he turned and fled from the grinning Bu, yelling, "**NEXT TIME, BU! NEXT TIME, YOU SCUM!**"

"**NEXT TIME YOU DIE!**" Lü Bu cackled as he turned and rode into the city; the gates closed behind him, and the distraction slowly came to an end.

"...So Bu and *all of Bu's generals* rode out and challenged...?" Cao Cao exclaimed as a messenger completed a report. "...From *every gate*...? ...He's sent a man out to go to someone, for certain."

"For all the good it'll do him," Guo Jia snickered. "His only choices are Zhang Yang – who is too far away – Zang Ba – who aids him anyway, and in the only way that he can or will, making the mission pointless – and Yuan Shu, who will refuse to help without some preposterous set of conditions that Bu cannot hope to meet, and has no means to help him anyway. All he's done is let one man escape death, and deprive himself of fodder."

"If he could hear you, Bu would cry," Xun Wenruo chuckled.

"I was magnificent!" Lü Bu declared as he returned to his living quarters with Chen Gong. "I am presuming that Wang Kai and Xu Si are safely away...?"

"The plan was a success, yes," Chen Gong replied. "We are sure to be sent aid soon, my lord."

"Cao Cao will die here!" Lü Bu cackled. "Yes... **Cao Cao, your doom is nigh!**"

Lady Yan watched her power-drunk husband and his adviser from the entrance to the sleeping quarters and sighed disdainfully.

At the northern frontier, the battle raged on. Gongsun Zan's ally Tian Kai led a force southwards to intercept Yuan Shao's officer Zhang Hè; the two small armies met on and around a road that would, if lost, provide Yuan Shao with a more efficient supply line and link his forces together.

"**He has Wuhuan cavalry!**" Tian Kai complained. "**How can the Wuhuan side with a man that will destroy them?**"

"**Because our lord has already led armies against them, and the violence bred resentment,**" the adviser-officer Tian Yu replied. "**Yuan Shao promises marriage alliances and autonomy, as the Southern Xiongnu enjoy.**"

"**...Perhaps we should have negotiated,**" Tian Kai sighed.

"**It is too late for that now,**" Tian Yu said. "**We must ready ourselves for the battle ahead and worry only about winning it.**"

Zhang Hè and his ally Gao Lan met in their command tent to discuss Tian Kai's competent defence plans.

"Tian held Yuan Tan at bay for quite a while," Zhang Hè noted. "He's a man that we should be wary of."

"But his sword is blunted," Gao Lan suggested. "Their cavalry is broken, and the majority of their regional support has gone; this once-great man is alone against us, and no man won a battle by himself."

"I don't doubt that he will be easy to push aside, but we want to minimise casualties for the battles ahead," Zhang Hè retorted. "A direct attack will incur losses; a patient stratagem will wear down our supplies. That is my dilemma."

Gao Lan hummed thoughtfully.

"...We have no choice," Zhang Hè decided. "Speed is a priority, since we have our back to the mountains and the Bandits might suddenly attack: in fact, he is probably here in order to facilitate some sort of reinforcement from this direction. Tian Kai must be removed from our path. We'll use a decoy force and..."

Tian Kai and Tian Yu waited for the inevitable surprise attack, but it did not come; a force advanced on their position in plain sight and formed a simple battle line.

"...So Zhang Hè plays a cautious game," Tian Yu mused. "That's unexpected."

"So what do we do?" Tian Kai wondered. "I'm hesitant to charge in case it's a decoy for a flanking attack... but if we just sit here, they could go around us if that's all that they're trying to do and leave us sitting here like fools, or they could pincer us anyway once we've lost our readiness."

"Then we charge," Tian Yu said. "At least we weaken them by attacking that line; we can wheel around if they attack our flanks."

Tian Kai issued the order, and the small militia charged at Zhang Hè's battle line; signalmen raised flags at each end of the line, and word was quickly carried to Zhang Hè and Gao Lan, who then attacked the charging force from north and south. Tian Yu and Tian Kai were separated during the skirmish, but both were able to get most of their men away unscathed and retreat to Yijing for what would be a protracted siege.

"Tian Kai's surrender or death would have been a great victory for our cause," Zhang Hè complained.

"At least the road is ours," Gao Lan replied.

"...True enough," Zhang Hè conceded. "We'll secure the area and proceed to Yijing. And we must send a man to notify Lord Yuan!"

****

84

Three days passed, and the siege of Xiapi went on.

In the Mount Tai Bandits' temporary camp to the north of Xiapi, Zang Ba, Sun Guan, Yin Li, Chang Xi and Wu Dun addressed their subordinates for one last time before they acted.
"...**Alright, friends, here's the plan,**" Zang Ba said. "**It's simple enough: we'll all go to a different place and make as much trouble as we can, which'll force Cao Cao to disperse his forces around Xiapi to deal with us; when Bu's advisers get word of what we're doing, they'll rush out and smash the Han forces while they're divided. It can't get any simpler than that.**"
"**What if Bu's advisers are as stupid as him?**" one man asked.
"Or what if Bu just *doesn't listen to them*...?" Yin Li said cuttingly.
"...**Then we just make a load of noise for as long as we can and hope Cao Cao runs out of food and goes home,**" Zang Ba replied desperately. "**Either way, we're doing *something*! COME ON, FRIENDS!**"
The Mount Tai Bandits filled themselves with false pride and courage and prepared to meet the Han Imperial army in a number of locations to the north and east of Xiapi City.

The embattled Yuan Shu welcomed Wang Kai and Xu Si into his reduced court in Shouchun within a week. When the two visitors were bowing in front of his host seat, Yuan Shu leaned forward, sneered at the envoys and said, "So, minions of the inconstant one... what does he want now...?"
"Aid, Your Majesty," Wang Kai replied.
Yuan Shu laughed at the idea.
"The first time we did business, Han Yin lost his head!" the adviser Yan Xiang said as he pointed at the envoys. "Your master deserves to die!"
"Our master is the victim of inconsistent advice from wicked, selfish men like Chen Gui," Wang Kai protested. "He was fine until he conquered Xu Province and brought those wretches into his trust! When Chen Gong, Xu Si and I invited him to Yan, we saw a different man, a hero! It was his new advisers that cause him trouble and make him appear inconstant, but they have fled, and their words are unheard now! Trust our lord again, Your Majesty! Save him from the evil Cao Cao!"
"He can rot," Yuan Shu said. "Now be gone."
"If he dies, what will become of *you*...?" Xu Si asked. "Isn't it true that Lord Lü is besieged now because he agreed to attack Liu Bei for you?"
Yuan Shu looked at his advisers and replied, "It is."
"Then his latest calamity is your concern!" Xu Si continued. "His loss is also yours... for if he fails to serve as a continued distraction to Cao's hordes, won't they come back here and finish what they started...?"
"...You will both remain here," Yuan Shu said irritably. "Help will be sent when it *can* be sent. A man will be sent to Xiapi to inform Bu of it; Qin Yilu, perhaps, so that he can aid his master in person."

"I would be glad to aid my lord at this critical hour," Qin Yilu declared tonelessly.

Wang Kai and Xu Si kowtowed and said, "Thank you, Majesty!"

"...Leave us," Yuan Shu ordered, and the envoys retreated.

"Mister Qin Yilu: go and prepare your retinue for departure," Yuan Shu ordered.

Qin Yilu kowtowed before he left the court.

"When shall we send help, Your Majesty?" Yan Xiang asked.

"...Not yet," Yuan Shu replied cagily.

Cao Cao was sat in his command tent with Guo Jia and Xun Gongda when he received an unexpected visit from Liu Bei's general Guan Yu; Xu Chu and the rest of Cao's guards raised their weapons and studied the lone warrior's every action.

"...General Guan Yunchang," Cao Cao murmured. "You are truly unlike any other man alive: your beard is truly magnificent, and your face carries no fear or shame!"

"I regret nothing," Guan Yu replied. "I-"

Xun Gongda suspected that Guan Yu was about to begin one of his notorious personal attacks, so he interrupted the general by asking, "Are you here to report something important...?"

"I am here to make a request," Guan Yu replied politely.

"...A request...?" Cao Cao said hesitantly.

"Lü Bu has a subordinate by the name of Qin Yilu, who is, it seems, a famous idiot that is blind to simple matters," Guan Yu explained. "I have heard that Qin Yilu has abandoned his wife, Lady Du, and gone to Yuan Shu in search of fame and fortune, despite her being the mother of his heir; I should like to take her as my consort, but I wanted to seek His Excellency's permission since she will be classed as spoils when this campaign ends."

Cao Cao hummed thoughtfully and said, "That's very honourable, Guan Yunchang. You would take a woman into your home that has the responsibility of the son and heir of another general... an enemy general that you were a party to slaying...?"

"Lady Du has publicly denounced her husband for his selfish behaviour, and her son will no doubt agree since he, too, has been abandoned by the fool Qin," Guan Yu replied. "She does not desire reconciliation, and I would take Qin's son as my own. My wife Lady Hu and my existing children will be happy with that."

"...I see," Cao Cao said. "Well, Guan Yunchang, I shall certainly consider your suggestion and ensure that Lady Du has her say if she survives this awful place; if none object, then I should certainly be happy to grant your request."

Guan Yu bowed humbly and replied, "I would be eternally grateful. Forgive my intrusion, and good evening to all."

Once Guan Yu had retreated, Guo Jia laughed and said, "Unbelievable. All that I have ever heard about that man is his loftiness, his rudeness, his terseness, and his inability to show discretion! Yet here, now, we have seen a very different man!"

"...Indeed," Cao Cao replied.

"If he would be eternally grateful to you for letting him wed this 'Lady Du', then you would surely stand a chance of gaining that fine man for your own army, Excellency!" Xun Gongda suggested.

"...Mm...? Oh, no, I doubt that," Cao Cao replied. "But seeing Guan Yu so desperate to win me over makes me wonder what sort of woman this 'Lady Du' is..."

"Ayah... Are you so eager to suffer more injury?" Guo Jia heckled. "Excellency, do not let this Lady Du be another Lady Zou! Just let Guan have-!"

"I will not empower Liu Bei's faction needlessly," Cao Cao retorted. "And I hardly think that a woman spurned is in any way similar to Lady Zou. Lady Du is an entirely different matter, and I look forward to finding out why Guan craves her."

"Even if doing what I suspect that you intend to do forever earns you Guan Yu as an enemy...?" Guo Jia challenged.

"If he is that petty, then why would I want him for an ally...?" Cao Cao replied. "Lady Du shall decide her own fate, as I promised."

"...With a little gentle persuasion, and an outline of all the facts, no doubt," Guo Jia sighed. "Very well, Excellency... very well."

"Where is Yue Jin?" Cao Cao asked.

"He's still on his way," Guo Jia replied tonelessly.

"...I am still unsure about bringing him here with the muddle-headed Zhang Yang – Bu's old colleague – still sat in Henei," Cao Cao admitted.

"Yue Jin's left capable men to watch Henei and the surrounding regions," Guo Jia replied. "And as for Zhang Yang... I'd not worry about him."

Cao Cao smirked and said, "You know something."

"I know a lot of things," Guo Jia chuckled. "I do not know Zhang Yang's motivations or final fate for certain because I am not a seer, but I can guess both and confidently say that he will not be a concern for us."

"...He should either help us put the rabid dog out of its misery – thus avenging his poor master Ding Yuan in the process – or stay away," Cao Cao replied. "So long as he does either of those things, I will be happy."

Chen Deng's army crossed the Guangling-Donghai prefectural border and began the last part of the march toward Xiapi.

"We will not stop at Ju City to rest, because speed is everything," Chen Deng said to his senior general.

"What will we be doing when we reach Xiapi?" the general asked.

"...I will tell you when we pass Ju," Chen Deng replied. "I am... waiting for something."

Cao Cao smiled when Chen Deng's approaching force was finally reported a day later.

"Will he keep his promise, I wonder...?" Guo Jia said once the messenger had left the command tent. "After all, isn't his brother in Xiapi...?"

"Such a man might fret for his kin and alter his plan if Bu were to threaten his life," Xun Gongda suggested.

"Do not doubt Chen Yuanlong," Cao Cao replied. "He is a great talent, and he'll have a plan..."

While Cao Cao continued his siege of Xiapi, his old acquaintance Yuan Shao was about to face the last defensive position held by Liu Bei's childhood friend Gongsun Zan. That fight would not be easy: Yijing Fortress was a gauntlet of challenges for even the best general to overcome. Ten moats separated the outside world from the structure; the city within was surrounded by towers that sat atop man-made hills and served as grain stores and defensive works that housed the leading officers, including Gongsun Zan himself; the city structure was guarded by the last of Gongsun Zan's White Horse Cavalry and several hundred infantry.

"...Such a place will not fall quickly," Yuan Shao sighed as he viewed Yijing from a hill near his camp. "What can we do...?"

"Every day, you ask that question," Liu Hè said. "Why don't your advisers find an answer? **Will I ever avenge my father???**"

"You will," Yuan Shao promised. "He'll make another mistake."

Yuan Shao's advisers agreed: while Gongsun Zan might have been nominated as a man of good and honest character by the educational system of the Han Dynasty, and while he might once have had a mighty cavalry and a terrifying reputation, he had not been proven to be an able tactician. Many reflected on his first significant mistake at the battle of Jie Bridge six years before, when he had ordered his cavalry to charge at an archery unit and lost hundreds of thoroughbred horses and elite riders; others recalled more recent errors, such as sending whole battalions out of Yijing to fight without support to harden their resolve, only for the soldiers to mutiny, kill their officers and desert. Most of Gongsun's tribal support had disappeared, including the sources of his once-proud cavalry: some were neutral, but others, like the Wuhuan chieftain Tadun, had chosen to side with Yuan Shao. While Yuan Shao had not distinguished himself as one of the finest military minds of the age, he had managed, to that point in time, to have more victories than defeats to his name: Gongsun Zan could not boast the same record at all, and the tribes were known to favour the strong.

"...We *waste time*," Liu Hè said as he turned and walked away.

"You won't let him provoke you into acting rashly, I hope," the adviser Tian Feng prompted.

Yuan Shao chuckled softly and said, "The poor lad has none of his father's wits; if I attack that place head-on, I'll lose everything. No, this will take time and patience..."

Gongsun Zan stood and stared at the swathe of enemy camps that were situated to the south of Yijing and growled angrily. His adviser Guan Jing approached him and asked, "What disturbs you, my lord...?"

"My son has been gone for a long time," Gongsun Zan replied. "I wonder if I should have gone to the Bandits in person."

"I advised against leaving the fortress for a reason, my lord," Guan Jing protested. "Your followers are following you and fighting only for you and their families, and-"

"I remember," Gongsun Zan interrupted. "And I took your advice to hold, but here we are, weeks later, and where are the reinforcements? Where is the retreat due to lack of supplies that you promised me?"

"Yuan Shao cannot hold out forever!" Guan Jing insisted.

"Word has reached me that the mighty Lü Bu is under siege in Xiapi," Gongsun Zan retorted. "He will soon be a memory; I don't want to be a memory, Guan Jing! I have to defeat Yuan Shao! I am not a capricious fool that fights because it is fun! I fight because I want to avenge my poor nephew that Yuan Shao's minions slaughtered so unnecessarily!"

Many of Gongsun's officials recalled the deal that their master had struck with Yuan Shao that had allowed the latter to seize Ji Province from Han Fu; they recalled the subsequent spat between the two over promises supposedly broken, and the secret deal with Yuan Shu that followed that; they recalled that Gongsun's nephew Yue had been sent to aid Sun Jian after Yuan Shao had sent a man to attack his brother's vassal, and that Gongsun Yue had died in battle. The trail of responsibility and blame was long and winding, but ultimately, every man had done another a wrong at some point: Gongsun Zan had killed Yòu Province's governor Liu Yu with very little evidence of necessity, and Yuan Shu had imprisoned Yu's son, so Yuan Shao's side had as much right to claim that the feud was about vengeance.

"He claims that he has tens of thousands of men," Gongsun Zan said. "I do not see such numbers; in fact, I think that he may only have six or seven thousand at this fortress, and he loses at least fifty men a day trying to get past my defences."

"So you see that there is still a hope of victory!" Guan Jing said.

"I... I do," Gongsun Zan replied. "I do, Mister Guan. He'll have lost a thousand men or more by the time he gets to the gates, and then he will lose even more trying to scale the walls. Energy will be spent filling in the moats, toppling the mounds and towers, and every strategist knows that a spent army cannot hope to vanquish a fresh one. My son will definitely return with the help I need, and... and... *aiee*."

Gongsun Zan's melancholy returned; his followers silently shared his pain.

****

85

An unpleasant week passed for the defenders of Xiapi, and there was no sign of the reinforcements that Yuan Shu had discussed. To make matters worse for the defenders, Chen Deng's Guangling army had not come to hinder Cao Cao: it had come to assist him. Lü Bu summoned Chen Gong to his residence to discuss it.
"Chen Deng will die a dog's death," Chen Gong promised.
"We have his brother, and his brother's family," Lü Bu said cruelly. "He shall die first and-!"
"Wait," Chen Gong said with a smile. "If that's the case, we can turn this around and make him work for us!"
"...*How so*?" Lü Bu growled.
"*Aiee*... I can hear the mistrust in every word!" Chen Gong replied as he turned his gaze to the sleeping quarters; Lady Yan smiled coldly and withdrew.
"I... have a good reason for my poor mood," Lü Bu replied.
"There are plenty of good reasons," Chen Gong said. "Which is it, my lord...?"
"...A man sent word that Zhang Yang is dead," Lü Bu continued.
"I know," Chen Gong admitted.
"I've caused the death of that good man too!" Lü Bu whined. "He was gullible, and I exploited it; I always thought he'd suffer for aiding me, but not that! I need Yuan Shu now, but... but there is no sign of his help. We both know why."
"...I'm afraid that I don't know," Chen Gong admitted.
"He expects the marriage alliance to be completed first!" Lü Bu said. "I must somehow get my daughter to Shouchun!"
"...I don't know if that's genuinely wise," Chen Gong replied.
"I must act!" Lü Bu said desperately. "I have a plan..."
Bu's wife, Lady Yan, tried to listen to the scheme that would potentially endanger their daughter; Lady Lü sat on her bed and sobbed, because she could guess that her lot would now be even more miserable.

"Ah! Mister Chen Yuanlong!" Cao Cao said as a miserable Chen Deng entered his busy command tent on the following morning.
"...Mister Chen," Liu Bei hailed coldly.
"I will come back," Chen Deng said.
"No, no!" Cao Cao chuckled. "Liu Xuande had come to report on siege supplies; he was leaving anyway."
"Indeed I was," Liu Bei said as he bowed to every other man – though only slightly when he came to Chen Deng – and began a retreat from the tent.
"...Now, Mister Chen, we can speak," Cao Cao said once Liu Bei was gone.
"Bu has threatened my brother," Chen Deng explained.
"I know of it," Cao Cao replied casually. "You are concerned...?"
"I... I know that he wouldn't dare harm him if he wants to live," Chen Deng chortled. "But if he becomes desperate, I worry that my newfound reputation won't be enough."
"Your triumphs against the Guangling pirates are every bit as impressive as Sun Ce's triumphs in southern Yang," Cao Cao suggested. "That's why Bu was looking forward to receiving your

help! ...And that's why one of his more cowardly subordinates will deliver your captured family members to you within the next three days. Your words, not mine."

"...'Do not panic at the critical hour'," Chen Deng sighed. "I'm a poor adviser, Excellency, if I can't abide by my own counsel."

"You're afraid for your family," Guo Jia said.

"Any of us would feel the same," Xun Gongda suggested.

"...I should make one more proclamation," Chen Deng decided.

"There is such a thing as saying too much," Cao Cao replied.

Chen Deng sighed, bowed humbly and said, "You are quite right, Excellency; silence will achieve more than empty protestations. I promise that my assistance will continue... I shall go now."

Cao Cao nodded, and Chen Deng retreated.

"...Poor fellow," Xun Gongda sighed.

"Chen Deng's more dangerous than he appears, and Bu knows it," Cao Cao said. "Thank the Heavens, gentlemen, that he is our ally and not our enemy."

Two nights later, Chen Deng's brother Ying and his family were escorted to a patch of ground near the western gates of Xiapi by one of Lü Bu's majors; they were dressed as soldiers, although their badly-fitting uniforms were barely convincing.

"What now, Major Zhang...?" Chen Ying asked.

"...I'll open the gates," Major Zhang replied. "Wait here."

Chen Ying's wife fought the urge to sob and hugged her eldest daughter tightly.

"We'll be fine, but stop doing that!" Chen Ying said as quietly as he could. "Do soldiers embrace each other...?"

Mother and daughter separated and tried to stand formally.

"...The rest of you straighten up as well," Chen Ying said to the rest of his family, who did their best to comply.

"Right, then," Major Zhang said as he returned. "They've opened the gates for us; try and look convincing, and you'll make it."

"...Thank you, Major," Chen Ying whispered.

"Thank me my securing me a pardon from His Excellency," Major Zhang replied. "Now go on, go, before they realise you're gone!"

Chen Ying and his family took advantage of the poor light as they marched out of the western gates; once they were clear of the city and the gates started to close, they turned and headed for the nearest camp, which was commanded by Chen Deng. Deng's men were easily convinced of who the visitors were, and Deng rushed to the gates to greet them.

"**Brother!**" Chen Deng cried.

"A thousand thanks to Major Zhang Hong," Chen Ying replied as he embraced his brother. "And a thousand thanks to you, Yuanlong, for being such a hero! Some of them are scared of you, genuinely scared! They call you 'The Pirate Slayer'!"

"They'll be more scared when they learn that I don't have to hold back now," Chen Deng said. "For threatening you, I swear that Bu and his wicked advisers will pay dearly."

"Enough!" Chen Ying pleaded. "Let us be glad we are free!"

Chen Deng invited his rescued family to his command tent and ensured that they were entertained as honoured guests as an apology for their ordeal.

Lü Bu and his associates could not hide their frustration at losing their valuable captives.

"*Aiee…* we needed them!" Chen Gong lamented.

"But someone helped them escape," Lü Bu growled. "Who was responsible for watching them…?"

"The prison officer said that he did not recognise the man that secured their escape," Gao Shun explained. "I do not know who it was, but I am doing my best to find out."

Lü Bu wanted to rebuke Gao Shun, but times were desperate; he smiled falsely and replied, "I know."

Gao Shun turned and left Bu's residence; Chen Gong sighed and said, "We'll have to proceed with your plan to get your daughter to Yuan Shu regardless."

"Yes, yes," Lü Bu scoffed. "What I want to know is why anyone would risk riling me by aiding Chen Ying."

"Chen Deng's proven to be a very persuasive man during his time in Guangling, my lord," Chen Gong replied. "His victories over the pirates were-"

"So I am now less intimidating than *Chen Deng*?" Lü Bu asked angrily. "I've fought a million Black Mountain Bandits! Every man with me knows that!"

"I… I cannot answer that rationally, my lord governor," Chen Gong replied. "Perhaps-"

"Perhaps some of my men prepare for a time when I am gone and Chen Deng remains," Lü Bu suggested. "Perhaps there are men that would do more than hand over Chen Ying… perhaps there are men that would hand *me* over to *Cao Cao*…!"

"No man can be sure of every person in his company," Chen Gong retorted. "Be sure of me, though, my lord; I have nothing to gain from such a scenario."

"…I should like to be alone with my family," Lü Bu ordered.

"As you wish," Chen Gong said as he retreated.

"…**Lady Yan!**" Lü Bu barked. "**We have to talk.**"

Lady Yan prepared to hear her husband's plans for their daughter, Lady Lü, who was already crying quietly.

The young scholar Mi Heng reached Jing Province after two weeks of travelling by cart, horse, boat, and on foot; he was welcomed into Liu Biao's northern capital Xiangyang by the adviser Kuai Liang, the politician Huan Jie and the adviser-politician Wang Can and immediately taken to Liu Biao's court.

"So now I have a good friend of Kong Rong in my court!" Liu Biao chuckled. "You are most welcome here, Mister Mi Heng."

"I am glad to be away from the fool's court that Cao Cao has constructed in Xuchang," Mi Heng replied. "No man is perfect, but there is no need to prove how imperfect they can be by surrounding yourself with the worst examples."

Liu Biao laughed, and many of his courtiers joined him.

"There are many good men, though, like Zhong Yao, Zheng Xuan, Kong Rong, Dong Zhao and the like," Wang Can suggested. "Are they not treated well?"

"Would you like my response as words or *brays*, Wang Can?" Mi Heng retorted.

Liu Biao and some of the other courtiers laughed; Wang Can laughed uncomfortably and replied, "I think words will be better understood, Mi Zhengping."

"Of course there are always some good ones in every bad court, just as there are bad ones in every good court," Mi Heng said as he turned his gaze to Huan Jie.

"...Why do you look in my direction...?" Huan Jie growled.

"Didn't you work for Sun Jian?" Mi Heng asked.

"Sun Jian was a fool that destroyed himself by stealing the Imperial Seal from the ruins of Luoyang and giving the heretic Yuan Shu the ability to make his treasonous claims that split the nation!" Huan Jie retorted. "He is also a touchy subject in this court that you would do well to *avoid*, Mister Mi Heng!"

"...I see," Mi Heng sniggered.

"Your humour will be most appreciated, Mister Mi Heng, though I should add that I don't much appreciate it when there is a crisis," Liu Biao declared. "Fortunately, we are spared disaster at present, though that won't last; Sun Ce is looming to the south, and my unwanted tenants in the north are going to bring more woe when Cao Cao's done with Lü Bu, I'll wager. Are you a strategist...?"

"I am a scholar, a poet and a musician," Mi Heng said proudly. "I am versed in the teachings of Confucius and Mencius, and of derived works such as that penned by Zheng Xuan and his friends, which I had the good fortune to see while I was in Xuchang."

"Oh...?" Liu Biao exclaimed. "Such great wisdom you shall bring to my court! You are a blessing, Mister Mi Heng!"

"...For now, maybe," Huan Jie muttered.

Huan Jie was one of many that sensed that Mi Heng would soon offend everyone, including Liu Biao, and that his irreverent nature would cost him his life one day; they were forced to admit that his talents were many and impressive, however, and Kong Rong was delighted by the letter that he received weeks later. But letters – even urgent ones – took time to travel, and by the time that Mi's correspondence arrived in Xuchang, the situation might have changed considerably; that would be the case as Mi Heng quickly tried the patience of his hosts yet again.

****

86

Two more days passed, and the siege of Xiapi continued.

As night fell, Cao Cao ordered his men to end their efforts to siege the city as he usually did, and the grounds around Xiapi City were silent save for the groans of dying men that had not been recovered. As midnight neared, Lü Bu hurried to the southern gates with his daughter, who was wrapped in leather armour: Chen Gong, Bu's wife Lady Yan and Bu's officers Wei Xu and Zhang Liao followed with a small group of trusted men.
"Reconsider!" Lady Yan pleaded.
"Be silent!" Lü Bu hissed. "Chen Gong: escort my lady home. Wei Xu: help me."
Chen Gong guided Lady Yan away from the gates while the others prepared for a daring mission. Lü Bu squatted, and Lady Lü pressed herself to her father's back as tightly as she could: Wei Xu then secured the young woman to her father's back with rope and added extra cuirasses to her defensive covering. Once Lady Lü was adequately secured, Lü Bu stood up and mounted a readied warhorse.
"This is insanity," Wei Xu muttered involuntarily.
"Oh, Father...!" Lady Lü gasped.
"You add to the misery, Wei Xu!" Lü Bu scolded. "Be silent!"
Wei Xu mumbled apologetically.
"Let's go," Lü Bu continued. "Open the gates."
Zhang Liao gave a signal, and the southern gates were opened: Lü Bu immediately galloped out of the gates with his halberd in one hand and the horse's reins in the other. Wei Xu and Zhang Liao followed on horseback, while the other men followed on foot. Cao Cao's scouts inevitably learned of the apparent escape attempt and reported it to their commanders: within a short time, Bu's small squad was beset by arrows from observation towers and their escape route was blocked by infantry, more wooden observation towers and hastily-erected barricades. Lü Bu cried with frustration as he tried to fight his way through, but the effort had been for naught, and he was forced to return to Xiapi with his squealing, hysterical daughter.
"**Those bastards!**" Lü Bu cried as the gates were closed behind him. "**We'll have to create a way through!**"
"**How do you propose doing that???**" Wei Xu asked.
"**I have to get her to Shouchun!**" Lü Bu screamed over his daughter's wailing. "**Everything depends upon it!**"
Wei Xu did not argue anymore, but he was no longer sure that Lü Bu was sane or likely to survive. A more manpower-intensive attempt to create a path to the south followed, but it resulted in the loss of horses and men, a further reduction in morale, and no more success than the first attempt. Lü Bu returned his shivering, traumatised daughter to their home and remained in his living quarters, desperately trying to conceive a plan to improve his ailing fortunes.

Days passed, and the siege dragged on.

"...Another letter from Guan Yu about this Lady Du," Cao Cao complained as he sat in his command tent with his advisers. "Has she enchanted him...?"

"Rumours have it that Lü Bu was enchanted by a maid, and that she coerced him into killing Dong Zhuo," Guo Jia replied. "Perhaps Lady Du is similarly cursed..."

"...Nice try!" Cao Cao chuckled. "I am still intent on seeing this woman for myself, Guo Jia. I can only think that she is as or more radiant than Lady Zou, and might be Heaven's compensation to me for my previous sufferings."

"Or a way to make another dangerous enemy," Guo Jia retorted. "But I can see that you are driven to pursue your current-"

"**REPORT!**"

Cao Cao and his advisers turned to the messenger, who added, **"Zang Ba and Chang Xi of the Mount Tai Bandits have been sighted to the east! Sun Guan and Yin Li of the Mount Tai Bandits are launching an attack from the north! Wu Dun of the Mount Tai Bandits attacks from the west!"**

"Thank you, soldier," Xun Gongda said. "You may go."

The messenger retreated.

"So Zang Ba is determined to die alongside Lü Bu, is he...?" Cao Cao said with anger. "Who shall we send to counter them...?"

"They're actually a greater threat than Bu now," Xun Gongda suggested. "We'll have to hope that some of Bu's better advisers and generals don't add their own men to this, or we might be pushed back across the Si River."

"I'm not going to be forced to leave here a third time because of a few bandits," Cao Cao growled. "If I'd knew Zang would become this much of a threat, I'd have annihilated him when I was near Kaiyang before! But enough of that: Cao Xiu and Han Hao will counter the eastern force; Yu Jin and Zhu Ling will oppose the northern force; Liu Bei can have one of his generals deal with Wu Dun. I want Yue Jin and Xu Huang to remain here."

"I'll ensure your orders are enacted," Xun Gongda replied.

"**Bastard Cao Cao, bossing us about like this!**" Zhang Fei shrieked as Liu Bei tried to decide who would go and confront the Mount Tai Bandits. "**If I didn't hate Bu and the bandits as much as I do, I'd-!**"

"We know what you'd do, and we know what it would lead to," Liu Bei interrupted.

Zhang Fei exhaled angrily.

"...I was stuck deciding who to send, but you've answered my question," Liu Bei continued. "You, Yide, will fight the Mount Tai Bandits and relieve some of your pent-up frustration. Go and show them why men fear you!"

"...But what if Bu challenges again?" Zhang Fei whined.

"He won't," Mi Zhu promised. "That was a distraction while he sent for help: this is probably the help."

"Oh, right, well, in that case, I'm happy to go!" Zhang Fei chuckled. "I'll shred them, and deliver them to Bu in bits!"

"That's the spirit!" Jian Yong teased. "Who's your adviser...?"

"I don't want to take any pedants!" Zhang Fei complained. "Please, Xuande, don't-!"

"Mi Zhu, Mister Sun: you'll both go," Liu Bei ordered.

"…***Two*??? …**For some *bandits*???**" Zhang Fei cried. "**I-!**"
"Just shut up and get ready, Yide," Liu Bei said.
Zhang Fei stormed out of Liu Bei's command tent, and the nervous Mi Zhu and Mister Sun followed at a distance.
"…I wish we still had *Zilong*," Liu Bei muttered.

More days passed.

"**Yet more bandits, Zhu Wenbo!**" Yu Jin complained as he finished chasing Yin Li and Sun Guan's followers away from the region north of Xiapi.
"**Indeed so!**" Zhu Ling replied. "**What fun this isn't.**"
Yu Jin laughed and said, "**I suspect a diversion!**"
"**But orders are orders…?**" Zhu Ling prompted.
"**Lord Cao loves or hates us, depending on his headaches,**" Yu Jin replied. "**I'd dared not suggest anything, not when he has the likes of Xun Yòu and Guo Jia to advise him!**"
"**Perhaps they know something we don't,**" Zhu Ling replied thoughtfully.

"**I'll tear you all apart!**" Zhang Fei screamed as he galloped around his appointed battlefield and hacked at the bandits with his pike. "**I'll rip you all to pieces! I'LL EAT YOUR FLESH!**"
Many of the bandits knew that Zhang Fei and his men had endured the siege of Haixi and all of its horrors; they wondered if his threats were genuine, and morale plummeted.
"…This won't take long," Mister Sun supposed.
"Yide is a demon," Mi Zhu replied. "With such men to aid us, only Lord Liu himself can ruin our cause."

And to the east of Xiapi – and the north of Ju City – Zang Ba retreated voluntarily from the force led by Cao Xiu and Han Hao; he and Chang Xi returned to their temporary base camp in the hills and met to discuss their next move.
"I still say that we should have gone and taken Ju City again!" Chang Xi protested.
"We've divided them, which was the intention," Zang Ba retorted. "If we'd have taken Ju, just us two without the others, then we'd be under siege as well, which is a pretty stupid idea."
"…Yeah, I s'pose," Chang Xi grumbled. "So what now…?"
"Now, if Chen Gong is more attentive than you are, Xiapi will send out everything they have to smash Cao Cao while he's understaffed," Zang Ba replied. "Chen's the mastermind of the takeover of Yan and then Xu; this should be nothing."

But Zang Ba's hopes were in vain: his support forces were repeatedly pushed back while the Xiapi defenders did nothing to improve their own situation. Zang Ba ordered a general retreat after several days and too many losses for his liking; that allowed the Han forces to return to the siege of Xiapi.

Lü Bu invited Chen Gong, Gao Shun and Zhang Liao to his home to inform them of another scheme, and the three men reluctantly abandoned their duties and complied.
"Chen Gong, Gao Shun: you will guard the city," Lü Bu said to his

weary lieutenants. "I know how to get rid of Cao Cao, and only I have the strength and skill to achieve it."

"Forgive my cynicism, but what do you intend to do?" Gao Shun asked. "Please do not tell me that you intend an attack on Cao Cao's command tent, or something."

"Don't heckle me!" Lü Bu retorted. "I know what I'm doing! I've been reading, and I know Cao Cao's weakness... his supply lines."

"Didn't I suggest that very thing four days ago?" Chen Gong protested. "Didn't I suggest that when we had Zang Ba distracting the bulk of his-"

"You wanted to do it in a different way to what I propose!" Lü Bu replied. "I will take a cavalry unit and strike at them, burning his food and demoralising his men!"

"We are running out of horses," Zhang Liao noted.

"And that is exactly the plan that I have already proposed and was ignored!" Chen Gong complained.

"Does it matter?" Lü Bu growled. "Zhang Liao, you'll provide support. Dismissed."

The three vassals bowed, turned, and left Lü Bu's home.

"...Cao Cao will die," Lü Bu muttered.

"Will he...?"

Lü Bu was startled by the light tones of his wife's voice and turned to her, asking, "Were you listening to my meetings?"

"Yes," Lady Yan replied honestly. "You've left two men in charge that cannot get along. How will they defend Xiapi together...?"

Lü Bu's eyes wandered.

"And what if you are surrounded, or forced to go into hiding before you can return to the city...?" Lady Yan continued. "I only ask for your own sake... not my own, or our daughter's. When you fled Chang'an, you did not take us with you, but we survived and came back to you because of noble Pang Shu, who was prepared to die for us if he had to. Now, we are here, so it is not us that I ask you to show consideration for... it is for yourself, my husband. If you can trust Chen Gong and the others, then so be it, but I urge you to be certain... for your own sake."

The thinly-disguised attempt to fill Lü Bu with guilt worked: he sighed, covered his head in his hands, and failed to leave his home to prepare for his daring attack.

After several hours had passed, Chen Gong suspected that Lü Bu had wavered again and returned to his home.

"Ah... Gongtai," Lü Bu said as Chen Gong approached him and bowed humbly.

"Why... have you not moved...?" Chen Gong asked; his eyes scanned the surroundings and caught sight of Lady Yan, who immediately disappeared into the sleeping quarters.

"I am muddled again," Lü Bu whimpered. "Help me find some clarity, Gongtai!"

"*Aiee*... I should not have to do this!" Chen Gong sighed. "My lord, the supply route idea is perhaps a little ambitious given our lack of horses: I am trying to find a way to get more. My interim suggestion is this: let's exhaust their supplies by forcing them to waste them!"

"How can we do that...?" Lü Bu asked.

"I will stay in the city, while you go outside and set up a large defensive camp," Chen Gong explained. "They'll have no choice but to attack the camp or attack the city else they risk losing ground, and Cao Cao knows it. If they attack the camp, I will pincer their forces with an attack from the city; if they attack the city, you can pincer them from the camp! They're tired, they're far from home, and their supplies are finite, even with Cao's impressive system for production. Follow this plan and they'll run out of supplies and retreat within a matter of days."

"Days...?" Lü Bu exclaimed.

"Yes, days," Chen Gong promised. "We can pursue them and chase them into the Si River, as you suggested... and then our lives are safe at last. We could go to Xuchang and join the Han, or we could find accord with Zang Ba, or we could cultivate our relationship with Yuan Shu: the choice would be ours."

"...Go and prepare," Lü Bu ordered. "I'll join you shortly!"

Chen Gong smiled, bowed, and left the house, content that he had swayed his master once again. Lü Bu smiled, laughed, got to his feet and prepared to follow Chen Gong, but his path to the sleeping quarters was barred by his wife.

"Don't try and muddle my head again!" Lü Bu said. "We have a plan now, and-!"

"I know, I heard it," Lady Yan sighed. "My dear husband, you're confusing what is being clear and what is being muddled."

"**Out of my way!**" Lü Bu ordered.

"When Cao Cao trusted Gongtai, and treated him like family, he still betrayed them," Bu's wife suggested. "Now you give him that same privileged position, but can you trust him anymore than the Caos could...? Now he hates them, and aims to destroy them; how does he feel about you?"

Lü Bu's face was robbed of certainty.

"When Cao trusted Gongtai with Dong Prefecture, he lost the whole of Yan Province," Bu's wife continued. "Now, you want to go and camp outside the city, and leave your family in his care...? Cao Cao did that. If he decided to betray you as he betrayed Cao Cao, would I be your wife...? What of our daughter?"

Lü Bu closed his eyes, lowered his head and placed a gentle hand on his wife's shoulder as a battle raged in his mind between her very plausible arguments and his trust in Chen Gong. That battle took several minutes: when it was over, Lü Bu opened his eyes, raised his head, smiled, and replied, "I shall stay."

Chen Gong would learn of Lü Bu's decision via an irreverent messenger: he sighed woefully and accepted that the siege of Xiapi was far from over.

✳✳✳✳✳✳✳✳✳✳✳✳

87

Yet more days passed.

After another day of overseeing the siege of Xiapi, Cao Cao asked his campaign advisers, Guo Jia and Xun Gongda, to meet with him privately in his command tent.

"Bu's defences are still robust, and my men are tired," Cao Cao complained. "I have written to your uncle for additional advice, Gongda, but he says that 'He is not here and therefore cannot know what is best'."

"And that is quite right," Xun Gongda replied. "You sound like you want to retreat."

"Honestly...? Yes, I do," Cao Cao sighed.

"A bad idea," Guo Jia insisted.

"...When I came here to Xu Province years ago, it was to destroy Tao Qian," Cao Cao mused. "I would never have contemplated retreat on that campaign willingly! But then that was personal; yet again I shirk by responsibility as a statesman."

"Yuan Shu is obviously not going to send any more aid to Lü Bu, not after the last attempt failed so badly," Guo Jia suggested. "As far-fetched an idea as it might have been, Li Jue might have helped him, but we know that he is dead, killed by a subordinate; Zhang Yang, Bu's old friend, is dead, also killed by his own men."

"Oh...?" Cao Cao exclaimed. "Zhang Yang is dead too...? I wasn't aware of it. How long have we known that?"

"A few days... I forgot to inform you," Guo Jia replied. "Grand Marshal Zhang's intention was either to come here and aid Lü Bu or to invade Yan."

"...Then I must not be saddened by his death, because he obviously chose to be a villain at the critical moment," Cao Cao said thoughtfully. "What happened...?"

"One general murdered him, and another avenged it," Guo Jia replied. "They've pledged allegience to Yuan Shao, sad to say; never mind, though, for their army is small."

"Even a small loss to Yuan Shao is a loss too many when considering the future," Cao Cao lamented.

"The point, my lord, is that Bu is isolated," Guo Jia continued. "Why lose this great opportunity to rid the land of a problem? With a little ingenuity, we can destroy him in a very short time or inspire others to do it for us."

"Guo Fengxiao is right," Xun Gongda insisted. "We must stay and see this matter concluded once and for all: don't let him become another Dong Zhuo or Li Jue that becomes harder to uproot as time goes on. Eliminate him now."

After a pause for thought, Cao Cao said, "You have both convinced me. But as you say, Fengxiao, we need a decisive blow against Bu. I had a thought, but I wondered if it was too much... might I share it...?"

Guo Jia smiled knowingly and replied, "You may, my lord."

Cao Cao unfurled a map of the region and pointed at the Si River; he moved his hand across the map to a smaller river – the Yi River – and held his finger there purposefully; after a pause, he moved to Xiapi, sighed, and said, "Is it too much?"

"...You... you mean to divert both rivers toward Xiapi?" Xun Gongda exclaimed.

"We think alike," Guo Jia chuckled. "No, it is the best solution."

"Gongda...?" Cao Cao prompted.

"It... it harms the civilians, but then a prolonged siege will do worse," Xun Gongda conceded. "We should do it quickly, and end it as soon as possible."

"Very good!" Cao Cao chuckled. "I'll send orders out immediately!"

"...I should have brought this up sooner as well," Guo Jia said suddenly, "but it seems that Yuan Shu might have sent aid after all; nothing impressive, mind. They'll soon be at Xiaopei."

Cao Cao frowned and turned to Xun Gongda, who smiled and said, "Guo Fengxiao has a wicked sense of humour, Lord Cao. We've already sent men to deal with that."

"...Don't scare me," Cao Cao chortled.

"Damn that Cao Cao! Damn him!"

Zhang Fei had to be restrained by Guan Yu and Chen Dao when the news of Cao Cao's plans reached Liu Bei's small camp to the west of Cao's.

"We have no choice, Yide!" Liu Bei insisted. "As he said, the siege does more harm! After Haixi, I am inclined to agree, and this must end soon!"

"All the same, it's going to make Xiapi uninhabitable for a while," Mister Sun said miserably. "As my home province, this place has emotional ties, and to see it harmed so..."

"It'll be over soon," Liu Bei said. "I know it will."

"Yeah, and then what...?" Zhang Fei growled. "Che Zhou becomes governor, Cao Cao said, and then what happens to us???"

"Yide has a point," Guan Yu suggested. "We will have to stay here as vassals to Cao Cao's puppet governor or go back to Xuchang."

"The latter is preferable, since that brings us closer to His Majesty, and allows us to watch over the throne," Liu Bei replied. "Xu Province needs a new start that I can't provide, and I think there will be some that will never forgive me for inviting Cao Cao back here anyway."

Zhang Fei grunted miserably and said, "I s'pose so."

"Let's be glad that Bu will soon be a terrible memory," Liu Bei continued. "Let Cao Cao atone for his actions here and rid this place of a worse menace. Then we can aid the Son of Heaven in his fight against Yuan Shu and pacify the land at last!"

Qin Yilu, Wang Kai and Xu Si's vanguard were halted at northern Xiaopei by a Han force led by the formidable Li Dian.

"We should hold and wait for the rest," Wang Kai suggested.

"...One general cannot be a problem!" Qin Yilu chuckled.

"They outnumber us," Wang Kai noted. "And all we have in the way of generals is you."

"You forget that I was trusted by Lord Lü to act as a general and later an envoy," Qin Yilu said as he prepared to charge at Li Dian. "Now I'll remind you why I was a trusted general!"

Qin Yilu charged with his small cavalry force.

"...A 'trusted envoy'," Xu Si scoffed. "We remember..."

"...And we remember that even his own wife couldn't trust him once he got there," Wang Kai said disdainfully. "He's done nothing to stay in shape since he's been hunting for a wife in Shouchun: look at him!"

Qin Yilu was quickly repelled by Li Dian's cavalrymen and archers.

"…**They're advancing!**" Wang Kai realised. "**What do we-**"

A series of loud horns signalled the arrival of more Han forces led by the officers Qi Ji and Qin Yi; most of Qin Yilu's men were seconded to him by Yuan Shu, and they retreated or deserted upon seeing two former allies serving the enemy.

"**We must turn back to Shouchun!**" Qin Yilu said as he returned to his main line.

"**For the Han!**" Li Dian bellowed. "**Let no one escape!**"

"*Aiee…* **we're routed!**" Qin Yilu lamented.

"**But what about Lord Lü???**" Wang Kai protested. "**We-!**"

"**I'll send a man ahead; you two take some cavalrymen and proceed to Xiapi!**" Qin Yilu ordered. "**Lord Lü will need your brains! I'll follow when I can!**"

Wang Kai and Xu Si knew that they had no choice but to follow Qin Yilu's suggestion; they waited for an opportunity to go northward while a rider hurried on to Xiapi.

Lü Bu's advisers suspected a ruse when some of Cao Cao's camps were relocated and additional trenches were dug in places that seemed to be strategically useless: one and all were taken by complete surprise when the Si and Yi Rivers suddenly surged toward Xiapi and left the city partially submerged. People were forced to move belongings onto the rooftops, and beasts of burden were led to higher ground to avoid the sudden risk of harm. Morale plummeted, and Chen Gong was forced to call an emergency meeting in the White Gate Tower.

"We must be united," Chen Gong said to Lü Bu, Chen Yuanfang, Chen Qun, Gao Shun, Zhang Liao, Wei Xu, Cao Xing, former General of the Household Xu Dan and a group of lower-ranked officers. "All of our past disagreements are meaningless now."

"What do you propose?" Chen Qun asked. "My father is old, and these conditions are going to kill him long before Cao Cao does."

Chen Yuanfang coughed uncomfortably and said, "My health is irrelevant, son."

"We must hold on," Chen Gong insisted. "Qin Yilu, Wang Kai and Xu Si have returned to Xu Province, and-"

"They bring reinforcements?" Lü Bu asked excitedly.

"…N-no… no, they do not," Chen Gong replied. "Yuan Shu's men were routed at Xiaopei and retreated, I understand. But Wang and Xu's minds will be a-"

"**I don't need more advisers, Chen Gong, for I have far too many bad ones as it is! I need food, dry ground, and soldiers!**" Lü Bu cried. "**Yuan Shu is a coward! Yuan Shu is a dog and a fool! Without me, he won't last a year!**"

The junior officers were chattering inanely and had to be silenced by Gao Shun and Zhang Liao; after that, a short silence descended on the gathering.

"We are isolated, then," Lü Bu said. "We must double our efforts."

"Against the entire Han army…?" one officer chortled.

"**Who spoke???**" Lü Bu shrieked. "**What wretch dares to ridicule me???**"

"Song Xian… meant no offence," Hou Cheng insisted.

"Who is 'Song Xian', anyway???" Lü Bu continued. **"Why are such low-ranking men here at such an important meeting??? Was that Hou Cheng that heckled me? Does he want to be demoted again?"**
"Song Xian and Hou Cheng are both very brave," Gao Shun said. "They have not betrayed or deserted you, as others have done."
"Brave or stupid...?" Lü Bu heckled. "Ridiculing my efforts to save us all isn't brave, Gao Shun!"
"I meant no offence to you, my lord," Song Xian pleaded.
"...In future, be quiet unless I address you," Lü Bu grumbled. "Chen Gong, you must have a plan; what is your plan?"
"My plan is to hold out," Chen Gong replied. "I have no specific method... if I can think of a way to get men out to channel the water away, I will, but-"
"So your plan, Mister Chen, is to tolerate having the Si River in our faces and up to our necks for as long as it takes to outlast Cao Cao's supplies?" Gao Shun scoffed.
"Xiapi is a grand city: Ze Rong made sure of that!" Chen Gong retorted. "We have large supply stores, a thriving market, a-!"
Gao Shun laughed disbelievingly and said, "It's all *underwater*, you cretin!"
"We've got the animals to high ground, like rooftops and steps along the walls," Zhang Liao said. "The weather is being kind, so diseases will not be as great a problem as at other times, but we can't afford to do this for long."
"We won't have to," Chen Gong promised.

But weeks passed, and nothing changed.

At around the same time, Kong Rong had become concerned about his young friend Mi Heng and sent an urgent letter to Wang Can in Jing's northern capital Xiangyang; the response, when it arrived in Xuchang, filled Kong Rong's heart with shame, sadness and anger.
"...Dead... *dead*...!" Kong Rong sobbed. "Liu Biao... you *fool*...! Huang Zu... you *thug*...! Cao... you *villain*...!"
Liu Biao had finally tired of Mi Heng's constant irreverence and frankness and sent him southward to Xiakou, more specifically to the court of his associate Huang Zu; Huang was not a patient man, but he had a bawdy sense of humour and, one way or another, it removed Mi Heng as a potential problem, just as Cao Cao had sought to do when he sent Mi to Liu. Huang Zu's son Huang Shè – who was closer to Mi Heng's age – had taken a liking to the young scholar, and was enjoying having an intellectual acquaintance for once; but when Mi Heng publicly ridiculed Huang Zu through song during a banquet, the drunken Zu ignored his son's pleas and ordered Mi Heng's immediate arrest and execution. Mi Heng was aged just 26.
"That's how all of us will go, isn't it...?" Kong Rong lamented as he lowered the letter to his lap. "That's how every man of the pen will die... by the swords of the fools that rule him."

∗∗∗∗∗∗∗∗∗∗∗∗

88

Chen Gong called another meeting in the White Gate Tower: Lü Bu, Gao Shun, Zhang Liao, Wei Xu, Wang Kai, Xu Si, Chen Qun and Hou Cheng sat and waited patiently for Chen Gong to begin.

"This had better be for a good reason," Gao Shun grumbled. "I have things to do!"

"Food supplies are still ample, and the floodwaters have not gotten higher, thank Heaven," Chen Gong began. "In fact, they've receded somewhat, and-"

"I can see that without being told!" Lü Bu shouted. **"Why are we here???"**

"Two months ago, you said 'A few more weeks'," Chen Qun heckled. "A month ago, you said, 'A matter of days'; now *three months* and *four days* have passed, Chen Gong. Has the siege ended yesterday, but nobody told us?"

"I have a plan," Chen Gong insisted. "We need horses. Cao will not expect a sudden retaliation at this point: let's surprise him!"

Chen Qun snorted a laugh and said, "Are we going to nail the horses to some driftwood and sail our cavalrymen out of the gates on their backs, Chen Gong...?"

"That isn't constructive!" Chen Gong retorted. "There are shallow areas that we can charge through at the west gate, and if the waters subside further, we'll want to be ready for it!"

"I know a man in the city that can procure horses, my lord," Hou Cheng volunteered.

"Oh, it's Hou Cheng," Lü Bu scoffed. "Why should I trust you?"

"I can vouch for him, my lord," Wei Xu said. "Mister Hou, what is your idea?"

"I'll help the man I spoke of to get past Cao Cao's lines, and he can try and get some horses from Ju or Donghai," Hou Cheng explained. "He's known in many places, so he'll get more help than any of us."

"Do it," Lü Bu ordered. "But remember: if you fail, and I lose the money I give you to do this, I'll hurt you."

All eyes turned to Hou Cheng, who said, "I will not fail, my lord."

Hou Cheng met with his colleague Song Xian, and the two men went to the partially-submerged marketplace to find the trader that would help them.

"Old Wu's son?" Song Xian exclaimed. "He's not like his father. Can you be sure that you can trust him?"

"Old Wu has been one of the most reliable traders we've bought from the whole time we've been here," Hou Cheng replied. "Alright, his son's got a shifty look about him, but I don't reckon he'll let his father down."

'Old Wu' watched as the two officers advanced toward the rooftop he was perched on and turned to his son, saying, "Heaven be with you, son."

The thin, malnourished 'Young Wu' nodded silently.

"Thanks for helping us out," Hou Cheng said as he reached the Wus. "Lord Lü gave us the money for about twenty horses."

Hou Cheng passed the money to Old Wu, who counted it and said, "We haven't been trapped in here long enough for a horse to have

455

devalued that much, I reckon. This will cover ten to fifteen horses at the most."
"Don't mess us about," Song Xian growled.
"No, no!" Hou Cheng said. "Calm down. Old Wu, you know better than to cross Lord Lü. Fifteen it is, and no less."
"Fine," Old Wu replied. "My son will go."
Hou Cheng turned to 'Young Wu' and said, "Let's be off then!"

Hou Cheng took 'Young Wu' out of Xiapi under cover of darkness and the two galloped east to Donghai Prefecture. Days passed, and the two did not return: Lu Bu became suspicious, but just as acquaintances like Song Xian were starting to doubt Hou Cheng, he returned to the eastern gates with 15 purchased horses and a hog-tied 'Young Wu'. Chen Gong ordered covering fire, and Hou Cheng re-entered the city safely.
"This trash should go back to his father for a beating... and if it can be proved, maybe his father deserves a beating as well," Hou Cheng complained as Lü Bu examined the horses.
"What happened?" Wei Xu asked.
"We found a horse trader in a small settlement just inside the Donghai border, and we got the horses easily enough," Hou Cheng explained as Song Xian glared at 'Young Wu'. "We were coming back, and then this little sneak waits 'til I needed to go for a pee and tries to make a run for it with the horses!"
Song Xian shoved the terrified 'Young Wu' and snarled at him.
"He got a good start on me, I'll give him that," Hou Cheng continued. "Halfway to Xiaopei, he got, before I caught up! He had a letter of surrender on him."
"Cao Cao...?" Chen Gong supposed.
"Liu Bei," Hou Cheng replied. "Bei, Cao, what's the difference? A traitor's a traitor."
Lü Bu eyed Hou Cheng with suspicion and said, "*Indeed*."
"You got us the horses: that deserves a celebration!" Wei Xu suggested. "What say you, my lord? We need a morale-booster, so why not have a feast tonight in the White Gate Tower keep?"
"...Alright," Lü Bu replied.
"Let me get the refreshments!" Hou Cheng declared. "Let it be another gift to you all, gentlemen!"
The officers cheered, but Lü Bu scowled: Chen Gong and Gao Shun knew Bu's mood, and they prayed that he would not ruin everything at a critical moment.

The banquet was an extravagance born of desperation: several jars of wine and several whole hogs were gathered for the event by Hou Cheng, who was then lavished with gifts by his grateful colleagues. Lü Bu was asked to surrender his host seat in honour of the hero of the hour, but Bu refused: that was the first mistake.
"...Bastard," Lü Bu muttered as he watched the smiling Hou Cheng and analysed every word of gratitude, warm laugh and bow that was exchanged between his cheerful vassals. The smell of roasting hog meat hit his nostrils, and he said, "How much meat do they prepare for this little nobody...?"
"Please be happy for our good fortune, my lord," Chen Gong said nervously. "Hou Cheng's actions might have saved us."
Hou Cheng laughed as he accepted yet another gift from the

reserved Zhang Liao: he then turned to smile at Lü Bu, but his master's angry expression robbed him of courage.

"Have I offended...?" Hou Cheng wondered.

"Take him some meat," Song Xian said. "He'll soon cheer up."

Hou Cheng nodded eagerly and collected a piece of roasted meat for his lord: he then went to the collection of wine jars that were near the entrance and filled a jug.

"...*Wine*...?" Zhang Liao exclaimed as Hou Cheng advanced toward Lü Bu with the food and drink.

"Hou Cheng doesn't know: he wasn't here...!" Gao Shun gasped.

Song Xian noticed the error as well, but too late: he hurried toward Hou Cheng, saying, "Uh, mate, don't-!"

"Some meat and wine for you, my lord," Hou Cheng said penitently as he presented the offerings. "Perhaps you would like to be the first to-"

"**WINE???**" Lü Bu shrieked: the room fell silent.

"I, uh... y-yes, my lord," Hou Cheng replied.

"**I banned all alcohol, Hou Cheng!**" Lü Bu shouted angrily. "**I tolerated this party, despite your meagre efforts being undeserving of it, and I did it because I am a kind lord: but being kind does not mean I am stupid!**"

"M-my lord, please," Wei Xu bumbled. "He didn't know, he was away when-"

"**All of you were so quick to throw this party, as if you had it all planned,**" Lü Bu continued. "He was gone for so long... and that story about defections, stolen horses, and the lad trying to run, but then he's spared... talk about letters of *surrender*... **even amongst the deepest lies, truth slips through! You meant to ply me with wine and betray me to Cao Cao! You're all in on it, all of you!**"

"My lord, no," Gao Shun pleaded. "Don't do this!"

"**All of you want me dead!**" Lü Bu shrieked. "**All of you! Every one of you!**"

"I... should leave," Hou Cheng said quietly.

"**Leave and go where? *Liu Bei*?**" Lü Bu retorted.

"Go, Hou Cheng," Wei Xu pleaded. "My lord, Hou Cheng will be in my barracks."

Hou Cheng fled quickly and quietly.

"**...Get out, all of you!**" Lü Bu ordered. "**Take your nonsense and GO!**"

The majority of the officials and officers got to their feet, bowed humbly, and left the keep: eventually, only Gao Shun, Chen Gong and Wei Xu were left.

"I want to be alone," Lü Bu growled. "**All of you GO!**"

The three men knew better than to argue: they made their way past the collection of wasted meat and wine and left the keep.

"...All of them... *all of them*...!" Lü Bu sobbed angrily.

Wei Xu hurried to his barracks, where he found Hou Cheng being consoled by Song Xian; Wei Xu bowed humbly and said, "Mister Hou, you saved us. He should not have reacted like that, and I cannot justify it."

"I've had enough," Hou Cheng admitted. "I paid for all that meat and wine! I rode across enemy territory for days looking for Young Wu and them horses, and-!"

"I know," Wei Xu sighed. "I... am tired too. He may be a relative, but what does that mean? He's threatened me twice in recent days. We have to end this."

"How...?" Song Xian asked.

"We can't challenge Zhang Liao, but we can get Gao Shun, because he's injured," Wei Xu explained. "If we can get Chen Gong, Wang Kai and Xu Si, then-"

"Wait, wait... You're suggesting that we...?" Song Xian exclaimed.

"It's over," Wei Xu replied. "Not tonight, but soon... we must act."

The group of men looked at one-another with shared unease: what they were about to do could potentially change the course of history, and they would at the very least run the risk of being remembered as the men that betrayed the most famous warlord of their age. But enough was enough; even Wei Xu, a relative of Lü Bu, could see when it was time to bring something to a conclusion, and that time was now.

But while Lü Bu was apparently nearing defeat, Gongsun Zan was about to enjoy a sudden improvement in his fortunes.

"We are to have a second chance, friends!" Gongsun Zan said to an audience of weary officials. "My son has been successful... help has come!"

"Really...?" Gongsun Zan's cousin Fan exclaimed. "The bandits, and Xu...?"

"Yes!" Gongsun Zan chuckled. "The bandits, brought by Xu! They are on their way right now, and they are forcing Yuan's western forces onto the defensive! We're about to be relieved!"

"How many?" Gongsun Fan asked.

"By all accounts, *all of them*!" Guan Jing reported. "That would be close to a hundred-thousand men!"

Gongsun's followers chattered excitedly.

"My son has saved us!" Gongsun Zan exclaimed. "Right: we must act quickly. Now the sides are even... and once the Xianbei, Wuhuan and Xiongnu see that I'm as strong as I ever was, they'll either flee or defect! Where will Yuan and his six-thousand-or-so be when that happens, mm...?"

Gongsun Zan's followers cheered at the news.

****

89

"It's as we feared," the adviser Guo Tu reported to a frustrated Yuan Shao. "The Black Mountain Bandits have reappeared in Changshan and Zhongshan: they number at least fifty-thousand."
"**Wretches!**" Yuan Shao cried. "I'm so close to breaking this fool, and now I must deal with these churls for the umpteenth time???"
"They'll have a plan to liaise with Gongsun, and the key to our victory is finding out what that plan is and turning it against them," the adviser Tian Feng insisted.
"Mightn't they just be planning to cause random havoc, as bandits always do…?" the adviser Pang Ji heckled. "Isn't the answer to prioritise and confront them, and-"
"You suggest relieving the siege, imbecile!" Yuan Shao scoffed. "We cannot give this fortress of Gongsun's even the slightest bit of breathing space! It took us long enough to get past the first moat! If he regained the mounds that we haven't toppled and the inner moats that we haven't filled in yet, we'd be here another year!"
"But I do have to admit that Pang Ji is correct," Tian Feng said. "We must still engage them, or we'll be overwhelmed."
"We have the men to match them," Yuan Shao retorted. "I've already written to Ju Shou and asked him to send more men, and now that we know that the bandits have been summoned here – I was worried that Gongsun might have the sense to attack Ji and force us to retreat – we can bring all of the men that we stationed on the border here, request Xiongnu men from Huchuquan, and call on Tadun and Budugen to provide more cavalry."
"In exchange for *what*…?" Tian Feng asked. "Surely you cannot intend to promise the Wuhuan more autonomy…! …And *Budugen*??? Budugen is the *Xianbei khan*! They harm the people that the Wuhuan do! They marched against us not more than-!"
"I am aware of all that, Mister Tian," Yuan Shao grumbled.
"We *can't* promise *anything* to the Xianbei, and we shouldn't promise more to the Wuhuan!" Tian Feng protested. "Lord Yuan, the court might argue that you do not have the authority to-"
"Whose court…? *Cao Cao's*…?" Yuan Shao chortled. "That villain's puppet court will certainly tell me such things, but I have no intention of heeding any of it. When this is over, I am going to demand a proper discussion regarding His Majesty's location and the composition of his court: if it is made up of nothing but Cao's toadies, then how is it any different to Dong Zhuo's…?"
Tian Feng scanned the command tent; Yuan and his advisers were the only ones present.
"You have something to say…?" Guo Tu prompted.
"…Have you *permanently* abandoned the idea of making Liu Hè emperor?" Tian Feng asked nervously.
"…Yes," Yuan Shao scoffed. "There is no swaying him. Like father, like son. And after my cousin's despicable proclamation, I daren't start suggesting alternative emperors anyway."
"…That's good," Tian Feng insisted.
"Nothing more from you about that or my alliances with the regional tribes," Yuan Shao ordered. "We must be pragmatic: even majesties concede that we had to show begrudging respect to the Qiang and Di in the west, the Xianbei and Xiongnu in the

north and the Wuhuan in the north and east, and Han princesses were and are wed to the Xiongnu and Xianbei chieftains. We must consider similar shows of respect, especially now that we have lost the appearance of overwhelming strength."

"… … …You want one of my daughters to marry off to those barbarians???" Tian Feng chortled. "Lord Yuan, you-!"

"We must all do our part!" Yuan Shao snapped. "Victory is all that matters right now, Mister Tian! There will be time enough to do what must be done about these uncultured peoples when we have the resources, but until that day we must be sensible! Surely a daughter or niece here and there is a small sacrifice for an alliance that will bring peace…? If princesses of the realm can be asked to give themselves over, why not our own girls…? Weren't you going to marry them off to whoever furthered your career anyway…?"

"…Their children will be barbarians like the fathers!" Tian Feng whined. "Guo Tu, Pang Ji, you don't-!"

"Pragmatism is the only way, Mister Tian," Pang Ji said. "The girls are as good as disowned and not our responsibility once they're married and gone; after all, are any of the barbarian sons of the princesses considered eligible for the throne…? Of course not!"

"I don't wish to discuss this any further," Yuan Shao grumbled.

Xu Yòu entered the tent and said, "My lord, Han Juzi reports."

"Bring it here, Mister Xu," Yuan Shao ordered.

"You heard the discussion, Mister Xu," Tian Feng prompted.

"…The end of it, including Lord Yuan's request to end it," Xu Yòu said as he handed a written report to Yuan Shao. "Necessity is often unpalatable. Such is life; such is war."

"…Well, at least Gongsun will get no help from the bandits around Zhou," Yuan Shao muttered as he finished reading the brief report. "We'll have scouts determine what Gongsun is up to, but in the meantime, we minimise our handling of the bandits and focus on this fortress. Not one moat is to be conceded… understand…?"

Yuan Shao's followers agreed silently.

"…**All of you out,**" Yuan Shao barked.

Xu Yòu was the last to turn to leave; Yuan Shao gestured toward him and said, "A moment."

"…I await your words, Lord Yuan," Xu Yòu prompted.

"Mm… to think that we once drank together and laughed as friends, and now we are lord and vassal," Yuan Shao said. "Xu Yòu, do you understand what I am trying to achieve…?"

"I do," Xu Yòu replied.

"And… and when the time comes… when I must do battle with Cao Cao… can I rely on you to understand *that*…?" Yuan Shao asked.

"…I have been with you for many years, and I have seen everything," Xu Yòu said. "If or when that day comes, I will accept it, Lord Yuan, and do as I have always done."

Yuan Shao nodded in response to the words; his secretary Chen Lin then entered the tent and said, "Another report."

"…You may go, Xu Yòu," Yuan Shao ordered.

Xu Yòu bowed humbly, but Yuan Shao had already turned his attention to the new report and missed the gesture; Xu smiled sadly, turned, and left the tent.

＊＊＊＊＊＊＊＊＊＊＊＊

90

Two days after the disastrous banquet in the White Gate Tower, a distressed General Cao Xing rushed into Lü Bu's rooftop tent and said, "Lord Lü: *mutiny*! Wei Xu, Hou Cheng and Song Xian, they've mutinied! They captured Chen Gong, Gao Shun, Wang-"

"**What???**" Lü Bu cried as he leapt to his feet; his wife Lady Yan cowered in fear as he added, "**They have Chen Gong???**"

Cao Xing nodded and said, "A-and Wang Kai… Xu Si… Gao Shun… they took them and went to Cao Cao."

Lü Bu groaned like a wounded animal and fell to his knees.

"Wei Xu…? *Wei Xu* betrayed us?" Lady Yan gasped.

"We… have about a hundred men left, but… that may be wrong soon, a lot are deserting," Cao Xing continued. "Zhang Liao has trusted men watching the gates to avoid them being opened to the enemy, but…"

"…But it's over," Lü Bu said. "My lady wife, I have to go. Cao Xing: tell Zhang Liao that I want him to come to the White Gate Tower. Anyone else that may still be with us… should come too."

Cao Xing hurried out of the tent.

Bu's wife reached out and whispered, "Husband…!"

"It's over," Lü Bu replied; he got to his feet, sighed loudly, and left the tent without looking at his wife or daughter again.

"…Over," Lady Yan murmured. She looked at the room around her and wondered what she should do and how she should do it: Lady Lü walked to her side, sat next to her, and smiled.

"Gentlemen, it's over," Lü Bu said to Zhang Liao, Chen Qun, Cao Xing and the few junior officers that he had left. "I asked you all here to make a request: I am a 'Man among men', therefore I must die like one."

"You want us to duel with you at a time like this, my lord…?" Cao Xing exclaimed.

"No, no…! …What an idiot's reputation I've earned for myself, and only now do I realise it," Lü Bu said. "No, I want you to kill me and take my head to Cao Cao for inspection. You must hate me, one and all: relieve your frustration."

"I cannot kill my own lord," Zhang Liao replied. "We should fight to the last man."

"Don't be a fool, Wenyuan!" Lü Bu chuckled. "You're a future hero: don't die with me here. Surrender, and serve a better lord."

Zhang Liao was about to reply when a cry rang out: a man ran into the room with his sword drawn and said, "**The west gate! The-!**"

"Enough," Lü Bu said softly. "It's over."

Lü Bu and his remaining men fought one last battle, but eventually, Zhang Liao succumbed to the inevitable and surrendered before his men were butchered. Lü Bu was caught by some of his own disgruntled bodyguards, who tied him firmly and brought him to Cao Cao's camp.

"So… the end has finally come," Cao Cao said thoughtfully. "I wonder if I have triumphed before dear old Benchu…?"

"I doubt that he has beaten Gongsun Zan just yet," Guo Jia

replied. "For now, focus on what you will do about Lü Bu."

"I am torn, gentlemen, between the urge to slay and the urge to tame such a powerful beast," Cao Cao admitted. "My sense tells me the former, my ego the latter. Am I more capable of gaining this man's service than Ding Yuan, Dong Zhuo, Wang Yun, Yuan Shu, Yuan Shao and Liu Bei before me...?"

"Only the first two of those men actually had a pledge of service, and he killed them both," Xun Gongda said. "One was good, the other evil; Bu knows no distinction and serves either willingly until he decides that he does not want to anymore."

"...I can volunteer no other counsel, merely the same worded differently," Guo Jia admitted.

"Then it is my decision alone," Cao Cao murmured.

Liu Bei and the other officials gathered to see what the Excellency of Works would do with the famous Lü Bu and his vassals.

"...What will he do...?" Liu Bei's adviser Mi Zhu wondered.

"I do not know Cao Mengde well enough to be sure," Liu Bei replied. "I just hope that Yide and Yunchang obey my orders and remain at the camp, or that Xianhe can get here before them if he can't dissuade them."

Mi Zhu nodded agreeably.

"Well, well... why do all the greatest warriors suffer the most ignominious ends...?" Cao Cao asked as Lü Bu squirmed in front of him. "Perhaps it is a way of balancing things. What do you think, Fengxian...?"

"Loosen my bonds," Lü Bu replied.

"Tigers must be restrained," Cao Cao retorted. "Answer my question: I'm intrigued to hear what you think. Sun Jian died under rocks or arrows, I hear: you wriggle like a worm in front of me, bound and deprived of dignity."

"I treated my people well, but they turned on me, and betrayed me when things became difficult," Lü Bu protested.

"I hear different things, Fengxian," Cao Cao teased. "I hear that you abandoned your family, mistreated your allies, and hankered for other men's women."

"...You've lost weight since we last met," Lü Bu replied; he was aware that Cao Cao was giving him an easy opportunity to retaliate with an accusation of hypocrisy, but he was keen to be diplomatic and prolong his life.

"I *have* lost weight!" Cao Cao said. "How long it's been since we were in Luoyang; perhaps I am distressed at the time it has taken to be here now, faced with the opportunity of recruiting you."

Xun Gongda, Liu Bei, Chen Deng, Mi Zhu and many others were horrified at the notion of Cao Cao recruiting Bu after all the things that he had done.

"You all fear me... but now I am tamed," Lü Bu said as he looked at the angry faces amongst his audience. "Let me go, and I will serve as I have never served before! I have atoned at last, and can render good service! Duke Huan of Qi forgave Guan Zhong and made him chancellor. Isn't now the time to emulate the actions of wise men?"

Cao Cao smiled.

"...Xuande," Lü Bu hailed as he turned slightly to face Liu Bei. "Xuande! You're a guest in my province. I'm a prisoner here, yet you say nothing. Didn't I save you and your allies from a beggar's death in Haixi, and then from Ji Ling with an arrow?"

"Why do you now turn to another man instead of addressing me?" Cao Cao asked.

"...**Xuande!**" Lü Bu cried. "Xuande, you know me: *vouch for me!*"

"A fine idea," Cao Cao said as he turned to Liu Bei. "Xuande, what is your thought when you hear talk of Bu working for the Han, or even just for me...?"

"...My only thought is the fates of Ding Yuan and Dong Zhuo," Liu Bei replied.

"**Dog!**" Lü Bu growled. "**I should have left you to die at Haixi!**"

"I think that Xuande remembers *Xiaopei*," Cao Cao chuckled.

"My lord, don't spare him," a young official said. "He is a famous villain: if he is released now, he'll harm us again in the future."

"Now my new registrar condemns you, and he hasn't even met you before!" Cao Cao snickered. "Oh dear... what should I do...?"

"...Release me!" Lü Bu pleaded. "I will never err again!"

"A worthless promise," Cao Cao scoffed as his false joviality finally gave way to his genuine anger. "Guards: death. And as we agreed... for a man with a woman's will, always swaying this way and that, a woman's death: *strangulation*."

"**No!**" Lü Bu screamed as two burly soldiers dragged him away. "**I am a man among men! Do not do this! Please, I beg of you! Not like this!**"

"Chen Gongtai; we meet again at last," Cao Cao said as he turned his attentions to Lü Bu's subordinates. "Have you anything to say to me?"

"Only that I still hate you for your many crimes, including those to come," Chen Gong replied. "Kill me and be done with it."

"...I do this reluctantly, but I see that you cannot be swayed," Cao Cao sighed. "Guards: death. A *man's death*."

Chen Gong smiled as he was dragged away.

"...Wang Kai, and Xu Si," Cao Cao chuckled softly. "Not with me as long as Gongtai, but your treachery hurt me all the same; have you words for me?"

"None that you'll want recorded," Wang Kai replied.

"We'll die knowing we opposed you!" Xu Si heckled.

"By trying to arrange a marriage between your lord and the son of a traitor to the world...?" Cao Cao chortled. "Any credibility you had is very much gone. Guards: death. They're men, but only just, I fear."

"**You'll die a dog's death!**" Wang Kai cried as he was led away.

"**We'll haunt you, Cao Cao!**" Xu Si promised.

"I'll look forward to it," Cao Cao said. "Now... Gao Shun."

Gao Shun sneered at Cao Cao, but he did not speak.

"Will a champion such as you not join me...?" Cao Cao asked.

"...As Zhang Liao has done...?" Gao Shun said as he looked at Zhang Liao and smiled accusingly; Zhang Liao lowered his head and exhaled miserably.

"...So you will not," Cao Cao lamented. "Very well. Guards: death."

"**See sense while you can!**" Zhang Liao shouted after Gao Shun, but the man did not reply.

"...Has Gao Shun's parting slight changed your mind?" Cao Cao asked as he turned to the unbound Zhang Liao.

"I was a fool to be blind to Bu's nature for so long, and yearn to make amends," Zhang Liao replied. "My only regret is being unable to help Gao Shun see the truth and serve a better cause, but... he was loyal to a fault, and could not be helped."

"A sad end, indeed," Liu Bei muttered.

"The worst of them are dealt with," Cao Cao decided. "Master Chen Yuanfang, Mister Chen Qun: you are, of course, spared; my thanks for your work."

The Chens bowed humbly and silently.

"Che Zhou, you are now Governor of Xu Province," Cao Cao said.

The tall, thin Che Zhou bowed silently.

"Xu Dan shall be restored as General of the Household," Cao Cao continued. "Liu Bei, Master Chen, Chen Qun: we must remain here until the Mount Tai Bandits are humbled and Zang Ba brought to heel. Once that is done, you shall then accompany me to Xuchang and aid me in presenting our victories to His Majesty. Chen Deng: return to Guangling, and carry on your marvellous work there. Xu Province is saved; how strange, yet how comforting it is to know that after all that I did to harm the place... I have atoned."

"But as you have said, Excellency, there are other enemies to defeat, so this is not over, and the province is not yet saved," Guo Jia suggested. "While Zang Ba and the other Mount Tai Bandit leaders are still to be pacified, we-"

"And pacified they will be, Fengxiao!" Cao Cao replied as he turned and walked away, clutching his head. He smiled, despite the pain: after a reputation spanning a decade, Lü Bu was dead, and very few obstacles now stood between Cao Cao and an end to the chaos.

But just as Cao Cao had finally defeated one of his greatest enemies, his next acts – though seemingly minor – earned him a future enemy, just as his advisers had feared.

"**That despicable man!**" Guan Yu cried as he received word that Lady Du, wife of Lü Bu's general Qin Yilu, had become part of Cao Cao's harem. "**He gave me his word that he would let me marry her! Time and again I wrote to confirm, and grovelled against my better nature, and time and again he assented! Now he has taken her for himself, just as he took Lady Zou against her will and condemned his heir to death at Wan! He is the greatest villain of them all!**"

"Calm down, Yunchang, she's just another woman, and there are many in the world," Zhang Fei suggested. "We've both got nice wives, and Xuande has as well; we get them all back after them all being trapped in Xiapi with that bastard Bu."

"I'm more annoyed about the change of orders," Liu Bei said.

"I agree," the adviser Mister Sun said. "He appointed you Governor of Yu Province, which should have meant that you would take office there and lead the assault against Yuan Shu: instead he keeps us here as vassals of his toady Che Zhou, and tasks us with rounding up Zang Ba's rabble!"

"I fear that Dong Cheng may have been right," Liu Bei said. "Sad to say, I may one day have to raise my sword against Cao Cao."

"I will do so gladly, for he and I are eternal foes," Guan Yu insisted. "I will haunt him, Lord Liu Xuande. In life, I will imperil him at every turn. When I am dead, I will ensure that he survives no more than ten days afterward!"

"Don't condemn yourself to die before that dishonest villain," Mi Zhu said.

"...Forgive me for saying so, Yunchang, but His Excellency might have simply put a better proposition to Lady Du and let her decide for herself," Liu Bei suggested. "We are hardly the happiest and wealthiest of men, and he is an Excellency; I might also add that she was shallow-minded enough to marry a fool like Qin Yilu, so perhaps it is better to forget the whole thing."

Guan Yu sighed sadly and replied, "Perhaps, Lord Liu... perhaps."

"Let's go smash some bandits, Yunchang," Zhang Fei said. "You'll feel better after you've cracked a few skulls."

Liu Bei shuddered and said, "Yide, you are truly unbelievable."

Emperor Xian was overjoyed at the news that the man whose actions had, in part, facilitated Dong Zhuo's rise to power was dead at last. But his elation was quickly tempered by uncertainty, and Empress Fu noted it with concern.

"You've had Consort Dong's father visit you twice, Your Majesty," Empress Fu said as she sat with her husband and sovereign.

"Do not fear for your position," Emperor Xian replied. "I have already told you that she is a consort, nothing more; her condition changes nothing."

"Then why are you now so distracted, Your Majesty...?" Empress Fu asked.

"...Cao Cao is now a hero," Emperor Xian replied. "That worries me; I have therefore taken steps to ensure that he does not hold all of the power."

"...You have promoted Dong Cheng...?" Empress Fu supposed.

"He has as much to lose as we have if Cao is another Dong Zhuo, now that he is tied to the Han," Emperor Xian replied. "Of course I worry about Cao's reaction, but he must be made to understand who is master... and who is subject."

The Emperor and the Empress then stared at one-another silently; both feared the possibility of their situation worsening.

Lü Bu's death marked the end of another era: he was the last of the famous generals that served Dong Zhuo, and the land would be a more predictable place for his passing. Governor Che Zhou and Liu Bei were two of many men that began a series of campaigns against the various leaders of the Mount Tai Bandits, who were the last great threat to stability in Xu Province; in the meantime, Cao Cao moved to the Xu-Yan provincial border and started to prepare for the final march against the isolated pretender Yuan Shu. The forces of Yuan Shu's sometimes-ally Gongsun Zan and his Black Mountain Bandit allies were now united in preventing Han Commander-in-Chief Yuan Shao from breaking Gongsun's fortified capital city of Yijing and seizing Yòu Province: the outcome would be the next significant event of the age, and that outcome was almost certain.

✱✱✱✱✱✱✱✱✱✱✱✱

ACT VIII: THE LAST OF THE DEFIANT

91

The politically-fragmented regions of Han Dynasty China were slowly being knitted back together, and an end to the chaos finally seemed to be possible. All of the men that had once plotted to commit regicide and supplant the Han Emperor – the self-styled Chancellor of State Dong Zhuo, and the self-appointed co-regents Li Jue and Guo Si – were now dead, and the majority of their aides were as dead as they were; only the adviser Jia Xu and the nephew of one of Dong Zhuo's generals remained, and they seemed to be trying to atone as they lived as unwanted yet well-behaved tenants in the north of the central province of Jing.

The power in the land was now centred in Xuchang, the supposedly temporary imperial capital in Yan Province; the actual capital, Luoyang, had been partially restored by loyalists, but it was still far from being habitable. That power rested mainly with Cao Cao – who served the Han as the Excellency of Works and Acting Excellency over the Masses – and his childhood friend, the Commander-in-Chief Yuan Shao. The two men were now defeating any of the warlord-governors and administrators that had not halted their territorial activities, and that task was almost done: only Gongsun Zan – who held the northern frontier province of Yòu – and Yuan Shao's brother Shu remained opposed to the rule of Emperor Xian.

Gongsun Zan had murdered a provincial governor and seized a province, but his crimes against the Han paled into insignificance when compared to Yuan Shu's. Shu was responsible for the collapse of the Eastern Pass Coalition that opposed Dong Zhuo, since he had slandered and militarily challenged Yuan Shao at a critical moment; after seven years of insisting that he was the rightful clan chief and not his 'illegitimate' half-brother Shao, Shu had – despite numerous defeats – decided that he was also worthy of the imperial throne, citing the well-known concept that any worthy man could become an emperor if they received the 'Mandate of Heaven' and the incumbent's mandate was deemed to be exhausted. Yuan Shu announced that he was 'First Emperor of the Zhong Dynasty', whereupon he lost almost all of his supporters, most notably the southern prodigy Sun Ce. Every other warlord except the famous athlete-warrior Lü Bu had either turned the other way or declared war upon Yuan Shu; Bu – who was famous for having first served and then killed Dong Zhuo – had proved an equally unreliable ally to Yuan Shu, but he was always an effective distraction: now Bu was gone, killed by a Han expedition force, and Yuan Shu was exposed, reviled by the court and running out of money and men to fight for him.

There would be no cooperation between Cao Cao and Yuan Shao, because the two were irreparably estranged: Yuan was determined to attack Cao as soon as Gongsun Zan was destroyed, and Cao knew it well. Bizarrely, one of Cao's main allies would be the minor warlord Liu Bei, who was secretly keen on regaining control of Xu Province after having lost it to Lü Bu. Cao and Liu had, only two years previously, been mortal enemies, but now they would be working together to rid Xu Province of the Mount Tai Bandits and Yu and Yang Provinces of what remained of

Yuan Shu's 'Zhong Dynasty' forces; but neither man trusted the other, despite their – admittedly forced – alliance against Lü Bu, and more changes in the political landscape were yet to come.

"You're all the same, you bandits!" Zhang Liao cried as he and his small force of cavalrymen chased a small group of Mount Tai Bandits; he was still in Xu Province, which had, until recently, been the base of his late master Lü Bu, but Zhang was now a Han officer serving Cao Cao, and he was very glad of it.
"Yield!" Wei Xu ordered. **"Yield to the Han or know no mercy!"**
"Hypocrites!" the bandit chief Wu Dun said as he tried to gesture retreat orders to his disorganised ranks. **"Weren't they just-"**
"There you are, Wu Dun!" Song Xian cackled as he charged at Wu Dun's command team. **"We've been looking for you!"**
Lü Bu's former officer was accompanied by his colleague Hou Cheng, who had attacked from the opposite side to catch Wu Dun in a pincer; the bandit had no choice but to lead his riders out of the trap and flee northwards while his infantry were cut down or forced to throw down their weapons.
"Spare us!" one bandit pleaded as Hou Cheng loomed over him.
"Do we spare them, General…?" Hou Cheng asked of Zhang Liao, who was approaching with Wei Xu and some elite riders.
"…**Yes,**" Zhang Liao replied. **"They can go, but only if they promise to pass on a message for Zang Ba."**
"We'll do as you ask!" the first bandit said.
"Zang Ba should know that surrender is the only option," Zhang Liao declared. **"If he surrenders to the Han, his case will be looked at properly; if he continues to resist, then our efforts to locate him will become less merciful. He should be told, 'If you know anything of my time serving Bing Inspector Ding Yuan, you'll know that I am very good at harming your kind and will do so gladly'."**
"We will, we will!" the second bandit promised.
Zhang Liao nodded to Hou Cheng and Song Xian, and the bandits were released. As the terrified bandits fled northward, Hou Cheng smiled and said, "Are we heroes now…?"
"We're on our way toward it," Zhang Liao replied as he stroked his beard thoughtfully. "We'd best report back to Governor Che."
"So we're not going to pursue Wu Dun?" Wei Xu exclaimed.
"Warnings are not much good if they are never delivered," Zhang Liao said; he was obviously haunted by something, and the others supposed it to be their former master or some fallen colleague.
"…You are thinking about Lord Lü," Wei Xu supposed.
"Not voluntarily," Zhang Liao replied. "I do so as I think about Gao Shun. He should be here, and he isn't, and for no good reason. He… … …well, it doesn't matter now, does it? He's dead."
Wei Xu smiled and said, "Bu and I were related, sort of, but I don't miss him, not after-"
"We need to get back," Zhang Liao said. "Let's check on the villagers first, though."
Wei Xu's smile disappeared; he nodded obediently, and the group of defected officers moved towards the nearby village, where a cheering crowd awaited them.

And in another part of Xu Province, the former White Wave Bandit associate Xu Huang was carrying out a similar exercise against Mount Tai Bandit leaders Chang Xi and Sun Guan.

"**Where is Zang Ba?**" Xu Huang bellowed as he hacked his way through a group of disordered bandits. "**WHERE IS THE MAN CALLED ZANG BA?**"

"**They ask with swords; can dead men answer???**" Chang Xi cried as he wheeled about and rode northward.

"*Aiee…* **Don't turn your back on them, idiot!**" Sun Guan scolded as he tried to follow Chang Xi; Yuan Shu's former general Qi Ji and Wang Zhong – one of Cao Cao's newly-promoted officers – blocked his way.

"**Where is your master?**" Qi Ji hollered.

Sun Guan turned a second time and rode eastward; Qi Ji followed Sun while Xu Huang, Liu Dai – who was another of Cao Cao's newly-promoted officers – and Qi Ji's colleague Qin Yi pursued Chang Xi. A group of bandits formed a doomed phalanx to block Xu Huang's advance while their leader, Chang Xi, completed his retreat; Qi Ji and Liu Dai halted their own pursuit of Sun Guan when Sun and his followers started to cross a shallow stream.

"**Tell Zang Ba to yield!**" Wang Zhong screamed. "**Tell Zang Ba that he should come to us bound or he will lose his head!**"

"**…Come back, Lü Bu: all is forgiven!**" Sun Guan sobbed.

Xu Huang and his allies regrouped after all of the bandits around Ju City had been scattered.

"They won't take this place again any time soon, so coming back here was a waste of time for them," Qin Yi said. "What now, General Xu?"

"I'll have a man report to Governor Che," Xu Huang replied. "All of this must force Zang Ba to surrender, or his allies to betray him; either will do. I just hope that the day comes soon, because we have to defeat-"

Xu Huang suddenly stopped talking.

"General Xu, we came here to get away from Yuan Shu, and we have no allegiance to him now," Qin Yi promised. "That was true before and even truer now that he is a disgusting heretic that claims to be the Son of Heaven."

"Indeed," Qi Ji said. "We are glad that we left before he made that awful proclamation, and have Master Liu Fu to thank for it; we are no more allied to Yuan than you are to the White Wave Bandits."

Xu Huang smiled and replied, "You are right to point out my folly, gentlemen. I must remember my own past faults when I presume to judge others."

"We are all now loyal followers of His Majesty, and destroying the wretched Yuan Shu will be a pleasure shared," Qin Yi said. "But as you say, how long will it take before Zang Ba understands the will of Heaven?"

General Yu Jin and his colleague Zhu Ling conducted their own bandit-quelling operation around the settlements to the north of Xiapi, near the intangible border between Xu Province and Qing Province's southernmost prefecture Langya; the Mount Tai Bandit chief Yin Li fled from a fierce attack by the Han army and camped in the hills to plan his next move.

"We're stuck," Yin Li said. "We need to co-operate a bit more."

"Why not turn in Zang Ba?" one man asked. "It's him they want."

"Don't make me answer that, idiot," Yin Li scoffed. "No, we need to show some solidarity; I just hope that Zang Ba's got the sense to call a meeting."

"We should just go to Kaiyang," another man suggested.

"...Agreed," Yin Li decided. "Alright, fellows, let's get ready to break out of this mess and go 'home'."

And in northeast Xiaopei, Liu Bei was leading forces against the White Wave Bandit remnants and Mount Tai Bandits that had strayed southward.

"Everywhere, there's bandits," Zhang Fei grumbled as he charged at a group of Mount Tai Bandits. "I'm *sick of bandits*."

Guan Yu was taking out his frustration at being deprived of General Qin Yilu's ex-wife Lady Du by Cao Cao; men fell left and right to his Green Dragon pole sword, and his callousness was conspicuous to his soldiers, his victims and even the most distant of observers.

"Yunchang's almost indistinguishable from Yide today," Mister Sun Qian said as he watched the battle from a vantage point near Liu Bei's main camp.

"Even Heaven should fear a Guan Yu that's denied a new wife," Jian Yong joked. "Cao Cao should try and stay away from him."

"Cao Cao was cruel to do that, and if Lady Du was ever made aware of Guan's infatuation, then that's also cruel, but at the same time, I understand," Mi Zhu admitted. "I feel for our families sometimes, thinking that they have to share our fate or even suffer worse fates; if Lady Du was watching how often our families ended up as hostages in Xiapi... Cao, on the other hand, offers stability and comfort."

"...A fair point," Liu Bei sighed.

The bandits finally retreated, and Liu Bei's men returned to their battle line.

"Another fine performance," Liu Bei praised.

"I want to fight Yuan Shu!" Zhang Fei said. "I'm sick of bandits!"

Guan Yu harrumphed angrily.

"...Are you ever going to cheer up, Yunchang?" Jian Yong asked.

Guan Yu harrumphed again.

"That's a 'no', I'll guess," Jian Yong chuckled. "But don't take it out on me. I'm not Cao Cao."

"Don't mention that despicable villain to me, Jian Yong," Guan Yu warned. "I might see him in my mind's eye, see him right where you stand, and-"

"*Yunchang*!" Liu Bei chortled.

Zhang Fei grinned and said, "Finally, someone else gets to be scolded! But I was saying, Xuande, that we should be-"

"I know, but our orders are to remain here!" Liu Bei retorted. "Until we're told otherwise, we have to stay and harass the Mount Tai Bandits."

"If Zang Ba doesn't surrender soon, I'll ride into Kaiyang and get his head for His Majesty by myself," Guan Yu growled. "I would take it to Xuchang, push that thief Cao Cao aside and present it to His Majesty."

"I'm sure that's what His Majesty wants, Yunchang; some bandit's mouldy head," Jian Yong chuckled. "Are you hoping to trade it for Lady Du?"

470

Guan Yu harrumphed and flicked his sleeve.

"*Aiee…*! Don't flick your sleeve at Xianhe!" Liu Bei whined. "He was joking, Yunchang! There's no need to be so offended!"

Guan Yu grunted tersely, turned to Jian Yong, bowed slightly and said, "Sorry, Mister Jian, for overreacting."

"It was a poor joke," Jian Yong replied. "And so is our mission here. Yide's right, Xuande: we shouldn't be here. We should be in Shouchun or Xuchang."

"…Patience," Liu Bei said with feigned cheer. "In time, gentlemen, all will be right."

Commander-in-Chief Yuan Shao finally learned of Lü Bu's death while pressing Gongsun Zan's new Yijing citadel in Yòu Province: the construction – which Gongsun Zan had made his new capital – had been holding Yuan Shao back for months, but it was also the last obstacle before Yòu Province was taken and Gongsun Zan was utterly destroyed.

"So Bu is finally dead," Yuan Shao said with delight.

"All that remains is the subjugation of Yuan Shu and the end of Gongsun Zan!" the adviser-general Chunyu Qiong suggested.

"My cousin… is not to be discussed at present," Yuan Shao ordered. "But yes, Mister Chunyu, Gongsun's destruction is necessary and nigh."

"Remember that I must be the one to kill him if the opportunity arises," one embittered young officer said: it was Liu Hè, the son of the murdered governor of Yòu Province, Liu Yu.

"Of course, Mister Liu," Yuan Shao promised. "He harmed you far more than me, and it is only right."

Liu Hè coughed deliberately and added, "Whether I am governor after this is over is no doubt open to debate, Lord Yuan; assure me, though, that your deal with Tadun of the Wuhuan does not include an independent state for the barbarians on lands that my father governed in the name of the Han."

"It is in exchange for more cordial relations," Yuan Shao replied. "I am loyal to the Han, and would not dare barter imperial territories for personal gain. I leave things like that for my treacherous former friend, Cao Cao."

"Yes… he'll need dealing with too," Liu Hè said. "And so will your cousin: I have not forgotten the time I spent as his prisoner, nor have I forgotten his claim to be a-"

"Please, Mister Liu, one thing at a time!" Yuan Shao interrupted. "Let us be glad that Lü Bu is gone, the deceitful Zhang Yang is no more and the wicked Gongsun Zan is on the verge of defeat!"

Liu Hè harrumphed quietly and withdrew.

"He fears that you'll renege," the adviser Tian Feng suggested.

"He can think what he wants," Yuan Shao scoffed. "My only concern right now is the elimination of the 'White Horse General' that has bitten at my heels these last six years or more."

The gaggle of advisers murmured agreeably.

****

92

The far west has home to two warlords that had once been allies; one, Governor Liu Zhang of Yi Province, feared that his northern neighbour, Zhang Lu of Han'ning, was planning an all-out war to avenge the family members that Liu had executed as punishment for Zhang's written declaration of defiance. The sudden removal of the imperial court in Chang'an had left a power vacuum in Liang Province that a court-appointed man was about to fill, but the future intent of the Xuchang imperial court was still a worry for Liu Zhang and Zhang Lu.

"I send tribute," Liu Zhang said as he paced back and forth along the floor of his governor's audience hall; he had dismissed all of his officials except for his late father's adviser Dong Fu, the politician Yang Hong, his brother-in-law Wu Yi and Yi's newest notable guest, the famous Han scholar and commentator Xu Jing.

"The Han court has not named you as a rebel," Dong Fu sighed.

"But they are not informing me of many of their movements!" Liu Zhang fretted. "I have a right to know who governs Liang Province! I have a right to know what they intend to do to my neighbour and relative Liu Biao, or to that wretched Zhang Lu!"

"...You fear isolation," Xu Jing supposed.

"I do, Master Xu," Liu Zhang replied humbly. "The Nanman barbarians hanker at my southern borders, and Zhang Lu and his deranged acolytes loom to the north; Liu Biao teeters between hero and villain, and if his province is seized by your old enemy Sun Ce I will have to call upon the court for aid for the inevitable invasion of Yi that will follow!"

"You should not have executed Zhang Lu's family for mere words, Governor," Xu Jing said honestly. "You should have waited until he actually tried to oppose you militarily, if that was ever his intent. Now you have no bargaining tools and a devoted enemy in that dangerous cult leader."

"Be my counsel, Mister Xu Jing, so that I might avoid similar mistakes later on!" Liu Zhang pleaded.

"I... am *tired*," Xu Jing replied. "I am a commentator and appraiser, like my poor brother Shao was... not an adviser. Did my counsel save Kuaiji from Sun Ce? Am I not now here in Yi because I had to abandon Wang Lang...?"

"You are being hard on yourself," Yang Hong suggested.

"I disagree, Mister Yang," Xu Jing replied. "I have been of no use to the empire: barbarians rule Liang and Yang, the Yuans tear up the east over matters that are better resolved by negotiation, and His Majesty has suffered great misfortune that neither me nor my poor brother could predict or prevent. Did we stop Dong Zhuo, mediate peace between the Yuans, or prevent the massacres in Xu Province...?"

"...Nonetheless, Mister Xu, you are welcome here as a respected guest for as long as you choose to remain... forever, hopefully," Liu Zhang said miserably.

"I shall leave you with the men that have the wits to aid you, Governor Liu," Xu Jing announced; he then bowed to each man in turn and left the hall.

"...*Aiee*... Xu Jing has borne much pain in his time in Yang

Province," Yang Hong said. "He was right about our response to Zhang Lu, but what's done is done. Zhang seems to be content with fortifying his borders, however, and refusing to answer our correspondence."

"So I needn't fear him at the moment...?" Liu Zhang asked as he looked at the frail, weary Dong Fu.

"He's not got the military means for a war," Dong Fu replied. "His entire regime's economy is based around bartering food; you need currency – coin, and a lot of it – to buy weapons and finance militias. The elderly and impaired that he supports cannot rise up and fight for him, and that's who much of the harvested food goes to. Any men that might have had the money to back him have fled to avoid his religion, either for the faith itself or because of the heavy taxation that the cult applies against the largest holders of wealth. And even if he did somehow foment the support for a war amongst his well-fed agricultural populace, he has to pass the mountains to get here, and we all know what a hassle that is."

"We certainly do," Wu Yi sighed.

"We'd get such an advantageous advance warning that he'd be walking into a trap, and he knows it," Dong Fu continued. "He'll just sit there for now; in the meantime, we'll ensure that we have a strong army to battle the Nanman people, Zhang Lu and anyone else that might threaten us and a strong economy that dissuades people closer to the Han'ning border from considering Zhang Lu's blasphemous doctrine."

"I agree wholeheartedly," Yang Hong said. "Winning hearts and strengthening our defences is the way to defeat Zhang Lu, not shedding blood."

"To best achieve this, you'll need more minds than ours," Dong Fu said with notable resignation. "I have a few suggestions; we must add to your counsel, Lord Liu, for time, age and such are our true masters, and I shall not be here forever."

"...I shall do as you say," Liu Zhang declared.

Zhang Lu of Han'ning did not confront Liu Zhang, just as many had predicted; he focussed on building walls, setting up defensive positions and keeping the majority of his observers facing north and eastward, as he feared attacks by the Qiang or the rejuvenated Han Dynasty. The region formerly known as Hanzhong was a symbol of Han's origins and future authority, and so Zhang Lu was right to worry: it was on the list of 'reputation-restoring measures' that Cao Cao and other government figures had drawn up for the near future, once Yuan Shu was vanquished. Liu Zhang could quietly build on what his father had left him, as no man would try to take Yi from him for many years to come.

＊＊＊＊＊＊＊＊＊＊＊＊

93

Zang Ba and the rest of the leaders of the Mount Tai Bandits gathered in the bandit-controlled city of Kaiyang – which was, in a way, a spiritual bìrthplace – to discuss the future.

"**Cao Cao has got men combing the northwest of Xu, arresting and killing men left, right and centre,**" Zang Ba complained. "**He says, friends, that he's after me, and only me: so, to save a lot o' blood being spilt, I'm going to surrender.**"

The dozens of bandit leaders responded angrily, although the recipient of their anger varied from man to man.

"**Who's your replacement?**" Chang Xi heckled.

"**Are we all supposed to surrender?**" Wu Dun asked.

"**What's the point when he'll just switch his focus to one of the rest of us?**" Yin Li protested.

"…Don't do it, Xuangao," Sun Guan pleaded.

"**Look, I expected some noise, so here's what we'll do,**" Zang Ba shouted.

"**Quiet!**" Wu Dun ordered.

Once the bandits were quiet enough that Zang Ba could be heard, he said, "**Let's put it to the vote. Cao Cao's deal is simple enough: he says that if I am handed over, then the rest of you will get amnesty.**"

"**Which is bollocks!**" Chang Xi heckled. "**This is Cao Cao *and* Liu Bei behind this: they'll kill us all!**"

"**…But 'can we fight them' is the question,**" Zang Ba retorted. "**Bu's dead, and anyone that didn't die with him joined Cao; that includes the likes of *Zhang Liao*, who used to make life quite hard for Zhang Yan's lot in Bing, and they number a lot more than we do.**"

The bandits mumbled nervously.

"**Zhang Liao, Yu Jin and Xu Huang are still here leading the 'pacification', and the people are actually *with them*,**" Zang Ba continued. "**Cao didn't hurt any civilians when he came here to get Bu: he actually ensured that they were protected from ours and Bu's raiding parties, and people are actually starting to ask stupid questions like 'Was it really him that came here before?', 'Maybe Tao Qian caused what happened?' and 'Perhaps he was possessed last time?'. If we don't have the people with us but they're neutral, bad enough; if the people are with Cao – or, to put it properly, they're with the Han government – then we won't hold here.**"

"**…Then we'll go back to Qing!**" Yin Li said.

"**And fight Yuan Tan for it…?**" Zang Ba retorted. "**We can certainly *try*, lads, but he's his father's son, and they don't much like bandits.**"

The bandits grumbled miserably.

"**Yuan Shu's done; Gongsun's done; Bu's dead; everywhere you look, it's Han officials turning it around,**" Zang Ba continued. "**Our options are to resist and surrender. What do you all want to do…?**"

The response was near-unanimous: the crowd roared, "**FIGHT!**"

"...**Alright,**" Zang Ba sighed. "**We fight.**"
The bandits cheered and chattered inanely.
"**We did the while amnesty thing before, remember...?**" Sun Guan said over the din. "**They lied last time, Xuangao, so why should we believe them now...?**"
Zang Ba nodded sadly and replied, "**True enough!**"

In the north, the Black Mountain Bandits and their ally Gongsun Xu enjoyed a brief advantage over the seemingly unprepared Yuan forces as they moved across western Yòu Province.
"We're making such a show of randomly causing havoc that they'll never expect our attack on the men 'round Yijing," Flying Swallow Zhang Yan explained to an audience of bandit leaders and Gongsun Xu. "We're waiting for more instructions, which we'll get once we're closer to the fort: isn't that right, Mister Gongsun...?"
"It is," Gongsun Xu said. "I'll have a man get into Yijing and inform my father of our numbers; our 'renegade' Xiongnu allies – the only sensible ones, if I may say – are Heaven-sent, as their cavalry make our plans even more likely to succeed."
"With six thousand elite horsemen that Yuan Shao's not expecting, how can we lose...?" Zhang Yan suggested.
"Yeah, but Zhang Hè is nearby, and he's doing a lot of damage," the bandit 'White Circles' said. "We need to hit back."
"And we will, mate, but the most important thing is relieving Yijing," Zhang Yan replied. "We need to get a move on. **You all have your instructions: good luck, lads.**"
The bandits hollered their support for Zhang Yan and Gongsun Xu.

Cao Cao was suffering from a crippling migraine on the day that an imperial messenger from Xuchang arrived in his camp; Cao Cao had the messenger taken to a guest tent for rest while he summoned Guo Jia, Xun Gongda and his newest acquisition – Chen Qun, the son of noted scholar Chen Yuanfang – to prepare for the announcements.
"Nice to see that I don't have to be in the capital for formalities to continue," Cao Cao grumbled. "What has been agreed to in my absence...?"
Xun Gongda smiled awkwardly and said, "My uncle sent a man ahead to warn me – or rather, us – that there have indeed been some potentially contentious administrative decisions made."
"Like *what*...?" Cao Cao growled.
"Wei Kang has been appointed Inspector of Liang Province," Xun Gongda reported.
"...I see no problem there," Cao Cao said. "Duan Wei and Wu Xi surrendered; Chang'an is back under government control; the 'Qiang trio' have retreated to their self-appointed kingdoms for now; and Zhang Xiu is isolated, and therefore ripe for picking from the tree of sedition and devouring at last. Appointing a man – and a very competent man at that – to be Inspector of Liang is fine by me. Stop delaying and tell me what the 'potentially contentious' decision is."
Xun Gongda exhaled noisily, took Xun Wenruo's letter from his baggy sleeve and passed it to the impatient Cao Cao.
"So I must read it myself," Cao Cao chortled. "It *must* be bad."
The advisers sat silently while Excellency Cao Cao read Xun

Wenruo's news.

"…What is this? Dong Cheng… promoted to **General of Chariots and Cavalry???**" Cao Cao exclaimed; he then threw down the letter and clutched his aching head.

"We expected a move like this," the adviser Guo Jia protested.

"Calm yourself, Excellency!" the adviser Xun Gongda pleaded.

"*Calm*…?" Cao Cao chortled.

Chen Qun coughed deliberately and said, "Yes, Excellency: calm. I am new to some of this, but as I come to understand it by talking to Mister Guo and Mister Xun, I can see that there are weak factions of ambitious mediocrities that pose minor problems. The-"

"Dong Cheng is no longer a powerless mediocrity!" Cao Cao retorted. "Bad enough that his daughter might one day carry an heir to the throne – perhaps she now *does*, come to think of it – but that document plainly states that he is now General of-!"

"'Chariots and Cavalry'… I heard it when it was read to me by Gongda, and I heard it again during your lament," Chen Qun interrupted. "Excellency, your most dangerous enemy, Yuan Shao, is Commander-in-Chief, but-"

"Yes, and now he has a powerful military ally in 'General of Chariots and Cavalry' Dong Cheng!" Cao Cao said. "My roles as Excellency of Works and *Acting* Excellency over the Masses – I wonder how long the later role will be mine – are both *civil posts*! This is done in the wake of my victory against Lü Bu – *Lü Bu*, the 'Man among men' that no other man could defeat!"

Guo Jia shook his head and said, "Excellency, you-"

"I have humbled the White Wave Bandits, the Yellow Turbans, Yufuluo's Xiongnu renegades, the Black Mountain Bandits and very soon the Mount Tai Bandits!" Cao Cao continued. "I've broken the mighty Yuan Shu and left him a shivering wreck, cowering in Shouchun! **Nobody has achieved what I have achieved!**"

"That is true," Xun Gongda said, "and-"

"I – and *I alone* – have brought stability to the central regions!" Cao Cao continued. "Even my defeats are more productive than other men's victories! My loss at Xingyang inspired Sun Jian to take Luoyang from Dong Zhuo! My loss at Wan, as bad as it was, was still punctuated by the subsequent deaths of both regents and the Qiang warlords suing for peace! Yuan Shao has achieved little more than cornering a former business partner in order to hide his criminal land deals, Liu Bei is an old joke that is no longer funny and Dong Cheng did *what* to earn this most prestigious role…? He fawned on Dong Zhuo's son-in-law, propped up Li Jue for three years, conspired with the White Wave Bandits to gain control of His Majesty and then had to beg me for help when his plan miscarried!"

"You overreact," Chen Qun protested. "This-"

"**I am the only competent military leader in the land: Yuan Shao, Liu Bei, Dong Cheng, Yuan Shu, Gongsun Zan, they are all guilty of strings of wrongdoings and failures that far outnumber mine!**" Cao Cao declared. "Why, then, do I sense that I am about to lose my military commissions and spend the rest of my life in court, being gradually demoted until I am either retired or assassinated while the first three of those aforementioned men rise ever higher…? **Ingrates, traitors, liars and fools! That's all there is, gentlemen, and I am doomed**

to suffer for it!"

"…When Zang Ba is captured – and I expect results within weeks or even days – we can return to Xuchang and assess Dong Cheng's motives," Xun Gongda suggested. "After that, Excellency, we'll react accordingly. But making yourself ill will achieve nothing save giving your rivals and enemies an advantage."

"…I… I know," Cao Cao conceded. "Forgive me, gentlemen, but I suffer from a second pain, a pain called loss. Every other day seems to be a day when I am reminded of someone dear to me being taken from the world. Age is a cruel thing: it becomes little more than a list of miseries if you're not careful."

"You have so many beautiful wives and consorts, Excellency, and you'll feel better when you are reunited with them," Guo Jia suggested. "You have many gifted children too, and-"

Guo Jia was forced to end his speech and cough violently.

"…*Aiee*… I suppose that's more self-inflicted sickness," Chen Qun grumbled.

"Indeed… yes!" Guo Jia replied through his fit of coughing.

"And every day that these wretched bandits waste my time here is another day that Yuan has to vanquish Gongsun and plan a march on Yan," Cao Cao fretted. "I must be out of here soon, gentlemen… I simply *must*."

"And you… shall be," Guo Jia rasped. "Patience… patience…"

Cao Cao's patience had already failed when it came to Zhang Xiu and Jia Xu: he intensified his attacks on the Wan City occupiers, despite Yuan Shu still being alive and Liang being pacified.

"…Will we survive, Mister Jia…?" Zhang Xiu asked of his adviser.

"That depends entirely on you now," Jia Xu replied as he looked around the private meeting room. "You have scrolls and paintings on every wall, my lord; each one tells a story or teaches a lesson. Many of those lessons and stories are timeless, because the spirits of men have not changed and probably never will."

"…I must 'surrender'," Zhang Xiu scoffed. "Why must I surrender…? Does Zhang Lu surrender…? Does Liu Zhang surrender…? Do the Qiang warlords surrender…?"

"In every case, there is no relevance," Jia Xu retorted. "Zhang Lu is a heretic, while you are happy to serve the Han if your given the chance; Liu Zhang is a court-appointed governor, while you have inherited a stolen city; the Qiang warlords are the court's original target, men who were seditious rebels long before Dong Zhuo ever wronged the empire, while you are the blameless nephew of a reluctant subordinate to a tyrant and therefore deserving of being judged in your own right. I, on the other hand, am more deserving of punishment, and if the court deems it necessary I will face it."

"But your words are contradictory!" Zhang Xiu complained. "Your words give me a reason to fight, to-!"

"My words give you a reason to protest and resist wrongful persecution," Jia Xu retorted. "You are not fighting the Han army, my lord; you are defending yourself from a misguided attack by the Han army as directed by certain officials. Be sure to understand and insist upon that distinction."

Zhang Xiu nodded silently.

"…Now that both Li Jue and Guo Si are gone, there is no 'enemy of the Han' to destroy in Liang other than mediocrities like Duan Wei and the barbarian lords like Ma Teng and Han Sui," Jia Xu noted. "What will they do, I wonder...?"

"When you say 'they', Mister Jia, do you mean the Liang rebel factions or the Han representatives like Cao Cao and Yuan Shao...?" Zhang Xiu asked.

"Both," Jia Xu replied. "Will Cao Cao really still march into Liang Province now, or is his attack on us a personal matter...? Will the Qiang warlords start fighting each other again, or will they accept their Han titles and the autonomy they've gained through the chaos in the east, or will they challenge the Han for more...? Will the remnants of Li Jue and Guo Si's forces surrender to the Han, or will they eventually try and carry on Dong Zhuo's legacy themselves...?"

"...Such times," Zhang Xiu sighed.

Liu Bei expected many people to visit him in his Xiaopei camp, but he did not expect a man that immediately riled his ally Guan Yu.

"**Damn that fool! Damn his idiocy!**" Guan Yu cried as he marched back and forth in front of his bemused – or in Zhang Fei's case, amused – colleagues.

"Why are you so annoyed, Yunchang...?" Liu Bei asked innocently.

"You haven't heard, then," Zhang Fei chuckled. "You'll never guess who showed up to make Yunchang angry!"

"...Xiahou Dun...?" Jian Yong supposed.

"Nope!" Zhang Fei snickered.

"...*Cao Cao*...?" Mister Sun chortled.

"**Don't mention him either!**" Guan Yu snapped. "**That man will swing from a noose tied by my own hand, the wife-stealing-!**"

"Wait... not... not *Qin Yilu*???" Mi Fang exclaimed.

Guan Yu screamed like a wounded animal and left the command tent without paying proper respects.

"Well done, Mi Fang, you guessed right!" Zhang Fei chuckled.

"*Seriously*...?" Liu Bei asked.

"*Seriously*, Xuande," Zhang Fei replied. "Qin Yilu."

"*Impossible... ridiculous...!*" Mi Zhu giggled.

"B-but was he not executed with the rest of Bu's unrepentant allies after the siege of Xiapi...?" Mister Sun asked.

"Qin Yilu was not among the men that died or surrendered," Mi Fang recalled.

"So the story that he was sent to Yuan Shu as an envoy and abandoned his family after a promise of ties to nobility is completely true, then," Liu Bei realised. "...And he didn't even get what he was promised. What an idiot."

"He was hiding right here in Xiaopei after being routed by one of Cao's generals," Zhang Fei explained. "He came back here with two of Bu's advisers and some men from Yuan Shu, he says, but he never got past Xiaopei. He tried to go back to Yuan Shu, but 'did not do so in the end'... I'm guessing that Yuan said 'sod off'."

"Yuan Shu turned down one of *Lü Bu's vanguard generals* at a time when he's lost almost every capable man he ever had?" Mi Zhu exclaimed.

"That's right," Zhang Fei replied. "So Qin's just been hiding here, doing nothing. No training, recruiting, planning, *nothing*. He's just found out Bu's dead, and now he's here wondering if we want to employ him!"

Liu Bei grinned and giggled like a child.

"No wonder Yunchang is acting like that," Jian Yong chuckled. "Qin's ex-wife is now in Cao Cao's harem – Heaven knows what'll happen to his son – and his lord was strangled to death after being humiliated in front of everyone; Qin knows that, right…?"

"He knows *everything*," Zhang Fei replied. "I admit that I'm annoyed with him too, just because of what having him here is doing to Yunchang, but he's so pathetic that I can't help laughing! He acts like he's got nothing to be ashamed of at all!"

"*Ayah*… Lord Liu, we can't have a useless man like that in our army!" Mister Sun protested. "Don't employ him!"

"Why would I do that?" Liu Bei sniggered. "Why would you think that I would? Mister Sun Qian, when did I take leave of my wits that you'd ask such a thing?"

"…Apologies," Mister Sun replied.

"**D'AAAAAAAGH! He is *still here*!**" Guan Yu screamed as he suddenly re-entered the tent. "**Why has he not gone and killed himself??? I could not live with myself if I were even *half* as wretched as he is right now!**"

Liu Bei laughed and said, "Calm down, Yunchang. He'll soon see that he is unwelcome and go away."

"I have hardly been *subtle*!" Guan Yu retorted. "Yide and I have already castigated him twice, and when I just shouted at him again he just replied by saying, 'Every man has bad times, Guan *Yunchang*'!"

"*Ooh*… that's not funny," Zhang Fei decided. "Was he holed up in Haixi for a year? He dared address you as though you were a *friend*…? And what 'bad times' are these, the little-!"

"He dares suggest that we – *me and him* – 'share the loss of a good woman to Cao Cao'…!" Guan Yu complained.

"**Bastard!**" Zhang Fei said. "**He-!**"

"So now you're both determined to attack him, gentlemen," Mi Zhu supposed. "Just tell him to go away; if he doesn't go, then I will rebuke him publicly."

"And if he *still won't go*…?" Guan Yu asked.

"Then *I* will tell him to go, Yunchang," Liu Bei promised. "But I'll only lower myself to speaking with this man if I absolutely *must*."

"**You'll do no such thing!**" Zhang Fei said. "**I'll kill him before he-!**"

"*Yide*, please *calm down* and stop threatening to kill such an unimpressive and unimportant man," Liu Bei scolded. "You don't want to have to admit that you wasted energy killing *Qin Yilu*, do you…? *Either of you…?*"

"…Was Lady Du *forced* to be with him, I wonder…?" Guan Yu said. "Why else would such a woman want to-"

"Yunchang, she's *Cao Cao's* now, and that's that," Jian Yong said bluntly. "Forget wondering why she married Qin Yilu."

"I was talking about her relationship with Cao Cao," Guan Yu replied icily. "Lord Liu, I should like to retire: we are still fighting the bandits, and-"

"Go and rest," Liu Bei said kindly.

Once Guan Yu had retreated, Zhang Fei grunted angrily and said, "I'll stay here, where you can all see me. I'm getting that feeling I

had before, when Cao Bao-"
"Say no more," Liu Bei chortled. "*Please*... say no more."

When two of the three Qiang 'super-warlords' – Ma Teng and Han Sui – heard the news that Cao Cao was once again attacking Nan County, they assembled their officials and pondered the move.
"Master, you should not fight the Son of Heaven," Han Sui's adviser, Chenggong Ying, protested. "To do so would anger-"
"**Han toady!**" one lesser Qiang chieftain heckled. "**Your kind always start grovelling to your emperor and-!**"
"**Enough!**" Han Sui barked. "I am the same 'kind', but I do not bow and stoop to a boy, not anymore. Mister Chenggong, we're not opposing the Han emperor right now – we just helped the Han emperor get rid of Li Jue and Guo Si and put an Inspector back in the province for the first time in eight years!"
"...Yes, and it was us that once prevented them being here, because they are corrupt and greedy!" a former rebel leader protested. "Have we all forgotten the string of thieves and eccentrics that they sent here to 'rule' us...? Why do we now-?"
"You serve me now, and I order you to be quiet," Ma Teng said. "Times have changed, and we must change with them."
Many of the rebel leaders and minor Qiang chieftains grumbled at the words.
"The point is still, as yet, unmade," Ma Teng continued. "We have not opposed the Han, and yet we are seeing Zhang Xiu under attack again, when the only reason for that last time was as a prerequisite of invading Liang Province to 'pacify' it. What game does Cao Cao play now...?"
"He obviously cannot be trusted!" Ma Teng's heir Ma Chao declared. "Let's oppose Cao Cao, and-!"
"No," Han Sui chortled. "We can barely sustain an alliance between us on most days, your father and I; Song Jian went home after Li Jue was killed and refused to have any further discussion. Without Dong Zhuo's old friends, we face the Han alone. Are we able to do that together, as we would have to...?"
"If you had not killed my father's sister, would such words be necessary?" Ma Chao retorted. "You-!"
"Don't you dare accuse me of starting our feud, Ma Chao!" Han Sui barked. "I've buried half of my own clan because of your father, and-!"
"So our differences are entirely my fault, are they, Han Sui?" Ma Teng heckled.
"*Aiee*... what about *Cao Cao*...?" a rebel leader groaned.
But the man's words were drowned out by an escalating argument; within weeks, Ma Teng and Han Sui would be fighting again, and the western half of Liang Province would once again suffer the horrors of indiscriminate and needless war between two former allies.

* * * * * * * * * * * *

94

The leader of the Mount Tai Bandits, Zang Ba, had fled Kaiyang and retreated to the hills to the south of the city in order to avoid a siege. Zang Ba was sat on his haunches by a fire in his open-air 'command centre' and silently thinking; Cao Cao's armies were closing in, and he knew that he would probably have to fight to the death.

"...Enemy sighted," Zang's ally Sun Guan said as he entered the 'command centre' and sat on his haunches. "Three thousand or so, we reckon. Banners read 'Liu Dai', 'Wang Zhong', 'Yu Jin', 'Zhu Ling' and 'Han Hao'."

"I'm honoured," Zang Ba snickered. "So many important men for little old me...! What's the mood...?"

"Unsurprisingly, they all want to fight," Sun Guan replied. "You're still very popular, Zang Xuangao."

"...I shouldn't be, Zhongtai," Zang Ba suggested. "I've made a right mess of everything. We should have stayed in Qing; we shouldn't have raided Ju; we shouldn't have sided with Lü Bu, or-"

"You made all the decisions that any of the rest of us would've made," Sun Guan insisted. "Anyhow; we outnumber them at least two-to-one, so we can send a few heads back to Xuchang."

"I'm for that," Zang Ba said as he got to his feet and brushed the dirt from his hands. "I've been a bandit for twenty years, and yet I reckon that not enough people have heard of me in the capital. It's time that changed!"

The Han generals arrayed their men on some flat ground to the west of the hills and consulted their campaign commander, Yu Jin.

"This ends now," Yu Jin declared. "The nation has more important problems, like Zhang Xiu, the Liang warlords and the heretics Zhang Lu and Yuan Shu. Don't hold back: we want Zang Ba, dead or alive, for presentation to the Excellency of Works."

"It shall be so," Han Hao said.

"Zhang Liao is ready to aid us, but Xu Huang will likely be sent back to Yu Province or down to the Xu-Yang border to liaise with his former White Wave Bandit allies that are still meandering around that area and resume attacks on Yuan Shu," Yu Jin continued. "I, too, should like to be out of here and reassigned to destroying the man that dares claim to be the Son of Heaven."

"As would we all," Zhu Ling said.

"We will deploy as one and use the tactics that our new friends from Bing Province have shared with us," Yu Jin continued. "We'll smash them once and for all! **Onward at once, gentlemen, to defeat Zang Ba!**"

"**For the Han!**" the officers replied as one.

Zang Ba's allies were deployed in a series of camps: some were in the hills, including the main camp, while others were based on flatter ground and served as bases for raiding parties, scouts and signalmen. The Han army's initial behaviour suggested that the commanders intended to challenge the bandits to field combat, but that would not be the case; Zhang Liao and the other veterans of campaigns against the Black Mountain Bandits had provided more effective approaches, and the Mount Tai Bandits were about to be unpleasantly surprised.

"ENEMY ATTACK!"

Zang Ba had been asleep when Yu Jin and Zhu Ling led a night attack on his outlying camps; the disorganised bandits scattered, allowing Zhu Ling to charge the main camp.

"Idiots! Where was the warning???" Zang Ba cried as he tried to prepare for the defence of the camp. Han cavalrymen were galloping about and cutting down many of the men that Zang hoped to be his main force; Zang forgot any fear and charged at one cavalry captain with his sword at the ready.

"HOLD ON MATES!" Sun Guan bellowed as he led a relief force into the main camp. **"WE CAN PULL THIS BACK!"**

Zhu Ling suddenly gave the order to retreat; the bandits were left dazed and demoralised as the Han forces disappeared as quickly as they had arrived. Sun Guan found Zang Ba, who had commandeered a horse and managed to gather some men for the now-unnecessary retaliation.

"...We... can't afford to rest a moment, then...!" Zang Ba chortled.

"I guess not," Sun Guan replied. "They're using Lü Bu's tactics."

"Not a surprise, I suppose," Zang Ba said. "They certainly work. We need to think about taking the fight to them before they do that again."

"More are angry than afraid," Sun Guan replied. "Let's hit back as soon as we can."

"Better yet, let's turn it against them," Zang Ba suggested.

While Cao Cao was reorganising his forces and preparing to eliminate the last of his opponents, the Xu Provincial nobleman and Chancellor of Pei, Chen Gui – a man that was, perhaps, more instrumental to the downfall of both Liu Bei and Lü Bu than any other – was finally settled into his new role and was doing his best to recruit as many good men to the Han cause as possible. One of the men that he sought more than, perhaps, any other was the scholar and noted physician Hua Tuo, but the aging polymath was uninterested in any of Chen Gui's propositions.

"I am nearly sixty, Chancellor, and have many things that I want to do before my time under Heaven expires," Hua Tuo explained as the two men shared a pot of tea in Hua Tuo's simple home. "I have no desire to serve in the government or be forced to practise my medical work in any specific place."

Chen Gui was unable to stop himself from studying the famous man time and again; his weathered features were almost foreign, and his expressive face was as mysterious as his chosen name and his medical breakthroughs.

"...You are silent, Chancellor," Hua Tuo prompted.

"Oh, uh... forgive my rudeness!" Chen Gui replied. "I, uh... I have heard so much about you, and have long wanted this moment to arrive, but you are a most elusive man in addition to being a most gifted one. Not since Cai Yong, perhaps, have I-"

"And it is Cai Yong that I think about, sad to say, when I consider your proposals, and he was not being 'asked of' as much as I am," Hua Tuo interrupted. "I am aware of the second reason why you want my service, and the answer is 'no'."

"But His Excellency's headaches are surely a challenge that stirs your natural curiosity, Mister Hua...?" Chen Gui pleaded. "He is a genius himself; his poetry, his writing, his musical work, his military skill, his-"

"His penchant for violence, his recklessness, his ambition," Hua Tuo retorted. "There are many that would react to my becoming his personal physician with violence of their own, and most likely against my kin and my friends and my students, Chancellor. I sympathise with his plight, but I doubt that I can help him with the little information that I have in my head."

"You are being mischievous," Chen Gui suggested. "I know of your studies of the animals and your derived 'Exercises', and of your 'Book of the Green Bag', and of your marvellous potions that relieve pain, and of your remarkable proficiency in the realm of acupuncture, and of your pioneering surgical work, and-"

"You know of it, and so do a lot of others, but what does that prove...?" Hua Tuo countered. "I meddle and dabble a little here and there, but what I know of His Excellency Cao Cao does not suggest itself to me as 'within my ability to resolve', Chancellor. I am, first and foremost, a scholar, and it is to that profession that I am most devoted. I think His Excellency has quite a few of them already; does he want one that practises unproven and experimental arts that might do more harm than good...? How would he react if I *failed* to help him...?"

"He is not an evil man!" Chen Gui protested. "He is the only man that raised a finger to help His Majesty escape from the barbarians, villains and bandits!"

"I would ask that you do not pass word of our brief meeting to your friends in Xuchang, Chancellor," Hua Tuo replied calmly. "I have a legacy that I am building that will, I hope, help all of humanity and perhaps the entire world under Heaven. I must continue with that legacy, for it is why I was born. One does not, if he is a true devotee of the Heavenly intent, abandon the many to favour the few."

Chen Gui exhaled loudly.

"...More tea...?" Hua Tuo asked.

"...Y-yes, Mister Hua... th-thank you," Chen Gui replied miserably.

Hua Tuo's refusal would not be his last, because word would – eventually – reach Xuchang that a possible solution to Cao Cao's lifelong problem had been found in Hua's revolutionary medical research; the outcome of that would be another unfortunate chapter in the history of the Han Empire's declining years.

Cao Cao received regular updates on the situations in and around the country; several days after his Xu Province forces were met by Zang Ba's counterattacks, he received one report from the northern region of Yijing in Yòu Province that startled him.

"The Black Mountain Bandits are coalescing in Yòu, but Gongsun is trapped in his city," Cao Cao mused as he stared at his three advisers. "Yuan Shao has the advantage, though: that much is clear. We're looking at a matter of weeks, maybe, before he defeats Gongsun Zan altogether."

"I'd say we have a little longer," Guo Jia insisted. "Gongsun's tougher than Yuan Shao likes to admit. All the same, though, we cannot stay in this region any longer. Dong Cheng's latest appointment aside, your presence in Xuchang is necessary to maintain order."

Cao Cao shook his head and said, "But can I afford to leave the province – and the responsibility of capturing Zang Ba – in the hands of Che Zhou, Liu Bei and-?"

"Oh, no-no-no, Excellency, you won't leave Liu Bei here," Guo Jia chuckled. "We do not need that ambitious man – especially unfettered and popular, as he is – in Xiaopei. He should be summoned here, to Xiapi, and then he – and all of his followers – will travel back to Xuchang with us."

"Too true, Fengxiao," Xun Gongda agreed. "I shall have him come to Xiapi at once with his entire entourage, and- ...Oh, wait, what about Guan Yu...?"

"Excellency...?" Guo Jia said as he turned his gaze to Cao Cao.

"...Guan will not attack me," Cao Cao replied as he turned his own gaze to his ever-present bodyguard Xu Chu, who smiled like a young child.

"He'd be most unwise to, admittedly," Xun Gongda said.

"...Fine!" Cao Cao replied. "I write to Xuande personally, so that he does not suspect the worst."

Cao Cao's messenger reached Xiaopei within a few days.

"...**D'AAAAAAAAAAAGH! Heaven _curse_ that man! Curse his women, his children, his _beard_!**" Guan Yu shrieked as Jian Yong finished reading the first part of Cao Cao's latest orders to Liu Bei's court.

"I don't know what to say, Xuande," Jian Yong sighed.

"I do: tell Cao Cao to bugger off!" Zhang Fei said.

"We... are ordered by the Han's _Excellency of Works_ to do this thing," Liu Bei said. "We are not in a position to bargain or refuse, else we'll be labelled as-"

"I want a chance to smite the villain Cao Cao, Lord Liu," Guan Yu protested. "Give me the order, and I will ride to his camp with some good cavalrymen and-!"

"You'll do _nothing of the sort_, Yunchang!" Liu Bei chortled. "We're going to do as we are asked by His Excellency."

"But why, Lord Liu, when so many enemies are not dealt with?" Guan Yu protested. "Yuan Shu lurks to the south, the remnants of the White Wave Bandits are still in the area, and Zang Ba is still a very powerful fugitive! We are one of his best militia forces, and yet we must go to _Xuchang_? What is there is Xuchang...? Why would he now want to have you in Xuchang when he did everything in his power to send you back here and get you away from Xuchang before...?"

"Perhaps I will go on to my governorship in Yu Province from there!" Liu Bei retorted. "I am as unaware of His Excellency's motives as you are, and-!"

"Those motives will be ominous, and that is all that matters," Guan Yu suggested.

"...I'm with Yunchang," Zhang Fei said. "Zang Ba's not the worry in the future, Xuande, and nor is Yuan Shu: it's-"

"I... cannot discuss this," Liu Bei insisted. "We must get ready to depart for Xiapi."

"...So we're all to leave Xiaopei and go to Xiapi, where we will then remain until we all depart for Xuchang," Jian Yong said with a resigned tone. "And we know _why_ as well."

"He fears *our* motives," Mi Zhu guessed.

"He's concerned that we'll rebel when he's gone," Mi Fang said.

"He'll regret forcing Lord Liu to bring me to Xiapi," Guan Yu suggested. "Had he trusted our lord, he'd live a long time; now that he demonstrates such fiendish and hypocritical mistrust, he will perish by my-!"

"Yunchang... no more threats," Liu Bei ordered. "We will gather our families and supporters, say our farewells, and go."

"This is truly a bad decision that he makes," Mister Sun said.

"...He leaves me with little choice but to comply with his wishes, though," Liu Bei replied.

Liu Bei's evacuation preparations were watched with interest by Lü Bu's former general Qin Yilu; when the moment for departure arrived, he dressed in his best civilian clothes and approached Liu Bei's vanguard.

"Oh, this is *unbelievable*," Jian Yong grumbled.

"What is...?" Liu Bei asked.

"That prick Qin Yilu is *actually*...!" Jian Yong exclaimed.

"'Actually' what...?" Liu Bei asked as he turned his horse to view the unfolding debacle; Guan Yu and Zhang Fei blocked Qin Yilu's path with their horses and raised their weapons.

"**Back, you bastard!**" Zhang Fei bellowed.

"I just want to speak to Lord Liu," Qin Yilu pleaded.

"**You DARE assume that you can approach Lord Liu, you worthless slug???**" Guan Yu heckled.

Qin Yilu smiled sheepishly, bowed humbly and said, "I know what you two gentlemen think of me, but I am a proven general! I could be of value to Lord Liu!"

"**He is not your lord, nor would he want to be!**" Guan Yu retorted. "**Be gone, you fool, before I lose my temper!**"

"...Should I just tell them to let him speak to me...?" Liu Bei asked.

"*No*," Jian Yong scoffed. "I wouldn't employ him to sweep dung from the road, let alone what he'll ask."

"He went to the heretic Yuan Shu for a role: he should rot," Mister Sun agreed.

"I'll go and tell him to go away," Mi Zhu said. "If I don't, Yunchang will kill him."

"Go at once," Liu Bei ordered.

"Please, friends, let me speak with Lord Liu!" Qin Yilu asked. "I could-"

"'Friends'???" Zhang Fei exclaimed. "You have a lot of nerve!"

"But I could be of use, I tell you!" Qin Yilu protested.

Guan Yu harrumphed.

"I was one of Lü Bu's best men!" Qin Yilu continued.

"Yes, and we all know what happened to him," Mi Zhu said as he stopped his horse beside Zhang Fei's. "Go away, Qin Yilu: you are not wanted."

"What have I done to deserve this scorn?" Qin Yilu pleaded.

"...Are you serious?" Zhang Fei cackled. "You abandoned your wife and your heir to go to a man that dared to claim he was emperor, hoping he'd get you something better, and you got *nothing*! And then, when you had to come back here, your lord was killed, you were defeated and lost all your men, and your wife was taken by another man, a man that has no shame about it and will treat her as just another of his women! The mother of your heir will be in Cao Cao's bed even though you're still alive, and you have no men, no job, no money and no friends, and yet you act as though everything's fine and good for you! Where's your son and heir, mm…? Do you even *know*, or *care*…? You're a man with no pride, and yet you think you have a right to follow us? Go away, you silly bastard, before I hurt you!"

Qin Yilu sighed and said, "Heaven heaps indignities on every man. But I will still follow Lord Liu until such time as I can be heard."

"Good luck," Zhang Fei scoffed as he turned his horse to move away. "C'mon, Yunchang; this idiot's not worth our time. If we killed him, it'd make us look bad, wasting our precious time on dogs and pigs."

Guan Yu was shaking violently.

"**Don't let him ruin your reputation!**" Zhang Fei pleaded. "**Ignore him!**"

Guan Yu finally lowered his weapon and reluctantly joined Zhang Fei's retreat.

"…**I can still be of value!**" Qin Yilu cried.

Mi Zhu glared at Qin Yilu and said, "Lord Liu will never give the likes of you his valuable time, so you might as well go back to Yuan Shu, or maybe ask your former comrades like Zhang Liao if they will recommend you to Cao Cao."

"I won't give up," Qin Yilu retorted. "I will join Lord Liu Bei!"

"…I've done my best," Mi Zhu sighed. "Your fate is in Heaven's hands now."

Mi Zhu turned his horse and returned to Liu Bei's side; Qin Yilu looked at the disdainful expression on the faces of the soldiers that surrounded him and exhaled loudly.

"**Go away!**" one infantryman heckled.

"…Truly, I am to walk a hard road," Qin Yilu murmured.

"'Walk' is right!" another infantryman said. "Did you think you'd get a horse?"

Qin Yilu stared at his weathered sandals and wondered if they – or he – would have the endurance for the walk to Xiapi.

Cao Cao made the journey from his battle camp to Xiapi City to speak with his chosen Governor of Xu Province, Che Zhou; the two met at the gates of the city and travelled to the governor's mansion to discuss the short-term future privately. After several minutes of talking over tea, the governor made his feelings clear to his master and the small collection of officials that had been deemed trustworthy enough to attend.

"You're *abandoning* Xu, Excellency…?" Che Zhou exclaimed.

"…I really don't see it that way, Governor Che, and neither should you," Cao Cao retorted. "Lü Bu is dead, the White Wave Bandits and crushed and Zang Ba is little more than a rat now, scurrying through tunnels and under floors in an effort to avoid inevitable capture. My priority now is Yuan Shu, and–"

"Forgive the interruption, but is it not the case that Yuan Shu might try and move into southern Xu to escape his current calamity, and perhaps forge an alliance with Zang Ba, as he tried to do with Lü Bu and the White Wave Bandits…?" Che Zhou said. "Shouldn't there be a pincer from all directions, with the pincer

force in Xu being commanded by your esteemed self…?"
Cao Cao smiled and replied, "I considered it. But right now I have much to deal with on all fronts, and I can only do that from the capital. There will be many fine officers leading our forces against both Yuan and Zang here in Xu, though some may need to be reallocated to other fronts if circumstances dictate it."
"…Like Liu Bei…?" Che Zhou supposed.
"No, Governor, not like Liu Bei," Cao Cao chuckled.
"…Good," Che Zhou grumbled. "Support for him has actually grown a little; some have 'had time to assess him in comparison to Lü Bu', and your own presence is still a contentious issue."
Cao Cao grunted ambiguously and said, "I am aware of that. That, in fact, is another reason why I am better off leaving, is it not…?"
Che Zhou's eyes wandered.
"Sometimes you need to think a little harder; sometimes more, you need to think harder still," Cao Cao continued. "It is better that I withdraw to Xuchang."
Che Zhou's officials looked at each other silently.
"And Liu Bei will be accompanying me on my journey," Cao Cao explained. "After all, gentlemen, he is the Governor of Yu Province, is he not…? So why would he stay here in Xu…?"
Che Zhou looked at Guo Jia, Xun Gongda and Chen Qun, smiled, and said, "This has, perhaps, been better considered by your minds than by mine, Excellency."
"I shall depart from here knowing that the situation is clear, then, Governor," Cao Cao replied.
"…Might *I* not need a clever strategist to aid me…?" Che Zhou asked nervously. "Mister Chen knows this region well from his time serving Liu Bei, or perhaps you could recall Chancellor Chen Gui back from Pei City; after all, Zang Ba and-or Yuan Shu might somehow-"
"If you need an adviser, Governor Che, I'll send you one," Cao Cao replied with a smile.

"…He's still following us," Guan Yu complained as Liu Bei's forces continued their reluctant advance to Xu Province's capital, Xiapi.
"And…?" Jian Yong retorted. "He's a joke, Yunchang."
"And by proxy, so am *I*!" Guan Yu cried. "Did I not ask for that fool's wife for my own home, believing him to be dead and her to be available…? His very *existence* makes my *blood boil*! His presence is a daily reminder that Lady Du is-!"
"We *know*," Liu Bei said involuntarily.
"…Forgive my lack of clarity, Lord Liu, but I am unable to resolve it!" Guan Yu admitted.
"I… I am sorry, Yunchang, that Cao Cao was so dishonest with regard to Lady Du," Liu Bei replied.
"But if he *had* been honest, what then???" Guan Yu cried. "This wretch would have appeared in Xiaopei, where she would have been my new bride, and-!"
"I… I know," Liu Bei replied. "Mi Fang, please go and tell the man to stop following us."
"I shall certainly try," Mi Fang chortled as he turned his horse and departed to carry out his instructions.
"…Well…?" Zhang Fei asked as soon as Mi Fang returned.
"H-he… uh… I…!" Mi Fang bumbled.

"What did he *dare* say now???" Guan Yu whined.

"Just tell us, Brother," Mi Zhu prompted.

"...He says that he regrets our stubbornness and inability to be sensible at the critical hour, and that he regrets having not seen 'the futility' sooner," Mi Fang said. "H-he says that he will withdraw and 'will seek another lord as we obviously desire', and that perhaps they will-"

Guan Yu halted his horse and bellowed like a wild animal; he was about to turn his mount and gallop toward Qin Yilu when Zhang Fei stayed him and shouted, "**No, Brother! This is my work!**"

Zhang Fei galloped toward the retreating Qin Yilu at speed before any could protest; there were gasps, yelps and even cheers as Zhang Fei tore into Lü Bu's former general with his customised pike and left him as a gory, headless mess by the side of the road.

"...It should have been me," Guan Yu murmured as Zhang Fei returned to the front of the convoy with Qin Yilu's head in one hand and his pike and reins in the other.

"*This*," Zhang Fei said as he held Qin's head aloft, "was not worth your time. You let this stupid, classless pig butcher deal with pigs and dogs like this, Brother Yunchang; you're supposed to fight worthy men."

Guan Yu smiled humbly, bowed low, and said, "To have a brother such as you... I am truly blessed, Zhang Yide!"

"...For once you're speechless, I see!" Liu Bei snickered as he stared at Jian Yong.

"Now we can carry on to Xiapi without any more sad faces!" Zhang Fei said as he tossed Qin Yilu's head aside.

"...General Qin's head should be sent ahead to His Excellency Cao Cao, for Qin's widow and heir's sakes," Guan Yu suggested.

Guan Yu then looked to Liu Bei for approval; Bei nodded silently.

"I like your thinking!" Zhang Fei sniggered; he then turned to a grinning infantryman and shouted, "**You there! Fetch me that head back!**"

Excellency Cao Cao frowned when a messenger brought word that Qin Yilu's battered, bruised head had been sent to him ahead of Liu Bei's arrival.

"It isn't too late to relinquish Lady Du!" Guo Jia joked.

"I'll do *nothing of the sort*," Cao Cao grumbled. "Xuande merely passes the head of an enemy of the state to me for approval."

"So he's 'Xuande' today," Guo Jia teased. "But yes, you're right, Excellency: he's merely doing his duty. It has nothing to do with-"

"Enough jokes, Guo Jia," Cao Cao ordered. "We've been in Xu Province long enough; we should quicken our pace."

"...And double our defences," Guo Jia suggested.

Cao Cao harrumphed in response, but he was only refusing to admit that he was nervous. Guan Yu was a very effective field general and mercenary, and the thought that he had angered him to the point of a possible attack was a worrying one; little did. either man know the strange and surprising twists of fate that the near future held.

✱✱✱✱✱✱✱✱✱✱✱✱

95

Cao Cao's return to Xuchang was, ostensibly, to plan for the final destruction of Yuan Shu; in truth, it was Shu's elder brother – Yuan Shao, Commander-in-Chief of the Han forces and self-styled Governor of Ji, Bing and Qing Provinces – that he was preparing to face. The man that had once stormed the imperial palace to slaughter the 'Ten Attendants' and free the current Han Emperor – then a prince – and his elder brother Emperor Shao from imprisonment by those corrupt eunuchs was now poised to destroy the rogue warlord Gongsun Zan, himself the self-styled Governor of Yòu Province. Two obstacles stood in Yuan Shao's path: one was Gongsun Zan's formidable Yijing fortress, and the other was the combined armies of rebel Wuhuan and Xiongnu tribes, Black Mountain Bandits and elite cavalry that Gongsun could still call upon despite a crippling reversal of fortune.

"He still has barbarian allies... but *how*...?" Yuan Shao complained during a private meeting with his senior campaign advisers. "They are only meant to respect strength and tribute; he surely proffers *neither* at this juncture, gentlemen!"

"Nonetheless, he's almost finished," Tian Feng suggested. "He can keep trying to push us back, but the outer moats are filled again and his cavalry is severely diminished. The bandits are providing a distraction that thins and spreads our forces, but our officers can deal with them. Our only enemies are supplies – which, at the moment, are ample – and time, which we have as well, I think."

"And now Dong Cheng – a man that is known as an outspoken critic of my treacherous former friend Cao Cao – is elevated to 'General of Chariots and Cavalry' by His Majesty," Yuan Shao mused. "Such a move can only benefit me."

"You definitely intend to challenge Cao," Tian Feng prompted.

"Oh, yes," Yuan Shao replied. "He is dishonest, incompetent, morally corrupt and quite obviously mad as well; we can't have another man like that as Chancellor of State, not after the horrors we endured with Dong Zhuo in that role. I owe it to His Majesty – and the state – to restore order after Gongsun is routed. I-"

"ATTACK!"

All eyes immediately turned to the soldier that had entered the tent and made the announcement.

"*Elaborate*, Captain," Yuan Shao ordered.

"**Gongsun's cavalry has surged out of the south gate and attacked our siege force!**" the messenger continued. "**They're pushing to retake the ground around the centre moats!**"

"Impossible...!" Yuan Shao exclaimed as his officers and advisers started to scurry around in preparation for Gongsun's forces.

"He's lost none of his courage," Tian Feng suggested. "You will not need to lead the counterattack, my lord, if-"

"I most certainly *will*!" Yuan Shao scoffed. "If Gongsun leads *his* men, then I must lead *mine*!"

Tian Feng resisted to the urge to sigh as he gave way for his lord to collect his gilded battle helmet.

But the battle was a distraction; a messenger from Gongsun Zan's son Xu was secreted into the fortress through the northern gates while Yuan Shao led his coalesced forces against Gongsun to the south. Once the messenger was safely within the walls, Gongsun Zan's adviser Guan Jing signalled from the battlements and the smirking Gongsun ordered a full retreat.

"…We must be vigilant and watch for messengers day and night, my lord," Tian Feng said as he followed the flustered Yuan Shao into his command tent.

"I, too, sense a distraction," Yuan Shao retorted. "All the same, he and his elite men fought with strength that should have long left them; his supplies must be as plentiful as he boasted after all."

"…Yes, it seems so," Tian Feng replied uneasily.

"Then we must strike at those supplies!" Chunyu Qiong suggested.

"*How*, General…?" Tian Feng scoffed. "They're in silos that are deep within that maze of moats, walls and traps that he's built! No, we have to hope that he makes a mistake… or, rather, that we do not. That was all to allow messengers to leave or enter; let us hope it was the latter, since a reply will be easier to intercept."

"If I have my way, a mouse or an insect wouldn't be able to get in or out of Yijing without us knowing," Liu Hè said. "I've waited for vengeance long enough."

Yuan Shao glared at Liu Hè and replied, "You are not the only man here that desires an end to it. Vigilance will be maximised."

At around the same time, Gongsun Zan listened with growing delight as his son's messenger relayed the strength of the support forces from within and beyond the western mountains.

"Zhang didn't let me down!" Gongsun Zan cackled. "With such an army, we can push back and turn the tide of battle at last! We-!"

Guan Jing coughed loudly and said, "We should act quickly."

"Oh! Yes," Gongsun chuckled. "I shall send a message to my son. We'll set a trap for Yuan Shao and destroy him!"

"Be sure and choose your man carefully," Guan Jing said.

"Agreed," Tian Kai said. "My lord, we need a man with the wits of a fox and the speed of a hare. If Yuan Shao expects us to be trying to sneak a man out-"

"We'll confound him with sudden attacks out of every gate and have decoy men make pointless lone sorties," Gongsun Zan suggested. "Even if Yuan knows that we have the intention of summoning help, does he know which way we'll send our messenger and be able to tell false from true…?"

"…I wouldn't recommend sending men out to die under torture as false spies," Guan Jing replied. "We'll do as you say with regard to the charging attacks from the gates, though."

"We'll begin at once!" Gongsun Zan declared.

For the next few days, Yuan Shao was repeatedly disturbed from meetings and attempts at sleep by night-time charges, duel challenges and small groups of men being sent to harass the defensive mounds and outer tents of Yuan's camp.

"This is intolerable!" Yuan Shao complained. "Not one of his bandit and barbarian allies has reached Yijing yet, and yet he's already exhausting our morale!"

"He's creating a smokescreen to hide an attempt at sending out a messenger, all with the intent of coordinating something; I'm almost sure of it," Tian Feng said.

"And if you're *wrong*...?" Xun Chen taunted. "Could this not be a simple case of renewed vigour in the wake of known reinforcements being nearby, and-?"

"We're being vigilant," Yuan Shao said. "If there's a messenger, we'll catch them."

That same night, a messenger left Yijing's western gates amid the chaos of a seemingly random charge from the eastern, western and northern gates: he hurried toward the northwest path that Gongsun Xu and Flying Swallow Zhang were taking to reach Yijing. The messenger did not get far, however, before he was caught by Yuan Shao's patrolmen, who brought him to the main camp for interrogation.

"Well...?" Yuan Shao asked impatiently; Xun Chen, Pang Ji, Guo Tu and Tian Feng were huddled over the interrogator's report.

"I can't believe that this is all that Gongsun's advisers could muster; that said, he is short of options," Tian Feng replied. "He-"

"He intends to draw our forces into an ambush and overwhelm our cavalry with arrows and sheer numbers," Guo Tu interrupted. "Many of the attacks elsewhere have been a cover for bringing almost all of the Black Mountain Bandits here, to Yijing."

"*Aiee*... that's a lot of bandits," Chunyu Qiong exclaimed. "The-"

"I will read it myself," Yuan Shao declared.

"...Here," Tian Feng said as he passed the report to his master.

"...Fool," Yuan Shao snickered as soon as he had finished reading. "So *he* plans to ambush *me*, eh...?"

"What will you do?" Pang Ji asked.

"The Bandits number a hundred-thousand," Xun Chen fretted.

"We've had to deal with more of those ruffians than that in the past," Yuan Shao scoffed. "We broke their backs last year, before this campaign: that hundred-thousand is far less than the half-a-million that their leader could muster years ago. The Bandits are finished, and so is Gongsun Zan. We'll need no committee to discuss this: Gongsun has given me my strategy!"

The officials gathered around their leader and awaited his orders.

Gongsun Zan smiled as he stared at the enemy encampment from the safety of the roof of his tower home in Yijing.

"**My lord, the signal!**" Gongsun's ally Tian Kai cried as he approached from the tower stairwell. "We're ready!"

"I must go!" Gongsun Zan replied excitedly. "This is the end!"

The signal that Tian Kai referred to was part of the message that had been intercepted by Yuan Shao: it signified that Yuan Shao had walked into a trap, and that the time had come for Gongsun Zan to ride out of the city and pincer Yuan Shao's demoralised forces. Gongsun's forces were smiling and laughing as they readied their weapons and prepared to charge out of the northern gates: bridges were lowered across the remaining moats to give a path to the defenders, and they charged toward the scene of what they expected to be a cavalry battle between Gongsun Xu's cavalry and Yuan Shao's army. What greeted them was nothing at all: the gulley that had been selected as the ambush point was completely quiet.

"What is this...?" Gongsun Zan exclaimed.

"...**Back! Back, my lord!**" Guan Jing cried. "**Hurry and retreat!**"

But Guan Jing's warning came too late: Yuan Shao's cavalry – led by Yan Liang, Wen Chou, Jiang Yiqu and Ju Hu – blocked the southern and northern ends of the path, and archers appeared on the high ground on either side.

"**We'll have to stage a fighting retreat!**" Tian Kai said. "**Tian Yu, you-! ...Tian Yu...?**"

The officer-official Tian Yu had been separated from his colleagues by the infantry forces that were now descending the slopes; Tian Kai was forced to abandon his ally and flee with Gongsun Zan.

"**I surrender, I surrender!**" Tian Yu pleaded as he and his small platoon became ever more entrenched. "**Throw down your arms, men! We're of no use to our lord now, dead or alive, and any more death is a waste!**"

"**Very sensible,**" Wen Chou said as he loomed over Tian Yu.

Gongsun Zan, Guan Jing and Tian Kai rallied some of their men and retreated to Yijing, but the cost of the ambush would be high, and they knew it. Gongsun had lost hundreds of men, and he knew that he would definitely lose many more over the next two weeks as Yuan Shao capitalised on his morale-boosting win.

"**We will have Zhang Hè and our other officers gather here for the final battle!**" Yuan Shao declared. "**Gongsun's end is nigh! Glory to our magnificent army!**"

Yuan Shao's soldiers chanted his name, and his arrogance peaked; the smile on his face was not only self-satisfied, but hungry for greater victories in the months and years to come.

The following days would bring more misery for Gongsun Zan.

"*...Decimated*, Guan Jing," Gongsun Zan sobbed as a medic tended to a wound on his arm. "Our forces have been *decimated*."

"I feel personally responsible," Guan Jing replied miserably.

"Don't," Gongsun Zan insisted. "This folly was mine: that last charge was another bad idea of mine. What's the latest situation?"

"Yuan has filled in all but two of the moats, but our archers are preventing progress," Guan Jing reported. "The Bandits were drawn into a second ambush using Yuan's knowledge of our signalling system; they have been crushed by Yuan's follow-up attacks and many of their leaders have gone back to Bing. Your son is here in Yijing now, but our external help is gone."

"Hah! Just like Lü Bu," Gongsun Zan noted. "What ignominy. So Yuan Shao is content to fill in my moats and goad me into futile charges? Are there any signs of his supplies running out? Are-"

A rumbling sound ended the conversation. Every man stopped what they were doing and looked about them for the source of the noise: it sounded like a peal of thunder, but it did not sound like it was coming from the sky.

"...Has he some new weapon...?" Gongsun Zan whispered.

Guan Jing was about to reply when a soldier shouted, "**Look! The tower falls!**"

Every man ran to see what was happening, and none could believe what they saw: the mounds of earth that supported Gongsun Zan's towers were collapsing and taking the defensive structures with them.

"*Ayah!* **He tunnelled under us!**" Guan Jing realised. "**He's-!**"

Screams ended Guan Jing's lament: a nearby tower was sinking and tilting, and the men that were underneath its obvious landing place were scattering.

"...It's over," Gongsun Zan whispered.

Over the next three hours, Yuan Shao's men burned the wooden supports that kept their secret tunnels from collapsing, and the structures above them – which included the officers' towers and the walls of the city – crumbled and fell. Gongsun Zan retreated to the governor's residence of Yijing, where his family was now gathered. He immediately set about gathering jars of oil while his son looked on with dread.

"Father, we must *fight*!" Gongsun Xu pleaded.

"We're dead," Gongsun Zan replied over the wailing of his sisters and wife. "Now we must preserve our dignity."

"I... I cannot stay!" Gongsun Xu cried.

Gongsun Zan's wife watched her son flee the house and said, "**Do it quickly, husband! End it now!**"

Gongsun Zan fought tears as he struck down each of his female family members: once they were dead, he whispered, "Join us quickly, son," and covered his body and those of his slaughtered relations with the oil. Within minutes, the White Horse General was burning alive, surrounded by most of those that he cared for.

Gongsun Xu joined Tian Kai and Guan Jing in a camp to the north of the shattered ruins of Yijing Fortress at the end of that day. Every man rued the loss, and every man regretted that they had not died with their lord and master. They had expected Yuan Shao to be content with the destruction of Gongsun Zan, but the Marquis of Yè was looking for absolute victory: the final approach of his formidable Han Chinese and Wuhuan army was reported to the survivors by a resigned Tian Kai.

"I'll fight," Guan Jing said. "It's my fault that he's gone: the least I can do is not outlive him any longer."

"We'll all fight," Gongsun Xu said. "My family's dead: I am lonely."

Tian Kai nodded silently: the trio would fight together for one last time. The hundred-or-so men met Yuan Shao's thousands and gave cries of defiance: they charged and died together.

"...Such a waste of fine warriors," Tian Feng said as he surveyed the battlefield with his lord and his colleagues.

"They were fools that deserved destruction," Yuan Shao scoffed.

"...But we've paid a high price," Tian Feng said. "Men's daughters now serve as concubines to barbarian chieftains, and–"

"**GENERAL YUAN!**"

"...I am Commander-in-Chief of the Han Imperial Armed Forces, Mister Liu," Yuan Shao said as he turned to face Liu Hè.

"It's 'Mister Liu' now, is it?" Liu Hè retorted. "My father's death is avenged, but where is the head of my enemy?"

"He immolated himself and his close family, Mister Liu," Yuan Shao replied coldly. "There isn't much of a head to present, or so I understand; I'm having it retrieved from the remains of his keep as we speak nonetheless."

"And now the province shall be ceded to me, since I am the son of its rightful governor; I hope that is your intent...?" Liu Hè asked.

"...The province is far from stable, Mister Liu," Yuan Shao replied. "It will take a long time to placate the tribes, pacify the rebels, chase down the remnants of Gongsun's–"

"So forcibly wedding your subordinates' daughters to the tribal chieftains didn't pacify them fully, then...?" Liu Hè retorted. "What rebels are left after this slaughter...? Where in this province are there men that still serve Gongsun Zan...? You are trying to rob me of my birth right, just like Gongsun, and-!"

"Since when is a provincial governorship a 'birth right', Mister Liu...?" Yuan Shao chortled. "Your father had the opportunity – an opportunity *I* afforded him – to become the ruler of the world under Heaven... and he declined. You also had the chance to give us a sovereign that was not tainted by Dong Zhuo and Cao Cao's meddling, but you also declined; now you are chasing a province and claiming 'birth right' to it...?"

"Treason such as that enacted by your brother is one thing; inheriting a role that is often inherited is something else entirely," Liu Hè growled. "You led me here on the pretext that I would gain the seat of Yòu and govern the province as my father did before your former business partner decided to kill him; are you reneging...? Was I nothing more to you than a way to recruit the hesitant in this place...?"

Yuan Shao fought gut-twisting rage as he said, "*You*... are *inexperienced* and *lacking vital understanding*, Mister Liu, since your education in state affairs was cut short by Dong Zhuo's usurpation of the court, and you will therefore need *support* to govern this province until it is *stable*. I-if your... 'cynicism', shall we say... would give way to *sense* for a moment... then you would *see that*. Your father needed Gongsun Zan, did he not...?"

Liu Hè lowered his head and said, "He did, unfortunately."

"I am not Gongsun Zan," Yuan Shao continued. "He was *not* my 'business partner', Mister Liu. You should know better than to listen to vicious slander about your friends and allies. *Remember*, for a moment, what we have just done. Do not sour a victory for the sake of venting groundless grievances."

"I must... go to my father's shrine, and prepare it for my offering of Gongsun's head," Liu Hè sighed. "I... I thank you, Commander-in-Chief Yuan, for your aid in bringing light to darkness."

Liu Hè exchanged bows and departed.

"*Ingrate*," Yuan Shao scoffed.

"You were right to say that we should not allow the occasion to be soured," Chunyu Qiong suggested. "My lord, you have pacified the northeast! You have tamed the Wuhuan, and earned the highest military rank in the land!"

"...Indeed," Yuan Shao said. "...And now... we turn southward."

The battle for the northeast of China was complete: Yuan Shao now governed – in all but name – the provinces of Ji, Bing, Qing and Yòu, and he was unmatched militarily by any man in the land. Many hoped that he would now set his sights on reconciliation with Excellency Cao Cao and an end to his brother Yuan Shu's failed attempts to seize power; instead, Shao quietly wondered if there was a way to save his wayward brother and wrest the Emperor from Cao Cao's grip in one tactical stroke.

✱✱✱✱✱✱✱✱✱✱✱✱

96

"…So Yuan Shao is lord of the northeast, then."

Cao Cao's assembled advisers knew his tone well: the Excellency of Works had a headache – or, to be more precise, one of his frequent and crippling migraines – and he was angered and perturbed by the news that Gongsun Zan was finally vanquished and Yòu Province was finally pacified.

"Barely have I got back here, and now this sudden victory!" Cao Cao continued. "Oh, I knew that he might have such a victory, we all did, but… but we hoped that he would be kept in the north a little longer, at least until I…!"

Cao Cao clutched his throbbing head and whimpered.

"…There's no guarantee that he'll declare war on you," Cheng Yu said. "How can he? He's got to feast the barbarians that helped him win, mop up resistance, decide how to dispose of Liu Hè-"

"*Ayah*… you think that he'd do that?" the adviser Tian Chou asked.

"Perhaps," Cheng Yu replied indifferently.

"He would not do such a thing in an obvious fashion," Guo Jia suggested. "Your former lord's son is, I think, quite safe, Mister Tian. No, he will not want to cede the province to him – as is correct – for two reasons: one, he hankers for Yòu Province for himself in the long term; two, he no doubt promised regional autonomy to the chieftains that aided his campaign. He may renege on a lot of things, but not promises made to a violent horde of thousands of horse-riding murderers… not unless all that alcohol he's consuming to help him cope with life – and many, many deaths – has finally pickled his brain completely."

Cao Cao laughed at the bold words and looked at Cheng Yu.

"…Youth beats experience," Cheng Yu grumbled. "I must concede that Guo Jia is probably – *probably*! – quite right in this instance."

"I am relieved," Tian Chou admitted. "My heart is still in my place of birth. Excellency, I may travel to Yòu to pay respects to Liu Yu's grave and also to his living son at some point, if you are comfortable with it."

"You wouldn't join Yuan Shao… and perhaps I wouldn't blame you if you did," Cao Cao replied. "You have my consent, Mister Tian."

Tian Chou bowed humbly.

"Are we turning our shields and weapons northward now, or do we continue with our plans to destroy Yuan Shu?" Cheng Yu asked.

"Yuan Shao would never openly support his brother's actions against the Han," Xun Wenruo suggested. "He *might* try to save him, but… he wouldn't do anything else."

"Agreed," Guo Jia said. "We can safely look southward; the only problem we have is our choice of allies."

"…Che Zhou, Chen Deng, Sun Ce, Liu Biao, and Liu Bei," Dong Gongren said.

"…Correctly recited, in order of trustworthiness!" Guo Jia chuckled. Cheng Yu grunted and said, "There is no safe place to put Liu Bei other than several spans under the ground."

"I agree," Guo Jia sighed. "He cannot remain in-"

"*Ayah*… 'Bring him to Xuchang'; 'Send him away'; 'Send him aid'; 'Let him die'; 'Bring him back to Xuchang'; *now* what must I do with the man???" Cao Cao cried.

"We cannot assassinate him, nor can we let him remain unfettered in Xuchang as a possible ally of Dong Cheng," Guo Jia said.

"But we cannot be seen to imprison or monitor him either," Cheng Yu complained.

"And if he goes to Yu Province, he'll cultivate alliances and grow," Guo Jia said. "I am thinking... *we must not let him grow*."

"...Is he really that much of a threat...?" Cao Cao protested. "He is simpering, buffoonish almost! He fawns and scrapes, whines and cries, and not one military effort has ended without serious harm being done to his cause! If he did not have Guan Yu, Zhang Fei and Mi Zhu, then... then surely he would be *nothing*!"

"He has a form of 'charisma', so I am to believe, that wins men to his 'cause'," Cheng Yu replied. "I would hope that a lot of this 'attractiveness' that he supposedly possesses is his tenuous royal connection; please let it not be his character, which is loathsomely wretched and pathetic."

Chen Qun coughed deliberately and said, "As a former follower of Liu Bei, I can say that his 'charisma' is, in fact, a 'believable sincerity' that some choose to believe more than others, Mister Cheng. I became gradually disenchanted because I was able to see his faults with increasing ease; others overlook them, maybe."

"Or they make comparisons," Cao Cao suggested miserably. "They look at his contemporaries – men like me – and they make a choice. To some, he is preferable to me as a lord because he is not a mass murderer, wife-stealer, widow-ravisher, apparent hegemon, crafty vill-"

"Perhaps," Guo Jia interrupted. "We have digressed, Excellency, and we cannot afford to. Liu Bei is, for whatever reason, viewed as a future hero; I don't dispute it, but not by choice. A future hero he is, but that future must not come to pass. He must be supressed, caged, controlled, subjugated or maybe even silenced... one way or the other, he must not grow or gain too many powerful allies, or he will be your greatest living rival."

Cao Cao laughed derisively and said, "Xuande the mat weaver? A man with a handful of borrowed troops...? I am the Excellency of Works! It is *Yuan Shao* – heir to the legacy of the Yuans of Ru County, Commander-in-Chief, ruler of four provinces and master of four-hundred-thousand men and horse – that I fear, Guo Jia, not *Liu Bei*! I fear 'General of Chariots and Cavalry' *Dong Cheng*, whose daughter carries a future prince – or, if Empress Fu is as unlucky as I, a future *Son of Heaven* – more than I could ever fear *Liu Bei*!"

"...Time will tell, Excellency... or at least it *will*, if we are not careful," Guo Jia retorted.

"*Fine*!" Cao Cao barked. "**So he is my greatest nemesis, this master of weaving mats and shoes out of straw, losing gifted rank and leading men to defeats! Tell me what to do with him, then!**"

"...I already told you: I cannot say," Guo Jia replied. "Yu, Xu, or right here in Yan, he is a menace. What we must ascertain is where he can do the least-"

"**REPORT!**"

"...Now what...?" Cao Cao complained as Xun Wenruo admitted the messenger into the private meeting room. "Has Lü Bu arisen from his grave to demand a better death from me...?"

Xun Wenruo dismissed the courier and read the letter.

"...Must I ask again...?" Cao Cao prompted.

"Yuan Shu's almost surrounded," Xun Wenruo reported. "Shouchun has all but fallen; his destruction is imminent."

"...It's *likely*," Cao Cao replied. "Yuan Shao can still save him."

"We can thwart that easily if we send the right men to prevent it," Cheng Yu said.

"...Yes," Guo Jia murmured. "But will we send the right men when the time comes...?"

Liu Bei was free to move as he pleased in Xuchang City, although he was denied easy access to Emperor Xian by a series of protocols and Cao Cao's carefully chosen intermediaries; he was approached by Dong Cheng as soon as he had returned, and the two quickly found common conversation.

"I am glad to see that you are more receptive since your last encounter with Excellency Cao, Governor Liu," Dong Cheng said as he shared tea with Liu Bei, Wang Fu and Zhong Ji.

"...I must admit that his behaviour irritates and confounds me more than it should," Liu Bei replied. "The personal affront against Yunchang – Guan Yu, I mean – has certainly 'muddied the waters', as much as it shouldn't."

"I am unfamiliar with the situation," Zhong Ji admitted.

"Cao Cao promised Lady Du – the widow of Qin Yilu – to Guan Yunchang, and then he took her for himself once Lü Bu was vanquished," Dong Cheng explained.

"Disgraceful!" Zhong Ji agreed.

"...Admittedly, waters were muddied further still when Qin Yilu turned up alive, but he's dead 'again', or rather 'definitely'; either way, Excellency Cao behaved in a manner most unbecoming a man of his rank," Liu Bei said.

"Unbecoming, yes, but not unusual for him," Dong Cheng said. "That business in Wan City that cost the army a victory, the business in Xu Province..."

"...Loath as I am to admit it, Cao Cao is a villain," Liu Bei declared. "He is a villain, and he cannot be allowed to retain his tightened grip on power. I worry that he will be another Wang Mang or Dong Zhuo... or maybe worse than either."

"We must act then, gentlemen," Dong Cheng said. "I am now a General, second only to Yuan Shao, who I am sure will be only too willing to smite his treacherous former friend, and-"

"Forgive my interruption, but isn't Yuan Shao's closeness to the traitor Yuan Shu a factor that must be considered...?" Liu Bei asked. "I have been forced to re-evaluate a lot of things in recent times, not least what a wretched – and, perhaps, deserved – end that my old school-friend Gongsun Zan suffered at the hands of that same Yuan Shao. Surely the brother of a man that tried to make an emperor of himself – and, if I recall, a man that himself tried to appoint Governor Liu Yu as an alternative sovereign without the proper authority – is not an ideal ally...?"

Dong Cheng laughed miserably and replied, "No, he isn't, but he's the one with the army, Governor Liu. You – no disrespect intended – have no army of your own; I'm a senior general, yes, but the army here in Xuchang is *Cao Cao's* army, and given a choice they'll most of them follow *him*, not *me*... unless they are given the *proper incentive*."

"...The 'proper incentive'...?" Liu Bei prompted.

Wang Fu and Zhong Ji exchanged pre-emptive, nervous glances.

"...His Majesty is as concerned about Cao Cao as we are, and I believe that His Majesty will provide us with the proper authority if the conditions were right," Dong Cheng explained. "If we had something that proved that we acted justly and in the name of the Son of Heaven, then I believe that a sizeable part of the army might turn from their evil master and serve the Han properly."

Liu Bei nodded to show his understanding and said, "You are the one that can achieve such things, General Dong. I shall await your word and hope that we are all properly placed and adequately resourced when the time comes."

"The right time to challenge Cao Cao is, surely, when Yuan Shu is destroyed, and not before," Zhong Ji said.

"Yes, else we'd be paving the way for Yuan to rebuild his strength and pose a threat greater than Cao Cao," Dong Cheng agreed.

"I hear that the heretic will soon be dead," Liu Bei said. "Months, maybe weeks."

"It could not happen soon enough, for then we can be rid of the other tyrant as well," Dong Cheng replied. "Remain safe and vigilant, Governor Liu Bei; our greatest gift to the Han is yet to come, but drawing ever closer!"

Liu Bei returned to his home an hour later with his guardian Chen Dao; Jian Yong, Mi Zhu, Mi Fang and Mister Sun were waiting for him in the living quarters.

"...So how was 'General Dong Cheng'...?" Mi Zhu asked as Liu Bei sat in his host seat.

"He speaks boldly," Liu Bei replied as he gestured to a servant that he would like some wine.

"He would," Mi Zhu snickered. "After all, is he not a father-in-law to the Son of Heaven...?"

"His daughter is a consort, not an empress," Liu Bei retorted.

"That's how a lot of them start," Mi Zhu suggested. "Dou Wu, Liang Ji, Hè Jin... their daughters all began their time in the Imperial harem as consorts."

"...True," Liu Bei admitted. "And Dong Cheng did serve Niu Fu for a time, didn't he...? I need to keep reminding myself of that."

"It is precisely because men keep forging alliances with monsters to fight other monsters that we have the sorry situation we have today," Mi Zhu said. "Hè Jin and Yuan Shao recruited Dong Zhuo to help them fight the eunuchs; Wang Yun recruited Lü Bu to help him fight Dong Zhuo, while Yuan Shao employed Yufuluo to do the same; Yuan Shao employed that same Lü Bu to help him fight the Black Mountain Bandits, while Dong Cheng was the one that asked Cao Cao to rescue the Son of Heaven after the Son of Heaven had mistakenly placed faith in the White Wave Bandits as saviours that could rescue the court from Li Jue and Guo Si."

"And – as you carefully and deliberately side-stepped, no doubt – I allowed Lü Bu to come into Xu to help us fight Cao Cao and Yuan Shu, which was especially disastrous for us," Liu Bei grumbled.

"And, like everyone else, we could not have known what would occur, only what might, and we took a chance based on his most recent record," Mister Sun said. "He was viewed as a hero, and-"

"So was Dong Zhuo when Hè Jin invited him to Luoyang," Jian Yong said. "We've all made mistakes; so was lending ourselves so readily to Gongsun Zan's seizure of Yòu Province; I only ask that-"
"We make as few as possible," Liu Bei chortled. "But I cannot say, gentlemen, what is a worse mistake: if I do not help Dong Cheng, will Cao Cao or his progeny destroy the Han...? ...But if I help Dong Cheng, do I simply elevate a new Liang Ji to replace the new Wang Mang, and harm the Han that way instead...?"
"It's a shame that we can't get rid of all of them and protect the emperor ourselves," Jian Yong said. "Why, if Heaven desires righteousness, does it keep empowering monsters and making mice of the honest people...?"
"...*Aiee*... another calamity, and again we are forced to make decisions that could cause great harm if we are wrong," Liu Bei muttered. "...Where are Yunchang and Yide...?"
"Readying our troops, like you ordered," Jian Yong chuckled. "Mind you, they did have a wander over to Cao's barracks first, and Yunchang had a run-in with Xiahou Dun that-"
"*Ayah*! But Yunchang intends harm to Cao Cao!" Liu Bei exclaimed. "He might deliberately injure Cao's officers! O Heaven, do not let Yunchang ruin us at this critical moment! O Heaven, you know I didn't bother mentioning Yide because that's obvious, but I'll mention him anyway! O Heaven, why are both of them now a potential burden??? Wasn't one enough???"
"... 'O Heaven, why did you make Xuande weave mats and make Chancellors out of Dong Zhuo and Cao Cao'...?" Jian Yong muttered. "'O Heaven, why did you make us eat bits of people and live in our own faeces for a year in Haixi while Lü Bu-?'"
"I *heard that*," Liu Bei chortled.
"You were *supposed to*," Jian Yong retorted.
"...Were it only that I still had Zilong," Liu Bei sighed. "Then I would not have to worry about Yunchang and Yide's antics."
"*Ayah*... we were discussing other things, like Gongsun Zan!" Jian Yong complained. "Do we have to start whinging about-?"
"Gongsun Zan?" Guan Yu said as he and Zhang Fei entered the room and joined Liu Bei's meeting.
"Ah! *Finally*," Liu Bei replied.
"We were preparing the men, like you ordered, so why are you angry?" Zhang Fei chuckled.
"You didn't... do anything to ruin us, either of you, when you 'wandered over to Cao's barracks'...?" Liu Bei asked.
"...Well... Yunchang made Xiahou Dun look like an arsehole in front of everyone, but he had it coming, as usual," Zhang Fei replied cheerfully. "The rest didn't seem too bothered, and are they scared of us now, after what Yunchang's told 'em...!"
Liu Bei and Mister Sun exchanged worried glances.
"Perhaps we should start packing our things," Jian Yong said.
"To go where? *Prison*...?" Liu Bei retorted.
"Nothing bad will come of it," Guan Yu insisted. "Your greatest weapon against Cao Cao is his fear of our collective strength. Is that not so, Mister Mi Zhu...?"
Mi Zhu smiled and said, "Great minds think alike, Yunchang."
"...Hopefully, Mister Mi and Lord Liu, our minds are in accord over Gongsun Zan," Guan Yu said. "He plundered his own ill-gotten province of all of its wealth and resources and secreted them in

silos within an impenetrable fortress, leaving almost all of his people – and his army – to starve and face Yuan's hordes without leadership or support – that would, quite possibly, have included us had we stayed, and even if it hadn't it would have been impossible to accept his plans. He surrounded his selfish fortress with unmanned moats that were quickly filled in, and when he needed help, the only ones left to turn to were an army of criminals; at the same time, Yuan smashed his way across southern Yòu almost unopposed, but he was so lofty and incompetent that he did not capitalise on any of the easy gains that Gongsun's selfishness had handed him.

"Time and again, two idiots rammed their heads together and missed opportunities to win, lose or make any positive difference; now Gongsun is dead – burned alive by his own hand, some say – but will that bring peace...? At the same time that Gongsun used the lives and well-being of Yòu's citizens as bargaining material for his shady deal with the Black Mountain Bandits, Yuan made whores of his subordinates' daughters in order to placate the tribes to whom he had already promised autonomy in exchange for their short-term help; in the long term they will turn Yòu into a hell above ground, just as the Bandits would have if Gongsun had won."

"...You are very *harsh*, Yunchang," Liu Bei suggested. "But yes, I hear your words as I have heard those of my advisers. I must be with Gongsun Zan as Yuan Shao now is with Cao Cao."

"Some people change," Guan Yu said. "Gongsun Zan became a greedy villain, like Cao Cao; forget him."

"I shall try, but should I also forget Zhao Zilong...?" Liu Bei replied. "I wonder what became of him..."

"Let's hope that Yunchang's antics didn't harm our survival," Mister Sun grumbled.

"All that my 'antics' will do, Mister Sun Qian, is make him think," Guan Yu retorted. "That, I assure you, will aid us."

Cao Cao was busy planning for future confrontations with his rival Yuan Shao: he had Xun Gongda, Xun Wenruo, Guo Jia and Cheng Yu meet in the chancellery's private study and presented a hand-drawn map of the region around the Yellow River that lay north of Xuchang.

"Ah! You pre-empted me," Guo Jia chuckled. "You are thinking that Yuan Shao needs to be prevented from moving freely from Li County to Xuchang...?"

"As we all know, gentlemen, the river's current is kinder to Boma – which sits between the Yellow and Puyang rivers – than other places, and that is where he will want to cross from Li County," Cao Cao said. "The Yingou waterway that intersects the Puyang River and flows into the Yellow River to the west is his next obstacle, since crossing the Puyang River to the south of Boma is not advantageous to marching. He'll want to take Wuchao, where the Yingou and Puyang intersect, and then cross to Yuanwu, from where he'll finally cross the Puyang and Bian Rivers... and end up at *Guandu*. That is where the river crossings end and the clear road to Xuchang begins."

"...You want to face him at Guandu," Xun Gongda said.

"After crossing rivers and stretching his forces, that is the place

500

that I can fight him and stand a chance of winning," Cao Cao replied. "I'll need to fortify other points too, of course... I intended Yan Ford, Meng Ford, Boma generally... putting a capable man in Juancheng in case Yuan tries to pincer us through Dong Prefecture to the east... have I missed anything...?"

"Nothing obvious," Cheng Yu said as he looked at the map.

"Who will guard what...?" Xun Gongda asked.

"That's where your keen minds come in," Cao Cao replied.

"...The current Administrator of Dong Prefecture, Liu Yan, is a good at what he does, and he excels at management," Cheng Yu suggested. "If I am posted back to Dong Prefecture immediately – and I strongly suggest that you do so – with a force of a few hundred men, then Mister Liu can be posted to Boma."

"Agreed," Cao Cao replied. "After your handling of the region in the wake of Lü Bu and Chen Gong's insurrection, I can think of nobody better suited. But is a few hundred men enough...?"

"I have my reasons," Cheng Yu insisted.

"...You'll have seven hundred good men assigned to you and leave within the next two days, Mister Cheng," Cao Cao decided.

"...Place Xiahou Dun at Meng," Guo Jia suggested, "and Yu Jin at Yan Ford."

"Yu Jin is an excellent choice," Cao Cao replied. "But having *Yuanrang* guard Meng Ford...? After the mess he made of guarding against Lü Bu...? I love him like a brother, but he's reckless, and his injury impedes him."

"He's good to his men," Guo Jia said. "What you need is men that inspire loyalty or enforce discipline correctly in such places: Xiahou is the former, Yu Jin is the latter. Zhu Ling should be retained here, in the capital, since he is proven to be good at pursuits and we might soon have such a mission to send him on."

"...Yuan Shu," Cao Cao supposed. "Very well: Yu Jin to Yan Ford. Do I recall Yue Jin from his current role, then...?"

"Leave him in his role near Henei, where he serves as a backup force to our army in Nan County and to any of the forces along the Yellow River, in addition to watching Sui Gu," Guo Jia replied. "Send Dong Zhao to him, in case there's an option to parley with Sui Gu or one of his subordinates."

"A wise move," Xun Gongda agreed.

"...I'll go and review the Yellow River region in person when the right moment presents itself," Cao Cao said. "Yuan Shu's destruction is important, but Yuan Shao's ambitions now scare me more. We must make no mistakes."

Guo Jia smiled and said, "No... we shouldn't."

Cao Cao knew that Guo Jia's real concern was Liu Bei. Cao Cao was being kept abreast of every move that Bei and his senior aides made and – as Guan Yu and Mi Zhu expected – he was left perturbed by the stories of Guan Yu's skill, Zhang Fei's might and Chen Dao's determination to remain at Bei's side and defend him at the critical hour. Guo Jia and Cheng Yu's constant warnings were starting to make more sense to him, but a solution to his 'Liu Bei problem' was still as elusive as ever.

✱✱✱✱✱✱✱✱✱✱✱✱

97

"...I am finished, aren't I...?"
Yuan Shu's remaining counsel stared at him silently. The court in Shouchun was drastically reduced, and the once-powerful younger brother of Yuan Shao was bankrupt and surrounded by enemies.
"Why do you not answer...?" Yuan Shu heckled. "Is it that you are afraid to tell me that my gambles have injured me, that all of my allies are turned or dead, and that I am soon to die a pauper...?"
"Liu Xun can't accommodate us at present," Yan Xiang said at last. "We must consider leaving here soon. Shouchun cannot be held."
"So that's the extent of your advice...?" Yuan Shu chortled. "Telling me I have nowhere to go, and then telling me that I should leave...? ...No wonder I lost."
The advisers looked at each other with weary eyes.
"I must leave, but I have nowhere to go...!" Yuan Shu continued. "Perhaps I will write to Lei Bo and Chen Lan: I can go and live with them in the Qian Hills, as a brigand! My brother-cousin likes bandits... he'll surely want me in his company again if I do that."
The officer Zhang Xun coughed deliberately and said, "Sun Ce is a friend of mine, and I'm sure that we could negotiate a-"
"I'll hear no more about that," Yuan Shu interrupted. "He betrayed me. He should not be a friend of yours anymore."
After a short silence, the adviser Yang Hong said, "My lord, we must go to the Qian Hills. We must destroy Shouchun so as to leave nothing for our enemies, and depart at once."
"...We're taking another example from Dong Zhuo's book, are we...?" Yuan Shu asked musically. "Oh, yes; insult the Han, loot and burn the capital, and then flee to the hills! I think it was Cai Yong that once said that we're doomed to repeat the same endless cycle of mistakes and wrongdoings; as a youth, I disagreed, but now I see that the old man was right."
Some of the junior officials started to whimper.
"...Begin at once," Yuan Shu continued. "I'll write to Chen Lan."

Yuan Shu's request reached the Qian Hills within days.
"Never," Chen Lan scoffed as he threw down Yuan Shu's letter. "Even now, he's trying to be pompous! Alright, he doesn't mention that he's an emperor, but look at this nonsense about 'you, as my vassals in the better days'!"
"Do I look like I need convincing...?" Lei Bo replied.
"What if he tries to come here anyway...?" a third man asked.
"Then we repel him, Mei Qian," Chen Lan replied. "I know you lot don't trust us because we were so loyal to Yuan before, but trust us, we're done with him."
The other bandit leaders chattered amongst themselves.
"Don't be worried!" Lei Bo insisted. "His army is smashed. Most of his best men have either done what we did and deserted, or they died. We outnumber him, so if comes here we'll chase him off."
"And will you reply to his letter?" Mei Qian asked.
"Yes," Chen Lan replied. "Politely, o' course...!"

Yuan Shu screamed when he read Chen Lan's response.
"We'll go there anyway and negotiate," Yan Xiang suggested.

"Negotiate...?" Yuan Shu chuckled desperately. "Me, a member of the prestigious Ru County Yuan clan, negotiating with trash like Chen Lan and Lei Bo...! ...Don't I have other choices...?"

"None that I can see," Yan Xiang replied.

"...Then we will go to the Qian Hills," Yuan Shu said tonelessly.

Chen Lan and Lei Bo were startled and angered by the announcement that Yuan Shu had ignored their rebuttal and advanced on the Qian Hills anyway; their bandit chieftain allies demanded an immediate meeting.

"So what now?" Mei Qian asked.

"I already said that he isn't our lord anymore," Chen Lan replied. "'Now', Mei Qian, we make that point clearer for our visitor."

"**AAAAAGH! I am your lord, you ingrates and scoundrels!**" Yuan Shu cried as his forces recoiled from a flurry of stones and arrows.

"**You're lord of *nothing*, you fool!**" Lei Bo retorted. "**Go back to your 'palace' and burn with it!**"

Yuan Shu screamed and threw his fist into the air; General Zhang Xun then guided him away as his screams gave way to tears.

"There's nobody...!" Yuan Shu sobbed. "Nobody... I can turn to...!"

But within weeks, Yuan Shu was sending a letter to a man that he thought that he would never need to speak to again.

"...Gonglu asks for aid...?" Yuan Shao gasped.

The entire throng of officials that stood within the command tent in Yijing were stunned into silence for a few moments.

"...He does, Lord Yuan," the courtier Chen Lin said. "He tried to seek refuge in the Qian Hills, but he was repelled by his former generals and forced to hide in various settlements."

"Can he not return to Shouchun?" Yuan Shao asked with genuine concern that rattled his advisers and officers.

"He cannot," Chen Lin replied. "The city was razed before he fled."

"My lord, I can sense a wavering in your voice and expression, but remember that Yuan Shu is now an enemy of the entire world under Heaven!" Tian Feng scolded. "By all means *think it*! By all means *say it*! But my lord, I *beseech you*, *do not do it*! *Forget* that he is your relation, and *remember* what he has inflicted upon you and upon this nation for the last *eight-*"

"He's... he's my brother," Yuan Shao said with as much strength as he could muster. "Yes, he's wronged me; yes, he's wronged the people; yes, I know, he's wronged the entire world. But I can't just let him perish. He and I were born of the same father, if not the same mother, and it would not be filial."

"*Filial*???" Ju Shou chortled. "He publicly ridiculed and condemned you, my lord, and became your worst enemy by choice!"

"Ju Shou is right," Xun Chen said. "I was expected to snub my older brother Wenruo for a lot less than treason. All blood ties between you and your brother were severed when he declared that he was the rightful sovereign, anyway: either ignore this craven plea or send someone to finish him off."

"'Finish him off', Xun Chen??? I'll do no such thing!" Yuan Shao cried. "He... he and I lived in the same house, ate at the same table! We loved each other once, until greed got in the way!"

"He's desperate, not reformed," Tian Feng warned. "His letter promises to bequeath the Imperial Seal to you, the Seal that he has already claimed to possess as a sign of his 'mandate to rule'."

Yuan Shao flinched violently.

"Of course, this promised article could be a worthless forgery," Tian Feng continued. "Or, alternatively, it could be the real Imperial Seal that so famously disappeared at around the time that Dong Zhuo destroyed Luoyang. Some say that the true Seal was lost when the then Son of Heaven and the incumbent were both abducted by the 'Ten' and that Dong Zhuo never saw it..."

Yuan Shao's eyes wandered.

"...So while some have accused Sun Jian of purloining it and then handing it to Yuan Shu, it could just as easily be that Yuan Shu found it during the purge of the eunuchs and decided to keep it," Tian Feng suggested. "The article he promises you is either stolen or forged: either way, he offers you the throne, and your being seen to accept that 'honour' – which you do by aiding him in response to that letter – would condemn you for eternity."

Yuan Shao whined miserably.

"Spare him, Lord Yuan, and he'll rebuild his support and challenge you again; that, and you'll know the fury of the Han," Ju Shou said. "He's offended Heaven, my lord; to help him is to-"

"Enough," Yuan Shao ordered. "Chen Lin!"

Yuan Shao's scribe awaited his instructions with dread.

"Write to my son Tan at once," Yuan Shao continued. "Write to my brother, telling him that- ...No, wait... I will do that. He needs to know that I am reconciled."

"Don't do it!" Tian Feng pleaded.

"We risk being labelled as traitors!" Chunyu Qiong cried.

The command tent was now filled with desperate protestations.

"I don't intend to accept his silly seal, nor his offer to rule!" Yuan Shao barked. **"I will be sure to castigate him for his actions! But...!** ...But... try and understand a brother's pain."

The officials fell silent; Yuan Shao then sighed and said, "As a Confucian, I know that I am duty-bound to serve the state, but... but as that same Confucian, I could not face our father's temple and tell him I killed my own brother."

The officials kept their silence for a host of reasons.

"Men make mistakes; I will let none but Heaven be his judge, and certainly not a hypocritical villain like *Cao Cao*," Yuan Shao insisted. "Chen Lin: go and write to my son Tan at once."

"...I shall," Chen Lin replied.

"And in the meantime, gentlemen, we have the final pacification of Yòu and our return to Yè to progress with," Yuan Shao said with feigned conviction. "After that, we make plans for dealing with the man that now controls the throne, despite a series of self-inflicted defeats and humiliations: I suggest we eliminate that true enemy of the Han before he has a chance to gain further strength."

Yuan Shao's words were forceful and, so far as he was concerned, intended to be the end of the matter; every man begrudgingly accepted that, but doubts with regard to Yuan's clarity were forming or growing stronger by the day.

＊＊＊＊＊＊＊＊＊＊＊＊

98

Cao Cao's court was making preparations for a final, decisive march against Yuan Shu when a spy brought word of the communications between the Yuan brothers. Cao Cao summoned some of his advisers to his private meeting room in the chancellery to discuss the development.

"This, I admit, is a shock: yes, it was not entirely unexpected, and yes, we have discussed it only recently, but... I am truly, genuinely shocked, gentlemen," Cao Cao said. "After *everything*..."

"Yuan Shao is a buffoon," Chen Qun replied. "The war *he* started – remember, Excellency, that he sent Zhou Renming to fight Sun Jian as the first response to mere *words* – was always mere words away from ending, no matter how much blood was shed, because when all was said and done, the entire feud was two overgrown children flexing their military might at everyone else's expense."

"Over-simplified, perhaps, but nonetheless it is a feeling that I share after so many years of misery," Cao Cao admitted. "Go on."

"The Yuans are on the verge of reconciliation, and that must not happen," Chen Qun continued. "Yuan Shu must be intercepted and destroyed. The information we have suggests that Yuan Tan – Shao's eldest, and a very competent general – has been asked to move south to rescue his uncle, while Shu heads north to meet him. Once Shu reaches Qing Province, we cannot touch him without confronting Yuan Shao: he must die before he gets there."

"I am convinced," Cao Cao said. "Whom do I send?"

"Send men that will not stray from the mission," Chen Qun replied. "Send men that will not seek glory or fall for cheap schemes, because our intelligence suggests that Yuan Shu probably still has Ji Ling and Zhang Xun for generals and Yan Xiang and Yang Hong for advice."

"...Guo Jia would agree," Cao Cao said. "How does he fare...?"

Chen Qun frowned and said, "He'll be back, but he is sick to the core of his bones. I concede that he is a clever man – a genius, in fact – but only when saving others from destruction. He seems content to destroy himself as well as his lord's enemies. Having once served Lü Bu, I-"

"Don't be hard on him, Chen Changwen!" Cao Cao chuckled. "Now... I have thought about it, and I think I shall send Zhu Ling and Liu Bei: the former excels at pursuits, as Fengxiao said, and Liu Bei has expressed interest in-"

"*Liu Bei*...?" Xun Gongda exclaimed. "Remember what Cheng Yu and Guo Jia have said: Bei will abscond the second you let him out of the capital!"

"But he's a greater threat if he stays in Xuchang and conspires with Dong Cheng, isn't he...?" Cao Cao countered.

"And sending him back to a place where he has tens of thousands of supporters is rational?" Chen Qun said. "I've worked for the man, and I tell you that if he is as much of a threat as Guo Jia seems to think he is – *if*, I stress – then he'll be a thousand times more dangerous if he gets to go back to Xiaopei."

"Cheng Yu and Guo Jia are right about Liu Bei, Excellency, and further to that, Zhu Ling is a former vassal of Yuan Shao," Xun Wenruo protested.

"So are you," Cao Cao snickered. "So are Guo Jia, Gongda and so many others! And yet you're all the right men for it. Yu Jin speaks highly of Zhu Ling, and so I trust him at long, long last. He will go after Yuan Shu and keep an eye on Liu Bei, who, as I have said, might be more dangerous if he is allowed to stay here in Xuchang for long periods of time. Such a man must be let out and reined in periodically so he cannot get a firm footing."

"They'll likely intercept Yuan Shu in *southern* Xu; Excellency, the interception is most likely to be near or actually in *Xiaopei*!" Chen Qun said. "That's precisely where we do *not* want Liu Bei!"

Cao Cao smiled and said, "He will think I trust him... in a way, I think that I do. He has no reason to betray me, gentlemen: I saved him from destruction, eliminated Lü Bu for him, rescued Xu Province and safeguarded the emperor from White Wave Bandits that he later executed as the worst of traitors. He and I, we're the heroes of future times; he and I will save the Han."

"...Guo Fengxiao! We need to get Guo Fengxiao and Cheng Zhongde back here to reason with you!" Xun Gongda cried. "You must not do this, Excellency! Liu Bei is-!"

"I am certain of my actions," Cao Cao insisted.

The majority of the Han officials were completely unaware of the purpose of the court gathering that they had been invited to: each man took his place amongst the sea of uniformly-dressed officials and awaited the arrival of Emperor Xian.

"...Any idea what's happening, Xuande...?" Kong Rong whispered.

"No," Liu Bei replied.

Excellency of Works Cao Cao and General of Chariots and Cavalry Dong Cheng took their places as two of the most important men in the land; they exchanged cold glances as Emperor Xian and his attendants shuffled into the meeting hall.

"...**We are to understand that an emergency – yet another, and so soon – has created the need for this meeting**," Emperor Xian said once he was seated.

Cao Cao was surprised that the young monarch had chosen to speak before all of the regular court protocols had been completed; many men were frantically kowtowing as a response to their ruler's words, and Cao Cao quickly joined them.

"...Y-yes, Majesty," Cao Cao replied after a noticeable hesitation. "It is not so much an emergency, but valuable information about the whereabouts and intentions of the villain and heretic Yuan Shu that should be acted upon at once."

"Oh...?" Emperor Xian exclaimed. "Is our enemy vulnerable...?"

"He has been 'vulnerable' for some time," Dong Cheng said.

"...He has, but he was inaccessible while he remained inside his defensive walls in Shouchun," Cao Cao replied. "He has abandoned – and, apparently, burned – those walls now, and after a failed attempt to occupy the Qian Hills he has turned about... and is headed for Xu Province, where he is apparently hoping to be met – and saved – by Yuan Tan, eldest son of Commander-in-Chief Yuan Shao."

The court was filled with involuntary gasps.

"This... is...!" Emperor Xian whispered.

"You make quite slanderous claims, Excellency," the elder statesman Zheng Xuan suggested. "Have you proof that

Commander-in-Chief Yuan Shao intends to save his wicked brother after so much has transpired between them…?"

"I… must contest any notion that Yuan Tan is without faults," Kong Rong said. "I and my family were held prisoner by that violent thug for some time. But we may not be certain that he acts with his father's permission or instruction."

"Quite right," Wang Lang said. "Every man is his own man: Yuan Shao and Yuan Shu are two very different men, so why should their children be any less the individuals…? Sun Jian was a true hero and example to us all, while his master Shu was a traitor and his son Sun Ce is a would-be king of the pirates in the south."

"That's unfair, Mister Wang, especially given your own history of fraternising with the unsavoury!" Sun Ce's ambassador to the court said angrily. "How *dare you* insult General Sun Ce, you… you lover of bandits and barbarians! Your conduct in Kuaiji was-!"

"We're not here to discuss Sun Ce: he's helping the court to fight Yuan Shu," Cao Cao insisted. "Yuan Tan's guidance is irrelevant; his actions are all that matter right now. He must not be allowed to intercept Yuan Shu and rescue him from Heaven's justice."

"We wholeheartedly agree, Mister Cao," Emperor Xian said. "An army must be sent at once to destroy Yuan Shu as he travels and punish Yuan Tan for his actions."

"If, indeed, it is Yuan Tan, and not some brigand faction that claims to act in the name of Yuan Shao to slander him," Dong Cheng suggested. "Who will go…?"

"In this case, the Commander-in-Chief is the last name on the list, I think," Cao Cao chortled. "He can hardly be ordered to destroy his own heir and brother! I ask the court to consider General Zhu Ling and General Liu Bei."

"…*Liu Bei*…?" Emperor Xian exclaimed. The young sovereign looked about and found Liu Bei amongst the courtiers; Bei was obviously as shocked at Cao Cao's announcement as he was. Emperor Xian then smiled and said, "We would be sad to see our relative leave Xuchang again, and so soon at that, but the mission is best carried out by such a man. We approve of our counsel."

Cao Cao turned to Liu Bei and said, "It is so, then. General Liu…?"

"…I-I, Bei, w-would be honoured to have the opportunity to smite the greatest villain in the land!" Liu Bei declared. "I have long regretted that my role against the Yellow Turbans was so small and my role in the fight against Dong Zhuo was even smaller; if I am allowed to undertake this mission, I will toil like a horse or dog until the task is completed, Your Majesty!"

Cao Cao turned to Zhu Ling and said, "You will accompany General Liu, General Zhu."

"I, Ling, relish the opportunity to be of such service to the Han!" Zhu Ling replied.

Cao Cao smiled and said, "Then you shall both depart within three days, and no more than that. I will provide everything that you both need."

When the court session ended, Liu Bei did not return to his own vassals: instead, he quickly relayed events to Mi Zhu and hurried to the home of 'General of Chariots and Cavalry' Dong Cheng, who was equally alarmed at the development and summoned his closest allies – Zhong Ji and Wang Fu – to discuss the matter.

"What Cao said... could it be true...?" Wang Fu wondered.

"Yuan Shao... would *aid* his evil brother...?" Zhong Ji exclaimed.

"Worse yet, we are to be separated, just as our cause has been given legitimacy," Dong Cheng fretted. "We were so *close*, gentlemen... so close to fulfilling the Son of Heaven's will...!"

Liu Bei hummed thoughtfully.

"...You still have conflicting thoughts about Cao Cao," Dong Cheng supposed.

"N-no... I am merely *concerned*, as you are," Liu Bei replied.

"...About the edict...?" Wang Fu guessed.

"Yes, Mister Wang... about the 'edict'," Liu Bei replied carefully.

"Don't mistake the Girdle Edict for a false document, Governor Liu," Dong Cheng said. "The Son of Heaven has taken my daughter for a consort, and he has elevated me to one of the highest military positions in the land. Would I then present a fraudulent edict that condemned his 'Chancellor of State in all but name' as a villain and risk disgracing myself...?"

"Excellency Cao has shown himself to be a sensible man," Liu Bei retorted. "It is not blind gratitude that fuels my words, General. He does not seem to be a threat, and His Majesty's tone today was not exactly that of a-"

"No, he does not visually present a threat: neither did Wang Mang," Dong Cheng suggested. "Dong Zhuo and Yuan Shu have become the new measurement for tyranny and sedition, but Dong Zhuo was a stupid thug that did things that no true schemer would do, and Yuan Shu is just stupid. Cao Cao is the Wang Mang we all feared: he is the 'Crafty Villain' Xu Shao promised."

"...Then this move is bad for our cause, as you say, despite my extended thoughts on the subject," Liu Bei sighed.

"Maybe, maybe not," Dong Cheng replied. "We will need external allies as well if we have a hope of destroying Cao Cao, and until this news arose, we thought Yuan Shao would be one of them. If he aids his wicked cousin, then he's another Cao Cao. Your mission places you in Xu Province, where you have strong support: perhaps your mission is fate."

"That was my own thought, General, or one of them at least," Liu Bei replied.

"Do not doubt the edict," Dong Cheng reiterated. "It is His Majesty's divine will that Cao Cao be destroyed, and our Heavenly mission to achieve it."

"...Gentlemen, I vow that I will build us a list of allies to purge the villains from the court," Liu Bei declared. "I will personally deliver His Majesty to a rebuilt Luoyang, where the Han will shine over the people once again!"

"You speak well," Zhong Ji said.

"You're the hero we needed," Wang Fu suggested.

"I promise, I won't forget our covenant and the true wishes of His Majesty," Liu Bei added. "When the proper moment arises, we will rise up and kill the villains!"

"...Well...?" Zhang Fei grumbled as Liu Bei and Chen Dao returned from General Dong Cheng's home.

"*Ayah*... that *tone*!" Liu Bei sighed as he took his host seat in his living quarters.

Zhang Fei scanned for any servants – potential spies – that might

be lurking before he said, "What do you expect me to think???
Your friend and his silly Belt Edict-"

"Firstly, he is not my friend, his is my ally in a great cause to
rescue and restore the Han," Liu Bei retorted. "Secondly, Yide, the
Girdle Edict is not 'silly'! I have thought about it, and-!"

"Welcome back," Mister Sun said as he entered the living quarters
with Mi Zhu, Mi Fang and Jian Yong.

"...*Aiee*... I can see that I am about to be criticised by five men
instead of one," Liu Bei complained. "Is Yunchang hiding
somewhere, waiting to add his own peerless chiding...?"

"Yunchang is 'conducting his own business', though I do not know
what that means, exactly," Mi Zhu replied. "I think I saw him with
a local criminal leader, but I convinced myself that I had maybe
drunk something that had affected my vision."

"I see," Liu Bei murmured. "Mi Zhu has informed you all of...?"

"...He has," Mister Sun sighed.

"...So are we going to go back to Xu, Lord Liu?" Mi Fang asked.

"We are," Liu Bei replied. "That is, of course, unless you have
some collective 'concern' that you wish to sway me with...?"

"It's your 'Belt Edict' that's a 'concern'," Zhang Fei heckled. "Dong
Cheng's just some bastard from Liang Province with a pretty
daughter! He's also a man that used to serve *Dong Zhuo*! He
could even be *related* to Dong Zhuo!"

Liu Bei shook his head and said, "H-he assures me that-"

"Nobody can get to the bottom of what Dong clan he's part of,
Xuande, and that should be scaring you," Zhang Fei continued.
"He says he's a Dong from the clan that Empress Dowager Dong
came from; what, the Dowager Dong that conspired against the
then Son of Heaven – with help from the 'Ten Attendants', some
reckon – and tried to murder his uncle Hè Jin?"

"You don't know anything about politics," Liu Bei heckled. "Who
told you that?"

"I did," Mi Zhu said. "We were discussing it, as advisers are
supposed to do."

"...B-but his daughter has the confidence of the Son of Heaven!"
Liu Bei protested. "I-it is His Majesty's will that-!"

"You're sure of that...?" Mi Zhu asked plainly. "We none of us can
endure another Haixi, Lord Liu... not, at least, without a just cause
to endure it for. Can we trust Dong Cheng completely?"

"His allies, Zhong Ji and Wang Fu, are good men and they trust
him fully," Liu Bei replied. "Of course I am scared of being wrong,
but I believe that His Majesty *does* want rid of Cao Cao! You are
not admitted to court sessions as I sometimes am, gentlemen!
Three times now, I have seen Zhong Ji, Kong Rong, Wang Fu,
Dong Cheng and Zheng Xuan criticise Cao Cao to collective,
agreeable murmurs from the majority of the court, and twice I
have heard the tone of His Majesty to be cold, suspicious and
dissatisfied when addressing Cao Cao! That is not a surprise at all!
What Majesty would want, for their Excellency of Works, a man
that lowers his guard to bed the aunts of surrendered generals –
in the general's own bed! – or destroys entire communities to
avenge an unconnected crime...?"

"...That is true," Mi Zhu conceded.

"I admit that the existence of a written condemnation is truly
incredible, but I have seen it, and its authenticity is almost beyond

question," Liu Bei continued. "The words are written as one would expect His Majesty to write: the language is regal, clear, superior, but... sad, lonely. When I saw it, gentlemen, I...!"
Tears filled Liu Bei's eyes.
"...Don't cry, Xuande," Zhang Fei pleaded. "If you say you saw it, and you say it looks real, then... then it's probably real."
"Sad... and lonely...!" Mister Sun whimpered. "His Majesty is the centre of our world! If His Majesty knows no peace or warmth, then we are all without them!"
The majority of the assembly were briefly too emotional to speak.
"...I think it's probably not real, because I don't trust Dong Cheng *at all*, but nobody cares what I think," Jian Yong said. "I do, however, think that the emperor is sick of being pushed about and being made to cower to villains, as any man would be: we've been pushed about and made to cower, and so we can all guess how bad being without a palace, servants or respect probably was, or what having to cower to men like Dong Zhuo and the regents was like. Cao Cao's made us all look stupid at some point, and there's no denying that he's got a really nasty side that's already harmed Xu Province twice and could, at some point, manifest toward the court or even the emperor. He's got to be got rid of for everyone's sakes, and if this edict is the only way to make that possible without everyone turning on us, then it doesn't matter if it's real or not, does it...?"
"...It *does* matter, Jian Yong!" Mister Sun protested. "If it isn't real and it's discovered that it isn't real, then-!"
"I... believe its content to be truthful, even if its creation was dubious, which is, I think, what Jian Yong was trying to say in his own strange way," Liu Bei declared. "I am prepared to act on it: whether it is genuine or not, Cao Cao will declare it to be a forgery if we are discovered, just as Yuan Shu would have made a genuine Imperial Seal of his cheap counterfeit if he had been victorious. Now, speaking of Yuan Shu..."
"...Yeah," Zhang Fei said. "We're being sent to go and destroy him by Cao Cao."
"Or, at least, to prevent him reaching safety in Ji or Qing, so that others can destroy him," Liu Bei replied. "I do not care who sends us to do that: destroying or ruining Yuan Shu is something personally gratifying, being a Liu and the progeny of a fallen prince. By this act, I surely pave the way for the redemption of my family line! We are meant to depart within three days."
"I'll have the men ready within *two*, my lord," Mi Zhu promised.

Cao Cao personally saw Liu Bei and Zhu Ling to the gates of Xuchang and wished them good fortune: little did he know that the 'Girdle Edict' – a document that Dong Cheng claimed to have been concealed within a belt that had been gifted to him by Emperor Xian himself – was now Liu Bei's guidance. That edict condemned Cao Cao as the worst of villains, and it called on every good man in the land to secretly prepare for a day of reckoning when the Excellency of Works – dubbed, in the document, as 'a would-be Chancellor of State' – would meet an end similar to his predecessor, Dong Zhuo.
"If Guo Fengxiao or Cheng Zhongde were here, they'd say as I say repeatedly, Excellency: this is *dangerous*!" Xun Gongda said as he

accompanied Cao Cao on his return visit to the Chancellery.

"But 'Guo Fengxiao' isn't here, is he?" Chen Qun heckled. "He's sick again, and-!"

"Quiet, please, both of you," Cao Cao ordered. "I am resolved that Liu Bei and Zhu Ling can be trusted to apprehend Yuan Shu: the former because Shu has been trying to overthrow the Han – of which he is a part by blood – and has been financing the Yellow Turbans in Yu Province; the latter will do so because – and if for no other reason, fine, for that will do – he will always strive to prove that Yuan Shao is no longer his master."

"And after that…?" Xun Gongda asked. "Forgive me, Excellency, but I must be Zhongde since Zhongde isn't here. When Yuan Shu is routed or forced to retreat, then we can expect *what* from Liu Bei…? Will he want to go into Yang Province and be the one to finish Shu off, thereby endearing himself to His Majesty yet further and guaranteeing that he will be elevated to some high rank – an *Excellence*, perhaps – or will he focus on personal ambition and set his roots back into Xiaopei's soil, with the aim of growing his support and forces again…?"

Cao Cao grunted irritably.

"Dong Cheng's expression was telling," Xun Wenruo suggested.

"He's scheming," Xun Gongda despaired. "Liu Bei spent more time in Dong Cheng's house than his own! The two are-!"

"Now *divided*, and the divided are easier to crush, *if needs be*," Cao Cao growled.

"Something was… *different*, Excellency," Xun Gongda said.

"A new atmosphere of unease," Xun Wenruo agreed.

"The enemies of the state are dwindling," Cao Cao retorted. "What you gentlemen are sensing is the unease that precedes *peace*."

"…Perhaps," Xun Wenruo murmured.

"Most likely, if not certainly," Cao Cao insisted. "Li Jue, Guo Si, Lü Bu, Gongsun Zan, Yufuluo, the White Wave Bandits and the Yellow Turbans are vanquished; Yuan Shu, the Black Mountain Bandits and the Mount Tai Bandits are close to destruction; Liu Zhang, Liu Xun, Liu Biao, Sun Ce and Yuan Shao will be made to accept that they are vassals of a strong Imperial court if they have not already realised it; Luoyang's reconstruction is continuing well, and the Qiang rebels in the northwest are destroying themselves for us; the isolated Zhang Lu of 'Han'ning' and the rebels Zhang Xiu and Jia Xu will capitulate or die. What we are seeing, gentlemen, is a long-overdue return to *order*."

"…What if the Mount Tai Bandits decide to help Yuan Shu?" Xun Wenruo asked.

"If this situation 'causes the head of the turtle to come out of the shell', then that can only benefit us, just as Zhang Yan's support of Gongsun Zan weakened the Black Mountain Bandits," Cao Cao retorted. "Zang Ba won't help, though… I strongly suspect that aiding a man that dared to be another Wang Mang is a step too far for that complicated man."

"I agree," Xun Gongda admitted.

"But we could get out of the mess we're in!" the bandit Chang Xi screamed over a chorus of voices; the Mount Tai Bandits had heard rumours that Yuan Shu was moving toward the Xu-Yang border, and they were divided over how they should react to the possibility of the self-styled 'First Emperor of Zhong' being so close and in definite need of friends.

"**How'd you see that, you idiot???**" Yin Li heckled. "**Everyone's out for his blood! Even Liu Biao and Sun Ce have put their personal problems aside to fight Yuan Shu!**"

"**Yuan Tan's moving south!**" Chang Xi protested. "**He's going to save his uncle Shu! If we helped, we-!**"

"**We stay out of it!**" Zang Ba ordered. "**We daren't be seen to help Yuan Shu!**"

Many voices were silenced by Zang Ba's authoritative tone.

"**…But he's our only chance of getting Cao Cao off our backs!**" Chang Xi suggested.

"**We're not fighting Cao Cao, we're fighting the *Han Dynasty*,**" Zang Ba retorted.

"**That's right: the same as Yuan Shu!**" Chang Xi countered.

"**No, fool, it isn't 'the same as Yuan Shu'!**" Zang Ba replied. "**We're bandits that were wronged by the Han in days gone by, looking for the right thing to be done; Shu's a spoiled brat that the Han treated extremely well that doesn't know the meanings of gratitude or being satisfied with a very nice lot! We didn't join the Yellow Turbans: we *fought them*, remember…? Shu's been *financing them*, even though they'd have turned on him as soon as he was on the imperial throne!**"

"**Zang's right,**" Sun Guan said. "**We'll carry on as we are; our fight is our fight, his fight is his. We're not on the same side, no matter how it looks.**"

Chang Xi sneered and left the meeting with his followers; the other bandit factions murmured amongst themselves and wondered whether their leaders were right.

"…Maybe the Han'll go easy on us while they have Yuan Shu to worry about," Sun Guan said optimistically.

"You'd like to think so," Zang Ba sighed.

And so one last chapter in the sorry affair of Yuan Shu's ambitions began: Yuan Tan led a force southward and into Xu Province at great speed, intent on rescuing the uncle that had, until only a short time before, been his father's worst nemesis; Liu Bei and Zhu Ling – whose agendas could not be more different – sped their own forces toward Xu Province in the hope of getting to Yuan Shu before Yuan Tan did; the Mount Tai Bandits looked on from their hiding places in the east of Xu Province, fearful of what the increase in Han forces would mean for them once Yuan Shu was vanquished; Yuan Shu himself hoped that he would survive a journey that would rob him of the last of his resources and his dignity. Yuan Shu's dreams of establishing his own imperial dynasty were over, but he did not know what his final fate would be; he dreaded the only possibilities that remained.

* * * * * * * * * * * *

99

The state-appointed Governor of Xu Province, Che Zhou, summoned his courtiers to the grand meeting hall in his Xiapi City mansion and told them, "I am unhappy with the news that Liu Bei has been asked to come back here."

"He is not going to be back here in any administrative capacity," General of the Household Xu Dan suggested. "Why worry?"

"…This hall has been the sight of much drama in recent years, and I should like to govern in a more peaceful time," Che Zhou retorted. "Tao Qian, Liu Bei and Lü Bu are my predecessors, and every one of them brought their own problems to this place."

"**Your master Cao Cao massacred people here!**" one young official heckled.

"…You are not being either pragmatic or impartial," Che Zhou replied. "Excellency Cao did not harm this place when he was here recently, did he…? No, he saved it from Lü Bu, who was invited here by Liu Bei after reducing neighbouring Yan Province to famine and hardship! Invited, yes, by Liu Bei, who – I am told, and by many of you – usurped the governorship from Tao Qian, whose own rule is tainted by Ze Rong's actions in this very region of Xiapi at the very least!"

Many of the local officials grumbled in response; without Chen Gui and Chen Deng to sway opinion, there was a growing feeling that Liu Bei had, perhaps, not been as bad as the Chens had depicted, and that betraying him to the spiteful and treacherous Lü Bu – even though Bei was the one to curse the province with Bu's presence in the first place – had been a mistake. Che Zhou was, to the eyes of many in Xu Province, Cao Cao's man, and the idea of being governed by a follower of a man that had attacked the province twice, killed a hundred-thousand of its inhabitants and forced the governor to relocate the capital before distressing him to an early grave was, at best, an uncomfortable one.

"I want regular reports on Bei's whereabouts," Che Zhou continued. "Additionally, I intend to write to His Excellency and request a greater force to deal with the Mount Tai Bandits once and for all. He withdrew Xu Huang, Zhang Liao, Zhu Ling and Han Hao from this area to concentrate on an attack on Shouchun that is now not happening: Zhu Ling should not be the only general coming back here. There isn't anyone else to send them after once Yuan Shu is gone, is there…?"

The officials continued their audible grumbling.

"…There isn't!" Che Zhou insisted. "Anyway, we should be ready for possible increases in activity by the Mount Tai Bandits… again, I want regular reports."

The court moved on to other matters, but most were still wondering what Liu Bei's return could or should mean and what Zang Ba might do.

An exhausted Cheng Yu entered the chancellery, went to his master's private meeting room – where Cao Cao and Xun Wenruo were discussing civil affairs – and said, "Am I too late…?"

"Mister Cheng!" Xun Wenruo exclaimed. "Has Dong Prefecture been-?"

"This... is not about Dong Prefecture," Cheng Yu said. "Lord Cao, am I too late to stop you from... from sending Bei to Xu...?"
Xun Wenruo exhaled loudly; Cao Cao was unreadable.
"...Then I am too late," Cheng Yu wheezed. "He's now our worst enemy, our greatest-"
"Don't be ridiculous!" Cao Cao scoffed. "His army is one that I gave him! He has perhaps a hundred men of his own!"
"You think that's an impediment to that crafty owl...?" Cheng Yu replied. "You know what an actor he is, Lord Cao, and what charismatic generals he has in Guan and Zhang: he'll fawn on them, cry, let the unmarried men mix with and marry the local women... he'll make Xiaopei men of them. Why didn't Guo Jia tell you all this???"
"...He's sick," Cao Cao replied numbly.
"*Ayah*... what a time for him to make himself ill," Cheng Yu grumbled. "Now Bei's off the leash, and there's nothing we can do about it."
"We can try and call them back!" Xun Wenruo suggested.
"...I'll have a man go after them," Cao Cao murmured.
"Do that, and do it *now*!" Cheng Yu snapped. "Undo this gross folly before it is too late!"
Cao Cao hurriedly prepared an order for Liu Bei to turn about and return to the capital, but it was too late: Liu Bei and Zhu Ling were already in Xu Province, and Liu Bei had no intention of turning back.

Yuan Tan passed the feeble Xu-Qing border defences and entered northern Xu Province with his cavalry force.
"We're allowing our army to thin dangrously, my lord," the adviser Xin Ping said.
"The infantry will catch up when we slow at Xiaopei," Yuan Tan retorted. "What are you really worried about?"
"Cao Cao must have learned of our advance," Xin Ping explained. "This will not be forgiven by the Han court if we are not clear on what-"
"We're intercepting Uncle: let Cao wonder why!" Yuan Tan insisted. "We already agreed on what to say to the Xuchang court whether we succeed or fail."
"But what if the Han government is able to send a force to intercept us as we intercept your uncle...?" Xin Ping asked.
"...That's unlikely," Yuan Tan replied. "They have further to travel, and can they know all of the shortcut roads and quickly pass every little obstacle between Xuchang and Xiaopei...? This province was controlled by Father before Lü Bu stole it and Cao Cao came here in the name of the Han: that's why we could pass the provincial border so easily, isn't it...?"
"...It depends on who is sent," Xin Ping suggested.

"I see now why you were chosen for this mission, General Liu," Zhu Ling admitted as the Han interception force reached western Xiaopei within a startling time. "Your hero Guan Yu has the respect of many of the former rebels and bandits, which I am not surprised about at all, and you and your followers must surely know every last dirt path and shortcut in the region!"
"We made this place our home, and got to know it as well as one

514

knows the back of one's own hand, General Zhu," Liu Bei replied. "I doubt that Yuan Tan will find the journey from Qing so easy, since he is not as popular as we are."

Zhu Ling hummed thoughtfully and said, "I doubt that he will endear himself either, General Liu; I remember him to be a stubborn, brash, violent man with little grace or intellect. His soldiers adore him for his generosity to them, but nobody else will. He can only have made such gains in Qing Province by having sound counsel in addition to military charisma."

"…I yearn for such counsel myself, General," Liu Bei admitted. "Perhaps I would be less prone to being beaten by the likes of Lü Bu and Ji Ling."

"One of my scouts approaches," Zhu Ling noted.

"Locals report a number of men attempting a river crossing close to the southern border with Yang Province, General Zhu," the scout reported.

"Yuan Shu, most likely," Liu Bei said.

"Agreed," Zhu Ling replied. "Let's advance quickly!"

Yuan Shu's small force crossed the river that separated the last of Yuan's loyal domains from Xu Province and stopped briefly.

"I urge haste," the adviser Yan Xiang said.

"We must rest!" Yuan Shu pleaded. "Food is scarce, and-!"

"If we dally, Che Zhou could send men after us or the Mount Tai Bandits could decide to attack us," Yan Xiang said. "We-"

"Why would Zang Ba attack me?" Yuan Shu chortled.

"Why did Chen Lan and Lei Bo not help us…?" Yan Xiang retorted.

"…Because I am a traitor to all men, even other traitors!" Yuan Shu chuckled miserably. "Why do you all stay at my side, then…?"

"The Han is doomed, and it seemed, for a while, that Heaven had, indeed, chosen you to replace them," Yan Xiang replied. "Perhaps our current situation is a setback designed to test you and show your courage and endurance."

"I, for one, do not abandon my lord," General Zhang Xun said.

"…Even after I demoted you for incompetence that you had not shown, General Zhang…?" Yuan Shu replied. "I do have very honourable vassals, don't I…?"

"And I, Father, will never abandon you," Yuan Yao declared.

Zhang Xun looked at the soldiers – who, like their leaders, were partially disguised as fishermen – and said, "Perhaps we should shed our armour. It might protect us if we're attacked, but we're less likely to be attacked if we don't look quite so much like soldiers pretending to be fishermen."

Yuan Shu laughed and said, "We shall keep our armour on and our weapons at the ready, General. Even the fish are likely to attack me for my treachery, and I expect the same of every tree and animal, never mind the locals!"

Yan Xiang turned his gaze westward as he said, "I agree, sad to- …**No! No, no, that's *impossible*!**"

Zhang Xun turned to the west, saw what Yan Xiang had seen, and drew his sword; others quickly followed, including the desperate Yuan Shu, who cried, "**For our lives, fight with every bit of strength you have!**"

"**You and your son must retreat at once, my lord!**" Zhang Xun insisted. "**The men will cover your escape!**"

Liu Bei and Zhu Ling led their men personally; the remnants of Yuan Shu's elite guard were still quite formidable despite malnutrition and exhaustion, so the battle would not be easily won. Yuan Shu protested inanely as Yuan Yao, Yan Xiang and Zhang Xun hurried him back to the abandoned fishing boats, but he was secretly eager to avoid the fate of his loyal men.

"The traitor escapes!" Zhu Ling cried. **"After him!"**

But Yuan Shu was already moving along the river when Liu Bei and Zhu Ling finally passed the gauntlet of brave defenders; the fallen noble sobbed and whimpered, "Now I am never to reach Qing… what now…?"

"We… we might be able to cross elsewhere," Yan Xiang said with false optimism. "Don't lose hope, my lord… d-do not… lose *hope*."

There would be no rendezvous with Yuan Tan for Yuan Shu's shrinking retinue. They tried to cross again and again, but they were met by Liu Bei and Zhu Ling's men at every point; when the leaders ran out of expendable men to serve as sacrificial blockades for future escape attempts, they gave up and began a desperate, pointless journey back to the ruins of Shouchun City.

"Victory can be ours!" Zhu Ling said to Liu Bei as they conferred in a temporary command tent in southern Xiaopei. "We should pursue him now!"

"Our orders were to intercept him, and we don't know how many followers he may be able to gather if we chase him into Yang Province," Liu Bei replied casually. "He might rally people by saying we've entered the province to ransack it. Additionally, Yuan Tan is on his way here: we can't leave our backs exposed to him if he's as dangerous as you so often say!"

"That's quite right," Liu Bei's adviser Mi Zhu said.

"Yuan Shao is Commander-in-Chief of the Han forces, and Tan is his son and heir: that all has meaning," Zhu Ling retorted. "When Tan learns Shu's fate, he'll turn around and go back to Pingyuan, and Shao will have some excuse for his son's actions."

"I *hope so*," Liu Bei sighed.

Yuan Tan grunted angrily when he learned that Yuan Shu's path had been blocked by Han forces.

"We have to go back now," Xin Ping insisted.

"I… I know that," Yuan Tan said reluctantly. "But that means that Uncle is dead, or as good as. I know that there are some that feel such a fate to be deserved, but he is kin! I failed to rescue kin, and my father's brother, no less! Father will be very displeased."

"We… we have to remember that rescuing him would have been far from simple," Xin Ping replied. "The plan involved sheltering him with all manner of stories about his true fate – perhaps pretending he had escaped, or that he had died or been executed – and if the chosen subterfuge had ever been discovered, then the Yuan clan as a whole would have been hunted to extinction, and their vassals with them. This is probably for the best, sad to say."

"…But I will never forgive Liu Bei or Zhu Ling for this… Zhu Ling especially, for he offends the clan he once worked for by doing this!" Yuan Tan said.

"Forgive my rudeness, but we have dallied enough," Xin Ping replied. "Turn the army at once, before we're targeted by those

men that you now decry."
"I am not afraid of them!" Yuan Tan scoffed.
"They're sanctioned by His Majesty to destroy your uncle and any who help him," Xin Ping noted.
"...I know, I know!" Yuan Tan cried. "I... I shall turn the army... I shall turn it at once!"

It did not take long for word of Yuan Tan's retreat to reach Liu Bei and Zhu Ling: within a week of that, rumours circulated around the Xu-Yang border region that Yuan Shu had died as he travelled back to what was left of his false imperial capital.
"I hope it's true," Liu Bei said to Zhu Ling as the two conferred in the latter's command tent. "It means that no great threats to the Han remain and peace is close to being found at last."
"...I am glad that you speak as you do," Zhu Ling admitted. "There are unfortunate rumours that some in the court consider Excellency Cao to be the 'last great threat to the Han'."
"It is under his guidance that we have pacified the land," Liu Bei replied. "...As a point, General Zhu... what do you think will happen next if it is confirmed that Yuan Shu is no more?"
"There's no reason to stay in Xu Province if he's dead... or, at least, not here by the Yang border," Zhu Ling said. "I'd imagine that we'll be sent into Yang to aid the pacification of the province, recalled to Xuchang or sent east to hasten the destruction of the Mount Tai Bandits."
"All will become clear soon, I imagine," Liu Bei replied.

And the situation did, in a very short time, become clear: Yuan Shu's attempted return to Shouchun ended with his death from exhaustion and malnutrition. From the moment that he had first opposed his half-brother Shao's right to be the Yuan clan chieftain 8 years before, Yuan Shu had become one of the most influential figures in China; his ambitions had pit the former members of the Eastern Pass Coalition against each other and brought seemingly endless war and chaos to Bing, Ji, Yòu, Qing, Yu, Yan, Xu, Yang and Jing Provinces, and in addition to that, many blamed him solely and specifically for the prolonged time that Dong Zhuo and, subsequently, the 'co-regents' had been able to hold Emperor Xian in Chang'an without proper opposition. Shu's declaration that he was the 'First Emperor of Zhong' only added to people's suspicions that Yuan Shu had always intended to destroy his 'rival' Emperor Xian and used Dong Zhuo to achieve it, but none of that mattered now. Yuan Shu was gone at last, and with him the most outrageous challenge to Imperial rule since the infamous Wang Mang; it was hoped that it would be the last such challenge, and that the House of Han was safe at last.

∗∗∗∗∗∗∗∗∗∗∗∗

100

Word of Yuan Shu's demise was reported and confirmed to Liu Bei, Zhu Ling and Che Zhou within a week; the news was quickly passed to Xuchang, whereupon Cao Cao called for a meeting of the Imperial court to discuss what to do next.

"I will recall Generals Liu Bei and Zhu Ling to the capital at once, so that they can be rewarded for their efforts and appropriately reassigned," Cao Cao explained. "I will additionally ensure that Commander-in-Chief Yuan Shao – the brother of the heretic seditionist – reaffirms his loyalty to the Han and publicly shares our relief that this sorry matter is brought to an end."

"We look forward to both of those things, Mister Cao," Emperor Xian said. "What of the Mount Tai Bandits that still occupy southern Qing and eastern Xu?"

"Their hold is diminishing, but we must be prepared to parley with some of their number if it means ending their threat quickly, Majesty," Cao Cao replied. "I am not the only one that found their refusal to support Yuan Shu's attempted retreat to be a sign of their ability to be 'assimilated', as it were, back into society rather than destroyed. They did – as I am reminded by my advisers – purge the Yellow Turbans from the parts of Qing Province that they controlled, rather than being derived from them as the White Wave and Black Mountain Bandits are."

The frail elder statesman Zheng Xuan motioned that he would like to speak and asked, "Has there been any explanation of Yuan Tan's actions, my question being aimed at whichever of Excellency Cao and General Dong is best suited to answer...?"

Dong Cheng glared at Cao Cao, who smiled and said, "I am not aware of any correspondence from Yuan Tan or his father, but as I have said, I intend to prompt the latter in his capacity as the nation's most important military figure."

Yuan Shao was concluding his return journey to his capital Yè in Ji Province when word of Yuan Shu's death reached him; Cao Cao's official correspondence followed soon afterward, and the enraged and emotional Shao summoned all of his advisers in order to discuss both as soon as he was back in his residence.

"They *killed him*," Yuan Shao said bitterly. "**They chased him like a wild animal and drove him to his death! He was *mine* to deal with, gentlemen! He was my brother, and it was my final decision to make as head of our clan!**"

Yuan Shao and Cao Cao's old friend, Xu Yòu, coughed deliberately and asked, "What will you tell the court, lord and friend...?"

"Your tone lacks emotion, which disgusts me!" Yuan Shao retorted. "Don't you *know* my brother, Xu Yòu? Don't you know his son and daughter, of whom there is no word...?"

"I did, and I never knew him more than when he publicly humiliated you and caused a protracted war that engulfed the entire east of the land," Xu Yòu replied. "His children are, unfortunately, victims of his folly, but folly it was, and there is no man here who would or could defend Yuan Shu right now, for to do so is to support a heretic that dared claim to be the Son of Heaven. And, furthermore, his most recent crimes were against the empire, against His Majesty, against all of the people and against the entire world under Heaven, and so his fate was the Imperial court's to decide. You know that, lord and friend, and you should also pay heed to that."

Yuan Shao scanned the room: every man lowered his gaze or showed accord with Xu Yòu.

"Your brother broke his covenants with your clan and with Heaven," Cui Yan said. "Do not ruin your own cause to avenge him after everything that he did to ruin you and the state."

"...Mister Xu and Mister Cui are right," Ju Shou said.

Yuan Shao eyed Xu Yòu bitterly and replied, "I do 'know that', gentlemen. And... and I will 'heed that' as suggested. To answer your question, Mister Xu, I... ... ...**Mister Chen Lin, relay my response to the court if you will!**"

Yuan Shao's secretary, Chen Lin, coughed nervously and said, "General Yuan Tan was moving south to intercept the traitor with the intention of returning him to Yè for trial as a heretic or, if needs be, sending him to Xuchang, after learning that he was fleeing to Xu to seek an alliance with other enemies of the state. When General Yuan Tan learned that Generals Liu Bei and Zhu Ling had already intercepted the traitor, Yuan Tan returned to Qing Province, since there was no longer a need to be in Xu. His failure to notify the court of his actions was due to a need to act on the intelligence quickly and reduce the risk of the traitor learning of his impending capture. It is good fortune that the court had its own intelligence – though, perhaps, clouded in its nature – and was able to act upon it so swiftly, thereby ridding the world under Heaven of a vile menace. Your Majesty can be assured that I, Shao, am your loyal servant, and that I always will be."

Yuan Shao glared at his officials and asked, "Will that do...?"

"It will, my lord," Tian Feng replied. "I will have people go to Yang and try to find your other relatives and bring them here, but current information suggests that your brother's son, Yuan Yao, has taken the coffin, what remains of the army, your brother's wealth and the family and gone to Lujiang, seat of Liu Xun."

"...A man that once was a friend to me, but also to *Cao Cao* before he chose to serve my brother," Yuan Shao said bitterly. "If he has them, then Liu Xun should be made to understand that I want my relatives and what is left of my brother's estate sent northward at the soonest opportunity."

"...And what of the plan to 'confront Cao Cao'...?" Xu Yòu asked. "Doesn't this latest incident make any attempt to challenge Cao more difficult to-?"

"Your concern for your old friend Cao Cao is touching, Xu Yòu!" Guo Tu heckled. "Or is it that you are worried that hostilities in this region might affect your 'private matters'...?"

Yuan Shao glared at Xu Yòu, who said, "*Ayah*! Don't listen to the slanderers, lord and friend! Time and again the likes of Guo and Chunyu slander me, just as they did to so many others!"

"You perhaps refer to Dong Zhao and Qu Yi...?" Chunyu Qiong retorted. "Where is 'Gongren' now, Xu Yòu...? Is he not serving Cao Cao, as he probably always was, striving every day to undermine our lord...?"

"And Qu Yi offended the lord, did he not, with his groundless arrogance!" Guo Tu said. "We didn't need to condemn him: the

fool condemned himself, as wrongdoers always do!"
Yuan Shao's judging gaze was fixed on Xu Yòu.
"...Present proof that I have done something, Guo Tu," Xu Yòu said. "Prove that I have in some way offended Lord Yuan or wronged the state, Chunyu Qiong, and I will willingly subject myself to a court of law."
"This serves no purpose!" Tian Feng cried.
"Indeed: it's a waste of valuable time!" Ju Shou said. "Lord Yuan, Xu Yòu asked a valid question: can we be seen to attack Cao Cao in any way now without being accused of sedition ourselves...?"
"There are... 'proofs', shall we say, of Cao's treachery and his threat to the land, and one particularly compelling one that I have recently been made aware of," Yuan Shao replied. "Regardless, though, I will make my case for the capital to be moved to Juancheng, to a region closer to Ji and farther from the pirate-ridden south than Xuchang, and I believe that my argument will be properly considered by the court... at which time I can march to Juancheng and wrest the Son of Heaven from Cao's grasp. If the idea is not accepted, then I will march on Xuchang and-"
"You shouldn't be attacking Cao Cao, at least not now," Tian Feng said. "You have too many problems to deal with: the army needs rest, the regions need stabilising, the-"
"When, then, 'Tian Yuanhao'...?" Guo Tu heckled.
"You were the one of the men that warned Lord Yuan of Cao years ago, Tian Feng: why do you now advocate leaving him to grow ever stronger?" Shen Pei asked.
"*Aiee*... **stop it!**" Ju Shou cried. "**You-!**"
"You and Tian Feng are cowards at best, Ju Shou!" Guo Tu said.
"If we are bickering over little things now, how can we fight Cao Cao?" Tian Feng asked. "His army is fed and well-organised, his advisers are united, he-"
"**Ayah! I am sick of you!**" Yuan Shao screamed. "**GUARDS! GUARDS! Arrest Tian Feng!**"
"**What???**" Tian Feng exclaimed as two soldiers took hold of his arms and started to drag him from the court. "**Lord Yuan! Lord Yuan, you can't-!**"
"**I am your master!**" Yuan Shao snapped. "**I can do with you as I please! Guards: take him to the prison!**"
"**On what charge, Lord Yuan??? On what charge???**" Tian Feng sobbed.
"...**Demoralising the army!**" Yuan Shao replied. "**Take him away, and quickly!**"
Tian Feng's protests were futile: Chunyu Qiong, Guo Tu, Shen Pei, Pang Ji and Xun Chen smirked as they watched Tian being led away, while others – such as Ju Shou and Xu Yòu – despaired at losing a colleague.
"I hope that Mister Tian uses his time in prison to *think*," Yuan Shao muttered. "Now, gentlemen, if we may continue...?"
Many of the officials that were present had their misgivings, but one – Xu Yòu – had more than many. He had remained at Yuan Shao's side for many years, but his allegiance wavered with every new decision that was being made.

Zhang Xiu – whose army still occupied Wan City and the surrounding areas of Nan County in northern Jing Province –

summoned his adviser Jia Xu and asked, "Is it true that Yuan Shao has sent a man to request an alliance against Cao Cao?"
"It is," Jia Xu replied solemnly.
"...Isn't this good...?" Zhang Xiu asked.
"Hardly," Jia Xu scoffed. "His brother's just been fighting the Han, and I'm hearing rumours that he tried to help him at the last!"
"*Help him...*?" Zhang Xiu exclaimed. "After all that-!"
"Exactly," Jia Xu said. "Yuan Tan had no other reason to be marching into Xu Province at speed while Yuan Shu journeyed northward into that same province. After everything that those brothers put the east of the country through, and after Shu outdid Dong Zhuo for temerity, Shao actually tried to help him. Such a man is not to be trusted or aided. I suggest that we turn his messenger back. Politely."
"...Alright," Zhang Xiu said miserably.
"We'll find a way to end our problems with the court," Jia Xu promised. "We just need to be open-minded and patient."

Zhu Ling received Cao Cao's order to withdraw to Xuchang and journeyed to Liu Bei's command tent to ensure that his ally intended to comply.
"How can I go back to Xuchang?" Liu Bei declared. "Is there peace just because Yuan Shu is dead?"
"His Excellency's orders are clear," Zhu Ling retorted.
"The Mount Tai Bandits are still here; the White Wave Bandits have fractured into smaller pockets of troublemakers that Governor Che Zhou is obviously unable to deal with; the local officials are mindful of my extensive knowledge of Xu Province – a fact that you also noted as we travelled here, General – and so ask that I stay to provide support," Liu Bei continued. "What use am I in Xuchang?"
"Didn't His Majesty desire your return?" Zhu Ling said as he glanced at each of Liu Bei's vassals in turn: Guan Yu was unreadable; Zhang Fei and Jian Yong were smirking; Mister Sun was noticeably uneasy; Mi Zhu and Mi Fang were solemn.
"I want nothing more than to bask in His Majesty's divine light, but can I do so when the task is so far from complete...?" Liu Bei said theatrically. "His Excellency Cao is wrong in this matter, if you'll forgive me for saying so: he should be leaving us both here to bring a swift end to the threat of the Bandits. I will exercise my judgement and do what I know to be right."
"Lord Cao has *ordered* us to return to Xuchang!" Zhu Ling cried.
"This province has suffered enough, General Zhu Ling," Liu Bei said. "I refuse to leave here until I am sure that its enemies are vanquished once and for all... you can do as you please."
Zhu Ling sighed angrily, bowed politely, and left the tent.
"We're staying, then," Jian Yong chuckled.
"I have a new mission now," Liu Bei replied.
"I guessed that when you sent Cao's man back before," Jian Yong teased. "I even know what your 'new mission' is, of course...!"
"We'll hold here, ostensibly to restore order," Liu Bei said. "And then, when the moment is right... we'll act."
Liu Bei, Guan Yu, Zhang Fei, Mi Zhu, Mi Fang and Mister Sun Qian nodded their heads purposefully and smiled as one.

Cao Cao harrumphed when Zhu Ling's advance report reached his personal court.

"I told you that we'd never get him out of there if we allowed him to go back; now he will not be removed without a fight," Guo Jia said disappointedly.

"His concerns about the province are valid," Cao Cao retorted. "We shall let him 'make his move' and react to it accordingly. He may, after all, be sincere."

"You know that he isn't," Cheng Yu scoffed. "He intends rebellion."

"**Enough!**" Cao Cao cried. "**Let us see what he does! If Liu Bei wants to remain in Xiaopei to fight Zang Ba, then we shall see what he does when Zang Ba is defeated! Until then, gentlemen, we have other worries! One of them is Dong Prefecture's security, Cheng Yu!**"

"Don't worry, I'm going back after this meeting," Cheng Yu replied. "And yes, you're right: we have a lot of other worries..."

"...Indeed," Xun Wenruo said. "Yang Province is a mess: Liu Xun retains control of Lujiang, but word is that he's not only taken Yuan Shu's surviving followers into his custody, he's trying to declare Lujiang as an independent state, and Sun Ce's forces – who, we now learn, had already started hostile military action against Huang Zu – are advancing to challenge Liu Xun without waiting for government authorisation."

"*What???*" Cao Cao exclaimed. "Why wasn't I told about this???"

"It isn't confirmed," Guo Jia replied.

"That's on top of 'General' Sun Ce's... how shall we say... 'ambiguous' status in Jiangdong," Cheng Yu scoffed. "Wang Lang's right, by the looks of things: he's after seizing the entire province now that his former master is dead."

"Liu Biao's not much better," Xun Wenruo sighed.

"I *must* have the peace I promised, gentlemen!" Cao Cao said. "This...! ...How *dare* the likes of Liu Xun, Liu Biao, Zang Ba, Liu Bei and Sun Ce: how *dare* they continue to threaten more chaos!"

"We must crush Zang Ba first, since that also gives us a way to remove the threat that Liu Bei poses," Guo Jia suggested. "After him, we try and put a good man in Lujiang to restore social order, control the 'Qian Hill Bandits' that have spilled into the area, and-"

Cao Cao groaned and muttered, "Not *another* army of bandits."

"Led by a motley bunch that includes two of Yuan Shu's former generals, Chen Lan and Lei Bo," Cheng Yu grumbled. "We may have to coordinate with Sun Ce... or fight him."

"...I had hoped that Yuan Shu's death meant more," Cao Cao admitted. "What a fool I was."

The destruction of the self-proclaimed 'First Emperor of Zhong', Yuan Shu, had left a power vacuum in northern Yang Province that Administrator Liu Xun of Lujiang and General Sun Ce of the Jiangdong region were as keen to fill as Cao Cao was; far from being an end to the chaos, Yuan Shu's death was the precursor to a battle for the whole of the Han Dynasty and a war that would precede its final decline.

✱✱✱✱✱✱✱✱✱✱✱✱

ACT IX: THE BATTLE OF GUANDU

101

Han Dynasty China was, at last, showing signs of returning to a form of stability. The Yellow Turbans that had technically started the chaos were reduced from a million-strong, nationwide threat to a few thousand Yu Province-based mercenaries led by long-time acolyte Liu Pi, and the derived 'White Wave Bandits' had been purged altogether; the enduring corrupt elements in the Han court – such as the eunuch faction known as the 'Ten Attendants' and certain influential families – had been eliminated or seen their power reduced; and, most importantly of all, several 'rogue warlords' – the most notorious of them being Yuan Shu in Yang Province, Gongsun Zan in Yòu Province and Lü Bu in Xu Province – had been defeated and killed by government forces. The first of those three had started a civil war during a national crisis and then declared as an alternative emperor, while the last had facilitated the rise of the tyrant Dong Zhuo, whose ambitions had left the capital Luoyang in ruins, led to the death of Emperor Shao and started the national crisis that Yuan Shu had then gone on to exploit; Gongsun Zan's crime of murdering and usurping a state-appointed governor was relatively minor, but he, like Yuan and Lü, would not be missed at all.

There were still several bandit armies and rebels, however: Zang Ba's 'Mount Tai Bandits' were still defying a government manhunt from their strongholds in Qing and Xu Provinces; the Qiang tribal warlords still had autonomy in Liang Province in the northwest; the cultist Zhang Lu still governed Hanzhong Province as Han'ning; the decimated Black Mountain Bandits still controlled parts of northern Bing Province; the Qian Hill Bandits were emerging as a potent but localised force in northern parts of Yang Province; various pirates and tribes still rampaged in southern parts of Yang Province; Yuan Shao's recent deals with the Wuhuan tribes of Yòu Province had given them autonomy that some were already abusing; Dong Zhuo's former subordinates Zhang Xiu and Jia Xu still controlled a county in Jing Province; and in Yu Province, the former cultist Liu Pi and the bandit Gong Du still caused trouble from time to time. They were, compared to past rebellions, minor worries; the Xuchang City government led by Cao Cao had dealt with many of the worst offenders after giving refuge and security to the young Emperor Xian. Cao Cao was Excellency of Works and Acting Excellency over the Masses; the last of the 'Ducal Minister' roles – Commander-in-Chief – was still held by friend-turned-rival Yuan Shao, who was now the uncontested chieftain of the influential Yuan clan of Ru County and brother to the treasonous Yuan Shu. Cao Cao and Yuan Shao were becoming increasingly estranged as their power grew, and Shao – having defeated the rebel warlord Gongsun Zan – now coveted the role of guardian of the emperor despite having rejected the opportunity three years earlier; that quest would now turn him from a rival to an enemy.

Cao Cao's advisers gathered on a daily basis to discuss the tasks that were yet to be still started or completed; Cao himself was plagued by his usual headaches and was therefore unpredictable from meeting to meeting.

"…Which brings us to *Sun Ce*," Xun Wenruo sighed at the end of a discussion about political affairs in southern Yang Province.

"The boy's a nuisance, unlike his father," Cao Cao growled. "Fengxiao, Wenruo and Gongda have all advocated marriage alliances; is that how we should proceed…?"

"Wait and see how the Lujiang debacle resolves itself," Guo Jia suggested. "Sun Ce's movements have been strange; at one point it seemed that he was intending to ally with Liu Xun against the government, but now it's unclear. His advisers, whoever they are, are quite good, I'd say."

"…I don't expect the boy to hand Lujiang Prefecture over to us if he seizes it," Chen Qun said.

"He might not seize it," Xun Gongda replied. "Liu Biao is sending a force to Lujiang to reinforce Liu Xun; Ce's father did not survive his confrontation with Biao, and Ce is not the hero his father was."

"We cannot be sure that he is 'inferior', especially if he has better counsel that dissuades him from reckless actions," Cao Cao said. "We'll wait and see, as Fengxiao recommends."

"What it all means is that Sun Ce is being kept busy, which is a good thing," Guo Jia chuckled. "Now: what about Yi Province?"

"Liu Zhang has sent more tributes, so we have nothing to fear from him," Chen Qun scoffed.

"Isn't his spineless toadying an improvement over his ambitious father…?" Xun Wenruo asked.

"Not enough of an improvement, Mister Xun: not when he has Zhang Lu sitting right next to him in Hanzhong and does nothing about him," Chen Qun retorted. "We must hope that Liang Province will be safe from harm from within and without."

"…I want to return to discussing Yuan Shao's 'suggestion'," Cao Cao said suddenly. "We can't afford to have the capital in Juancheng! It's an easy target for his army in comparison to Xuchang, which is why-!"

"We've done all that can be done," Xun Wenruo protested.

"But it will be put to the court!" Cao Cao cried. "I have too many enemies in that court, men that-!"

"Zheng Xuan is ill, and at over seventy years old we're unlikely to see him again," Guo Jia interrupted. "Kong Rong is dithering, mainly because he cannot reconcile confronting you – his saviour – and supporting Yuan Shao, the man whose son he was saved from; Dong Cheng and his little band are doing a lot of posturing, but nothing we're not used to by now; others, like Wang Lang, Zhong Yao, Yang Biao, Liu Fu and so on are either won over to you or neutral, Lord Cao."

"So I would not be humiliated…?" Cao Cao prompted.

"Who'd advocate the Son of Heaven moving to Juancheng and hence closer to a man whose brother was so recently destroyed for high treason and heresy, a man whose son abducted state governors and tried to save traitors…?" Chen Qun asked.

"…Fine," Cao Cao said. "I'll let it be discussed."

An altogether different battle – the military struggle between the Han Imperial armed forces and Zang Ba's Mount Tai Bandits – still raged in the east of Xu Province, although there were signs that it was nearing a conclusion. Each day or night would see a raid on one camp or the other, a land battle or a thwarted attempt at severing supply lines. All the while, Zang Ba was planning for the moment when timings were correctly predicted and he could deal a serious blow to the morale of the Han army. It seemed that his moment had come on one moonlit night: scouts reported that the Han camps were close to empty, which had typically signalled another series of raids on the camps of the Mount Tai Bandits.

"We've got them," Zang Ba said. "Let them attack our camps again! We'll be attacking their camps and their supply lines at the same time, and that'll be the end of them!"

"We can't be sure that we're getting the right information," Yin Li warned. "Has Cao really moved his best generals elsewhere…?"

"It's either this plan or wait for their attack and hope it doesn't break us, Yin," Zang Ba retorted. "What do you want to do…?"

"…We'll try it," Yin Li replied.

"Right then, let's get to it!" Zang Ba said.

Zang Ba, Sun Guan and Yin Li took their men to attack the Han camps; Chang Xi led his own force to attack the Han supply line, while Wu Dun coordinated the reduced defences in the camps in order to fool the Han forces for as long as possible. Wu Dun was delighted when Han cavalry attacked the camps yet again; he awaited the inevitable attack on the main camp and smiled as he thought about the effect that his colleagues' countermeasures would have on enemy morale.

"We'll make them suffer…!" Wu Dun muttered.

"**THEY'RE HERE!**" a bandit shouted.

"**Stay calm!**" Wu Dun said. "**They have to think that-!**"

"**Did you think we'd be fooled…?**" Qin Yi bellowed as he rode to the outer boundary of the bandits' main camp. "**Our leader, General Zhang Liao, made his living fighting your kind! How long will it be before we have Zang Ba, who was kind enough to deliver himself to our camp…?**"

"**AIEE! We're finished!**" Wu Dun cried.

When Zang Ba's force reached the Han camp, they were not even given the chance to realise the situation and retreat; Han soldiers surrounded them, and Zhang Liao rode to the front to issue a stark warning.

"**YOU CANNOT FLEE,**" the Han general declared. "**YOU HAVE TWO CHOICES: FIGHT – AND THEN *DIE* – OR SURRENDER.**"

"**THIS CAN'T BE IT!**" Sun Guan cried. "**THIS IS-!**"

"**This is it,**" Zang Ba retorted. "**WEAPONS DOWN, LADS!**"

Some bandits refused to follow Zang Ba's command, but Zhang Liao's soldiers were not in a forgiving mood; every man that resisted was quickly felled by a blade.

"**I SAID 'WEAPONS DOWN'!**" Zang Ba screeched. "**DON'T WASTE YOUR LIVES!**"

"**…They'll kill you, Xuangao!**" Sun Guan said.

"**Prob'ly,**" Zang Ba replied. "**But I've had a good run.**"

Zang Ba slapped Sun Guan's arm, smiled, and turned to approach the nearest group of Han soldiers so that he could surrender; the soldiers shoved and heckled him before they forced him to his knees and tied his hands behind his back with coarse rope.

"Go easy!" Zang Ba chuckled nervously.

"**We should cut your throat!**" one Han captain said.
"**DO NOT KILL HIM!**" Zhang Liao barked.
"They're making a fool of him!" Sun Guan complained.
"But we'll live," Yin Li retorted. "They'll likely spare him too."
Zhang Liao turned to the main group of surrounded and disarmed bandits and said, "**You'll all be escorted to a corral: your leader has an appointment with the Excellency of Works.**"
"**And a sword!**" Sun Guan heckled.
"**...That is for Excellency Cao to decide,**" Zhang Liao replied.
Zang Ba heard the words and murmured, "I'm dead, then."

Cao Cao smiled when a messenger told him of Zang Ba's defeat.
"At *last*...!" Cao Cao whispered.
Chen Qun said, "You may go, messenger," as he read the written report from Zhang Liao; the messenger smiled reflexively, bowed to Cao Cao, and retreated.
"This is splendid!" Cao Cao chuckled. "Inform Governor Che Zhou that I shall be in Xiapi personally for this man's surrender."
"...And we must recall Liu Bei at once," Guo Jia suggested. "Now that Zang Ba is apprehended, he has no plausible excuse for remaining in Xiaopei."
"Quite right, Fengxiao," Xun Gongda said. "We should have him come back to Xuchang at once."
"And this time, Bei should *not be allowed to leave here again*," Guo Jia continued.
"...But did we not just discuss how he strengthens Dong Cheng...?" Cao Cao asked desperately.
"He's more dangerous in Xiaopei," Chen Qun said.
"Might I see the letter, Mister Chen...?" Guo Jia asked.
Chen Qun harrumphed and handed the letter to Guo Jia.
"...Zang Ba, leader of the Mount Tai Bandits, broken at last...! This is ideal!" Cao Cao said. "What should our final terms be?"
"Spare Zang Ba, since he surrendered, and allow him to return to his allies in order to have him placate them and win them to our cause," Guo Jia replied as he read the letter.
Chen Qun scowled and said, "Should a man that's guilty of such weakness of will and selfishness be allowed to live another day...?"
"...Toward who was that slight aimed, Mister Chen: Zang or me...?" Guo Jia chuckled.
"You celebrated the victory at Xiapi with a trip to a brothel, Mister Guo, and became so intoxicated from the range of vile substances that you ingested that you could barely walk or speak," Chen Qun heckled. "Such behaviour is-!"
"We are none of us perfect, Changwen," Cao Cao interrupted. "I care nothing for criticisms of a man that has delivered me victory: I care about how we best deal with the bandit king Zang Ba."
"I agree with Guo Fengxiao," Xun Gongda said.
"...As do I," Chen Qun admitted. "Zang's past is infamously complex; had the state not been corrupt and thereafter failed to reward his loyalty during the Yellow Turban Rebellion, there would be no Mount Tai Bandits: that leader of men was pushed to villainy by circumstance, and he long desires a return to the light."
"...You've convinced me of the need to try and negotiate with Zang," Cao Cao replied thoughtfully. "But we must test this man's word; any thoughts...?"

Guo Jia smiled and said, "There are the two officers that 'defected' during the siege of Xiapi, Excellency. They fled and joined the Mount Tai Bandits, did they not...?"

"...But that poses him with a dilemma," Xun Gongda suggested. "Zang's of no use to us if we force him to betray allies, because he'll then lose the rest and be overthrown."

"We have very little choice," Guo Jia insisted. "If Zang has 'lost his way' in more recent times, he'll rise up again when it least suits us, as the Yellow Turban leaders did in Runan; we must be sure, and that means testing his loyalty to the Han."

"A man with integrity must be sent to do this, *after* we have formally accepted his surrender," Xun Gongda suggested.

"...Bei," Chen Qun said. "Send Liu Bei."

Guo Jia and Xun Wenruo exchanged unreadable glances.

"...I am disturbed by the silence, gentlemen," Cao Cao said at last.

"I needed a moment to think," Guo Jia replied. "Changwen is correct; I pondered sending Xu Huang, since he is a former White Wave associate, but this is better. Liu Bei has a reputation for disliking bandits, and he is the man that executed Yang Feng and Han Xian; Zang Ba will be aware of Bei's seriousness, and his reaction will, one way or another, benefit us."

Xun Gongda smirked and said, "Well put, Fengxiao...!"

"...Aha! I see your devious scheme, Fengxiao and Changwen," Cao Cao chuckled. "If Zang is genuine, we have his loyalty affirmed; if he is confused, Bei is the one to lose his head and we get Bei's former associates to use as guardians of Xu Province and a scourge of bandits near and far. Very good!"

"I'll be honest and admit that I hope that Bei is convincing on our behalf," Chen Qun said. "I may not respect him anymore, but Zang *must* be pacified."

"...Very good, very good!" Cao Cao cackled. "I shall put this to 'Xuande' myself, and in my own hand! Quick: a pen, and paper...!"

Cao Cao's messenger reached Xiaopei within a week; Mister Sun read Cao Cao's latest orders to Liu Bei's assembled court with obvious timidity.

"Really, Xuande, this is the worst yet," Jian Yong suggested. "He's sending us to the lair of the wolves, and-"

"We should be more worried by the fact that he comes here in person," Liu Bei said. "Does he intend to force us to return once he accepts Zang Ba's-?"

"Heaven provides us with a chance – perhaps the last easy one – to kill the villain, Lord Liu," Guan Yu suggested. "You refused last time, but I beseech you not to do so again: give me the order, and I will ride to his camp and-!"

"*No*, Yunchang!" Liu Bei chortled. "We're going to speak with Zang Ba, who has come down to Xiapi's county border with his subordinate chieftains to formally surrender. Governor Che and General Xu will be very close."

"...I'm with Yunchang," Zhang Fei said. "This is a chance to-!"

"I... I won't discuss this," Liu Bei insisted. "We must go to Xiapi."

"*Aiee*... sometimes, life feels like a big circular road," Jian Yong complained. "I swear that this conversation is one that we've had before. All that we seem to do is get sent to places and then get a letter telling us to-"

"**Not now, Xianhe!**" Liu Bei cried desperately.

"The journey will take many days," Mi Zhu said. "Who will stay here, in case Cao Cao intends to march an army here…?"

"…Mi Fang, and Zhang Fei," Liu Bei decided. "For once, it is Yunchang that I do not want to leave alone."

Guan Yu harrumphed quietly.

"…Cao Cao's going to Xu Province again," Dong Cheng said to a small gathering of allies that included the officials Zhong Ji and Wang Fu. "I asked you all to come here to my home, under the guise of a banquet, to discuss how we might-"

"We shouldn't do anything," Zhong Ji protested. "He is only going to accept Zang Ba's surrender; most of the army – *his* army – is still here in the capital, commanded by the likes of Cao Ren, Xiahou Dun and Zhu Ling."

Dong Cheng sighed desperately and said, "But we have the-!"

"We should not make our most important move until we are sure that every other piece on the board is placed favourably," Wang Fu interrupted. "Keeping knowledge of our 'possession' from Cao's allies while ascertaining who will be our own allies is proving difficult enough; let Cao go and come back. We need to know what he does with-or-to Liu Bei, don't we, before we act…?"

"…True," Dong Cheng grumbled. "We wait, then."

At around the same time, Emperor Xian dismissed all of his attendants so that he could speak privately with Empress Fu.

"These 'Mount Tai Bandits' are meant to be the last obstacle, my love," Emperor Xian began. "Now that they are defeated, perhaps the empire can start to breathe again!"

"…Perhaps," Empress Fu sighed.

"I know that we have spoken like this before and been disappointed, but there are no more difficult obstacles," Emperor Xian continued.

"…Rumours abound, Your Majesty… rumours of unrest in the court, of Dong Cheng opposing Cao Cao and planning things," Empress Fu replied.

Emperor Xian frowned and said, "Dong Cheng…? …Do you allow these 'rumours' to affect you because his daughter carries a prince in her belly…?"

"No, Majesty, I do not," Empress Fu insisted. "It is the consorts' role to bear princes, as it is mine; I worry that more scheming might undo us, intentionally or not."

Emperor Xian was visibly unnerved as he replied, "There isn't anything to worry about. There is no scheme that can harm us now: almost all of the worst of the villains and heretics are gone, and soon there will be peace."

Empress Fu smiled unconvincingly.

✴✴✴✴✴✴✴✴✴✴✴✴

102

Within a week of his defeat, the leader of the Mount Tai Bandits, Zang Ba, was met at the gates of Xiapi City by Xu Provincial Governor Che Zhou, Excellency Cao Cao and a large collection of senior officials and officers.

"So many big names for one scruffy little bandit," Zang Ba suggested as he glared at the smiling Cao Cao.

"You should count yourself lucky that you were spared, you uncouth ruffian!" Che Zhou heckled. "You-!"

"I can answer for myself, Governor Che," Cao Cao chuckled.

"I hear that I'm to be spared," Zang Ba noted.

"You are," Cao Cao replied. "I know all about you, Zang Ba, and I can only say that I am sorry that so many men – men deemed 'talented' by the state – failed to see that you belong with them, at the side of righteousness, and not as a willing agent of the underworld, as corrupt officials drove you to so many years ago."

Zang Ba frowned.

"I was stationed in Ji'nan for a while, which is not far from where you were," Cao Cao continued. "I saw what it was like in that region, Zang Ba; telling the good from the bad, or the law from the lawless, was as telling one grain of rice from another. The 'Ten', Heaven curse them, placed their vile allies everywhere, and no man could truly say that their choice would have been any different to yours."

"...S'at so...?" Zang Ba muttered.

"It is," Cao Cao continued. "Your choices were limited by your status; mine were far greater in number, because of my father's wealth and status."

"And was this man not a bandit in the area where your father was killed???" one Xu official cried. **"Do not spare him, Excellency, for *there* is the likely murderer, the man that the people of this province suffered so greatly for! Kill him! His kind are evil, Excellency, and incapable of redemption!"**

Others added their own protestations; Zang Ba was suddenly very nervous, as everyone in the land knew what had happened to those that had been accused – rightly or wrongly – of any part in Cao Song's death.

"I never had nothing to do with that, you troublemaking bastards!" Zang Ba screamed at the hecklers. **"Do I look stupid enough to-?"**

"BE SILENT! *NOW!*" Cao Cao barked.

The officials fell silent immediately.

"...I *swear*, Your Excellency, that I had nothing to do with what happened to your father," Zang Ba said.

"You... do not have to defend yourself," Cao Cao replied calmly. "The crime was carried out by others and has been punished enough, I think."

Many of the local officials quietly harrumphed at Cao Cao's words.

"Your surrender is accepted, Zang Ba," Cao Cao said. "Your allies were brought here in another convoy: go back to them and extend my wish that you return to the Han as loyal followers, as you were in past days, and put your banditry behind you."

Zang Ba fell to one knee and said, "For your kindness, Excellency,

I shall do as you ask: it is my desire to return to the light."

"…You do so as a 'figure of authority' within Qing and Xu provinces both," Cao Cao continued. "Your precise appointments are yet to be decided, but you will enjoy high rank in exchange for your service. Your knowledge of the region and its problems will prove invaluable to the restoration of the Han Empire's lustre."

Many of Xiapi's officials were exasperated and angered by Cao Cao's words, but they restricted their protestations to muttering and discreet sleeve-flicking.

"You… are too generous!" Zang Ba said as he kowtowed.

"Go, then, Mister Zang, and reassure and coerce your friends," Cao Cao ordered.

Zang Ba got to his feet, bowed humbly, and turned to flee; Zhang Liao, Qin Yi and Qu Ji ordered their confused forces to part and allow Zang Ba to pass them unmolested.

"…Get him a horse," Cao Cao said. "Where is Liu Bei…?"

"On his way here, though not entirely as asked," Guo Jia replied.

"I don't like the idea of Bei being in Xiapi," Che Zhou said.

"…I will return to Xuchang and make preparations for both of the two possible outcomes of this next encounter," Cao Cao declared. "Governor Che, fortify the city; Yu Jin, Qu Ji, Qin Yi: monitor Zang Ba closely; Guo Jia, Xun Yòu, Chen Qun: with me, please."

"Might I not need a clever strategist to aid me…?" Che Zhou asked nervously. "Surely, you can spare *one*-"

"If you need an adviser, Governor, I'll send you one," Cao Cao chuckled. "Did I not tell you that before…?"

Days passed; Cao Cao retreated to Xuchang and Liu Bei reached Xiapi City.

Zang Ba's encampment learned of Liu Bei's approach and reacted angrily; Zang was forced to assemble his allies in the centre of the undefended sea of tents and reason with them once again.

"*Liu Bei*, **of all people!**" Yin Li cried. "**I tell you, Zang, that he comes for our heads!**"

"**That's right!**" Chang Xi said. "**Cao Cao's double-crossed us!**"

"**If he's double-crossed anyone, it's Bei,**" Zang Ba argued. "**Cao's not reinstated him as governor, has he…? He's sent him here, yes, but** *why*…?"

"**Like I said, he's come to deal with us in the same way that he dealt with Yang Feng and Han Xian!**" Yin Li replied.

"**We should never have surrendered!**" Chang Xi suggested. "**The Han lot are liars, same as they've always been!**"

"**Give them a** *chance*!" Zang Ba pleaded. "**It's that or fight them until we die anyway, remember…?**"

The disaffected bandits grumbled quietly.

"**…Any that wants to turn back to Kaiyang, go ahead,**" Zang Ba continued. "**I'll speak to Bei, find out what he wants.**"

"**I'll join you, Xuangao,**" Sun Guan said.

"**…So will I,**" Yin Li said.

A day later, Liu Bei and his followers were welcomed at the outskirts of the Mount Tai Bandit camp by Zang Ba, Sun Guan, Yin Li, Wu Dun and Chang Xi.

"…General Liu Bei," Zang Ba said as he bowed humbly; the other bandit leaders reluctantly followed his example.

"Let us not be too formal!" Liu Bei chuckled as he bowed slightly. "For this discussion, Mister Zang, please call me Mister Liu."

The bandit leaders exchanged bemused glances.

"Forgive my frankness, but... why are you here, Mister Liu...?" Zang Ba asked warily.

"Excellency Cao has asked that I come here and request from you two things of minor importance that you can easily part with," Liu Bei replied.

"...I know that language," Chang Xi said worriedly. "That means *heads*! **That means that he wants our heads!**"

"Not yours, gentlemen," Liu Bei insisted. "There are two men – both of them former Han officers – that deserted with their men and joined your confederacy during the recent siege of the capital. Their heads are what His Excellency seeks, gentlemen, as a sign of your commitment to serving the Han."

"...That's a lot to ask a man of his word to do," Zang Ba replied. "Yes, I gave my word that I would surrender, but I also promised those men that I would never betray them. I give that promise to every man that joins us, and to break it would be-"

"Immoral...?" Guan Yu scoffed. "A bandit king has the nerve to lecture loyal Han officers about morals...?"

Chang Xi had to be restrained by Sun Guan and Wu Dun; Zang Ba looked at Guan Yu and smiled, saying, "You might have a point there, Mister Guan Yunchang. Oh, yes, I know you: the green robes, the long beard... you're known for your appearance alone, and you're quite famous. A lot of my associates look up to you as a man that knows the times for *right* and *necessity*."

Guan Yu grunted tersely and replied, "Indeed, Mister Zang, and you quite rightly note that nothing is simple."

"No, it isn't, else I'd be a Han official," Zang Ba said. "Who do I reply to, and how long do I have?"

"Excellency Cao has asked that you send the heads to him," Liu Bei explained. "He asks for a speedy response."

"...And you...?" Zang Ba asked. "Are you staying here with us...?"

"We are returning to Xiaopei," Liu Bei replied. "My task as I understand it is completed."

The two factions exchanged polite bows, and Liu Bei's group retreated peacefully.

"That's it...?" Wu Dun chortled.

"Seems so," Yin Li replied.

"What will you do, Xuangao...?" Sun Guan asked.

"...You know the answer to that," Zang Ba replied. "So does Cao: the question, then, is 'Why ask'...?"

Over the next four days, Cao Cao received letters from Xu Governor Che Zhou and Zang Ba.

"Understandably enough, Che Zhou frets that Liu Bei did not obey the order to leave the province," Cao Cao grumbled.

"What's done is done," Guo Jia said. "We'll just have to watch Bei carefully now."

"But what about Zang Ba, Excellency...?" Xun Wenruo asked. "He has refused to hand over the two men you asked for!"

"We knew that he wouldn't," Guo Jia chuckled. "It's not his refusal that we feared; it was how he put that refusal. He has put it into very agreeable words, I think."

"Indeed," Cao Cao conceded. "It frees me to place more forces to the north, where they are more likely to be needed. Sun Ce's also being agreeable, so we can probably go ahead with the marriage alliance idea as well."

"...So at long, long last, our only worthy opponent is Yuan Shao," Guo Jia said. "An army of up to four-hundred thousand, men like Yuan Tan, Chunyu Qiong, Zhang Hè, Gao Lan, Yan Liang and Wen Chou to call his vanguard generals; men like Tian Feng, Pang Ji, Ju Shou, Xu Yòu, Xin Pi, Guo Tu, Gao Gan and Xun Chen to look to for military counsel and local government; a vast domain comprising four entire Han provinces, access to vast wealth, a noble lineage and a Wuhuan cavalry that some say is better than Gongsun Zan's ever was. That makes him quite the foe, should he choose to act and have the 'right cause' to do so for."

"...Was that supposed to inspire us???" Cao Cao exclaimed.

"We know him, therefore we are halfway to defeating him," Guo Jia chuckled. "And that is *if* he acts... for he would need a very grand cause indeed."

"...Let us hope he is not given some excuse by others," Cao Cao said. "Now... now you, Gongda and I must go to Guandu and oversee the work there, Fengxiao."

"I am ready to go when you are," Guo Jia promised.

"As am I, Excellency," Xun Gongda said.

"Watch Dong Cheng and the others while I am gone, Wenruo," Cao Cao ordered. "Changwen, you make use of any contacts you still have to watch Liu Bei."

Xun Wenruo and Chen Qun bowed silently.

"...May Heaven be with us," Cao Cao muttered.

Yuan Shao's adviser Tian Feng had developed a good relationship with the prison warders while incarcerated for 'demoralising the army'; one of them came to him on one dull morning and said, "Lord Yuan Shao has sent word that you are to be released immediately, Mister Tian!"

"...Is that so...?" Tian Feng replied.

"You are pardoned and allowed to return to the court, he says!" the warder continued as he fumbled for the key to the cell. "Isn't that good news, Mister Tian...?"

"...So we are once again preparing for something," Tian Feng murmured. "But I will retain my opinions and continue to express them, for that is why I am an adviser. What a pity it is that so many of my peers put personal advancement before the needs of their lord and the nation."

Tian Feng returned to Yuan Shao's side, much to the dismay of his rivals at court: no more was said about his imprisonment, since plans for an attack on Cao Cao were still uppermost in Yuan Shao's mind and Tian's views had – to Yuan's irritation – been proven correct. His counsel was sought once again, but for how long, nobody could guess.

＊＊＊＊＊＊＊＊＊＊＊

103

Over the next few weeks, Cao Cao divided his attention between military and diplomatic measures to bring order to the country.

The military plans were simple enough in principle: militias were stationed at key points along the southern bank of the Yellow River – with the largest contingent at Boma – and a main headquarters was established at Guandu, a settlement on what was, effectively, the road to Xuchang.

Cao's diplomatic efforts were numerous: he strengthened his ties to the Sun clan of Jiangdong by arranging two marriages with his own clan; he accepted the defeated Administrator of Lujiang, Liu Xun, into Xuchang and rewarded him with a civil post; he sent a letter to Zhang Xiu in Nan County that hinted at a possible truce for discussions; he wrote to the warring Qiang tribal chieftains in Liang Province and hinted at greater autonomy in exchange for cooperation; he sent a letter to Liu Biao in Jing Province that suggested that he should try and find accord with Sun Ce; he opened dialogue with Xu Gong, a voice of civil opposition to Sun Ce that held a small amount of power in Wu Prefecture in eastern Yang Province; he wrote a reply to the former bandit Zang Ba – who moved back to southern Qing Province after his surrender – and reassured him that his loyalty to his followers was acceptable and that his faction would have the autonomy that had been promised if they 'harassed' Yuan Tan's interests in Qing Province; and lastly, he sent Liu Bei a series of orders to leave Xiaopei and return to the capital.

"The orders become ever more stern in their wording," Mister Sun fretted; he then turned to Liu Bei and added, "My lord, we must either act against him or comply with his wishes: the time for ignoring these demands is over."
"We must act," Guan Yu said. "Cao Cao's end is already overdue."
Liu Bei turned to Mi Zhu and smiled strangely.
"Dong Cheng's correspondence is fraught," Mi Zhu said. "He wonders what the 'right moment' is, and frankly I do too. If we sit here and wait for Dong Cheng to have the backing of enough courtiers and officers to stage a revolt in the capital, as he suggests, then we'll probably be attacked by Cao Cao 'in the name of the Han' and be dead before a single cry of defiance is uttered in Xuchang; if we act on Dong Cheng's edict now, it risks outing the conspirators in the capital and condemning them to death... and, besides that, there's the fact that, without significant external help, we will lose and lose badly."
"...And the only man that has the strength to oppose Cao Cao is *Yuan Shao*," Liu Bei supposed.
"Sun Ce is also formidable, but his motives are questionable," Mi Zhu replied.
"And Yuan Shao's are *not*...?" Mi Fang asked.
"...Of *course they are*, Brother, but Yuan has a noble background and wealth that Sun Ce does not possess," Mi Zhu retorted. "If Yuan challenged Cao, it would be as the descendant of countless Han loyalists, whereas Sun Ce does so as the son of a rustic lesser marquis and the former subordinate of a traitor and heretic. In

addition, Sun's forces probably only number sixty-to-eighty thousand – including former river pirates and the like – which matches Cao's force in size but not experience of the mountain-and-plain warfare that will face them; Yuan Shao can call upon an army four times that size, even without the Wuhuan, and such a force would overwhelm Cao's forces completely."

"...Then we must act at once, and at the same time alert Yuan Shao – and, perhaps, others, like Liu Biao, Sun Ce, and Liu Zhang – to the existence of the Girdle Edict so that we will have powerful allies!" Liu Bei said enthusiastically. "Imagine it! Liu Biao and Liu Zhang to the west, our force to the east, Sun Ce's to the south and Yuan Shao's to the north: what could Cao Cao do against hundreds of thousands of men on all sides...?"

"Act, yes, but we must warn Dong Cheng and his allies of it *sufficiently beforehand*, Lord Liu, and I might add that we should not mention the 'Girdle Edict' in any of our proclamations either," Mi Zhu said. "There are lives at stake if we do not."

"B-but that edict is the only proper sanction that we would have for seizing Xu Province!" Mister Sun protested. "If we acted without citing it, we'd just be rebels!"

"If it's 'proven' to be false – after all, could the Son of Heaven admit to its authenticity with Cao's blade at his throat – what then...?" Mi Zhu retorted.

"...Then perhaps I *should* wait, after all," Liu Bei murmured.

"Ayah... we'll dither ourselves to death!" Zhang Fei complained.

Yuan Shao was also making preparations and sending letters to prospective allies; Jing Province Governor Liu Biao summoned his allies and courtiers to his southern capital, Jiangling, so that they might discuss the situation properly.

"We should not be too hasty," the adviser Wang Can suggested.

"Who do we ally ourselves with, donkey boy, if not Yuan Shao?" the warlord Huang Zu scoffed. "Isn't Cao Cao pursuing marriage alliances with Sun Ce...?"

"Cao Cao is treacherous, while Yuan Shao is, at the worst, bumbling and naïve," the adviser Kuai Liang suggested.

"That is quite true, Brother," the adviser Kuai Yue said. "In my time as a junior official serving Hè Jin, I saw a lot of Yuan Shao as he came and went from the offices. He was the only man to stand up to the eunuchs, and he opposed his brother's plans."

"...But sent his son to rescue Shu, so I hear," Liu Biao replied.

"There are many reasons why Yuan Shao might have sent his son to meet his brother, and one of them is apprehending him, as he claims," Kuai Liang said. "We have been threatened by Cao Cao repeatedly, not least for our 'inaction' against our squatters in Nan County that-"

"That I can do nothing about while I need most of my army here and in Jiangxia to repel the Sun family that he is so keen to be a part of!" Liu Biao cried. "Does he not see the truth of things???"

"Cao Cao's done little that tells me that he's anything more than another Wang Mang," Huang Zu scoffed. "Face facts, Jingsheng: we're going to have to-"

Liu Biao coughed deliberately and said, "In court, I am *Governor Liu*, Mister Huang. We *must observe protocol*."

Huang Zu smiled dryly.

"But yes, I admit that you're right, and that we have little choice but so side with Yuan Shao," Liu Biao continued. "I'll admit that I am tired of it all, as well. I'm nearly sixty, and can well do without this. In fact, Shao's brother and the Suns have worn me out and made a premature eighty-year-old of me."

"So we are to write to Yuan Shao and agree to this 'alliance'…?" Wang Can prompted.

"…Your tone implies concern, and we'd be right to accord with that concern," Liu Biao replied. "An alliance for *what*, exactly…?"

"He made it clear enough," Kuai Liang said. "It is an alliance against Cao Cao, who plots sedition, like Dong Zhuo before him."

"Yes, yes, I see that!" Liu Biao grumbled. "But what will my involvement entail…? What guarantees do I have that I won't have Sun Ce coming over the border as soon as my back is turned…?"

"None, by the sounds of things," Huang Zu chortled. "In fact, you can bet that Cao Cao's marriage alliances are being done to counter Yuan Shao's posturing. The point is that you're being given an ultimatum, Governor: surrender to Cao Cao and face losing half the province – my half – to Sun Ce, or join Yuan Shao's effort to uproot Cao Cao, which will involve attacking Cao's western border while I defend Jiangxia against whatever Cao asks Sun to send here."

Liu Biao looked to Kuai Liang, who said, "That is the situation, more or less. It's a simple choice between fighting to retain your autonomy and quietly capitulating."

Liu Biao looked at his eldest son Qi and said, "I cannot simply capitulate… so I must join Yuan Shao. Get me paper, pen and- …No, wait, I'll write it in my private study. Everyone is dismissed and ordered to prepare for what is to come."

Huang Zu rubbed his bearded chin and said, "As you wish."

Yuan Shao received Liu Biao's cautious response and excitedly summoned his officials to his audience hall.

"We have our allies!" Yuan Shao began. "The Wuhuan, the remnants of Gongsun Zan's army from Yòu Province, converts from the Black Mountain Bandits and sensible Xiongnu tribes in Bing Province, Sui Gu's force in Henei, and now the men of Jing! I can muster at least a hundred-thousand, for certain, while Cao can barely manage a fraction of that, and-!"

"Lord Yuan, numbers are meaningless in war," the adviser Tian Feng protested. "The army may be large, but it is fractured, with many yet to be fully integrated and none yet recovered fully from the war in Yòu. We cannot rely on bribed tribespeople, 'reformed' criminals and defeated enemies as a vanguard!"

"We're yet to implement many of the necessary improvements to living conditions in the provinces that were suggested by the likes of Mister Cui Yan, and those suggestions were made before we marched," the adviser Ju Shou ventured. "Matters are unchanged in many places, and-"

"It is now or never, gentlemen!" Yuan Shao insisted. "Can I afford to give Cao Cao the time to integrate the remnants of Lü Bu's forces, my brother's forces, Chen Lan and Lei Bo's band of criminals in the Qian Hills, Zang Ba's Mount Tai Bandits and the Yellow Turbans of Runan into *his* army…? You speak of Cao Cao's army as a tiny rock and mine as a giant dragon's egg that will shatter on contact with his! Is his army any less fractured, poorly rested or disorderly in remote areas...?"

"Cao Cao's implemented '*tuntian*' to feed the populace of Yan Province and make them loyal and content, which will make every man fight twice as hard as a demoralised one," Cui Yan suggested. "In fact, I should like to take this opportunity to declare my complete opposition to your plan, Lord Yuan. His Majesty is in Xuchang, and peace is a frantic grasp away, if only we would reach for it. Why risk such an opportunity...?"

"Your benign approach is nice but inappropriate, Cui Yan," Tian Feng said. "I am not opposed to fighting Cao, merely the method and timing."

"Why do we want this goody-goody pacifist here for such things...?" Chunyu Qiong heckled. "Lord Yuan, dismiss Cui Yan!"

"Cui Yan's a dreamer with eyes wide shut!" Guo Tu chuckled. "We need men who are awake and see the way of things!"

"Do you not have some slander to hurl at him...?" Xu Yòu scoffed. "I speak and get abuse and accusations in return."

"...Perhaps he is better at hiding his wrongdoings!" Guo Tu retorted. "You could learn from him, Xu Yòu, since you can plot little better than having your wife serve as a conduit for your-!"

"**ENOUGH!**" Yuan Shao bellowed. "**I DON'T CARE ABOUT YOUR SILLY, PETTY DEALINGS!**"

The heckling died away immediately.

"...I do not intend to challenge Cao Cao publicly," Yuan Shao continued. "He will know that I am preparing to march on the capital anyway, since he has spies everywhere."

"Like *Xu Yòu*," Xun Chen taunted. "Isn't 'Mengde' an old friend...?"

"Aren't your older brother and an older nephew two of his closest aides?" Xu Yòu retorted. "Stop heckling and let Lord Yuan speak!"

"...He'll know, one way or the other," Yuan Shao said coldly. "I will continue my preparations, amass my men, maintain contact with my allies, and strike as soon as the weather is favourable and all is ready. Enough is enough, gentlemen: Cao Cao must die, and the empire must be restored, and it is my duty – as slayer of the 'Ten', Commander of the Eastern Pass Coalition, Commander-in-Chief of the Han Imperial Army, descendant of the loyal Yuan An and brother of a man that must be atoned for – to lead the charge on Xuchang."

Cavalry Commandant Cui Yan was posted to Li County for a time to oversee troop movements; he took the opportunity to visit the home of the famous Sima family, who were noticeably on edge and contemplating another move to flee the chaos.

"Mister Cui Yan!" the eldest of the 'Eight Simas', Sima Lang, cried excitedly. "Cui Yan! Cui Jigui!"

"It's good to see you, Boda," Cui Yan replied. "Your father is well?"

"He's away on a trip to the capital," Sima Lang explained as he guided Cui Yan into the house and had him sit in a guest place in the living quarters. "Excellency Cao wants him to take up a post, and us as well of course."

Sima Lang paused to give silent orders to a servant.

"All eight of you...?" Cui Yan asked as the servant retreated.

"Naturally," Sima Lang replied. "We're the 'Eight Simas', so we have little choice, really. Yi has no interest whatsoever, but I keep telling him that it's an inevitability."

"…A truly marvellous young man, young Zhongda," Cui Yan suggested. "He'll surpass many a man… maybe all of the rest of you brothers."

The servant returned with a tea kettle and dishes.

"Yi…?" Sima Lang chuckled as he oversaw the servant's placement of the tea-drinking implements. "No, no, Jigui; Yi's too stubborn, opinionated and limited in his thinking."

"I think that he's more flexible in his thinking than you give him credit," Cui Yan retorted as he took a proffered tea dish. "I spoke with him when he was a boy, and his mind was as sharp as a man twice his age; he's a future prodigy."

"Don't tell him that, Jigui, I implore you," Sima Lang chortled. "He's recalcitrant enough as it is. So, to move on… why are you here…? It isn't for 'business', as with so many of Yuan Shao's other officials; you're probably the most honest man in the land."

Sima Lang poured tea into Cui Yan's dish and awaited a reply.

"…I couldn't be in Li County and say nothing," Cui Yan replied.

"*Ah*… Yuan Shao is preparing for war with Cao Cao," Sima Lang guessed. "You're here to mass forces. You wanted to ensure that we knew."

Cui Yan nodded silently.

"…Father also went to Xuchang to assess the situation there, but can we risk being there when Yuan intends a march of a hundred-thousand men – a lot of them disreputable – in that direction?" Sima Lang mused. "Dare we stay here either…?"

"The Simas are survivors," Cui Yan replied. "You've survived the Yellow Turbans, Dong Zhuo, the regents, the Black Mountain Bandits and Lü Bu: this is just another thing that's happening."

"…We all want to be neutral, not just Yi, if I'm honest," Sima Lang said. "Neither Cao nor Yuan is easy to truly fathom; Yi says that he considers them both to be a danger to the Han under the right – or rather *wrong* – circumstances, and- …You're smiling."

"Yi's words *do* move you," Cui Yan chuckled; his mood darkened as he added, "If Elder Zheng Xuan were still able to take students, then Yi… … …alas, I hear that Elder Zheng's ill, maybe dying."

"I heard the same," Sima Lang sighed.

"But in amidst all of this chaos, will anyone mourn his passing as grandly as they should…?" Cui Yan asked. "When Elder Qiao Xuan passed away, his name was quickly forgotten as the nation was overrun by the Yellow Turbans; will Lord Yuan and Excellency Cao now deny another great scholar a famous funeral…?"

"At least he'll not die a dog's death like Cai Yong," Sima Lang replied. "It is better to be a forgotten light in the darkness that to die disgraced… especially when it is not deserved."

The scholar Zheng Xuan – whose inclusive, balanced approach to the Confucian studies of his time made him a pioneer of thinking that influenced studies for centuries to come – did die of old age and illness at the age of 73. He was one of the few famous men that would meet his end naturally over the coming years.

****

104

Xu Province Governor Che Zhou was alarmed when a messenger brought word of a force approaching Xiapi City from the south.

"They're Bei's men!" Che Zhou said to his divided court. "They intend insurrection!"

"We don't know that," General of the Household Xu Dan replied.

"**Reinforce the city anyway!**" Che Zhou cried. "**We must not let him get close!**"

The courtiers grumbled for varying reasons; there were many that disliked Cao Cao's chosen governor and many more that resented the fact that Cao Cao had any jurisdiction at all.

"...Why did His Excellency have to withdraw every decent officer he had to Xuchang???" Che Zhou lamented. "Even if I had just one – Yu Jin, Xu Huang, even one of Bu's former officers like Zhang Liao – I'd at least survive until he got here! What can I do against Guan Yu and Zhang Fei???"

Liu Bei's small army had crossed the Si River at its narrowest point and was preparing for the final march on Xiapi.

"This is not wise," Mister Sun grumbled.

"Cao Cao's most direct route into the province is through the mountains and Xiaopei, and by the same thinking, so is any messenger's," Liu Bei retorted. "We've got that route blocked, so they'd need to go through northeast Yan to get to Xuchang, which is a longer journey. I've written to Yuan Shao, so-"

"He's not dependable," Mister Sun said.

"He's the most dependable of them all!" Liu Bei insisted. "He's the only one that did anything against the 'Ten', against Dong Zhuo, against the Black Mountain Bandits, and-!"

"And Gongsun Zan," Jian Yong chuckled. "He wasn't so fast to act against Yuan Shu, Lü Bu, the Qiang warlords and the Yellow Turbans, and he didn't rescue the emperor when he was rummaging for food on the plains to the southwest of his capital either... that's how Cao Cao ended up with him."

"...**Who else is there???**" Liu Bei screamed. "**Sooner or later, Dong Cheng will demand action, and Yuan Shao will be involved! Isn't that true???**"

"Che Zhou will expect us," Guan Yu suggested. "I recommend sending an advance force to surprise and kill him before he can fortify the city properly."

"It should be you, Yunchang," Zhang Fei said soberly. "People probably remember me and that Cao Bao: they know you're more 'business-like' than me."

"Agreed," Liu Bei said. "Guan Yunchang, you should do the deed."

Guan Yu smiled and prepared for the attack.

"**Excellency Cao! Excellency Cao!**"

Xun Gongda ran into the command tent of Cao Cao's Guandu base and fell to his knees in penitence; his desperate cries – which were now being followed by exhausted wheezing – left Cao Cao perturbed.

"Speak as soon as you can, Gongda," Cao Cao ordered.

Guo Jia frowned and muttered, "I know what this is."

Xun Gongda coughed and said, "Ch-Cheng... Yu... sends word from Xuchang, that-"
"Cheng Yu is in Xuchang again?" Cao Cao exclaimed. "Has Yuan Shao attacked-?"
"N-no... not Yuan!" Xun Gongda said. "Bei... Liu Bei!"
Cao Cao scowled angrily.
"Liu Bei... has... h-has attacked Xiapi!" Xun Gongda reported.
Cao Cao's face contorted, and he let out a hollow, booming cry.
"Excellency!" Xun Gongda sobbed.
"...We must go back to Xuchang at once," Guo Jia suggested.
Xun Gongda looked at Cao Cao – whose head was now hung low – and asked, "Your Excellency, are you alright...?"
"...Bei... will know *pain*," Cao Cao growled. "Call everyone... and... and have my carriage readied *at once*."

Cao Cao made the relatively short journey back to Xuchang and convened an emergency meeting of his closest advisers and allies in the private meeting room in the chancellery.
"We must go and deal with Bei at once," Guo Jia insisted.
"We daren't risk it," Xun Wenruo protested. "The generals agree, Excellency, that the mobilisation that would be necessary to siege Bei would leave us at the very least understaffed in the capital, if not everywhere that-"
"But I cannot do nothing!" Cao Cao interrupted. "Yes, I worry for the capital, but at the same time, we can't afford to lose the province; I'd never have tolerated Zang Ba's defiant attitude if that weren't the case."
"He'll definitely have written to Yuan Shao, who was his master when he was running the province before," Cheng Yu said. "Yuan must be planning to pincer Yan Province."
"Well then why are you here instead of guarding Dong Prefecture...?" Cao Cao asked.
"Because I had to inform you of Bei's actions in person and be here to proffer my advice," Cheng Yu retorted. "I've left capable men there, and-"
"If I may... I have thwarted Yuan's southern pincer by mediating with Sun Ce," Cao Cao said. "Liu Biao is too timid to act, even if he does ally with Yuan Shao; no, it is Bei that is the real threat now... just as I was warned by you both, Cheng Zhongde and Guo Fengxiao, and I regret not heeding you before."
"Bei seemed weak; that's his strength," Guo Jia chuckled. "He lulls enemies into thinking that he's harmless while earning sympathy and loyalty from fellow dissidents and self-pitying types. I'd be lying if I said that I wasn't disappointed that you ignored us, of course... but you've ignored advice and suffered for it before, so I'm used to it."
Cao Cao smiled sadly and said, "That was a deserved rebuke, Fengxiao; at least this only costs me an expendable toady and not another son."
"So are you marching on Xu or not...?" Cheng Yu asked frankly.
"There are two factors that affect that decision: the first is the likelihood of Yuan Shao marching on Xuchang as soon as we march on Xiapi, and the second is the likelihood of Bei's little rebellion being supported either locally or nationally," Guo Jia explained. "I say that Yuan will hesitate and do nothing or be

impeded by our forces at Boma and Yan Ford, which answers the first concern: the second is difficult to answer, because it may involve an internal rebellion – related or unrelated – right here in Xuchang if we miscalculate."

"...The notion that Bei is part of a larger scheme is entirely plausible to me," Cao Cao replied as he clutched his head.

"You're... getting a headache...?" Cheng Yu fretted.

"I was getting the signs anyway, long before this news... please, gentlemen, continue," Cao Cao insisted.

"But if your head ails you, we might be better discussing this without you," Cheng Yu suggested. "After all, the-"

"**I am the Excellency of Works!**" Cao Cao snapped. "**I am Acting Excellency over the Masses too, for what it's worth, and Acting Commander-in-Chief too, because of Yuan Shao's enduring idiocy! How can a national emergency be discussed without my involvement???**"

Cheng Yu smiled humbly – an action that surprised his peers – and said, "But at least until it gets a little better, Lord Cao, you-"

"**From here, it only gets *worse*! It *ALWAYS* GETS *WORSE*!**" Cao Cao screamed. "**This will be my constant companion for *DAYS*, CHENG YU! You *KNOW THAT*! There IS NO CURE! There IS NO RESPITE! And your supposed miracle-worker, 'Hua Tuo', will not come and help me! He'll not come here unless I have the rat dragged here from Pei, which I daren't do right for fear of earning more enemies, so what is the point of discussing it???**"

Even Cheng Yu was unnerved by Cao Cao's rant.

"...I... forgive me, gentlemen," Cao Cao sighed. "Please continue."

"...Guo Fengxiao was quite right when he said that we must discover Bei's allies in the capital," Cheng Yu said. "Dong Cheng, Zhong Ji and Wang Fu are obvious enough; the question is how many more are of a like mind."

"How many want rid of *wicked old Mengde*...!" Cao Cao chortled.

"It isn't just who and how many," Guo Jia suggested. "Bei's brave in his own way, but only when he can cite some sort of justification for his actions. Yes, he could say that he's the 'rightful Governor of Xu Province', the man chosen by Tao Qian, that was deposed by Lü Bu and never reinstated as justice dictated, but is that enough...? He's got to convince the people of Xu Province of that; he's got to convince Zang Ba of that; he's got to convince the nation of that. To some, he usurped the governorship from a dying man in a time of crisis, and it was only Yuan Shao and the regency government that nominally accepted Bei as governor, and neither really wanted to; the Xiapi court colluded with Bu to oust him, so why would they want him now...?"

"That's a very good point," Chen Qun admitted.

"Perhaps because they resent having a man chosen by 'The Butcher of Xu' as their governor, and because time has shown them that their alliance with Bu was a mistake...?" Cao Cao suggested bitterly.

"Yes, but doesn't his action now guarantee your return for a fourth time...?" Guo Jia countered. "Last time, you were there to oust the tyrannical Lü Bu and save the place in your capacity as Excellency of Works; who would you be this time...? Are you there to punish Bei or everyone, and punish them for what...? What could Bei have

as his mandate for this that is so compelling that he'd risk it...?
What thing does he have – his 'authority', if you will – to tell the
people of Xu if they are afraid of your return...?"
"...Dong Cheng's little clique of troublemakers has contrived
something," Cao Cao said.
"They must have," Guo Jia replied. "We cannot march anywhere
or defend anything if we do not discover the nature of the plot and
destroy the heart of it."
"But what of Xiapi...?" Chen Qun asked.
"We can't save Che Zhou," Cheng Yu replied. "Xu Province isn't
ready for what Bei's done, unfortunately... and that's Yuan Shao's
fault for forcing us to withdraw so much of our forces."
"...Forget Yuan for now," Cao Cao said. "Focus on Dong Cheng."

General of Chariots and Cavalry Dong Cheng arranged a meeting
of his senior allies at the home of Zhong Ji.
"We shouldn't be meeting at all now!" Wang Fu hissed.
"We have to, just this once, because this is serious," Dong Cheng
replied. "Bei's attacked Che Zhou and sieged Xiapi."
"*Ayah*... we're not ready!" Zhong Ji whimpered.
"As he said in his letter, he had no choice," Dong Cheng
continued. "Cao's been threatening to send a force to Xiaopei to
make him come back to Xuchang, and that would have ended in
blood. He's promised to do this without mentioning 'it', so we're
free to continue with our own plan."
"But Cao will probably march on Xu Province and not be here or in
Guandu!" Wang Fu protested. "Bei's ruined everything!"
"Cao can't leave here, not with Yuan Shao amassing forces at the
Yellow River," Dong Cheng explained. "He'll want to take Xiapi
back, but any forces that he sends will weaken him here."
"But he'll expect attacks now!" Zhong Ji whined.
"He expected them anyway, since he's so suspicious," Dong Cheng
insisted. "This doesn't really hamper us."
"What if Cao guesses that Bei's acting on a higher authority?"
Wang Fu asked.
"...Can he?" Dong Cheng replied defensively.
"It would have to be you," Wang Fu continued. "We've no choice:
we have to advance our plan and try to get Cao before his
advisers guess our plans or slander us anyway to weaken Bei's
allies in the capital."
"...Alright," Dong Cheng agreed. "I'll talk to everyone individually.
Be ready."

Guan Yu's raid on Xiapi was successful: the city's defences had
not been finalised, and the inhabitants were not prepared to hold
without the proper resources for a siege; the gates were wide
open, and the defiant governor, Che Zhou, met his end at the
hands of Guan Yu's elite cavalrymen.
"...So now what...?" Mister Sun heckled as Liu Bei took what he felt
to be his rightful place as the master of the governor's mansion.
"How long do we have before Cao Cao sends an army here for
what will be the fourth time in six years, and with us as his target
for the second time...?"
"He'll hesitate because he fears Yuan Shao," Mi Zhu insisted.
"And Yuan Shao is not a fool," Liu Bei replied. "He'll receive my

letter soon enough and act upon it. With Liu Biao of Jing as a powerful third arm, Cao Cao and his new in-law, Sun Ce, will either die as allies or live on as enemies, depending on whether Sun Ce wants to be seen to join yet another seditionist that intends to harm the Son of Heaven. If Sun Ce does the right thing – and, from what I hear of him, I think that he will – then Cao Cao will be surrounded, and his death will quickly follow!"

"If Yuan Shao procrastinates – which is something that he is known for – then it is us for whom 'death will quickly follow', Lord Liu," Mister Sun retorted. "Is the defensive force that we left in Xiaopei going to be enough…?"

"Of course it isn't," Liu Bei scoffed. "Yunchang will remain here and guard Xiapi from Cao Cao and Zang Ba; the rest of us will go back to Xiaopei and reinforce it."

"May Heaven be with us," Mister Sun muttered.

But while tensions grew in Xuchang and the pace of events quickened in Xu Province, Yuan Shao's court in Yè City was struck by paralysis.

"**What sense is there in this???**" the adviser Tian Feng cried as he stared at his quiet, emotionless lord with utter disbelief; the rest of the Yè court was bitterly divided over the general situation and Yuan's reaction to the most recent development.

"Liu Bei is a seditionist, and an incompetent one at that," Yuan Shao replied. "He betrayed and usurped Tao Qian; he came crawling to me when Cao Cao attacked him and tricked me into giving him my support and protection, thus giving Cao the excuse that he needed to betray me; Bei then broke our covenant by giving shelter to Lü Bu, who was fleeing not just from Cao Cao but from me; after that, he allowed Bu to seize the province and yielded to him in exchange for his worthless life; he then ran to Cao – whom he had once called his 'greatest enemy under Heaven' – and sought shelter when Bu chased him out of Xiaopei, rather than come to me, which thereby gave Cao's regime undeserved credibility at the same time that he betrayed Xu Province; he then pledged loyalty to Cao, served the role of loyal dog and chased my brother back to Yang, thereby denying me the chance to ensure that his estate and fate were managed appropriately; then, after all that, he parleyed with Zang Ba on Cao's behalf, when he is supposed to hate bandits; and *now*, gentlemen, he has stolen an army from Cao and used it to betray Cao and conquer Xu for his own ends!"

The officials were quiet and ponderous.

"Bei is deceitful, dishonest and self-serving in a way that is almost casually self-destructive," Yuan Shao continued. "To help him would be foolish indeed."

"But he's an ally of Dong Cheng, who is the Son of Heaven's appointed General of Chariots and Cavalry, and a man with whom you have enjoyed cordial correspondence!" Tian Feng protested. "General Dong has hinted at the Son of Heaven's willingness to grant a formal decree that condemns Cao Cao: Liu Bei has, perhaps, seen such a decree already and simply acts upon it! Does he not hint at it in his letter…?"

"He speaks of 'having established purpose' or some nonsense or other," Yuan Shao replied. "He's a delusional hankerer that has dreamt of being an emperor since he was a youth, and he no doubt believes that his time as a sandal weaver was a 'test from Heaven' rather than the inherited punishment that it was. Liu Bei's line fell from favour because of his ancestor's arrogance and ambition: he's inherited the faults, so the inherited punishment is obviously deserved."

"That's right!" Guo Tu said.

"But he's a valuable ally, at least for now, and we should 'do him a favour' in this matter," Ju Shou pleaded. "If we divide Cao's inferior force between three fronts, that's even more effective than two!"

"*Aiee...* you and Tian Feng are the two men that have most protested against my intent to fight Cao Cao!" Yuan Shao complained. "Are you just intent on being meddlesome...? Will you advocate caution again when I finally relent?"

"This is the critical moment," Tian Feng insisted. "Act now, and Cao will have nowhere to run; wait, and we lose an ally, a province and an advantage."

"Liu Bei is no ally, Xu Province is mostly in the hands of Zang Ba's bandits, and we already have enough advantages against Cao Cao," Guo Tu heckled.

"You were for *attacking*, Guo Tu!" Tian Feng despaired. "Why do you now champion doing nothing...? Is it just to spite the men that you consider to be your rivals rather than your peers...?"

"You imply that I am a poor servant of my lord, but at least I reflect his inner thoughts rather than those of his enemies and rivals!" Guo Tu retorted. "Who in his right mind would want to aid *Liu Bei*...?"

"**Enough, enough!**" Yuan Shao cried. "**Silence, all of you! The matter is closed!**"

The court started to disperse; once Yuan Shao was alone save for his secretary Chen Lin, Xu Yòu approached him and said, "Forgive me, lord and friend, for asking this, but... do you only refuse to aid Liu Bei because he pursued your brother and thwarted your plan to bring him to Yè...?"

"**WRETCH!**" Yuan Shao shrieked. "**How *dare* you ask such a thing! GET AWAY FROM ME!**"

Xu Yòu bowed humbly, turned and retreated.

"*...Wretch,*" Yuan Shao muttered.

"Are you replying to Liu Bei...?" Chen Lin asked.

"...I'll send something cordial but dismissive," Yuan Shao replied. "I'll say that he can come here if he falters. I will not march until I am ready; I will not let Liu Bei, of all men, dictate my schedule."

The days passed: Liu Bei received Yuan Shao's response and silently lamented the obvious outcome, and the Han government continued to prepare for its own response.

****

105

Cao Cao was at home when Xun Gongda arrived with more urgent news; Cao dismissed his family and asked his adviser to explain everything.

"Guo Jia was right: Yuan's just sitting there, and no signs of collaboration with Liu Bei are evident!" Xun Gongda said excitedly. "But that isn't why I'm here: Excellency, we… we have uncovered the truth of Dong Cheng's plot."

"You told me about Yuan first because the 'plot' is so unpalatable," Cao Cao guessed. "I have a headache already, so nothing you tell me can make me suffer any more."

"…I hope so," Xun Gongda replied uneasily.

Cao Cao's eyes became slits: he leant forward, frowned and asked, "What does that dog Dong Cheng intend for me, Gongda…? What has he done…?"

Xun Gongda stammered incoherently.

"…So he's labelled me as a villain, has he…?" Cao Cao growled.

"My lord, it… it's worse, far worse!" Xun Gongda whimpered.

Cao Cao snorted angrily and got to his feet: Xun Gongda knew that the next move was to go to the chancellery, where the rest of Cao's advisers were already waiting.

"What has happened, Mother…?" Cao Pi asked as he watched his father retreat from the house.

"Something terrible," Lady Bian replied.

Cao Cao bit his hand and fought the urge to scream like a wild animal as Xun Wenruo nervously relayed the results of his investigation into Dong Cheng.

"An edict from the Son of Heaven…?" the adviser Tian Chou exclaimed. "After everything that Excellency Cao did to rescue His Majesty from the White Wave Bandits and reconstruct the court here in Xuchang…?"

"…It must be a fake," Chen Qun chuckled. "Excellency, I highly doubt that His Majesty would give such a thing to the father of one of the consorts."

"Were it real – and I am not saying that it is – then it would be given to someone who openly defies Lord Cao," Guo Jia said. "It doesn't matter whether it is real or not in the end: it's each man's choice to believe its authenticity or not. Xun Wenruo would not believe it to be real even if His Majesty declared it so in court."

"That is right," Xun Wenruo said. "If it in His Majesty's hand, then it was fraudulently obtained: Lord Cao – *His Excellency Cao* – has never wronged the Son of Heaven, and Dong Cheng has either forged it or fraudulently obtained it. Either way, gentlemen, it is worthless, because it is founded on lies."

"But as you say, Guo Fengxiao, its authenticity is irrelevant," Cheng Yu chortled. "There are men in this court – fools, all of them – that would insist that it was real even if the Son of Heaven decried it."

"They would say that His Majesty was threatened," Guo Jia replied. "What matters, in the end, is what each man does. What we must do first is apprehend Dong Cheng, Zhong Ji, Wang Fu, Liu Bei and all of their family, servants and close associates. They are one and all guilty of treason."

"Liu Bei is in Xu Province," Cheng Yu scoffed. "The craven, devious old owl made sure that not even a loyal dog was left here, and now we know why."

"But his allies will die and die horribly," Guo Jia said emotionlessly.

"But Dong Cheng is the father of a favourite consort, a consort that carries a future prince or princess," Cheng Yu grumbled. "That will ensure him amnesty for sure when-"

"It will *not*, gentlemen," Cao Cao declared; he stood up, tightened the cloth belt that secured his robes and turned to look at his sword of authority.

"What do you hope to do...?" Cheng Yu asked.

"The 'old mistake' will not be repeated," Cao Cao said as he ran his finger along the ceremonial sword and pondered his next move – a move that would forever immortalise him in history were he to act – one last time. "I will learn one lesson from my former friend Yuan Shao: when a problem presents itself, you deal with it, giving no thought to 'protocol' and 'taboos'."

"My lord, Lord Cao, *Excellency*, what... what are you planning...?" Cheng Yu asked with uncharacteristic feebleness.

"...Xun Yòu: you will personally oversee the apprehension of Dong Cheng, Zhong Ji, Wang Fu, and the others that are listed in Xun Yu's report," Cao Cao ordered. "Xun Yu, Tian Chou: I want the city placed on alert and any suspicious persons arrested, since their assassins might already be awaiting a moment to attack us. Cheng Yu: you're best placed in Dong Prefecture and should go back there. The other matter... is mine to deal with personally."

"What 'other matter'...?" Xun Wenruo asked.

"...Do not do it," Cheng Yu croaked.

"He has no choice," Guo Jia suggested.

Cao Cao smiled slightly and said, "I am glad that someone understands. Kindly carry out your duties, gentlemen... while I carry out mine."

Less than an hour later, a eunuch attendant ran into Emperor Xian's personal quarters, fell to his knees and kowtowed, saying, "Your Majesty, men from the chancellery are on their way here to take possession of Consort Dong!"

"...What nonsense is this...?" Emperor Xian asked disbelievingly.

"...Majesty, Cao Cao intends to harm her," Empress Fu said as she looked at the young and beautiful Consort Dong with sympathy.

"He would not *dare*!" Emperor Xian chortled. "She is with child! She carries a prince, a light of the realm!"

Empress Fu shook her head and said, "She must be hidden, or she'll die, and so will the prince she carries."

"Majesty, we must hurry!" the attendant pleaded. "The-!"

But it was too late: Cao Cao entered the living quarters with a group of gate guards, his bodyguard Xu Chu and three of his other loyal retainers.

"You are trespassing in a place that forbids the bearing of arms!" Emperor Xian said as bravely as he could.

Cao Cao smiled coldly, turned his irreverent gaze to Consort Dong and said, "Your father's plot is exposed."

"Plot...?" Empress Fu exclaimed as she turned her gaze to her unreadable husband and sovereign.

"A plot, Empress, to label me as a seditionist, assassinate me and take control of the capital, while Yuan Shao – the brother of the traitor Yuan Shu – and Liu Bei – an ambitious sandal weaver that covets the throne for himself – prepared their own armies to attack the capital from outside of the province," Cao Cao explained. "And it was all to be carried out in the name of an edict – an Imperial edict – that, they claim, was written in His Majesty's hand, concealed within a girdle and passed to Dong Cheng."

Emperor Xian silently fought tears as he stared at the shivering Consort Dong.

"But the plot is exposed: they will all be dead this very night, convicted of treason one and all," Cao Cao continued. "But to ensure the end of the matter, the families must be executed to the third degree… and that includes Consort Dong."

"**She carries our child: she carries a *prince*!**" Emperor Xian said angrily.

"**You forget who is master and who is servant, Mister Cao!**" Empress Fu cried. "**Get out of here at once!**"

Cao Cao shook his head and said, "In this case, Majesty, I must refuse: what I do, I do not do gladly. Her child, should it survive, will be a threat to Your Majesty, for that was the intent all along. If we are to have peace, then this deed must be done."

"…We *forbid it*," Emperor Xian whimpered powerlessly.

Cao Cao snorted irritably and turned to his nervous guards; they did nothing, so he was forced to say, "Take Consort Dong from this room, to a place more fitting, wherein she will meet her end by strangulation."

"**Save me, Majesty!**" Consort Dong screamed.

Emperor Xian's head fell forward as he realised that he was as powerless as he had ever been.

"**Save me! You are the Son of Heaven! SAVE ME!!!**" Consort Dong pleaded as she was dragged from the room.

"…I do what I do because I desire an end to the chaos, Majesty," Cao Cao insisted. "Dong Cheng and his allies – including Liu Bei – will soon be no more, and then Your Majesty can be restored to Luoyang, and all will be well."

Cao Cao bowed, turned, and retreated.

"…We are doomed," Empress Fu sobbed.

Emperor Xian did not reply.

Cao Cao's forces apprehended and exterminated everyone and everything that was in any way connected to Dong Cheng's plot: the 'Girdle Edict' was now in Cao Cao's possession, but the extent of the knowledge of its existence was not his to decide. Liu Bei and a few others that were fortunate enough to survive the purge were now the champions of that controversial document, and it would be one of their main reasons for opposing Cao Cao for years to come.

****

106

Cao Cao had narrowly avoided a rebellion in the capital, but his purge had not removed the dual threats of Yuan Shao and Liu Bei. "If Yuan Shao knew of that edict, he'd have acted when Bei seized Xiapi," Guo Jia said to a sober audience of fellow officials: many were haunted by the news that their master, Cao Cao, had personally overseen the execution of a pregnant imperial consort.

"Ah! I see that you have all decided to stay," Cao Cao said as he entered the chancellery meeting hall with Xu Chu and six guards. "Even Mister Cheng Yu is here: are you not supposed to return to Juancheng City…?"

"We… were just discussing Liu Bei, Lord Cao," Cheng Yu replied meekly. "I… I was going back as soon as that was discussed."

"I can hear it in your tone, Mister Cheng," Cao Cao chortled as he took his host seat. "I can see it in most of your faces! You despise my decision to remove Consort Dong as a threat."

"…It is an unprecedented move, Excellency, but what's done is done," Cheng Yu replied.

"All the same, I can see that it's left you feeling afraid of me," Cao Cao said as he clutched his head. "Perhaps that's good, perhaps that's bad."

"I… I understand, Excellency, for I have been willing to make difficult decisions that were unpopular but necessary," Cheng Yu replied. "Nothing has changed."

"Except, perhaps, your willingness to be blunt and frank," Cao Cao noted. "I hope that does not diminish your usefulness as my counsel. Guo Fengxiao, I believe that you were making a point."

"I was," Guo Jia replied. "Yuan did not know of Dong Cheng's edict, but he will probably learn of it once Bei hears about Dong Cheng's death. Bei did kill Che Zhou, and he has since returned to Xiaopei to fortify the passes."

"Who guards Xiapi?" Cao Cao asked.

"Guan Yu… guards Xiapi," Cheng Yu reported.

"…Bei's forces are weak, and they have far from full support," Cao Cao mused. "I will send Generals Liu Dai and Wang Zhong to Xiaopei and-"

"Send better men than them," Guo Jia said. "Send Yue Jin, Xu Huang, or even send Zhu Ling back there if you must, but-"

"Bei's army is made up of my men, and many of them will realise that they've made a mistake," Cao Cao insisted. "We have no need to summon the Imperial court to authorise this: Xun Yu, please have Generals Liu Dai and Wang Zhong come to the chancellery at once to receive their orders."

"As… as you wish, Excellency," Xun Wenruo replied.

"I can see that there will be no reasoning with you about who to send," Guo Jia sighed. "But at least have them attack *quickly*!"

"It shall be as you suggest," Cao Cao replied.

Liu Bei was not surprised when a messenger brought word of an army from the capital; the second part of the message, however, was a crushing blow to morale.

"Dong Cheng… Zhong Ji… Wang Fu… and *Consort Dong as well*???" Liu Bei cried as he read the report.

"Wait: Cao killed an *imperial consort*...?" Jian Yong exclaimed.
"A... a *pregnant* imperial consort," Liu Bei replied miserably.
The news was met with fear, surprise and disgust.
"This man *is* another Dong Zhuo," Mi Fang said.
"This proves it," Mi Zhu agreed.
"I have caused the death of good men, an innocent girl and an unborn prince!" Liu Bei cried. "My actions here have-!"
"Stop that *right now*, Xuande!" Zhang Fei barked. "It's nothing that he wouldn't have done when he found out about the edict eventually anyway!"
"And our first concern should be preventing further loss," Mi Zhu said. "Cao's terrified of Yuan Shao, so he sends two mediocrities to face us, and they're not even rushing to get here so as to catch us off guard, the fools. We should dispatch this Liu Dai fellow quickly, as soon as his army arrives."
"Leave them to me," Zhang Fei declared.
"Should I hurry word of Wang Zhong's advance to Guan Yu...?" Mister Sun asked.
"He'll know," Liu Bei replied.

Messengers hurried news to Cao Cao's office a week later.
"...Both *defeated*," Cao Cao complained.
"I did try to warn you," Guo Jia sighed.
"At least they were captured rather than killed, Excellency," Xun Wenruo suggested.
"Do you think I want such useless men back???" Cao Cao retorted. "When I do have them returned to me, Wenruo, their first duty will be to go to the executioner for gross incompetence!"
"Neither man was a match for Guan Yu or Zhang Fei, and the outcome would have been the same if you'd done as I suggested and sent both to one location," Guo Jia said. "You do not send such men to fight champions."
"...So I am once again forced to make a snap decision," Cao Cao said. "Do I sit and await Yuan Shao's march from Ji that might never come, or do I attack Bei and recover Xu Province...?"
"Yuan Shao cannot and will not attack," Guo Jia insisted.
"But he might try if we dally," Xun Wenruo said. "If, as Fengxiao suggests, he does not know of Dong Cheng's collection of lies, then he will be content to sit in Yè, drink, and watch his advisers bicker as they always do. As soon as he learns of it – as soon as all of the other warlords learn of it – then we won't have manoeuvring room to attack Liu Bei."
"And we must be swift and merciless," Guo Jia suggested. "We must hit Xu Province on two fronts simultaneously: we must hit Xiaopei and break Bei's defences there, and at the same time we must hit Xiapi with full force and frighten the inhabitants into surrendering and giving us Guan Yu's head."
"...If it is at all possible, Fengxiao, I want him alive to serve me," Cao Cao admitted.
"He *hates you*!" Guo Jia said. "He craved Qin Yilu's wife, who-!"
"Who is now in my household, and part of my family," Cao Cao interrupted. "He will have to accept that. What worries me is the numbers: to hit Xiaopei and Xiapi simultaneously with all of the forces that we have at our immediate disposal will leave the capital exposed."

"There are no more seditionists," Guo Jia replied. "Yuan Shao will just sit there or he'll be stalled at the riverbank by Yu Jin or Liu Yan; and not waiting for Zang Ba will surprise Bei, as he'll expect any further attack to be months away from now. Hit him now, hit him hard, and *destroy him* so that he is no longer a threat."
"...This time, it shall really be as you suggest," Cao Cao said. "Who should go...?"
"Yue Jin and Dong Zhao have just sent a memorial and a tribute to the capital," Guo Jia replied. "Gongren intercepted an attempt by Zhang Yang's former subordinate, Sui Gu, to leave Henei and take his men to Yè. Yue Jin ambushed and defeated Sui Gu, sent us his head and added Sui's forces to his own after Gongren was able, as Zhang Yang's old friend and adviser, to persuade the rest to submit."
"That's the men that should go to Xu!" Cao Cao said excitedly.
"Take everyone that isn't guarding against Yuan Shao at the Yellow River," Guo Jia suggested. "Send so much that it will not only destroy Bei, but remind Zang Ba that he was wise to surrender to you and should not change his mind."
"...That's what we'll do!" Cao Cao replied. "Bei will be ground to meat paste! I want every available man mobilised at once!"

Cheng Yu was surprised by the next piece of correspondence that he received from Cao Cao.

> "Mister Cheng Zhongde,
>
> I am moving against Liu Bei, but I worry for your safety. You only have 700 men, and if Yuan Shao were to attack Juancheng you would be destroyed. I intend to send 2,000 men to you as I move toward Xu Province. Will that be enough?
>
> Cao Cao, Excellency of Works"

"...Wrong, wrong, wrong," Cheng Yu muttered as he took up a pen and prepared to send a reply that would reach Cao Cao on the eve of his march.

"Mister Cheng has said that I must not give him any other men," Cao Cao explained to his officials. "He says that a show of strength would lead to Yuan attacking him with a large force and destroying him, whereas Yuan would simply pass him by and leave himself exposed to a pincer or be apprehensive about attacking at all if the defences appear to be weak."
"And he's quite right," Guo Jia insisted. "Think no more about Juancheng: we'll be closer to that than to the Yellow River, which will be Yuan's target if he targets anything and doesn't just flounder. We must move at once!"
Cao Cao laughed and said, "And so we shall!"

****

107

Liu Bei's divided forces were utterly unprepared for what happened next, as none could have considered that Guo Jia's idea – that the capital should be left under the supervision of a small force led by Cao Ren while the entire army marched eastward at 'double-time' to attack both fronts at once – would ever be proffered or adopted.

"**REPORT!**" a battered messenger cried as he almost fell into the Xiaopei home of the self-appointed provincial governor Liu Bei.

"…What happened to you?" Liu Bei asked numbly.

"**Thousands, Lord Liu! THOUSANDS!**" the messenger screamed. "Th-they… **THOUSANDS…!**"

"…**Mister Sun! Mi Zhu! Yide!**" Liu Bei cried desperately. "**Where are they??? We have to do something!**"

"How he's done it, I don't know," Mi Zhu admitted as he addressed an emergency meeting in Liu Bei's military camp command tent a short time later. "But it's true: he's brought an army of thousands here, perhaps of half of what we thought he had. They'll be here in… I don't know, maybe hours."

"How did they sneak up on us like that???" Zhang Fei complained. "Where'd he get all these men from???"

"Then… then he *lied*… he must have an *enormous army*!" Liu Bei exclaimed. "How did he hide such an army from us when we were in Xuchang???"

"Or he's actually brought half of his army here," Mi Zhu replied. "We can't fight such a large- …Oh no."

"**What???**" Zhang Fei cried.

"…He can't have… he can't have sent a similarly sized force to the northeast, and struck at Xiapi as well?!" Mi Zhu fretted.

"Yunchang hasn't got a large enough army for that either!" Liu Bei said. "How can Cao Cao do this???"

"Does it bloody matter???" Zhang Fei replied. "Aren't we dead if we just sit here and talk about it???"

"But our families are in Xiapi!" Liu Bei said. "We can't lose them again! **How can this be happening again???**"

"They're on their way! We have no time to think about that!" Mi Zhu urged.

"…Then… then we fight," Liu Bei said. "We fight our way out, and-"

"**ENEMY ATTACK!**"

The response to the external cry was sudden panic.

"*Already*???" Liu Bei screamed.

"We have to leave, Lord Liu," Chen Dao said.

"I'll cover the rear!" Zhang Fei declared.

Liu Bei fled his command tent with Chen Dao's security force as his vanguard and Zhang Fei, Mister Sun, Mi Zhu and Mi Fang each taking up rear guard positions: the enemy force tore into the western side of the camp and killed or maimed any man that failed to surrender immediately.

"**NO MERCY!**" Qi Ji bellowed.

"**LIU BEI MUST BE FOUND!**" Han Hao ordered.

Cao Xiu, Xu Huang, Li Dian, Han Hao, Qi Ji, Qin Yi and a force of several thousand men and horse overwhelmed and all but flattened Liu Bei's camps.

"**East! Move east, toward Ju City!**" Liu Bei ordered.
"**No! We have to go *north*, Lord Liu, via the mountain roads!**" Mi Zhu retorted.
Liu Bei could see that Mi Zhu had a plan and did not argue.

The battle for Xiaopei was over within an hour; those that successfully fled with Liu Bei – and they numbered less than a hundred – were forced to move along treacherous mountain roads that a large army would not risk.
"Why north…?" Mi Fang asked. "Are we headed for Xiapi…?"
"We're not going to Xiapi… we daren't try," Mi Zhu replied. "We must go to Yè, and seek an audience with Yuan Shao. I've sent a man on to see if Yuan can take advantage of what's happening."
"But what of Yunchang… and our families…?" Liu Bei whimpered.
"…Yunchang'll be alright," Zhang Fei insisted. "He's smart, smarter than me… he'll do whatever has to be done."

Tian Feng received Liu Bei's latest messenger and hurried to the home of his lord Yuan Shao; the Commander-in-Chief made his adviser wait for almost half an hour before he agreed to speak to him, and he was noticeably forlorn when he finally invited Tian to the private study.
"What is it, Mister Tian…?" Yuan Shao sighed.
"Cao Cao has made a grave error, Lord Yuan, and the moment of victory is here!" Tian Feng said excitedly. "He's attacked Liu Bei with what sounds like his entire army!"
Yuan Shao frowned and said, "Nonsense."
"No, Lord, not 'nonsense'!" Tian Feng insisted. "We must capitalise on this at once and-!"
"I may hate Cao Cao, but I do not underestimate him," Yuan Shao interrupted. "He'd never do such a reckless thing, even if he didn't fear me. Look at the forces that he's placed along the Yellow River! How am I supposed to believe that he'd then abandon the capital to be attacked by the Qian Hill Bandits or the former Yellow Turbans that still haunt Runan as mercenaries, let alone me…?"
"But he has done so!" Tian Feng insisted. "He's gone mad, Lord Yuan… we know that he's murdered General Dong Cheng, and now we're hearing that he had Dong's daughter – a pregnant imperial consort – strangled to death in a room in the palace, in direct defiance of His Majesty's will!"
Yuan Shao was visibly perplexed.
"That's confirmed by trusted sources!" Tian Feng continued. "Cao must surely be considered the greatest villain under Heaven! Rumours of a secret edict abound, and that it was the edict that condemned Dong Cheng and the others and brought Cao's wrath down on Liu Bei!"
"I… I can't risk it," Yuan Shao said after a long pause. "My son is still sick, and-"
Tian Feng struck the ground at his feet with his staff and cried, "*Ayah*! This is a historic opportunity, perhaps the only one that we'll get! How can you throw it away for a sick child???"
"…You want me to abandon my family and jeopardise everything for rumours and suppositions?" Yuan Shao retorted. "Dong Zhuo had Jia Xu and Li Ru, and he did rather well; Cao Cao has Xun Yu, Xun Yòu, Guo Jia, Dong Zhao, Chen Qun, and goodness knows

how many more, and you expect me to believe that he'd be allowed to leave the capital undefended to fight an irrelevant wretch like Liu Bei, that not one of them would remonstrate...?"

"Perhaps they even suggested this stratagem, precisely because it is so risky!" Tian Feng said. "The information is good, my lord: march the army on two fronts, against Dong Prefecture to the east and to Yuanwu to the west, and His Majesty will be in Yè within a week and Cao Cao defeated within a month or less."

"...Such a grand endeavour requires my personal involvement, and I'll not leave my son," Yuan Shao said as he glanced sideways and met the judging gaze of his wife Lady Liu. "I'll permit the use of small detachments to harass his lines along the Yellow River and test his defences, but nothing more until I'm sure that he's as weak as the rumours – rumours that he himself might be responsible for – are proved correct. You may go and see to that now, Mister Tian... I should like to get back to my son now."

Tian Feng groaned disdainfully, got to his feet and left the house, muttering, "Why bother...? The moment is already gone!"

Guan Yu stared at the sea of men that were massed in front of the western gates of Xiapi City and grunted irritably; the generals' standards included Yue Jin, Zhu Ling, Zhang Liao, Wei Xu, Song Xian, Cao Hong and Excellency Cao Cao himself.

"You're not going to try and fight, are you, Yunchang...?" General of the Household Xu Dan asked. "The militia that we have in the city is barely adequate for such a task."

"I'm not a fool," Guan Yu replied. "You respect me, perhaps, for my military prowess, as many do, but you were part of the Chens' conspiracy to oust Lord Liu Xuande. I have to think of Lord Liu's wives when I act, and also of the city's inhabitants; they will not forgive me if I condemn them to a siege like that which I experienced at Haixi and, more relevantly, like that which they endured when Lü Bu refused to surrender not so long ago."

"...That is very true," Xu Dan admitted. "If nobody else threw the gates open after a week of that, I would do it myself."

"Though it pains me to do so, I surrender," Guan Yu continued. "Make that known to everyone so that we can avoid unnecessary hostage-taking and assassination attempts. Release Wang Zhong and return him to Cao Cao."

"I shall," Xu Dan replied.

Guan Yu turned to his 20-year-old son Ping and said, "You'll watch over our families for me."

"...You fear that Cao will kill you...?" Ping asked.

"No, but I shall be unable to do what I now ask of you," Guan Yu replied. "Can you do that, son...?"

"I am the son of Guan Yu," Guan Ping said.

Guan Yu smiled and said, "A good answer."

"Well, well... Guan Yunchang!" Cao Cao said as Guan Yu was brought before him.

"Governor Cao," Guan Yu replied with false politeness.

"**Governor???**" Cao Hong exclaimed. "**Cur! You will-**"

"Enough," Cao Cao insisted. "Guan Yunchang, you are defeated, and the people of Xiapi are now under my jurisdiction."

"I trust you will not massacre them this time," Guan Yu retorted.

Cao Cao stifled his rage, smiled, and said, "I will harm not a man, woman or child, Guan Yunchang; my past rage is satisfied, and perhaps regretted also. Yunchang, I have long admired you; I have heard of your valiant first action against the bully in your hometown... they speak of you as a hero in Xie County, a man of the highest moral values and strength that defies belief. Your battles with the Yellow Turbans are also impressive to hear of... choosing to reason, yet when you were pushed, you bested them against ridiculous odds. You are of a calibre matching my Xu Huang, my Xu Chu, my Zhang Liao and Li Dian... and yet you serve Liu Bei, who has now strayed from the light, following a falsified edict and rebelling against the court. It is truly sad that a man such as you should be fated thus."

"Spare me, Governor of Yan," Guan Yu scoffed. "I was in Xu when you slaughtered the innocents by the thousand... you claim to be a Zhang Liang, when you are, in fact, another Wang Mang, another Dong Zhuo, that covets all others' wealth and women and, no doubt, the throne as well."

"**I'll kill him!**" Cao Hong shrieked.

"You'll do nothing of the sort!" Cao Cao chuckled. "Yunchang is being his usual self... I understand. I receive the blows with dignity, and look forward to redeeming myself in his eyes."

Cao Hong harrumphed angrily.

Cao Cao turned to Guan Yu once again and said, "Yunchang, you are captured. Liu Bei... I do not know. Perhaps he is dead; perhaps he has fled north, in an effort to join Yuan Shao; but he can't run forever. You, too, have nowhere to run; what will you do...?"

"What would *you* have me do...?" Guan Yu retorted.

"I would have you surrender fully, and serve me," Cao Cao explained. "I would have you become a willing vassal of His Majesty once again, as you were when you quelled the Yellow Turbans and fought at my side against Lü Bu. Can you do that...?"

Guan Yu hummed thoughtfully and closed his eyes, but he did not reply to the question.

"... ... ...**Say something, you dog!**" Cao Hong bellowed.

Guan Yu opened his eyes, looked at Cao Hong, and harrumphed.

"*You*...! Mengde, why do you tolerate this from a defeated general?" Cao Hong pleaded. "He should *die*, as Lü Bu did!"

"It is unfair to compare my former master to Guan Yunchang," Zhang Liao suggested. "Lü Bu was the opposite of Guan Yunchang in every way, save strength... Lü Bu knew nothing of loyalty, morals or conviction, and he was a coward at the critical hour. I am ashamed that I must admit that I ever knew him."

"...All the same, Guan should die for his insolence!" Cao Hong said with anger as he pointed at Guan Yu, who was calm in contrast.

"Will you challenge me to a duel, cousin of Cao Cao...?" Guan Yu taunted. "Or will you simply behead me here, while I am defenceless, since that will be easy for you...?"

Cao Hong was too angry to respond.

"How can you be so confident, Guan Yu?" Wei Xu heckled. "You're a nobody now!"

"As Governor Cao has said, I am a hero in the world," Guan Yu retorted. "Killing me now cannot undo my exploits thus far... I can die here having done enough. What have *you* done, Lü Bu's self-serving cousin, that you call me a 'nobody'...?"

Wei Xu scowled silently.

"Enough, please!" Cao Cao chuckled. "Guan Yunchang is not to be challenged. Yunchang, you may answer when you are ready."

"I am ready *now*," Guan Yu replied. "I will surrender, but only according to certain terms."

Cao Hong laughed disbelievingly and said, "You dare set *terms*???"

Cao Cao hushed his cousin with a gesture before turning back to Guan Yu and asking, "What terms…?"

"It shall obviously be understood that I 'surrender' to His Majesty, not to you," Guan Yu began. "I already tender my service to His Majesty, in fact, so nothing has changed… but I will take your word as His Majesty's will until such time as I know otherwise or perform adequate feats to demand release from that service. When I demand that release, I will be free to pursue my own path. I also insist that any of the families of vassals of Lord Liu Xuande that you have in your custody will be placed under my care, and that they will be free to go when my service has ended."

"And where would you go…?" Cao Cao wondered.

"If Lord Liu Xuande is alive, I will go to him," Guan Yu replied. "If he is dead, then by staying, I would be in the immediate service of his killer; if you would have me do that, would *you* then be content to serve Governor Tao Qian, were he alive…?"

Cao Cao stifled anger before he replied, "I could not."

"I would seek a quiet life somewhere perhaps, or choose another lord," Guan Yu continued. "The families of vanquished men would not wish to stay either, for certain, and I would devote my life to their care, to atone for my failure to hold this city."

Cao Cao sighed and said, "You are truly a man of conviction, sure of every word you say, and strong in the face of great peril; I cannot truly rebuke any of your terms, and in exchange for your undoubtedly marvellous service… I accept them all."

"Do not do this," Cao Hong said. "He shows *contempt*! Do not-"

"**My word is final!**" Cao Cao snapped. "Guan Yunchang, I have accepted your terms… do you yield…?"

"I 'yield' to nobody but His Majesty," Guan Yu replied defiantly. "I acknowledge your acceptance of my terms, and offer myself to the empire, answering only to you until such time as I have rendered great service, and can honourably take my leave."

Many of Cao Cao's retainers were visibly and audibly irritated at Guan Yu's haughty attitude.

Cao Cao bowed slightly, and said, "It shall be so."

And with those words, one of the most bizarre – if short-lived – alliances of the era was formed: Guan Yu – whose friend and lord, Liu Bei, had been routed and, so far as he knew, perhaps killed by Cao Cao, and whose intended consort, Lady Du, was now in Cao Cao's harem – was now forced to serve as a vanguard general in Cao's army. Liu Bei, meanwhile, continued his journey to Ji Province, unaware that Guan Yu was now, by circumstance, fighting for his sworn enemy, and that the two would soon be on opposing sides in one of the most famous battles of the age.

****

108

General Yu Jin was surprised when a scout ran into his Yan Ford camp command tent and said, "Yuan Shao's forces are attacking!"

"*Ayah*... we only have two thousand men!" Yu Jin exclaimed. "How many has he sent? What great generals command them...?"

"I don't know, there's maybe... maybe a thousand men, I don't know!" the scout replied. "The officers' standards read 'Sui Yuanjin', 'Lü Weihuang', 'Hè Mao', 'Wang Mo'-"

"Either Yuan Shao's stupid, or this is part of some larger scheme," Yu Jin mused. "They're none of them his best officers... I've never heard of most of them. Where's Yan Liang, Wen Chou, Zhang Hè...? ...Wait, I don't have time for this. Help me with my armour!"

Yu Jin led an elite force of infantry and cavalry to counter the attack by Yuan Shao's suspiciously small army: their robust defence was reported to Tian Feng and Guo Tu, who then reported it to Yuan Shao.

"The men have retreated to their camps on the northern bank," Tian Feng said glumly.

"*Aha*! I can hear it in your voice, Mister Tian: you were *wrong*!" Yuan Shao heckled.

"I was *not wrong*!" Tian Feng protested. "You threw an egg at a rock! The officers had at best the same number of men, and they were attacking a well-defended camp full of rested men on unfamiliar ground! Furthermore, it's *Yu Jin*, one of Cao's champions, guarding the ground south of Yan Ford, and you sent the likes of *Wang Mo*?"

"Wang Mo served well during the campaigns against the Bandits and Gongsun Zan!" Guo Tu said. "You're just covering your own-!"

"Enough," Yuan Shao chuckled. "I'm just glad that I didn't leave my son for this nonsense. We'll make more preparations and attack when Cao isn't trying to bait us with false shows of weakness. Yan Ford's defences will be the norm, I imagine."

"Attack again, but with a proper army!" Tian Feng pleaded. "Do that, Lord Yuan, before Cao can return to Guandu, and we'll have a clear path to-!"

"The men will hold their positions, and we'll attack when I sense the time to be right," Yuan Shao said with a menacing tone. "Your constant objections to whatever I say are starting to grate, Tian Feng; go back to your duties."

Guo Tu smirked at Tian Feng, who bowed low and retreated from the private meeting room without another word.

"...To think that I almost committed my entire army!" Yuan Shao chortled. "No, no... Cao Cao is too clever to risk it all... far too... clever..."

But Yuan Shao was haunted: something told him that there might have been some truth in the information that Tian Feng had brought to him, and that an opportunity had not only been squandered but turned into an opportunity for Cao Cao to gain an otherwise implausible advantage. He knew, though, that only time would tell.

Cao Cao finished listening to a report on Yuan Shao's obvious test of Yan Ford's defences and laughed; Guo Jia dismissed the messenger and asked, "What will you do, I wonder...?"

"Yuan's lost his nerve!" Cao Cao cackled. "What else can I do but play on his timidity with a genuine scare! Gongda: fetch Yue Jin!"

"...A sound choice," Guo Jia said as Xun Gongda left the command tent. "In the meantime, you'll be marching: where, I wonder...?"

"I must report to the court in Xuchang before I return to Guandu," Cao Cao replied. "It's obvious that I won't be attacked by this pathetic drunk, not yet at least: but just to make sure, I'll have Yu Jin and Yue Jin smash all of his main camps along the river to impede any more attempts to harass me. I'll go back to Guandu immediately after my report."

"I agree completely," Guo Jia said. "I have no suggestions."

Cao Cao frowned and asked, "None...? So you don't worry about Juancheng, or Meng Ford, or...?"

"Liu Biao didn't move; the mercenaries in Runan didn't move; the Qian Hill Bandits didn't move; nobody moved except Yuan Shao, who might as well have coughed or scratched his leg for the amount of damage it did us," Guo Jia replied. "We'll have Zang Ba's friends intensify their harassment campaign in Qing Province, maybe, but besides that I can offer nothing."

"...Excellent," Cao Cao murmured. "I almost pity the senile fool..."

The short, stocky Yue Jin took an army of 4,000 men and travelled back to the southern bank of the Yellow River, where he met with his triumphant colleague Yu Jin at the gates of the Yan Ford camp. "His Excellency couldn't be happier, Wenze," Yue Jin said. "As you can see, I've been sent here for us both to do some serious damage to Yuan Shao now. The men are happy after our victory over Liu Bei, and they're keen to do more."

"Then let's waste no time, Wenqian!" Yu Jin replied. "Once every man and horse has had a brief rest and some food, let's strike all of Yuan's encampments!"

Yu Jin left 1,000 of his men to guard the Yan Ford base and, together with Yue Jin, led the 5,000-strong army to the nearest enemy camp.

"**Cao Cao's army's actually attacking us!**" a captain said to his commanding officer, General Hè Mao. "**We're outnumbered at least three-to-one!**"

"**Don't let them overrun us!**" Hè Mao ordered. "**Every one of us is worth ten of theirs!**"

But Hè Mao's rhetoric could not turn the battle in his favour: Yu Jin and Yue Jin had ordered their seasoned infantry and cavalrymen to be merciless to any that would not surrender, and the fatalities quickly mounted.

"**We have to retreat northward!**" Hè Mao decided.

"**By all means, your body can go northward!**" Yu Jin shouted as he charged at Hè Mao. "**But your head's going to Guandu for inspection!**"

Hè Mao barely survived Yu Jin's attack; he turned about and fled while Cao's forces continued their assault on his decimated army.

"**He'll warn the next camp,**" Yu Jin said to a cavalry captain. "**We'll need to pursue until there's nobody left.**"

Hè Mao was only able to give an hour's warning, at best,

to the neighbouring camp: Yu Jin had wasted no time, and the carnage was repeated.

"**We're not equipped for this!**" General Wang Mo complained.

"**Lü Weihuang and Lü Kuang are too far away,**" Hè Mao replied. "**We should regroup with Sui Yuanjin and join Jiang Yiqu to the north!**"

The generals and their weary, frightened men defied the attacking forces, but their morale was spent following the failed attack on Yan Ford a week earlier; Yu Jin was now on the offensive after a fearsome show of defensive skill, and that left the northern men without hope.

"**Show no mercy!**" Yu Jin ordered. "**Let Yuan Shao know that he is doomed!**"

Headless corpses were piling up as the Han forces collected the customary trophies; Hè Mao fled with Wang Mo, leaving another camp to be reduced to smouldering ruins.

"**Keep moving!**" Yue Jin ordered. "**We're not done yet!**"

A day later, an exhausted Wang Mo reached General Sui Yuanjin's camp with less than a dozen men; he had witnessed the destruction of over a dozen camps and lost contact with his colleague Hè Mao.

"...*Ayah*... what happened...?" Sui Yuanjin asked. "You're covered in gore, and your horse is close to death! What's going on?"

"They've... they've stopped, perhaps to rest... I was beginning to wonder if... if they were demons," Wang Mo replied. "They... they've destroyed everything south of here, General Sui...!"

"*Aiee*...! We're exposed, then, if we stay here!" Sui Yuanjin exclaimed. "We have to go north to Ji, and-!"

"They're... they're frenzied, and they're obviously tasked with getting rid of every camp on the southern bank of the river... we'll not survive if we try and fight," Wang Mo insisted. "They've taken hundreds, maybe thousands of heads, and we'll lose ours if we don't cross the river and get to Huojia."

"...That's a defeatist attitude, but I can understand that I suppose," Sui Yuanjin replied. "Alright: I'll hold the ground here while you-"

"I'll hold ground," Wang Mo insisted. "You get to Huojia and warn Lord Yuan of what's happening. You're rested... you'll make it."

More survivors of the camp attacks were starting to arrive, but Wang Mo and Sui Yuanjin knew that they would soon be followed by the attackers.

"Go," Wang Mo said. "I'll keep going north if I can, to warn the camps going toward Ji. Go on!"

Sui Yuanjin fled the camp and crossed the river while Wang Mo did his best to warn and defend the remaining camps; Yu Jin and Yue Jin completed their task, incinerating another dozen camps and taking heads or prisoners where necessary. Wang Mo was one of many who eventually surrendered.

★★★★★★★★★★★★

558

109

Cao Cao's return to the capital was met with surprise: his newfound lack of accountability meant that many were unaware that he had even left, never mind to go on a campaign with the entire army. An urgent meeting of the Imperial court was arranged – the first since Dong Cheng's plot had been foiled – so that the Excellency of Works could explain his actions before he sped northward to Guandu. Emperor Xian was like a ghost: he had none of his usual calmness and dry wit, and he could barely bring himself to meet the gaze of the man that had so recently defied his will and killed one of his pregnant consorts.

"I am newly returned from Xu Province, where I have dealt a fatal blow to the traitor Liu Bei, and appointed Dong Zhao – a very capable man, and former subordinate of the loyal Zhang Yang that toiled to rebuild the palace in Luoyang – as the acting Governor, pending approval to have him take the role properly," Cao Cao reported. "As many of you will now be aware, Liu Bei sieged Xiapi, murdered the appointed Governor Che Zhou and established an independent regime, citing in his own defence that he had been granted the permanent governorship on two separate occasions… the first by Tao Qian – which many in Xu can testify as being 'not verifiable by a long way', if not an outright lie – and then by Yuan Shao, who had – and has – no right to bestow titles."

"Such behaviour is intolerable," Wang Lang said. "He's obviously as disloyal and destructive as his school-friend Gongsun Zan turned out to be."

Kong Rong got to his feet and said, "So Liu Bei is dead…?"

"There has been no word of his capture, nor has there been word of a sighting since he was routed at Xiaopei," Cao Cao replied. "It is my understanding that the force in Xiaopei was very thorough. But I had good cause to be thorough: he murdered Che Zhou, and when Liu Dai and Wang Zhong were sent to demand that he surrendered without fuss, he ambushed them, destroyed their forces and took them prisoner."

"And what of those generals now…?" Kong Rong asked.

"Both men are returned to us, but their incompetence is unforgivable," Cao Cao said with a sigh. "Wang Zhong is particularly embarrassing, and so he will face execution for-"

"I beseech you, Excellency, not to do that," Kong Rong interrupted. "If, as rumours suggest, a war with the duplicitous Yuan Shao is imminent, then you will need every man you have. Have him atone with service."

There were many muted voices that agreed with Kong Rong, and Cao Cao could sense it.

"…He shall be spared as you suggest," Cao Cao said. "But the time for talking is over: Yuan Shao continues to amass troops at provincial borders in a threatening manner, Jing Governor Liu Biao had ceased friendly communications with the capital, and word now reaches me that there is unrest in Runan."

"Not the Yellow Turbans…!" Wang Lang exclaimed.

"It might well be, but the news is patchy at present," Cao Cao replied. "Yuan Shao's brother employed them in his own treacherous gambit, so why would Yuan Shao not do so…?"

"So Yuan *Shao* plots sedition now," Zhong Yao prompted.

"What else?" Cao Cao replied. "But he will regret it... he will, and so will Liu Biao, Jia Xu, Zhang Xiu and anyone else that is fool enough to ally with him."

Cao Cao left the meeting and returned to the chancellery, where more news awaited him.

"It's amazing, isn't it, how busy a day can become!" Cao Cao chuckled. "What news from Yan Ford, Wenruo...?"

"Yu Jin has sped word of a series of routs along the riverbank," Xun Wenruo explained. "Yuan's forces were repelled to the northern bank, with every camp from Yan Ford to Boma being left a ruin, and... and..."

"...And...?" Guo Jia prompted.

"...And they intend to pursue the enemy across the river to Huojia," Xun Wenruo said. "This was sent before the attempt."

"They'll be fine," Guo Jia insisted. "Yu Jin and Yue Jin are two of the best generals that we have, Wenruo, and Yuan's feeble men are no match for ours. I expect that we'll receive word of their continued success within a day or so."

"And when we do, I want a camp set up at Yuanwu and an attack made on Dushi Ford, as you suggested," Cao Cao ordered. "It's better defended than the others, but a sudden, unexpected attack will break it and leave Yuan Shao wondering what happened."

"By the time that we get to Guandu, half of the battle will have already been won," Guo Jia suggested.

The lord of Wan City, Zhang Xiu, summoned his adviser Jia Xu and said, "Cao's intensified his attacks on us."

"He has, and unsurprisingly so," Jia Xu replied. "My lord, the news from the east is not good for us: Liu Bei has tried – and failed – to take Xu Province and defy Cao Cao, while this province's governor, Liu Biao, has 'secretly' decided to side with Yuan Shao in the upcoming battle between Yè and Xuchang. Sui Gu's dead, and the Henei forces absorbed into Cao's, who is also courting the Qiang warlords with apparent success."

"*Aiee*... so... so we *must* pick a side...?" Zhang Xiu said.

"I'm glad that you responded in that way," Jia Xu replied. "You now understand, as I do, that we cannot automatically side with Yuan Shao because of our past 'disagreements' with Cao Cao. In fact, I suggest that we surrender to the Xuchang court at the soonest opportunity."

"...But won't Cao simply kill me and start molesting my aunt again...?" Zhang Xiu asked plainly.

"He's learned his lesson," Jia Xu insisted. "The tone of his letters says as much. He'll not touch Lady Zou again, and he'll spare you because he needs the men that you command, men like Huche'er, in his fight against Yuan Shao's much larger army."

"...And he'll want you as well, for certain," Zhang Xiu supposed.

Jia Xu rubbed his bearded chin and said, "I doubt he'll want the man that made a king out of Dong Zhuo and killed his heir and bodyguard, but my perceived role – and that of your uncle – in the extermination of the Yuan clan in Luoyang won't endear us to Yuan Shao either, will it...? And now we're caught in a pincer between Liu Biao – who still resents us – and Yuan, who are now allies. We haven't much time."

Zhang Xiu exhaled loudly and said, "Write to Cao at once."

Yuan Shao's camp at Dushi Ford had been reinforced in the wake of the attacks on Huojia and the camps on the southern bank; Jiang Yiqu, Sui Yuanjin, Lü Kuang and Lü Weihuang kept the base on full alert at all times, but none truly believed that such a reckless effort would be undertaken.
"In fact," Lü Kuang said as the generals discussed matters on one glum afternoon, "I reckon that we should have been given the order to retaliate, since they must be completely spent. Where are the proper orders…? Why haven't Yan Liang, Wen Chou, Zhang-"
"You're implying that we're incapable of dealing with one or two of Cao's mangy generals," Jiang Yiqu interrupted. "Let them come here when they've rested! The camps that they attacked were understaffed, demoralised, ill-advised, unprepared and isolated: we're none of those things!"
"We're isolated," Sui Yuanjin said. "We have no adviser either."
"We're ready for them, which is all that matters!" Jiang Yiqu insisted. "They'll never get close to us without-"
Jiang Yiqu was interrupted by a sudden commotion outside the tent; a messenger ran into the tent moments later and shouted, "**ENEMY ATTACK!**"
"**What???**" Jiang Yiqu exclaimed. "**That's *impossible*!**"
"**Do they not need *food, sleep*???**" Sui Yuanjin complained as he hurriedly tried to put his helmet on. "**What way are they coming from?**"
"***Everywhere*!**" the messenger replied.
Yu Jin and Yue Jin had split their army – which still numbered close to 5,000 – into four and surrounded the camp. The unguarded ring of outer camps – a sea of tents that was supposed to provide ample warning in additional defence for the fenced inner camp – was already in flames, and many of the infantrymen that Yuan's officers were depending upon for victory were already dead or seriously injured.
"**We're already finished!**" Lü Weihuang cried. "**This is *humiliating*! Lord Yuan will probably execute us for-!**"
"**Worry about that later!**" Jiang Yiqu barked. "**Let's survive so that we can beg for a chance to redeem ourselves!**"
Yuan Shao's officers fought their way out of the Dushi Ford camp and fled the region, leaving Yu Jin and Yue Jin's forces with a small supply depot, thousands of enemy prisoners and yet another unexpected victory.
"**Back to Yuanwu!**" Yue Jin said. "**But let nobody doubt who won here today, and who will win in the end!**"
The soldiers chanted: some chanted for their generals, others chanted for the Han, but most chanted for their lord Cao Cao.

"**This is *ridiculous*!**" Yuan Shao screamed as he read the reports from the Yellow River. "**It is also *intolerable*!**"
The vast majority of Yuan Shao's court was silent and desperate to distance itself from Tian Feng, who sighed angrily and said, "You didn't listen to Ju Shou and I, that's why this has happened! We said that you should-!"
"**Listen to *what*???**" Yuan Shao retorted. "**Which advice am I guilty of not heeding??? Do I hear the silken tones of a man**

that advocated doing nothing when Cao Cao was powerless, and then wanted to engage him only when he had established impenetrable defences???"

Tian Feng exhaled loudly.

"If only that was the only noise you ever made, Tian Feng!" Yuan Shao continued. "Who is it that said 'Do Liu Bei a favour', mm...? That's the advice heeded – yours and Ju Shou's – and look what doing him a favour has done! All of my riverside camps are now ash, thousands dead, generals and men captured and killed!"

Tian Feng shook his head and said, "Only because you sent a weak force, Lord Yuan! If you had sent your entire army as Ju Shou and I suggested, then-!"

"They'd have all *drowned*, probably!" Yuan Shao heckled. "Oh yes, what good fortune I've had by siding with *Liu Bei*! I've got that fool coming here to Yè now: he'll be here in a few days, and him being the hex that he is, he'll probably cause the city to sink into a hole in the ground and my army to turn into beans!"

"...So are we to refuse him...?" Tian Feng asked calmly.

"No, no... I want to hear more about this 'Girdle Edict', since I need to get more to my side," Yuan Shao replied. "I need Sun Ce, and I need Liu Biao to be doing more than sitting there, especially now that Cao's said to be making peace with *Zhang Xiu*."

"I don't believe that's possible!" Chunyu Qiong said. "Zhang and his evil adviser, Jia Xu, are criminals, former Dong Zhuo collaborators that murdered his son!"

"Cao Cao's not to be underestimated," Xu Yòu said.

"What a surprise, *you* saying that," Xun Chen heckled. "You flatter our enemy at every opportunity!"

"How am I flattering him by suggesting that he'd ally with the likes of them?" Xu Yòu retorted. "Stop taking every opportunity to make cheap slights when-!"

"**STOP IT!**" Yuan Shao screamed. "**STOP IT! I...!** I... I need you to stop bickering and advise me, gentlemen! I have lost a valuable morale advantage... what must I do...?"

Tian Feng tried to answer, but the court was soon drowned in the noise of conflicting and contradictory arguments between the dozens of officials that Yuan Shao now had; the lord of the northeast slumped forward, groaned miserably, and awaited the right moment to try and demand silence once again.

The majority of Cao Cao's officials were shocked when Zhang Xiu's desire to surrender was reported to the main camp at Guandu.

"Perfect timing!" Cao Cao said. "Now we have Guan Yu in the vanguard and Jia Xu for advice."

"My, my... what a motley crew we have aboard this rickety ship!" Guo Jia joked. "First, Liu Bei's loyal 'brother', and now we have Dong Zhuo's schemer..."

"I know you're teasing, else I'd rebuke you," Cao Cao chuckled. "I shall have to return to Wan and accept his surrender personally."

"You just got back here," Xiahou Dun said. "Aren't you tired?"

"I must do this, Yuanrang," Cao Cao replied. "It will prove my reformed ways to Zhang Xiu and Guan Yu in one stroke."

"...You're so keen to impress Guan Yu," Xiahou Dun complained.

"If I can prove that I am a worthy lord, Yuanrang, then he will forget Liu Bei and serve me sincerely, and I will have another great general," Cao Cao explained. "I have future champions in Yue Jin, Xu Huang, Li Dian, Yu Jin and Zhang Liao, but I have a champion of today in Guan Yu. He actually survived a duel with Lü Bu, and none of my officers can match his abilities yet: yes, he's rude to those he disrespects, but he is a hero to the fighting men because of his skill, strength, honesty and generosity. He's a man that we must try and win over."

"And Jia Xu...?" Xun Wenruo asked. "Members of my family – members of almost every noble family in the land – were slaughtered by Dong Zhuo. I've heard the arguments: 'Jia Xu was not there, it was Li Ru', and 'Nobody tells Dong Zhuo not to commit evil acts'... Dong Zhuo could only do those things because of Jia Xu's scheming."

"His time as adviser to the regents paints a different picture, that of a man who is aware that his choice of master was flawed," Cao Cao retorted. "He'll now serve the Han properly, as he obviously wishes, and with his great mind on our side, how can we lose a battle of wits against a fool like Yuan Shao...? With Guan Yu in our vanguard, how can he beat us on the battlefield...?"

"But what if Liu Bei survived...?" Cheng Yu asked.

"...I admit that would be a problem," Cao Cao replied. "If he turns up alive, then we must do all that we can to supress the fact for as long as we can, in order to get as much service from Guan as possible before we lose him."

"By 'lose', I hope you mean 'kill'," Xiahou Dun grumbled.

"...I cannot do that," Cao Cao said. "He is too much respected."

Guo Jia coughed uncomfortably and said, "I agree with your recruitment of Jia Xu, especially since you'll need advisers in the years to come and I won't necessarily be here."

"Only because you insist on destroying yourself, you fool!" Chen Qun cried.

Guo Jia laughed and said, "I cannot do anything else. At thirty, I have seen everything this tedious, repetitive world has to offer. Life is boring, and the only things that make it even slightly bearable are also fatal. That's Heaven's fault, not mine."

"...Do not talk of your life as being short, Fengxiao," Cao Cao pleaded. "I need you to finish our great task."

"These men – and Jia Xu – will be there," Guo Jia replied. "Now, to move on, if we may...? If you insist on leaving here to meet this man in Nan County, then do so now while Yuan Shao is reeling from his recent defeats and the news of our action in Xu: go there, do what you must to earn their trust, and return at once, leaving them in Nan County to prevent Liu Biao – on the off-chance that relic should actually decide to do something – from being able to properly coordinate with Yuan Shao."

"More wisdom," Chen Qun said. "If only you'd learn to love life..."

"Indeed," Xun Wenruo sighed.

"It shall be as you say, Fengxiao," Cao Cao promised. "I'll leave at once: ready my carriage."

Over two years had passed since Cao Cao had fled from Nan County; he stared at the scenery as he travelled and pondered the events that had led to his earlier defeat.

"Are you alright, Master Cao Cao...?" Xu Chu asked suddenly.

"Mm...? ...Oh, yes, yes I'm fine, Xu Chu," Cao Cao replied. "I met

you just before I came to Nan County last time, didn't I...? ...I had
Dian Wei then. I must show him the proper respect... and Ang,
and Anmin too."
"...Your son was very brave," Xu Chu said.
"He was," Cao Cao replied as he thought of Ang's last noble deed.
"He... was."

Zhang Xiu and Jia Xu met Cao Cao at the gates of Wan City: they
were surrounded by guards that wore no armour, and an official
carried the Administrator's seal, which was wrapped in silk and
mounted on a wooden tray. Cao Cao was not wearing armour or
carrying a sword as he approached Zhang Xiu, took his hands and
said, "Last time, Mister Zhang, I was rude, disrespectful, and
brought misfortune on myself. This time I am a better man."
"I would prefer that we forgot past transgressions," Zhang Xiu
replied uneasily.
Xu Chu looked at the cautious Huche'er and smiled cheerfully.
"I insist that we have a banquet that I will pay for," Cao Cao
continued. "There will be no prostitutes, no rowdiness... just
civilised men enjoying a drink and good conversation. After that,
Mister Zhang – *Administrator* Zhang – you must forgive that I
must leave you and return to Guandu."
Jia Xu hid a smile.
"You came all this way... for a banquet, Excellency...?" Zhang Xiu
exclaimed.
"I 'came all this way', Administrator, because I am aware that I
wronged you before and had to be seen to do things right this
time," Cao Cao replied. "You have a daughter, do you not...? When
she and my son Jun are both of the right age, they should be
married, so that our houses are one."
Zhang Xiu frowned silently.
"...You still do not trust me," Cao Cao sighed. "Please, ask your
man to take your seal of office back to where it belongs...? I have
already made it clear that I do not want it."
Zhang Xiu turned to his aides and ordered them to retreat to his
office with the Administrator's seal.
"If I may," Cao Cao said hesitantly, "I... I shall mention Lady Zou
once and once only, just to say that I was wrong to approach her
in the way that I did, and I apologise for the offence that I
caused."
"It is difficult to ascertain which aspects of your relationship that
she found problematic, for she prefers not to speak of it," Zhang
Xiu replied. "I am truly sorry that our last encounter cost you your
heir and so many trusted men."
"We have both lost things," Cao Cao said. "Let's strive for accord
from now on."
Jia Xu was silently pleased: he knew that Cao Cao's apparent
redemption – whether it was false or true – was an indication that
he was trying to forge future alliances. Jia Xu could sense that he
would one day be approached to serve in Cao's court, and that
was exactly what he wanted.

* * * * * * * * * * * *

110

Yuan Shao met the remnants of Liu Bei's army at the gates of Yè City: Bei was visibly mortified and angry.

"I tried to send support as soon as your man arrived, but the way was blocked and it was already too late to save you," Yuan Shao explained. "Nobody expected Cao Cao to do what he did."

"His advisers are obviously extraordinary thinkers that are prepared to take ridiculous risks," Liu Bei replied. "In this case, Commander-in-Chief, the risk was worth it for them. I know that you did what you could."

Yuan Shao was noticeably awkward: Liu Bei's allies suspected that he might be inwardly guilt-ridden and felt foolish for having failed to act when Liu Bei had originally asked him to.

"What do you hope for now, Mister Liu?" Guo Tu asked.

"Nothing more than working in concert with Commander-in-Chief Yuan in order to bring about the end of the villain Cao Cao," Liu Bei replied. "I am willing to do whatever it takes: I will do whatever I am asked to do and go wherever I am asked to go. I am Commander-in-Chief Yuan's ally and subordinate."

Yuan Shao nodded and said, "I appreciate your humble support in this grand endeavour, Mister Liu. As you may or may not be aware, I have suffered some… 'setbacks', shall we say, against Cao Cao, primarily because I lack a mandate that satisfies the more recalcitrant or ambivalent elements in our fractured nation."

"…I don't like this idiot already," Zhang Fei grumbled quietly.

"Don't make that too obvious, Yide," Jian Yong whispered.

"…I see," Liu Bei said as Guo Tu finished detailing the losses at the Yellow River. "I have lost my finest warrior, my 'brother' Guan Yunchang, who was isolated at Xiapi: I have had no word of him, so I can only assume that he was captured or… or killed."

Liu Bei's eyes filled with tears.

"That's unfortunate," Yuan Shao sighed.

"But… but his sacrifice, along with the others who have been taken from our cause, is not in vain," Liu Bei insisted. "Your 'mandate' will be strengthened by what we can tell the nation about Cao Cao: if we were to make the 'Girdle Edict' public knowledge, who would want to stand with the villain…?"

Yuan Shao hid an involuntary smile as he said, "I have heard stories of an edict; you were said to be a signatory in the alliance that intended to act upon this edict. You and your closest aides should come with me to my private meeting room, so that you might fully enlighten me."

Liu Bei bowed humbly and turned to his allies.

"I won't be wanted at the meeting," Zhang Fei supposed.

"Yide: you and Mi Fang should take what's left of our poor army and set up a small camp outside Yè, somewhere that Commander-in-Chief Yuan can have us carefully watched," Liu Bei ordered. "I say that not just because he might have reservations about us… I say it because some of our men came from Cao Cao, and we must be jointly cautious. Mister Sun, Mister Jian, Mister Mi Zhu: you shall accompany me… Commander Yuan, may my security force accompany me…?"

Guo Tu harrumphed.

"I trust you," Yuan Shao promised. "Now you must join me, you, your advisers, and yes, bring your security, for I have my own that I never part with, as no sensible lord should! Let us plan Cao's destruction together!"

Zhang Fei watched Liu Bei and Yuan Shao's withdrawal to the meeting hall of the latter's mansion and said, "I'm worried about Yunchang."

"...I cannot believe that he is dead," Mi Fang replied. "But why have we heard nothing...? Where is he...?"

"AAAAGH! Such defences!" Zhu Ling cried as he retreated in the wake of a series of failed attempts to break Guan Yu's guard; a large number of junior officers and soldiers looked on in awe of the contests of strength that were taking place between the champions of the day.

"Truly impressive, Guan Yunchang," Xu Huang said.

Guan Yu nodded silently.

"Have you no manners?" Xiahou Dun heckled as he watched from the side of the makeshift arena. "You were just complimented by a Han officer, you vagrant! Bloody say something! Show some gratitude!"

"...Don't call me a vagrant, Xiahou Dun," Guan Yu replied icily. "I have had a number of homes; my last was in Xu until circumstance forced me to vacate it."

Xiahou Dun started to advance, but Xu Huang hurried to his side and restrained him.

"...You intended to attack me, Xiahou Dun?" Guan Yu chuckled. "Your colleague has two eyes and more skill than you ever had, and he didn't land a single blow. What did you hope to achieve?"

"BASTARD!" Xiahou Dun screamed. **"I LOST MY EYE PROTECTING YOUR TREACHEROUS, MAT-WEAVING PEASANT MASTER LIU BEI!"**

"You lost it fighting Gao Shun, your cause at the time being to protect Xu Province, ironically enough," Guan Yu retorted. "To try and blame Lord Liu for your misfortune is petty and ridiculous."

"That's enough, both of you," Han Hao ordered. "General Guan, you are right to say that your master is blameless; General Xiahou, you are right to be distressed, but your anger is not aimed at the right men."

"Maybe you're right," Xiahou Dun growled. "Maybe I should ask Mengde if I can have Zhang Liao and the rest of Bu's generals for target practice."

Zhang Liao smiled and said, "I thought that we were all on the same side now, General Xiahou."

"...We are," Xiahou Dun grumbled. "...I'm going."

"Do as you please," Guan Yu retorted. "It's not as though you can do much beyond heckling, is it...?"

Xiahou Dun pointed at Guan Yu and tried to mouth words, but no sound emanated save for hoarse croaking; anger and distress enveloped him, and he walked away with his fists clenched tightly.

"I should like to try and challenge you again soon, Yunchang," Zhang Liao said.

"Of course," Guan Yu replied. "You broke my guard, if only briefly: still, that's no surprise. You were Lü Bu's second, and only the most impressive warrior could achieve such a status."

Zhang Liao bowed and said, "You are too kind."

Guan Yu smiled, turned to Xu Huang, and said, "General Zhu Ling was unable to break my defence, but I imagine that he'll learn once he has studied me further, for he is a true warrior; you, I think, might already know how, for I saw how you watched our bout. Would you like to try…?"

Xu Huang readied his halberd and said, "I should like to try, Guan Yunchang."

Guan Yu and Xu Huang began a cautious bout with their long-handled training weapons: each man studied the other intently, looking for an opening; it was Xu Huang who made the first move, and after a series of strikes, he managed to tap Guan Yu's right arm with the butt of his halberd. Guan Yu backed away rather than exploit an obvious hole in Xu Huang's own defences; Zhang Liao noted it and hummed thoughtfully.

"Very good!" Guan Yu chuckled. "I shall have to improve upon my right-side defence, Xu Gongming!"

The bout resumed: Guan Yu took the initiative this time, and Xu Huang was forced to defend against a relentless series of attacks that broke his guard on several occasions, though Guan Yu did not capitalise on a single opportunity.

"…I… give up…!" Xu Huang panted.

"Impressive… only Lü Bu has impressed me more," Zhang Liao admitted.

"I am no match for you, Yunchang, and surely never will be," Xu Huang lamented.

"Perhaps, perhaps not, but I knew nothing once," Guan Yu said. "You broke my guard this time, did you not…?"

"Once," Xu Huang replied. "You're very formidable, Yunchang. I could not hit you with the bladed end, such is your skill. I know that I also left myself open to make my strike, but that you did not exploit it. I have much to learn from you."

"And Zhang Wenyuan is a man that you can learn from as well," Guan Yu said. "In life, a man must sometimes place himself at risk for a cause, and that's what you did: hitting me was more important than maintaining your own defence. Sometimes that's reckless; sometimes, it's what's necessary to give openings to others. Our business is to work as a team, achieving victory alongside – and always above – the quest for personal glory."

"…The inability to do that was Lü Bu's biggest weakness," Zhang Liao noted.

"But in hand-to-hand combat, he was unparalleled, Wenyuan," Guan Yu replied. "I despise his character, yes, but his ability must be admired. He had no difficulty finding his way past my guard… but was incapable of surviving because he was incapable of thinking clearly or showing loyalty."

"What about Zhang Fei?" Zhu Ling asked suddenly. "Could he break your guard…?"

"…Yes, often," Guan Yu replied forlornly. "Sometimes, Yide scared me with his power. He broke many a training weapon with his lunges… what he lacked in tactics, he more than made up for with power that I truly envy. Lord Liu's bodyguard, Chen Dao, could break my guard quite often as well; that's why he serves as Lord Liu's last line of defence. That's why I know that Lord Liu lives… for there are few men alive that could – perhaps – pass Yide *and*

Chen Dao, and I am one of them."

Xu Huang, Han Hao and Zhu Ling exchanged nervous glances.

"…I must go," Guan Yu decided. "I must go and visit Lord Liu's family and ensure them that I am still watching over them."

"…It's been an education," Zhu Ling said as he bowed to Guan Yu.

"We should do this again soon, Yunchang," Zhang Liao suggested.

"Indeed… it is an honour to train with you all," Guan Yu said.

Guan Yu exchanged polite bows with each of Cao Cao's generals and withdrew.

"Yunchang is a true hero," Zhang Liao said. "His rebukes of those that he does not respect are admittedly harsh… but his humility and cordiality when speaking of or to those that he does respect shows that he is not merely arrogant, as some suggest."

"Indeed," Xu Huang replied.

"…*Aiee*… so Zhang Fei 'scares' Guan Yu…?" Zhu Ling exclaimed. "When we were routing Yuan Shu's men in Xu, I saw how Zhang knocked six men over at once with a *shove*; his elite men are like smaller versions of him, as well."

"And Yunchang was *holding back*," Xu Huang noted. "If he is *scared* by Zhang Fei, with whom he does *not* hold back…"

"Anyone that can 'scare' Guan Yu does more than scare me," Zhu Ling admitted.

"…And then there is 'Chen Dao', Liu Bei's 'last line of defence', who sounds like the best of Guan Yunchang and Zhang Fei in one man," Xu Huang mused.

"…Such men that Liu Bei had – or has, if he still lives," Han Hao sighed. "Let's hope that we never have to fight them."

Guan Yu could not hear the discussions as he walked away, but he could guess their tone: he smiled as he thought of the caution that Cao Cao's men would show in future conflicts.

Yuan Shao summoned his officials to his main audience hall and declared, "I have spoken to Liu Bei, the last survivor of the brave group that sought to challenge the vile, wicked Cao Cao in the name of the Son of Heaven. He has told me of the 'Girdle Edict' – a document that is now either confiscated or destroyed – that was written in His Majesty's own hand and told of the misery inflicted by the seditionist, the defiler of women, the thief and liar and murderer Cao Cao!"

The officials gasped and muttered at the words; the adviser Shen Pei said, "How will we proceed, Lord Yuan…?"

"We must make everyone aware of the extent of the evil that is carried out by the 'Excellency of Works'," Yuan Shao replied. "I will have my secretary, Chen Lin, compose a written condemnation that will be distributed in every part of the country. I will ensure that Liu Biao, Liu Zhang, Sun Ce, Chen Deng, the Qiang warlords of Liang, the Southern Xiongnu Chanyu Huchuquan, the Wuhuan, the Shanyue and, most importantly of all, Cao's own subordinates face what this monster has done. We will bring them all to our side, and then we will lead the charge that smites him!"

"You intend to attack him directly…?" Tian Feng said. "You had your moment to do that when Cao was in Xu Province, Lord Yuan, but you sent an insufficient force; now that Cao is back in Guandu with his best advisers and a seasoned army of forty-thousand to call upon at a moment's notice, you want to throw everything you have at him?"

Yuan Shao scowled angrily.

"The answer is to grow food, cultivate goodwill amongst the people of the vast region that you now rule, and prepare for a long, patient battle with Cao Cao," Tian Feng continued. "When the army is well-fed, well-paid, reorganised and invigorated in body and spirit, we can unleash a series of fierce pincer attacks on Cao's positions with elite troops, whittling his men and morale down slowly but effectively. In two years or so, we–"

"*Two years…?*" Guo Tu scoffed.

"We cannot rush this," Ju Shou suggested.

"Mister Cui writes from Li County to say the men are unhappy," Tian Feng said. "All over the region, we're still suffering the effects of bad management, and–"

"You accuse good men of being corrupt," Shen Pei heckled, "while saying nothing about others."

Some eyes turned to Xu Yòu, who said, "What am I being dragged into this again for???"

"Problems must be dealt with!" Xun Chen said.

"That's what we're trying to do!" Ju Shou retorted, "but as usual, the–!"

"The army is being misrepresented!" Chunyu Qiong cried. "I–!"

"**Can we stay on the subject???**" Tian Feng protested. "Lord Yuan, we must–!"

"**ENOUGH!**" Yuan Shao bellowed. "**Tian Feng, I am sick of your floundering! I walk, you say 'Run'; I run, you say 'Stop'; I stop, and you ask why I am not walking! You are fast becoming a man that is best ignored!**"

Tian Feng sighed woefully; Liu Bei – who had been invited, along with his close aides, as a guest – exchanged cynical glances with Jian Yong and Mi Zhu.

"We will strike quickly and attack relentlessly, not wait until Cao Cao has had time to double the size of his army," Yuan Shao grumbled. "I will not wait for two years! The nation had to endure Dong Zhuo for two years, and then Li Jue and Guo Si for another three! The succession of tyrants will end here!"

Guo Tu, Shen Pei, Chunyu Qiong and many of the other officials voiced approval of Yuan Shao's words.

"This is a mistake," Tian Feng insisted. "You'll be putting your head into the tiger's mouth if you attack head-on, no matter how many men you have! You have to–!"

"**You dare to question me again???**" Yuan Shao exclaimed. "**GUARDS!**"

"*Aiee…* now what's this fool doing…?" Jian Yong muttered as four soldiers advanced toward the exasperated Tian Feng and prepared to drag him from the hall.

"No, Lord Yuan, stop!" Tian Feng protested. "I am only trying to serve you!"

"**You'll serve me better in a prison cell!**" Yuan Shao retorted. "**Take him away!**"

"**What charge???**" Tian Feng cried. "**What charge???**"

"…Malicious mischief!" Yuan Shao said. "**Guards, remove him!**"

"**My lord, you must not do this!**" Tian Feng pleaded as the soldiers dragged him away. "**Somebody say something! My** only 'crime' was to proffer advice that was not heeded! Ju Shou! JU SHOU!"

Ju Shou turned his gaze and sighed sadly.

"**Stop whining, Tian Feng!**" Guo Tu heckled. "**You get to keep your head, which is more than you deserve!**"

Once Tian Feng was gone, Yuan Shao turned to Chen Lin and said, "Now we are rid of that pest, there will be no more dallying; Mister Chen, compose the document at once."

Chen Lin bowed humbly and replied, "At once, Lord Yuan."

Yuan Shao's actions were eventually reported to Cao Cao's camp in Guandu by spies.

"...He arrested and imprisoned Tian Feng *again*...?" Cao Cao said with a laugh. "There was one of the few men that would save him... I'm glad of it."

"Yes, but the other matter... the 'condemnation' written by Chen Lin... is no laughing matter," Xun Gongda suggested. "This, my lord, is what is being distributed."

Cao Cao took a piece of cloth paper from Xun Gongda and started to read.

"To all men that desire order and know Heaven,

We are once again threatened by a great evil. The peoples of the world under Heaven collectively sighed with relief when Dong Zhuo perished, just as it was when Wang Mang met his end in times long gone; but that was then, and little did the world know that there would be a second great evil after the first! Li Jue and Guo Si, however, have come and gone, and now we have a third, even more despicable villain in Cao Cao, the man that now holds the Son of Heaven hostage in his domain in Yan Province.

Cao Cao, son of a man adopted by court eunuchs; his father, Cao Song, enjoyed privilege because of the vast wealth and influence enjoyed by the court attendants at that time, and there are few that do not know the damage that they did to our country. Cao Song was one of the wealthiest men in the land, though few could explain how: Cao Cao then enjoyed status far in excess of what should have been correct, receiving a great education and court employment that he repeatedly neglected in favour of drinking, women and song. Regardless, his peers showed him friendship and goodwill.

When Dong Zhuo seized the capital, Cao Cao fled, and his family somehow survived the purge that followed; when Yuan Shao called upon the heroes of the age to aid him against the tyrant, Cao Cao showed poor judgement and cost the Eastern Pass Coalition a considerable amount of its forces stationed in Yan Province. Some could say that this loss at Xingyang partially contributed to the collapse of the alliance. After abandoning Liu Dai, Governor of Yan Province, Cao somehow managed, through subterfuge, to 'inherit' the province, wherein he began a merciless campaign against neighbouring Xu Province, ostensibly to avenge the 'murder' of his father but, in truth, to seize the region and add it to his own domains! It is only because of the actions of Commander-in-Chief Yuan that the province was spared, but since then Cao has held a grudge that now plays out.

When the Son of Heaven was finally able to escape the wicked villains Li Jue and Guo Si, he was captured by bandits: General of Chariots and Cavalry Dong Cheng asked help of every hero in the land, but Commander Yuan was affected by constant assaults by Black Mountain Bandits, and was therefore unable to promise safe shelter; Cao Cao fought any who opposed his own bid and brought the Son of Heaven to Xuchang, where he built a palace – a palace for his own descendants to rule from – and surrounded His Majesty with his own cronies to ensure that he would have complete control of all affairs. The Son of Heaven attempted to create an alternative power base, but Cao ensured that he was Excellency of Works and Excellency over the Masses – a Chancellor of State in all but name – and tried to deny the title 'Commander-in-Chief' to the one man that was fit to hold it. His next action – to abuse his power by raping the aunt of surrendered rebel Zhang Xiu in Zhang's own bed – culminated in the loss of a fine army and for the misguided rebel, Yuan Shu, to mistake Cao's incompetence as a sign that the Han Dynasty was exhausted. Yuan Shu's wicked acts are unforgivable, and his death a relief to clan and state, but were his acts possible if Cao had been a better man?

With the nation close to stable, Cao Cao had the option to sue for peace, but he has instead sought to undermine and destroy every man that is his social peer: he seeks alliances with bandits, forces the widows of defeated generals to become his concubines and inflicts savage working conditions on his soldiers, who must be unpaid farmers when they are not bearing arms! The people are still miserable, and who else can they look to as the guilty party but Cao, who has concentrated all power in his greedy hands?

General of Chariots and Cavalry Dong Cheng – whose daughter was a consort of the Son of Heaven – was approached by loyal vassals and presented with the 'Girdle Edict' – written by His Majesty – that called upon all good men to take up arms against the villain; the truth emerged, and Cao Cao purged not only the heroes but their families, just like Dong Zhuo before him. But that was not enough! Cao then journeyed to the palace – armed and with evil intent – and strangled to death the pregnant daughter of the hero Dong Cheng: the unborn child that he killed was a prince, perhaps a future sovereign, and that is regicide! Nothing else need be said.

Act now or there will never be peace. For Heaven, take up arms! This most wicked of all villains must be destroyed quickly, before the world is enveloped in eternal suffering! Commander-in-Chief Yuan will lead, if only you will follow!"

The dumbstruck Cao Cao lowered the pamphlet to his lap and shook his head silently.
"...Are you alright, Lord Cao...?" Guo Jia asked.
Cao Cao shook his head again and said, "I'm not sure."
"He is truly a hypocrite," Xun Gongda said. "I remember his reaction when Yuan Shu wrote something that was far less vitriolic than *this*!"
"So do I, Gongda," Cao Cao replied numbly. "He... he actually mentions my father...! He actually slanders my poor father...!"
"Are you... going to start screaming, Mengde...?" Cao Hong asked nervously.
"No," Cao Cao chortled. "This has made me far too angry for that. I... it has made my head clearer, strangely, but... but I am stiff inside, my stomach is churning, I feel like I am being crushed..."
"He's massing more troops at Li County," Guo Jia reported. "He wants a full confrontation, which is, of course, what Tian Feng objected to. Word also reaches us that Liu Bei is alive... and with Yuan, as a field general."
Cao Cao smiled dryly and said, "That doesn't surprise me at all."
"We'll do what we can to keep it from Guan Yu," Xun Gongda promised.
Cao Cao raised the written condemnation for a second time and read most of it again: after a pause, he lowered it to his lap for a second time, laughed strangely, and started to speak.

"All men, they walk a cyclic path that leads unto itself;
War and peace, love and hate; the selfish quests for boundless wealth.
And every man that turns the rest to seek some better routes
Is confounded by a greedy few whose cause that looped path suits.

Oh how I tried and tried to pull the line of men
Draw them to a path that I had seen,
Such peace was there ahead, a world serene!
But they resisted my attempts and turned again.

I tried so hard and lost the fight, but still,
My given fate has always been to fail;
What a fool I was to challenge Heaven's will!
That line of men must *always* chase its tail!"

"...Ah, so your faith is finally shattered," Guo Jia chuckled. "But did you ensure that we had fine wine and a brothel to drown our sorrows, as I suggested...?"
Cao Cao shook his head and said, "You misunderstand. I-"
"I was joking, Lord Cao," Guo Jia insisted. "You have seen that there is no way back or forward, no matter how much your heart yearned for one. The only way to proceed now is to complete the circle."
"...Yes," Cao Cao replied. "Yuan has, as you say, created another loop: he began as a man that meant well enough, a man that was born complicated but quickly simplified things so that he could be pompous. We all pinned our hopes on him: the champion of the 'Partisans', the slayer of the 'Ten', the leader of the Eastern Pass Coalition... but in the end, the only thing separating him from Yuan Shu was that he became the head of the clan. As soon as he had an excuse to feel sorry for himself and focus all of his hatred on a man that he could reinvent as some sort of 'obstruction to his preordained supremacy' he grasped it with both hands, even going so far as to mimic the written condemnation; will he also one day mimic the claim to the throne...? He's so demented, so convinced of his own cause that he has become a hankering, spiteful, hypocritical tyrant without even realising it... a man devoid of reason that must be destroyed."
Guo Jia hummed ambiguously.
"Yes, Guo Fengxiao, I intend to 'close the circle'," Cao Cao continued. "I will face the impact of this filth that Chen Lin has written on Yuan's behalf, and I shall rise above it. There will be no peace between Yuan Shao and I now; this ends with the death of one or both of us, for we cannot share the world under Heaven now... not after this. If I have my way, Guandu will be where his world ends, and we can finish what we started... bringing peace to the nation."

Yuan Shao's propaganda campaign did have consequences, but Cao Cao would not be an easy man to defeat; in the end, the outcome would be decided with action rather than words, although that outcome depended more on capable minds than abundance of muscle. If Yuan Shao was to win, he would have to unite his remaining advisers and ensure complete discipline within his bloated, factional army such that it matched Cao Cao's organised military machine, and he did not have long to achieve it.

✳✳✳✳✳✳✳✳✳✳✳✳

111

The damning denunciation letter that Yuan Shao's followers distributed throughout the country took time to reach places like Yi Province in the far west and Yang Province in the farthest south, but the response – wherever and whenever it was read – was unavoidably immediate.

"We'll need to act now," Jing Governor Liu Biao said to his Jiangling court. "Cao is now Sun Ce's in-law, which gives us personal cause to oppose him, but this is for the nation! I reason that if I am not seen to act again – after already being castigated for not joining Yuan's Eastern Pass Coalition against Dong Zhuo – then I might suffer later. Am I correct in my thinking, gentlemen?"
"I agree, my lord, but only because we have little choice," the adviser Kuai Liang replied. "Cao Cao will certainly come for us if he defeats Yuan Shao."
"Shao has a *hundred-thousand men*!" the politician Huan Jie chortled. "Cao has a third of that at best!"
"If Yuan Shao were competent, that would matter," Wang Can retorted. "He isn't."
"So what do you suggest, then, Mister Wang…?" Liu Biao asked.
"The Kuai brothers and I – to name but a few – agree that cautious support is advised," Wang Can replied.
"Indeed," Kuai Yue said. "We should act only if Cao Cao is visibly distracted, and our aim should not be to attack Guandu as Yuan implies; we should march upon Xuchang and rescue the Son of Heaven from the sparsely-defended city."
"…I shall do as you say, and wait," Liu Biao declared.

Xuchang had suddenly stopped receiving correspondence from the Yang Province official Xu Gong; Gong had previously dubbed Sun Ce 'A hero comparable to Xiang Yu, the conqueror of old times' – which led to Ce being dubbed 'The Little Conqueror' by some in later times – and advised the court to force Ce to leave his large following in Jiangdong and move to Xuchang. Cao Cao suspected that something was wrong and had Guangling Administrator Chen Deng investigate the matter; the response that Cao eventually received was not to his liking.
"…Dead…?" Cao Cao exclaimed.
"Dead, and for a few weeks, perhaps," Xun Gongda replied. "Xu Gong's correspondence was intercepted: Ce knows everything Gong's been saying, it seems, and he had him killed. In addition, Chen Yuanlong warns us that Sun Ce's now massing troops in 'suspicious ways'… we might consider reinforcing Xuchang."
"Sun Ce won't march on Xuchang," Guo Jia said calmly.
"…You seem awfully certain of that," Xun Gongda prompted.
"Groundlessly certain," a new addition to Cao's court – Liu Xun, the former Administrator of Lujiang – said coldly. "Sun Ce and his adviser, Zhou Yu, who is the son of Luoyang's former Magistrate Zhou Yi, are greedy and ambitious. They took Lujiang from me and Jiangdong from Liu Yao, so why wouldn't they try and take Xuchang from His Excellency? Am I not right, Liu Yè…?"
Liu Xun's long-time adviser, Liu Yè, smiled and replied, "I think

that Mister Guo has considered his case very carefully, Lord Liu. We should hear him out."

Liu Xun harrumphed and said, "Very well."

"Xu Gong was very popular in Wu Prefecture," Guo Jia explained. "He overthrew the court-appointed administrator, Sheng Xian, with an army of disaffected locals. Sun Ce was not so popular when he overthrew Xu Gong in turn; Ce's been reluctantly allied to Xu Gong ever since. There will be men that will want Ce dead for this, and given Ce's reckless streak... I imagine that we will not have to wait long for the 'Little Conqueror' to join his famous father in death."

"And then what...?" Xun Gongda asked.

"The third brother, Sun Yi, is similarly reckless but popular; the second brother, Sun Quan, is less popular and a proven liability," Guo Jia replied. "If Sun Quan replaces his brother, then many will desert the Sun clan and Jiangdong will either descend into chaos, be invaded by Liu Biao or come back under court control. If Sun Yi replaces Sun Ce, then we might have slightly more trouble, but that's unlikely: he'll probably be too busy purging Xu Gong's allies and waging war on Liu Biao and Huang Zu to march on Xuchang."

"...I had hoped for Sun Ce's support against my enemies," Cao Cao admitted.

"You won't get that support you want now," Guo Jia replied. "Sun Ce will not support another man that's been branded as a villain, not after being shackled to Yuan Shu."

"...At least we have Guan Yu," Cao Cao sighed. "It leaves Yuan Shao and Liu Bei with one less hero..."

But fate had a surprise for Liu Bei: one day, as he was rueing the loss of Guan Yu – as he did every day – Mi Fang entered his private study and said, "Lord Liu, it is a miracle! It is unbelievable! He is here! He is here!"

"...Yunchang???" Liu Bei exclaimed.

Mi Fang's face fell, and he said, "I... I had not thought... forgive me, Lord Liu, that I was so foolish as to-"

"If it isn't Yunchang, then who is it?" Zhang Fei asked gruffly. "Speak up, speak up!"

"...Zhao Zilong," Mi Fang replied.

"Zilong???" Liu Bei exclaimed. "Zilong is alive, and here in Yè???"

"That's a surprise and a half!" Jian Yong chuckled. "He was serving Tian Kai when we last saw him, Mi Zifang; how is he in Yè?"

"His men came here only a few days ago!" Mi Fang explained. "They surrendered to Yuan's forces during the attack on Yòu Province, and now they're here, serving Yuan Shao!"

"...It isn't Yunchang, but it's good," Zhang Fei conceded. "Zhao Yun, here in Yè...! After all this time... he was pretty good!"

"He was magnificent!" Liu Bei said. "He is a future hero, like Yunchang! This is a sign from Heaven! Heaven has given us Zilong to reassure us that we are not yet finished, and soon Heaven will return Yunchang to us as well!"

"He's anxious to see you, Lord Liu," Mi Fang said.

"And I am equally anxious!" Liu Bei replied. "We must be reunited at once! Zilong will never leave my side again! I will have Yuan Shao assign him to me at the soonest opportunity! Bring him here, bring him here!"

Mi Fang turned and left the house to fetch Zhao Yun.

"…Zilong… *Zilong*…!" Liu Bei sobbed. "Such an unexpected reunion can only be a *sign*… Yunchang will be back with us soon as well, I'm sure of it! This is a new beginning!"

Jian Yong smiled and said, "I… I actually think that it *might be*…!"

When Liu Bei and Zhao Yun saw one-another, they took each other's hands and smiled smiles of genuine satisfaction: Zhao Yun saw Liu Bei as an older brother or uncle as well as a kindly lord, while Liu Bei treasured Zhao Yun's honesty, loyalty and military talent. The two were then virtually inseparable: Yuan Shao grudgingly allowed Liu Bei to regain a man that had once been his cavalry commander during their shared time in Pingyuan, and another historic alliance was born.

"We mustn't react to this 'denunciation' sent by Yuan Shao," the veteran adviser Dong Fu said to his lord, the Governor of Yi Province Liu Zhang.

"B-but it states that Cao Cao is a villain!" Liu Zhang replied worriedly. "Am I the only man that frets…?"

Most of the rest of the Chengdu court was close to silent; Liu Zhang's brother-in-law, Wu Yi, shook his head and said, "Of course not, Lord Liu, but is Yuan Shao to be believed? We're ignorant of detail, being so remote; news that we get via travellers and Liang Province is not helpful, but what we do know for certain is that Yuan Shu – Shao's brother – was recently hunted down by Cao Cao and driven to death for daring to claim that he was an emperor. Is it then wise to listen to the brother of a traitor that tried to bring down the Han Dynasty…?"

"…As you say, we're ignorant of detail," Liu Zhang replied. "We'll stay out of this matter… we'll continue to send tribute to His Majesty in Xuchang, since that is a neutral and proper thing, but we'll refrain from being seen to support Cao or Yuan."

"That is best," Dong Fu agreed.

Liu Zhang sighed and said, "I wonder what the Qiang and the other rebels in Liang province will do…? What will Zhang Lu do…?"

The answers to Liu Zhang's questions were soon evident: of the three Qiang warlords, Han Sui and Ma Teng were alternating their time between short truces, long periods of fighting and contemplating the offers that Cao Cao's Han court and Yuan Shao's 'Yè court' made; the third Qiang warlord, Song Jian, ignored the situation altogether; the rebel groups in did Liang did very little, as their new governor Wei Kang was a vast improvement over his predecessors; and Zhang Lu was content to avoid riling either Yuan or Cao, who made no attempt to ally with him. The choices had been made, the initial manoeuvres had been made, and now the moment had arrived: Yuan Shao and Cao Cao were finally going to confront each other and decide who would govern the nation on behalf of the cynical Han Emperor.

****

112

"The time to fight Cao Cao is here," Yuan Shao said to his assembled court. "Pang Ji will stay and manage affairs here in Yè; I will personally journey to Li County to oversee the mobilisation of my grand army while a detachment of considerable size begins hostilities at Boma."

"…Who do you intend to send…?" the adviser Ju Shou asked.

"Your friend Tian Feng criticised me for sending 'mediocrities' to challenge Cao's force at Yan Ford, Mister Ju, but this time I will send my best," Yuan Shao replied coldly. "General Yan Liang – supported by Chunyu Qiong and advised by Guo Tu – will cross the river and march on Boma. I will ensure that my main forces are ready for a river crossing as soon as Boma falls!"

"I can't recommend General Yan for this," Ju Shou said. "He is brave and strong, yes, but he is also impatient and prone to acting prematurely and without proper thought: Zhang Hè is more cautious and the better choice here, Lord Yuan."

Yan Liang grunted angrily and flicked his sleeve.

"Am I not sending counsel in the form of Mister Guo Tu and Mister Chunyu Qiong?" Yuan Shao heckled. "Or are you also slandering their ability…?"

Guo Tu and Chunyu Qiong joined Yan Liang in glaring at Ju Shou, who sighed miserably and said, "I will remonstrate no further."

"That would be wise," Yuan Shao replied. "No more talk: we begin at once!"

Cao Cao's base at Boma – which was close to a strategically important river crossing – was made up of a walled city and a series of camps, but it was only manned by 1,500 men: the base commander, Dong Prefecture Administrator Liu Yan, watched with horror as General Yan Liang's elite cavalry tore into the outer ring of camps with ease and isolated the city almost completely.

"**Contact His Excellency!**" Liu Yan said to an adviser. "**We can't hold out! We need assistance at once!**"

"…So the dithering fool moves at last," Cao Cao said as he read Liu Yan's urgent letter for a second time. "I wonder how long Boma will hold…?"

"If I may…?" Xun Gongda asked.

"…Go on," Cao Cao prompted.

"We didn't intend Boma to be more than an impediment to Yuan reaching Guandu, but the place is now seen by a lot of the men as a symbol of our authority on the south bank of the Yellow River," Xun Gongda explained. "If they hold for longer than another week, then the men will start to demand that we act."

"…And in that case, we should," Guo Jia agreed.

"And do what…?" Cao Cao chortled.

"…I'll be blunt: if Yuan takes Boma, he'll have a clear path to march his hundred-thousand over the river and toward Guandu," Xun Gongda said. "Our men will be so demoralised that we'll see desertions and defections by the hundreds. We cannot let him."

"So we should wait and see what Yan Liang does," Guo Jia suggested. "If he doesn't retreat after three weeks, then he has

ample supplies to break Boma and we'll have to relieve the city."
"...Alright," Cao Cao said. "One way or another, it has begun."

Yan Liang's siege of Boma lasted for three weeks without any sign of pause or intent to retreat: Cao Cao summoned Xun Gongda to his tent and said, "Guo Jia is ill, which is bad timing, but there isn't anything that I can do. The siege continues, and Liu Yan is breaking: what advice do you have?"
"The only way to defeat Yan Liang is to weaken the support that Yuan Shao can provide from his camps across the river," Xun Gongda explained. "I have a suggestion, but it is risky..."
"Losing the men and supplies at Boma is a greater risk to morale," Cao Cao replied. "Tell me your plan."

Yuan Shao was startled when a scout brought word of an enemy mobilisation near Yan Ford, which was to the west of Boma.
"The knave!" Yuan Shao exclaimed. "The churl! He intends a crossing at Yan Ford to outflank me!"
"We don't know that he doesn't do this to draw forces away from Li County!" Ju Shou protested. "We-!"
"So am I to just let him send an army over the river?" Yuan Shao retorted. "Keep your silence, imbecile! **Wen Chou, Han Juzi, Lü Kuang, Sui Yuanjin!**"
"I await your orders, Lord Yuan!" General Wen Chou said.
"You will take your forces to Yan Ford and meet Cao Cao's forces at once!" Yuan Shao ordered. "Smash them! **Crush them!**"
Wen Chou and his aides bowed, turned and retreated to ready their armies.
"...We needed Wen Chou for the crossing!" Ju Shou complained.
"Did I not tell you to shut up???" Yuan Shao retorted.

Wen Chou took a force of thousands and sped toward the northern side of Yan Ford; Xun Gongda learned of the move and reported it to Cao Cao, saying, "The moment is upon us."
"Who will relieve Boma?" Cao Cao asked.
"We need men that are experts at 'camp smashing'," Xun Gongda said. "There are only two senior generals that are competent enough... Zhang Liao, and..."
"...And...?" Cao Cao prompted impatiently.
"...Guan Yu," Xun Gongda replied.
"*Aiee*... I'd hoped that I could keep Guan as a surprise asset for the end of the campaign!" Cao Cao said. "I have not given him gold, silk, rank, tolerated his slights and his feuds with Yuanrang and Zilian and made every little concession he's demanded in order to lose him this early! He's a long-term investment!"
"Lose Boma, and having Guan is meaningless," Xun Gongda retorted. "He'll find out about Liu Bei soon anyway, so why not use him while he's still ignorant...?"
"...Alright, alright!" Cao Cao grumbled. "It is Heaven's will... send Guan Yu."

Zhang Liao and Guan Yu's army crossed the numerous rivers that separated the main base at Guandu from Boma and marched to the besieged city at speed; they stopped short of the city and had scouts survey the area.

"We'll be reported to Yan Liang soon," Guan Yu suggested.

"What do you want to do?" Zhang Liao asked.

"We were not selected at random," Guan Yu replied. "You're a student of Gao Shun's camp-smashing tactics, and I have similar experience. We're to charge Yan's main camp with everything we have, which will force Yan's men to abandon the siege and defend the camp. I don't intend to disobey orders."

Zhang Liao looked at the clothes that Guan Yu wore under his armour and said, "They're not the fine silk robes that His Excellency gave you… they're the tired robes that you wear to train… nor is that the fine halberd that he gave to you."

"They're the robes that were gifted to me by Lord Liu Xuande," Guan Yu explained. "I wear them always, Zhang Wenyuan; the weapon I carry is the Green Dragon that was forged with monies raised to fight the Yellow Turbans sixteen years ago."

"…There is no buying you, is there, Yunchang…?" Zhang Liao said.

Guan Yu smiled and replied, "There isn't, Wenyuan: I appreciate your honesty."

"You know His Excellency's intent," Zhang Liao said. "I'd not patronise you by acting as though you couldn't have guessed."

A scout returned and said, "**Their camp is to the northwest!**"

"Let's turn it to ashes," Guan Yu declared.

Zhang Liao turned to the army and shouted, "**FORWARD!**"

Yan Liang was taken aback when Zhang Liao and Guan Yu began their attack.

"**Where is Guo Tu?**" Yan Liang asked desperately. "**Where is Chunyu Qiong?**"

"**They're both at the city walls!**" a major replied.

"…**Okay! Raise standards and prepare to counterattack!**" Yan Liang ordered.

Yan Liang had every one of his officers raise their standards and ready their men, but the action gave Guan Yu a clear indication of where Yan Liang was: he left his attack on the outer camps and charged at Yan Liang with a small group of elite cavalrymen.

"…Who's this…?" Yan Liang asked as he caught sight of Guan Yu; the valiant general was confused at the sight of a group of riders charging straight through his defensive lines, and he did not have time to react to a swipe that knocked him from his horse and killed him instantly. Guan Yu leapt from the decorated saddle of his Arabic steed and severed Yan Liang's head with a second swipe of his Green Dragon pole sword: the men that surrounded him could scarce believe what was happening as they fought off attacks by Guan's riders.

"**BACK TO THE OUTER CAMPS!**" Guan Yu ordered as he mounted his horse and galloped away with the head and standard of the commanding officer; the riders were gone as quickly as they had appeared.

"…General Yan…!" a captain sobbed as he joined a group of men that were gathered around the headless corpse of Yan Liang.

Zhang Liao was amazed and impressed when Guan Yu approached him with his trophies: he laughed and said, "**You have no peer, Yunchang!**"

"**Yan Liang is dead!**" Guan Yu declared. "**Let us end this!**"

A messenger sped word of Cao Cao's counterattack to Guo Tu and Chunyu Qiong, who ordered a general retreat from the walls of Boma to relieve their camp: Guo Tu cried out when they learned that Zhang Liao and Guan Yu were long gone and little was left of their camp or their morale.

"...Yan Liang... *dead*...?" Chunyu Qiong bleated.

"**Who did this???**" Guo Tu screamed.

"Their standards read 'Wei Xu', 'Cao Xing', 'Guan Yu', and 'Zhang Liao'!" one survivor replied.

"*Guan Yu*???" Chunyu Qiong exclaimed. "He's Liu Bei's man!"

"**Liu Bei must die for this!**" Guo Tu declared. "**Our campaign is stalled on account of that duplicitous sandal-weaver!**"

"...**We must retreat to Li County!**" Chunyu Qiong said. "**We're exposed now... we must retreat at once!**"

Within a day, Cao Cao was inspecting the head of Yan Liang.

"...Magnificent," Cao Cao murmured.

"You don't sound happy," Guo Jia noted. "Boma is relieved, Yan Liang is dead..."

"...And Guan Yu is soon to be lost," Cao Cao replied. "This man was one of Yuan's best warriors, but Guan charged at him and killed him as easily as taking something from a sack! Imagine what he could have achieved had Liu Bei been able to participate in the Eastern Pass Coalition! Would the likes of Xu Rong and Hua Xiong been so troublesome...?"

"Many have suggested that Yan Liang might have hesitated because Guan's appearance is well-known and Liu Bei is an ally of his lord," Xun Gongda said. "Perhaps he thought that Guan Yu was sent to reinforce him."

"...Yes, but such suppositions have reached Guan, have they not, along with word that Bei is in Li County...?" Cao Cao retorted. "He knows Bei is alive now..."

"But will Bei be alive for much longer...?" Guo Jia asked. "Won't Yuan Shao want him dead for what Guan Yu's done...?"

"...In which case, Guan will blame me for the death," Cao Cao suggested. "I will still appoint him a marquis anyway, and give him more gifts..."

"...Is this true?" Yuan Shao said as he looked at Chunyu Qiong's hand-delivered report. "*Guan Yu* killed my Yan Liang?"

"Almost certainly," Chunyu Qiong replied.

"That's what we're being told," Guo Tu said.

"...Summon Bei here at once," Yuan Shao ordered.

Yuan Shao's officials wondered what their lord would do with the luckless warlord whose famous subordinate had been blamed for such a catastrophic setback; Yuan's face betrayed anger and desperation, and that could mean anything.

****

113

Liu Bei was confronted with the reports from the siege of Boma within the hour.

"...Yunchang...?" Liu Bei exclaimed; he looked at the angry faces of Yuan Shao's officials and added, "This must be a mistake or a misunderstanding...!"

"He killed my Yan Liang, charged and beheaded him!" Yuan Shao said. "The dog didn't even engage him in a fair fight, so I hear! My sword is blunted, Liu Bei, and I again have you to thank for it!"

"B-but Guan Yunchang *hates* Cao Cao!" Liu Bei chuckled nervously. "Cao Cao humbled us repeatedly, destroyed our homes, and stole the woman that Yunchang wanted to wed! If it really is him, it's because he thinks that I am dead and Cao's got our families as hostages!"

Yuan Shao turned his gaze to his advisers: Xin Pi frowned and said, "Guan Yu is known to be fiercely devoted to Liu Bei; we haven't made Liu Bei's presence particularly public, so it's entirely possible that Guan is ignorant of it and protecting the families as Liu Bei suggests."

"**Execute him!**" Guo Tu cried.

"No!" Yuan Shao said. "If... if Guan can be brought to our side..."

"If it really is he, and not some attempt at slandering me, then I will write to him and make him see that he is on the wrong side," Liu Bei promised. "Even if our families are placed at risk, I will not let Yunchang jeopardise our cause. I beseech you, let me discover the truth of this and atone for past mistakes!"

"...Alright," Yuan Shao said. "You have a week."

Liu Bei returned to his camp and informed his shocked allies of what he had just heard.

"**Yunchang???**" Zhang Fei cried. "**Yunchang has betrayed us??? The bastard! How??? How can he serve Cao Cao???**"

"Calm down, Yide," Liu Bei pleaded.

"**How can I calm down???**" Zhang Fei screamed. "**He tricked me, the bastard! He really convinced me that we were brothers forever, all of us, and-!**"

"I mean it, Yide... shut up," Liu Bei ordered.

Zhang Fei whined like a wounded animal.

"...If it's him, there's a reason for this," Jian Yong suggested. "We were together at Haixi... no, the man we know cannot serve Cao Cao willingly. What are you going to do, Xuande...?"

"I'll find out the truth," Liu Bei insisted. "I believe in Yunchang... we must all believe in him. If it's him, we'll get him back..."

Days passed: Cao Cao evacuated Boma, gave retreat orders to his forces at Yan Ford and started to consolidate his forces in and around his main base at Guandu.

"...I cannot let what has happened stall us," Yuan Shao said to an audience of officials. "Liu Bei informs me that Guan Yu can be brought over to us, and that he will not aid Cao Cao anymore."

"Where is Bei now...?" Guo Tu asked. "He is not here."

"He is on his way to the west to support Wen Chou," Yuan Shao replied. "We're going to cross the river: Boma is abandoned, which means that Cao Cao doesn't have the resources to keep the city, which means that he is, despite outward appearances, almost defeated. We'll occupy Boma, destroy his decoy force at Yan Ford and overrun him at Guandu: he will soon die a dog's death!"

Cao Cao knew that he would probably have to face Yuan Shao at Yan Ford, but he was quietly hopeful that Guan Yu would be his vanguard once again.
"You... are too kind," Guan Yu said as he received a bundle of expensive silk from the desperate Excellency of Works.
"I would give you the sun in the sky if I could, Yunchang," Cao Cao replied. "Your heroic action saved the servants of the Son of Heaven that were defending Boma."
"I am glad that my actions are considered so," Guan Yu said.
Cao Cao could sense a change in Guan Yu's tone: he smiled uneasily and asked, "Are you digesting Yuan Shao's rumours that Liu Bei is alive...?"
"I am," Guan Yu replied.
"...And... and if they were true...?" Cao Cao asked.
"I cannot answer that because I do not know if they are true," Guan Yu replied. "If they are proved true, then I will answer you in writing, Excellency."
"In writing...?" Cao Cao prompted.
"I owe you a great deal," Guan Yu explained. "You have cared for the captured families of my lord and his vassals well, and you have provided me with fine clothes, a fine horse, silks and gold, and now a marquisate. Such a debt is not easily repaid, but my honour obliges me to do so."
"...A true hero," Cao Cao sighed. "Will you aid my efforts to protect the retreat from Yan Ford...?"
"I shall certainly journey there," Guan Yu replied: he had heard that Liu Bei was close to Yan Ford, but he had to be sure. Cao Cao tried to feign cheer, but he knew that – despite his best efforts – his brief alliance with Guan Yu was soon to come to an end.

General Wen Chou received Liu Bei at the gates of his camp and said, "It is good to have you here, General Liu."
"You are not aggrieved...?" Liu Bei asked.
"If Guan Yu is responsible for the death of my colleague, then it was due to deceit by Cao Cao," Wen Chou replied. "This much I have been told or guessed."
"Then let's waste no more time," Liu Bei suggested. "Cao Cao's forces retreat from Boma and Yan Ford, and his baggage train is there for the taking at the very least."
"Agreed," Wen Chou said. "We'll start immediately!"

Cao Cao's retreating forces camped at the base of a slope that was close to the southern side of Yan Ford and south of Boma: Cao joined his force with Xun Gongda and ordered an immediate investigation of Yuan Shao's new camps as they were set up.
"The civilian evacuees from Boma are travelling down the rivers and roads, and that goes well," Liu Yan reported. "The military supplies are another matter: we couldn't secure enough boats to save them that way, so they're coming by road, and Yuan's forces are getting closer."

"Isn't that why we're here...?" Xun Gongda replied. "The scouts report a cavalry advance force of about six hundred riders coming from Yan Ford, nothing from Boma... Yuan's probably sent infantry, but they will move more slowly."

"Only six hundred...?" Cao Cao said. "...Yuan Shao surprises me."

"It's an initial estimate," Xun Gongda said. "I also expect more."

"...Who leads this cavalry...?" Cao Cao asked.

Xun Gongda sighed and said, "I had hoped that you wouldn't ask... Yuan Shao's sent Wen Chou and Liu Bei."

Cao Cao nodded slowly and silently.

"...A scout approaches," Xun Gongda announced.

"**Report!**" the scout said. "**The cavalry numbers at least two thousand, but-**"

"*Aiee*...! We can't repel those sorts of numbers!" Yu Jin said.

"Let the man finish," Cao Cao scolded. "We have not heard the infantry count."

"...The infantry are innumerable," the scout said fearfully.

"We should probably forget about the supplies, return to our camp and prepare to defend it," Zhu Ling suggested.

"No, General: that would be missing an opportunity!" Xun Gongda insisted. "The baggage train is the bait for a marvellous trap: how can we leave here?"

"But the odds are insurmountable, Excellency!" Han Hao said.

Cao Cao looked at Xun Gongda, smiled, and said, "Really...?"

Wen Chou and Liu Bei led their massive cavalry force to the road that lay north of Cao Cao's hidden South Slope camp: Cao Cao's scouts were ordered to retreat, and no effort was made to send men to assist the approaching baggage train.

"Cao Cao's weakness is evident!" Wen Chou suggested. "My men report a bounty of weapons, food, oxen and horses approaching from Boma, but where is the large escort that should be supplied...? All I see is a force of a few hundred infantry and a handful of riders!"

Liu Bei looked to the tall slope to the south and asked, "Might there be more forces hiding over there, General Wen...?"

"There has been no move to stop our approach!" Wen Chou said. "Besides, Cao could hide no more than a few hundred men behind that slope: what good would that be if he did...?"

"...Then our victory is assured," Liu Bei replied uneasily.

Cao Cao joined his hidden cavalry force and watched the attack on the baggage train: his cousin Cao Hong grunted angrily and asked, "Why did you leave Guan Yu behind?"

"His lord is here," Cao Cao replied. "How could I risk them meeting? But if Bei dies here, then Guan Yu must choose to serve me, defect to Yuan Shao or die. I think that his sense of honour will compel him to remain with me."

"**Excellency: the enemy approaches the baggage train!**" Yu Jin reported. "**Permission to mount horses and-?**"

"**No, General,**" Cao Cao interrupted. "**Not yet...!**"

Wen Chou's men descended on the Boma soldiers like a storm: the men discarded their horses and weapons and fled in all directions, leaving the baggage train undefended.

"**My lord, the baggage train is theirs if we don't act!**" Yu Jin said impatiently.

"Yes, the men did abandon all of their belongings and flee without putting up any fight at all, didn't they...?" Xun Gongda snickered.
"...**We must charge!**" Cao Hong protested.
"**Wait!**" Cao Cao insisted.
"The baggage train is ours!" Wen Chou cackled. "And where is mighty Cao Cao, mm...?"
"...The men are losing their order," Liu Bei fretted.
Wen Chou frowned: many of his cavalrymen were breaking ranks, getting off of their horses and looting rather than pursuing the fleeing soldiers.
"**FORGET THE GOODS!**" Wen Chou cried. "**CHASE THE ENEMY!**"
Liu Bei watched Wen Chou chase his men around the roadside and sighed disdainfully.
"**Wen Chou has no control over his men!**" Mi Zhu said.
"...**Our men aren't any better!**" Jian Yong replied. "**Does Yuan Shao not pay them?**"
"They've almost all of them dismounted to loot the baggage train!" Yu Jin exclaimed.
"**As I expected,**" Cao Cao said. "**The time is now! CHARGE!**"
Cao Cao's 600 riders wheeled around the slope and charged at the distracted cavalry force: most of Yuan Shao's men had dropped their weapons in addition to abandoning their horses, and that left them defenceless.
"**FOOLS!**" Wen Chou cried. "**Your greed has doomed us!**"
"**We'd better get out of here, Xuande!**" Jian Yong said.
Liu Bei nodded, turned to Chen Dao and said, "**You, Yide and Zilong are the rear guard! Let's save as many as we can!**"
Liu Bei's retreat began immediately, but Wen Chou was trapped and forced to fight his way out.
"**DAMN YOU, CAO CAO!**" Wen Chou screamed. "**DAMN YOU!**"
"**Leave nobody alive!**" Cao Cao ordered.

"...What's going on...?" General Sui Yuanjin asked as Liu Bei approached him with the remnants of his cavalry contingent.
"General Wen is captured or killed," Liu Bei reported. "The baggage train was another trap. We should turn the infantry and retreat to Yan Ford."
"*Ayah*! **How can this be???**" Sui Yuanjin exclaimed. "**Was this your man Guan Yu's work as well???**"
"**Little bastard, I'll gut you!**" Zhang Fei bellowed.
"No, Yide!" Liu Bei pleaded. "We must stand united!"
Zhang Fei lowered his pike and snorted angrily.
"Yunchang was not there, I'm sure of it," Liu Bei promised. "I will go to Li County and report to Commander Yuan personally."
"...Alright," Sui Yuanjin conceded. "We'll retreat."

Cao Cao had inflicted a crushing blow on Yuan Shao's forces: he saved his baggage train and killed or captured thousands of Yuan Shao's better men, including Wen Chou, who perished during the failed retreat. Cao Cao did not celebrate, however; he knew that Liu Bei had not been captured or killed, and that would mean the loss of a valuable asset in the formidable, unbending Guan Yu.

****

114

Yuan Shao was distressed and enraged by the news from Yan Ford and Qing Province.

"**I have barely begun, and already I've lost Yan Liang and Wen Chou!**" Yuan Shao cried. "**Does Heaven favour tyrants?!**"

"Perhaps we should summon your son from Qing Province, lord and friend," Xu Yòu said.

"We can't do that, idiot!" Xun Chen heckled. "Zang Ba's 'Mount Tai Bandits' have pinned him down!"

"Why would Cao risk an alliance with them when his reputation is already at stake...?" Xu Yòu wondered. "Why-?"

"Sometimes criminals are the only choice found," Shen Pei chided.

"That was aimed at me!" Xu Yòu cried. "This isn't the time for-!"

"Like it or not, the point is valid," Yuan Shao declared. "Once my forces complete their retreat from Yan Ford, I'm advancing to Yangwu; the army will consolidate there, opposite Cao's base at Guandu, and Liu Bei can-"

"You're placing too much faith in Liu Bei, missing a vital opportunity, failing to address internal problems in order to give us greater resources to work with and neglecting a threat to our position, Lord Yuan," Ju Shou said. "You-"

"So I am an incompetent fool that does *nothing right*, am I, Ju Shou...?" Yuan Shao retorted.

"...No, that is not what I meant to imply," Ju Shou insisted. "We must leave a force in Yan Ford, or Cao can still outflank us. We must take the advice of men like Cui Yan and order strict, incorrupt government to pacify the rural territories so that we can divert more of our vast army here. And Lord Yuan, we have very reliable information that suggests that Cao Cao has left a mere seven-hundred men at Juancheng, under the command of Cheng Yu – *seven-hundred* – in order to concentrate his forces in Guandu. We should-"

"By consolidating our army at Yangwu, we force Cao to consolidate at Guandu, which ensures that he cannot risk trying to outflank us," Shen Pei said.

Ju Shou shook his head disdainfully and said, "Wrong, wrong, wrong! That-!"

"And, furthermore, by consolidating his forces at Guandu, he has also left his capital Xuchang understaffed, which is a far better target than Dong Prefecture," Yuan Shao countered. "I have no desire to lose another general by cheerfully walking into another trap, which is what Juancheng will be. No, Mister Ju, I intend to follow Cao's example and coordinate with 'rebel elements' in order to exploit the lack of forces in Xuchang instead."

"...Gong Du?" Ju Shou asked.

"Of *course not*!" Yuan Shao chortled. "His are a mindless rabble!"

"The Qian Hill Bandits...?" Ju Shou asked.

"Of *course not*!" Yuan Shao chortled. "They are faithless!"

"...Then who...?" Ju Shou wondered.

"Liu Pi's mercenaries in Runan," Shen Pei said.

"Liu Pi's not a mercenary!" Ju Shou cried. "He's a Yellow Turban!"

"**Not anymore!**" Yuan Shao snapped.

"Liu Pi worked for Yuan Shu!" Ju Shou protested. "They're-!"

"I'll hear no more random remonstrance from you, Ju Shou!" Yuan Shao barked.

Ju Shou exhaled loudly and lowered his head.

"...I am now lacking capable generals, so I will need to assign men to you advisers and promote some of the promising majors ahead of time," Yuan Shao continued. "I don't want to work with some of the undesirables that fate thrusts upon me, believe me, but I am left with little choice."

"...Might I be excused...?" Ju Shou asked meekly.

"The meeting's as good as over," Yuan Shao replied coldly. "Do as you please."

Ju Shou retreated quietly.

"...I want another meeting as soon as Liu Bei and my Yan Ford forces return," Yuan Shao ordered.

"It shall be as you say, Lord Yuan," Xun Chen replied.

Cao Cao read the reports from around Yan Province and smiled.

"Every county magistrate and prefectural administrator heeded your demand for lenient government," Xun Gongda said cheerfully. "We're already seeing a reduction in civil disobedience and can afford to move more militias here."

"And Yuan is making no move to attack Juancheng, just as Cheng Yu predicted!" Cao Cao replied. "Our only problem, so far as I see it, is the uprisings in Runan..."

"A bandit named Gong Du," Guo Jia said.

"...But I'm hearing word of something altogether more worrying," Cao Cao replied. "Isn't there talk of that accursed mantra being chanted amongst them...?"

"...Yes," Guo Jia admitted. "That's an altogether different group of troublemakers, if it's true."

"That's *Liu Pi*, by the sounds of things," Xun Gongda sighed. "And it's true."

"I warned that fool that I'd crush him if he did this," Cao Cao said. "When Yuan Shao is defeated, Liu Pi will suffer for putting that heretic turban on again!"

"Our only concerns now are the size of Yuan Shao's army and supply stores," Guo Jia suggested. "We've expended a lot in our campaigns against Zhang Xiu, Yuan Shu, Lü Bu, Zang Ba and Liu Bei in succession, and had little opportunity to grow more, even with *tuntian* in place: we must end this in a month or so."

"A *month*...? ...That would require a *miracle*," Cao Cao muttered.

"The deaths of Yan Liang and Wen Chou within a week of fighting are miracles, so do not rule out anything," Guo Jia retorted.

"...Perhaps we can utilise Guan Yu again," Cao Cao said hopefully.

"I'd not place too much faith in that," Xun Gongda replied.

Guan Yu sat in his tent and stared at the desk in front of him: he had placed an expensive robe that Cao Cao had given him next to a tatty green robe that Liu Bei had gifted him long ago.

"...Now that I know for certain," Guan Yu murmured, "it ends..."

Guan Yu's only company – his son Ping – nodded purposefully.

Yuan Shao called another meeting that Liu Bei attended with his senior aides.

"...I am in the process of restoring order after my unforeseen losses," Yuan Shao explained. "Yan Liang and Wen Chou are a loss, but they are not irreplaceable. My next move is to advance the army to Yangwu and face Cao Cao directly."

The officials chattered anxiously.

"...I do not hear the honey tones of Mister Ju Shou!" Yuan Shao said sarcastically.

"He is not here," Shen Pei replied dryly. "He has asked that you forgive his absence, but he has been struck down by illness."

"...Is that so?" Yuan Shao scoffed. "Well, then, he is unreliable: Guo Tu and Chunyu Qiong will each take half of the men that I had intended to assign to him, and he can remain at the rear of the field, the coward that he is."

Guo Tu and Chunyu Qiong hid satisfied smirks.

"I have written to Liu Pi in Runan," Yuan Shao continued. "I think that he will be a valuable ally now that he has reformed and seeks to atone for his past actions. My only concern is his ability to command that rabble effectively and remind them that the Girdle Edict – not the yellow turban – is their motivation now."

"Indeed," Liu Bei said. "Forgive my intervention, Commander, but it is so that I might note that General Wen Chou was not defeated by Cao Cao: he was defeated by the fact that his cavalry was comprised mostly of barbarian tribes that disobeyed his orders and followed their greedy chieftains instead, abandoning their horses and weapons to loot the baggage train."

"I can vouch for that observation," the officer Han Meng said. "I saw it, Lord Yuan, as did many others."

Several captains murmured to show agreement with Han Meng.

"...Then a man that commands authority must be sent to aid Liu Pi," Yuan Shao decided. "Who can I spare...?"

"Nobody!" Xu Yòu insisted. "We must focus on Guandu!"

"I will not miss a chance to strike Xuchang!" Yuan Shao snapped.

"...I, Bei, would gladly go to Runan," Liu Bei announced.

"You...?" Shen Pei scoffed.

"Hear him out," Yuan Shao ordered.

"I was able to save most of my contingent of cavalry, small as it was," Liu Bei continued. "My men are feared by the Yellow Turbans and bandits, and my connection – though slight – to the royal line gives greater weight to their mission to save, rather than depose, the Son of Heaven. His Majesty knows that I was a signatory of the edict, and that I want to save him."

"...I cannot argue with that," Guo Tu said.

"He's right," Shen Pei conceded.

"Like it or not, he's the right man," Chunyu Qiong said.

"Very well," Yuan Shao said. "Liu Bei: you will take an army and reinforce Liu Pi. You'll coordinate with him in an attack on the capital. Hopefully, your Guan Yu will join you: if he's half as effective against Cao as he was against me, we'll rescue the Son of Heaven in a stroke."

"I have made efforts to reach Yunchang," Liu Bei promised. "But whether he is with me or not, I have Zhang Yide and Zhao Zilong: I shall give you this victory or die in the attempt."

Yuan Shao smiled and said, "Cao will die! It is Heaven's will!"

"...So he is gone," Cao Cao said as he read a note from Guan Yu.

"We should chase him and kill him!" Xiahou Dun barked.

"Don't let him go back to Liu Bei!" Cao Hong protested.

"He's a future threat," Guo Jia said.

"We must act quickly," Xun Gongda urged.

"No, gentlemen," Cao Cao replied. "Guan Yunchang is a hero: the men that could at least harry him – if they could be persuaded to kill him, which I doubt – are needed here, and the rest would die if they challenged him. Besides, I admire him too much, and I promised to let him go if he performed great service. He killed Yan Liang, which destabilised Yuan's army and gave us early, otherwise unlikely victories at Boma and Yan Ford: let him go."

"You made the ungrateful bastard a marquis!" Xiahou Dun said.

"Have you any idea what sort of man he is…?" Cao Cao asked. "He took the families that were captured in Xiapi, but he didn't keep a single thing that I gave him, Yuanrang… not a thing."

Cao Hong and Xiahou Dun were both surprised.

"He left every bit of gold and silk, the marquis seal, the halberd, the horse, the clothes… everything," Cao Cao continued. "He cannot be bought."

"That's why he must die!" Cao Hong said. "He-!"

"I'll hear no more said," Cao Cao insisted. "Guan is gone… and life goes on."

Xiahou Dun grunted angrily, but he did not argue.

A few days later, Cao Cao's cousin Cao Ren – who had been tasked with the defence of Xuchang alongside Xun Wenruo – received word of Liu Bei's arrival in Runan.

"He slipped past our border forces???" Cao Ren exclaimed.

"We can't leave him in Yinjiang," Xun Wenruo fretted. "That's too close to the capital."

"But we lack the forces to defend against an attack on the city," Cao Ren mused. "Lord Cao must be notified."

**"Han's mandate has passed!
Yellow Sky, soon here!
In this renewing year,
Prosperous all, at last!"**

Liu Bei's army was horrified by the words that were being chanted by some of Liu Pi's followers as they made their way through his main camp.

"That's the Yellow Turban mantra!" Zhang Fei shrieked.

"Keep it down!" Liu Bei hissed.

"No I won't 'keep it down'!" Zhang Fei retorted. "How can we-!"

"Hush, I said!" Liu Bei ordered.

"…Yide's right," Jian Yong said. "We can't work with these people, Xuande: as soon as they're in Xuchang, they'll start looting and kill the emperor."

"It isn't all of them!" Liu Bei insisted. "Look at how many of them are visibly disgusted!"

"Or worried that their friends shouldn't be 'giving the game away' in front of Yuan Shao's men," Jian Yong countered.

Liu Bei was unable to find the words to reply: the group continued until they reached the command tent.

"Ah! General Liu Bei!" Liu Pi said boldly.

Liu Bei bowed slightly and said, "I am glad that we can meet like this in a joint endeavour against the villain Cao Cao."

"He's our common enemy," Liu Pi agreed.

"...But why do you rise up against him, if you do not mind me asking...?" Liu Bei said cautiously. "It's just that... I heard, from some of your followers, as we went through the camp... the mantra taught by Zhang Jue."

Liu Pi's smile disappeared, and he replied, "Some of my followers are not as easy to re-educate as others. I can control them, just as I have done for years, General."

"...I certainly hope so," Liu Bei replied.

Cao Cao was as amused as he was angry when he read Cao Ren's letter, which arrived in the late hours of the night: he summoned Guo Jia and Xun Gongda to his command tent to discuss it.

"...Liu Bei's utterly discredited himself!" Cao Cao chuckled. "His alliance with Lü Bu was bad enough, but now he fights side-by-side with heretics that seek an end to his family's rule! Has this man no dignity at all...?"

"You don't sound as worried as you should be," Xun Gongda said.

"I received this a few hours ago, and yes, I was worried at first," Cao Cao admitted. "But Cousin Zixiao makes a valid point: Liu Bei's men are mostly a mixture of Yuan's vassals, tribal cavalry, conscripts and hired thugs, and Liu Pi's heretics won't take orders from him. Zixiao wants permission to attack them with the city defence force before they can do any serious damage, and I intend to give him consent unless you two have other ideas."

"...That leaves the city completely undefended," Xun Gongda said.

"Ah! But that's precisely why it will succeed!" Guo Jia chuckled. "Liu Bei and Liu Pi will not expect such an action, so their camp will not be well designed enough to survive such an attack."

"That's what I thought you'd say, Fengxiao," Cao Cao said. "I'll write back at once!"

But by the time that Cao Cao's letter reached Cao Ren, Liu Bei and Liu Pi had already made a failed attempt to enter Xuchang: Emperor Xian and Empress Fu sat in their private quarters and stared at each other blankly.

"...Should we not have guards...?" Empress Fu asked.

The question was followed by an uncomfortable silence.

"...I have never heard the mantra," Emperor Xian said at last.

"You should not want to, Majesty," Empress Fu replied.

"...I have never heard it, but I have read it," Emperor Xian admitted. "The azure sky – a metaphor for my mandate, my reign – is passed, it said, and 'yellow sky' – their time, a time of 'prosperous all' – will replace it in the 'renewing year'."

"Say no more, Majesty!" Empress Fu pleaded.

"The 'Ten Attendants' manipulated my father, and then abducted me and my brother; Dong Zhuo killed my brother; Yuan Shao tried to supplant me with Liu Yu; the regents treated me as their puppet; the bandits looted my convoy as I travelled to the ruins of my capital; Cao Cao brought me here, and then he killed Consort Dong, who carried my unborn child," Emperor Xian continued. "The governors do as they please; Yuan and Cao openly fight for control of me; and now, this place that is meant to be the capital is easily breached by the Yellow Turbans... the ones that once said that they would depose the Han and rule 'for the people'. Maybe

the prophecy is about to be fulfilled."
Empress Fu tried to reply, but started to sob involuntarily instead:
Emperor Xian wanted to comfort her, but he could not move.

Liu Bei and Liu Pi had returned to their base in the meantime.
**"Your people were chanting that mantra when they were
attacking!"** Liu Bei screamed at the indifferent Liu Pi. **"You lied
to me!"**
"Some of them, Bei: *some of them*!" Liu Pi retorted. "Did all of
your men do as you asked them...?"
Liu Bei snorted angrily.
"Anyway, we'll try and get a bit more organisation before we try
again," Liu Pi continued. "We gave them a scare; next time we'll
take the city!"
"For *what*, and for *whom*...?" Liu Bei muttered as he left Liu Pi's
command tent with his disconcerted allies.
Liu Pi turned to his senior aides Hè Man and Hè Yi and said, "We'll
need more food: go and get us some from the locals."

But Liu Pi would not get the chance to launch his second attack:
Cao Ren led a force of 1,500 men against the rebel camp within
two days. The attack was, as Cao Ren had predicted, completely
unexpected; most of Liu Pi's followers were frolicking or doing
daily chores at the time, and by the time that they realised what
was going on, Cao Ren's dozens of able cavalrymen were deep
within the camp and slaying everyone that they saw, regardless of
whether they were armed or not.
"ENEMY ATTACK!" Hè Man cried as he ran into Liu Pi's command
tent. **"Cao Cao's sent men to-!"**
"You're wrong," Liu Pi chuckled nervously. "It *can't be*! The-!"
"It's Cao Ren!" Hè Man insisted. **"He's killing *everyone*!"**
Liu Pi finally realised the extent of the threat and left the tent to
do battle with Cao Ren: Liu Bei's encampment was also alerted to
the attack, but it was already too late to save Liu Pi's camp.
"We outnumber the enemy, Lord Liu!" Mister Sun suggested.
Liu Bei stared at the approaching force and said, **"All the same,
we must fight our way out and retreat!"**
"Back to Yuan Shao...?" Zhang Fei exclaimed.
"Yes, Yide: back to Yuan Shao!" Liu Bei replied.
"I shall cover the rear, Lord Liu!" Zhao Yun declared.
"I'm with you!" Zhang Fei cried.
"No, Yide, take the vanguard!" Liu Bei ordered. **"Zilong can
repel Cao Ren!"**
Zhao Yun's cavalry met Cao Ren's force and provided a formidable
barrier while Liu Bei made good his escape; Liu Pi and hundreds of
his followers were killed, and the most formidable of the rebel
forces in Runan was quelled with frightening ease. Cao Cao smiled
when he heard the news: he genuinely started to believe that
ultimate victory would be his.

****

590

115

Yuan Shao glared at the humbled Liu Bei as he walked into the Yangwu command tent.

"…Well…?" Yuan Shao scoffed. "Did you not promise victory…?"

"I, Bei, offer my sincerest apologies for the outcome," Liu Bei said. "But defeat was inevitable."

"Really, 'General'…?" Guo Tu heckled.

"Yes," Liu Bei insisted. "Liu Pi's men were not at all remorseful: many of my men – your men, Lord Yuan, men that you assigned to me – will testify that Liu Pi was not in full control of his 'army', and that many chanted Zhang Jue's mantra for comfort."

Yuan Shao scowled and said, "He promised me that he was…!"

"…Such people are not reliable," Ju Shou said. "I-"

"You cried off sick, you craven wretch!" Chunyu Qiong heckled. "Else how have I got half of your men? You should be in Runan!"

"*Enough*, General Chunyu," Yuan Shao ordered. "Now, I do not think that General Liu Bei can be held responsible for a poor choice of ally on our part."

Ju Shou snorted irritably.

"…The question is how we try and go forward," Yuan Shao continued. "General Liu, is it your view that the Runan situation is still exploitable…?"

"If I had a capable second and a less disreputable local force to work with, I might make ground," Liu Bei replied. "Cao Ren is obviously understaffed: he relies on a 'Cai Yang' to lead his force in Runan, and he can muster no more than two-thousand to guard the capital and attack external threats."

"He didn't have any trouble swatting you and Liu Pi aside, and Pi had thousands of men!" Guo Tu said.

"I agree with Guo Tu," Ju Shou admitted. "We shouldn't waste any more time trying to send more men into Runan."

"I meant no such thing, you coward!" Guo Tu retorted. "I asked whether we were doing enough, not that we-!"

"I… get the idea, Mister Guo," Yuan Shao sighed. "Gentlemen, I implore you to *advise me*."

"I suggest involving Liu Biao of Jing," Liu Bei said. "He has an impressive army and navy, and he has no love for Cao Cao."

"He's afraid of the Suns and Zhang Xiu," Ju Shou replied. "He'll sit there and do nothing."

"We should contact him nonetheless," Liu Bei protested. "If he lent aid, and Sun Ce could put petty grievances aside to serve the nation…!"

"I've written to Sun Ce personally, but I have received no response as yet," Yuan Shao admitted. "I wonder if something has happened in Jiangdong… but enough about him. I'll write to Liu Biao and ask him to act; Liu Bei, I shall give you Han Meng and another army, so that you can return to Runan and coordinate with the local leader Gong Du."

Jian Yong stifled laughter.

"…Gong Du," Liu Bei murmured. "…Very well, Commander Yuan."

"*Gong Du*…?" Jian Yong snickered as Liu Bei's retinue travelled back to their Yangwu camp. "Alright, he's better than Liu Pi, but-!"

"He's a bandit," Liu Bei sighed. "I know, Xianhe, I know."
"Yuan Shao's a bloody idiot," Zhang Fei complained. "He's going to lose, I can sense it in my-!"
"We *can't afford to lose*!" Liu Bei said. "Yuan Shao must prevail, Yide, else Cao Cao will rule the land and the Han will be extinguished! If stopping him means working with Gong Du, then... then we work with Gong Du."
Mister Sun coughed deliberately.
"Speak up, old man," Zhang Fei grumbled.
"...Guan Yunchang's left word that he's sent our families on to Xiangyang in Jing Province, since the region is fairly safe," Mister Sun said. "He's been trying to find us since he left Cao Cao."
"...That's splendid!" Liu Bei said.
"He's got questions to answer," Zhang Fei suggested. "He-!"
"We'll ask them when we see him," Liu Bei interrupted. "For now, let's ready ourselves for the journey back to Runan."

Jing Governor Liu Biao had moved his main government back to Xiangyang in the north of the region once Sun Ce was rumoured to have severed ties with Cao Cao: he received Yuan Shao's request for support and summoned his officials.
"We'll send an army to take Xuchang from Cao Cao," Liu Biao declared. "Cao's entire army is distracted by Yuan at Guandu, so we have a clear path through Yu Province; Liu Bei and Gong Du are providing their own distractions for Cao's defence force in Xuchang, so we're certain to win and win quickly."
"What about Zhang Xiu?" the adviser Wang Can asked. "The-"
"**Go and listen to some donkeys, Wang Can!**" the navy commander Cai Mao heckled. "**We have to act now!**"
"I agree with General Cai," the adviser Kuai Liang said. "We must be seen to support the initiative against Cao Cao."
Wang Can sighed woefully and muttered, "Yuan Shao will lose."
"We march at once!" Liu Biao said. "**For the Han!**"

Cao Ren learned of Han Meng's army camping at Mount Jiluo and said to Xun Wenruo, "Again, Yuan Shao sends people to fraternise with criminals and cultists in Yu Province: I'll join Cai Yang personally and smash this little 'army' before they get settled."
"Be certain that Han Meng is the only threat," Xun Wenruo replied.

But while Cai Yang was readying his force for the attack on Mount Jiluo, a second force appeared that was led by Liu Bei and the local bandit chieftain Gong Du; Cai Yang's camp was unprepared and poorly defended.
"**KILL THEM ALL!**" Gong Du screamed as he led his army of bandits and rebels into battle.
"*Aiee*...! Most of the men have already advanced to the mountain!" Cai Yang lamented. "**We'll have to retreat!**"
Zhao Yun led Liu Bei's cavalry as support for Gong Du's infantry: Liu Bei watched the scene with Jian Yong, Mi Zhu, Zhang Fei and Guan Yu.
"...**Shouldn't we be helping?**" Zhang Fei asked.
"**We're to chase Cai Yang away and press on to Xuchang,**" Liu Bei replied.
"...**Cai Yang's strangely understaffed,**" Mi Zhu noted. "**Can Cao

Ren know about our camp at Mount Jiluo...?"
"...We must support it as soon as possible!" Liu Bei said.
"Gong Du's beaten Cai Yang; let's go and save our camp!"

Cai Yang travelled to Mount Jiluo, met with Cao Ren and said, "It was a disaster, Commander."
"I heard," Cao Ren replied. "Never fear: Bei's army was accounted for in the end. I heeded Xun Yu's advice and sent out more scouting parties; I learned of Liu Bei and Gong Du, but I didn't have time to warn you. I've already taken Mount Jiluo, so Bei and Gong Du are already losing!"

"AYAH! We're too late!" Liu Bei cried as he surveyed the remains of the Mount Jiluo camp; Han Meng had already fled.
"...We must go and join Gong Du at once," Guan Yu suggested.
"Perhaps *you* informed Cao of our plans!" Zhang Fei said as he pointed at Guan Yu.
"Yide, *please*!" Liu Bei scolded. "Yunchang has explained everything three or four times now!"
Zhang Fei lowered his gaze and muttered curses.
"...I'll prove that you can trust me, Yide, if it takes my entire lifetime," Guan Yu said. "I refuse to leave this world until I have regained your faith."
Zhang Fei looked up at Guan Yu: his eyes were filled with tears as he replied, "You don't need to, alright...? I... if I didn't trust you, I'd have killed you the second I-"
"YIDE!" Liu Bei screamed.
Guan Yu smiled and said, "Or *tried to*, Yide."
"We don't have time for this!" Jian Yong protested. "Cao Ren's probably attacking Gong Du now!"
"...That's right," Liu Bei realised. "We must hurry to Gong Du's camp and warn them at once!"
        But Liu Bei was only able to reach Gong Du in time to assist the bandit's retreat; many of Gong's followers deserted him, and Cao Ren won the day.
"I'll report to Lord Cao at once!" Cao Ren said. "Xuchang is safe!"

And within days, Liu Biao halted his advance: he received word of Liu Bei and Gong Du's defeat, but it was the other pieces of news that swayed him most.
"The Suns... are massing troops near Jiangxia again...?" Liu Biao exclaimed.
"And Zhang Xiu is harassing us, as expected," Wang Can reported. "In addition, it seems that the Qiang warlords Ma Teng and Han Sui have sent small armies to aid Cao Cao, and they'll-"
"I've heard enough," Liu Biao said. "I'll not risk losing Jing to attack Xuchang. Call back the vanguard at once!"

"D'AAAAAAGH! That bloody fool Liu Bei's cost me another army!" Yuan Shao shrieked when he read the report from Yu Province. **"Curse Liu Biao as well, the craven old dodderer!"**
"Liu Bei's vowed that he will help Gong Du reassemble his forces and continue their efforts," Ju Shou said.
"What good is it, though?" the adviser Guo Tu scoffed. "Tickling Cao Cao's back every now and then isn't going to beat him, is it?

Bei's incompetent: he-"

"**Enough about Liu Bei!**" Yuan Shao ordered. "I won't waste any more resources on Yu Province: this is going to be resolved by Cao and I facing each other on the field, not by petty intrigue. I defeated the 'Ten', the Black Mountain Bandits and Gongsun Zan by engaging them directly."

"Cao Cao will have limited grain in comparison to us!" Ju Shou said. "Exhaust him with a protracted siege!"

"Even better, whittle him down with sieges and send another army to outflank him and take the capital via Dong Prefecture," Xu Yòu said. "Or, maybe, Runan if-"

"**ENOUGH, BOTH OF YOU!**" Yuan Shao boomed. "**No more about flanks and whittling! Cao Cao will be smashed! Cao Cao will be overwhelmed and destroyed in a simple, straightforward battle! Don't make me tell you again, or I swear that you'll join Tian Feng in prison!**"

Xu Yòu and Ju Shou exchanged weary, resigned glances; their patience was, at last, expended.

"Something's odd about Liu Biao's retreat," Xun Chen said.

"I think it might have something to do with a rumour that's coming out of Jiangdong," Ju Shou replied.

"Rumour...?" Yuan Shao asked. "What rumour...?"

"...Dead...?" Cao Cao exclaimed. "Sun Ce... is *dead*...?"

Guo Jia and Xun Gongda nodded as one.

"...I am less surprised than disappointed," Cao Cao admitted. "When I heard that he was considering sending an army northward, it worried me: Sun Ce might have tipped the balance in Yuan's favour if it was not to aid me."

"But, as we guessed, the 'Little Conqueror' was assassinated by embittered associates of Xu Gong," Guo Jia said. "In the end, he was just an ambitious young man with many friends and just as many enemies, and such men die like all others do... some sooner than others."

Cao Cao hummed thoughtfully and asked, "If Sun Ce is dead, then another rules Jiangdong: do we know who...?"

Guo Jia smiled and said, "We do: Sun Ce's younger brother, Sun Quan, now 'rules' Jiangdong. He is – if you'll excuse this hypocritical comment – ruined by vice, and not at all popular. Some of his own family will probably desert him, in fact. In the meantime, he's pledged allegiance to the Son of Heaven – and, by proxy, shown deference to you – and turned his attentions to an attack on Jiangxia, which will also rid us of the need to worry about Liu Biao."

Cao Cao smiled and said, "Heaven favours us! Jing and Yang will be handed back to us once Yuan Shao is vanquished!"

"It's just you and Yuan Shao now," Guo Jia said. "The outcome will be decided by armies... or, perhaps, by the actions of an individual. Let's wait and see."

****

116

Yuan Shao wasted no more time: he ordered a full-scale attack against his friend-turned-enemy Cao Cao and threw every resource that he could spare at Guandu. The land around the fortified city became a sea of trenches and men, and both sides employed every weapon that the age had to offer: Yuan Shao had immense wooden siege towers moved to his front lines that allowed him to fire downward on Cao Cao's infantry, which in turn forced Cao Cao's men to move about with their shields – or whatever they could find as a useable defence – raised over their heads. The impact to morale was devastating, and the casualties started to mount.

"We'll need a solution to this," Xun Gongda said as he watched an attempt to move Yuan Shao's siege towers closer to the fortress.

Guo Jia fought against a coughing fit and said, "Cat- ...*Catapults*."

"We have some, but they'll need defending once established," Xun Gongda said.

"Fine, but do it if that's what must be done!" Cao Cao ordered.

Cao Cao had his giant catapults brought to the front line to attack Yuan Shao's siege towers with stones; as soon as the archers within the towers were prevented from firing, Cao's men set the wooden towers ablaze with fire-tipped arrows.

"**Zhang Hè! Provide support to the towers!**" Guo Tu ordered.

"**Why? They're wrecked!**" Zhang Hè protested.

"**Not all of them!**" Guo Tu retorted. "**Go on! Go!**"

Xun Gongda approached Cao Cao and said, "They're sending men to support the siege tower positions."

"Then send men to oppose them!" Cao Cao replied. "If they are trying to get to the catapults then they must be thwarted!"

Cao Cao's generals Yue Jin and Zhang Liao led their weary cavalrymen against Zhang Hè and Gao Lan; the two forces clashed without any clear winner. Yue Jin fought his way through a line of supporting infantrymen and tried to attack the rear line: Zhang Hè blocked his path and raised his halberd to chest height.

"**Do you challenge me?**" Zhang Hè bellowed.

Yue Jin's riders backed away; Yue Jin charged at Zhang Hè, and the two generals had a brief clash before Cao's archers turned their weapons against Yuan Shao's ground forces and scared them into a fighting retreat.

"What a mess," Zhang Hè muttered as he finally halted his retreat: the siege towers were lost, and some of his surviving men were badly injured.

"...**They're not unskilled,**" Gao Lan said as he approached the exhausted Zhang Hè. "...**And... we lost the position.**"

"**We did, yes,**" Zhang Hè replied. "**But we're not beaten yet...**"

There were limited yet costly confrontations on a daily basis. Yuan's infantry were regularly forced to charge out of their trenches and brave stones, arrows and Cao's own infantry in an effort to gain ground, and there was the occasional cavalry battle as one side or the other tried a desperate offensive: lives and grain were lost with every encounter, and despite a lack of visible progress it was Yuan Shao that seemed to have the advantage at every point due to sheer overwhelming numbers, experienced field generals such as Chunyu Qiong, Han Juzi, Zhang Hè and Gao Lan, and healthy stocks of supplies.

The days turned to weeks, and the situation worsened for Cao Cao's forces. There were daily reports from around the region that Excellency Cao was forced to receive and lament; Guo Jia was ill once again, so Xun Gongda was his only reliable counsel.
"I think that I've finally found Yuan Shao's supply base!" Xun Gongda reported on one grey morning. "I'd not normally recommend it, Lord Cao, but if it is confirmed, we should attack it: our own supplies are limited, and we need some sort of crippling strike on his men or supplies, and the former is highly unlikely."
"And Liu Bei continues his feeble efforts to harass Xuchang," Cao Cao grumbled. "He's realigned with Gong Du and what's left of Liu Pi's Yellow Turbans..."
"I know: I told you," Xun Gongda sighed.
"...I was pondering it," Cao Cao replied. "We have almost every capable officer we have here in Guandu: Zhang Liao, Xu Huang, Yu Jin, Yue Jin, Zhu Ling, Han Hao... Xiahou Yuan guards Yingchuan against Liu Bei for me, while Zhang Xiu prevents that pathetic coward Liu Biao from moving..."
"Liu Biao was actually moving against the capital!" Xun Gongda said disdainfully. "He must be made to answer for that later on. But to return to our current plight, if we may, Excellency...?"
Cao Cao nodded and said, "You're right, Gongda, that we would need to destroy Yuan's morale in order to win... preferably before our own plummets any lower."
"...Your tone and your words lead me to infer that you're contemplating a retreat," Xun Gongda said.
"Naturally," Cao Cao replied. "I am tired; my men are tired; Guo Fengxiao's health is deteriorating; my headaches continue to impede my thinking; my officers, competent though they are, are matched by Yuan's, but the men and resources that they can utilise are exceeded by Yuan; I must contemplate fortifying Xuchang and-"
"That's exactly what Yuan wants," Xun Gongda interrupted. "He'll surround you in Xuchang, just as he did to Gongsun Zan in Yijing, and we'll not survive. You must hold Guandu."
"...It isn't that I do not trust your judgement, but... I have written to your uncle in Xuchang and Mister Cheng in Juancheng to see what they think," Cao Cao declared. "I cannot do this alone, and if my advisers do not unanimously agree on me staying here, then I must not try and force accord. We'll only succeed if we collectively believe that we can win."
"...We're with you until the end," Xun Gongda promised. "I think that Uncle and Mister Cheng will urge you to fight on..."
Cao Cao smiled and said, "We'll see."

Yuan Shao stared at a map of Cao Cao's defensive positions and grimaced; his advisers watched silently until he said, "I will act."
"What do you intend...?" Ju Shou asked. "You keep looking at the city; are you planning to go under Cao as you did with Gongsun-"
"I am," Yuan Shao replied.
"...My lord, Cao Cao is not Gongsun Zan," Ju Shou sighed. "Such

an effort to speed up the outcome won't-"

"I will not plod along just because I have the resources to wait him out!" Yuan Shao barked. "I want no more 'patience, patience' advice from you, Ju Shou!"

Ju Shou looked at Xun Chen, Shen Pei, Xu Yòu and Guo Tu and asked, "My lord, you have ample counsel. I-"

"Stop trying to get out of being part of this, Ju Shou!" Guo Tu heckled. "Either defect to Cao Cao or be of use!"

"*Aiee*... sometimes I think that you *want* everyone else to defect, Guo Tu, so that you can be our lord's sole counsel," Xu Yòu said.

"**Stop arguing!**" Yuan Shao ordered. "I want to begin at once..."

Days later, a trench captain ran into Cao Cao's command tent and said, "Forgive my impertinence, but there is strange activity in the trench directly opposite us, Excellency!"

"Oh...?" Cao Cao exclaimed.

"...Conspicuously large and apparently perfunctory defences, constant supply deliveries, and high levels of staffing even at night...?" the frail Guo Jia asked.

The captain nodded quietly.

"Your trench is in line with a city wall, Captain," Xun Gongda said.

"It is, Mister Xun," the captain replied.

"Yuan's a fool!" Cao Cao chuckled. "Tunnelling under me, eh...? Am I Gongsun Zan? ...Captain, you will go back to your position with Mister Xun, who will help your men to manage this."

Guo Jia turned to Cao Cao once Xun Gongda and the captain had gone and asked, "Have you heard from Xun Wenruo yet...?"

Cao Cao produced a cloth letter and waved it back and forth.

"He obviously... advised you to remain," Guo Jia said. "Out of curiosity, what... was his argument...?"

Cao Cao handed the letter to Guo Jia, who started to read it.

> "Excellency,
>
> I have read your report and pondered your question. Your resources are indeed dwindling, but when I compare it to the time when the kingdoms of Chu and Han contested, I do not see a situation that places you beyond victory. In that great conflict, neither lord wanted to retreat first, since 'first flight means no might', as it were, and to flee indicates weakness. You, Excellency, have maybe a tenth of what Yuan can muster and yet you have stood fast, throttled his advance and stalled him for half a year. While his military strength remains formidable, his repeated defeats will have caused him harm and that will almost certainly lead to internal strife. Do not surrender your ground yet: now is the time for using unexpected stratagems and exploiting every small opportunity.
>
> Remember that it is a fool that you face!
>
> Your faithful servant, Xun Yu"

"I... agree," Guo Jia croaked. "Might I... make another suggestion?"
"Please do, Fengxiao," Cao Cao prompted.
Guo Jia smiled and said, "Send for... Jia Xu."
"Jia Xu...?" Cao Cao exclaimed. "Why do I want him here?"
Guo Jia coughed painfully.
"...I will send for Jia Xu," Cao Cao continued. "I... see that I must."

Within days, Jia Xu was saying farewell to Zhang Xiu after spending over 4 years as his adviser.
"I'll be alright," Zhang Xiu insisted. "You've taught me a lot: Liu Biao will not be getting the better of me!"
"Yes, well... be careful of the Qiang, in case their sudden generosity has some ulterior motive," Jia Xu replied. "...Farewell for now, Lord Zhang."
"It's 'Mister Zhang' now, I think, Jia Wenhe," Zhang Xiu chuckled. "...Good luck."

Jia Xu left Wan City and travelled to the battle-torn Guandu. Yuan Shao's tunnelling attempts had just been thwarted when he arrived: the angry Yuan Shao had sent an infantry force to attack, but that was being repelled with surprising ease.
"Welcome, Mister Jia!" Cao Cao said. "The accommodation will not be pleasant, but you are a man that enjoys being useful, so I know you won't mind."
"...I was stagnating in Wan," Jia Xu replied honestly.
"Not enough intrigue...?" Cao Hong heckled.
Jia Xu sighed miserably.
"**Jia Xu, you bastard!**" Xiahou Dun barked. "**Mengde, his hands are covered in the blood of Ang, Dian Wei, Wei Zi-!**"
"**Silence, all of you!**" Cao Cao ordered. "Mister Jia was doing what was necessary for his lords; he will now do that for me."
Xiahou Dun and Cao Hong harrumphed and left the tent.
"...Forgive my relations, Mister Jia," Cao Cao said.
"I deserve such things," Jia Xu replied. "My life will be spent atoning for a list of mistakes, I fear. What can I do to help...?"
"Right now, just listen," Cao Cao replied. "Xun Yòu – whom you can call 'Gongda' if he permits it – has something to tell us!"
"Firstly, welcome to you, Jia Wenhe," Xun Gongda said. "You are here to serve Lord Cao, which makes us colleagues."
Jia Xu clasped his hands together and bowed humbly.
"...We've found Yuan's supply base," Xun Gongda continued. "They're in Gushi Village... a weak position, but that's probably why it was chosen. He has left only one general – Han Meng, a man that we recently defeated in Runan – to guard the place. We must attack it to destroy Yuan Shao's morale."
"Who should go...?" Cao Cao asked. "Zhang Liao...? Yu Jin...?"
"Xu Huang is best suited to this," Xun Gongda replied. "Shi Huan can go as well to provide support."
"...Do it," Cao Cao ordered. "Destroy the depot at Gushi: we must leave nothing!"

Xu Huang's assault force – which was mainly comprised of cavalry – waited until a new convoy of supplies was delivered before they attacked Gushi Village.
"*Ayah*! **I am once again unlucky!**" Han Meng cried as he

hurriedly equipped his armour and prepared to leave his command tent. "**We must notify Lord Yuan at once!**"

Xu Huang's assistant officer, Shi Huan, led a small unit in a direct charge on Han Meng's command tent; the two men clashed briefly before Xu Huang arrived and used his own superior expertise to overwhelm Han Meng.

"**Cao Cao has demons for generals!**" Han Meng said as he turned and fled.

"**Don't pursue him, Shi Huan!**" Xu Huang ordered. "**Let him run: our job is to raze this place to the ground and leave nothing for Yuan's men, and he only makes it easier!**"

Shi Huan laughed and said, "**As you command!**"

Cao's saboteurs demolished Han Meng's small battalion and destroyed the supply train and the entire storage depot before they retreated. The news was quickly reported to Yuan Shao, whose rage was close to uncontrollable.

"**This is intolerable!**" Yuan Shao screamed. "**My cause is almost ruined again on account of Han Meng's bungling!**"

"Don't blame Han Meng for being short-staffed," Ju Shou said. "I am not the only one that protested against you only putting one capable man in charge of-"

"**The problem, Mister Ju, is that he *wasn't* capable,**" Yuan Shao retorted. "**Chunyu Qiong!**"

General Chunyu awaited his orders.

"Chunyu Qiong, you will personally oversee the delivery of new supplies to a new depot," Yuan Shao continued. "The new depot will be a better kept secret and enjoy greater defences, since they will be overseen by you."

"I lament being taken away from the front line, but I will serve diligently," Chunyu Qiong promised. "Where-?"

"*Ayah*... one general again?" Ju Shou cried. "My lord, General Jiang Qi should-!"

"**Shut up!**" Yuan Shao barked. "**Chunyu Qiong, you will go and prepare to leave at once! I'll inform you of your destination when you are ready!**"

Chunyu Qiong sneered at Ju Shou as he left the tent.

"...Where, lord and friend...?" Xu Yòu asked. "Where will our depot be now...?"

Yuan Shao smirked and said, "*Wuchao*."

✳✳✳✳✳✳✳✳✳✳✳✳

117

General Chunyu Qiong collected the new supplies and started the return journey to the front line near Guandu: he halted at a defensive encampment commanded by fellow General Jiang Yiqu and said, "All is well, I hope?"
"It is, General," Jiang Yiqu replied. "No aid has been sought."
"Then the supply problem hasn't harmed our campaign too badly!" Chunyu Qiong said. "I'll continue on to the supply depot, then: farewell for now, General!"
The two colleagues parted, and Chunyu Qiong continued his fateful journey to the new supply fort near Wuchao Village.

Yuan Shao received word of Chunyu Qiong's return and said, "Our problems are at an end! We now have enough supplies to outlast Cao and end this once and for all!"
"I'm telling you, Lord Yuan, that we need to reinforce Wuchao!" Ju Shou protested.
"I agree, lord and friend," Xu Yòu said. "We must-!"
"I have already had a proper camp constructed – despite that making it more obvious – and provided thousands of men to guard the place!" Yuan Shao retorted. "What more would you two have me do?"
"Send General Jiang Qi," Ju Shou suggested. "Have General Jiang set up a perimeter guard to-"
"Aren't we fighting a war...?" Shen Pei taunted.
"That's right!" Xun Chen said. "Don't we need every available man to fight here at Guandu?"
"Your plans for slow action are wasteful and futile, Ju Shou!" Guo Tu heckled. "My lord, do not send Jiang Qi – or anybody else – away from the front line to follow the advice of this fool Ju Shou!"
"My lord, please!" Ju Shou cried. "I don't wish to see us falter!"
Yuan Shao was about to retort when Xu Yòu clasped his hands together and said, "Lord and friend, we only mean you well!"
"...**Enough!**" Yuan Shao snapped. "There will be no 'perimeter guard'! Cao Cao cannot possibly learn of Wuchao before it is too late! Jiang Qi will stay on the front line to hasten the end of this already-far-too-long campaign! Xu Yòu, Ju Shou: go and inspect the supplies and ready the depot for replenishing!"
Xu Yòu and Ju Shou did as they were asked. A moment later, a scout entered the tent: Yuan Shao turned to the young soldier and said, "You're from Zhang Hè...? Tell me everything."
The scout began his report; Shen Pei seized the moment in order to turn to Guo Tu and whisper, "Lord Yuan hesitated."
"Xu Yòu swayed him, if only momentarily," Guo Tu replied.
"...Then he must be made impossible to listen to," Shen Pei said.

A week passed.

Cao Cao's forces started to buckle under the pressure of Yuan Shao's constant attacks, and everyone in Cao's administration knew that nothing short of a miracle was needed to turn the tide: it would be Yuan Shao's own divided counsel that would now provide that miracle.

"...So if we move troops to the west, we can exploit that weakness in his line, you say...?" Yuan Shao asked of the assembly in his command tent. "I see the-"

Xu Yòu ran into the command tent at that moment and cried, **"Lord Yuan! Lord Yuan, I beg you to hear me out! A great wrong has been committed!"**

Yuan Shao's eyes steeled: he turned to Xu Yòu – who had fallen to his knees in penitence – and said, "Ah! Mister Xu Yòu. So you have finally arrived for work, have you...? And I see that you have adopted the proper countenance."

"You... you *know*...!" Xu Yòu gasped.

"Yes, I 'know', Mister Xu Yòu," Yuan Shao replied icily. "After all of the favour I've shown you, Mister Xu... and at such a critical moment... your greed is insatiable beyond belief."

Xu Yòu looked at Shen Pei and said, "You selfish hankerer! You know there isn't-!"

"I am addressing you, Mister Xu Yòu!" Yuan Shao barked. **"Me, your lord and master! How dare you avert your gaze!"**

"I... I have done nothing, lord and friend!" Xu Yòu protested. "My wife has done nothing! How can she be arrested when-?"

"I'll hear no more out of you," Yuan Shao ordered. "You *disgust me*, Xu Yòu... you truly disgust me. After Zhang Miao – and especially after Cao Cao – I had thought that I had seen the end of untrustworthy friends... get out."

Shen Pei, Xun Chen and Guo Tu made no effort to hide their satisfied smirks: Xu Yòu was no better at hiding his frustrated, desperate tears as he got to his feet, bowed to his lord as etiquette dictated, and left the command tent.

"...That isn't appropriate, especially not *now*," Ju Shou sighed.

"Ju Shou is right: Xu Yòu should be watched," Guo Tu suggested.

"He should be told that his wife is to be released!" Ju Shou retorted. "Yes, I've heard the rumours about their 'business dealings', but now isn't the time to-!"

"Be silent," Yuan Shao ordered. "I have lost another friend... which hurts. I'd like to return to military matters, if I may."

Ju Shou's protest went unheard, and the meeting continued.

Xu Yòu fled to his personal tent, stared at the collection of military texts and other personal belongings within, and started to weep uncontrollably. He knew that Shen Pei and Guo Tu would push for him to be removed from Yuan Shao's inner counsel and, perhaps, arrested as well: inner voices told him that he had only one place that he could turn to, despite the fear that he might be empowering a tyrant.

"I... must go to Mengde," Xu Yòu sobbed.

✱✱✱✱✱✱✱✱✱✱✱✱

118

Another day of fighting ended, and the evening came: Cao Cao was genuinely surprised when a gate captain brought word of Xu You's arrival at his main camp.

"...Xu Ziyuan...? Here...? Alone...?" Cao Cao murmured. "What can his purpose be...?"

"...Perhaps he is the answer to our prayers," Jia Xu replied.

"He probably comes on Yuan's orders to suggest surrender," Xun Gongda scoffed. "Isn't that usually why familiar faces are sent alone to enemy camps...?"

"...Regardless of my feelings, I'll hear him out," Cao Cao decided. "Wenhe, Gongda, bring him to me: I'll speak to him alone."

The captain retreated with Jia Xu and Xun Gongda.

"Is that wise?" Cao Hong asked. "He may be here to attempt an assassination."

"*Ziyuan*...?" Cao Cao chuckled. "He's a wily tongue at best, sent here to urge surrender, as Gongda said. Besides, when I say 'alone', I mean without advisers present: Xu Chu will be here, and I doubt that a mouse like Xu Yòu will want to rile my Crazy Tiger."

The enormous Xu Chu smiled at the notion.

Within the hour, Cao Cao and Xu Yòu were sat together in Cao Cao's command tent with a pot of tea between them.

"...I'll get to the point," Xu Yòu said after a few polite words were exchanged. "You probably think I'm here on Yuan Shao's behalf to ask you to surrender; I'm here to provide information that I think you will find useful in bringing this sorry matter to an end."

Cao Cao frowned and asked, "Such as...? And *why*...?"

"I... have selfish reasons, Mengde, I admit that," Xu Yòu replied. "Shen Pei, Chunyu Qiong, Guo Tu and Xun Chen have long been the leaders of a faction within Yuan's counsel that wants to be his sole 'voices of reason'. They conspired against Dong Zhao, who now serves you as Governor of Xu Province; they tried to destroy Cui Yan, have successfully goaded Yuan into arresting Tian Feng, and now they're after me... Ju Shou will be next. They... they arrested my wife, Mengde, and she is being treated like a dog! The accusations are groundless, Mengde! My private business dealings should be above suspicion! They-!"

"Forgive my rudeness, Ziyuan, but what is the information that you've brought me...?" Cao Cao interrupted. "I cannot save your wife if I am defeated, can I...?"

"Oh, yes, of course, sorry!" Xu Yòu bumbled. "The location of Yuan's supply depot; it's at Wuchao."

Cao Cao hid an excited smile.

"It's reasonably fortified, but despite the fiercest protestations from me and Ju Shou, the fool wouldn't reinforce the place with capable men!" Xu Yòu continued. "He insists upon using Chunyu Qiong, who is an incompetent braggart with a drink problem! Ju Shou repeatedly suggested Jiang Qi, who is level-headed and serious, but-! ...I can see that you want more *useful* information."

Cao Cao nodded slowly.

"...The supply train between Wuchao and Yangwu is managed at various points by Lü Kuang, Ju Hu and Han Juzi," Xu Yòu continued. "Chunyu is the only depot general."

"You should rest in the tent that I have provided for you, Ziyuan," Cao Cao said warmly.

Xu Yòu looked at Xu Chu and said, "*Ayah…* your new bodyguard is even bigger than the old one! The-!"

"I must consult my advisers," Cao Cao interrupted.

"…You can trust me," Xu Yòu insisted.

"I'm certain that I can," Cao Cao replied. "**CAO HONG!**"

Cao Hong entered the tent with two guards.

"Please escort Xu Ziyuan to his accommodation," Cao Cao said. "I should like Jia Xu, Xun Yòu and Guo Jia to return here as well… and the senior generals."

"It shall be so," Cao Hong replied.

Cao Cao waited until all of his advisers and officers had arrived and the surrounding area had been cleared of non-essential personnel before he reported Xu Yòu's information.

"…Can we trust this little man, Lord Cao…?" Yu Jin asked.

"As a relatively short man myself, Yu Wenze, I care nothing for his height," Yue Jin said. "But he's served Yuan Shao for all this time; why now, Excellency, and should we really trust him…?"

"Shen Pei has had his wife arrested for 'corrupt business dealings', and it is only a matter of time before he too is arrested," Cao Cao replied. "He's done it to save himself."

"It's Qu Yi all over again," Zhu Ling scoffed.

"And Dong Gongren as well," Xun Gongda noted. "He was slandered too, after all of his loyal service."

"Guo Tu, Pang Ji, Chunyu Qiong and Shen Pei are hankering cretins," Guo Jia said. "They're the reason for most of the defections to our cause thus far, including me."

"I believe that Xu Yòu has seen the light," Xun Gongda declared. "What say you, Jia Wenhe…?"

All eyes turned to Jia Xu.

"…I think we should trust him," Jia Xu replied. "My instincts tell me that his timing makes him highly believable. Yuan Shao is, if you'll excuse my frankness, winning: Xu Yòu knows that he will be destroyed by his rivals as soon as Guandu falls, so he acts now while his information has value. Wuchao is a very plausible place for Yuan Shao to relocate his depot, and as for the suspicion that it is a trap… well, Lord Cao, you'd have to send a lot of capable men to attack the place and leave Guandu close to unguarded for such a trap to have a point."

Guo Jia smiled dryly; Jia Xu had included a veiled military suggestion in his answer that perfectly accorded with his own thinking. Cao Cao noted Guo Jia's expression, formulated his own conclusions and prepared to speak.

"…Then it's decided," Cao Cao said. "Xun Gongda, Cao Hong: you will stay here and guard Guandu against any possible attacks. Guo Jia: you should retire, for I see that you are still frail. Jia Xu: you will be my counsel on this mission. Xu Yòu will come with me so that I can keep an eye on him and-"

"You're going to Wuchao?" Xiahou Dun exclaimed.

"I am," Cao Cao said. "This is a desperate gambit, which Wenruo predicted as being necessary: let us completely succeed or completely fail. I intend to do exactly what a successful trap would

entail: Yu Jin, Yue Jin, Xu Huang, Zhang Liao, Zhu Ling, Cao Xiu and you, Yuanrang, will ride with me. I shall take five-thousand men and-"
"But that leaves Guandu understaffed!" Cao Hong exclaimed.
"If we fail, it's probably over anyway," Cao Cao replied. "Let us begin this very night. Yuan Shao must not have time to guess that he has been betrayed!"
"I have formulated a plan with Gongda and Fengxiao that was designed for a situation such as this," Jia Xu said. "We'll need the uniforms and standards of the captives, and..."

Under cover of darkness, Cao Cao's saboteur force of 5,000 crossed the Bian and Puyang Rivers and reached the outskirts of the region where Wuchao was located. The depot's guardian, Chunyu Qiong, was as serious as he could be about his task: he remained fairly sober and ensured that he was given regular reports from the supply train. A scout reported the situation to Cao Cao, who said, "If he's not got more than two thousand men at his disposal, and they're spread thinly, then we can do some serious damage before anyone is alerted."
Cao's men were already disguised in the uniform of Yuan Shao's army: they would, in the dark, easily pass as Yuan forces.
"If we are discovered too quickly and reinforcements are sent, escape will be difficult," Jia Xu suggested.
"Then we will have to be merciless," Cao Cao replied. "Once we are entrenched, we will start to do our work. Spare nobody; captives are not a priority. Let us move!"

Cao Cao led his force to the outer ring of camps that surrounded the depot: the major in charge of security looked Cao and his men up and down and said, "Why are you here...?"
"Reinforcements authorised by Lord Yuan at the suggestion of Mister Ju Shou, who worries about an attack," Cao Cao replied.
"...An attack...?" the major chuckled. "Well, alright, go through..."
Cao Cao's 5,000 passed that checkpoint and two others before they sensed that the proper moment had arrived: once they were within striking distance of the main depot, Cao Cao cried, "**CHARGE!**" and began his attack.
"What in the...!" Chunyu Qiong exclaimed as the sounds of battle became clearer; he threw down his wine dish, abandoned the military text that he had been reading and ran out of his command tent.
"**We're under attack!**" a captain reported. "**We don't know how many!**"
"...**That's *ridiculous*!**" Chunyu Qiong said. "**How have they found us so quickly???**"
"**They have, and they're here!**" the captain retorted. "**The outer camps were surprised, General; they're gone!**"
The air carried the smell of smoke to Chunyu Qiong's nose: he grimaced and said, "**We'll have to hold the forts and send for assistance, then! Get a good man to Yangwu at once!**"

"...Say... say that *again*, soldier."
Yuan Shao loomed over the messenger from Wuchao in a way that almost robbed the man of his powers of speech: the young man

finally found the courage and replied to his lord's demand by saying, "W-Wuchao has been attacked by four-to-five-thousand men and horse and-!"

"**D'AAAAAGH! This is-! …Get out!**" Yuan Shao bellowed. "**GET OUT OF MY SIGHT!**"

Ju Shou watched the messenger flee and said, "It wasn't his fault! And you didn't wait for more information!"

"We need to do something, my lord," Zhang Hè said; his words were ignored.

"What else is there to know, Ju Shou?" Guo Tu heckled. "Your friend Xu Yòu – who is nowhere to be found – has gone and given our greatest secrets to Cao Cao, just as we feared that he would!"

"**We have to help Wuchao!**" Zhang Hè protested; again, his words were ignored.

"**You manipulative cretin, Guo Tu!**" Ju Shou retorted. "**You and Shen Pei *created* this situation, just as you drove away Dong Zhao! You won't be happy until our lord is surrounded by none but you and your useless friends! Every time you do this, you weaken our lord and empower his enemies!**"

"**We haven't got time for this!**" Zhang Hè cried; again, the general was ignored.

"**So the response to slander is *betrayal*, is it, Ju Shou?**" Shen Pei asked snidely.

"**Wuchao will be lost!**" Zhang Hè complained.

"…**No, of course it isn't, Shen Pei,**" Ju Shou replied, "**but-!**"

"**SILENCE!**"

Yuan Shao's order was immediately obeyed.

"…We need to save Wuchao at once, Lord Yuan," Zhang Hè pleaded. "If this second depot is lost, morale will plummet and-"

"Such short-sightedness!" Guo Tu heckled. "Zhang Hè, this is why you are not an adviser! Cao Cao has given us a way to destroy him this very night, and you'd forsake that to save some grain…?"

"Oh…?" Yuan Shao exclaimed. "What plan have you, Mister Guo?"

"*Aiee*… don't listen to that fool!" Ju Shou pleaded. "It's his fault that Wuchao's in flames in the first place!"

Zhang Hè groaned angrily and said, "But if we hurry, something might be-!"

"Wuchao cannot be saved now, not entirely, but by taking such a large force, Cao leaves his main camp understaffed!" Guo Tu suggested. "If we send a large force to attack his main camp, then he'll be forced to break off his attack on Wuchao to try and save it! What will it matter then, Lord Yuan, if Wuchao is lost? We'll have a large army that-!"

"**That will *starve*, you idiot!**" Ju Shou cried.

"…Wait, wait, I understand Mister Guo's point," Yuan Shao said. "Zhang Hè, you and Gao Lan will take a large army – ten-thousand to start with – and attack Guandu at once!"

"But what about *Wuchao*?" Zhang Hè asked. "Lord Yuan, I do not normally like to speak out against advisers, but Guo Tu suggests a strategy that is-!"

"Do as you are *told*, General Zhang," Yuan Shao ordered.

Zhang Hè bowed to Yuan Shao, glared at Guo Tu and Shen Pei, cast a sympathetic glance in Ju Shou's direction and left the tent.

"…I want five-hundred riders sent to Wuchao as a relief force," Yuan Shao said to Guo Tu. "Allow Cao to learn of the attack on his-"

"*Ayah*! Five-*hundred*??? Is that it?" Ju Shou exclaimed. "Cao has five-*thousand*! The-!"

"They will be *elite* riders, Mister Ju, led by Generals Sui Yuanjin, Lü Weihuang, Zhao Rui and Han Juzi," Yuan Shao continued. "Such skilful men will overwhelm Cao's rabble!"

"...We're *lost*!" Ju Shou sobbed.

"On the contrary, Mister Ju, we've *won*!" Yuan Shao insisted. "Let Cao burn my food! Will he have a cause left to return to...?"

The Wuchao relief force set out at speed and met with a sight that horrified them: the outer camps were destroyed, the supply depot was already in flames, and most of Chunyu Qiong's fortifications were in ruins.

"**We're too late!**" Han Juzi cried. "**We-!**"

"**ATTACK!**"

Cao Cao's yell preceded a sudden strike: his forces descended on the Yuan militia and dealt a fierce blow. General Sui Yuanjin was killed in the initial skirmish, and Han Juzi was forced to reorganise the militia and flee to the remaining fortress.

"**IT'S GENERAL HAN!**" Han Juzi screamed at the fenced enclosure. "**WE'RE OUTNUMBERED! ASSIST AT ONCE!**"

Chunyu Qiong learned of the request and added his own decimated militia to Han Juzi's, but they were forced to fight Cao Cao's larger force on treacherous open ground with nothing but flames and the moon for light.

"**Is this it?**" Cao Cao cackled as he met with Jia Xu.

"**...Apparently!**" Jia Xu replied as he wiped blood from his sword.

"**That can't be right!**" Cao Cao suggested.

"**...Agreed,**" Jia Xu replied cagily.

The fighting continued; a short time later, a messenger from Guandu arrived with word of the attack on the main camp.

"*Ayah*! **Yuan's outfoxed us!**" Cao Cao exclaimed.

"**I swear I know nothing of his plans, Mengde!**" Xu Yòu said. "**There's no way he'd have guessed that you'd-!**"

"*Ayah*! **Yuan's going to triumph!**" Cao Cao cried.

"**Not so, my lord!**" Jia Xu replied. "**What good is sieging our camp if he has no food to finish the campaign?**"

"**But Gongda requests aid!**" Cao Cao noted.

"**Will you send aid...?**" Jia Xu asked.

"**...No!**" Cao Cao decided. "**Yuan's done this to try and force me to spare his depot! But I'll do no such thing! Gongda and Zilian must be brave! Every man at Guandu must fight as though they were ten men!**"

"**...You're a true hero, Lord Cao!**" Jia Xu replied. "**I've met my true lord at last!**"

Cao Cao laughed and raised his sword; he and Jia Xu then returned to the battle to inspire their subordinates and bring a swift end to the rout.

＊＊＊＊＊＊＊＊＊＊＊＊

119

Morning came: Yuan Shao staggered out of his command tent and started a slow, mournful journey to the gates of his camp, accompanied by some of his advisers and a desperate, sobbing messenger.

"A-and… and *Han Juzi*…! A-and *Sui Yuanjin*!" the messenger explained. "*Dead*, Lord Yuan! *Dead*!"

Yuan Shao reached the gates and stared in the direction of Wuchao: a great plume of smoke was rising from where his depot once stood, and the sobbing that could be heard throughout the camp was an indication that most knew just how bad things were.

"It… is all *dust*…!" Yuan Shao whimpered.

"We must be fearful," Guo Tu whispered to Shen Pei. "Ju Shou and Zhang Hè will surely blame us for this."

"…Then they must not be listened to," Shen Pei replied.

Cao Cao's soldiers celebrated as they rounded up the survivors of the Wuchao massacre: Cao Cao ordered the captives to be gathered in front of the main fortress while he waited for news of the whereabouts of Chunyu Qiong.

"**Would you like to see something…?**" Cao Cao asked of the captives. "**BRING THE BOWLS!**"

Several of Cao's soldiers brought large bowls and placed them in front of the captives: many of the prisoners started to howl and wail as they realised that the bowls contained the severed ears, noses and lips of their dead comrades, and their distress was intensified when they realised that Cao Cao had ordered his men to add the severed lips and noses of slaughtered oxen and horses that had once been part of the supply train.

"**You're all afraid!**" Cao Cao cackled. "…**You *should be*.**"

"**Look what I found, my lord!**" Yue Jin said as he approached: Chunyu Qiong was stumbling along in front of Yue's horse, bound tightly with rope.

"Ah! Mister Chunyu Qiong!" Cao Cao said. "How long it's been since we last met! You and I once served the Han together as Colonels of the Western Garden… but now, you're a rebel. What should I do with you, I wonder…?"

Chunyu Qiong had his head lowered; when he finally raised it, Cao Cao realised that his face was bandaged tightly and that he had no nose.

"He was trying to escape," Yue Jin reported. "My apologies, my lord, that one of my men taking his nose for a trophy; I can have him punished if-"

"Unnecessary," Cao Cao chuckled. "So, Chunyu Qiong, there are your allies…"

Cao Cao gestured to a makeshift table to his left, where the severed heads of Sui Yuanjin, Lü Weihuang, Zhao Rui and Han Juzi were on display.

"Do you have anything to say…?" Cao Cao asked.

"It was Heaven's will that you won," Chunyu Qiong replied. "What else can I say?"

"…A fine answer, General Chunyu," Cao Cao said. "Perhaps you have suffered enough…"

"**No!**" Xu Yòu said. "Mengde, you must-!"

"*You*???" Chunyu Qiong exclaimed. "So it was you that-!"

"If you spare Chunyu Qiong, you'll regret it," Xu Yòu insisted. "He'll make friends, gain sympathy, and be another Dong Cheng!"

"Traitor!" Chunyu Qiong heckled. "You'll die a dog's death, you faithless man!"

Cao Cao sighed and said, "I wanted to let you live, Chunyu Qiong... but Ziyuan is quite right. There can be no more Dong Chengs: **guards**...!"

Zhang Hè broke off his attack on Guandu when word arrived from Wuchao; many men started to sob as they thought of starvation, and the desertions began almost immediately amongst the tribal elements from Yòu Province.

"...So Wuchao is lost," Zhang Hè sighed as he entered his front line command tent.

"And we've got nowhere, just as you expected," Gao Lan said.

"That... that idiot, Guo Tu, will die a woman's death for his bad advice if I have my way," Zhang He growled. "His spiteful, pointless intriguing has-!"

"**General Zhang! General Zhang!**"

Zhang Hè turned to the excited captain that had barged into his tent and asked, "What is it, Guan...?"

"There are rumours that Guo Tu is calling for your arrest!" the captain replied.

"What...!" Gao Lan exclaimed.

"Is he deranged?" Zhang Hè chortled. "*Explain*, Captain!"

The captain sighed and said, "He's saying that you were slandering Lord Yuan and calling him 'a senile old fool', and that you were contemplating defecting to-!"

"General Zhang!"

The second visitor – a junior official from Yuan Shao's command post – was noticeably smug and disdainful: he glared at Zhang Hè and said, "You and Gao Lan are to return to Yangwu *at once*, General Zhang."

Zhang Hè nodded slowly, and the official retreated.

"...He believes Guo Tu," Gao Lan murmured.

"...Then we have no choice," Zhang Hè replied.

Zhang Hè ordered his men to throw down their arms and surrender to Cao Hong; unbeknownst to Zhang, he was now to become the fifth and, perhaps, most important of Cao Cao's great generals. Having served Han Fu and Yuan Shao in succession with little of the recognition that his skill deserved, Zhang would now go on to be in the vanguard on many of Cao Cao's future campaigns and be a thorn in the side of the famous strategist Zhuge Liang. At that moment, however, he was just another crushing blow to Yuan Shao's morale and a military loss from which Yuan could not truly recover.

"Wuchao is completely destroyed! Cao Cao has taken the heads of Sui Yuanjin, Lü Weihuang, Zhao Rui, Han Juzi and close to a thousand other men!"

Yuan Shao fought the urge to scream as a messenger relayed a series of distressing reports to his silent command tent.

"...Zhang Hè and Gao Lan have surrendered, and Guandu is

relieved! Chunyu Qiong was captured and executed by-!"

"Enough," Ju Shou ordered. "You may go."

The messenger turned and fled.

"...In the end, after everything, Heaven wanted Cao to win!" Yuan Shao chortled. "*Why...?*"

"All is not lost," Guo Tu insisted. "We can-!"

"You've undone us, Guo Tu," Ju Shou growled. "You and your friends, you're the ones that brought about this defeat. Zhang Hè surrendered because he found out that you were trying to have him arrested in order to stop him complaining about you; Xu Yòu defected to Cao Cao because Shen Pei slandered him and had his wife arrested; Dong Zhao is with Cao Cao because-"

"You are trying to blame every failure on me, but you advocated a slow, 'patient' campaign, and wouldn't Cao have found Gushi and Wuchao early into such a campaign and ruined it...?" Guo Tu retorted. "Zhang Hè did as we predicted! Xu Yòu did as we predicted! Dong Zhao did as we predicted! Our advice purged Lord Yuan's court of obvious traitors!"

"...I can see now that there will be no happy ending," Ju Shou sighed. "You-"

The sounds of battle halted Ju Shou's lament; Yuan Shao reached for his sword of authority and said, "We are under attack!"

A captain ran into the tent and shouted, "**Cao Cao's forces have launched a-!**"

"**I can hear that, you fool!**" Yuan Shao cried. "**Everyone: ready yourselves! We must defend our camp and rout them as quickly as possible!**"

Yuan Shao led his advisers and officers in a desperate retaliation, but Cao Cao's attack had already blunted the resolve of the Yangwu defenders; the outer defensive positions were destroyed, hundreds if not thousands were already dead or had surrendered, and most of the main camp's enclosures were on fire, including the weapon and supply stores.

"**We can't win now!**" Ju Shou said. "**Lord Yuan, you must flee! My son Hu will aid your flight: I will take up the rear and ensure they do not reach you!**"

Yuan Shao knew that he could trust Ju Shou, and although he also knew that the suggestion all but guaranteed Ju Shou's capture or death, he silently agreed to it.

"**I'll support the vanguard!**" Guo Tu said.

"**So will I!**" Shen Pei said. "**We will not leave your side, Lord Yuan Shao!**"

"**We will preserve your life!**" Xun Chen said.

"You'll remain at my side too, Chen Lin," Yuan Shao said to his weary, cynical secretary. "Your skill with the pen must not be lost. Let us go."

Yuan Shao, Chen Lin, Guo Tu, Shen Pei, Xun Chen, Ju Hu, Yuan's bodyguard force and an additional force of several hundred elite cavalrymen began a retreat toward the Yellow River while Ju Shou oversaw a general retreat within the ruins of the Yangwu camp; Cao Cao had once again given the order that none that resisted were to be shown mercy, and the corpses were quickly piling up.

In Qing Province, the frustrated Yuan Tan received word from his father and said to his adviser Xin Ping, "I am stuck here fighting

Zang Ba while my father needs me! Why are the Mount Tai
Bandits managing to do what Tian Kai never could?"
"Tian Kai had few men," Xin Ping replied. "Zang Ba is clever,
resourceful and in possession of an army of tens of thousands."
"...**We _must_ win!**" Yuan Tan cried. "**I am needed in Yangwu!**"

Zang Ba, meanwhile, celebrated another successful attack on
Yuan Tan's outer defensive positions.
"I swear that Yuan was crying as he fled from that last battle!"
Zang Ba said. "Tomorrow, friends, we'll press the capital again!"
"...But then there's the stuff that's being said about Cao," Sun
Guan noted. "He's really unpopular in Ji'nan already, Xuangao; we
might lose support with 'The Families' if we're seen to side with
him too much."
"We're fighting for the Han, Zhongtai, not Cao," Zang Ba insisted.
"They know that: when Yuan Shao is beaten, Cao's bound to be
overthrown by someone else, like..."
Zang Ba paused for thought.
"..._Like_...?" Yin Li prompted.
Zang Ba could not think of a plausible answer: it suddenly became
very obvious to him that once Yuan Shao was gone, Cao Cao was
the most formidable warlord in the land.
"...I hope that's not a bad thing," Zang Ba murmured.

Yuan Shao reached and crossed the Yellow River without incident,
whereupon he continued towards General Jiang Yiqu's camp at the
border with Ji Province. Yuan Shao's 800-strong retinue was a
sorry sight that surprised Jiang Yiqu and the scholar-turned-
Cavalry Commandant Cui Yan.
"Lord Yuan!" Cui Yan exclaimed.
"So you're here, Mister Cui," Yuan Shao grumbled.
"...I am," Cui Yan said. "Cao launched an attack on the Li County
camp, and we retreated in order to regroup and- ...Is Yangwu
lost...?"
"_Everything_ is lost!" Yuan Shao cried. "Chunyu Qiong, Han Juzi,
Yan Liang, Wen Chou and countless others are dead, my army
probably consists of little more than what you see with me, Xu
Yòu and Zhang Hè betrayed me and defected to Cao Cao, our
storage depots are gone, our main camp is gone, Ju Shou is
gone... everything... is gone...!"
Jiang Yiqu sighed and said, "We must go back to Yè, then."
"...We can turn things around if we do the right things, Lord Yuan,"
Cui Yan suggested.
"Like what?" Guo Tu heckled. "You advocated-!"
"Please, Guo Tu, do not castigate Mister Cui Yan," Yuan Shao said
wearily. "I am aware that my defeat would probably have come
even quicker had I procrastinated and that my failure to act more
quickly is why I was beaten; Mister Cui, Mister Tian and Mister Ju
are entitled to their opinions."
"Is that how you see it?" Cui Yan exclaimed.
"It is," Yuan Shao replied. "Let us retreat to Yè and see what can
be done to reverse our fortunes, gentlemen... there's no sense in
us staying here now."
"B-but you only have what, a thousand with you at the most!" Cui
Yan said. "Aren't we waiting for the other survivors to-?"

"**There probably *won't be any*, Cui Yan!**" Yuan Shao snapped. "Now *please*... let us go."

Cao Cao's army captured the majority of Yuan Shao's army as it fled; among the caught was the adviser Ju Shou. Cao Cao had Ju Shou brought before him and said, "Well, well... Mister Ju, you've served two fools in succession. You first served Han Fu, who was his own undoing, and then you served Yuan Shao until this day; why die needlessly when you could serve me, as others have chosen to...?"

"See sense and turn away from Yuan Shao, Mister Ju!" Zhang Hè pleaded. "I have come to understand much since I have spoken to His Excellency's followers, and I now *truly* serve the Han! We both served Han Fu once, and turned to Yuan when Han proved unreliable and foolish; we are faced with the same dilemma again, you and I, and your choice, like mine, should be the same! You're an able man that always saw the right way to do things, and so you could too!"

"Don't throw your life away," Xu Yòu pleaded. "Yuan Shao's deluded and easily swayed by spiteful slurs: if you were to somehow get back to him, he'd only let Guo Tu and Shen Pei talk him into locking you up, as he's done with Tian Feng."

"Yuan Shao was once a good man at heart, but in recent times he's become a foolish hankerer," Xun Gongda said. "My uncle and I abandoned him, as did Guo Jia, because we saw that he was no longer the same hero, and we believe that my other uncle, Chen, will eventually do the same; Zhu Ling is here, Zhang Hè is here, Gao Lan is here, I am here, Xu Yòu is here... join us, Ju Shou, and let your talent serve the Han!"

"I pledged allegiance to Lord Yuan, and it is to Lord Yuan – who serves the Han as the appointed Commander-in-Chief – that I remain loyal," Ju Shou replied. "My son is still with him, and so am I, in spirit. It is my hope that I can return to him and save him from Guo Tu and Shen Pei."

"I can't allow that," Cao Cao said. "You know that."

"I can give you no other answer," Ju Shou insisted.

"...I was too quick to give up on Gao Shun, and I won't make the same mistake again," Cao Cao decided. "You'll be kept here in Guandu under light security, and treated as a guest-prisoner; please think carefully, Mister Ju Shou, and we'll talk again in a few days, before I return to Xuchang."

Ju Shou sensed an opportunity to escape and said, "Very well."

Xu Yòu visited Ju Shou that night and said, "See sense."

"Don't talk to me, traitor," Ju Shou growled. "You – more than *anyone*, perhaps – know what Cao is! You only turned away from Yuan Shao because your freedom was at stake! Tian Feng was imprisoned for a second time and yet he stays loyal: he could be locked up another hundred times and never betray Lord Yuan!"

Xu Yòu averted his gaze.

"You've rescued a villain," Ju Shou heckled. "I hope you're proud of yourself."

Xu Yòu turned and left without saying another word.

"...I must try and get back to my lord," Ju Shou whispered.

The next night, Ju Shou waited for his two complacent guards to show signs of laxity, as they had done the night before: he seized the opportunity to pad his bed, leave the tent by passing under the back of it and starting for a horse corral that he had noted while being escorted to his accommodation. He managed to secure a horse, but he had alerted a soldier to his presence while doing so.

"**YOU THERE!**" the soldier cried.

"...**It's over, then!**" Ju Shou cried; he then ran at the soldier, who ran him through with his spear.

"...So sad," Cao Cao said when Ju Shou's death was reported to him less than an hour later. "I had hoped to recruit such an able man."

"He was too *stubborn*," Xu Yòu grumbled. "I tried, Mengde, but he wouldn't see sense!"

"He'll be buried with honours," Cao Cao declared. "And I'll say this, gentlemen: it is causing the deaths of able men like Ju Shou, Chunyu Qiong, Yan Liang, Wen Chou and Qu Yi that Yuan Shao should be most reviled for."

"Agreed," Xun Gongda said. "What a pity that such loyalty is wasted on the undeserving."

"What about any others that tried or will try to escape...?" Xu Yòu asked. "I hear that a quite a few men have-"

"Ju Shou was an exception; all others must suffer a severe punishment for such escape attempts," Cao Cao replied. "Xun Gongda, I want any man that is caught trying to escape now to be buried alive – in front of their fellow captives – as a warning."

Xun Gongda shuddered and said, "As you wish."

Jia Xu was silent; he wondered whether this latest order was one of many that would herald a new era of tyranny that he had, yet again, facilitated, or whether it was just another 'necessity'.

Yuan Shao continued his humiliating retreat into Ji Province: Yuan's imprisoned adviser, Tian Feng, was told of the defeat by a prison warder, who then added, "Your words were prophetic, Mister Tian! Lord Yuan is magnanimous in the end; he freed you before, and he's sure to free you again!"

"I'm afraid not," Tian Feng replied. "Commander-in-Chief Yuan, defender of the Han Empire, might appear to be 'magnanimous', warder, but on the inside he is vain, stubborn and prone to heeding bad advice in addition to ignoring good advice. If he'd won, he'd have released me in order to gloat; now that he's lost, I expect that he'll order my death."

"...That would be wrong, Mister Tian!" the warder said.

"But I am right once again, sad to say," Tian Feng retorted. "I'm sad not for myself, but for the Empire, for his muddle-headedness has allowed another Wang Mang to take power; I'm sad that my lord could *hear* the good advice, but refused to *listen*. I'll gladly die for failing to make him understand."

The emotional warder said no more.

****

120

The so-called 'Battle of Guandu' was over, and the Excellency of Works, Cao Cao, had overcome seemingly insurmountable odds to become the definitive victor.

"We estimate that as many as seventy-thousand of Yuan Shao's men were killed, and thousands more captured!" Cao Cao said to the silent Imperial court. **"Yuan himself has fled to his base in Yè, and his son Tan has retreated from Qing Province to support him; it is only a matter of time before the army is ready to pursue Yuan Shao and bring an end to his insidious plotting once and for all."**

Emperor Xian sat motionlessly on his throne and listened to Cao Cao's words; every syllable cut into him like a knife.

"For now, we must concentrate on eliminating the threats closer to the capital," Cao Cao continued. **"The rebel Liu Bei and the bandit Gong Du are still attempting to cause trouble in Runan and attack the outskirts of Xuchang at Yuan's behest; we must rid ourselves of this threat to the capital, no matter how insignificant it may appear to be."**

Kong Rong shook his head sadly as he thought of Liu Bei's fall from grace and the fate that probably awaited him.

"The Qiang warlords in the northwest will be rewarded for supporting the government rather than the rebels on this occasion," Cao Cao continued. **"The current protector of the Jiangdong region, Sun Quan, should also be commended for not allowing the slanders spread by Yuan Shao to sway him from the correct path."**

Sun Quan's ambassador, Zhang Hong, was grateful for the conciliatory comment.

"Governor Liu Biao of Jing, by contrast, aided the rebel Yuan Shao, and so he must be punished," Cao Cao said. **"When Liu Bei, Gong Du and Yuan Shao are no longer a threat, then Zhang Lu's cultist regime in Hanzhong, Liu Biao's governorship of Jing and Yuan Shao's despicable granting of autonomy to the Wuhuan barbarians in Yòu Province can be dealt with, and then, at last, I think that we can start to say that peace is within our grasp!"**

The words were met with silence. The court was divided as always, but few would challenge Cao Cao: he was now a fearsome figure, a true hero of the times that had felled giants and left his mark on history.

The adviser Pang Ji met Yuan Shao at the gates of Yè City and said, "I am glad that you are alive and well, Lord Yuan."

"We have much to do," Yuan Shao replied. "My defeat is a setback, nothing more! I can rebuild the army, grow new crops, and fight again! It just requires… … …a little patience."

Yuan Shao's thoughts turned to Tian Feng, Ju Shou and Cui Yan's constant remonstrations and repeated insistence on embarking upon a slow, cautious campaign.

"…We must begin at once," Yuan Shao said in a more subdued tone. "I should really let Tian Feng out of prison again, as much I cannot bear to see that man again after- …You have something to say, Mister Pang...?"

"Mister Tian... has been gloating since hearing of your defeat," Pang Ji replied. "It has been reported to me that he has been laughing, saying 'I told him so, the fool!' and other such–"

"He *dares*...!" Yuan Shao growled.

Guo Tu shook his head and said, "It is so like Tian Feng to see your defeat as a victory, Lord Yuan."

"He'll gloat no more!" Yuan Shao barked. **"I want him dead!"**

Yuan Shao strode into his city with false pride; Guo Tu, Pang Ji, Xun Chen and Shen Pei exchanged self-satisfied glances as they quietly celebrated the fact that Ju Shou and Tian Feng would not be able to blame them for the string of defeats. From now on, their words and their words alone would guide their lord; Cui Yan knew as much and sighed woefully.

Yuan Shao's order was quickly relayed to the prison.

"...So I am to die," Tian Feng murmured.

"Mister Tian...! Mister Tian...!" the warder sobbed.

"...But I expected this, so why am I acting so surprised?" Tian Feng chuckled. "If I may ask a favour of you, warder...?"

"I... I cannot help you to escape!" the warder replied fearfully. "I have family, I–!"

"I would not dare ask," Tian Feng insisted. "No, I would like for you to give me a knife of some kind... so that I might be my own executioner."

The warder produced a knife and said, "I... thought you'd ask."

"You, too, have the power of insight!" Tian Feng joked. "But I warn you to keep it to yourself."

"...Mister Tian...!" the warder bleated.

"Don't mourn me," Tian Feng insisted. "An able man that is born into this world but does not have the ability to see or serve a good lord is, in truth, no better than a fool. I'll die needlessly today, but I don't deserve your pity or anyone else's."

The warder walked away from the cell so that Tian Feng could have some privacy; within the hour, the adviser was dead by his own hand, and Yuan Shao had lost yet another of his counsel.

"We should not invite Liu Bei here!"

The politician Huan Jie's words were lost amid the arguments that dominated Jing Governor Liu Biao's court in Xiangyang.

"He'll be a useful asset, a buffer to use against Cao Cao!" Kuai Liang insisted.

"Bei's a hankerer!" General Cai Mao heckled. **"He'll want to seize Jing Province, just as he seized power in Xu Province! Do not be another Tao Qian, Lord Liu!"**

"Liu Bei is incompetent!" Wang Can said. **"He couldn't keep Jing if he gained it, and he's unlikely to do that any–"**

"SILENCE!" Liu Biao ordered; once the room has quietened, he sighed and said, "I am old, and I tire of the intrigue. Liu Bei is a distant cousin, and I am not anything like Tao Qian. I have only invited him here as a guest in the event that he is defeated in Runan; if he is defeated then his army will be broken and any new army that he has will be Jing men that are loyal to me. I will use him as a buffer against Cao Cao, who... who will now, it seems, be all-powerful. Like it or not, I must confront Cao Cao, and–"

"Surrender to Cao Cao and he might let you keep what you have, as he has done with the less deserving Zhang Xiu," Wang Can suggested.

"I will do no such thing!" Liu Biao snapped. "Jing Province is mine to govern, and after me, my son Qi…"

Cai Mao – whose sister was now Liu Biao's principal wife – shorted irritably as he glared at the sickly Liu Qi; his clan were forging ties with Biao's younger son Cong, and that would have ramification in the near future.

"I must fight on, and so must Huang Zu," Liu Biao continued. "We must hold onto Jing, resist Cao Cao and Sun Quan, and fight for the true restoration of the Han. Liu Xuande is my relation and my ally in that cause… so if he needs to come here… he will. Let no one oppose it: the matter is closed."

No more was said, but every man in the court had already made their choices; Liu Biao was a sick man with two potential heirs and a lot of enemies, so there was no choice but to plan for the future.

Within weeks, the resistance in Runan was crushed: Cao Cao had a large force decimate Liu Bei's army, all but exterminate Gong Du's bandits and arrest any that still had sympathy with the Yuan clan that had once had so much influence in the region. Liu Bei collected what remained of his followers – civilian and military – and began the tiring journey to Xiangyang, the northern capital of Jing Province.

"So now we're going to Liu Biao," Zhang Fei grumbled.

"At least Governor Liu has a large army and fears Cao Cao," Liu Bei retorted.

"But we've been beaten *again*!" Zhang Fei complained.

"We're together, Yide; that's what matters," Liu Bei replied.

"…I feel partly responsible," Guan Yu admitted. "I hate Cao Cao, yet I slew Yan Liang and gave him his first victory at Boma. Would he have won if-?"

"There's no point asking that, Yunchang," Jian Yong said. "In the end, Cao won because he has good advisers that worked together and Yuan Shao's did nothing but try and destroy each other."

"But I have good advisers that work together, Xianhe, and yet I am repeatedly trounced!" Liu Bei cried. "I have Mi Ziheng, Mi Zifang and Sun Gongyou!"

"I'm not a strategist," Mi Zhu replied. "Neither is my brother; Mister Sun Gongyou is a politician and envoy, not a master of the art of war."

"…You're right," Mi Fang sighed.

"We do alright!" Mister Sun insisted. "We don't have an army, that's the problem! Yes, we have Yunchang, Yide and Zilong, but we need more men to-!"

"We could have a million men, but we don't have a Xun Yu, Cheng Yu, Guo Jia or Jia Xu to make proper use of them," Mi Zhu said. "What we need is a man that can scheme and weave stratagems… we must hope that such a man can be found in Jing Province or somewhere nearby."

"If Heaven truly wants to preserve the Han, he will be," Liu Bei declared. "Jing Province – especially northern Jing – is seen as a place where wise men can think freely; if such a man exists, he will be there."

Liu Bei was quietly optimistic, despite yet another defeat, that fate had preserved his life for some greater purpose: he would be proved correct, for his time in Jing would introduce him to Zhuge Liang, who was the man that would turn Bei's fortunes around in ways that few thought possible.

"…So Yuan is defeated, and the rebellion in Runan is over."
Emperor Xian uttered the words as he stared at Empress Fu; the empress was weeping silently, for she feared that her fate would be similar to that of Consort Dong as Cao Cao gradually moulded the court and the royal house into the image that best suited him.
"Cao Cao is the law now," Emperor Xian continued. "To think that I plotted my way out of Chang'an to escape Dong Zhuo's cronies, endured the wilderness with my loyal vassals, and suffered the 'protection' of bandits, only to… to… *aiee*."
Emperor Xian could think of nothing else to say: the couple sat silently and alone while the Excellency of Works plotted his next military manoeuvres with his growing inner circle of loyal advisers, officials and officers – men that were loyal, it seemed, to Cao before the Han Emperor. In fact, the civil war between the western regents, the long time spent in the wastelands of Central Province, the court's relocation to Cao Cao's Yan Province and Dong Cheng's rebellion had left the Imperial court as a whole comprised almost entirely of Cao Cao's loyalists, and that would, in less than two decades, spell the end of 400 years of Han rule.

There would be many battles over the coming years: the Jing Governor Liu Biao and the warlord Liu Bei would briefly withstand Cao Cao together, and then Liu Bei and Sun Quan of Jiangdong would famously confront Cao Cao on the Great River; the three factions would then continue to fight for decades, although the alliances would change from moment to moment as strategy and scheming continued to dominate decision-making. In a little over two decades from the end of the Battle of Guandu, the Empire of Cao Wei would supplant the Han in the north, and loyalists would found the 'preserving' Empire of Shu Han in the east; the peoples of the south would enjoy the status of an independent state, an independent kingdom and finally an empire as the political climate evolved. Upon the fall of the Han, the era known as 'Three Kingdoms' was born: that era would end almost 100 years after the Yellow Turban Rebellion, and the progeny of another famous man would rule a unified China until chaos inevitably split the country once again. The great unifier was not and could not be a Yuan: that once-dominant Ru County clan did not recover its wealth or its influence, and although its sons did their best to resist the winds of change after Guandu, Yuan Shu's controversial ambitions and Yuan Shao's strategic errors at Guandu had undone everything that their ancestors had achieved.

"…If Yuan Shao truly was our last hope, and not just another hankerer, then… … …but now, we'll never know," Emperor Xian said. "Now… now, we must wait for… the end."

****

EPILOGUE: A PAUSE FOR THOUGHT

"...**Why did you stop...?**"
"**What happened to Liu Bei?**"
"**Cao Cao did all that???**"
"**Lü Bu couldn't have just died like that!**"
"**What happened after Guandu?**"
"**After Guan Yu what...?**"
"**I said 'Guandu'! And-!**"
"**Yeah! Yuan Shao never died! What happened to him?**"
"**When is Red Cliffs?**"
The middle-aged traveller did not answer any of the questions and statements that his audience was throwing at him; he was thinking about the past and how so many of those stories were frighteningly familiar when one swapped the old names and places for the new.
"**Hey!**" one woman shrieked.
"Oh! ...Sorry!" the traveller chuckled. "That's it for now, I think."
"But what happened to Yuan Shao and the Han Emperor?" one boy asked.
"...The Han Emperor...?" the traveller said. "Well, he lost his throne later on... else we'd still have the Han. Yuan Shao and his followers went north and-"
"Never mind," the boy said. "Did Liu Bei meet Zhuge Liang next?"
"**Yeah!**" another boy cried. "**Tell us 'bout Zhuge Liang an' Liu Bei! Tell us 'bout-!**"
"Another time," the traveller pleaded.
The crowd gradually dispersed to a chorus of mumbles, groans and excited chattering.
"...**I shall come back tomorrow,**" the traveller promised.
"If you could," a middle-aged man said. "It's Zhuge Liang, Red Cliffs and Jing next, isn't it?"
The traveller nodded silently. Once the crowd of villagers had fully dispersed, the traveller slowly made his way to a tavern. News about the collapse of the current empire was coming in quickly now, as were descriptions of the foreigners that would soon be the new masters in China.
"...Going further means talking about... the *end*... but is that really what people want to hear right now...?" the traveller murmured.
The years after Cao Cao defeated Yuan Shao at Guandu were busy and famous ones. There would be yet more rebellions, uprisings, betrayals, coups, pretenders and disasters, and – as in any era – talking about some of them in a particular way was dangerous. History could be a source of entertainment, but it could also be a source of lessons, warnings and ideas: some were more welcome than others.
"What to do... what to say...?"
But whatever he chose to say, that traveller – and many others like him – would continue to tell the expansive story of the Han Dynasty's end and the birth of the Three Kingdoms for generations to come, and there would always be an audience willing to listen: such was the power of that story and the characters within.

****

CHARACTER PROFILES AND NAME PRONUNCIATION GUIDE

It may or may not come as a surprise that the author of a novel about China cannot actually read, write or converse in Chinese (yes, that is still the case for anyone that read my previous works): that could be seen as an indication of how interesting this era can be regardless of knowing the language or culture well, but it severely reduces what you can find in the way of further reading or information. The Three Kingdoms era is very popular in Far East Asia, so there are a lot of works based on the period, although there are only a few that have been translated to English and other European languages. But even when you find the work in your language, there is the pronunciation hurdle to jump; this is a (admittedly simplistic) guide for the completely uninitiated to at least get started, although I should note that I am not a professional historian, language teacher or linguist of any kind and that my guide is not meant to be a professional start of a Chinese language course. That said, here we go.

Pronunciation of Chinese names can be very awkward, since the spellings generated by the Hanyu-Pinyin system are sometimes misleading. Cao Cao, for example, is often thought to be 'Cow Cow' at first. The first attempt at translating *Three Kingdoms* by C. H. Brewitt-Taylor used a different method for pronunciation, known as the Wade-Giles system, wherein Cao Cao was spelt T'sao T'sao: the modern approach assumes awareness of 'C' never being used as a 'K' (as in, say, *continue*), but always as an 'Ts' (similar to its usage in *central*). The pronunciation guide below does not use either Wade-Giles or Pinyin, and might itself be open to interpretation: hopefully, it will serve as a rough guide for English speakers. The characters are ordered alphabetically rather than by order of appearance or affiliation. Place names are completely translated or partially translated depending on what I felt worked best.

In every case, the family name is first, the given name second: nobles often take on a 'style name' in addition, which is often used to differentiate the friend, focus of respect, or ally from a stranger or enemy in conversation, hence I say 'in familiar terms' after the style name. Some of the details have been rewritten or corrected where mistakes were found post-publishing (yet again, I'll say this and no more: I'm only human).

Some of the information provided along with the name – intended as a refresher, as an explanation as to what happened to them after they disappeared from the narrative, or to elaborate where the person was only mentioned in some context – can sometimes spoil surprises for a first-time reader. **You have been warned.**

NB: 'ow' on its own or after an apostrophe in a compound should be pronounced as it is in 'cow', 'ay' as in 'pay' and 'eye' as is. 'X' is a tough one, as is 'J': I vary my approach to the latter quite a bit, since it is a soft 'ch' that's almost a 'j' (just as 'B' is a soft 'P' and 'G' is a soft 'k'), but 'X' can be seen as 'Sh' or 'Hs' (I use 'Sh' because it best reflected it so far as my research went).

Name [Pronunciation] – *brief refresher on who the person was.*
*Any other name they were known by, typically their style name.

PEOPLE

'Big Eyes' – *Black Mountain Bandit 'lesser chieftain'*

Bo Cai [P'oh Ts'eye] – *Yellow Turban rebel general that was based in Yu Province during the original uprising.*

Budugen [Boo-t'oo-k'ern] – *the khan of the Xianbei tribal confederacy at the time of the Battles of Yijing and Guandu*

Cai Mao [Ts'eye Mah-oh] – *high-ranking military officer and official in Jing Province whose sister married Governor Liu Biao; he was later pivotal in the surrender of the province to Cao Cao after Liu Biao's death.*
*Known by the courtesy name Degui [T'er-k'oo-ee]

Cai Yan [Ts'eye Yan] – *highly intelligent eldest daughter of Cai Yong that was kidnapped by Southern Xiongnu prince Liu Bao and became his unwilling consort; she was later brought back to the court (by Cao Cao) to act as the last link to her father's works, which she had committed to memory.*
*Known in adult life by the courtesy name Wenji [Wern-jee]

Cai Yang [Ts'eye Yarng] – *Han military officer that aided Cao Ren's defence of Xuchang during the Guandu campaign.*

Cai Yong [Ts'eye Yong] – *famous polymath and Han official that was responsible for saving the unaltered works of many classical literati by petitioning the court for the creation of the Xiping Stones; he later earned the ire of the 'Ten Attendants' and suffered a long period of exile in the north and east of the country. During his stay in the east, he educated Gu Yong, one of the men that helped the Sun family to found the state of Eastern Wu. He is responsible for launching the careers of many other men, including the calligrapher Zhong Yao (whose son, Zhong Hui, was famous in his own right later on) and scholar-prodigy Wang Can, author of the Cao Wei Empire's official histories.*
*Known by the courtesy name Bojie [Boh-jee-eh]

Cao Ang [Ts'ao Arng] – *Cao Cao's eldest son and heir.*
*Known by the courtesy name Zixiu [Tz'ee-shee-oo]

Cao Anmin [Ts'ao Arn-min] - *Cao Cao's nephew*

Cao Bao [Ts'ao P'ah-oh] – *the Chancellor of Xiapi*

Cao Cao [Ts'ao Ts'ao] – *one of the main characters and a significant figure of the era*
*Known by the courtesy name Mengde [Mung-der].
*Also known as A'Man [Ah-Marn] as a child and for varying reasons in adulthood, from affectionate to derisive.
*Once labelled a *jianxiong* [jee-arn-shee-ong] (which the author

translates at various points as 'Crafty Villain' and 'Hero of Chaos', as either might apply) by the appraiser Xu Shao.

Cao Chong [Ts'ao T'ong] – *son of Cao Cao by Lady Huan that went on to be an extraordinary polymath but died young.*
*Known as an adult by the courtesy name Cangshu [Ts'arng-s'oo]

Cao Hong [Ts'ao Hong] – *cousin of Cao Cao that served as a senior officer on many of Cao Cao's campaigns*
*Known by the courtesy name Zilian [Zee-lee-arn]

Cao Pi [Ts'ao Pee] – *eldest of Cao Cao's sons by Lady Bian*
*Known by the courtesy name Zihuan [Tz'ee-hoo-arn]
*Known as/for many things later on, but he is a child at this point

Cao Ren [Ts'ao Rern] – *cousin of Cao Cao that joined his army as a senior-ranking subordinate*
*Known by the courtesy name Zixiao [Zee-shee-ow]

Cao Shuo [Ts'ao Shoo-oh] – *Cao Cao's second son*

Cao Song [Ts'ao Song] – *hereditary marquis, Cao Cao's father, adopted son of the influential eunuch attendant Cao Teng. He held a range of posts including Director of Retainers, Minister Herald and Commander-in-Chief, but he retired to his ancestral home in Pei County with his wealth when Dong Zhuo became Chancellor of State and was later robbed and murdered as he travelled through Xu Province, triggering a violent war between his son and Xu Governor Tao Qian. He was idolised by Cao Cao.*

Cao Teng [Ts'ao Tung] – *a favourite eunuch of at least one Han Emperor (prior to Emperor Ling) that adopted Cao Cao's father*

Cao Xing [Ts'ao Shing] – *officer serving Lü Bu*

Cao Xiong [Ts'ao See-ong] – *son of Cao Cao by Lady Bian*

Cao Xiu [Ts'ao Shee-oo] – *cousin of Cao Cao that served as a senior officer*
*Known by the courtesy name Wenlie [Wern-lee-er]

Cao Zhang [Ts'ao Ch'arng] – *son of Cao Cao by Lady Bian*
*Known by the courtesy name Ziwen [Tz'ee-wern]

Cao Zhi [Ts'ao Ch'ee] – *son of Cao Cao by his consort Lady Bian*
*Known by the courtesy name Zijian [Tz'ee-jee-arn]

Captain Guan – *officer that notifies Generals Zhang Hè and Gao Lan of slander against them during the Battle of Guandu* ('FICTIONAL' CHARACTER CREATED FOR NARRATIVE COHESION)

Chang Xi [T'arng Shee] – *ally of Mount Tai Bandit leader Zang Ba*

Che Zhou [T'er Ch'oh] – *official serving Cao Cao/the Han that Cao appointed as Governor of Xu Province after the Battle of Xiapi*

Chen Dao [Ch'en T'ow] – *possibly a former Danyang Brigade member; regardless of his origins, he became Liu Bei's trusted bodyguard. His fictional role is either minimal or non-existent, with Zhao Yun adopting many of his duties.*
*Known by the courtesy name Shuzhi [S'oo-ch'ee]

Chen Deng [Ch'en T'erng] – *eldest son and heir of Chen Gui, the chieftain of the wealthy and influential Chen clan of Xiapi in Xu Province and a pivotal figure*
*Known by the courtesy name Yuanlong [Yoo-arn-long]

Chen Fan [Ch'en Farn] – *Commander-in-Chief at the end of the reign of Emperor Huan and Grand Tutor for the first few months of the reign of Emperor Ling; he lost the first role when he defended Partisans like Li Ying and gained the second when his ally Dou Wu took over the court through his daughter the Empress Dowager. He then joined Dou Wu's failed plot to oust the 'Ten Attendants'.*
*Known by the courtesy name Zhongju [Ch'ong-joo]

Chen Gong [Ch'en K'ong] – *adviser that initially served Cao Cao; he later staged a consequence-ridden 'protest' in Yan Province and went on to serve as an adviser to Lü Bu.*
*Known by the courtesy name Gongtai [K'ong-t'eye]

Chen Gui [Ch'en K'oo-ee] – *the chieftain of the wealthy and influential Chen clan of Xiapi in Xu Province and father to Chen Deng; he is instrumental to the many regime changes that occur in Xu Province and briefly advised Lü Bu.*
*Known by the courtesy name Hanyu [Harn-yoo]

Chen Ji [Ch'en Jee] – *Yuan Shu's Administrator of Jiujiang*

Chen Ji [Ch'en Jee] – *known as Chen Yuanfang throughout the work (with the exception of certain dialogue) to make him stand out and also to distinguish him from the Chen Ji that served Yuan Shu. The scholar and author Chen Ji was the son of disgraced statesman Chen Shi and father of Chen Qun. He studied diligently whilst in exile in his youth, and when the 'Partisan Crisis' ended he became an official in the Han Court. He briefly served Dong Zhuo in the capital before fleeing to Qing Province with his family and serving Liu Bei. He then followed Liu Bei to Xu Province and served in successive provincial governments.*
*Known by the courtesy name Yuanfang [Yoo-arn-farng]

Chen Lan [Ch'en Larn] – *officer serving Yuan Shu, later a 'Qian Hills Bandit'*

Chen Lin [Ch'en Lin] – *Han official and later secretary to Hè Jin and then Yuan Shao. He is famous for a document that he authored prior to the Battle of Guandu.*
*Known by the courtesy name Kongzhang [Kong-ch'arng]

Chen Qun [Ch'en Choon] – *the eldest son of the respected author, scholar and statesman Chen Ji (Yuanfang). He served Liu Bei in Pingyuan alongside his father, and then he travelled to Xu*

Province and served successive provincial governors and then the Han court in Xuchang.
*Known by the courtesy name Changwen [T'arng-wern]

Chen Ying [Ch'en Ying] – *younger brother of Chen Deng that was trapped in Xiapi during the government campaign against Lü Bu*

Chen Ying's family [Ch'en]

Cheng Yu [Ch'erng Yoo] – *an adviser to Cao Cao. He was quite old, relatively speaking, when he joined Cao Cao (around 50), and he was known in earlier years of service for being cantankerous, frank and devoid of conscience when matters required it; the author gradually 'softens' his character in the wake of Cao Cao's reaction to Dong Cheng's plot being uncovered, since Cheng Yu is notably quieter, more humble and less influential by the time that he is chief adviser to Cao Cao during the infamous Red Cliffs campaign against Liu Bei and Sun Quan.*
*Known by the courtesy name Zhongde [Ch'ong-der]

Chenggong Ying [Ch'erng-k'ong Ying] – *adviser to Han Sui*

Chunyu Qiong [T'oon-yoo Chee-ong] – *Han official and colonel of the short-lived 'Army of the Western Garden'; he later joined Yuan Shao as a general and adviser. He was famously trusted to guard the Wuchao storage depot during the Battle of Guandu. In fiction he was an absent-minded alcoholic (this was given as the cause of his loss at Wuchao) and so the author hints at him having a love of drink, although he is depicted as closer to the historical figure generally.*
*Known by the courtesy name Zhongjian [Ch'ong-jee-arn]

Consort Dong [T'ong] – *one of Emperor Xian's consorts and daughter of the official Dong Cheng*

Cui Yan [Ts'oo-ee Yarn] – *a scholar and student of the elder statesman Zheng Xuan that wandered the country after the Yellow Turban Rebellion; he later served Yuan Shao and the Han court.*

Dian Wei [Dee-arn Way] – *bodyguard to Cao Cao that also acts as a field general on occasion; the narrative makes use of his popular epithet 'The Coming Evil', regardless of its historical accuracy, since Dian Wei is conspicuously violent and intimidating. He is most famous for his defence of Cao Cao during the so-called 'Battle of Wan City' that occurred between Cao and the warlord Zhang Xiu.*

Ding Yuan [T'ing Yoo-arn] – *a Han official and Inspector of Bing Province at the time of the Liang Province Rebellion and the Black Mountain Bandit attacks in the north; he later discovered and recruited the warrior Lü Bu. He became a known force of benevolence: his other notable subordinate was Zhang Yang, the Administrator of Henei that provided support to Emperor Xian after the collapse of Li Jue and Guo Si's 'Regency' regime.*
*Known by the courtesy name Jianyang [Jee-arn-yarng]

Dong Cheng [T'ong Cherng] – *a subordinate of Dong Zhuo (how and why is not known at the time of writing) that may have been a relative of Dong Zhuo or the late Grand Empress Dowager Dong, or another Dong clan altogether (to elaborate: there were many families with the name Dong, just as there are many Zhangs, Huangs, Wangs, Zhous, Chens, Patels, Smiths, Kims and a lot more besides around the world. Dong Cheng may have been related to Dong Zhuo, or he may have been a relative of Grand Empress Dowager Dong – Emperor Xian's grandmother – that had been forced to serve Dong Zhuo. As with many historical conundrums, we may never know: Dong Cheng was trusted by figures on all sides, which does not aid deduction). Regardless, he served Dong Zhuo and became a Han Dynasty officer during Li Jue and Guo Si's regency, and later served in the Han court in Xuchang; he is a major figure in throughout this work, not least due to the consequences of his actions.*

Dong Fu [T'ong Foo] – *an adviser to Yi Governor Liu Zhang. Dong Fu served Zhang's father Liu Yan in the same capacity and was probably succeeded by others at this point historically, but he is kept in order to minimise the number of characters that are introduced within a faction that serves as little more than observers in this work. The men that Liu Zhang was probably relying upon by this point are all featured in 'Crouching Dragon' as Liu Bei campaigns in Yi.*

Dong Min [T'ong Min] – *Dong Zhuo's brother*

Dong Zhao [T'ong Ch'ow] – *known as Dong Gongren throughout to avoid confusion, with the exception of certain dialogue (his name is so similar at a glance to that of the more famous Dong Zhuo that the author felt it wise); he was a prodigious, promising subordinate of Yuan Shao that later joined Administrator Zhang Yang in Henei after a series of 'misunderstandings' and went on to serve the Han court in Xuchang.*
*Known by the courtesy name Gongren [K'ong-rern]

Dong Zhuo [T'ong Ch'oo-oh] – *the infamous Liang Province warlord-general that seized control of the capital after the deaths of Emperor Ling, Commander Hè Jin and the 'Ten Attendants' and ruled with cruelty, protected by his foster son Lü Bu and a host of formidable allies. His actions – which included pillaging, treason, torture and regicide – inspired Yuan Shao to form the Eastern Pass Coalition and challenge him militarily. Dong Zhuo is an unpleasant memory during the timeframe of this work, although his subordinates Li Jue and Guo Si dominate the political landscape in the early acts; his exploits are covered extensively in "Yellow Sky".*
*Known by the courtesy name Zhongying [Ch'ong-ying]

Dou Wu [T'oh Woo] – *a respected scholar and father to Emperor Huan's last empress, Lady Dou. He tried to purge the 'Ten Attendants', but his plan had serious and far-reaching consequences.*
*Known by the courtesy name Youping [Yoh-ping]

Duan Wei [T'oo-arn Way] – *officer that served Dong Zhuo and then the regents*

'Eighty-foot Moustache' Zuo [Tz'oo-oh] – *Black Mountain Bandit 'lesser chieftain'*

Emperor Huan of the Han [Hoo-arn] – *predecessor to Emperor Ling (but not his father: Huan died without issue).*

Emperor Ling of the Han [Ling] – *formerly known as Liu Hong, Marquis of Jieduting. He was selected – at the age of 12 – as the successor to Emperor Huan, who had no issue. Some blame Ling for the fall of the Han; he was emperor during the 'Yellow Turban Rebellion' and 'Liang Province Rebellion', both of which were blamed on government mismanagement. His death was followed by the rise of Dong Zhuo and the fission that resulted from that.*
*Also known as (Han) Lingdi [(Harn) Ling-t'ee] (lit. Han Emperor Ling) when Lingdi is a better option for conciseness.
*Known as Liu Hong [Lee-oo Hong], Marquis of Jieduting [Jee-er-doo-ting]) before being created Emperor.

Emperor Shao of Han [S'ah-oh] – *Emperor Ling's eldest son, born to Empress Hè. There were a lot of inauspicious prognostications being made at that point in time, so Emperor Ling had his sons 'adopted' to others prior to their coming of age; Liu Bian was entrusted to a nobleman vassal and known to the outside world as Marquis Shi. Bian became Emperor shortly after the death of his father (after a short but unpleasant conflict between his grandmother's clan and his mother's clan that resulted in the purge of his grandmother's clan from the court), but when Dong Zhuo came to power in the capital the young emperor was deposed, created the Prince of Hongnong and replaced by his younger brother Liu Xie, who became Emperor Xian, the last Emperor of the Han Dynasty. Liu Bian and his mother were then murdered by Dong Zhuo's allies.*
*Known alternatively within the text as (Han) Shaodi [(Harn) S'ah-oh-t'ee] (lit. Han Emperor Shao) when Shaodi is a better option for conciseness.
*Known as Marquis Shi [S'ee] while 'adopted'.
*Known as Liu Bian [Lee-oo P'ee-arn], Prince of Hongnong [Hong-nong] after being deposed by Dong Zhuo.

Emperor Xian of Han [Shee-an] – *Emperor Ling's second son, Liu Xie was born to Consort Wang rather than Empress Hè: the jealous empress then poisoned his mother. There were a lot of inauspicious prognostications being made at that point in time, so Emperor Ling had his sons 'adopted' to others prior to their coming of age; Liu Xie was entrusted to his grandmother, Empress Dowager Dong. He was first created the Prince of Bohai and then the Prince of Chenliu after the 'adoption' period ended, but despite being a second son by a consort, he would later become Emperor Xian after a series of extraordinary events in the court, but he was never truly accepted by some. It is no secret or 'plot spoiler' that the Han Dynasty was finally eradicated in the early 3rd Century; Xiandi was the last Han Emperor and had the*

'privilege' of overseeing the final years of the decline. He is said to have lived for over a decade after abdicating as the Duke of Shanyang; his given date of death is unusually close to – as in not long after – the death of Zhuge Liang, Chancellor/Prime Minister of the independent state of Shu Han, whose mission it was to restore the Han in some form.
*Also known as (Han) Xiandi [(Harn) Shee-an-t'ee] (lit. Han Emperor Xian) when Xiandi is a better option for conciseness.
*Known as Marquis Dong [T'ong] while in the care of his grandmother.
*Known as Liu Xie [Lee-oo Shee-er], Prince of Bohai [P'oh-high] after leaving his grandmother's direct care.
*Known as Liu Xie [Lee-oo Shee-er], Prince of Chenliu [Ch'en-lee-oo] prior to his ascension.

(Grand) Empress Dowager Dong [T'ong] – *the mother of Emperor Ling; she was initially marginalised because of the designs of the Dou family. When the Dous were destroyed by the 'Ten Attendants', Emperor Ling gratefully installed his mother as Dowager in place of Dowager Dou, wherein she started to meddle in the affairs of state. She raised Liu Xie, her younger grandson, when court superstition dictated that her son's heirs should not be raised as princes. When her son died Lady Dong became Grand Dowager, but she and her Hejian Dong clan were then forced to contest the rival Hè family's plans for the succession: the Dongs of Hejian lost, and Lady Dong paid a heavy price for failure. She was later lauded by Dong Zhuo of Longxi, who did so, some said, for little more than their shared clan name.*

Empress Dowager Dou [T'oh] – *the daughter of Han official Dou Wu and principal spouse of Emperor Huan; after Huan's death, she briefly became a regent that assisted in the selection of the next emperor.*

Empress Dowager Hè [Her] – *the second empress taken by Emperor Ling; her brother, Hè Jin, would go on to become Commander-in-Chief. She was the mother of Liu Bian, later Emperor Shao and Prince of Hongnong.*

Empress Fu [Foo] – *daughter of Han official Fu Wan and (one of, if not the) first consort to Emperor Xian; she was then made Empress when Li Jue and Guo Si founded their 'co-regency' government. Empress Fu was said to be a confidante to Emperor Xian; the author takes the liberty of portraying the relationship between the young monarchs as frank, affectionate and relatively informal in order to give the audience an idea of what they might think about events at any given point.*

Empress Dowager Liang [Lee-arng] – *sister of the influential Liang Ji and stepmother to Emperor Huan; she was purged along with her brother by the 'Ten Attendants' and Emperor Huan.*

Fan Chou [Farn T'ou] – *a general that served Dong Zhuo and then the regents Li Jue and Guo Si; he grew up in the same region as the Liang Province rebel-turned-Qiang warlord Han Sui. He was initially highly trusted by the regents, and was promoted to one of the highest military ranks, but was later 'executed' by Li Jue at a banquet for his failure to capture Han Sui in the wake of a failed attempt by Han, Ma Teng and Yi Governor Li Yan to seize the then imperial capital Chang'an.*

'Fixed Gaze' – *Black Mountain Bandit 'lesser chieftain'; it is entirely possible that he and Zhang Yang's vassal Sui Gu are one and the same (the author has Fixed Gaze disappear from the narrative as Sui Gu is introduced).*

'Floating Cloud' – *Black Mountain Bandit 'lesser chieftain'*

'Flying Swallow' Zhang Yan [Ch'arng Yarn] – *known as 'Flying Swallow' for his great speed and dexterity, Chu Yan (as he was first known) was a bandit leader that formed an uneasy alliance with 'Oxhorn Zhang' to raid a village; Oxhorn was mortally wounded by the defending forces, but to the surprise of all, Chu Yan helped his temporary ally to safety. Oxhorn saw in Chu Yan a man that could do something amazing, and he bequeathed his bandit army to Chu Yan as he lay dying. Chu Yan then changed his named to Zhang Yan in honour of Oxhorn, and went on to become the charismatic leader of a million-strong coalition known as the Black Mountain Bandits.*
*Formerly known as Chu Yan [T'oo Yarn]

Fu Wan [Foo Wahn] – *a Han official and descendant of the scholar Fu Sheng and the Han loyalist official Fu Dan; he became father-in-law to Emperor Xian when his daughter Lady Fu became a royal consort and then Empress.*

Fu Xie [Foo Shee-er] – *a senior official in the Han court. In history, he earned merit fighting the Yellow Turbans and was made a 'Gentleman Scholar'; he was then consulted on matters that included the Qiang uprising in Liang Province. His advice did not always produce positive results, and he was eventually humiliated and posted to Liang Province to serve the current Governor; he died fighting the rebels Ma Teng and Han Sui, who went on to become prominent Qiang warlords.*

Gao Gan [K'ao K'arn] – *nephew/vassal of Yuan Shao*

Gao Lan [K'ao Larn] – *military officer that served Yuan Shao and worked with future legend Zhang Hè*

Gao Shun [K'ao S'oon] – *a subordinate of Lü Bu that remained with Bu until his death; the two men had a difficult working relationship. Gao Shun was known for his honesty and attempts at giving advice that was rarely wanted or heeded. He was also a very competent field commander. He (or one of his subordinates) was likely responsible for the infamous arrow that robbed Xiahou Dun of one of his eyes.*

Gong Du [K'ong T'oo] – *bandit in Yu Province that collaborated with Yuan Shao's forces during the Guandu campaign.*

Gongsun Xu [K'ong-soon Shoo] – *son of Gongsun Zan*

Gongsun Yue [K'ong-soon Yoo-er] – *a much-loved nephew of Gongsun Zan; he was sent to assist Sun Jian at the Battle of Yang City, but he was struck down during that conflict. Gongsun Zan held Yuan Shao personally responsible for the incident.*

Gongsun Zan [K'ong-soon Tz'arn] – *a military officer, county magistrate, self-appointed governor and warlord in the last two decades of the 2nd Century; he was a friend of the warlord Liu Bei, and was known for his tumultuous relationship with the Ru County Yuan clan. He collaborated with Yuan Shu from time to time and briefly worked with Yuan Shao, but he later became fiercely antagonistic toward the latter for a number of reasons. He then fought Yuan Shao for control of Ji, Qing and Yòu provinces; Gongsun took the last of those provinces from its governor, Liu Yu, and was directly responsible for Yu's death.*
*Known by the courtesy name Bogui [P'oh-goo-ee]

Guan Jing [K'oo-arn Ch'ing] – *a subordinate of Gongsun Zan that served as an adviser*

Guan Ping [K'oo-arn Ping] – *eldest son of Guan Yu*

Guan Yu [K'oo-arn Yoo] – *an early ally of Liu Bei who would gain a magnitude of fame and worship after his death that exceeded that enjoyed by his master; he is known for his long beard, his green robes, his learnedness, his lofty demeanour, his 'Green Dragon' weapon (which the author has retained despite its being a possible fiction), his fictional inheritance of the equally-fictional 'Red Hare' warhorse from Lü Bu, and his similarly fictional unmatched skill in battle, although his historical skill is still quite impressive. He is revered by the lawful and the lawless alike, since he is seen as a man that applied morals when and where appropriate to achieve an ultimate end. His early career is covered in "Yellow Sky" and this work, while his later career is depicted in 'Crouching Dragon'.*
*Known by the courtesy name Yunchang [Yoon-charng]

Guo Jia [K'oo-oh Jee-ah] – *senior adviser to Cao Cao that briefly served Yuan Shao; he is one of the most important advisers that Cao Cao ever had, and his absence from the first major campaign after his untimely death – the acquisition of Jing Province and subsequent 'Battle of Red Cliffs' – is largely blamed – and by none more than Cao Cao himself – for the disastrous outcome.*
*Known by the courtesy name Fengxiao [Fung-shee-ow]

Guo Si [K'oo-oh See] – *a general serving Dong Zhuo; he cooperated with fellow Liang Province general Li Jue and became 'co-regent' after Dong Zhuo's death. Guo and Li's joint rise to power is depicted in the last acts of "Yellow Sky".*

Guo Tu [K'oo-oh Too] – *an adviser to Yuan Shao that once served – and then betrayed – Ji Province governor Han Fu, allowing Yuan to seize Ji and begin building his strength.*
*Known by the courtesy name Gongze [K'ong-tz'er]

'Haixi Chen' [Ch'ern] – *a bandit chieftain in the Haixi region of Xu Province; his name was Chen Yu, but the author uses an epithet to make him more distinct. He fought against – and was soundly beaten by – the southern warlord Sun Ce at one point in his career, an event that is covered in 'East of the River'.*

Han Fu – *the Governor of Ji Province; Han Fu later lent his forces to the campaign against Dong Zhuo. He had many vassals that were notable in their own right, such as Qu Yi and Zhang Hè: the former was a hero of the Yellow Turban suppression campaign, while the latter would go on to serve Yuan Shao and Cao Cao in succession and become one of the most famous generals of the 'Three Kingdoms' era. After trying to escape his obligations to the Eastern Pass Coalition, he was attacked by Gongsun Zan (who was acting at Yuan Shao's behest), betrayed by a large number of his vassals and forced to cede his post to Yuan Shao and go into exile in Yan Province; he committed suicide whilst living under the protection of Cao Cao's friend Zhang Miao, Administrator of Chenliu (presumably because he suspected that he and his family would be killed by Yuan Shao's agents otherwise).*
*Known by the courtesy name Wenjie [Wern-jee-er]

Han Hao [Harn Ha-oh] – *an officer serving Cao Cao; he was a subordinate of Wang Kuang at the time of the 'Dong Zhuo crisis' and joined Cao Cao after Wang Kuang retired.*
*Known by the courtesy name Yuansi [Yoo-arn-see]

Han Juzi [Harn Ch'oo-tz'ee] – *an officer serving Yuan Shao.*

Han Meng [Harn Mung] – *an officer serving Yuan Shao.*

Han Sui [Harn Soo-ee] – *Attendant Official of the Liang Province administration at the time of the major rebellion in the year 185; he was captured and convinced that he should join the rebellion. Within a year, Han Sui was a senior commander of the rebel forces, and he even married into the Qiang, becoming a senior chieftain. He had a stormy political relationship and tribal rivalry with fellow rebel-turned-tribal leader Ma Teng and his more famous son Ma Chao.*
*Known by the courtesy name Wenyue [Wern-yoo-er]

Han Xian [Harn Shee-an] - *the leader of the White Wave Bandits; he was a good friend of the Han officer Yang Feng. He and his allies briefly 'protected' Emperor Xian from the co-regents.*

Han Yin [Harn Yin] – *adviser to the warlord Yuan Shu*

Hao Meng [Ha-oh Mung] – *an officer serving the warlord Lü Bu*

Hè Jin [Her Jin] – *the brother of Emperor Ling's second Empress, Lady Hè; Jin enjoyed a rapid rise from butcher to Commander-in-Chief of the Imperial army once his sister was elevated. He earned great acclaim when he led the army against the Yellow Turban rebels, and quickly earned equally-substantial ire from the 'Ten Attendants', who convinced Emperor Ling to form a second force,*

the 'Army of the Western Garden', to counter Jin's influence. When Emperor Ling died he had a brief political battle against Grand Empress Dowager Dong and secured his nephew as Emperor Shao. Jin then tried to purge the 'Ten Attandants', but he was forced to threaten his own sister, Empress Dowager Hè (who was, in turn,being blackmailed by the eunuchs) and invite Yuan Shao and, more disastrously, Dong Zhuo to empower his cause. Jin was killed by the 'Ten' before Dong Zhuo reached the capital, which allowed Dong – who was now the highest-ranking officer – to seize power.
*Known by the courtesy name Suigao [Soo-ee-gah-oh]

Hè Man [Her Marn] – *Yellow Turban rebel in Yu Province.*

Hè Mao [Her Mah-oh] – *an officer serving Yuan Shao*

Hè Xian [Her Shee-an] – *son of Hè Jin by his principal wife; Xian died young, and Cao Cao took his widow Lady Yin into his own home as a consort.*

Hè Yi [Her Yee] – *Yellow Turban rebel in Yu Province.*

Hou Cheng [Hoh T'erng] – *an officer serving Lü Bu*

Hu Guang [Hoo K'oo-arng] – *a famous calligrapher that lived in earlier times*

Hu Zhen [Hoo Ch'ern] – *an influential Liang Province general serving Dong Zhuo; he had a minor rivalry with Lü Bu that was not always friendly. He put his differences with Bu aside to plot Dong Zhuo's assassination with Director of the Imperial Secretariat Wang Yun, but when his fellow conspirator Xu Rong was defeated by Li Jue and Guo Si he switched sides yet again and aided the two in defeating Lü Bu and Wang Yun. He was rewarded with rank but died suddenly; many blamed Regent Li Jue.*
*Known by the courtesy name Wencai [Wern-ts'eye]

Hua Tuo [Hoo-ah Too-oh] – *a famous scholar and doctor that lived and worked through the time of the last three Han Emperors; he is already in his sixties at the time that he is briefly introduced in this work. He was said to have created beneficial exercises based on the physical postures and movements of several animals and practised a range of medicinal treatments including anaesthesia, surgery and the more traditional acupuncture. He and his 'Book of the Green Bag' were lost to time when he refused to abandon his free-roaming ways and become the Cao family's personal physician – primarily to deal with Cao Cao's recurring migraines – and died a pitiful death in prison.*
*Known by the courtesy name Yuanhua [Yoo-arn-hoo-ah]

Hua Xiong [Hoo-ah Shee-ong] – *a general serving Dong Zhuo; he is most famous for how he was killed in fiction. In 'Sanguo Yanyi' (Romance of the Three Kingdoms), Hua Xiong was depicted as second only to Lü Bu (whose strength is also greatly exaggerated); he bests every general sent to challenge him, including the formidable Sun Jian (who had the most to do with his historical defeat), but he is finally killed with ease during a duel with Guan Yu. Historically, Hua Xiong is far less exciting, and it is this Hua Xiong that the author chose for the sake of producing more factual works, namely his appearances in "Yellow Sky" and 'East of the River'. Hua is briefly mentioned in this work.*

Huan Jie [Hoo-arn Jee-er] – *a politician that briefly served the Sun clan of Jiangdong and accompanied the family patriarch Sun Jian on his fateful campaign to Jing Province; when Sun Jian was killed in an ambush, Huan successfully lobbied Liu Biao to have the body returned to the family and then remained in Jing as a vassal to Liu Biao. Huan Jie joined the new Han regime when Liu Biao died and went on to serve Cao Cao and then the Cao Wei Empire.*
*Known by the courtesy name Boxu [P'oh-shoo]

Huang Shao [Hoo-arng S'ow] – *a Yellow Turban officer; in "Yellow Sky", he was introduced as a vanguard general under Bo Cai. He surrendered to the loyalist forces and formed a mercenary confederacy with fellow Yellow Turban Liu Pi; they briefly worked with Sun Jian (as depicted in 'East of the River') before returning to their old ways and working against Cao Cao's court in Xuchang.*

Huang She [Hoo-arng S'er] – *the son of the Jiangxia (southern Jing Province) warlord Huang Zu*

Huang Wan [Hoo-arng Wahn] – *a Han official and loyalist that contributed to plots to rid the capital of Dong Zhuo and his allies; in this novel, he is only briefly depicted and shown as being uninvolved in the plot to oust the regents*

Huang Zu [Hoo-arng Tz'oo] – *ostensibly a vassal of Jing Province Governor Liu Biao, but Huang Zu was autonomous in the southeast Jiangxia region and had immense influence besides that.*

Huangfu Song [Hoo-arng-foo Song] – *a prominent general of the Han Dynasty army; he was extremely effective against the Yellow Turbans, and he was renowned for his upstanding moral values and generous nature. He challenged the 'Ten Attendants' and suffered a temporary downturn in his career, but he had one last significant victory against the Qiang rebels in that was then impacted by concurrent events in the capital. He is retired and in poor health at the start of this work and dies 'off-stage' during the civil war between the co-regents Li Jue and Guo Si.*
*Known by the courtesy name Yizhen [Yee-ch'ern]

Huche'er [Hoo-cher Er] – *a man of non-Chinese origin that serves as an officer to the Liang Province warlord Zhang Ji and later his nephew Zhang Xiu; he is said to have been strong and resourceful, and he was pivotal to the ambush-based victory over Cao Cao's forces during the so-called 'Battle of Wan City'. He disappears from history after that encounter.*

Huchuquan [Hoo-t'oo-chooarn] – *brother of Southern Xiongnu renegade chieftain Yufuluo and elected Chanyu (supreme chieftain) of the Southern Xiongnu*

Hui Qu [Hoo-ee Choo] – *only mentioned during this work; Hui is Yuan Shu's chosen 'Inspector of Yang Province', but he never truly takes up the role. He briefly features in 'East of the River'.*

Ji Jian [Jee Jee-arn] – *an official serving Xiao Jian*

Ji Ling [Jee Ling] – *a high-ranking officer serving Yuan Shu*

Jia Xu [Jee-ah Shoo] – *an adviser and politician; Jia Xu served the infamous Dong Zhuo until the latter's death, at which point he aided Dong's generals Li Jue and Guo Si when they tried to govern as co-regents to the emperor. When the regents faltered, Jia Xu realigned to their former vassal Zhang Xiu in Wan City, whereupon he inflicted one of the most famous and costly defeats of Cao Cao's career upon him; he later served Cao Cao and the Cao Wei Empire. He is probably one of the most divisive and decisive figures of the period, and is, it might be argued, one of the greatest strategists of the time, an equal or perhaps superior to more famous figures such as Zhuge Liang, Pang Tong, Zhou Yu, Lü Meng, Lu Xun, Sima Yi and Guo Jia.*
*Known by the courtesy name Wenhe [Wern-her]

Jian Shuo [Jee-arn S'oo-oh] – *a member (and later leader) of the 'Ten Attendants'; he would go on to become the appointed commander of the militia-based 'Army of the Western Garden'. He is never mentioned by name, but his overall command of Cao Cao, Yuan Shao and Chunyu Qiong (amongst others) is remembered by those men with obvious bitterness; he met his end when his fellow 'Ten Attendants' failed to support him after a failed attempt to assassinate Hè Jin.*

Jian Shuo's uncle – *never referred to by name, he is the uncle of the eunuch (and senior member of the 'Ten Attendants') Jian Shuo. He was arrested and flogged by the then-District Captain of Luoyang, Cao Cao, for flouting a curfew law, which led to Cao being 'exiled' to Ji'nan by the 'Ten Attendants'.*

Jian Yong [Jee-arn Yong] – *an ally of imperial scion Liu Bei who is said, in some accounts, to have travelled with him from the earliest days of his career; he was said to be vulgar and direct, so the author tends to use Jian Yong as a means for lightening the mood (and he is, as always, depicted as a near-constant companion to Liu Bei).*
*Known by the courtesy name Xianhe [Shee-an-her]

Jiang Qi [Jee-arng Chee] – *an officer serving Yuan Shao*

Jiang Yiqu [Jee-arng Yee-choo] – *an officer serving the warlord Yuan Shao*

Ju Hu [Joo Hoo] – *son of Ju Shou and an officer serving the warlord Yuan Shao*

Ju Shou [Joo S'oh] – *an official and adviser to Yuan Shao; he was formerly a subordinate official of Ji Province governor Han Fu, and was one of the men that convinced Han that he should cede the province quietly. He is one of Yuan Shao's most important advisers, although his advice was frequently ignored.*

Kong Rong [Kong Rong] – *a descendant of the famous philosopher Confucius; he assumed many respectable roles, including Governor of Qing Province, and was an acquaintance of men such as Cai Yong, Liu Bei and Yuan Shao.*
*Known by the courtesy name Wenju [Wern-joo]

Kuai Liang [Koo-eye Lee-arng] – *Jing Governor Liu Biao's senior adviser*
*Known by the courtesy name Zirou [Tz'ee-roh]

Kuai Yue [Koo-eye Yoo-er] – *brother of Kuai Liang, official in southern Jing Province and former subordinate of Hè Jin*
*Known by the courtesy name Yidu [Yee-t'oo]

Lady Bian [P'ee-arn] – *favourite consort to Cao Cao and mother of Cao Pi*

Lady Cai [Ts'eye] – *sister of Jing officer Cai Mao and second wife of Governor Liu Biao; she is only mentioned, but she is instrumental in the final fate of the province after Liu Biao's death*

Lady Cao [Ts'ao] – *eldest daughter of Cao Cao by Lady Liu*

Lady Ding [T'ing] – *Cao Cao's second wife and carer to his first 3 children after the early death of Lady Liu*

Lady Du [T'oo] – *the beautiful wife of Lü Bu's general Qin Yilu; she later becomes a consort to Cao Cao.*

Lady Hu [Hoo] – *Guan Yu's principal wife*

Lady Huan [Hoo-arn] – *one of Cao Cao's consorts and mother to his favourite son, the short-lived prodigy Cao Chong*

Lady Liu (1) [Lee-oo] – *Cao Cao's first wife and mother to his first 3 children*

Lady Liu (2) [Lee-oo] – *Yuan Shao's principal wife in later years and mother to his favourite third son Yuan Shang*

Lady Lü [L'] – *daughter of Lü Bu by Lady Yan*

Lady Qiong [Chee-ong] – *wife of the warlord Guo Si*

Lady Mi [Mee] – *sister of Donghai Mi clan leader Mi Zhu; she married Liu Bei*

Lady Yan [Yarn] – *Lü Bu's principal wife*

Lady Yin [Yin] – *widow of Hè Jin's son Xian that became a consort to Cao Cao*

Lady Zou [Tz'oh] – *incredibly beautiful wife of Zhang Ji; like Qin Yilu's wife Lady Du, she becomes an involuntary source of contention between warlords*

Lei Bo [Lay P'oh] – *military officer serving Yuan Shu*

Li Cheng [Lee T'erng] – *official serving Yuan Shao that was appointed as Administrator of Wei Prefecture in Ji Province*

Li Dian [Lee T'ee-an] –*Han official that later became a noted general in Cao Cao's army*
*Known by the courtesy name Mancheng [Man-t'eng]

Li Feng (1) [Lee Fung] – *subordinate of Lü Bu that tried, unsuccessfully, to convince Li Qian and his family to abandon Cao Cao and aid Bu's takeover of Yan Province; he and his allies murdered Li Qian and were subsequently killed by forces led by Qian's sons Zheng and Dian*

Li Feng (2) [Lee Fung] – *an officer serving the warlord Yuan Shu*

Li Jue [Lee Joo-er] – *one of Dong Zhuo's subordinate officers; he sometimes served in an advisory or emissary capacity in addition to having a personal army and acting as one of Dong Zhuo's most trusted generals. He later took charge of Chang'an with fellow officer Guo Si after Dong Zhuo's death and became a co-regent (he is already a regent at the start of this work; his rise to power is depicted in "Yellow Sky"). He claimed to be descended from two famous historical figures: one was Lao Tzu, founder of Taoism, and the other was Li Guang, a Han commander known as the 'Flying General'.*
*Known by the courtesy name Zhiran [Ch'ee-rarn]

Li Li [Lee Lee] – *the nephew of the Liang general Li Jue; he was given much of the real military power by his uncle.*

Li Qian [Lee Chee-arn] – *Han official serving Cao Cao and father of future general Li Dian; Li Qian was a popular native of Chengshi (in Juye County, Yan Province). He featured briefly in "Yellow Sky", but he has been murdered, avenged and succeeded in his role by the start of this work.*

Li Ru [Lee Roo] – *an adviser to the warlord Dong Zhuo that assisted him in the overthrow of the Imperial court in Luoyang and advised on matters such as the succession to the throne; he usually worked alongside the more famous Jia Xu. He has already 'retired' (his final fate is debatable) at the start of this work after being publicly castigated by the Emperor and all but threatened for his role in the regicide of Emperor Shao.*
*Known by the courtesy name Wenyou [Wern-yoh]

Li Su [Lee Soo] – *a cavalry officer serving Dong Zhuo; he later allied with Lü Bu when relations strained between Bu and their lord Dong Zhuo. He is never mentioned by name in this work.*

Li Zheng [Lee Ch'erng] – *the eldest son and heir of Han official Li Qian and the elder brother of future Han general Li Dian*

Liang Gang [Lee-arng Garng] – *officer serving Yuan Shu*

Liang Ji [Lee-arng Jee] – *controlled the court of Emperor Huan until he was outwitted by Huan and his eunuchs and executed for sedition. A highly divisive figure, praised for reforms by some but vilified for moral corruption by others*

Liu Bao [Lee-oo P'ao] – *eldest son of exiled Southern Xiongnu chieftain Yufuluo, later the chosen Southern Xiongnu Chanyu*

Liu Bei [Lee-oo P'ay] – *a historically famous scion of the ruling Liu family; his ancestors were disinherited after committing an offence, so Bei was forced into a life of weaving straw shoes and mats with his mother. He was later pitied and advanced by a wealthier relative, and quickly made friends in high places. He gained initial fame for his victories against the Yellow Turbans and made many acquaintances that would become famous in their own right. He rose to become 'King of Hanzhong' and First Emperor of the western state of Shu Han, which was one of the famous 'Three Kingdoms'. He famously aided the state of Eastern Wu during the conflict known as the Battle of Red Cliffs, and then he had an uneasy alliance with Eastern Wu's founding family for over a decade. He left his mission to reunify the country to his trusted Prime Minister, Zhuge Liang. Liu Bei's early career is a story thread in this work and "Yellow Sky" before it, but he is dealt with more specifically in 'Crouching Dragon'.*
*Known by the courtesy name Xuande [Shoo-arn-der]

Liu Biao [Lee-oo P'ee-ow] – *the Governor of Jing Province. Liu Biao is one of the major figures within the time period, despite being relatively inactive; he had a famous feud with the Sun family, and his province was craved by Yuan Shu in the years after the collapse of the Eastern Pass Coalition against Dong Zhuo. His final years and the fate of his strategically important province are a central story thread in 'Crouching Dragon'.*
*Known by the courtesy name Jingsheng [Jing-s'ung]

Liu Cong [Lee-oo Ts'ong] – *the second son of Jing Provincial Governor Liu Biao; he was the one that inherited the province after Biao's death due to the actions of Biao's second wife, Lady Cai and her brother General Cai Mao. The Jing court then advised Cong to cede the province to Cao Cao, which led in turn to the 'Battle of Steepslope', Liu Bei's famous flight from Jing with a horde of 100,000 civilians that feared Cao's intentions for them.*

Liu Dai (1) [Lee-oo T'eye] – *an officer serving Cao Cao*

Liu Dai (2) [Lee-oo T'eye] – *scion of the royal house and Governor of Yan Province before Cao Cao; he once defended the elder*

statesman Lu Kang when the latter was slandered by allies of the 'Ten Attendants'. He later became a leading member of the Eastern Pass Coalition against Dong Zhuo. He died fighting an army of Yellow Turban rebels, whereupon Cao Cao successfully petitioned Yuan Shao for the role of governor.
*Known by the courtesy name Gongshan [K'ong-s'arn]

Liu Fan [Lee-oo Farn], Liu Dan [Lee-oo T'arn], Liu Mao [Lee-oo Mah-oh] – *the eldest sons of Yi Governor Liu Yan (from eldest to youngest), none of whom are mentioned by name in this work; they all died (Fan and Dan were killed whilst fighting Li Jue and Guo Si, Liu Mao died of illness), leaving Liu Yan's timid fourth son Zhang to inherit the provincial governorship*

Liu Fu [Lee-oo Foo] – *Han official that left Lujiang Prefecture, Yu Province prior to Yuan Shu's declaration as emperor and joined the court in Xuchang; he later returned to Lujiang, pacified the region by improving education and employment, and was the architect behind the famous Hefei fortress that repelled the Sun clan of Jiangdong on numerous occasions*
*Known by the courtesy name Yuanying [Yoo-arn-ying]

Liu Hè [Lee-oo Her] – *the eldest son of Yòu Governor Liu Yu; he served as a close attendant to Emperor Xian during the early months of Dong Zhuo's rule. When Liu Yu refused to allow Yuan Shao to declare him as an alternative emperor, Emperor Xian sent Hè to request aid from Yu, but he was captured en route by Yuan Shu and taken hostage. He is released during the course of this work and aids Yuan Shao's persecution of Gongsun Zan, who murdered his father Yu. His final fate is unknown by the author at the time of writing: he disappears after the Battle of Yijing, when he should have, by rights, been appointed as Governor of Yòu Province.*

Liu Pi [Lee-oo Pee] – *a Yellow Turban officer during the initial rebellion; he initially fought in Runan Prefecture, Yu Province under the command of Bo Cai, but when the initial uprising ended he surrendered and acted as a mercenary for warlords like Yuan Shu and Sun Ce. He collaborated with fellow acolyte Huang Shao in a new, localised rebellion in Runan a decade later, and – depending on which accounts are to be believed – either died then or undertook one last campaign against Cao Cao during the Battle of Guandu four years after that (the author chose the latter).*

Liu Qi [Lee-oo Chee] – *the eldest son of Jing Provincial Governor Liu Biao; he is depicted as being in poor health due to vice in 'Crouching Dragon'. He was cheated out of inheriting the province by his stepmother Lady Cai and her brother Cai Mao, who ensured that his younger brother Cong became Governor. Liu Qi fled to avoid assassination and allied with Liu Bei; the province was then ceded to Cao Cao, and Liu Qi became a rebel in his own region. He died a year after the famous Battle of Red Cliffs, and Liu Bei – who had already been made 'Inspector of Jing Province' by Sun Quan – absorbed Qi's army into his own.*

Liu Xun [Lee-oo Shoon] – *an official serving Yuan Shu that was appointed as Administrator of Lujiang Prefecture; he later joined the court in Xuchang.*
*Known by the courtesy name Zitai [Tz'ee-t'eye]

Liu Yan (1) [Lee-oo Yarn] – *a relative of the emperor who served as a court official in the imperial capital; in the year 187, he was given an opportunity to suggest upgrading certain inspectors to regional governors to reduce pressure on the capital's administration, and he was subsequently made Governor of Yi Province. He quickly forged an alliance with Zhang Lu, leader of the 'Way of Five Pecks' cult. His fourth son Liu Zhang – his fourth and only surviving son after a series of mishaps – inherited his position when he died shortly after a failed attempt to overthrow Li Jue and Guo Si and seize Chang'an with the aid of the Qiang warlords Han Sui and Ma Teng.*
*Known by the courtesy name Junlang [Joon-larng]

Liu Yan (2) [Lee-oo Yarn] – *an official serving Cao Cao that was appointed as Administrator of Dong Prefecture, Yan Province and went on to defend Boma against Yuan Shao during the early stages of the Guandu campaign.*
*Known by the courtesy name Junlang [Joon-larng]

Liu Yao [Lee-oo Yah-oh] – *a distant member of the imperial ruling family and brother of Yan Province Governor Liu Dai; he was later made Governor of Yang Province when the court wanted to curb the ambitions of Yuan Shu and his allies. His main adviser was Xu Shao, the man that famously appraised Cao Cao.*
*Known by the courtesy name Zhengli [Ch'erng-lee]

Liu Yè [Lee-oo Yer] – *an official in Liujiang Prefecture that served as an adviser to Liu Xun; he later served Cao Cao.*
*Known by the courtesy name Ziyang [Tz'ee-yarng]

Liu Yu [Lee-oo Yoo] – *a distant member of the imperial ruling family; he was made Governor of Yòu Province and given the responsibility of pacifying the tribes and rebels in that frontier region, which he did with the essential support of his vassal Gongsun Zan. Liu Yu was considered as an alternative emperor after the demise of Emperor Shao, but he refused the appointment. In later years, his relationship with Gongsun Zan – who was, by now, a warlord – deteriorated, and when he challenged Gongsun's 'business activities', Gongsun murdered him and seized the province as an independent territory.*
*Known by the courtesy name Bo'an [P'oh An]

Liu Zhang [Lee-oo Ch'arng] – *fourth son of the Governor of Yi Province, Liu Yan (1); he inherited his father's role, since his elder brothers had all died. Liu Zhang is only visited rarely and briefly in this work: his controversial governorship of Yi and his strained relationship with his distant relative Liu Bei are important elements in 'Crouching Dragon'.*
*Known by the courtesy name Jiyu [Jee-yoo]

Lu Kang [Loo Karng] – *Han official, respected pacifier of troublemakers and future Administrator of Lujiang; he was one of the first men to experience the military might of Sun Ce, and the experience ended his long career. He was, ironically enough, closely related to the famous strategist Lu Xun, who would later be a cornerstone of the Sun clan's regime in the south. His battle with Sun Ce is only mentioned in this work; it is actually depicted in 'East of the River'.*
*Known by the courtesy name Jining [Jee-ning]

Lu Zhi [Loo Ch'ee] – *a scholar of the Han court; he tutored the warlords Liu Bei and Gongsun Zan and was lauded for his military efforts against the Yellow Turbans. He had a turbulent career, veering between high rank and imprisonment due to his opposition to the 'Ten Attendants' He is already retired at the start of this work and is never seen.*
*Known by the courtesy name Zigan [Tz'ee-garn]

Lü Boshe [L' P'oh-sher] – *friend of Cao Cao; the story of the fate of his family is recorded in certain historical documents, although it is a very vivid and perhaps fictional event. It does offer a vision of Cao Cao that fits with his later actions in Xu Province however, so despite the controversy surrounding this story, the author chose to keep it. Boshe may be the man's courtesy name: so little is known of him (at the time of writing) that it is difficult to say.*

Lü Bu [L'Boo] – *one of the most famous men of the era; he is known particularly for his disloyalty, inconstancy, and inevitable downfall. In fiction, he is portrayed as a near-invincible warrior that rides a similarly unparalleled horse, 'Red Hare'; famous scenes include him successfully keeping Liu Bei, Guan Yu and Zhang Fei at Bei simultaneously and with ease, retreating only when the three attacked at exactly the same time (this took place during the Campaign against Dong Zhuo, whereas Liu Bei and his followers were historically absent from this campaign; the author chose to reference the scene during the Battle of Xiapi). Historically and in fiction, Lü Bu is a poor tactician, but in history that serves as a greater handicap since he is not an invincible warrior. He began his career as the adopted son to Bing Province Inspector Ding Yuan, but he quickly gains notoriety for betraying Ding Yuan and becoming the bodyguard and foster son of the tyrant Dong Zhuo. The loyalist courtier Wang Yun persuaded Bu to betray Dong Zhuo less than three years later, but Lü Bu was then chased from the capital by former allies Li Jue and Guo Si. Bu then drifted from place to place, gaining greater notoriety as he went; he has just failed to seize Yan Province from Cao Cao at the start of this work.*
*Known by the courtesy name Fengxian [Ferng-shee-arn]

Lü Kuang [L'Koo-arng] – *an officer serving Yuan Shao.*

Lü Weihuang [L'Way-hoo-arng] – *an officer serving Yuan Shao.*

Lü Xiang [L'Shee-arng] – *an officer serving Yuan Shao.*

Ma Chao [Mah T'ao] – *son of Ma Teng and future tribal leader in Liang Province; he is relatively unimportant during the time frame of this work, but later becomes the leader of a rebellion in Liang that threatens to undo all of Cao Cao's efforts. He later joined the warlord Liu Bei and assisted his takeover of Yi Province*
*Known by the courtesy name Mengqi [Mung-chee]

Ma Midi [Mah Mee-t'ee] – *Han official that is noted for two things: he assisted the career of Sun clan ally Zhu Zhi, and he was one of only a very small number of men – possibly two – that paid respects to Dong Zhuo after the latter's death.*

Ma Rong [Mah Rong] – *deceased tutor of the scholars Zhang Xuan and Lu Zhi*

Ma Teng [Mah Tung] – *a mid-ranking officer in the Han imperial army that defected to the Liang Province rebels during the siege of Didao; he later married a Qiang woman and became the father of the famous Qiang warlord Ma Chao.*
*Known by the courtesy name Shoucheng [S'oh-t'ung]

Ma Tie [Mah Tee-er] – *younger son of the warlord Ma Teng*

Major Deng [T'erng] – *a Qing Corps officer that slandered Yu Jin in order to avoid punishment for crimes against colleagues after the Battle of Wan; based on unnamed historical person or persons* ('FICTIONAL' CHARACTER CREATED FOR NARRATIVE COHESION)

Man Chong [Marn T'ong] – *an official serving Cao Cao that becomes an important adviser in later years*
*Known by the courtesy name Boning [P'oh-ning]

Mao Jie [Mah-oh Chee-er] – *official serving Cao Cao*
*Known by the courtesy name Xiaoxian [Shee-ow-shee-arn]

Mei Qian [May Chee-arn] – *a leader of the Qian Hill Bandits*

Mi Fang [Mee Farng] - *the younger brother of Mi Zhu; he became an early supporter of Liu Bei. Some of his complicated later career – including his role in Guan Yu's famous loss of Jing Province – is covered in 'Crouching Dragon'.*
*Known by the courtesy name Zifang [Tz'ee-farng]

Mi Heng [Mee Herng] – *prodigious but irreverent young scholar that was recommended to Cao Cao by Kong Rong in a letter that survives; his fate is dramatized in this work*
*Known by the courtesy name Zhengping [Ch'erng-ping]

Mi Zhu [Mee Ch'oo] – *an influential clan chieftain in Xu Province that became an early supporter of Liu Bei; he led the faction in the Xu Province court that favoured Liu Bei as Tao Qian's successor rather than Tao Qian's eldest son. His later career is covered in 'Crouching Dragon'.*
*Known by the courtesy name Zizhong [Tz'ee-ch'ong]

Niu Fu [Nee-oo Foo] – *Dong Zhuo's son-in-law and minor warlord in his own right; Jia Xu briefly served him in order to escape being part of the evacuation of Luoyang*

'Old Wu' [Woo] – *a trader in Xiapi that is called upon to help with procuring horses; based on unnamed historical person or persons* ('FICTIONAL' CHARACTER CREATED FOR NARRATIVE COHESION)

'Oxhorn' Zhang [Ch'arng] – *a bandit leader; he was mortally wounded during a raid, and – to the surprise of all – passed the authority of his band of men to a rival, Chu Yan. Chu Yan was so touched by the gesture that he changed his name to Zhang Yan; he then went on to inspire all of the small bandit groups in the region to unite under his leadership, forming the million-strong Black Mountain Bandits.*

Pang Ji [Parng Jee] – *an adviser to Yuan Shao*
*Known by the courtesy name Yuantu [Yoo-arn-too]

Pang Shu [Parng S'oo] – *a friend, ally or vassal of Lü Bu (his exact connection was unclear to the author at the time of writing, and therefore left vague) that protected Bu's family when he left the capital after Wang Yun's coup was countered.*

'Poison Yu' [Yoo] – *a Black Mountain Bandit chieftain that riled Yuan Shao with one of his more audacious and costly attacks on Ji Province's capital*

Qi Ji [Chee Jee] – *military officer serving Yuan Shu; he later defected to Cao Cao*

Qiao Long [Chee-ow Long] – *an officer serving Lü Bu that has already met his end (during Bu's failed Yan Province campaign) at the start of the work*

Qiao Rui [Chee-ow Roo-ee] – *an officer serving Yuan Shu*

Qiao Xuan [Chee-ow Shoo-arn] – *an infamous scholar and senior government official of the later years of the Han Dynasty; he was said to have been so certain of the importance of law over all that when his closest family were held for ransom, he went ahead with an armed assault on the kidnappers despite the risk and gave no thought to payment. His wife and children perished shortly before their desperate and vengeful captors, but Qiao Xuan was publicly unapologetic, saying that future kidnappers could expect no money or mercy; the number of kidnappings – which had been increasing exponentially to that point – was reduced to next to nothing as a result. He held almost every important court rank that there was at one time or another, and was one of the men that launched the career of the prodigy Cai Yong. He also endorsed Cao Cao, calling him 'A hero of future times', and the two remained friends until Qiao Xuan's death.*
*Known by the courtesy name Gongzu [K'ong-tz'oo]

Qin Bonan [Chin P'oh-narn] – *an old acquaintance of Cao Cao's that gives his life for him during Cao's campaign against Yufuluo in Act I of this work; he may, like Lü Boshe, be an invention or be used to create an apocryphal tale: the author chose to include the story, despite that uncertainty, as it provides a contrast to the earlier Boshe story and develops Cao's complicated character. Some accounts suggest that Qin was the natural father of Cao Zhen (who later served as Commander-in-Chief to the Cao Wei Emperor and fought against Shu Han Prime Minister Zhuge Liang on a number of occasions), and that Cao adopted Zhen as a way of honouring Qin's sacrifice; alternative accounts have Cao Zhen as an actual relation, however.*

Qin Yi [Chin Yee] – *military officer serving Yuan Shu; he later defected to Cao Cao*

Qin Yilu [Chin Yee-loo] – *officer and official serving Lü Bu; he later abandoned his wife, Lady Du, and became an envoy to Yuan Shu's court in Shouchun*

Qu Yi [Choo Yee] – *a military officer during the time of the Yellow Turban Rebellion, Qu already had experience fighting rebels and tribes and lent his experience to the loyalist cause. He later worked for the Ji Governor Han Fu and his successor Yuan Shao. Qu Yi served Yuan Shao at the Battle of Jie Bridge, where he faced the challenge of overcoming Gongsun Zan's famed cavalry.*

Shen Pei [S'ern Pay] – *an adviser to Yuan Shao*
*Known by the courtesy name Zhengnan [Ch'erng-narn]

Sheng Xian [S'erng Shee-arn] – *appointed Administrator of Wu Prefecture that was overthrown by Xu Gong and forced into exile; he is only referred to in this work, but is a secondary character in 'East of the River'*
*Known by the courtesy name Xiaozhang [Shee-ow-ch'arng]

Shi Huan [S'ee Hoo-arn] – *an officer serving Cao Cao*
*Known by the courtesy name Gongliu [K'ong-lee-oo]

Shisun Rui [S'ee-soon Roo-ee] – *Han Dynasty politician; he was a staunch Han loyalist that became involved in many plots to remove Dong Zhuo and his allies.*
*Known by the courtesy name Junrong [Ch'oon-rong]

Sima brothers, "The 8 Simas" [Ss-mah] – *the 8 sons of Han official Sima Fang that included Sima Yi*

Sima Fang [Ss-mah Farng] – *Han official and father of Sima Yi*
*Known by the courtesy name Jiangong [Jee-arn-k'ong]

Sima Lang [Ss-mah Larng] – *elder brother of Sima Yi*
*Known by the courtesy name Boda [P'oh-t'ah]

Sima Yi [Ss-mah Yee] – *a famous official that served Cao Cao and several successive members of the Cao clan; he is also the father*

of Sima Shi and Sima Zhao and the grandfather of Sima Yan, who were all historically significant in their own right as the founders of the Jin Dynasty. He is only referred to in this work, but his famous rivalry with Zhuge Liang is depicted in 'Crouching Dragon'.
*Known by the courtesy name Zhongda [Ch'ong-t'ah]

Song Jian [Song Jee-arn] – *a former Han official that defected to the Liang Province rebels at some point before the death of Emperor Ling; he became one of three men that ruled Liang Province when the Han court finally gave up trying to reclaim it (the other two were the more ambitious Han Sui and Ma Teng), and his autonomous state lasted for decades.*

Song Xian [Song Shee-arn] – *an officer serving the warlord Lü Bu*

Sui Gu [Soo-ee K'oo] – *an officer serving Zhang Yang; he may have been a former Black Mountain Bandit.*
*Known by the courtesy name Baitu [P'eye-too]

Sui Yuanjin [Soo-ee Yoo-arn-jin] – *an officer serving Yuan Shao*

Sun Ben [Soon P'ern] – *cousin of Sun Ce and briefly the head of the Fuchun Sun clan; officer serving Yuan Shu*
*Known by the courtesy name Boyang [P'oh-yarng]

Sun Ce [Soon Ts'er] – *the eldest son of the warrior-prodigy Sun Jian and the true founder of the state of Eastern Wu. The Sun clan's exploits during the timeframe of "Yellow Sky" and this work (as far as Yuan Shu's death) are covered in 'East of the River'.*
*Known by the courtesy name Bofu [P'oh-foo]

Sun Guan [Soon Ts'er] – *a Black Mountain Bandit cheiftain*
*Known by the courtesy name Zhongtai [Ch'ong-T'eye]

Sun Jian [Soon Jee-arn] – *a southern man whose military career began during the Yellow Turban Rebellion and continued with a sizeable role in the campaigns against the Liang Province rebels and Dong Zhuo; his progeny founded the state of Eastern Wu.*
*Known by the courtesy name Wentai [Wern-T'eye]

Sun Qian [Soon Chee-arn] – *known throughout as 'Mister Sun' (in-keeping with a practice started in the author's earlier work 'Crouching Dragon' to differentiate members of the southern Sun clan from this separate figure whose name is represented by a completely different glyph); he – along with the heads of the influential Mi and Chen clans of Xu Province – turned their allegiances from Tao Qian to Liu Bei and remained with him thereafter. Some of his early career is covered here, and the end of his career is covered in 'Crouching Dragon'.*
*Known by the courtesy name Gongyou [K'ong-yoh]

Sun Quan [Soon Choo-arn] – *the second son of Sun Jian and future ruler of Eastern Wu; he is mentioned only briefly when he inherits his clan's legacy 'off-stage' during the Guandu campaign.*
*Known by the courtesy name Zhongmou [Ch'ong-moh]

Sun Yi [Soon Yee] – *younger son of Sun Jian that was considered, by some, to be a better choice for a successor to his elder brother Sun Ce's legacy; Yi conceded the role to his older brother Quan and happily served under him until his untimely death at the hands of assassins.*
*Known by the courtesy name Shubi [S'oo-p'ee]

Tadun [Tah-doon] – *Wuhuan chieftain in the northeast that allied with Yuan Shao against Gongsun Zan and then Cao Cao's Xuchang government*

Taishi Ci [T'eye-sher Ts'er] – *a 'lone wolf' that has become legendary for acts of great heroism: he supposedly travelled from the northeast tip of China to the capital to deliver a petition to the capital, and then duped a rival petitioner into handing his own letter over to be destroyed; he is then said to have rescued Kong Rong from a horde of Yellow Turbans using a combination of ruses and a militia borrowed from none other than Liu Bei. He then travelled to Yang Province to aid fellow townsman (and provincial governor) Liu Yao in his battle against Yuan Shu; that initially pitted him against Sun Ce, but the two later became allies.*
*Known by the courtesy name Ziyi [Tz'ee-yee]

Tao Qian [Tah-oh Chee-an] – *the Inspector and then Governor of Xu Province during the reign of Emperor Ling; he was a friend of the prominent Han official Zhu Jun. Tao Qian is revered in some fiction as a morally upstanding man, but historical accounts suggest a more multifaceted man that hankered for talented subordinates and reacted badly to any that rejected his work offers. He is famous for being held responsible for the death of Cao Cao's father, Cao Song. Xu Province later passed to Liu Bei instead of one of Tao's sons; some popular fiction explicitly states that Tao made this decision, but history is less clear.*
*Known by the courtesy name Gongzu [K'ong-tz'oo]

Tao Shang [Tah-oh S'arng] – *one of Tao Qian's sons*

Tao Ying [Tah-oh Ying] – *one of Tao Qian's sons*

'Thin Wang' [Warng] – *a Black Mountain Bandit chieftain* ('FICTIONAL' CHARACTER CREATED FOR NARRATIVE COHESION)

'Thunder Lord Zhang' [Ch'arng] – *Black Mountain Bandit chieftain*

Tian Chou [Tee-an T'oh] – *official that once served Yòu Province Governor Liu Yu and then joined Cao Cao*
*Known by the courtesy name Zitai [Tz'ee-t'eye]

Tian Feng [Tee-an Fung] – *an adviser to Yuan Shao*
*Known by the courtesy name Yuanhao [Yoo-arn-ha-oh]

Tian Kai [Tee-an K'eye] – *officer and trusted offical serving Gongsun Zan; Gongsun made him Inspector of Qing Province.*

Tian Yu [Tee-an K'eye] – *an offical serving Gongsun Zan; the author always places him with Tian Kai.*

Wang Can [Warng Ts'arn] – *a Han Dynasty official that served Liu Biao and then Cao Cao; his family were prestigious enough for his grandfather and great-grandfather to be Excellences alongside the Yuan clan. He was said to possess an eidetic memory and have a fascination with donkeys, among other things, and the famed polymath Cai Yong was a vocal sponsor. Wang Can wrote a historical work, 'Record of Heroes', that serves as an alternative biographical compendium to the more famous 'Record of the Three Kingdoms', though it might be seen as biased toward Cao Cao's faction. It includes alternate fates (or even dates of death) for some notable figures, such as Sun Jian.*
*Known by the courtesy name Zhongxuan [Ch'ong-shoo-arn]

Wang Fang [Warng Farng] – *officer serving Dong Zhuo; he is notable for opening the gates of Chang'an to Li Jue and Guo Si toward the end of Wang Yun's coup and facing a young Ma Chao.*

Wang Fu [Warng Foo] – *Han official that was part of Dong Cheng's plot to oust Cao Cao*

Wang Kai [Warng K'eye] – *an official that served Cao Cao when he was Governor of Yan Province and later joined Lü Bu as a senior adviser and envoy*

Wang Kuang [Warng Koo-arng] – *a subordinate of Commander-in-Chief Hè Jin at the end of Emperor Ling's reign; he later became the Administrator of Henei at the suggestion of Han loyalist Zhou Bi and joined the Eastern Pass Coalition. His subordinate Han Hao went on to serve Cao Cao.*
*Known by the courtesy name Gongjie [K'ong-Jee-er]

Wang Lang [Warng Larng] – *official that served Han and Cao Wei, great-grandfather of first Jin Emperor Sima Yan. He was a friend of Kong Rong. His time in Yang Province – where he opposed Sun Ce – is depicted in 'East of the River'.*
*Known by the courtesy name Jingxing [Jing-shing]

Wang Men [Warng Mern] – *military officer serving Gongsun Zan that defected prior to the siege of Yijing*

Wang Mo [Warng Moh] – *an officer serving Yuan Shao*

Wang Yun [Warng Yoon] – *an official of the Han; he was Director of the Imperial Secretariat when Dong Zhuo seized the court and relocated the capital to Chang'an. Wang Yun plotted to oust Dong Zhuo: in fiction, he used an exceptionally beautiful young palace maiden (and in some versions, adopted daughter) known as Diaochan to sow discord between Dong Zhuo and Lü Bu: historically, some accounts speak of Dong Zhuo and Lü Bu having fallen out over their interest in the same serving maid, and the author adapted this version of events in "Yellow Sky". Regardless of the exact circumstances, Wang Yun managed to convince Lü Bu*

to betray Dong Zhuo, and once Dong was dead, Wang Yun took charge in Chang'an, although his success was short-lived and he was killed by the faction of Dong Zhuo's vassals that he had refused to offer amnesty to; he famously executed the polymath Cai Yong for serving and then mourning Dong Zhuo.
*Known by the courtesy name Zishi [Tz'ee-shee]

Wang Zhong [Warng Ch'ong] – *an officer serving Cao Cao*

Wei Kang [Way Karng] – *a Han official that was appointed as Governor of Liang Province prior to the Battle of Guandu.*
*Known by the courtesy name Yuanjiang [Yoo-arn-ch'ee-arng]

Wei Xu [Way Shoo] – *a trusted relative of Lü Bu that served him as a military officer*

Wei Zi [Way Tz'ee] – *a friend of Cao Cao, and the only man to join Cao Cao's assault against Dong Zhuo's retreating army at Xingyang; he met his end during that battle and is shown (by the author) to have left Cao Cao with a sense of guilt.*

Wen Chou [Wern T'oh] – *military officer serving Yuan Shao; he is famous for his death in fiction, as he is said to be yet another victim of Guan Yu's near-peerless talent as a general. Historically, information about his fate is vague; the author chose to be similarly vague as to how he died during the Guandu campaign.*

'White Circles' – *a Black Mountain Bandit chieftain*

'Wild Fox' – *a Southern Xiongnu warrior that is allied to Yufuluo* ('FICTIONAL' CHARACTER CREATED FOR NARRATIVE COHESION)

Wu Dun [Woo T'oon] – *a Mount Tai Bandit chieftain*

Wu Jing [Woo Jing] – *the maternal uncle of Sun Ce and vassal of the warlord Yuan Shu*

Wu Xi [Woo Shee] – *a subordinate of Dong Zhuo that served as an officer; he then served the regents Li Jue and Guo Si.*

Wu Yi [Woo Yee] – *the brother-in-law of Yi Province's Governor Liu Zhang, whose father was a friend of Zhang's father Yan. Wu Yi is a recurring character in 'Crouching Dragon'.*
*Known by the courtesy name Ziyuan [Tz'ee-yoo-arn]

Xi Zhicai [Shee Ch'ee-ts'eye] - *briefly served Cao Cao as an adviser; he is notable for his similarity 'health-wise' to the more famous Guo Jia. Zhicai is possibly his courtesy name rather than his given name.*

Xiahou Dun [Shee-ah-hoh T'oon] – *a close ally (and possible relative) of Cao Cao; he serves Cao as an officer, and it is during his time aiding Liu Bei against Lü Bu that he suffers the injury – the loss of his eye to an arrow – that he is most famous for. In fiction, he is said to have removed the arrow from his eye socket*

– with the eye attached to it – and consumed the eye before continuing to fight; the author has settled on something less dramatic but more likely.
*Known by the courtesy name Yuanrang [Yoo-arn-ranrng]

Xiahou Yuan [Shee-ah-hoh Yoo-arn] – *a close associate (and possible relative) of Cao Cao. He supposedly took the blame for one of Cao Cao's misdemeanours at an early age. He was highly trusted and was often given heavy responsibilities during his career. One of his later roles – the protector of the Hanzhong region – brought him into conflict with Liu Bei, and the resultant Battle of Dingjun Mountain – a famous and oft-recounted event that has many interesting fictional variations – is covered in 'Crouching Dragon'.*
*Known by the courtesy name Miaocai [Mee-ow-ts'eye]

Xiao Jian [Shee-ow Ch'ee-arn] – *an official in Xu Province that took his appointment as Administrator of Langya in Qing Province by opponents of Yuan Shao very seriously, although he never actually managed to get into Qing.*

Xin Pi [Shin Pee] – *an official that served Ji Province Governor Yuan Shao as an adviser after the death of the previous governor Han Fu; brother of Xin Ping*
*Known by the courtesy name Zuozhi [Tz'oo-oh-ch'ee]

Xin Ping [Shin Ping] – *an official that served Ji Province Governor Han Fu; he later served Yuan Shao and his son Yuan Tan as an adviser and brought his brother Xin Pi into Yuan Shao's court.*
*Known by the courtesy name Zhongzhi [Ch'ong-ch'ee]

Xu Chu [Shoo T'oo] – *a purportedly simple-minded man that served voluntarily as the guardian of his village and supposedly repelled an army of 10,000 Yellow Turbans with a combination of prowess and bluff. He later surrendered to Cao Cao, becoming a member of Cao's elite Tiger Guard: when the role of Cao Cao's bodyguard was vacated by the death of Dian Wei, Xu Chu took the role. His quiet, affable, dopey nature outside of combat contrasted heavily with the violent powerhouse that he would become when faced with those that were designated as his enemies.*
*Known by the courtesy name Zhognkang [Ch'ong-karng]
*Known by the moniker Hu Chi [Hoo T'ee] (lit. 'Tiger Fool') by some; the author uses 'Crazy Tiger' instead when Cao Cao refers to him

Xu Dan [Shoo T'arn] – *General of the Household in Xiapi City; the author uses him far beyond historical reference as a force of continuity in Xu Province*

Xu Gong [Shoo K'ong] – *a difficult-to-fathom figure that some accounts depict as a rebel that overthrew the Administrator of Wu Prefecture in Yang Province and then received recognition by the Han due to his competence; this is the Xu Gong that the author has used. Xu Gong opposed and then reluctantly collaborated with Sun Ce in his last years; he began to correspond with Cao Cao's* court in Xuchang and unintentionally gave Sun Ce his famous epithet 'Little Conqueror' whilst describing the threat that Ce supposedly posed. Sun Ce learned of the exchanges and had Xu Gong assassinated, but Gong's followers repaid the action and fatally attacked Sun Ce months later. Xu Gong is a recurring character in 'East of the River'

Xu Huang [Shoo Hoo-arng] – *a comrade-vassal of the Han officer and White Wave Bandit collaborator Yang Feng; Xu went on to serve Cao Cao and become one of his most famous generals. He had a friendly rivalry with Guan Yu.*
*Known by the courtesy name Gongming [K'ong-ming]

Xu Jing [Shoo Jing] – *an official in the Han court that aided Yuan Shao and secretly conspired against Dong Zhuo; he was the brother of the famous appraiser Xu Shao that supposedly appraised Cao Cao. He fled Luoyang when Dong Zhuo began his purge of the intelligentsia and went to the south to Yu Province and then to serve Wang Lang in Kuaiji. He fled to the far south after Wang Lang's defeat and eventually travelled to Yi Province, where he served in Liu Zhang's government. When Liu Zhang ceded Yi to Liu Bei, Xu Jing held a high degree of respect and authority, even demanding deference from the likes of the Shu Han Prime Minister Zhuge Liang (a fact that is mentioned in passing in chapter 101 of Crouching Dragon', although Xu Jing does not feature prominently otherwise).*
*Known by the courtesy name Wenxiu [Wern-shee-oo]

Xu Rong [Shoo Rong] – *a general serving Dong Zhuo. Historically his ability is considerable, as he defeats many notable figures during the siege of Luoyang. Xu decided to aid Wang Yun and Lü Bu's plot to oust Dong Zhuo and his loyalist faction led by Li Jue and Guo Si; he then died fighting against those loyalists.*

Xu Shao [Shoo S'ao] – *a famous appraiser who was known for fearless frankness; it was said that men feared his judgement and would try to curry favour with him in the hope that it would result in a career-boosting response. He is famous for having supposedly judged Cao Cao to be 'An able statesman in times of peace, and a "jianxiong" (meaning a "crafty villain", more or less) in chaotic times'. He later travelled to Xu Province, where he supposedly rated its governor Tao Qian poorly; after that, he went to Yang Province and served the court-appointed governor Liu Yao until his untimely death from illness and despair at failing to halt the progress of the talented warlord Sun Ce (his tenure in Yang is depicted in 'East of the River').*
*Known by the courtesy name Zijiang [Tz'ee-jee-arng]

Xu Si [Shoo See] – *an official that served Cao Cao when he was Governor of Yan Province and later defected to Lü Bu*

Xu Yòu [Shoo Yoh] – *a friend of Yuan Shao and Cao Cao, and later an adviser to both in turn; his advice and information ultimately decide the outcome of the Guandu campaign*
*Known by the courtesy name Ziyuan [Tz'ee-yoo-arn]

Xue Lan [Shoo-er Larn] – *subordinate of Lü Bu that tried, unsuccessfully, to convince Li Qian and his family to abandon Cao Cao and aid Bu's takeover of Yan Province; he then conspired to kill Li Qian but died at the hands of Qian's sons. He is already dead at the start of this work.*

Xue Li [Shoo-er Lee] – *Chancellor of Peng City in Xu Province and then an ally to Yang Governor Liu Yao; he forged close ties with the cultist cleric Ze Rong, who then betrayed him and stole his men and supplies (this is depicted in 'East of the River')*

Xue Ti [Shoo-er Tee] – *Han official serving Cao Cao*

Xun Chen [Shoon T'ern] – *official serving Ji Governor Han Fu that later served Yuan Shao; the brother of Xun Yu (Wenruo)*
*Known by the courtesy name Youruo [Yoh-roo-oh]

Xun Yòu [Shoon Yoh] – *known through the text as 'Xun Gongda' to differentiate his name from that of Cao Cao's old friend Xu Yòu; he is an adviser to Cao Cao and nephew of Xun Yu (Wenruo)*
*Known by the courtesy name Gongda [K'ong-t'ah]

Xun Yu [Shoon Yoo] – *known as 'Xun Wenruo' throughout the text; he was an official in the Han court before joining Yuan Shao as an emissary and adviser. He later 'defected' to Cao Cao and started to find more officials to serve his new lord, including Xi Zhicai, his own nephew Xun Gongda and Guo Jia.*
*Known by the courtesy name Wenruo [Wern-roo-oh]

Yan Liang [Yarn Lee-arng] – *military officer serving Yuan Shao; he is famous for his fictional prowess and death at the hands of Guan Yu, much like Hua Xiong before him and Wen Chou after him. The one difference is that Yan Liang was actually said to have been killed by Guan Yu (Hua Xiong was killed by Sun Jian's forces, while Wen Chou's death is attributed to Cao Cao's forces in general); his historical death is less majestic and could – as the author has noted – be attributed to Yan's thinking that Guan had come to support him rather than kill him (since Liu Bei – Guan Yu's liege lord – was serving Yan's lord Yuan Shao at the time).*

Yan Pu [Yarn Poo] – *an adviser to the 'Way of Five Pecks' leader Zhang Lu*

Yan Xiang [Yarn Shee-arng] – *an adviser to Yuan Shu*

Yang Biao [Yarng P'ee-ow] – *a senior Han Dynasty politician; he was said to have come up with the scheme that divided Li Jue and Guo Si and effectively ended their co-regency. He was the father of the more famous Yang Xiu that worked for Cao Cao.*
*Known by the courtesy name Wenxian [Wern-shee-arn]

Yang Bo [Yarng P'oh] – *an adviser to the 'Way of Five Pecks' leader Zhang Lu*

Yang Chou [Yarng T'oh] – *an officer serving the warlord Zhang Yang that ultimately betrayed him*

Yang Ding [Yarng T'ing] – *a subordinate of the White Wave Bandit collaborator and Han officer Yang Feng*

Yang Feng [Yarng Fung] – *a subordinate of Dong Zhuo that had connections to the leader of the White Wave Bandits, Han Xian*

Yang Hong (1) [Yarng Hong] – *an adviser to Yuan Shu*

Yang Hong (2) [Yarng Hong] – *Yi Province politician that served Liu Zhang and later served Liu Bei; he advised Zhuge Liang on how to deal with a resource crisis during the Hanzhong Campaign*
*Known by the courtesy name Jixiu [Ch'ee-shee-oo]

Yang Zan [Yarng Tz'arn] – *a Han official and loyalist that contributed to plots to rid the capital of Dong Zhuo and his allies*

'Yellow Dragon' – *a Black Mountain Bandit chieftain*

Yin Li [Yin Lee] – *a Mount Tai Bandit chieftain*

'Young Wolf' – *a Southern Xiongnu warrior allied to Yufuluo* ('FICTIONAL' CHARACTER CREATED FOR NARRATIVE COHESION)

'Young Wu' [Woo] – *a trader in Xiapi that is called upon to help with procuring horses; based on unnamed historical person* ('FICTIONAL' CHARACTER CREATED FOR NARRATIVE COHESION)

Yu Jin [Yoo Ch'in] – *a former subordinate officer to Wang Lang that was given to Cao Cao by Wang. He was initially mistrusted, but he went on to become one of the most renowned generals in Cao Cao's army. Some of Yu Jin's later exploits, including the Battle of Fan City at the end of his career, are covered in 'Crouching Dragon'.*
*Known by the courtesy name Wenze [Wern-tz'er]

Yuan Huan [Yoo-arn Hoo-arn] – *an adviser to Yuan Shu*
*Known by the courtesy name Yaoqing [Yah-oh-ching]

Yuan Shao [Yoo-arn S'ao] – *head of the influential Yuan clan of Ru County in Yu Province and famous 'Super Warlord' of the period leading up the 'Three Kingdoms' era; he was a friend of Cao Cao, Zhang Miao and other noted up-and-coming figures in the later 2nd Century. He became a colonel in the ill-fated 'Army of the Western Garden', befriended the Commander-in-Chief Hè Jin, and personally led the purge of the 'Ten Attendants' in Luoyang. He would later lead the Eastern Pass Coalition against Dong Zhuo when the latter seized power. When that coalition ended, Shao was pitched against his own brother in a power-struggle that lasted for 6 years. He conquered 4 provinces in the north and was one of the two warlords that fought the famous Battle of Guandu.*
*Known by the courtesy name Benchu [P'ern-t'oo]

Yuan Shu [Yoo-arn S'oo] – *a senior member of the Yuan clan of Ru County in Yu Province: he always felt that his inheritance was snatched from him when his father – whose elder brother was the head of the clan – allowed his elder brother, Yuan Shao, to be adopted by his heirless older brother, placing Shao as the new heir to the clan fortune. As Yuan Shao was technically illegitimate, Yuan Shu felt that he should have been the next in line, and that he was before Shao's adoption took place: Yuan Shu never forgot that 'outrage' and had a very strained relationship with Yuan Shao, who he held personally responsible for being adopted. Yuan Shu is often under-represented, but his actions are, perhaps, the most important triggers for defining events in the period, even if others are the ones to directly benefit or suffer the consequences of them.*
*Known by the courtesy name Gonglu [K'ong-loo]

Yuan Tan [Yoo-arn Tarn] – *the eldest of Yuan Shao's sons; he served his father as a general.*
*Known by the courtesy name Xiansi [Shee-an-see]

Yuan Yao [Yoo-arn Yah-oh] – *the eldest of Yuan Shu's sons*

Yuan Yi [Yoo-arn Yee] – *a cousin of Yuan Shao and Yuan Shu that later served as Administrator of Shanyang Prefecture, Yan Province; he was a founder member of Yuan Shao's Eastern Pass Coalition against Dong Zhuo, serving under his provincial governor Liu Dai. Cao Cao was said to respect him greatly. He was killed in action not long after the Eastern Pass Coalition collapsed.*
*Known by the courtesy name Boye [P'oh-yer]

Yuan Yin [Yoo-arn Yin] – *an adviser to Yuan Shu*

Yue Jin [Yoo-er Ch'in] – *a subordinate of Cao Cao that became one of his most famous generals*
*Known by the courtesy name Wenqian [Wern-chee-an]

Yue Jiu [Yoo-er Jee-oo] – *an officer serving Yuan Shu*

Yufuluo [Yoo-foo-loo-oh] – *the chieftain of a breakaway faction of Southern Xiongnu; he had been selected as the Chanyu (king) of his people by a meddling Han court, but instead of accepting Yufuluo the Southern Xiongnu exiled him and his followers (although his brother Huchuquan stayed and was actually elected as the next Chanyu by the Xiongnu themselves). Yufuluo then became a wandering warlord of sorts, but he joined Yuan Shao's Eastern Pass Coalition very briefly; he tired of the inactivity and rebelled, capturing Shangdang Administrator Zhang Yang and forging alliances with the Black Mountain Bandits and groups of Yellow Turbans at varying points in time. He was the father of future Southern Xiongnu Chanyu Liu Bao, whose progeny would enjoy great power in northern China.*

Zang Ba [Tz'arng P'ah] – *resident of northeast Xu Province that began his career as a Yellow Turban suppressor in Qing Province but later took over an entire region of Xu and ruled it as an*

independent 'crime haven'. His confederacy evolved into the Mount Tai Bandits, but he later surrendered to the Han and became a powerful subordinate of Cao Cao and Cao Pi.
*Known by the courtesy name Xuangao [Shoo-arng-k'ao]

Zao Zhi [Ch'ao Ch'ee] – *Han official serving Cao Cao; proposed the 'tuntian' military-agricultural system*

Ze Rong [Tz'er Rong] – *a so-called 'Buddhist cleric' that was a cult leader in Xu Province: he was the trusted Administrator of the northeast region of Xiapi – which later became the capital region – and turned the main city into a stronghold and sanctuary for his followers, who eventually numbered in the tens of thousands. He was accused of funding his 'Buddhist Utopia' with monies that should have been used for a range of purposes. He later travelled to Yang Province to join the state-appointed governor Liu Yao's struggle against Yuan Shu, but he was accused of looting prefectures and counties along the way; he repeated his self-serving activities whilst in Yang and eventually suffered defeat by the remnants of Liu Yao's forces and death at the hands of local tribesmen. He is a major antagonist to Sun Ce in one act of 'East of the River'.*

Zhang Chao [Ch'arng T'ao] – *brother of Zhang Miao that died defending Chenliu's capital against the vengeful Cao Cao's forces after Miao's coup attempt collapsed*

Zhang Fei [Ch'arng Fay] – *an early ally and sponsor of Liu Bei who is frequently paired with Guan Yu. In fiction he is typically portrayed as a brash, slow-witted, violent drunk, but in reality he was smart enough to run his pig-butchery business, rally troops and inspire men to action, so while the author has retained his usual outspokenness and comic relief aspects from fiction, Zhang Fei is also shown to be more intelligent and not an alcoholic. His early career is covered in "Yellow Sky" and this work, while his later career is chronicled in 'Crouching Dragon'.*
*Known by the courtesy name Yide [Yee-der]

Zhang Hè [Ch'arng Her] – *a subordinate of Ji Governor Han Fu that went on to serve Yuan Shao but defected to Cao Cao during the latter stages of the Guandu campaign. His later career pitted him against Liu Bei's faction many times, and is consequently covered in 'Crouching Dragon'.*
*Known by the courtesy name Junyi [Joon-yee]

Zhang Hong (1) [Ch'arng Hong] – *an officer serving Lü Bu that allowed Chen Deng's brother and his family to escape Xiapi during the famous siege.*

Zhang Hong (2) [Ch'arng Hong] – *a senior adviser and envoy that served Sun Ce and then Sun Quan; he features more prominently in 'East of the River' but has a late cameo in Cao Cao's court in this work, since he has taken up the role of ambassador at this point in time*

Zhang Ji [Ch'arng Jee] – *a general serving Dong Zhuo; he was envied for his beautiful wife, Lady Zou. He later left the service of the regents Li Jue and Guo Ji and travelled to Nan County, Jing Province with his nephew Zhang Xiu.*

Zhang Jue [Ch'arng J'oo-er] – *The founder of the Taoist sect 'The Way of Peace' (his name is sometimes Romanised to Zhang Jiao [Ch'arng J'ee-ao], but the author has chosen the older, more traditional version); he travelled the country performing benevolent 'miracles' and spreading word of a new era of peace and enlightenment that required the removal of the eroded ruling house of Han. As discontent amongst the peasant populace grew, Zhang Jue and his allies turned their rhetoric toward outright insurrection and started to plan a nationwide revolution. When their allies within the capital were exposed, Zhang Jue ordered his followers to adopt a common symbol of a yellow turban and form armies to fight the emperor. That uprising – which was known as the Yellow Turban Rebellion – began the careers of many future 'heroes' such as Cao Cao, Liu Bei and Sun Jian, who would then become important to the 'Three Kingdoms' era that followed over 30 years later. Zhang Jue did not live to see the end of the initial uprising; in fact, he died quite some time before it ended. However, new factions and evolutions of the Yellow Turbans would continue to plague the Han government for over a decade.*

Zhang Kai [Ch'arng K'eye] – *a briefly mentioned but never seen 'associate' of Xu Province Governor Tao Qian that is historically suspected as one of the men that might have led the fatal attack on Cao Song's travelling party (and caused Song's son, Cao Cao, to launch his Xu Province Campaign).*

Zhang Kuang [Ch'arng Koo-arng] – *a military officer serving in Xu Province. He took the news to the tenant-warlord Lü Bu that Governor Liu Bei's vassal Zhang Fei had killed Chancellor Cao Bao; that news was accompanied by an invitation to oust Liu Bei and seize control of Xu Province, which Bu then did without hesitation.*

Zhang Liao [Ch'arng Lee-ow] – *a subordinate of Lü Bu; he went on to serve Cao Cao and earn greater fame as a defender of Hefei.*
*Known by the courtesy name Wenyuan [Wern-yoo-arn]

Zhang Lu [Ch'arng Loo] – *the leader of the 'Way of Five Pecks' in Yi Province and Hanzhong. He was approached by the newly-appointed governor of Yi Province and asked to assist in the defeat of influential clans and the governor of neighbouring Hanzhong. He did as he was asked until Hanzhong was seized, at which point he killed his campaign ally and seized Hanzhong, turning it into a theocratic state called Han'ning and declaring independence from Han rule. His relationship with Liu Yan's successor Liu Zhang was less cordial and evolved into direct conflict; Liu Zhang fatefully invited Liu Bei to Yi Province to guard against Zhang Lu, which led in turn to Bei seizing the province. Zhang Lu later surrendered to Cao Cao (the later events are depicted in 'Crouching Dragon').*
*Known by the courtesy name Gongqi [K'ong-chee]

Zhang Miao [Ch'arng Mee-ow] – *friend of Cao Cao and Yuan Shao; he is later made Administrator of Chenliu Prefecture/Principality. He was said to be very generous and kind, but he was also naively outspoken. His criticism of Yuan Shao's conduct during the blockade of Luoyang irks Yuan to the point where the two are not speaking, and he is very hesitant to support Cao Cao's Xu Province campaign: he eventually allies himself with Chen Gong, which has irreversible consequences.*
*Known by the courtesy name Mengzhuo [Mung-ch'oo-oh]

Zhang Ren [Ch'arng Rern] – *an officer serving Yi Governor Liu Zhang; he later acted as the senior general during Liu Zhang's bid to keep Liu Bei from seizing Yi, and his defence of Luo City led to the death of Liu Bei's famous strategist Pang Tong (depicted in 'Crouching Dragon')*

Zhang Xiu [Ch'arng Shee-oo] – *nephew of Dong Zhuo's ally Zhang Ji; he later received Jia Xu's service after occupying Wan City in Jing Province, and the two had an encounter with Cao Cao thereafter that is a pivotal moment in this work.*

Zhang Xun [Ch'arng Shoon] – *an officer serving Yuan Shu; he is said to have been a friend of Sun Ce and recommended seeking refuge in Jiangdong after Yuan Shu's regime collapsed.*

Zhang Yang [Ch'arng Yarng] – *a general serving Ding Yuan during the time of the Liang Province Rebellion; he was once forced to act as the eunuch Jian Shuo's vice-marshal in the 'Army of the Western Garden', but returned to Bing Province after Commander-in-Chief Hè Jin disbanded the militia. His colleague Lü Bu betrayed their master Ding Yuan, but he never lost faith in Lü Bu, and defended him many times, despite also lending his army to the Eastern Pass Coalition, which was dedicated to the destruction of Lü Bu's new master Dong Zhuo. His contribution to the coalition ended when he was captured by his own ally Yufuluo, who had tired of aiding Yuan Shao (who then had to rescue Zhang Yang). He was then made Administrator of Henei by Dong Zhuo's court in Chang'an, and later gave safe haven to the fugitive official Dong Zhao (Gongren): neither aided his professional relationship with Yuan Shao. He later played a key role in the restoration of the imperial palace in the capital Luoyang and was rewarded for it with high rank; he then undid everything by deciding to march against Cao Cao when Lü Bu was besieged in Xiapi, and he was murdered by his own subordinate Yang Chou.*
*Known by the courtesy name Zhishu [Ch'ee-s'oo]

Zhao Qi [Ch'ao Chee] – *famous scholar and Han official*

Zhao Rong [Ch'ao Rong] – *an officer serving Cao Cao*

Zhao Rui [Ch'ao Roo-ee] – *an officer serving Yuan Shao*

Zhao Yu [Ch'ao Yoo] – *the Administrator of Guangling, Yang Province when Cao Cao began his Xu Province Campaign. It appears that he was a vassal of Xu Province Governor Tao Qian in some accounts, as certain people were held in Guangling at Tao's pleasure; that suggests that Guangling was a part of Yang Province that Tao Qian seized while in collusion with Yuan Shu. Zhao Yu was said to be too trusting, and that he respected the cultist Ze Rong, mistaking him for a Buddhist saint as many did.*

Zhao Yun [Ch'ao Yoon] – *a subordinate of Gongsun Zan; after Gongsun Zan's loss at the Battle of Jie Bridge, Zhao Yun was sent to Pingyuan and seconded to Liu Bei, who took an instant liking to him. Zhao was forced to go home to bury a relation, and he and Liu Bei would not work together again for some time: when they did reunite, Zhao Yun remained a vassal of Liu Bei and his successors for his entire life. The majority of his career and life forms part of 'Crouching Dragon'.*
*Known by the courtesy name Zilong [Tz'il-ong]

Zheng Tai [Ch'erng T'eye] – *an official in the Han court; he, along with the scholar Lu Zhi, opposed the decision to invite Dong Zhuo to the capital when Hè Jin planned to kill the 'Ten Attendants', but his protestations were disregarded.*

Zheng Xuan [Ch'erng Shoo-arn] – *famous commentator and Confucian philosopher; he is included in the text, despite the instinct to lower what is an already mentally-exhausting number of characters, because the author wanted to emphasise the importance of 'the minds behind the swords'. He shares a mentor with Lu Zhi, who is, in turn, Liu Bei and Gongsun Zan's mentor.*

Zhong Ji [Ch'ong Jee] – *Han official and ally of Dong Cheng*

Zhong Yao [Ch'ong Yao] – *Han official, student of Cai Yong, calligrapher and father of famous Cao Wei general Zhong Hui*
*Known by the courtesy name Yuanchang [Yoo-arn-ch'arng]

Zhou Bi [Ch'oh P'ee] – *an official in the Han court; he secretly supported Yuan Shao and aided his escape from the capital after Dong Zhuo seized power. Dong trusted Zhou Bi, and made him a high-ranking minister, but all the while Zhou Bi used his influence to appoint Han loyalists to key positions. He met his end when the product of his efforts – the Eastern Pass Coalition – publicly opposed Dong Zhuo.*

Zhou Yi [Ch'oh Yee] – *Magistrate of Luoyang at the time of Emperor Ling's death; he took his family, fled the capital and went to his ancestral home in Lujiang Prefecture, Yang Province when Dong Zhuo started to enforce his rule. He was the father of the famous strategist and general Zhou Yu (Gongjin), and the flight from Luoyang ensured that Zhou Yu would meet his future lord and friend Sun Ce when the latter travelled from the south with his father, who was on his way to confront Dong Zhuo as part of the Eastern Pass Coalition.*

Zhou Yu (1) [Ch'oh Yoo] – *younger son of Luoyang Magistrate Zhou Yi; he was evacuated and taken to Lujiang Prefecture, Yang Province when Dong Zhuo started to purge his supposed enemies.*

He then met Sun Ce, the son of the famous prodigy Sun Jian, and the two became friends and sworn brothers. Their exploits created an independent state in the south that endured for decades; the earlier exploits are the main events in 'East of the River'.
*Known by the courtesy name Gongjin [K'ong-jin]

Zhou Yu (2) [Ch'oh Yoo] – *an adviser to Cao Cao that defected to Yuan Shao; he was later appointed Inspector of Yu Province as a rival to Sun Jian, which led to the Battle of Yang City. His brothers also served Yuan Shao. Not to be confused with the more famous Zhou Yu (Gongjin) that was an ally of the Sun clan. His brothers Ang [Arng] and Xin [Shin] also served in key military and civil posts; Xin is a tertiary character in 'East of the River', where he serves Wang Lang and opposes Sun Ce.*
*Known by the courtesy name Renming [Rern-ming]

Zhu Jun [Ch'oo J'oon] – *a prominent Han official; he was a 'sponsor' of the southern prodigy Sun Jian, and recommended him to good effect whenever he could. His career was affected by his opposition to the 'Ten Attendants': although he was handsomely rewarded for his role in defeating the Yellow Turban rebels, he also suffered slander and endured periods of hardship. He is only mentioned in this work; he has already seen his lands pillaged by Li Jue and Guo Si and suffered illness at the start of the work and dies 'off-stage' during the Regency civil war.*
*Known by the courtesy name Gongwei [K'ong-way]

Zhu Ling [Ch'oo Ling] – *an officer that initially served Yuan Shao; he was later sent to aid Cao Cao but decided to remain with Cao.*
*Known by the courtesy name Wenbo [Wern-p'oh]

Zhuge Jin [Ch'oo-ker Jin] – *a civil official that travelled from the family home in Jing Province to serve Sun Ce, who was an enemy of Jing Province's governor Liu Biao; he did not enjoy high rank until Sun Ce was replaced by Sun Quan, who elevated him to a senior adviser and envoy. He is the brother of the more famous Zhuge Liang and features prominently in 'Crouching Dragon'.*
*Known by the courtesy name Ziyu [Tz'ee-yoo]

Zhuge Liang [Ch'oo-ker Lee-arng] – *a famous polymath that served the warlord Liu Bei and was pivotal to elevating him from minor player to ruler of his own kingdom; he is the protagonist of 'Crouching Dragon' – which is named for one of his Taoist soubriquets – and one of the most famous figures of the era.*
* Known by the courtesy name Kongming [Kong-ming]
* Known by the Taoist name 'Crouching Dragon'
* Known by the Taoist name 'Sleeping Dragon'

Zu Lang [Tz'oo Larng] – *a 'bandit king' in southern Yang Province; he is a major antagonist to Sun Ce that almost bested Ce before he had earned the support of his father's vassals and then opposed him for a second time when Sun Ce declared independence from Yuan Shu. Zu Lang eventually joined Sun Ce. He is a prominent character in 'East of the River'.*

UNNAMED MAGISTRATE OF NAN COUNTY IN JING PROVINCE –
cedes Wan City to Zhang Ji

UNNAMED TRAVELLER – *appears in the prologue and epilogue*

HISTORICAL CHINESE FIGURES

Confucius (Romanisation of Kong Fusha, lit. Master Kong) – *a
famous scholar and philosopher whose beliefs and teachings
became a philosophy in their own right, with many noted figures
throughout Chinese history adopting 'Confucianism' as a way of
life. Confucius' 'analects' were seen as the model for a morally
correct way of living: their teachings usually sat alongside any
other moral or spiritual beliefs that the practitioner had.*

Fan Kuai [Farn Koo-eye] – *a legendary strongman that was often
used to compare a man's strength; Xu Chu was supposedly
likened to him by Cao Cao when they first met.*

Fu Sheng [Foo S'erng] – *famed Confucian scholar ancestor of
Empress Fu and Fu Wan*

Guan Zhong [K'oo-arn Ch'ong] – *a famous adviser from the
'Spring and Autumn Period' of Chinese history. His military
achievements are significant, but his administrative reforms are
what really allowed his master Duke Huan's state of Qi to grow
and prosper beyond all of its rivals. Like Zhang Liang and Jiang
Ziya, being likened to Guan Zhong was seen as a great
compliment, as the recipient of the praise was seen as a great
state builder. Lü Bu compares himself to Guan Zhong and Cao Cao
to Duke Huan when he is captured, hoping that Cao will relent and
recruit him.*

Duke Huan [Hoo-arn] of Qi [Chee] – *ruler of the state of Qi in the
7th/8th Century BC, during the era known as the 'Spring and
Autumn Period'. He relied very heavily on the advice of his Prime
Minister Guan Zhong, whose words turned the Qi into one of the
most efficient and self-sufficient at that time.*

Jiang Ziya [Jee-arng Tz'ee-yah] (a.k.a. Taigong Wang [T'eye-
k'ong Warng]) – *a famous genius in ancient China that served as
a strategist and adviser to King Wen [Wern] and King Wu [Woo]
of Zhou [Ch'oh] in succession, preventing them from prematurely
challenging the immoral King Zhou [Ch'oh], whose rule was
supposedly tainted further by the sadistic whims of his concubine
Daji [T'ah-jee]. King Zhou's Shang [S'arng] Dynasty collapsed and
was replaced by the King Wu's Zhou [Ch'oh] Dynasty; Jiang Ziya
then served as Prime Minister. A fantastical version of the fall of
the Shang Dynasty/rise of the Zhou Dynasty was written during
the Ming Dynasty: it is called 'Fengshen Yanyi' (a.k.a. Fengshen
Bang, known sometimes as 'Creation/Investiture/ of the Gods' or
'Apotheosis of Heroes' in english).*

Lao Tzu [Lao Tz'oo] (sometimes Romanised to Laozi [Lao-tz-er], but the author has opted for the older form) – *famous philosopher and founder of Taoism (again, this can be Romanised to Daoism, but the author has opted for one over the other). Li Jue apparently claimed to be his descendant.*

Li Guang [Lee K'oo-arng] – *a Han officer that served an earlier generation of the Han Dynasty, although his service record was apparently questionable: he was known by some as 'The Flying General'. Li Jue apparently claimed to be his descendant.*

Liu Bang [Lee-oo P'arng] – *the founder of the Han Dynasty; his region of influence, Hanzhong, gave his dynasty its name. One of his descendants was eventually overthrown by the chancellor Wang Mang; Wang was defeated in turn by a popular uprising led by Liu clan members, and the Han Dynasty was restored. The second of the new line of Han Emperors, Liu Xiu/Emperor Guangwu, moved the capital to the eastern city of Luoyang to create distance between his government and the foreign tribes that threatened to devour the western provinces. As such, some historians tend refer to a Western Han (pre-Wang Mang) and an Eastern Han (post-Wang Mang).*

Liu Xiu [Lee-oo Shee-oo] – *an official that rose up against the Xin Dynasty founder Wang Mang and contributed to his defeat and the subsequent restoration of the Han Dynasty. He initially served a relative that had been named as the first in a new line of Han Emperors, but within two years he had taken the throne as Emperor Guangwu. He was primarily responsible for moving the capital from the imperilled western city of Chang'an to the safer eastern city of Luoyang, which was just south of the vibrant Yellow River.*

Red Eyebrows – *a peasant rebel confederacy that rose up against the government of the Xin Dynasty that was founded by the Han usurper Wang Mang.*

Sima Qian [Ss-mah Chee-an] – *the author of 'Records of the Grand Historian', which was an account of the reign of Emperor Wu [Woo] of Han. Sima Qian was sentenced to death for a perceived crime (slandering a relative of Emperor Wu) before 'Records of the Grand Historian' was completed: he famously opted for castration and life as a eunuch (which would have been seen as ignominious as well as painful, since he would no longer be classed as a man) rather than execution, since he could not bear to die before completing it. The finished work contained a relatively scathing account of Emperor Wu.*

Sun Tzu [Soon Tz'oo] (sometimes Romanised to Sunzi [Soon-tz'er], but the author has opted for the older form) – *a legendary scholar, famed for his work 'The Art of War'; while new technologies outdated some strategies and forced later scholars such as Zhuge Liang to annotate the work, his understanding of the psychological aspects of warfare were used to great effect, and unlike technology, those references remained relevant since people, unlike their inventions, did not and do not change. The 2nd*

Century warlord Sun Jian and his progeny claimed descent from Sun Tzu, though this was never completely proven or disputed.

Tian Dan [Tee-arn T'arn] – one of many famous statesmen from the Warring States period that many 'Three Kingdoms period' figures look back to for inspiration. He is referred to by Lü Bu during this work for his famous surprise victory at Ju City in Xu Province. Tian's lord, the unpopular King Min of Qi, had been isolated and humbled by surrounding kingdoms after annexing another state; Tian was part of the forces that the great strategist of the Yan Kingdom, Yue Yi, had trapped in Ju City. Tian had 1,000 oxen decorated to resemble dragons, had blades affixed to their horns and flammable reeds applied to make them look like they were emitting fire and smoke from their tails; the oxen were then panicked into charging out of gates and holes in the walls on one dark night, followed by a 5,000-strong army of burly men and accompanied by the sounds of drums and pots being struck by the civilians in the city. The result was a rout; the so-called 'Fire Cattle Columns' stratagem reversed the Qi kingdom's fortunes and all but destroyed Yue Yi's Yan forces. Lü Bu tells Ju City's guardian Xiao Jian 'I am not Yue Yi, but then you are not Tian Dan', meaning that if Bu were to attack the city (which is, of course, a threat that he will if not shown deference), that Xiao was not capable enough to prevail.

Wang Mang [Warng Marng] – the regent and Chancellor to the last Chang'an-based Han Emperor and founder of his own short-lived Xin Dynasty. He created the idea of the Mandate of Heaven that later regimes kept despite the reputation of its conceptualist. He was eventually overthrown by members of Liu clan, who revived the Han Dynasty. Wang Mang is treated as a villain by Han loyalists and subsequent imperial regimes, while some historians argue that his government was not entirely malevolent. His name was typically used in Han times as a slander to imply that a person was seditious – or, more typically, make a specific accusation of evil ambition.

Xun Kuang [Shoon Koo-arng] – referred to by Cui Yan as 'Master Xun' (Xunzi, [Shoon-tz'er]) in this work; he was a Warring States era scholar that professed to be a Confucian but actually believed, unlike other Confucians such as Mencius, that humans as inherently evil, rather than good, and many of his 'solutions' to this dilemma involved an approach to civil governance that is, in truth, closer to the dictatorial legal framework that is now known as Legalism (although he stated that his harsh approach was to improve men and redeem them). He produced a set of essays that are also known as Xunzi. Two of his students became the founders of the doctrine that evolved into Legalism.

Yuan An [Yoo-arn Arn] – an ancestor of Yuan Shao that provided much support to the Han Dynasty; he was rewarded with grand titles that his descendants inherited, and there were many statues erected to honour him.

Yue Yi [Yoo-er Yee] – a famous strategist that was an able

statesman in addition, forming alliances with other small nations to defeat the state of Qi during the 'Warring States' era; likening a man to him implies an intention to unite lesser lords against corrupt officials or an evil ruler.

Zhang Liang – a famous adviser and strategist that aided the future Han founder Liu Bang; likening men to him was a great compliment that also implied that they would make their lord a future hero at the very least.
*Known by the courtesy name Zifang [Tz'ee-farng]

PLACES

In this book, land locations are sorted by their provincial-level location and other landmarks – rivers and such – trail the list. In '"Yellow Sky', every part of the nation is covered in some way save for south of Yang Province (a.k.a. Jiangdong); this work follows the pattern.

Luoyang [Loo-oh-yarng] – *the eastern and current capital, used by Han Emperor Guangwu (Liu Xiu) onwards during the second phase of the Han Dynasty; at the start of this work, it has already been looted and left a gutted shell by Dong Zhuo and his allies (prior to their move to the former capital Chang'an). Luoyang does not enjoy a revival until the early 3rd Century, when it becomes the seat of a new dynasty, Cao Wei.*

Chang'an [T'arng Arn] – *the western and former capital, designated so by the Han Dynasty founder Liu Bang and used until the usurper Wang Mang temporarily ended the Han Dynasty and founded his own Xin [Shin] Dynasty. It was still considered to be the capital for a very short time after the restoration of the Han, but for a number of reasons (primarily that the Qiang and other tribes in the west were a constant threat, and Emperor Guangwu had an established power base in the east), a new capital – Luoyang – was created. Dong Zhuo moved the court back to Chang'an during his time as Chancellor of State, and this text begins with the regency court maintaining Chang'an as their capital with Emperor Xian as a hostage.*

Central Province – *known at the time as 'Sili' [See-lee], but the author chose to refer to the province by its political purpose and geographical location. Luoyang is to the east of the region, and Chang'an is to the west, bordering (and also inhabiting, technically) Liang Province. Notable places include White Wave Gorge, the base of operations of the White Wave Bandits, who are obviously named for the place.*
  Other places that are mentioned during the narrative include (or may include, due to boundary changes): Xingyang [Shing-yarng] (where Cao Cao fought Xu Rong after Dong Zhuo fled the capital); Suanzao [Soo-arn-tz'ao] where Yan Governor Liu Dai camped (it may be in Central Province, or it may be in Yan); Anyi [Arn-yee] (located in western Central Province) which becomes a strategic base for Dong Zhuo's son-in-law Niu Fu after

the end of the Dong Zhuo Campaign; and Zhongmu [Ch'ong-moo] (located in eastern Central Province, to the southeast of Luoyang and near the Yan Province border), where Dong Zhuo's followers defeat Zhu Jun and subsequently attack Yan after the end of the Dong Zhuo Campaign.

Henei [Her-nay] Prefecture – the capital prefecture of Central Province; Zhang Yang is prefectural administrator at the start of the text and runs the region from Henei City, the northern capital of Henei Prefecture. Luoyang, the overall capital until Dong Zhuo moves Emperor Xian to Chang'an, is in Henei.

Liang [Lee-arng] Province – *located in the far northwest of China; Ji [Jee] County was the capital of the province, and later suffered a siege by the warlord Ma Chao. The region is home to the Qiang and Yuezhi peoples, who rose up against the Han government in semi-organised revolt; many of the local Han Chinese people in the region were as dissatisfied with the government as the Qiang, so they joined the uprising, turning it into a full-blown rebellion that would take many decades for the Han government to fully quell. The northernmost region, Xiliang, is the region most associated with the QIang rebels and their famous prodigy Ma Chao. Tong Pass is mentioned briefly; this crossing point between Central and Liang Provinces is a later 'flash point' in the conflict between Ma Chao and the Han regime.*

Notable places include: Mei [May] County – located in the southeast of Liang Province; it was Dong Zhuo's power base, though it appears to have been ceded to Ma Teng after Dong's death; Longxi [Long-shee] Prefecture – located in western Liang Province; Han Sui and Ma Teng contend for the region; Guzang [K'oo-tz'arng] Village – located in Xiliang [Shee-lee-arng] in the far northwest of China, on the frontier; it the hometown of the adviser Jia Xu.

Yu [Yoo] Province – *located south and east of Central Province; the Yuan clan's ancestral home, Ru County, is here. The famous warlord Sun Jian was once made Inspector of the province by his lord Yuan Shu, and Wang Yun held the role at some point. Yang [Yarng] City in the west of the province was the site of the first battle between the forces of the feuding Yuan brothers.*

Runan [Roo-narn] Prefecture – the capital prefecture of Yu Province, located in its centre; the Yuan clan's ancestral home, Ru [Roo] County, is located here; the warlord Liu Bei, Liu Pi and the bandit Gong Du are all active in this region at varying points. When Yuan Shu was trying to seize Yu Province, he initially targeted Chen [T-ern] County in Runan; when Liu Bei was fighting Cao Cao on behalf of Yuan Shao, Yinjiang [Yin-ch'ee-arng] and Mount Jiluo [Ch'ee-loo-oh] were sites of skirmishes with Cao Ren. Cao Cao's future bodyguard Xu Chu defended his townspeople's fortress in the region at one point.

Yòu [Yoh] Province – *located in the northeast of China, on the frontier; it is therefore prone to frequent attacks by Northern Xiongnu, Wuhuan and other tribes. Liu Yu was made Governor; the famous warlord Gongsun Zan killed Yu and usurped control. Its capital is Fanyang [Farn-yarng].*

660

Notable places include: Yijing [Yee-ch'ing] City in the northwest, which was Gongsun Zan's last stronghold when Yuan Shao finally attacked him; Magistrate of Anxi [Arn-shee] County was future 'super-warlord' Liu Bei's first official post, awarded to him after the original Yellow Turban rebellion; Yòubeiping [Yoh-p'ay-ping]/Right Beiping [P'ay-ping] is a strategic point in the northeast of the province.

Zhuo [Ch'oo-oh] County – located in the northwest of Yòu Province; Gongsun Zan was appointed as the Magistrate after the Yellow Turban Rebellion. It is the ancestral home of Zhang Fei and home to Liu Bei's recent ancestors.

Zhongshan [Ch'ong-s'arn] Prefecture – located in the west-southwest of Yòu Province; this became a regular target for the Black Mountain Bandits and is home to Zhao Yun

Ji [Jee] Province – *located in the northeast of China, south of Yòu Province, east of Bing Province and west of Qing Province; this later becomes Yuan Shao's power base. Its first capital is Xindu [Shin-t'oo] in the centre of the province, but Yuan Shao relocated the centre of power to the southern city of Yè after becoming Governor.*

Hejian [Her-jee-an] – which is located in northern Ji Province – is the ancestral home of the Dong clan that Empress Dowager Dong (mother of Emperor Ling) belonged to. The Qing [Ching] River runs north of Yè, and it is close to a prominent crossing here Jie [Jee-er] Bridge – that Gongsun Zan and Yuan Shao fought of their most important early battles.

Bohai Prefecture/Principality – located in the central-east of Ji Province; Yuan Shao was made Administrator of Bohai by Dong Zhuo (at Minister Zhou Bi's suggestion) when he first arrived in Ji Province.

Changshan [T'arng-s'arn] Prefecture – located in the west of Ji Province, to the west of Xindu; the Black Mountain Bandits were very active here. The wandering warlord Lü Bu once confronted the Black Mountain Bandits at their base in Changshan at Yuan Shao's request.

Zhao [Ch'ao] Prefecture – located in the west of Ji Province, west of Julu and adjacent to the mountains; its location made it a frequent target for the Black Mountain Bandits.

Yan [Yarn] Province – *located in central China, to the east of Central and Jing Provinces, west of Xu Province and south of Ji Province; Cao Cao is Governor at the start of the text. The Guandu [K'oo-arn-t'oo] Campaign, which is better known as The Battle of Guandu – which is one of the most important battles of the Later Han period and takes places over the last act of this text – was centred around the place it is named for and several surrounding points in Yan Province. Guandu City is close to a number of rivers and a 'road' that an army can take to attack Cao Cao's temporary imperial capital, Xuchang [Shoo-t'arng] City; Cao Cao chose it to be his last line of defence and sent other forces at Boma [P'oh-mah] City, Meng [Mung] Ford, Yan [Yarn] Ford and Dushi [T'oo-s'ee] Ford to either guard against Yuan Shao's army or harry established military camps. Boma was the site of Yan Liang's famous death at the hands of Guan Yu (who was, at the* *time, being forced to work for Cao Cao) and 'South Slope' (which is more of an author's naming choice than an actual name) was sued to hide Cao Cao's cavalry from the advancing forces of Wen Chou, whose death is fictionally attributed to Guan Yu as well.*

Dong [T'ong] Prefecture – *located in northeast Yan Province; it is the provincial capital. Juancheng [Joo-arn-t'erng] City appears to be the capital or at the very least a preferred base, since Cao Cao always seems to place great emphasis on holding it (the author has gone with the former for cohesion). Cangting [Ts'arng-ting] Ford is located in Dong Prefecture: Cheng Yu fortified this region before Chen Gong could during the former's failed coup, thus causing the latter to retreat and fail in his mission to take Dong Prefecture. Cheng Yu was also forced to travel to Fan [Farn] County (located north of Juancheng) in order to reason with the Magistrate and ensure that the region did not yield to Chen Gong during the uprising.*

Chenliu [T'ern-lee-oo] Prefecture/Principality – *located in southwest Yan Province, on the border with Central Province; Cao Cao's friend Zhang Miao became the administrator prior to the campaign against Dong Zhuo. The city of Yongqiu [Yong-chee-oo] was where Zhang Miao's brother Zhang Chao made his last stand during the Yan Province uprising*

Juye [Joo-yer] – *located in Yan Province, west of Shanyang and southeast of Juancheng; Lü Bu prioritised attacking this county during Chen Gong's uprising. The village/town of Chengshi [T'erng-s'ee] was the ancestral home of Cao Cao's trusted vassal Li Qian (and his more famous son Li Dian)*

Shanyang [S'arn-yarng] Prefecture – *located in eastern Yan Province; Cao Cao once told Lü Bu that an awaited seal of office was somehow 'misplaced' in this region*

Yingchuan [Ying-t'oo-arn] – *located in southwest Yan Province and northeast Yu Province; it straddles the border between the provinces. Xiahou Yuan was posted here as it is strategically important; he spends the entire text defending the region against Yellow Turbans, Yuan Shu's mercenaries, Yuan Shao's mercenaries, bandits and Liu Bei.*

Fengqiu [Ferng-chee-oo] – *located in northwest Yan Province; the Black Mountain Bandits and the Southern Xiongu exile Yufuluo repeated attacked and settled in this region, and Yuan Shu tried – and failed – to occupy this region after being chased out of Jing Province by Liu Biao. Notable locations include Kuang [Koo-arng] Town, which saw action during the Battle of Fengqiu and Yufuluo's attempts to seize the region.*

Xuchang [Shoo-t'arng] – *located in northwest Yan Province; Cao Cao's chosen imperial capital while Luoyang was being rebuilt (sometimes known as Xu [Shoo] but the author was concerned that it would lead to confusion with Xu Province)*

Qing [Ching] Province – *located in the northeast of China, east of Ji Province and south of Yòu Province; there is a large 'information hole' when it comes to Qing Province. The region seems to suffer from high crime and corruption, despite several principalities. The region spends most of the narrative under dome form of siege, be it Yellow Turbans or the war between Yuan Shao and Gongsun Zan. Linzi [Lin-tz'er] – located in the centre-north of*

Qing Province – served as the provincial capital, although the fighting places Pingyuan at the centre of politics at times

Beihai [P'ay-high] – *located in the centre-north of Qing Province, south of Linzi; Kong Rong was made Chancellor of the capital around the time of the death of Emperor Ling. Kong Rong famously required rescuing when an army of Yellow Turbans sieged the city; the hero Taishi Ci borrowed an army from Liu Bei and saved him.*

Mount Tai [Tigh] Prefecture – *located in the northwest of Qing Province, near the actual Mount Tai; some historical records state that members of Zhuge Liang's clan held government roles here (including at least one administrator, which might raise questions, since there was a lot of corruption here). This was the home region of future minor warlord Zang Ba: at one point in time prior to the Yellow Turban Rebellion, Zang Ba's father was arrested after criticising the corrupt administrator, leading to his son 'crossing the floor' and becoming a criminal to free him.*

Ji'nan [Jee Narn] Prefecture – *located in the west of Qing Province, near the Ji River; Cao Cao was sent here by the court, but he could not cope with the pressure and retired*

Langya [Larng-yah] Prefecture – *located in the centre of Qing Province, southeast of Beihai; Yangdu [Yarng-t'oo], located in the southwest of Langya Prefecture, was the famous Zhuge clan's ancestral home. Cao Cao's consort Lady Bian also hails from this prefecture. Ju City governor Xiao Jian was appointed as Langya's Administrator by either Tao Qian or Gongsun Zan, but he never actually inhabited the role or the place.*

Pingyuan [Ping-yoo-arn] County – *located in the far northwest of Qing Province, near the border with Yòu Province; Gongsun Zan's appointed Inspector of Qing, Tian Kai, and Yuan Shao's son Yuan Tan fought here for years. Liu Bei was invited to Pingyuan by Gongsun Zan; it was here that he first met his future ally Zhao Yun and recruited the father-and-son scholars Chen Ji (Yuanfang) and Chen Qun.*

Yang [Yarng] Province – *located in the southeast of China, east of southern Jing and south of everything else; it is quite a large province, and can be divided into two as the Yangtze/Great River bisects the province. The southern part is also considered to be east of the Great River, and is sometimes known as Jiangdong [Jee-arng-t'ong] (lit. river-east, or 'east of the river'). Lujiang and Jiujiang Prefectures comprise the majority of the northern part, although Guangling and Danyang could be partially included (and were often considered as annexed into Xu Province as well). The northern part of the province is the only part featured.*

Jiujiang [Jee-oo-jee-arng] Prefecture – *located in the northeast of Yang Province, 'above' the Great River; the provincial capital Shouchun [S'oh-t'oon] – which is also Yuan Shu's chosen capital for his 'Zhong Dynasty' – is based here. There are land borders with Yan and Xu Provinces to the north.*

Lujiang [Loo-jiang] Prefecture – *located in the northwest of Yang Province, 'above' the Great River; there are land borders with Jing, Yu and Yan Provinces. Yuan Shu's vassal Liu Xun is the Administrator at the start of the text. The famous strategist Zhou Yu (Gongjin) hailed from Lujiang. Hefei [Her-fay] is located in the south of Lujiang Prefecture; this strategically useful area was under constant threat of attack by forces in the so-called 'Jiangdong region' (southern Yang Province), and it was eventually fortified by Cao Cao's vassal Liu Fu. The resultant fortress was a major obstacle to the Sun clan's plans to reclaim northern Yang.*

Wu [Woo] Prefecture – located in the east of Yang Province, south of Guangling and west of Wu Prefecture, 'below' the Yangtze/Great River; the Sun clan hailed from this region, and the scholar Cai Yong hid here for 12 years. The rebel-turned-official Xu Gong – who was one of the warlord Sun Ce's most vocal critics – resided here.

Danyang [T'arn-yarng] Prefecture – located in the centre of Yang Province, south of Jiujiang and 'below' the Yangtze/Great River; Tao Qian hailed from here, and the region was famous for producing good cavalrymen.

Guangling [K'oo-arng-ling] Prefecture – located in the east of Yang Province, on the coast, north of Wu Prefecture and south of Xiapi in eastern Xu Province; it appears to be controlled by various warlords (Tao Qian and whoever controls most of the rest of Yang) most of the time, and Chen Deng is eventually assigned here by Cao Cao (which implies it to be part of Xu Province, rather than Yang).

Kuaiji [Koo-eye-jee] Prefecture – located in the southeast of Yang Province, on the coast, south of Wu Prefecture; Wang Lang (grandfather to future Jin founder Sima Yan) administrated this prefecture at one point and contested Sun Ce to no avail.

Xu [Shoo] Province *– located in the centre-east of China, south of Qing Province and east of Yan Province; it was governed by Tao Qian until Cao Cao's campaign, at which point the role passed to Liu Bei. Lu Bu usurps the role during the course of the text, and Che Zhou inherits the role after Bu; Liu Bei then usurps Che Zhou and is then defeated and replaced by Dong Zhao (Gongren). The capital prior to Cao Cao's campaigns was Peng [Perng] City; Tao Qian later abandoned this city and fled to Tan [Tarn], which offered greater defence; that also yielded, and Tao moved the capital to Xiapi [Shee-ah-pee] City in Xiapi Prefecture, which was located in the east of Xu Province, to the east of the Si River. The prefecture was, prior to Cao Cao's campaign, administrated by the Buddhist cult leader Ze Rong, who turned the city into a 'Buddhist Utopia'; Ze fled the city when Cao invaded, leaving it vacant for Tao Qian to turn it into his new provincial capital. Ju [Ch'oo] City is located to the east of Xiapi City, and was the site of many battles throughout history, including one between Warring States legends Yue Yi and Tian Dan and another between Lü Bu and Mount Tai Bandits led by Zang Ba. Haixi [High-shee] – where Liu Bei suffered a year-long siege – is located to the north of Xiapi.*

Kaiyang [K-eye-yarng] County – located somewhere in the far north-northeast of Xu Province; in the wake of the Yellow Turban Rebellion, the minor warlord Zang Ba occupied this place and made it into an independent state with few rules.

Pei [Pay] County – located in the west of Xu Province; it was Cao Cao's clan's ancestral home

Donghai [T'ong-h'eye] Prefecture – located in the east of Xu Province, north of Xiapi; Cao Cao's forces attacked this region during his campaign

Xiaopei [Shee-ow-pay] County – *located in the southwest of Xu Province; Liu Bei stationed here many times*

Bing [P'ing] Province – *located in the centre-north of China, north of Central Province; it is relatively unimportant to the narrative. Lü Bu's mentor and first foster father Ding Yuan was Inspector of the province; the Southern Xiongnu mainly live in Bing, and the Black Mountain Bandits are very active here.*

Shangdang [S'arn-t'arng] Prefecture – *located in the centre-east of Bing Province; there is a vast mountain range to the east of this place that harbours various bandit groups.*

Wuyuan [Woo-yoo-arn] Prefecture – *located north of the Great Wall in northernmost Bing Prefecture (it is certainly considered to be frontier territory); Jiuyuan [Jee-oo-yoo-arn] County in Wuyuan was where the warlord Lü Bu hailed from*

Yi [Yee] Province – *a province located in the centre-west of Han China, south of Hanzhong and west of Jing; it is a relatively harsh and unforgiving place at this point (now it is Szechuan), but Liu Yan (1) craved the governorship precisely because it was isolated enough for him to have complete autonomy. Liu Bei later sets his sights on making Yi his first base (after the loaned piece of Jing that he has obtained by that point) and seizes it from Liu Yan's son Zhang after a long campaign that robbed Bei of his adviser Pang Tong (the entire affair is chronicled in 'Crouching Dragon'). Its first capital was Mianzhu [Mee-an-ch'oo], a city located in the centre-west of Yi Prefecture; it is protected by mountains, hills and valleys. After a series of events that Governor Liu Yan deemed inauspicious, he moved the capital to Chengdu [T'erng-doo], in the south of Yi Province; that place was protected by a complex natural defensive barrier of rivers, hills and mountains. The province is governed by Liu Zhang throughout this text.*

Hanzhong [Harn-ch'ong] Province – *interchangeably known throughout this text as (The Taoist/Theocratic State of) Han'ning [Harn Ning]; this region was the fief of sorts of Liu Bang, founder of the Han Dynasty, and he named his dynasty for this region. When Zhang Lu occupied Hanzhong, he renamed it: if Hanzhong is read as meaning 'Amidst/In Han', Han'ning could, when taking individual characters, mean 'Tranqil Han' or, possibly, 'Rather than Han/Preferable to Han', which fits perfectly with Zhang Lu's beliefs. The region serves as little more than a place that people must journey through in this text, but it becomes a battleground for Cao Cao and Liu Bei in later years. The province barely features in this text but is very important to past and future events in the later Han and Three Kingdoms periods.*

Jing [Jing] Province – *a province located in the centre of Han China; it has borders with Yi, Hanzhong, Yu, Yan and Central provinces, which makes it strategically desirable to a would-be conqueror. Jing does not play a large part in the main narrative, but Yuan Shu tries to seize it in the middle acts with little success (or rather, little success once Sun Jian is dead).*

Nan [Narn] County – *a county located in the far north of*

Jing Province; it borders Yan Province, Yu Province and Central Province, making it strategically invaluable for conquering the north of China. The Yellow Turbans prioritised Nan County and almost took it during their first rebellion; Yuan Shu's vassal Sun Jian seized it for his lord, and Zhang Xiu later governed from the capital Wan [Wahn] City with surprising popularity. Wan [Wahn] City has its own story. Sun Jian liberated Wan from the Yellow Turbans during their rebellion, but later returned to the province to seize it for Yuan Shu; Shu then lost it and fled to Fengqiu in Yan Province. Dong Zhuo's former vassal Zhang Ji seized the city after leaving Chang'an, but died and left the place in the hands of his nephew Zhang Xiu and the adviser Jia Xu. The two fugitives were then forced to fight Cao Cao's army with days or perhaps hours of an amicable surrender: that event – which is depicted in Act V of this work – is famous for its outcome.

Xiangyang [Shee-arng-yarng] – a county (and city named for the county) located in the lower north of Jing Province; it straddles the south bank of the River Han. The city of Xiangyang was the location of numerous sieges: Sun Jian sieged the city and fought land battles here before his death, and Guan Yu sieged the city as part of his attack on neighbouring Fan County, a campaign that became his last great exploit before he was famously betrayed and destroyed (as depicted in 'Crouching Dragon').

Jiangxia [Jee-arng-shee-ah] Prefecture – located in southeast Jing Province; this is Huang Zu's power base, and is the site of many battles between Huang Zu and the Sun clan.

Great Wall [a.k.a. 'The Endless Wall'] – *commissioned by various rulers throughout history to repel the Xiongnu and other tribal invaders; it spans the entire northern border. Some Han Chinese lived north of the wall by the end of the Han Dynasty: Lü Bu and many of his followers hail from such settlements. Conversely, the 'Southern Xiongnu' settled south of the wall (primarily in Bing Province) and contributed to Han society. The early iterations of the wall were mostly earthworks, signal towers and garrisons, and provided limited and ultimately futile defence against the Mongols (successors to the Xianbei that were first led by the infamous Genghis Khan), who went on to conquer China and found the Yuan [Yoo-arn] Dynasty.*

After the Mongol Yuans were replaced by the Chinese Ming Dynasty, the wall was rebuilt in stone to try and prevent further incursions; this is the more famous wall of modern times. The wall was not completely breached again until the end of the Ming Dynasty, during a popular peasant uprising (that bore great similarity to the Yellow Turban Rebellion in terms of magnitude, cause and purpose). That rebellion had led to the suicide of the last Ming emperor and left the loyalist military generals stationed at the wall with two choices: allow an invasion by the Mongol-Manchu alliance or submit to the will of their own frustrated people. The generals ultimately chose to open the gates to the Manchus, who overran and conquered China (and were, incidentally, the last imperial rulers of China – the 'Last Emperor', Puyi, was Manchurian, not Han Chinese); this is the on-going event that is alluded to in the prologue and epilogue.

Ji [Jee] River – *ran parallel to (and east of) the Yellow River from the coast to Chenliu.*

Qing [Ching] River – *located in Ji Province, to the north of Yè*

Si [See] River – *located in Qing and Xu Provinces; it flows south and east toward the east coast. Xiapi is east of its banks.*

Yangtze [Yarng-tz'ee] River – *spoken of in the text as the Great River, it runs from the west of China to the east, separating the land naturally into north and south.*

Yellow River – *located in the centre-north of China; this vibrant river – which literally runs yellow with sand – runs south and west from the northeast coast to the lands east of Luoyang, whereupon it turns west and runs north of Luoyang as far as the lands east of Chang'an, whereupon it splits and runs north and west.*

MISCELLANEOUS

Di [Dee] – *a northern, non-Han Chinese race, broken down further into tribes; they were indigenous to the mountains of Hanzhong.*

Hongmen [Hong-mern] – *a commonly-recalled event in Chinese literature, specifically referring to a sword dance or fencing exhibition performed by one or more assassins during a banquet. The host is typically the author of the plot, and they will use a signal – usually dropping or dashing their wine cup – to tell the assassin(s) to strike at the intended victim, who is usually a guest that is blissfully enjoying the proceedings. Any time that a person enters a gathering and notes the host holding a wine cup with caution, they fear a variation of a Hongmen-style assassination, the main variant being hidden assassins (usually behind the hall curtains, or posing as guards). There are several examples in fictional versions of Three Kingdoms: Liu Bei's strategist Pang Tong tries to kill Liu Zhang using this ruse, prior to the hostilities in Yi Province, and Wu General Ling Tong tries to kill fellow general and former enemy Gan Ning during a victory banquet with a spontaneous lone performance. In this work, the closest equivalent is Fan Chou's execution, which is still a fairly recent event; Hongmen is also referred to.*

Nan(man) [Narn(-marn)] – *a southern, non-Chinese race, broken down further into tribes; they were indigenous to Nanzhong, which once included Yi Province until the Han Chinese expanded into their territory. They play no role in this book, but they are mentioned by Yi Province Governor Liu Zhang.*

Qiang [Chee-arng] – *non-Chinese ethnic tribes that lived in the northwest on either side of the Great Wall. The various tribes were typically enemies of the Han Dynasty. Ma Teng and Han Sui famously joined the tribes, and the eldest son of the former, Ma Chao, became a notorious historical warrior king.*

Shanyue [S'arn-yoo-er] – *non-Chinese tribes that lived in and around various regions: they lived in Yang Province in large numbers. They resented Han rule, but their allegiances shifted dramatically through the eras.*

The 'Ten Attendants' – *a clique of eunuchs in the imperial capital Luoyang; they began life as loyalists that helped Emperor Huan to purge Liang Ji and Empress Dowager Liang's influence, but over time they formed a power base of their own. By the year 166, they were almost untouchable, and anyone that crossed them, deliberately or otherwise, was dealt with in the harshest fashion: hundreds of non-compliant intelligentsia were labelled as traitors and persecuted, an event known as the 'Partisan Crisis'. They were finally purged after thwarted political action by Commander-in-Chief Hè Jin and decisive military action by his ally Yuan Shao.*

'The Way of Five Pecks' – *a religious cult that was led by Zhang Lu, the ruler of Han'ning; their doctrine was based around a non-monetary system where rice was the currency and community was paramount, although many decried the way that potentially troublesome elements were kept loyal by providing them with whatever they needed at the expense of others.*

'The Way of Peace' – *the religious group that started the Yellow Turban Rebellion; although it can probably be said that many of those that fought were not followers of this Taoist cult, their 16-character mantra was a simple, inspirational way to gather followers and rally other forms of support.*

Wuhuan [Woo-hoo-arn] – *non-Chinese tribes that lived across China and the surrounding territories*

Xiongnu [Shee-ong-noo] – *non-Chinese ethnic tribes that lived in the north on either side of the Great Wall; the various tribes were enemies, economic trading partners or allies of the Han Dynasty. The Southern Xiongnu provided troops to the Han army.*

Xianbei [Shee-an-p'ay] – *a confederacy of mostly Xiongnu tribes that became a powerful force in the lands north of the Great Wall.*

Yellow Turbans – *a common army that earned their name from the yellow scarves that they used to cover their hair. They were mostly made up of peasants that were tired of heavy taxation and poor treatment by the state. The founder was a Taoist cultist, Zhang Jue. The rebellion was eventually crushed by a combination of government forces and local militias, but they reappeared many times over the next decade before they were finally suppressed by the Han government.*

****